DIGITAL FORTRESS

Dan Brown

CORGI BOOKS

DIGITAL FORTRESS
A CORGI BOOK: 0 552 15169 6

First publication in Great Britain

PRINTING HISTORY
Corgi edition published 2004

33

Set in 10/12 pt Palatino by
Falcon Oast Graphic Art Ltd

Corgi Books are published by Transworld Publishers,
61–63 Uxbridge Road, London W5 5SA,
a division of The Random House Group Ltd,
in Australia by Random House Australia (Pty) Ltd,
20 Alfred Street, Milsons Point, Sydney, NSW 2061, Australia,
in New Zealand by Random House New Zealand Ltd,
18 Poland Road, Glenfield, Auckland 10, New Zealand
and in South Africa by Random House (Pty) Ltd,
Endulini, 5a Jubilee Road, Parktown 2193, South Africa.

Printed and bound in Great Britain by
Cox & Wyman Ltd, Reading, Berkshire.

Papers used by Transworld Publishers are natural, recyclable products
made from wood grown in sustainable forests. The manufacturing processes
conform to the environmental regulations of the country of origin.

Dan Brown is the bestselling author of *Digital Fortress*, *Deception Point*, *Angels and Demons* and *The Da Vinci Code*. He is a graduate of Amherst College and Phillips Exeter Academy, where he has taught English and creative writing. He lives with his wife in New England and can be found on the web at www.danbrown.com

Acclaim for *The Da Vinci Code*:

'The word for *The Da Vinci Code* is a rare invertible palindrome. Rotated 180 degrees on a horizontal axis so that it is upside down, it denotes the maternal essence that is sometimes linked to the sport of soccer. Read right side up, it concisely conveys the kind of extreme enthusiasm with which this riddle-filled, code-breaking, exhilaratingly brainy thriller can be recommended. That word is wow. The author is Dan Brown (a name you will want to remember). In this gleefully erudite suspense novel, Mr Brown takes the format he has been developing through three earlier novels and fine-tunes it to blockbuster perfection. Not since the advent of Harry Potter has an author so flagrantly delighted in leading readers on a breathless chase and coaxing them through hoops ... The book moves at a breakneck pace, with the author seeming thoroughly to enjoy his contrivances. Virtually every chapter ends with a cliffhanger' Janet Maslin, *New York Times*

'Intrigue and menace mingle in one of the finest mysteries I've ever read. An amazing tale with enigma piled on secrets stacked on riddles' *New York Times* bestselling author, Clive Cussler

'*The Da Vinci Code* is a fascinating and absorbing read – perfect for history buffs, conspiracy nuts, puzzle lovers or anyone who appreciates a great, riveting read. Dan Brown is my new must-read. I loved this book' *New York Times* bestselling author, Harlan Coben

'I would never have believed that this is my kind of thriller, but I'm going to tell you something – the more I read, the more I had to read. In *The Da Vinci Code*, Dan Brown has built a world that is rich in fascinating detail, and I could not get enough of it. Mr Brown, I am your fan' *New York Times* bestselling author, Robert Crais

'*The Da Vinci Code* sets the hook-of-all-hooks. This novel takes off down a road that is as eye-opening as it is page-turning. You simply cannot put it down. Thriller readers everywhere will soon realize Dan Brown is a master'
New York Times bestselling author, Vince Flynn

'This is pure genius. Dan Brown has to be one of the best, smartest, and most accomplished writers in the country' Nelson DeMille

'Thriller writing doesn't get any better than this' *Denver Post*

'A heart-racing thriller. This story has so many twists – all satisfying, most unexpected – that it would be a sin to reveal too much of the plot in advance. Let's just say that if this novel doesn't get your pulse racing, you need to check your meds' *San Francisco Chronicle*

'Exceedingly clever. Both fascinating and fun ... a considerable achievement' *Washington Post*

'This masterpiece should be mandatory reading. Brown solidifies his reputation as one of the most skilled thriller writers on the planet with his best book yet, a compelling blend of history and page-turning suspense. Highly recommended' *Library Journal*

'A new master of smart thrills. A pulse-quickening, brain-teasing adventure' *People* magazine

'A thundering, tantalizing, extremely smart fun ride. Brown doesn't slow down his tremendously powerful narrative engine despite transmitting several doctorates' worth of fascinating history and learned speculation, *The Da Vinci Code* is brain candy of the highest quality – which is a reviewer's code meaning, "Put this on top of your pile"' *Chicago Tribune*

'One hell of a read. A gripping mix of murder and myth' *New York Daily News*

'An international chase ... a quest ... codes within codes. Brown's novel is a page-turner ... and you'll never view "The Last Supper" the same way again' *The Christian Science Monitor*

'Dan Brown's conspiracy-theory thriller is the pulp must-read of the season ... an ingenious mixture of paranoid thriller, art history lesson, chase story, religious symbology lecture and anti-clerical screed, and it's the most fun you can have between the sort of covers that aren't 300-count Egyptian cotton' *Salon.com*

'Far more than the average thriller. Intellectually satisfying ... page-turning suspense' *Houston Chronicle*

'Brown has assembled a whopper of a plot that will please conspiracy buffs and thriller addicts alike' *Publishers Weekly*

'A dazzling performance by Brown ... a delightful display of erudition. Brown delivers a crackling, intricate mystery, complete with breathtaking escapes and several stunning surprises. It's challenging, exciting, and a whole lot more. The race across France and the United Kingdom leads us on a fascinating journey through a covert, enigmatic world revealed through a seemingly endless collection of codes, puzzles, anagrams, cryptograms, and messages hidden not only in Da Vinci's art but in things we think we know well' *Boston Globe*

'Brainy stuff. The standard car chases and intrigues are leavened with Crichtonesque discursions on medieval iconography, the formation of the early Christian church, and history's suppression of the "sacred feminine"' *Entertainment Weekly*

'A stunning new thriller that will provoke much debate. Dan Brown's extensive research on secret societies and symbology adds intellectual depth to this page-turning thriller. His surprising revelations on Da Vinci's penchant for hiding codes in his paintings will lead the reader to search out such renowned artistic icons as The Mona Lisa, The Madonna of the Rocks and The Last Supper. The Last Supper holds the most astonishing coded secrets of all and, after reading *The Da Vinci Code*, you will never see this famous painting in quite the same way again' Bookreporter.com

'Some readers spurn genre fiction, often due to a misguided belief that mass entertainment is always mindless dribble. For those of you who know better, *The Da Vinci Code* will make you feel justifiably smug. It's that rare book that manages to both entertain and educate simultaneously. Dan Brown has managed to outdo the best of Robert Ludlum in this byzantine . . . and engrossing story. There is enough medieval history to please any historian and enough action to satisfy a hardcore thrill-seeker . . . an early favorite for thriller of the year' *Rocky Mountain News*

'Enthralling . . . Dan Brown masterfully concocts an intelligent and lucid thriller that marries the gusto of an international murder mystery with a collection of fascinating esoterica culled from 2,000 years of Western history. Brown's hero and heroine embark on a lofty and intriguing exploration of some of culture's greatest mysteries – from the nature of the Mona Lisa's smile to the secret of the Holy Grail . . . rich food for thought' amazon.com

'*The Da Vinci Code* shines – brilliantly – in its exploration of cryptology, particularly the encoding methods developed by Leonardo Da Vinci, whose art and manuscripts are packed with mystifying symbolism and quirky codes' *Wired* magazine

'Brown's intricate plot delivers more satisfying twists than a licorice factory' *Booklist*

'A blockbuster with brains. *The Da Vinci Code* is a thrill-a-minute adventure as well as an educational tour of France and England, symbology 101, riddle-breaking for dummies, the magical powers of anagrams, numerical codes to die for and navigational factoids' *The Ottawa Citizen*

'Brown's scholarship never slows down the sizzling action [of this] absorbing new novel . . . a labyrinth of intricate schemes, sidetracks, and deceptions' *Bookpage*

Also by Dan Brown

DECEPTION POINT
ANGELS AND DEMONS
THE DA VINCI CODE

For my parents . . .
my mentors and heroes

A debt of gratitude: to my editors at St Martin's Press, Thomas Dunne and the exceptionally talented Melissa Jacobs. To my agents in New York, George Wieser, Olga Wieser, and Jake Elwell. To all those who read and contributed to the manuscript along the way. And especially to my wife, Blythe, for her enthusiasm and patience.

Also . . . a quiet thank you to the two faceless ex-NSA cryptographers who made invaluable contributions via anonymous remailers. Without them this book would not have been written.

PROLOGUE

PLAZA DE ESPAÑA
SEVILLE, SPAIN
11:00 A.M.

It is said that in death, all things become clear; Ensei Tankado now knew it was true. As he clutched his chest and fell to the ground in pain, he realized the horror of his mistake.

People appeared, hovering over him, trying to help. But Tankado did not want help – it was too late for that.

Trembling, he raised his left hand and held his fingers outward. *Look at my hand!* The faces around him stared, but he could tell they did not understand.

On his finger was an engraved golden ring. For an instant, the markings glimmered in the Andalusian sun. Ensei Tankado knew it was the last light he would ever see.

11

CHAPTER 1

They were in the Smoky Mountains at their favorite bed-and-breakfast. David was smiling down at her. 'What do you say, gorgeous? Marry me?'

Looking up from their canopy bed, she knew he was the one. Forever. As she stared into his deep-green eyes, somewhere in the distance a deafening bell began to ring. It was pulling him away. She reached for him, but her arms clutched empty air.

It was the sound of the phone that fully awoke Susan Fletcher from her dream. She gasped, sat up in bed, and fumbled for the receiver. 'Hello?'

'Susan, it's David. Did I wake you?'

She smiled, rolling over in bed. 'I was just dreaming of you. Come over and play.'

He laughed. 'It's still dark out.'

'Mmm.' She moaned sensuously. 'Then *definitely* come over and play. We can sleep in before we head north.'

David let out a frustrated sigh. 'That's why I'm calling. It's about our trip. I've got to postpone.'

Susan was suddenly wide awake. 'What!'

'I'm sorry. I've got to leave town. I'll be back by

tomorrow. We can head up first thing in the morning. We'll still have two days.'

'But I made reservations,' Susan said, hurt. 'I got our old room at Stone Manor.'

'I know, but—'

'Tonight was supposed to be *special* – to celebrate six months. You *do* remember we're engaged, don't you?'

'Susan.' He sighed. 'I really can't go into it now, they've got a car waiting. I'll call you from the plane and explain everything.'

'*Plane?*' she repeated. 'What's going on? Why would the university . . . ?'

'It's not the university. I'll phone and explain later. I've really got to go; they're calling for me. I'll be in touch. I promise.'

'David!' she cried. 'What's—'

But it was too late. David had hung up.

Susan Fletcher lay awake for hours waiting for him to call back. The phone never rang.

Later that afternoon Susan sat dejected in the tub. She submerged herself in the soapy water and tried to forget Stone Manor and the Smoky Mountains. *Where could he be?* she wondered. *Why hasn't he called?*

Gradually the water around her went from hot to lukewarm and finally to cold. She was about to get out when her cordless phone buzzed to life. Susan bolted upright, sloshing water on the floor as she grappled for the receiver she'd left on the sink.

'David?'

'It's Strathmore,' the voice replied.

Susan slumped. 'Oh.' She was unable to hide her disappointment. 'Good afternoon, Commander.'

'Hoping for a younger man?' The voice chuckled.

'No, sir,' Susan said, embarrassed. 'It's not how it—'

'Sure it is.' He laughed. 'David Becker's a good man. Don't ever lose him.'

'Thank you, sir.'

The commander's voice turned suddenly stern. 'Susan, I'm calling because I need you in here. Pronto.'

She tried to focus. 'It's Saturday, sir. We don't usually—'

'I know,' he said calmly. 'It's an emergency.'

Susan sat up. *Emergency?* She had never heard the word cross Commander Strathmore's lips. *An emergency? In Crypto?* She couldn't imagine. 'Y-yes, sir.' She paused. 'I'll be there as soon as I can.'

'Make it sooner.' Strathmore hung up.

Susan Fletcher stood wrapped in a towel and dripped on the neatly folded clothes she'd set out the night before – hiking shorts, a sweater for the cool mountain evenings, and the new lingerie she'd bought for the nights. Depressed, she went to her closet for a clean blouse and skirt. *An emergency? In Crypto?*

As she went downstairs, Susan wondered how the day could get much worse.

She was about to find out.

CHAPTER 2

Thirty thousand feet above a dead-calm ocean, David Becker stared miserably from the Learjet 60's small, oval window. He'd been told the phone on board was out of order, and he'd never had a chance to call Susan.

'What am I doing here?' he grumbled to himself. But the answer was simple – there were men to whom you just didn't say no.

'Mr Becker,' the loudspeaker crackled. 'We'll be arriving in half an hour.'

Becker nodded gloomily to the invisible voice. *Wonderful.* He pulled the shade and tried to sleep. But he could only think of her.

CHAPTER 3

Susan's Volvo sedan rolled to a stop in the shadow of the ten-foot-high, barbed Cyclone fence. A young guard placed his hand on the roof.

'ID, please.'

Susan obliged and settled in for the usual half-minute wait. The officer ran her card through a computerized scanner. Finally he looked up. 'Thank you, Ms Fletcher.' He gave an imperceptible sign, and the gate swung open.

Half a mile ahead Susan repeated the entire procedure at an equally imposing electrified fence. *Come on, guys . . . I've only been through here a million times.*

As she approached the final checkpoint, a stocky sentry with two attack dogs and a machine gun glanced down at her license plate and waved her through. She followed Canine Road for another 250 yards and pulled into Employee Lot C. Unbelievable, she thought. *Twenty-six thousand employees and a twelve-billion-dollar budget; you'd think they could make it through the weekend without me.* Susan gunned the car into her reserved spot and killed the engine.

After crossing the landscaped terrace and entering

16

the main building, she cleared two more internal checkpoints and finally arrived at the windowless tunnel that led to the new wing. A voice-scan booth blocked her entry.

The armed guard looked up. 'Afternoon, Ms Fletcher.'

Susan smiled tiredly. 'Hi, John.'

'Didn't expect you today.'

'Yeah, me neither.' She leaned toward the parabolic microphone. 'Susan Fletcher,' she stated clearly. The computer instantly confirmed the frequency concentrations in her voice, and the gate clicked open. She stepped through.

The guard admired Susan as she began her walk down the cement causeway. He noticed that her strong hazel eyes seemed distant today, but her cheeks had a flushed freshness, and her shoulder-length, auburn hair looked newly blown dry. Trailing her was the faint scent of Johnson's Baby Powder. His eyes fell the length of her slender torso – to her white blouse with the bra barely visible beneath, to her knee-length khaki skirt, and finally to her legs . . . Susan Fletcher's legs.

Hard to imagine they support a 170 IQ, he mused to himself.

He stared after her a long time. Finally he shook his head as she disappeared in the distance.

*

17

As Susan reached the end of the tunnel, a circular, vaultlike door blocked her way. The enormous letters read: CRYPTO.

Sighing, she placed her hand inside the recessed cipher box and entered her five-digit PIN. Seconds later the twelve-ton slab of steel began to revolve. She tried to focus, but her thoughts reeled back to him.

David Becker. The only man she'd ever loved. The youngest full professor at Georgetown University and a brilliant foreign-language specialist, he was practically a celebrity in the world of academia. Born with an eidetic memory and a love of languages, he'd mastered six Asian dialects as well as Spanish, French, and Italian. His university lectures on etymology and linguistics were standing-room-only, and he invariably stayed late to answer a barrage of questions. He spoke with authority and enthusiasm, apparently oblivious to the adoring gazes of his star-struck coeds.

Becker was dark – a rugged, youthful thirty-five with sharp green eyes and a wit to match. His strong jaw and taut features reminded Susan of carved marble. Over six feet tall, Becker moved across a squash court faster than any of his colleagues could comprehend. After soundly beating his opponent, he would cool off by dousing his head in a drinking fountain and soaking his tuft of thick, black hair. Then, still dripping, he'd treat his opponent to a fruit shake and a bagel.

As with all young professors, David's university salary was modest. From time to time, when he needed to renew his squash club membership or restring his old Dunlop with gut, he earned extra money by doing translating work for government agencies in and around Washington. It was on one of those jobs that he'd met Susan.

It was a crisp morning during fall break when Becker returned from a morning jog to his three-room faculty apartment to find his answering machine blinking. He downed a quart of orange juice as he listened to the playback. The message was like many he received – a government agency requesting his translating services for a few hours later that morning. The only strange thing was that Becker had never heard of the organization.

'They're called the National Security Agency,' Becker said, calling a few of his colleagues for background.

The reply was always the same. 'You mean the National Security *Council?'*

Becker checked the message. 'No. They said *Agency.* The NSA.'

'Never heard of 'em.'

Becker checked the GAO Directory, and it showed no listing either. Puzzled, Becker called one of his old squash buddies, an ex-political analyst turned research clerk at the Library of Congress. David was shocked by his friend's explanation.

Apparently, not only did the NSA exist, but it was considered one of the most influential government organizations in the world. It had been gathering global electronic intelligence data and protecting U.S. classified information for over half a century. Only 3 percent of Americans were even aware it existed.

'NSA,' his buddy joked, 'stands for "No Such Agency."'

With a mixture of apprehension and curiosity, Becker accepted the mysterious agency's offer. He drove the thirty-seven miles to their eighty-six-acre headquarters hidden discreetly in the wooded hills of

Fort Meade, Maryland. After passing through endless security checks and being issued a six-hour, holographic guest pass, he was escorted to a plush research facility where he was told he would spend the afternoon providing 'blind support' to the Cryptography Division – an elite group of mathematical brainiacs known as the code-breakers.

For the first hour, the cryptographers seemed unaware Becker was even there. They hovered around an enormous table and spoke a language Becker had never heard. They spoke of stream ciphers, self-decimated generators, knapsack variants, zero knowledge protocols, unicity points. Becker observed, lost. They scrawled symbols on graph paper, pored over computer printouts, and continuously referred to the jumble of text on the overhead projector.

```
JHDJA3JKHDHMADO/ERTWTJLW+JGJ328
5JHALSFNHKHHHFAFOHHDFGAF/FJ37WE
OHI93450S9DJFD2H/HHRTYFHLF89303
95JSPJF2JO890IHJ98YHFIO8OEWRT03
JOJR845HDROQ+JTDEU4TQEFQE//OUJW
O8UYOIHO934JTPWFIAJERO9QU4JR9GU
IVJP$DUW4H95PE8RTUGVJW3P4E/IKKC
MFFUERHFGVDQ394IKJRMG+UNHVS9OER
IRK/O956Y7UOPOIKIOJP9F876OQWERQI
```

Eventually one of them explained what Becker had already surmised. The scrambled text was a code – a 'ciphertext' – groups of numbers and letters representing encrypted words. The cryptographers' job was to study the code and extract from it the original message, or 'cleartext.' The NSA had called Becker because they suspected the original message was written in Mandarin Chinese; he was to translate the symbols as the cryptographers decrypted them.

For two hours, Becker interpreted an endless stream of Mandarin symbols. But each time he gave them a translation, the cryptographers shook their heads in despair. Apparently the code was not making sense. Eager to help, Becker pointed out that all the characters they'd shown him had a common trait – they were also part of the Kanji language. Instantly the bustle in the room fell silent. The man in charge, a lanky chain-smoker named Morante, turned to Becker in disbelief.

'You mean these symbols have multiple meanings?'

Becker nodded. He explained that Kanji was a Japanese writing system based on modified Chinese characters. He'd been giving Mandarin translations because that's what they'd asked for.

'Jesus Christ.' Morante coughed. 'Let's try the Kanji.'

Like magic, everything fell into place.

The cryptographers were duly impressed, but nonetheless, they still made Becker work on the characters out of sequence. 'It's for your own safety,' Morante said. 'This way, you won't know what you're translating.'

Becker laughed. Then he noticed nobody else was laughing.

When the code finally broke, Becker had no idea what dark secrets he'd helped reveal, but one thing was for certain – the NSA took code-breaking seriously; the check in Becker's pocket was more than an entire month's university salary.

On his way back out through the series of security checkpoints in the main corridor, Becker's exit was blocked by a guard hanging up a phone. 'Mr Becker, wait here, please.'

'What's the problem?' Becker had not expected the meeting to take so long, and he was running late for his standing Saturday afternoon squash match.

The guard shrugged. 'Head of Crypto wants a word. She's on her way out now.'

'*She?*' Becker laughed. He had yet to see a female inside the NSA.

'Is that a problem for you?' a woman's voice asked from behind him.

Becker turned and immediately felt himself flush. He eyed the ID card on the woman's blouse. The head of the NSA's Cryptography Division was not only a woman, but an attractive woman at that.

'No,' Becker fumbled. 'I just . . .'

'Susan Fletcher.' The woman smiled, holding out her slender hand.

Becker took it. 'David Becker.'

'Congratulations, Mr Becker. I hear you did a fine job today. Might I chat with you about it?'

Becker hesitated. 'Actually, I'm in a bit of a rush at the moment.' He hoped spurning the world's most powerful intelligence agency wasn't a foolish act, but his squash match started in forty-five minutes, and he had a reputation to uphold: David Becker was never late for squash . . . class maybe, but *never* squash.

'I'll be brief.' Susan Fletcher smiled. 'Right this way, please.'

Ten minutes later, Becker was in the NSA's commissary enjoying a popover and cranberry juice with the NSA's lovely head cryptographer, Susan Fletcher. It quickly became evident to David that the thirty-eight-year-old's high-ranking position at the NSA was no fluke – she was one of the brightest women he had ever met. As they discussed codes and code-breaking, Becker found himself struggling to keep up – a new and exciting experience for him.

An hour later, after Becker had obviously missed his squash match and Susan had blatantly ignored three pages on the intercom, both of them had to laugh. There they were, two highly analytical minds, presumably immune to irrational infatuations – but somehow, while they sat there discussing linguistic morphology and pseudo-random number generators, they felt like a couple of teenagers – everything was fireworks.

Susan never did get around to the real reason she'd wanted to speak to David Becker – to offer him a trial post in their Asiatic Cryptography Division. It was clear from the passion with which the young professor spoke about teaching that he would never leave the university. Susan decided not to ruin the mood by talking business. She felt like a schoolgirl all over again; nothing was going to spoil it. And nothing did.

Their courtship was slow and romantic – stolen escapes whenever their schedules permitted, long walks through the Georgetown campus, late-night cappuccinos at Merlutti's, occasional lectures and concerts. Susan found herself laughing more than she'd ever thought possible. It seemed there was nothing David couldn't twist into a joke. It was a welcome release from the intensity of her post at the NSA.

One crisp, autumn afternoon they sat in the bleachers watching Georgetown soccer get pummeled by Rutgers.

'What sport did you say you play?' Susan teased.

'Zucchini?'

Becker groaned. 'It's called *squash*.'

She gave him a dumb look.

'It's *like* zucchini,' he explained, 'but the court's smaller.'

Susan pushed him.

Georgetown's left wing sent a corner-kick sailing out of bounds, and a boo went up from the crowd. The defensemen hurried back downfield.

'How about you?' Becker asked. 'Play any sports?'

'I'm a black belt in StairMaster.'

Becker cringed. 'I prefer sports you can win.'

Susan smiled. 'Overachiever, are we?'

Georgetown's star defenseman blocked a pass, and there was a communal cheer in the stands. Susan leaned over and whispered in David's ear. 'Doctor.'

He turned and eyed her, lost.

'Doctor,' she repeated. 'Say the first thing that comes to mind.'

Becker looked doubtful. 'Word associations?'

'Standard NSA procedure. I need to know who I'm with.' She eyed him sternly. 'Doctor.'

Becker shrugged. 'Seuss.'

Susan gave him a frown. 'Okay, try this one . . . "kitchen."'

He didn't hesitate. 'Bedroom.'

Susan arched her eyebrows coyly. 'Okay, how about this . . . "cat."'

'Gut,' Becker fired back.

'Gut?'

'Yeah. Catgut. Squash racquet string of champions.'

'That's pleasant.' She groaned.

'Your diagnosis?' Becker inquired.

24

Susan thought a minute. 'You're a childish, sexually frustrated squash fiend.'

Becker shrugged. 'Sounds about right.'

It went on like that for weeks. Over dessert at all-night diners Becker would ask endless questions.

Where had she learned mathematics?

How did she end up at the NSA?

How did she get so captivating?

Susan blushed and admitted she'd been a late bloomer. Lanky and awkward with braces through her late teens, Susan said her Aunt Clara had once told her God's apology for Susan's plainness was to give her brains. A premature apology, Becker thought.

Susan explained that her interest in cryptography had started in junior high school. The president of the computer club, a towering eighth grader named Frank Gutmann, typed her a love poem and encrypted it with a number-substitution scheme. Susan begged to know what it said. Frank flirtatiously refused. Susan took the code home and stayed up all night with a flashlight under her covers until she figured out the secret – every number represented a letter. She carefully deciphered the code and watched in wonder as the seemingly random digits turned magically into beautiful poetry. In that instant, she knew she'd fallen in love – codes and cryptography would become her life.

Almost twenty years later, after getting her master's in mathematics from Johns Hopkins and studying number theory on a full scholarship from MIT, she submitted her doctoral thesis, *Cryptographic Methods, Protocols, and Algorithms for Manual Applications*. Apparently her professor was not the only one who read it; shortly afterward, Susan received a phone call and a plane ticket from the NSA.

Everyone in cryptography knew about the NSA; it was home to the best cryptographic minds on the planet. Each spring, as the private-sector firms descended on the brightest new minds in the workforce and offered obscene salaries and stock options, the NSA watched carefully, selected their targets, and then simply stepped in and doubled the best standing offer. What the NSA wanted, the NSA bought. Trembling with anticipation, Susan flew to Washington's Dulles International Airport where she was met by an NSA driver, who whisked her off to Fort Meade.

There were forty-one others who had received the same phone call that year. At twenty-eight, Susan was the youngest. She was also the only female. The visit turned out to be more of a public relations bonanza and a barrage of intelligence testing than an informational session. In the week that followed, Susan and six others were invited back. Although hesitant, Susan returned. The group was immediately separated. They underwent individual polygraph tests, background searches, handwriting analyses, and endless hours of interviews, including taped inquiries into their sexual orientations and practices. When the interviewer asked Susan if she'd ever engaged in sex with animals, she almost walked out, but somehow the mystery carried her through – the prospect of working on the cutting edge of code theory, entering 'The Puzzle Palace,' and becoming a member of the most secretive club in the world – the National Security Agency.

Becker sat riveted by her stories. 'They actually asked you if you'd had sex with animals?'

Susan shrugged. 'Part of the routine background check.'

'Well . . .' Becker fought off a grin. 'What did you say?'

She kicked him under the table. 'I told them no!' Then she added, 'And until last night, it was true.'

In Susan's eyes, David was as close to perfect as she could imagine. He only had one unfortunate quality: Every time they went out, he insisted on picking up the check. Susan hated seeing him lay down a full day's salary on dinner for two, but Becker was immovable. Susan learned not to protest, but it still bothered her. *I make more money than I know what to do with,* she thought. *I should be paying.*

Nonetheless, Susan decided that aside from David's outdated sense of chivalry, he was ideal. He was compassionate, smart, funny, and best of all, he had a sincere interest in her work. Whether it was during trips to the Smithsonian, bike rides, or burning spaghetti in Susan's kitchen, David was perpetually curious. Susan answered what questions she could and gave David the general, unclassified overview of the National Security Agency. What David heard enthralled him.

Founded by President Truman at 12:01 A.M. on November 4, 1952, the NSA had been the most clandestine intelligence agency in the world for almost fifty years. The NSA's seven-page inception doctrine laid out a very concise agenda: to protect U.S. government communications and to intercept the communications of foreign powers.

The roof of the NSA's main operations building was littered with over five hundred antennas, including two large radomes that looked like enormous golf balls. The building itself was mammoth – over two million square feet, twice the size of CIA headquarters. Inside were eight million feet of telephone wire and eighty thousand square feet of permanently sealed windows.

Susan told David about COMINT, the agency's global reconnaissance division – a mind-boggling collection of listening posts, satellites, spies, and wiretaps around the globe. Thousands of communiqués and conversations were intercepted every day, and they were all sent to the NSA's analysts for decryption. The FBI, CIA, and U.S. foreign policy advisors all depended on the NSA's intelligence to make their decisions.

Becker was mesmerized. 'And code-breaking? Where do *you* fit in?'

Susan explained how the intercepted transmissions often originated from dangerous governments, hostile factions, and terrorist groups, many of whom were inside U.S. borders. Their communications were usually encoded for secrecy in case they ended up in the wrong hands – which, thanks to COMINT, they usually did. Susan told David her job was to study the codes, break them by hand, and furnish the NSA with the deciphered messages. This was not entirely true.

Susan felt a pang of guilt over lying to her new love, but she had no choice. A few years ago it would have been accurate, but things had changed at the NSA. The whole world of cryptography had changed. Susan's new duties were classified, even to many in the highest echelons of power.

'Codes,' Becker said, fascinated. 'How do you know where to start? I mean . . . how do you break them?'

Susan smiled. 'You of all people should know. It's like studying a foreign language. At first the text looks like gibberish, but as you learn the rules defining its structure, you can start to extract meaning.'

Becker nodded, impressed. He wanted to know more.

With Merlutti's napkins and concert programs as her chalkboard, Susan set out to give her charming new pedagogue a minicourse in cryptography. She began with Julius Caesar's 'perfect square' cipher box.

Caesar, she explained, was the first code-writer in history. When his foot-messengers started getting ambushed and his secret communiqués stolen, he devised a rudimentary way to encrypt his directives. He rearranged the text of his messages such that the correspondence looked senseless. Of course, it was not. Each message always had a letter-count that was a perfect square – sixteen, twenty-five, one hundred – depending on how much Caesar needed to say. He secretly informed his officers that when a random message arrived, they should transcribe the text into a square grid. If they did, and read top-to-bottom, a secret message would magically appear.

Over time Caesar's concept of rearranging text was adopted by others and modified to become more difficult to break. The pinnacle of noncomputer-based encryption came during World War II. The Nazis built a baffling encryption machine named Enigma. The device resembled an old-fashioned typewriter with brass interlocking rotors that revolved in intricate ways and shuffled cleartext into confounding arrays of seemingly senseless character groupings. Only by having another Enigma machine, calibrated the exact same way, could the recipient break the code.

Becker listened, spellbound. The teacher had become the student.

One night, at a university performance of *The Nutcracker*, Susan gave David his first basic code to break. He sat through the entire intermission, pen in hand, puzzling over the eleven-letter message:

HL FKZC VD LDS

Finally, just as the lights dimmed for the second half, he got it. To encode, Susan had simply replaced each letter of her message with the letter preceding it in the alphabet. To decrypt the code, all Becker had to do was shift each letter one space forward in the alphabet – 'A' became 'B,' 'B' became 'C,' and so on. He quickly shifted the remaining letters. He never imagined four little syllables could make him so happy:

IM GLAD WE MET

He quickly scrawled his response and handed it to her:

LD SNN

Susan read it and beamed.

Becker had to laugh; he was thirty-five years old, and his heart was doing backflips. He'd never been so attracted to a woman in his life. Her delicate European features and soft brown eyes reminded him of an ad for Estée Lauder. If Susan's body had been lanky and awkward as a teenager, it sure wasn't now. Somewhere along the way, she had developed a willowy grace – slender and tall with full, firm breasts and a perfectly flat abdomen. David often joked that she was the first swimsuit model he'd ever met with a doctorate in applied mathematics and number theory. As the months passed, they both started to suspect they'd found something that could last a lifetime.

They'd been together almost two years when, out of the blue, David proposed to her. It was on a weekend trip to the Smoky Mountains. They were lying on a big canopy bed at Stone Manor. He had no ring – he just blurted it out. That's what she loved about him – he was so spontaneous. She kissed him long and hard. He took her in his arms and slipped off her nightgown.

'I'll take that as a yes,' he said, and they made love all night by the warmth of the fire.

That magical evening had been six months ago – before David's unexpected promotion to chairman of the Modern Language Department. Their relationship had been in a downhill slide ever since.

CHAPTER 4

The Crypto door beeped once, waking Susan from her depressing reverie. The door had rotated past its fully open position and would be closed again in five seconds, having made a complete 360-degree rotation. Susan gathered her thoughts and stepped through the opening. A computer made note of her entry.

Although she had practically lived in Crypto since its completion three years ago, the sight of it still amazed her. The main room was an enormous circular chamber that rose five stories. Its transparent, domed ceiling towered 120 feet at its central peak. The Plexiglas cupola was embedded with a polycarbonate mesh – a protective web capable of withstanding a two-megaton blast. The screen filtered the sunlight into delicate lacework across the walls. Tiny particles of dust drifted upward in wide unsuspecting spirals – captives of the dome's powerful deionizing system.

The room's sloping sides arched broadly at the top and then became almost vertical as they approached eye level. Then they became subtly translucent and graduated to an opaque black as they reached the floor – a shimmering expanse of polished black tile that shone with an eerie luster, giving one the unsettling sensation that the floor was transparent. Black ice.

Pushing through the center of the floor like the tip of a colossal torpedo was the machine for which the dome had been built. Its sleek black contour arched twenty-three feet in the air before plunging back into the floor below. Curved and smooth, it was as if an enormous killer whale had been frozen midbreach in a frigid sea.

This was TRANSLTR, the single most expensive piece of computing equipment in the world – a machine the NSA swore did not exist.

Like an iceberg, the machine hid 90 percent of its mass and power deep beneath the surface. Its secret was locked in a ceramic silo that went six stories straight down – a rocketlike hull surrounded by a winding maze of catwalks, cables, and hissing exhaust from the freon cooling system. The power generators at the bottom droned in a perpetual low-frequency hum that gave the acoustics in Crypto a dead, ghostlike quality.

TRANSLTR, like all great technological advancements, had been a child of necessity. During the 1980s, the NSA witnessed a revolution in telecommunications that would change the world of intelligence reconnaissance forever – public access to the Internet. More specifically, the arrival of E-mail.

Criminals, terrorists, and spies had grown tired of having their phones tapped and immediately embraced this new means of global communication. E-mail had the security of conventional mail and the speed of the telephone. Since the transfers traveled through underground fiber-optic lines and were never transmitted into the airwaves, they were entirely intercept-proof – at least that was the perception.

In reality, intercepting E-mail as it zipped across the Internet was child's play for the NSA's techno-gurus. The Internet was not the new home computer revelation that most believed. It had been created by the Department of Defense three decades earlier – an enormous network of computers designed to provide secure government communication in the event of nuclear war. The eyes and ears of the NSA were old Internet pros. People conducting illegal business via E-mail quickly learned their secrets were not as private as they'd thought. The FBI, DEA, IRS, and other U.S. law enforcement agencies – aided by the NSA's staff of wily hackers – enjoyed a tidal wave of arrests and convictions.

Of course, when the computer users of the world found out the U.S. government had open access to their E-mail communications, a cry of outrage went up. Even pen pals, using E-mail for nothing more than recreational correspondence, found the lack of privacy unsettling. Across the globe, entrepreneurial programmers began working on a way to keep E-mail more secure. They quickly found one and public-key encryption was born.

Public-key encryption was a concept as simple as it was brilliant. It consisted of easy-to-use, home-computer software that scrambled personal E-mail messages in such a way that they were totally unreadable. A user could write a letter and run it through the encryption software, and the text would come out the other side looking like random nonsense – totally illegible – a code. Anyone intercepting the transmission found only an unreadable garble on the screen.

34

The only way to unscramble the message was to enter the sender's 'pass-key' – a secret series of characters that functioned much like a PIN number at an automatic teller. The pass-keys were generally quite long and complex; they carried all the information necessary to instruct the encryption algorithm exactly what mathematical operations to follow to re-create the original message.

A user could now send E-mail in confidence. Even if the transmission was intercepted, only those who were given the key could ever decipher it.

The NSA felt the crunch immediately. The codes they were facing were no longer simple substitution ciphers crackable with pencil and graph paper – they were computer-generated hash functions that employed chaos theory and multiple symbolic alphabets to scramble messages into seemingly hopeless randomness.

At first, the pass-keys being used were short enough for the NSA's computers to 'guess.' If a desired pass-key had ten digits, a computer was programmed to try every possibility between 0000000000 and 9999999999. Sooner or later the computer hit the correct sequence. This method of trial-and-error guessing was known as 'brute force attack.' It was time-consuming but mathematically guaranteed to work.

As the world got wise to the power of brute-force code-breaking, the pass-keys started getting longer and longer. The computer time needed to 'guess' the correct key grew from weeks to months and finally to years.

By the 1990s, pass-keys were over fifty characters long and employed the full 256-character ASCII alphabet of letters, numbers, and symbols. The number of different possibilities was in the neighborhood of 10^{120} – one with 120 zeros after it. Correctly guessing a pass-key was as mathematically unlikely as choosing the correct grain of sand from a three-mile beach. It was estimated that a successful brute-force attack on a standard sixty-four-bit key would take the NSA's fastest computer – the top-secret Cray/Josephson II – over nineteen years to break. By the time the computer guessed the key and broke the code, the contents of the message would be irrelevant.

Caught in a virtual intelligence blackout, the NSA passed a top-secret directive that was endorsed by the President of the United States. Buoyed by federal funds and a carte blanche to do whatever was necessary to solve the problem, the NSA set out to build the impossible: the world's first universal code-breaking machine.

Despite the opinion of many engineers that the newly proposed code-breaking computer was impossible to build, the NSA lived by its motto: Everything is possible. The impossible just takes longer.

Five years, half a million man-hours, and $1.9 billion later, the NSA proved it once again. The last of the three million stamp-size processors was hand-soldered in place, the final internal programming was finished, and the ceramic shell was welded shut. TRANSLTR had been born.

Although the secret internal workings of TRANSLTR were the product of many minds and were not fully understood by any one individual, its basic principle was simple: Many hands make light work.

Its three million processors would all work in

parallel – counting upward at blinding speed, trying every new permutation as they went. The hope was that even codes with unthinkably colossal pass-keys would not be safe from TRANSLTR's tenacity. This multibillion-dollar masterpiece would use the power of parallel processing as well as some highly classified advances in cleartext assessment to guess pass-keys and break codes. It would derive its power not only from its staggering number of processors but also from new advances in quantum computing – an emerging technology that allowed information to be stored as quantum-mechanical states rather than solely as binary data.

The moment of truth came on a blustery Thursday morning in October. The first live test. Despite uncertainty about how fast the machine would be, there was one thing on which the engineers agreed – if the processors all functioned in parallel, TRANSLTR would be powerful. The question was *how* powerful.

The answer came twelve minutes later. There was a stunned silence from the handful in attendance when the printout sprang to life and delivered the cleartext – the broken code. TRANSLTR had just located a sixty-four-character key in a little over ten minutes, almost a million times faster than the two decades it would have taken the NSA's second-fastest computer.

Led by the deputy director of operations, Commander Trevor J. Strathmore, the NSA's Office of Production had triumphed. TRANSLTR was a success. In the interest of keeping their success a secret, Commander Strathmore immediately leaked information that the project had been a complete failure. All the activity in the Crypto wing was supposedly an attempt to salvage their $2 billion fiasco. Only the

NSA elite knew the truth – TRANSLTR was cracking hundreds of codes every day.

With word on the street that computer-encrypted codes were entirely unbreakable – even by the all-powerful NSA – the secrets poured in. Drug lords, terrorists, and embezzlers alike – weary of having their cellular phone transmissions intercepted – were turning to the exciting new medium of encrypted E-mail for instantaneous global communications. Never again would they have to face a grand jury and hear their own voice rolling off tape, proof of some long-forgotten cellular phone conversation plucked from the air by an NSA satellite.

Intelligence gathering had never been easier. Codes intercepted by the NSA entered TRANSLTR as totally illegible ciphers and were spat out minutes later as perfectly readable cleartext. No more secrets.

To make their charade of incompetence complete, the NSA lobbied fiercely against all new computer encryption software, insisting it crippled them and made it impossible for lawmakers to catch and prosecute the criminals. Civil rights groups rejoiced, insisting the NSA shouldn't be reading their mail anyway. Encryption software kept rolling off the presses. The NSA had lost the battle – exactly as it had planned. The entire electronic global community had been fooled . . . or so it seemed.

CHAPTER 5

Where is everyone? Susan wondered as she crossed the deserted Crypto floor. *Some emergency.*

Although most NSA departments were fully staffed seven days a week, Crypto was generally quiet on Saturdays. Cryptographic mathematicians were by nature high-strung workaholics, and there existed an unwritten rule that they take Saturdays off except in emergencies. Code-breakers were too valuable a commodity at the NSA to risk losing them to burnout.

As Susan traversed the floor, TRANSLTR loomed to her right. The sound of the generators eight stories below sounded oddly ominous today. Susan never liked being in Crypto during off hours. It was like being trapped alone in a cage with some grand, futuristic beast. She quickly made her way toward the commander's office.

Strathmore's glass-walled workstation, nicknamed 'the fishbowl' for its appearance when the drapes were open, stood high atop a set of catwalk stairs on the back wall of Crypto. As Susan climbed the grated steps, she gazed upward at Strathmore's thick, oak door. It bore the NSA seal – a bald eagle fiercely clutching an ancient skeleton key. Behind that door sat one of the greatest men she'd ever met.

Commander Strathmore, the fifty-six-year-old deputy director of operations, was like a father to Susan. He was the one who'd hired her, and he was the one who'd made the NSA her home. When Susan joined the NSA over a decade ago, Strathmore was heading the Crypto Development Division – a training ground for new cryptographers – new *male* cryptographers. Although Strathmore never tolerated the hazing of anyone, he was especially protective of his sole female staff member. When accused of favoritism, he simply replied with the truth: Susan Fletcher was one of the brightest young recruits he'd ever seen, and he had no intention of losing her to sexual harassment. One of the senior cryptographers foolishly decided to test Strathmore's resolve.

One morning during her first year, Susan dropped by the new cryptographers' lounge to get some paperwork. As she left, she noticed a picture of herself on the bulletin board. She almost fainted in embarrassment. There she was, reclining on a bed and wearing only panties.

As it turned out, one of the cryptographers had digitally scanned a photo from a pornographic magazine and edited Susan's head onto someone else's body. The effect had been quite convincing.

Unfortunately for the cryptographer responsible, Commander Strathmore did not find the stunt even remotely amusing. Two hours later, a landmark memo went out:

EMPLOYEE CARL AUSTIN TERMINATED FOR
INAPPROPRIATE CONDUCT

From that day on, nobody messed with her; Susan Fletcher was Commander Strathmore's golden girl.

But Strathmore's young cryptographers were not the only ones who learned to respect him; early in his career Strathmore made his presence known to his superiors by proposing a number of unorthodox and highly successful intelligence operations. As he moved up the ranks, Trevor Strathmore became known for his cogent, reductive analyses of highly complex situations. He seemed to have an uncanny ability to see past the moral perplexities surrounding the NSA's difficult decisions and to act without remorse in the interest of the common good.

There was no doubt in anyone's mind that Strathmore loved his country. He was known to his colleagues as a patriot and a visionary . . . a decent man in a world of lies.

In the years since Susan's arrival at the NSA, Strathmore had skyrocketed from head of Crypto Development to second-in-command of the entire NSA. Now only one man outranked Commander Strathmore there – Director Leland Fontaine, the mythical overlord of the Puzzle Palace – never seen, occasionally heard, and eternally feared. He and Strathmore seldom saw eye to eye, and when they met, it was like the clash of the titans. Fontaine was a giant among giants, but Strathmore didn't seem to care. He argued his ideas to the director with all the restraint of an impassioned boxer. Not even the President of the United States dared challenge Fontaine the way Strathmore did. One needed political immunity to do that – or, in Strathmore's case, political indifference.

Susan arrived at the top of the stairs. Before she could knock, Strathmore's electronic door lock buzzed. The door swung open, and the commander waved her in.

'Thanks for coming, Susan. I owe you one.'

'Not at all.' She smiled as she sat opposite his desk.

Strathmore was a rangy, thick-fleshed man whose muted features somehow disguised his hard-nosed efficiency and demand for perfection. His gray eyes usually suggested a confidence and discretion born from experience, but today they looked wild and unsettled.

'You look beat,' Susan said.

'I've been better.' Strathmore sighed.

I'll say, she thought.

Strathmore looked as bad as Susan had ever seen him. His thinning gray hair was disheveled, and even in the room's crisp air-conditioning, his forehead was beaded with sweat. He looked like he'd slept in his suit. He was sitting behind a modern desk with two recessed keypads and a computer monitor at one end. It was strewn with computer printouts and looked like some sort of alien cockpit propped there in the center of his curtained chamber.

'Tough week?' she inquired.

Strathmore shrugged. 'The usual. The EFF's all over me about civilian privacy rights again.'

Susan chuckled. The EFF, or Electronics Frontier Foundation, was a worldwide coalition of computer users who had founded a powerful civil liberties coalition aimed at supporting free speech on-line and educating others to the realities and dangers of living in an electronic world. They were constantly lobbying against what they called 'the Orwellian eavesdropping capabilities of government agencies' – particularly the NSA. The EFF was a perpetual thorn in Strathmore's side.

'Sounds like business as usual,' she said. 'So what's this big emergency you got me out of the tub for?'

Strathmore sat a moment, absently fingering the computer trackball embedded in his desktop. After a long silence, he caught Susan's gaze and held it. 'What's the longest you've ever seen TRANSLTR take to break a code?'

The question caught Susan entirely off guard. It seemed meaningless. *This is what he called me in for?*

'Well . . .' She hesitated. 'We hit a COMINT intercept a few months ago that took about an hour, but it had a ridiculously long key – ten thousand bits or something like that.'

Strathmore grunted. 'An hour, huh? What about some of the boundary probes we've run?'

Susan shrugged. 'Well, if you include diagnostics, it's obviously longer.'

'How *much* longer?'

Susan couldn't imagine what Strathmore was getting at. 'Well, sir, I tried an algorithm last March with a segmented million-bit key. Illegal looping functions, cellular automata, the works. TRANSLTR still broke it.'

'How long?'

'Three hours.'

Strathmore arched his eyebrows. 'Three hours? That long?'

Susan frowned, mildly offended. Her job for the last three years had been to fine-tune the most secret computer in the world; most of the programming that made TRANSLTR so fast was hers. A million-bit key was hardly a realistic scenario.

'Okay,' Strathmore said. 'So even in extreme conditions, the longest a code has ever survived inside TRANSLTR is about three hours?'

Susan nodded. 'Yeah. More or less.'

Strathmore paused as if afraid to say something he might regret. Finally he looked up. 'TRANSLTR's hit something . . .' He stopped.

Susan waited. 'More than three hours?'

Strathmore nodded.

She looked unconcerned. 'A new diagnostic? Something from the Sys-Sec Department?'

Strathmore shook his head. 'It's an outside file.'

Susan waited for the punch line, but it never came. 'An outside file? You're joking, right?'

'I wish. I queued it last night around eleven thirty. It hasn't broken yet.'

Susan's jaw dropped. She looked at her watch and then back at Strathmore. 'It's *still* going? Over fifteen hours?'

Strathmore leaned forward and rotated his monitor toward Susan. The screen was black except for a small, yellow text box blinking in the middle.

TIME ELAPSED: 15:09:33
AWAITING KEY: _____

Susan stared in amazement. It appeared TRANSLTR had been working on one code for over fifteen hours. She knew the computer's processors auditioned thirty million keys per second – one hundred billion per hour. If TRANSLTR was still counting, that meant the key had to be enormous –

44

over ten billion digits long. It was absolute insanity.

'It's impossible!' she declared. 'Have you checked for error flags? Maybe TRANSLTR hit a glitch and—'

'The run's clean.'

'But the pass-key must be huge!'

Strathmore shook his head. 'Standard commercial algorithm. I'm guessing a sixty-four-bit key.'

Mystified, Susan looked out the window at TRANSLTR below. She knew from experience that it could locate a sixty-four-bit key in under ten minutes. 'There's got to be some explanation.'

Strathmore nodded. 'There is. You're not going to like it.'

Susan looked uneasy. 'Is TRANSLTR malfunctioning?'

'TRANSLTR's fine.'

'Have we got a virus?'

Strathmore shook his head. 'No virus. Just hear me out.'

Susan was flabbergasted. TRANSLTR had never hit a code it couldn't break in under an hour. Usually the cleartext was delivered to Strathmore's printout module within minutes. She glanced at the high-speed printer behind his desk. It was empty.

'Susan,' Strathmore said quietly. 'This is going to be hard to accept at first, but just listen a minute.' He chewed his lip. 'This code that TRANSLTR's working on – it's unique. It's like nothing we've ever seen before.' Strathmore paused, as if the words were hard for him to say. 'This code is unbreakable.'

Susan stared at him and almost laughed. *Unbreakable? What was THAT supposed to mean?* There was no such thing as an unbreakable code – some took longer than others, but every code was breakable. It was mathematically guaranteed that sooner or later TRANSLTR would guess the right key. 'I *beg* your pardon?'

'The code's unbreakable,' he repeated flatly.

Unbreakable? Susan couldn't believe the word had been uttered by a man with twenty-seven years of code analysis experience.

'Unbreakable, sir?' she said uneasily. 'What about the Bergofsky Principle?'

Susan had learned about the Bergofsky Principle early in her career. It was a cornerstone of brute-force technology. It was also Strathmore's inspiration for building TRANSLTR. The principle clearly stated that if a computer tried enough keys, it was mathematically guaranteed to find the right one. A code's security was not that its pass-key was unfindable but rather that most people didn't have the time or equipment to try.

Strathmore shook his head. 'This code's different.'

'Different?' Susan eyed him askance. *An unbreakable code is a mathematical impossibility! He knows that!*

Strathmore ran a hand across his sweaty scalp. 'This code is the product of a brand-new encryption algorithm – one we've never seen before.'

Now Susan was even more doubtful. Encryption algorithms were just mathematical formulas, recipes for scrambling text into code. Mathematicians and programmers created new algorithms every day. There were hundreds of them on the market – PGP, Diffie-Hellman, ZIP, IDEA, El Gamal. TRANSLTR broke all of their codes every day, no problem. To TRANSLTR all codes looked identical, regardless of which algorithm wrote them.

'I don't understand,' she argued. 'We're not talking

about reverse-engineering some complex function, we're talking brute force. PGP, Lucifer, DSA – it doesn't matter. The algorithm generates a key it thinks is secure, and TRANSLTR keeps guessing until it finds it.'

Strathmore's reply had the controlled patience of a good teacher. 'Yes, Susan, TRANSLTR will *always* find the key – even if it's huge.' He paused a long moment. 'Unless . . .'

Susan wanted to speak, but it was clear Strathmore was about to drop his bomb. *Unless what?*

'Unless the computer doesn't know when it's broken the code.'

Susan almost fell out of her chair. 'What!'

'Unless the computer guesses the correct key but just keeps guessing because it doesn't realize it found the right key.' Strathmore looked bleak. 'I think this algorithm has got a rotating cleartext.'

Susan gaped.

The notion of a rotating cleartext function was first put forth in an obscure, 1987 paper by a Hungarian mathematician, Josef Harne. Because brute-force computers broke codes by examining cleartext for identifiable word patterns, Harne proposed an encryption algorithm that, in addition to encrypting, shifted decrypted cleartext over a time variant. In theory, the perpetual mutation would ensure that the attacking computer would never locate recognizable word patterns and thus never know when it had found the proper key. The concept was somewhat like the idea of colonizing Mars – fathomable on an intellectual level, but, at present, well beyond human ability.

'Where did you get this thing?' she demanded.

The commander's response was slow. 'A public sector programmer wrote it.'

'What?' Susan collapsed back in her chair. 'We've got the best programmers in the world downstairs! All of us working together have never even come *close* to writing a rotating cleartext function. Are you trying to tell me some punk with a PC figured out how to do it?'

Strathmore lowered his voice in an apparent effort to calm her. 'I wouldn't call this guy a punk.'

Susan wasn't listening. She was convinced there had to be some other explanation: A glitch. A virus. Anything was more likely than an unbreakable code.

Strathmore eyed her sternly. 'One of the most brilliant cryptographic minds of all time wrote this algorithm.'

Susan was more doubtful than ever; the most brilliant cryptographic minds of all time were in her department, and she certainly would have heard about an algorithm like this.

'Who?' she demanded.

'I'm sure you can guess,' Strathmore said. 'He's not too fond of the NSA.'

'Well, that narrows it down!' she snapped sarcastically.

'He worked on the TRANSLTR project. He broke the rules. Almost caused an intelligence nightmare. I deported him.'

Susan's face was blank only an instant before going white. 'Oh my God . . .'

Strathmore nodded. 'He's been bragging all year about his work on a brute-force-resistant algorithm.'

'B-but . . .' Susan stammered. 'I thought he was bluffing. He actually *did* it?'

48

'He did. The ultimate unbreakable code-writer.'

Susan was silent a long moment. 'But . . . that means . . .'

Strathmore looked her dead in the eye. 'Yes. Ensei Tankado just made TRANSLTR obsolete.'

49

CHAPTER 6

Although Ensei Tankado was not alive during the Second World War, he carefully studied everything about it – particularly about its culminating event, the blast in which 100,000 of his countrymen where incinerated by an atomic bomb.

Hiroshima, 8:15 A.M. August 6, 1945 – a vile act of destruction. A senseless display of power by a country that had already won the war. Tankado had accepted all that. But what he could never accept was that the bomb had robbed him of ever knowing his mother. She had died giving birth to him – complications brought on by the radiation poisoning she'd suffered so many years earlier.

In 1945, before Ensei was born, his mother, like many of her friends, traveled to Hiroshima to volunteer in the burn centers. It was there that she became one of the hibakusha – the radiated people. Nineteen years later, at the age of thirty-six, as she lay in the delivery room bleeding internally, she knew she was finally going to die. What she did not know was that death would spare her the final horror – her only child was to be born deformed.

Ensei's father never even saw his son. Bewildered by the loss of his wife and shamed by the arrival of what the nurses told him was an imperfect child who probably would not survive the night, he disappeared from the hospital and never came back. Ensei Tankado was placed in a foster home.

Every night the young Tankado stared down at the twisted fingers holding his daruma wish-doll and swore he'd have revenge – revenge against the country that had stolen his mother and shamed his father into abandoning him. What he didn't know was that destiny was about to intervene.

In February of Ensei's twelfth year, a computer manufacturer in Tokyo called his foster family and asked if their crippled child might take part in a test group for a new keyboard they'd developed for handicapped children. His family agreed.

Although Ensei Tankado had never seen a computer, it seemed he instinctively knew how to use it. The computer opened worlds he had never imagined possible. Before long it became his entire life. As he got older, he gave classes, earned money, and eventually earned a scholarship to Doshisha University. Soon Ensei Tankado was known across Tokyo as *fugusha kisai* – the crippled genius.

Tankado eventually read about Pearl Harbor and Japanese war crimes. His hatred of America slowly faded. He became a devout Buddhist. He forgot his childhood vow of revenge; forgiveness was the only path to enlightenment.

By the time he was twenty, Ensei Tankado was somewhat of an underground cult figure among programmers. IBM offered him a work visa and a post in Texas. Tankado jumped at the chance. Three years later he had left IBM, was living in New York, and was writing software on his own. He rode the new wave of public-key encryption. He wrote algorithms and made a fortune.

Like many of the top authors of encryption algorithms, Tankado was courted by the NSA. The irony was not lost on him – the opportunity to work in the heart of the government in a country he had once vowed to hate. He decided to go on the interview. Whatever doubts he had disappeared when he met Commander Strathmore. They talked frankly about Tankado's background, the potential hostility he might feel toward the U.S., his plans for the future. Tankado took a polygraph test and underwent five weeks of rigorous psychological profiles. He passed them all. His hatred had been replaced by his devotion to Buddha. Four months later Ensei Tankado went to work in the Cryptography Department of the National Security Agency.

Despite his large salary, Tankado went to work on an old moped and ate a bag lunch alone at his desk instead of joining the rest of the department for prime rib and vichyssoise in the commissary. The other cryptographers revered him. He was brilliant – as creative a programmer as any of them had ever seen. He was kind and honest, quiet, and of impeccable ethics. Moral integrity was of paramount importance to him. It was for this reason that his dismissal from the NSA and subsequent deportation had been such a shock.

Tankado, like the rest of the Crypto staff, had been working on the TRANSLTR project with the understanding that if successful, it would be used to decipher E-mail only in cases preapproved by the

Justice Department. The NSA's use of TRANSLTR was to be regulated in much the same way the FBI needed a federal court order to install a wiretap. TRANSLTR was to include programming that called for passwords held in escrow by the Federal Reserve and the Justice Department in order to decipher a file. This would prevent the NSA from listening indiscriminately to the personal communications of law-abiding citizens around the globe.

However, when the time came to enter that programming, the TRANSLTR staff was told there had been a change of plans. Because of the time pressures often associated with the NSA's antiterrorist work, TRANSLTR was to be a free-standing decryption device whose day-to-day operation would be regulated solely by the NSA.

Ensei Tankado was outraged. This meant the NSA would, in effect, be able to open everyone's mail and reseal it without their knowing. It was like having a bug in every phone in the world. Strathmore attempted to make Tankado see TRANSLTR as a law-enforcement device, but it was no use; Tankado was adamant that it constituted a gross violation of human rights. He quit on the spot and within hours violated the NSA's code of secrecy by trying to contact the Electronic Frontier Foundation. Tankado stood poised to shock the world with his story of a secret machine capable of exposing computer users around the world to unthinkable government treachery. The NSA had had no choice but to stop him.

Tankado's capture and deportation, widely publicized among on-line newsgroups, had been an unfortunate public shaming. Against Strathmore's wishes, the NSA damage-control specialists – nervous that Tankado would try to convince people of TRANSLTR's existence – generated rumors that destroyed his credibility. Ensei Tankado was shunned by the global computer community – nobody trusted a cripple accused of spying, particularly when he was trying to buy his freedom with absurd allegations about a U.S. code-breaking machine.

The oddest thing of all was that Tankado seemed to understand; it was all part of the intelligence game. He appeared to harbor no anger, only resolve. As security escorted him away, Tankado spoke his final words to Strathmore with a chilling calm.

'We all have a right to keep secrets,' he'd said. 'Someday I'll see to it we can.'

CHAPTER 7

Susan's mind was racing – *Ensei Tankado wrote a program that creates unbreakable codes!* She could barely grasp the thought.

'Digital Fortress,' Strathmore said. 'That's what he's calling it. It's the ultimate counterintelligence weapon. If this program hits the market, every third grader with a modem will be able to send codes the NSA can't break. Our intelligence will be shot.'

But Susan's thoughts were far removed from the political implications of Digital Fortress. She was still struggling to comprehend its existence. She'd spent her life breaking codes, firmly denying the existence of the ultimate code. *Every code is breakable – the Bergofsky Principle!* She felt like an atheist coming face to face with God.

'If this code gets out,' she whispered, 'cryptography will become a dead science.'

Strathmore nodded. 'That's the least of our problems.'

'Can we pay Tankado off? I know he hates us, but can't we offer him a few million dollars? Convince him not to distribute?'

Strathmore laughed. 'A few million? Do you know what this thing is worth? Every government in the world will bid top dollar. Can you imagine telling the President that we're still cable-snooping the Iraqis but we can't read the intercepts anymore? This isn't just about the NSA, it's about the entire intelligence community. This facility provides support for everyone – the FBI, CIA, DEA; they'd all be flying blind. The drug cartels' shipments would become untraceable, major corporations could transfer money with no paper trail and leave the IRS out in the cold, terrorists could chat in total secrecy – it would be chaos.'

'The EFF will have field day,' Susan said, pale.

'The EFF doesn't have the first clue about what we do here,' Strathmore railed in disgust. 'If they knew how many terrorist attacks we've stopped because we can decrypt codes, they'd change their tune.'

Susan agreed, but she also knew the realities; the EFF would never know how important TRANSLTR was. TRANSLTR had helped foil dozens of attacks, but the information was highly classified and would never be released. The rationale behind the secrecy was simple: The government could not afford the mass hysteria caused by revealing the truth; no one knew how the public would react to the news that there had been two nuclear close calls by fundamentalist groups on U.S. soil in the last year.

Nuclear attack, however, was not the only threat. Only last month TRANSLTR had thwarted one of the most ingeniously conceived terrorist attacks the NSA had ever witnessed. An antigovernment organization had devised a plan, code-named Sherwood Forest. It targeted the New York Stock Exchange with the intention of 'redistributing the wealth.' Over the course of six days, members of the group placed twenty-seven nonexplosive flux pods in the buildings surrounding the Exchange. These devices, when detonated, create a powerful blast of magnetism. The simultaneous discharge of these carefully placed pods would create a magnetic field so powerful that all magnetic media in the Stock Exchange would be erased – computer hard drives, massive ROM storage banks, tape backups, and even floppy disks. All records of who owned what would disintegrate permanently.

Because pinpoint timing was necessary for simultaneous detonation of the devices, the flux pods were interconnected over Internet telephone lines. During the two-day countdown, the pods' internal clocks exchanged endless streams of encrypted synchronization data. The NSA intercepted the data-pulses as a network anomaly but ignored them as a seemingly harmless exchange of gibberish. But after TRANSLTR decrypted the data streams, analysts immediately recognized the sequence as a network-synchronized countdown. The pods were located and removed a full three hours before they were scheduled to go off.

Susan knew that without TRANSLTR the NSA was helpless against advanced electronic terrorism. She eyed the Run-Monitor. It still read over fifteen hours. Even if Tankado's file broke right now, the NSA was sunk. Crypto would be relegated to breaking less than two codes a day. Even at the present rate of 150 a day, there was still a backlog of files awaiting decryption.

'Tankado called me last month,' Strathmore said, interrupting Susan's thoughts.

Susan looked up. 'Tankado called *you*?'

He nodded. 'To warn me.'

'*Warn* you? He hates you.'

'He called to tell me he was perfecting an algorithm that wrote unbreakable codes. I didn't believe him.'

'But why would he tell you about it?' Susan demanded. 'Did he want you to buy it?'

'No. It was blackmail.'

Things suddenly began falling into place for Susan. 'Of course,' she said, amazed. 'He wanted you to clear his name.'

'No,' Strathmore frowned. 'Tankado wanted TRANSLTR.'

'TRANSLTR?'

'Yes. He ordered me to go public and tell the world we have TRANSLTR. He said if we admitted we can read public E-mail, he would destroy Digital Fortress.'

Susan looked doubtful.

Strathmore shrugged. 'Either way, it's too late now. He's posted a complimentary copy of Digital Fortress at his Internet site. Everyone in the world can download it.'

Susan went white. 'He *what!*'

'It's a publicity stunt. Nothing to worry about. The copy he posted is encrypted. People can download it, but nobody can open it. It's ingenious, really. The source code for Digital Fortress has been encrypted, locked shut.'

Susan looked amazed. 'Of course! So everybody can *have* a copy, but nobody can open it.'

'Exactly. Tankado's dangling a carrot.'

'Have you seen the algorithm?'

The commander looked puzzled. 'No, I told you it's encrypted.'

Susan looked equally puzzled. 'But we've got TRANSLTR; why not just decrypt it?' But when Susan saw Strathmore's face, she realized the rules had changed. 'Oh my God.' She gasped, suddenly understanding. 'Digital Fortress is encrypted with *itself*?'

Strathmore nodded. 'Bingo.'

Susan was amazed. The formula for Digital Fortress had been encrypted using Digital Fortress. Tankado had posted a priceless mathematical recipe, but the text of the recipe had been scrambled. And it had used *itself* to do the scrambling.

'It's Biggleman's Safe,' Susan stammered in awe.

Strathmore nodded. Biggleman's Safe was a hypothetical cryptography scenario in which a safe builder wrote blueprints for an unbreakable safe. He wanted to keep the blueprints a secret, so he built the safe and locked the blueprints inside. Tankado had done the same thing with Digital Fortress. He'd protected his blueprints by encrypting them with the formula outlined in his blueprints.

'And the file in TRANSLTR?' Susan asked.

'I downloaded it from Tankado's Internet site like everyone else. The NSA is now the proud owner of the Digital Fortress algorithm; we just can't open it.'

Susan marveled at Ensei Tankado's ingenuity. Without revealing his algorithm, he had proven to the NSA that it was unbreakable.

Strathmore handed her a newspaper clipping. It was a translated blurb from the *Nikkei Shimbun*, the Japanese equivalent of the *Wall Street Journal*, stating that the Japanese programmer Ensei Tankado had completed a mathematical formula he claimed could write unbreakable codes. The formula was called Digital Fortress and was available for review on the Internet. The programmer would be auctioning it off to the highest bidder. The column went on to say that although there was enormous interest in Japan, the few U.S. software companies who had heard about Digital Fortress deemed the claim preposterous, akin to turning lead to gold. The formula, they said, was a hoax and not to be taken seriously.

Susan looked up. 'An auction?'

Strathmore nodded. 'Right now every software company in Japan has downloaded an encrypted copy of Digital Fortress and is trying to crack it open. Every second they can't, the bidding price climbs.'

'That's absurd,' Susan shot back. 'All the new encrypted files are uncrackable unless you have TRANSLTR. Digital Fortress could be nothing more than a generic, public-domain algorithm, and none of these companies could break it.'

'But it's a brilliant marketing ploy,' Strathmore said. 'Think about it – all brands of bulletproof glass stop bullets, but if a company dares you to put a bullet through *theirs,* suddenly everybody's trying.'

'And the Japanese actually *believe* Digital Fortress is different? Better than everything else on the market?'

'Tankado may have been shunned, but everybody knows he's a genius. He's practically a cult icon among hackers. If Tankado says the algorithm's unbreakable, it's unbreakable.'

'But they're *all* unbreakable as far as the public knows!'

'Yes . . .' Strathmore mused. 'For the moment.'

'What's *that* supposed to mean?'

Strathmore sighed. 'Twenty years ago no one imagined we'd be breaking twelve-bit stream ciphers. But technology progressed. It always does. Software manufacturers assume at some point computers like TRANSLTR will exist. Technology is progressing exponentially, and eventually current public-key algorithms will lose their security. Better algorithms will be needed to stay ahead of tomorrow's computers.'

'And Digital Fortress is it?'

'Exactly. An algorithm that resists brute force will never become obsolete, no matter how powerful code-breaking computers get. It could become a world standard overnight.'

Susan pulled in a long breath. 'God help us,' she whispered. 'Can we make a bid?'

Strathmore shook his head. 'Tankado gave us our chance. He made that clear. It's too risky anyway; if we get caught, we're basically admitting that we're afraid of his algorithm. We'd be making a public confession not only that we have TRANSLTR but that Digital Fortress is immune.'

'What's the time frame?'

Strathmore frowned. 'Tankado planned to announce the highest bidder tomorrow at noon.'

Susan felt her stomach tighten. 'Then what?'

'The arrangement was that he would give the winner the pass-key.'

'The *pass-key*?'

'Part of the ploy. Everybody's already got the algorithm, so Tankado's auctioning off the pass-key that unlocks it.'

Susan groaned. 'Of course.' It was perfect. Clean and simple. Tankado had encrypted Digital Fortress, and he alone held the pass-key that unlocked it. She found it hard to fathom that somewhere out there – probably scrawled on a piece of paper in Tankado's pocket – there was a sixty-four-character pass-key that could end U.S. intelligence gathering forever.

Susan suddenly felt ill as she imagined the scenario.

Tankado would give his pass-key to the highest bidder, and that company would unlock the Digital Fortress file. Then it probably would embed the algorithm in a tamper-proof chip, and within five years every computer would come preloaded with a Digital Fortress chip. No commercial manufacturer had ever dreamed of creating an encryption chip because normal encryption algorithms eventually become obsolete. But Digital Fortress would never become obsolete; with a rotating cleartext function, no brute-force attack would ever find the right key. A new digital encryption standard. From now until forever. Every code unbreakable. Bankers, brokers, terrorists, spies. One world – one algorithm.

Anarchy.

'What are the options?' Susan probed. She was well aware that desperate times called for desperate measures, even at the NSA.

'We can't remove him, if that's what you're asking.'

It was exactly what Susan was asking. In her years with the NSA, Susan had heard rumors of its loose affiliations with the most skilled assassins in the world – hired hands brought in to do the intelligence community's dirty work.

Strathmore shook his head. 'Tankado's too smart to leave us an option like that.'

Susan felt oddly relieved. 'He's protected?'

'Not exactly.'

'In hiding?'

Strathmore shrugged. 'Tankado left Japan. He planned to check his bids by phone. But we know where he is.'

'And you don't plan to make a move?'

'No. He's got insurance. Tankado gave a copy of his

pass-key to an anonymous third party . . . in case anything happened.'

Of course, Susan marveled. *A guardian angel.* 'And I suppose if anything happens to Tankado, the mystery man sells the key?'

'Worse. Anyone hits Tankado, and his partner publishes.'

Susan looked confused. 'His partner *publishes* the key?'

Strathmore nodded. 'Posts it on the Internet, puts it in newspapers, on billboards. In effect, he *gives* it away.'

Susan's eyes widened. 'Free downloads?'

'Exactly. Tankado figured if he was dead, he wouldn't need the money – why not give the world a little farewell gift?'

There was a long silence. Susan breathed deeply as if to absorb the terrifying truth. *Ensei Tankado has created an unbreakable algorithm. He's holding us hostage.*

She suddenly stood. Her voice was determined. 'We must contact Tankado! There must be a way to convince him not to release! We can offer him triple the highest bid! We can clear his name! Anything!'

'Too late,' Strathmore said. He took a deep breath. 'Ensei Tankado was found dead this morning in Seville, Spain.'

CHAPTER 8

The twin-engine Learjet 60 touched down on the scorching runway. Outside the window, the barren landscape of Spain's lower Extremadura blurred and then slowed to a crawl.

'Mr Becker?' a voice crackled. 'We're here.'

Becker stood and stretched. After unlatching the overhead compartment, he remembered he had no luggage. There had been no time to pack. It didn't matter – he'd been promised the trip would be brief, in and out.

As the engines wound down, the plane eased out of the sun and into a deserted hangar opposite the main terminal. A moment later the pilot appeared and popped the hatch. Becker tossed back the last of his cranberry juice, put the glass on the wet bar, and scooped up his suit coat.

The pilot pulled a thick manila envelope from his flight suit. 'I was instructed to give you this.' He handed it to Becker. On the front, scrawled in blue pen, were the words:

KEEP THE CHANGE

Becker thumbed through the thick stack of reddish bills. 'What the . . . ?'

'Local currency,' the pilot offered flatly.

'I know what it is,' Becker stammered. 'But it's . . . it's too much. All I need is taxi fare.' Becker did the conversion in his head. 'What's in here is worth *thousands* of dollars!'

'I have my orders, sir.' The pilot turned and hoisted himself back into the cabin. The door slid shut behind him.

Becker stared up at the plane and then down at the money in his hand. After standing a moment in the empty hangar, he put the envelope in his breast pocket, shouldered his suit coat, and headed out across the runway. It was a strange beginning. Becker pushed it from his mind. With a little luck he'd be back in time to salvage some of his Stone Manor trip with Susan.

In and out, he told himself. *In and out.*

There was no way he could have known.

CHAPTER 9

Systems security technician Phil Chartrukian had only intended to be inside Crypto a minute – just long enough to grab some paperwork he'd forgotten the day before. But it was not to be.

After making his way across the Crypto floor and stepping into the Sys-Sec lab, he immediately knew something was not right. The computer terminal that perpetually monitored TRANSLTR's internal workings was unmanned and the monitor was switched off.

Chartrukian called out, 'Hello?'

There was no reply. The lab was spotless – as if no one had been there for hours.

Although Chartrukian was only twenty-three and relatively new to the Sys-Sec squad, he'd been trained well, and he knew the drill: There was *always* a Sys-Sec on duty in Crypto ... especially on Saturdays when no cryptographers were around.

He immediately powered up the monitor and turned to the duty board on the wall. 'Who's on watch?' he demanded aloud, scanning the list of names. According to the schedule, a young rookie named Seidenberg was supposed to have started a

66

double shift at midnight the night before. Chartrukian glanced around the empty lab and frowned. 'So where the hell is he?'

As he watched the monitor power up, Chartrukian wondered if Strathmore knew the Sys-Sec lab was unmanned. He had noticed on his way in that the curtains of Strathmore's workstation were closed, which meant the boss was in – not at all uncommon for a Saturday; Strathmore, despite requesting his cryptographers take Saturdays off, seemed to work 365 days a year.

There was one thing Chartrukian knew for certain – if Strathmore found out the Sys-Sec lab was unmanned, it would cost the absent rookie his job. Chartrukian eyed the phone, wondering if he should call the young techie and bail him out; there was an unspoken rule among Sys-Sec that they would watch each other's backs. In Crypto, Sys-Secs were second-class citizens, constantly at odds with the lords of the manor. It was no secret that the cryptographers ruled this multibillion-dollar roost; Sys-Secs were tolerated only because they kept the toys running smoothly.

Chartrukian made his decision. He grabbed the phone. But the receiver never reached his ear. He stopped short, his eyes transfixed on the monitor now coming into focus before him. As if in slow motion, he set down the phone and stared in open-mouthed wonder.

In eight months as a Sys-Sec, Phil Chartrukian had never seen TRANSLTR's Run-Monitor post anything other than a double zero in the *hours* field. Today was a first.

TIME ELAPSED: 15:17:21

67

'Fifteen hours and seventeen minutes?' he choked. 'Impossible!'

He rebooted the screen, praying it hadn't refreshed properly. But when the monitor came back to life, it looked the same.

Chartrukian felt a chill. Crypto's Sys-Secs had only one responsibility: Keep TRANSLTR 'clean' – virus free.

Chartrukian knew that a fifteen-hour run could only mean one thing – infection. An impure file had gotten inside TRANSLTR and was corrupting the programming. Instantly his training kicked in; it no longer mattered that the Sys-Sec lab had been unmanned or the monitors switched off. He focused on the matter at hand – TRANSLTR. He immediately called up a log of all the files that had entered TRANSLTR in the last forty-eight hours. He began scanning the list.

Did an infected file get through? he wondered. *Could the security filters have missed something?*

As a precaution, every file entering TRANSLTR had to pass through what was known as Gauntlet – a series of powerful circuit-level gateways, packet filters, and disinfectant programs that scanned inbound files for computer viruses and potentially dangerous subroutines. Files containing programming 'unknown' to Gauntlet were immediately rejected. They had to be checked by hand. Occasionally Gauntlet rejected entirely harmless files on the basis that they contained programming the filters had never seen before. In that case, the Sys-Secs did a scrupulous manual inspection, and only then, on confirmation that the file was clean, did they bypass Gauntlet's filters and send the file into TRANSLTR.

Computer viruses were as varied as bacterial viruses. Like their physiological counterparts, computer viruses had one goal – to attach themselves to a host system and replicate. In this case, the host was TRANSLTR.

Chartrukian was amazed the NSA hadn't had problems with viruses before. Gauntlet was a potent sentry, but still, the NSA was a bottom feeder, sucking in massive amounts of digital information from systems all over the world. Snooping data was a lot like having indiscriminate sex – protection or no protection, sooner or later you caught something.

Chartrukian finished examining the file list before him. He was now more puzzled than before. Every file checked out. Gauntlet had seen nothing out of the ordinary, which meant the file in TRANSLTR was totally clean.

'So what the hell's taking so long?' he demanded of the empty room. Chartrukian felt himself break a sweat. He wondered if he should go disturb Strathmore with the news.

'A virus probe,' Chartrukian said firmly, trying to calm himself down. 'I should run a virus probe.'

Chartrukian knew that a virus probe would be the first thing Strathmore would request anyway. Glancing out at the deserted Crypto floor, Chartrukian made his decision. He loaded the viral probe software and launched it. The run would take about fifteen minutes.

'Come back clean,' he whispered. 'Squeaky clean. Tell Daddy it's nothing.'

But Chartrukian sensed it was *not* 'nothing.' Instinct told him something very unusual was going on inside the great decoding beast.

CHAPTER 10

'Ensei Tankado is dead?' Susan felt a wave of nausea. 'You killed him? I thought you said—'

'We didn't touch him,' Strathmore assured her. 'He died of a heart attack. COMINT phoned early this morning. Their computer flagged Tankado's name in a Seville police log through Interpol.'

'Heart attack?' Susan looked doubtful. 'He was thirty years old.'

'Thirty-two,' Strathmore corrected. 'He had a congenital heart defect.'

'I'd never heard that.'

'Turned up in his NSA physical. Not something he bragged about.'

Susan was having trouble accepting the serendipity of the timing. 'A defective heart could kill him – just like that?' It seemed too convenient.

Strathmore shrugged. 'Weak heart ... combine it with the heat of Spain. Throw in the stress of blackmailing the NSA . . .'

Susan was silent a moment. Even considering the conditions, she felt a pang of loss at the passing of such a brilliant fellow cryptographer. Strathmore's gravelly voice interrupted her thoughts.

'The only silver lining on this whole fiasco is that Tankado was traveling alone. Chances are good his partner doesn't know yet he's dead. The Spanish authorities said they'd contain the information for as long as possible. We only got the call because COMINT was on the ball.' Strathmore eyed Susan closely. 'I've got to find the partner before he finds out Tankado's dead. That's why I called you in. I need your help.'

Susan was confused. It seemed to her that Ensei Tankado's timely demise had solved their entire problem. 'Commander,' she argued, 'if the authorities are saying he died of a heart attack, we're off the hook; his partner will know the NSA is not responsible.'

'Not responsible?' Strathmore's eyes widened in disbelief. 'Somebody blackmails the NSA and turns up dead a few days later – and we're *not responsible*? I'd bet big money Tankado's mystery friend won't see it that way. Whatever happened, we look guilty as hell. It could easily have been poison, a rigged autopsy, any number of things.' Strathmore paused. 'What was your first reaction when I told you Tankado was dead?'

She frowned. 'I thought the NSA had killed him.'

'Exactly. If the NSA can put five Rhyolite satellites in geosynchronous orbit over the Mideast, I think it's safe to assume we have the resources to pay off a few Spanish policemen.' The commander had made his point.

Susan exhaled. *Ensei Tankado is dead. The NSA will be blamed.* 'Can we find his partner in time?'

'I think so. We've got a good lead. Tankado made numerous public announcements that he was working

71

with a partner. I think he hoped it would discourage software firms from doing him any harm or trying to steal his key. He threatened that if there was any foul play, his partner would publish the key, and all firms would suddenly find themselves in competition with free software.'

'Clever.' Susan nodded.

Strathmore went on. 'A few times, in public, Tankado referred to his partner by name. He called him North Dakota.'

'North Dakota? Obviously an alias of some sort.'

'Yes, but as a precaution I ran an Internet inquiry using North Dakota as a search string. I didn't think I'd find anything, but I turned up an E-mail account.' Strathmore paused. 'Of course I assumed it wasn't the North Dakota we were looking for, but I searched the account just to be sure. Imagine my shock when I found the account was full of E-mail from Ensei Tankado.' Strathmore raised his eyebrows. 'And the messages were full of references to Digital Fortress and Tankado's plans to blackmail the NSA.'

Susan gave Strathmore a skeptical look. She was amazed the commander was letting himself be played with so easily. 'Commander,' she argued, 'Tankado knows full well the NSA can snoop E-mail from the Internet; he would *never* use E-mail to send secret information. It's a trap. Ensei Tankado *gave* you North Dakota. He *knew* you'd run a search. Whatever information he's sending, he *wanted* you to find – it's a false trail.'

'Good instinct,' Strathmore fired back, 'except for a couple of things. I couldn't find anything under North Dakota, so I tweaked the search string. The account I found was under a variation – NDAKOTA.'

Susan shook her head. 'Running permutations is standard procedure. Tankado knew you'd try variations until you hit something. NDAKOTA's far too easy an alteration.'

'Perhaps,' Strathmore said, scribbling words on a piece of paper and handing it to Susan. 'But look at this.'

Susan read the paper. She suddenly understood the commander's thinking. On the paper was North Dakota's E-mail address.

NDAKOTA@ARA.ANON.ORG

It was the letters ARA in the address that had caught Susan's eye. ARA stood for American Remailers Anonymous, a well-known anonymous server.

Anonymous servers were popular among Internet users who wanted to keep their identities secret. For a fee, these companies protected an E-mailer's privacy by acting as a middleman for electronic mail. It was like having a numbered post office box – a user could send and receive mail without ever revealing his true address or name. The company received E-mail addressed to aliases and then forwarded it to the client's real account. The remailing company was bound by contract never to reveal the identity or location of its real users.

'It's not proof,' Strathmore said. 'But it's pretty suspicious.'

Susan nodded, suddenly more convinced. 'So you're saying Tankado didn't care if anybody searched for North Dakota because his identity and location are protected by ARA.'

'Exactly.'

Susan schemed for a moment. 'ARA services mainly U.S. accounts. You think North Dakota might be over here somewhere?'

Strathmore shrugged. 'Could be. With an American partner, Tankado could keep the two pass-keys separated geographically. Might be a smart move.'

Susan considered it. She doubted Tankado would have shared his pass-key with anyone except a very close friend, and as she recalled, Ensei Tankado didn't have many friends in the States.

'North Dakota,' she mused, her cryptological mind mulling over the possible meanings of the alias. 'What does his E-mail to Tankado sound like?'

'No idea. COMINT only caught Tankado's outbound. At this point all we have on North Dakota is an anonymous address.'

Susan thought a minute. 'Any chance it's a decoy?'

Strathmore raised an eyebrow. 'How so?'

'Tankado could be sending bogus E-mail to a dead account in hopes we'd snoop it. We'd think he's protected, and he'd never have to risk sharing his pass-key. He could be working alone.'

Strathmore chuckled, impressed. 'Tricky idea, except for one thing. He's not using any of his usual home or business Internet accounts. He's been dropping by Doshisha University and logging on to their mainframe. Apparently he's got an account there that he's managed to keep secret. It's a very well-hidden account, and I found it only by chance.' Strathmore paused. 'So . . . if Tankado wanted us to snoop his mail, why would he use a secret account?'

Susan contemplated the question. 'Maybe he used a secret account so you wouldn't suspect a ploy? Maybe

Tankado hid the account just deep enough that you'd stumble on to it and think you got lucky. It gives his E-mail credibility.'

Strathmore chuckled. 'You should have been a field agent. The idea's a good one. Unfortunately, every letter Tankado sends gets a response. Tankado writes, his partner responds.'

Susan frowned. 'Fair enough. So, you're saying North Dakota's for real.'

'Afraid so. And we've got to find him. And *quietly*. If he catches wind that we're on to him, it's all over.'

Susan now knew exactly why Strathmore had called her in. 'Let me guess,' she said. 'You want me to snoop ARA's secure database and find North Dakota's real identity?'

Strathmore gave her a tight smile. 'Ms Fletcher, you read my mind.'

When it came to discreet Internet searches, Susan Fletcher was the woman for the job. A year ago, a senior White House official had been receiving E-mail threats from someone with an anonymous E-mail address. The NSA had been asked to locate the individual. Although the NSA had the clout to demand the remailing company reveal the user's identity, it opted for a more subtle method – a 'tracer.'

Susan had created, in effect, a directional beacon disguised as a piece of E-mail. She could send it to the user's phony address, and the remailing company, performing the duty for which it had been contracted, would forward it to the user's real address. Once there, the program would record its Internet location and send word back to the NSA. Then the program would disintegrate without a trace. From that day on, as far as the NSA was concerned, anonymous remailers were nothing more than a minor annoyance.

'Can you find him?' Strathmore asked.

'Sure. Why did you wait so long to call me?'

'Actually' – he frowned – 'I hadn't planned on calling you at all. I didn't want anyone else in the loop. I tried to send a copy of your tracer myself, but you wrote the damn thing in one of those new hybrid languages; I couldn't get it to work. It kept returning nonsensical data. I finally had to bite the bullet and bring you in.'

Susan chuckled. Strathmore was a brilliant cryptographic programmer, but his repertoire was limited primarily to algorithmic work; the nuts and bolts of less lofty 'secular' programming often escaped him. What was more, Susan had written her tracer in a new, crossbreed programming language called LIMBO; it was understandable that Strathmore had encountered problems. 'I'll take care of it.' She smiled, turning to leave. 'I'll be at my terminal.'

'Any idea on a time frame?'

Susan paused. 'Well . . . it depends on how efficiently ARA forwards their mail. If he's here in the States and uses something like AOL or Compuserve, I'll snoop his credit card and get a billing address within the hour. If he's with a university or corporation, it'll take a little longer.' She smiled uneasily. 'After that, the rest is up to you.'

Susan knew that 'the rest' would be an NSA strike team, cutting power to the guy's house and crashing through his windows with stun guns. The team would probably think it was on a drug bust. Strathmore would undoubtedly stride through the rubble himself and locate the sixty-four-character pass-key. Then he would destroy it. Digital Fortress would languish forever on the Internet, locked for all eternity.

'Send the tracer carefully,' Strathmore urged. 'If North Dakota sees we're on to him, he'll panic, and I'll never get a team there before he disappears with the key.'

'Hit and run,' she assured. 'The moment this thing finds his account, it'll dissolve. He'll never know we were there.'

The commander nodded tiredly. 'Thanks.'

Susan gave him a soft smile. She was always amazed how even in the face of disaster Strathmore could muster a quiet calm. She was convinced it was this ability that had defined his career and lifted him to the upper echelons of power.

As Susan headed for the door, she took a long look down at TRANSLTR. The existence of an unbreakable algorithm was a concept she was still struggling to grasp. She prayed they'd find North Dakota in time.

'Make it quick,' Strathmore called, 'and you'll be in the Smoky Mountains by nightfall.'

Susan froze in her tracks. She knew she had never mentioned her trip to Strathmore. She wheeled. *Is the NSA tapping my phone?*

Strathmore smiled guiltily. 'David told me about your trip this morning. He said you'd be pretty ticked about postponing it.'

Susan was lost. 'You talked to David this *morning?*'

'Of course.' Strathmore seemed puzzled by Susan's reaction. 'I had to brief him.'

'Brief him?' she demanded. 'For *what?*'

'For his trip. I sent David to Spain.'

CHAPTER 11

Spain. *I sent David to Spain.* The commander's words stung.

'David's in Spain?' Susan was incredulous. 'You sent him to Spain?' Her tone turned angry. *'Why?'*

Strathmore looked dumbfounded. He was apparently not accustomed to being yelled at, even by his head cryptographer. He gave Susan a confused look. She was flexed like a mother tiger defending her cub.

'Susan,' he said. 'You spoke to him, didn't you? David *did* explain?'

She was too shocked to speak. *Spain? That's why David postponed our Stone Manor trip?*

'I sent a car for him this morning. He said he was going to call you before he left. I'm sorry. I thought—'

'Why would you send David to Spain?'

Strathmore paused and gave her an obvious look. 'To get the other pass-key.'

'What other pass-key?'

'Tankado's copy.'

Susan was lost. 'What are you talking about?'

Strathmore sighed. 'Tankado surely would have

had a copy of the pass-key on him when he died. I sure as hell didn't want it floating around the Seville morgue.'

'So you sent David Becker?' Susan was beyond shock. Nothing was making sense. 'David doesn't even work for you!'

Strathmore looked startled. No one ever spoke to the deputy director of the NSA that way. 'Susan,' he said, keeping his cool, 'that's the point. I needed—'

The tiger lashed out. 'You've got twenty thousand employees at your command! What gives you the right to send my fiancé?'

'I needed a civilian courier, someone totally removed from government. If I went through regular channels and someone caught wind—'

'And David Becker is the only civilian you know?'

'No! David Becker is *not* the only civilian I know! But at six this morning, things were happening quickly! David speaks the language, he's smart, I trust him, and I thought I'd do him a favor!'

'A favor?' Susan sputtered. 'Sending him to Spain is a favor?'

'Yes! I'm paying him ten thousand for one day's work. He'll pick up Tankado's belongings, and he'll fly home. That's a favor!'

Susan fell silent. She understood. It was all about money.

Her thoughts wheeled back five months to the night the president of Georgetown University had offered David a promotion to the language department chair. The president had warned him that his teaching hours would be cut back and that there would be increased paperwork, but there was also a substantial raise in salary. Susan had wanted to cry out *David, don't do it!*

You'll be miserable. We have plenty of money – who cares which one of us earns it? But it was not her place. In the end, she stood by his decision to accept. As they fell asleep that night, Susan tried to be happy for him, but something inside kept telling her it would be a disaster. She'd been right – but she'd never counted on being *so* right.

'You paid him ten thousand dollars?' she demanded. 'That's a dirty trick!'

Strathmore was fuming now. 'Trick? It wasn't any goddamn trick! I didn't even tell him about the money. I asked him as a personal favor. He agreed to go.'

'Of course he agreed! You're my boss! You're the deputy director of the NSA! He couldn't say no!'

'You're right,' Strathmore snapped. 'Which is why I called him. I didn't have the luxury of—'

'Does the director know you sent a civilian?'

'Susan,' Strathmore said, his patience obviously wearing thin, 'the director is not involved. He knows nothing about this.'

Susan stared at Strathmore in disbelief. It was as if she no longer knew the man she was talking to. He had sent her fiancé – a teacher – on an NSA mission and then failed to notify the director about the biggest crisis in the history of the organization.

'Leland Fontaine *hasn't* been notified?'

Strathmore had reached the end of his rope. He exploded. 'Susan, now listen here! I called you in here because I need an ally, not an inquiry! I've had one hell of a morning. I downloaded Tankado's file last night and sat here by the output printer for hours praying TRANSLTR could break it. At dawn I swallowed my pride and dialed the director – and let me tell you, *that* was a conversation I was *really* looking forward to. Good morning, sir. I'm sorry to wake you. Why am I calling? I just found out TRANSLTR is obsolete. It's because of an algorithm my entire top-dollar Crypto team couldn't come close to writing!' Strathmore slammed his fist on the desk.

Susan stood frozen. She didn't make a sound. In ten years, she had seen Strathmore lose his cool only a handful of times, and never once with her.

Ten seconds later neither one of them had spoken. Finally Strathmore sat back down, and Susan could hear his breathing slowing to normal. When he finally spoke, his voice was eerily calm and controlled.

'Unfortunately,' Strathmore said quietly, 'it turns out the director is in South America meeting with the President of Colombia. Because there's absolutely nothing he could do from down there, I had two options – request he cut his meeting short and return, or handle this myself.' There was a long silence. Strathmore finally looked up, and his tired eyes met Susan's. His expression softened immediately. 'Susan, I'm sorry. I'm exhausted. This is a nightmare come true. I know you're upset about David. I didn't mean for you to find out this way. I thought you knew.'

Susan felt a wave of guilt. 'I overreacted. I'm sorry. David is a good choice.'

Strathmore nodded absently. 'He'll be back tonight.'

Susan thought about everything the commander was going through – the pressure of overseeing TRANSLTR, the endless hours and meetings. It was rumored his wife of thirty years was leaving him. Then on top of it, there was Digital Fortress – the biggest intelligence threat in the history of the NSA, and the poor guy was flying solo. No wonder he looked about to crack.

'Considering the circumstances,' Susan said, 'I think you should probably call the director.'

Strathmore shook his head, a bead of sweat dripping on his desk. 'I'm not about to compromise the director's safety or risk a leak by contacting him about a major crisis he can do nothing about.'

Susan knew he was right. Even in moments like these, Strathmore was clear-headed. 'Have you considered calling the President?'

Strathmore nodded. 'Yes. I've decided against it.'

Susan had figured as much. Senior NSA officials had the right to handle verifiable intelligence emergencies without executive knowledge. The NSA was the only U.S. intelligence organization that enjoyed total immunity from federal accountability of any sort. Strathmore often availed himself of this right; he preferred to work his magic in isolation.

'Commander,' she argued, 'this is too big to be handled alone. You've got to let somebody else in on it.'

'Susan, the existence of Digital Fortress has major implications for the future of this organization. I have no intention of informing the President behind the director's back. We have a crisis, and I'm handling it.' He eyed her thoughtfully. 'I *am* the deputy director of operations.' A weary smile crept across his face. 'And besides, I'm not alone. I've got Susan Fletcher on my team.'

In that instant, Susan realized what she respected so much about Trevor Strathmore. For ten years, through thick and thin, he had always led the way for her. Steadfast. Unwavering. It was his dedication that amazed her – his unshakable allegiance to his principles, his country, and his ideals. Come what may, Commander Trevor Strathmore was a guiding light in a world of impossible decisions.

'You *are* on my team, aren't you?' he asked.

Susan smiled. 'Yes, sir, I am. One hundred percent.'

'Good. Now can we get back to work?'

CHAPTER 12

David Becker had been to funerals and seen dead bodies before, but there was something particularly unnerving about this one. It was not an immaculately groomed corpse resting in a silk-lined coffin. This body had been stripped naked and dumped unceremoniously on an aluminum table. The eyes had not yet found their vacant, lifeless gaze. Instead they were twisted upward toward the ceiling in an eerie freeze-frame of terror and regret.

'Dónde están sus efectos?' Becker asked in fluent Castillian Spanish. 'Where are his belongings?'

'Allí,' replied the yellow-toothed lieutenant. He pointed to a counter of clothing and other personal items.

'Es todo? Is that all?'

'Sí.'

Becker asked for a cardboard box. The lieutenant hurried off to find one.

It was Saturday evening, and the Seville morgue was technically closed. The young lieutenant had let Becker in under direct orders from the head of the Seville Guardia – it seemed the visiting American had powerful friends.

Becker eyed the pile of clothes. There was a passport, wallet, and glasses stuffed in one of the shoes. There was also a small duffel the Guardia had taken from the man's hotel. Becker's directions were clear: Touch nothing. Read nothing. Just bring it all back. Everything. Don't miss anything.

Becker surveyed the pile and frowned. *What could the NSA possibly want with this junk?*

The lieutenant returned with a small box, and Becker began putting the clothes inside.

The officer poked at the cadaver's leg. 'Quien es? Who is he?'

'No idea.'

'Looks Chinese.'

Japanese, Becker thought.

'Poor bastard. Heart attack, huh?'

Becker nodded absently. 'That's what they told me.'

The lieutenant sighed and shook his head sympathetically. 'The Seville sun can be cruel. Be careful out there tomorrow.'

'Thanks,' Becker said. 'But I'm headed home.'

The officer looked shocked. 'You just got here!'

'I know, but the guy paying my airfare is waiting for these items.'

The lieutenant looked offended in the way only a Spaniard can be offended. 'You mean you're not going to *experience* Seville?'

'I was here years ago. Beautiful city. I'd love to stay.'

'So you've seen La Giralda?'

Becker nodded. He'd never actually climbed the ancient Moorish tower, but he'd seen it.

'How about the Alcazar?'

Becker nodded again, remembering the night he'd

heard Paco de Lucia play guitar in the courtyard – flamenco under the stars in a fifteenth-century fortress. He wished he'd known Susan back then.

'And of course there's Christopher Columbus.' The officer beamed. 'He's buried in our cathedral.'

Becker looked up. 'Really? I thought Columbus was buried in the Dominican Republic.'

'Hell no! Who starts these rumors? Columbus's body is here in Spain! I thought you said you went to college.'

Becker shrugged. 'I must have missed that day.'

'The Spanish church is very proud to own his relics.'

The Spanish church. Becker knew there was only one church in Spain – the Roman Catholic church. Catholicism was bigger here than in Vatican City.

'We don't, of course, have his entire body,' the lieutenant added. 'Solo el escroto.'

Becker stopped packing and stared at the lieutenant. *Solo el escroto?* He fought off a grin. 'Just his scrotum?'

The officer nodded proudly. 'Yes. When the church obtains the remains of a great man, they saint him and spread the relics to different cathedrals so everyone can enjoy their splendor.'

'And you got the . . .' Becker stifled a laugh.

'Oye! It's a pretty important part!' the officer defended. 'It's not like we got a rib or a knuckle like those churches in Galicia! You should really stay and see it.'

Becker nodded politely. 'Maybe I'll drop in on my way out of town.'

'Mala suerte.' The officer sighed. 'Bad luck. The cathedral's closed till sunrise mass.'

'Another time then.' Becker smiled, hoisting the box. 'I should probably get going. My flight's waiting.' He made a final glance around the room.

'You want a ride to the airport?' the officer asked. 'I've got a Moto Guzzi out front.'

'No thanks. I'll catch a cab.' Becker had driven a motorcycle once in college and nearly killed himself on it. He had no intention of getting on one again, regardless of who was driving.

'Whatever you say,' the officer said, heading for the door. 'I'll get the lights.'

Becker tucked the box under his arm. *Have I got everything?* He took a last look at the body on the table. The figure was stark naked, faceup under fluorescent lights, clearly hiding nothing. Becker found his eyes drawn again to the strangely deformed hands. He gazed a minute, focusing more intently.

The officer killed the lights, and the room went dark.

'Hold on,' Becker said. 'Turn those back on.'

The lights flickered back on.

Becker set his box on the floor and walked over to the corpse. He leaned down and squinted at the man's left hand.

The officer followed Becker's gaze. 'Pretty ugly, huh?'

But the deformity was not what had caught Becker's eye. He'd seen something else. He turned to the officer. 'You're sure everything's in this box?'

The officer nodded. 'Yeah. That's it.'

Becker stood for a moment with his hands on his hips. Then he picked up the box, carried it back over to the counter, and dumped it out. Carefully, piece by piece, he shook out the clothing. Then he emptied the shoes and tapped them as if trying to remove a pebble. After going over everything a second time, he stepped back and frowned.

'Problem?' asked the lieutenant.

'Yeah,' Becker said. 'We're missing something.'

CHAPTER 13

Tokugen Numataka stood in his plush, penthouse office and gazed out at the Tokyo skyline. His employees and competitors knew him as *akuta same* – the deadly shark. For three decades he'd outguessed, outbid, and outadvertised all the Japanese competition; now he was on the brink of becoming a giant in the world market as well.

He was about to close the biggest deal of his life – a deal that would make his Numatech Corp. the Microsoft of the future. His blood was alive with the cool rush of adrenaline. Business was war – and war was exciting.

Although Tokugen Numataka had been suspicious when the call had come three days ago, he now knew the truth. He was blessed with *myouri* – good fortune. The gods had chosen him.

'I have a copy of the Digital Fortress pass-key,' the American accent had said. 'Would you like to buy it?'

Numataka had almost laughed aloud. He knew it was a ploy. Numatech Corp. had bid generously for Ensei Tankado's new algorithm, and now one of

89

Numatech's competitors was playing games, trying to find out the amount of the bid.

'You have the pass-key?' Numataka feigned interest.

'I do. My name is North Dakota.'

Numataka stifled a laugh. Everyone knew about North Dakota. Tankado had told the press about his secret partner. It had been a wise move on Tankado's part to have a partner; even in Japan, business practices had become dishonorable. Ensei Tankado was not safe. But one false move by an overeager firm, and the pass-key would be published; every software firm on the market would suffer.

Numataka took a long pull on his Umami cigar and played along with the caller's pathetic charade. 'So you're selling your pass-key? Interesting. How does Ensei Tankado feel about this?'

'I have no allegiance to Mr Tankado. Mr Tankado was foolish to trust me. The pass-key is worth hundreds of times what he is paying me to handle it for him.'

'I'm sorry,' Numataka said. 'Your pass-key alone is worth nothing to me. When Tankado finds out what you've done, he will simply publish his copy, and the market will be flooded.'

'You will receive both pass-keys,' the voice said. 'Mr Tankado's *and* mine.'

Numataka covered the receiver and laughed aloud. He couldn't help asking, 'How much are you asking for both keys?'

'Twenty million U.S. dollars.'

Twenty million was almost exactly what Numataka had bid. 'Twenty million?' He gasped in mock horror. 'That's outrageous!'

'I've seen the algorithm. I assure you it's well worth it.'

No shit, thought Numataka. *It's worth ten times that.* 'Unfortunately,' he said, tiring of the game, 'we both know Mr Tankado would never stand for this. Think of the legal repercussions.'

The caller paused ominously. 'What if Mr Tankado were no longer a factor?'

Numataka wanted to laugh, but he noted an odd determination in the voice. 'If Tankado were no longer a factor?' Numataka considered it. 'Then you and I would have a deal.'

'I'll be in touch,' the voice said. The line went dead.

CHAPTER 14

Becker gazed down at the cadaver. Even hours after death, the Asian's face radiated with a pinkish glow of a recent sunburn. The rest of him was a pale yellow – all except the small area of purplish bruising directly over his heart.

Probably from the CPR, Becker mused. *Too bad it didn't work.*

He went back to studying the cadaver's hands. They were like nothing Becker had ever seen. Each hand had only three digits, and they were twisted and askew. The disfigurement, however, was not what Becker was looking at.

'Well, I'll be.' The lieutenant grunted from across the room. 'He's Japanese, not Chinese.'

Becker looked up. The officer was thumbing through the dead man's passport. 'I'd rather you didn't look at that,' Becker requested. *Touch nothing. Read nothing.*

'Ensei Tankado . . . born January—'

'Please,' Becker said politely. 'Put it back.'

The officer stared at the passport a moment longer and then tossed it back on the pile. 'This guy's got a class-3 visa. He could have stayed here for years.'

Becker poked at the victim's hand with a pen. 'Maybe he lived here.'

'Nope. Date of entry was last week.'

'Maybe he was *moving* here,' Becker offered curtly.

'Yeah, maybe. Crummy first week. Sunstroke and a heart attack. Poor bastard.'

Becker ignored the officer and studied the hand. 'You're positive he wasn't wearing any jewelry when he died?'

The officer looked up, startled. 'Jewelry?'

'Yeah. Take a look at this.'

The officer crossed the room.

The skin on Tankado's left hand showed traces of sunburn, everywhere except a narrow band of flesh around the smallest finger.

Becker pointed to the strip of pale flesh. 'See how this isn't sunburned here? Looks like he was wearing a ring.'

The officer seemed surprised. 'A *ring*?' His voice sounded suddenly perplexed. He studied the corpse's finger. Then he flushed sheepishly. 'My God.' He chuckled. 'The story was *true*?'

Becker had a sudden sinking feeling. 'I beg your pardon?'

The officer shook his head in disbelief. 'I would have mentioned it before . . . but I thought the guy was nuts.'

Becker was not smiling. 'What guy?'

'The guy who phoned in the emergency. Some Canadian tourist. Kept talking about a ring. Babbling in the worst damn Spanish I ever heard.'

'He said Mr Tankado was wearing a *ring*?'

93

The officer nodded. He pulled out a Ducado ciga-rette, eyed the NO FUMAR sign, and lit up anyway. 'Guess I should have said something, but the guy sounded totally loco.'

Becker frowned. Strathmore's words echoed in his ears. *I want everything Ensei Tankado had with him. Everything. Leave nothing. Not even a tiny scrap of paper.*

'Where is the ring now?' Becker asked.

The officer took a puff. 'Long story.'

Something told Becker this was *not* good news. 'Tell me anyway.'

CHAPTER 15

Susan Fletcher sat at her computer terminal inside Node 3. Node 3 was the cryptographers' private, soundproofed chamber just off the main floor. A two-inch sheet of curved one-way glass gave the cryptographers a panorama of the Crypto floor while prohibiting anyone else from seeing inside.

At the back of the expansive Node 3 chamber, twelve terminals sat in a perfect circle. The annular arrangement was intended to encourage intellectual exchange between cryptographers, to remind them they were part of a larger team – something like a code-breaker's Knights of the Round Table. Ironically, secrets were frowned on inside Node 3.

Nicknamed the Playpen, Node 3 had none of the sterile feel of the rest of Crypto. It was designed to feel like home – plush carpets, high-tech sound system, fully stocked fridge, kitchenette, a Nerf basketball hoop. The NSA had a philosophy about Crypto: Don't drop a couple billion bucks into a code-breaking computer without enticing the best of the best to stick around and use it.

Susan slipped out of her Salvatore Ferragamo flats

and dug her stockinged toes into the thick pile carpet. Well-paid government employees were encouraged to refrain from lavish displays of personal wealth. It was usually no problem for Susan – she was perfectly happy with her modest duplex, Volvo sedan, and conservative wardrobe. But shoes were another matter. Even when Susan was in college, she'd budgeted for the best.

You can't jump for the stars if your feet hurt, her aunt had once told her. *And when you get where you're going, you darn well better look great!*

Susan allowed herself a luxurious stretch and then settled down to business. She pulled up her tracer and prepared to configure it. She glanced at the E-mail address Strathmore had given her.

NDAKOTA@ARA.ANON.ORG

The man calling himself North Dakota had an anonymous account, but Susan knew it would not remain anonymous for long. The tracer would pass through ARA, get forwarded to North Dakota, and then send information back containing the man's real Internet address.

If all went well, it would locate North Dakota soon, and Strathmore could confiscate the pass-key. That would leave only David. When he found Tankado's copy, both pass-keys could be destroyed; Tankado's little time bomb would be harmless, a deadly explosive without a detonator.

Susan double-checked the address on the sheet in front of her and entered the information in the correct datafield. She chuckled that Strathmore had encountered difficulty sending the tracer himself. Apparently he'd sent it twice, both times receiving Tankado's address back rather than North Dakota's. It was a simple mistake, Susan thought; Strathmore had probably interchanged the datafields, and the tracer had searched for the wrong account.

Susan finished configuring her tracer and queued it for release. Then she hit return. The computer beeped once.

TRACER SENT

Now came the waiting game.

Susan exhaled. She felt guilty for having been hard on the commander. If there was anyone qualified to handle this threat single-handed, it was Trevor Strathmore. He had an uncanny way of getting the best of all those who challenged him.

Six months ago, when the EFF broke a story that an NSA submarine was snooping underwater telephone cables, Strathmore calmly leaked a conflicting story that the submarine was actually illegally burying toxic waste. The EFF and the oceanic environmentalists spent so much time bickering over which version was true, the media eventually tired of the story and moved on.

Every move Strathmore made was meticulously planned. He depended heavily on his computer when devising and revising his plans. Like many NSA employees, Strathmore used NSA-developed software called BrainStorm – a risk-free way to carry out 'what-if' scenarios in the safety of a computer.

BrainStorm was an artificial intelligence experiment described by its developers as a Cause & Effect Simulator. It originally had been intended for use in political campaigns as a way to create real-time models of a given 'political environment.' Fed by enormous amounts of data, the program created a relationary web – a hypothesized model of interaction between political variables, including current prominent figures, their staffs, their personal ties to each other, hot issues, individuals' motivations weighted by variables like sex, ethnicity, money, and power. The user could then enter any hypothetical event and BrainStorm would predict the event's effect on 'the environment.'

Commander Strathmore worked religiously with BrainStorm – not for political purposes, but as a TFM device; Time-Line, Flowchart, & Mapping software was a powerful tool for outlining complex strategies and predicting weaknesses. Susan suspected there were schemes hidden in Strathmore's computer that someday would change the world.

Yes, Susan thought, *I was too hard on him.*

Her thoughts were jarred by the hiss of the Node 3 doors.

Strathmore burst in. 'Susan,' he said. 'David just called. There's been a setback.'

CHAPTER 16

'A ring?' Susan looked doubtful. 'Tankado's missing a ring?'

'Yes. We're lucky David caught it. It was a real heads-up play.'

'But you're after a pass-key, not jewelry.'

'I know,' Strathmore said, 'but I think they might be one and the same.'

Susan looked lost.

'It's a long story.'

She motioned to the tracer on her screen. 'I'm not going anywhere.'

Strathmore sighed heavily and began pacing. 'Apparently, there were witnesses to Tankado's death. According to the officer at the morgue, a Canadian tourist called the Guardia this morning in a panic – he said a Japanese man was having a heart attack in the park. When the officer arrived, he found Tankado dead and the Canadian there with him, so he radioed the paramedics. While the paramedics took Tankado's body to the morgue, the officer tried to get the Canadian to tell him what happened. All the old guy did was babble about some ring Tankado had given away right before he died.'

Susan eyed him skeptically. 'Tankado *gave away* a ring?'

'Yeah. Apparently he forced it in this old guy's face – like he was begging him to take it. Sounds like the old guy got a close look at it.' Strathmore stopped pacing and turned. 'He said the ring was engraved – with some sort of lettering.'

'Lettering?'

'Yes, and according to him, it wasn't English.' Strathmore raised his eyebrows expectantly.

'Japanese?'

Strathmore shook his head. 'My first thought too. But get this – the Canadian complained that the letters didn't spell anything. Japanese characters could never be confused with our Roman lettering. He said the engraving looked like a cat had gotten loose on a typewriter.'

Susan laughed. 'Commander, you don't really think—'

Strathmore cut her off. 'Susan, it's crystal clear. Tankado engraved the Digital Fortress pass-key on his ring. Gold is durable. Whether he's sleeping, showering, eating – the pass-key would always be with him, ready at a moment's notice for instant publication.'

Susan looked dubious. 'On his finger? In the open like that?'

'Why not? Spain isn't exactly the encryption capital of the world. Nobody would have any idea what the letters meant. Besides, if the key is a standard sixty-four-bit – even in broad daylight, nobody could possibly read and memorize all sixty-four characters.'

Susan looked perplexed. 'And Tankado gave this

100

ring to a total stranger moments before he died? Why?'

Strathmore's gaze narrowed. 'Why do you think?'

It took Susan only a moment before it clicked. Her eyes widened.

Strathmore nodded. 'Tankado was trying to get rid of it. He thought we'd killed him. He felt himself dying and logically assumed we were responsible. The timing was too coincidental. He figured we'd gotten to him, poison or something, a slow-acting cardiac arrestor. He knew the only way we'd dare kill him is if we'd found North Dakota.'

Susan felt a chill. 'Of course,' she whispered. 'Tankado thought that we neutralized his insurance policy so we could remove *him* too.'

It was all coming clear to Susan. The timing of the heart attack was so fortunate for the NSA that Tankado had assumed the NSA was responsible. His final instinct was revenge. Ensei gave away his ring as a last-ditch effort to publish the pass-key. Now, incredibly, some unsuspecting Canadian tourist held the key to the most powerful encryption algorithm in history.

Susan sucked in a deep breath and asked the inevitable question. 'So where is the Canadian now?'

Strathmore frowned. 'That's the problem.'

'The officer doesn't know where he is?'

'No. The Canadian's story was so absurd that the officer figured he was either in shock or senile. So he put the old guy on the back of his motorcycle to take him back to his hotel. But the Canadian didn't know enough to hang on; he fell off before they'd gone three feet – cracked his head and broke his wrist.'

'What!' Susan choked.

'The officer wanted to take him to a hospital, but the Canadian was furious – said he'd walk back to Canada before he'd get on the motorcycle again. So all the officer could do was walk him to a small public clinic near the park. He left him there to get checked out.'

Susan frowned. 'I assume there's no need to ask where David is headed.'

CHAPTER 17

David Becker stepped out onto the scorching tile concourse of Plaza de España. Before him, El Ayuntamiento – the ancient city council building – rose from the trees on a three-acre bed of blue and white azulejo tiles. Its Arabic spires and carved facade gave the impression it had been intended more as a palace than a public office. Despite its history of military coups, fires, and public hangings, most tourists visited because the local brochures plugged it as the English military headquarters in the film *Lawrence of Arabia*. It had been far cheaper for Columbia Pictures to film in Spain than in Egypt, and the Moorish influence on Seville's architecture was enough to convince moviegoers they were looking at Cairo.

Becker reset his Seiko for local time: 9:10 P.M. – still afternoon by local standards; a proper Spaniard never ate dinner before sunset, and the lazy Andalusian sun seldom surrendered the skies before ten.

Even in the early-evening heat, Becker found himself walking across the park at a brisk clip. Strathmore's tone had sounded a lot more urgent this time than it had that morning. His new orders left no room for misinterpretation: Find the Canadian, get the ring. Do whatever is necessary, just get that ring.

Becker wondered what could possibly be so important about a ring with lettering all over it. Strathmore hadn't offered, and Becker hadn't asked. *NSA,* he thought. *Never Say Anything.*

On the other side of Avenida Isabela Católica, the clinic was clearly visible – the universal symbol of a red cross in a white circle painted on the roof. The Guardia officer had dropped the Canadian off hours ago. Broken wrist, bumped head – no doubt the patient had been treated and discharged by now. Becker just hoped the clinic had discharge information – a local hotel or phone number where the man could be reached. With a little luck, Becker figured he could find the Canadian, get the ring, and be on his way home without any more complications.

Strathmore had told Becker, 'Use the ten thousand cash to buy the ring if you have to. I'll reimburse you.'

'That's not necessary,' Becker had replied. He'd intended to return the money anyway. He hadn't gone to Spain for money, he'd gone for Susan. Commander Trevor Strathmore was Susan's mentor and guardian. Susan owed him a lot; a one-day errand was the least Becker could do.

Unfortunately, things this morning hadn't gone quite as Becker had planned. He'd hoped to call Susan from the plane and explain everything. He considered having the pilot radio Strathmore so he could pass along a message but was hesitant to involve the deputy director in his romantic problems.

Three times Becker had tried to call Susan himself – first from a defunct cellular on board the jet, next from a pay phone at the airport, then again from the morgue. Susan was not in. David wondered where she could be. He'd gotten her answering machine but had not left a message; what he wanted to say was not a message for an answering machine.

As he approached the road, he spotted a phone booth near the park entrance. He jogged over, snatched up the receiver, and used his phone card to place the call. There was a long pause as the number connected. Finally it began to ring.

Come on. Be there.

After five rings the call connected.

'Hi. This is Susan Fletcher. Sorry I'm not in right now, but if you leave your name . . .'

Becker listened to the message. *Where is she?* By now Susan would be panicked. He wondered if maybe she'd gone to Stone Manor without him. There was a beep.

'Hi. It's David.' He paused, unsure what to say. One of the things he hated about answering machines was that if you stopped to think, they cut you off. 'Sorry I didn't call,' he blurted just in time. He wondered if he should tell her what was going on. He thought better of it. 'Call Commander Strathmore. He'll explain every-thing.' Becker's heart was pounding. *This is absurd,* he thought. 'I love you,' he added quickly and hung up.

Becker waited for some traffic to pass on Avenida Borbolla. He thought about how Susan undoubtedly would have assumed the worst; it was unlike him not to call when he'd promised to.

Becker stepped out onto the four-lane boulevard. 'In and out,' he whispered to himself. 'In and out.' He was too preoccupied to see the man in wire-rim glasses watching from across the street.

CHAPTER 18

Standing before the huge plate-glass window in his Tokyo skyrise, Numataka took a long pull on his cigar and smiled to himself. He could scarcely believe his good fortune. He had spoken to the American again, and if all was going according to the timetable, Ensei Tankado had been eliminated by now, and his copy of the pass-key had been confiscated.

It was ironic, Numataka thought, that he himself would end up with Ensei Tankado's pass-key. Tokugen Numataka had met Tankado once many years ago. The young programmer had come to Numatech Corp. fresh out of college, searching for a job. Numataka had denied him. There was no question that Tankado was brilliant, but at the time there were other considerations. Although Japan was changing, Numataka had been trained in the old school; he lived by the code of menboko – honor and face. Imperfection was not to be tolerated. If he hired a cripple, he would bring shame on his company. He had disposed of Tankado's résumé without a glance.

Numataka checked his watch again. The American, North Dakota, should have called by now. Numataka felt a tinge of nervousness. He hoped nothing was wrong.

If the pass-keys were as good as promised, they would unlock the most sought-after product of the computer age – a totally invulnerable digital encryption algorithm. Numataka could embed the algorithm in tamper-proof, spray-sealed VSLI chips and mass market them to world computer manufacturers, governments, industries, and perhaps, even the darker markets . . . the black market of world terrorists.

Numataka smiled. It appeared, as usual, that he had found favor with the shichigosan – the seven deities of good luck. Numatech Corp. was about to control the only copy of Digital Fortress that would ever exist. Twenty million dollars was a lot of money – but considering the product, it was the steal of the century.

CHAPTER 19

'What if someone else is looking for the ring?' Susan asked, suddenly nervous. 'Could David be in danger?'

Strathmore shook his head. 'Nobody else knows the ring exists. That's why I sent David. I wanted to keep it that way. Curious spooks don't usually tail Spanish teachers.'

'He's a professor,' Susan corrected, immediately regretting the clarification. Every now and again Susan got the feeling David wasn't good enough for the commander, that he thought somehow she could do better than a schoolteacher.

'Commander,' she said, moving on, 'if you briefed David by car phone this morning, someone could have intercepted the—'

'One-in-a-million shot,' Strathmore interrupted, his tone reassuring. 'Any eavesdropper had to be in the immediate vicinity and know exactly what to listen for.' He put his hand on her shoulder. 'I would never have sent David if I thought it was dangerous.' He smiled. 'Trust me. Any sign of trouble, and I'll send in the pros.'

Strathmore's words were punctuated by the sudden

sound of someone pounding on the Node 3 glass. Susan and Strathmore turned.

Sys-Sec Phil Chartrukian had his face pressed against the pane and was pounding fiercely, straining to see through. Whatever he was excitedly mouthing was not audible through the soundproofed glass. He looked like he'd seen a ghost.

'What the hell is Chartrukian doing here?' Strathmore growled. 'He's not on duty today.'

'Looks like trouble,' Susan said. 'He probably saw the Run-Monitor.'

'Goddamn it!' the commander hissed. 'I specifically called the scheduled Sys-Sec last night and told him not to come in!'

Susan was not surprised. Canceling a Sys-Sec duty was irregular, but Strathmore undoubtedly had wanted privacy in the dome. The last thing he needed was some paranoid Sys-Sec blowing the lid off Digital Fortress.

'We better abort TRANSLTR,' Susan said. 'We can reset the Run-Monitor and tell Phil he was seeing things.'

Strathmore appeared to consider it, then shook his head. 'Not yet. TRANSLTR is fifteen hours into this attack. I want to run it a full twenty-four – just to be sure.'

This made sense to Susan. Digital Fortress was the first-ever use of a rotating cleartext function. Maybe Tankado had overlooked something; maybe TRANSLTR would break it after twenty-four hours. Somehow Susan doubted it.

'TRANSLTR keeps running,' Strathmore resolved. 'I need to know for sure this algorithm is untouchable.'

Chartrukian continued pounding on the pane.

'Here goes nothing.' Strathmore groaned. 'Back me up.'

The commander took a deep breath and then strode to the sliding glass doors. The pressure plate on the floor activated, and the doors hissed open.

Chartrukian practically fell into the room. 'Commander, sir. I . . . I'm sorry to bother you, but the Run-Monitor . . . I ran a virus probe and—'

'Phil, Phil, Phil,' the commander gushed pleasantly as he put a reassuring hand on Chartrukian's shoulder. 'Slow down. What seems to be the problem?'

From the easygoing tone in Strathmore's voice, nobody would ever have guessed his world was falling in around him. He stepped aside and ushered Chartrukian into the sacred walls of Node 3. The Sys-Sec stepped over the threshold hesitantly, like a well-trained dog that knew better.

From the puzzled look on Chartrukian's face, it was obvious he'd never seen the inside of this place. Whatever had been the source of his panic was momentarily forgotten. He surveyed the plush interior, the line of private terminals, the couches, the bookshelves, the soft lighting. When his gaze fell on the reigning queen of Crypto, Susan Fletcher, he quickly looked away. Susan intimidated the hell out of him. Her mind worked on a different plane. She was unsettlingly beautiful, and his words always seemed to get jumbled around her. Susan's unassuming air made it even worse.

'What seems to be the problem, Phil?' Strathmore said, opening the refrigerator. 'Drink?'

'No, ah – no, thank you, sir.' He seemed tongue-tied, not sure he was truly welcome. 'Sir . . . I think there's a problem with TRANSLTR.'

Strathmore closed the refrigerator and looked at Chartrukian casually. 'You mean the Run-Monitor?'

Chartrukian looked shocked. 'You mean you've *seen* it?'

'Sure. It's running at about sixteen hours, if I'm not mistaken.'

Chartrukian seemed puzzled. 'Yes, sir, sixteen hours. But that's not all, sir. I ran a virus probe, and it's turning up some pretty strange stuff.'

'Really?' Strathmore seemed unconcerned. 'What kind of stuff?'

Susan watched, impressed with the commander's performance.

Chartrukian stumbled on. 'TRANSLTR's processing something very advanced. The filters have never seen anything like it. I'm afraid TRANSLTR may have some sort of virus.'

'A virus?' Strathmore chuckled with just a hint of condescension. 'Phil, I appreciate your concern, I really do. But Ms Fletcher and I are running a new diagnostic, some very advanced stuff. I would have alerted you to it, but I wasn't aware you were on duty today.'

The Sys-Sec did his best to cover gracefully. 'I switched with the new guy. I took his weekend shift.'

Strathmore's eyes narrowed. 'That's odd. I spoke to him last night. I told him not to come in. He said nothing about switching shifts.'

Chartrukian felt a knot rise in his throat. There was a tense silence.

'Well.' Strathmore finally sighed. 'Sounds like an unfortunate mix-up.' He put a hand on the Sys-Sec's shoulder and led him toward the door. 'The good news is you don't have to stay. Ms Fletcher and I will

111

be here all day. We'll hold the fort. You just enjoy your weekend.'

Chartrukian was hesitant. 'Commander, I really think we should check the—'

'Phil,' Strathmore repeated a little more sternly, 'TRANSLTR is fine. If your probe saw something strange, it's because *we* put it there. Now if you don't mind . . .' Strathmore trailed off, and the Sys-Sec understood. His time was up.

'A diagnostic, my ass!' Chartrukian muttered as he fumed back into the Sys-Sec lab. 'What kind of looping function keeps three million processors busy for sixteen hours?'

Chartrukian wondered if he should call the Sys-Sec supervisor. *Goddamn cryptographers*, he thought. *They just don't understand security!*

The oath Chartrukian had taken when he joined Sys-Sec began running through his head. He had sworn to use his expertise, training, and instinct to protect the NSA's multibillion-dollar investment.

'Instinct,' he said defiantly. *It doesn't take a psychic to know this isn't any goddamn diagnostic!*

Defiantly, Chartrukian strode over to the terminal and fired up TRANSLTR's complete array of system assessment software.

'Your baby's in trouble, Commander,' he grumbled. 'You don't trust instinct? I'll get you proof!'

CHAPTER 20

La Clínica de Salud Pública was actually a converted elementary school and didn't much resemble a hospital at all. It was a long, one-story brick building with huge windows and a rusted swing set out back. Becker headed up the crumbling steps.

Inside, it was dark and noisy. The waiting room was a line of folding metal chairs that ran the entire length of a long narrow corridor. A cardboard sign on a sawhorse read OFICINA with an arrow pointing down the hall.

Becker walked the dimly lit corridor. It was like some sort of eerie set conjured up for a Hollywood horror flick. The air smelled of urine. The lights at the far end were blown out, and the last forty or fifty feet revealed nothing but muted silhouettes. A bleeding woman . . . a young couple crying . . . a little girl praying . . . Becker reached the end of the darkened hall. The door to his left was slightly ajar, and he pushed it open. It was entirely empty except for an old, withered woman naked on a cot struggling with her bedpan.

Lovely. Becker groaned. He closed the door. *Where the hell is the office?*

Around a small dog-leg in the hall, Becker heard voices. He followed the sound and arrived at a translucent glass door that sounded as if a brawl were going on behind it. Reluctantly, Becker pushed the door open. The office. *Mayhem.* Just as he'd feared.

The line was about ten people deep, everyone pushing and shouting. Spain was not known for its efficiency, and Becker knew he could be there all night waiting for discharge info on the Canadian. There was only one secretary behind the desk, and she was fending off disgruntled patients. Becker stood in the doorway a moment and pondered his options. There was a better way.

'Con permiso!' an orderly shouted. A fast-rolling gurney sailed by.

Becker spun out of the way and called after the orderly 'Dónde está el teléfono?'

Without breaking stride, the man pointed to a set of double doors and disappeared around the corner. Becker walked over to the doors and pushed his way through.

The room before him was enormous – an old gymnasium. The floor was a pale green and seemed to swim in and out of focus under the hum of the fluorescent lights. On the wall, a basketball hoop hung limply from its backboard. Scattered across the floor were a few dozen patients on low cots. In the far corner, just beneath a burned-out scoreboard, was an old pay phone. Becker hoped it worked.

As he strode across the floor, he fumbled in his pocket for a coin. He found 75 pesetas in cinco-duros coins, change from the taxi – just enough for two local calls. He smiled politely to an exiting nurse and made his way to the phone. Scooping up the receiver, Becker

114

dialed Directory Assistance. Thirty seconds later he had the number for the clinic's main office.

Regardless of the country, it seemed there was one universal truth when it came to offices: Nobody could stand the sound of an unanswered phone. It didn't matter how many customers were waiting to be helped, the secretary would always drop what she was doing to pick up the phone.

Becker punched the six-digit exchange. In a moment he'd have the clinic's office. There would undoubtedly be only one Canadian admitted today with a broken wrist and a concussion; his file would be easy to find. Becker knew the office would be hesitant to give out the man's name and discharge address to a total stranger, but he had a plan.

The phone began to ring. Becker guessed five rings was all it would take. It took nineteen.

'Clínica de Salud Pública,' barked the frantic secretary.

Becker spoke in Spanish with a thick Franco-American accent. 'This is David Becker. I'm with the Canadian Embassy. One of our citizens was treated by you today. I'd like his information such that the embassy can arrange to pay his fees.'

'Fine,' the woman said. 'I'll send it to the embassy on Monday.'

'Actually,' Becker pressed, 'it's important I get it immediately.'

'Impossible,' the woman snapped. 'We're very busy.'

Becker sounded as official as possible. 'It is an urgent matter. The man had a broken wrist and a head injury. He was treated sometime this morning. His file should be right on top.'

Becker thickened the accent in his Spanish – just clear enough to convey his needs, just confusing enough to be exasperating. People had a way of bending the rules when they were exasperated.

Instead of bending the rules, however, the woman cursed self-important North Americans and slammed down the phone.

Becker frowned and hung up. Strikeout. The thought of waiting hours in line didn't thrill him; the clock was ticking – the old Canadian could be anywhere by now. Maybe he had decided to go back to Canada. Maybe he would sell the ring. Becker didn't have hours to wait in line. With renewed determination, Becker snatched up the receiver and redialed. He pressed the phone to his ear and leaned back against the wall. It began to ring. Becker gazed out into the room. One ring . . . two rings . . . three—

A sudden surge of adrenaline coursed through his body.

Becker wheeled and slammed the receiver back down into its cradle. Then he turned and stared back into the room in stunned silence. There on a cot, directly in front of him, propped up on a pile of old pillows, lay an elderly man with a clean white cast on his right wrist.

CHAPTER 21

The American on Tokugen Numataka's private line sounded anxious.

'Mr Numataka – I only have a moment.'

'Fine. I trust you have both pass-keys.'

'There will be a small delay,' the American answered.

'Unacceptable,' Numataka hissed. 'You said I would have them by the end of today!'

'There is one loose end.'

'Is Tankado dead?'

'Yes,' the voice said. 'My man killed Mr Tankado, but he failed to get the pass-key. Tankado gave it away before he died. To a tourist.'

'Outrageous!' Numataka bellowed. 'Then how can you promise me exclusive—'

'Relax,' the American soothed. 'You will have exclusive rights. That is my guarantee. As soon as the missing pass-key is found, Digital Fortress will be yours.'

'But the pass-key could be copied!'

'Anyone who has seen the key will be eliminated.'

There was a long silence. Finally Numataka spoke. 'Where is the key now?'

'All you need to know is that it *will* be found.'

'How can you be so certain?'

'Because I am not the only one looking for it. American intelligence has caught wind of the missing key. For obvious reasons they would like to prevent the release of Digital Fortress. They have sent a man to locate the key. His name is David Becker.'

'How do you know this?'

'That is irrelevant.'

Numataka paused. 'And if Mr Becker locates the key?'

'My man will take it from him.'

'And after that?'

'You needn't be concerned,' the American said coldly. 'When Mr Becker finds the key, he will be properly rewarded.'

CHAPTER 22

David Becker strode over and stared down at the old man asleep on the cot. The man's right wrist was wrapped in a cast. He was between sixty and seventy years old. His snow-white hair was parted neatly to the side, and in the center of his forehead was a deep purple welt that spread down into his right eye.

A little bump? he thought, recalling the lieutenant's words. Becker checked the man's fingers. There was no gold ring anywhere. Becker reached down and touched the man's arm. 'Sir?' He shook him lightly. 'Excuse me . . . sir?'

The man didn't move.

Becker tried again, a little louder. 'Sir?'

The man stirred. 'Qu'est-ce . . . quelle heure est—' He slowly opened his eyes and focused on Becker. He scowled at having been disturbed. 'Qu'est-ce-que vous voulez?'

Yes, Becker thought, *a French Canadian!* Becker smiled down at him. 'Do you have a moment?'

Although Becker's French was perfect, he spoke in what he hoped would be the man's weaker language, English. Convincing a total stranger to hand over a gold ring might be a little tricky; Becker figured he could use any edge he could get.

There was a long silence as the man got his bearings. He surveyed his surroundings and lifted a long finger to smooth his limp white mustache. Finally he spoke. 'What do you want?' His English carried a thin, nasal accent.

'Sir,' Becker said, overpronouncing his words as if speaking to a deaf person, 'I need to ask you a few questions.'

The man glared up at him with a strange look on his face. 'Do you have some sort of problem?'

Becker frowned; the man's English was impeccable. He immediately lost the condescending tone. 'I'm sorry to bother you, sir, but were you by any chance at the Plaza de España today?'

The old man's eyes narrowed. 'Are you from the City Council?'

'No, actually I'm—'

'Bureau of Tourism?'

'No, I'm—'

'Look, I know why you're here!' The old man struggled to sit up. 'I'm not going to be intimidated! If I've said it once, I've said it a thousand times – Pierre Cloucharde writes the world the way he *lives* the world. Some of your corporate guidebooks might sweep this under the table for a free night on the town, but the *Montreal Times* is *not* for hire! I refuse!'

'I'm sorry, sir. I don't think you under—'

'Merde alors! I understand perfectly!' He wagged a bony finger at Becker, and his voice echoed through the gymnasium. 'You're not the first! They tried the same thing at the Moulin Rouge, Brown's Palace, and the Golfigno in Lagos! But *what* went to press? The truth! The worst Wellington I've ever eaten! The filthiest tub I've ever seen! And the rockiest beach I've ever walked! My readers expect no less!'

Patients on nearby cots began sitting up to see what was going on. Becker looked around nervously for a nurse. The last thing he needed was to get kicked out.

Cloucharde was raging. 'That miserable excuse for a police officer works for *your* city! He made me get on his motorcycle! Look at me!' He tried to lift his wrist. '*Now* who's going to write my column?'

'Sir, I—'

'I've never been so uncomfortable in my forty-three years of travel! Look at this place! You know, my column is syndicated in over—'

'Sir!' Becker held up both hands urgently signaling truce. 'I'm not interested in your column; I'm from the Canadian Consulate. I'm here to make sure you're okay!'

Suddenly there was a dead quiet in the gymnasium. The old man looked up from his bed and eyed the intruder suspiciously.

Becker ventured on in almost a whisper. 'I'm here to see if there's anything I can do to help.' *Like bring you a couple of Valium.*

After a long pause, the Canadian spoke. 'The consulate?' His tone softened considerably.

Becker nodded.

'So, you're *not* here about my column?'

'No, sir.'

It was as if a giant bubble had burst for Pierre Cloucharde. He settled slowly back down onto his mound of pillows. He looked heartbroken. 'I thought you were from the city . . . trying to get me to . . .' He

121

faded off and then looked up. 'If it's not about my column, then why *are* you here?'

It was a good question, Becker thought, picturing the Smoky Mountains. 'Just an informal diplomatic courtesy,' he lied.

The man looked surprised. 'A diplomatic courtesy?'

'Yes, sir. As I'm sure a man of your stature is well aware, the Canadian government works hard to protect its countrymen from the indignities suffered in these, er – shall we say – less *refined* countries.'

Cloucharde's thin lips parted in a knowing smile. 'But of course . . . how pleasant.'

'You *are* a Canadian citizen, aren't you?'

'Yes, of course. How silly of me. Please forgive me. Someone in my position is often approached with . . . well . . . you understand.'

'Yes, Mr Cloucharde, I certainly do. The price one pays for celebrity.'

'Indeed.' Cloucharde let out a tragic sigh. He was an unwilling martyr tolerating the masses. 'Can you believe this hideous place?' He rolled his eyes at the bizarre surroundings. 'It's a mockery. And they've decided to keep me overnight.'

Becker looked around. 'I know. It's terrible. I'm sorry it took me so long to get here.'

Cloucharde looked confused. 'I wasn't even aware you were coming.'

Becker changed the subject. 'Looks like a nasty bump on your head. Does it hurt?'

'No, not really. I took a spill this morning – the price one pays for being a good Samaritan. The wrist is the thing that's hurting me. Stupid Guardia. I mean, really! Putting a man of *my* age on a motorcycle. It's reprehensible.'

122

'Is there anything I can get for you?'

Cloucharde thought a moment, enjoying the attention. 'Well, actually . . .' He stretched his neck and tilted his head left and right. 'I *could* use another pillow if it's not too much trouble.'

'Not at all.' Becker grabbed a pillow off a nearby cot and helped Cloucharde get comfortable.

The old man sighed contentedly. 'Much better . . . thank you.'

'Pas du tout,' Becker replied.

'Ah!' The man smiled warmly. 'So you *do* speak the language of the civilized world.'

'That's about the extent of it,' Becker said sheepishly.

'Not a problem,' Cloucharde declared proudly. 'My column is syndicated in the U.S.; my English is first rate.'

'So I've heard.' Becker smiled. He sat down on the edge of Cloucharde's cot. 'Now, if you don't mind my asking, Mr Cloucharde, why would a man such as yourself come to a place like *this*? There are far better hospitals in Seville.'

Cloucharde looked angry. 'That police officer . . . he bucked me off his motorcycle and then left me bleeding in the street like a stuck pig. I had to walk over here.'

'He didn't offer to take you to a better facility?'

'On that godawful bike of his? No thanks!'

'What exactly happened this morning?'

'I told it all to the lieutenant.'

'I've spoken to the officer and—'

'I hope you reprimanded him!' Cloucharde interrupted.

Becker nodded. 'In the severest terms. My office will be following up.'

'I should hope so.'

'Monsieur Cloucharde.' Becker smiled, pulling a pen out of his jacket pocket. 'I'd like to make a formal complaint to the city. Would you help? A man of your reputation would be a valuable witness.'

Cloucharde looked buoyed by the prospect of being quoted. He sat up. 'Why, yes . . . of course. It would be my pleasure.'

Becker took out a small note pad and looked up. 'Okay, let's start with this morning. Tell me about the accident.'

The old man sighed. 'It was sad really. The poor Asian fellow just collapsed. I tried to help him – but it was no use.'

'You gave him CPR?'

Cloucharde looked ashamed. 'I'm afraid I don't know how. I called an ambulance.'

Becker remembered the bluish bruises on Tankado's chest. 'Did the paramedics administer CPR?'

'Heavens, no!' Cloucharde laughed. 'No reason to whip a dead horse – the fellow was long gone by the time the ambulance got there. They checked his pulse and carted him off, leaving me with that horrific policeman.'

That's strange, Becker thought, wondering where the bruise had come from. He pushed it from his mind and got to the matter at hand. 'What about the ring?' he said as nonchalantly as possible.

Cloucharde looked surprised. 'The lieutenant told you about the ring?'

'Yes, he did.'

Cloucharde seemed amazed. 'Really? I didn't think he believed my story. He was so rude – as if he thought I were lying. But my story was accurate, of course. I pride myself on accuracy.'

'Where is the ring?' Becker pressed.

Cloucharde didn't seem to hear. He was glassy-eyed, staring into space. 'Strange piece really, all those letters – looked like no language I'd ever seen.'

'Japanese, maybe?' Becker offered.

'Definitely not.'

'So you got a good look at it?'

'Heavens, yes! When I knelt down to help, the man kept pushing his fingers in my face. He wanted to give me the ring. It was most bizarre, horrible really – his hands were quite dreadful.'

'And that's when you took the ring?'

Cloucharde went wide-eyed. 'That's what the officer told you! That *I* took the ring?'

Becker shifted uneasily.

Cloucharde exploded. 'I knew he wasn't listening! That's how rumors get started! I told him the Jap fellow gave away the ring – but not to *me!* There's no way I would take anything from a dying man! My heavens! The thought of it!'

Becker sensed trouble. 'So you don't have the ring?'

'Heavens, no!'

A dull ache crept through the pit of his stomach. 'Then who has it?'

Cloucharde glared at Becker indignantly. 'The German! The German has it!'

Becker felt like the floor had been pulled out from under him. 'German? What German?'

'The German in the park! I told the officer about him! I refused the ring but the fascist swine accepted it!'

Becker set down his pen and paper. The charade was over. This was trouble. 'So a *German* has the ring?'

'Indeed.'

125

'Where did he go?'

'No idea. I ran to call the police. When I got back, he was gone.'

'Do you know who he was?'

'Some tourist.'

'Are you sure?'

'My life is tourists,' Cloucharde snapped. 'I know one when I see one. He and his lady friend were out strolling the park.'

Becker was more and more confused every moment. 'Lady friend? There was somebody *with* the German?'

Cloucharde nodded. 'An escort. Gorgeous redhead. Mon dieu! Beautiful.'

'An escort?' Becker was stunned. 'As in . . . a prostitute?'

Cloucharde grimaced. 'Yes, if you must use the vulgar term.'

'But . . . the officer said nothing about—'

'Of course not! I never mentioned the escort.' Cloucharde dismissed Becker with a patronizing wave of his good hand. 'They aren't criminals – it's absurd that they're harassed like common thieves.'

Becker was still in a mild state of shock. 'Was there anyone else there?'

'No, just the three of us. It was hot.'

'And you're positive the woman was a prostitute?'

'Absolutely. No woman that beautiful would be with a man like that unless she were well paid! Mon dieu! He was fat, fat, *fat!* A loud-mouthed, over-weight, obnoxious German!' Cloucharde winced momentarily as he shifted his weight, but he ignored the pain and plowed on. 'This man was a beast – three hundred pounds at least. He locked on to that poor dear like she was about to run away – not that I'd blame her. I mean really! Hands all over her. Bragged that he had her all weekend for three hundred dollars! *He's* the one who should have dropped dead, not that poor Asian fellow.' Cloucharde came up for air, and Becker jumped in.

'Did you get his name?'

Cloucharde thought for a moment and then shook his head. 'No idea.' He winced in pain again and settled slowly back into his pillows.

Becker sighed. The ring had just evaporated before his eyes. Commander Strathmore was not going to be happy.

Cloucharde dabbed at his forehead. His burst of enthusiasm had taken its toll. He suddenly looked ill.

Becker tried another approach. 'Mr Cloucharde, I'd like to get a statement from the German and his escort as well. Do you have any idea where they're staying?'

Cloucharde closed his eyes, his strength fading. His breathing grew shallow.

'Anything at all?' Becker pressed. 'The escort's name?'

There was a long silence.

Cloucharde rubbed his right temple. He was suddenly looking pale. 'Well . . . ah . . . no. I don't believe . . .' His voice was shaky.

Becker leaned toward him. 'Are you all right?'

Cloucharde nodded lightly. 'Yes, fine . . . just a little . . . the excitement maybe . . .' He trailed off.

'Think, Mr Cloucharde,' Becker urged quietly. 'It's important.'

Cloucharde winced. 'I don't know . . . the woman . . . the man kept calling her . . .' He closed his eyes and groaned.

'What was her name?'

'I really don't recall . . .' Cloucharde was fading fast.

'Think,' Becker prodded. 'It's important that the consular file be as complete as possible. I'll need to support your story with statements from the other witnesses. Any information you can give me to help locate them . . .'

But Cloucharde was not listening. He was dabbing his forehead with the sheet. 'I'm sorry . . . perhaps tomorrow . . .' He looked nauseated.

'Mr Cloucharde, it's important you remember this *now.*' Becker suddenly realized he was speaking too loudly. People on nearby cots were still sitting up watching what was going on. On the far side of the room a nurse appeared through the double doors and strode briskly toward them.

'Anything at all,' Becker pressed urgently.

'The German called the woman—'

Becker lightly shook Cloucharde, trying to bring him back.

Cloucharde's eyes flickered momentarily. 'Her name . . .'

Stay with me, old fella . . .

'Dew . . .' Cloucharde's eyes closed again. The nurse was closing in. She looked furious.

'Dew?' Becker shook Cloucharde's arm.

The old man groaned. 'He called her . . .' Cloucharde was mumbling now, barely audible.

The nurse was less than ten feet away yelling at Becker in angry Spanish. Becker heard nothing. His eyes were fixed on the old man's lips. He shook Cloucharde one last time as the nurse bore down on him.

The nurse grabbed David Becker's shoulder. She

pulled him to his feet just as Cloucharde's lips parted. The single word leaving the old man's mouth was not actually spoken. It was softly sighed – like a distant sensual remembrance. 'Dewdrop . . .'

The scolding grasp yanked Becker away.

Dewdrop? Becker wondered. *What the hell kind of name is Dewdrop?* He spun away from the nurse and turned one last time to Cloucharde. 'Dewdrop? Are you *sure?*'

But Pierre Cloucharde was fast asleep.

CHAPTER 23

Susan sat alone in the plush surroundings of Node 3. She nursed a lemon mist herb tea and awaited the return of her tracer.

As senior cryptographer, Susan enjoyed the terminal with the best view. It was on the back side of the ring of computers and faced the Crypto floor. From this spot, Susan could oversee all of Node 3. She could also see, on the other side of the one-way glass, TRANSLTR standing dead-center of the Crypto floor.

Susan checked the clock. She had been waiting almost an hour. American Remailers Anonymous was apparently taking their time forwarding North Dakota's mail. She sighed heavily. Despite her efforts to forget her morning conversation with David, the words played over and over in her head. She knew she'd been hard on him. She prayed he was okay in Spain.

Her thoughts were jarred by the loud hiss of the glass doors. She looked up and groaned. Cryptographer Greg Hale stood in the opening.

Greg Hale was tall and muscular with thick blond hair and a deep cleft chin. He was loud, thick-fleshed, and perpetually overdressed. His fellow cryptographers had nicknamed him 'Halite' – after the mineral. Hale had always assumed it referred to some rare gem – paralleling his unrivaled intellect and rock-hard physique. Had his ego permitted him to consult an encyclopedia, he would have discovered it was nothing more than the salty residue left behind when oceans dried up.

Like all NSA cryptographers, Hale made a solid salary. However, he had a hard time keeping that fact to himself. He drove a white Lotus with a moon roof and a deafening subwoofer system. He was a gadget junkie, and his car was his showpiece; he'd installed a global positioning computer system, voice-activated door locks, a five-point radar jammer, and a cellular fax/phone so he'd never be out of touch with his message services. His vanity plate read MEGABYTE and was framed in violet neon.

Greg Hale had been rescued from a childhood of petty crime by the U.S. Marine Corps. It was there that he'd learned about computers. He was one of the best programmers the Marines had ever seen, well on his way to a distinguished military career. But two days before the completion of his third tour of duty, his future suddenly changed. Hale accidentally killed a fellow Marine in a drunken brawl. The Korean art of self-defense, Taekwondo, proved more deadly than defensive. He was promptly relieved of his duty.

After serving a brief prison term, Halite began looking for work in the private sector as a programmer. He was always up front about the incident in the Marines, and he courted prospective employers by offering a month's work without pay to prove his worth. He had no shortage of takers, and once they found out what he could do with a computer, they never wanted to let him go.

As his computer expertise grew, Hale began making Internet connections all over the world. He was one of the new breed of cyberfreaks with E-mail friends in every nation, moving in and out of seedy electronic bulletin boards and European chat groups. He'd been fired by two different employers for using their business accounts to upload pornographic photos to some of his friends.

'What are *you* doing here?' Hale demanded, stopping in the doorway and staring at Susan. He'd obviously expected to have Node 3 to himself today.

Susan forced herself to stay cool. 'It's Saturday, Greg. I could ask you the same question.' But Susan knew what Hale was doing there. He was the consummate computer addict. Despite the Saturday rule, he often slipped into Crypto on weekends to use the NSA's unrivalled computing power to run new programs he was working on.

'Just wanted to re-tweak a few lines and check my E-mail,' Hale said. He eyed her curiously. 'What was it you said *you*'re doing here?'

'I didn't,' Susan replied.

Hale arched a surprised eyebrow. 'No reason to be coy. We have no secrets here in Node 3, remember? All for one and one for all.'

Susan sipped her lemon mist and ignored him. Hale shrugged and strode toward the Node 3 pantry. The pantry was always his first stop. As Hale crossed the room, he sighed heavily and made a point of ogling Susan's legs stretched out beneath her terminal.

Susan, without looking up, retracted her legs and kept working. Hale smirked.

Susan had gotten used to Hale hitting on her. His favorite line was something about interfacing to check the compatibility of their hardware. It turned Susan's stomach. She was too proud to complain to Strathmore about Hale; it was far easier just to ignore him.

Hale approached the Node 3 pantry and pulled open the lattice doors like a bull. He slid a Tupperware container of tofu out of the fridge and popped a few pieces of the gelatinous white substance in his mouth. Then he leaned on the stove and smoothed his gray Bellvienne slacks and well-starched shirt. 'You gonna be here long?'

'All night,' Susan said flatly.

'Hmm . . .' Halite cooed with his mouth full. 'A cozy Saturday in the playpen, just the two of us.'

'Just the *three* of us,' Susan interjected. 'Commander Strathmore's upstairs. You might want to disappear before he sees you.'

Hale shrugged. 'He doesn't seem to mind *you* here. He must really enjoy your company.'

Susan forced herself to keep silent.

Hale chuckled to himself and put away his tofu. Then he grabbed a quart of virgin olive oil and took a few swigs. He was a health fiend and claimed olive oil cleaned out his lower intestine. When he wasn't pushing carrot juice on the rest of the staff, he was preaching the virtues of high colonics.

Hale replaced the olive oil and went to down his computer directly opposite Susan. Even across the wide ring of terminals, Susan could smell his cologne. She crinkled her nose.

'Nice cologne, Greg. Use the entire bottle?'

Hale flicked on his terminal. 'Only for you, dear.'

As he sat there waiting for his terminal to warm up, Susan had a sudden unsettling thought. What if Hale accessed TRANSLTR's Run-Monitor? There was no logical reason why he would, but nonetheless Susan knew he would never fall for some half-baked story about a diagnostic that stumped TRANSLTR for sixteen hours. Hale would demand to know the truth. The truth was something Susan had no intention of telling him. She did not trust Greg Hale. He was not NSA material. Susan had been against hiring him in the first place, but the NSA had had no choice. Hale had been the product of damage control.

The Skipjack fiasco.

Four years ago, in an effort to create a single, public-key encryption standard, Congress charged the nation's best mathematicians, those at the NSA, to write a new superalgorithm. The plan was for Congress to pass legislation that made the new algorithm the nation's standard, thus alleviating the incompatibilities now suffered by corporations that used different algorithms.

Of course, asking the NSA to lend a hand in improving public-key encryption was somewhat akin to asking a condemned man to build his own coffin. TRANSLTR had not yet been conceived, and an encryption standard would only help to proliferate the use of code-writing and make the NSA's already difficult job that much harder.

The EFF understood this conflict of interest and lobbied vehemently that the NSA might create an algorithm of poor quality – something it could break. To appease these fears, Congress announced that

134

when the NSA's algorithm was finished, the formula would be published for examination by the world's mathematicians to ensure its quality.

Reluctantly, the NSA's Crypto team, led by Commander Strathmore, created an algorithm they christened Skipjack. Skipjack was presented to Congress for their approval. Mathematicians from all over the world tested Skipjack and were unanimously impressed. They reported that it was a strong, untainted algorithm and would make a superb encryption standard. But three days before Congress was to vote their certain approval of Skipjack, a young programmer from Bell Laboratories, Greg Hale, shocked the world by announcing he'd found a back door hidden in the algorithm.

The back door consisted of a few lines of cunning programming that Commander Strathmore had inserted into the algorithm. It had been added in so shrewd a way that nobody, except Greg Hale, had seen it. Strathmore's covert addition, in effect, meant that any code written by Skipjack could be decrypted via a secret password known only to the NSA. Strathmore had come within inches of turning the nation's proposed encryption standard into the biggest intelligence coup the NSA had ever seen; the NSA would have held the master key to every code written in America.

The computer-savvy public was outraged. The EFF descended on the scandal like vultures, ripping Congress to shreds for their naïveté and proclaiming the NSA the biggest threat to the free world since Hitler. The encryption standard was dead.

It had come as little surprise when the NSA hired Greg Hale two days later. Strathmore felt it was better to have him on the inside working for the NSA than on the outside working against it.

Strathmore faced the Skipjack scandal head-on. He defended his actions vehemently to Congress. He argued that the public's craving for privacy would come back to haunt them. He insisted the public needed someone to watch over them; the public needed the NSA to break codes in order to keep the peace. Groups like the EFF felt differently. And they'd been fighting him ever since.

CHAPTER 24

David Becker stood in a phone booth across the street from La Clínica de Salud Pública; he'd just been ejected for harassing patient number 104, Monsieur Cloucharde.

Things were suddenly more complicated than he'd anticipated. His little favor to Strathmore – picking up some personal belongings – had turned into a scavenger hunt for some bizarre ring.

He'd just called Strathmore and told him about the German tourist. The news had not been received well. After demanding the specifics, Strathmore had fallen silent for a long time. 'David,' he had finally said very gravely, 'finding that ring is a matter of national security. I'm leaving it in your hands. Don't fail me.' The phone had gone dead.

David stood in the phone booth and sighed. He picked up the tattered Guía Telefónica and began scanning the yellow pages. 'Here goes nothing,' he muttered to himself.

There were only three listings for Escort Services in the directory, and he didn't have much to go on. All he knew was that the German's date had red hair, which conveniently was rare in Spain. The delirious Cloucharde had recalled the escort's name as Dewdrop. Becker cringed – Dewdrop? It sounded more like a cow than a beautiful girl. Not a good Catholic name at all; Cloucharde must have been mistaken.

Becker dialed the first number.

'Servicio Social de Sevilla,' a pleasant female voice answered.

Becker affected his Spanish with a thick German accent. 'Hola, hablas aleman?'

'No. But I speak English' came the reply.

Becker continued in broken English. 'Thank you. I wondering if you to help me?'

'How can we be of service?' The woman spoke slowly in an effort to aid her potential client. 'Perhaps you would like an escort?'

'Yes, please. Today my brother, Klaus, he has girl, very beautiful. Red hair. I want same. For tomorrow, please.'

'Your brother Klaus comes here?' The voice was suddenly effervescent, like they were old friends.

'Yes. He very fat. You remember him, no?'

'He was here today, you say?'

Becker could hear her checking the books. There would be no Klaus listed, but Becker figured clients seldom used their real names.

'Hmm, I'm sorry,' she apologized. 'I don't see him here. What was the girl's name your brother was with?'

'Had red hair,' Becker said, avoiding the question.

'Red hair?' she repeated. There was a pause. 'This is Servicio Social de Sevilla. Are you sure your brother comes here?'

'Sure, yes.'

'Señor, we have no redheads. We have only pure Andalusian beauties.'

'Red hair,' Becker repeated, feeling stupid.

'I'm sorry, we have no redheads at all, but if you—'

'Name is Dewdrop,' Becker blurted, feeling even stupider.

The ridiculous name apparently meant nothing to the woman. She apologized, suggested Becker was confusing her with another agency, and politely hung up.

Strike one.

Becker frowned and dialed the next number. It connected immediately.

'Buenas noches, Mujeres España. May I help you?'

Becker launched into his same spiel, a German tourist who was willing to pay top dollar for the red-haired girl who was out with his brother today.

This time the response was in polite German, but again no redheads. 'Keine Rotköpfe, I'm sorry.' The woman hung up.

Strike two.

Becker looked down at the phone book. There was only one number left. The end of the rope already.

He dialed.

'Escortes Belén,' a man answered in a very slick tone.

Again Becker told his story.

'Sí, sí, señor. My name is Señor Roldán. I would be pleased to help. We have two redheads. Lovely girls.'

Becker's heart leapt. 'Very beautiful?' he repeated in his German accent. 'Red hair?'

'Yes, what is your brother's name? I will tell you

who was his escort today. And we can send her to you tomorrow.'

'Klaus Schmidt.' Becker blurted a name recalled from an old textbook.

A long pause. 'Well, sir . . . I don't see a Klaus Schmidt on our registry, but perhaps your brother chose to be discreet – perhaps a wife at home?' He laughed inappropriately.

'Yes, Klaus married. But he very fat. His wife no lie with him.' Becker rolled his eyes at himself reflected in the booth. *If Susan could hear me now,* he thought. 'I fat and lonely too. I want lie with her. Pay lots of money.'

Becker was giving an impressive performance, but he'd gone too far. Prostitution was illegal in Spain, and Señor Roldán was a careful man. He'd been burned before by Guardia officials posing as eager tourists. *I want lie with her.* Roldán knew it was a setup. If he said yes, he would be heavily fined and, as always, forced to provide one of his most talented escorts to the police commissioner free of charge for an entire weekend.

When Roldán spoke, his voice was not quite as friendly. 'Sir, this is Escortes Belén. May I ask who's calling?'

'Aah . . . Sigmund Schmidt,' Becker invented weakly.

'Where did you get our number?'

'La Guía Telefónica – yellow pages.'

'Yes, sir, that's because we are an escort service.'

'Yes. I want escort.' Becker sensed something was wrong.

'Sir, Escortes Belén is a service providing escorts to businessmen for luncheons and dinners. This is why

140

we are listed in the phone book. What we do is legal. What you are looking for is a *prostitute*.' The word slid off his tongue like a vile disease.

'But my brother . . .'

'Sir, if your brother spent the day kissing a girl in the park, she was not one of ours. We have strict regulations about client–escort contact.'

'But . . .'

'You have us confused with someone else. We only have two redheads, Inmaculada and Rocío, and neither would allow a man to sleep with them for money. That is called prostitution, and it is illegal in Spain. Good night, sir.'

'But—'

CLICK.

Becker swore under his breath and dropped the phone back into its cradle. Strike three. He was certain Cloucharde had said the German had hired the girl for the entire weekend.

Becker stepped out of the phone booth at the intersection of Calle Salado and Avenida Asunción. Despite the traffic, the sweet scent of Seville oranges hung all around him. It was twilight – the most romantic hour. He thought of Susan. Strathmore's words invaded his mind: *Find the ring*. Becker flopped miserably on a bench and pondered his next move.

What move?

CHAPTER 25

Inside the Clínica de Salud Pública, visiting hours were over. The gymnasium lights had been turned out. Pierre Cloucharde was fast asleep. He did not see the figure hunched over him. The needle of a stolen syringe glinted in the dark. Then it disappeared into the IV tube just above Cloucharde's wrist. The hypodermic contained 30 cc of cleaning fluid stolen from a janitor's cart. With great force, a strong thumb rammed the plunger down and forced the bluish liquid into the old man's veins.

Cloucharde was awake only for a few seconds. He might have screamed in pain had a strong hand not been clamped across his mouth. He lay trapped on his cot, pinned beneath a seemingly immovable weight. He could feel the pocket of fire searing its way up his arm. There was an excruciating pain traveling through his armpit, his chest, and then, like a million shattering pieces of glass, it hit his brain. Cloucharde saw a brilliant flash of light . . . and then nothing.

The visitor released his grip and peered through the darkness at the name on the medical chart. Then he slipped silently out.

On the street, the man in wire-rim glasses reached to a tiny device attached to his belt. The rectangular pack was about the size of a credit card. It was a prototype of the new Monocle computer. Developed by the U.S. Navy to help technicians record battery voltages in cramped quarters on submarines, the miniature computer packed a cellular modem and the newest advances in microtechnology. Its visual monitor was a transparent liquid crystal display, mounted in the left lens of a pair of eyeglasses. The Monocle reflected a whole new age in personal computing; the user could now look *through* his data and still interact with the world around him.

The Monocle's real coup, though, was not its miniature display but rather its data entry system. A user entered information via tiny contacts fixed to his fingertips; touching the contacts together in sequence mimicked a shorthand similar to court stenography. The computer would then translate the shorthand into English.

The killer pressed a tiny switch, and his glasses flickered to life. His hands inconspicuously at his sides, he began touching different fingertips together in rapid succession. A message appeared before his eyes.

SUBJECT: P. CLOUCHARDE – TERMINATED

He smiled. Transmitting notification of kills was part of his assignment. But including victims' names . . . that, to the man in the wire-rim glasses, was elegance. His fingers flashed again, and his cellular modem activated.

MESSAGE SENT

CHAPTER 26

Sitting on the bench across from the public clinic, Becker wondered what he was supposed to do now. His calls to the escort agencies had turned up nothing. The commander, uneasy about communication over unsecured public phones, had asked David not to call again until he had the ring. Becker considered going to the local police for help – maybe they had a record of a red-headed hooker – but Strathmore had given strict orders about that too. *You are invisible. No one is to know this ring exists.*

Becker wondered if he was supposed to wander the drugged-out district of Triana in search of this mystery woman. Or maybe he was supposed to check all the restaurants for an obese German. Everything seemed like a waste of time.

Strathmore's words kept coming back: *It's a matter of national security . . . you must find that ring.*

A voice in the back of Becker's head told him he'd missed something – something crucial – but for the life of him, he couldn't think what it would be. *I'm a teacher, not a damned secret agent!* He was beginning to wonder why Strathmore hadn't sent a professional.

Becker stood up and walked aimlessly down Calle Delicias pondering his options. The cobblestone sidewalk blurred beneath his gaze. Night was falling fast.

Dewdrop.

There was something about that absurd name that nagged at the back of his mind. *Dewdrop.* The slick voice of Señor Roldán at Escortes Belén was on endless loop in his head. *'We only have two redheads . . . Two redheads, Inmaculada and Rocío . . . Rocío . . . Rocío . . .'*

Becker stopped short. He suddenly knew. *And I call myself a language specialist?* He couldn't believe he'd missed it.

Rocío was one of the most popular girl's names in Spain. It carried all the right implications for a young Catholic girl – purity, virginity, natural beauty. The connotations of purity all stemmed from the name's literal meaning – *Drop of Dew!*

The old Canadian's voice rang in Becker's ears. *Dewdrop.* Rocío had translated her name to the only language she and her client had in common – English. Excited, Becker hurried off to find a phone.

Across the street, a man in wire-rim glasses followed just out of sight.

CHAPTER 27

On the Crypto floor, the shadows were growing long and faint. Overhead, the automatic lighting gradually increased to compensate. Susan was still at her terminal silently awaiting news from her tracer. It was taking longer than expected.

Her mind had been wandering – missing David and willing Greg Hale to go home. Although Hale hadn't budged, thankfully he'd been silent, engrossed in whatever he was doing at his terminal. Susan couldn't care less what Hale was doing, as long as he didn't access the Run-Monitor. He obviously hadn't – sixteen hours would have brought an audible yelp of disbelief.

Susan was sipping her third cup of tea when it finally happened – her terminal beeped once. Her pulse quickened. A flashing envelope icon appeared on her monitor announcing the arrival of E-mail. Susan shot a quick glance toward Hale. He was absorbed in his work. She held her breath and double-clicked the envelope.

'North Dakota,' she whispered to herself. 'Let's see who you are.'

When the E-mail opened, it was a single line. Susan read it. And then she read it again.

DINNER AT ALFREDO'S? 8 PM?

Across the room, Hale muffled a chuckle. Susan checked the message header.

FROM: GHALE@CRYPTO.NSA.GOV

Susan felt a surge of anger but fought it off. She deleted the message. 'Very mature, Greg.'

'They make a great carpaccio.' Hale smiled. 'What do you say? Afterward we could—'

'Forget it.'

'Snob.' Hale sighed and turned back to his terminal. That was strike eighty-nine with Susan Fletcher. The brilliant female cryptographer was a constant frustration to him. Hale had often fantasized about having sex with her – pinning her against TRANSLTR's curved hull and taking her right there against the warm black tile. But Susan would have nothing to do with him. In Hale's mind, what made things worse was that she was in love with some university teacher who slaved for hours on end for peanuts. It would be a pity for Susan to dilute her superior gene pool procreating with some geek – particularly when she could have Greg. *We'd have perfect children*, he thought.

'What are you working on?' Hale asked, trying a different approach.

Susan said nothing.

'Some team player *you* are. Sure I can't have a peek?' Hale stood and started moving around the circle of terminals toward her.

Susan sensed that Hale's curiosity had the potential to cause some serious problems today. She made a snap decision. 'It's a diagnostic,' she offered, falling back on the commander's lie.

Hale stopped in his tracks. 'Diagnostic?' He sounded doubtful. 'You're spending Saturday running a diagnostic instead of playing with the prof?'

'His name is David.'

'Whatever.'

Susan glared at him. 'Haven't you got anything better to do?'

'Are you trying to get rid of me?' Hale pouted.

'Actually, yes.'

'Gee, Sue, I'm hurt.'

Susan Fletcher's eyes narrowed. She hated being called Sue. She had nothing against the nickname, but Hale was the only one who'd ever used it.

'Why don't I help you?' Hale offered. He was suddenly circling toward her again. 'I'm great with diagnostics. Besides, I'm dying to see what diagnostic could make the mighty Susan Fletcher come to work on a Saturday.'

Susan felt a surge of adrenaline. She glanced down at the tracer on her screen. She knew she couldn't let Hale see it – he'd have too many questions. 'I've got it covered, Greg,' she said.

But Hale kept coming. As he circled toward her terminal, Susan knew she had to act fast. Hale was only a few yards away when she made her move. She stood to meet his towering frame, blocking his way. His cologne was overpowering.

She looked him straight in the eye. 'I said no.'

Hale cocked his head, apparently intrigued by her odd display of secrecy. He playfully stepped closer.

Greg Hale was not ready for what happened next.

With unwavering cool, Susan pressed a single index finger against his rock-hard chest, stopping his forward motion.

Hale halted and stepped back in shock. Apparently Susan Fletcher was serious; she had *never* touched him before, ever. It wasn't quite what Hale had had in mind for their first contact, but it was a start. He gave her a long puzzled look and slowly returned to his terminal. As he sat back down, one thing became perfectly clear: The lovely Susan Fletcher was working on something important, and it sure as hell wasn't any diagnostic.

CHAPTER 28

Señor Roldán was sitting behind his desk at Escortes Belén congratulating himself for deftly sidestepping the Guardia's newest pathetic attempt to trap him. Having an officer fake a German accent and request a girl for the night – it was entrapment; what would they think of next?

The phone on his desk buzzed loudly. Señor Roldán scooped up the receiver with a confident flair. 'Buenas noches, Escortes Belén.'

'Buenas noches,' a man's voice said in lightning-fast Spanish. He sounded nasal, like he had a slight cold. 'Is this a hotel?'

'No, sir. What number are you dialing?' Señor Roldán was not going to fall for any more tricks this evening.

'34-62-10,' the voice said.

Roldán frowned. The voice sounded vaguely familiar. He tried to place the accent – Burgos, maybe? 'You've dialed the correct number,' Roldán offered cautiously, 'but this is an escort service.'

There was a pause on the line. 'Oh . . . I see. I'm sorry. Somebody wrote down this number; I thought it was a hotel. I'm visiting here, from Burgos. My apologies for disturbing you. Good nigh—'

'Espére! Wait!' Señor Roldán couldn't help himself; he was a salesman at heart. Was this a referral? A new client from up north? He wasn't going to let a little paranoia blow a potential sale.

'My friend,' Roldán gushed into the phone. 'I thought I recognized a bit of a Burgos accent on you. I myself am from Valencia. What brings you to Seville?'

'I sell jewelry. Majórica pearls.'

'Majóricas, reeaally! You must travel quite a bit.'

The voice coughed sickly. 'Well, yes, I do.'

'In Seville on business?' Roldán pressed. There was no way in hell this guy was Guardia; he was a customer with a capital C. 'Let me guess – a friend gave you our number? He told you to give us a call. Am I right?'

The voice was obviously embarrassed. 'Well, no, actually, it's nothing like that.'

'Don't be shy, señor. We are an escort service, nothing to be ashamed of. Lovely girls, dinner dates, that is all. Who gave you our number? Perhaps he is a regular. I can give you a special rate.'

The voice became flustered. 'Ah . . . nobody actually *gave* me this number. I found it with a passport. I'm trying to find the owner.'

Roldán's heart sank. This man was not a customer after all. 'You *found* the number, you say?'

'Yes, I found a man's passport in the park today. Your number was on a scrap of paper inside. I thought perhaps it was the man's hotel; I was hoping to return his passport to him. My mistake. I'll just drop it off at a police station on my way out of—'

'Perdón,' Roldán interrupted nervously. 'Might I

suggest a better idea?' Roldán prided himself on discretion, and visits to the Guardia had a way of making his customers ex-customers. 'Consider this,' he offered. 'Because the man with the passport had our number, he is most likely a client here. Perhaps I could save you a trip to the police.'

The voice hesitated. 'I don't know. I should probably just—'

'Do not be too hasty, my friend. I'm ashamed to admit that the police here in Seville are not always as efficient as the police up north. It could be *days* before this man's passport is returned to him. If you tell me his name, I could see that he gets his passport *immediately*.'

'Yes, well . . . I suppose there's no harm . . .' Some paper rustled, and the voice returned. 'It's a German name. I can't quite pronounce it . . . Gusta . . . Gustafson?'

Roldán didn't recognize the name, but he had clients from all over the world. They never left their real names. 'What does he look like – in his photo? Perhaps I will recognize him.'

'Well . . .' the voice said. 'His face is very, very fat.'

Roldán immediately knew. He remembered the obese face well. It was the man with Rocío. It was odd, he thought, to have two calls about the German in one night.

'Mr Gustafson?' Roldán forced a chuckle. 'Of course! I know him well. If you bring me his passport, I'll see he gets it.'

'I'm downtown without a car,' the voice interrupted. 'Maybe you could come to me?'

'Actually,' Roldán hedged, 'I can't leave the phone. But it's really not that far if you—'

'I'm sorry, it's late to be out wandering about. There's a Guardia precinct nearby. I'll drop it there, and when you see Mr Gustafson, you can tell him where it is.'

'No, wait!' Roldán cried. 'The police really needn't be involved. You said you're downtown, right? Do you know the Alfonso XIII Hotel? It's one of the city's finest.'

'Yes,' the voice said. 'I know the Alfonso XIII. It's nearby.'

'Wonderful! Mr Gustafson is a guest there tonight. He's probably there now.'

The voice hesitated. 'I see. Well, then . . . I suppose it would be no trouble.'

'Superb! He's having dinner with one of our escorts in the hotel restaurant.' Roldán knew they were probably in bed by now, but he needed to be careful not to offend the caller's refined sensibilities. 'Just leave the passport with the concierge, his name is Manuel. Tell him I sent you. Ask him to give it to Rocío. Rocío is Mr Gustafson's date for the evening. She will see that the passport is returned. You might slip your name and address inside – perhaps Mr Gustafson will send you a little thank you.'

'A fine idea. The Alfonso XIII. Very well, I'll take it over right now. Thank you for your help.'

David Becker hung up the phone. 'Alfonso XIII.' He chuckled. 'Just have to know how to ask.'

Moments later a silent figure followed Becker up Calle Delicias into the softly settling Andalusian night.

CHAPTER 29

Still unnerved from her encounter with Hale, Susan gazed out through the one-way glass of Node 3. The Crypto floor was empty. Hale was silent again, engrossed. She wished he would leave.

She wondered if she should call Strathmore; the commander could simply kick Hale out – after all, it *was* Saturday. Susan knew, however, that if Hale got kicked out, he would immediately become suspicious. Once dismissed, he probably would start calling other cryptographers asking what they thought was going on. Susan decided it was better just to let Hale be. He would leave on his own soon enough.

An unbreakable algorithm. She sighed, her thoughts returning to Digital Fortress. It amazed her that an algorithm like that could really be created – then again, the proof was right there in front of her; TRANSLTR appeared useless against it.

Susan thought of Strathmore, nobly bearing the weight of this ordeal on his shoulders, doing what was necessary, staying cool in the face of disaster.

Susan sometimes saw David in Strathmore. They had many of the same qualities – tenacity, dedication, intelligence. Sometimes Susan thought Strathmore would be lost without her; the purity of her love for cryptography seemed to be an emotional lifeline to Strathmore, lifting him from the sea of churning politics and reminding him of his early days as a code-breaker.

Susan relied on Strathmore too; he was her shelter in a world of power-hungry men, nurturing her career, protecting her, and, as he often joked, making all her dreams come true. There was some truth to that, she thought. As unintentional as it may have been, the commander was the one who'd made the call that brought David Becker to the NSA that fateful afternoon. Her mind reeled back to him, and her eyes fell instinctively to the pull-slide beside her keyboard. There was a small fax taped there.

The fax had been there for seven months. It was the only code Susan Fletcher had yet to break. It was from David. She read it for the five-hundredth time.

PLEASE ACCEPT THIS HUMBLE FAX
MY LOVE FOR YOU IS WITHOUT WAX

He'd sent it to her after a minor tiff. She'd begged him for months to tell her what it meant, but he had refused. *Without wax.* It was David's revenge. Susan had taught David a lot about code-breaking, and to keep him on his toes, she had taken to encoding all of her messages to him with some simple encryption scheme. Shopping lists, love notes – they were all encrypted. It was a game, and David had become quite a good cryptographer. Then he'd decided to return the favor. He'd started signing all his letters 'Without wax, David.' Susan had over two dozen notes from David. They were all signed the same way. *Without wax.*

Susan begged to know the hidden meaning, but David wasn't talking. Whenever she asked, he simply smiled and said, *'You're* the code-breaker.'

The NSA's head cryptographer had tried everything – substitutions, cipher boxes, even anagrams. She'd run the letters 'without wax' through her computer and asked for rearrangements of the letters into new phrases. All she'd gotten back was: TAXI HUT WOW. It appeared Ensei Tankado was not the only one who could write unbreakable codes.

Her thoughts were interrupted by the sound of the pneumatic doors hissing open. Strathmore strode in.

'Susan, any word yet?' Strathmore saw Greg Hale and stopped short. 'Well, good evening, Mr Hale.' He frowned, his eyes narrowing. 'On a Saturday, no less. To what do we owe the honor?'

Hale smiled innocently. 'Just making sure I pull my weight.'

'I see.' Strathmore grunted, apparently weighing his options. After a moment, it seemed he too decided not to rock Hale's boat. He turned coolly to Susan. 'Ms Fletcher, could I speak to you for a moment? *Outside?'*

Susan hesitated. 'Ah . . . yes, sir.' She shot an uneasy glance at her monitor and then across the room at Greg Hale. 'Just a minute.'

With a few quick keystrokes, she pulled up a program called ScreenLock. It was a privacy utility. Every terminal in Node 3 was equipped with it. Because the terminals stayed on around the clock, ScreenLock enabled cryptographers to leave their stations and know that nobody would tamper with their files.

Susan entered her five-character privacy code, and her screen went black. It would remain that way until she returned and typed the proper sequence.

Then she slipped on her shoes and followed the commander out.

'What the hell is *he* doing here?' Strathmore demanded as soon as he and Susan were outside Node 3.

'His usual,' Susan replied. 'Nothing.'

Strathmore looked concerned. 'Has he said anything about TRANSLTR?'

'No. But if he accesses the Run-Monitor and sees it registering seventeen hours, he'll have something to say all right.'

Strathmore considered it. 'There's no reason he'd access it.'

Susan eyed the commander. 'You want to send him home?'

'No. We'll let him be.' Strathmore glanced over at the Sys-Sec office. 'Has Chartrukian left yet?'

'I don't know. I haven't seen him.'

'Jesus.' Strathmore groaned. 'This is a circus.' He ran a hand across the beard stubble that had darkened his face over the past thirty-six hours. 'Any word yet on the tracer? I feel like I'm sitting on my hands up there.'

'Not yet. Any word from David?'

Strathmore shook his head. 'I asked him not to call me until he has the ring.'

Susan looked surprised. 'Why not? What if he needs help?'

Strathmore shrugged. 'I can't help him from here – he's on his own. Besides, I'd rather not talk on un-secured lines just in case someone's listening.'

Susan's eyes widened in concern. 'What's *that* supposed to mean?'

Strathmore immediately looked apologetic. He gave her a reassuring smile. 'David's fine. I'm just being careful.'

Thirty feet away from their conversation, hidden behind the one-way glass of Node 3, Greg Hale stood at Susan's terminal. Her screen was black. Hale glanced out at the commander and Susan. Then he reached for his wallet. He extracted a small index card and read it.

Double-checking that Strathmore and Susan were still talking, Hale carefully typed five keystrokes on Susan's keyboard. A second later her monitor sprang to life.

'Bingo.' He chuckled.

Stealing the Node 3 privacy codes had been simple. In Node 3, every terminal had an identical detachable keyboard. Hale had simply taken his keyboard home one night and installed a chip that kept a record of every keystroke made on it. Then he had come in early, swapped his modified keyboard for someone else's, and waited. At the end of the day, he switched back and viewed the data recorded by the chip. Even though there were millions of keystrokes to sort through, finding the access code was simple; the first thing a cryptographer did every morning was type the privacy code that unlocked his terminal. This, of course, made Hale's job effortless – the privacy code always appeared as the first five characters on the list.

It was ironic, Hale thought as he gazed at Susan's monitor. He'd stolen the privacy codes just for kicks.

He was happy now he'd done it; the program on Susan's screen looked significant.

Hale puzzled over it for a moment. It was written in LIMBO – not one of his specialties. Just by looking at it, though, Hale could tell one thing for certain – this was *not* a diagnostic. He could make sense of only two words. But they were enough.

TRACER SEARCHING . . .

'Tracer?' he said aloud. 'Searching for *what?*' Hale felt suddenly uneasy. He sat a moment studying Susan's screen. Then he made his decision.

Hale understood enough about the LIMBO programming language to know that it borrowed heavily from two other languages – C and Pascal – both of which he knew cold. Glancing up to check that Strathmore and Susan were still talking outside, Hale improvised. He entered a few modified Pascal commands and hit RETURN. The tracer's status window responded exactly as he had hoped.

TRACER ABORT?

He quickly typed: YES

ARE YOU SURE?

Again he typed: YES
After a moment the computer beeped.

TRACER ABORTED

Hale smiled. The terminal had just sent a message

telling Susan's tracer to self-destruct prematurely. Whatever she was looking for would have to wait.

Mindful to leave no evidence, Hale expertly navigated his way into her system activity log and deleted all the commands he'd just typed. Then he reentered Susan's privacy code.

The monitor went black.

When Susan Fletcher returned to Node 3, Greg Hale was seated quietly at his terminal.

CHAPTER 30

Alfonso XIII was a small four-star hotel set back from the Puerta de Jerez and surrounded by a thick wrought-iron fence and lilacs. David made his way up the marble stairs. As he reached for the door, it magically opened, and a bellhop ushered him inside.

'Baggage, señor? May I help you?'

'No, thanks. I need to see the concierge.'

The bellhop looked hurt, as if something in their two-second encounter had not been satisfactory. 'Por aquí, señor.' He led Becker into the lobby, pointed to the concierge, and hurried off.

The lobby was exquisite, small and elegantly appointed. Spain's Golden Age had long since passed, but for a while in the mid-1600s, this small nation had ruled the world. The room was a proud reminder of that era – suits of armor, military etchings, and a display case of gold ingots from the New World.

Hovering behind the counter marked CONSERJE was a trim, well-groomed man smiling so eagerly that it appeared he'd waited his entire life to be of assistance. 'En qué puedo servirle, señor? How may I serve you?'

He spoke with an affected lisp and ran his eyes up and down Becker's body.

Becker responded in Spanish. 'I need to speak to Manuel.'

The man's well-tanned face smiled even wider. 'Sí, sí, señor. I am Manuel. What is it you desire?'

'Señor Roldán at Escortes Belén told me you would—'

The concierge silenced Becker with a wave and glanced nervously around the lobby. 'Why don't you step over here?' He led Becker to the end of the counter. 'Now,' he continued, practically in a whisper. 'How may I help you?'

Becker began again, lowering his voice. 'I need to speak to one of his escorts whom I believe is dining here. Her name is Rocío.'

The concierge let out his breath as though overwhelmed. 'Aaah, Rocío – a beautiful creature.'

'I need to see her immediately.'

'But, señor, she is with a client.'

Becker nodded apologetically. 'It's important.' *A matter of national security.*

The concierge shook his head. 'Impossible. Perhaps if you left a—'

'It will only take a moment. Is she in the dining room?'

The concierge shook his head. 'Our dining room closed half an hour ago. I'm afraid Rocío and her guest have retired for the evening. If you'd like to leave me a message, I can give it to her in the morning.' He motioned to the bank of numbered message boxes behind him.

'If I could just call her room and—'

'I'm sorry,' the concierge said, his politeness

evaporating. 'The Alfonso XIII has strict policies regarding client privacy.'

Becker had no intention of waiting ten hours for a fat man and a prostitute to wander down for breakfast.

'I understand,' Becker said. 'Sorry to bother you.' He turned and walked back into the lobby. He strode directly to a cherry roll-top desk that had caught his eye on his way in. It held a generous supply of Alfonso XIII postcards and stationery as well as pens and envelopes. Becker sealed a blank piece of paper in an envelope and wrote one word on the envelope.

ROCÍO.

Then he went back to the concierge.

'I'm sorry to trouble you again,' Becker said approaching sheepishly. 'I'm being a bit of a fool, I know. I was hoping to tell Rocío personally how much I enjoyed our time together the other day. But I'm leaving town tonight. Perhaps I'll just leave her a note after all.' Becker laid the envelope on the counter.

The concierge looked down at the envelope and clucked sadly to himself. *Another lovesick heterosexual,* he thought. *What a waste.* He looked up and smiled. 'But of course, Mr . . . ?'

'Buisán,' Becker said. 'Miguel Buisán.'

'Of course. I'll be sure Rocío gets this in the morning.'

'Thank you.' Becker smiled and turned to go.

The concierge, after discreetly checking out Becker's backside, scooped up the envelope off the counter and turned to the bank of numbered slots on the wall behind him. Just as the man slipped the envelope into one of the slots, Becker spun with one final inquiry.

'Where might I call a taxi?'

The concierge turned from the wall of cubbyholes and answered. But Becker did not hear his response. The timing had been perfect. The concierge's hand was just emerging from a box marked Suite 301.

Becker thanked the concierge and slowly wandered off looking for the elevator.

In and out, he repeated to himself.

CHAPTER 31

Susan returned to Node 3. Her conversation with Strathmore had made her increasingly anxious about David's safety. Her imagination was running wild.

'So,' Hale spouted from his terminal. 'What did Strathmore want? A romantic evening alone with his head cryptographer?'

Susan ignored the comment and settled in at her terminal. She typed her privacy code and the screen came to life. The tracer program came into view; it still had not returned any information on North Dakota.

Damn, Susan thought. *What's taking so long?*

'You seem uptight,' Hale said innocently. 'Having trouble with your diagnostic?'

'Nothing serious,' she replied. But Susan wasn't so sure. The tracer was overdue. She wondered if maybe she'd made a mistake while writing it. She began scanning the long lines of LIMBO programming on her screen, searching for anything that could be holding things up.

Hale observed her smugly. 'Hey, I meant to ask you,' he ventured. 'What do you make of that unbreakable algorithm Ensei Tankado said he was writing?'

Susan's stomach did a flip. She looked up. 'Unbreakable algorithm?' She caught herself. 'Oh, yeah . . . I think I read something about that.'

'Pretty incredible claim.'

'Yeah,' Susan replied, wondering why Hale had suddenly brought it up. 'I don't buy it, though. Everyone knows an unbreakable algorithm is a mathematical impossibility.'

Hale smiled. 'Oh, yeah . . . the Bergofsky Principle.'

'And common sense,' she snapped.

'Who knows . . .' Hale sighed dramatically. 'There are more things in heaven and earth than are dreamt of in your philosophy.'

'I beg your pardon?'

'Shakespeare,' Hale offered. *'Hamlet.'*

'Read a lot while you were in jail?'

Hale chuckled. 'Seriously, Susan, did you ever think that maybe it *is* possible, that maybe Tankado really *did* write an unbreakable algorithm?'

This conversation was making Susan uneasy. 'Well, *we* couldn't do it.'

'Maybe Tankado's better than we are.'

'Maybe.' Susan shrugged, feigning disinterest.

'We corresponded for a while,' Hale offered casually. 'Tankado and me. Did you know that?'

Susan looked up, attempting to hide her shock. 'Really?'

'Yeah. After I uncovered the Skipjack algorithm, he wrote me – said we were brothers in the global fight for digital privacy.'

Susan could barely contain her disbelief. *Hale knows Tankado personally!* She did her best to look uninterested.

Hale went on. 'He congratulated me for proving

that Skipjack had a back door – called it a coup for privacy rights of civilians all over the world. You gotta admit, Susan, the back door in Skipjack was an underhanded play. Reading the world's E-mail? If you ask me, Strathmore *deserved* to get caught.'

'Greg,' Susan snapped, fighting her anger, 'that back door was so the NSA could decode E-mail that threatened this nation's security.'

'Oh, really?' Hale sighed innocently. 'And snooping the average citizen was just a lucky by-product?'

'We don't snoop average citizens, and you know it. The FBI can tap telephones, but that doesn't mean they listen to *every* call that's ever made.'

'If they had the manpower, they would.'

Susan ignored the remark. 'Governments should have the right to gather information that threatens the common good.'

'Jesus Christ' – Hale sighed – 'you sound like you've been brainwashed by Strathmore. You know damn well the FBI can't listen in whenever they want – they've got to get a warrant. A spiked encryption standard would mean the NSA could listen in to *anyone, anytime, anywhere.*'

'You're right – as we *should* be able to!' Susan's voice was suddenly harsh. 'If you hadn't uncovered the back door in Skipjack, we'd have access to *every* code we need to break, instead of just what TRANSLTR can handle.'

'If I hadn't found the back door,' Hale argued, 'someone else would have. I saved your asses by uncovering it when I did. Can you imagine the fallout if Skipjack had been in circulation when the news broke?'

'Either way,' Susan shot back, 'now we've got a

paranoid EFF who think we put back doors in *all* our algorithms.'

Hale asked smugly, 'Well, don't we?'

Susan eyed him coldly.

'Hey,' he said, backing off, 'the point is moot now anyway. You built TRANSLTR. You've got your instant information source. You can read *what* you want, *when* you want – no questions asked. You win.'

'Don't you mean *we* win? Last I heard, you worked for the NSA.'

'Not for long,' Hale chirped.

'Don't make promises.'

'I'm serious. Someday I'm getting out of here.'

'I'll be crushed.'

In that moment, Susan found herself wanting to curse Hale for everything that wasn't going right. She wanted to curse him for Digital Fortress, for her troubles with David, for the fact that she wasn't in the Smokies – but none of it was his fault. Hale's only fault was that he was obnoxious. Susan needed to be the bigger person. It was her responsibility as head cryptographer to keep the peace, to educate. Hale was young and naïve.

Susan looked over at him. It was frustrating, she thought, that Hale had the talent to be an asset in Crypto, but he still hadn't grasped the importance of what the NSA did.

'Greg,' Susan said, her voice quiet and controlled, 'I'm under a lot of pressure today. I just get upset when you talk about the NSA like we're some kind of high-tech peeping Tom. This organization was founded for one purpose – to protect the security of this nation. That may involve shaking a few trees and looking for the bad apples from time to time. I think most citizens would gladly sacrifice some privacy to know that the bad guys can't maneuver unchecked.'

Hale said nothing.

'Sooner or later,' Susan argued, 'the people of this nation need to put their trust somewhere. There's a lot of good out there – but there's also a lot of bad mixed in. Someone has to have access to all of it and separate the right from wrong. That's our job. That's our duty. Whether we like it or not, there is a frail gate separating democracy from anarchy. The NSA guards that gate.'

Hale nodded thoughtfully. 'Quis custodiet ipsos custodes?'

Susan looked puzzled.

'It's Latin,' Hale said. 'From *Satires* of Juvenal. It means "Who will guard the guards?" '

'I don't get it,' Susan said. '"Who will guard the guards?"'

'Yeah. If *we're* the guards of society, then who will watch *us* and make sure that *we're* not dangerous?'

Susan nodded, unsure how to respond.

Hale smiled. 'It's how Tankado signed all his letters to me. It was his favorite saying.'

CHAPTER 32

David Becker stood in the hallway outside suite 301. He knew that somewhere behind the ornately carved door was the ring. *A matter of national security.*

Becker could hear movement inside the room. Faint talking. He knocked. A deep German accent called out.

'Ja?'

Becker remained silent.

'Ja?'

The door opened a crack, and a rotund Germanic face gazed down at him.

Becker smiled politely. He did not know the man's name. 'Deutscher, ja?' he asked. 'German, right?'

The man nodded, uncertain.

Becker continued in perfect German. 'May I speak to you a moment?'

The man looked uneasy. 'Was wollen Sie? What do you want?'

Becker realized he should have rehearsed this before brazenly knocking on a stranger's door. He searched for the right words. 'You have something I need.'

These were apparently not the right words. The German's eyes narrowed.

'Ein ring,' Becker said. 'Du hast einen Ring. You have a ring.'

'Go away,' the German growled. He started to close the door. Without thinking, Becker slid his foot into the crack and jammed the door open. He immediately regretted the action.

The German's eyes went wide. 'Was tust du?' he demanded. 'What are you doing?'

Becker knew he was in over his head. He glanced nervously up and down the hall. He'd already been thrown out of the clinic; he had no intention of going two for two.

'Nimm deinen Fuß weg!' the German bellowed. 'Remove your foot!'

Becker scanned the man's pudgy fingers for a ring. Nothing. *I'm so close*, he thought. 'Ein Ring!' Becker repeated as the door slammed shut.

David Becker stood a long moment in the well-furnished hallway. A replica of a Salvador Dali hung nearby. 'Fitting,' Becker groaned. *Surrealism. I'm trapped in an absurd dream.* He'd woken up that morning in his own bed but had somehow ended up in Spain breaking into a stranger's hotel room on a quest for some magical ring.

Strathmore's stern voice pulled him back to reality: *You must find that ring.*

Becker took a deep breath and blocked out the words. He wanted to go home. He looked back to the door marked 301. His ticket home was just on the other side – a gold ring. All he had to do was get it.

He exhaled purposefully. Then he strode back to

suite 301 and knocked loudly on the door. It was time to play hardball.

The German yanked open the door and was about to protest, but Becker cut him off. He flashed his Maryland squash club ID and barked, 'Polizei!' Then Becker pushed his way into the room and threw on the lights.

Wheeling, the German squinted in shock. 'Was machst—'

'Silence!' Becker switched to English. 'Do you have a prostitute in this room?' Becker peered around the room. It was as plush as any hotel room he'd ever seen. Roses, champagne, a huge canopy bed. Rocío was nowhere to be seen. The bathroom door was closed.

'Prostituiert?' The German glanced uneasily at the closed bathroom door. He was larger than Becker had imagined. His hairy chest began right under his triple chin and sloped outward to his colossal gut. The drawstring of his white terry-cloth Alfonso XIII bathrobe barely reached around his waist.

Becker stared up at the giant with his most intimidating look. 'What is your name?'

A look of panic rippled across the German's corpulent face. 'Was willst du? What do you want?'

'I am with the tourist relations branch of the Spanish Guardia here in Seville. Do you have a prostitute in this room?'

The German glanced nervously at the bathroom door. He hesitated. 'Ja,' he finally admitted.

'Do you know this is illegal in Spain?'

'Nein,' the German lied. 'I did not know. I'll send her home right now.'

172

'I'm afraid it's too late for that,' Becker said with authority. He strolled casually into the room. 'I have a proposition for you.'

'Ein Vorschlag?' The German gasped. 'A proposition?'

'Yes. I can take you to headquarters right now . . .' Becker paused dramatically and cracked his knuckles.

'Or what?' the German asked, his eyes widening in fear.

'Or we make a deal.'

'What kind of deal?' The German had heard stories about the corruption in the Spanish Guardia Civil.

'You have something I want,' Becker said.

'Yes, of course!' the German effused, forcing a smile. He went immediately to the wallet on his dresser. 'How much?'

Becker let his jaw drop in mock indignation. 'Are you trying to bribe an officer of the law?' he bellowed.

'No! Of course not! I just thought . . .' The obese man quickly set down his wallet. 'I . . . I . . .' He was totally flustered. He collapsed on the corner of the bed and wrung his hands. The bed groaned under his weight. 'I'm sorry.'

Becker pulled a rose from the vase in the center of the room and casually smelled it before letting it fall to the floor. He spun suddenly. 'What can you tell me about the murder?'

The German went white. 'Mord? Murder?'

'Yes. The Asian man this morning? In the park? It was an assassination – Ermordung.' Becker loved the German word for assassination. Ermordung. It was so chilling.

'Ermordung? He . . . he was . . . ?'

'Yes.'

'But . . . but that's impossible,' the German choked. 'I was there. He had a heart attack. I saw it. No blood. No bullets.'

Becker shook his head condescendingly. 'Things are not always as they seem.'

The German went whiter still.

Becker gave an inward smile. The lie had served its purpose. The poor German was sweating profusely.

'Wh-wh-at do you want?' he stammered. 'I know nothing.'

Becker began pacing. 'The murdered man was wearing a gold ring. I need it.'

'I-I don't have it.'

Becker sighed patronizingly and motioned to the bathroom door. 'And Rocío? Dewdrop?'

The man went from white to purple. 'You know Dewdrop?' He wiped the sweat from his fleshy forehead and drenched his terry-cloth sleeve. He was about to speak when the bathroom door swung open.

Both men looked up.

Rocío Eva Granada stood in the doorway. A vision. Long flowing red hair, perfect Iberian skin, deep-brown eyes, a high smooth forehead. She wore a white terry-cloth robe that matched the German's. The tie was drawn snugly over her wide hips, and the neck fell loosely open to reveal her tanned cleavage. She stepped into the bedroom, the picture of confidence.

'May I help you?' she asked in throaty English.

Becker gazed across the room at the stunning woman before him and did not blink. 'I need the ring,' he said coldly.

'Who are you?' she demanded.

Becker switched to Spanish with a dead-on Andalusian accent. 'Guardia Civil.'

She laughed. 'Impossible,' she replied in Spanish.

Becker felt a knot rise in his throat. Rocío was clearly a little tougher than her client. 'Impossible?' he repeated, keeping his cool. 'Shall I take you downtown to prove it?'

Rocío smirked. 'I will not embarrass you by accepting your offer. Now, who are you?'

Becker stuck to his story. 'I am with the Seville Guardia.'

Rocío stepped menacingly toward him. 'I know every police officer on the force. They are my best clients.'

Becker felt her stare cutting right through him. He regrouped. 'I am with a special tourist task force. Give me the ring, or I'll have to take you down to the precinct and—'

'And what?' she demanded, raising her eyebrows in mock anticipation.

Becker fell silent. He was in over his head. The plan was backfiring. *Why isn't she buying this?*

Rocío came closer. 'I don't know who you are or what you want, but if you don't get out of this suite right now, I will call hotel security, and the *real* Guardia will arrest you for impersonating a police officer.'

Becker knew that Strathmore could have him out of jail in five minutes, but it had been made very clear to him that this matter was supposed to be handled discreetly. Getting arrested was not part of the plan.

Rocío had stopped a few feet in front of Becker and was glaring at him.

'Okay.' Becker sighed, accentuating the defeat in his voice. He let his Spanish accent slip. 'I am not with the Seville police. A U.S. government organization sent

175

me to locate the ring. That's all I can reveal. I've been authorized to pay you for it.'

There was a long silence.

Rocío let his statement hang in the air a moment before parting her lips in a sly smile. 'Now that wasn't so hard, was it?' She sat down on a chair and crossed her legs. 'How much can you pay?'

Becker muffled his sigh of relief. He wasted no time getting down to business. 'I can pay you 750,000 pesetas. Five thousand American dollars.' It was half what he had on him but probably ten times what the ring was actually worth.

Rocío raised her eyebrows. 'That's a lot of money.'

'Yes it is. Do we have a deal?'

Rocío shook her head. 'I wish I could say yes.'

'A million pesetas?' Becker blurted. 'It's all I have.'

'My, my.' She smiled. 'You Americans don't bargain very well. You wouldn't last a day in our markets.'

'Cash, right now,' Becker said, reaching for the envelope in his jacket. *I just want to go home.*

Rocío shook her head. 'I can't.'

Becker bristled angrily. 'Why not?'

'I no longer have the ring,' she said apologetically. 'I've already sold it.'

CHAPTER 33

Tokugen Numataka stared out his window and paced like a caged animal. He had not yet heard from his contact, North Dakota. *Damn Americans! No sense of punctuality!*

He would have called North Dakota himself, but he didn't have a phone number for him. Numataka hated doing business this way – with someone else in control.

The thought had crossed Numataka's mind from the beginning that the calls from North Dakota could be a hoax – a Japanese competitor playing him for the fool. Now the old doubts were coming back. Numataka decided he needed more information.

He burst from his office and took a left down Numatech's main hallway. His employees bowed reverently as he stormed past. Numataka knew better than to believe they actually loved him – bowing was a courtesy Japanese employees offered even the most ruthless of bosses.

Numataka went directly to the company's main switchboard. All calls were handled by a single operator on a Corenco 2000, twelve-line switchboard terminal.

The woman was busy but stood and bowed as Numataka entered.

'Sit down,' he snapped.

She obeyed.

'I received a call at four forty-five on my personal line today. Can you tell me where it came from?' Numataka kicked himself for not having done this earlier.

The operator swallowed nervously. 'We don't have caller identification on this machine, sir. But I can contact the phone company. I'm sure they can help.'

Numataka had no doubt the phone company could help. In this digital age, privacy had become a thing of the past; there was a record of everything. Phone companies could tell you exactly who had called you and how long you'd spoken.

'Do it,' he commanded. 'Let me know what you find out.'

CHAPTER 34

Susan sat alone in Node 3, waiting for her tracer. Hale had decided to step outside and get some air – a decision for which she was grateful. Oddly, however, the solitude in Node 3 provided little asylum. Susan found herself struggling with the new connection between Tankado and Hale.

'Who will guard the guards?' she said to herself. *Quis custodiet ipsos custodes.* The words kept circling in her head. Susan forced them from her mind.

Her thoughts turned to David, hoping he was all right. She still found it hard to believe he was in Spain. The sooner they found the pass-keys and ended this, the better.

Susan had lost track of how long she'd been sitting there waiting for her tracer. Two hours? Three? She gazed out at the deserted Crypto floor and wished her terminal would beep. There was only silence. The late-summer sun had set. Overhead, the automatic fluorescents had kicked on. Susan sensed time was running out.

She looked down at her tracer and frowned. 'Come on,' she grumbled. 'You've had plenty of time.' She palmed her mouse and clicked her way into her tracer's status window. 'How long have you been running, anyway?'

Susan opened the tracer's status window – a digital clock much like the one on TRANSLTR; it displayed the hours and minutes her tracer had been running. Susan gazed at the monitor expecting to see a readout of hours and minutes. But she saw something else entirely. What she saw stopped the blood in her veins.

TRACER ABORTED

'Tracer aborted!' she choked aloud. 'Why?'

In a sudden panic, Susan scrolled wildly through the data, searching the programming for any commands that might have told the tracer to abort. But her search went in vain. It appeared her tracer had stopped all by itself. Susan knew this could mean only one thing – her tracer had developed a bug.

Susan considered 'bugs' the most maddening asset of computer programming. Because computers followed a scrupulously precise order of operations, the most minuscule programming errors often had crippling effects. Simple syntactical errors – such as a programmer mistakenly inserting a comma instead of a period – could bring entire systems to their knees. Susan had always thought the term 'bug' had an amusing origin:

It came from the world's first computer – the Mark 1 – a room-size maze of electromechanical circuits built in 1944 in a lab at Harvard University. The computer developed a glitch one day, and no one was able to locate the cause. After hours of searching, a lab assistant finally spotted the problem. It seemed a moth had landed on one of the computer's circuit boards and shorted it out. From that moment on, computer glitches were referred to as bugs.

'I don't have time for this,' Susan cursed.

Finding a bug in a program was a process that could take days. Thousands of lines of programming needed to be searched to find a tiny error – it was like inspecting an encyclopedia for a single typo.

Susan knew she had only one choice – to send her tracer again. She also knew the tracer was almost guaranteed to hit the same bug and abort all over again. Debugging the tracer would take time, time she and the commander didn't have.

But as Susan stared at her tracer, wondering what error she'd made, she realized something didn't make sense. She had used this exact same tracer last month with no problems at all. Why would it develop a glitch all of a sudden?

As she puzzled, a comment Strathmore made earlier echoed in her mind. *Susan, I tried to send the tracer myself, but the data it returned was nonsensical.*

Susan heard the words again. *The data it returned . . .*

She cocked her head. Was it possible? The data it returned?

If Strathmore had received data back from the tracer, then it obviously was working. His data was nonsensical, Susan assumed, because he had entered the wrong search strings – but nonetheless, the tracer was working.

Susan immediately realized that there was one other possible explanation for why her tracer aborted. Internal programming flaws were not the only reasons programs glitched; sometimes there were *external* forces – power surges, dust particles on circuit boards, faulty cabling. Because the hardware in Node 3 was so well tuned, she hadn't even considered it.

Susan stood and strode quickly across Node 3 to a large bookshelf of technical manuals. She grabbed a spiral binder marked SYS-OP and thumbed through. She found what she was looking for, carried the manual back to her terminal, and typed a few commands. Then she waited while the computer raced through a list of commands executed in the past three hours. She hoped the search would turn up some sort of external interrupt – an abort command generated by a faulty power supply or defective chip.

Moments later Susan's terminal beeped. Her pulse quickened. She held her breath and studied the screen.

ERROR CODE 22

Susan felt a surge of hope. It was good news. The fact that the inquiry had found an error code meant her tracer was fine. The trace had apparently aborted due to an external anomaly that was unlikely to repeat itself.

ERROR CODE 22. Susan racked her memory trying to remember what code 22 stood for. Hardware failures were so rare in Node 3 that she couldn't remember the numerical codings.

Susan flipped through the SYS-OP manual, scanning the list of error codes.

19: CORRUPT HARD PARTITION
20: DC SPIKE
21: MEDIA FAILURE

When she reached number 22, she stopped and stared a long moment. Baffled, she double-checked her monitor.

ERROR CODE 22

Susan frowned and returned to the SYS-OP manual. What she saw made no sense. The explanation simply read:

22: MANUAL ABORT

CHAPTER 35

Becker stared in shock at Rocío. 'You *sold* the ring?'

The woman nodded, her silky red hair falling around her shoulders.

Becker willed it not to be true. 'Pero . . . but . . .'

She shrugged and said in Spanish, 'A girl near the park.'

Becker felt his legs go weak. *This can't be!*

Rocío smiled coyly and motioned to the German. 'Él quería que lo guardará. He wanted to keep it, but I told him no. I've got Gitana blood in me, Gypsy blood; we Gitanas, in addition to having red hair, are very superstitious. A ring offered by a dying man is not a good sign.'

'Did you know the girl?' Becker interrogated.

Rocío arched her eyebrows. 'Vaya. You really want this ring, don't you?'

Becker nodded sternly. 'Who did you sell it to?'

The enormous German sat bewildered on the bed. His romantic evening was being ruined, and he apparently had no idea why. 'Was passiert?' he asked nervously. 'What's happening?'

Becker ignored him.

'I didn't actually sell it,' Rocío said. 'I tried to, but she was just a kid and had no money. I ended up giving it to her. Had I known about your generous offer, I would have saved it for you.'

'Why did you leave the park?' Becker demanded. 'Somebody had died. Why didn't you wait for the police? And give *them* the ring?'

'I solicit many things, Mr Becker, but *trouble* is not one of them. Besides, that old man seemed to have things under control.'

'The Canadian?'

'Yes, he called the ambulance. We decided to leave. I saw no reason to involve my date or myself with the police.'

Becker nodded absently. He was still trying to accept this cruel twist of fate. *She gave the damn thing away!*

'I tried to help the dying man,' Rocío explained. 'But he didn't seem to want it. He started with the ring – kept pushing it in our faces. He had these three crippled fingers sticking up. He kept pushing his hand at us – like we were supposed to take the ring. I didn't want to, but my friend here finally did. Then the guy died.'

'And you tried CPR?' Becker guessed.

'No. We didn't touch him. My friend got scared. He's big, but he's a wimp.' She smiled seductively at Becker. 'Don't worry – he can't speak a word of Spanish.'

Becker frowned. He was wondering again about the bruises on Tankado's chest. 'Did the paramedics give CPR?'

'I have no idea. As I told you, we left before they arrived.'

185

'You mean after you *stole* the ring.' Becker scowled.

Rocío glared at him. 'We did not steal the ring. The man was dying. His intentions were clear. We gave him his last wish.'

Becker softened. Rocío was right; he probably would have done the same damn thing. 'But then you gave the ring to some girl?'

'I told you. The ring made me nervous. The girl had lots of jewelry on. I thought she might like it.'

'And she didn't think it was strange? That you'd just *give* her a ring?'

'No. I told her I found it in the park. I thought she might offer to pay me for it, but she didn't. I didn't care. I just wanted to get rid of it.'

'When did you give it to her?'

Rocío shrugged. 'This afternoon. About an hour after I got it.'

Becker checked his watch: 11:48 P.M. The trail was eight hours old. *What the hell am I doing here? I'm supposed to be in the Smokys.* He sighed and asked the only question he could think of. 'What did the girl look like?'

'Era un punqui,' Rocío replied.

Becker looked up, puzzled. 'Un punqui?'

'Sí. Punqui.'

'A punk?'

'Yes, a punk,' she said in rough English, and then immediately switched back to Spanish. 'Mucha joyería. Lots of jewelry. A weird pendant in one ear. A skull, I think.'

'There are punk rockers in Seville?'

Rocío smiled. 'Todo bajo el sol. Everything under the sun.' It was the motto of Seville's Tourism Bureau.

'Did she give you her name?'

'No.'

'Did she say where she was going?'

'No. Her Spanish was poor.'

'She wasn't Spanish?' Becker asked.

'No. She was English, I think. She had wild hair – red, white, and blue.'

Becker winced at the bizarre image. 'Maybe she was American,' he offered.

'I don't think so,' Rocío said. 'She was wearing a T-shirt that looked like the British flag.'

Becker nodded dumbly. 'Okay. Red, white, and blue hair, a British flag T-shirt, a skull pendant in her ear. What else?'

'Nothing. Just your average punk.'

Average punk? Becker was from a world of collegiate sweatshirts and conservative haircuts – he couldn't even picture what the woman was talking about. 'Can you think of anything else at all?' he pressed.

Rocío thought a moment. 'No. That's it.'

Just then the bed creaked loudly. Rocío's client shifted his weight uncomfortably. Becker turned to him and spoke in fluent German. 'Noch etwas? Anything else? Anything to help me find the punk rocker with the ring?'

There was a long silence. It was as if the giant man had something he wanted to say, but he wasn't sure how to say it. His lower lip quivered momentarily, there was a pause, and then he spoke. The four words that came out were definitely English, but they were barely intelligible beneath his thick German accent. 'Fock off und die.'

Becker gaped in shock. 'I beg your pardon?'

'Fock off und die,' the man repeated, patting his left palm against his fleshy right forearm – a crude approximation of the Italian gesture for 'fuck you.'

Becker was too drained to be offended. *Fuck off and die? What happened to Das Wimp?* He turned back to Rocío and spoke in Spanish. 'Sounds like I've overstayed my welcome.'

'Don't worry about him.' She laughed. 'He's just a little frustrated. He'll get what's coming to him.' She tossed her hair and winked.

'Is there anything else?' Becker asked. 'Anything you can tell me that might help?'

Rocío shook her head. 'That's all. But you'll never find her. Seville is a big city – it can be very deceptive.'

'I'll do the best I can.' *It's a matter of national security . . .*

'If you have no luck,' Rocío said, eyeing the bulging envelope in Becker's pocket, 'please stop back. My friend will be sleeping, no doubt. Knock quietly. I'll find us an extra room. You'll see a side of Spain you'll never forget.' She pouted lusciously.

Becker forced a polite smile. 'I should be going.' He apologized to the German for interrupting his evening.

The giant smiled timidly. 'Keine Ursache.'

Becker headed out the door. *No problem? Whatever happened to 'Fuck off and die'?*

CHAPTER 36

'Manual abort?' Susan stared at her screen, mystified.

She knew she hadn't typed any manual abort command – at least not intentionally. She wondered if maybe she'd hit the wrong sequence of keys by mistake.

'Impossible,' she muttered. According to the headers, the abort command had been sent less than twenty minutes ago. Susan knew the only thing she'd typed in the last twenty minutes was her privacy code when she'd stepped out to talk to the commander. It was absurd to think the privacy code could have been misinterpreted as an abort command.

Knowing it was a waste of time, Susan pulled up her ScreenLock log and double-checked that her privacy code had been entered properly. Sure enough, it had.

'Then *where*,' she demanded angrily, 'where did it get a *manual* abort?'

Susan scowled and closed the ScreenLock window. Unexpectedly, however, in the split second as the window blipped away, something caught her eye. She reopened the window and studied the data. It made no sense. There was a proper 'locking' entry when she'd left Node 3, but the timing of the subsequent 'unlock' entry seemed strange. The two entries were less than one minute apart. Susan was certain she'd been outside with the commander for more than one minute.

Susan scrolled down the page. What she saw left her aghast. Registering three minutes later, a *second* set of lock-unlock entries appeared. According to the log, someone had unlocked her terminal while she was gone.

'Not possible!' she choked. The only candidate was Greg Hale, and Susan was quite certain she'd never given Hale her privacy code. Following good cryptographic procedure, Susan had chosen her code at random and never written it down; Hale's guessing the correct five-character alphanumeric was out of the question – it was thirty-six to the fifth power, over sixty million possibilities.

But the ScreenLock entries were as clear as day. Susan stared at them in wonder. Hale had somehow been on her terminal while she was gone. He had sent her tracer a manual abort command.

The questions of *how* quickly gave way to questions of *why?* Hale had no motive to break into her terminal. He didn't even know Susan was running a tracer. Even if he did know, Susan thought, why would he object to her tracking some guy named North Dakota?

The unanswered questions seemed to be multiplying in her head. 'First things first,' she said aloud. She would deal with Hale in a moment. Focusing on the matter at hand, Susan reloaded her tracer and hit the ENTER key. Her terminal beeped once.

Susan knew the tracer would take hours to return. She cursed Hale, wondering how in the world he'd gotten her privacy code, wondering what interest he had in her tracer.

Susan stood up and strode immediately for Hale's terminal. The screen was black, but she could tell it was not locked – the monitor was glowing faintly around the edges. Cryptographers seldom locked their terminals except when they left Node 3 for the night. Instead, they simply dimmed the brightness on their monitors – a universal, honor-code indication that no one should disturb the terminal.

Susan reached for Hale's terminal. 'Screw the honor code,' she said. 'What the hell are you up to?'

Throwing a quick glance out at the deserted Crypto floor, Susan turned up Hale's brightness controls. The monitor came into focus, but the screen was entirely empty. Susan frowned at the blank screen. Uncertain how to proceed, she called up a search engine and typed:

SEARCH FOR: 'TRACER'

It was a long shot, but if there were any references to Susan's tracer in Hale's computer, this search would find them. It might shed some light on why Hale had manually aborted her program. Seconds later the screen refreshed.

NO MATCHES FOUND

Susan sat a moment, unsure what she was even looking for. She tried again.

191

The monitor refreshed and provided a handful of innocuous references – no hint that Hale had any copies of Susan's privacy code on his computer.

Susan sighed loudly. *So what programs has he been using today?* She went to Hale's 'recent applications' menu to find the last program he had used. It was his E-mail server. Susan searched his hard drive and eventually found his E-mail folder hidden discreetly inside some other directories. She opened the folder, and additional folders appeared; it seemed Hale had numerous E-mail identities and accounts. One of them, Susan noticed with little surprise, was an anonymous account. She opened the folder, clicked one of the old, inbound messages, and read it.

She instantly stopped breathing. The message read:

TO: NDAKOTA@ARA.ANON.ORG
FROM: ET@DOSHISHA.EDU
GREAT PROGRESS! DIGITAL FORTRESS IS ALMOST DONE.
THIS THING WILL SET THE NSA BACK DECADES!

As if in a dream, Susan read the message over and over. Then, trembling, she opened another.

TO: NDAKOTA@ARA.ANON.ORG
FROM: ET@DOSHISHA.EDU
ROTATING CLEARTEXT WORKS! MUTATION STRINGS ARE THE TRICK!

It was unthinkable, and yet there it was. E-mail from Ensei Tankado. He had been writing to Greg Hale. They were working together. Susan went numb as the impossible truth stared up at her from the terminal.

Greg Hale is NDAKOTA?

Susan's eyes locked on the screen. Her mind searched desperately for some other explanation, but there was none. It was proof – sudden and inescapable: Tankado had used mutation strings to create a rotating cleartext function, and Hale had conspired with him to bring down the NSA.

'It's . . .' Susan stammered. 'It's . . . not possible.'

As if to disagree, Hale's voice echoed from the past: *Tankado wrote me a few times . . . Strathmore took a gamble hiring me . . . I'm getting out of here someday.*

Still, Susan could not accept what she was seeing. True, Greg Hale was obnoxious and arrogant – but he wasn't a traitor. He knew what Digital Fortress would do to the NSA; there was no way he was involved in a plot to release it!

And yet, Susan realized, there was nothing to stop him – nothing except honor and decency. She thought of the Skipjack algorithm. Greg Hale had ruined the NSA's plans once before. What would prevent him from trying again?

'But Tankado . . .' Susan puzzled. *Why would someone as paranoid as Tankado trust someone as unreliable as Hale?*

She knew that none of it mattered now. All that mattered was getting to Strathmore. By some ironic stroke of fate, Tankado's partner was right there under their noses. She wondered if Hale knew yet that Ensei Tankado was dead.

She quickly began closing Hale's E-mail files in order to leave the terminal exactly as she had found it. Hale could suspect nothing – not yet. The Digital

Fortress pass-key, she realized in amazement, was probably hidden somewhere inside that very computer.

But as Susan closed the last of the files, a shadow passed outside the Node 3 window. Her gaze shot up, and she saw Greg Hale approaching. Her adrenaline surged. He was almost to the doors.

'Damn!' she cursed, eyeing the distance back to her seat. She knew she'd never make it. Hale was almost there.

She wheeled desperately, searching Node 3 for options. The doors behind her clicked. Then they engaged. Susan felt instinct take over. Digging her shoes into the carpet, she accelerated in long, reaching strides toward the pantry. As the doors hissed open, Susan slid to a stop in front of the refrigerator and yanked open the door. A glass pitcher on top tipped precariously and then rocked to a stop.

'Hungry?' Hale asked, entering Node 3 and walking toward her. His voice was calm and flirtatious. 'Want to share some tofu?'

Susan exhaled and turned to face him. 'No thanks,' she offered. 'I think I'll just—' But the words got caught in her throat. She went white.

Hale eyed her oddly. 'What's wrong?'

Susan bit her lip and locked eyes with him. 'Nothing,' she managed. But it was a lie. Across the room, Hale's terminal glowed brightly. She'd forgotten to dim it.

CHAPTER 37

Downstairs at the Alfonso XIII, Becker wandered tiredly over to the bar. A dwarf-like bartender laid a napkin in front of him. 'Qué bebe usted? What are you drinking?'

'Nothing, thanks,' Becker replied. 'I need to know if there are any clubs in town for punk rockers?'

The bartender eyed him strangely. 'Clubs? For punks?'

'Yeah. Is there anyplace in town where they all hang out?'

'No lo sé, señor. I don't know. But certainly not here!' He smiled. 'How about a drink?'

Becker felt like shaking the guy. Nothing was going quite the way he'd planned.

'Quiere Vd. algo?' The bartender repeated. 'Fino? Jerez?'

Faint strains of classical music were being piped in overhead. *Brandenburg Concertos,* Becker thought. *Number four.* He and Susan had seen the Academy of St Martin in the Fields play the Brandenburgs at the university last year. He suddenly wished she were with him now. The breeze from an overhead air-conditioning vent reminded Becker what it was like outside. He pictured himself walking the sweaty, drugged-out streets of Triana looking for some punk in a British flag T-shirt. He thought of Susan again. 'Zumo de arándano,' he heard himself say. 'Cranberry juice.'

The bartender looked baffled. 'Solo?' Cranberry juice was a popular drink in Spain, but drinking it alone was unheard of.

'Sí,' Becker said. 'Solo.'

'Echo un poco de Smirnoff?' The bartender pressed. 'A splash of vodka?'

'No, gracias.'

'Gratis?' he coaxed. 'On the house?'

Through the pounding in his head, Becker pictured the filthy streets of Triana, the stifling heat, and the long night ahead of him. *What the hell*. He nodded. 'Sí, échame un poco de vodka.'

The bartender seemed much relieved and hustled off to make the drink.

Becker glanced around the ornate bar and wondered if he was dreaming. Anything would make more sense than the truth. *I'm a university teacher*, he thought, *on a secret mission*.

The bartender returned with a flourish and presented Becker's beverage. 'A su gusto, señor. Cranberry with a splash of vodka.'

Becker thanked him. He took a sip and gagged. *That's a splash?*

CHAPTER 38

Hale stopped halfway to the Node 3 pantry and stared at Susan. 'What's wrong, Sue? You look terrible.'

Susan fought her rising fear. Ten feet away, Hale's monitor glowed brightly. 'I'm . . . I'm okay,' she managed, her heart pounding.

Hale eyed her with a puzzled look on his face. 'You want some water?'

Susan could not answer. She cursed herself. *How could I forget to dim his damn monitor?* Susan knew the moment Hale suspected her of searching his terminal, he'd suspect she knew his real identity, North Dakota. She feared Hale would do anything to keep that information inside Node 3.

Susan wondered if she should make a dash for the door. But she never got the chance. Suddenly there was a pounding at the glass wall. Both Hale and Susan jumped. It was Chartrukian. He was banging his sweaty fists against the glass again. He looked like he'd seen Armageddon.

Hale scowled at the crazed Sys-Sec outside the window, then turned back to Susan. 'I'll be right back. Get yourself a drink. You look pale.' Hale turned and went outside.

Susan steadied herself and moved quickly to Hale's terminal. She reached down and adjusted the brightness controls. The monitor went black.

Her head was pounding. She turned and eyed the conversation now taking place on the Crypto floor. Apparently, Chartrukian had not gone home, after all. The young Sys-Sec was now in a panic, spilling his guts to Greg Hale. Susan knew it didn't matter – Hale knew everything there was to know.

I've got to get to Strathmore, she thought. *And fast*.

CHAPTER 39

Room 301. Rocío Eva Granada stood naked in front of the bathroom mirror. This was the moment she'd been dreading all day. The German was on the bed waiting for her. He was the biggest man she'd ever been with.

Reluctantly, she took an ice cube from the water bucket and rubbed it across her nipples. They quickly hardened. This was her gift – to make men feel wanted. It's what kept them coming back. She ran her hands across her supple, well-tanned body and hoped it would survive another four or five more years until she had enough to retire. Señor Roldán took most of her pay, but without him she knew she'd be with the rest of the hookers picking up drunks in Triana. These men at least had money. They never beat her, and they were easy to satisfy. She slipped into her lingerie, took a deep breath, and opened the bathroom door.

As Rocío stepped into the room, the German's eyes bulged. She was wearing a black negligee. Her chestnut skin radiated in the soft light, and her nipples stood at attention beneath the lacy fabric.

199

'Komm doch hierher,' he said eagerly, shedding his robe and rolling onto his back.

Rocío forced a smile and approached the bed. She gazed down at the enormous German. She chuckled in relief. The organ between his legs was tiny.

He grabbed at her and impatiently ripped off her negligee. His fat fingers groped at every inch of her body. She fell on top of him and moaned and writhed in false ecstasy. As he rolled her over and climbed on top of her, she thought she would be crushed. She gasped and choked against his puttylike neck. She prayed he would be quick.

'Sí! Sí!' she gasped in between thrusts. She dug her fingernails into his backside to encourage him.

Random thoughts cascaded through her mind – faces of the countless men she'd satisfied, ceilings she'd stared at for hours in the dark, dreams of having children . . .

Suddenly, without warning, the German's body arched, stiffened, and almost immediately collapsed on top of her. *That's all?* she thought, surprised and relieved.

She tried to slide out from under him. 'Darling,' she whispered huskily. 'Let me get on top.' But the man did not move.

She reached up and pushed at his massive shoulders. 'Darling, I . . . I can't breathe!' She began feeling faint. She felt her ribs cracking. 'Despiértate!' Her fingers instinctively started pulling at his matted hair. *Wake up!*

It was then that she felt the warm sticky liquid. It was matted in his hair – flowing onto her cheeks, into her mouth. It was salty. She twisted wildly beneath him. Above her, a strange shaft of light illuminated the German's contorted face. The bullet hole in his temple was gushing blood all over her. She tried to scream, but there was no air left in her lungs. He was crushing her. Delirious, she clawed toward the shaft of light coming from the doorway. She saw a hand. A gun with a silencer. A flash of light. And then nothing.

CHAPTER 40

Outside Node 3, Chartrukian looked desperate. He was trying to convince Hale that TRANSLTR was in trouble. Susan raced by them with only one thought in mind – to find Strathmore.

The panicked Sys-Sec grabbed Susan's arm as she passed. 'Ms Fletcher! We have a virus! I'm positive! You have to—'

Susan shook herself free and glared ferociously. 'I thought the commander told you to go home.'

'But the Run-Monitor! It's registering eighteen—'

'Commander Strathmore told you to go home!'

'FUCK STRATHMORE!' Chartrukian screamed, the words resounding throughout the dome.

A deep voice boomed from above. 'Mr Chartrukian?'

The three Crypto employees froze.

High above them, Strathmore stood at the railing outside his office.

For a moment, the only sound inside the dome was the uneven hum of the generators below. Susan tried desperately to catch Strathmore's eye. *Commander! Hale is North Dakota!*

But Strathmore was fixated on the young Sys-Sec. He descended the stairs without so much as a blink, keeping his eyes trained on Chartrukian the whole way down. He made his way across the Crypto floor and stopped six inches in front of the trembling technician. '*What* did you say?'

'Sir,' Chartrukian choked, 'TRANSLTR's in trouble.'

'Commander?' Susan interjected. 'If I could—'

Strathmore waved her off. His eyes never left the Sys-Sec.

Phil blurted, 'We have an infected file, sir. I'm sure of it!'

Strathmore's complexion turned a deep red. 'Mr Chartrukian, we've been through this. There is *no* file infecting TRANSLTR!'

'Yes, there is!' he cried. 'And if it makes its way to the main databank—'

'Where the hell is this infected file?' Strathmore bellowed. 'Show it to me!'

Chartrukian hesitated. 'I can't.'

'Of course you can't! It doesn't exist!'

Susan said, 'Commander, I must—'

Again Strathmore silenced her with an angry wave.

Susan eyed Hale nervously. He seemed smug and detached. *It makes perfect sense,* she thought. *Hale wouldn't be worried about a virus; he knows what's really going on inside TRANSLTR.*

Chartrukian was insistent. 'The infected file *exists,* sir. But Gauntlet never picked it up.'

'If Gauntlet never picked it up,' Strathmore fumed, 'then how the hell do you know it exists?'

Chartrukian suddenly sounded more confident. 'Mutation strings, sir. I ran a full analysis, and the probe turned up mutation strings!'

203

Susan now understood why the Sys-Sec was so concerned. *Mutation strings*, she mused. She knew mutation strings were programming sequences that corrupted data in extremely complex ways. They were very common in computer viruses, particularly viruses that altered large blocks of data. Of course, Susan also knew from Tankado's E-mail that the mutation strings Chartrukian had seen were harmless – simply part of Digital Fortress.

The Sys-Sec went on. 'When I first saw the strings, sir, I thought Gauntlet's filters had failed. But then I ran some tests and found out . . .' He paused, looking suddenly uneasy. 'I found out that somebody manually *bypassed* Gauntlet.'

The statement met with a sudden hush. Strathmore's face turned an even deeper shade of crimson. There was no doubt whom Chartrukian was accusing; Strathmore's terminal was the only one in Crypto with clearance to bypass Gauntlet's filters.

When Strathmore spoke, his voice was like ice. 'Mr Chartrukian, not that it is any concern of yours, but *I* bypassed Gauntlet.' He went on, his temper hovering near the boiling point. 'As I told you earlier, I'm running a very advanced diagnostic. The mutation strings you see in TRANSLTR are part of that diagnostic; they are there because *I* put them there. Gauntlet refused to let me load the file, so I bypassed its filters.' Strathmore's eyes narrowed sharply at Chartrukian. 'Now, will there be anything else before you go?'

In a flash, it all clicked for Susan. When Strathmore had downloaded the encrypted Digital Fortress algorithm from the Internet and tried to run it through TRANSLTR, the mutation strings had tripped

Gauntlet's filters. Desperate to know whether Digital Fortress was breakable, Strathmore decided to bypass the filters.

Normally, bypassing Gauntlet was unthinkable. In this situation, however, there was no danger in sending Digital Fortress directly into TRANSLTR; the commander knew exactly what the file was and where it came from.

'With all due respect, sir,' Chartrukian pressed, 'I've never heard of a diagnostic that employs mutation—'

'Commander,' Susan interjected, not able to wait another moment. 'I really need to—'

This time her words were cut short by the sharp ring of Strathmore's cellular phone. The commander snatched up the receiver. 'What is it!' he barked. Then he fell silent and listened to the caller.

Susan forgot about Hale for an instant. She prayed the caller was David. *Tell me he's okay,* she thought. *Tell me he found the ring!* But Strathmore caught her eye and he gave her a frown. It was not David.

Susan felt her breath grow short. All she wanted to know was that the man she loved was safe. Strathmore, Susan knew, was impatient for other reasons; if David took much longer, the commander would have to send backup – NSA field agents. It was a gamble he had hoped to avoid.

'Commander?' Chartrukian urged. 'I really think we should check—'

'Hold on,' Strathmore said, apologizing to his caller. He covered his mouthpiece and leveled a fiery stare at his young Sys-Sec. 'Mr Chartrukian,' he growled, 'this discussion is over. You are to leave Crypto. *Now.* That's an order.'

Chartrukian stood stunned. 'But, sir, mutation str—'

'NOW!' Strathmore bellowed.

Chartrukian stared a moment, speechless. Then he stormed off toward the Sys-Sec lab.

Strathmore turned and eyed Hale with a puzzled look. Susan understood the commander's mystification. Hale had been quiet – too quiet. Hale knew very well there was no such thing as a diagnostic that used mutation strings, much less one that could keep TRANSLTR busy eighteen hours. And yet Hale hadn't said a word. He appeared indifferent to the entire commotion. Strathmore was obviously wondering *why*. Susan had the answer.

'Commander,' she said insistently, 'if I could just speak—'

'In a minute,' he interjected, still eyeing Hale quizzically. 'I need to take this call.' With that, Strathmore turned on his heel and headed for his office.

Susan opened her mouth, but the words stalled on the tip of her tongue. *Hale is North Dakota!* She stood rigid, unable to breathe. She felt Hale staring at her. Susan turned. Hale stepped aside and swung his arm graciously toward the Node 3 door. 'After you, Sue.'

CHAPTER 41

In a linen closet on the third floor of the Alfonso XIII, a maid lay unconscious on the floor. The man with wire-rim glasses was replacing a hotel master key in her pocket. He had not sensed her scream when he struck her, but he had no way of knowing for sure – he had been deaf since he was twelve.

He reached to the battery pack on his belt with a certain kind of reverence; a gift from a client, the machine had given him new life. He could now receive his contracts anywhere in the world. All communications arrived instantaneously and untraceably.

He was eager as he touched the switch. His glasses flickered to life. Once again his fingers carved into the empty air and began clicking together. As always, he had recorded the names of his victims – a simple matter of searching a wallet or purse. The contacts on his fingers connected, and the letters appeared in the lens of his glasses like ghosts in the air.

SUBJECT: ROCIO EVA GRANADA – TERMINATED
SUBJECT: HANS HUBER – TERMINATED

Three stories below David Becker paid his tab and wandered across the lobby, his half-finished drink in hand. He headed toward the hotel's open terrace for some fresh air. *In and out*, he mused. Things hadn't panned out quite as he expected. He had a decision to make. Should he just give up and go back to the airport? *A matter of national security*. He swore under his breath. So why the hell had they sent a schoolteacher?

Becker moved out of sight of the bartender and dumped the remaining drink in a potted jasmine. The vodka had made him light-headed. *Cheapest drunk in history*, Susan often called him. After refilling the heavy crystal glass from a water fountain, Becker took a long swallow.

He stretched a few times trying to shake off the light haze that had settled over him. Then he set down his glass and walked across the lobby.

As he passed the elevator, the doors slid open. There was a man inside. All Becker saw were thick wire-rim glasses. The man raised a handkerchief to blow his nose. Becker smiled politely and moved on . . . out into the stifling Sevillian night.

CHAPTER 42

Inside Node 3, Susan caught herself pacing frantically. She wished she'd exposed Hale when she'd had the chance.

Hale sat at his terminal. 'Stress is a killer, Sue. Something you want to get off your chest?'

Susan forced herself to sit. She had thought Strathmore would be off the phone by now and return to speak to her, but he was nowhere to be seen. Susan tried to keep calm. She gazed at her computer screen. The tracer was still running – for the second time. It was immaterial now. Susan knew whose address it would return: GHALE@crypto.nsa.gov.

Susan gazed up toward Strathmore's workstation and knew she couldn't wait any longer. It was time to interrupt the commander's phone call. She stood and headed for the door.

Hale seemed suddenly uneasy, apparently noticing Susan's odd behavior. He strode quickly across the room and beat her to the door. He folded his arms and blocked her exit.

'Tell me what's going on,' he demanded. 'There's something going on here today. What is it?'

'Let me out,' Susan said as evenly as possible, feeling a sudden twinge of danger.

'Come on,' Hale pressed. 'Strathmore practically fired Chartrukian for doing his job. What's going on inside TRANSLTR? We don't have any diagnostics that run eighteen hours. That's bullshit, and you know it. Tell me what's going on.'

Susan's eyes narrowed. *You know damn well what's going on!* 'Back off, Greg,' she demanded. 'I need to use the bathroom.'

Hale smirked. He waited a long moment and then stepped aside. 'Sorry, Sue. Just flirting.'

Susan pushed by him and left Node 3. As she passed the glass wall, she sensed Hale's eyes boring into her from the other side.

Reluctantly, she circled toward the bathrooms. She would have to make a detour before visiting the Commander. Greg Hale could suspect nothing.

CHAPTER 43

A jaunty forty-five, Chad Brinkerhoff was well-pressed, well-groomed, and well-informed. His summer-weight suit, like his tan skin, showed not a wrinkle or hint of wear. His hair was thick, sandy blond, and – most importantly – all his own. His eyes were a brilliant blue – subtly enhanced by the miracle of tinted contact lenses.

He surveyed the wood-paneled office around him and knew he had risen as far as he would rise in the NSA. He was on the ninth floor – Mahogany Row. Office 9A197. The Directorial Suite.

It was a Saturday night, and Mahogany Row was all but deserted, its executives long gone – off enjoying whatever pastimes influential men enjoyed in their leisure. Although Brinkerhoff had always dreamed of a 'real' post with the agency, he had somehow ended up as a 'personal aide' – the official cul de sac of the political rat race. The fact that he worked side by side with the single most powerful man in American intelligence was little consolation. Brinkerhoff had graduated with honors from Andover and Williams, and yet here he was, middle-aged, with no real power

– no real stake. He spent his days arranging someone else's calendar.

There were definite benefits to being the director's personal aide – Brinkerhoff had a plush office in the directorial suite, full access to all the NSA departments, and a certain level of distinction that came from the company he kept. He ran errands for the highest echelons of power. Deep down Brinkerhoff knew he was born to be a PA – smart enough to take notes, handsome enough to give press conferences, and lazy enough to be content with it.

The sticky-sweet chime of his mantel clock accented the end of another day of his pathetic existence. *Shit*, he thought. *Five o'clock on a Saturday. What the hell am I doing here?*

'Chad?' A woman appeared in his doorway.

Brinkerhoff looked up. It was Midge Milken, Fontaine's internal security analyst. She was sixty, slightly heavy, and, much to the puzzlement of Brinkerhoff, quite appealing. A consummate flirt and an ex-wife three times over, Midge prowled the six-room directorial suite with a saucy authority. She was sharp, intuitive, worked ungodly hours, and was rumored to know more about the NSA's inner workings than God himself.

Damn, Brinkerhoff thought, eyeing her in her gray cashmere dress. *Either I'm getting older, or she's looking younger.*

'Weekly reports.' She smiled, waving a fanfold of paper. 'You need to check the figures.'

Brinkerhoff eyed her body. 'Figures look good from here.'

'Really, Chad,' she laughed. 'I'm old enough to be your mother.'

Don't remind me, he thought.

Midge strode in and sidled up to his desk. 'I'm on my way out, but the director wants these compiled by the time he gets back from South America. That's Monday, bright and early.' She dropped the printouts in front of him.

'What am I, an accountant?'

'No, hon, you're a cruise director. Thought you knew that.'

'So what am I doing crunching numbers?'

She ruffled his hair. 'You wanted more responsibility. Here it is.'

He looked up at her sadly. 'Midge . . . I have no life.'

She tapped her finger on the paper. '*This* is your life, Chad Brinkerhoff.' She looked down at him and softened. 'Anything I can get you before I go?'

He eyed her pleadingly and rolled his aching neck. 'My shoulders are tight.'

Midge didn't bite. 'Take an aspirin.'

He pouted. 'No back rub?'

She shook her head. '*Cosmopolitan* says two-thirds of backrubs end in sex.'

Brinkerhoff looked indignant. '*Ours* never do!'

'Precisely.' She winked. 'That's the problem.'

'Midge—'

'Night, Chad.' She headed for the door.

'You're leaving?'

'You know I'd stay,' Midge said, pausing in the doorway, 'but I do have *some* pride. I just can't see playing second fiddle – particularly to a teenager.'

'My wife's *not* a teenager,' Brinkerhoff defended. 'She just acts like one.'

Midge gave him a surprised look. 'I wasn't talking about your wife.' She batted her eyes innocently. 'I

213

was talking about *Carmen.'* She spoke the name with a thick Puerto Rican accent.

Brinkerhoff's voice cracked slightly. 'Who?'

'Carmen? In food services?'

Brinkerhoff felt himself flush. Carmen Huerta was a twenty-seven-year-old pastry chef who worked in the NSA commissary. Brinkerhoff had enjoyed a number of presumably secret after-hours flings with her in the stockroom.

She gave him a wicked wink. 'Remember, Chad . . . Big Brother knows all.'

Big Brother? Brinkerhoff gulped in disbelief. *Big Brother watches the STOCKROOMS too?*

Big Brother, or 'Brother' as Midge often called it, was a Centrex 333 that sat in a small closetlike space off the suite's central room. Brother was Midge's whole world. It received data from 148 closed circuit video cameras, 399 electronic doors, 377 phone taps, and 212 free-standing bugs in the NSA complex.

The directors of the NSA had learned the hard way that 26,000 employees were not only a great asset but a great liability. Every major security breach in the NSA's history had come from within. It was Midge's job as internal security analyst, to watch everything that went on within the walls of the NSA . . . including, apparently, the commissary stockroom.

Brinkerhoff stood to defend himself, but Midge was already on her way out.

'Hands *above* the desk,' she called over her shoulder. 'No funny stuff after I go. The walls have eyes.'

Brinkerhoff sat and listened to the sound of her heels fading down the corridor. At least he knew Midge would never tell. She was not without her weaknesses. Midge had indulged in a few indiscretions of her own – mostly wandering back rubs with Brinkerhoff.

His thoughts turned back to Carmen. He pictured her lissome body, those dark thighs, that AM radio she played full blast – hot San Juan salsa. He smiled. *Maybe I'll drop by for a snack when I'm done.*

He opened the first printout.

CRYPTO – PRODUCTION/EXPENDITURE

His mood immediately lightened. Midge had given him a freebie; the Crypto report was always a piece of cake. Technically he was supposed to compile the whole thing, but the only figure the director ever asked for was the MCD – the mean cost per decryption. The MCD represented the estimated amount it cost TRANSLTR to break a single code. As long as the figure was below $1,000 per code, Fontaine didn't flinch. *A grand a pop.* Brinkerhoff chuckled. *Our tax dollars at work.*

As he began plowing through the document and checking the daily MCDs, images of Carmen Huerta smearing herself with honey and confectioner's sugar began playing in his head. Thirty seconds later he was almost done. The Crypto data was perfect – as always.

But just before moving on to the next report, something caught his eye. At the bottom of the sheet, the last MCD was off. The figure was so large that it had carried over into the next column and made a mess of the page. Brinkerhoff stared at the figure in shock.

999,999,999? He gasped. *A billion dollars?* The images of Carmen vanished. A *billion*-dollar code?

Brinkerhoff sat there a minute, paralyzed. Then in a burst of panic, he raced out into the hallway. 'Midge! Come back!'

215

CHAPTER 44

Phil Chartrukian stood fuming in the Sys-Sec lab. Strathmore's words echoed in his head: *Leave now! That's an order!* He kicked the trash can and swore in the empty lab.

'Diagnostic, my ass! Since when does the deputy director bypass Gauntlet's filters!?'

The Sys-Secs were well paid to protect the computer systems at the NSA, and Chartrukian had learned that there were only two job requirements: be utterly brilliant and exhaustively paranoid.

Hell, he cursed, *this isn't paranoia! The fucking Run-Monitor's reading eighteen hours!*

It was a virus. Chartrukian could feel it. There was little doubt in his mind what was going on: Strathmore had made a mistake by bypassing Gauntlet's filters, and now he was trying to cover it up with some half-baked story about a diagnostic.

Chartrukian wouldn't have been quite so edgy had TRANSLTR been the only concern. But it wasn't. Despite its appearance, the great decoding beast was by no means an island. Although the cryptographers believed Gauntlet was constructed for the sole purpose of protecting their code-breaking masterpiece, the Sys-Secs understood the truth. The Gauntlet filters served a much higher god. The NSA's main databank.

The history behind the databank's construction had always fascinated Chartrukian. Despite the efforts of the Department of Defense to keep the Internet to themselves in the late 1970s, it was too useful a tool not to attract the public sector. Eventually universities pried their way in. Shortly after that came the commercial servers. The floodgates opened, and the public poured in. By the early 90s, the government's once-secure 'Internet' was a congested wasteland of public E-mail and cyberporn.

Following a number of unpublicized, yet highly damaging computer infiltrations at the Office of Naval Intelligence, it became increasingly clear that government secrets were no longer safe on computers connected to the burgeoning Internet. The President, in conjunction with the Department of Defense, passed a classified decree that would fund a new, totally secure government network to replace the tainted Internet and function as a link between U.S. intelligence agencies. To prevent further computer pilfering of government secrets, all sensitive data was relocated to one highly secure location – the newly constructed NSA databank – the Fort Knox of U.S. intelligence data.

Literally millions of the country's most classified photos, tapes, documents, and videos were digitized and transferred to the immense storage facility and then the hard copies were destroyed. The databank was protected by a triple-layer power relay and a tiered digital backup system. It was also 214 feet underground to shield it from magnetic fields and possible explosions. Activities within the control room were designated *Top Secret Umbra* ... the country's highest level of security.

The secrets of the country had never been safer. This impregnable databank now housed blueprints for advanced weaponry, witness protection lists, aliases of field agents, detailed analyses and proposals for covert operations. The list was endless. There would be no more black-bag jobs damaging U.S. intelligence.

Of course, the officers of the NSA realized that stored data had value only if it was accessible. The real coup of the databank was not getting the classified data off the streets, it was making it accessible only to the correct people. All stored information had a security rating and, depending on the level of secrecy, was accessible to government officials on a compartmentalized basis. A submarine commander could dial in and check the NSA's most recent satellite photos of Russian ports, but he would not have access to the plans for an antidrug mission in South America. CIA analysts could access histories of known assassins but could not access launch codes reserved for the President.

Sys-Secs, of course, had no clearance for the information in the databank, but they were responsible for its safety. Like all large databanks – from insurance companies to universities – the NSA facility was constantly under attack by computer hackers trying to sneak a peek at the secrets waiting inside. But the NSA security programmers were the best in the world. No one had ever come close to infiltrating the NSA databank – and the NSA had no reason to think anybody ever would.

*

Inside the Sys-Sec lab, Chartrukian broke into a sweat trying to decide whether to leave. Trouble in TRANSLTR meant trouble in the databank too. Strathmore's lack of concern was bewildering.

Everyone knew that TRANSLTR and the NSA main databank were inextricably linked. Each new code, once broken, was fired from Crypto through 450 yards of fiber-optic cable to the NSA databank for safe keeping. The sacred storage facility had limited points of entry – and TRANSLTR was one of them. Gauntlet was supposed to be the impregnable threshold guardian. And Strathmore had bypassed it.

Chartrukian could hear his own heart pounding. *TRANSLTR's been stuck eighteen hours!* The thought of a computer virus entering TRANSLTR and then running wild in the basement of the NSA proved too much. 'I've got to report this,' he blurted aloud.

In a situation like this, Chartrukian knew there was only one person to call: the NSA's senior Sys-Sec officer, the short-fused, 400-pound computer guru who had built Gauntlet. His nickname was Jabba. He was a demigod at the NSA – roaming the halls, putting out virtual fires, and cursing the feeblemindedness of the inept and the ignorant. Chartrukian knew that as soon as Jabba heard Strathmore had bypassed Gauntlet's filters, all hell would break loose. *Too bad,* he thought, *I've got a job to do.* He grabbed the phone and dialed Jabba's twenty-four-hour cellular.

CHAPTER 45

David Becker wandered aimlessly down Avenida del Cid and tried to collect his thoughts. Muted shadows played on the cobblestones beneath his feet. The vodka was still with him. Nothing about his life seemed in focus at the moment. His mind drifted back to Susan, wondering if she'd gotten his phone message yet.

Up ahead, a Seville Transit Bus screeched to a halt in front of a bus stop. Becker looked up. The bus's doors cranked open, but no one disembarked. The diesel engine roared back to life, but just as the bus was pulling out, three teenagers appeared out of a bar up the street and ran after it, yelling and waving. The engines wound down again, and the kids hurried to catch up.

Thirty yards behind them, Becker stared in utter incredulity. His vision was suddenly focused, but he knew what he was seeing was impossible. It was a one-in-a-million chance.

I'm hallucinating.

But as the bus doors opened, the kids crowded around to board. Becker saw it again. This time he was certain. Clearly illuminated in the haze of the corner streetlight, he'd seen her.

The passengers climbed on, and the bus's engines revved up again. Becker suddenly found himself at a full sprint, the bizarre image fixed in his mind – black lipstick, wild eye shadow, and that hair . . . spiked straight up in three distinctive spires. Red, white, and blue.

As the bus started to move, Becker dashed up the street into a wake of carbon monoxide.

'Espera!' he called, running behind the bus.

Becker's cordovan loafers skimmed the pavement. His usual squash agility was not with him, though; he felt off balance. His brain was having trouble keeping track of his feet. He cursed the bartender and his jet lag.

The bus was one of Seville's older diesels, and fortunately for Becker, first gear was a long, arduous climb. Becker felt the gap closing. He knew he had to reach the bus before it downshifted.

The twin tailpipes choked out a cloud of thick smoke as the driver prepared to drop the bus into second gear. Becker strained for more speed. As he surged even with the rear bumper, Becker moved right, racing up beside the bus. He could see the rear doors – and as on all Seville buses, it was propped wide open: cheap air-conditioning.

Becker fixed his sights on the opening and ignored the burning sensation in his legs. The tires were beside him, shoulder-high, humming at a higher and higher pitch every second. He surged toward the door, missing the handle and almost losing his balance. He pushed harder. Underneath the bus, the clutch clicked as the driver prepared to change gears.

He's shifting! I won't make it!

But as the engine cogs disengaged to align the larger gears, the bus let up ever so slightly. Becker lunged. The engine reengaged just as his fingertips curled around the door handle. Becker's shoulder almost ripped from its socket as the engine dug in, catapulting him up onto the landing.

David Becker lay collapsed just inside the vehicle's doorway. The pavement raced by only inches away. He was now sober. His legs and shoulder ached. Wavering, he stood, steadied himself, and climbed into the darkened bus. In the crowd of silhouettes, only a few seats away, were the three distinctive spikes of hair.

Red, white, and blue! I made it!

Becker's mind filled with images of the ring, the waiting Learjet 60, and at the end of it all, Susan.

As Becker came even with the girl's seat wondering what to say to her, the bus passed beneath a street-light. The punk's face was momentarily illuminated.

Becker stared in horror. The makeup on her face was smeared across a thick stubble. She was not a girl at all, but a young man. He wore a silver stud in his upper lip, a black leather jacket, and no shirt.

'What the fuck do *you* want?' the hoarse voice asked. His accent was New York.

With the disoriented nausea of a slow-motion free fall, Becker gazed at the busload of passengers staring back at him. They were all punks. At least half of them had red, white, and blue hair.

'Siéntate!' the driver yelled.

Becker was too dazed to hear.

'*Siéntate!*' The driver screamed. '*Sit down!*'

222

Becker turned vaguely to the angry face in the rearview mirror. But he had waited too long.

Annoyed, the driver slammed down hard on the brakes. Becker felt his weight shift. He reached for a seat back but missed. For an instant, David Becker was airborne. Then he landed hard on the gritty floor.

On Avenida del Cid, a figure stepped from the shadows. He adjusted his wire-rim glasses and peered after the departing bus. David Becker had escaped, but it would not be for long. Of all the buses in Seville, Mr Becker had just boarded the infamous number 27.

Bus 27 had only one destination.

223

CHAPTER 46

Phil Chartrukian slammed down his receiver. Jabba's line was busy; Jabba spurned call-waiting as an intrusive gimmick that was introduced by AT&T to increase profits by connecting every call; the simple phrase 'I'm on the other line, I'll call you back' made phone companies millions annually. Jabba's refusal of call-waiting was his own brand of silent objection to the NSA's requirement that he carry an emergency cellular at all times.

Chartrukian turned and looked out at the deserted Crypto floor. The hum of the generators below sounded louder every minute. He sensed that time was running out. He knew he was supposed to leave, but from out of the rumble beneath Crypto, the Sys-Sec mantra began playing in his head: *Act first, explain later.*

In the high-stakes world of computer security, minutes often meant the difference between saving a system or losing it. There was seldom time to justify a defensive procedure before taking it. Sys-Secs were paid for their technical expertise . . . and their instinct.

Act first, explain later. Chartrukian knew what he

had to do. He also knew that when the dust settled, he would be either an NSA hero or in the unemployment line.

The great decoding computer had a virus – of that, the Sys-Sec was certain. There was one responsible course of action. Shut it down.

Chartrukian knew there were only two ways to shut down TRANSLTR. One was the commander's private terminal, which was locked in his office – out of the question. The other was the manual kill-switch located on one of the sublevels beneath the Crypto floor.

Chartrukian swallowed hard. He hated the sub-levels. He'd only been there once, during training. It was like something out of an alien world with its long mazes of catwalks, freon ducts, and a dizzy 136-foot drop to the rumbling power supplies below . . .

It was the last place he felt like going, and Strathmore was the last person he felt like crossing, but duty was duty. *They'll thank me tomorrow*, he thought, wondering if he was right.

Taking a deep breath, Chartrukian opened the senior Sys-Sec's metal locker. On a shelf of disassembled computer parts, hidden behind a media concentrator and LAN tester, was a Stanford alumni mug. Without touching the rim, he reached inside and lifted out a single Medeco key.

'It's amazing,' he grumbled, 'what System-Security officers *don't* know about security.'

CHAPTER 47

'A billion-dollar code?' Midge snickered, accompanying Brinkerhoff back up the hallway. 'That's a good one.'

'I swear it,' he said.

She eyed him askance. 'This better not be some ploy to get me out of this dress.'

'Midge, I would never—' he said self-righteously.

'I know, Chad. Don't remind me.'

Thirty seconds later, Midge was sitting in Brinkerhoff's chair and studying the Crypto report.

'See?' he said, leaning over her and pointing to the figure in question. 'This MCD? A billion dollars!'

Midge chuckled. 'It *does* appear to be a touch on the high side, doesn't it?'

'Yeah.' He groaned. 'Just a touch.'

'Looks like a divide-by-zero.'

'A who?'

'A divide-by-zero,' she said, scanning the rest of the data. 'The MCD's calculated as a fraction – total expense divided by number of decryptions.'

'Of course.' Brinkerhoff nodded blankly and tried not to peer down the front of her dress.

'When the denominator's zero,' Midge explained, 'the quotient goes to infinity. Computers hate infinity, so they type all nines.' She pointed to a different column. 'See this?'

'Yeah.' Brinkerhoff refocused on the paper.

'It's today's raw production data. Take a look at the number of decryptions.'

Brinkerhoff dutifully followed her finger down the column.

NUMBER OF DECRYPTIONS = 0

Midge tapped on the figure. 'It's just as I suspected. Divide-by-zero.'

Brinkerhoff arched his eyebrows. 'So everything's okay?'

She shrugged. 'Just means we haven't broken any codes today. TRANSLTR must be taking a break.'

'A break?' Brinkerhoff looked doubtful. He'd been with the director long enough to know that 'breaks' were not part of his preferred modus operandi – particularly with respect to TRANSLTR. Fontaine had paid $2 billion for the code-breaking behemoth, and he wanted his money's worth. Every second TRANSLTR sat idle was money down the toilet.

'Ah . . . Midge?' Brinkerhoff said. 'TRANSLTR doesn't take any breaks. It runs day and night. You know that.'

She shrugged. 'Maybe Strathmore didn't feel like hanging out last night to prepare the weekend run. He probably knew Fontaine was away and ducked out early to go fishing.'

'Come on, Midge.' Brinkerhoff gave her a disgusted look. 'Give the guy a break.'

It was no secret Midge Milken didn't like Trevor Strathmore. Strathmore had attempted a cunning maneuver rewriting Skipjack, but he'd been caught. Despite Strathmore's bold intentions, the NSA had paid dearly. The EFF had gained strength, Fontaine had lost credibility with Congress, and worst of all, the agency had lost a lot of its anonymity. There were suddenly housewives in Minnesota complaining to America Online and Prodigy that the NSA might be reading their E-mail – like the NSA gave a damn about a secret recipe for candied yams.

Strathmore's blunder had cost the NSA, and Midge felt responsible – not that she could have anticipated the commander's stunt, but the bottom line was that an unauthorized action had taken place behind Director Fontaine's back, a back Midge was paid to cover. Fontaine's hands-off attitude made him susceptible; and it made Midge nervous. But the director had learned long ago to stand back and let smart people do their jobs; that's exactly how he handled Trevor Strathmore.

'Midge, you know damn well Strathmore's not slacking,' Brinkerhoff argued. 'He runs TRANSLTR like a fiend.'

Midge nodded. Deep down, she knew that accusing Strathmore of shirking was absurd. The commander was as dedicated as they came – dedicated to a fault. He bore the evils of the world as his own personal cross. The NSA's Skipjack plan had been Strathmore's brainchild – a bold attempt to change the world. Unfortunately, like so many divine quests, this crusade ended in crucifixion.

'Okay,' she admitted, 'so I'm being a little harsh.'

'A little?' Brinkerhoff's eyes narrowed. 'Strathmore's

got a backlog of files a mile long. He's not about to let TRANSLTR sit idle for a whole weekend.'

'Okay, okay.' Midge sighed. 'My mistake.' She furrowed her brow and puzzled why TRANSLTR hadn't broken any codes all day. 'Let me double-check something,' she said, and began flipping through the report. She located what she was looking for and scanned the figures. After a moment she nodded. 'You're right, Chad. TRANSLTR's been running full force. Raw consumables are even a little on the high side; we're at over half a million kilowatt-hours since midnight last night.'

'So where does that leave us?'

Midge was puzzled. 'I'm not sure. It's odd.'

'You want to rerun the data?'

She gave him a disapproving stare. There were two things one never questioned about Midge Milken. One of them was her data. Brinkerhoff waited while Midge studied the figures.

'Huh,' she finally grunted. 'Yesterday's stats look fine: 237 codes broken. MCD, $874. Average time per code, a little over six minutes. Raw consumables, average. Last code entering TRANSLTR—' She stopped.

'What is it?'

'That's funny,' she said. 'Last file on yesterday's queue log ran at 11:37 P.M.'

'So?'

'So, TRANSLTR breaks codes every six minutes or so. The last file of the day usually runs closer to midnight. It sure doesn't look like—' Midge suddenly stopped short and gasped.

Brinkerhoff jumped. 'What!'

Midge was staring at the readout in disbelief. 'This file? The one that entered TRANSLTR last night?'

'Yeah?'

'It hasn't broken yet. It's queue time was 23:37:08 – but it lists *no* decrypt time.' Midge fumbled with the sheets. 'Yesterday *or* today!'

Brinkerhoff shrugged. 'Maybe those guys are running a tough diagnostic.'

Midge shook her head. *'Eighteen hours tough?'* She paused. 'Not likely. Besides, the queue data says it's an outside file. We should call Strathmore.'

'At home?' Brinkerhoff swallowed. 'On a Saturday night?'

'No,' Midge said. 'If I know Strathmore, he's on top of this. I'll bet good money he's here. Just a hunch.' Midge's hunches were the other thing one never questioned. 'Come on,' she said, standing up. 'Let's see if I'm right.'

Brinkerhoff followed Midge to her office, where she sat down and began to work Big Brother's keypads like a virtuoso pipe organist.

Brinkerhoff gazed up at the array of closed-caption video monitors on her wall, their screens all freeze frames of the NSA seal. 'You're gonna snoop Crypto?' he asked nervously.

'Nope,' Midge replied. 'Wish I could, but Crypto's a sealed deal. It's got no video. No sound. No nothing. Strathmore's orders. All I've got is approach stats and basic TRANSLTR stuff. We're lucky we've even got *that*. Strathmore wanted total isolation, but Fontaine insisted on the basics.'

Brinkerhoff looked puzzled. 'Crypto hasn't got video?'

'Why?' she asked, without turning from her monitor. 'You and Carmen looking for a little more privacy?'

Brinkerhoff grumbled something inaudible.

Midge typed some more keys. 'I'm pulling Strathmore's elevator log.' She studied her monitor a moment and then rapped her knuckle on the desk. 'He's here,' she said matter-of-factly. 'He's in Crypto right now. Look at this. Talk about long hours – he went in yesterday morning bright and early, and his elevator hasn't budged since. I'm showing no magnocard use for him on the main door. So he's definitely in there.'

Brinkerhoff breathed a slight sigh of relief. 'So, if Strathmore's in there, everything's okay, right?'

Midge thought a moment. 'Maybe,' she finally decided.

'Maybe?'

'We should call him and double-check.'

Brinkerhoff groaned. 'Midge, he's the deputy director. I'm sure he has everything under control. Let's not second-guess—'

'Oh, come on, Chad – don't be such a child. We're just doing our job. We've got a snag in the stats, and we're following up. Besides,' she added, 'I'd like to remind Strathmore that Big Brother's watching. Make him think twice before planning any more of his harebrained stunts to save the world.' Midge picked up the phone and began dialing.

Brinkerhoff looked uneasy. 'You really think you should bother him?'

'I'm not bothering him,' Midge said, tossing him the receiver. '*You* are.'

CHAPTER 48

'What?' Midge sputtered in disbelief. 'Strathmore claims our data is wrong?'

Brinkerhoff nodded and hung up the phone.

'Strathmore *denied* that TRANSLTR's been stuck on one file for eighteen hours?'

'He was quite pleasant about the whole thing.' Brinkerhoff beamed, pleased with himself for surviving the phone call. 'He assured me TRANSLTR was working fine. Said it was breaking codes every six minutes even as we speak. Thanked me for checking up on him.'

'He's lying,' Midge snapped. 'I've been running these Crypto stats for two years. The data is never wrong.'

'First time for everything,' he said casually.

She shot him a disapproving look. 'I run all data *twice*.'

'Well . . . you know what they say about computers. When they screw up, at least they're consistent about it.'

Midge spun and faced him. 'This isn't funny, Chad! The DDO just told a blatant lie to the director's office. I want to know why!'

Brinkerhoff suddenly wished he hadn't called her back in. Strathmore's phone call had set her off. Ever since Skipjack, whenever Midge had a sense that something suspicious was going on, she made an eerie transition from flirt to fiend. There was no stopping her until she sorted it out.

'Midge, it *is* possible our data is off,' Brinkerhoff said firmly. 'I mean, think about it – a file that ties up TRANSLTR for eighteen hours? It's unheard of. Go home. It's late.'

She gave him a haughty look and tossed the report on the counter. 'I trust the data. Instinct says it's right.'

Brinkerhoff frowned. Not even the director questioned Midge Milken's instincts anymore – she had an uncanny habit of always being right.

'Something's up,' she declared. 'And I intend to find out what it is.'

CHAPTER 49

Becker dragged himself off the floor of the bus and collapsed in an empty seat.

'Nice move, dipshit.' The kid with the three spikes sneered. Becker squinted in the stark lighting. It was the kid he'd chased onto the bus. He glumly surveyed the sea of red, white, and blue coiffures.

'What's with the hair?' Becker moaned, motioning to the others. 'It's all . . .'

'Red, white, and blue?' the kid offered.

Becker nodded, trying not to stare at the infected perforation in the kid's upper lip.

'Judas Taboo,' the kid said matter-of-factly.

Becker looked bewildered.

The punk spat in the aisle, obviously disgusted with Becker's ignorance. 'Judas Taboo? Greatest punk since Sid Vicious? Blew his head off here a year ago today. It's his anniversary.'

Becker nodded vaguely, obviously missing the connection.

'Taboo did his hair this way the day he signed off.' The kid spat again. 'Every fan worth his weight in piss has got red, white, and blue hair today.'

234

For a long moment, Becker said nothing. Slowly, as if he had been shot with a tranquilizer, he turned and faced front. Becker surveyed the group on the bus. Every last one was a punk. Most were staring at him.

Every fan has red, white, and blue hair today.

Becker reached up and pulled the driver-alert cord on the wall. It was time to get off. He pulled again. Nothing happened. He pulled a third time, more frantically. Nothing.

'They disconnect 'em on bus 27.' The kid spat again. 'So we don't fuck with 'em.'

Becker turned. 'You mean, I can't get off?'

The kid laughed. 'Not till the end of the line.'

Five minutes later, the bus was barreling along an unlit Spanish country road. Becker turned to the kid behind him. 'Is this thing ever going to stop?'

The kid nodded. 'Few more miles.'

'Where are we going?'

He broke into a sudden wide grin. 'You mean you don't know?'

Becker shrugged.

The kid started laughing hysterically. 'Oh, shit. You're gonna love it.'

CHAPTER 50

Only yards from TRANSLTR's hull, Phil Chartrukian stood over a patch of white lettering on the Crypto floor.

CRYPTO SUBLEVELS

AUTHORIZED PERSONNEL ONLY

He knew he was definitely *not* authorized personnel. He shot a quick glance up at Strathmore's office. The curtains were still pulled. Chartrukian had seen Susan Fletcher go into the bathrooms, so he knew she wasn't a problem. The only other question was Hale. He glanced toward Node 3, wondering if the cryptographer were watching.

'Fuck it,' he grumbled.

Below his feet the outline of a recessed trapdoor was barely visible in the floor. Chartrukian palmed the key he'd just taken from the Sys-Sec lab.

He knelt down, inserted the key in the floor, and turned. The bolt beneath clicked. Then he unscrewed the large external butterfly latch and freed the door. Checking once again over his shoulder, he squatted down and pulled. The panel was small, only three feet by three feet, but it was heavy. When it finally opened, the Sys-Sec stumbled back.

A blast of hot air hit him in the face. It carried with it the sharp bite of freon gas. Billows of steam swirled out of the opening, illuminated by the red utility lighting below. The distant hum of the generators became a rumble. Chartrukian stood up and peered into the opening. It looked more like the gateway to hell than a service entrance for a computer. A narrow ladder led to a platform under the floor. Beyond that, there were stairs, but all he could see was swirling red mist.

Greg Hale stood behind the one-way glass of Node 3. He watched as Phil Chartrukian eased himself down the ladder toward the sublevels. From where Hale was standing, the Sys-Sec's head appeared to have been severed from his body and left out on the Crypto floor. Then, slowly, it sank into the swirling mist.

'Gutsy move,' Hale muttered. He knew where Chartrukian was headed. An emergency manual abort of TRANSLTR was a logical action if he thought the computer had a virus. Unfortunately, it was also a sure way to have Crypto crawling with Sys-Secs in about ten minutes. Emergency actions raised alert flags at the main switchboard. A Sys-Sec investigation of Crypto was something Hale could not afford. Hale left Node 3 and headed for the trapdoor. Chartrukian had to be stopped.

CHAPTER 51

Jabba resembled a giant tadpole. Like the cinematic creature for whom he was nicknamed, the man was a hairless spheroid. As resident guardian angel of all NSA computer systems, Jabba marched from department to department, tweaking, soldering, and reaffirming his credo that prevention was the best medicine. No NSA computer had ever been infected under Jabba's reign; he intended to keep it that way.

Jabba's home base was a raised workstation overlooking the NSA's underground, ultra-secret databank. It was there that a virus would do the most damage and there that he spent the majority of his time. At the moment, however, Jabba was taking a break and enjoying pepperoni calzones in the NSA's all-night commissary. He was about to dig into his third when his cellular phone rang.

'Go,' he said, coughing as he swallowed a mouthful.

'Jabba,' a woman's voice cooed. 'It's Midge.'

'Data Queen!' the huge man gushed. He'd always had a soft spot for Midge Milken. She was sharp, and she was also the only woman Jabba had ever met who flirted with him. 'How the hell are you?'

'No complaints.'

Jabba wiped his mouth. 'You on site?'

'Yup.'

'Care to join me for a calzone?'

'Love to, Jabba, but I'm watching these hips.'

'Really?' He snickered. 'Mind if I join you?'

'You're bad.'

'You have no idea. . . .'

'Glad I caught you in,' she said. 'I need some advice.'

He took a long swallow of Dr Pepper. 'Shoot.'

'It might be nothing,' Midge said, 'but my Crypto stats turned up something odd. I was hoping you could shed some light.'

'What ya got?' He took another sip.

'I've got a report saying TRANSLTR's been running the same file for eighteen hours and hasn't cracked it.'

Jabba sprayed Dr Pepper all over his calzone. 'You *what?*'

'Any ideas?'

He dabbed at his calzone with a napkin. 'What report is this?'

'Production report. Basic cost analysis stuff.' Midge quickly explained what she and Brinkerhoff had found.

'Have you called Strathmore?'

'Yes. He said everything's fine in Crypto. Said TRANSLTR's running full speed ahead. Said our data's wrong.'

Jabba furrowed his bulbous forehead. 'So what's the problem? Your report glitched.' Midge did not

239

respond. Jabba caught her drift. He frowned. 'You don't think your report glitched?'

'Correct.'

'So you think Strathmore's lying?'

'It's not that,' Midge said diplomatically, knowing she was on fragile ground. 'It's just that my stats have never been wrong in the past. I thought I'd get a second opinion.'

'Well,' Jabba said, 'I hate to be the one to break it to you, but your data's fried.'

'You think so?'

'I'd bet my job on it.' Jabba took a big bite of soggy calzone and spoke with his mouth full. 'Longest a file has ever lasted inside TRANSLTR is three hours. That includes diagnostics, boundary probes, everything. Only thing that could lock it down for eighteen hours would have to be viral. Nothing else could do it.'

'Viral?'

'Yeah, some kind of redundant cycle. Something that got into the processors, created a loop, and basically gummed up the works.'

'Well,' she ventured, 'Strathmore's been in Crypto for about thirty-six hours straight. Any chance he's fighting a virus?'

Jabba laughed. 'Strathmore's been in there for thirty-six hours? Poor bastard. His wife probably said he can't come home. I hear she's bagging his ass.'

Midge thought a moment. She'd heard that too. She wondered if maybe she was being paranoid.

'Midge.' Jabba wheezed and took another long drink. 'If Strathmore's toy had a virus, he would have called me. Strathmore's sharp, but he doesn't know shit about viruses. TRANSLTR's all he's got. First sign of trouble, he would have pressed the panic button –

and around here, that means *me*.' Jabba sucked in a long strand of mozzarella. 'Besides, there's no way in hell TRANSLTR has a virus. Gauntlet's the best set of package filters I've ever written. Nothing gets through.'

After a long silence, Midge sighed. 'Any other thoughts?'

'Yup. Your data's fried.'

'You already said that.'

'Exactly.'

She frowned. 'You haven't caught wind of anything? Anything at all?'

Jabba laughed harshly. 'Midge . . . listen up. Skipjack sucked. Strathmore blew it. But move on – it's over.' There was a long silence on the line, and Jabba realized he'd gone too far. 'Sorry, Midge. I know you took heat over that whole mess. Strathmore was wrong. I know how you feel about him.'

'This has nothing to do with Skipjack,' she said firmly.

Yeah, sure, Jabba thought. 'Listen, Midge, I don't have feelings for Strathmore one way or another. I mean, the guy's a cryptographer. They're basically all self-centered assholes. They need their data yesterday. Every damn file is the one that could save the world.'

'So what are you saying?'

Jabba sighed. 'I'm saying Strathmore's a psycho like the rest of them. But I'm also saying he loves TRANSLTR more than his own goddamn wife. If there were a problem, he would have called me.'

Midge was quiet a long time. Finally she let out a reluctant sigh. 'So you're saying my data's fried?'

Jabba chuckled. 'Is there an echo in here?'

She laughed.

241

'Look, Midge. Drop me a work order. I'll be up on Monday to double-check your machine. In the meantime, get the hell out of here. It's Saturday night. Go get yourself laid or something.'

She sighed. 'I'm trying, Jabba. Believe me, I'm trying.'

CHAPTER 52

Club Embrujo – 'Warlock' in English – was situated in the suburbs at the end of the number 27 bus line. Looking more like a fortification than a dance club, it was surrounded on all sides by high stucco walls into which were embedded shards of shattered beer bottles – a crude security system preventing anyone from entering illegally without leaving behind a good portion of flesh.

During the ride, Becker had resolved himself to the fact that he'd failed. It was time to call Strathmore with the bad news – the search was hopeless. He had done the best he could; now it was time to go home.

But now, gazing out at the mob of patrons pushing their way through the club's entrance, Becker was not so sure his conscience would allow him to give up the search. He was staring at the biggest crowd of punks he'd ever seen; there were coiffures of red, white, and blue everywhere.

Becker sighed, weighing his options. He scanned the crowd and shrugged. *Where else would she be on a Saturday night?* Cursing his good fortune, Becker climbed off the bus.

The access to Club Embrujo was a narrow stone corridor. As Becker entered he immediately felt himself caught up in the inward surge of eager patrons.

'Outta my way, faggot!' A human pincushion pawed past him, giving Becker an elbow in the side.

'Nice tie.' Someone gave Becker's necktie a hard yank.

'Wanna fuck?' A teenage girl stared up at him looking like something out of *Dawn of the Dead*.

The darkness of the corridor spilled out into a huge cement chamber that reeked of alcohol and body odor. The scene was surreal – a deep mountain grotto in which hundreds of bodies moved as one. They surged up and down, hands pressed firmly to their sides, heads bobbing like lifeless bulbs on top of rigid spines. Crazed souls took running dives off a stage and landed on a sea of human limbs. Bodies were passed back and forth like human beach balls. Overhead, the pulsating strobes gave the whole thing the look of an old, silent movie.

On the far wall, speakers the size of minivans shook so deeply that not even the most dedicated dancers could get closer than thirty feet from the pounding woofers.

Becker plugged his ears and searched the crowd. Everywhere he looked was another red, white, and blue head. The bodies were packed so closely together that he couldn't see what they were wearing. He saw no hint of a British flag anywhere. It was obvious he'd never be able to enter the crowd without getting trampled. Someone nearby started vomiting.

Lovely. Becker groaned. He moved off down a spray-painted hallway.

The hall turned into a narrow mirrored tunnel,

which opened to an outdoor patio scattered with tables and chairs. The patio was crowded with punk rockers, but to Becker it was like the gateway to Shangri-La – the summer sky opened up above him and the music faded away.

Ignoring the curious stares, Becker walked out into the crowd. He loosened his tie and collapsed into a chair at the nearest unoccupied table. It seemed like a lifetime since Strathmore's early-morning call.

After clearing the empty beer bottles from his table, Becker laid his head in his hands. *Just for a few minutes*, he thought.

Five miles away, the man in wire-rim glasses sat in the back of a Fiat taxi as it raced headlong down a country road.

'Embrujo,' he grunted, reminding the driver of their destination.

The driver nodded, eyeing his curious new fare in the rearview mirror. 'Embrujo,' he grumbled to himself. 'Weirder crowd every night.'

CHAPTER 53

Tokugen Numataka lay naked on the massage table in his penthouse office. His personal masseuse worked out the kinks in his neck. She ground her palms into the fleshy pockets surrounding his shoulder blades, slowly working her way down to the towel covering his backside. Her hands slipped lower . . . beneath his towel. Numataka barely noticed. His mind was elsewhere. He had been waiting for his private line to ring. It had not.

There was a knock at the door.

'Enter,' Numataka grunted.

The masseuse quickly pulled her hands from beneath the towel.

The switchboard operator entered and bowed. 'Honored chairman?'

'Speak.'

The operator bowed a second time. 'I spoke to the phone exchange. The call originated from country code 1 – the United States.'

Numataka nodded. This was good news. *The call came from the States.* He smiled. *It was genuine.*

'Where in the U.S.?' he demanded.

'They're working on it, sir.'

'Very well. Tell me when you have more.'

The operator bowed again and left.

Numataka felt his muscles relax. Country code 1. Good news indeed.

Susan Fletcher paced impatiently in the Crypto bathroom and counted slowly to fifty. Her head was throbbing. *Just a little longer,* she told herself. *Hale is North Dakota!*

Susan wondered what Hale's plans were. Would he announce the pass-key? Would he be greedy and try to sell the algorithm? Susan couldn't bear to wait any longer. It was time. She had to get to Strathmore.

Cautiously she cracked the door and peered out at the reflective wall on the far side of Crypto. There was no way to know if Hale was still watching. She'd have to move quickly to Strathmore's office. Not too quickly, of course – she could not let Hale suspect she was on to him. She reached for the door and was about to pull it open when she heard something. Voices. Men's voices.

The voices were coming through the ventilation shaft near the floor. She released the door and moved toward the vent. The words were muffled by the dull hum of the generators below. The conversation sounded like it was coming up from the sublevel cat-walks. One voice was shrill, angry. It sounded like Phil Chartrukian.

'You don't believe me?'

The sound of more arguing rose.

'We have a virus!'

Then the sound of harsh yelling.

'We need to call Jabba!'

Then there were sounds of a struggle.

'Let me go!'

The noise that followed was barely human. It was a long wailing cry of horror, like a tortured animal about to die. Susan froze beside the vent. The noise ended as abruptly as it had begun. Then there was a silence.

An instant later, as if choreographed for some cheap horror matinee, the lights in the bathroom slowly dimmed. Then they flickered and went out. Susan Fletcher found herself standing in total blackness.

CHAPTER 55

'You're in my seat, asshole.'

Becker lifted his head off his arms. *Doesn't anyone speak Spanish in this damn country?*

Glaring down at him was a short, pimple-faced teenager with a shaved head. Half of his scalp was red and half was purple. He looked like an Easter egg. 'I said you're in my seat, asshole.'

'I heard you the first time,' Becker said, standing up. He was in no mood for a fight. It was time to go.

'Where'd you put my bottles?' the kid snarled. There was a safety pin in his nose.

Becker pointed to the beer bottles he'd set on the ground. 'They were empty.'

'They were *my* fuckin' empties!'

'My apologies,' Becker said, and turned to go.

The punk blocked his way. 'Pick 'em up!'

Becker blinked, not amused. 'You're kidding, right?' He was a full foot taller and outweighed the kid by about fifty pounds.

'Do I fuckin' *look* like I'm kidding?'

Becker said nothing.

'Pick 'em up!' The kid's voice cracked.

Becker attempted to step around him, but the teenager blocked his way. 'I said, fuckin' pick 'em up!'

Stoned punks at nearby tables began turning to watch the excitement.

'You don't want to do this, kid,' Becker said quietly.

'I'm warning you!' The kid seethed. 'This is my table! I come here every night. Now *pick 'em up!*'

Becker's patience ran out. Wasn't he supposed to be in the Smokys with Susan? What was he doing in Spain arguing with a psychotic adolescent?

Without warning, Becker caught the kid under the armpits, lifted him up, and slammed his rear end down on the table. 'Look, you runny-nosed little runt. You're going to back off right now, or I'm going to rip that safety pin out of your nose and pin your mouth shut.'

The kid's face went pale.

Becker held him a moment, then he released his grip. Without taking his eyes off the frightened kid, Becker stooped down, picked up the bottles, and returned them to the table. 'What do you say?' he asked.

The kid was speechless.

'You're welcome,' Becker snapped. *This kid's a walking billboard for birth control.*

'Go to hell!' the kid yelled, now aware of his peers laughing at him. 'Ass-wipe!'

Becker didn't move. Something the kid had said suddenly registered. *I come here every night.* Becker wondered if maybe the kid could help him. 'I'm sorry,' Becker said, 'I didn't catch your name.'

'Two-Tone,' he hissed, as if he were giving a death sentence.

'Two-Tone?' Becker mused. 'Let me guess . . . because of your hair?'

'No shit, Sherlock.'

'Catchy name. Make that up yourself?'

'Damn straight,' he said proudly. 'I'm gonna *patent* it.'

Becker scowled. 'You mean *trademark it?*'

The kid looked confused.

'You'd need a trademark for a name,' Becker said. 'Not a patent.'

'Whatever!' the punk screamed in frustration.

The motley assortment of drunken and drugged-out kids at the nearby tables were now in hysterics. Two-Tone stood up and sneered at Becker. 'What the fuck do you want from me?'

Becker thought a moment. *I want you to wash your hair, clean up your language, and get a job.* Becker figured it was too much to ask on a first meeting. 'I need some information,' he said.

'Fuck you.'

'I'm looking for someone.'

'I ain't seen him.'

'Haven't seen him,' Becker corrected as he flagged a passing waitress. He bought two Aguila beers and handed one to Two-Tone. The boy looked shocked. He took a swig of beer and eyed Becker warily.

'You hitting on me, mister?'

Becker smiled. 'I'm looking for a girl.'

Two-Tone let out a shrill laugh. 'You sure as hell ain't gonna get any action dressed like that!'

Becker frowned. 'I'm not looking for action. I just need to talk to her. Maybe you could help me find her.'

Two-Tone set down his beer. 'You a cop?'

Becker shook his head.

The kid's eyes narrowed. 'You look like a cop.'

'Kid, I'm from Maryland. If I were a cop, I'd be a little out of my jurisdiction, don't you think?'

The question seemed to stump him.

'My name's David Becker.' Becker smiled and offered his hand across the table.

The punk recoiled in disgust. 'Back off, fag boy.'

Becker retracted the hand.

The kid sneered. 'I'll help you, but it'll cost you.'

Becker played along. 'How much?'

'A hundred bucks.'

Becker frowned. 'I've only got pesetas.'

'Whatever! Make it a hundred *pesetas*.'

Foreign currency exchange was obviously not one of Two-Tone's fortes; a hundred pesetas was about eighty-seven cents. 'Deal,' Becker said, rapping his bottle on the table.

The kid smiled for the first time. 'Deal.'

'Okay,' Becker continued in his hushed tone. 'I figure the girl I'm looking for might hang out here. She's got red, white, and blue hair.'

Two-Tone snorted. 'It's Judas Taboo's anniversary. Everybody's got—'

'She's also wearing a British flag T-shirt and has a skull pendant in one ear.'

A faint look of recognition crossed Two-Tone's face. Becker saw it and felt a surge of hope. But a moment later Two-Tone's expression turned stern. He slammed his bottle down and grabbed Becker's shirt.

'She's Eduardo's, you asshole! I'd watch it! You touch her, and he'll kill you!'

CHAPTER 56

Midge Milken prowled angrily into the conference room across from her office. In addition to the thirty-two-foot mahogany table with the NSA seal inlaid in black cherry and walnut, the conference room contained three Marion Pike watercolors, a Boston fern, a marble wet bar, and of course, the requisite Sparkletts water cooler. Midge helped herself to a glass of water, hoping it might calm her nerves.

As she sipped at the liquid, she gazed across at the window. The moonlight was filtering through the open venetian blind and playing on the grain of the table. She'd always thought this would make a nicer director's office than Fontaine's current location on the front of the building. Rather than looking out over the NSA parking lot, the conference room looked out over an impressive array of NSA outbuildings – including the Crypto dome, a high-tech island floating separate from the main building on three wooded acres. Purposefully situated behind the natural cover of a grove of maples, Crypto was difficult to see from most windows in the NSA complex, but the view from the directorial suite was perfect. To Midge the conference room seemed the perfect vantage point for a king to survey his domain. She had suggested once that Fontaine move his office, but the director had simply replied, 'Not on the rear.' Fontaine was not a man to be found on the back end of anything.

Midge pulled apart the blinds. She stared out at the hills. Sighing ruefully, she let her eyes fall toward the spot where Crypto stood. Midge had always felt comforted by the sight of the Crypto dome – a glowing beacon regardless of the hour. But tonight, as she gazed out, there was no comfort. Instead she found herself staring into a void. As she pressed her face to the glass, she was gripped by a wild, girlish panic. Below her there was nothing but blackness. Crypto had disappeared!

CHAPTER 57

The Crypto bathrooms had no windows, and the darkness surrounding Susan Fletcher was absolute. She stood dead still for a moment trying to get her bearings, acutely aware of the growing sense of panic gripping her body. The horrible cry from the ventilation shaft seemed to hang all around her. Despite her effort to fight off a rising sense of dread, fear swept across her flesh and took control.

In a flurry of involuntary motion, Susan found herself groping wildly across stall doors and sinks. Disoriented, she spun through the blackness with her hands out in front of her and tried to picture the room. She knocked over a garbage can and found herself against a tiled wall. Following the wall with her hand, she scrambled toward the exit and fumbled for the door handle. She pulled it open and stumbled out onto the Crypto floor.

There she froze for a second time.

The Crypto floor looked nothing like it had just moments ago. TRANSLTR was a gray silhouette against the faint twilight coming in through the dome. All of the overhead lighting was dead. Not even the electronic keypads on the doors were glowing.

As Susan's eyes became accustomed to the dark, she saw that the only light in Crypto was coming through the open trapdoor – a faint red glow from the utility lighting below. She moved toward it. There was the faint smell of ozone in the air.

When she made it to the trapdoor, she peered into the hole. The freon vents were still belching swirling mist through the redness, and from the higher-pitched drone of the generators, Susan knew Crypto was running on backup power. Through the mist she could make out Strathmore standing on the platform below. He was leaning over the railing and staring into the depths of TRANSLTR's rumbling shaft.

'Commander!'

There was no response.

Susan eased onto the ladder. The hot air from below rushed in under her skirt. The rungs were slippery with condensation. She set herself down on the grated landing.

'Commander?'

Strathmore did not turn. He continued staring down with a blank look of shock, as if in a trance. Susan followed his gaze over the banister. For a moment she could see nothing except wisps of steam. Then suddenly she saw it. A figure. Six stories below. It appeared briefly in the billows of steam. There it was again. A tangled mass of twisted limbs. Lying ninety feet below them, Phil Chartrukian was sprawled across the sharp iron fins of the main generator. His body was darkened and burned. His fall had shorted out Crypto's main power supply.

But the most chilling image of all was not of Chartrukian but of someone else, another body, halfway down the long staircase, crouched, hiding in the shadows. The muscular frame was unmistakable. It was Greg Hale.

CHAPTER 58

The punk screamed at Becker, 'Megan belongs to my friend Eduardo! You stay away from her!'

'Where is she?' Becker's heart was racing out of control.

'Fuck you!'

'It's an emergency!' Becker snapped. He grabbed the kid's sleeve. 'She's got a ring that belongs to me. I'll pay her for it! A lot!'

Two-Tone stopped dead and burst into hysterics. 'You mean that ugly, gold piece of shit is yours?'

Becker's eyes widened. 'You've seen it?'

Two-Tone nodded coyly.

'Where is it?' Becker demanded.

'No clue.' Two-Tone chuckled. 'Megan was up here trying to hock it.'

'She was trying to *sell* it?'

'Don't worry, man, she didn't have any luck. You've got shitty taste in jewelry.'

'Are you sure nobody bought it?'

'Are you shitting me? For four hundred bucks? I told her I'd give her fifty, but she wanted more. She was trying to buy a plane ticket – standby.'

Becker felt the blood drain from his face. 'Where to?'

'Fuckin' Connecticut,' Two-tone snapped. 'Eddie's bummin'.'

'Connecticut?'

'Shit, yeah. Going back to Mommy and Daddy's mansion in the burbs. Hated her Spanish homestay family. Three Spic brothers always hitting on her. No fucking hot water.'

Becker felt a knot rise in his throat. 'When is she leaving?'

Two-Tone looked up. 'When?' He laughed. 'She's long gone by now. Went to the airport hours ago. Best spot to hock the ring – rich tourists and shit. Once she got the cash, she was flying out.'

A dull nausea swept through Becker's gut. *This is some kind of sick joke, isn't it?* He stood a long moment. 'What's her last name?'

Two-Tone pondered the question and shrugged.

'What flight was she taking?'

'She said something about the Roach Coach.'

'Roach Coach?'

'Yeah. Weekend red-eye – Seville, Madrid, La Guardia. That's what they call it. College kids take it 'cause it's cheap. Guess they sit in back and smoke roaches.'

Great. Becker groaned, running a hand through his hair. 'What time did it leave?'

'Two A.M. sharp, every Saturday night. She's somewhere over the Atlantic by now.'

Becker checked his watch. It read 1:45 A.M. He turned to Two-Tone, confused. 'You said it's a two A.M. flight?'

The punk nodded, laughing. 'Looks like you're fucked, ol' man.'

Becker pointed angrily to his watch. 'But it's only quarter to two!'

Two-Tone eyed the watch, apparently puzzled. 'Well, I'll be damned.' He laughed. 'I'm usually not this buzzed till four A.M.!'

'What's the fastest way to the airport?' Becker snapped.

'Taxi stand out front.'

Becker grabbed a 1,000-peseta note from his pocket and stuffed it in Two-Tone's hand.

'Hey, man, thanks!' the punk called after him. 'If you see Megan, tell her I said hi!' But Becker was already gone.

Two-Tone sighed and staggered back toward the dance floor. He was too drunk to notice the man in wire-rim glasses following him.

Outside, Becker scanned the parking lot for a taxi. There was none. He ran over to a stocky bouncer. 'Taxi!'

The bouncer shook his head. 'Demasiado temprano. Too early.'

Too early? Becker swore. *It's two o'clock in the morning!* 'Pídame uno! Call me one!'

The man pulled out a walkie-talkie. He said a few words and then signed off. 'Veinte minutos,' he offered.

'Twenty minutes?!' Becker demanded. 'Y el autobus?'

The bouncer shrugged. 'Forty-five minutos.'

Becker threw up his hands. *Perfect!*

The sound of a small engine turned Becker's head. It sounded like a chainsaw. A big kid and his chain-clad date pulled into the parking lot on an old Vespa 250 motorcycle. The girl's skirt had blown high on her

260

thighs. She didn't seem to notice. Becker dashed over. *I can't believe I'm doing this,* he thought. *I hate motorcycles.* He yelled to the driver. 'I'll pay you ten thousand pesetas to take me to the airport!'

The kid ignored him and killed the engine.

'Twenty thousand!' Becker blurted. 'I need to get to the airport!'

The kid looked up. 'Scusi?' He was Italian.

'Aeropórto! Per favore. Sulla Vespa! Venti mille pesete!'

The Italian eyed his crummy, little bike and laughed. 'Venti mille pesete? La Vespa?'

'Cinquanta mille! Fifty thousand!' Becker offered. It was about four hundred dollars.

The Italian laughed doubtfully. 'Dov'é la plata? Where's the cash?'

Becker pulled five 10,000-peseta notes from his pocket and held them out. The Italian looked at the money and then at his girlfriend. The girl grabbed the cash and stuffed it in her blouse.

'*Grazie!*' the Italian beamed. He tossed Becker the keys to his Vespa. Then he grabbed his girlfriend's hand, and they ran off laughing into the building.

'Aspetta!' Becker yelled. 'Wait! I wanted a *ride!*'

CHAPTER 59

Susan reached for Commander Strathmore's hand as he helped her up the ladder onto the Crypto floor. The image of Phil Chartrukian lying broken on the generators was burned into her mind. The thought of Hale hiding in the bowels of Crypto had left her dizzy. The truth was inescapable – Hale had pushed Chartrukian.

Susan stumbled past the shadow of TRANSLTR back toward Crypto's main exit – the door she'd come through hours earlier. Her frantic punching on the unlit keypad did nothing to move the huge portal. She was trapped; Crypto was a prison. The dome sat like a satellite, 109 yards away from the main NSA structure, accessible only through the main portal. Since Crypto made its own power, the switchboard probably didn't even know they were in trouble.

'The main power's out,' Strathmore said, arriving behind her. 'We're on aux.'

The backup power supply in Crypto was designed so that TRANSLTR and its cooling systems took precedence over all other systems, including lights and doorways. That way an untimely power outage would not interrupt TRANSLTR during an important run. It also meant TRANSLTR would never run without its freon cooling system; in an uncooled enclosure, the heat generated by three million processors would rise to treacherous levels – perhaps even igniting the silicon chips and resulting in a fiery meltdown. It was an image no one dared consider.

Susan fought to get her bearings. Her thoughts were consumed by the single image of the Sys-Sec on the generators. She stabbed at the keypad again. Still no response. 'Abort the run!' she demanded. Telling TRANSLTR to stop searching for the Digital Fortress pass-key would shut down its circuits and free up enough backup power to get the doors working again.

'Easy, Susan,' Strathmore said, putting a steadying hand on her shoulder.

The commander's reassuring touch lifted Susan from her daze. She suddenly remembered why she had been going to get him. She wheeled, 'Commander! Greg Hale is North Dakota!'

There was a seemingly endless beat of silence in the dark. Finally Strathmore replied. His voice sounded more confused than shocked. 'What are you talking about?'

'Hale . . .' Susan whispered. 'He's North Dakota.'

There was more silence as Strathmore pondered Susan's words. 'The tracer?' He seemed confused. 'It fingered Hale?'

'The tracer isn't back yet. Hale aborted it!'

Susan went on to explain how Hale had stopped her tracer and how she'd found E-mail from Tankado in Hale's account. Another long moment of silence followed. Strathmore shook his head in disbelief.

'There's no way *Greg Hale* is Tankado's insurance! It's absurd! Tankado would never trust Hale.'

'Commander,' she said, 'Hale sank us once before – Skipjack. Tankado trusted him.'

Strathmore could not seem to find words.

'Abort TRANSLTR,' Susan begged him. 'We've got North Dakota. Call building security. Let's get out of here.'

Strathmore held up his hand requesting a moment to think.

Susan looked nervously in the direction of the trapdoor. The opening was just out of sight behind TRANSLTR, but the reddish glow spilled out over the black tile like fire on ice. *Come on, call Security, Commander! Abort TRANSLTR! Get us out of here!*

Suddenly Strathmore sprang to action. 'Follow me,' he said. He strode toward the trapdoor.

'Commander! Hale is dangerous! He—'

But Strathmore disappeared into the dark. Susan hurried to follow his silhouette. The commander circled around TRANSLTR and arrived over the opening in the floor. He peered into the swirling, steaming pit. Silently he looked around the darkened Crypto floor. Then he bent down and heaved the heavy trapdoor. It swung in a low arc. When he let go, it slammed shut with a deadening thud. Crypto was once again a silent, blackened cave. It appeared North Dakota was trapped.

Strathmore knelt down. He turned the heavy butterfly lock. It spun into place. The sublevels were sealed.

Neither he nor Susan heard the faint steps in the direction of Node 3.

CHAPTER 60

Two-Tone headed through the mirrored corridor that led from the outside patio to the dance floor. As he turned to check his safety pin in the reflection, he sensed a figure looming up behind him. He spun, but it was too late. A pair of rocklike arms pinned his body face-first against the glass.

The punk tried to twist around. 'Eduardo? Hey, man, is that you?' Two-Tone felt a hand brush over his wallet before the figure leaned firmly into his back. 'Eddie!' the punk cried. 'Quit fooling around! Some guy was lookin' for Megan.'

The figure held him firmly.

'Hey, Eddie, man, cut it out!' But when Two-Tone looked up into the mirror, he saw the figure pinning him was not his friend at all.

The face was pockmarked and scarred. Two lifeless eyes stared out like coal from behind wire-rim glasses. The man leaned forward, placing his mouth against Two-Tone's ear. A strange, voice choked, '*Adónde fué?* Where'd he go?' The words sounded somehow mis-shapen.

The punk froze, paralyzed with fear.

'*Adónde fué?*' the voice repeated. 'El Americano.'

'The . . . the airport. Aeropuerto,' Two-Tone stammered.

'Aeropuertó?' the man repeated, his dark eyes watching Two-Tone's lips in the mirror.

The punk nodded.

'Tenía el anillo? Did he have the ring?'

Terrified, Two-Tone shook his head. 'No.'

'Viste el anillo? Did you see the ring?'

Two-Tone paused. What was the right answer?

'Viste el anillo?' the muffled voice demanded.

Two-Tone nodded affirmatively, hoping honesty would pay. It did not. Seconds later he slid to the floor, his neck broken.

CHAPTER 61

Jabba lay on his back lodged halfway inside a dismantled mainframe computer. There was a penlight in his mouth, a soldering iron in his hand, and a large schematic blueprint propped on his belly. He had just finished attaching a new set of attenuators to a faulty motherboard when his cellular phone sprang to life.

'Shit,' he swore, groping for the receiver through a pile of cables. 'Jabba here.'

'Jabba, it's Midge.'

He brightened. 'Twice in one night? People are gonna start talking.'

'Crypto's got problems.' Her voice was tense.

Jabba frowned. 'We been through this already. Remember?'

'It's a *power* problem.'

'I'm not an electrician. Call Engineering.'

'The dome's dark.'

'You're seeing things. Go home.' He turned back to his schematic.

'*Pitch black!*' she yelled.

Jabba sighed and set down his penlight. 'Midge, first of all, we've got aux power in there. It would

267

never be *pitch* black. Second, Strathmore's got a slightly better view of Crypto than I do right now. Why don't you call *him?*'

'Because this has to do with *him*. He's hiding something.'

Jabba rolled his eyes. 'Midge, sweetie, I'm up to my armpits in serial cable here. If you need a date, I'll cut loose. Otherwise, call Engineering.'

'Jabba, this is *serious*. I can *feel* it.'

She can feel it? It was official, Jabba thought, Midge was in one of her *moods*. 'If Strathmore's not worried, *I'm* not worried.'

'Crypto's pitch black, dammit!'

'So maybe Strathmore's stargazing.'

'Jabba! I'm not kidding around here!'

'Okay, okay,' he grumbled, propping himself up on an elbow. 'Maybe a generator shorted out. As soon as I'm done here, I'll stop by Crypto and—'

'What about aux power!' Midge demanded. 'If a generator blew, why is there no aux power?'

'I don't know. Maybe Strathmore's got TRANSLTR running and aux power is tapped out.'

'So why doesn't he abort? Maybe it's a virus. You said something earlier about a virus.'

'Damn it, Midge!' Jabba exploded. 'I told you, there's *no* virus in Crypto! Stop being so damned *paranoid!*'

There was a long silence on the line.

'Aw, shit, Midge,' Jabba apologized. 'Let me explain.' His voice was tight. 'First of all, we've got Gauntlet – no virus could possibly get through. Second, if there's a power failure, it's *hardware*-related – viruses don't kill *power*, they attack software and data. Whatever's going on in Crypto, it's *not* a virus.'

Silence.

'Midge? You there?'

Midge's response was icy. 'Jabba, I have a job to do. I don't expect to be yelled at for doing it. When I call to ask why a multibillion-dollar facility is in the dark, I expect a professional response.'

'Yes, ma'am.'

'A simple yes or no will suffice. Is it possible the problem in Crypto is virus-related?'

'Midge . . . I told you—'

'Yes or no. Could TRANSLTR have a virus?'

Jabba sighed. 'No, Midge. It's totally impossible.'

'Thank you.'

He forced a chuckle and tried to lighten the mood. 'Unless you think Strathmore wrote one himself and bypassed my filters.'

There was a stunned silence. When Midge spoke, her voice had an eerie edge. 'Strathmore can *bypass* Gauntlet?'

Jabba sighed. 'It was a *joke*, Midge.' But he knew it was too late.

CHAPTER 62

The Commander and Susan stood beside the closed trapdoor and debated what to do next.

'We've got Phil Chartrukian dead down there,' Strathmore argued. 'If we call for help, Crypto will turn into a circus.'

'So what do you propose we do?' Susan demanded, wanting only to leave.

Strathmore thought a moment. 'Don't ask me how it happened,' he said, glancing down at the locked trapdoor, 'but it looks like we've inadvertently located and neutralized North Dakota.' He shook his head in disbelief. 'Damn lucky break if you ask me.' He still seemed stunned by the idea that Hale was involved in Tankado's plan. 'My guess is that Hale's got the pass-key hidden in his terminal somewhere – maybe he's got a copy at home. Either way, he's trapped.'

'So why not call building security and let them cart him away?'

'Not yet,' Strathmore said. 'If the Sys-Secs uncover stats of this endless TRANSLTR run, we've got a whole new set of problems. I want all traces of Digital Fortress deleted before we open the doors.'

Susan nodded reluctantly. It was a good plan. When Security finally pulled Hale from the sublevels and charged him with Chartrukian's death, he probably would threaten to tell the world about Digital Fortress. But the proof would be erased – Strathmore could play dumb. *An endless run? An unbreakable algorithm? But that's absurd! Hasn't Hale heard of the Bergofsky Principle?*

'Here's what we need to do.' Strathmore coolly outlined his plan. 'We erase all of Hale's correspondence with Tankado. We erase all records of my bypassing Gauntlet, all of Chartrukian's Sys-Sec analysis, the Run-Monitor records, everything. Digital Fortress disappears. It was never here. We bury Hale's key and pray to God David finds Tankado's copy.'

David, Susan thought. She forced him from her mind. She needed to stay focused on the matter at hand.

'I'll handle the Sys-Sec lab,' Strathmore said. 'Run-Monitor stats, mutation activity stats, the works. You handle Node 3. Delete all of Hale's E-mail. Any records of correspondence with Tankado, anything that mentions Digital Fortress.'

'Okay,' Susan replied, focusing. 'I'll erase Hale's whole drive. Reformat everything.'

'No!' Strathmore's response was stern. 'Don't do that. Hale most likely has a copy of the pass-key in there. I want it.'

Susan gaped in shock. 'You want the pass-key? I thought the whole point was to *destroy* the pass-keys!'

'It is. But I want a copy. I want to crack open this damn file and have a look at Tankado's program.'

Susan shared Strathmore's curiosity, but instinct told her unlocking the Digital Fortress algorithm was

271

not wise, regardless of how interesting it would be. Right now, the deadly program was locked safely in its encrypted vault – totally harmless. As soon as he decrypted it. . . . 'Commander, wouldn't we be better off just to—'

'I want the key,' he replied.

Susan had to admit, ever since hearing about Digital Fortress, she'd felt a certain academic curiosity to know how Tankado had managed to write it. Its mere existence contradicted the most fundamental rules of cryptography. Susan eyed the commander. 'You'll delete the algorithm immediately after we see it?'

'Without a trace.'

Susan frowned. She knew that finding Hale's key would not happen instantly. Locating a random pass-key on one of the Node 3 hard drives was somewhat like trying to find a single sock in a bedroom the size of Texas. Computer searches only worked when you knew what you were looking for; this pass-key was random. Fortunately, however, because Crypto dealt with so much random material, Susan and some others had developed a complex process known as a nonconformity search. The search essentially asked the computer to study every string of characters on its hard drive, compare each string against an enormous dictionary, and flag any strings that seemed nonsensical or random. It was tricky work to refine the parameters continually, but it was possible.

Susan knew she was the logical choice to find the pass-key. She sighed, hoping she wouldn't regret it. 'If all goes well, it will take me about half an hour.'

'Then let's get to work,' Strathmore said, putting a hand on her shoulder and leading her through the darkness toward Node 3.

Above them, a star-filled sky had stretched itself across the dome. Susan wondered if David could see the same stars from Seville.

As they approached the heavy glass doors of Node 3, Strathmore swore under his breath. The Node 3 keypad was unlit, and the doors were dead.

'Damn it,' he said. 'No power. I forgot.'

Strathmore studied the sliding doors. He placed his palms flat against the glass. Then he leaned sideways trying to slide them open. His hands were sweaty and slipped. He wiped them on his pants and tried again. This time the doors slid open a tiny crack.

Susan, sensing progress, got in behind Strathmore and they both pushed together. The doors slid open about an inch. They held it a moment, but the pressure was too great. The doors sprang shut again.

'Hold on,' Susan said, repositioning herself in front of Strathmore. 'Okay, now try.'

They heaved. Again the door opened only about an inch. A faint ray of blue light appeared from inside Node 3; the terminals were still on; they were considered critical to TRANSLTR and were receiving aux power.

Susan dug the toe of her Ferragamo into the floor and pushed harder. The door started to move. Strathmore moved to get a better angle. Centering his palms on the left slider, he pushed straight back. Susan pushed the right slider in the opposite direction. Slowly, arduously, the doors began to separate. They were now almost a foot apart.

'Don't let go,' Strathmore said, panting as they pushed harder. 'Just a little farther.'

Susan repositioned herself with her shoulder in the crack. She pushed again, this time with a better angle. The doors fought back against her.

Before Strathmore could stop her, Susan squeezed her slender body into the opening. Strathmore protested, but she was intent. She wanted out of Crypto, and she knew Strathmore well enough to know she wasn't going anywhere until Hale's passkey was found.

She centered herself in the opening and pushed with all her strength. The doors seemed to push back. Suddenly Susan lost her grip. The doors sprang toward her. Strathmore fought to hold them off, but it was too much. Just as the doors slammed shut, Susan squeezed through and collapsed on the other side.

The commander fought to reopen the door a tiny sliver. He put his face to the narrow crack. 'Jesus, Susan – are you okay?'

Susan stood up and brushed herself off. 'Fine.'

She looked around. Node 3 was deserted, lit only by the computer monitors. The bluish shadows gave the place a ghostly ambiance. She turned to Strathmore in the crack of the door. His face looked pallid and sickly in the blue light.

'Susan,' he said. 'Give me twenty minutes to delete the files in Sys-Sec. When all traces are gone, I'll go up to my terminal and abort TRANSLTR.'

'You *better*,' Susan said, eyeing the heavy glass doors. She knew that until TRANSLTR stopped hoarding aux power, she was a prisoner in Node 3.

Strathmore let go of the doors, and they snapped shut. Susan watched through the glass as the commander disappeared into the Crypto darkness.

CHAPTER 63

Becker's newly purchased Vespa motorcycle struggled up the entry road to Aeropuerto de Sevilla. His knuckles had been white the whole way. His watch read just after 2:00 A.M. local time.

As he approached the main terminal, he rode up on the sidewalk and jumped off the bike while it was still moving. It clattered to the pavement and sputtered to a stop. Becker dashed on rubbery legs through the revolving door. *Never again,* he swore to himself.

The terminal was sterile and starkly lit. Except for a janitor buffing the floor, the place was deserted. Across the concourse, a ticket agent was closing down the Iberia Airlines counter. Becker took it as a bad sign.

He ran over. 'El vuelo a los Estados Unidos?'

The attractive Andalusian woman behind the counter looked up and smiled apologetically. 'Acaba de salir. You just missed it.' Her words hung in the air for a long moment.

I missed it. Becker's shoulders slumped. 'Was there standby room on the flight?'

'Plenty,' the woman smiled. 'Almost empty. But tomorrow's eight A.M. also has—'

'I need to know if a friend of mine made that flight. She was flying standby.'

The woman frowned. 'I'm sorry, sir. There were several standby passengers tonight, but our privacy clause states—'

'It's very important,' Becker urged. 'I just need to know if she made the flight. That's all.'

The woman gave a sympathetic nod. 'Lovers' quarrel?'

Becker thought a moment. Then he gave her a sheepish grin. 'It's *that* obvious?'

She gave him a wink. 'What's her name?'

'Megan,' he replied sadly.

The agent smiled. 'Does your lady friend have a last name?'

Becker exhaled slowly. *Yes, but I don't know it!* 'Actually, it's kind of a complicated situation. You said the plane was almost empty. Maybe you could—'

'Without a last name I really can't . . .'

'Actually,' Becker interrupted, having another idea. 'Have you been on all night?'

The woman nodded. 'Seven to seven.'

'Then maybe you saw her. She's a young girl. Maybe fifteen or sixteen? Her hair was—' Before the words left his mouth, Becker realized his mistake.

The agent's eyes narrowed. 'Your lover is fifteen years old?'

'No!' Becker gasped. 'I mean . . .' *Shit.* 'If you could just help me, it's very important.'

'I'm sorry,' the woman said coldly.

'It's not the way it sounds. If you could just—'

'Good night, sir.' The woman yanked the metal grate down over the counter and disappeared into a back room.

Becker groaned and stared skyward. *Smooth*, David. Very smooth. He scanned the open concourse. Nothing. *She must have sold the ring and made the flight.* He headed for the custodian. 'Has visto a una niña?' he called over the sound of the tile buffer. 'Have you seen a girl?'

The old man reached down and killed the machine. 'Eh?'

'Una niña?' Becker repeated. 'Pelo rojo, azul, y blanco. Red white and blue hair.'

The custodian laughed. 'Qué fea. Sounds ugly.' He shook his head and went back to work.

David Becker stood in the middle of the deserted airport concourse and wondered what to do next. The evening had been a comedy of errors. Strathmore's words pounded in his head: Don't call until you have the ring. A profound exhaustion settled over him. If Megan had sold the ring and made the flight, there was no telling who had the ring now.

Becker closed his eyes and tried to focus. *What's my next move?* He decided to consider it in a moment. First, he needed to make a long-overdue trip to a rest room.

CHAPTER 64

Susan stood alone in the dimly lit silence of Node 3. The task at hand was simple: Access Hale's terminal, locate his key, and then delete all of his communication with Tankado. There could be no hint of Digital Fortress anywhere.

Susan's initial fears of saving the key and unlocking Digital Fortress were nagging at her again. She felt uneasy tempting fate; they'd been lucky so far. North Dakota had miraculously appeared right under their noses and been trapped. The only remaining question was David; he had to find the other pass-key. Susan hoped he was making progress.

As she made her way deeper into Node 3, Susan tried to clear her mind. It was odd that she felt uneasy in such a familiar space. Everything in Node 3 seemed foreign in the dark. But there was something else. Susan felt a momentary hesitation and glanced back at the inoperable doors. There was no escape. *Twenty minutes*, she thought.

As she turned toward Hale's terminal, she noticed a strange, musky odor – it was definitely not a Node 3 smell. She wondered if maybe the deionizer was malfunctioning. The smell was vaguely familiar, and with it came an unsettling chill. She pictured Hale locked below in his enormous steaming cell. *Did he set something on fire?* She looked up at the vents and sniffed. But the odor seemed to be coming from nearby.

Susan glanced toward the latticed doors of the kitchenette. And in an instant she recognized the smell. It was *cologne . . . and sweat.*

She recoiled instinctively, not prepared for what she saw. From behind the lattice slats of the kitchenette, two eyes stared out at her. It only took an instant for the horrifying truth to hit her. Greg Hale was not locked on the sublevels – he was in Node 3! He'd slipped upstairs before Strathmore closed the trap-door. He'd been strong enough to open the doors all by himself.

Susan had once heard that raw terror was paralyz-ing – she now knew that was a myth. In the same instant her brain grasped what was happening, she was in motion – stumbling backward through the dark with a single thought in mind: escape.

The crash behind her was instantaneous. Hale had been sitting silently on the stove and extended his legs like two battering rams. The doors exploded off their hinges. Hale launched himself into the room and thundered after her with powerful strides.

Susan knocked over a lamp behind her, attempting to trip Hale as he moved toward her. She sensed him vault it effortlessly. Hale was gaining quickly.

When his right arm circled her waist from behind, it felt like she'd hit a steel bar. She gasped in pain as the wind went out of her. His biceps flexed against her rib cage.

Susan resisted and began twisting wildly. Somehow

279

her elbow struck cartilage. Hale released his grip, his hands clutching his nose. He fell to his knees, hands cupped over his face.

'Son of a—' He screamed in pain.

Susan dashed onto the door's pressure plates saying a fruitless prayer that Strathmore would in that instant restore power and the doors would spring open. Instead, she found herself pounding against the glass.

Hale lumbered toward her, his nose covered with blood. In an instant, his hands were around her again – one of them clamped firmly on her left breast and the other on her midsection. He yanked her away from the door.

She screamed, her hand outstretched in a futile attempt to stop him.

He pulled her backward, his belt buckle digging into her spine. Susan couldn't believe his strength. He dragged her back across the carpet, and her shoes came off. In one fluid motion, Hale lifted her and dumped her on the floor next to his terminal.

Susan was suddenly on her back, her skirt bunched high on her hips. The top button of her blouse had released, and her chest was heaving in the bluish light. She stared up in terror as Hale straddled her, pinning her down. She couldn't decipher the look in his eyes. It looked like fear. Or was it anger? His eyes bore into her body. She felt a new wave of panic.

Hale sat firmly on her midsection, staring down at her with an icy glare. Everything Susan had ever learned about self-defense was suddenly racing through her mind. She tried to fight, but her body did not respond. She was numb. She closed her eyes.

Oh, please, God. No!

CHAPTER 65

Brinkerhoff paced Midge's office. '*Nobody* bypasses Gauntlet. It's impossible!'

'Wrong,' she fired back. 'I just talked to Jabba. He said he installed a bypass switch last year.'

The PA looked doubtful. 'I never heard that.'

'Nobody did. It was hush-hush.'

'Midge,' Brinkerhoff argued, 'Jabba's compulsive about security! He would never put in a switch to bypass—'

'Strathmore made him do it,' she interrupted.

Brinkerhoff could almost hear her mind clicking.

'Remember last year,' she asked, 'when Strathmore was working on that anti-Semitic terrorist ring in California?'

Brinkerhoff nodded. It had been one of Strathmore's major coups last year. Using TRANSLTR to decrypt an intercepted code, he had uncovered a plot to bomb a Hebrew school in Los Angeles. He decrypted the terrorists' message only twelve minutes before the bomb went off, and using some fast phone work, he saved three hundred schoolchildren.

'Get this,' Midge said, lowering her voice unnecessarily.

'Jabba said Strathmore intercepted that terrorist code *six hours* before that bomb went off.'

Brinkerhoff's jaw dropped. 'But . . . then why did he wait—'

'Because he couldn't get TRANSLTR to decrypt the file. He tried, but Gauntlet kept rejecting it. It was encrypted with some new public key algorithm that the filters hadn't seen yet. It took Jabba almost six hours to adjust them.'

Brinkerhoff looked stunned.

'Strathmore was furious. He made Jabba install a bypass switch in Gauntlet in case it ever happened again.'

'Jesus.' Brinkerhoff whistled. 'I had no idea.' Then his eyes narrowed. 'So what's your point?'

'I think Strathmore used the switch today . . . to process a file that Gauntlet rejected.'

'So? That's what the switch is for, right?'

Midge shook her head. 'Not if the file in question is a virus.'

Brinkerhoff jumped. 'A virus? Who said anything about a virus!'

'It's the only explanation,' she said. 'Jabba said a virus is the only thing that could keep TRANSLTR running this long, so—'

'Wait a minute!' Brinkerhoff flashed her the time-out sign. 'Strathmore said everything's fine!'

'He's lying.'

Brinkerhoff was lost. 'You're saying Strathmore *intentionally* let a virus into TRANSLTR?'

'No,' she snapped. 'I don't think he *knew* it was a virus. I think he was tricked.'

Brinkerhoff was speechless. Midge Milken was definitely losing it.

282

'It explains a lot,' she insisted. 'It explains what he's been doing in there all night.'

'Planting viruses in his own computer?'

'No,' she said, annoyed. 'Trying to cover up his mistake! And now he can't abort TRANSLTR and get aux power back because the virus has the processors locked down!'

Brinkerhoff rolled his eyes. Midge had gone nuts in the past, but never like this. He tried to calm her. 'Jabba doesn't seem to be too worried.'

'Jabba's a fool,' she hissed.

Brinkerhoff looked surprised. Nobody had ever called Jabba a fool – a pig maybe, but never a fool. 'You're trusting feminine intuition over Jabba's advanced degrees in anti-invasive programming?'

She eyed him harshly.

Brinkerhoff held up his hands in surrender. 'Never mind. I take it back.' He didn't need to be reminded of Midge's uncanny ability to sense disaster. 'Midge,' he begged. 'I know you hate Strathmore, but—'

'This has nothing to do with Strathmore!' Midge was in overdrive. 'The first thing we need to do is confirm Strathmore bypassed Gauntlet. Then we call the director.'

'Great.' Brinkerhoff moaned. 'I'll call Strathmore and ask him to send us a signed statement.'

'No,' she replied, ignoring his sarcasm. 'Strathmore's lied to us once already today.' She glanced up, her eyes probing his. 'Do you have keys to Fontaine's office?'

'Of course. I'm his PA.'

'I need them.'

Brinkerhoff stared in disbelief. 'Midge, there's no way in hell I'm letting you into Fontaine's office.'

'You have to!' she demanded. Midge turned and

started typing on Big Brother's keyboard. 'I'm requesting a TRANSLTR queue list. If Strathmore manually bypassed Gauntlet, it'll show up on the printout.'

'What does that have to do with Fontaine's office?'

She spun and glared at him. 'The queue list only prints to Fontaine's printer. You know that!'

'That's because it's *classified*, Midge!'

'This is an emergency. I need to see that list.'

Brinkerhoff put his hands on her shoulders. 'Midge, please settle down. You know I can't—'

She huffed loudly and spun back to her keyboard. 'I'm printing a queue list. I'm going to walk in, pick it up, and walk out. Now give me the key.'

'Midge . . .'

She finished typing and spun back to him. 'Chad, the report prints in thirty seconds. Here's the deal. You give me the key. If Strathmore bypassed, we call Security. If I'm wrong, I leave, and you can go smear marmalade all over Carmen Huerta.' She gave him a malicious glare and held out her hands for the keys. 'I'm waiting.'

Brinkerhoff groaned, regretting that he had called her back to check the Crypto report. He eyed her outstretched hand. 'You're talking about classified information inside the director's private quarters. Do you have any idea what would happen if we got caught?'

'The director is in South America.'

'I'm sorry. I just can't.' Brinkerhoff crossed his arms and walked out.

Midge stared after him, her gray eyes smoldering. 'Oh, yes you can,' she whispered. Then she turned back to Big Brother and called up the video archives.

*

Midge'll get over it, Brinkerhoff told himself as he settled in at his desk and started going over the rest of his reports. He couldn't be expected to hand out the director's keys whenever Midge got paranoid.

He had just begun checking the COMSEC breakdowns when his thoughts were interrupted by the sound of voices coming from the other room. He set down his work and walked to his doorway.

The main suite was dark – all except a dim shaft of grayish light from Midge's half-open door. He listened. The voices continued. They sounded excited. 'Midge?'

No response.

He strode through the darkness to her workspace. The voices were vaguely familiar. He pushed the door open. The room was empty. Midge's chair was empty. The sound was coming from overhead. Brinkerhoff looked up at the video monitors and instantly felt ill. The same image was playing on each one of the twelve screens – a kind of perversely choreographed ballet. Brinkerhoff steadied himself on the back of Midge's chair and watched in horror.

'Chad?' The voice was behind him.

He spun and squinted into the darkness. Midge was standing kitty-corner across the main suite's reception area in front of the director's double doors. Her palm was outstretched. 'The key, Chad.'

Brinkerhoff flushed. He turned back to the monitors. He tried to block out the images overhead, but it was no use. He was everywhere, groaning with pleasure and eagerly fondling Carmen Huerta's small, honey-covered breasts.

285

CHAPTER 66

Becker crossed the concourse toward the rest room doors only to find the door marked CABALLEROS blocked by an orange pylon and a cleaning cart filled with detergent and mops. He eyed the other door. DAMAS. He strode over and rapped loudly.

'Hola?' he called, pushing the ladies' room door open an inch. 'Con permiso?'

Silence.

He went in.

The rest room was typical, Spanish institutional – perfectly square, white tile, one incandescent bulb overhead. As usual, there was one stall and one urinal. Whether the urinals were ever used in the women's bathrooms was immaterial – adding them saved the contractors the expense of having to build the extra stall.

Becker peered into the rest room in disgust. It was filthy. The sink was clogged with murky brown water. Dirty paper towels were strewn everywhere. The floor was soaked. The old electric handblower on the wall was smeared with greenish fingerprints.

Becker stepped in front of the mirror and sighed.

The eyes that usually stared back with fierce clarity were not so clear tonight. *How long have I been running around over here?* he wondered. The math escaped him. Out of professorial habit, he shimmied his necktie's Windsor knot up on his collar. Then he turned to the urinal behind him.

As he stood there, he found himself wondering if Susan was home yet. *Where could she have gone? To Stone Manor without me?*

'Hey!' a female voice behind him said angrily.

Becker jumped. 'I-I'm . . .' he stammered, hurrying to zip up. 'I'm sorry . . . I . . .'

Becker turned to face the girl who had just entered. She was a young sophisticate, right off the pages of *Seventeen* magazine. She wore conservative plaid pants and a white sleeveless blouse. In her hand was a red L.L. Bean duffel. Her blond hair was perfectly blow-dried.

'I'm sorry.' Becker fumbled, buckling his belt. 'The men's room was . . . anyway . . . I'm leaving.'

'Fuckin' weirdo!'

Becker did a double-take. The profanity seemed inappropriate coming from her lips – like sewage flowing from a polished decanter. But as Becker studied her, he saw that she was not as polished as he'd first thought. Her eyes were puffy and bloodshot, and her left forearm was swollen. Underneath the reddish irritation on her arm, the flesh was blue.

Jesus, Becker thought. *Intravenous drugs. Who would have guessed?*

'Get out!' she yelled. 'Just get out!'

Becker momentarily forgot all about the ring, the NSA, all of it. His heart went out to the young girl. Her parents had probably sent her over here with

some prep school study program and a VISA card –
and she'd ended up all alone in a bathroom in the
middle of the night doing drugs.

'Are you okay?' he asked, backing toward the door.

'I'm fine.' Her voice was haughty. 'You can leave
now!'

Becker turned to go. He shot her forearm a last sad
glance. *There's nothing you can do, David. Leave it alone.*

'Now!' she hollered.

Becker nodded. As he left he gave her a sad smile.
'Be careful.'

CHAPTER 67

'Susan?' Hale panted, his face in hers.

He was sitting, one leg on either side of her, his full weight on her midsection. His tailbone ground painfully into her pubis through the thin fabric of her skirt. His nose was dripping blood all over her. She tasted vomit in the back of her throat. His hands were at her chest.

She felt nothing. *Is he touching me?* It took a moment for Susan to realize Hale was buttoning her top button and covering her up.

'Susan.' Hale gasped, breathless. 'You've got to get me out of here.'

Susan was in a daze. Nothing made sense.

'Susan, you've got to help me! Strathmore killed Chartrukian! I saw it!'

It took a moment for the words to register. *Strathmore killed Chartrukian?* Hale obviously had no idea Susan had seen him downstairs.

'Strathmore knows I saw him!' Hale spat. 'He'll kill me too!'

Had Susan not been breathless with fear, she would have laughed in his face. She recognized the divide-and-conquer mentality of an ex-Marine. Invent lies – pit your enemies against each other.

'It's true!' he yelled. 'We've got to call for help! I think we're both in danger!'

She did not believe a word he said.

Hale's muscular legs were cramping, and he rolled up on his haunches to shift his weight slightly. He opened his mouth to speak, but he never got the chance.

As Hale's body rose, Susan felt the circulation surge back into her legs. Before she knew what had happened, a reflex instinct jerked her left leg back hard into Hale's crotch. She felt her kneecap crush the soft sac of tissue between his legs.

Hale whimpered in agony and instantly went limp. He rolled onto his side, clutching himself. Susan twisted out from under his dead weight. She staggered toward the door, knowing she'd never be strong enough to get out.

Making a split-second decision, Susan positioned herself behind the long maple meeting table and dug her feet into the carpet. Mercifully the table had casters. She strode with all her might toward the arched glass wall, pushing the table before her. The casters were good, and the table rolled well. Halfway across Node 3, she was at a full sprint.

Five feet from the glass wall, Susan heaved and let go. She leapt to one side and covered her eyes. After a sickening crack, the wall exploded in a shower of glass. The sounds of Crypto rushed into Node 3 for the first time since its construction.

Susan looked up. Through the jagged hole, she could see the table. It was still rolling. It spun wide circles out across the Crypto floor and eventually disappeared into the darkness.

Susan rammed her mangled Ferragamo back on her feet, shot a last glance at the still-writhing Greg Hale, and dashed across the sea of broken glass out onto the Crypto floor.

CHAPTER 68

'Now wasn't that easy?' Midge said with a sneer as Brinkerhoff handed over the key to Fontaine's office.

Brinkerhoff looked beaten.

'I'll erase it before I go,' Midge promised. 'Unless you and your wife want it for your private collection.'

'Just get the damned printout,' he snapped. 'And then get out!'

'Sí, señor,' Midge cackled in a thick Puerto Rican accent. She winked and headed across the suite to Fontaine's double doors.

Leland Fontaine's private office looked nothing like the rest of the directorial suite. There were no paintings, no overstuffed chairs, no ficus plants, no antique clocks. His space was streamlined for efficiency. His glass-topped desk and black leather chair sat directly in front of his enormous picture window. Three file cabinets stood in the corner next to a small table with a French press coffeepot. The moon had risen high over Fort Meade, and the soft light filtering through the window accentuated the starkness of the director's furnishings.

What the hell am I doing? Brinkerhoff wondered.

Midge strode to the printer and scooped up the queue list. She squinted in the darkness. 'I can't read the data,' she complained. 'Turn on the lights.'

'You're reading it *outside*. Now come on.'

But Midge was apparently having too much fun. She toyed with Brinkerhoff, walking to the window and angling the readout for a better view.

'Midge . . .'

She kept reading.

Brinkerhoff shifted anxiously in the doorway. 'Midge . . . come on. These are the director's private quarters.'

'It's here somewhere,' she muttered, studying the printout. 'Strathmore bypassed Gauntlet, I know it.' She moved closer to the window.

Brinkerhoff began to sweat. Midge kept reading.

After a few moments, she gasped. 'I knew it! Strathmore did it! He really did! The idiot!' She held up the paper and shook it. 'He bypassed Gauntlet! Have a look!'

Brinkerhoff stared dumbfounded a moment and then raced across the director's office. He crowded in next to Midge in front of the window. She pointed to the end of the readout.

Brinkerhoff read in disbelief. 'What the . . . ?'

The printout contained a list of the last thirty-six files that had entered TRANSLTR. After each file was a four-digit Gauntlet clearance code. However, the last file on the sheet had no clearance code – it simply read: MANUAL BYPASS.

Jesus, Brinkerhoff thought. *Midge strikes again.*

'The idiot!' Midge sputtered, seething. 'Look at this! Gauntlet rejected the file twice! Mutation strings! And he *still* bypassed! What the hell was he thinking?'

293

Brinkerhoff felt weak-kneed. He wondered why Midge was always right. Neither of them noticed the reflection that had appeared in the window beside them. A massive figure was standing in Fontaine's open doorway.

'Jeez,' Brinkerhoff choked. 'You think we have a virus?'

Midge sighed. 'Nothing else it could be.'

'Could be none of your damn business!' the deep voice boomed from behind them.

Midge knocked her head against the window. Brinkerhoff tipped over the director's chair and wheeled toward the voice. He immediately knew the silhouette.

'Director!' Brinkerhoff gasped. He strode over and extended his hand. 'Welcome home, sir.'

The huge man ignored it.

'I-I thought,' Brinkerhoff stammered, retracting his hand, 'I thought you were in South America.'

Leland Fontaine glared down at his aide with eyes like bullets. 'Yes . . . and now I'm back.'

CHAPTER 69

'Hey, mister!'

Becker had been walking across the concourse toward a bank of pay phones. He stopped and turned. Coming up behind him was the girl he'd just surprised in the bathroom. She waved for him to wait. 'Mister, wait!'

Now what? Becker groaned. *She wants to press invasion-of-privacy charges?*

The girl dragged her duffel toward him. When she arrived, she was now wearing a huge smile. 'Sorry to yell at you back there. You just kind of startled me.'

'No problem,' Becker assured, somewhat puzzled. 'I was in the wrong place.'

'This will sound crazy,' she said, batting her blood-shot eyes. 'But you wouldn't happen to have some money you can lend me, would you?'

Becker stared at her in disbelief. 'Money for what?' he demanded. *I'm not funding your drug habit if that's what you're asking.*

'I'm trying to get back home,' the blonde said. 'Can you help?'

'Miss your flight?'

She nodded. 'Lost my ticket. They wouldn't let me

295

get on. Airlines can be such assholes. I don't have the cash to buy another.'

'Where are your parents?' Becker asked.

'States.'

'Can you reach them?'

'Nope. Already tried. I think they're weekending on somebody's yacht.'

Becker scanned the girl's expensive clothing. 'You don't have a credit card?'

'Yeah, but my dad canceled it. He thinks I'm on drugs.'

'*Are* you on drugs?' Becker asked, deadpan, eyeing her swollen forearm.

The girl glared, indignant. 'Of course not!' She gave Becker an innocent huff, and he suddenly got the feeling he was being played.

'Come on,' she said. 'You look like a rich guy. Can't you spot me some cash to get home? I could send it to you later.'

Becker figured any cash he gave this girl would end up in the hands of some drug dealer in Triana. 'First of all,' he said, 'I'm not a rich guy – I'm a teacher. But I'll tell you what I'll do . . .' *I'll call your bluff, that's what I'll do.* 'Why don't I *charge* the ticket for you?'

The blonde stared at him in utter shock. 'You'd do that?' she stammered, eyes wide with hope. 'You'd buy me a ticket home? Oh, God, thank you!'

Becker was speechless. He had apparently misjudged the moment.

The girl threw her arms around him. 'It's been a shitty summer,' she choked, almost bursting into tears. 'Oh, thank you! I've got to get out of here!'

Becker returned her embrace halfheartedly. The girl let go of him, and he eyed her forearm again.

She followed his gaze to the bluish rash. 'Gross, huh?'

Becker nodded. 'I thought you said you weren't on drugs.'

The girl laughed. 'It's Magic Marker! I took off half my skin trying to scrub it off. The ink smeared.'

Becker looked closer. In the fluorescent light, he could see, blurred beneath the reddish swelling on her arm, the faint outline of writing – words scrawled on flesh.

'But . . . but your *eyes*,' Becker said, feeling dumb. 'They're all red.'

She laughed. 'I was crying. I told you, I missed my flight.'

Becker looked back at the words on her arm.

She frowned, embarrassed. 'Oops, you can still kind of read it, can't you?'

Becker leaned closer. He could read it all right. The message was crystal clear. As he read the four faint words, the last twelve hours flashed before his eyes.

David Becker found himself back in the Alfonso XIII hotel room. The obese German was touching his own forearm and speaking broken English: Fock off und die.

'You okay?' the girl asked, eyeing the dazed Becker.

Becker did not look up from her arm. He was dizzy. The four words smeared across the girl's flesh carried a very simple message: FUCK OFF AND DIE.

The blonde looked down at it, embarrassed. 'This friend of mine wrote it . . . pretty stupid, huh?'

Becker couldn't speak. *Fock off und die.* He couldn't believe it. The German hadn't been insulting him, he'd been trying to help. Becker lifted his gaze to the girl's face. In the fluorescent light of the concourse, he

297

could see faint traces of red and blue in the girl's blond hair.

'Y-you . . .' Becker stammered, staring at her unpierced ears. 'You wouldn't happen to wear earrings, would you?'

The girl eyed him strangely. She fished a tiny object from her pocket and held it out. Becker gazed at the skull pendant dangling in her hand.

'A clip-on?' he stammered.

'Hell, yes,' the girl replied. 'I'm scared shitless of needles.'

CHAPTER 70

David Becker stood in the deserted concourse and felt his legs go weak. He eyed the girl before him and knew his search was over. She had washed her hair and changed clothes – maybe in hopes of having better luck selling the ring – but she'd never boarded for New York.

Becker fought to keep his cool. His wild journey was about to end. He scanned her fingers. They were bare. He gazed down at her duffel. *It's in there*, he thought. *It's got to be!*

He smiled, barely containing his excitement. 'This is going to sound crazy,' he said, 'but I think you've got something I need.'

'Oh?' Megan seemed suddenly uncertain.

Becker reached for his wallet. 'Of course I'd be happy to pay you.' He looked down and started sorting through the cash in his billfold.

As Megan watched him count out his money, she drew a startled gasp, apparently misunderstanding his intentions. She shot a frightened glance toward the revolving door . . . measuring the distance. It was fifty yards.

'I can give you enough to buy your ticket home if—'

'Don't say it,' Megan blurted, offering a forced smile. 'I think I know exactly what you need.' She bent down and started rifling through her duffel.

Becker felt a surge of hope. *She's got it!* he told himself. *She's got the ring!* He didn't know how the hell she knew what it was he wanted, but he was too tired to care. Every muscle in his body relaxed. He pictured himself handing the ring to the beaming deputy director of the NSA. Then he and Susan would lie in the big canopy bed at Stone Manor and make up for lost time.

The girl finally found what she was looking for – her PepperGard – the environmentally safe alternative to Mace, made from a potent blend of cayenne and chili peppers. In one swift motion, she swung around and fired a direct stream into Becker's eyes. She grabbed her duffel and dashed for the door. When she looked back, David Becker was on the floor, holding his face, writhing in agony.

CHAPTER 71

Tokugen Numataka lit his fourth cigar and kept pacing. He snatched up his phone and buzzed the main switchboard.

'Any word yet on that phone number?' he demanded before the operator could speak.

'Nothing yet, sir. It's taking a bit longer than expected – it came from a cellular.'

A cellular, Numataka mused. *Figures.* Fortunately for the Japanese economy, the Americans had an insatiable appetite for electronic gadgets.

'The boosting station,' the operator added, 'is in the 202 area code. But we have no number yet.'

'202? Where's that?' *Where in the vast American expanse is this mysterious North Dakota hiding?*

'Somewhere near Washington, D.C., sir.'

Numataka arched his eyebrows. 'Call me as soon as you have a number.'

CHAPTER 72

Susan Fletcher stumbled across the darkened Crypto floor toward Strathmore's catwalk. The commander's office was as far from Hale as Susan could get inside the locked complex.

When Susan reached the top of the catwalk stairs, she found the commander's door hanging loosely, the electronic lock rendered ineffective by the power outage. She barged in.

'Commander?' The only light inside was the glow of Strathmore's computer monitors. 'Commander!' she called once again. *'Commander!'*

Susan suddenly remembered that the commander was in the Sys-Sec lab. She turned circles in his empty office, the panic of her ordeal with Hale still in her blood. She had to get out of Crypto. Digital Fortress or no Digital Fortress, it was time to act – time to abort the TRANSLTR run and escape. She eyed Strathmore's glowing monitors, then dashed to his desk. She fumbled with his keypad. *Abort TRANSLTR!* The task was simple now that she was on an authorized terminal. Susan called up the proper command window and typed:

Her finger hovered momentarily over the ENTER key.

'Susan!' a voice barked from the doorway. Susan wheeled scared, fearing it was Hale. But it was not, it was Strathmore. He stood, pale and eerie in the electronic glow, his chest heaving. 'What the hell's going on!'

'Com . . . mander!' Susan gasped. 'Hale's in Node 3! He just attacked me!'

'What? Impossible! Hale's locked down in—'

'No, he's not! He's loose! We need security in here now! I'm aborting TRANSLTR!' Susan reached for the keypad.

'DON'T TOUCH THAT!' Strathmore lunged for the terminal and pulled Susan's hands away.

Susan recoiled, stunned. She stared at the commander and for the second time that day did not recognize him. Susan felt suddenly alone.

Strathmore saw the blood on Susan's shirt and immediately regretted his outburst. 'Jesus, Susan. Are you okay?'

She didn't respond.

He wished he hadn't jumped on her unnecessarily. His nerves were frayed. He was juggling too much. There were things on his mind – things Susan Fletcher did not know about – things he had not told her and prayed he'd never have to.

'I'm sorry,' he said softly. 'Tell me what happened.'

She turned away. 'It doesn't matter. The blood's not mine. Just get me out of here.'

'Are you hurt?' Strathmore put a hand on her shoulder. Susan recoiled. He dropped his hand and looked away. When he looked back at Susan's face, she seemed to be staring over his shoulder at something on the wall.

There, in the darkness, a small keypad glowed full force. Strathmore followed her gaze and frowned. He'd hoped Susan wouldn't notice the glowing control panel. The illuminated keypad controlled his private elevator. Strathmore and his high-powered guests used it to come and go from Crypto without advertising the fact to the rest of the staff. The personal lift dropped down fifty feet below the Crypto dome and then moved laterally 109 yards through a reinforced underground tunnel to the sublevels of the main NSA complex. The elevator connecting Crypto to the NSA was powered from the main complex; it was on-line despite Crypto's power outage.

Strathmore had known all along it was on-line, but even as Susan had been pounding on the main exit downstairs, he hadn't mentioned it. He could not afford to let Susan out – not yet. He wondered how much he'd have to tell her to make her want to stay.

Susan pushed past Strathmore and raced to the back wall. She jabbed furiously at the illuminated buttons.

'Please,' she begged. But the door did not open.

'Susan,' Strathmore said quietly. 'The lift takes a password.'

'A password?' she repeated angrily. She glared at the controls. Below the main keypad was a second keypad – a smaller one, with tiny buttons. Each button was marked with a letter of the alphabet. Susan wheeled to him. 'What is the password!' she demanded.

Strathmore thought a moment and sighed heavily. 'Susan, have a seat.'

Susan looked as if she could hardly believe her ears.

'Have a seat,' the commander repeated, his voice firm.

'Let me out!' Susan shot an uneasy glance toward the commander's open office door.

Strathmore eyed the panicked Susan Fletcher. Calmly he moved to his office door. He stepped out onto the landing and peered into the darkness. Hale was nowhere to be seen. The commander stepped back inside and pulled the door shut. Then he propped a chair in front to keep it closed, went to his desk, and removed something from a drawer. In the pale glow of the monitors Susan saw what he was holding. Her face went pale. It was a gun.

Strathmore pulled two chairs into the middle of the room. He rotated them to face the closed office door. Then he sat. He lifted the glittering Beretta semi-automatic and aimed steadily at the slightly open door. After a moment he laid the gun back in his lap.

He spoke solemnly. 'Susan, we're safe here. We need to talk. If Greg Hale comes through that door . . .' He let it hang.

Susan was speechless.

Strathmore gazed at her in the dim light of his office. He patted the seat beside him. 'Susan, sit. I have something to tell you.' She did not move. 'When I'm done,' he said, 'I'll give you the password to the elevator. You can decide whether to leave or not.'

There was a long silence. In a daze, Susan moved across the office and sat next to Strathmore.

'Susan,' he began, 'I haven't been entirely honest with you.'

305

CHAPTER 73

David Becker felt as if his face had been doused in turpentine and ignited. He rolled over on the floor and squinted through bleary tunnel vision at the girl halfway to the revolving doors. She was running in short, terrified bursts, dragging her duffel behind her across the tile. Becker tried to pull himself to his feet, but he could not. He was blinded by red-hot fire. *She can't get away!*

He tried to call out, but there was no air in his lungs, only a sickening pain. 'No!' He coughed. The sound barely left his lips.

Becker knew the second she went through the door, she would disappear forever. He tried to call out again, but his throat was searing.

The girl had almost reached the revolving door. Becker staggered to his feet, gasping for breath. He stumbled after her. The girl dashed into the first compartment of the revolving door, dragging her duffel behind her. Twenty yards back, Becker was staggering blindly toward the door.

'Wait!' He gasped. *'Wait!'*

The girl pushed furiously on the inside of the door.

The door began to rotate, but then it jammed. She wheeled in terror and saw her duffel snagged in the opening. She knelt and pulled furiously to free it.

Becker fixed his bleary vision on the fabric protruding through the door. As he dove, the red corner of nylon protruding from the crack was all he could see. He flew toward it, arms outstretched.

As David Becker fell toward the door, his hands only inches away, the fabric slipped into the crack and disappeared. His fingers clutched empty air as the door lurched into motion. The girl and the duffel tumbled into the street outside.

'Megan!' Becker wailed as he hit the floor. White-hot needles shot through the back of his eye sockets. His vision tunneled to nothing, and a new wave of nausea rolled in. His own voice echoed in the blackness. *Megan!*

David Becker wasn't sure how long he'd been lying there before he became aware of the hum of fluorescent bulbs overhead. Everything else was still. Through the silence came a voice. Someone was calling. He tried to lift his head off the floor. The world was cockeyed, watery. *Again the voice.* He squinted down the concourse and saw a figure twenty yards away.

'Mister?'

Becker recognized the voice. It was the girl. She was standing at another entrance farther down the concourse, clutching her duffel to her chest. She looked more frightened now than she had before.

'Mister?' she asked, her voice trembling. 'I never told you my name. How come you know my name?'

CHAPTER 74

Director Leland Fontaine was a mountain of a man, sixty-three years old, with a close-cropped military haircut and a rigid demeanor. His jet-black eyes were like coal when he was irritated, which was almost always. He'd risen through the ranks of the NSA through hard work, good planning, and the well-earned respect of his predecessors. He was the first African American director of the National Security Agency, but nobody ever mentioned the distinction; Fontaine's politics were decidedly color-blind, and his staff wisely followed suit.

Fontaine had kept Midge and Brinkerhoff standing as he went through the silent ritual of making himself a mug of Guatemalan java. Then he'd settled at his desk, left them standing, and questioned them like schoolchildren in the principal's office.

Midge did the talking – explaining the unusual series of events that led them to violate the sanctity of Fontaine's office.

'A virus?' the director asked coldly. 'You two think we've got a virus?'

Brinkerhoff winced.

'Yes, sir,' Midge snapped.

'Because Strathmore bypassed Gauntlet?' Fontaine eyed the printout in front of him.

'Yes,' she said. 'And there's a file that hasn't broken in over twenty hours!'

Fontaine frowned. 'Or so your data says.'

Midge was about to protest, but she held her tongue. Instead she went for the throat. 'There's a blackout in Crypto.'

Fontaine looked up, apparently surprised.

Midge confirmed with a curt nod. 'All power's down. Jabba thought maybe—'

'You called Jabba?'

'Yes, sir, I—'

'Jabba?' Fontaine stood up, furious. 'Why the hell didn't you call Strathmore?'

'We did!' Midge defended. 'He said everything was fine.'

Fontaine stood, his chest heaving. 'Then we have no reason to doubt him.' There was closure in his voice. He took a sip of coffee. 'Now if you'll excuse me, I have work to do.'

Midge's jaw dropped. 'I beg your pardon?'

Brinkerhoff was already headed for the door, but Midge was cemented in place.

'I said good night, Ms Milken,' Fontaine repeated. 'You are excused.'

'But – but sir,' she stammered, 'I . . . I have to protest. I think—'

'*You* protest?' the director demanded. He set down his coffee. '*I* protest! I protest to your presence in my office. I protest to your insinuations that the deputy director of this agency is lying. I protest—'

'We have a virus, sir! My instincts tell me—'

'Well, your instincts are wrong, Ms. Milken! For once, they're wrong!'

Midge stood fast. 'But, sir! Commander Strathmore bypassed Gauntlet!'

Fontaine strode toward her, barely controlling his anger. 'That is *his* prerogative! I pay you to watch analysts and service employees – not spy on the deputy director! If it weren't for him we'd still be breaking codes with pencil and paper! Now leave me!' He turned to Brinkerhoff, who stood in the doorway colorless and trembling. 'Both of you.'

'With all due respect, sir,' Midge said. 'I'd like to recommend we send a Sys-Sec team to Crypto just to ensure—'

'We will do no such thing!'

After a tense beat, Midge nodded. 'Very well. Good night.' She turned and left. As she passed, Brinkerhoff could see in her eyes that she had no intention of letting this rest – not until her intuition was satisfied.

Brinkerhoff gazed across the room at his boss, massive and seething behind his desk. This was not the director he knew. The director he knew was a stickler for detail, for neatly tied packages. He always encouraged his staff to examine and clarify any inconsistencies in daily procedure, no matter how minute. And yet here he was, asking them to turn their backs on a very bizarre series of coincidences.

The director was obviously hiding something, but Brinkerhoff was paid to assist, not to question. Fontaine had proven over and over that he had everyone's best interests at heart; if assisting him now meant turning a blind eye, then so be it. Unfortunately, Midge was paid to question, and Brinkerhoff feared she was headed for Crypto to do just that.

Time to get out the résumés, Brinkerhoff thought as he turned to the door.

'Chad!' Fontaine barked, from behind him. Fontaine had seen the look in Midge's eyes when she left. 'Don't let her out of this suite.'

Brinkerhoff nodded and hustled after Midge.

Fontaine sighed and put his head in his hands. His sable eyes were heavy. It had been a long, unexpected trip home. The past month had been one of great anticipation for Leland Fontaine. There were things happening right now at the NSA that would change history, and ironically, Director Fontaine had found out about them only by chance.

Three months ago, Fontaine had gotten news that Commander Strathmore's wife was leaving him. He'd also heard reports that Strathmore was working absurd hours and seemed about to crack under the pressure. Despite differences of opinion with Strathmore on many issues, Fontaine had always held his deputy director in the highest esteem; Strathmore was a brilliant man, maybe the best the NSA had. At the same time, ever since the Skipjack fiasco, Strathmore had been under tremendous stress. It made Fontaine uneasy; the commander held a lot of keys around the NSA – and Fontaine had an agency to protect.

Fontaine needed someone to keep tabs on the wavering Strathmore and make sure he was 100 percent – but it was not that simple. Strathmore was a proud and powerful man; Fontaine needed a way to check up on the commander without undermining his confidence or authority.

Fontaine decided, out of respect for Strathmore, to

do the job himself. He had an invisible tap installed on Commander Strathmore's Crypto account – his E-mail, his interoffice correspondence, his brainstorms, all of it. If Strathmore was going to crack, the director would see warning signs in his work. But instead of signs of a breakdown, Fontaine uncovered the groundwork for one of the most incredible intelligence schemes he'd ever encountered. It was no wonder Strathmore was busting his ass; if he could pull this plan off, it would make up for the Skipjack fiasco a hundred times over.

Fontaine had concluded Strathmore was fine, working at 110 percent – as sly, smart, and patriotic as ever. The best thing the director could do would be to stand clear and watch the commander work his magic. Strathmore had devised a plan . . . a plan Fontaine had no intention of interrupting.

CHAPTER 75

Strathmore fingered the Beretta in his lap. Even with the rage boiling in his blood, he was programmed to think clearly. The fact that Greg Hale had dared lay a finger on Susan Fletcher sickened him, but the fact that it was his own fault made him even sicker; Susan going into Node 3 had been his idea. Strathmore knew enough to compartmentalize his emotion – it could in no way affect his handling of Digital Fortress. He was the deputy director of the National Security Agency. And today his job was more critical than it had ever been.

Strathmore slowed his breathing. 'Susan.' His voice was efficient and unclouded. 'Did you delete Hale's E-mail?'

'No,' she said, confused.

'Do you have the pass-key?'

She shook her head.

Strathmore frowned, chewing his lip. His mind was racing. He had a dilemma. He could easily enter his elevator password, and Susan would be gone. But he needed her there. He needed her help to find Hale's pass-key. Strathmore hadn't told her yet, but finding that pass-key was far more than a matter of academic interest – it was an absolute necessity. Strathmore suspected he could run Susan's nonconformity search and find the pass-key himself, but he'd already encountered problems running her tracer. He was not about to risk it again.

'Susan.' He sighed resolutely. 'I'd like you to help me find Hale's pass-key.'

'What!' Susan stood up, her eyes wild.

Strathmore fought off the urge to stand along with her. He knew a lot about negotiating – the position of power was always seated. He hoped she would follow suit. She did not.

'Susan, sit down.'

She ignored him.

'Sit down.' It was an order.

Susan remained standing. 'Commander, if you've still got some burning desire to check out Tankado's algorithm, you can do it alone. I want out.'

Strathmore hung his head and took a deep breath. It was clear she would need an explanation. *She deserves one*, he thought. Strathmore made his decision – Susan Fletcher would hear it all. He prayed he wasn't making a mistake.

'Susan,' he began, 'it wasn't supposed to come to this.' He ran his hand across his scalp. 'There are some things I haven't told you. Sometimes a man in my position . . .' The commander wavered as if making a painful confession. 'Sometimes a man in my position is forced to lie to the people he loves. Today was one of those days.' He eyed her sadly. 'What I'm about to tell you, I never planned to have to say . . . to you . . . or to anyone.'

Susan felt a chill. The commander had a deadly

serious look on his face. There was obviously some aspect of his agenda to which she was not privy. Susan sat down.

There was a long pause as Strathmore stared at the ceiling, gathering his thoughts. 'Susan,' he finally said, his voice frail. 'I have no family.' He returned his gaze to her. 'I have no marriage to speak of. My life has been my love for this country. My life has been my work here at the NSA.'

Susan listened in silence.

'As you may have guessed,' he continued, 'I planned to retire soon. But I wanted to retire with pride. I wanted to retire knowing that I'd truly made a difference.'

'But you *have* made a difference,' Susan heard herself say. 'You built TRANSLTR.'

Strathmore didn't seem to hear. 'Over the past few years, our work here at the NSA has gotten harder and harder. We've faced enemies I never imagined would challenge us. I'm talking about our own citizens. The lawyers, the civil rights fanatics, the EFF – they've all played a part, but it's more than that. It's the *people*. They've lost faith. They've become paranoid. They suddenly see *us* as the enemy. People like you and me, people who truly have the nation's best interests at heart, we find ourselves having to fight for our right to serve our country. We're no longer peacekeepers. We're eavesdroppers, peeping Toms, violators of people's rights.' Strathmore heaved a sigh. 'Unfortunately, there are naive people in the world, people who can't imagine the horrors they'd face if we didn't intervene. I truly believe it's up to us to save them from their own ignorance.'

Susan waited for his point.

The commander stared wearily at the floor and then looked up. 'Susan, hear me out,' he said, smiling tenderly at her. 'You'll want to stop me, but hear me out. I've been decrypting Tankado's E-mail for about two months now. As you can imagine, I was shocked when I first read his messages to North Dakota about an unbreakable algorithm called Digital Fortress. I didn't believe it was possible. But every time I intercepted a new message, Tankado sounded more and more convincing. When I read that he'd used mutation strings to write a rotating key-code, I realized he was light-years ahead of us; it was an approach no one here had ever tried.'

'Why *would* we?' Susan asked. 'It barely makes sense.'

Strathmore stood up and started pacing, keeping one eye on the door. 'A few weeks ago, when I heard about the Digital Fortress auction, I finally accepted the fact that Tankado was serious. I knew if he sold his algorithm to a Japanese software company, we were sunk, so I tried to think of any way I could stop him. I considered having him killed, but with all the publicity surrounding the algorithm and all his recent claims about TRANSLTR, we would be prime suspects. That's when it dawned on me.' He turned to Susan. 'I realized that Digital Fortress should *not* be stopped.'

Susan stared at him, apparently lost.

Strathmore went on. 'I suddenly saw Digital Fortress as the opportunity of a lifetime. It hit me that with a few changes, Digital Fortress could work *for* us instead of against us.'

Susan had never heard anything so absurd. Digital Fortress was an unbreakable algorithm; it would destroy them.

'If,' Strathmore continued, 'if I could just make a small modification in the algorithm . . . before it was released . . .' He gave her a cunning glint of the eye.

It took only an instant.

Strathmore saw the amazement register in Susan's eyes. He excitedly explained his plan. 'If I could get the pass-key, I could unlock our copy of Digital Fortress and insert a modification.'

'A back door,' Susan said, forgetting the commander had ever lied to her. She felt a surge of anticipation. 'Just like Skipjack.'

Strathmore nodded. 'Then we could replace Tankado's give-away file on the Internet with our *altered* version. Because Digital Fortress is a Japanese algorithm, no one will ever suspect the NSA had any part in it. All we have to do is make the switch.'

Susan realized the plan was beyond ingenious. It was pure . . . Strathmore. He planned to facilitate the release of an algorithm the NSA could break!

'Full access,' Strathmore said. 'Digital Fortress will become the encryption standard overnight.'

'Overnight?' Susan said. 'How do you figure *that?* Even if Digital Fortress becomes available everywhere for free, most computer users will stick with their old algorithms for convenience. Why would they switch to Digital Fortress?'

Strathmore smiled. 'Simple. We have a security leak. The whole world finds out about TRANSLTR.'

Susan's jaw dropped.

'Quite simply, Susan, we let the truth hit the street. We tell the world that the NSA has a computer that can break every algorithm except Digital Fortress.'

Susan was amazed. 'So everyone jumps ship to Digital Fortress . . . not knowing we can break it!'

Strathmore nodded. 'Exactly.' There was a long silence. 'I'm sorry I lied to you. Trying to rewrite Digital Fortress is a pretty big play, I didn't want you involved.'

'I . . . understand,' she replied slowly, still reeling from the brilliance of it all. 'You're not a bad liar.'

Strathmore chuckled. 'Years of practice. Lying was the only way to keep you out of the loop.'

Susan nodded. 'And how big a loop is it?'

'You're looking at it.'

Susan smiled for the first time in an hour. 'I was afraid you'd say that.'

He shrugged. 'Once Digital Fortress is in place, I'll brief the director.'

Susan was impressed. Strathmore's plan was a global intelligence coup the magnitude of which had never before been imagined. And he'd attempted it single-handedly. It looked like he might pull it off too. The pass-key was downstairs. Tankado was dead. Tankado's partner had been located.

Susan paused.

Tankado is dead. That seemed very convenient. She thought of all the lies that Strathmore had told her and felt a sudden chill. She looked uneasily at the commander. 'Did you kill Ensei Tankado?'

Strathmore looked surprised. He shook his head. 'Of course not. There was no need to kill Tankado. In fact, I'd prefer he were alive. His death could cast suspicion on Digital Fortress. I wanted this switch to go as smoothly and inconspicuously as possible. The original plan was to make the switch and let Tankado sell his key.'

Susan had to admit it made sense. Tankado would have no reason to suspect the algorithm on the

318

Internet was not the original. Nobody had access to it except himself and North Dakota. Unless Tankado went back and studied the programming after it was released, he'd never know about the back door. He'd slaved over Digital Fortress for long enough that he'd probably never want to see the programming again.

Susan let it all soak in. She suddenly understood the commander's need for privacy in Crypto. The task at hand was time-consuming and delicate – writing a concealed back door in a complex algorithm and making an undetected Internet switch. Concealment was of paramount importance. The simple suggestion that Digital Fortress was tainted could ruin the commander's plan.

Only now did she fully grasp why he had decided to let TRANSLTR keep running. *If Digital Fortress is going to be the NSA's new baby, Strathmore wanted to be sure it was unbreakable!*

'Still want out?' he asked.

Susan looked up. Somehow sitting there in the dark with the great Trevor Strathmore, her fears were swept away. Rewriting Digital Fortress was a chance to make history – a chance to do incredible good – and Strathmore could use her help. Susan forced a reluctant smile. 'What's our next move?'

Strathmore beamed. He reached over and put a hand on her shoulder. 'Thanks.' He smiled and then got down to business. 'We'll go downstairs together.' He held up his Beretta. 'You'll search Hale's terminal. I'll cover you.'

Susan bristled at the thought of going downstairs. 'Can't we wait for David to call with Tankado's copy?'

Strathmore shook his head. 'The sooner we make the switch, the better. We have no guarantees that

319

David will even find the other copy. If by some fluke the ring falls into the wrong hands over there, I'd prefer we'd already made the algorithm switch. That way, whoever ends up with the key will download *our* version of the algorithm.' Strathmore fingered his gun and stood. 'We need to go for Hale's key.'

Susan fell silent. The commander had a point. They needed Hale's pass-key. And they needed it now.

When Susan stood, her legs were jittery. She wished she'd hit Hale harder. She eyed Strathmore's weapon and suddenly felt queasy. 'You'd actually shoot Greg Hale?'

'No.' Strathmore frowned, striding to the door. 'But let's hope *he* doesn't know that.'

CHAPTER 76

Outside the Seville airport terminal, a taxi sat idle, the meter running. The passenger in the wire-rim glasses gazed through the plate-glass windows of the well-lit terminal. He knew he'd arrived in time.

He could see a blond girl. She was helping David Becker to a chair. Becker was apparently in pain. *He does not yet know pain,* the passenger thought. The girl pulled a small object from her pocket and held it out. Becker held it up and studied it in the light. Then he slipped it on his finger. He pulled a stack of bills from his pocket and paid the girl. They talked a few minutes longer, and then the girl hugged him. She waved, shouldered her duffel, and headed off across the concourse.

At last, the man in the taxi thought. *At last.*

CHAPTER 77

Strathmore stepped out of his office onto the landing with his gun leveled. Susan trailed close behind, wondering if Hale was still in Node 3.

The light from Strathmore's monitor behind them threw eerie shadows of their bodies out across the grated platform. Susan inched closer to the commander.

As they moved away from the door, the light faded, and they were plunged into darkness. The only light on the Crypto floor came from the stars above and the faint haze from behind the shattered Node 3 window.

Strathmore inched forward, looking for the place where the narrow staircase began. Switching the Beretta to his left hand, he groped for the banister with his right. He figured he was probably just as bad a shot with his left, and he needed his right for support. Falling down this particular set of stairs could cripple someone for life, and Strathmore's dreams for his retirement did not involve a wheelchair.

Susan, blinded by the blackness of the Crypto dome, descended with a hand on Strathmore's shoulder. Even at the distance of two feet, she could not see the commander's outline. As she stepped onto each metal tread, she shuffled her toes forward looking for the edge.

Susan began having second thoughts about risking a visit to Node 3 to get Hale's pass-key. The commander insisted Hale wouldn't have the guts to touch them, but Susan wasn't so sure. Hale was desperate. He had two options: Escape Crypto or go to jail.

A voice kept telling Susan they should wait for David's call and use *his* pass-key, but she knew there was no guarantee he would even find it. She wondered what was taking David so long. Susan swallowed her apprehension and kept going.

Strathmore descended silently. There was no need to alert Hale they were coming. As they neared the bottom, Strathmore slowed, feeling for the final step. When he found it, the heel of his loafer clicked on hard black tile. Susan felt his shoulder tense. They'd entered the danger zone. Hale could be anywhere.

In the distance, now hidden behind TRANSLTR, was their destination – Node 3. Susan prayed Hale was still there, lying on the floor, whimpering in pain like the dog he was.

Strathmore let go of the railing and switched the gun back to his right hand. Without a word, he moved out into the darkness. Susan held tight to his shoulder. If she lost him, the only way she'd find him again was to speak. Hale might hear them. As they moved away from the safety of the stairs, Susan recalled late-night games of tag as a kid – she'd left home base, she was in the open. She was vulnerable.

TRANSLTR was the only island in the vast black sea. Every few steps Strathmore stopped, gun poised, and listened. The only sound was the faint hum from below. Susan wanted to pull him back, back to safety, back to home base. There seemed to be faces in the dark all around her.

Halfway to TRANSLTR, the silence of Crypto was broken. Somewhere in the darkness, seemingly right on top of them, a high-pitched beeping pierced the night. Strathmore spun, and Susan lost him. Fearful, Susan shot her arm out, groping for him. But the commander was gone. The space where his shoulder had been was now just empty air. She staggered forward into the emptiness.

The beeping noise continued. It was nearby. Susan wheeled in the darkness. There was a rustle of clothing, and suddenly the beeping stopped. Susan froze. An instant later, as if from one of her worst childhood nightmares, a vision appeared. A face materialized directly in front of her. It was ghostly and green. It was the face of a demon, sharp shadows jutting upward across deformed features. She jumped back. She turned to run, but it grabbed her arm.

'Don't move!' it commanded.

For an instant, she thought she saw Hale in those two burning eyes. But the voice was not Hale's. And the touch was too soft. It was Strathmore. He was lit from beneath by a glowing object that he'd just pulled from his pocket. Her body sagged with relief. She felt herself start breathing again. The object in Strathmore's hand had some sort of electronic LED that was giving off a greenish glow.

'Damn,' Strathmore cursed under his breath. 'My new pager.' He stared in disgust at the SkyPager in his palm. He'd forgotten to engage the silent-ring feature. Ironically, he'd gone to a local electronics store to buy the device. He'd paid cash to keep it anonymous;

nobody knew better than Strathmore how closely the NSA watched their own – and the digital messages sent and received from this pager were something Strathmore definitely needed to keep private.

Susan looked around uneasily. If Hale hadn't known they were coming, he knew now.

Strathmore pressed a few buttons and read the incoming message. He groaned quietly. It was more bad news from Spain – not from David Becker, but from the *other* party Strathmore had sent to Seville.

Three thousand miles away, a mobile surveillance van sped along the darkened Seville streets. It had been commissioned by the NSA under 'Umbra' secrecy from a military base in Rota. The two men inside were tense. It was not the first time they'd received emergency orders from Fort Meade, but the orders didn't usually come from so high up.

The agent at the wheel called over his shoulder. 'Any sign of our man?'

The eyes of his partner never left the feed from the wide-angle video monitor on the roof. 'No. Keep driving.'

CHAPTER 78

Underneath the twisting mass of cables, Jabba was sweating. He was still on his back with a penlight clenched in his teeth. He'd gotten used to working late on weekends; the less hectic NSA hours were often the only times he could perform hardware maintenance. As he maneuvered the red-hot soldering iron through the maze of wires above him, he moved with exceptional care; singeing any of the dangling sheaths would be disaster.

Just another few inches, he thought. The job was taking far longer than he'd imagined.

Just as he brought the tip of the iron against the final thread of raw solder, his cellular phone rang sharply. Jabba started, his arm twitched, and a large glob of sizzling, liquefied lead fell on his arm.

'*Shit!*' He dropped the iron and practically swallowed his penlight. 'Shit! Shit! Shit!'

He scrubbed furiously at the drop of cooling solder. It rolled off, leaving an impressive welt. The chip he was trying to solder in place fell out and hit him in the head.

'Goddamn it!'

Jabba's phone summoned him again. He ignored it.

'Midge,' he cursed under his breath. *Damn you! Crypto's fine!* The phone rang on. Jabba went back to work reseating the new chip. A minute later the chip was in place, but his phone was still ringing. *For Christ's sake, Midge! Give it up!*

The phone rang another fifteen seconds and finally stopped. Jabba breathed a sigh of relief.

Sixty seconds later the intercom overhead crackled. 'Would the chief Sys-Sec please contact the main switchboard for a message?'

Jabba rolled his eyes in disbelief. *She just doesn't give up, does she?* He ignored the page.

CHAPTER 79

Strathmore replaced his SkyPager in his pocket and peered through the darkness toward Node 3.

He reached for Susan's hand. 'Come on.'

But their fingers never touched.

There was a long guttural cry from out of the darkness. A thundering figure loomed – a Mack truck bearing down with no headlights. An instant later, there was a collision and Strathmore was skidding across the floor.

It was Hale. The pager had given them away.

Susan heard the Beretta fall. For a moment she was planted in place, unsure where to run, what to do. Her instincts told her to escape, but she didn't have the elevator code. Her heart told her to help Strathmore, but how? As she spun in desperation, she expected to hear the sounds of a life-and-death struggle on the floor, but there was nothing. Everything was suddenly silent – as if Hale had hit the commander and then disappeared back into the night.

Susan waited, straining her eyes into the darkness, hoping Strathmore wasn't hurt. After what seemed like an eternity, she whispered, 'Commander?'

Even as she said it, she realized her mistake. An instant later Hale's odor welled up behind her. She turned too late. Without warning, she was twisting, gasping for air. She found herself crushed in a familiar headlock, her face against Hale's chest.

'My balls are killing me,' Hale panted in her ear.

Susan's knees buckled. The stars in the dome began to spin above her.

CHAPTER 80

Hale clamped down on Susan's neck and yelled into the darkness. 'Commander, I've got your sweetheart. I want out!'

His demands were met with silence.

Hale's grip tightened. 'I'll break her neck!'

A gun cocked directly behind them. Strathmore's voice was calm and even. 'Let her go.'

Susan winced in pain. 'Commander!'

Hale spun Susan's body toward the sound. 'You shoot and you'll hit your precious Susan. You ready to take that chance?'

Strathmore's voice moved closer. 'Let her go.'

'No way. You'll kill me.'

'I'm not going to kill anyone.'

'Oh, yeah? Tell that to Chartrukian!'

Strathmore moved closer. 'Chartrukian's dead.'

'No shit. You killed him. I saw it!'

'Give it up, Greg,' Strathmore said calmly.

Hale clutched at Susan and whispered in her ear, 'Strathmore pushed Chartrukian – I swear it!'

'She's not going to fall for your divide-and-conquer technique,' Strathmore said, moving closer. 'Let her go.'

Hale hissed into the darkness, 'Chartrukian was just a *kid*, for Christ's sake! Why'd you do it? To protect your little secret?'

Strathmore stayed cool. 'And what little secret is that?'

'You know damn-fucking-well what secret that is! Digital Fortress!'

'My, my,' Strathmore muttered condescendingly, his voice like an iceberg. 'So you *do* know about Digital Fortress. I was starting to think you'd deny *that* too.'

'Fuck you.'

'A witty defense.'

'You're a fool,' Hale spat. 'For your information, TRANSLTR is overheating.'

'Really?' Strathmore chuckled. 'Let me guess – I should open the doors and call in the Sys-Secs?'

'Exactly,' Hale fired back. 'You'd be an idiot not to.'

This time Strathmore laughed out loud. 'That's your big play? TRANSLTR's overheating, so open the doors and let us out?'

'It's true, dammit! I've been down to the sublevels! The aux power isn't pulling enough freon!'

'Thanks for the tip,' Strathmore said. 'But TRANSLTR's got automatic shutdown; if it's overheating, Digital Fortress will quit all by itself.'

Hale sneered. 'You're insane. What the fuck do I care if TRANSLTR blows? The damn machine should be outlawed anyway.'

Strathmore sighed. 'Child psychology only works on children, Greg. Let her go.'

'So you can shoot me?'

'I won't shoot you. I just want the pass-key.'

'What pass-key?'

Strathmore sighed again. 'The one Tankado sent you.'

'I have no idea what you're talking about.'

'Liar!' Susan managed. 'I saw Tankado's mail in your account!'

Hale went rigid. He spun Susan around. 'You went in my account?'

'And *you* aborted my tracer,' she snapped.

Hale felt his blood pressure skyrocket. He thought he'd covered his tracks; he had no idea Susan knew what he'd done. It was no wonder she wasn't buying a word he said. Hale felt the walls start to close in. He knew he could never talk his way out of that one – not in time. He whispered to her in desperation, 'Susan . . . Strathmore killed Chartrukian!'

'Let her go,' the commander said evenly. 'She doesn't believe you.'

'Why *should* she?' Hale fired back. 'You lying bastard! You've got her brainwashed! You only tell her what suits your needs! Does she know what you *really* plan to do with Digital Fortress?'

'And what's that?' Strathmore taunted.

Hale knew what he was about to say would either be his ticket to freedom or his death warrant. He took a deep breath and went for broke. 'You plan to write a back door in Digital Fortress.'

The words met with a bewildered silence from the darkness. Hale knew he had hit a bull's-eye.

Apparently Strathmore's unflappable cool was being put to the test. 'Who told you that?' he demanded, his voice rough around the edges.

'I read it,' Hale said smugly, trying to capitalize on the change of momentum. 'In one of your brainstorms.'

'Impossible. I *never* print my brainstorms.'

'I know. I read it directly off your account.'

Strathmore seemed doubtful. 'You got into my office?'

'No. I snooped you from Node 3.' Hale forced a self-assured chuckle. He knew he'd need all the negotiating skills he'd learned in the Marines to get out of Crypto alive.

Strathmore edged closer, the Beretta leveled in the darkness. 'How do you know about my back door?'

'I told you, I snooped your account.'

'Impossible.'

Hale forced a cocky sneer. 'One of the problems of hiring the best, Commander – sometimes they're better than you.'

'Young man,' Strathmore seethed, 'I don't know where you get your information, but you're in way over your head. You will let Ms Fletcher go right now or I'll call in Security and have you thrown in jail for life.'

'You won't do it,' Hale stated matter-of-factly. 'Calling Security ruins your plans. I'll tell them everything.' Hale paused. 'But let me out clean, and I'll never say a word about Digital Fortress.'

'No deal,' Strathmore fired back. 'I want the pass-key.'

'I don't have any fucking pass-key!'

'Enough lies!' Strathmore bellowed. 'Where is it?'

Hale clamped down on Susan's neck. 'Let me out, or she dies!'

Trevor Strathmore had done enough high-stakes bargaining in his life to know that Hale was in a very dangerous state of mind. The young cryptographer had backed himself into a corner, and a cornered opponent was always the most dangerous kind – desperate and unpredictable. Strathmore knew his next move was a critical one. Susan's life depended on it – and so did the future of Digital Fortress.

Strathmore knew the first thing he had to do was release the tension of the situation. After a long moment, he sighed reluctantly. 'Okay, Greg. You win. What do you want me to do?'

Silence. Hale seemed momentarily unsure how to handle the commander's cooperative tone. He let up a bit on Susan's neck.

'W-well . . .' he stammered, his voice wavering suddenly. 'First thing you do is give me your gun. You're both coming with me.'

'Hostages?' Strathmore laughed coldly. 'Greg, you'll have to do better than that. There are about a dozen armed guards between here and the parking lot.'

'I'm not a fool,' Hale snapped. 'I'm taking your elevator. Susan comes with me! *You* stay!'

'I hate to tell you this,' Strathmore replied, 'but there's no power to the elevator.'

'Bullshit!' Hale snapped. 'The lift runs on power from the main building! I've seen the schematics!'

'We tried it already,' Susan choked, trying to help. 'It's dead.'

'You're both so full of shit, it's incredible.' Hale tightened his grip. 'If the elevator's dead, I'll abort TRANSLTR and restore power.'

'The elevator takes a password,' Susan managed feistily.

'Big deal.' Hale laughed. 'I'm sure the commander will share. Won't you, Commander?'

'No chance,' Strathmore hissed.

Hale boiled over. 'Now you listen to me, old man – here's the deal! You let Susan and me out through your elevator, we drive a few hours, and then I let her go.'

Strathmore felt the stakes rising. He'd gotten Susan into this, and he needed to get her out. His voice stayed steady as a rock. 'What about my plans for Digital Fortress?'

Hale laughed. 'You can write your back door – I won't say a word.' Then his voice turned ominous. 'But the day I think you're tracking me, I go to the press with the whole story. I tell them Digital Fortress is tainted, and I sink this whole fucking organization!'

Strathmore considered Hale's offer. It was clean and simple. Susan lived, and Digital Fortress got its back door. As long as Strathmore didn't chase Hale, the back door stayed a secret. Strathmore knew Hale couldn't keep his mouth shut for long. But still . . . the knowledge of Digital Fortress was Hale's only insurance – maybe he'd be smart. Whatever happened, Strathmore knew Hale could be removed later if necessary.

'Make up your mind, old man!' Hale taunted. 'Are we leaving or not?' Hale's arms tightened around Susan like a vise.

Strathmore knew that if he picked up the phone right now and called Security, Susan would live. He'd bet his life on it. He could see the scenario clearly. The call would take Hale completely by surprise. He would panic, and in the end, faced with a small army, Hale would be unable to act. After a brief standoff, he

335

would give in. *But if I call Security*, Strathmore thought, *my plan is ruined.*

Hale clamped down again. Susan cried out in pain. 'What's it gonna be?' Hale yelled. 'Do I kill her?'

Strathmore considered his options. If he let Hale take Susan out of Crypto, there were no guarantees. Hale might drive for a while, park in the woods. He'd have a gun. . . . Strathmore's stomach turned. There was no telling what would happen before Hale set Susan free . . . *if* he set her free. *I've got to call Security*, Strathmore decided. *What else can I do?* He pictured Hale in court, spilling his guts about Digital Fortress. *My plan will be ruined. There must be some other way.*

'Decide!' Hale yelled, dragging Susan toward the staircase.

Strathmore wasn't listening. If saving Susan meant his plans were ruined, then so be it – nothing was worth losing her. Susan Fletcher was a price Trevor Strathmore refused to pay.

Hale had Susan's arm twisted behind her back and her neck bent to one side. 'This is your last chance, old man! Give me the gun!'

Strathmore's mind continued to race, searching for another option. *There are always other options!* Finally he spoke – quietly, almost sadly. 'No, Greg, I'm sorry. I just can't let you go.'

Hale choked in apparent shock. 'What!'

'I'm calling Security.'

Susan gasped. 'Commander! No!'

Hale tightened his grip. 'You call Security, and she dies!'

Strathmore pulled the cellular off his belt and flicked it on. 'Greg, you're bluffing.'

'You'll never do it!' Hale yelled. 'I'll talk! I'll ruin your plan! You're only hours away from your dream! Controlling all the data in the world! No more TRANSLTR. No more limits – just free information. It's a chance of a lifetime! You won't let it slip by!'

Strathmore's voice was like steel. 'Watch me.'

'But – but what about Susan?' Hale stammered. 'You make that call, and she dies!'

Strathmore held firm. 'That's a chance I'm ready to take.'

'Bullshit! You've got a bigger hard-on for her than you do for Digital Fortress! I know you! You won't risk it!'

Susan began to make an angry rebuttal, but Strathmore beat her to it. 'Young man! You *don't* know me! I take risks for a living. If you're looking to play hardball, let's play!' He started punching keys on his phone. 'You misjudged me, son! Nobody threatens the lives of my employees and walks out!' He raised the phone and barked into the receiver, 'Switchboard! Get me Security!'

Hale began to torque Susan's neck. 'I-I'll kill her. I swear it!'

'You'll do no such thing!' Strathmore proclaimed. 'Killing Susan will just make things wor—' He broke off and rammed the phone against his mouth. 'Security! This is Commander Trevor Strathmore. We've got a hostage situation in Crypto! Get some men in here! Yes, *now*, goddamn it! We also have a generator failure. I want power routed from all available external sources. I want all systems on-line in five minutes! Greg Hale killed one of my junior Sys-Secs. He's holding my senior cryptographer hostage. You're cleared to use tear gas on all of us if necessary! If Mr

337

Hale doesn't cooperate, have snipers shoot him dead. I'll take full responsibility. Do it now!'

Hale stood motionless – apparently limp in disbelief. His grip on Susan eased.

Strathmore snapped his phone shut and shoved it back onto his belt. 'Your move, Greg.'

CHAPTER 81

Becker stood bleary-eyed beside the telephone booth on the terminal concourse. Despite his burning face and a vague nausea, his spirits were soaring. It was over. Truly over. He was on his way home. The ring on his finger was the grail he'd been seeking. He held his hand up in the light and squinted at the gold band. He couldn't focus well enough to read, but the inscription didn't appear to be in English. The first symbol was either a Q, an O, or a zero, his eyes hurt too much to tell. Becker studied the first few characters. They made no sense. *This was a matter of national security?*

Becker stepped into the phone booth and dialed Strathmore. Before he had finished the international prefix, he got a recording. 'Todos los circuitos están ocupados,' the voice said. 'Please hang up and try your call later.' Becker frowned and hung up. He'd forgotten: Getting an international connection from Spain was like roulette, all a matter of timing and luck. He'd have to try again in a few minutes.

Becker fought to ignore the waning sting of the pepper in his eyes. Megan had told him rubbing his eyes would only make them worse; he couldn't imagine. Impatient, he tried the phone again. Still no circuits. Becker couldn't wait any longer – his eyes were on fire; he had to flush them with water. Strathmore would have to wait a minute or two. Half blind, Becker made his way toward the bathrooms.

The blurry image of the cleaning cart was still in front of the men's room, so Becker turned again toward the door marked DAMAS. He thought he heard sounds inside. He knocked. 'Hola?'

Silence.

Probably Megan, he thought. She had five hours to kill before her flight and had said she was going to scrub her arm till it was clean.

'Megan?' he called. He knocked again. There was no reply. Becker pushed the door open. 'Hello?' He went in. The bathroom appeared empty. He shrugged and walked to the sink.

The sink was still filthy, but the water was cold. Becker felt his pores tighten as he splashed the water in his eyes. The pain began to ease, and the fog gradually lifted. Becker eyed himself in the mirror. He looked like he'd been crying for days.

He dried his face on the sleeve of his jacket, and then it suddenly occurred to him. In all the excitement, he'd forgotten where he was. He was at the airport! Somewhere out there on the tarmac, in one of the Seville airport's three private hangars, there was a Learjet 60 waiting to take him home. The pilot had stated very clearly, *I have orders to stay here until you return.*

It was hard to believe, Becker thought, that after all this, he had ended up right back where he'd started. *What am I waiting for?* he laughed. *I'm sure the pilot can radio a message to Strathmore!*

Chuckling to himself, Becker glanced in the mirror and straightened his tie. He was about to go when the reflection of something behind him caught his eye. He turned. It appeared to be one end of Megan's duffel, protruding from under a partially open stall door.

'Megan?' he called. There was no reply. *'Megan?'*

Becker walked over. He rapped loudly on the side of the stall. No answer. He gently pushed the door. It swung open.

Becker fought back a cry of horror. Megan was on the toilet, her eyes rolled skyward. Dead center of her forehead, a bullet hole oozed bloody liquid down her face.

'Oh, Jesus!' Becker cried in shock.

'Está muerta,' a barely human voice croaked behind him. 'She's dead.'

It was like a dream. Becker turned.

'Señor Becker?' the eerie voice asked.

Dazed, Becker studied the man stepping into the rest room. He looked oddly familiar.

'Soy Hulohot,' the killer said. 'I am Hulohot.' The misshapen words seemed to emerge from the depths of his stomach. Hulohot held out his hand. 'El anillo. The ring.'

Becker stared blankly.

The man reached in his pocket and produced a gun. He raised the weapon and trained it on Becker's head. 'El anillo.'

In an instant of clarity, Becker felt a sensation he had never known. As if cued by some subconscious survival instinct, every muscle in his body tensed simultaneously. He flew through the air as the shot spat out. Becker crashed down on top of Megan. A bullet exploded against the wall behind him.

'Mierda!' Hulohot seethed. Somehow, at the last possible instant, David Becker had dived out of the way. The assassin advanced.

Becker pulled himself off the lifeless teenager. There were approaching footsteps. Breathing. The cock of a weapon.

'Adiós,' the man whispered as he lunged like a panther, swinging his weapon into the stall.

The gun went off. There was a flash of red. But it was not blood. It was something else. An object had materialized as if out of nowhere, sailing out of the stall and hitting the killer in the chest, causing his gun to fire a split second early. It was Megan's duffel.

Becker exploded from the stall. He buried his shoulder in the man's chest and drove him back into the sink. There was a bone-crushing crash. A mirror shattered. The gun fell free. The two men collapsed to the floor. Becker tore himself away and dashed for the exit. Hulohot scrambled for his weapon, spun, and fired. The bullet ripped into the slamming bathroom door.

The empty expanse of the airport concourse loomed before Becker like an uncrossable desert. His legs surged beneath him faster than he'd ever known they could move.

As he skidded into the revolving door, a shot rang out behind him. The glass panel in front of him exploded in a shower of glass. Becker pushed his shoulder into the frame and the door rotated forward. A moment later he stumbled onto the pavement outside.

A taxi stood waiting.

'Déjame entrar!' Becker screamed, pounding on the locked door. 'Let me in!' The driver refused; his fare with the wire-rim glasses had asked him to wait. Becker turned and saw Hulohot streaking across he concourse, gun in hand. Becker eyed his little Vespa on the sidewalk. *I'm dead.*

Hulohot blasted through the revolving doors just in time to see Becker trying in vain to kickstart his Vespa. Hulohot smiled and raised his weapon.

The choke! Becker fumbled with the levers under the gas tank. He jumped on the starter again. It coughed and died.

'El anillo. The ring.' The voice was close.

Becker looked up. He saw the barrel of a gun. The chamber was rotating. He rammed his foot on the starter once again.

Hulohot's shot just missed Becker's head as the little bike sprang to life and lurched forward. Becker hung on for his life as the motorcycle bounced down a grassy embankment and wobbled around the corner of the building onto the runway.

Enraged, Hulohot raced toward his waiting taxi. Seconds later, the driver lay stunned on the curb watching his taxi peel out in a cloud of dust.

CHAPTER 82

As the implications of the commander's phone call to Security began to settle on the dazed Greg Hale, he found himself weakened by a wave of panic. *Security is coming!* Susan began to slip away. Hale recovered, clutching at her midsection, pulling her back.

'Let me go!' she cried, her voice echoing through the dome.

Hale's mind was in overdrive. The commander's call had taken him totally by surprise. *Strathmore phoned Security! He's sacrificing his plans for Digital Fortress!*

Not in a million years had Hale imagined the commander would let Digital Fortress slip by. This back door was the chance of a lifetime.

As the panic rushed in, Hale's mind seemed to play tricks on him. He saw the barrel of Strathmore's Beretta everywhere he looked. He began to spin, holding Susan close, trying to deny the commander a shot. Driven by fear, Hale dragged Susan blindly toward the stairs. In five minutes the lights would come on, the doors would open, and a SWAT team would pour in.

'You're hurting me!' Susan choked. She gasped for

breath as she stumbled through Hale's desperate pirouettes.

Hale considered letting her go and making a mad dash for Strathmore's elevator, but it was suicide. He had no password. Besides, once outside the NSA without a hostage, Hale knew he was as good as dead. Not even his Lotus could outrun a fleet of NSA helicopters. *Susan is the only thing that will keep Strathmore from blowing me off the road!*

'Susan,' Hale blurted, dragging her toward the stairs. 'Come with me! I swear I won't hurt you!'

As Susan fought him, Hale realized he had new problems. Even if he somehow managed to get Strathmore's elevator open and take Susan with him, she would undoubtedly fight him all the way out of the building. Hale knew full well that Strathmore's elevator made only one stop: 'the Underground Highway,' a restricted labyrinth of underground access tunnels through which NSA powerbrokers moved in secrecy. Hale had no intention of ending up lost in the basement corridors of the NSA with a struggling hostage. It was a death trap. Even if he got out, he realized, he had no gun. How would he get Susan across the parking lot? How would he drive?

It was the voice of one of Hale's Marine, military-strategy professors that gave him his answer:

Force a hand, the voice warned, *and it will fight you. But convince a mind to think as you want it to think, and you have an ally.*

'Susan,' Hale heard himself saying, 'Strathmore's a killer! You're in danger here!'

Susan didn't seem to hear. Hale knew it was an absurd angle anyway; Strathmore would never hurt Susan, and she knew it.

345

Hale strained his eyes into the darkness, wondering where the commander was hidden. Strathmore had fallen silent suddenly, which made Hale even more panicky. He sensed his time was up. Security would arrive at any moment.

With a surge of strength, Hale wrapped his arms around Susan's waist and pulled her hard up the stairs. She hooked her heels on the first step and pulled back. It was no use, Hale overpowered her.

Carefully, Hale backed up the stairs with Susan in tow. Pushing her up might have been easier, but the landing at the top was illuminated from Strathmore's computer monitors. If Susan went first, Strathmore would have a clear shot at Hale's back. Pulling Susan behind him, Hale had a human shield between himself and the Crypto floor.

About a third of the way up, Hale sensed movement at the bottom of the stairs. *Strathmore's making his move!* 'Don't try it, Commander,' he hissed. 'You'll only get her killed.'

Hale waited. But there was only silence. He listened closely. Nothing. The bottom of the stairs was still. Was he imagining things? It didn't matter. Strathmore would never risk a shot with Susan in the way.

But as Hale backed up the stairs dragging Susan behind him, something unexpected happened. There was a faint thud on the landing behind him. Hale stopped, adrenaline surging. Had Strathmore slipped upstairs? Instinct told him Strathmore was at the *bottom* of the stairs. But then, suddenly, it happened again – louder this time. A distinct step on the upper landing!

In terror, Hale realized his mistake. *Strathmore's on the landing behind me! He has a clear shot of my back!* In desperation, he spun Susan back to his uphill side and started retreating backwards down the steps.

As he reached the bottom step, he stared wildly up at the landing and yelled, 'Back off, Commander! Back off, or I'll break her—'

The butt of a Beretta came slicing through the air at the foot of the stairs and crashed down into Hale's skull.

As Susan tore free of the slumping Hale, she wheeled in confusion. Strathmore grabbed her and reeled her in, cradling her shaking body. 'Shhh,' he soothed. 'It's me. You're okay.'

Susan was trembling. 'Com . . . mander,' she gasped, disoriented. 'I thought . . . I thought you were upstairs . . . I heard . . .'

'Easy now,' he whispered. 'You heard me toss my loafers up onto the landing.'

Susan found herself laughing and crying at the same time. The commander had just saved her life. Standing there in the darkness, Susan felt an overwhelming sense of relief. It was not, however, without guilt; Security was coming. She had foolishly let Hale grab her, and he had used her against Strathmore. Susan knew the commander had paid a huge price to save her. 'I'm sorry,' she said.

'What for?'

'Your plans for Digital Fortress . . . they're ruined.'

Strathmore shook his head. 'Not at all.'

'But . . . but what about Security? They'll be here any minute. We won't have time to—'

'Security's not coming, Susan. We've got all the time in the world.'

Susan was lost. *Not coming?* 'But you phoned . . .'

Strathmore chuckled. 'Oldest trick in the book. I faked the call.'

CHAPTER 83

Becker's Vespa was no doubt the smallest vehicle ever to tear down the Seville runway. Its top speed, a whining 50 mph, sounded more like a chainsaw than a motorcycle and was unfortunately well below the necessary power to become airborne.

In his side mirror, Becker saw the taxi swing out onto the darkened runway about four hundred yards back. It immediately started gaining. Becker faced front. In the distance, the contour of the airplane hangars stood framed against the night sky about a half mile out. Becker wondered if the taxi would overtake him in that distance. He knew Susan could do the math in two seconds and calculate his odds. Becker suddenly felt fear like he had never known.

He lowered his head and twisted the throttle as far as it would go. The Vespa was definitely topped out. Becker guessed the taxi behind him was doing almost ninety, twice his speed. He set his sights on the three structures looming in the distance. *The middle one. That's where the Learjet is.* A shot rang out.

The bullet buried itself in the runway yards behind him. Becker looked back. The assassin was hanging out the window taking aim. Becker swerved and his side mirror exploded in a shower of glass. He could feel the impact of the bullet all the way up the handlebars. He lay his body flat on the bike. *God help me, I'm not going to make it!*

The tarmac in front of Becker's Vespa was growing brighter now. The taxi was closing, the headlights throwing ghostly shadows down the runway. A shot fired. The bullet ricocheted off the hull of the bike.

Becker struggled to keep from going into a swerve. *I've got to make the hangar!* He wondered if the Learjet pilot could see them coming. *Does he have a weapon? Will he open the cabin doors in time?* But as Becker approached the lit expanse of the open hangars, he realized the question was moot. The Learjet was nowhere to be seen. He squinted through blurred vision and prayed he was hallucinating. He was not. The hangar was bare. *Oh my God! Where's the plane!*

As the two vehicles rocketed into the empty hangar, Becker desperately searched for an escape. There was none. The building's rear wall, an expansive sheet of corrugated metal, had no doors or windows. The taxi roared up beside him, and Becker looked left to see Hulohot raising his gun.

Reflex took over. Becker slammed down on his brakes. He barely slowed. The hangar floor was slick with oil. The Vespa went into a headlong skid.

Beside him there was a deafening squeal as the taxi's brakes locked and the balding tires hydroplaned on the slippery surface. The car spun around in a cloud of smoke and burning rubber only inches to the left of Becker's skidding Vespa.

Now side by side, the two vehicles skimmed out of control on a collision course with the rear of the hangar. Becker desperately pumped his brakes, but there was no traction; it was like driving on ice. In front of him, the metal wall loomed. It was coming fast. As the taxi spiraled wildly beside him, Becker faced the wall and braced for the impact.

There was an earsplitting crash of steel and corrugated metal. But there was no pain. Becker found himself suddenly in the open air, still on his Vespa, bouncing across a grassy field. It was as if the hangar's back wall had vanished before him. The taxi was still beside him, careening across the field. An enormous sheet of corrugated metal from the hangar's back wall billowed off the taxi's hood and sailed over Becker's head.

Heart racing, Becker gunned the Vespa and took off into the night.

CHAPTER 84

Jabba let out a contented sigh as he finished the last of his solder points. He switched off the iron, put down his penlight, and lay a moment in the darkness of the mainframe computer. He was beat. His neck hurt. Internal work was always cramped, especially for a man of his size.

And they just keep building them smaller, he mused.

As he closed his eyes for a well-deserved moment of relaxation, someone outside began pulling on his boots.

'Jabba! Get out here!' a woman's voice yelled.

Midge found me. He groaned.

'Jabba! Get out here!'

Reluctantly he slithered out. 'For the love of God, Midge! I told you—' But it was not Midge. Jabba looked up, surprised. 'Soshi?'

Soshi Kuta was a ninety-pound live wire. She was Jabba's right-hand assistant, a razor-sharp Sys-Sec techie from MIT. She often worked late with Jabba and was the one member of his staff who seemed unintimidated by him. She glared at him and demanded, 'Why the hell didn't you answer your phone? Or my page?'

'*Your* page,' Jabba repeated. 'I thought it was—'

'Never mind. There's something strange going on in the main databank.'

Jabba checked his watch. 'Strange?' Now he was growing concerned. 'Can you be any more specific?'

Two minutes later Jabba was dashing down the hall toward the databank.

CHAPTER 85

Greg Hale lay curled on the Node 3 floor. Strathmore and Susan had just dragged him across Crypto and bound his hands and feet with twelve-gauge printer cable from the Node 3 laser-printers.

Susan couldn't get over the artful maneuver the commander had just executed. *He faked the call!* Somehow Strathmore had captured Hale, saved Susan, and bought himself the time needed to rewrite Digital Fortress.

Susan eyed the bound cryptographer uneasily. Hale was breathing heavily. Strathmore sat on the couch with the Beretta propped awkwardly in his lap. Susan returned her attention to Hale's terminal and continued her random-string search.

Her fourth string search ran its course and came up empty. 'Still no luck.' She sighed. 'We may need to wait for David to find Tankado's copy.'

Strathmore gave her a disapproving look. 'If David fails, and Tankado's key falls into the wrong hands . . .'

Strathmore didn't need to finish. Susan understood. Until the Digital Fortress file on the Internet had been

353

replaced with Strathmore's modified version, Tankado's pass-key was dangerous.

'After we make the switch,' Strathmore added, 'I don't care how many pass-keys are floating around; the more the merrier.' He motioned for her to continue searching. 'But until then, we're playing beat-the-clock.'

Susan opened her mouth to acknowledge, but her words were drowned out by a sudden deafening blare. The silence of Crypto was shattered by a warning horn from the sublevels. Susan and Strathmore exchanged startled looks.

'What's *that*?' Susan yelled, timing her question between the intermittent bursts.

'TRANSLTR!' Strathmore called back, looking troubled. 'It's too hot! Maybe Hale was right about the aux power not pulling enough freon.'

'What about the auto-abort?'

Strathmore thought a moment, then yelled, 'Something must have shorted.' A yellow siren light spun above the Crypto floor and swept a pulsating glare across his face.

'You better abort!' Susan called.

Strathmore nodded. There was no telling what would happen if three million silicon processors overheated and decided to ignite. Strathmore needed to get upstairs to his terminal and abort the Digital Fortress run – particularly before anyone outside of Crypto noticed the trouble and decided to send in the cavalry.

Strathmore shot a glance at the still-unconscious Hale. He laid the Beretta on a table near Susan and yelled over the sirens, 'Be right back!' As he disappeared through the hole in the Node 3 wall,

Strathmore called over his shoulder, 'And find me that pass-key!'

Susan eyed the results of her unproductive pass-key search and hoped Strathmore would hurry up and abort. The noise and lights in Crypto felt like a missile launch.

On the floor, Hale began to stir. With each blast of the horn, he winced. Susan surprised herself by grabbing the Beretta. Hale opened his eyes to Susan Fletcher standing over him with the gun leveled at his crotch.

'Where's the pass-key?' Susan demanded.

Hale was having trouble getting his bearings. 'Wh-what happened?'

'You blew it, that's what happened. Now, where's the pass-key?'

Hale tried to move his arms but realized he was tied. His face became taut with panic. 'Let me go!'

'I need the pass-key,' Susan repeated.

'I don't have it! Let me go!' Hale tried to get up. He could barely roll over.

Susan yelled between blasts of the horn. 'You're North Dakota, and Ensei Tankado gave you a copy of his key. I need it now!'

'You're crazy!' Hale gasped. 'I'm not North Dakota!' He struggled unsuccessfully to free himself.

Susan charged angrily, 'Don't lie to me. Why the hell is all of North Dakota's mail in *your* account?'

'I told you before!' Hale pleaded as the horns blared on. 'I snooped Strathmore! That E-mail in my account was mail I copied out of *Strathmore's* account – E-mail COMINT stole from Tankado!'

'Bull! You could never snoop the commander's account!'

355

'You don't understand!' Hale yelled. 'There was *already* a tap on Strathmore's account!' Hale delivered his words in short bursts between the sirens. 'Someone else put the tap there. I think it was Director Fontaine! I just piggybacked! You've got to believe me! That's how I found out about his plan to rewrite Digital Fortress! I've been reading Strathmore's brainstorms!'

BrainStorms? Susan paused. Strathmore had undoubtedly outlined his plans for Digital Fortress using his BrainStorm software. If anyone had snooped the commander's account, all the information would have been available . . .

'Rewriting Digital Fortress is *sick!*' Hale cried. 'You know damn well what it implies – *total* NSA access!' The sirens blasted, drowning him out, but Hale was possessed. 'You think we're ready for that responsibility? You think *anyone* is? It's fucking shortsighted! You say our government has the people's best interests at heart? Great! But what happens when some future government *doesn't* have our best interests at heart! This technology is *forever!*'

Susan could barely hear him; the noise in Crypto was deafening.

Hale struggled to get free. He looked Susan in the eye and kept yelling. 'How the hell do civilians defend themselves against a police state when the guy at the top has access to *all* their lines of communication? How do they plan a revolt?'

Susan had heard this argument many times. The future-governments argument was a stock EFF complaint.

'Strathmore *had* to be stopped!' Hale screamed as the sirens blasted. 'I swore *I'd* do it. That's what I've

356

been doing here all day – watching his account, waiting for him to make his move so I could record the switch in progress. I needed proof – evidence that he'd written in a back door. That's why I copied all his E-mail into my account. It was evidence that he'd been watching Digital Fortress. I planned to go to the press with the information.'

Susan's heart skipped. Had she heard correctly? Suddenly this did sound like Greg Hale. *Was it possible?* If Hale had known about Strathmore's plan to release a tainted version of Digital Fortress, he could wait until the whole world was using it and then drop his bombshell – complete with proof!

Susan imagined the headlines: CRYPTOGRAPHER GREG HALE UNVEILS SECRET U.S. PLAN TO CONTROL GLOBAL INFORMATION!

Was it Skipjack all over again? Uncovering an NSA back door a second time would make Greg Hale famous beyond his wildest dreams. It would also sink the NSA. She suddenly found herself wondering if maybe Hale was telling the truth. *No!* she decided. *Of course not!*

Hale continued to plead. 'I aborted your tracer because I thought you were looking for *me!* I thought you suspected Strathmore was being snooped! I didn't want you to find the leak and trace it back to me!'

It was plausible but unlikely. 'Then why'd you kill Chartrukian?' Susan snapped.

'I didn't!' Hale screamed over the noise. 'Strathmore was the one who pushed him! I saw the whole thing from downstairs! Chartrukian was about to call the Sys-Secs and ruin Strathmore's plans for the back door!'

Hale's good, Susan thought. *He's got an angle for everything.*

'Let me go!' Hale begged. 'I didn't do anything!'

'Didn't *do* anything?' Susan shouted, wondering what was taking Strathmore so long. 'You and Tankado were holding the NSA hostage. At least until you double-crossed him. Tell me,' she pressed, 'did Tankado really die of a heart attack, or did you have one of your buddies take him out?'

'You're so blind!' Hale yelled. 'Can't you see I'm not involved? Untie me! Before Security gets here!'

'Security's not coming,' she snapped flatly.

Hale turned white. 'What?'

'Strathmore faked the phone call.'

Hale's eyes went wide. He seemed momentarily paralyzed. Then he began writhing fiercely. 'Strathmore'll kill me! I know he will! I know too much!'

'Easy, Greg.'

The sirens blared as Hale yelled out, 'But I'm innocent!'

'You're lying! And I have proof!' Susan strode around the ring of terminals. 'Remember that tracer you aborted?' she asked, arriving at her own terminal. 'I sent it again! Shall we see if it's back yet?'

Sure enough, on Susan's screen, a blinking icon alerted her that her tracer had returned. She palmed her mouse and opened the message. *This data will seal Hale's fate*, she thought. *Hale is North Dakota.* The data-box opened. *Hale is—*

Susan stopped. The tracer materialized, and Susan stood in stunned silence. There had to be some mistake; the tracer had fingered someone else – a most unlikely person.

Susan steadied herself on the terminal and reread the databox before her. It was the same information Strathmore said *he'd* received when *he* ran the tracer! Susan had figured Strathmore had made a mistake, but she knew she'd configured the tracer perfectly.

And yet the information on the screen was unthinkable:

NDAKOTA = ET@DOSHISHA.EDU

'ET?' Susan demanded, her head swimming. 'Ensei Tankado is North Dakota?'

It was inconceivable. If the data was correct, Tankado and his partner were the *same* person. Susan's thoughts were suddenly disconnected. She wished the blaring horn would stop. *Why doesn't Strathmore turn that damn thing off?*

Hale twisted on the floor, straining to see Susan. 'What does it say? Tell me!'

Susan blocked out Hale and the chaos around her. *Ensei Tankado is North Dakota. . . .*

She reshuffled the pieces trying to make them fit. If Tankado was North Dakota, then he was sending E-mail to *himself* . . . which meant North Dakota didn't exist. Tankado's partner was a hoax.

North Dakota is a ghost, she said to herself. *Smoke and mirrors.*

The ploy was a brilliant one. Apparently Strathmore had been watching only one side of a tennis match. Since the ball kept coming back, he assumed there was someone on the other side of the net. But Tankado had been playing against a wall. He had been proclaiming the virtues of Digital Fortress in E-mail he'd sent to himself. He had written letters, sent them to an anonymous remailer, and a few hours later, the remailer had sent them right back to him.

Now, Susan realized, it was all so obvious. Tankado had *wanted* the commander to snoop him . . . he'd *wanted* him to read the E-mail. Ensei Tankado had created an imaginary insurance policy without ever having to trust another soul with his pass-key. Of course, to make the whole farce seem authentic, Tankado had used a secret account . . . just secret enough to allay any suspicions that the whole thing was a setup. Tankado was his own partner. North Dakota did not exist. Ensei Tankado was a one-man show.

A one-man show.

A terrifying thought gripped Susan. *Tankado could have used his fake correspondence to convince Strathmore of just about anything.*

She remembered her first reaction when Strathmore told her about the unbreakable algorithm. She'd sworn it was impossible. The unsettling potential of the situation settled hard in Susan's stomach. What proof did they actually have that Tankado had *really* created Digital Fortress? Only a lot of hype in his E-mail. And of course . . . TRANSLTR. The computer had been locked in an endless loop for almost twenty hours. Susan knew, however, that there were other programs that could keep TRANSLTR busy that long, programs far easier to create than an unbreakable algorithm.

Viruses.

The chill swept across her body.

But how could a virus get into TRANSLTR?

Like a voice from the grave, Phil Chartrukian gave the answer. *Strathmore bypassed Gauntlet!*

In a sickening revelation, Susan grasped the truth. Strathmore had downloaded Tankado's Digital Fortress file and tried to send it into TRANSLTR to break it. But Gauntlet had rejected the file because it contained dangerous mutation strings. Normally Strathmore would have been concerned, but he had seen Tankado's E-mail – *Mutation strings are the trick!* Convinced Digital Fortress was safe to load, Strathmore bypassed Gauntlet's filters and sent the file into TRANSLTR.

Susan could barely speak. 'There *is* no Digital Fortress,' she choked as the sirens blared on. Slowly, weakly, she leaned against her terminal. Tankado had gone fishing for fools . . . and the NSA had taken the bait.

Then, from upstairs, came a long cry of anguish. It was Strathmore.

CHAPTER 86

Trevor Strathmore was hunched at his desk when Susan arrived breathless at his door. His head was down, his sweaty head glistening in the light of his monitor. The horns on the sublevels blared.

Susan raced over to his desk. 'Commander?'

Strathmore didn't move.

'Commander! We've got to shut down TRANSLTR! We've got a—'

'He got us,' Strathmore said without looking up. 'Tankado fooled us all . . .'

She could tell by the tone of his voice he understood. All of Tankado's hype about the unbreakable algorithm . . . auctioning off the pass-key – it was all an act, a charade. Tankado had tricked the NSA into snooping his mail, tricked them into believing he had a partner, and tricked them into downloading a very dangerous file.

'The mutation strings—' Strathmore faltered.

'I know.'

The commander looked up slowly. 'The file I downloaded off the Internet . . . it was a . . .'

Susan tried to stay calm. All the pieces in the game

362

had shifted. There had never been any unbreakable algorithm – never any Digital Fortress. The file Tankado had posted on the Internet was an encrypted virus, probably sealed with some generic, mass-market encryption algorithm, strong enough to keep everyone out of harm's way – everyone except the NSA. TRANSLTR had cracked the protective seal and released the virus.

'The mutation strings,' the commander croaked. 'Tankado said they were just part of the algorithm.' Strathmore collapsed back onto his desk.

Susan understood the commander's pain. He had been completely taken in. Tankado had never intended to let any computer company buy his algorithm. There *was* no algorithm. The whole thing was a charade. Digital Fortress was a ghost, a farce, a piece of bait created to tempt the NSA. Every move Strathmore had made, Tankado had been behind the scenes, pulling the strings.

'I bypassed Gauntlet.' The commander groaned. 'You didn't know.'

Strathmore pounded his fist on his desk. 'I *should* have known! His screen name, for Christ's sake! NDAKOTA! Look at it!'

'What do you mean?'

'He's laughing at us! It's a goddamn anagram!'

Susan puzzled a moment. *NDAKOTA is an anagram?* She pictured the letters and began reshuffling them in her mind. *Ndakota . . . Kado-tan . . . Oktadan . . . Tandoka . . .* Her knees went weak. Strathmore was right. It was as plain as day. How could they have missed it? North Dakota wasn't a reference to the U.S. state at all – it was Tankado rubbing salt in the wound! He'd even sent the NSA a warning, a blatant clue that he himself was NDAKOTA. The letters spelled TANKADO. But the best code-breakers in the world had missed it, just as he had planned.

'Tankado was mocking us,' Strathmore said.

'You've got to abort TRANSLTR,' Susan declared.

Strathmore stared blankly at the wall.

'Commander. Shut it down! God only knows what's going on in there!'

'I tried,' Strathmore whispered, sounding as faint as she'd ever heard him.

'What do you mean you *tried?*'

Strathmore rotated his screen toward her. His monitor had dimmed to a strange shade of maroon. At the bottom, the dialogue box showed numerous attempts to shut down TRANSLTR. They were all followed by the same response:

SORRY. UNABLE TO ABORT.
SORRY. UNABLE TO ABORT.
SORRY. UNABLE TO ABORT.

Susan felt a chill. *Unable to abort? But why?* She feared she already knew the answer. *So this is Tankado's revenge? Destroying TRANSLTR!* For years Ensei Tankado had wanted the world to know about TRANSLTR, but no one had believed him. So he'd decided to destroy the great beast himself. He'd fought to the death for what he believed – the individual's right to privacy.

Downstairs the sirens blared.

'We've got to kill all power,' Susan demanded. 'Now!'

Susan knew that if they hurried, they could save the great parallel processing machine. Every computer in the world – from Radio Shack PCs to NASA's satellite control systems – had a built-in fail-safe for situations like this. It wasn't a glamorous fix, but it always worked. It was known as 'pulling the plug.'

By shutting off the remaining power in Crypto, they could force TRANSLTR to shut down. They could remove the virus later. It would be a simple matter of reformatting TRANSLTR's hard drives. Reformatting would completely erase the computer's memory – data, programming, virus, *everything*. In most cases, reformatting resulted in the loss of thousands of files, sometimes years of work. But TRANSLTR was different – it could be reformatted with virtually no loss at all. Parallel processing machines were designed to think, not to remember. Nothing was actually stored inside TRANSLTR. Once it broke a code, it sent the results to the NSA's main databank in order to—

Susan froze. In a stark instant of realization, she brought her hand to her mouth and muffled a scream. 'The main databank!'

Strathmore stared into the darkness, his voice disembodied. He'd apparently already made this realization. 'Yes, Susan. The main databank. . . .'

Susan nodded blankly. *Tankado used TRANSLTR to put a virus in our main databank.*

Strathmore motioned sickly to his monitor. Susan returned her gaze to the screen in front of her and looked beneath the dialogue box. Across the bottom of the screen were the words:

> TELL THE WORLD ABOUT TRANSLTR
> ONLY THE TRUTH WILL SAVE YOU NOW . . .

Susan felt cold. The nation's most classified information was stored at the NSA: military communication protocols, SIGINT confirmation codes, identities of foreign spies, blueprints for advanced weaponry, digitized documents, trade agreements – the list was unending.

'Tankado wouldn't dare!' she declared. 'Corrupting a country's classified records?' Susan couldn't believe even Ensei Tankado would dare attack the NSA databank. She stared at his message.

ONLY THE TRUTH WILL SAVE YOU NOW

'The truth?' she asked. 'The truth about what?'

Strathmore was breathing heavily. 'TRANSLTR,' he croaked. 'The truth about TRANSLTR.'

Susan nodded. It made perfect sense. Tankado was forcing the NSA to tell the world about TRANSLTR. It was blackmail after all. He was giving the NSA a choice – either tell the world about TRANSLTR or lose your databank. She stared in awe at the text before her. At the bottom of the screen, a single line blinked menacingly.

ENTER PASS-KEY

Staring at the pulsating words, Susan understood – the virus, the pass-key, Tankado's ring, the ingenious blackmail plot. The pass-key had nothing to do with unlocking an algorithm; it was an *antidote*. The pass-key stopped the virus. Susan had read a lot about viruses like this – deadly programs that included a built-in cure, a secret key that could be used to deactivate them. *Tankado never planned to destroy the NSA*

databank – he just wanted us go public with TRANSLTR!
Then he would give us the pass-key, so we could stop the
virus!

It was now clear to Susan that Tankado's plan had
gone terribly wrong. He had not planned on dying.
He'd planned on sitting in a Spanish bar and listening
to the CNN press conference about America's top-
secret code-breaking computer. Then he'd planned
on calling Strathmore, reading the pass-key off the
ring, and saving the databank in the nick of time.
After a good laugh, he'd disappear into oblivion, an
EFF hero.

Susan pounded her fist on the desk. 'We need that
ring! It's the *only* pass-key!' She now understood –
there *was* no North Dakota, no second pass-key. Even
if the NSA went public with TRANSLTR, Tankado
was no longer around to save the day.

Strathmore was silent.

The situation was more serious than Susan had ever
imagined. The most shocking thing of all was that
Tankado had allowed it to go this far. He had obviously known what would happen if the NSA didn't
get the ring – and yet, in his final seconds of life, he'd
given the ring away. He had deliberately tried to keep
it from them. Then again, Susan realized, what could
she *expect* Tankado to do – save the ring for them,
when he thought the NSA had killed him?

Still, Susan couldn't believe that Tankado would
have allowed this to happen. He was a pacifist. He
didn't want to wreak destruction; all he wanted was
to set the record straight. This was about TRANSLTR.
This was about everyone's right to keep a secret. This
was about letting the world know that the NSA was
listening. Deleting the NSA's databank was an act of

aggression Susan could not imagine Ensei Tankado committing.

The sirens pulled her back to reality. Susan eyed the debilitated commander and knew what he was thinking. Not only were his plans for a back door in Digital Fortress shot, but his carelessness had put the NSA on the brink of what could turn out to be the worst security disaster in U.S. history.

'Commander, this is *not* your fault!' she insisted over the blare of the horns. 'If Tankado hadn't died, we'd have bargaining power – we'd have options!'

But Commander Strathmore heard nothing. His life was over. He'd spent thirty years serving his country. This was supposed to be his moment of glory, his pièce de résistance – a back door in the world encryption standard. But instead, he had sent a virus into the main databank of the National Security Agency. There was no way to stop it – not without killing power and erasing every last one of the billions of bytes of irretrievable data. Only the ring could save them, and if David hadn't found the ring by now . . .

'I need to shut down TRANSLTR!' Susan took control. 'I'm going down to the sublevels to throw the circuit breaker.'

Strathmore turned slowly to face her. He was a broken man. 'I'll do it,' he croaked. He stood up, stumbling as he tried to slide out from behind his desk.

Susan sat him back down. 'No,' she barked. 'I'*m* going.' Her tone left no room for debate.

Strathmore put his face in his hands. 'Okay. Bottom floor. Beside the freon pumps.'

Susan spun and headed for the door. Halfway there, she turned and looked back. 'Commander,' she yelled.

'This is *not* over. We're not beaten yet. If David finds the ring in time, we can save the databank!'

Strathmore said nothing.

'Call the databank!' Susan ordered. 'Warn them about the virus! You're the deputy director of the NSA. You're a survivor!'

In slow motion, Strathmore looked up. Like a man making the decision of a lifetime, he gave her a tragic nod.

Determined, Susan tore into the darkness.

CHAPTER 87

The Vespa lurched into the slow lane of the Carretera de Huelva. It was almost dawn, but there was plenty of traffic – young Sevillians returning from their all-night beach verbenas. A van of teenagers laid on its horn and flew by. Becker's motorcycle felt like a toy out there on the freeway.

A quarter of a mile back, a demolished taxi swerved out onto the freeway in a shower of sparks. As it accelerated, it sideswiped a Peugeot 504 and sent it careening onto the grassy median.

Becker passed a freeway marker: SEVILLA CENTRO – 2 KM. If he could just reach the cover of downtown, he knew he might have a chance. His speedometer read 60 kilometers per hour. *Two minutes to the exit.* He knew he didn't have that long. Somewhere behind him, the taxi was gaining. Becker gazed out at the nearing lights of downtown Seville and prayed he would reach them alive.

He was only halfway to the exit when the sound of scraping metal loomed up behind him. He hunched on his bike, wrenching the throttle as far as it would go. There was a muffled gunshot, and a bullet sailed by. Becker cut left, weaving back and forth across the lanes in hopes of buying more time. It was no use. The exit ramp was still three hundred yards when the taxi roared to within a few car lengths behind him. Becker knew that in a matter of seconds he would be either shot or run down. He scanned ahead for any possible escape, but the highway was bounded on both sides by steep gravel slopes. Another shot rang out. Becker made his decision.

In a scream of rubber and sparks, he leaned violently to his right and swerved off the road. The bike's tires hit the bottom of the embankment. Becker strained to keep his balance as the Vespa threw up a cloud of gravel and began fish-tailing its way up the slope. The wheels spun wildly, clawing at the loose earth. The little engine whimpered pathetically as it tried to dig in. Becker urged it on, hoping it wouldn't stall. He didn't dare look behind him, certain at any moment the taxi would be skidding to a stop, bullets flying.

The bullets never came.

Becker's bike broke over the crest of the hill, and he saw it – the centro. The downtown lights spread out before him like a star-filled sky. He gunned his way through some underbrush and out over the curb. His Vespa suddenly felt faster. The Avenue Luis Montoto seemed to race beneath his tires. The soccer stadium zipped past on the left. He was in the clear.

It was then that Becker heard the familiar screech of metal on concrete. He looked up. A hundred yards ahead of him, the taxi came roaring up the exit ramp. It skidded out onto Luis Montoto and accelerated directly toward him.

Becker knew he should have felt a surge of panic.

But he did not. He knew exactly where he was going. He swerved left on Menendez Pelayo and opened the throttle. The bike lurched across a small park and into the cobblestoned corridor of Mateus Gago – the narrow one-way street that led to the portal of Barrio Santa Cruz.

Just a little farther, he thought.

The taxi followed, thundering closer. It trailed Becker through the gateway of Santa Cruz, ripping off its side mirror on the narrow archway. Becker knew he had won. Santa Cruz was the oldest section of Seville. It had no roads between the buildings, only mazes of narrow walkways built in Roman times. They were only wide enough for pedestrians and the occasional moped. Becker had once been lost for hours in the narrow caverns.

As Becker accelerated down the final stretch of Mateus Gago, Seville's eleventh-century Gothic cathedral rose like a mountain before him. Directly beside it, the Giralda tower shot 419 feet skyward into the breaking dawn. This was Santa Cruz, home to the second largest cathedral in the world as well as Seville's oldest, most pious Catholic families.

Becker sped across the stone square. There was a single shot, but it was too late. Becker and his motorcycle disappeared down a tiny passageway – Callita de la Virgen.

CHAPTER 88

The headlight of Becker's Vespa threw stark shadows on the walls of the narrow passageways. He struggled with the gear shift and roared between the white-washed buildings, giving the inhabitants of Santa Cruz an early wake-up call this Sunday morning.

It had been less than thirty minutes since Becker's escape from the airport. He'd been on the run ever since, his mind grappling with endless questions: *Who's trying to kill me? What's so special about this ring? Where is the NSA jet?* He thought of Megan dead in the stall, and the nausea crept back.

Becker had hoped to cut directly across the barrio and exit on the other side, but Santa Cruz was a bewildering labyrinth of alleyways. It was peppered with false starts and dead ends. Becker quickly became disoriented. He looked up for the tower of the Giralda to get his bearings, but the surrounding walls were so high he could see nothing except a thin slit of breaking dawn above him.

Becker wondered where the man in wire-rim glasses was; he knew better than to think the assailant had given up. The killer probably was after him on

373

foot. Becker struggled to maneuver his Vespa around tight corners. The sputtering of the engine echoed up and down the alleys. Becker knew he was an easy target in the silence of Santa Cruz. At this point, all he had in his favor was speed. *Got to get to the other side!*

After a long series of turns and straightaways, Becker skidded into a three-way intersection marked Esquina de los Reyes. He knew he was in trouble – he had been there already. As he stood straddling the idling bike, trying to decide which way to turn, the engine sputtered to a stop. The gas gauge read VACIO. As if on cue, a shadow appeared down an alley on his left.

The human mind is the fastest computer in existence. In the next fraction of a second, Becker's mind registered the shape of the man's glasses, searched his memory for a match, found one, registered danger, and requested a decision. He got one. He dropped the useless bike and took off at a full sprint.

Unfortunately for Becker, Hulohot was now on solid ground rather than in a lurching taxi. He calmly raised his weapon and fired.

The bullet caught Becker in the side just as he stumbled around the corner out of range. He took five or six strides before the sensation began to register. At first it felt like a muscle pull, just above the hip. Then it turned to a warm tingling. When Becker saw the blood, he knew. There was no pain, no pain anywhere, just a headlong race through the winding maze of Santa Cruz.

Hulohot dashed after his quarry. He had been tempted to hit Becker in the head, but he was a professional; he played the odds. Becker was a moving target, and aiming at his midsection provided the greatest margin of error both vertically and horizontally. The odds had paid off. Becker had shifted at the last instant, and rather than missing his head, Hulohot had caught a piece of his side. Although he knew the bullet had barely grazed Becker and would do no lasting damage, the shot had served its purpose. Contact had been made. The prey had been touched by death. It was a whole new game.

Becker raced forward blindly. Turning. Winding. Staying out of the straightaways. The footsteps behind him seemed relentless. Becker's mind was blank. Blank to everything – where he was, who was chasing him – all that was left was instinct, self preservation, no pain, only fear, and raw energy.

A shot exploded against the azulejo tile behind him. Shards of glass sprayed across the back of his neck. He stumbled left, into another alley. He heard himself call for help, but except for the sound of footsteps and strained breathing, the morning air remained deathly still.

Becker's side was burning now. He feared he was leaving a crimson trail on the whitewashed walks. He searched everywhere for an open door, an open gate, any escape from the suffocating canyons. Nothing. The walkway narrowed.

'Socorro!' Becker's voice was barely audible. 'Help!'

The walls grew closer on each side. The walkway curved. Becker searched for an intersection, a tributary, any way out. The passageway narrowed. Locked doors. Narrowing. Locked gates. The footsteps were closing. He was in a straightaway, and suddenly the alley began to slope upward. Steeper. Becker felt his legs straining. He was slowing.

And then he was there.

Like a freeway that had run out of funding, the alley just stopped. There was a high wall, a wooden bench, and nothing else. No escape. Becker looked up three stories to the top of the building and then spun and started back down the long alley, but he had only taken a few steps before he stopped short.

At the foot of the inclined straightaway, a figure appeared. The man moved toward Becker with a measured determination. In his hand, a gun glinted in the early morning sun.

Becker felt a sudden lucidity as he backed up toward the wall. The pain in his side suddenly registered. He touched the spot and looked down. There was blood smeared across his fingers and across Ensei Tankado's golden ring. He felt dizzy. He stared at the engraved band, puzzled. He'd forgotten he was wearing it. He'd forgotten why he had come to Seville. He looked up at the figure approaching. He looked down at the ring. Was this why Megan had died? Was this why *he* would die?

The shadow advanced up the inclined passageway. Becker saw walls on all sides – a dead end behind him. A few gated entryways between them, but it was too late to call for help.

Becker pressed his back against the dead end. Suddenly he could feel every piece of grit beneath the soles of his shoes, every bump in the stucco wall behind him. His mind was reeling backward, his childhood, his parents . . . Susan.

Oh, God . . . Susan.

For the first time since he was a kid, Becker prayed.

He did not pray for deliverance from death; he did not believe in miracles. Instead he prayed that the woman he left behind would find strength, that she would know without a doubt that she had been loved. He closed his eyes. The memories came like a torrent. They were not memories of department meetings, university business, and the things that made up 90 percent of his life; they were memories of her. Simple memories: teaching her to use chopsticks, sailing on Cape Cod. *I love you,* he thought. *Know that . . . forever.*

It was as if every defense, every facade, every insecure exaggeration of his life had been stripped away. He was standing naked – flesh and bones before God. *I am a man,* he thought. And in a moment of irony he thought, *A man without wax.* He stood, eyes closed, as the man in wire-rim glasses drew nearer. Somewhere nearby, a bell began to toll. Becker waited in darkness, for the sound that would end his life.

CHAPTER 89

The morning sun was just breaking over the Seville rooftops and shining down into the canyons below. The bells atop the Giralda cried out for sunrise mass. This was the moment inhabitants had all been waiting for. Everywhere in the ancient barrio, gates opened and families poured into the alleyways. Like lifeblood through the veins of old Santa Cruz, they coursed toward the heart of their pueblo, toward the core of their history, toward their God, their shrine, their cathedral.

Somewhere in Becker's mind, a bell was tolling. *Am I dead?* Almost reluctantly, he opened his eyes and squinted into the first rays of sunlight. He knew exactly where he was. He leveled his gaze and searched the alley for his assailant. But the man in wire-rims was not there. Instead, there were others. Spanish families, in their finest clothes, stepping from their gated portals into the alleyways, talking, laughing.

At the bottom of the alley, hidden from Becker's view, Hulohot cursed in frustration. At first there had been only a single couple separating him from his quarry. Hulohot had been certain they would leave. But the sound of the bells kept reverberating down the alley, drawing others from their homes. A second couple, with children. They greeted each other. Talking, laughing, kissing three times on the cheek. Another group appeared, and Hulohot could no longer see his prey. Now, in a boiling rage, he raced into the quickly growing crowd. He had to get to David Becker!

The killer fought his way toward the end of the alley. He found himself momentarily lost in a sea of bodies – coats and ties, black dresses, lace mantles over hunched women. They all seemed oblivious to Hulohot's presence; they strolled casually, all in black, shuffling, moving as one, blocking his way. Hulohot dug his way through the crowd and dashed up the alley into the dead end, his weapon raised. Then he let out a muted, inhuman scream. David Becker was gone.

Becker stumbled and sidestepped his way through the crowd. *Follow the crowd*, he thought. *They know the way out*. He cut right at the intersection and the alley widened. Everywhere gates were opening and people were pouring out. The pealing of the bells grew louder.

Becker's side was still burning, but he sensed the bleeding had stopped. He raced on. Somewhere behind him, closing fast, was a man with a gun.

Becker ducked in and out of the groups of church-goers and tried to keep his head down. It was not much farther. He could sense it. The crowd had thickened. The alley had widened. They were no longer in a little tributary, this was the main river. As he

379

rounded a bend, Becker suddenly saw it, rising before them – the cathedral and Giralda tower.

The bells were deafening, the reverberations trapped in the high-walled plaza. The crowds converged, everyone in black, pushing across the square toward the gaping doors of the Seville Cathedral. Becker tried to break away toward Mateus Gago, but he was trapped. He was shoulder to shoulder, heel to toe with the shoving throngs. The Spaniards had always had a different idea of closeness than the rest of the world. Becker was wedged between two heavy-set women, both with their eyes closed, letting the crowd carry them. They mumbled prayers to themselves and clutched rosary beads in their fingers.

As the crowd closed on the enormous stone structure, Becker tried to cut left again, but the current was stronger now. The anticipation, the pushing and shoving, the blind, mumbled prayers. He turned into the crowd, trying to fight backward against the eager throngs. It was impossible, like swimming upstream in a mile-deep river. He turned. The cathedral doors loomed before him – like the opening to some dark carnival ride he wished he hadn't taken. David Becker suddenly realized he was going to church.

CHAPTER 90

The Crypto sirens were blaring. Strathmore had no idea how long Susan had been gone. He sat alone in the shadows, the drone of TRANSLTR calling to him. *You're a survivor . . . you're a survivor. . . .*

Yes, he thought. *I'm a survivor – but survival is nothing without honor. I'd rather die than live in the shadow of disgrace.*

And disgrace was what was waiting for him. He had kept information from the director. He had sent a virus into the nation's most secure computer. There was no doubt he would be hung out to dry. His intentions had been patriotic, but nothing had gone as he'd planned. There had been death and treachery. There would be trials, accusations, public outrage. He had served his country with honor and integrity for so many years, he couldn't allow it to end this way.

I'm a survivor, he thought.

You're a liar, his own thoughts replied.

It was true. He *was* a liar. There were people he hadn't been honest with. Susan Fletcher was one of them. There were so many things he hadn't told her – things he was now desperately ashamed of. For years

381

she'd been his illusion, his living fantasy. He dreamed of her at night; he cried out for her in his sleep. He couldn't help it. She was as brilliant and as beautiful as any woman he could imagine. His wife had tried to be patient, but when she finally met Susan, she immediately lost hope. Bev Strathmore never blamed her husband for his feelings. She tried to endure the pain as long as possible, but recently it had become too much. She'd told him their marriage was ending; another woman's shadow was no place to spend the rest of her life.

Gradually the sirens lifted Strathmore from his daze. His analytical powers searched for any way out. His mind reluctantly confirmed what his heart had suspected. There was only one true escape, only one solution.

Strathmore gazed down at the keyboard and began typing. He didn't bother to turn the monitor so he could see it. His fingers pecked out the words slowly and decisively.

Dearest friends, I am taking my life today . . .

This way, no one would ever wonder. There would be no questions. There would be no accusations. He would spell out for the world what had happened. Many had died . . . but there was still one life to take.

CHAPTER 91

In a cathedral, it is always night. The warmth of the day turns to damp coolness. The traffic is silenced behind thick granite walls. No number of candelabra can illuminate the vast darkness overhead. Shadows fall everywhere. There's only the stained glass, high above, filtering the ugliness of the outside world into rays of muted reds and blues.

The Seville Cathedral, like all great cathedrals of Europe, is laid out in the shape of a cross. The sanctuary and altar are located just above the midpoint and open downward onto the main sanctuary. Wooden pews fill the vertical axis, a staggering 113 yards from the altar to the base of the cross. To the left and right of the altar, the transept of the cross houses confessionals, sacred tombs, and additional seating.

Becker found himself wedged in the middle of a long pew about halfway back. Overhead, in the dizzying empty space, a silver censer the size of a refrigerator swung enormous arcs on a frayed rope, leaving a trail of frankincense. The bells of the Giralda kept ringing, sending low rumbling shock waves through the stone. Becker lowered his gaze to the gilded wall behind the altar. He had a lot to be thankful for. He was breathing. He was alive. It was a miracle.

As the priest prepared to give the opening prayer, Becker checked his side. There was a red stain on his shirt, but the bleeding had stopped. The wound was small, more of a laceration than a puncture. Becker tucked his shirt back in and craned his neck. Behind him, the doors were cranking shut. He knew if he'd been followed, he was now trapped. The Seville Cathedral had a single functional entrance, a design popularized in the days when churches were used as fortresses, a safe haven against Moorish invasion. With a single entrance, there was only one door to barricade. Now the single entrance had another function – it ensured all tourists entering the cathedral had purchased a ticket.

The twenty-two-foot-high gilded doors slammed with a decisive crash. Becker was sealed in the house of God. He closed his eyes and slid low in his pew. He was the only one in the building not dressed in black. Somewhere voices began to chant.

Toward the back of the church, a figure moved slowly up the side aisle, keeping to the shadows. He had slipped in just before the doors closed. He smiled to himself. The hunt was getting interesting. *Becker is here . . . I can feel it.* He moved methodically, one row at a time. Overhead the frankincense decanter swung its long, lazy arcs. *A fine place to die*, Hulohot thought. *I hope I do as well.*

Becker knelt on the cold cathedral floor and ducked his head out of sight. The man seated next to him glared down – it was most irregular behavior in the house of God.

'Enfermo,' Becker apologized. 'Sick.'

Becker knew he had to stay low. He had glimpsed a familiar silhouette moving up the side aisle. *It's him! He's here!*

Despite being in the middle of an enormous congregation, Becker feared he was an easy target – his khaki blazer was like a roadside flare in the crowd of black. He considered removing it, but the white oxford shirt underneath was no better. Instead he huddled lower.

The man beside him frowned. 'Turista.' He grunted. Then he whispered, half sarcastically, 'Llamo un médico? Shall I call a doctor?'

Becker looked up at the old man's mole-ridden face. 'No, gracias. Estoy bien.'

The man gave him an angry look. 'Pues siéntate! Then sit down!' There were scattered shushes around them, and the old man bit his tongue and faced front.

Becker closed his eyes and huddled lower, wondering how long the service would last. Becker, raised Protestant, had always had the impression Catholics were long-winded. He prayed it was true – as soon as the service ended, he would be forced to stand and let the others out. In khaki he was dead.

Becker knew he had no choice at the moment. He simply knelt there on the cold stone floor of the great cathedral. Eventually, the old man lost interest. The congregation was standing now, singing a hymn. Becker stayed down. His legs were starting to cramp. There was no room to stretch them. *Patience,* he thought. *Patience.* He closed his eyes and took a deep breath.

It felt like only minutes later that Becker felt someone kicking him. He looked up. The mole-faced man was standing to his right, waiting impatiently to leave the pew.

Becker panicked. *He wants to leave already? I'll have to stand up!* Becker motioned for the man to step over him. The man could barely control his anger. He grabbed the tails of his black blazer, pulled them down in a huff, and leaned back to reveal the entire row of people waiting to leave. Becker looked left and saw that the woman who had been seated there was gone. The length of pew to his left was empty all the way to the center aisle.

The service can't be over! It's impossible! We just got here!

But when Becker saw the altar boy at the end of the row and the two single-file lines moving up the center aisle toward the altar, he knew what was happening.

Communion. He groaned. *The damn Spaniards do it first!*

CHAPTER 92

Susan climbed down the ladder into the sublevels. Thick steam was now boiling up around TRANSLTR's hull. The catwalks were wet with condensation. She almost fell, her flats providing very little traction. She wondered how much longer TRANSLTR would survive. The sirens continued their intermittent warning. The emergency lights spun in two-second intervals. Three stories below, the aux generators shook in a taxed whine. Susan knew somewhere at the bottom in the foggy dimness there was a circuit breaker. She sensed time was running out.

Upstairs, Strathmore held the Beretta in his hand. He reread his note and laid it on the floor of the room where he was standing. What he was about to do was a cowardly act, there was no doubt. *I'm a survivor*, he thought. He thought of the virus in the NSA databank, he thought of David Becker in Spain, he thought of his plans for a back door. He had told so many lies. He was guilty of so much. He knew this was the only way to avoid accountability . . . the only way to avoid the shame. Carefully he aimed the gun. Then he closed his eyes and pulled the trigger.

Susan had only descended six flights when she heard the muffled shot. It was far off, barely audible over the generators. She had never heard a gunshot except on television, but she had no doubt what it was.

She stopped short, the sound resounding in her ears. In a wave of horror, she feared the worst. She pictured the commander's dreams – the back door in Digital Fortress, the incredible coup it would have been. She pictured the virus in the databank, his failing marriage, that eerie nod he had given her. Her footing faltered. She spun on the landing, grappling for the banister. *Commander! No!*

Susan was momentarily frozen, her mind blank. The echo of the gunshot seemed to drown out the chaos around her. Her mind told her to keep on going, but her legs refused. *Commander!* An instant later she found herself stumbling back up the stairs, entirely forgetting the danger around her.

She ran blindly, slipping on the slick metal. Above her the humidity fell like rain. When she reached the ladder and began climbing, she felt herself lifted from below by a tremendous surge of steam that practically jettisoned her through the trapdoor. She rolled onto the Crypto floor and felt the cool air wash over her. Her white blouse clung to her body, soaked through.

It was dark. Susan paused, trying to get her bearings. The sound of the gunshot was on endless loop in her head. Hot steam billowed up through the trapdoor like gases from a volcano about to explode.

Susan cursed herself for leaving the Beretta with Strathmore. She *had* left it with him, hadn't she? *Or was it in Node 3?* As her eyes adjusted to the dark, she glanced toward the gaping hole in the Node 3 wall.

The glow from the monitors was faint, but in the distance she could see Hale lying motionless on the floor where she'd left him. There was no sign of Strathmore. Terrified of what she'd find, she turned toward the commander's office.

But as she began to move, something registered as strange. She backpedaled a few steps and peered into Node 3 again. In the soft light she could see Hale's arm. It was not at his side. He was no longer tied like a mummy. His arm was up over his head. He was sprawled backward on the floor. Had he gotten free? There was no movement. Hale was deathly still.

Susan gazed up at Strathmore's workstation perched high on the wall. 'Commander?'

Silence.

Tentatively she moved toward Node 3. There was an object in Hale's hand. It glimmered in the light of the monitors. Susan moved closer . . . closer. Suddenly she could see what Hale was holding. It was the Beretta.

Susan gasped. Following the arch of Hale's arm, her eyes moved to his face. What she saw was grotesque. Half of Greg Hale's head was soaked in blood. The dark stain had spread out across the carpet.

Oh my God! Susan staggered backward. It wasn't the commander's shot she'd heard, it was *Hale's!*

As if in a trance, Susan moved toward the body. Apparently, Hale had managed to free himself. The printer cables were piled on the floor beside him. *I must have left the gun on the couch,* she thought. The blood flowing through the hole in his skull looked black in the bluish light.

On the floor beside Hale was a piece of paper. Susan went over unsteadily, and picked it up. It was a letter.

*Dearest friends, I am taking my life today in penance for
the following sins . . .*

In utter disbelief, Susan stared at the suicide note in
her hand. She read slowly. It was surreal – so unlike
Hale – a laundry list of crimes. He was admitting to
everything – figuring out that NDAKOTA was a hoax,
hiring a mercenary to kill Ensei Tankado and take the
ring, pushing Phil Chartrukian, planning to sell
Digital Fortress.

Susan reached the final line. She was not prepared
for what she read. The letter's final words delivered a
numbing blow.

*Above all, I'm truly sorry about David Becker. Forgive
me, I was blinded by ambition.*

As Susan stood trembling over Hale's body, the
sound of running footsteps approached behind her. In
slow motion, she turned.

Strathmore appeared in the broken window, pale
and out of breath. He stared down at Hale's body in
apparent shock.

'Oh my God!' he said. 'What happened?'

CHAPTER 93

Communion.

Hulohot spotted Becker immediately. The khaki blazer was impossible to miss, particularly with the small bloodstain on one side. The jacket was moving up the center aisle in a sea of black. *He must not know I'm here.* Hulohot smiled. *He's a dead man.*

He fanned the tiny metal contacts on his fingertips, eager to tell his American contact the good news. *Soon,* he thought, *very soon.*

Like a predator moving downwind, Hulohot moved to the back of the church. Then he began his approach – straight up the center aisle. Hulohot was in no mood to track Becker through the crowds leaving the church. His quarry was trapped, a fortunate turn of events. Hulohot just needed a way to eliminate him quietly. His silencer, the best money could buy, emitted no more than a tiny spitting cough. That would be fine.

As Hulohot closed on the khaki blazer, he was unaware of the quiet murmurs coming from those he was passing. The congregation could understand this man's excitement to receive the blessing of God, but nevertheless, there were strict rules of protocol – two lines, single file.

Hulohot kept moving. He was closing quickly. He thumbed the revolver in his jacket pocket. The moment had arrived. David Becker had been exceptionally fortunate so far; there was no need to tempt fortune any further.

The khaki blazer was only ten people ahead, facing front, head down. Hulohot rehearsed the kill in his mind. The image was clear – cutting in behind Becker, keeping the gun low and out of sight, firing two shots into Becker's back, Becker slumping, Hulohot catching him and helping him into a pew like a concerned friend. Then Hulohot would move quickly to the back of the church as if going for help. In the confusion, he would disappear before anyone knew what had happened.

Five people. Four. Three.

Hulohot fingered the gun in his pocket, keeping it low. He would fire from hip level upward into Becker's spine. That way the bullet would hit either the spine or a lung before finding the heart. Even if the bullet missed the heart, Becker would die. A punctured lung was fatal, maybe not in more medically advanced parts of the world, but in *Spain*, it was fatal.

Two people . . . one. And then Hulohot was there. Like a dancer performing a well-rehearsed move, he turned to his right. He laid his hand on the shoulder of the khaki blazer, aimed the gun, and . . . fired. Two muffled spats.

Instantly the body was rigid. Then it was falling. Hulohot caught his victim under the armpits. In a single motion, he swung the body into a pew before any bloodstains spread across his back. Nearby, people turned. Hulohot paid no heed – he would be gone in an instant.

He groped the man's lifeless fingers for the ring. Nothing. He felt again. The fingers were bare. Hulohot spun the man around angrily. The horror was instantaneous. The face was not David Becker's.

Rafael de la Maza, a banker from the suburbs of Seville, had died almost instantly. He was still clutching the 50,000 pesetas the strange American had paid him for a cheap black blazer.

CHAPTER 94

Midge Milken stood fuming at the water cooler near the entrance to the conference room. *What the hell is Fontaine doing?* She crumpled her paper cup and threw it forcefully into the trash can. *There's something happening in Crypto! I can feel it!* Midge knew there was only one way to prove herself right. She'd go check out Crypto herself – track down Jabba if need be. She spun on her heel and headed for the door.

Brinkerhoff appeared out of nowhere, blocking her way. 'Where are you headed?'

'Home!' Midge lied.

Brinkerhoff refused to let her pass.

Midge glared. 'Fontaine told you not to let me out, didn't he?'

Brinkerhoff looked away.

'Chad, I'm telling you, there's something happening in Crypto – something big. I don't know why Fontaine's playing dumb, but TRANSLTR's in trouble. Something is not right down there tonight!'

'Midge,' he soothed, walking past her toward the curtained conference room windows, 'let's let the director handle it.'

Midge's gaze sharpened. 'Do you have any idea what happens to TRANSLTR if the cooling system fails?'

Brinkerhoff shrugged and approached the window. 'Power's probably back on-line by now anyway.' He pulled apart the curtains and looked.

'Still dark?' Midge asked.

But Brinkerhoff did not reply. He was spellbound. The scene below in the Crypto dome was unimaginable. The entire glass cupola was filled with spinning lights, flashing strobes, and swirling steam. Brinkerhoff stood transfixed, teetering light-headed against the glass. Then, in a frenzy of panic, he raced out. 'Director! *Director!*'

CHAPTER 95

The blood of Christ . . . the cup of salvation . . .

People gathered around the slumped body in the pew. Overhead, the frankincense swung its peaceful arcs. Hulohot wheeled wildly in the center aisle and scanned the church. *He's got to be here!* He spun back toward the altar.

Thirty rows ahead, holy communion was proceeding uninterrupted. Padre Gustaphes Herrera, the head chalice bearer, glanced curiously at the quiet commotion in one of the center pews; he was not concerned. Sometimes some of the older folks were overcome by the Holy Spirit and passed out. A little air usually did the trick.

Meanwhile, Hulohot was searching frantically. Becker was nowhere in sight. A hundred or so people were kneeling at the long altar receiving communion. Hulohot wondered if Becker was one of them. He scanned their backs. He was prepared to shoot from fifty yards away and make a dash for it.

El cuerpo de Jesus, el pan del cielo.

The young priest serving Becker communion gave

him a disapproving stare. He could understand the stranger's eagerness to receive communion, but it was no excuse to cut in line.

Becker bowed his head and chewed the wafer as best he could. He sensed something was happening behind him, some sort of disturbance. He thought of the man from whom he'd bought the jacket and hoped he had listened to his warning and not taken Becker's in exchange. He started to turn and look, but he feared the wire-rim glasses would be staring back. He crouched in hopes his black jacket was covering the back of his khaki pants. It was not.

The chalice was coming quickly from his right. People were already swallowing their wine, crossing themselves, and standing to leave. *Slow down!* Becker was in no hurry to leave the altar. But with two thousand people waiting for communion and only eight priests serving, it was considered bad form to linger over a sip of wine.

The chalice was just to the right of Becker when Hulohot spotted the mismatched khaki pants. 'Estás ya muerto,' he hissed softly. 'You're already dead.' Hulohot moved up the center aisle. The time for subtlety had passed. Two shots in the back, and he would grab the ring and run. The biggest taxi stand in Seville was half a block away on Mateus Gago. He reached for his weapon.

Adiós, Señor Becker . . .

La sangre de Cristo, la copa de la salvación.

The thick scent of red wine filled Becker's nostrils as Padre Herrera lowered the hand-polished, silver chalice. *Little early for drinking,* Becker thought as he leaned forward. But as the silver goblet dropped past eye level, there was a blur of movement. A figure, coming fast, his shape warped in the reflection of the cup.

Becker saw a flash of metal, a weapon being drawn. Instantly, unconsciously, like a runner from a starting block at the sound of a gun, Becker was vaulting forward. The priest fell back in horror as the chalice sailed through the air, and red wine rained down on white marble. Priests and altar boys went scattering as Becker dove over the communion rail. A silencer coughed out a single shot. Becker landed hard, and the shot exploded in the marble floor beside him. An instant later he was tumbling down three granite stairs into the valle, a narrow passageway through which the clergy entered, allowing them to rise onto the altar as if by divine grace.

At the bottom of the steps, he stumbled and dove. Becker felt himself sliding out of control across the slick polished stone. A dagger of pain shot through his gut as he landed on his side. A moment later he was stumbling through a curtained entryway and down a set of wooden stairs.

Pain. Becker was running through a dressing room. It was dark. There were screams from the altar. Loud footsteps in pursuit. Becker burst through a set of double doors and stumbled into some sort of study. It was dark, furnished with rich Oriental rugs and polished mahogany. On the far wall was a life-size crucifix. Becker staggered to a stop. Dead end. He was at the tip of the cross. He could hear Hulohot closing fast. Becker stared at the crucifix and cursed his bad luck.

'*Goddamn it!*' he screamed.

There was the sudden sound of breaking glass to Becker's left. He wheeled. A man in red robes gasped and turned to eye Becker in horror. Like a cat caught with a canary, the holy man wiped his mouth and tried to hide the broken bottle of holy communion wine at his feet.

'*Salida!*' Becker demanded. '*Salida!* Let me out!'

Cardinal Guerra reacted on instinct. A demon had entered his sacred chambers screaming for deliverance from the house of God. Guerra would grant him that wish – immediately. The demon had entered at a most inopportune moment.

Pale, the cardinal pointed to a curtain on the wall to his left. Hidden behind the curtain was a door. He'd installed it three years ago. It led directly to the courtyard outside. The cardinal had grown tired of exiting the church through the front door like a common sinner.

CHAPTER 96

Susan was wet and shivering, huddled on the Node 3 couch. Strathmore draped his suit coat over her shoulders. Hale's body lay a few yards away. The sirens blared. Like ice thawing on a frozen pond, TRANSLTR's hull let out a sharp crack.

'I'm going down to kill power,' Strathmore said, laying a reassuring hand on her shoulder. 'I'll be right back.'

Susan stared absently after the commander as he dashed across the Crypto floor. He was no longer the catatonic man she'd seen ten minutes before. Commander Trevor Strathmore was back – logical, controlled, doing whatever was necessary to get the job done.

The final words of Hale's suicide note ran through her mind like a train out of control: *Above all, I'm truly sorry about David Becker. Forgive me, I was blinded by ambition.*

Susan Fletcher's nightmare had just been confirmed. David was in danger ... or worse. Maybe it was already too late. *I'm truly sorry about David Becker.*

She stared at the note. Hale hadn't even signed it – he'd just typed his name at the bottom: *Greg Hale*. He'd poured out his guts, pressed PRINT, and then shot himself – just like that. Hale had sworn he'd never go back to prison; he'd kept his vow – he'd chosen death instead.

'David . . .' She sobbed. *David!*

At that moment, ten feet below the Crypto floor, Commander Strathmore stepped off the ladder onto the first landing. It had been a day of fiascos. What had started out as a patriotic mission had swerved wildly out of control. The commander had been forced to make impossible decisions, commit horrific acts – acts he'd never imagined himself capable of.

It was a solution! It was the only *damn solution!*

There was duty to think of: country and honor. Strathmore knew there was still time. He could shut down TRANSLTR. He could use the ring to save the country's most valuable databank. *Yes*, he thought, *there was still time.*

Strathmore looked out over the disaster around him. The overhead sprinklers were on. TRANSLTR was groaning. The sirens blared. The spinning lights looked like helicopters closing in through dense fog. With every step, all he could see was Greg Hale – the young cryptographer gazing up, his eyes pleading, and then, the shot. Hale's death was for country . . . for honor. The NSA could not afford another scandal. Strathmore needed a scapegoat. Besides, Greg Hale was a disaster waiting to happen.

Strathmore's thoughts were jarred free by the sound of his cellular. It was barely audible over the sirens and hissing fumes. He snatched it off his belt without breaking stride.

'Speak.'

'Where's my pass-key?' a familiar voice demanded.

'Who is this?' Strathmore yelled over the din.

'It's Numataka!' the angry voice bellowed back. 'You promised me a pass-key!'

Strathmore kept moving.

'I want Digital Fortress!' Numataka hissed.

'There *is* no Digital Fortress!' Strathmore shot back.

'What?'

'There is no unbreakable algorithm!'

'Of course there is! I've seen it on the Internet! My people have been trying to unlock it for days!'

'It's an encrypted virus, you fool – and you're damn lucky you can't open it!'

'But—'

'The deal is off!' Strathmore yelled. 'I'm not North Dakota. There *is* no North Dakota! Forget I ever mentioned it!' He clamped the cellular shut, turned off the ringer, and rammed it back on his belt. There would be no more interruptions.

Twelve thousand miles away, Tokugen Numataka stood stunned at his plate-glass window. His Umami cigar hung limply in his mouth. The deal of his lifetime had just disintegrated before his eyes.

Strathmore kept descending. *The deal is off.* Numatech Corp. would never get the unbreakable algorithm . . . and the NSA would never get its back door.

Strathmore's dream had been a long time in the planning – he'd chosen Numatech carefully. Numatech was wealthy, a likely winner of the pass-key auction.

No one would think twice if it ended up with the key. Conveniently there was no company less likely to be suspected of consorting with the U.S. government. Tokugen Numataka was old-world Japan – death before dishonor. He hated Americans. He hated their food, he hated their customs, and most of all, he hated their grip on the world's software market.

Strathmore's vision had been bold – a world encryption standard with a back door for the NSA. He'd longed to share his dream with Susan, to carry it out with her by his side, but he knew he could not. Even though Ensei Tankado's death would save thousands of lives in the future, Susan would never have agreed; she was a pacifist. *I'm a pacifist too,* thought Strathmore, *I just don't have the luxury of acting like one.*

There had never been any doubt in the commander's mind who would kill Tankado. Tankado was in Spain – and Spain meant Hulohot. The forty-two-year-old Portuguese mercenary was one of the commander's favorite pros. He'd been working for the NSA for years. Born and raised in Lisbon, Hulohot had done work for the NSA all over Europe. Never once had his kills been traced back to Fort Meade. The only catch was that Hulohot was deaf; telephone communication was impossible. Recently Strathmore had arranged for Hulohot to receive the NSA's newest toy, the Monocle computer. Strathmore bought himself a SkyPager and programmed it to the same frequency. From that moment on, his communication with Hulohot was not only instantaneous but also entirely untraceable.

The first message Strathmore had sent Hulohot left

little room for misunderstanding. They had already discussed it. Kill Ensei Tankado. Obtain pass-key.

Strathmore never asked how Hulohot worked his magic, but somehow he had done it again. Ensei Tankado was dead, and the authorities were convinced it was a heart attack. A textbook kill – except for one thing. Hulohot had misjudged the location. Apparently Tankado dying in a public place was a necessary part of the illusion. But unexpectedly, the public had appeared too soon. Hulohot was forced into hiding before he could search the body for the pass-key. When the dust settled, Tankado's body was in the hands of Seville's coroner.

Strathmore was furious. Hulohot had blown a mission for the first time ever – and he'd picked an inauspicious time to do it. Getting Tankado's pass-key was critical, but Strathmore knew that sending a deaf assassin into the Seville morgue was a suicide mission. He had pondered his other options. A second scheme began to materialize. Strathmore suddenly saw a chance to win on two fronts – a chance to realize two dreams instead of just one. At six-thirty that morning, he had called David Becker.

CHAPTER 97

Fontaine burst into the conference room at a full sprint. Brinkerhoff and Midge were close at his heels.

'Look!' Midge choked, motioning frantically to the window.

Fontaine looked out the window at the strobes in the Crypto dome. His eyes went wide. This was definitely *not* part of the plan.

Brinkerhoff sputtered. 'It's a goddamn disco down there!'

Fontaine stared out, trying to make sense of it. In the few years TRANSLTR had been operational, it had never done this. *It's overheating,* he thought. He wondered why the hell Strathmore hadn't shut it down. It took Fontaine only an instant to make up his mind.

He snatched an interoffice phone off the conference table and punched the extension for Crypto. The receiver began beeping as if the extension were out of order.

Fontaine slammed down the receiver. 'Damn it!' He immediately picked up again and dialed Strathmore's private cellular line. This time the line began to ring.

Six rings went by.

Brinkerhoff and Midge watched as Fontaine paced the length of his phone cable like a tiger on a chain. After a full minute, Fontaine was crimson with rage.

He slammed down the receiver again. 'Unbelievable!' he bellowed. 'Crypto's about to blow, and Strathmore won't answer his goddamn phone!'

CHAPTER 98

Hulohot burst out of Cardinal Guerra's chambers into the blinding morning sun. He shielded his eyes and cursed. He was standing outside the cathedral in a small patio, bordered by a high stone wall, the west face of the Giralda tower, and two wrought-iron fences. The gate was open. Outside the gate was the square. It was empty. The walls of Santa Cruz were in the distance. There was no way Becker could have made it so far so quickly. Hulohot turned and scanned the patio. *He's in here. He must be!*

The patio, Jardin de los Naranjos, was famous in Seville for its twenty blossoming orange trees. The trees were renowned in Seville as the birthplace of English marmalade. An eighteenth-century English trader had purchased three dozen bushels of oranges from the Seville church and taken them back to London only to find the fruit inedibly bitter. He tried to make jam from the rinds and ended up having to add pounds of sugar just to make it palatable. Orange marmalade had been born.

Hulohot moved forward through the grove, gun leveled. The trees were old, and the foliage had

407

moved high on their trunks. Their lowest branches were unreachable, and the thin bases provided no cover. Hulohot quickly saw the patio was empty. He looked straight up. The Giralda.

The entrance to the Giralda's spiral staircase was cordoned off by a rope and small wooden sign. The rope hung motionless. Hulohot's eyes climbed the 419-foot tower and immediately knew it was a ridiculous thought. There was no way Becker would have been that stupid. The single staircase wound straight up to a square stone cubicle. There were narrow slits in the wall for viewing, but there was no way out.

David Becker climbed the last of the steep stairs and staggered breathless into a tiny stone cubicle. There were high walls all around him and narrow slits in the perimeter. No exit.

Fate had done Becker no favors this morning. As he'd dashed from the cathedral into the open courtyard, his jacket had caught on the door. The fabric had stopped him midstride and swung him hard left before tearing. Becker was suddenly stumbling off balance into the blinding sun. When he'd looked up, he was heading straight for a staircase. He'd jumped over the rope and dashed up. By the time he realized where it led, it was too late.

Now he stood in the confined cell and caught his breath. His side burned. Narrow slats of morning sun streamed through the openings in the wall. He looked out. The man in the wire-rim glasses was far below, his back to Becker, staring out at the plaza. Becker shifted his body in front of the crack for a better view. *Cross the plaza*, he willed him.

*

The shadow of the Giralda lay across the square like a giant felled sequoia. Hulohot stared the length of it. At the far end, three slits of light cut through the tower's viewing apertures and fell in crisp rectangles on the cobblestone below. One of those rectangles had just been blotted out by the shadow of a man. Without so much as a glance toward the top of the tower, Hulohot spun and dashed toward the Giralda stairs.

CHAPTER 99

Fontaine pounded his fist into his hand. He paced the conference room and stared out at the spinning Crypto lights. 'Abort! Goddamn it! Abort!'

Midge appeared in the doorway waving a fresh readout. 'Director! Strathmore *can't* abort!'

'What!' Brinkerhoff and Fontaine gasped in unison.

'He tried, sir!' Midge held up the report. 'Four times already! TRANSLTR's locked in some sort of endless loop.'

Fontaine spun and stared back out the window. 'Jesus Christ!'

The conference room phone rang sharply. The director threw up his arms. 'It's got to be Strathmore! About goddamn time!'

Brinkerhoff scooped up the phone. 'Director's office.'

Fontaine held out his hand for the receiver.

Brinkerhoff looked uneasy and turned to Midge. 'It's Jabba. He wants *you.*'

The director swung his gaze over to Midge, who was already crossing the room. She activated the speaker phone. 'Go ahead, Jabba.'

Jabba's metallic voice boomed into the room. 'Midge, I'm in the main databank. We're showing some strange stuff down here. I was wondering if—'

'Dammit, Jabba!' Midge came unglued. 'That's what I've been trying to tell you!'

'It could be nothing,' Jabba hedged, 'but—'

'Stop saying that! It's *not* nothing! Whatever's going on down there, take it seriously, *very* seriously. My data isn't fried – never has been, never will.' She started to hang up and then added, 'Oh, and Jabba? Just so there aren't any surprises . . . Strathmore bypassed Gauntlet.'

CHAPTER 100

Hulohot took the Giralda stairs three at a time. The only light in the spiral passage was from small open-air windows every 180 degrees. *He's trapped! David Becker will die!* Hulohot circled upward, gun drawn. He kept to the outside wall in case Becker decided to attack from above. The iron candle poles on each landing would make good weapons if Becker decided to use one. But by staying wide, Hulohot would be able to spot him in time. Hulohot's gun had a range significantly longer than a five-foot candle pole.

Hulohot moved quickly but carefully. The stairs were steep; tourists had died here. This was not America – no safety signs, no handrails, no insurance disclaimers. This was Spain. If you were stupid enough to fall, it was your own damn fault, regardless of who built the stairs.

Hulohot paused at one of the shoulder-high openings and glanced out. He was on the north face and, from the looks of things, about halfway up.

The opening to the viewing platform was visible around the corner. The staircase to the top was empty. David Becker had not challenged him. Hulohot realized maybe Becker had not seen him enter the tower. That meant the element of surprise was on Hulohot's side as well – not that he'd need it. Hulohot held all the cards. Even the layout of the tower was in his favor; the staircase met the viewing platform in the southwest corner – Hulohot would have a clear line of fire to every point of the cell with no possibility that Becker could get behind him. And to top things off, Hulohot would be moving out of the dark into the light. *A killing box*, he mused.

Hulohot measured the distance to the doorway. Seven steps. He practiced the kill in his mind. If he stayed right as he approached the opening, he would be able to see the leftmost corner of the platform before he reached it. If Becker was there, Hulohot would fire. If not, he would shift inside and enter moving east, facing the right corner, the only place remaining that Becker could be. He smiled.

SUBJECT: DAVID BECKER – TERMINATED

The time had come. He checked his weapon.

With a violent surge, Hulohot dashed up. The platform swung into view. The left corner was empty. As rehearsed, Hulohot shifted inside and burst through the opening facing right. He fired into the corner. The bullet ricocheted back off the bare wall and barely missed him. Hulohot wheeled wildly and let out a muted scream. There was no one there. David Becker had vanished.

Three flights below, suspended 325 feet over the Jardin de los Naranjos, David Becker hung on the outside of the Giralda like a man doing chin-ups on a

413

window ledge. As Hulohot had been racing up the staircase, Becker had descended three flights and lowered himself out one of the openings. He'd dropped out of sight just in time. The killer had run right by him. He'd been in too much of a hurry to notice the white knuckles grasping the window ledge.

Hanging outside the window, Becker thanked God that his daily squash routine involved twenty minutes on the Nautilus machine to develop his biceps for a harder overhead serve. Unfortunately, despite his strong arms, Becker was now having trouble pulling himself back in. His shoulders burned. His side felt as if it were tearing open. The rough-cut stone ledge provided little grip, grating into his fingertips like broken glass.

Becker knew it was only a matter of seconds before his assailant would come running down from above. From the higher ground, the killer would undoubtedly see Becker's fingers on the ledge.

Becker closed his eyes and pulled. He knew he would need a miracle to escape death. His fingers were losing their leverage. He glanced down, past his dangling legs. The drop was the length of a football field to the orange trees below. Unsurvivable. The pain in his side was getting worse. Footsteps now thundered above him, loud leaping footsteps rushing down the stairs. Becker closed his eyes. It was now or never. He gritted his teeth and pulled.

The stone tore against the skin on his wrists as he yanked himself upward. The footsteps were coming fast. Becker grappled at the inside of the opening, trying to secure his hold. He kicked his feet. His body felt like lead, as if someone had a rope tied to his legs and were pulling him down. He fought it. He surged up onto his elbows. He was in plain view now, his head half through the window like a man in a guillotine. He wriggled his legs, kicking himself into the opening. He was halfway through. His torso now hung into the stairwell. The footsteps were close. Becker grabbed the sides of the opening and in a single motion launched his body through. He hit the staircase hard.

Hulohot sensed Becker's body hit the floor just below him. He leapt forward, gun leveled. A window spun into view. *This is it!* Hulohot moved to the outside wall and aimed down the staircase. Becker's legs dashed out of sight just around the curve. Hulohot fired in frustration. The bullet ricocheted down the stairwell.

As Hulohot dashed down the stairs after his prey, he kept to the outside wall for the widest angle view. As the staircase revolved into view before him, it seemed Becker was always 180 degrees ahead of him, just out of sight. Becker had taken the inside track, cutting off the angle and leaping four or five stairs at a time. Hulohot stayed with him. It would take only a single shot. Hulohot was gaining. He knew that even if Becker made the bottom, there was nowhere to run; Hulohot could shoot him in the back as he crossed the open patio. The desperate race spiraled downward.

Hulohot moved inside to the faster track. He sensed he was gaining. He could see Becker's shadow every time they passed an opening. Down. Down. Spiraling. It seemed that Becker was always just around the corner. Hulohot kept one eye on his shadow and one eye on the stairs.

Suddenly it appeared to Hulohot that Becker's

shadow had stumbled. It made an erratic lurch left and then seemed to spin in midair and sail back toward the center of the stairwell. Hulohot leapt forward. *I've got him!*

On the stairs in front of Hulohot, there was a flash of steel. It jabbed into the air from around the corner. It thrust forward like a fencer's foil at ankle level. Hulohot tried to shift left, but it was too late. The object was between his ankles. His back foot came forward, caught it hard, and the post slammed across his shin. Hulohot's arms went out for support but found only empty air. He was abruptly airborne, turning on his side. As Hulohot sailed downward, he passed over David Becker, prone on his stomach, arms outstretched. The candle pole in his hands was now caught up in Hulohot's legs as he spun downward.

Hulohot crashed into the outside wall before he hit the staircase. When he finally found the floor, he was tumbling. His gun clattered to the floor. Hulohot's body kept going, head over heels. He spiraled five complete 360-degree rotations before he rolled to a stop. Twelve more steps, and he would have tumbled out onto the patio.

CHAPTER 101

David Becker had never held a gun, but he was holding one now. Hulohot's body was twisted and mangled in the darkness of the Giralda staircase. Becker pressed the barrel of the gun against his assailant's temple and carefully knelt down. One twitch and Becker would fire. But there was no twitch. Hulohot was dead.

Becker dropped the gun and collapsed on the stairs. For the first time in ages he felt tears well up. He fought them. He knew there would be time for emotion later; now it was time to go home. Becker tried to stand, but he was too tired to move. He sat a long while, exhausted, on the stone staircase.

Absently, he studied the twisted body before him. The killer's eyes began to glaze over, gazing out at nothing in particular. Somehow, his glasses were still intact. They were odd glasses, Becker thought, with a wire protruding from behind the earpiece and leading to a pack of some sort on his belt. Becker was too exhausted to be curious.

As he sat alone in the staircase and collected his thoughts, Becker shifted his gaze to the ring on his

417

finger. His vision had cleared somewhat, and he could finally read the inscription. As he had suspected, it was not English. He stared at the engraving a long moment and then frowned. *This is worth killing for?*

The morning sun was blinding when Becker finally stepped out of the Giralda onto the patio. The pain in his side had subsided, and his vision was returning to normal. He stood a moment, in a daze, enjoying the fragrance of the orange blossoms. Then he began moving slowly across the patio.

As Becker strode away from the tower, a van skidded to a stop nearby. Two men jumped out. They were young and dressed in military fatigues. They advanced on Becker with the stiff precision of well-tuned machines.

'David Becker?' one demanded.

Becker stopped short, amazed they knew his name. 'Who . . . who are you?'

'Come with us, please. Right away.'

There was something unreal about the encounter – something that made Becker's nerve endings start to tingle again. He found himself backing away from them.

The shorter man gave Becker an icy stare. 'This way, Mr Becker. *Right now.*'

Becker turned to run. But he only took one step. One of the men drew a weapon. There was a shot.

A searing lance of pain erupted in Becker's chest. It rocketed to his skull. His fingers went stiff, and Becker fell. An instant later, there was nothing but blackness.

CHAPTER 102

Strathmore reached the TRANSLTR floor and stepped off the catwalk into an inch of water. The giant computer shuddered beside him. Huge droplets of water fell like rain through the swirling mist. The warning horns sounded like thunder.

The commander looked across at the failed main generators. Phil Chartrukian was there, his charred remains splayed across a set of coolant fins. The scene looked like some sort of perverse Halloween display.

Although Strathmore regretted the man's death, there was no doubt it had been 'a warranted casualty.' Phil Chartrukian had left Strathmore no choice. When the Sys-Sec came racing up from the depths, screaming about a virus, Strathmore met him on the landing and tried to talk sense to him. But Chartrukian was beyond reason. *We've got a virus! I'm calling Jabba!* When he tried to push past, the commander blocked his way. The landing was narrow. They struggled. The railing was low. It was ironic, Strathmore thought, that Chartrukian had been right about the virus all along.

The man's plunge had been chilling – a momentary

howl of terror and then silence. But it was not half as chilling as the next thing Commander Strathmore saw. Greg Hale was staring up at him from the shadows below, a look of utter horror on his face. It was then that Strathmore knew Greg Hale would die.

TRANSLTR crackled, and Strathmore turned his attention back to the task at hand. Kill power. The circuit breaker was on the other side of the freon pumps to the left of the body. Strathmore could see it clearly. All he had to do was pull a lever and the remaining power in Crypto would die. Then, after a few seconds, he could restart the main generators; all doorways and functions would come back on-line; the freon would start flowing again, and TRANSLTR would be safe.

But as Strathmore slogged toward the breaker, he realized there was one final obstacle: Chartrukian's body was still on the main generator's cooling fins. Killing and then restarting the main generator would only cause another power failure. The body had to be moved.

Strathmore eyed the grotesque remains and made his way over. Reaching up, he grabbed a wrist. The flesh was like Styrofoam. The tissue had been fried. The whole body was devoid of moisture. The commander closed his eyes, tightened his grip around the wrist, and pulled. The body slid an inch or two. Strathmore pulled harder. The body slid again. The commander braced himself and pulled with all his might. Suddenly he was tumbling backward. He landed hard on his backside up against a power casement. Struggling to sit up in the rising water, Strathmore stared down in horror at the object in his fist. It was Chartrukian's forearm. It had broken off at the elbow.

Upstairs, Susan continued her wait. She sat on the Node 3 couch feeling paralyzed. Hale lay at her feet. She couldn't imagine what was taking the commander so long. Minutes passed. She tried to push David from her thoughts, but it was no use. With every blast of the horns, Hale's words echoed inside her head: *I'm truly sorry about David Becker.* Susan thought she would lose her mind.

She was about to jump up and race onto the Crypto floor when finally it happened. Strathmore had thrown the switch and killed all power.

The silence that engulfed Crypto was instantaneous. The horns choked off midblare, and the Node 3 monitors flickered to black. Greg Hale's corpse disappeared into the darkness, and Susan instinctively yanked her legs up onto the couch. She wrapped Strathmore's suitcoat around her.

Darkness.

Silence.

She had never heard such quiet in Crypto. There'd always been the low hum of the generators. But now there was nothing, only the great beast heaving and sighing in relief. Crackling, hissing, slowly cooling down.

Susan closed her eyes and prayed for David. Her prayer was a simple one – that God protect the man she loved.

Not being a religious woman, Susan had never expected to hear a response to her prayer. But when there was a sudden shuddering against her chest, she jolted upright. She clutched her chest. A moment later she understood. The vibrations she felt were not the hand of God at all – they were coming from the commander's jacket pocket. He had set the vibrating silent-ring feature on his SkyPager. Someone was sending Commander Strathmore a message.

Six stories below, Strathmore stood at the circuit breaker. The sublevels of Crypto were now as dark as the deepest night. He stood a moment enjoying the blackness. The water poured down from above. It was a midnight storm. Strathmore tilted his head back and let the warm droplets wash away his guilt. *I'm a survivor.* He knelt and washed the last of Chartrukian's flesh from his hands.

His dreams for Digital Fortress had failed. He could accept that. Susan was all that mattered now. For the first time in decades, he truly understood that there was more to life than country and honor. *I sacrificed the best years of my life for country and honor. But what about love?* He had deprived himself for far too long. *And for what?* To watch some young professor steal away his dreams? Strathmore had nurtured Susan. He had protected her. He had *earned* her. And now, at last, he would have her. Susan would seek shelter in his arms when there was nowhere else to turn. She would come to him helpless, wounded by loss, and in time, he would show her that love heals all.

Honor. Country. Love. David Becker was about to die for all three.

CHAPTER 103

The commander rose through the trapdoor like Lazarus back from the dead. Despite his soggy clothes, his step was light. He strode toward Node 3 – toward Susan. Toward his future.

The Crypto floor was again bathed in light. Freon was flowing downward through the smoldering TRANSLTR like oxygenated blood. Strathmore knew it would take a few minutes for the coolant to reach the bottom of the hull and prevent the lowest processors from igniting, but he was certain he'd acted in time. He exhaled in victory, never suspecting the truth – that it was already too late.

I'm a survivor, he thought. Ignoring the gaping hole in the Node 3 wall, he strode to the electronic doors. They hissed open. He stepped inside.

Susan was standing before him, damp and tousled in his blazer. She looked like a freshman coed who'd been caught in the rain. He felt like the senior who'd lent her his varsity sweater. For the first time in years, he felt young. His dream was coming true.

But as Strathmore moved closer, he felt he was staring into the eyes of a woman he did not recognize. Her gaze was like ice. The softness was gone. Susan Fletcher stood rigid, like an immovable statue. The only perceptible motion were the tears welling in her eyes.

'Susan?'

A single tear rolled down her quivering cheek.

'What is it?' the commander pleaded.

The puddle of blood beneath Hale's body had spread across the carpet like an oil spill. Strathmore glanced uneasily at the corpse, then back at Susan. *Could she possibly know?* There was no way. Strathmore knew he had covered every base.

'Susan?' he said, stepping closer. 'What is it?'

Susan did not move.

'Are you worried about David?'

There was a slight quiver in her upper lip.

Strathmore stepped closer. He was going to reach for her, but he hesitated. The sound of David's name had apparently cracked the dam of grief. Slowly at first – a quiver, a tremble. And then a thundering wave of misery seemed to course through her veins. Barely able to control her shuddering lips, Susan opened her mouth to speak. Nothing came.

Without ever breaking the icy gaze she'd locked on Strathmore, she took her hand from the pocket of his blazer. In her hand was an object. She held it out, shaking.

Strathmore half expected to look down and see the Beretta leveled at his gut. But the gun was still on the floor, propped safely in Hale's hand. The object Susan was holding was smaller. Strathmore stared down at it, and an instant later, he understood.

As Strathmore stared, reality warped, and time slowed to a crawl. He could hear the sound of his own

424

heart. The man who had triumphed over giants for so many years had been outdone in an instant. Slain by love – by his own foolishness. In a simple act of chivalry, he had given Susan his jacket. And with it, his SkyPager.

Now it was Strathmore who went rigid. Susan's hand was shaking. The pager fell at Hale's feet. With a look of astonishment and betrayal that Strathmore would never forget, Susan Fletcher raced past him out of Node 3.

The commander let her go. In slow motion, he bent and retrieved the pager. There were no new messages – Susan had read them all. Strathmore scrolled desperately through the list.

SUBJECT: ENSEI TANKADO – TERMINATED
SUBJECT: PIERRE CLOUCHARDE – TERMINATED
SUBJECT: HANS HUBER – TERMINATED
SUBJECT: ROCÍO EVA GRANADA – TERMINATED . . .

The list went on. Strathmore felt a wave of horror. *I can explain! She will understand! Honor! Country!* But there was one message he had not yet seen – one message he could never explain. Trembling, he scrolled to the final transmission.

SUBJECT: DAVID BECKER – TERMINATED

Strathmore hung his head. His dream was over.

CHAPTER 104

Susan staggered out of node 3.

SUBJECT: DAVID BECKER — TERMINATED

As if in a dream, she moved toward Crypto's main exit. Greg Hale's voice echoed in her mind: *Susan, Strathmore's going to kill me! Susan, the commander's in love with you!*

Susan reached the enormous circular portal and began stabbing desperately at the keypad. The door did not move. She tried again, but the enormous slab refused to rotate. Susan let out a muted scream – apparently the power outage had deleted the exit codes. She was still trapped.

Without warning, two arms closed around her from behind, grasping her half-numb body. The touch was familiar yet repulsive. It lacked the brute strength of Greg Hale, but there was a desperate roughness to it, an inner determination like steel.

Susan turned. The man restraining her was desolate, frightened. It was a face she had never seen.

'Susan,' Strathmore begged, holding her. 'I can explain.' She tried to pull away.

426

The commander held fast.

Susan tried to scream, but she had no voice. She tried to run, but strong hands restrained her, pulling her backward.

'I love you,' the voice was whispering. 'I've loved you forever.'

Susan's stomach turned over and over.

'Stay with me.'

Susan's mind whirled with grisly images – David's bright-green eyes, slowly closing for the last time; Greg Hale's corpse seeping blood onto the carpet; Phil Chartrukian's burned and broken on the generators.

'The pain will pass,' the voice said. 'You'll love again.'

Susan heard nothing.

'Stay with me,' the voice pleaded. 'I'll heal your wounds.'

She struggled, helpless.

'I did it for us. We're made for each other. Susan, I love you.' The words flowed as if he had waited a decade to speak them. 'I love you! *I love you!*'

In that instant, thirty yards away, as if rebutting Strathmore's vile confession, TRANSLTR let out a savage, pitiless hiss. The sound was an entirely new one – a distant, ominous sizzling that seemed to grow like a serpent in the depths of the silo. The freon, it appeared, had not reached its mark in time.

The commander let go of Susan and turned toward the $2 billion computer. His eyes went wide with dread. 'No!' He grabbed his head. 'No!'

The six-story rocket began to tremble. Strathmore staggered a faltering step toward the thundering hull. Then he fell to his knees, a sinner before an angry god. It was no use. At the base of the silo, TRANSLTR's titanium-strontium processors had just ignited.

CHAPTER 105

A fireball racing upward through three million silicon chips makes a unique sound. The crackling of a forest fire, the howling of a tornado, the steaming gush of a geyser . . . all trapped within a reverberant hull. It was the devil's breath, pouring through a sealed cavern, looking for escape. Strathmore knelt transfixed by the horrific noise rising toward them. The world's most expensive computer was about to become an eight-story inferno.

In slow motion, Strathmore turned back toward Susan. She stood paralyzed beside the Crypto door. Strathmore stared at her tear-streaked face. She seemed to shimmer in the fluorescent light. *She's an angel,* he thought. He searched her eyes for heaven, but all he could see was death. It was the death of trust. Love and honor were gone. The fantasy that had kept him going all these years was dead. He would never have Susan Fletcher. Never. The sudden emptiness that gripped him was overwhelming.

Susan gazed vaguely toward TRANSLTR. She knew that trapped within the ceramic shell, a fireball was racing toward them. She sensed it rising faster and faster, feeding on the oxygen released by the burning chips. In moments the Crypto dome would be a blazing inferno.

Susan's mind told her to run, but David's dead weight pressed down all around her. She thought she heard his voice calling to her, telling her to escape, but there was nowhere to go. Crypto was a sealed tomb. It didn't matter; the thought of death did not frighten her. Death would stop the pain. She would be with David.

The Crypto floor began to tremble, as if below it an angry sea monster were rising out of the depths. David's voice seemed to be calling. *Run, Susan! Run!*

Strathmore was moving toward her now, his face a distant memory. His cool gray eyes were lifeless. The patriot who had lived in her mind a hero had died – a murderer. His arms were suddenly around her again, clutching desperately. He kissed her cheeks. 'Forgive me,' he begged. Susan tried to pull away, but Strathmore held on.

TRANSLTR began vibrating like a missile preparing to launch. The Crypto floor began to shake. Strathmore held tighter. 'Hold me, Susan. I need you.'

A violent surge of fury filled Susan's limbs. David's voice called out again. *I love you! Escape!* In a sudden burst of energy, Susan tore free. The roar from TRANSLTR became deafening. The fire was at the silo's peak. TRANSLTR groaned, straining at its seams.

David's voice seemed to lift Susan, guide her. She dashed across the Crypto floor and started up Strathmore's catwalk stairs. Behind her, TRANSLTR let out a deafening roar.

As the last of the silicon chips disintegrated, a tremendous updraft of heat tore through the upper casing of the silo and sent shards of ceramic thirty feet into the air. Instantly the oxygen-rich air of Crypto rushed in to fill the enormous vacuum.

Susan reached the upper landing and grabbed the banister when the tremendous rush of wind ripped at her body. It spun her around in time to see the deputy director of operations, far below, staring up at her from beside TRANSLTR. There was a storm raging all around him, and yet there was peace in his eyes. His lips parted, and he mouthed his final word. 'Susan.'

The air rushing into TRANSLTR ignited on contact. In a brilliant flash of light, Commander Trevor Strathmore passed from man, to silhouette, to legend.

When the blast hit Susan, it blew her back fifteen feet into Strathmore's office. All she remembered was a searing heat.

CHAPTER 106

In the window of the director's conference room, high above the Crypto dome, three faces appeared, breathless. The explosion had shaken the entire NSA complex. Leland Fontaine, Chad Brinkerhoff, and Midge Milken all stared out in silent horror.

Seventy feet below, the Crypto dome was blazing. The polycarbonate roof was still intact, but beneath the transparent shell, a fire raged. Black smoke swirled like fog inside the dome.

The three stared down without a word. The spectacle had an eerie grandeur to it.

Fontaine stood a long moment. He finally spoke, his voice faint but unwavering. 'Midge, get a crew down there . . . now.'

Across the suite, Fontaine's phone began to ring.

It was Jabba.

CHAPTER 107

Susan had no idea how much time had passed. A burning in her throat pulled her to her senses. Disoriented, she studied her surroundings. She was on a carpet behind a desk. The only light in the room was a strange orange flickering. The air smelled of burning plastic. The room she was standing in was not really a room at all; it was a devastated shell. The curtains were on fire, and the Plexiglas walls were smoldering.

Then she remembered it all.

David.

In a rising panic, she pulled herself to her feet. The air felt caustic in her windpipe. She stumbled to the doorway looking for a way out. As she crossed the threshold, her leg swung out over an abyss; she grabbed the door frame just in time. The catwalk had disappeared. Fifty feet below was a twisted collapse of steaming metal. Susan scanned the Crypto floor in horror. It was a sea of fire. The melted remains of three million silicon chips had erupted from TRANSLTR like lava. Thick, acrid smoke billowed upward. Susan knew the smell. Silicon smoke. Deadly poison.

Retreating into the remains of Strathmore's office, she began to feel faint. Her throat burned. The entire place was filled with a fiery light. Crypto was dying. *So will I*, she thought.

For a moment, she considered the only possible exit – Strathmore's elevator. But she knew it was useless; the electronics never would have survived the blast.

But as Susan made her way through the thickening smoke, she recalled Hale's words. *The elevator runs on power from the main building! I've seen the schematics!* Susan knew that was true. She also knew the entire shaft was encased in reinforced concrete.

The fumes swirled all around her. She stumbled through the smoke toward the elevator door. But when she got there, she saw that the elevator's call button was dark. Susan jabbed fruitlessly at the darkened panel, then she fell to her knees and pounded on the door.

She stopped almost instantly. Something was whirring behind the doors. Startled, she looked up. It sounded like the carriage was right there! Susan stabbed at the button again. Again, a whirring behind the doors.

Suddenly she saw it.

The call button was not dead – it had just been covered with black soot. It now glowed faintly beneath her smudged fingerprints.

There's power!

With a surge of hope, she punched at the button. Over and over, something behind the doors engaged. She could hear the ventilation fan in the elevator car. *The carriage is here! Why won't the damn doors open?*

Through the smoke she spied the tiny secondary keypad – lettered buttons, A through Z. In a wave of despair, Susan remembered. The password.

The smoke was starting to curl in through the melted window frames. Again she banged on the elevator doors. They refused to open. *The password!* she thought. *Strathmore never told me the password!* Silicon smoke was now filling the office. Choking, Susan fell against the elevator in defeat. The ventilation fan was running just a few feet away. She lay there, dazed, gulping for air.

She closed her eyes, but again David's voice woke her. *Escape, Susan! Open the door! Escape!* She opened her eyes expecting to see his face, those wild green eyes, that playful smile. But the letters A–Z came into focus. *The password . . .* Susan stared at the letters on the keypad. She could barely keep them in focus. On the LED below the keypad, five empty spots awaited entry. *A five-character password*, she thought. She instantly knew the odds: twenty-six to the fifth power; 11,881,376 possible choices. At one guess every second, it would take nineteen weeks . . .

As Susan Fletcher lay choking on the floor beneath the keypad, the commander's pathetic voice came to her. He was calling to her again. *I love you, Susan! I've always loved you! Susan! Susan! Susan . . .*

She knew he was dead, and yet his voice was relentless. She heard her name over and over.

Susan . . . Susan . . .

Then, in a moment of chilling clarity, she knew.

Trembling weakly, she reached up to the keypad and typed the password.

S . . . U . . . S . . . A . . . N

An instant later, the doors slid open.

CHAPTER 108

Strathmore's elevator dropped fast. Inside the carriage, Susan sucked deep breaths of fresh air into her lungs. Dazed, she steadied herself against the wall as the car slowed to a stop. A moment later some gears clicked, and the conveyor began moving again, this time horizontally. Susan felt the carriage accelerate as it began rumbling toward the main NSA complex. Finally it whirred to a stop, and the doors opened.

Coughing, Susan Fletcher stumbled into a darkened cement corridor. She found herself in a tunnel – low-ceilinged and narrow. A double yellow line stretched out before her. The line disappeared into an empty, dark hollow.

The Underground Highway . . .

She staggered toward the tunnel, holding the wall for guidance. Behind her, the elevator door slid shut. Once again Susan Fletcher was plunged into darkness.

Silence.

Nothing except a faint humming in the walls.

A humming that grew louder.

Suddenly it was as if dawn were breaking. The

435

blackness thinned to a hazy gray. The walls of the tunnel began to take shape. All at once, a small vehicle whipped around the corner, its headlight blinding her. Susan stumbled back against the wall and shielded her eyes. There was a gust of air, and the transport whipped past.

An instant later there was a deafening squeal of rubber on cement. The hum approached once again, this time in reverse. Seconds later the vehicle came to a stop beside her.

'Ms Fletcher!' an astonished voice exclaimed.

Susan gazed at a vaguely familiar shape in the driver's seat of an electric golf cart.

'Jesus.' The man gasped. 'Are you okay? We thought you were dead!'

Susan stared blankly.

'Chad Brinkerhoff,' he sputtered, studying the shellshocked cryptographer. 'Directorial PA.'

Susan could only manage a dazed whimper. 'TRANSLTR . . .'

Brinkerhoff nodded. 'Forget it. Get on!'

The beam of the golf cart's headlights whipped across the cement walls.

'There's a virus in the main databank,' Brinkerhoff blurted.

'I know,' Susan heard herself whisper.

'We need you to help us.'

Susan was fighting back the tears. 'Strathmore . . . he . . .'

'We know,' Brinkerhoff said. 'He bypassed Gauntlet.'

'Yes . . . and . . .' The words got stuck in her throat. *He killed David!*

Brinkerhoff put a hand on her shoulder. 'Almost there, Ms Fletcher. Just hold on.'

The high-speed Kensington golf cart rounded a corner and skidded to a stop. Beside them, branching off perpendicular to the tunnel, was a hallway, dimly lit by red floor lighting.

'Come on,' Brinkerhoff said, helping her out.

He guided her into the corridor. Susan drifted behind him in a fog. The tiled passageway sloped downward at a steep incline. Susan grabbed the handrail and followed Brinkerhoff down. The air began to grow cooler. They continued their descent.

As they dropped deeper into the earth, the tunnel narrowed. From somewhere behind them came the echo of footsteps – a strong, purposeful gait. The footsteps grew louder. Both Brinkerhoff and Susan stopped and turned.

Striding toward them was an enormous black man. Susan had never seen him before. As he approached, he fixed her with a penetrating stare.

'Who's this?' he demanded.

'Susan Fletcher,' Brinkerhoff replied.

The enormous man arched his eyebrows. Even sooty and soaked, Susan Fletcher was more striking than he had imagined. 'And the commander?' he demanded.

Brinkerhoff shook his head.

The man said nothing. He stared off a moment. Then he turned back to Susan. 'Leland Fontaine,' he said, offering her his hand. 'Glad you're okay.'

Susan stared. She'd always known she'd meet the director someday, but this was not the introduction she'd envisioned.

'Come along, Ms Fletcher,' Fontaine said, leading the way. 'We'll need all the help we can get.'

Looming in the reddish haze at the bottom of the tunnel, a steel wall blocked their way. Fontaine approached and typed an entry code into a recessed cipher box. He then placed his right hand against a small glass panel. A strobe flashed. A moment later the massive wall thundered left.

There was only one NSA chamber more sacred than Crypto, and Susan Fletcher sensed she was about to enter it.

CHAPTER 109

The command center for the NSA's main databank looked like a scaled-down NASA mission control. A dozen computer workstations faced the thirty-foot by forty-foot video wall at the far end of the room. On the screen, numbers and diagrams flashed in rapid succession, appearing and disappearing as if someone were channel surfing. A handful of technicians raced wildly from station to station trailing long sheets of printout paper and yelling commands. It was chaos.

Susan stared at the dazzling facility. She vaguely remembered that 250 metric tons of earth had been excavated to create it. The chamber was located 214 feet below ground, where it would be totally impervious to flux bombs and nuclear blasts.

On a raised workstation in the center of the room stood Jabba. He bellowed orders from his platform like a king to his subjects. Illuminated on the screen directly behind him was a message. The message was all too familiar to Susan. The billboard-size text hung ominously over Jabba's head:

As if trapped in some surreal nightmare, Susan followed Fontaine toward the podium. Her world was a slow-motion blur.

Jabba saw them coming and wheeled like an enraged bull. 'I built Gauntlet for a reason!'

'Gauntlet's gone,' Fontaine replied evenly.

'Old news, Director,' Jabba spat. 'The shock wave knocked me on my ass! Where's Strathmore?'

'Commander Strathmore is dead.'

'Poetic fucking justice.'

'Cool it, Jabba,' the director ordered. 'Bring us up to speed. How bad is this virus?'

Jabba stared at the director a long moment, and then without warning, he burst out laughing. 'A *virus?*' His harsh guffaw resonated through the underground chamber. 'Is that what you think this is?'

Fontaine kept his cool. Jabba's insolence was way out of line, but Fontaine knew this was not the time or place to handle it. Down here, Jabba outranked God himself. Computer problems had a way of ignoring the normal chain of command.

'It's *not* a virus?' Brinkerhoff exclaimed hopefully.

Jabba snorted in disgust. '*Viruses* have replication strings, pretty boy! *This* doesn't!'

Susan hovered nearby, unable to focus.

'Then what's going on?' Fontaine demanded. 'I thought we had a virus.'

Jabba sucked in a long breath and lowered his voice. 'Viruses . . .' he said, wiping sweat from his face. 'Viruses reproduce. They create clones. They're vain and stupid – binary egomaniacs. They pump out babies faster than rabbits. That's their weakness – you can cross-breed them into oblivion if you know what you're doing. Unfortunately, this program has no ego, no need to reproduce. It's clear-headed and focused. In fact, when it's accomplished its objective here, it will probably commit digital suicide.' Jabba held out his arms reverently to the projected havoc on the enormous screen. 'Ladies and gentlemen.' He sighed. 'Meet the kamikaze of computer invaders . . . the *worm*.'

'*Worm*?' Brinkerhoff groaned. It seemed like a mundane term to describe the insidious intruder.

'Worm.' Jabba smoldered. 'No complex structures, just instinct – eat, shit, crawl. That's it. Simplicity. Deadly simplicity. It does what it's programmed to do and then checks out.'

Fontaine eyed Jabba sternly. 'And what is this worm programmed to do?'

'No clue,' Jabba replied. 'Right now, it's spreading out and attaching itself to all our classified data. After that, it could do anything. It might decide to delete all the files, or it might just decide to print smiley faces on certain White House transcripts.'

Fontaine's voice remained cool and collected. 'Can you stop it?'

Jabba let out a long sigh and faced the screen. 'I have no idea. It all depends on how pissed off the author is.' He pointed to the message on the wall. 'Anybody want to tell me what the hell *that* means?'

ONLY THE TRUTH WILL SAVE YOU NOW
ENTER PASS-KEY _____

441

Jabba waited for a response and got none. 'Looks like someone's messing with us, Director. Blackmail. This is a ransom note if I ever saw one.'

Susan's voice was a whisper, empty and hollow. 'It's . . . Ensei Tankado.'

Jabba turned to her. He stared a moment, wide-eyed. '*Tankado?*'

Susan nodded weakly. 'He wanted our confession . . . about TRANSLTR . . . but it cost him his—'

'Confession?' Brinkerhoff interrupted, looking stunned. 'Tankado wants us to confess we have TRANSLTR? I'd say it's a bit late for *that!*'

Susan opened her mouth to speak, but Jabba took over. 'Looks like Tankado's got a kill-code,' he said, gazing up at the message on the screen.

Everyone turned.

'Kill code?' Brinkerhoff demanded.

Jabba nodded. 'Yeah. A pass-key that stops the worm. Simply put, if we admit we have TRANSLTR, Tankado gives us a kill-code. We type it in and save the databank. Welcome to digital extortion.'

Fontaine stood like rock, unwavering. 'How long have we got?'

'About an hour,' Jabba said. 'Just time enough to call a press conference and spill our guts.'

'Recommendation,' Fontaine demanded. 'What do you propose we do?'

'A *recommendation?*' Jabba blurted in disbelief. 'You want a recommendation? I'll give you a recommendation! You quit fucking around, *that's* what you do!'

'Easy,' the director warned.

'Director,' Jabba sputtered. 'Right now, Ensei Tankado *owns* this databank! Give him *whatever* he wants. If he wants the world to know about TRANSLTR, call CNN, and drop your shorts. TRANSLTR's a hole in the ground now anyway – what the hell do *you* care?'

There was a silence. Fontaine seemed to be considering his options. Susan began to speak, but Jabba beat her to it.

'What are you waiting for, Director! Get Tankado on the phone! Tell him you'll play ball! We need that kill-code, or this whole place is going down!'

Nobody moved.

'Are you all insane?' Jabba screamed. 'Call Tankado! Tell him we fold! Get me that kill-code! NOW!' Jabba whipped out his cellular phone and switched it on. 'Never mind! Get me his number! I'll call the little prick *myself!*'

'Don't bother,' Susan said in a whisper. 'Tankado's dead.'

After a moment of confused astonishment, the implications hit Jabba like a bullet to the gut. The huge Sys-Sec looked like he was about to crumble. *'Dead? But then . . . that means . . . we can't . . .'*

'That means we'll need a new plan,' Fontaine said matter-of-factly.

Jabba's eyes were still glazed with shock when someone in the back of the room began shouting wildly.

'Jabba! Jabba!'

It was Soshi Kuta, his head techie. She came running toward the podium trailing a long printout. She looked terrified.

'Jabba!' She gasped. 'The worm . . . I just found out what it's programmed to do!' Soshi thrust the paper into Jabba's hands. 'I pulled this from the

443

system-activity probe! We isolated the worm's execute commands – have a look at the programming! Look what it's planning to do!'

Dazed, the chief Sys-Sec read the printout. Then he grabbed the handrail for support.

'Oh, Jesus,' Jabba gasped. 'Tankado . . . you *bastard!*'

CHAPTER 110

Jabba stared blankly at the printout Soshi had just handed him. Pale, he wiped his forehead on his sleeve. 'Director, we have no choice. We've got to kill power to the databank.'

'Unacceptable,' Fontaine replied. 'The results would be devastating.'

Jabba knew the director was right. There were over three thousand ISDN connections tying into the NSA databank from all over the world. Every day military commanders accessed up-to-the-instant satellite photos of enemy movement. Lockheed engineers downloaded compartmentalized blueprints of new weaponry. Field operatives accessed mission updates. The NSA databank was the backbone of thousands of U.S. government operations. Shutting it down without warning would cause life-and-death intelligence blackouts all over the globe.

'I'm aware of the implications, sir,' Jabba said, 'but we have no choice.'

'Explain yourself,' Fontaine ordered. He shot a quick glance at Susan standing beside him on the podium. She seemed miles away.

Jabba took a deep breath and wiped his brow again. From the look on his face, it was clear to the group on the podium that they were not going to like what he had to say.

'This worm,' Jabba began. 'This worm is not an ordinary degenerative cycle. It's a *selective* cycle. In other words, it's a worm with *taste*.'

Brinkerhoff opened his mouth to speak, but Fontaine waved him off.

'Most destructive applications wipe a databank clean,' Jabba continued, 'but this one is more complex. It deletes only those files that fall within certain parameters.'

'You mean it won't attack the *whole* databank?' Brinkerhoff asked hopefully. 'That's *good*, right?'

'No!' Jabba exploded. 'It's bad! It's *very* fucking *bad!*'

'Cool it!' Fontaine ordered. 'What parameters is this worm looking for? Military? Covert ops?'

Jabba shook his head. He eyed Susan, who was still distant, and then Jabba's eyes rose to meet the director's. 'Sir, as you know, anyone who wants to tie into this databank from the outside has to pass a series of security gates before they're admitted.'

Fontaine nodded. The databank's access hierarchies were brilliantly conceived; authorized personnel could dial in via the Internet and World Wide Web. Depending on their authorization sequence, they were permitted access to their own compartmentalized zones.

'Because we're tied to the global Internet,' Jabba explained, 'hackers, foreign governments, and EFF sharks circle this databank twenty-four hours a day and try to break in.'

'Yes,' Fontaine said, 'and twenty-four hours a day, our security filters keep them out. What's your point?'

Jabba gazed down at the printout. 'My point is this. Tankado's worm is not targeting our *data*.' He cleared his throat. 'It's targeting our *security filters*.'

Fontaine blanched. Apparently he understood the implications – this worm was targeting the filters that kept the NSA databank confidential. Without filters, all of the information in the databank would become accessible to everyone on the outside.

'We need to shut down,' Jabba repeated. 'In about an hour, every third grader with a modem is going to have top U.S. security clearance.'

Fontaine stood a long moment without saying a word.

Jabba waited impatiently and finally turned to Soshi. 'Soshi! VR! NOW!'

Soshi dashed off.

Jabba relied on VR often. In most computer circles, VR meant 'virtual reality,' but at the NSA it meant *vis-rep* – visual representation. In a world full of technicians and politicians all having different levels of technical understanding, a graphic representation was often the only way to make a point; a single plummeting graph usually aroused ten times the reaction inspired by volumes of spreadsheets. Jabba knew a VR of the current crisis would make its point instantly.

'VR!' Soshi yelled from a terminal at the back of the room.

A computer-generated diagram flashed to life on the wall before them. Susan gazed up absently, detached from the madness around her. Everyone in the room followed Jabba's gaze to the screen.

The diagram before them resembled a bull's-eye. In the center was a red circle marked DATA. Around the center were five concentric circles of differing thickness and color. The outermost circle was faded, almost transparent.

'We've got a five-tier level of defense,' Jabba explained. 'A primary Bastion Host, two sets of packet filters for FTP and X-eleven, a tunnel block, and finally a PEM-based authorization window right off the Truffle project. The outside shield that's disappearing represents the exposed host. It's practically gone. Within the hour, all five shields will follow. After that, the world pours in. Every byte of NSA data becomes public domain.'

Fontaine studied the VR, his eyes smoldering.

Brinkerhoff let out a weak whimper. 'This worm can open our databank to the world?'

'Child's play for Tankado,' Jabba snapped. 'Gauntlet was our fail-safe. Strathmore blew it.'

'It's an act of war,' Fontaine whispered, an edge in his voice.

Jabba shook his head. 'I really doubt Tankado ever meant for it to go this far. I suspect he intended to be around to stop it.'

Fontaine gazed up at the screen and watched the first of the five walls disappear entirely.

'Bastion Host is toast!' a technician yelled from the back of the room. 'Second shield's exposed!'

'We've got to start shutting down,' Jabba urged. 'From the looks of the VR, we've got about forty-five minutes. Shutdown is a complex process.'

It was true. The NSA databank had been constructed in such a way as to ensure it would never lose power – accidentally or if attacked. Multiple fail-safes for phone and power were buried in reinforced steel canisters deep underground, and in addition to the feeds from within the NSA complex, there were multiple backups off main public grids. Shutting down involved a complex series of confirmations and protocols – significantly more complicated than the average nuclear submarine missile launch.

'We have time,' Jabba said, 'if we hurry. Manual shutdown should take about thirty minutes.'

Fontaine continued staring up at the VR, apparently pondering his options.

'Director!' Jabba exploded. 'When these firewalls fall, every user on the planet will be issued top-security clearance! And I'm talking *upper level!* Records of covert ops! Overseas agents! Names and locations of everyone in the federal witness protection program! Launch code confirmations! We must shut down! Now!'

The director seemed unmoved. 'There must be some other way.'

'Yes,' Jabba spat, 'there is! The kill-code! But the only guy who knows it happens to be dead!'

'How about brute force?' Brinkerhoff blurted. 'Can we guess the kill-code?'

Jabba threw up his arms. 'For Christ's sake! Kill-codes are like encryption keys – random! Impossible to guess! If you think you can type 600 trillion entries in the next forty-five minutes, be my guest!'

'The kill-code's in Spain,' Susan offered weakly.

Everyone on the podium turned. It was the first thing she had said in a long time.

Susan looked up, bleary-eyed. 'Tankado gave it away when he died.'

Everyone looked lost.

'The pass-key . . .' Susan shivered as she spoke. 'Commander Strathmore sent someone to find it.'

'And?' Jabba demanded. 'Did Strathmore's man *find* it?'

Susan tried to fight it, but the tears began to flow. 'Yes,' she choked. 'I think so.'

CHAPTER 111

An earsplitting yell cut through the control room. *'Sharks!'* It was Soshi.

Jabba spun toward the VR. Two thin lines had appeared outside the concentric circles. They looked like sperm trying to breach a reluctant egg.

'Blood's in the water, folks!' Jabba turned back to the director. 'I need a decision. Either we start shutting down, or we'll never make it. As soon as these two intruders see the Bastion Host is down, they'll send up a war cry.'

Fontaine did not respond. He was deep in thought. Susan Fletcher's news of the pass-key in Spain seemed promising to him. He shot a glance toward Susan in the back of the room. She appeared to be in her own world, collapsed in a chair, her head buried in her hands. Fontaine was unsure exactly what had triggered the reaction, but whatever it was, he had no time for it now.

'I need a decision!' Jabba demanded. 'Now!'

Fontaine looked up. He spoke calmly. 'Okay, you've got one. We are *not* shutting down. We're going to wait.'

Jabba's jaw dropped. *'What?* But that's—'

'A gamble,' Fontaine interrupted. 'A gamble we just might win.' He took Jabba's cellular and punched a few keys. 'Midge,' he said. 'It's Leland Fontaine. Listen carefully. . . .'

CHAPTER 112

'You better know what the hell you're doing, Director,' Jabba hissed. 'We're about to lose shutdown capability.'

Fontaine did not respond.

As if on cue, the door at the back of the control room opened, and Midge came dashing in. She arrived breathless at the podium. 'Director! The switchboard is patching it through right now!'

Fontaine turned expectantly toward the screen on the front wall. Fifteen seconds later the screen crackled to life.

The image on screen was snowy and stilted at first, and gradually grew sharper. It was a QuickTime digital transmission – only five frames per second. The image revealed two men. One was pale with a buzz cut, the other a blond all-American. They were seated facing the camera like two newscasters waiting to go on the air.

'What the hell is this?' Jabba demanded.

'Sit tight,' Fontaine ordered.

The men appeared to be inside a van of some sort. Electronic cabling hung all around them. The audio connection crackled to life. Suddenly there was background noise.

'Inbound audio,' a technician called from behind them. 'Five seconds till two-way.'

'Who are they?' Brinkerhoff asked, uneasily.

'Eye in the sky,' Fontaine replied, gazing up at the two men he had sent to Spain. It had been a necessary precaution. Fontaine had believed in almost every aspect of Strathmore's plan – the regrettable but necessary removal of Ensei Tankado, rewriting Digital Fortress – it was all solid. But there was one thing that made Fontaine nervous: the use of Hulohot. Hulohot was skilled, but he was a mercenary. Was he trustworthy? Would he take the pass-key for himself? Fontaine wanted Hulohot covered, just in case, and he had taken the requisite measures.

CHAPTER 113

'Absolutely not!' the man with the buzz cut yelled into the camera. 'We have orders! We report to Director Leland Fontaine and Leland Fontaine only!'

Fontaine looked mildly amused. 'You don't know who I am, do you?'

'Doesn't matter, does it?' the blond fired hotly.

'Let me explain,' Fontaine interjected. 'Let me explain something right now.'

Seconds later, the two men were red-faced, spilling their guts to the director of the National Security Agency. 'D-director,' the blond stammered, 'I'm Agent Coliander. This is Agent Smith.'

'Fine,' Fontaine said. 'Just brief us.'

At the back of the room, Susan Fletcher sat and fought the suffocating loneliness that pressed down around her. Eyes closed, and ears ringing, she wept. Her body had gone numb. The mayhem in the control room faded to a dull murmur.

The gathering on the podium listened, restless, as Agent Smith began his briefing.

'On your orders, Director,' Smith began, 'we've

455

been here in Seville for two days, trailing Mr Ensei Tankado.'

'Tell me about the kill,' Fontaine said impatiently.

Smith nodded. 'We observed from inside the van at about fifty meters. The kill was smooth. Hulohot was obviously a pro. But afterward his directive went awry. Company arrived. Hulohot never got the item.'

Fontaine nodded. The agents had contacted him in South America with news that something had gone wrong, so Fontaine had cut his trip short.

Coliander took over. 'We stayed with Hulohot as you ordered. But he never made a move for the morgue. Instead, he picked up the trail of some other guy. Looked private. Coat and tie.'

'Private?' Fontaine mused. It sounded like a Strathmore play – wisely keeping the NSA out of it.

'FTP filters failing!' a technician called out.

'We need the item,' Fontaine pressed. 'Where is Hulohot now?'

Smith looked over his shoulder. 'Well . . . he's with us, sir.'

Fontaine exhaled. 'Where?' It was the best news he'd heard all day.

Smith reached toward the lens to make an adjustment. The camera swept across the inside of the van to reveal two limp bodies propped against the back wall. Both were motionless. One was a large man with twisted wire-rim glasses. The other was young with a shock of dark hair and a bloody shirt.

'Hulohot's the one on the left,' Smith offered.

'Hulohot's dead?' the director demanded.

'Yes, sir.'

Fontaine knew there would be time for explanations

later. He glanced up at the thinning shields. 'Agent Smith,' he said slowly and clearly. 'The item. I need it.'

Smith looked sheepish. 'Sir, we still have no idea *what* the item is. We're on a need-to-know.'

CHAPTER 114

'Then look again!' Fontaine declared.

The director watched in dismay as the stilted image of the agents searched the two limp bodies in the van for a list of random numbers and letters.

Jabba was pale. 'Oh my God, they can't find it. We're dead!'

'Losing FTP filters!' a voice yelled. 'Third shield's exposed!' There was a new flurry of activity.

On the front screen, the agent with the buzz cut held out his arms in defeat. 'Sir, the pass-key isn't here. We've searched both men. Pockets. Clothing. Wallets. No sign at all. Hulohot was wearing a Monocle computer, and we've checked that too. It doesn't look like he ever transmitted anything remotely resembling random characters – only a list of kills.'

'Dammit!' Fontaine seethed, suddenly losing his cool. 'It's got to be there! Keep looking!'

Jabba had apparently seen enough – Fontaine had gambled and lost. Jabba took over. The huge Sys-Sec descended from his pulpit like a storm off a mountain. He swept through his army of programmers calling out commands. 'Access auxiliary kills! Start shutting it down! Do it now!'

'We'll never make it!' Soshi yelled. 'We need a half hour! By the time we shut down, it will be too late!'

Jabba opened his mouth to reply, but he was cut short by a scream of agony from the back of the room.

Everyone turned. Like an apparition, Susan Fletcher rose from her crouched position in the rear of the chamber. Her face was white, her eyes transfixed on the freeze-frame of David Becker, motionless and bloody, propped up on the floor of the van.

'You killed him!' she screamed. *'You killed him!'* She stumbled toward the image and reached out. 'David . . .'

Everyone looked up in confusion. Susan advanced, still calling, her eyes never leaving the projection of David's body. 'David,' she gasped, staggering forward. 'Oh, David . . . how could they—'

Fontaine seemed lost. 'You know this man?'

Susan swayed unsteadily as she passed the podium. She stopped a few feet in front of the enormous projection and stared up, bewildered and numb, calling over and over to the man she loved.

CHAPTER 115

The emptiness in David Becker's mind was absolute. *I am dead.* And yet there was a sound. A distant voice . . .

'David.'

There was a dizzying burning beneath his arm. His blood was filled with fire. *My body is not my own.* And yet there was a voice, calling to him. It was thin, distant. But it was part of him. There were other voices too – unfamiliar, unimportant. Calling out. He fought to block them out. There was only one voice that mattered. It faded in and out.

'David . . . I'm sorry . . .'

There was a mottled light. Faint at first, a single slit of grayness. Growing. Becker tried to move. Pain. He tried to speak. Silence. The voice kept calling.

Someone was near him, lifting him. Becker moved toward the voice. Or was he being moved? It was calling. He gazed absently at the illuminated image. He could see her on a small screen. It was a woman, staring up at him from another world. *Is she watching me die?*

'David . . .'

460

The voice was familiar. She was an angel. She had come for him. The angel spoke. 'David, I love you.'

Suddenly he knew.

Susan reached out toward the screen, crying, laughing, lost in a torrent of emotions. She wiped fiercely at her tears. 'David, I – I thought . . .'

Field Agent Smith eased David Becker into the seat facing the monitor. 'He's a little woozy, ma'am. Give him a second.'

'B-but,' Susan was stammering, 'I saw a transmission. It said . . .'

Smith nodded. 'We saw it too. Hulohot counted his chickens a little early.'

'But the blood . . .'

'Flesh wound,' Smith replied. 'We slapped a gauze on it.'

Susan couldn't speak.

Agent Coliander piped in from off camera. 'We hit him with the new J23 – long-acting stun gun. Probably hurt like hell, but we got him off the street.'

'Don't worry, ma'am,' Smith assured. 'He'll be fine.'

David Becker stared at the TV monitor in front of him. He was disoriented, light-headed. The image on the screen was of a room – a room filled with chaos. Susan was there. She was standing on an open patch of floor, gazing up at him.

She was crying and laughing. 'David. Thank God! I thought I had lost you!'

He rubbed his temple. He moved in front of the screen and pulled the gooseneck microphone toward his mouth. 'Susan?'

Susan gazed up in wonder. David's rugged features

461

now filled the entire wall before her. His voice boomed.

'Susan, I need to ask you something.' The resonance and volume of Becker's voice seemed to momentarily suspend the action in the databank. Everyone stopped midstride and turned.

'Susan Fletcher,' the voice resonated, 'will you marry me?'

A hush spread across the room. A clipboard clattered to the floor along with a mug of pencils. No one bent to pick them up. There was only the faint hum of the terminal fans and the sound of David Becker's steady breathing in his microphone.

'D-David . . .' Susan stammered, unaware that thirty-seven people stood riveted behind her. 'You already asked me, remember? Five months ago. I said yes.'

'I know.' He smiled. 'But this time' – he extended his left hand into the camera and displayed a golden band on his fourth finger – 'this time I have a ring.'

462

CHAPTER 116

'Read it, Mr Becker!' Fontaine ordered.

Jabba sat sweating, hands poised over his keyboard. 'Yes,' he said, 'read the blessed inscription!'

Susan Fletcher stood with them, weak-kneed and aglow. Everyone in the room had stopped what they were doing and stared up at the enormous projection of David Becker. The professor twisted the ring in his fingers and studied the engraving.

'And read *carefully!*' Jabba commanded. 'One typo, and we're *screwed!*'

Fontaine gave Jabba a harsh look. If there was one thing the director of the NSA knew about, it was pressure situations; creating additional tension was never wise. 'Relax, Mr Becker. If we make a mistake, we'll reenter the code till we get it right.'

'Bad advice, Mr Becker,' Jabba snapped. 'Get it right the first time. Kill-codes usually have a penalty clause – to prevent trial-and-error guessing. Make an incorrect entry, and the cycle will probably accelerate. Make *two* incorrect entries, and it will lock us out permanently. Game over.'

The director frowned and turned back to the screen.

'Mr Becker? My mistake. Read carefully – read *extremely* carefully.'

Becker nodded and studied the ring for a moment. Then he calmly began reciting the inscription. 'Q . . . U . . . I . . . S . . . space . . . C . . .'

Jabba and Susan interrupted in unison. '*Space?*' Jabba stopped typing. 'There's a *space?*'

Becker shrugged, checking the ring. 'Yeah. There's a bunch of them.'

'Am I missing something?' Fontaine demanded. 'What are we waiting for?'

'Sir,' Susan said, apparently puzzled. 'It's . . . it's just . . .'

'I agree,' Jabba said. 'It's strange. Passwords *never* have spaces.'

Brinkerhoff swallowed hard. 'So, what are you saying?'

'He's saying,' Susan interjected, 'that this may not be a kill-code.'

Brinkerhoff cried out, 'Of course it's the kill-code! What else could it be? Why else would Tankado give it away? Who the hell inscribes a bunch of random letters on a ring?'

Fontaine silenced Brinkerhoff with a sharp glare.

'Ah . . . folks?' Becker interjected, appearing hesitant to get involved. 'You keep mentioning *random* letters. I think I should let you know . . . the letters on this ring *aren't* random.'

Everyone on the podium blurted in unison. 'What!'

Becker looked uneasy. 'Sorry, but there are definitely words here. I'll admit they're inscribed pretty close together; at first glance it appears random, but if you look closely you'll see the inscription is actually . . . well . . . it's *Latin*.'

Jabba gaped. 'You're shitting me!'

Becker shook his head. 'No. It reads, *"Quis custodiet ipsos custodes."* It translates roughly to—'

'Who will guard the guards!' Susan interrupted, finishing David's sentence.

Becker did a double-take. 'Susan, I didn't know you could—'

'It's from *Satires* of Juvenal,' she exclaimed. 'Who will guard the guards? Who will guard the NSA while we guard the world? It was Tankado's favorite saying!'

'So,' Midge demanded, 'is it the pass-key, or not?'

'It *must* be the pass-key,' Brinkerhoff declared.

Fontaine stood silent, apparently processing the information.

'I don't know if it's the key,' Jabba said. 'It seems unlikely to me that Tankado would use a nonrandom construction.'

'Just omit the spaces,' Brinkerhoff cried, 'and type the damn code!'

Fontaine turned to Susan. 'What's *your* take, Ms Fletcher?'

She thought a moment. She couldn't quite put her finger on it, but something didn't feel right. Susan knew Tankado well enough to know he thrived on simplicity. His proofs and programming were always crystalline and absolute. The fact that the spaces needed to be removed seemed odd. It was a minor detail, but it was a flaw, definitely not *clean* – not what Susan would have expected as Ensei Tankado's crowning blow.

'It doesn't feel right,' Susan finally said. 'I don't think it's the key.'

Fontaine sucked in a long breath, his dark eyes probing hers. 'Ms Fletcher, in your mind, if this is not the key, why would Ensei Tankado have given it away? If he knew we'd murdered him – don't you assume he'd want to punish us by making the ring disappear?'

A new voice interrupted the dialogue. 'Ah . . . Director?'

All eyes turned to the screen. It was Agent Coliander in Seville. He was leaning over Becker's shoulder and speaking into the mic. 'For whatever it's worth, I'm not so sure Mr Tankado *knew* he was being murdered.'

'I beg your pardon?' Fontaine demanded.

'Hulohot was a pro, sir. We saw the kill – only fifty meters away. All evidence suggests Tankado was unaware.'

'Evidence?' Brinkerhoff demanded. '*What* evidence? Tankado gave away this ring. That's proof enough!'

'Agent Smith,' Fontaine interrupted. 'What makes you think Ensei Tankado was unaware he was being killed?'

Smith cleared his throat. 'Hulohot killed him with an NTB – a noninvasive trauma bullet. It's a rubber pod that strikes the chest and spreads out. Silent. Very clean. Mr Tankado would only have felt a sharp thump before going into cardiac arrest.'

'A trauma bullet,' Becker mused to himself. 'That explains the bruising.'

'It's doubtful,' Smith added, 'that Tankado associated the sensation with a gunman.'

'And yet he gave away his ring,' Fontaine stated.

'True, sir. But he never looked for his assailant. A victim *always* looks for his assailant when he's been shot. It's instinct.'

Fontaine puzzled. 'And you're saying Tankado didn't look for Hulohot?'

'No, sir. We have it on film if you'd like—'

'X-eleven filter's going!' a technician yelled. 'The worm's halfway there!'

'Forget the film,' Brinkerhoff declared. 'Type in the damn kill-code and finish this!'

Jabba sighed, suddenly the cool one. 'Director, if we enter the wrong code . . .'

'Yes,' Susan interrupted, 'if Tankado didn't suspect we killed him, we've got some questions to answer.'

'What's our time frame, Jabba?' Fontaine demanded.

Jabba looked up at the VR. 'About twenty minutes. I suggest we use the time wisely.'

Fontaine was silent a long moment. Then sighed heavily. 'All right. Run the film.'

CHAPTER 117

'Transmitting video in ten seconds,' Agent Smith's voice crackled. 'We're dropping every other frame as well as audio – we'll run as close to real time as possible.'

Everyone on the podium stood silent, watching, waiting. Jabba typed a few keys and rearranged the video wall. Tankado's message appeared on the far left:

ONLY THE TRUTH WILL SAVE YOU NOW

On the right of the wall was the static interior shot of the van with Becker and the two agents huddled around the camera. In the center, a fuzzy frame appeared. It dissolved into static and then into a black and white image of a park.

'Transmitting,' Agent Smith announced.

The shot looked like an old movie. It was stilted and jerky – a by-product of frame-dropping, a process that halved the amount of information sent and enabled faster transmission.

The shot panned out across an enormous concourse enclosed on one end by a semicircular facade – the

Seville Ayuntamiento. There were trees in the foreground. The park was empty.

'X-eleven's are down!' a technician called out. 'This bad boy's hungry!'

Smith began to narrate. His commentary had the detachment of a seasoned agent. 'This is shot from the van,' he said, 'about fifty meters from the kill zone. Tankado is approaching from the right. Hulohot's in the trees to the left.'

'We've got a time crunch here,' Fontaine pressed. 'Let's get to the meat of it.'

Agent Coliander touched a few buttons, and the frame speed increased.

Everyone on the podium watched in anticipation as their former associate, Ensei Tankado, came into the frame. The accelerated video made the whole image seem comic. Tankado shuffled jerkily out onto the concourse, apparently taking in the scenery. He shielded his eyes and gazed up at the spires of the huge facade.

'This is it,' Smith warned. 'Hulohot's a pro. He took his first open shot.'

Smith was right. There was a flash of light from behind the trees on the left of the screen. An instant later Tankado clutched his chest. He staggered momentarily. The camera zoomed in on him, unstable – in and out of focus.

As the footage rolled in high speed, Smith coldly continued his narration. 'As you can see, Tankado is instantly in cardiac arrest.'

Susan felt ill watching the images. Tankado clutched at his chest with crippled hands, a confused look of terror on his face.

'You'll notice,' Smith added, 'his eyes are focused downward, at himself. Not once does he look around.'

'And that's important?' Jabba half stated, half inquired.

'Very,' Smith said. 'If Tankado suspected foul play of any kind, he would instinctively search the area. But as you can see, he does not.'

On the screen, Tankado dropped to his knees, still clutching his chest. He never once looked up. Ensei Tankado was a man alone, dying a private, natural death.

'It's odd,' Smith said, puzzled. 'Trauma pods usually won't kill this quickly. Sometimes, if the target's big enough, they don't kill at all.'

'Bad heart,' Fontaine said flatly.

Smith arched his eyebrows, impressed. 'Fine choice of weapon, then.'

Susan watched as Tankado toppled from his knees to his side and finally onto his back. He lay, staring upward, grabbing at his chest. Suddenly the camera wheeled away from him back toward the grove of trees. A man appeared. He was wearing wire-rim glasses and carrying an oversize briefcase. As he approached the concourse and the writhing Tankado, his fingers began tapping in a strange silent dance on a mechanism attached to his hand.

'He's working his Monocle,' Smith announced. 'Sending a message that Tankado is terminated.' Smith turned to Becker and chuckled. 'Looks like Hulohot had a bad habit of transmitting kills before his victim actually expired.'

Coliander sped the film up some more, and the camera followed Hulohot as he began moving toward his victim. Suddenly an elderly man rushed out of a nearby courtyard, ran over to Tankado, and knelt beside him. Hulohot slowed his approach. A moment later two more people appeared from the courtyard – an obese man and a red-haired woman. They also came to Tankado's side.

'Unfortunate choice of kill zone,' Smith said. 'Hulohot thought he had the victim isolated.'

On the screen, Hulohot watched for a moment and then shrank back into the trees, apparently to wait.

'Here comes the handoff,' Smith prompted. 'We didn't notice it the first time around.'

Susan gazed up at the sickening image on the screen. Tankado was gasping for breath, apparently trying to communicate something to the Samaritans kneeling beside him. Then, in desperation, he thrust his left hand above him, almost hitting the old man in the face. He held the crippled appendage outward before the old man's eyes. The camera tightened on Tankado's three deformed fingers, and on one of them, clearly glistening in the Spanish sun, was the golden ring. Tankado thrust it out again. The old man recoiled. Tankado turned to the woman. He held his three deformed fingers directly in front of her face, as if begging her to understand. The ring glinted in the sun. The woman looked away. Tankado, now choking, unable to make a sound, turned to the obese man and tried one last time.

The elderly man suddenly stood and dashed off, presumably to get help. Tankado seemed to be weakening, but he was still holding the ring in the fat man's face. The fat man reached out and held the dying man's wrist, supporting it. Tankado seemed to gaze upward at his own fingers, at his own ring, and then to the man's eyes. As a final plea before death, Ensei

Tankado gave the man an almost imperceptible nod, as if to say *yes*.

Then Tankado fell limp.

'Jesus,' Jabba moaned.

Suddenly the camera swept to where Hulohot had been hiding. The assassin was gone. A police motorcycle appeared, tearing up Avenida Firelli. The camera wheeled back to where Tankado was lying. The woman kneeling beside him apparently heard the police sirens; she glanced around nervously and then began pulling at her obese companion, begging him to leave. The two hurried off.

The camera tightened on Tankado, his hands folded on his lifeless chest. The ring on his finger was gone.

CHAPTER 118

'It's proof,' Fontaine said decidedly. 'Tankado dumped the ring. He wanted it as far from himself as possible – so we'd never find it.'

'But, Director,' Susan argued, 'it doesn't make sense. If Tankado was unaware he'd been murdered, *why* would he give away the kill code?'

'I agree,' Jabba said. 'The kid's a rebel, but he's a rebel with a conscience. Getting us to admit to TRANSLTR is one thing; revealing our classified databank is another.'

Fontaine stared, disbelieving. 'You think Tankado *wanted* to stop this worm? You think his dying thoughts were for the poor NSA?'

'Tunnel-block corroding!' a technician yelled. 'Full vulnerability in fifteen minutes, maximum!'

'I'll tell you what,' the director declared, taking control. 'In fifteen minutes, every Third World country on the planet will learn how to build an intercontinental ballistic missile. If someone in this room thinks he's got a better candidate for a kill code than this ring, I'm all ears.' The director waited. No one spoke. He returned his gaze to Jabba and locked eyes. 'Tankado

473

dumped that ring for a reason, Jabba. Whether he was trying to bury it, or whether he thought the fat guy would run to a pay phone and call us with the information, I really don't care. But I've made the decision. We're entering that quote. Now.'

Jabba took a long breath. He knew Fontaine was right – there was no better option. They were running out of time. Jabba sat. 'Okay . . . let's do it.' He pulled himself to the keyboard. 'Mr Becker? The inscription, please. Nice and easy.'

David Becker read the inscription, and Jabba typed. When they were done, they double-checked the spelling and omitted all the spaces. On the center panel of the view wall, near the top, were the letters:

QUISCUSTODIETIPSOSCUSTODES

'I don't like it,' Susan muttered softly. 'It's not clean.'

Jabba hesitated, hovering over the ENTER key.

'Do it,' Fontaine commanded.

Jabba hit the key. Seconds later the whole room knew it was a mistake.

CHAPTER 119

'It's accelerating!' Soshi yelled from the back of the room. 'It's the wrong code!'

Everyone stood in silent horror.

On the screen before them was the error message:

ILLEGAL ENTRY. NUMERIC FIELD ONLY.

'Damn it!' Jabba screamed. 'Numeric *only!* We're looking for a goddamn number! We're fucked! This ring is shit!'

'Worm's at double speed!' Soshi shouted. 'Penalty round!'

On the center screen, right beneath the error message, the VR painted a terrifying image. As the third firewall gave way, the half-dozen or so black lines representing marauding hackers surged forward, advancing relentlessly toward the core. With each passing moment, a new line appeared. Then another.

'They're swarming!' Soshi yelled.

'Confirming overseas tie-ins!' cried another technician. 'Word's out!'

Susan averted her gaze from the image of the

475

collapsing firewalls and turned to the side screen. The footage of Ensei Tankado's kill was on endless loop. It was the same every time – Tankado clutching his chest, falling, and with a look of desperate panic, forcing his ring on a group of unsuspecting tourists. *It makes no sense,* she thought. *If he didn't know we'd killed him . . .* Susan drew a total blank. It was too late. *We've missed something.*

On the VR, the number of hackers pounding at the gates had doubled in the last few minutes. From now on, the number would increase exponentially. Hackers, like hyenas, were one big family, always eager to spread the word of a new kill.

Leland Fontaine had apparently seen enough. 'Shut it down,' he declared. 'Shut the damn thing down.'

Jabba stared straight ahead like the captain of a sinking ship. 'Too late, sir. We're going down.'

CHAPTER 120

The four-hundred-pound Sys-Sec stood motionless, hands resting atop his head in a freeze-frame of disbelief. He'd ordered a power shutdown, but it would be a good twenty minutes too late. Sharks with high-speed modems would be able to download staggering quantities of classified information in that window.

Jabba was awakened from his nightmare by Soshi rushing to the podium with a new printout. 'I've found something, sir!' she said excitedly. 'Orphans in the source! Alpha groupings. All over the place!'

Jabba was unmoved. 'We're looking for a numeric, dammit! Not an alpha! The kill-code is a *number!*'

'But we've got orphans! Tankado's too good to leave orphans – especially this many!'

The term 'orphans' referred to extra lines of programming that didn't serve the program's objective in any way. They fed nothing, referred to nothing, led nowhere, and were usually removed as part of the final debugging and compiling process.

Jabba took the printout and studied it.

Fontaine stood silent.

Susan peered over Jabba's shoulder at the printout. 'We're being attacked by a *rough draft* of Tankado's worm?'

'Polished or not,' Jabba retorted, 'it's kicking our ass.'

'I don't buy it,' Susan argued. 'Tankado was a perfectionist. You know that. There's no way he left bugs in his program.'

'There are lots of them!' Soshi cried. She grabbed the printout from Jabba and pushed it in front of Susan. 'Look!'

Susan nodded. Sure enough, after every twenty or so lines of programming, there were four free-floating characters. Susan scanned them.

```
PFEE
SESN
RETM
```

'Four-bit alpha groupings,' she puzzled. 'They're definitely not part of the programming.'

'Forget it,' Jabba growled. 'You're grabbing at straws.'

'Maybe not,' Susan said. 'A lot of encryption uses four-bit groupings. This could be a code.'

'Yeah.' Jabba groaned. 'It says – "Ha, ha. You're fucked."' He looked up at the VR. 'In about nine minutes.'

Susan ignored Jabba and locked in on Soshi. 'How many orphans are there?'

Soshi shrugged. She commandeered Jabba's terminal and typed all the groupings. When she was done, she pushed back from the terminal. The room looked up at the screen.

PFEE SESN RETM MFHA IRWE OOIG MEEN NRMA
ENET SHAS DCNS IIAA IEER BRNK FBLE LODI

Susan was the only one smiling. 'Sure looks familiar,' she said. 'Blocks of four – just like Enigma.'

The director nodded. Enigma was history's most famous code-writing machine – the Nazis' twelve-ton encryption beast. It had encrypted in blocks of four.

'Great.' He moaned. 'You wouldn't happen to have one lying around, would you?'

'That's not the point!' Susan said, suddenly coming to life. This was her specialty. 'The point is that this is a code. Tankado left us a clue! He's taunting us, daring us to figure out the pass-key in time. He's laying hints just out of our reach!'

'Absurd,' Jabba snapped. 'Tankado gave us only one out – revealing TRANSLTR. That was it. That was our escape. We blew it.'

'I have to agree with him,' Fontaine said. 'I doubt there's any way Tankado would risk letting us off the hook by hinting at his kill-code.'

Susan nodded vaguely, but she recalled how Tankado had given them NDAKOTA. She stared up at the letters wondering if he were playing another one of his games.

'Tunnel block half gone!' a technician called.

On the VR, the mass of black tie-in lines surged deeper into the two remaining shields.

David had been sitting quietly, watching the drama unfold on the monitor before them. 'Susan?' he offered. 'I have an idea. Is that text in sixteen groupings of four?'

'Oh, for Christ's sake,' Jabba said under his breath. 'Now everyone wants to play?'

Susan ignored Jabba and counted the groupings. 'Yes. Sixteen.'

'Take out the spaces,' Becker said firmly.

'David,' Susan replied, slightly embarrassed. 'I don't think you understand. The groupings of four are—'

'Take out the spaces,' he repeated.

Susan hesitated a moment and then nodded to Soshi. Soshi quickly removed the spaces. The result was no more enlightening.

PFEESESNRETMMFHAIRWEOOIGMEENNRM
AENETSHASDCNSIIAAIEERBRNKFBLELODI

Jabba exploded. 'ENOUGH! Playtime's over! This thing's on double-speed! We've got about eight minutes here! We're looking for a *number*, not a bunch of half-baked letters!'

'Four by sixteen,' David said calmly. 'Do the math, Susan.'

Susan eyed David's image on the screen. *Do the math? He's terrible at math!* She knew David could memorize verb conjugations and vocabulary like a Xerox machine, but math? . . .

'Multiplication tables,' Becker said.

Multiplication tables, Susan wondered. *What is he talking about?*

'Four by sixteen,' the professor repeated. 'I had to memorize multiplication tables in fourth grade.'

Susan pictured the standard grade school multiplication table. *Four by sixteen.* 'Sixty-four,' she said blankly. 'So what?'

David leaned toward the camera. His face filled the frame. 'Sixty-four letters . . .'

480

Susan nodded. 'Yes, but they're—' Susan froze.

'Sixty-four letters,' David repeated.

Susan gasped. 'Oh my God! David, you're a genius!'

CHAPTER 121

'Seven minutes!' a technician called out.

'Eight rows of eight!' Susan shouted, excited.

Soshi typed. Fontaine looked on silently. The second to last shield was growing thin.

'Sixty-four letters!' Susan was in control. 'It's a perfect square!'

'Perfect square?' Jabba demanded. 'So *what?*'

Ten seconds later Soshi had rearranged the seemingly random letters on the screen. They were now in eight rows of eight. Jabba studied the letters and threw up his hands in despair. The new layout was no more revealing than the original.

P	F	E	E	S	E	S	N
R	E	T	M	P	F	H	A
I	R	W	E	O	O	I	G
M	E	E	N	N	R	M	A
E	N	E	T	S	H	A	S
D	C	N	S	I	I	A	A
I	E	E	R	B	R	N	K
F	B	L	E	L	O	D	I

'Clear as shit.' Jabba groaned.

'Ms Fletcher,' Fontaine demanded, 'explain yourself.' All eyes turned to Susan.

Susan was staring up at the block of text. Gradually she began nodding, then broke into a wide smile. 'David, I'll be damned!'

Everyone on the podium exchanged baffled looks.

David winked at the tiny image of Susan Fletcher on the screen before him. 'Sixty-four letters. Julius Caesar strikes again.'

Midge looked lost. 'What are you talking about?'

'Caesar box.' Susan beamed. 'Read top to bottom. Tankado's sending us a message.'

CHAPTER 122

'Six minutes!' a technician called out.

Susan shouted orders. 'Retype top to bottom! Read down, not across!'

Soshi furiously moved down the columns, retyping the text.

'Julius Caesar sent codes this way!' Susan blurted. 'His letter count was always a perfect square!'

'Done!' Soshi yelled.

Everyone looked up at the newly arranged, single line of text on the wall-screen.

'Still garbage,' Jabba scoffed in disgust. 'Look at it. It's totally random bits of—' The words lodged in his throat. His eyes widened to saucers. 'Oh . . . oh my . . .'

Fontaine had seen it too. He arched his eyebrows, obviously impressed.

Midge and Brinkerhoff both cooed in unison. 'Holy . . . shit.'

The sixty-four letters now read:

PRIMEDIFFERENCEBETWEENELEMENTS
RESPONSIBLEFORHIROSHIMAANDNAGASAKI

484

'Put in the spaces,' Susan ordered. 'We've got a puzzle to solve.'

CHAPTER 123

An ashen technician ran to the podium. 'Tunnel block's about to go!'

Jabba turned to the VR onscreen. The attackers surged forward, only a whisker away from their assault on the fifth and final wall. The databank was running out of time.

Susan blocked out the chaos around her. She read Tankado's bizarre message over and over.

PRIME DIFFERENCE BETWEEN ELEMENTS

RESPONSIBLE FOR HIROSHIMA AND NAGASAKI

'It's not even a question!' Brinkerhoff cried. 'How can it have an answer?'

'We need a number,' Jabba reminded. 'The kill-code is *numeric*.'

'Silence,' Fontaine said evenly. He turned and addressed Susan. 'Ms Fletcher, you've gotten us this far. I need your best guess.'

Susan took a deep breath. 'The kill-code entry field accepts numerics *only*. My guess is that this is some sort of clue as to the correct number. The text

486

mentions Hiroshima and Nagasaki – the two cities that were hit by atomic bombs. Maybe the kill-code is related to the number of casualties, the estimated dollars of damage . . .' She paused a moment, rereading the clue. 'The word "difference" seems important. The prime *difference* between Nagasaki and Hiroshima. Apparently Tankado felt the two incidents differed somehow.'

Fontaine's expression did not change. Nonetheless, hope was fading fast. It seemed the political backdrops surrounding the two most devastating blasts in history needed to be analyzed, compared, and translated into some magic number . . . and all within the next five minutes.

CHAPTER 124

'Final shield under attack!'

On the VR, the PEM authorization programming was now being consumed. Black, penetrating lines engulfed the final protective shield and began forcing their way toward its core.

Prowling hackers were now appearing from all over the world. The number was doubling almost every minute. Before long, anyone with a computer – foreign spies, radicals, terrorists – would have access to all of the U.S. government's classified information.

As technicians tried vainly to sever power, the assembly on the podium studied the message. Even David and the two NSA agents were trying to crack the code from their van in Spain.

PRIME DIFFERENCE BETWEEN ELEMENTS
RESPONSIBLE FOR HIROSHIMA AND NAGASAKI

Soshi thought aloud. 'The elements responsible for Hiroshima and Nagasaki . . . Pearl Harbor? Hirohito's refusal to . . .'

'We need a *number*,' Jabba repeated, 'not political theories. We're talking *mathematics* – not history!'

Soshi fell silent.

'How about payloads?' Brinkerhoff offered. 'Casualties? Dollars damage?'

'We're looking for an *exact* figure,' Susan reminded. 'Damage estimates vary.' She stared up at the message. 'The elements responsible . . .'

Three thousand miles away, David Becker's eyes flew open. 'Elements!' he declared. 'We're talking math, not history!'

All heads turned toward the satellite screen.

'Tankado's playing word games!' Becker spouted. 'The word "elements" has multiple meanings!'

'Spit it out, Mr Becker,' Fontaine snapped.

'He's talking about *chemical* elements – not socio-political ones!'

Becker's announcement met blank looks.

'Elements!' he prompted. 'The periodic table! *Chemical* elements! Didn't any of you see the movie *Fat Man and Little Boy* – about the Manhattan Project? The two atomic bombs were different. They used different fuel – different *elements!*'

Soshi clapped her hands. 'Yes! He's right! I read that! The two bombs used different fuels! One used uranium and one used plutonium! Two *different* elements!'

A hush swept across the room.

'Uranium and plutonium!' Jabba exclaimed, suddenly hopeful. 'The clue asks for the *difference* between the two elements!' He spun to his army of workers. 'The difference between uranium and plutonium! Who knows what it is?'

Blank stares all around.

'Come on!' Jabba said. 'Didn't you kids go to college? Somebody! Anybody! I need the difference between plutonium and uranium!'

No response.

Susan turned to Soshi. 'I need access to the Web. Is there a browser here?'

Soshi nodded. 'Netscape's sweetest.'

Susan grabbed her hand. 'Come on. We're going surfing.'

CHAPTER 125

'How much time?' Jabba demanded from the podium.

There was no response from the technicians in the back. They stood riveted, staring up at the VR. The final shield was getting dangerously thin.

Nearby, Susan and Soshi pored over the results of their Websearch. 'Outlaw Labs?' Susan asked. 'Who are they?'

Soshi shrugged. 'You want me to open it?'

'Damn right,' she said. 'Six hundred forty-seven text references to uranium, plutonium, and atomic bombs. Sounds like our best bet.'

Soshi opened the link. A disclaimer appeared.

The information contained in this file is strictly for academic use only. Any layperson attempting to construct any of the devices described runs the risk of radiation poisoning and/or self-explosion.

'Self-explosion?' Soshi said. 'Jesus.'

'Search it,' Fontaine snapped over his shoulder. 'Let's see what we've got.'

Soshi plowed into the document. She scrolled past a

recipe for urea nitrate, an explosive ten times more powerful than dynamite. The information rolled by like a recipe for butterscotch brownies.

'Plutonium and uranium,' Jabba repeated. 'Let's focus.'

'Go back,' Susan ordered. 'The document's too big. Find the table of contents.'

Soshi scrolled backward until she found it.

'Section two!' Susan cried. 'Uranium and plutonium! Go!'

Everyone waited while Soshi found the right section. 'This is it,' she said. 'Hold on.' She quickly scanned the data. 'There's a lot of information here. A

492

whole chart. How do we know which difference we're looking for? One occurs naturally, one is man-made. Plutonium was first discovered by—'

'A *number*,' Jabba reminded. 'We need a *number*.'

Susan reread Tankado's message. *The prime difference between the elements . . . the difference between . . . we need a number . . .* 'Wait!' she said. 'The word "difference" has multiple meanings. We need a *number* – so we're talking *math*. It's another of Tankado's word games – "difference" means *subtraction*.'

'Yes!' Becker agreed from the screen overhead. 'Maybe the elements have different numbers of protons or something? If you subtract—'

'He's right!' Jabba said, turning to Soshi. 'Are there any *numbers* on that chart? Proton counts? Half-lives? Anything we can subtract?'

'Three minutes!' a technician called.

'How about supercritical mass?' Soshi ventured. 'It says the supercritical mass for plutonium is 35.2 pounds.'

'Yes!' Jabba said. 'Check uranium! What's the supercritical mass of uranium?'

Soshi searched. 'Um . . . 110 pounds.'

'One hundred ten?' Jabba looked suddenly hopeful. 'What's 35.2 from 110?'

'Seventy-four point eight,' Susan snapped. 'But I don't think—'

'Out of my way,' Jabba commanded, plowing toward the keyboard. 'That's got to be the kill-code! The difference between their critical masses! Seventy-four point eight!'

'Hold on,' Susan said, peering over Soshi's shoulder. 'There's more here. Atomic weights. Neutron counts. Extraction techniques.' She skimmed the chart. 'Uranium splits into barium and krypton; plutonium does something else. Uranium has 92 protons and 146 neutrons, but—'

'We need the most *obvious* difference,' Midge chimed in. 'The clue reads "the *primary* difference between the elements." '

'Jesus Christ!' Jabba swore. 'How do we know what Tankado considered the *primary* difference?'

David interrupted. 'Actually, the clue reads *prime*, not *primary.*'

The word hit Susan right between the eyes. *'Prime!'* she exclaimed. *'Prime!'* She spun to Jabba. 'The kill-code is a *prime* number! Think about it! It makes perfect sense!'

Jabba instantly knew Susan was right. Ensei Tankado had built his career on prime numbers. Primes were the fundamental building blocks of all encryption algorithms – unique values that had no factors other than one and themselves. Primes worked well in code writing because they were impossible for computers to guess using typical number-tree factoring.

Soshi jumped in. 'Yes! It's perfect! Primes are essential to Japanese culture! Haiku uses primes. *Three* lines and syllable counts of *five, seven, five*. All primes. The temples of Kyoto all have—'

'Enough!' Jabba said. 'Even if the kill-code *is* a prime, so what! There are endless possibilities!'

Susan knew Jabba was right. Because the number line was infinite, one could always look a little farther and find another prime number. Between zero and a million, there were over 70,000 choices. It all depended on how large a prime Tankado decided to use. The bigger it was, the harder it was to guess.

'It'll be huge,' Jabba groaned. 'Whatever prime Tankado chose is sure to be a monster.'

A call went up from the rear of the room. *'Two-minute warning!'*

Jabba gazed up at the VR in defeat. The final shield was starting to crumble. Technicians were rushing everywhere.

Something in Susan told her they were close. 'We can do this!' she declared, taking control. 'Of all the differences between uranium and plutonium, I bet only one can be represented as a *prime* number! That's our final clue. The number we're looking for is prime!'

Jabba eyed the uranium/plutonium chart on the monitor and threw up his arms. 'There must be a hundred entries here! There's no way we can subtract them all and check for primes.'

'A lot of the entries are *nonnumeric,*' Susan encouraged. 'We can ignore them. Uranium's natural, plutonium's man-made. Uranium uses a gun barrel detonator, plutonium uses implosion. They're not numbers, so they're irrelevant!'

'Do it,' Fontaine ordered. On the VR, the final wall was eggshell thin.

Jabba mopped his brow. 'All right, here goes nothing. Start subtracting. I'll take the top quarter. Susan, you've got the middle. Everybody else split up the rest. We're looking for a prime difference.'

Within seconds, it was clear they'd never make it. The numbers were enormous, and in many cases the units didn't match up.

'It's apples and goddamn oranges,' Jabba said. 'We've got gamma rays against electromagnetic pulse. Fissionable against unfissionable. Some is pure. Some is percentage. It's a mess!'

'It's got to be here,' Susan said firmly. 'We've got to think. There's some difference between plutonium and uranium that we're missing! Something simple!'

'Ah . . . guys?' Soshi said. She'd created a second document window and was perusing the rest of the Outlaw Labs document.

'What is it?' Fontaine demanded. 'Find something?'

'Um, sort of.' She sounded uneasy. 'You know how I told you the Nagasaki bomb was a plutonium bomb?'

'Yeah,' they all replied in unison.

'Well . . .' Soshi took a deep breath. 'Looks like I made a mistake.'

'What!' Jabba choked. 'We've been looking for the wrong thing?'

Soshi pointed to the screen. They huddled around and read the text:

. . . the common misconception that the Nagasaki bomb was a plutonium bomb. In fact, the device employed uranium, like its sister bomb in Hiroshima.

'But—' Susan gasped. 'If both elements were uranium, how are we supposed to find the difference between the two?'

'Maybe Tankado made a mistake,' Fontaine ventured. 'Maybe he didn't know the bombs were the same.'

'No.' Susan sighed. 'He was a cripple because of those bombs. He'd know the facts cold.'

CHAPTER 126

'One minute!'

Jabba eyed the VR. 'PEM authorization's going fast. Last line of defense. And there's a crowd at the door.'

'Focus!' Fontaine commanded.

Soshi sat in front of the Web browser and read aloud.

'. . . Nagasaki bomb did not use plutonium but rather an artificially manufactured, neutron-saturated isotope of uranium 238.'

'Damn!' Brinkerhoff swore. 'Both bombs used uranium. The elements responsible for Hiroshima and Nagasaki were both uranium. There *is* no difference!'

'We're dead,' Midge moaned.

'Wait,' Susan said. 'Read that last part again!'

Soshi repeated the text. '. . . . artificially manufactured, neutron-saturated isotope of uranium 238.'

'238?' Susan exclaimed. 'Didn't we just see something that said Hiroshima's bomb used some other isotope of uranium?'

They all exchanged puzzled glances. Soshi frantically

scrolled backward and found the spot. *'Yes!* It says here that the Hiroshima bomb used a different isotope of uranium!'

Midge gasped in amazement. 'They're both uranium – but they're different kinds!'

'Both uranium?' Jabba muscled in and stared at the terminal. 'Apples and apples! Perfect!'

'How are the two isotopes different?' Fontaine demanded. 'It's got to be something basic.'

Soshi scrolled through the document. 'Hold on . . . looking . . . okay . . .'

'Forty-five seconds!' a voice called out.

Susan looked up. The final shield was almost invisible now.

'Here it is!' Soshi exclaimed.

'Read it!' Jabba was sweating. 'What's the difference! There must be some difference between the two!'

'Yes!' Soshi pointed to her monitor. 'Look!'

They all read the text:

. . . two bombs employed two different fuels . . . precisely identical chemical characteristics. No ordinary chemical extraction can separate the two isotopes. They are, with the exception of minute differences in weight, perfectly identical.

'Atomic weight!' Jabba said, excitedly. 'That's it! The only difference is their *weights!* That's the key! Give me their weights! We'll subtract them!'

'Hold on,' Soshi said, scrolling ahead. 'Almost there! *Yes!'* Everyone scanned the text.

. . . difference in weight very slight . . .

. . . gaseous diffusion to separate them . . .

. . . 10,032498X10^134 as compared to 19,39484X10 ^23.**

'There they are!' Jabba screamed. 'That's it! Those are the weights!'

'*Thirty seconds!*'

'Go,' Fontaine whispered. 'Subtract them. Quickly.'

Jabba palmed his calculator and started entering numbers.

'What's the asterisk?' Susan demanded. 'There's an asterisk after the figures!'

Jabba ignored her. He was already working his calculator keys furiously.

'Careful!' Soshi urged. 'We need an *exact* figure.'

'The asterisk,' Susan repeated. 'There's a footnote.'

Soshi clicked to the bottom of the paragraph.

Susan read the asterisked footnote. She went white. 'Oh . . . dear God.'

Jabba looked up. 'What?'

They all leaned in, and there was a communal sigh of defeat. The tiny footnote read:

**12% margin of error. Published figures vary from lab to lab.

CHAPTER 127

There was a sudden and reverent silence among the group on the podium. It was as if they were watching an eclipse or volcanic eruption – an incredible chain of events over which they had no control. Time seemed to slow to a crawl.

'We're losing it!' a technician cried. 'Tie-ins! All lines!'

On the far-left screen, David and Agents Smith and Coliander stared blankly into their camera. On the VR, the final firewall was only a sliver. A mass of blackness surrounded it, hundreds of lines waiting to tie in. To the right of that was Tankado. The stilted clips of his final moments ran by in an endless loop. The look of desperation – fingers stretched outward, the ring glistening in the sun.

Susan watched the clip as it went in and out of focus. She stared at Tankado's eyes – they seemed filled with regret. *He never wanted it to go this far*, she told herself. *He wanted to save us*. And yet, over and over, Tankado held his fingers outward, forcing the ring in front of people's eyes. He was trying to speak but could not. He just kept thrusting his fingers forward.

In Seville, Becker's mind still turned it over and over. He mumbled to himself, 'What did they say those two isotopes were? U238 and U . . .?' He sighed heavily – it didn't matter. He was a language teacher, not a physicist.

'Incoming lines preparing to authenticate!'

'Jesus!' Jabba bellowed in frustration. 'How do the damn isotopes *differ?* Nobody knows how the hell they're different?!' There was no response. The roomful of technicians stood helplessly watching the VR. Jabba spun back to the monitor and threw up his arms. 'Where's a nuclear fucking physicist when you need one!'

Susan stared up at the QuickTime clip on the wall screen and knew it was over. In slow motion, she watched Tankado dying over and over. He was trying to speak, choking on his words, holding out his deformed hand . . . trying to communicate something. *He was trying to save the databank,* Susan told herself. *But we'll never know how.*

'Company at the door!'

Jabba stared at the screen. 'Here we go!' Sweat poured down his face.

On the center screen, the final wisp of the last firewall had all but disappeared. The black mass of lines surrounding the core was opaque and pulsating. Midge turned away. Fontaine stood rigid, eyes front. Brinkerhoff looked like he was about to get sick.

'Ten seconds!'

Susan's eyes never left Tankado's image. The desperation. The regret. His hand reached out, over and over, ring glistening, deformed fingers arched crookedly in strangers' faces. *He's telling them something. What is it?*

On the screen overhead, David looked deep in thought. 'Difference,' he kept muttering to himself. 'Difference between U238 and U235. It's got to be something simple.'

A technician began the countdown. *'Five! Four! Three!'*

The word made it to Spain in just under a tenth of a second. *Three ... three.*

It was as if David Becker had been hit by the stun gun all over again. His world slowed to a stop. *Three ... three ... three. 238 minus 235! The difference is three!* In slow motion, he reached for the microphone ...

At that very instant, Susan was staring at Tankado's outstretched hand. Suddenly, she saw past the ring ... past the engraved gold to the flesh beneath ... to his fingers. *Three* fingers. It was not the ring at all. It was the flesh. Tankado was not telling them, he was *showing* them. He was telling his secret, revealing the kill-code – begging someone to understand ... praying his secret would find its way to the NSA in time.

'Three,' Susan whispered, stunned.

'Three!' Becker yelled from Spain.

But in the chaos, no one seemed to hear.

'We're down!' a technician yelled.

The VR began flashing wildly as the core succumbed to a deluge. Sirens erupted overhead.

'Outbound data!'

'High-speed tie-ins in all sectors!'

Susan moved as if through a dream. She spun toward Jabba's keyboard. As she turned, her gaze fixed on her fiancé, David Becker. Again his voice exploded overhead.

'Three! The difference between 235 and 238 is three!'

Everyone in the room looked up.

'Three!' Susan shouted over the deafening cacophony of sirens and technicians. She pointed to the screen. All eyes followed, to Tankado's hand, outstretched, three fingers waving desperately in the Sevillian sun.

Jabba went rigid. 'Oh my God!' He suddenly realized the crippled genius had been giving them the answer all the time.

'Three's prime!' Soshi blurted. 'Three's a *prime* number!'

Fontaine looked dazed. 'Can it be that simple?'

'Outbound data!' a technician cried. *'It's going fast!'*

Everyone on the podium dove for the terminal at the same instant – a mass of outstretched hands. But through the crowd, Susan, like a shortstop stabbing a line drive, connected with her target. She typed the number 3. Everyone wheeled to the wallscreen. Above the chaos, it simply read.

ENTER PASS-KEY? 3

'Yes!' Fontaine commanded. 'Do it now!'

Susan held her breath and lowered her finger on the ENTER key. The computer beeped once.

Nobody moved.

Three agonizing seconds later, nothing had happened.

The sirens kept going. Five seconds. Six seconds.

'Outbound data!'

'No change!'

503

Suddenly Midge began pointing wildly to the screen above. 'Look!'

On it, a message had materialized.

KILL CODE CONFIRMED

'Upload the firewalls!' Jabba ordered.

But Soshi was a step ahead of him. She had already sent the command.

'*Outbound interrupt!*' a technician yelled.

'*Tie-ins severed!*'

On the VR overhead, the first of the five firewalls began reappearing. The black lines attacking the core were instantly severed.

'Reinstating!' Jabba cried. 'The damn thing's reinstating!'

There was a moment of tentative disbelief, as if at any instant, everything would fall apart. But then the second firewall began reappearing ... and then the third. Moments later the entire series of filters reappeared. The databank was secure.

The room erupted. Pandemonium. Technicians hugged, tossing computer printouts in the air in celebration. Sirens wound down. Brinkerhoff grabbed Midge and held on. Soshi burst into tears.

'Jabba,' Fontaine demanded. 'How much did they get?'

'Very little,' Jabba said, studying his monitor. 'Very little. And nothing complete.'

Fontaine nodded slowly, a wry smile forming in the corner of his mouth. He looked around for Susan Fletcher, but she was already walking toward the front of the room. On the wall before her, David Becker's face filled the screen.

'David?'

'Hey, gorgeous.' He smiled.

'Come home,' she said. 'Come home, right now.'

'Meet you at Stone Manor?' he asked.

She nodded, the tears welling. 'Deal.'

'Agent Smith?' Fontaine called.

Smith appeared onscreen behind Becker. 'Yes, sir?'

'It appears Mr Becker has a date. Could you see that he gets home immediately?'

Smith nodded. 'Our jet's in Málaga.' He patted Becker on the back. 'You're in for a treat, Professor. Ever flown in a Learjet 60?'

Becker chuckled. 'Not since yesterday.'

CHAPTER 128

When Susan awoke, the sun was shining. The soft rays sifted through the curtains and filtered across her goosedown feather bed. She reached for David. *Am I dreaming?* Her body remained motionless, spent, still dizzy from the night before.

'David?' she moaned.

There was no reply. She opened her eyes, her skin still tingling. The mattress on the other side of the bed was cold. David was gone.

I'm dreaming, Susan thought. She sat up. The room was Victorian, all lace and antiques – Stone Manor's finest suite. Her overnight bag was in the middle of the hardwood floor . . . her lingerie on a Queen Anne chair beside the bed.

Had David really arrived? She had memories – his body against hers, his waking her with soft kisses. Had she dreamed it all? She turned to the bedside table. There was an empty bottle of champagne, two glasses . . . and a note.

Rubbing the sleep from her eyes, Susan drew the comforter around her naked body and read the message.

Dearest Susan,
I love you.
Without wax, David

She beamed and pulled the note to her chest. It was David, all right. *Without wax* ... it was the one code she had yet to break.

Something stirred in the corner, and Susan looked up. On a plush divan, basking in the morning sun, wrapped in a thick bathrobe, David Becker sat quietly watching her. She reached out, beckoning him to come to her.

'Without wax?' she cooed, taking him in her arms.

'Without wax.' He smiled.

She kissed him deeply. 'Tell me what it means.'

'No chance.' He laughed. 'A couple needs secrets – it keeps things interesting.'

Susan smiled coyly. 'Any more interesting than last night and I'll never walk again.'

David took her in his arms. He felt weightless. He had almost died yesterday, and yet here he was, as alive as he had ever felt in his life.

Susan lay with her head on his chest, listening to the beat of his heart. She couldn't believe that she had thought he was gone forever.

'David,' she sighed, eyeing the note beside the table. 'Tell me about "without wax." You know I hate codes I can't break.'

David was silent.

'Tell me.' Susan pouted. 'Or you'll never have me again.'

'Liar.'

Susan hit him with a pillow. 'Tell me! Now!'

But David knew he would never tell. The secret behind 'without wax' was too sweet. Its origins were ancient.

During the Renaissance, Spanish sculptors who made mistakes while carving expensive marble often patched their flaws with *cera* – 'wax.' A statue that had no flaws and required no patching was hailed as a 'sculpture *sin cera*' or a 'sculpture without wax.' The phrase eventually came to mean anything honest or true. The English word 'sincere' evolved from the Spanish *sin cera* – 'without wax.' David's secret code was no great mystery – he was simply signing his letters 'Sincerely.' Somehow he suspected Susan would not be amused.

'You'll be pleased to know,' David said, attempting to change the subject, 'that during the flight home, I called the president of the university.'

Susan looked up, hopeful. 'Tell me you resigned as department chair.'

David nodded. 'I'll be back in the classroom next semester.'

She sighed in relief. 'Right where you belonged in the first place.'

David smiled softly. 'Yeah, I guess Spain reminded me what's important.'

'Back to breaking coeds' hearts?' Susan kissed his cheek. 'Well, at least you'll have time to help me edit my manuscript.'

'Manuscript?'

'Yes. I've decided to publish.'

'Publish?' David looked doubtful. 'Publish *what*?'

'Some ideas I have on variant filter protocols and quadratic residues.'

He groaned. 'Sounds like a real best-seller.'

She laughed. 'You'd be surprised.'

David fished inside the pocket of his bathrobe and pulled out a small object. 'Close your eyes. I have something for you.'

Susan closed her eyes. 'Let me guess – a gaudy gold ring with Latin all over it?'

'No.' David chuckled. 'I had Fontaine return that to Ensei Tankado's estate.' He took Susan's hand and slipped something onto her finger.

'Liar.' Susan laughed, opening her eyes. 'I knew—'

But Susan stopped short. The ring on her finger was not Tankado's at all. It was a platinum setting that held a glittering diamond solitaire.

Susan gasped.

David looked her in the eye. 'Will you marry me?'

Susan's breath caught in her throat. She looked at him and then back to the ring. Her eyes suddenly welled up. 'Oh, David . . . I don't know what to say.'

'Say yes.'

Susan turned away and didn't say a word.

David waited. 'Susan Fletcher, I love you. Marry me.'

Susan lifted her head. Her eyes were filled with tears. 'I'm sorry, David,' she whispered. 'I . . . I can't.'

David stared in shock. He searched her eyes for the playful glimmer he'd come to expect from her. It wasn't there. 'S-Susan,' he stammered. 'I – I don't understand.'

'I can't,' she repeated. 'I can't marry you.' She turned away. Her shoulders started trembling. She covered her face with her hands.

David was bewildered. 'But, Susan . . . I thought . . .' He held her trembling shoulders and turned her body toward him. It was then that he understood. Susan Fletcher was not crying at all; she was in hysterics.

'I won't marry you!' She laughed, attacking again with the pillow. 'Not until you explain "without wax"! You're driving me *crazy!*'

EPILOGUE

They say in death, all things become clear. Tokugen Numataka now knew it was true. Standing over the casket in the Osaka customs office, he felt a bitter clarity he had never known. His religion spoke of circles, of the interconnectedness of life, but Numataka had never had time for religion.

The customs officials had given him an envelope of adoption papers and birth records. 'You are this boy's only living relative,' they had said. 'We had a hard time finding you.'

Numataka's mind reeled back thirty-two years to that rain-soaked night, to the hospital ward where he had deserted his deformed child and dying wife. He had done it in the name of menboku – honor – an empty shadow now.

There was a golden ring enclosed with the papers. It was engraved with words Numataka did not understand. It made no difference; words had no meaning for Numataka anymore. He had forsaken his only son. And now, the cruelest of fates had reunited them.

128-10-93-85-10-128-98-112-6-6-25-126-39-1-68-78

DAN BROWN

THE
DA VINCI CODE

SPECIAL ILLUSTRATED COLLECTOR'S EDITION

Go behind the scenes of the bestselling thriller of all time

Breaking the mould of traditional suspense novels, *The Da Vinci Code* is simultaneously lightning-paced, intelligent and intricately layered with remarkable research and detail. And in this exclusive edition Dan Brown allows the reader behind the scenes of the novel, which now incorporates over 150 photographs and illustrations throughout the text, showing the rich historical tapestry from which he drew his inspiration. The visual sources, which provide both the backdrop and the stimulus for the novel's action, are revealed for the first time and uniquely complement the reading experience.

'Wow... Blockbuster perfection...
An exhilaratingly brainy thriller'
New York Times

'Fascinating and absorbing...
A great, riveting read. I loved this book'
Harlan Coben

'Intrigue and menace mingle in
one of the finest mysteries I've ever read'
Clive Cussler

'Dan Brown has built a world that is rich in
fascinating detail, and I could not get enough of it'
Robert Crais

0 593 05425 3

Dan Brown is the bestselling author of *Digital Fortress*, *Deception Point*, *Angels and Demons* and *The Da Vinci Code*. He is a graduate of Amherst College and Phillips Exeter Academy, where he has taught English and creative writing. He lives in New England and can be found on the web at www.danbrown.com.

ANGELS
AND
DEMONS

Dan Brown

CORGI BOOKS

ANGELS AND DEMONS
A CORGI BOOK : 0 552 15073 8

First publication in Great Britain

PRINTING HISTORY
Corgi edition published 2001

34 36 38 40 39 37 35

Set in 10/12 Palatino by
Falcon Oast Graphic Art Ltd.

Corgi Books are published by Transworld Publishers,
61-63 Uxbridge Road, London W5 5SA,
a division of The Random House Group Ltd,
in Australia by Random House Australia (Pty) Ltd,
20 Alfred Street, Milsons Point, Sydney, NSW 2061, Australia,
and in New Zealand by Random House New Zealand Ltd,
18 Poland Road, Glenfield, Auckland 10, New Zealand
and in South Africa by Random House (Pty) Ltd,
Endulini, 5a Jubilee Road, Parktown 2193, South Africa.

Printed and bound in Germany by
GGP Media GmbH, Pößneck.

Papers used by Transworld Publishers are natural, recyclable
products made from wood grown in sustainable forests.
The manufacturing processes conform to the environmental
regulations of the country of origin.

For Blythe . . .

ACKNOWLEDGMENTS

A debt of gratitude to Emily Bestler, Jason Kaufman, Ben Kaplan, and everyone at Pocket Books for their belief in this project.

To my friend and agent, Jake Elwell, for his enthusiasm and unflagging effort.

To the legendary George Wieser, for convincing me to write novels.

To my dear friend Irv Sittler, for facilitating my audience with the Pope, secreting me into parts of Vatican City few ever see, and making my time in Rome unforgettable.

To one of the most ingenious and gifted artists alive, John Langdon, who rose brilliantly to my impossible challenge and created the ambigrams for this novel.

To Stan Planton, head librarian, Ohio University – Chillicothe, for being my number one source of information on countless topics.

To Sylvia Cavazzini, for her gracious tour through the secret *Passetto*.

And to the best parents a kid could hope for, Dick and Connie Brown . . . for everything.

Thanks also to CERN, Henry Beckett, Brett Trotter, the Pontifical Academy of Science, Brookhaven Institute,

FermiLab Library, Olga Wieser, Don Ulsch of the National Security Institute, Caroline H. Thompson at University of Wales, Kathryn Gerhard and Omar Al Kindi, John Pike and the Federation of American Scientists, Heimlich Viserholder, Corinna and Davis Hammond, Aizaz Ali, the Galileo Project of Rice University, Julie Lynn and Charlie Ryan at Mockingbird Pictures, Gary Goldstein, Dave (Vilas) Arnold and Andra Crawford, the Global Fraternal Network, the Phillips Exeter Academy Library, Jim Barrington, John Maier, the exceptionally keen eye of Margie Wachtel, alt.masonic. members, Alan Wooley, the Library of Congress Vatican Codices Exhibit, Lisa Callamaro and the Callamaro Agency, Jon A. Stowell, Musei Vaticani, Aldo Baggia, Noah Alireza, Harriet Walker, Charles Terry, Micron Electrics, Mindy Renselaer, Nancy and Dick Curtin, Thomas D. Nadeau, NuvoMedia and Rocket E-books, Frank and Sylvia Kennedy, Simon Edwards, Rome Board of Tourism, Maestro Gregory Brown, Val Brown, Werner Brandes, Paul Krupin at Direct Contact, Paul Stark, Tom King at Computalk Network, Sandy and Jerry Nolan, Web guru Linda George, the National Academy of Art in Rome, physicist and fellow scribe Steve Howe, Robert Weston, the Water Street Bookstore in Exeter, New Hampshire, and the Vatican Observatory.

FACT

The world's largest scientific research facility – Switzerland's *Conseil Européen pour la Recherche Nucléaire* (CERN) – recently succeeded in producing the first particles of antimatter. Antimatter is identical to physical matter except that it is composed of particles whose electric charges are *opposite* to those found in normal matter.

Antimatter is the most powerful energy source known to man. It releases energy with 100 per cent efficiency (nuclear fission is 1.5 per cent efficient). Antimatter creates no pollution or radiation, and a droplet could power New York City for a full day.

There is, however, one catch . . .

Antimatter is highly unstable. It ignites when it comes in contact with absolutely anything . . . even air. A single gram of antimatter contains the energy of a 20-kiloton nuclear bomb – the size of the bomb dropped on Hiroshima.

Until recently antimatter has been created only in very small amounts (a few atoms at a time). But CERN has now broken ground on its new Antiproton Decelerator – an advanced antimatter production facility that promises to create antimatter in much larger quantities.

One question looms: Will this highly volatile substance save the world, or will it be used to create the most deadly weapon ever made?

AUTHOR'S NOTE

References to all works of art, tombs, tunnels, and architecture in Rome are entirely factual (as are their exact locations). They can still be seen today.

The brotherhood of the Illuminati is also factual.

MODERN ROME

VATICAN CITY

1 St Peter's Basilica	7 Office of the Swiss Guard	11 Courtyard of the Belvedere
2 St Peter's Square	8 heliport	12 Central Post Office
3 Sistine Chapel	9 gardens	13 Papal Audience Hall
4 Borgia Courtyard	10 the *Passetto*	14 Government Palace
5 Office of the Pope		
6 Vatican Museums		

ANGELS
AND
DEMONS

PROLOGUE

Physicist Leonardo Vetra smelled burning flesh, and he knew it was his own. He stared up in terror at the dark figure looming over him. 'What do you want!'

'*La chiave*,' the raspy voice replied. 'The password.'

'But . . . I don't—'

The intruder pressed down again, grinding the white hot object deeper into Vetra's chest. There was the hiss of broiling flesh.

Vetra cried out in agony. 'There *is* no password!' He felt himself drifting toward unconsciousness.

The figure glared. '*Ne avevo paura*. I was afraid of that.'

Vetra fought to keep his senses, but the darkness was closing in. His only solace was in knowing his attacker would never obtain what he had come for. A moment later, however, the figure produced a blade and brought it to Vetra's face. The blade hovered. Carefully. Surgically.

'For the love of God!' Vetra screamed. But it was too late.

1

High atop the steps of the Great Pyramid of Giza, a young woman laughed and called down to him. 'Robert, hurry up! I knew I should have married a younger man!' Her smile was magic.

He struggled to keep up, but his legs felt like stone. 'Wait,' he begged. 'Please . . .'

As he climbed, his vision began to blur. There was a thundering in his ears. *I must reach her!* But when he looked up again, the woman had disappeared. In her place stood an old man with rotting teeth. The man stared down, curling his lips into a lonely grimace. Then he let out a scream of anguish that resounded across the desert.

Robert Langdon awoke with a start from his nightmare. The phone beside his bed was ringing. Dazed, he picked up the receiver.

'Hello?'

'I'm looking for Robert Langdon,' a man's voice said.

Langdon sat up in his empty bed and tried to clear his mind. 'This . . . is Robert Langdon.' He squinted at his digital clock. It was 5.18 a.m.

'I must see you immediately.'

'Who is this?'

'My name is Maximilian Kohler. I'm a discrete particle physicist.'

'A *what*?' Langdon could barely focus. 'Are you sure you've got the right Langdon?'

'You're a professor of religious iconology at Harvard University. You've written three books on symbology and—'

'Do you know what time it is?'

'I apologize. I have something you need to see. I can't discuss it on the phone.'

A knowing groan escaped Langdon's lips. This had happened before. One of the perils of writing books about religious symbology was the calls from religious zealots who wanted him to confirm their latest sign from God. Last month, a stripper from Oklahoma had promised Langdon the best sex of his life if he would fly down and verify the authenticity of a cruciform that had magically appeared on her bed sheets. *The Shroud of Tulsa*, Langdon had called it.

'How did you get my number?' Langdon tried to be polite, despite the hour.

'On the Worldwide Web. The site for your book.'

Langdon frowned. He was damn sure his book's site did not include his home phone number. The man was obviously lying.

'I need to see you,' the caller insisted. 'I'll pay you well.'

Now Langdon was getting mad. 'I'm sorry, but I really—'

'If you leave immediately, you can be here by—'

'I'm not going anywhere! It's five o'clock in the morning!' Langdon hung up and collapsed back in bed. He closed his eyes and tried to fall back asleep. It

20

was no use. The dream was emblazoned in his mind. Reluctantly, he put on his robe and went downstairs.

Robert Langdon wandered barefoot through his deserted Massachusetts Victorian home and nursed his ritual insomnia remedy – a mug of steaming Nestlé's Quik. The April moon filtered through the bay windows and played on the oriental carpets. Langdon's colleagues often joked that his place looked more like an anthropology museum than a home. His shelves were packed with religious artifacts from around the world – an *ekuaba* from Ghana, a gold cross from Spain, a cycladic idol from the Aegean, and even a rare woven *boccus* from Borneo, a young warrior's symbol of perpetual youth.

As Langdon sat on his brass Maharishi's chest and savored the warmth of the chocolate, the bay window caught his reflection. The image was distorted and pale . . . like a ghost. *An aging ghost*, he thought, cruelly reminded that his youthful spirit was living in a mortal shell.

Although not overly handsome in a classical sense, the forty-five-year-old Langdon had what his female colleagues referred to as an 'erudite' appeal – wisps of gray in his thick brown hair, probing blue eyes, an arrestingly deep voice, and the strong, carefree smile of a collegiate athlete. A varsity diver in prep school and college, Langdon still had the body of a swimmer, a toned, six-foot physique that he vigilantly maintained with fifty laps a day in the university pool.

Langdon's friends had always viewed him as a bit of an enigma – a man caught between centuries. On weekends he could be seen lounging on the quad in blue jeans, discussing computer graphics or religious history with students; other times he could be spotted in his Harris tweed and paisley vest, photographed in the pages of upscale art magazines at museum openings where he had been asked to lecture.

Although a tough teacher and strict disciplinarian, Langdon was the first to embrace what he hailed as the 'lost art of good clean fun.' He relished recreation with an infectious fanaticism that had earned him a fraternal acceptance among his students. His campus nickname – 'The Dolphin' – was a reference both to his affable nature and his legendary ability to dive into a pool and outmaneuver the entire opposing squad in a water polo match.

As Langdon sat alone, absently gazing into the darkness, the silence of his home was shattered again, this time by the ring of his fax machine. Too exhausted to be annoyed, Langdon forced a tired chuckle.

God's people, he thought. *Two thousand years of waiting for their Messiah, and they're still persistent as hell.*

Wearily, he returned his empty mug to the kitchen and walked slowly to his oak-paneled study. The incoming fax lay in the tray. Sighing, he scooped up the paper and looked at it.

Instantly, a wave of nausea hit him.

The image on the page was that of a human corpse. The body had been stripped naked, and its head had been twisted, facing completely backward. On the victim's chest was a terrible burn. The man had been branded ... imprinted with a single word. It was a word Langdon knew well. Very well. He stared at the ornate lettering in disbelief.

Illuminati

'Illuminati,' he stammered, his heart pounding. *It can't be . . .*

In slow motion, afraid of what he was about to witness, Langdon rotated the fax 180 degrees. He looked at the word upside down.

Instantly, the breath went out of him. It was like he had been hit by a truck. Barely able to believe his eyes, he rotated the fax again, reading the brand right-side up and then upside down.

'Illuminati,' he whispered.

Stunned, Langdon collapsed in a chair. He sat a moment in utter bewilderment. Gradually, his eyes were drawn to the blinking red light on his fax machine. Whoever had sent this fax was still on the line . . . waiting to talk. Langdon gazed at the blinking light a long time.

Then, trembling, he picked up the receiver.

2

'Do I have your attention now?' the man's voice said when Langdon finally answered the line.

'Yes, sir, you damn well do. You want to explain yourself?'

'I tried to tell you before.' The voice was rigid,

mechanical. 'I'm a physicist. I run a research facility. We've had a murder. You saw the body.'

'How did you find me?' Langdon could barely focus. His mind was racing from the image on the fax.

'I already told you. The Worldwide Web. The site for your book, *The Art of the Illuminati*.'

Langdon tried to gather his thoughts. His book was virtually unknown in mainstream literary circles, but it had developed quite a following on-line. Nonetheless, the caller's claim still made no sense. 'That page has no contact information,' Langdon challenged. 'I'm certain of it.'

'I have people here at the lab very adept at extracting user information from the Web.'

Langdon was skeptical. 'Sounds like your lab knows *a lot* about the Web.'

'We should,' the man fired back. 'We *invented* it.'

Something in the man's voice told Langdon he was not joking.

'I must see you,' the caller insisted. 'This is not a matter we can discuss on the phone. My lab is only an hour's flight from Boston.'

Langdon stood in the dim light of his study and analyzed the fax in his hand. The image was overpowering, possibly representing the epigraphical find of the century, a decade of his research confirmed in a single symbol.

'It's urgent,' the voice pressured.

Langdon's eyes were locked on the brand. *Illuminati*, he read over and over. His work had always been based on the symbolic equivalent of fossils – ancient documents and historical hearsay – but this image before him was today. Present tense. He felt like a paleontologist coming face to face with a living dinosaur.

'I've taken the liberty of sending a plane for you,' the voice said. 'It will be in Boston in twenty minutes.'

Langdon felt his mouth go dry. *An hour's flight . . .*

'Please forgive my presumption,' the voice said. 'I need you here.'

Langdon looked again at the fax – an ancient myth confirmed in black and white. The implications were frightening. He gazed absently through the bay window. The first hint of dawn was sifting through the birch trees in his backyard, but the view looked somehow different this morning. As an odd combination of fear and exhilaration settled over him, Langdon knew he had no choice.

'You win,' he said. 'Tell me where to meet the plane.'

3

Thousands of miles away, two men were meeting. The chamber was dark. Medieval. Stone.

'*Benvenuto,*' the man in charge said. He was seated in the shadows, out of sight. 'Were you successful?'

'*Si,*' the dark figure replied. '*Perfettamente.*' His words were as hard as the rock walls.

'And there will be no doubt who is responsible?'

'None.'

'Superb. Do you have what I asked for?'

The killer's eyes glistened, black like oil. He produced a heavy electronic device and set it on the table.

The man in the shadows seemed pleased. 'You have done well.'

'Serving the brotherhood is an honor,' the killer replied.

'Phase two begins shortly. Get some rest. Tonight we change the world.'

4

Robert Langdon's Saab 900S tore out of the Callahan Tunnel and emerged on the east side of Boston Harbor near the entrance to Logan Airport. Checking his directions Langdon found Aviation Road and turned left past the old Eastern Airlines Building. Three hundred yards down the access road a hangar loomed in the darkness. A large number '4' was painted on it. He pulled into the parking lot and got out of his car.

A round-faced man in a blue flight suit emerged from behind the building. 'Robert Langdon?' he called. The man's voice was friendly. He had an accent Langdon couldn't place.

'That's me,' Langdon said, locking his car.

'Perfect timing,' the man said. 'I've just landed. Follow me, please.'

As they circled the building, Langdon felt tense. He was not accustomed to cryptic phone calls and secret rendezvous with strangers. Not knowing what to expect he had donned his usual classroom attire – a pair of chinos, a turtleneck, and a Harris tweed suit jacket. As they walked, he thought about the fax in his jacket pocket, still unable to believe the image it depicted.

The pilot seemed to sense Langdon's anxiety. 'Flying's not a problem for you, is it, sir?'

'Not at all,' Langdon replied. *Branded corpses are a problem for me. Flying I can handle.*

The man led Langdon the length of the hangar. They rounded the corner onto the runway.

Langdon stopped dead in his tracks and gaped at the aircraft parked on the tarmac. 'We're riding in *that*?'

The man grinned. 'Like it?'

Langdon stared a long moment. 'Like it? What the hell *is* it?'

The craft before them was enormous. It was vaguely reminiscent of the space shuttle except that the top had been shaved off, leaving it perfectly flat. Parked there on the runway, it resembled a colossal wedge. Langdon's first impression was that he must be dreaming. The vehicle looked as airworthy as a Buick. The wings were practically nonexistent – just two stubby fins on the rear of the fuselage. A pair of dorsal guiders rose out of the aft section. The rest of the plane was hull – about 200 feet from front to back – no windows, nothing but hull.

'Two hundred fifty thousand kilos fully fueled,' the pilot offered, like a father bragging abut his newborn. 'Runs on slush hydrogen. The shell's a titanium matrix with silicon carbide fibers. She packs a 20:1 thrust/weight ratio; most jets run at 7:1. The director must be in one helluva hurry to see you. He doesn't usually send the big boy.'

'This thing *flies*?' Langdon said.

The pilot smiled. 'Oh yeah.' He led Langdon across the tarmac toward the plane. 'Looks kind of startling, I know, but you better get used to it. In five years, all you'll see are these babies – HSCT's – High Speed Civil Transports. Our lab's one of the first to own one.'

Must be one hell of a lab, Langdon thought.

'This one's a prototype of the Boeing X-33,' the pilot continued, 'but there are dozens of others – the National Aero Space Plane, the Russians have Scramjet, the Brits have HOTOL. The future's here, it's just taking some time to get to the public sector. You can kiss conventional jets good-bye.'

Langdon looked up warily at the craft. 'I think I'd prefer a conventional jet.'

The pilot motioned up the gangplank. 'This way, please, Mr Langdon. Watch your step.'

Minutes later, Langdon was seated inside the empty cabin. The pilot buckled him into the front row and disappeared toward the front of the aircraft.

The cabin itself looked surprisingly like a wide-body commercial airliner. The only exception was that it had no windows, which made Langdon uneasy. He had been haunted his whole life by a mild case of claustrophobia – the vestige of a childhood incident he had never quite overcome.

Langdon's aversion to closed spaces was by no means debilitating, but it had always frustrated him. It manifested itself in subtle ways. He avoided enclosed sports like racquetball or squash, and he had gladly paid a small fortune for his airy, high-ceilinged Victorian home even though economical faculty housing was readily available. Langdon had often suspected his attraction to the art world as a young boy sprang from his love of museums' wide open spaces.

The engines roared to life beneath him, sending a deep shudder through the hull. Langdon swallowed hard and waited. He felt the plane start taxiing. Piped-in country music began playing quietly overhead.

A phone on the wall beside him beeped twice. Langdon lifted the receiver.

'Hello?'

'Comfortable, Mr Langdon?'

'Not at all.'

'Just relax. We'll be there in an hour.'

'And where exactly is *there*?' Langdon asked, realizing he had no idea where he was headed.

'Geneva,' the pilot replied, revving the engines. 'The lab's in Geneva.'

'Geneva,' Langdon repeated, feeling a little better. 'Upstate New York. I've actually got family near Seneca Lake. I wasn't aware Geneva had a physics lab.'

The pilot laughed. 'Not Geneva, *New York*, Mr Langdon. Geneva, *Switzerland*.'

The word took a long moment to register. 'Switzerland?' Langdon felt his pulse surge. 'I thought you said the lab was only an hour away!'

'It is, Mr Langdon.' The pilot chuckled. 'This plane goes Mach fifteen.'

5

On a busy European street, the killer serpentined through a crowd. He was a powerful man. Dark and potent. Deceptively agile. His muscles still felt hard from the thrill of his meeting.

It went well, he told himself. Although his employer had never revealed his face, the killer felt honored to be in his presence. *Had it really been only fifteen days since his employer had first made contact?* The killer

29

still remembered every word of that call . . .

'My name is Janus,' the caller had said. 'We are kins-men of a sort. We share an enemy. I hear your skills are for hire.'

'It depends whom you represent,' the killer replied.

The caller told him.

'Is this your idea of a joke?'

'You have heard our name, I see,' the caller replied.

'Of course. The brotherhood is legendary.'

'And yet you find yourself doubting I am genuine.'

'Everyone knows the brothers have faded to dust.'

'A devious ploy. The most dangerous enemy is that which no one fears.'

The killer was skeptical. 'The brotherhood endures?'

'Deeper underground than ever before. Our roots infiltrate everything you see . . . even the sacred fortress of our most sworn enemy.'

'Impossible. They are invulnerable.'

'Our reach is far.'

'No one's reach is that far.'

'Very soon, you will believe. An irrefutable demon-stration of the brotherhood's power has already transpired. A single act of treachery and proof.'

'What have you done?'

The caller told him.

The killer's eyes went wide. 'An impossible task.'

The next day, newspapers around the globe carried the same headline.The killer became a believer.

Now, fifteen days later, the killer's faith had solidi-fied beyond the shadow of a doubt. *The brotherhood endures*, he thought. *Tonight they will surface to reveal their power.*

As he made his way through the streets, his black

eyes gleamed with foreboding. One of the most covert and feared fraternities ever to walk the earth had called on him for service. *They have chosen wisely*, he thought. His reputation for secrecy was exceeded only by that of his deadliness.

So far, he had served them nobly. He had made his kill and delivered the item to Janus as requested. Now, it was up to Janus to use his power to ensure the item's placement.

The placement . . .

The killer wondered how Janus could possibly handle such a staggering task. The man obviously had connections on the inside. The brotherhood's dominion seemed limitless.

Janus, the killer thought. *A code name, obviously*. Was it a reference, he wondered, to the Roman two-faced god . . . or to the moon of Saturn? Not that it made any difference. Janus wielded unfathomable power. He had proven that beyond a doubt.

As the killer walked, he imagined his ancestors smiling down on him. Today he was fighting *their* battle, he was fighting the same enemy they had fought for ages, as far back as the eleventh century . . . when the enemy's crusading armies had first pillaged his land, raping and killing his people, declaring them unclean, defiling their temples and gods.

His ancestors had formed a small but deadly army to defend themselves. The army became famous across the land as protectors – skilled executioners who wandered the countryside slaughtering any of the enemy they could find. They were renowned not only for their brutal killings, but also for celebrating their slayings by plunging themselves into drug-induced stupors. Their drug of choice was a potent intoxicant they called *hashish*.

As their notoriety spread, these lethal men became known by a single word – *Hassassin* – literally 'the followers of hashish.' The name *Hassassin* became synonymous with death in almost every language on earth. The word was still used today, even in modern English ... but like the craft of killing, the word had evolved.

It was now pronounced *assassin*.

6

Sixty-four minutes had passed when an incredulous and slightly airsick Robert Langdon stepped down the gangplank onto the sun-drenched runway. A crisp breeze rustled the lapels of his tweed jacket. The open space felt wonderful. He squinted out at the lush green valley rising to snowcapped peaks all around them.

I'm dreaming, he told himself. *Any minute now I'll be waking up.*

'Welcome to Switzerland,' the pilot said, yelling over the roar of the X-33's misted-fuel HEDM engines winding down behind them.

Langdon checked his watch. It read 7.07 a.m.

'You just crossed six time zones,' the pilot offered. 'It's a little past 1 p.m. here.'

Langdon reset his watch.

'How do you feel?'

He rubbed his stomach. 'Like I've been eating Styrofoam.'

The pilot nodded. 'Altitude sickness. We were at

sixty thousand feet. You're thirty per cent lighter up there. Lucky we only did a puddle jump. If we'd gone to Tokyo I'd have taken her all the way up – a hundred miles. Now *that'll* get your insides rolling.'

Langdon gave a wan nod and counted himself lucky. All things considered, the flight had been remarkably ordinary. Aside from a bone-crunching acceleration during take off, the plane's motion had been fairly typical – occasional minor turbulence, a few pressure changes as they'd climbed, but nothing at all to suggest they had been hurtling through space at the mind-numbing speed of 11,000 miles per hour.

A handful of technicians scurried onto the runway to tend to the X-33. The pilot escorted Langdon to a black Peugeot sedan in a parking area beside the control tower. Moments later they were speeding down a paved road that stretched out across the valley floor. A faint cluster of buildings rose in the distance. Outside, the grassy plains tore by in a blur.

Langdon watched in disbelief as the pilot pushed the speedometer up around 170 kilometers an hour – over 100 miles per hour. *What is it with this guy and speed?* he wondered.

'Five kilometers to the lab,' the pilot said. 'I'll have you there in two minutes.'

Langdon searched in vain for a seat belt. *Why not make it three and get us there alive?*

The car raced on.

'Do you like Reba?' the pilot asked, jamming a cassette into the tape deck.

A woman started singing. 'It's just the fear of being alone . . .'

No fear here, Langdon thought absently. His female colleagues often ribbed him that his collection of

33

museum-quality artifacts was nothing more than a transparent attempt to fill an empty home, a home they insisted would benefit greatly from the presence of a woman. Langdon always laughed it off, reminding them he already had three loves in his life – symbology, water polo, and bachelorhood – the latter being a freedom that enabled him to travel the world, sleep as late as he wanted, and enjoy quiet nights at home with a brandy and a good book.

'We're like a small city,' the pilot said, pulling Langdon from his daydream. 'Not just labs. We've got supermarkets, a hospital, even a cinema.'

Langdon nodded blankly and looked out at the sprawling expanse of buildings rising before them.

'In fact,' the pilot added, 'we possess the largest machine on earth.'

'Really?' Langdon scanned the countryside.

'You won't see it out there, sir.' The pilot smiled. 'It's buried six stories below the earth.'

Langdon didn't have time to ask. Without warning the pilot jammed on the brakes. The car skidded to a stop outside a reinforced sentry booth.

Langdon read the sign before them. SECURITE. ARRETEZ. He suddenly felt a wave of panic, realizing where he was. 'My God! I didn't bring my passport!'

'Passports are unnecessary,' the driver assured. 'We have a standing arrangement with the Swiss government.'

Langdon watched dumbfounded as his driver gave the guard an ID. The sentry ran it through an electronic authentication device. The machine flashed green.

'Passenger name?'

'Robert Langdon,' the driver replied.

'Guest of?'

'The director.'

The sentry arched his eyebrows. He turned and checked a computer printout, verifying it against the data on his computer screen. Then he returned to the window. 'Enjoy your stay, Mr Langdon.'

The car shot off again, accelerating another 200 yards around a sweeping rotary that led to the facility's main entrance. Looming before them was a rectangular, ultramodern structure of glass and steel. Langdon was amazed by the building's striking transparent design. He had always had a fond love of architecture.

'The Glass Cathedral,' the escort offered.

'A church?'

'Hell, no. A church is the one thing we *don't* have. Physics is the religion around here. Use the Lord's name in vain all you like,' he laughed, 'just don't slander any quarks or mesons.'

Langdon sat bewildered as the driver swung the car around and brought it to a stop in front of the glass building. *Quarks and mesons? No border control? Mach 15 jets? Who the hell ARE these guys?* The engraved granite slab in front of the building bore the answer:

(CERN)
*Conseil Européen pour la
Recherche Nucléaire*

'Nuclear Research?' Langdon asked, fairly certain his translation was correct.

The driver did not answer. He was leaning forward, busily adjusting the car's cassette player. 'This is your stop. The director will meet you at this entrance.'

Langdon noted a man in a wheelchair exiting the building. He looked to be in his early sixties. Gaunt and totally bald with a sternly set jaw, he wore a white lab coat and dress shoes propped firmly on the wheelchair's footrest. Even at a distance his eyes looked lifeless – like two gray stones.

'Is that him?' Langdon asked.

The driver looked up. 'Well, I'll be.' He turned and gave Langdon an ominous smile. 'Speak of the devil.'

Uncertain what to expect, Langdon stepped from the vehicle.

The man in the wheelchair accelerated toward Langdon and offered a clammy hand. 'Mr Langdon? We spoke on the phone. My name is Maximilian Kohler.'

7

Maximilian Kohler, director general of CERN, was known behind his back as *König* – King. It was a title more of fear than reverence for the figure who ruled over his dominion from a wheelchair throne. Although few knew him personally, the horrific story of how he had been crippled was lore at CERN, and there were few there who blamed him for his bitterness . . . nor for his sworn dedication to pure science.

Langdon had only been in Kohler's presence a few moments and already sensed the director was a man who kept his distance. Langdon found himself practically jogging to keep up with Kohler's electric wheelchair as it sped silently toward the main entrance. The wheelchair was like none Langdon had ever seen – equipped with a bank of electronics including a multiline phone, a paging system, computer screen, even a small, detachable video camera. King Kohler's mobile command center.

Langdon followed through a mechanical door into CERN's voluminous main lobby.

The Glass Cathedral, Langdon mused, gazing upward toward heaven.

Overhead, the bluish glass roof shimmered in the afternoon sun, casting rays of geometric patterns in the air and giving the room a sense of grandeur. Angular shadows fell like veins across the white tiled walls and down to the marble floors. The air smelled clean, sterile. A handful of scientists moved briskly about, their footsteps echoing in the resonant space.

'This way, please, Mr Langdon.' His voice sounded almost computerized. His accent was rigid and precise, like his stern features. Kohler coughed and wiped his mouth on a white handkerchief as he fixed his dead gray eyes on Langdon. 'Please hurry.' His wheelchair seemed to leap across the tiled floor.

Langdon followed past what seemed to be countless hallways branching off the main atrium. Every hallway was alive with activity. The scientists who saw Kohler seemed to stare in surprise, eyeing Langdon as if wondering who he must be to command such company.

'I'm embarrassed to admit,' Langdon ventured, trying to make conversation, 'that I've never heard of CERN.'

'Not surprising,' Kohler replied, his clipped response sounding harshly efficient. 'Most Americans do not see Europe as the world leader in scientific research. They see us as nothing but a quaint shopping district – an odd perception if you consider the nationalities of men like Einstein, Galileo, and Newton.'

Langdon was unsure how to respond. He pulled the fax from his pocket. 'This man in the photograph, can you—'

Kohler cut him off with a wave of his hand. 'Please. Not here. I am taking you to him now.' He held out his hand. 'Perhaps I should take that.'

Langdon handed over the fax and fell silently into step.

Kohler took a sharp left and entered a wide hallway adorned with awards and commendations. A particularly large plaque dominated the entry. Langdon slowed to read the engraved bronze as they passed.

ARS ELECTRONICA AWARD
For Cultural Innovation in the Digital Age
Awarded to Tim Berners Lee and CERN
for the invention of the
WORLDWIDE WEB

Well I'll be damned, Langdon thought, reading the text. *This guy wasn't kidding.* Langdon had always thought of the Web as an American invention. Then again, his knowledge was limited to the site for his own book and the occasional on-line exploration of the Louvre or El Prado on his old Macintosh.

'The Web,' Kohler said, coughing again and wiping his mouth, 'began here as a network of in-house computer sites. It enabled scientists from different departments to share daily findings with one another. Of course, the entire world is under the impression the Web is U.S. technology.'

38

Langdon followed down the hall. 'Why not set the record straight?'

Kohler shrugged, apparently disinterested. 'A petty misconception over a petty technology. CERN is far greater than a global connection of computers. Our scientists produce miracles almost daily.'

Langdon gave Kohler a questioning look. '*Miracles?*' The word 'miracle' was certainly not part of the vocabulary around Harvard's Fairchild Science Building. *Miracles* were left for the School of Divinity.

'You sound skeptical,' Kohler said. 'I thought you were a religious symbologist. Do you not believe in miracles?'

'I'm undecided on miracles,' Langdon said. *Particularly those that take place in science labs.*

'Perhaps miracle is the wrong word. I was simply trying to speak your language.'

'My language?' Langdon was suddenly uncomfortable. 'Not to disappoint you, sir, but I study religious *symbology* – I'm an academic, not a priest.'

Kohler slowed suddenly and turned, his gaze softening a bit. 'Of course. How simple of me. One does not need to have cancer to analyze its symptoms.'

Langdon had never heard it put quite that way.

As they moved down the hallway, Kohler gave an accepting nod. 'I suspect you and I will understand each other perfectly, Mr Langdon.'

Somehow Langdon doubted it.

As the pair hurried on, Langdon began to sense a deep rumbling up ahead. The noise got more and more pronounced with every step, reverberating through the walls. It seemed to be coming from the end of the hallway in front of them.

'What's that?' Langdon finally asked, having to yell. He felt like they were approaching an active volcano.

'Free Fall Tube,' Kohler replied, his hollow voice cutting the air effortlessly. He offered no other explanation.

Langdon didn't ask. He was exhausted, and Maximilian Kohler seemed disinterested in winning any hospitality awards. Langdon reminded himself why he was here. *Illuminati*. He assumed somewhere in this colossal facility was a body . . . a body branded with a symbol he had just flown 3,000 miles to see.

As they approached the end of the hall, the rumble became almost deafening, vibrating up through Langdon's soles. They rounded the bend, and a viewing gallery appeared on the right. Four thick-paned portals were embedded in a curved wall, like windows in a submarine. Langdon stopped and looked through one of the holes.

Professor Robert Langdon had seen some strange things in his life, but this was the strangest. He blinked a few times, wondering if he was hallucinating. He was staring into an enormous circular chamber. Inside the chamber, floating as though weightless, were *people*. Three of them. One waved and did a somersault in midair.

My God, he thought. *I'm in the land of Oz.*

The floor of the room was a mesh grid, like a giant sheet of chicken wire. Visible beneath the grid was the metallic blur of a huge propeller.

'Free fall tube,' Kohler said, stopping to wait for him. 'Indoor skydiving. For stress relief. It's a vertical wind tunnel.'

Langdon looked on in amazement. One of the free fallers, an obese woman, maneuvered toward the window. She was being buffeted by the air currents but grinned and flashed Langdon the thumbs-up sign. Langdon smiled weakly and returned the gesture, wondering if she knew it was the ancient phallic symbol for masculine virility.

The heavyset woman, Langdon noticed, was the only one wearing what appeared to be a miniature parachute. The swathe of fabric billowed over her like a toy. 'What's her little chute for?' Langdon asked Kohler. 'It can't be more than a yard in diameter.'

'Friction,' Kohler said. 'Decreases her aerodynamics so the fan can lift her.' He started down the corridor again. 'One square yard of drag will slow a falling body almost twenty percent.'

Langdon nodded blankly.

He never suspected that later that night, in a country hundreds of miles away, the information would save his life.

8

When Kohler and Langdon emerged from the rear of CERN's main complex into the stark Swiss sunlight, Langdon felt as if he'd been transported home. The scene before him looked like an Ivy League campus.

A grassy slope cascaded downward onto an expansive lowlands where clusters of sugar maples dotted quadrangles bordered by brick dormitories and footpaths. Scholarly looking individuals with stacks of books hustled in and out of buildings. As if to accentuate the collegiate atmosphere, two longhaired hippies hurled a Frisbee back and forth while enjoying Mahler's Fourth Symphony blaring from a dorm window.

'These are our residential dorms,' Kohler explained as he accelerated his wheelchair down the path toward the buildings. 'We have over three thousand physicists here. CERN single-handedly employs more than half of the world's particle physicists – the brightest minds on earth – Germans, Japanese, Italians, Dutch, you name it. Our physicists represent over five hundred universities and sixty nationalities.'

Langdon was amazed. 'How do they all communicate?'

'English, of course. The universal language of science.'

Langdon had always heard *math* was the universal language of science, but he was too tired to argue. He dutifully followed Kohler down the path.

Halfway to the bottom, a young man jogged by. His T-shirt proclaimed the message: NO GUT, NO GLORY!

Langdon looked after him, mystified. 'Gut?'

'General Unified Theory,' Kohler quipped. 'The theory of everything.'

'I see,' Langdon said, not seeing at all.

'Are you familiar with particle physics, Mr Langdon?'

Langdon shrugged. 'I'm familiar with general physics – falling bodies, that sort of thing.' His years of high-diving experience had given him a profound respect for the awesome power of gravitational acceleration. 'Particle physics is the study of atoms, isn't it?'

Kohler shook his head. 'Atoms look like planets compared to what we deal with. Our interests lie with an atom's *nucleus* – a mere ten-thousandth the size of the whole.' He coughed again, sounding sick. 'The men and women of CERN are here to find answers to the same questions man has been asking since the beginning of time. Where did we come from? What are we made of?'

'And these answers are in a physics lab?'

'You sound surprised.'

'I am. The questions seem spiritual.'

'Mr Langdon, all questions were once spiritual. Since the beginning of time, spirituality and religion have been called on to fill in the gaps that science did not understand. The rising and setting of the sun was once attributed to *Helios* and a flaming chariot. Earthquakes and tidal waves were the wrath of Poseidon. Science has now proven those gods to be false idols. Soon *all* Gods will be proven to be false idols. Science has now provided answers to almost every question man can ask. There are only a few questions left, and they are the esoteric ones. Where do we come from? What are we doing here? What is the meaning of life and the universe?'

Langdon was amazed. 'And these are questions CERN is trying to answer?'

'Correction. These are questions we *are* answering.'

Langdon fell silent as the two men wound through the residential quadrangles. As they walked, a Frisbee sailed overhead and skidded to a stop directly in front of them. Kohler ignored it and kept going.

A voice called out from across the quad. '*S'il vous plaît!*'

Langdon looked over. An elderly white-haired man in a COLLEGE PARIS sweatshirt waved to him. Langdon picked up the Frisbee and expertly threw it back. The old man caught it on one finger and bounded it a few

43

times before whipping it over his shoulder to his partner. 'Merci!' he called to Langdon.

'Congratulations,' Kohler said when Langdon finally caught up. 'You just played toss with a Nobel prize-winner, Georges Charpak, inventor of the multi-wire proportional chamber.'

Langdon nodded. *My lucky day.*

It took Langdon and Kohler three more minutes to reach their destination – a large, well-kept dormitory sitting in a grove of aspens. Compared to the other dorms, this structure seemed luxurious. The carved stone sign in front read BUILDING C.

Imaginative title, Langdon thought.

But despite its sterile name, Building C appealed to Langdon's sense of architectural style – conservative and solid. It had a red brick facade, an ornate balustrade, and sat framed by sculpted symmetrical hedges. As the two men ascended the stone path toward the entry, they passed under a gateway formed by a pair of marble columns. Someone had put a sticky-note on one of them.

THIS COLUMN IS IONIC

Physicist graffiti? Langdon mused, eyeing the column and chuckling to himself. 'I'm relieved to see that even brilliant physicists make mistakes.'

Kohler looked over. 'What do you mean?'

'Whoever wrote that note made a mistake. That column isn't Ionic. Ionic columns are uniform in width. That one's tapered. It's Doric – the Greek counterpart. A common mistake.'

Kohler did not smile. 'The author meant it as a joke,

Mr Langdon. *Ionic* means containing ions – electrically charged particles. Most objects contain them.'

Langdon looked back at the column and groaned.

Langdon was still feeling stupid when he stepped from the elevator on the top floor of Building C. He followed Kohler down a well-appointed corridor. The decor was unexpected – traditional colonial French – a cherry divan, porcelain floor vase, and scrolled woodwork.

'We like to keep our tenured scientists comfortable,' Kohler explained.

Evidently, Langdon thought. 'So the man in the fax lived up here? One of your upper-level employees?'

'Quite,' Kohler said. 'He missed a meeting with me this morning and did not answer his page. I came up here to locate him and found him dead in his living room.'

Langdon felt a sudden chill realizing that he was about to see a dead body. His stomach had never been particularly stalwart. It was a weakness he'd discovered as an art student when the teacher informed the class that Leonardo da Vinci had gained his expertise in the human form by exhuming corpses and dissecting their musculature.

Kohler led the way to the far end of the hallway. There was a single door. 'The Penthouse, as you would say,' Kohler announced, dabbing a bead of perspiration from his forehead.

Langdon eyed the lone oak door before them. The name plate read:

LEONARDO VETRA

'Leonardo Vetra,' Kohler said, 'would have been

fifty-eight next week. He was one of the most brilliant scientists of our time. His death is a profound loss for science.'

For an instant Langdon thought he sensed emotion in Kohler's hardened face. But as quickly as it had come, it was gone. Kohler reached in his pocket and began sifting through a large key ring.

An odd thought suddenly occurred to Langdon. The building seemed deserted. 'Where is everyone?' he asked. The lack of activity was hardly what he expected considering they were about to enter a murder scene.

'The residents are in their labs,' Kohler replied, finding the key.

'I mean the *police*,' Langdon clarified. 'Have they left already?'

Kohler paused, his key halfway into the lock. 'Police?'

Langdon's eyes met the director's. 'Police. You sent me a fax of a homicide. You *must* have called the police.'

'I most certainly have not.'

'What?'

Kohler's gray eyes sharpened. 'The situation is complex, Mr Langdon.'

Langdon felt a wave of apprehension. 'But . . . certainly someone else knows about this!'

'Yes. Leonardo's adopted daughter. She is also a physicist here at CERN. She and her father share a lab. They are partners. Ms Vetra has been away this week doing field research. I have notified her of her father's death, and she is returning as we speak.'

'But a man has been murd—'

'A formal investigation,' Kohler said, his voice firm,

'will take place. However, it will most certainly involve a search of Vetra's lab, a space he and his daughter hold most private. Therefore, it will wait until Ms Vetra has arrived. I feel I owe her at least that modicum of discretion.'

Kohler turned the key.

As the door swung open, a blast of icy air hissed into the hall and hit Langdon in the face. He fell back in bewilderment. He was gazing across the threshold of an alien world. The flat before him was immersed in a thick, white fog. The mist swirled in smoky vortexes around the furniture and shrouded the room in opaque haze.

'What the . . .?' Langdon stammered.

'Freon cooling system,' Kohler replied. 'I chilled the flat to preserve the body.'

Langdon buttoned his tweed jacket against the cold. *I'm in Oz*, he thought. *And I forgot my magic slippers.*

9

The corpse on the floor before Langdon was hideous. The late Leonardo Vetra lay on his back, stripped naked, his skin bluish-gray. His neck bones were jutting out where they had been broken, and his head was twisted completely backward, pointing the wrong way. His face was out of view, pressed against the floor. The man lay in a frozen puddle of his own urine, the hair around his shriveled genitals spidered with frost.

Fighting a wave of nausea, Langdon let his eyes fall to the victim's chest. Although Langdon had stared at the symmetrical wound a dozen times on the fax, the burn was infinitely more commanding in real life. The raised, broiled flesh was perfectly delineated ... the symbol flawlessly formed.

Langdon wondered if the intense chill now raking through his body was the air-conditioning or his utter amazement with the significance of what he was now staring at.

His heart pounded as he circled the body, reading the word upside down, reaffirming the genius of the symmetry. The symbol seemed even less conceivable now that he was staring at it.

'Mr Langdon?'

Langdon did not hear. He was in another world ... his world, his element, a world where history, myth, and fact collided, flooding his senses. The gears turned.

'Mr Langdon?' Kohler's eyes probed expectantly.

Langdon did not look up. His disposition now intensified, his focus total. 'How much do you already know?'

'Only what I had time to read on your website. The word *Illuminati* means "the enlightened ones." It is the name of some sort of ancient brotherhood.'

Langdon nodded. 'Had you heard the name before?'

'Not until I saw it branded on Mr Vetra.'

'So you ran a web search for it?'

'Yes.'

'And the word returned hundreds of references, no doubt.'

'Thousands,' Kohler said. 'Yours, however, contained references to Harvard, Oxford, a reputable publisher, as well as a list of related publications. As a scientist I have come to learn that information is only as valuable as its source. Your credentials seemed authentic.'

Langdon's eyes were still riveted on the body.

Kohler said nothing more. He simply stared, apparently waiting for Langdon to shed some light on the scene before them.

Langdon looked up, glancing around the frozen flat. 'Perhaps we should discuss this in a warmer place?'

'This room is fine.' Kohler seemed oblivious to the cold. 'We'll talk here.'

Langdon frowned. The Illuminati history was by no means a simple one. *I'll freeze to death trying to explain it.* He gazed again at the brand, feeling a renewed sense of awe.

Although accounts of the Illuminati emblem were legendary in modern symbology, no academic had ever actually *seen* it. Ancient documents described the symbol as an *ambigram* – *ambi* meaning 'both' – signifying it was legible *both* ways. And although ambigrams were common in symbology – swastikas, yin yang, Jewish stars, simple crosses – the idea that a *word* could be crafted into an ambigram seemed utterly impossible. Modern symbologists had tried for years to forge the word 'Illuminati' into a perfectly symmetrical style, but they had failed miserably. Most academics had now decided the symbol's existence was a myth.

'So who are the Illuminati?' Kohler demanded.

Yes, Langdon thought, *who indeed*? He began his tale.

'Since the beginning of history,' Langdon explained, 'a deep rift has existed between science and religion. Outspoken scientists like Giordano Bruno—'

'Were murdered,' Kohler interjected. 'Murdered by the church for revealing scientific truths. Religion has always persecuted science.'

'Yes. But in the 1500s, a group of men in Rome fought back against the church. Some of Italy's most enlightened men – physicists, mathematicians, astronomers – began meeting secretly to share their concerns about the church's inaccurate teachings. They feared that the church's monopoly on "truth" threatened academic enlightenment around the world. They founded the world's first scientific think tank, calling themselves "the enlightened ones."'

'The Illuminati.'

'Yes,' Langdon said. 'Europe's most learned minds . . . dedicated to the quest for scientific truth.'

Kohler fell silent.

'Of course, the Illuminati were hunted ruthlessly by the Catholic Church. Only through rites of extreme secrecy did the scientists remain safe. Word spread through the academic underground, and the Illuminati brotherhood grew to include academics from all over Europe. The scientists met regularly in Rome at an ultrasecret lair they called the *Church of Illumination*.'

Kohler coughed and shifted in his chair.

'Many of the Illuminati,' Langdon continued, 'wanted to combat the church's tyranny with acts of violence, but their most revered member persuaded

50

them against it. He was a pacifist, as well as one of history's most famous scientists.'

Langdon was certain Kohler would recognize the name. Even nonscientists were familiar with the ill-fated astronomer who had been arrested and almost executed by the church for proclaiming that the *sun*, not the earth, was the center of the solar system. Although his data were incontrovertible, the astronomer was severely punished for implying that God had placed mankind somewhere other than at the *center* of His universe.

'His name was Galileo Galilei,' Langdon said.

Kohler looked up. 'Galileo?'

'Yes. Galileo was an Illuminatus. And he was also a devout Catholic. He tried to soften the church's position on science by proclaiming that science did not undermine the existence of God, but rather *reinforced* it. He wrote once that when he looked through his telescope at the spinning planets, he could hear God's voice in the music of the spheres. He held that science and religion were not enemies, but rather *allies* – two different languages telling the same story, a story of symmetry and balance ... heaven and hell, night and day, hot and cold, God and Satan. Both science and religion rejoiced in God's symmetry ... the end-less contest of light and dark.' Langdon paused, stamping his feet to stay warm.

Kohler simply sat in his wheelchair and stared.

'Unfortunately,' Langdon added, 'the unification of science and religion was not what the church wanted.'

'Of course not,' Kohler interrupted. 'The union would have nullified the church's claim as the *sole* vessel through which man could understand God. So the church tried Galileo as a heretic, found him guilty,

51

and put him under permanent house arrest. I am quite aware of scientific history, Mr Langdon. But this was all centuries ago. What does it have to do with Leonardo Vetra?'

The million dollar question. Langdon cut to the chase. 'Galileo's arrest threw the Illuminati into upheaval. Mistakes were made, and the church discovered the identities of four members, whom they captured and interrogated. But the four scientists revealed nothing . . . even under torture.'

'Torture?'

Langdon nodded. 'They were branded alive. On the chest. With the symbol of a cross.'

Kohler's eyes widened, and he shot an uneasy glance at Vetra's body.

'Then the scientists were brutally murdered, their dead bodies dropped in the streets of Rome as a warning to others thinking of joining the Illuminati. With the church closing in, the remaining Illuminati fled Italy.'

Langdon paused to make his point. He looked directly into Kohler's eyes. 'The Illuminati went deep underground, where they began mixing with other refugee groups fleeing the Catholic purges – mystics, alchemists, occultists, Muslims, Jews. Over the years, the Illuminati began absorbing new members. A new Illuminati emerged. A darker Illuminati. A deeply anti-Christian Illuminati. They grew very powerful, employing mysterious rites, deadly secrecy, vowing someday to rise again and take revenge on the Catholic Church. Their power grew to the point where the church considered them the single most dangerous anti-Christian force on earth. The Vatican denounced the brotherhood as *Shaitan*.'

'Shaitan?'

'It's Islamic. It means "adversary" ... *God's* adversary. The church chose Islam for the name because it was a language they considered dirty.' Langdon hesitated. '*Shaitan* is the root of an English word ... *Satan.*'

An uneasiness crossed Kohler's face.

Langdon's voice was grim. 'Mr Kohler, I do not know how this marking appeared on this man's chest ... or why ... but you are looking at the long-lost symbol of the world's oldest and most powerful satanic cult.'

10

The alley was narrow and deserted. The Hassassin strode quickly now, his black eyes filling with anticipation. As he approached his destination, Janus's parting words echoed in his mind. *Phase two begins shortly. Get some rest.*

The Hassassin smirked. He had been awake all night, but sleep was the last thing on his mind. Sleep was for the weak. He was a warrior like his ancestors before him, and his people never slept once a battle had begun. This battle had most definitely begun, and he had been given the honor of spilling first blood. Now he had two hours to celebrate his glory before going back to work.

Sleep? There are far better ways to relax ...

An appetite for hedonistic pleasure was something bred into him by his ancestors. His ascendants had indulged in hashish, but he preferred a different kind of gratification. He took pride in his body – a well-tuned, lethal machine, which, despite his heritage, he refused to pollute with narcotics. He had developed a more nourishing addiction than drugs . . . a far more healthy and satisfying reward.

Feeling a familiar anticipation swelling within him, the Hassassin moved faster down the alley. He arrived at the nondescript door and rang the bell. A view slit in the door opened, and two soft brown eyes studied him appraisingly. Then the door swung open.

'Welcome,' the well-dressed woman said. She ushered him into an impeccably furnished sitting room where the lights were low. The air was laced with expensive perfume and musk. 'Whenever you are ready.' She handed him a book of photographs. 'Ring me when you have made your choice.' Then she disappeared.

The Hassassin smiled.

As he sat on the plush divan and positioned the photo album on his lap, he felt a carnal hunger stir. Although his people did not celebrate Christmas, he imagined that this is what it must feel like to be a Christian child, sitting before a stack of Christmas presents, about to discover the miracles inside. He opened the album and examined the photos. A lifetime of sexual fantasies stared back at him.

Marisa. An Italian goddess. Fiery. A young Sophia Loren.

Sachiko. A Japanese geisha. Lithe. No doubt skilled.

Kanara. A stunning black vision. Muscular. Exotic.

He examined the entire album twice and made his choice. He pressed a button on the table beside him. A minute later the woman who had greeted him re-

54

appeared. He indicated his selection. She smiled. 'Follow me.'

After handling the financial arrangements, the woman made a hushed phone call. She waited a few minutes and then led him up a winding marble staircase to a luxurious hallway. 'It's the gold door on the end,' she said. 'You have expensive taste.'

I should, he thought. *I am a connoisseur.*

The Hassassin padded the length of the hallway like a panther anticipating a long overdue meal. When he reached the doorway he smiled to himself. It was already ajar . . . welcoming him in. He pushed, and the door swung noiselessly open.

When he saw his selection, he knew he had chosen well. She was exactly as he had requested . . . nude, lying on her back, her arms tied to the bedposts with thick velvet cords.

He crossed the room and ran a dark finger across her ivory abdomen. *I killed last night,* he thought. *You are my reward.*

11

'Satanic?' Kohler wiped his mouth and shifted uncomfortably. 'This is the symbol of a *satanic* cult?'

Langdon paced the frozen room to keep warm. 'The Illuminati were satanic. But not in the modern sense.'

Langdon quickly explained how most people pictured satanic cults as devil-worshiping fiends, and yet Satanists historically were educated men who stood as adversaries to the church. *Shaitan*. The rumors of satanic black-magic animal sacrifices and the pentagram ritual were nothing but lies spread by the church as a smear campaign against their adversaries. Over time, opponents of the church, wanting to emulate the Illuminati, began believing the lies and acting them out. Thus, modern Satanism was born.

Kohler grunted abruptly. 'This is all ancient history. I want to know how this symbol got *here*.'

Langdon took a deep breath. 'The symbol itself was created by an anonymous sixteenth-century Illuminati artist as a tribute to Galileo's love of symmetry – a kind of sacred Illuminati logo. The brotherhood kept the design secret, allegedly planning to reveal it only when they had amassed enough power to resurface and carry out their final goal.'

Kohler looked unsettled. 'So this symbol means the Illuminati brotherhood is resurfacing?'

Langdon frowned. 'That would be impossible. There is one chapter of Illuminati history that I have not yet explained.'

Kohler's voice intensified. 'Enlighten me.'

Langdon rubbed his palms together, mentally sorting through the hundreds of documents he'd read or written on the Illuminati. 'The Illuminati were survivors,' he explained. 'When they fled Rome, they traveled across Europe looking for a safe place to regroup. They were taken in by another secret society . . . a brotherhood of wealthy Bavarian stone craftsmen called the Freemasons.'

Kohler looked startled. 'The Masons?'

Langdon nodded, not at all surprised that Kohler had heard of the group. The brotherhood of the Masons currently had over five million members worldwide, half of them residing in the United States, and over one million of them in Europe.

'Certainly the Masons are not satanic,' Kohler declared, sounding suddenly skeptical.

'Absolutely not. The Masons fell victim of their own benevolence. After harboring the fleeing scientists in the 1700s, the Masons unknowingly became a front for the Illuminati. The Illuminati grew within their ranks, gradually taking over positions of power within the lodges. They quietly reestablished their scientific brotherhood deep within the Masons – a kind of secret society within a secret society. Then the Illuminati used the worldwide connection of Masonic lodges to spread their influence.'

Langdon drew a cold breath before racing on. 'Obliteration of Catholicism was the Illuminati's central covenant. The brotherhood held that the super-stitious dogma spewed forth by the church was mankind's greatest enemy. They feared that if religion continued to promote pious myth as absolute fact, scientific progress would halt, and mankind would be doomed to an ignorant future of senseless holy wars.'

'Much like we see today.'

Langdon frowned. Kohler was right. Holy wars were still making headlines. *My God is better than your God.* It seemed there was always close correlation between true believers and high body counts.

'Go on,' Kohler said.

Langdon gathered his thoughts and continued. 'The Illuminati grew more powerful in Europe and set their sights on America, a fledgling government many of whose leaders were Masons – George Washington, Ben Franklin – honest, God-fearing men who were unaware of the Illuminati stronghold on the Masons.

The Illuminati took advantage of the infiltration and helped found banks, universities, and industry to finance their ultimate quest.' Langdon paused. 'The creation of a single unified world state – a kind of secular New World Order.'

Kohler did not move.

'A New World Order,' Langdon repeated, 'based on scientific enlightenment. They called it their Luciferian Doctrine. The church claimed Lucifer was a reference to the devil, but the brotherhood insisted Lucifer was intended in its literal Latin meaning – *bringer of light*. Or *Illuminator*.'

Kohler sighed, and his voice grew suddenly solemn. 'Mr Langdon, please sit down.'

Langdon sat tentatively on a frost-covered chair.

Kohler moved his wheelchair closer. 'I am not sure I understand everything you have just told me, but I do understand this. Leonardo Vetra was one of CERN's greatest assets. He was also a friend. I need you to help me locate the Illuminati.'

Langdon didn't know how to respond. 'Locate the Illuminati?' *He's kidding, right?* 'I'm afraid, sir, that will be utterly impossible.'

Kohler's brow creased. 'What do you mean? You won't—'

'Mr Kohler,' Langdon leaned toward his host, uncertain how to make him understand what he was about to say. 'I did not finish my story. Despite appearances, it is extremely unlikely that this brand was put here by the Illuminati. There has been no evidence of their existence for over half a century, and most scholars agree the Illuminati have been defunct for many years.'

The words hit silence. Kohler stared through the fog

with a look somewhere between stupefaction and anger. 'How the hell can you tell me this group is extinct when their name is seared into this man!'

Langdon had been asking himself that question all morning. The appearance of the Illuminati ambigram was astonishing. Symbologists worldwide would be dazzled. And yet, the academic in Langdon understood that the brand's reemergence proved absolutely nothing about the Illuminati.

'Symbols,' Langdon said, 'in no way confirm the presence of their original creators.'

'What is *that* supposed to mean?'

'It means that when organized philosophies like the Illuminati go out of existence, their symbols remain . . . available for adoption by other groups. It's called *transference*. It's very common in symbology. The Nazis took the swastika from the Hindus, the Christians adopted the cruciform from the Egyptians, the—'

'This morning,' Kohler challenged, 'when I typed the word "Illuminati" into the computer, it returned thousands of current references. Apparently a lot of people think this group is still active.'

'Conspiracy buffs,' Langdon replied. He had always been annoyed by the plethora of conspiracy theories that circulated in modern pop culture. The media craved apocalyptic headlines, and self-proclaimed 'cult specialists' were still cashing in on millennium hype with fabricated stories that the Illuminati were alive and well and organizing their New World Order. Recently the *New York Times* had reported the eerie Masonic ties of countless famous men – Sir Arthur Conan Doyle, the Duke of Kent, Peter Sellers, Irving Berlin, Prince Philip, Louis Armstrong, as well as a pantheon of well-known modern-day industrialists and banking magnates.

Kohler pointed angrily at Vetra's body. 'Considering the evidence, I would say perhaps the conspiracy buffs are correct.'

'I realize how it appears,' Langdon said as diplomatically as he could. 'And yet a far more plausible explanation is that some *other* organization has taken control of the Illuminati brand and is using it for their own purposes.'

'What purposes? What does this murder prove?'

Good question, Langdon thought. He was also having trouble imagining where anyone could have turned up the Illuminati brand after 400 years. 'All I can tell you is that even if the Illuminati were still active today, which I am virtually positive they are not, they would never be involved in Leonardo Vetra's death.'

'No?'

'No. The Illuminati may have believed in the abolition of Christianity, but they wielded their power through political and financial means, not through terrorist acts. Furthermore, the Illuminati had a strict code of morality regarding who they saw as enemies. They held men of science in the highest regard. There is no way they would have murdered a fellow scientist like Leonardo Vetra.'

Kohler's eyes turned to ice. 'Perhaps I failed to mention that Leonardo Vetra was anything but an ordinary scientist.'

Langdon exhaled patiently. 'Mr Kohler, I'm sure Leonardo Vetra was brilliant in many ways, but the fact remains—'

Without warning, Kohler spun in his wheelchair and accelerated out of the living room, leaving a wake of swirling mist as he disappeared down a hallway.

For the love of God, Langdon groaned. He followed. Kohler was waiting for him in a small alcove at the end of the hallway.

'This is Leonardo's study,' Kohler said, motioning to the sliding door. 'Perhaps when you see it you'll understand things differently.' With an awkward grunt, Kohler heaved, and the door slid open.

Langdon peered into the study and immediately felt his skin crawl. *Holy mother of Jesus*, he said to himself.

12

In another country, a young guard sat patiently before an expansive bank of video monitors. He watched as images flashed before him – live feeds from hundreds of wireless video cameras that surveyed the sprawling complex. The images went by in an endless procession.

An ornate hallway.

A private office.

An industrial-size kitchen.

As the pictures went by, the guard fought off a daydream. He was nearing the end of his shift, and yet he was still vigilant. Service was an honor. Someday he would be granted his ultimate reward.

As his thoughts drifted, an image before him registered alarm. Suddenly, with a reflexive jerk that startled even himself, his hand shot out and hit a button on the control panel. The picture before him froze.

His nerves tingling, he leaned toward the screen for

a closer look. The reading on the monitor told him the image was being transmitted from camera #86 – a camera that was supposed to be overlooking a hallway.

But the image before him was most definitely *not* a hallway.

13

Langdon stared in bewilderment at the study before him. 'What *is* this place?' Despite the welcome blast of warm air on his face, he stepped through the door with trepidation.

Kohler said nothing as he followed Langdon inside.

Langdon scanned the room, not having the slightest idea what to make of it. It contained the most peculiar mix of artifacts he had ever seen. On the far wall, dominating the decor, was an enormous wooden crucifix, which Langdon placed as fourteenth-century Spanish. Above the cruciform, suspended from the ceiling, was a metallic mobile of the orbiting planets. To the left was an oil painting of the Virgin Mary, and beside that was a laminated periodic table of elements. On the side wall, two additional brass cruciforms flanked a poster of Albert Einstein, his famous quote reading, GOD DOES NOT PLAY DICE WITH THE UNIVERSE.

Langdon moved into the room, looking around in astonishment. A leather-bound Bible sat on Vetra's desk beside a plastic Bohr model of an atom and a miniature replica of Michelangelo's Moses.

Talk about eclectic, Langdon thought. The warmth

felt good, but something about the decor sent a new set of chills through his body. He felt like he was witnessing the clash of two philosophical titans . . . an unsettling blur of opposing forces. He scanned the titles on the bookshelf:

The God Particle
The Tao of Physics
God: The Evidence

One of the bookends was etched with a quote:

> TRUE SCIENCE DISCOVERS GOD
> WAITING BEHIND EVERY DOOR.
> —POPE PIUS XII

'Leonardo was a Catholic priest,' Kohler said.

Langdon turned. 'A priest? I thought you said he was a physicist.'

'He was both. Men of science and religion are not unprecedented in history. Leonardo was one of them. He considered physics "God's natural law". He claimed God's handwriting was visible in the natural order all around us. Through science he hoped to prove God's existence to the doubting masses. He considered himself a theo-physicist.'

Theo-physicist? Langdon thought it sounded impossibly oxymoronic.

'The field of particle physics,' Kohler said, 'has made some shocking discoveries lately – discoveries quite spiritual in implication. Leonardo was responsible for many of them.'

Langdon studied CERN's director, still trying to process the bizarre surroundings. 'Spirituality and physics?' Langdon had spent his career studying religious history, and if there was one recurring theme, it was that science and religion had been oil and water since day one . . . archenemies . . . unmixable.

'Vetra was on the cutting edge of particle physics,' Kohler said. 'He was starting to fuse science and religion . . . showing that they complement each other in most unanticipated ways. He called the field *New Physics*.' Kohler pulled a book from the shelf and handed it to Langdon.

Langdon studied the cover. *God, Miracles, and the New Physics* – by Leonardo Vetra.

'The field is small,' Kohler said, 'but it's bringing fresh answers to some old questions – questions about the origin of the universe and the forces that bind us all. Leonardo believed his research had the potential to convert millions to a more spiritual life. Last year he categorically proved the existence of an energy force that unites us all. He actually demonstrated that we are all physically connected . . . that the molecules in your body are intertwined with the molecules in mine . . . that there is a single force moving within all of us.'

Langdon felt disconcerted. *And the power of God shall unite us all.* 'Mr Vetra actually found a way to *demonstrate* that particles are connected?'

'Conclusive evidence. A recent *Scientific American* article hailed *New Physics* as a surer path to God than religion itself.'

The comment hit home. Langdon suddenly found himself thinking of the antireligious Illuminati. Reluctantly, he forced himself to permit a momentary intellectual foray into the impossible. If the Illuminati were indeed still active, would they have killed Leonardo to stop him from bringing his religious message to the masses? Langdon shook off the thought. *Absurd! The Illuminati are ancient history! All academics know that!*

'Vetra had plenty of enemies in the scientific world,' Kohler went on. 'Many scientific purists despised him. Even here at CERN. They felt that using analytical physics to support religious principles was a treason against science.'

'But aren't scientists today a bit less defensive about the church?'

Kohler grunted in disgust. 'Why *should* we be? The church may not be burning scientists at the stake anymore, but if you think they've released their reign over science, ask yourself why half the schools in your country are not allowed to teach evolution. Ask yourself why the U.S. Christian Coalition is the most influential lobby against scientific progress in the world. The battle between science and religion is still raging, Mr Langdon. It has moved from the battlefields to the boardrooms, but it is still raging.'

Langdon realized Kohler was right. Just last week the Harvard School of Divinity had marched on the Biology Building, protesting the genetic engineering taking place in the graduate program. The chairman of the Bio Department, famed ornithologist Richard Aaronian, defended his curriculum by hanging a huge banner from his office window. The banner depicted the Christian 'fish' modified with four little feet – a tribute, Aaronian claimed, to the African lung-fishes' evolution onto dry land. Beneath the fish, instead of the word 'Jesus', was the proclamation 'DARWIN!'

A sharp beeping sound cut the air, and Langdon looked up. Kohler reached down into the array of electronics on his wheelchair. He slipped a beeper out of its holder and read the incoming message.

'Good. That is Leonardo's daughter. Ms Vetra is arriving at the helipad right now. We will meet her there. I think it best she not come up here and see her father this way.'

Langdon agreed. It would be a shock no child deserved.

'I will ask Ms Vetra to explain the project she and her father have been working on . . . perhaps shedding light on why he was murdered.'

'You think Vetra's *work* is why he was killed?'

'Quite possibly. Leonardo told me he was working on something groundbreaking. That is all he said. He had become very secretive about the project. He had a private lab and demanded seclusion, which I gladly afforded him on account of his brilliance. His work had been consuming huge amounts of electric power lately, but I refrained from questioning him.' Kohler rotated toward the study door. 'There is, however, one more thing you need to know before we leave this flat.'

Langdon was not sure he wanted to hear it.

'An item was stolen from Vetra by his murderer.'

'An item?'

'Follow me.'

The director propelled his wheelchair back into the fog-filled living room. Langdon followed, not knowing what to expect. Kohler maneuvered to within inches of Vetra's body and stopped. He ushered Langdon to join him. Reluctantly, Langdon came close, bile rising in his throat at the smell of the victim's frozen urine.

'Look at his face,' Kohler said.

Look at his face? Langdon frowned. *I thought you said something was stolen.*

Hesitantly, Langdon knelt down. He tried to see Vetra's face, but the head was twisted 180 degrees backward, his face pressed into the carpet.

Struggling against his handicap Kohler reached down and carefully twisted Vetra's frozen head. Cracking loudly, the corpse's face rotated into view, contorted in agony. Kohler held it there for a moment.

'Sweet Jesus!' Langdon cried, stumbling back in horror. Vetra's face was covered in blood. A single hazel eye stared lifelessly back at him. The other socket was tattered and empty. 'They stole his *eye*?'

14

Langdon stepped out of Building C into the open air, grateful to be outside Vetra's flat. The sun helped dissolve the image of the empty eye socket emblazoned into his mind.

'This way, please,' Kohler said, veering up a steep path. The electric wheelchair seemed to accelerate effortlessly. 'Ms Vetra will be arriving any moment.'

Langdon hurried to keep up.

'So,' Kohler asked. 'Do you still doubt the Illuminati's involvement?'

Langdon had no idea what to think anymore. Vetra's religious affiliations were definitely troubling, and yet Langdon could not bring himself to abandon every shred of academic evidence he had ever researched. Besides, there was the eye . . .

'I still maintain,' Langdon said, more forcefully than

he intended, 'that the Illuminati are *not* responsible for this murder. The missing eye is proof.'

'What?'

'Random mutilation,' Langdon explained, 'is very ... *un*-Illuminati. Cult specialists see desultory defacement from inexperienced fringe sects – zealots who commit random acts of terrorism – but the Illuminati have always been more deliberate.'

'Deliberate? Surgically removing someone's eyeball is not deliberate?'

'It sends no clear message. It serves no higher purpose.'

Kohler's wheelchair stopped short at the top of the hill. He turned. 'Mr Langdon, believe me, that missing eye does *indeed* serve a higher purpose ... a much higher purpose.'

As the two men crossed the grassy rise, the beating of helicopter blades became audible to the west. A chopper appeared, arching across the open valley toward them. It banked sharply, then slowed to a hover over a helipad painted on the grass.

Langdon watched, detached, his mind churning circles like the blades, wondering if a full night's sleep would make his current disorientation any clearer. Somehow, he doubted it.

As the skids touched down, a pilot jumped out and started unloading gear. There was a lot of it – duffels, vinyl wet bags, scuba tanks, and crates of what appeared to be high-tech diving equipment.

Langdon was confused. 'Is that Ms Vetra's gear?' he yelled to Kohler over the roar of the engines.

Kohler nodded and yelled back, 'She was doing biological research in the Balearic Sea.'

'I thought you said she was a *physicist*!'

'She is. She's a Bio Entanglement Physicist. She studies the interconnectivity of life systems. Her work ties closely with her father's work in particle physics. Recently she disproved one of Einstein's fundamental theories by using atomically synchronized cameras to observe a school of tuna fish.'

Langdon searched his host's face for any glint of humor. *Einstein and tuna fish?* He was starting to wonder if the X-33 space plane had mistakenly dropped him off on the wrong planet.

A moment later, Vittoria Vetra emerged from the fuselage. Robert Langdon realized today was going to be a day of endless surprises. Descending from the chopper in her khaki shorts and white sleeveless top, Vittoria Vetra looked nothing like the bookish physicist he had expected. Lithe and graceful, she was tall with chestnut skin and long black hair that swirled in the backwind of the rotors. Her face was unmistakably Italian – not overly beautiful, but possessing full, earthy features that even at twenty yards seemed to exude a raw sensuality. As the air currents buffeted her body, her clothes clung, accentuating her slender torso and small breasts.

'Ms Vetra is a woman of tremendous personal strength,' Kohler said, seeming to sense Langdon's captivation. 'She spends months at a time working in dangerous ecological systems. She is a strict vegetarian and CERN's resident guru of Hatha yoga.'

Hatha yoga? Langdon mused. The ancient Buddhist art of meditative stretching seemed an odd proficiency for the physicist daughter of a Catholic priest.

Langdon watched Vittoria approach. She had obviously been crying, her deep sable eyes filled with emotions Langdon could not place. Still, she moved toward them with fire and command. Her limbs were strong and toned, radiating the healthy luminescence of Mediterranean flesh that had enjoyed long hours in the sun.

'Vittoria,' Kohler said as she approached. 'My deepest condolences. It's a terrible loss for science . . . for all of us here at CERN.'

Vittoria nodded gratefully. When she spoke, her voice was smooth – a throaty, accented English. 'Do you know who is responsible yet?'

'We're still working on it.'

She turned to Langdon, holding out a slender hand. 'My name is Vittoria Vetra. You're from Interpol, I assume?'

Langdon took her hand, momentarily spellbound by the depth of her watery gaze. 'Robert Langdon.' He was unsure what else to say.

'Mr Langdon is not with the authorities,' Kohler explained. 'He is a specialist from the U.S. He's here to help us locate who is responsible for this situation.'

Vittoria looked uncertain. 'And the police?'

Kohler exhaled but said nothing.

'Where is his body?' she demanded.

'Being attended to.'

The white lie surprised Langdon.

'I want to see him,' Vittoria said.

'Vittoria,' Kohler urged, 'your father was brutally murdered. You would be better to remember him as he was.'

Vittoria began to speak but was interrupted.

'Hey, Vittoria!' voices called from the distance. 'Welcome home!'

70

She turned. A group of scientists passing near the helipad waved happily.

'Disprove any more of Einstein's theories?' one shouted.

Another added, 'Your dad must be proud!'

Vittoria gave the men an awkward wave as they passed. Then she turned to Kohler, her face now clouded with confusion. 'Nobody *knows* yet?'

'I decided discretion was paramount.'

'You haven't told the staff my father was *murdered*?' Her mystified tone was now laced with anger.

Kohler's tone hardened instantly. 'Perhaps you forget, Ms Vetra, as soon as I report your father's murder, there will be an investigation of CERN. Including a thorough examination of his lab. I have always tried to respect your father's privacy. Your father has told me only two things about your current project. One, that it has the potential to bring CERN millions of francs in licensing contracts in the next decade. And two, that it is not ready for public disclosure because it is still hazardous technology. Considering these two facts, I would prefer strangers not poke around inside his lab and either steal his work or kill themselves in the process and hold CERN liable. Do I make myself clear?'

Vittoria stared, saying nothing. Langdon sensed in her a reluctant respect and acceptance of Kohler's logic.

'Before we report anything to the authorities,' Kohler said, 'I need to know what you two were working on. I need you to take us to your lab.'

'The lab is irrelevant,' Vittoria said. 'Nobody knew what my father and I were doing. The experiment could not possibly have anything to do with my father's murder.'

Kohler exhaled a raspy, ailing breath. 'Evidence suggests otherwise.'

'Evidence? What evidence?'

Langdon was wondering the same thing.

Kohler was dabbing his mouth again. 'You'll just have to trust me.'

It was clear, from Vittoria's smoldering gaze, that she did not.

15

Langdon strode silently behind Vittoria and Kohler as they moved back into the main atrium where Langdon's bizarre visit had begun. Vittoria's legs drove in fluid efficiency – like an Olympic diver – a potency, Langdon figured, no doubt born from the flexibility and control of yoga. He could hear her breathing slowly and deliberately, as if somehow trying to filter her grief.

Langdon wanted to say something to her, offer his sympathy. He too had once felt the abrupt hollowness of unexpectedly losing a parent. He remembered the funeral mostly, rainy and gray. Two days after his twelfth birthday. The house was filled with gray-suited men from the office, men who squeezed his hand too hard when they shook it. They were all mumbling words like *cardiac* and *stress*. His mother joked through teary eyes that she'd always been able to follow the stock market simply by holding her husband's hand . . . his pulse her own private ticker tape.

Once, when his father was alive, Langdon had heard his mom begging his father to 'stop and smell the roses'. That year, Langdon bought his father a tiny blown-glass rose for Christmas. It was the most beautiful thing Langdon had ever seen . . . the way the sun caught it, throwing a rainbow of colours on the wall. 'It's lovely,' his father had said when he opened it, kissing Robert on the forehead. 'Let's find a safe spot for it.' Then his father had carefully placed the rose on a high dusty shelf in the darkest corner of the living room. A few days later, Langdon got a stool, retrieved the rose, and took it back to the store. His father never noticed it was gone.

The ping of an elevator pulled Langdon back to the present. Vittoria and Kohler were in front of him, boarding the lift. Langdon hesitated outside the open doors.

'Is something wrong?' Kohler asked, sounding more impatient than concerned.

'Not at all,' Langdon said, forcing himself toward the cramped carriage. He only used elevators when absolutely necessary. He preferred the more open spaces of stairwells.

'Dr Vetra's lab is subterranean,' Kohler said.

Wonderful, Langdon thought as he stepped across the cleft, feeling an icy wind churn up from the depths of the shaft. The doors closed, and the car began to descend.

'Six stories,' Kohler said blankly, like an analytical engine.

Langdon pictured the darkness of the empty shaft below them. He tried to block it out by staring at the numbered display of changing floors. Oddly, the elevator showed only two stops. GROUND LEVEL and LHC.

73

'What's LHC stand for?' Langdon asked, trying not to sound nervous.

'Large Hadron Collider,' Kohler said. 'A particle accelerator.'

Particle accelerator? Langdon was vaguely familiar with the term. He had first heard it over dinner with some colleagues at Dunster House in Cambridge. A physicist friend of theirs, Bob Brownell, had arrived for dinner one night in a rage.

'The bastards canceled it!' Brownell cursed.

'Canceled what?' they all asked.

'The SSC!'

'The what?'

'The Superconducting Super Collider!'

Someone shrugged. 'I didn't know Harvard was building one.'

'Not Harvard!' he exclaimed. 'The U.S.! It was going to be the world's most powerful particle accelerator! One of the most important scientific projects of the century! Two *billion* dollars into it and the Senate sacks the project! Damn Bible-Belt lobbyists!'

When Brownell finally calmed down, he explained that a particle accelerator was a large, circular tube through which subatomic particles were accelerated. Magnets in the tube turned on and off in rapid succession to 'push' particles around and around until they reached tremendous velocities. Fully accelerated particles circled the tube at over 180,000 miles per *second*.

'But that's almost the speed of light,' one of the professors exclaimed.

'Damn right,' Brownell said. He went on to say that by accelerating two particles in opposite directions around the tube and then colliding them, scientists could shatter the particles into their constituent parts and get a glimpse of nature's most fundamental components. 'Particle accelerators,' Brownell declared, 'are critical to the future of science. Colliding particles is the key to understanding the building blocks of the universe.'

Harvard's *Poet in Residence*, a quiet man named Charles Pratt, did not look impressed. 'It sounds to me,' he said, 'like a rather Neanderthal approach to science . . . akin to smashing clocks together to discern their internal workings.'

Brownell dropped his fork and stormed out of the room.

So CERN has a particle accelerator? Langdon thought, as the elevator dropped. *A circular tube for smashing particles.* He wondered why they had buried it underground.

When the elevator thumped to a stop, Langdon was relieved to feel terra firma beneath his feet. But when the doors slid open, his relief evaporated. Robert Langdon found himself standing once again in a totally alien world.

The passageway stretched out indefinitely in both directions, left and right. It was a smooth cement tunnel, wide enough to allow passage of an eighteen wheeler. Brightly lit where they stood, the corridor turned pitch black further down. A damp wind rustled out of the darkness – an unsettling reminder that they were now deep in the earth. Langdon could almost sense the weight of the dirt and stone now hanging above his head. For an instant he was nine years old . . . the darkness forcing him back . . . back to the five hours of crushing blackness that haunted him still. Clenching his fists, he fought it off.

Vittoria remained hushed as she exited the elevator

and strode off without hesitation into the darkness without them. Overhead the fluorescents flickered on to light her path. The effect was unsettling, Langdon thought, as if the tunnel were alive . . . anticipating her every move. Langdon and Kohler followed, trailing a distance behind. The lights extinguished automatically behind them.

'This particle accelerator,' Langdon said quietly. 'It's down this tunnel someplace?'

'That's it there.' Kohler motioned to his left where a polished, chrome tube ran along the tunnel's inner wall.

Langdon eyed the tube, confused. '*That's* the accelerator?' The device looked nothing like he had imagined. It was perfectly straight, about three feet in diameter, and extended horizontally the visible length of the tunnel before disappearing into the darkness. *Looks more like a high-tech sewer*, Langdon thought. 'I thought particle accelerators were *circular*.'

'This accelerator *is* a circle,' Kohler said. 'It appears straight, but that is an optical illusion. The circumference of this tunnel is so large that the curve is imperceptible – like that of the earth.'

Langdon was flabbergasted. *This is a circle?* 'But . . . it must be enormous!'

'The LHC is the largest machine in the world.'

Langdon did a double take. He remembered the CERN driver saying something about a huge machine buried in the earth. *But—*

'It is over eight kilometers in diameter . . . and twenty-seven kilometres long.'

Langdon's head whipped around. 'Twenty-seven kilometers?' He stared at the director and then turned and looked into the darkened tunnel before him. 'This

tunnel is twenty-seven kilometers long? That's . . .
that's over sixteen miles!'

Kohler nodded. 'Bored in a perfect circle. It extends
all the way into France before curving back here to this
spot. Fully accelerated particles will circle the tube
more than ten thousand times in a single second before
they collide.'

Langdon's legs felt rubbery as he stared down the
gaping tunnel. 'You're telling me that CERN dug out
millions of tons of earth just to smash tiny particles?'

Kohler shrugged. 'Sometimes to find truth, one
must move mountains.'

16

Hundreds of miles from CERN, a voice crackled
through a walkie-talkie. 'Okay, I'm in the hallway.'

The technician monitoring the video screens
pressed the button on his transmitter. 'You're looking
for camera #86. It's supposed to be at the far end.'

There was a long silence on the radio. The waiting
technician broke a light sweat. Finally his radio
clicked.

'The camera isn't here,' the voice said. 'I can see
where it was mounted, though. Somebody must have
removed it.'

The technician exhaled heavily. 'Thanks. Hold on a
second, will you?'

Sighing, he redirected his attention to the bank of
video screens in front of him. Huge portions of the
complex were open to the public, and wireless

cameras had gone missing before, usually stolen by visiting pranksters looking for souvenirs. But as soon as a camera left the facility and was out of range, the signal was lost, and the screen went blank. Perplexed, the technician gazed up at the monitor. A crystal clear image was still coming from camera #86.

If the camera was stolen, he wondered, *why are we still getting a signal?* He knew, of course, there was only one explanation. The camera was still inside the complex, and someone had simply moved it. *But who? And why?*

He studied the monitor a long moment. Finally he picked up his walkie-talkie. 'Are there any closets in that stairwell? Any cupboards or dark alcoves?'

The voice replying sounded confused. 'No. Why?'

The technician frowned. 'Never mind. Thanks for your help.' He turned off his walkie-talkie and pursed his lips.

Considering the small size of the video camera and the fact that it was wireless, the technician knew that camera #86 could be transmitting from just about *anywhere* within the heavily guarded compound – a densely packed collection of thirty-two separate buildings covering a half-mile radius. The only clue was that the camera seemed to have been placed somewhere dark. Of course, that wasn't much help. The complex contained endless dark locations – maintenance closets, heating ducts, gardening sheds, bedroom wardrobes, even a labyrinth of underground tunnels. Camera #86 could take weeks to locate.

But that's the least of my problems, he thought.

Despite the dilemma posed by the camera's relocation, there was another far more unsettling matter at hand. The technician gazed up at the image the lost camera was transmitting. It was a stationary

78

object. A modern-looking device like nothing the technician had ever seen. He studied the blinking electronic display at its base.

Although the guard had undergone rigorous training preparing him for tense situations, he still sensed his pulse rising. He told himself not to panic. There had to be an explanation. The object appeared too small to be of significant danger. Then again, its presence inside the complex was troubling. *Very troubling, indeed.*

Today of all days, he thought.

Security was always a top priority for his employer, but *today,* more than any other day in the past twelve years, security was of the utmost importance. The technician stared at the object for a long time and sensed the rumblings of a distant gathering storm.

Then, sweating, he dialed his superior.

17

Not many children could say they remembered the day they met their father, but Vittoria Vetra could. She was eight years old, living where she always had, *Orfanotrofio di Siena*, a Catholic orphanage near Florence, deserted by parents she never knew. It was raining that day. The nuns had called for her twice to come to dinner, but as always she pretended not to hear. She lay outside in the courtyard, staring up at the raindrops . . . feeling them hit her body . . . trying to guess where one would land next. The nuns called again, threatening that pneumonia might make an insufferably headstrong child a lot less curious about nature.

I can't hear you, Vittoria thought.

She was soaked to the bone when the young priest came out to get her. She didn't know him. He was new there. Vittoria waited for him to grab her and drag her back inside. But he didn't. Instead, to her wonder, he lay down beside her, soaking his robes in a puddle.

'They say you ask a lot of questions,' the young man said.

Vittoria scowled. 'Are questions bad?'

He laughed. 'Guess they were right.'

'What are you doing out here?'

'Same thing you're doing . . . wondering why raindrops fall.'

'I'm not wondering why they fall! I already know!'

The priest gave her an astonished look. 'You *do*?'

'Sister Francisca says raindrops are angels' tears coming down to wash away our sins.'

'Wow!' he said, sounding amazed. 'So *that* explains it.'

'No it doesn't!' the girl fired back. 'Raindrops fall because *everything* falls! *Everything* falls! Not just rain!'

The priest scratched his head, looking perplexed. 'You know, young lady, you're right. Everything *does* fall. It must be gravity.'

'It must be *what*?'

He gave her an astonished look. 'You haven't heard of *gravity*?'

'No.'

The priest shrugged sadly. 'Too bad. Gravity answers a *lot* of questions.'

80

Vittoria sat up. 'What's gravity?' she demanded. 'Tell me!'

The priest gave her a wink. 'What do you say I tell you over dinner.'

The young priest was Leonardo Vetra. Although he had been an award-winning physics student while in university, he'd heard another call and gone into the seminary. Leonardo and Vittoria became unlikely best friends in the lonely world of nuns and regulations. Vittoria made Leonardo laugh, and he took her under his wing, teaching her that beautiful things like rainbows and the rivers had many explanations. He told her about light, planets, stars, and all of nature through the eyes of both God and science. Vittoria's innate intellect and curiosity made her a captivating student. Leonardo protected her like a daughter.

Vittoria was happy too. She had never known the joy of having a father. When every other adult answered her questions with a slap on the wrist, Leonardo spent hours showing her books. He even asked what *her* ideas were. Vittoria prayed Leonardo would stay with her forever. Then one day, her worst nightmare came true. Father Leonardo told her he was leaving the orphanage.

'I'm moving to Switzerland,' Leonardo said. 'I have a grant to study physics at the University of Geneva.'

'Physics?' Vittoria cried. 'I thought you loved *God*!'

'I do, very much. Which is why I want to study his divine rules. The laws of physics are the canvas God laid down on which to paint his masterpiece.'

Vittoria was devastated. But Father Leonardo had some other news. He told Vittoria he had spoken to his superiors, and they said it was okay if Father Leonardo adopted her.

'Would you *like* me to adopt you?' Leonardo asked.

'What's *adopt* mean?' Vittoria said.

Father Leonardo told her.

Vittoria hugged him for five minutes, crying tears of joy. 'Oh yes! Yes!'

Leonardo told her he had to leave for a while and get their new home settled in Switzerland, but he promised to send for her in six months. It was the longest wait of Vittoria's life, but Leonardo kept his word. Five days before her ninth birthday, Vittoria moved to Geneva. She attended Geneva International School during the day and learned from her father at night.

Three years later Leonardo Vetra was hired by CERN. Vittoria and Leonardo relocated to a wonderland the likes of which the young Vittoria had never imagined.

Vittoria Vetra's body felt numb as she strode down the LHC tunnel. She saw her muted reflection in the LHC and sensed her father's absence. Normally she existed in a state of deep calm, in harmony with the world around her. But now, very suddenly, nothing made sense. The last three hours had been a blur.

It had been 10 a.m. in the Balearic Islands when Kohler's call came through. *Your father has been murdered. Come home immediately.* Despite the sweltering heat on the deck of the dive boat, the words had chilled her to the bone. Kohler's emotionless tone hurting as much as the news.

Now she had returned home. *But home to what?* CERN, her world since she was twelve, seemed suddenly foreign. Her father, the man who had made it magical, was gone.

Deep breaths, she told herself, but she couldn't calm her mind. The questions circled faster and faster. Who killed her father? And why? Who was this American 'specialist'? Why was Kohler insisting on seeing the lab?

Kohler had said there was evidence that her father's murder was related to the current project. *What evidence? Nobody knew what we were working on! And even if someone found out, why would they kill him?*

As she moved down the LHC tunnel toward her father's lab, Vittoria realized she was about to unveil her father's greatest achievement without him there. She had pictured this moment much differently. She had imagined her father calling CERN's top scientists to his lab, showing them his discovery, watching their awestruck faces. Then he would beam with fatherly pride as he explained to them how it had been one of *Vittoria's* ideas that had helped him make the project a reality . . . that his *daughter* had been integral in his breakthrough. Vittoria felt a lump in her throat. *My father and I were supposed to share this moment together.* But here she was alone. No colleagues. No happy faces. Just an American stranger and Maximilian Kohler.

Maximilian Kohler. Der König.

Even as a child, Vittoria had disliked the man. Although she eventually came to respect his potent intellect, his icy demeanor always seemed inhuman, the exact antithesis of her father's warmth. Kohler pursued science for its immaculate logic . . . her father for its spiritual wonder. And yet oddly there had always seemed to be an unspoken respect between the two men. *Genius,* someone had once explained to her, *accepts genius unconditionally.*

Genius, she thought. *My father . . . Dad. Dead.*

The entry to Leonardo Vetra's lab was a long sterile hallway paved entirely in white tile. Langdon felt like he was entering some kind of underground insane asylum. Lining the corridor were dozens of framed, black-and-white images. Although Langdon had made a career of studying images, these were entirely alien to him. They looked like chaotic negatives of random streaks and spirals. *Modern art?* he mused. *Jackson Pollock on amphetamines?*

'Scatter plots,' Vittoria said, apparently noting Langdon's interest. 'Computer representations of particle collisions. That's the Z-particle,' she said, pointing to a faint track that was almost invisible in the confusion. 'My father discovered it five years ago. Pure energy – no mass at all. It may well be the smallest building block in nature. Matter is nothing but trapped energy.'

Matter is energy? Langdon cocked his head. *Sounds pretty Zen.* He gazed at the tiny streak in the photograph and wondered what his buddies in the Harvard physics department would say when he told them he'd spent the weekend hanging out in a Large Hadron Collider admiring Z-particles.

'Vittoria,' Kohler said, as they approached the lab's imposing steel door, 'I should mention that I came down here this morning looking for your father.'

Vittoria flushed slightly. 'You did?'

'Yes. And imagine my surprise when I discovered he had replaced CERN's standard keypad security with something else.' Kohler motioned to an intricate electronic device mounted beside the door.

'I apologize,' she said. 'You know how he was about privacy. He didn't want anyone but the two of us to have access.'

Kohler said, 'Fine. Open the door.'

Vittoria stood for a long moment. Then, pulling a deep breath, she walked to the mechanism on the wall.

Langdon was in no way prepared for what happened next.

Vittoria stepped up to the device and carefully aligned her right eye with a protruding lens that looked like a telescope. Then she pressed a button. Inside the machine, something clicked. A shaft of light oscillated back and forth, scanning her eyeball like a copy machine.

'It's a retina scan,' she said. 'Infallible security. Authorized for two retina patterns only. Mine and my father's.'

Robert Langdon stood in horrified revelation. The image of Leonardo Vetra came back in grisly detail – the bloody face, the solitary hazel eye staring back, and the empty eye socket. He tried to reject the obvious truth, but then he saw it . . . beneath the scanner on the white tile floor . . . faint droplets of crimson. Dried blood.

Vittoria, thankfully, did not notice.

The steel door slid open and she walked through.

Kohler fixed Langdon with an adamant stare. His message was clear: *As I told you . . . the missing eye serves a higher purpose.*

18

The woman's hands were tied, her wrists now purple and swollen from chafing. The mahogany-skinned

Hassassin lay beside her, spent, admiring his naked prize. He wondered if her current slumber was just a deception, a pathetic attempt to avoid further service to him.

He did not care. He had reaped sufficient reward. Sated, he sat up in bed.

In *his* country women were possessions. Weak. Tools of pleasure. Chattel to be traded like livestock. And they understood their place. But *here*, in Europe, women feigned a strength and independence that both amused and excited him. Forcing them into physical submission was a gratification he always enjoyed.

Now, despite the contentment in his loins, the Hassassin sensed another appetite growing within him. He had killed last night, killed and mutilated, and for him killing was like heroin . . . each encounter satisfying only temporarily before increasing his longing for more. The exhilaration had worn off. The craving had returned.

He studied the sleeping woman beside him. Running his palm across her neck, he felt aroused with the knowledge that he could end her life in an instant. What would it matter? She was subhuman, a vehicle only of pleasure and service. His strong fingers encircled her throat, savoring her delicate pulse. Then, fighting desire, he removed his hand. There was work to do. Service to a higher cause than his own desire.

As he got out of bed, he reveled in the honor of the job before him. He still could not fathom the influence of this man named Janus and the ancient brotherhood he commanded. Wondrously, the brotherhood had chosen *him*. Somehow they had learned of his loathing . . . and of his skills. How, he would never know. *Their roots reach wide.*

Now they had bestowed on him the ultimate honor. He would be their hands and their voice. Their assassin and their messenger. The one his people knew as *Malk al-haq* – the Angel of Truth.

19

Vetra's lab was wildly futuristic.

Stark white and bounded on all sides by computers and specialized electronic equipment, it looked like some sort of operating room. Langdon wondered what secrets this place could possibly hold to justify cutting out someone's eye to gain entrance.

Kohler looked uneasy as they entered, his eyes seeming to dart about for signs of an intruder. But the lab was deserted. Vittoria moved slowly too . . . as if the lab felt unknown without her father there.

Langdon's gaze landed immediately in the center of the room, where a series of short pillars rose from the floor. Like a miniature Stonehenge, a dozen or so columns of polished steel stood in a circle in the middle of the room. The pillars were about three feet tall, reminding Langdon of museum displays for valuable gems. These pillars, however, were clearly not for precious stones. Each supported a thick, transparent canister about the size of a tennis ball can. They appeared empty.

Kohler eyed the canisters, looking puzzled. He apparently decided to ignore them for the time being. He turned to Vittoria. 'Has anything been stolen?'

'Stolen? *How?*' she argued. 'The retina scan only allows entry to us.'

'Just look around.'

Vittoria sighed and surveyed the room for a few moments. She shrugged. 'Everything looks as my father always leaves it. Ordered chaos.'

Langdon sensed Kohler weighing his options, as if wondering how far to push Vittoria . . . how much to tell her. Apparently he decided to leave it for the moment. Moving his wheelchair toward the center of the room, he surveyed the mysterious cluster of seemingly empty canisters.

'Secrets,' Kohler finally said, 'are a luxury we can no longer afford.'

Vittoria nodded in acquiescence, looking suddenly emotional, as if being here brought with it a torrent of memories.

Give her a minute, Langdon thought.

As though preparing for what she was about to reveal, Vittoria closed her eyes and breathed. Then she breathed again. And again. And again . . .

Langdon watched her, suddenly concerned. *Is she okay?* He glanced at Kohler, who appeared unfazed, apparently having seen this ritual before. Ten seconds passed before Vittoria opened her eyes.

Langdon could not believe the metamorphosis. Vittoria Vetra had been transformed. Her full lips were lax, her shoulders down, and her eyes soft and assenting. It was as though she had realigned every muscle in her body to accept the situation. The resentful fire and personal anguish had been quelled somehow beneath a deeper, watery cool.

'Where to begin . . .' she said, her accent unruffled.

'At the beginning,' Kohler said. 'Tell us about your father's experiment.'

'Rectifying science with religion has been my father's life dream,' Vittoria said. 'He hoped to prove that science and religion are two totally compatible fields – two different approaches to finding the same truth.' She paused as if unable to believe what she was about to say. 'And recently . . . he conceived of a way to do that.'

Kohler said nothing.

'He devised an experiment, one he hoped would settle one of the most bitter conflicts in the history of science and religion.'

Langdon wondered which conflict she could mean. There were so many.

'Creationism,' Vittoria declared. 'The battle over how the universe came to be.'

Oh, Langdon thought. *THE debate.*

'The Bible, of course, states that God created the universe,' she explained. 'God said, "Let there be light," and everything we see appeared out of a vast emptiness. Unfortunately, one of the fundamental laws of physics states that matter cannot be created out of nothing.'

Langdon had read about this stalemate. The idea that God allegedly created 'something from nothing' was totally contrary to accepted laws of modern physics and therefore, scientists claimed, Genesis was scientifically absurd.

'Mr Langdon,' Vittoria said, turning, 'I assume you are familiar with the Big Bang Theory?'

Langdon shrugged. 'More or less.' The Big Bang, he knew, was *the* scientifically accepted model for the creation of the universe. He didn't really understand it, but according to the theory, a single point of intensely focused energy erupted in a cataclysmic explosion, expanding outward to form the universe. Or something like that.

Vittoria continued. 'When the Catholic Church first proposed the Big Bang Theory in 1927, the—'

'I'm sorry?' Langdon interrupted, before he could stop himself. 'You say the Big Bang was a *Catholic* idea?'

Vittoria looked surprised by his question. 'Of course. Proposed by a Catholic monk, Georges Lemaître in 1927.'

'But, I thought . . .' he hesitated. 'Wasn't the Big Bang proposed by Harvard astronomer Edwin Hubble?'

Kohler glowered. 'Again, American scientific arrogance. Hubble published in 1929, two years *after* Lemaître.'

Langdon scowled. *It's called the Hubble Telescope, sir – I've never heard of any Lemaître Telescope!*

'Mr Kohler is right,' Vittoria said, 'the idea belonged to Lemaître. Hubble only *confirmed* it by gathering the hard evidence that proved the Big Bang was scientifically probable.'

'Oh,' Langdon said, wondering if the Hubble-fanatics in the Harvard Astronomy Department ever mentioned Lemaître in their lectures.

'When Lemaître first proposed the Big Bang Theory,' Vittoria continued, 'scientists claimed it was utterly ridiculous. Matter, science said, could not be created out of nothing. So, when Hubble shocked the world by scientifically proving the Big Bang was accurate, the church claimed victory, heralding this as *proof* that the Bible was scientifically accurate. The divine truth.'

Langdon nodded, focusing intently now.

'Of course scientists did not appreciate having their discoveries used by the church to promote religion, so they immediately mathematicized the Big Bang Theory, removed all religious overtones, and claimed it as their own. Unfortunately for science, however, their equations, even today, have one serious deficiency that the church likes to point out.'

Kohler grunted. 'The *singularity*.' He spoke the word as if it were the bane of his existence.

'Yes, the singularity,' Vittoria said. 'The exact moment of creation. Time zero.' She looked at Langdon. 'Even today, science cannot grasp the initial moment of creation. Our equations explain the *early* universe quite effectively, but as we move back in time, approaching time zero, suddenly our mathematics disintegrates, and everything becomes meaningless.'

'Correct,' Kohler said, his voice edgy, 'and the church holds up this deficiency as proof of God's miraculous involvement. Come to your point.'

Vittoria's expression became distant. 'My point is that my father had always believed in God's involvement in the Big Bang. Even though science was unable to comprehend the divine moment of creation, he believed someday it *would*.' She motioned sadly to a laser-printed memo tacked over her father's work area. 'My dad used to wave that in my face every time I had doubts.'

Langdon read the message:

SCIENCE AND RELIGION ARE NOT AT ODDS.
SCIENCE IS SIMPLY TOO YOUNG TO UNDERSTAND.

'My dad wanted to bring science to a higher level,'

Vittoria said, 'where science supported the concept of God.' She ran a hand through her long hair, looking melancholy. 'He set out to do something no scientist had ever thought to do. Something that no one has ever had the *technology* to do.' She paused, as though uncertain how to speak the next words. 'He designed an experiment to prove Genesis was possible.'

Prove Genesis? Langdon wondered. *Let there be light? Matter from nothing?*

Kohler's dead gaze bore across the room. 'I beg your pardon?'

'My father created a universe ... from nothing at all.'

Kohler snapped his head around. 'What!'

'Better said, he recreated the Big Bang.'

Kohler looked ready to jump to his feet.

Langdon was officially lost. *Creating a universe? Recreating the Big Bang?*

'It was done on a much smaller scale, of course,' Vittoria said, talking faster now. 'The process was remarkably simple. He accelerated two ultrathin particle beams in opposite directions around the accelerator tube. The two beams collided head-on at enormous speeds, driving into one another and compressing all their energy into a single pinpoint. He achieved extreme energy densities.' She started rattling off a stream of units, and the director's eyes grew wider.

Langdon tried to keep up. *So Leonardo Vetra was simulating the compressed point of energy from which the universe supposedly sprang.*

'The result,' Vittoria said, 'was nothing short of wondrous. When it is published, it will shake the very foundation of modern physics.' She spoke slowly now, as though savoring the immensity of her news. 'Without warning, inside the accelerator tube, at this point of highly focused energy, particles of matter began appearing out of nowhere.'

Kohler made no reaction. He simply stared.

'*Matter*,' Vittoria repeated. 'Blossoming out of nothing. An incredible display of subatomic fireworks. A miniature universe springing to life. He proved not only that matter *can* be created from nothing, but that the Big Bang *and* Genesis can be explained simply by accepting the presence of an enormous source of energy.'

'You mean *God*?' Kohler demanded.

'God, Buddha, The Force, Yahweh, the singularity, the unicity point – call it whatever you like – the result is the same. Science and religion support the same truth – pure *energy* is the father of creation.'

When Kohler finally spoke, his voice was somber. 'Vittoria, you have me at a loss. It sounds like you're telling me your father *created* matter . . . out of nothing?'

'Yes.' Vittoria motioned to the canisters. 'And there is the proof. In those canisters are specimens of the matter he created.'

Kohler coughed and moved towards the canisters like a wary animal circling something he instinctively sensed was wrong. 'I've obviously missed something,' he said. 'How do you expect anyone to believe these canisters contain particles of matter your father actually *created*? They could be particles from anywhere at all.'

'Actually,' Vittoria said, sounding confident, 'they couldn't. These particles are unique. They are a type of matter that does not exist anywhere on earth . . . hence they *had* to be created.'

Kohler's expression darkened. 'Vittoria, what do you mean a certain *type* of matter? There is only *one* type of matter, and it—' Kohler stopped short.

Vittoria's expression was triumphant. 'You've lectured on it yourself, director. The universe contains *two* kinds of matter. Scientific fact.' Vittoria turned to Langdon. 'Mr Langdon, what does the Bible say about the Creation? What did God create?'

Langdon felt awkward, not sure what this had to do with anything. 'Um, God created . . . light and dark, heaven and hell—'

'Exactly,' Vittoria said. 'He created everything in opposites. Symmetry. Perfect balance.' She turned back to Kohler. 'Director, science claims the same thing as religion, that the Big Bang created everything in the universe with an opposite.'

'Including *matter* itself,' Kohler whispered, as if to himself.

Vittoria nodded. 'And when my father ran his experiment, sure enough, *two* kinds of matter appeared.'

Langdon wondered what this meant. *Leonardo Vetra created matter's opposite?*

Kohler looked angry. 'The substance you're referring to only exists *elsewhere* in the universe. Certainly not on earth. And possibly not even in our galaxy!'

'Exactly,' Vittoria replied, 'which is proof that the particles in these canisters had to be *created*.'

Kohler's face hardened. 'Vittoria, surely you can't be saying those canisters contain actual specimens?'

'I am.' She gazed proudly at the canisters. 'Director, you are looking at the world's first specimens of *anti-matter*.'

Phase two, the Hassassin thought, striding into the darkened tunnel.

The torch in his hand was overkill. He knew that. But it was for effect. Effect was everything. Fear, he had learned, was his ally. *Fear cripples faster than any implement of war.*

There was no mirror in the passage to admire his disguise, but he could sense from the shadow of his billowing robe that he was perfect. Blending in was part of the plan . . . part of the depravity of the plot. In his wildest dreams he had never imagined playing this part.

Two weeks ago, he would have considered the task awaiting him at the far end of this tunnel impossible. A suicide mission. Walking naked into a lion's lair. But Janus had changed the definition of impossible.

The secrets Janus had shared with the Hassassin in the last two weeks had been numerous . . . this very tunnel being one of them. Ancient, and yet still perfectly passable.

As he drew closer to his enemy, the Hassassin wondered if what awaited him inside would be as easy as Janus had promised. Janus had assured him someone on the inside would make the necessary arrangements. *Someone on the inside. Incredible.* The more he considered it, the more he realized it was child's play.

Wahad . . . tintain . . . thalatha . . . arbaa, he said to himself in Arabic as he neared the end. *One . . . two . . . three . . . four . . .*

'I sense you've heard of antimatter, Mr Langdon?' Vittoria was studying him, her dark skin in stark contrast to the white lab.

Langdon looked up. He felt suddenly numb. 'Yes. Well . . . sort of.'

A faint smile crossed her lips. 'You watch *Star Trek*.'

Langdon flushed. 'Well, my students enjoy . . .' He frowned. 'Isn't antimatter what fuels the *U.S.S. Enterprise*?'

She nodded. 'Good science fiction has its roots in good science.'

'So antimatter is *real*?'

'A fact of nature. Everything has an opposite. Protons have electrons. Up-quarks have down-quarks. There is a cosmic symmetry at the subatomic level. Antimatter is *yin* to matter's *yang*. It balances the physical equation.'

Langdon thought of Galileo's belief of duality.

'Scientists have known since 1918,' Vittoria said, 'that *two* kinds of matter were created in the Big Bang. One matter is the kind we see here on earth, making up rocks, trees, people. The other is its inverse – identical to matter in all respects except that the charges of its particles are reversed.'

Kohler spoke as though emerging from a fog. His voice sounded suddenly precarious. 'But there are enormous technological barriers to actually *storing* antimatter. What about neutralization?'

'My father built a reverse polarity vacuum to pull the antimatter positrons out of the accelerator before they could decay.'

Kohler scowled. 'But a vacuum would pull out the *matter* also. There would be no way to separate the particles.'

'He applied a magnetic field. Matter arced right, and antimatter arced left. They are polar opposites.'

At that instant, Kohler's wall of doubt seemed to crack. He looked up at Vittoria in clear astonishment and then without warning was overcome by a fit of coughing. 'Incred ... ible ...' he said, wiping his mouth, 'and yet ...' It seemed his logic was still resisting. 'Yet even if the vacuum *worked*, these canisters are made of matter. Antimatter cannot be stored inside canisters made out of *matter*. The antimatter would instantly react with—'

'The specimen is not touching the canister,' Vittoria said, apparently expecting the question. 'The antimatter is suspended. The canisters are called "antimatter traps" because they literally trap the antimatter in the center of the canister, suspending it at a safe distance from the sides and bottom.'

'Suspended? But ... *how*?'

'Between two intersecting magnetic fields. Here, have a look.'

Vittoria walked across the room and retrieved a large electronic apparatus. The contraption reminded Langdon of some sort of cartoon ray gun – a wide canonlike barrel with a sighting scope on top and a tangle of electronics dangling below. Vittoria aligned the scope with one of the canisters, peered into the eyepiece, and calibrated some knobs. Then she stepped away, offering Kohler a look.

Kohler looked nonplussed. 'You collected *visible* amounts?'

'Five thousand nanograms,' Vittoria said. 'A

liquid plasma containing millions of positrons.'

'Millions? But a few *particles* is all anyone has ever detected . . . *anywhere.*'

'Xenon,' Vittoria said flatly. 'He accelerated the particle beam through a jet of xenon, stripping away the electrons. He insisted on keeping the exact procedure a secret, but it involved simultaneously injecting raw electrons into the accelerator.'

Langdon felt lost, wondering if their conversation was still in English.

Kohler paused, the lines in his brow deepening. Suddenly he drew a short breath. He slumped like he'd been hit with a bullet. 'Technically that would leave . . .'

Vittoria nodded. 'Yes. *Lots* of it.'

Kohler returned his gaze to the canister before him. With a look of uncertainty, he hoisted himself in his chair and placed his eye to the viewer, peering inside. He stared a long time without saying anything. When he finally sat down, his forehead was covered with sweat. The lines on his face had disappeared. His voice was a whisper. 'My God . . . you really did it.'

Vittoria nodded. 'My *father* did it.'

'I . . . I don't know what to say.'

Vittoria turned to Langdon. 'Would you like a look?' She motioned to the viewing device.

Uncertain what to expect, Langdon moved forward. From two feet away, the canister appeared empty. Whatever was inside was infinitesimal. Langdon placed his eye to the viewer. It took a moment for the image before him to come into focus.

Then he saw it.

The object was not on the bottom of the container as he expected, but rather it was floating in the center –

suspended in midair – a shimmering globule of mercurylike liquid. Hovering as if by magic, the liquid tumbled in space. Metallic wavelets rippled across the droplet's surface. The suspended fluid reminded Langdon of a video he had once seen of a water droplet in zero G. Although he knew the globule was microscopic, he could see every changing gorge and undulation as the ball of plasma rolled slowly in suspension.

'It's . . . floating,' he said.

'It had better be,' Vittoria replied. 'Antimatter is highly unstable. Energetically speaking, antimatter is the mirror of matter, so the two instantly cancel each other out if they come in contact. Keeping antimatter isolated from matter is a challenge, of course, because *everything* on earth is made of matter. The samples have to be stored without ever touching anything at all – even air.'

Langdon was amazed. *Talk about working in a vacuum.*

'These antimatter traps?' Kohler interrupted, looking amazed as he ran a pallid finger around one's base. 'They are your father's design?'

'Actually,' she said, 'they are mine.'

Kohler looked up.

Vittoria's voice was unassuming. 'My father produced the first particles of antimatter but was stymied by how to store them. I suggested these. Airtight nanocomposite shells with opposing electromagnets at each end.'

'It seems your father's genius has rubbed off.'

'Not really. I borrowed the idea from nature. Portuguese man-o'-wars trap fish between their tentacles using nematocystic charges. Same principle here. Each canister has two electromagnets, one at each end. Their opposing magnetic fields intersect in the center of the canister and hold the antimatter there, suspended in midvacuum.'

Langdon looked again at the canister. Antimatter floating in a vacuum, not touching anything at all. Kohler was right. It was genius.

'Where's the power source for the magnets?' Kohler asked.

Vittoria pointed. 'In the pillar beneath the trap. The canisters are screwed into a docking port that continuously recharges them so the magnets never fail.'

'And if the field fails?'

'The obvious. The antimatter falls out of suspension, hits the bottom of the trap, and we see an annihilation.'

Langdon's ears pricked up. 'Annihilation?' He didn't like the sound of it.

Vittoria looked unconcerned. 'Yes. If antimatter and matter make contact, both are destroyed instantly. Physicists call the process "annihilation".'

Langdon nodded. 'Oh.'

'It is nature's simplest reaction. A particle of matter and a particle of antimatter combine to release two *new* particles – called photons. A photon is effectively a tiny puff of light.'

Langdon had read about photons – light particles – the purest form of energy. He decided to refrain from asking about Captain Kirk's use of photon torpedoes against the Klingons. 'So if the antimatter falls, we see a tiny puff of light?'

Vittoria shrugged. 'Depends what you call tiny. Here, let me demonstrate.' She reached for the canister and started to unscrew it from its charging podium.

Without warning, Kohler let out a cry of terror and lunged forward, knocking her hands away. 'Vittoria! Are you insane!'

22

Kohler, incredibly, was standing for a moment, teetering on two withered legs. His face was white with fear. 'Vittoria! You can't remove that trap!'

Langdon watched, bewildered by the director's sudden panic.

'Five hundred nanograms!' Kohler said. 'If you break the magnetic field—'

'Director,' Vittoria assured, 'it's perfectly safe. Every trap has a failsafe – a back-up battery in case it is removed from its recharger. The specimen remains suspended even if I remove the canister.'

Kohler looked uncertain. Then, hesitantly, he settled back into his chair.

'The batteries activate automatically,' Vittoria said, 'when the trap is moved from the recharger. They work for twenty-four hours. Like a reserve tank of gas.' She turned to Langdon, as if sensing his discomfort. 'Antimatter has some astonishing characteristics, Mr Langdon, which make it quite dangerous. A ten milligram sample – the volume of a grain of sand – is hypothesized to hold as much energy as about two hundred metric tons of conventional rocket fuel.'

Langdon's head was spinning again.

'It is the energy source of tomorrow. A thousand times more powerful than nuclear energy. One hundred percent efficient. No byproducts. No radiation. No pollution. A few grams could power a major city for a week.'

Grams? Langdon stepped uneasily back from the podium.

'Don't worry,' Vittoria said. '*These* samples are minuscule fractions of a gram – *millionths*. Relatively harmless.' She reached for the canister again and twisted it from its docking platform.

Kohler twitched but did not interfere. As the trap came free, there was a sharp bleep, and a small LED display activated near the base of the trap. The red digits blinked, counting down from twenty-four hours.

24:00:00 . . .
23:59:59 . . .
23:59:58 . . .

Langdon studied the descending counter and decided it looked unsettlingly like a bomb.

'The battery,' Vittoria explained, 'will run for the full twenty-four hours before dying. It can be recharged by placing the trap back on the podium. It's designed as a safety measure, but it's also convenient for transport.'

'Transport?' Kohler looked thunderstruck. 'You take this stuff out of the lab?'

'Of course not,' Vittoria said. 'But the mobility allows us to study it.'

Vittoria led Langdon and Kohler to the far end of the room. She pulled a curtain aside to reveal a window, beyond which was a large room. The walls, floors, and ceiling were entirely plated in steel. The room reminded Langdon of the holding tank of an oil freighter he had once taken to Papua New Guinea to study *Hanta* body graffiti.

'It's an annihilation tank,' Vittoria declared.

Kohler looked up. 'You actually *observe* annihilations?'

'My father was fascinated with the physics of the Big Bang – large amounts of energy from minuscule kernels of matter.' Vittoria pulled open a steel drawer beneath the window. She placed the trap inside the drawer and closed it. Then she pulled a lever beside the drawer. A moment later, the trap appeared on the other side of the glass, rolling smoothly in a wide arc across the metal floor until it came to a stop near the center of the room.

Vittoria gave a tight smile. 'You're about to witness your first antimatter-matter annihilation. A few millionths of a gram. A relatively minuscule specimen.'

Langdon looked out at the antimatter trap sitting alone on the floor of the enormous tank. Kohler also turned toward the window, looking uncertain.

'Normally,' Vittoria explained, 'we'd have to wait the full twenty-four hours until the batteries died, but this chamber contains magnets beneath the floor that can override the trap, pulling the antimatter out of suspension. And when the matter and antimatter touch . . .'

'Annihilation,' Kohler whispered.

'One more thing,' Vittoria said. 'Antimatter releases pure energy. A one hundred per cent conversion of mass to photons. So don't look directly at the sample. Shield your eyes.'

Langdon was wary, but he now sensed Vittoria was being overly dramatic. *Don't look directly at the canister?* The device was more than thirty yards away, behind an ultrathick wall of tinted Plexiglas. Moreover, the speck in the canister was invisible, microscopic. *Shield my eyes?* Langdon thought. *How much energy could that speck possibly —*

Vittoria pressed the button.

Instantly, Langdon was blinded. A brilliant point of light shone in the canister and then exploded outward in a shock wave of light that radiated in all directions, erupting against the window before him with thunderous force. He stumbled back as the detonation rocked the vault. The light burned bright for a moment, searing, and then, after an instant, it rushed back inward, absorbing in on itself, and collapsing into a tiny speck that disappeared to nothing. Langdon blinked in pain, slowly recovering his eyesight. He squinted into the smoldering chamber. The canister on the floor had entirely disappeared. Vaporized. Not a trace.

He stared in wonder. 'G . . . God.'

Vittoria nodded sadly. 'That's precisely what my father said.'

23

Kohler was staring into the annihilation chamber with a look of utter amazement at the spectacle he had just seen. Robert Langdon was beside him, looking even more dazed.

'I want to see my father,' Vittoria demanded. 'I showed you the lab. Now I want to see my father.'

Kohler turned slowly, apparently not hearing her. 'Why did you wait so long, Vittoria? You and your father should have told me about this discovery immediately.'

Vittoria stared at him. *How many reasons do you want?* 'Director, we can argue about this later. Right now, I want to see my father.'

'Do you know what this technology implies?'

'Sure,' Vittoria shot back. 'Revenue for CERN. A lot of it. Now I want—'

'Is that why you kept it secret?' Kohler demanded, clearly baiting her. 'Because you feared the board and I would vote to license it out?'

'It *should* be licensed,' Vittoria fired back, feeling herself dragged into the argument. 'Antimatter is important technology. But it's also dangerous. My father and I wanted time to refine the procedures and make it safe.'

'In other words, you didn't trust the board of directors to place prudent science before financial greed.'

Vittoria was surprised by the indifference in Kohler's tone. 'There were other issues as well,' she said. 'My father wanted time to present antimatter in the appropriate light.'

'Meaning?'

What do you think I mean? 'Matter from energy? Something from nothing? It's practically proof that Genesis is a scientific possibility.'

'So he didn't want the religious implications of his discovery lost in an onslaught of commercialism?'

'In a manner of speaking.'

'And you?'

Vittoria's concerns, ironically, were somewhat the opposite. Commercialism was critical for the success of any new energy source. Although antimatter technology had staggering potential as an efficient and nonpolluting energy source – if unveiled prematurely, antimatter ran the risk of being vilified by the politics and PR fiascoes that had killed nuclear and solar power. Nuclear had proliferated before it was safe, and there were accidents. Solar had proliferated before it was efficient, and people lost money. Both technologies got bad reputations and withered on the vine.

'My interests,' Vittoria said, 'were a bit less lofty than uniting science and religion.'

'The environment,' Kohler ventured assuredly.

'Limitless energy. No strip mining. No pollution. No radiation. Antimatter technology could save the planet.'

'Or destroy it,' Kohler quipped. 'Depending on who uses it for what.' Vittoria felt a chill emanating from Kohler's crippled form. 'Who else knew about this?' he asked.

'No one,' Vittoria said. 'I told you that.'

'Then why do you think your father was killed?'

Vittoria's muscles tightened. 'I have no idea. He had enemies here at CERN, you know that, but it couldn't have had anything to do with antimatter. We swore to each other to keep it between us for another few months, until we were ready.'

'And you're certain your father kept his vow of silence?'

Now Vittoria was getting mad. 'My father has kept tougher vows than that!'

'And *you* told no one?'

'Of course not!'

Kohler exhaled. He paused, as though choosing his next words carefully. 'Suppose someone *did* find out. And suppose someone gained access to this lab. What do you imagine they would be after? Did your father have notes down here? Documentation of his processes?'

'Director, I've been patient. I need some answers now. You keep talking about a break-in, but you saw the retina scan. My father has been vigilant about secrecy and security.'

'Humor me,' Kohler snapped, startling her. 'What would be missing?'

'I have no idea.' Vittoria angrily scanned the lab. All the antimatter specimens were accounted for. Her father's work area looked in order. 'Nobody came in here,' she declared. 'Everything up here looks fine.'

Kohler looked surprised. '*Up* here?'

Vittoria had said it instinctively. 'Yes, here in the upper lab.'

'You're using the lower lab too?'

'For storage.'

Kohler rolled towards her, coughing again. 'You're using the Haz-Mat chamber for storage? Storage of *what*?'

Hazardous material, what else! Vittoria was losing her patience. 'Antimatter.'

Kohler lifted himself on the arms of his chair. 'There are *other* specimens? Why the hell didn't you tell me!'

'I just did,' Vittoria fired back. 'And you've barely given me a chance!'

'We need to check those specimens,' Kohler said. 'Now.'

'Specimen,' Vittoria corrected. 'Singular. And it's fine. Nobody could ever—'

'Only one?' Kohler hesitated. 'Why isn't it up here?'

'My father wanted it below the bedrock as a precaution. It's larger than the others.'

The look of alarm that shot between Kohler and Langdon was not lost on Vittoria. Kohler rolled toward her again. 'You created a specimen *larger* than five hundred nanograms?'

'A necessity,' Vittoria defended. 'We had to prove the input/yield threshold could be safely crossed.' The question with new fuel sources, she knew, was always one of input vs. yield – how much money one had to expend to harvest the fuel. Building an oil rig to yield a single barrel of oil was a losing endeavour. However, if that same rig, with minimal added expense, could deliver millions of barrels, then you were in business. Antimatter was the same way. Firing up sixteen miles of electromagnets to create a tiny specimen of antimatter expended more energy than the resulting antimatter contained. In order to prove antimatter efficient and viable, one had to create specimens of a larger magnitude.

Although Vittoria's father had been hesitant to create a large specimen, Vittoria had pushed him hard. She argued that in order for antimatter to be taken seriously, she and her father had to prove two things. First, that cost-effective amounts could be produced. And second, that the specimens could be safely stored. In the end she had won, and her father had acquiesced against his better judgment. Not, however, without some firm guidelines regarding secrecy and access. The antimatter, her father had insisted, would be stored in Haz-Mat – a small granite hollow, an additional seventy-five feet below ground. The specimen would be their secret. And only the two of them would have access.

'Vittoria?' Kohler insisted, his voice tense. 'How large a specimen did you and your father create?'

Vittoria felt a wry pleasure inside. She knew the amount would stun even the great Maximilian Kohler.

She pictured the antimatter below. An incredible sight. Suspended inside the trap, perfectly visible to the naked eye, danced a tiny sphere of antimatter. This was no microscopic speck. This was a droplet the size of a BB.

Vittoria took a deep breath. 'A full quarter of a gram.'

The blood drained from Kohler's face. 'What!' He broke into a fit of coughing. 'A quarter of a gram? That converts to . . . almost five kilotons!'

Kilotons. Vittoria hated the word. It was one she and her father never used. A kiloton was equal to 1,000 metric tons of TNT. Kilotons were for weaponry. Payload. Destructive power. She and her father spoke in electron volts and joules – constructive energy output.

'That much antimatter could literally liquidate everything in a half-mile radius!' Kohler exclaimed.

'Yes, if annihilated all at once,' Vittoria shot back, 'which nobody would ever do!'

'Except someone who didn't know better. Or if your power source failed!' Kohler was already heading for the elevator.

'Which is why my father kept it in Haz-Mat under a fail-safe power and a redundant security system.'

Kohler turned, looking hopeful. 'You have additional security on Haz-Mat?'

'Yes. A second retina-scan.'

Kohler spoke only two words. 'Downstairs. Now.'

The freight elevator dropped like a rock.

Another seventy-five feet into the earth.

Vittoria was certain she sensed fear in both men as the elevator fell deeper. Kohler's usually emotionless face was taut. *I know,* Vittoria thought, *the sample is enormous, but the precautions we've taken are—*

They reached the bottom.

The elevator opened, and Vittoria led the way down the dimly lit corridor. Up ahead the corridor dead-ended at a huge steel door. HAZ-MAT. The retina device beside the door was identical to the one upstairs. She approached. Carefully, she aligned her eye with the lens.

She pulled back. Something was wrong. The usually spotless lens was splattered . . . smeared with something that looked like . . . *blood?* Confused she turned to the two men, but her gaze met waxen faces. Both Kohler and Langdon were white, their eyes fixed on the floor at her feet.

Vittoria followed their line of sight . . . down.

'No!' Langdon yelled, reaching for her. But it was too late.

Vittoria's vision locked on the object on the floor. It was both utterly foreign and intimately familiar to her.

It took only an instant.

Then, with a reeling horror, she knew. Staring up at her from the floor, discarded like a piece of trash, was an eyeball. She would have recognized that shade of hazel anywhere.

24

The security technician held his breath as his commander leaned over his shoulder, studying the bank of security monitors before them. A minute passed.

The commander's silence was to be expected, the technician told himself. The commander was a man of rigid protocol. He had not risen to command one of the world's most elite security forces by talking first and thinking second.

But what is he thinking?

The object they were pondering on the monitor was a canister of some sort – a canister with transparent sides. That much was easy. It was the rest that was difficult.

Inside the container, as if by some special effect, a small droplet of metallic liquid seemed to be *floating* in midair. The droplet appeared and disappeared in the robotic red blinking of a digital LED descending resolutely, making the technician's skin crawl.

'Can you lighten the contrast?' the commander asked, startling the technician.

The technician heeded the instruction, and the image lightened somewhat. The commander leaned forward, squinting closer at something that had just come visible on the base of the container.

The technician followed his commander's gaze. Ever so faintly, printed next to the LED was an acronym. Four capital letters gleaming in the intermittent spurts of light.

'Stay here,' the commander said. 'Say nothing. I'll handle this.'

25

Haz-Mat. Fifty meters below ground.

Vittoria Vetra stumbled forward, almost falling into

the retina scan. She sensed the American rushing to help her, holding her, supporting her weight. On the floor at her feet, her father's eyeball stared up. She felt the air crushed from her lungs. *They cut out his eye!* Her world twisted. Kohler pressed close behind, speaking. Langdon guided her. As if in a dream, she found herself gazing into the retina scan. The mechanism beeped.

The door slid open.

Even with the terror of her father's eye boring into her soul, Vittoria sensed an additional horror awaited inside. When she leveled her blurry gaze into the room, she confirmed the next chapter of the nightmare. Before her, the solitary recharging podium was empty.

The canister was gone. They had cut out her father's eye to steal it. The implications came too fast for her to fully comprehend. Everything had backfired. The specimen that was supposed to prove antimatter was a safe and viable energy source had been stolen. *But nobody knew this specimen even existed!* The truth, however, was undeniable. Someone had found out. Vittoria could not imagine who. Even Kohler, whom they said knew everything at CERN, clearly had no idea about the project.

Her father was dead. Murdered for his genius.

As the grief strafed her heart, a new emotion surged into Vittoria's conscious. This one was far worse. Crushing. Stabbing at her. The emotion was guilt. Uncontrollable, relentless guilt. Vittoria knew it had been *she* who convinced her father to create the specimen. Against his better judgment. And he had been killed for it.

A quarter of a gram . . .

Like any technology – fire, gunpowder, the combustion engine – in the wrong hands, antimatter could be deadly. Very deadly. Antimatter was a lethal weapon. Potent, and unstoppable. Once removed from its recharging platform at CERN, the canister would count down inexorably. A runaway train.

And when time ran out . . .

A blinding light. The roar of thunder. Spontaneous incineration. Just the flash . . . and an empty crater. A *big* empty crater.

The image of her father's quiet genius being used as a tool of destruction was like poison in her blood. Antimatter was the ultimate terrorist weapon. It had no metallic parts to trip metal detectors, no chemical signature for dogs to trace, no fuse to deactivate if the authorities located the canister. The countdown had begun . . .

Langdon didn't know what else to do. He took his handkerchief and laid it on the floor over Leonardo Vetra's eyeball. Vittoria was standing now in the doorway of the empty Haz-Mat chamber, her expression wrought with grief and panic. Langdon moved toward her again, instinctively, but Kohler intervened.

'Mr Langdon?' Kohler's face was expressionless. He motioned Langdon out of earshot. Langdon reluctantly followed, leaving Vittoria to fend for herself. 'You're the specialist,' Kohler said, his whisper intense. 'I want to know what these Illuminati bastards intend to do with this antimatter.'

Langdon tried to focus. Despite the madness around him, his first reaction was logical. Academic rejection. Kohler was still making assumptions. Impossible assumptions. 'The Illuminati are defunct,

113

Mr Kohler. I stand by that. This crime could be any-thing – maybe even another CERN employee who found out about Mr Vetra's breakthrough and thought the project was too dangerous to continue.'

Kohler looked stunned. 'You think this is a crime of *conscience*, Mr Langdon? Absurd. Whoever killed Leonardo wanted one thing – the antimatter specimen. And no doubt they have plans for it.'

'You mean terrorism.'

'Plainly.'

'But the Illuminati were not terrorists.'

'Tell that to Leonardo Vetra.'

Langdon felt a pang of truth in the statement. Leonardo Vetra had indeed been branded with the Illuminati symbol. Where had it come from? The sacred brand seemed too difficult a hoax for someone trying to cover his tracks by casting suspicion else-where. There had to be another explanation.

Again, Langdon forced himself to consider the implausible. *If the Illuminati were still active, and if they stole the antimatter, what would be their intention? What would be their target?* The answer furnished by his brain was instantaneous. Langdon dismissed it just as fast. True, the Illuminati had an obvious enemy, but a wide-scale terrorist attack against that enemy was inconceivable. It was entirely out of character. Yes, the Illuminati had killed people, but *individuals*, carefully conscripted targets. Mass destruction was somehow heavy-handed. Langdon paused. Then again, he thought, there would be a rather majestic eloquence to it – antimatter, the ultimate scientific achievement, being used to vaporize—

He refused to accept the preposterous thought.

'There is,' he said suddenly, 'a logical explanation other than terrorism.'

Kohler stared, obviously waiting.

Langdon tried to sort out the thought. The Illuminati had always wielded tremendous power through *financial* means. They controlled banks. They owned gold bullion. They were even rumoured to possess the single most valuable gem on earth – the Illuminati Diamond, a flawless diamond of enormous proportions. 'Money,' Langdon said. 'The antimatter could have been stolen for financial gain.'

Kohler looked incredulous. 'Financial gain? Where does one sell a droplet of antimatter?'

'Not the specimen,' Langdon countered. 'The technology. Antimatter technology must be worth a mint. Maybe someone stole the specimen to do analysis and R and D.'

'Industrial espionage? But that canister has twenty-four hours before the batteries die. The researchers would blow themselves up before they learned anything at all.'

'They could recharge it before it explodes. They could build a compatible recharging podium like the ones here at CERN.'

'In twenty-four hours?' Kohler challenged. 'Even if they stole the schematics, a recharger like that would take *months* to engineer, not hours!'

'He's right.' Vittoria's voice was frail.

Both men turned. Vittoria was moving toward them, her gait as tremulous as her words.

'He's right. Nobody could reverse engineer a recharger in time. The interface alone would take weeks. Flux filters, servo-coils, power conditioning alloys, all calibrated to the specific energy grade of the locale.'

Langdon frowned. The point was taken. An antimatter trap was not something one could simply plug into a wall socket. Once removed from CERN, the canister was on a one-way, twenty-four-hour trip to oblivion.

Which left only one, very disturbing, conclusion.

'We need to call Interpol,' Vittoria said. Even to herself, her voice sounded distant. 'We need to call the proper authorities. Immediately.'

Kohler shook his head. 'Absolutely not.'

The words stunned her. 'No? What do you mean?'

'You and your father have put me in a very difficult position here.'

'Director, we need help. We need to find that trap and get it back here before someone gets hurt. We have a responsibility!'

'We have a responsibility to *think*,' Kohler said, his tone hardening. 'This situation could have very, very serious repercussions for CERN.'

'You're worried about CERN's *reputation*? Do you know what that canister could do to an urban area? It has a blast radius of a half mile! Nine city blocks!'

'Perhaps you and your father should have considered that before you created the specimen.'

Vittoria felt like she'd been stabbed. 'But . . . we took every precaution.'

'Apparently, it was not enough.'

'But nobody *knew* about the antimatter.' She realized, of course, it was an absurd argument. Of course somebody knew. Someone had found out.

Vittoria had told no one. That left only two explanations. Either her father had taken someone into his confidence without telling her, which made no sense

116

because it was her *father* who had sworn them both to secrecy, or she and her father had been monitored. The cell phone maybe? She knew they had spoken a few times while Vittoria was traveling. Had they said too much? It was possible. There was also their E-mail. But they had been discreet, hadn't they? CERN's security system? Had they been monitored somehow without their knowledge? She knew none of that mattered anymore. What was done, was done. *My father is dead.*

The thought spurred her to action. She pulled her cell phone from her shorts pocket.

Kohler accelerated toward her, coughing violently, eyes flashing anger. 'Who . . . are you calling?'

'CERN's switchboard. They can connect us to Interpol.'

'Think!' Kohler choked, screeching to a halt in front of her. 'Are you really so naïve? That canister could be anywhere in the world by now. No intelligence agency on earth could possibly mobilize to find it in time.'

'So we do *nothing*?' Vittoria felt compunction challenging a man in such frail health, but the director was so far out of line she didn't even know him anymore.

'We do what is *smart*,' Kohler said. 'We don't risk CERN's reputation by involving the authorities who cannot help anyway. Not yet. Not without thinking.'

Vittoria knew there was logic somewhere in Kohler's argument, but she also knew that logic, by definition, was bereft of moral responsibility. Her father had *lived* for moral responsibility – careful science, accountability, faith in man's inherent goodness. Vittoria believed in those things too, but she saw them in terms of *karma*. Turning away from Kohler, she snapped open her phone.

117

'You can't do that,' he said.

'Just try and stop me.'

Kohler did not move.

An instant later, Vittoria realized why. This far underground, her cell phone had no dial tone.

Fuming, she headed for the elevator.

26

The Hassassin stood at the end of the stone tunnel. His torch still burned bright, the smoke mixing with the smell of moss and stale air. Silence surrounded him. The iron door blocking his way looked as old as the tunnel itself, rusted but still holding strong. He waited in the darkness, trusting.

It was almost time.

Janus had promised someone on the inside would open the door. The Hassassin marveled at the betrayal. He would have waited all night at that door to carry out his task, but he sensed it would not be necessary. He was working for determined men.

Minutes later, exactly at the appointed hour, there was a loud clank of heavy keys on the other side of the door. Metal scraped on metal as multiple locks disengaged. One by one, three huge deadbolts ground open. The locks creaked as if they had not been used in centuries. Finally all three were open.

Then there was silence.

The Hassassin waited patiently, five minutes, exactly as he had been told. Then, with electricity in his blood, he pushed. The great door swung open.

'Vittoria, I will not allow it!' Kohler's breath was labored and getting worse as the Haz-Mat elevator ascended.

Vittoria blocked him out. She craved sanctuary, something familiar in this place that no longer felt like home. She knew it was not to be. Right now, she had to swallow the pain and act. *Get to a phone.*

Robert Langdon was beside her, silent as usual. Vittoria had given up wondering who the man was. *A specialist?* Could Kohler be any less specific? *Mr Langdon can help us find your father's killer.* Langdon was being no help at all. His warmth and kindness seemed genuine, but he was clearly hiding something. They both were.

Kohler was at her again. 'As director of CERN, I have a responsibility to the future of science. If you amplify this into an international incident and CERN suffers—'

'Future of science?' Vittoria turned on him. 'Do you really plan to escape accountability by never admitting this antimatter came from CERN? Do you plan to ignore the people's lives we've put in danger?'

'Not *we*,' Kohler countered. '*You.* You and your father.'

Vittoria looked away.

'And as far as endangering lives,' Kohler said, '*life* is exactly what this is about. You know antimatter technology has enormous implications for life on this planet. If CERN goes bankrupt, destroyed by scandal, *everybody* loses. Man's future is in the hands of places like CERN, scientists like you and your father, working to solve tomorrow's problems.'

Vittoria had heard Kohler's Science-as-God lecture before, and she never bought it. Science *itself* caused half the problems it was trying to solve. 'Progress' was Mother Earth's ultimate malignancy.

'Scientific advancement carries risk,' Kohler argued. 'It always has. Space programs, genetic research, medicine – they all make mistakes. Science needs to survive its own blunders, at any cost. For *everyone's* sake.'

Vittoria was amazed at Kohler's ability to weigh moral issues with scientific detachment. His intellect seemed to be the product of an icy divorce from his inner spirit. 'You think CERN is so critical to the earth's future that we should be immune from moral responsibility?'

'Do not argue *morals* with me. You crossed a line when you made that specimen, and you have put this entire facility at risk. I'm trying to protect not only the jobs of the three thousand scientists who work here, but also your father's reputation. Think about *him*. A man like your father does not deserve to be remembered as the creator of a weapon of mass destruction.'

Vittoria felt his spear hit home. *I am the one who convinced my father to create that specimen. This is my fault!*

When the door opened, Kohler was still talking. Vittoria stepped out of the elevator, pulled out her phone, and tried again.

Still no dial tone. *Damn!* She headed for the door.

'Vittoria, stop.' The director sounded asthmatic now, as he accelerated after her. 'Slow down. We need to talk.'

'*Basta di parlare!*'

'Think of your father,' Kohler urged. 'What would he do?'

She kept going.

'Vittoria, I haven't been totally honest with you.'

Vittoria felt her legs slow.

'I don't know what I was thinking,' Kohler said. 'I was just trying to protect you. Just tell me what you want. We need to work together here.'

Vittoria came to a full stop halfway across the lab, but she did not turn. 'I want to find the antimatter. And I want to know who killed my father.' She waited.

Kohler sighed. 'Vittoria, we already know who killed your father. I'm sorry.'

Now Vittoria turned. 'You what?'

'I didn't know how to tell you. It's a difficult—'

'You *know* who killed my father?'

'We have a very good idea, yes. The killer left somewhat of a calling card. That's the reason I called Mr Langdon. The group claiming responsibility is his specialty.'

'The group? A terrorist group?'

'Vittoria, they stole a quarter *gram* of antimatter.'

Vittoria looked at Robert Langdon standing there across the room. Everything began falling into place. *That explains some of the secrecy.* She was amazed it hadn't occurred to her earlier. Kohler had called the authorities after all. *The* authorities. Now it seemed obvious. Robert Langdon was American, clean-cut, conservative, obviously very sharp. Who else could it be? Vittoria should have guessed from the start. She felt a newfound hope as she turned to him.

'Mr Langdon, I want to know who killed my father. And I want to know if your agency can find the antimatter.'

121

Langdon looked flustered. 'My agency?'

'You're with U.S. Intelligence, I assume.'

'Actually . . . no.'

Kohler intervened. 'Mr Langdon is a professor of art history at Harvard University.'

Vittoria felt like she had been doused with ice water. 'An art teacher?'

'He is a specialist in cult symbology.' Kohler sighed. 'Vittoria, we believe your father was killed by a satanic cult.'

Vittoria heard the words in her mind, but she was unable to process them. *A satanic cult.*

'The group claiming responsibility calls themselves the Illuminati.'

Vittoria looked at Kohler and then at Langdon, wondering if this was some kind of perverse joke. 'The Illuminati?' she demanded.'As in the *Bavarian Illuminati?*'

Kohler looked stunned. 'You've *heard* of them?'

Vittoria felt the tears of frustration welling right below the surface. '*Bavarian Illuminati: New World Order.* Steve Jackson computer games. Half the techies here play it on the Internet.' Her voice cracked. 'But I don't understand . . .'

Kohler shot Langdon a confused look.

Langdon nodded. 'Popular game. Ancient brother-hood takes over the world. Semihistorical. I didn't know it was in Europe too.'

Vittoria was bewildered. 'What are you talking about? The Illuminati? It's a computer game!'

'Vittoria,' Kohler said, 'the Illuminati is the group claiming responsibility for your father's death.'

Vittoria mustered every bit of courage she could find to fight the tears. She forced herself to hold on and assess the situation logically. But the harder she focused, the less she understood. Her father had been murdered. CERN had suffered a major breach of security. There was a bomb counting down somewhere that *she* was responsible for. And the director had nominated an art teacher to help them find a mythical fraternity of Satanists.

Vittoria felt suddenly all alone. She turned to go, but Kohler cut her off. He reached for something in his pocket. He produced a crumpled piece of fax paper and handed it to her.

Vittoria swayed in horror as her eyes hit the image. 'They branded him,' Kohler said. 'They branded his goddamn chest.'

28

Secretary Sylvie Baudeloque was now in a panic. She paced outside the director's empty office. *Where the hell is he? What do I do?*

It had been a bizarre day. Of course, any day working for Maximilian Kohler had the potential to be strange, but Kohler had been in rare form today.

'Find me Leonardo Vetra!' he had demanded when Sylvie arrived this morning.

Dutifully, Sylvie paged, phoned, and E-mailed Leonardo Vetra.

Nothing.

So Kohler had left in a huff, apparently to go find Vetra himself. When he rolled back in a few hours later, Kohler looked decidedly not well . . . not that he ever actually looked *well*, but he looked worse than usual. He locked himself in his office, and she could hear him on his modem, his phone, faxing, talking. Then Kohler rolled out again. He hadn't been back since.

Sylvie had decided to ignore the antics as yet another Kohlerian melodrama, but she began to get concerned when Kohler failed to return at the proper time for his daily injections; the director's physical condition required regular treatment, and when he decided to push his luck, the results were never pretty – respiratory shock, coughing fits, and a mad dash by the infirmary personnel. Sometimes Sylvie thought Maximilian Kohler had a death wish.

She considered paging him to remind him, but she'd learned charity was something Kohler's pride despised. Last week, he had become so enraged with a visiting scientist who had shown him undue pity that Kohler clambered to his feet and threw a clipboard at the man's head. King Kohler could be surprisingly agile when he was *pissé*.

At the moment, however, Sylvie's concern for the director's health was taking a back burner . . . replaced by a much more pressing dilemma. The CERN switchboard had phoned five minutes ago in a frenzy to say they had an urgent call for the director.

'He's not available,' Sylvie had said.

Then the CERN operator told her who was calling.

Sylvie half laughed aloud. 'You're kidding, right?' She listened, and her face clouded with disbelief. 'And your caller ID confirms—' Sylvie was frowning. 'I see. Okay. Can you ask what the—' She sighed. 'No. That's fine. Tell him to hold. I'll locate the director right away. Yes, I understand. I'll hurry.'

But Sylvie had not been able to find the director. She had called his cell line three times and each time gotten the same message: 'The mobile customer you are trying to reach is out of range.' *Out of range? How far could he go?* So Sylvie had dialed Kohler's beeper. Twice. No response. Most unlike him. She'd even E-mailed his mobile computer. Nothing. It was like the man had disappeared off the face of the earth.

So what do I do? she now wondered.

Short of searching CERN's entire complex herself, Sylvie knew there was only one other way to get the director's attention. He would not be pleased, but the man on the phone was not someone the director should keep waiting. Nor did it sound like the caller was in any mood to be told the director was unavailable.

Startled with her own boldness, Sylvie made her decision. She walked into Kohler's office and went to the metal box on his wall behind his desk. She opened the cover, stared at the controls, and found the correct button.

Then she took a deep breath and grabbed the microphone.

29

Vittoria did not remember how they had gotten to the main elevator, but they were there. Ascending. Kohler was behind her, his breathing labored now. Langdon's concerned gaze passed through her like a ghost. He had taken the fax from her hand and slipped it in his jacket pocket away from her sight, but the image was still burned into her memory.

As the elevator climbed, Vittoria's world swirled into darkness. *Papa!* In her mind she reached for him. For just a moment, in the oasis of her memory, Vittoria was with him. She was nine years old, rolling down hills of edelweiss flowers, the Swiss sky spinning over-head.

Papa! Papa!

Leonardo Vetra was laughing beside her, beaming. 'What is it, angel?'

'Papa!' she giggled, nuzzling close to him. 'Ask me what's the matter!'

'But you look happy, sweetie. Why would I ask you what's the matter?'

'Just ask me.'

He shrugged. 'What's the matter?'

She immediately started laughing. 'What's the matter? *Everything* is the matter! Rocks! Trees! Atoms! Even anteaters! Everything is the matter!'

He laughed. 'Did you make that up?'

'Pretty smart, huh?'

'My little Einstein.'

She frowned. 'He has stupid hair. I saw his picture.'

'He's got a smart head, though. I told you what he proved, right?'

Her eyes widened with dread. 'Dad! No! You *promised*!'

'$E=MC^2$!' He tickled her playfully. '$E=MC^2$!'

'No *math*! I told you! I hate it!'

'I'm glad you hate it. Because girls aren't even *allowed* to do math.'

Vittoria stopped short. 'They *aren't*?'

'Of course not. Everyone knows that. Girls play with dollies. Boys do math. No math for girls. I'm not even *permitted* to talk to little girls about math.'

'What! But that's not fair!'

'Rules are rules. Absolutely no math for little girls.'

Vittoria looked horrified. 'But dolls are boring!'

'I'm sorry,' her father said. 'I could tell you about math, but if I got caught . . .' He looked nervously around the deserted hills.

Vittoria followed his gaze. 'Okay,' she whispered, 'just tell me quietly.'

The motion of the elevator startled her. Vittoria opened her eyes. He was gone.

Reality rushed in, wrapping a frosty grip around her. She looked to Langdon. The earnest concern in his gaze felt like the warmth of a guardian angel, especially in the aura of Kohler's chill.

A single sentient thought began pounding at Vittoria with unrelenting force.

Where is the antimatter?

The horrifying answer was only a moment away.

30

'Maximilian Kohler. Kindly call your office immediately.'

Blazing sunbeams flooded Langdon's eyes as the elevator doors opened into the main atrium. Before the echo of the announcement on the intercom overhead faded, every electronic device on Kohler's wheelchair started beeping and buzzing simultaneously. His pager. His phone. His E-mail. Kohler glanced down at the blinking lights in apparent bewilderment. The director had resurfaced, and he was back in range.

'Director Kohler. Please call your office.'

The sound of his name on the PA seemed to startle Kohler.

He glanced up, looking angered and then almost immediately concerned. Langdon's eyes met his, and Vittoria's too. The three of them were motionless a moment, as if all the tension between them had been erased and replaced by a single, unifying foreboding.

Kohler took his cell phone from the armrest. He dialed an extension and fought off another coughing fit. Vittoria and Langdon waited.

'This is . . . Director Kohler,' he said, wheezing. 'Yes? I was subterranean, out of range.' He listened, his gray eyes widening. *'Who?* Yes, patch it through.' There was a pause. 'Hello? This is Maximilian Kohler. I am the director of CERN. With whom am I speaking?'

Vittoria and Langdon watched in silence as Kohler listened.

'It would be unwise,' Kohler finally said, 'to speak of this by phone. I will be there immediately.' He was coughing again. 'Meet me . . . at Leonardo da Vinci Airport. Forty minutes.' Kohler's breath seemed to be failing him now. He descended into a fit of coughing and barely managed to choke out the words. 'Locate the canister immediately . . . I am coming.' Then he clicked off his phone.

Vittoria ran to Kohler's side, but Kohler could no longer speak. Langdon watched as Vittoria pulled out her cell phone and paged CERN's infirmary. Langdon felt like a ship on the periphery of a storm . . . tossed but detached.

Meet me at Leonardo da Vinci Airport. Kohler's words echoed.

The uncertain shadows that had fogged Langdon's mind all morning, in a single instant, solidified into a vivid image. As he stood there in the swirl of confusion, he felt a door inside him open . . . as if some mystic threshold had just been breached. *The ambigram. The murdered priest/scientist. The antimatter. And now . . . the target.* Leonardo da Vinci Airport could only mean one thing. In a moment of stark realization, Langdon knew he had just crossed over. He had become a believer.

Five kilotons. Let there be light.

Two paramedics materialized, racing across the atrium in white smocks. They knelt by Kohler, putting an oxygen mask on his face. Scientists in the hall stopped and stood back.

Kohler took two long pulls, pushed the mask aside, and still gasping for air, looked up at Vittoria and Langdon. 'Rome.'

'Rome?' Vittoria demanded. 'The antimatter is in Rome? Who called?'

Kohler's face was twisted, his gray eyes watering. 'The Swiss . . .' He choked on the words, and the paramedics put the mask back over his face. As they prepared to take him away, Kohler reached up and grabbed Langdon's arm.

Langdon nodded. He knew.

'Go . . .' Kohler wheezed beneath his mask. 'Go . . . call me . . .' Then the paramedics were rolling him away.

Vittoria stood riveted to the floor, watching him go. Then she turned to Langdon. 'Rome? But . . . what was that about *the Swiss*?'

Langdon put a hand on her shoulder, barely whispering the words. 'The Swiss Guard,' he said. 'The sworn sentinels of Vatican City.'

31

The X-33 space plane roared into the sky and arched south toward Rome. On board, Langdon sat in silence. The last fifteen minutes had been a blur. Now that he had finished briefing Vittoria on the Illuminati and their covenant against the Vatican, the scope of this situation was starting to sink in.

What the hell am I doing? Langdon wondered. *I should have gone home when I had the chance!* Deep down, though, he knew he'd never had the chance.

Langdon's better judgment had screamed at him to return to Boston. Nonetheless, academic astonishment had somehow vetoed prudence. Everything he had ever believed about the demise of the Illuminati was suddenly looking like a brilliant sham. Part of him craved proof. Confirmation. There was also a question of conscience. With Kohler ailing and Vittoria on her own, Langdon knew that if his knowledge of the Illuminati could assist in any way, he had a moral obligation to be here.

There was more, though. Although Langdon was ashamed to admit it, his initial horror on hearing about the antimatter's location was not only the danger to human life in Vatican City, but for something else as well.

Art.

The world's largest art collection was now sitting on a time bomb. The Vatican Museum housed over 60,000 priceless pieces in 1,407 rooms – Michelangelo, da Vinci, Bernini, Botticelli. Langdon wondered if all of the art could possibly be evacuated if necessary. He knew it was impossible. Many of the pieces were sculptures weighing tons. Not to mention, the greatest treasures were architectural – the Sistine Chapel, St Peter's Basilica, Bramante's famed spiral staircase leading to the *Museo Vaticano* – priceless testaments to man's creative genius. Langdon wondered how much time was left on the canister.

'Thanks for coming,' Vittoria said, her voice quiet.

Langdon emerged from his daydream and looked up. Vittoria was sitting across the aisle. Even in the stark fluorescent light of the cabin, there was an aura of composure about her – an almost magnetic radiance of wholeness. Her breathing seemed deeper now, as if a spark of self-preservation had ignited within her . . . a craving for justice and retribution, fueled by a daughter's love.

Vittoria had not had time to change from her shorts and sleeveless top, and her tawny legs were now goose-bumped in the cold of the plane. Instinctively Langdon removed his jacket and offered it to her.

'American chivalry?' She accepted, her eyes thanking him silently.

The plane jostled across some turbulence, and Langdon felt a surge of danger. The windowless cabin felt cramped again, and he tried to imagine himself in an open field. The notion, he realized, was ironic. He had been in an open field when it had happened. *Crushing darkness.* He pushed the memory from his mind. *Ancient history.*

Vittoria was watching him. 'Do you believe in God, Mr Langdon?'

The question startled him. The earnestness in Vittoria's voice was even more disarming than the inquiry. *Do I believe in God?* He had hoped for a lighter topic of conversation to pass the trip.

A spiritual conundrum, Langdon thought. *That's what my friends call me.* Although he studied religion for years, Langdon was not a religious man. He respected the power of faith, the benevolence of churches, the strength religion gave so many people . . . and yet, for him, the intellectual suspension of disbelief that was imperative if one were truly going to 'believe' had always proved too big an obstacle for his academic mind. 'I *want* to believe,' he heard himself say.

Vittoria's reply carried no judgment or challenge. 'So why *don't* you?'

He chuckled. 'Well, it's not that easy. *Having* faith requires *leaps* of faith, cerebral acceptance of miracles – immaculate conceptions and divine interventions. And then there are the codes of conduct. The Bible, the Koran, Buddhist scripture . . . they all carry similar requirements – and similar penalties. They claim that if I don't live by a specific code I will go to hell. I can't imagine a God who would rule that way.'

'I hope you don't let your students dodge questions that shamelessly.'

The comment caught him off guard. 'What?'

'Mr Langdon, I did not ask if you believe what *man* says about God. I asked if you believe in God. There is a difference. Holy scripture is stories . . . legends and history of man's quest to understand his own need for meaning. I am not asking you to pass judgment on literature. I am asking if you believe in *God*. When you lie out under the stars, do you sense the divine? Do you feel in your gut that you are staring up at the work of God's hand?'

Langdon took a long moment to consider it.

'I'm prying,' Vittoria apologized.

'No, I just . . .'

'Certainly you must debate issues of faith with your classes.'

'Endlessly.'

'And you play devil's advocate, I imagine. Always fueling the debate.'

Langdon smiled. 'You must be a teacher too.'

'No, but I learned from a master. My father could argue two sides of a Möbius Strip.'

Langdon laughed, picturing the artful crafting of a Möbius Strip – a twisted ring of paper, which technically possessed only *one* side. Langdon had first seen the single-sided shape in the artwork of M. C. Escher. 'May I ask you a question, Ms Vetra?'

'Call me Vittoria. Ms Vetra makes me feel old.'

He sighed inwardly, suddenly sensing his own age. 'Vittoria, I'm Robert.'

'You had a question.'

'Yes. As a scientist and the daughter of a Catholic priest, what do *you* think of religion?'

Vittoria paused, brushing a lock of hair from her eyes. 'Religion is like language or dress. We gravitate toward the practices with which we were raised. In the end, though, we are all proclaiming the same thing. That life has meaning. That we are grateful for the power that created us.'

Langdon was intrigued. 'So you're saying that whether you are a Christian or a Muslim simply depends on where you were born?'

'Isn't it obvious? Look at the diffusion of religion around the globe.'

'So faith is random?'

'Hardly. Faith is universal. Our specific methods for understanding it are arbitrary. Some of us pray to Jesus, some of us go to Mecca, some of us study subatomic particles. In the end we are all just searching for truth, that which is greater than ourselves.'

Langdon wished his students could express themselves so clearly. Hell, he wished *he* could express himself so clearly. 'And God?' he asked. 'Do you believe in God?'

Vittoria was silent for a long time. 'Science tells me God must exist. My mind tells me I will never understand God. And my heart tells me I am not meant to.'

How's that for concise, he thought. 'So you believe God is fact, but we will never understand Him.'

'*Her,*' she said with a smile. 'Your Native Americans had it right.'

Langdon chuckled. 'Mother Earth.'

'*Gaea*. The planet is an organism. All of us are cells with different purposes. And yet we are intertwined. Serving each other. Serving the whole.'

Looking at her, Langdon felt something stir within him that he had not felt in a long time. There was a bewitching clarity in her eyes . . . a purity in her voice. He felt drawn.

'Mr Langdon, let me ask you another question.'

'Robert,' he said. *Mr Langdon makes me feel old. I am old!*

'If you don't mind my asking, Robert, how did you get involved with the Illuminati?'

Langdon thought back. 'Actually, it was money.'

134

Vittoria looked disappointed. 'Money? Consulting, you mean?'

Langdon laughed, realizing how it must have sounded. 'No. Money as in *currency*.' He reached in his pants pocket and pulled out some money. He found a one-dollar bill. 'I became fascinated with the cult when I first learned that U.S. currency is covered with Illuminati symbology.'

Vittoria's eyes narrowed, apparently not knowing whether or not to take him seriously.

Langdon handed her the bill. 'Look at the back. See the Great Seal on the left?'

Vittoria turned the one-dollar bill over. 'You mean the pyramid?'

'The pyramid. Do you know what pyramids have to do with U.S. history?'

Vittoria shrugged.

'Exactly,' Langdon said. 'Absolutely *nothing*.'

Vittoria frowned. 'So why is it the *central* symbol of your Great Seal?'

'An eerie bit of history,' Langdon said. 'The pyramid is an occult symbol representing a convergence upward, toward the ultimate source of Illumination. See what's above it?'

Vittoria studied the bill. 'An eye inside a triangle.'

'It's called the *trinacria*. Have you ever seen that eye in a triangle anywhere else?'

Vittoria was silent a moment. 'Actually, yes, but I'm not sure . . .'

'It's emblazoned on Masonic lodges around the world.'

'The symbol is Masonic?'

'Actually, no. It's Illuminati. They called it their "shining delta". A call for enlightened change. The eye

135

signifies the Illuminati's ability to infiltrate and watch all things. The shining triangle represents enlightenment. And the triangle is also the Greek letter delta, which is the mathematical symbol for—'

'Change. Transition.'

Langdon smiled. 'I forgot I was talking to a scientist.'

'So you're saying the U.S. Great Seal is a call for enlightened, all-seeing change?'

'Some would call it a New World Order.'

Vittoria seemed startled. She glanced down at the bill again. 'The writing under the pyramid says *Novus . . . Ordo . . .*'

'*Novus Ordo Seclorum*,' Langdon said. 'It means New Secular Order.'

'Secular as in *non*religious?'

'Nonreligious. The phrase not only clearly states the Illuminati objective, but it also blatantly contradicts the phrase beside it. In God We Trust.'

Vittoria seemed troubled. 'But how could all this symbology end up on the most powerful currency in the world?'

'Most academics believe it was through Vice President Henry Wallace. He was an upper echelon Mason and certainly had ties to the Illuminati. Whether it was as a member or innocently under their influence, nobody knows. But it was Wallace who sold the design of the Great Seal to the president.'

'How? Why would the president have agreed to—'

'The president was Franklin D. Roosevelt. Wallace simply told him *Novus Ordo Seclorum* meant *New Deal*.'

Vittoria seemed skeptical. 'And Roosevelt didn't have anyone *else* look at the symbol before telling the Treasury to print it?'

'No need. He and Wallace were like brothers.'

'Brothers?'

'Check your history books,' Langdon said with a smile. 'Franklin D. Roosevelt was a well-known Mason.'

32

Langdon held his breath as the X-33 spiraled into Rome's Leonardo da Vinci International Airport. Vittoria sat across from him, eyes closed as if trying to will the situation into control. The craft touched down and taxied to a private hangar.

'Sorry for the slow flight,' the pilot apologized, emerging from the cockpit. 'Had to trim her back. Noise regulations over populated areas.'

Langdon checked his watch. They had been airborne thirty-seven minutes.

The pilot popped the outer door. 'Anybody want to tell me what's going on?'

Neither Vittoria nor Langdon responded.

'Fine,' he said, stretching. 'I'll be in the cockpit with the air-conditioning and my music. Just me and Garth.'

The late-afternoon sun blazed outside the hangar. Langdon carried his tweed jacket over his shoulder. Vittoria turned her face skyward and inhaled deeply, as if the sun's rays somehow transferred to her some mystical replenishing energy.

Mediterraneans, Langdon mused, already sweating.

'Little old for cartoons, aren't you?' Vittoria asked, without opening her eyes.

'I'm sorry?'

'Your wristwatch. I saw it on the plane.'

Langdon flushed slightly. He was accustomed to having to defend his timepiece. The collector's edition Mickey Mouse watch had been a childhood gift from his parents. Despite the contorted foolishness of Mickey's outstretched arms designating the hour, it was the only watch Langdon had ever worn. Waterproof and glow-in-the-dark, it was perfect for swimming laps or walking unlit college paths at night. When Langdon's students questioned his fashion sense, he told them he wore Mickey as a daily reminder to stay young at heart.

'It's six o'clock,' he said.

Vittoria nodded, eyes still closed. 'I think our ride's here.'

Langdon heard the distant whine, looked up, and felt a sinking feeling. Approaching from the north was a helicopter, slicing low across the runway. Langdon had been on a helicopter once in the Andean Palpa Valley looking at the *Nazca* sand drawings and had not enjoyed it one bit. *A flying shoebox*. After a morning of space plane rides, Langdon had hoped the Vatican would send a car.

Apparently not.

The chopper slowed overhead, hovered a moment, and dropped toward the runway in front of them. The craft was white and carried a coat of arms emblazoned on the side – two skeleton keys crossing a shield and papal crown. He knew the symbol well. It was the traditional seal of the Vatican – the sacred symbol of the *Holy See* or 'holy seat' of government, the *seat* being literally the ancient throne of St Peter.

138

The Holy Chopper, Langdon groaned, watching the craft land. He'd forgotten the Vatican owned one of these things, used for transporting the Pope to the airport, to meetings, or to his summer palace in Gandolfo. Langdon definitely would have preferred a car.

The pilot jumped from the cockpit and strode toward them across the tarmac.

Now it was Vittoria who looked uneasy. '*That's* our pilot?'

Langdon shared her concern. 'To fly, or not to fly. That is the question.'

The pilot looked like he was festooned for a Shakespearean melodrama. His puffy tunic was vertically striped in brilliant blue and gold. He wore matching pantaloons and spats. On his feet were black flats that looked like slippers. On top of it all, he wore a black felt beret.

'Traditional Swiss Guard uniforms,' Langdon explained. 'Designed by Michelangelo himself.' As the man drew closer, Langdon winced. 'I admit, *not* one of Michelangelo's better efforts.'

Despite the man's garish attire, Langdon could tell the pilot meant business. He moved toward them with all the rigidity and dignity of a U.S. Marine. Langdon had read many times about the rigorous requirements for becoming one of the elite Swiss Guard. Recruited from one of Switzerland's four Catholic cantons, applicants had to be Swiss males between nineteen and thirty years old, at least 5 feet 6 inches, trained by the Swiss Army, and unmarried. This imperial corps was envied by world governments as the most allegiant and deadly security force in the world.

'You are from CERN?' the guard asked, arriving before them. His voice was steely.

'Yes, sir,' Langdon replied.

'You made remarkable time,' he said, giving the X-33 a mystified stare. He turned to Vittoria. 'Ma'am, do you have any other clothing?'

'I beg your pardon?'

He motioned to her legs. 'Short pants are not permitted inside Vatican City.'

Langdon glanced down at Vittoria's legs and frowned. He had forgotten. Vatican City had a strict ban on visible legs above the knee – both male and female. The regulation was a way of showing respect for the sanctity of God's city.

'This is all I have,' she said. 'We came in a hurry.'

The guard nodded, clearly displeased. He turned next to Langdon. 'Are you carrying any weapons?'

Weapons? Langdon thought. *I'm not even carrying a change of underwear!* He shook his head.

The officer crouched at Langdon's feet and began patting him down, starting at his socks. *Trusting guy*, Langdon thought. The guard's strong hands moved up Langdon's legs, coming uncomfortably close to his groin. Finally they moved up to his chest and shoulders. Apparently content Langdon was clean, the guard turned to Vittoria. He ran his eyes up her legs and torso.

Vittoria glared. 'Don't even think about it.'

The guard fixed Vittoria with a gaze clearly intended to intimidate. Vittoria did not flinch.

'What's that?' the guard said, pointing to a faint square bulge in the front pocket of her shorts.

Vittoria removed an ultrathin cell phone. The guard took it, clicked it on, waited for a dial tone, and then, apparently satisfied that it was indeed nothing more than a phone, returned it to her. Vittoria slid it back into her pocket.

'Turn around, please,' the guard said.

Vittoria obliged, holding her arms out and rotating a full 360 degrees.

The guard carefully studied her. Langdon had already decided that Vittoria's form-fitting shorts and blouse were not bulging anywhere they shouldn't have been. Apparently the guard came to the same conclusion.

'Thank you. This way please.'

The Swiss Guard chopper churned in neutral as Langdon and Vittoria approached. Vittoria boarded first, like a seasoned pro, barely even stooping as she passed beneath the whirling rotors. Langdon held back a moment.

'No chance of a car?' he yelled, half-joking to the Swiss Guard, who was climbing in the pilot's seat.

The man did not answer.

Langdon knew that with Rome's maniacal drivers, flying was probably safer anyway. He took a deep breath and boarded, stooping cautiously as he passed beneath the spinning rotors.

As the guard fired up the engines, Vittoria called out, 'Have you located the canister?'

The guard glanced over his shoulder, looking confused. 'The what?'

'The canister. You called CERN about a canister?'

The man shrugged. 'No idea what you're talking about. We've been busy today. My commander told me to pick you up. That's all I know.'

Vittoria gave Langdon an unsettled look.

'Buckle up, please,' the pilot said as the engine revved.

Langdon reached for his seat belt and strapped himself in. The tiny fuselage seemed to shrink around him. Then with a roar, the craft shot up and banked sharply north toward Rome.

Rome . . . the *caput mundi*, where Caesar once ruled, where St Peter was crucified. The cradle of modern civilization. And at its core . . . a ticking bomb.

33

Rome from the air is a labyrinth – an indecipherable maze of ancient roadways winding around buildings, fountains, and crumbling ruins.

The Vatican chopper stayed low in the sky as it sliced northwest through the permanent smog layer coughed up by the congestion below. Langdon gazed down at the mopeds, sight-seeing buses, and armies of miniature Fiat sedans buzzing around rotaries in all directions. *Koyaanisqatsi*, he thought, recalling the Hopi term for 'life out of balance.'

Vittoria sat in silent determination in the seat beside him.

The chopper banked hard.

His stomach dropping, Langdon gazed farther into the distance. His eyes found the crumbling ruins of the Roman Coliseum. The Coliseum, Langdon had always thought, was one of history's greatest ironies. Now a dignified symbol for the rise of human culture and civilization, the stadium had been built to host centuries of barbaric events – hungry lions shredding prisoners, armies of slaves battling to the death, gang rapes of exotic women captured from far-off lands, as well as public beheadings and castrations. It was ironic, Langdon thought, or perhaps fitting, that the Coliseum had served as the architectural blueprint for Harvard's Soldier Field – the football stadium where the ancient traditions of savagery were reenacted every fall ... crazed fans screaming for bloodshed as Harvard battled Yale.

As the chopper headed north, Langdon spied the Roman Forum – the heart of pre-Christian Rome. The decaying columns looked like toppled gravestones in a cemetery that had somehow avoided being swallowed by the metropolis surrounding it.

To the west the wide basin of the Tiber River wound enormous arcs across the city. Even from the air Langdon could tell the water was deep. The churning currents were brown, filled with silt and foam from heavy rains.

'Straight ahead,' the pilot said, climbing higher.

Langdon and Vittoria looked out and saw it. Like a mountain parting the morning fog, the colossal dome rose out of the haze before them: St Peter's Basilica.

'Now *that*,' Langdon said to Vittoria, 'is something Michelangelo got right.'

Langdon had never seen St Peter's from the air. The marble façade blazed like fire in the afternoon sun. Adorned with 140 statues of saints, martyrs, and angels, the Herculean edifice stretched two football fields wide and a staggering *six* long. The cavernous interior of the basilica had room for over 60,000 worshipers ... over one hundred times the population of Vatican City, the smallest country in the world.

143

Incredibly, though, not even a citadel of this magnitude could dwarf the piazza before it. A sprawling expanse of granite, St Peter's Square was a staggering open space in the congestion of Rome, like a classical Central Park. In front of the basilica, bordering the vast oval common, 284 columns swept outward in four concentric arcs of diminishing size . . . an architectural *trompe l'oeil* used to heighten the piazza's sense of grandeur.

As he stared at the magnificent shrine before him, Langdon wondered what St Peter would think if he were here now. The Saint had died a gruesome death, crucified upside down on this very spot. Now he rested in the most sacred of tombs, buried five stories down, directly beneath the central cupola of the basilica.

'Vatican City,' the pilot said, sounding anything but welcoming.

Langdon looked out at the towering stone bastions that loomed ahead – impenetrable fortifications surrounding the complex . . . a strangely earthly defense for a spiritual world of secrets, power and mystery.

'Look!' Vittoria said suddenly, grabbing Langdon's arm. She motioned frantically downward toward St Peter's Square directly beneath them. Langdon put his face to the window and looked.

'Over there,' she said, pointing.

Langdon looked. The rear of the piazza looked like a parking lot crowded with a dozen or so trailer trucks. Huge satellite dishes pointed skyward from the roof of every truck. The dishes were emblazoned with familiar names:

TELEVISOR EUROPEA
VIDEO ITALIA
BBC
UNITED PRESS INTERNATIONAL

Langdon felt suddenly confused, wondering if the news of the antimatter had already leaked out.

Vittoria seemed suddenly tense. 'Why is the press here? What's going on?'

The pilot turned and gave her an odd look over his shoulder. 'What's going on? You don't know?'

'No,' she fired back, her accent husky and strong.

'*Il Conclave*,' he said. 'It is to be sealed in about an hour. The whole world is watching.'

Il Conclave.

The word rang a long moment in Langdon's ears before dropping like a brick to the pit of his stomach. *Il Conclave. The Vatican Conclave.* How could he have forgotten? It had been in the news recently.

Fifteen days ago, the Pope, after a tremendously popular twelve-year reign, had passed away. Every paper in the world had carried the story about the Pope's fatal stroke while sleeping – a sudden and unexpected death many whispered was suspicious. But now, in keeping with the sacred tradition, fifteen days after the death of a Pope, the Vatican was holding *Il Conclave* – the sacred ceremony in which the 165 cardinals of the world – the most powerful men in Christendom – gathered in Vatican City to elect the new Pope.

Every cardinal on the planet is here today, Langdon thought as the chopper passed over St Peter's Basilica. The expansive inner world of Vatican City spread out

145

beneath him. *The entire power structure of the Roman Catholic Church is sitting on a time bomb.*

34

Cardinal Mortati gazed up at the lavish ceiling of the Sistine Chapel and tried to find a moment of quiet reflection. The frescoed walls echoed with the voices of cardinals from nations around the globe. The men jostled in the candlelit tabernacle, whispering excitedly and consulting with one another in numerous languages, the universal tongues being English, Italian and Spanish.

The light in the chapel was usually sublime – long rays of tinted sun slicing through the darkness like rays from heaven – but not today. As was the custom, all of the chapel's windows had been covered in black velvet in the name of secrecy. This ensured that no one on the inside could send signals or communicate in any way with the outside world. The result was a profound darkness lit only by candles . . . a shimmering radiance that seemed to purify everyone it touched, making them all ghostly . . . like saints.

What privilege, Mortati thought, *that I am to oversee this sanctified event.* Cardinals over eighty years of age were too old to be eligible for election and did not attend conclave, but at seventy-nine years old, Mortati was the most senior cardinal here and had been appointed to oversee the proceedings.

Following tradition, the cardinals gathered here two hours before conclave to catch up with friends and engage in last-minute discussion. At 7 p.m., the late Pope's chamberlain would arrive, give opening prayer, and then leave. Then the Swiss Guard would seal the doors and lock all the cardinals inside. It was then that the oldest and most secretive political ritual in the world would begin. The cardinals would not be released until they decided who among them would be the next Pope.

Conclave. Even the name was secretive. '*Con clave*' literally meant 'locked with a key.' The cardinals were permitted no contact whatsoever with the outside world. No phone calls. No messages. No whispers through doorways. Conclave was a vacuum, not to be influenced by anything in the outside world. This would ensure that the cardinals kept *Solum Dum prae oculis* . . . only God before their eyes.

Outside the walls of the chapel, of course, the media watched and waited, speculating as to which of the cardinals would become the ruler of one billion Catholics worldwide. Conclaves created an intense, politically charged atmosphere, and over the centuries they had turned deadly; poisonings, fist fights, and even murder had erupted within the sacred walls. *Ancient history*, Mortati thought. *Tonight's conclave will be unified, blissful, and above all . . . brief.*

Or at least that had been his speculation.

Now, however, an unexpected development had emerged. Mystifyingly, four cardinals were absent from the chapel. Mortati knew that all the exits to Vatican City were guarded, and the missing cardinals could not have gone far, but still, with less than an hour before opening prayer, he was feeling disconcerted. After all, the four missing men were no *ordinary* cardinals. They were *the* cardinals.

The chosen four.

As overseer of the conclave, Mortati had already sent word through the proper channels to the Swiss Guard alerting them to the cardinals' absence. He had yet to hear back. Other cardinals had now noticed the puzzling absence. The anxious whispers had begun. Of *all* cardinals, these *four* should be on time! Cardinal Mortati was starting to fear it might be a long evening after all.

He had no idea.

35

The Vatican's helipad, for reasons of safety and noise control, is located in the northwest tip of Vatican City, as far from St Peter's Basilica as possible.

'Terra firma,' the pilot announced as they touched down. He exited and opened the sliding door for Langdon and Vittoria.

Langdon descended from the craft and turned to help Vittoria, but she had already dropped effortlessly to the ground. Every muscle in her body seemed tuned to one objective – finding the antimatter before it left a horrific legacy.

After stretching a reflective sun tarp across the cockpit window, the pilot ushered them to an oversized electric golf cart waiting near the helipad. The cart whisked them silently alongside the country's western border – a fifty-foot-tall cement bulwark thick enough to ward off attacks even by tanks. Lining the interior of the wall, posted at fifty-meter intervals, Swiss Guards stood at attention, surveying the interior of the grounds. The cart turned sharply right onto Via della Osservatorio. Signs pointed in all directions:

PALAZZO GOVERNATORIO
COLLEGIO ETIOPE
BASILICA SAN PIETRO
CAPELLA SISTINA

They accelerated up the manicured road past a squat building marked RADIO VATICANA. This, Langdon realized to his amazement, was the hub of the world's most listened-to radio programming – *Radio Vaticana* – spreading the word of God to millions of listeners around the globe.

'*Attenzione,*' the pilot said, turning sharply into a rotary.

As the cart wound round, Langdon could barely believe the sight now coming into view. *Giardini Vaticani*, he thought. The heart of Vatican City. Directly ahead rose the rear of St Peter's Basilica, a view, Langdon realized, most people never saw. To the right loomed the Palace of the Tribunal, the lush papal residence rivaled only by Versailles in its baroque embellishment. The severe-looking Governatorato building was now behind them, housing Vatican City's administration. And up ahead on the left, the massive rectangular edifice of the Vatican Museum. Langdon knew there would be no time for a museum visit this trip.

'Where is everyone?' Vittoria asked, surveying the deserted lawns and walkways.

The guard checked his black, military-style chrono-graph – an odd anachronism beneath his puffy sleeve.

'The cardinals are convened in the Sistine Chapel. Conclave begins in a little under an hour.'

Langdon nodded, vaguely recalling that before conclave the cardinals spent two hours inside the Sistine Chapel in quiet reflection and visitations with their fellow cardinals from around the globe. The time was meant to renew old friendships among the cardinals and facilitate a less heated election process. 'And the rest of the residents and staff?'

'Banned from the city for secrecy and security until the conclave concludes.'

'And when does it conclude?'

The guard shrugged. 'God only knows.' The words sounded oddly literal.

After parking the cart on the wide lawn directly behind St Peter's Basilica, the guard escorted Langdon and Vittoria up a stone escarpment to a marble plaza off the back of the basilica. Crossing the plaza, they approached the rear wall of the basilica and followed it through a triangular courtyard, across Via Belvedere, and into a series of buildings closely huddled together. Langdon's art history had taught him enough Italian to pick out signs for the Vatican Printing Office, the Tapestry Restoration Lab, Post Office Management, and the Church of St Ann. They crossed another small square and arrived at their destination.

The Office of the Swiss Guard is housed adjacent to Il Corpo di Vigilanza, directly northeast of St Peter's Basilica. The office is a squat, stone building. On either side of the entrance, like two stone statues, stood a pair of guards.

Langdon had to admit, these guards did not look

quite so comical. Although they also wore the blue and gold uniform, each wielded the traditional 'Vatican long sword' – an eight-foot spear with a razor-sharp scythe – rumored to have decapitated countless Muslims while defending the Christian crusaders in the fifteenth century.

As Langdon and Vittoria approached, the two guards stepped forward, crossing their long swords, blocking the entrance. One looked up at the pilot in confusion. '*I pantaloni,*' he said, motioning to Vittoria's shorts.

The pilot waved them off. '*Il comandante vuole vederli subito.*'

The guards frowned. Reluctantly they stepped aside.

Inside, the air was cool. It looked nothing like the administrative security offices Langdon would have imagined. Ornate and impeccably furnished, the hallways contained paintings Langdon was certain any museum worldwide would gladly have featured in its main gallery.

The pilot pointed down a steep set of stairs. 'Down, please.'

Langdon and Vittoria followed the white marble treads as they descended between a gauntlet of nude male sculptures. Each statue wore a fig leaf that was lighter in color than the rest of the body.

The Great Castration, Langdon thought.

It was one of the most horrific tragedies in Renaissance art. In 1857, Pope Pius IX decided that the accurate representation of the male form might incite lust inside the Vatican. So he got a chisel and mallet and hacked off the genitalia of every single male statue inside Vatican City. He defaced works by Michel-angelo, Bramante, and Bernini. Plaster fig leaves were used to patch the damage. Hundreds of sculptures had been emasculated. Langdon had often wondered if there was a huge crate of stone penises someplace.

'Here,' the guard announced.

They reached the bottom of the stairs and dead-ended at a heavy, steel door. The guard typed an entry code, and the door slid open. Langdon and Vittoria entered.

Beyond the threshold was absolute mayhem.

36

The Office of the Swiss Guard.

Langdon stood in the doorway, surveying the collision of centuries before them. *Mixed media.* The room was a lushly adorned Renaissance library com-plete with inlaid bookshelves, oriental carpets, and colorful tapestries . . . and yet the room bristled with high-tech gear – banks of computers, faxes, electronic maps of the Vatican complex, and televisions tuned to CNN. Men in colorful pantaloons typed feverishly on computers and listened intently in futuristic head-phones.

'Wait here,' the guard said.

Langdon and Vittoria waited as the guard crossed the room to an exceptionally tall, wiry man in a dark blue military uniform. He was talking on a cellular phone and stood so straight he was almost bent back-ward. The guard said something to him, and the man shot a glance over at Langdon and Vittoria. He nodded, then turned his back on them and continued his phone call.

The guard returned. 'Commander Olivetti will be with you in a moment.'

'Thank you.'

The guard left and headed back up the stairs.

Langdon studied Commander Olivetti across the room, realizing he was actually the Commander in Chief of the armed forces of an entire country. Vittoria and Langdon waited, observing the action before them. Brightly dressed guards bustled about yelling orders in Italian.

'Continua cercando!' one yelled into a telephone.

'Probasti il museo?' another asked.

Langdon did not need fluent Italian to discern that the security center was currently in intense search mode. This was the good news. The bad news was that they obviously had not yet found the antimatter.

'You okay?' Langdon asked Vittoria.

She shrugged, offering a tired smile.

When the commander finally clicked off his phone and approached across the room, he seemed to grow with each step. Langdon was tall himself and not accustomed to looking up at many people, but Commander Olivetti demanded it. Langdon sensed immediately that the commander was a man who had weathered tempests, his face hale and steeled. His dark hair was cropped in a military buzz cut, and his eyes burned with the kind of hardened determination only attainable through years of intense training. He moved with ramrod exactness, the earpiece hidden discreetly behind one ear making him look more like U.S. Secret Service than Swiss Guard.

The commander addressed them in accented English. His voice was startlingly quiet for such a large man, barely a whisper. It bit with a tight, military efficiency. 'Good afternoon,' he said. 'I am Commander Olivetti – *Comandante Principale* of the Swiss Guard. I'm the one who called your director.'

Vittoria gazed upward. 'Thank you for seeing us, sir.'

The commander did not respond. He motioned for them to follow and led them through the tangle of electronics to a door in the side wall of the chamber. 'Enter,' he said, holding the door for them.

Langdon and Vittoria walked through and found themselves in a darkened control room where a wall of video monitors was cycling lazily through a series of black-and-white images of the complex. A young guard sat watching the images intently.

'*Fuori,*' Olivetti said.

The guard packed up and left.

Olivetti walked over to one of the screens and pointed to it. Then he turned toward his guests. 'This image is from a remote camera hidden somewhere inside Vatican City. I'd like an explanation.'

Langdon and Vittoria looked at the screen and inhaled in unison. The image was absolute. No doubt. It was CERN's antimatter canister. Inside, a shimmering droplet of metallic liquid hung ominously in the air, lit by the rhythmic blinking of the LED digital clock. Eerily, the area around the canister was almost entirely dark, as if the antimatter were in a closet or darkened room. At the top of the monitor flashed superimposed text: LIVE FEED – CAMERA #86.

Vittoria looked at the time remaining on the flashing indicator on the canister. 'Under six hours,' she whispered to Langdon, her face tense.

Langdon checked his watch. 'So we have until . . .' He stopped, a knot tightening in his stomach.

'Midnight,' Vittoria said, with a withering look.

Midnight, Langdon thought. *A flair for the dramatic.* Apparently whoever stole the canister last night had timed it perfectly. A stark foreboding set in as he realized he was currently sitting at ground zero.

Olivetti's whisper now sounded more like a hiss. 'Does this object belong to your facility?'

Vittoria nodded. 'Yes, sir. It was stolen from us. It contains an extremely combustible substance called antimatter.'

Olivetti looked unmoved. 'I am quite familiar with incendiaries, Ms Vetra. I have not heard of antimatter.'

'It's new technology. We need to locate it immediately or evacuate Vatican City.'

Olivetti closed his eyes slowly and reopened them, as if refocusing on Vittoria might change what he just heard. 'Evacuate? Are you aware what is going on here this evening?'

'Yes, sir. And the lives of your cardinals are in danger. We have about six hours. Have you made any headway locating the canister?'

Olivetti shook his head. 'We haven't started looking.'

Vittoria choked. 'What? But we expressly heard your guards talking about searching the—'

'Searching, *yes*,' Olivetti said, 'but not for your canister. My men are looking for something else that does not concern you.'

Vittoria's voice cracked. 'You haven't even *begun* looking for this canister?'

Olivetti's pupils seemed to recede into his head. He had the passionless look of an insect. 'Ms Vetra, is it?

Let me explain something to you. The director of your faculty refused to share any details about this object with me over the phone except to say that I needed to find it immediately. We are exceptionally busy, and I do not have the luxury of dedicating manpower to a situation until I get some facts.'

'There is only one relevant fact at this moment, sir,' Vittoria said, 'that being that in six hours that device is going to vaporize this entire complex.'

Olivetti stood motionless. 'Ms Vetra, there is something you need to know.' His tone hinted at patronizing. 'Despite the archaic appearance of Vatican City, every single entrance, both public and private, is equipped with the most advanced sensing equipment known to man. If someone tried to enter with any sort of incendiary device it would be detected instantly. We have radioactive isotope scanners, olfactory filters designed by the American DEA to detect the faintest chemical signatures of combustibles and toxins. We also use the most advanced metal detectors and X-ray scanners available.'

'Very impressive,' Vittoria said, matching Olivetti's cool. 'Unfortunately, antimatter is nonradioactive, its chemical signature is that of pure hydrogen, and the canister is plastic. None of those devices would have detected it.'

'But the device has an energy source,' Olivetti said, motioning to the blinking LED. 'Even the smallest trace of nickel-cadmium would register as—'

'The batteries are also plastic.'

Olivetti's patience was clearly starting to wane. 'Plastic batteries?'

'Polymer gel electrolyte with Teflon.'

Olivetti leaned towards her, as if to accentuate his

height advantage. '*Signorina*, the Vatican is the target of dozens of bomb threats a month. I personally train every Swiss Guard in modern explosive technology. I am well aware that there is no substance on earth powerful enough to do what you are describing unless you are talking about a nuclear warhead with a fuel core the size of a baseball.'

Vittoria framed him with a fervent stare. 'Nature has many mysteries yet to unveil.'

Olivetti leaned closer. 'Might I ask exactly *who* you are? What is your position at CERN?'

'I am a senior member of the research staff and appointed liaison to the Vatican for this crisis.'

'Excuse me for being rude, but if there is indeed a *crisis*, why am I dealing with *you* and not your director? And what disrespect do you intend by coming into Vatican City in short pants?'

Langdon groaned. He couldn't believe that under the circumstances the man was being a stickler for dress code. Then again, he realized, if stone penises could induce lustful thoughts in Vatican residents, Vittoria Vetra in shorts could *certainly* be a threat to national security.

'Commander Olivetti,' Langdon intervened, trying to diffuse what looked like a second bomb about to explode. 'My name is Robert Langdon. I'm a professor of religious studies in the U.S. and unaffiliated with CERN. I have seen an antimatter demonstration and will vouch for Ms Vetra's claim that it is exceptionally dangerous. We have reason to believe it was placed inside your complex by an antireligious cult hoping to disrupt your conclave.'

Olivetti turned, peering down at Langdon. 'I have a woman in shorts telling me that a droplet of liquid is going to blow up Vatican City, and I have an American professor telling me we are being targeted by some antireligious cult. What exactly is it you expect me to do?'

'Find the canister,' Vittoria said. 'Right away.'

'Impossible. That device could be anywhere. Vatican City is enormous.'

'Your cameras don't have GPS locators on them?'

'They are not generally *stolen*. This missing camera will take days to locate.'

'We don't have *days*,' Vittoria said adamantly. 'We have six hours.'

'Six hours until what, Ms Vetra?' Olivetti's voice grew louder suddenly. He pointed to the image on the screen. 'Until these numbers count down? Until Vatican City disappears? Believe me, I do not take kindly to people tampering with my security system. Nor do I like mechanical contraptions appearing mysteriously inside my walls. I *am* concerned. It is my *job* to be concerned. But what you have told me here is unacceptable.'

Langdon spoke before he could stop himself. 'Have you heard of the Illuminati?'

The commander's icy exterior cracked. His eyes went white, like a shark about to attack. 'I am warning you. I do not have time for this.'

'So you *have* heard of the Illuminati?'

Olivetti's eyes stabbed like bayonets. 'I am a sworn defendant of the Catholic Church. *Of course* I have heard of the Illuminati. They have been dead for decades.'

Langdon reached in his pocket and pulled out the fax image of Leonardo Vetra's branded body. He handed it to Olivetti.

'I am an Illuminati scholar,' Langdon said as Olivetti studied the picture. 'I am having a difficult time accepting that the Illuminati are still active, and yet the appearance of this brand combined with the fact that the Illuminati have a well-known covenant against Vatican City has changed my mind.'

'A computer-generated hoax.' Olivetti handed the fax back to Langdon.

Langdon stared, incredulous. 'Hoax? Look at the symmetry! You of all people should realize the authenticity of—'

'Authenticity is precisely what you lack. Perhaps Ms Vetra has not informed you, but CERN scientists have been criticizing Vatican policies for decades. They regularly petition us for retraction of Creationist theory, formal apologies for Galileo and Copernicus, repeal of our criticism against dangerous or immoral research. What scenario seems more likely to you – that a four-hundred-year-old satanic cult has re-surfaced with an advanced weapon of mass destruction, or that some prankster at CERN is trying to disrupt a sacred Vatican event with a well-executed fraud?'

'That photo,' Vittoria said, her voice like boiling lava, 'is of my father. *Murdered*. You think this is my idea of a *joke*?'

'I don't know, Ms Vetra. But I do know until I get some answers that make *sense*, there is no way I will raise any sort of alarm. Vigilance and discretion are my duty . . . such that spiritual matters can take place here with clarity of mind. Today of all days.'

Langdon said, 'At least postpone the event.'

'Postpone?' Olivetti's jaw dropped. 'Such arrogance! A conclave is not some American baseball game you call off on account of rain. This is a sacred event with a strict code and process. Never mind that one billion Catholics in the world are waiting for a leader. Never mind that the world media is outside. The protocols for this event are holy – *not* subject to modification. Since 1179, conclaves have survived earthquakes, famines, and even the plague. Believe me, it is not about to be canceled on account of a murdered scientist and a droplet of God knows what.'

'Take me to the person in charge,' Vittoria demanded.

Olivetti glared. 'You've got him.'

'No,' she said. 'Someone in the *clergy*.'

The veins on Olivetti's brow began to show. 'The clergy has gone. With the exception of the Swiss Guard, the only ones present in Vatican City at this time are the College of Cardinals. And they are inside the Sistine Chapel.'

'How about the *chamberlain*?' Langdon stated flatly.

'Who?'

'The late Pope's *chamberlain*.' Langdon repeated the word self-assuredly, praying his memory served him. He recalled reading once about the curious arrangement of Vatican authority following the death of a Pope. If Langdon was correct, during the interim between Popes, complete autonomous power shifted temporarily to the late Pope's personal assistant – his chamberlain – a secretarial underling who oversaw conclave until the cardinals chose the new Holy Father. 'I believe the *chamberlain* is the man in charge at the moment.'

'*Il camerlengo*?' Olivetti scowled. 'The camerlengo is only a priest here. He is the late Pope's hand servant.'

160

'But he is here. And you answer to him.'

Olivetti crossed his arms. 'Mr Langdon, it is true that Vatican rule dictates the camerlengo assume chief executive office during conclave, but it is only because his lack of eligibility for the papacy ensures an unbiased election. It is as if your president died, and one of his aides temporarily sat in the oval office. The camerlengo is young, and his understanding of security, or anything else for that matter, is extremely limited. For all intents and purposes, I am in charge here.'

'Take us to him,' Vittoria said.

'Impossible. Conclave begins in forty minutes. The camerlengo is in the Office of the Pope preparing. I have no intention of disturbing him with matters of security.'

Vittoria opened her mouth to respond but was interrupted by a knocking at the door. Olivetti opened it.

A guard in full regalia stood outside, pointing to his watch. '*É l'ora, comandante.*'

Olivetti checked his own watch and nodded. He turned back to Langdon and Vittoria like a judge pondering their fate. 'Follow me.' He led them out of the monitoring room across the security center to a small clear cubicle against the rear wall. 'My office.' Olivetti ushered them inside. The room was unspecial – a cluttered desk, file cabinets, folding chairs, a water cooler. 'I will be back in ten minutes. I suggest you use the time to decide how you would like to proceed.'

Vittoria wheeled. 'You can't just leave! That canister is—'

'I do not have time for this,' Olivetti seethed. 'Perhaps I should detain you until after the conclave when I *do* have time.'

'Signore,' the guard urged, pointing to his watch again. '*Spazzare di cappella.*'

161

Olivetti nodded and started to leave.

'*Spazzare di cappella?*' Vittoria demanded. 'You're leaving to *sweep* the chapel?'

Olivetti turned, his eyes boring through her. 'We sweep for electronic bugs, Miss Vetra – a matter of *discretion.*' He motioned to her legs. 'Not something I would expect you to understand.'

With that he slammed the door, rattling the heavy glass. In one fluid motion he produced a key, inserted it, and twisted. A heavy deadbolt slid into place.

'*Idiòta!*' Vittoria yelled. 'You can't keep us in here!'

Through the glass, Langdon could see Olivetti say something to the guard. The sentinel nodded. As Olivetti strode out of the room, the guard spun and faced them on the other side of the glass, arms crossed, a large sidearm visible on his hip.

Perfect, Langdon thought. *Just bloody perfect.*

37

Vittoria glared at the Swiss Guard standing outside Olivetti's locked door. The sentinel glared back, his colorful costume belying his decidedly ominous air.

Che fiasco, Vittoria thought. *Held hostage by an armed man in pajamas.*

Langdon had fallen silent, and Vittoria hoped he was using that Harvard brain of his to think them out of this. She sensed, however, from the look on his face, that he was more in shock than in thought. She regretted getting him so involved.

Vittoria's first instinct was to pull out her cell phone

and call Kohler, but she knew it was foolish. First, the guard would probably walk in and take her phone. Second, if Kohler's episode ran its usual course, he was probably still incapacitated. Not that it mattered . . . Olivetti seemed unlikely to take anybody's word on anything at the moment.

Remember! she told herself. *Remember the solution to this test!*

Remembrance was a Buddhist philosopher's trick. Rather than asking her mind to search for a solution to a potentially impossible challenge, Vittoria asked her mind simply to remember it. The presupposition that one once *knew* the answer created the mindset that the answer must *exist* . . . thus eliminating the crippling conception of hopelessness. Vittoria often used the process to solve scientific quandaries . . . those that most people thought had no solution.

At the moment, however, her remembrance trick was drawing a major blank. So she measured her options . . . her needs. She needed to warn someone. Someone at the Vatican needed to take her seriously. But who? The camerlengo? How? She was in a glass box with one exit.

Tools, she told herself. *There are always tools. Reevaluate your environment.*

Instinctively she lowered her shoulders, relaxed her eyes, and took three deep breaths into her lungs. She sensed her heart rate slow and her muscles soften. The chaotic panic in her mind dissolved. *Okay*, she thought, *let your mind be free. What makes this situation positive? What are my assets?*

The analytical mind of Vittoria Vetra, once calmed, was a powerful force. Within seconds she realized their incarceration was actually their key to escape.

'I'm making a phone call,' she said suddenly.

Langdon looked up. 'I was about to suggest you call Kohler, but—'

'Not Kohler. Someone else.'

'Who?'

'The camerlengo.'

Langdon looked totally lost. 'You're calling the chamberlain? How?'

'Olivetti said the camerlengo was in the Pope's office.'

'Okay. You know the Pope's private number?'

'No. But I'm not calling on *my* phone.' She nodded to a high-tech phone system on Olivetti's desk. It was riddled with speed dial buttons. 'The head of security *must* have a direct line to the Pope's office.'

'He also has a weight lifter with a gun planted six feet away.'

'And we're locked in.'

'I was actually aware of that.'

'I mean the *guard* is locked out. This is Olivetti's private office. I doubt anyone else has a key.'

Langdon looked out at the guard. 'This is pretty thin glass, and that's a pretty big gun.'

'What's he going to do, shoot me for using the phone?'

'Who the hell knows! This is a pretty strange place, and the way things are going—'

'Either that,' Vittoria said, 'or we can spend the next five hours and forty-eight minutes in Vatican Prison. At least we'll have a front-row seat when the anti-matter goes off.'

Langdon paled. 'But the guard will get Olivetti the second you pick up that phone. Besides, there are twenty buttons on there. And I don't see any identification. You going to try them all and hope to get lucky?'

'Nope,' she said, striding to the phone. 'Just one.' Vittoria picked up the phone and pressed the top button. 'Number *one*. I bet you one of those Illuminati U.S. dollars you have in your pocket that this is the Pope's office. What else would take primary importance for a Swiss Guard commander?'

Langdon did not have time to respond. The guard outside the door started rapping on the glass with the butt of his gun. He motioned for her to set down the phone.

Vittoria winked at him. The guard seemed to inflate with rage.

Langdon moved away from the door and turned back to Vittoria. 'You damn well better be right, 'cause this guy does not look amused!'

'Damn!' she said, listening to the receiver. 'A recording.'

'Recording?' Langdon demanded. 'The Pope has an answering machine?'

'It wasn't the Pope's office,' Vittoria said, hanging up. 'It was the damn weekly menu for the Vatican commissary.'

Langdon offered a weak smile to the guard outside who was now glaring angrily through the glass while he hailed Olivetti on his walkie-talkie.

38

The Vatican switchboard is located in the Ufficio di Communicazione behind the Vatican post office. It is a relatively small room containing an eight-line Corelco 141 switchboard. The office handles over 2,000 calls a day, most routed automatically to the recording information system.

Tonight, the sole communications operator on duty sat quietly sipping a cup of caffeinated tea. He felt proud to be one of only a handful of employees still allowed inside Vatican City tonight. Of course the honor was tainted somewhat by the presence of the Swiss Guards hovering outside his door. *An escort to the bathroom*, the operator thought. *Ah, the indignities we endure in the name of Holy Conclave.*

Fortunately, the calls this evening had been light. Or maybe it was not so *fortunate*, he thought. World interest in Vatican events seemed to have dwindled in the last few years. The number of press calls had thinned, and even the crazies weren't calling as often. The press office had hoped tonight's event would have more of a festive buzz about it. Sadly, though, despite St Peter's Square being filled with press trucks, the vans looked to be mostly standard Italian and Euro press. Only a handful of global cover-all networks were there . . . no doubt having sent their *giornalisti secondarii*.

The operator gripped his mug and wondered how long tonight would last. *Midnight or so*, he guessed. Nowadays, most insiders already knew who was favored to become Pope well before conclave convened, so the process was more of a three- or four-hour ritual than an actual election. Of course, last-minute dissension in the ranks could prolong the ceremony through dawn . . . or beyond. The conclave of 1831 had lasted fifty-four days. *Not tonight*, he told himself; rumor was *this* conclave would be a 'smoke-watch'.

The operator's thoughts evaporated with the buzz

of an inside line on his switchboard. He looked at the blinking red light and scratched his head. *That's odd,* he thought. *The zero-line. Who on the inside would be calling operator information tonight? Who is even inside?*

'*Città del Vaticano, prego?*' he said, picking up the phone.

The voice on the line spoke in rapid Italian. The operator vaguely recognized the accent as that common to Swiss Guards – fluent Italian tainted by the Franco-Swiss influence. This caller, however, was most definitely not Swiss Guard.

On hearing the woman's voice, the operator stood suddenly, almost spilling his tea. He shot a look back down at the line. He had not been mistaken. *An internal extension.* The call was from the inside. *There must be some mistake!* he thought. *A woman inside Vatican City? Tonight?*

The woman was speaking fast and furiously. The operator had spent enough years on the phones to know when he was dealing with a *pazzo*. This woman did not sound crazy. She was urgent but rational. Calm and efficient. He listened to her request, bewildered.

'*Il camerlengo?*' the operator said, still trying to figure out where the hell the call was coming from. 'I cannot possibly connect . . . yes, I am aware he is in the Pope's office but . . . who are you again? . . . and you want to warn him of . . .' He listened, more and more unnerved. *Everyone is in danger? How? And where are you calling from?* 'Perhaps I should contact the Swiss . . .' The operator stopped short. 'You say you're *where? Where?*'

He listened in shock, then made a decision. 'Hold, please,' he said, putting the woman on hold before she could respond. Then he called Commander

Olivetti's direct line. *There is no way that woman is really—*

The line picked up instantly.

'Per l'amore di Dio!' a familiar woman's voice shouted at him. 'Place the damn call!'

The door of the Swiss Guards' security center hissed open. The guards parted as Commander Olivetti entered the room like a rocket. Turning the corner to his office, Olivetti confirmed what his guard on the walkie-talkie had just told him; Vittoria Vetra was standing at his desk talking on the commander's private telephone.

Che coglioni che ha questa! he thought. *The balls on this one!*

Livid, he strode to the door and rammed the key into the lock. He pulled open the door and demanded, 'What are you doing!'

Vittoria ignored him. 'Yes,' she was saying into the phone. 'And I must warn—'

Olivetti ripped the receiver from her hand, and raised it to his ear. 'Who the hell is this!'

For the tiniest of an instant, Olivetti's inelastic posture slumped. 'Yes, camerlengo . . .' he said. 'Correct, signore . . . but questions of security demand . . . of course not . . . I am holding her here for . . . certainly, but . . .' He listened. 'Yes, sir,' he said finally. 'I will bring them up immediately.'

39

The Apostolic Palace is a conglomeration of buildings located near the Sistine Chapel in the northeast corner of Vatican City. With a commanding view of St Peter's Square, the palace houses both the Papal Apartments and the Office of the Pope.

Vittoria and Langdon followed in silence as Commander Olivetti led them down a long rococo corridor, the muscles in his neck pulsing with rage. After climbing three sets of stairs, they entered a wide, dimly lit hallway.

Langdon could not believe the artwork on the walls – mint-condition busts, tapestries, friezes – works worth hundreds of thousands of dollars. Two-thirds of the way down the hall they passed an alabaster fountain. Olivetti turned left into an alcove and strode to one of the largest doors Langdon had ever seen.

'*Ufficio di Papa*,' the commander declared, giving Vittoria an acrimonious scowl. Vittoria didn't flinch. She reached over Olivetti and knocked loudly on the door.

Office of the Pope, Langdon thought, having difficulty fathoming that he was standing outside one of the most sacred rooms in all of world religion.

'*Avanti!*' someone called from within.

When the door opened, Langdon had to shield his eyes. The sunlight was blinding. Slowly, the image before him came into focus.

The Office of the Pope seemed more of a ballroom than an office. Red marble floors sprawled out in all directions to walls adorned with vivid frescoes. A colossal chandelier hung overhead, beyond which a bank of arched windows offered a stunning panorama of the sun-drenched St Peter's Square.

My God, Langdon thought. *This is a room with a view.*

At the far end of the hall, at a carved desk, a man sat writing furiously. '*Avanti*,' he called out again, setting down his pen and waving them over.

Olivetti led the way, his gait military. *'Signore,'* he said apologetically. *'No ho potuto—'*

The man cut him off. He stood and studied his two visitors.

The camerlengo was nothing like the images of frail, beatific old men Langdon usually imagined roaming the Vatican. He wore no rosary beads or pendants. No heavy robes. He was dressed instead in a simple black cassock that seemed to amplify the solidity of his substantial frame. He looked to be in his late-thirties, indeed a child by Vatican standards. He had a surprisingly handsome face, a swirl of coarse brown hair, and almost radiant green eyes that shone as if they were somehow fueled by the mysteries of the universe. As the man drew nearer, though, Langdon saw in his eyes a profound exhaustion – like a soul who had been through the toughest fifteen days of his life.

'I am Carlo Ventresca,' he said, his English perfect. 'The late Pope's camerlengo.' His voice was unpretentious and kind, with only the slightest hint of Italian inflection.

'Vittoria Vetra,' she said, stepping forward and offering her hand. 'Thank you for seeing us.'

Olivetti twitched as the camerlengo shook Vittoria's hand.

'This is Robert Langdon,' Vittoria said. 'A religious historian from Harvard University.'

'Padre,' Langdon said, in his best Italian accent. He bowed his head as he extended his hand.

'No, no,' the camerlengo insisted, lifting Langdon back up. 'His Holiness's office does not make me holy. I am merely a priest – a chamberlain serving in a time of need.'

Langdon stood upright.

'Please,' the camerlengo said, 'everyone sit.' He arranged some chairs around his desk. Langdon and Vittoria sat. Olivetti apparently preferred to stand.

The camerlengo seated himself at the desk, folded his hands, sighed, and eyed his visitors.

'Signore,' Olivetti said. 'The woman's attire is my fault. I—'

'Her attire is *not* what concerns me,' the camerlengo replied, sounding too exhausted to be bothered. 'When the Vatican operator calls me a half hour before I begin conclave to tell me a woman is calling from *your* private office to warn me of some sort of major security threat of which I have not been informed, *that* concerns me.'

Olivetti stood rigid, his back arched like a soldier under intense inspection.

Langdon felt hypnotized by the camerlengo's presence. Young and wearied as he was, the priest had the air of some mythical hero – radiating charisma and authority.

'Signore,' Olivetti said, his tone apologetic but still unyielding. 'You should not concern yourself with matters of security. You have other responsibilities.'

'I am well aware of my other responsibilities. I am also aware that as *direttore intermediario*, I have a responsibility for the safety and wellbeing of everyone at this conclave. What is going on here?'

'I have the situation under control.'

'Apparently not.'

'Father,' Langdon interrupted, taking out the crumpled fax and handing it to the camerlengo, 'please.'

Commander Olivetti stepped forward, trying to intervene. 'Father, please do not trouble your thoughts with—'

The camerlengo took the fax, ignoring Olivetti for a long moment. He looked at the image of the murdered Leonardo Vetra and drew a startled breath. 'What is this?'

'That is my father,' Vittoria said, her voice wavering. 'He was a priest and a man of science. He was murdered last night.'

The camerlengo's face softened instantly. He looked up at her. 'My dear child. I'm so sorry.' He crossed himself and lookèd again at the fax, his eyes seeming to pool with waves of abhorrence. 'Who would . . . and this burn on his . . .' The camerlengo paused, squinting closer at the image.

'It says *Illuminati*,' Langdon said. 'No doubt you are familiar with the name.'

An odd look came across the camerlengo's face. 'I have heard the name, yes, but . . .'

'The Illuminati murdered Leonardo Vetra so they could steal a new technology he was—'

'Signore,' Olivetti interjected. 'This is absurd. The Illuminati? This is clearly some sort of elaborate hoax.'

The camerlengo seemed to ponder Olivetti's words. Then he turned and contemplated Langdon so fully that Langdon felt the air leave his lungs. 'Mr Langdon, I have spent my life in the Catholic Church. I am familiar with the Illuminati lore . . . and the legend of the brandings. And yet I must warn you, I am a man of the present tense. Christianity has enough real enemies without resurrecting ghosts.'

'The symbol is authentic,' Langdon said, a little too defensively he thought. He reached over and rotated the fax for the camerlengo.

The camerlengo fell silent when he saw the symmetry.

'Even modern computers,' Langdon added, 'have been unable to forge a symmetrical ambigram of this word.'

The camerlengo folded his hands and said nothing for a long time. 'The Illuminati are dead,' he finally said. 'Long ago. That is historical fact.'

Langdon nodded. 'Yesterday, I would have agreed with you.'

'Yesterday?'

'Before today's chain of events. I believe the Illuminati have resurfaced to make good on an ancient pact.'

'Forgive me. My history is rusty. What ancient pact is this?'

Langdon took a deep breath. 'The destruction of Vatican City.'

'*Destroy* Vatican City?' The camerlengo looked less frightened than confused. 'But that would be impossible.'

Vittoria shook her head. 'I'm afraid we have some more bad news.'

40

'Is this *true*?' the camerlengo demanded, looking amazed as he turned from Vittoria to Olivetti.

'Signore,' Olivetti assured, 'I'll admit there is some sort of device here. It is visible on one of our security monitors, but as for Ms Vetra's claims as to the power of this substance, I cannot possibly—'

'Wait a minute,' the camerlengo said. 'You can *see* this thing?'

'Yes, signore. On wireless camera #86.'

'Then why haven't you recovered it?' The camerlengo's voice echoed anger now.

'Very difficult, signore.' Olivetti stood straight as he explained the situation.

The camerlengo listened, and Vittoria sensed his growing concern. 'Are you certain it is inside Vatican City?' the camerlengo asked. 'Maybe someone took the camera out and is transmitting from somewhere else.'

'Impossible,' Olivetti said. 'Our external walls are shielded electronically to protect our internal communications. This signal can *only* be coming from the inside or we would not be receiving it.'

'And I assume,' he said, 'that you are now looking for the missing camera with all available resources?'

Olivetti shook his head. 'No, signore. Locating that camera could take hundreds of man hours. We have a number of other security concerns at the moment, and with all due respect to Ms Vetra, this droplet she talks about is very small. It could not possibly be as explosive as she claims.'

Vittoria's patience evaporated. 'That droplet is enough to level Vatican City! Did you even listen to a word I told you?'

'Ma'am,' Olivetti said, his voice like steel, 'my experience with explosives is extensive.'

'Your experience is obsolete,' she fired back, equally tough. 'Despite my attire, which I realize you find troublesome, I am a senior level physicist at the world's most advanced subatomic research facility. I personally designed the antimatter trap that is keeping that sample from annihilating right now. And I am warning you that unless you find that canister in the next six hours, your guards will have nothing to protect for the next century but a big hole in the ground.'

Olivetti wheeled to the camerlengo, his insect eyes flashing rage. 'Signore, I cannot in good conscience allow this to go any further. Your time is being wasted by pranksters. The Illuminati? A droplet that will destroy us all?'

'*Basta*,' the camerlengo declared. He spoke the word quietly and yet it seemed to echo across the chamber. Then there was silence. He continued in a whisper. 'Dangerous or not, Illuminati or no Illuminati, whatever this thing is, it most certainly should not be inside Vatican City . . . no less on the eve of the conclave. I want it found and removed. Organize a search immediately.'

Olivetti persisted. 'Signore, even if we used all the guards to search the complex, it could take days to find this camera. Also, after speaking to Ms Vetra, I had one of my guards consult our most advanced ballistics guide for any mention of this substance called antimatter. I found no mention of it anywhere. Nothing.'

Pompous ass, Vittoria thought. *A ballistics guide? Did you try an encyclopedia? Under A!*

Olivetti was still talking. 'Signore, if you are suggesting we make a naked-eye search of the entirety of Vatican City then I must object.'

'Commander.' The camerlengo's voice simmered with rage. 'May I remind you that when you address me, you are addressing this office. I realize you do not take my position seriously – nonetheless, by law, I am in charge. If I am not mistaken, the cardinals are now safely within the Sistine Chapel, and your security concerns are at a minimum until the conclave breaks. I do not understand why you are hesitant to look

175

for this device. If I did not know better it would appear that you are causing this conclave intentional danger.'

Olivetti looked scornful. 'How dare you! I have served your Pope for twelve years! And the Pope before that for fourteen years! Since 1438 the Swiss Guard have—'

The walkie-talkie on Olivetti's belt squawked loudly, cutting him off. '*Comandante?*'

Olivetti snatched it up and pressed the transmitter. '*Sono occupato! Cosa voi!!*'

'*Scusi,*' the Swiss Guard on the radio said. 'Communications here. I thought you would want to be informed that we have received a bomb threat.'

Olivetti could not have looked less interested. 'So handle it! Run the usual trace, and write it up.'

'We did, sir, but the caller . . .' The guard paused. 'I would not trouble you, commander, except that he mentioned the substance you just asked me to research. *Antimatter.*'

Everyone in the room exchanged stunned looks.

'He mentioned *what*?' Olivetti stammered.

'Antimatter, sir. While we were trying to run a trace, I did some additional research on his claim. The information on antimatter is . . . well, frankly, it's quite troubling.'

'I thought you said the ballistics guide showed no mention of it.'

'I found it on-line.'

Alleluia, Vittoria thought.

'The substance appears to be quite explosive,' the guard said. 'It's hard to imagine this information is accurate but it says here that pound for pound antimatter carries about a hundred times more

176

payload than a nuclear warhead.'

Olivetti slumped. It was like watching a mountain crumble. Vittoria's feeling of triumph was erased by the look of horror on the camerlengo's face.

'Did you trace the call?' Olivetti stammered.

'No luck. Cellular with heavy encryption. The SAT lines are interfused, so triangulation is out. The IF signature suggests he's somewhere in Rome, but there's really no way to trace him.'

'Did he make demands?' Olivetti said, his voice quiet.

'No sir. Just warned us that there is antimatter hidden inside the complex. He seemed surprised I didn't know. Asked me if I'd *seen* it yet. You'd asked me about antimatter, so I decided to advise you.'

'You did the right thing,' Olivetti said. 'I'll be down in a minute. Alert me immediately if he calls back.'

There was a moment of silence on the walkie-talkie. 'The caller is still on the line, sir.'

Olivetti looked like he'd just been electrocuted. 'The line is open?'

'Yes, sir. We've been trying to trace him for ten minutes, getting nothing but splayed ferreting. He must know we can't touch him because he refuses to hang up until he speaks to the camerlengo.'

'Patch him through,' the camerlengo commanded. 'Now!'

Olivetti wheeled. 'Father, no. A trained Swiss Guard negotiator is much better suited to handle this.'

'*Now!*'

Olivetti gave the order.

A moment later, the phone on Camerlengo Ventresca's desk began to ring. The camerlengo rammed his fingers down on the speaker-phone button. 'Who in the name of God do you think you are?'

41

The voice emanating from the camerlengo's speaker phone was metallic and cold, laced with arrogance. Everyone in the room listened.

Langdon tried to place the accent. *Middle Eastern, perhaps?*

'I am a messenger of an ancient brotherhood,' the voice announced in an alien cadence. 'A brotherhood you have wronged for centuries. I am a messenger of the Illuminati.'

Langdon felt his muscles tighten, the last shreds of doubt withering away. For an instant he felt the familiar collision of thrill, privilege, and dead fear that he had experienced when he first saw the ambigram this morning.

'What do you want?' the camerlengo demanded.

'I represent men of science. Men who like yourselves are searching for the answers. Answers to man's destiny, his purpose, his creator.'

'Whoever you are,' the camerlengo said, 'I—'

'*Silenzio.* You will do better to listen. For two millennia your church has dominated the quest for truth. You have crushed your opposition with lies and prohesies of doom. You have manipulated the truth to serve your needs, murdering those whose discoveries did not serve your politics. Are you surprised you are the target of enlightened men from around the globe?'

'Enlightened men do not resort to blackmail to further their causes.'

'Blackmail?' The caller laughed. 'This is not blackmail. We have no demands. The abolition of the Vatican is nonnegotiable. We have waited four hundred years for this day. At midnight, your city will be destroyed. There is nothing you can do.'

Olivetti stormed toward the speaker phone. 'Access to this city is impossible! You could not possibly have planted explosives in here!'

'You speak with the ignorant devotion of a Swiss Guard. Perhaps even an officer? Surely you are aware that for centuries the Illuminati have infiltrated elitist organizations across the globe. Do you really believe the Vatican is immune?'

Jesus, Langdon thought, *they've got someone on the inside.* It was no secret that infiltration was the Illuminati trademark of power. They had infiltrated the Masons, major banking networks, government bodies. In fact, Churchill had once told reporters that if English spies had infiltrated the Nazis to the degree the Illuminati had infiltrated English Parliament, the war would have been over in one month.

'A transparent bluff,' Olivetti snapped. 'Your influence cannot possibly extend so far.'

'Why? Because your Swiss Guards are vigilant? Because they watch every corner of your private world? How about the Swiss Guards themselves? Are they not men? Do you truly believe they stake their lives on a fable about a man who walks on water? Ask yourself how else the canister could have entered your city. Or how four of your most precious assets could have disappeared this afternoon.'

'Our assets?' Olivetti scowled. 'What do you mean?'

'One, two, three, four. You haven't missed them by now?'

'What the hell are you talk—' Olivetti stopped short, his eyes rocketing wide as though he'd just been punched in the gut.

'Light dawns,' the caller said. 'Shall I read their names?'

'What's going on?' the camerlengo said, looking bewildered.

The caller laughed. 'Your officer has not yet informed you? How sinful. No surprise. Such pride. I imagine the disgrace of telling you the truth . . . that four cardinals he had sworn to protect seem to have disappeared . . .'

Olivetti erupted. 'Where did you get this information!'

'Camerlengo,' the caller gloated, 'ask your commander if *all* your cardinals are present in the Sistine Chapel.'

The camerlengo turned to Olivetti, his green eyes demanding an explanation.

'Signore,' Olivetti whispered in the camerlengo's ear, 'it is true that four of our cardinals have not yet reported to the Sistine Chapel, but there is no need for alarm. Every one of them checked into the residence hall this morning, so we know they are safely inside Vatican City. You yourself had tea with them only hours ago. They are simply late for the fellowship preceding conclave. We are searching, but I'm sure they just lost track of time and are still out enjoying the grounds.'

'Enjoying the grounds?' The calm departed from the camerlengo's voice. 'They were due in the chapel over an hour ago!'

Langdon shot Vittoria a look of amazement. *Missing cardinals? So that's what they were looking for downstairs?*

'Our inventory,' the caller said, 'you will find quite convincing. There is Cardinal Lamassé from Paris, Cardinal Guidera from Barcelona, Cardinal Ebner from Frankfurt . . .'

Olivetti seemed to shrink smaller and smaller after each name was read.

The caller paused, as though taking special pleasure in the final name. 'And from Italy . . . Cardinal Baggia.'

The camerlengo loosened like a tall ship that had just run sheets first into a dead calm. His frock billowed, and he collapsed in his chair. '*I preferiti*,' he whispered. 'The four favorites . . . including Baggia . . . the most likely successor as Supreme Pontiff . . . how is it possible?'

Langdon had read enough about modern papal elections to understand the look of desperation on the camerlengo's face. Although technically *any* cardinal under eighty years old could become Pope, only a very few had the respect necessary to command a two-thirds majority in the ferociously partisan balloting procedure. They were known as the *preferiti*. And they were all gone.

Sweat dripped from the camerlengo's brow. 'What do you intend with these men?'

'What do you think I intend? I am a descendant of the Hassassin.'

Langdon felt a shiver. He knew the name well. The church had made some deadly enemies through the years – the Hassassin, the Knights Templar, armies that had been either hunted by the Vatican or betrayed by them.

'Let the cardinals go,' the camerlengo said. 'Isn't threatening to destroy the City of God enough?'

'Forget your four cardinals. They are lost to you. Be assured their deaths will be remembered though . . . by millions. Every martyr's dream. I will make them media luminaries. One by one. By midnight the Illuminati will have everyone's attention. Why change

181

the world if the world is not watching? Public killings have an intoxicating horror about them, don't they? You proved that long ago ... the inquisition, the torture of the Knights Templar, the Crusades.' He paused. 'And of course, *la purga.*'

The camerlengo was silent.

'Do you not recall *la purga*?' the caller asked. 'Of course not, you are a child. Priests are poor historians, anyway. Perhaps because their history shames them?'

'*La purga,*' Langdon heard himself say. 'Sixteen sixty-eight. The church branded four Illuminati scientists with the symbol of the cross. To purge their sins.'

'Who is speaking?' the voice demanded, sounding more intrigued than concerned. 'Who else is there?'

Langdon felt shaky. 'My name is not important,' he said, trying to keep his voice from wavering. Speaking to a living Illuminatus was disorienting for him ... like speaking to George Washington. 'I am an academic who has studied the history of your brotherhood.'

'Superb,' the voice replied. 'I am pleased there are still those alive who remember the crimes against us.'

'Most of us think you are dead.'

'A misconception the brotherhood has worked hard to promote. What else do you know of *la purga*?'

Langdon hesitated. *What else do I know? That this whole situation is insanity, that's what I know!* 'After the brandings, the scientists were murdered, and their bodies were dropped in public locations around Rome as a warning to other scientists not to join the Illuminati.'

'Yes. So we shall do the same. *Quid pro quo.* Consider it symbolic retribution for our slain bothers. Your four cardinals will die, one every hour starting at eight. By midnight the whole world will be enthralled.'

Langdon moved toward the phone. 'You actually intend to *brand* and kill these four men?'

'History repeats itself, does it not? Of course, we will be more elegant and bold than the church was. They killed privately, dropping bodies when no one was looking. It seems so cowardly.'

'What are you saying?' Langdon asked. 'That you are going to brand and kill these men in *public*?'

'Very good. Although it depends what you consider public. I realize not many people go to church anymore.'

Langdon did a double take. 'You're going to kill them in *churches*?'

'A gesture of kindness. Enabling God to commend their souls to heaven more expeditiously. It seems only right. Of course the press will enjoy it too, I imagine.'

'You're bluffing,' Olivetti said, the cool back in his voice. 'You cannot kill a man in a church and expect to get away with it.'

'Bluffing? We move among your Swiss Guard like ghosts, remove four of your cardinals from within your walls, plant a deadly explosive at the heart of your most sacred shrine, and you think this is a bluff? As the killings occur and the victims are found, the media will swarm. By midnight the world will know the Illuminati cause.'

'And if we stake guards in every church?' Olivetti said.

The caller laughed. 'I fear the prolific nature of your religion will make that a trying task. Have you not counted lately? There are over four hundred Catholic churches in Rome. Cathedrals, chapels, tabernacles, abbeys, monasteries, convents, parochial schools . . .'

Olivetti's face remained hard.

'In ninety minutes it begins,' the caller said with a note of finality. 'One an hour. A mathematical progression of death. Now I must go.'

'Wait!' Langdon demanded. 'Tell me about the brands you intend to use on these men.'

The killer sounded amused. 'I suspect you know what the brands will be already. Or perhaps you are a skeptic? You will see them soon enough. Proof the ancient legends are true.'

Langdon felt light-headed. He knew exactly what the man was claiming. Langdon pictured the brand on Leonardo Vetra's chest. Illuminati folklore spoke of five brands in all. *Four brands are left*, Langdon thought, *and four missing cardinals.*

'I am sworn,' the camerlengo said, 'to bring a new Pope tonight. Sworn by God.'

'Camerlengo,' the caller said, 'the world does not need a new Pope. After midnight he will have nothing to rule over but a pile of rubble. The Catholic Church is finished. Your run on earth is done.'

Silence hung.

The camerlengo looked sincerely sad. 'You are misguided. A church is more than mortar and stone. You cannot simply erase two thousand years of faith ... *any* faith. You cannot crush faith simply by removing its earthly manifestations. The Catholic Church will continue with or without Vatican City.'

'A noble lie. But a lie all the same. We both know the truth. Tell me, why is Vatican City a walled citadel?'

'Men of God live in a dangerous world,' the camerlengo said.

'How young *are* you? The Vatican is a fortress

184

because the Catholic Church holds half of its equity *inside* its walls – rare paintings, sculpture, devalued jewels, priceless books ... then there is the gold bullion and the real estate deeds inside the Vatican Bank vaults. Inside estimates put the raw value of Vatican City at 48.5 billion dollars. Quite a nest egg you're sitting on. Tomorrow it will be ash. Liquidated assets as it were. You will be bankrupt. Not even men of cloth can work for nothing.'

The accuracy of the statement seemed to be reflected in Olivetti's and the camerlengo's shell-shocked looks. Langdon wasn't sure what was more amazing, that the Catholic Church had that kind of money, or that the Illuminati somehow knew about it.

The camerlengo sighed heavily. 'Faith, not money, is the backbone of this church.'

'More lies,' the caller said. 'Last year you spent 183 million dollars trying to support your struggling dioceses worldwide. Church attendance is at an all-time low – down forty-six per cent in the last decade. Donations are half what they were only seven years ago. Fewer and fewer men are entering the seminary. Although you will not admit it, your church is dying. Consider this a chance to go out with a bang.'

Olivetti stepped forward. He seemed less combative now, as if he now sensed the reality facing him. He looked like a man searching for an out. Any out. 'And what if some of that bullion went to fund *your* cause?'

'Do not insult us both.'

'We have money.'

'As do we. More than you can fathom.'

Langdon flashed on the alleged Illuminati fortunes, the ancient wealth of the Bavarian stone masons, the

Rothschilds, the Bilderbergers, the legendary Illuminati Diamond.

'*I preferiti*,' the camerlengo said, changing the subject. His voice was pleading. 'Spare them. They are old. They—'

'They are virgin sacrifices.' The caller laughed. 'Tell me, do you think they are *really* virgins? Will the little lambs squeal when they die? *Sacrifici vergini nell' altare di scienza.*'

The camerlengo was silent for a long time. 'They are men of faith,' he finally said. 'They do not fear death.'

The caller sneered. 'Leonardo Vetra was a man of faith, and yet I saw fear in his eyes last night. A fear I removed.'

Vittoria, who had been silent, was suddenly air-borne, her body taut with hatred. '*Asino!* He was my father!'

A cackle echoed from the speaker. 'Your father? What is this? Vetra has a daughter? You should know your father whimpered like a child at the end. Pitiful really. A pathetic man.'

Vittoria reeled as if knocked backward by the words. Langdon reached for her, but she regained her balance and fixed her dark eyes on the phone. 'I swear on my life, before this night is over, I will find you.' Her voice sharpened like a laser. 'And when I do . . .'

The caller laughed coarsely. 'A woman of spirit. I am aroused. Perhaps before this night is over, I will find *you*. And when I do . . .'

The words hung like a blade. Then he was gone.

Cardinal Mortati was sweating now in his black robe. Not only was the Sistine Chapel starting to feel like a sauna, but conclave was scheduled to begin in twenty minutes, and there was still no word on the four missing cardinals. In their absence, the initial whispers of confusion among the other cardinals had turned to outspoken anxiety..

Mortati could not imagine where the truant men could be. *With the camerlengo perhaps?* He knew the camerlengo had held the traditional private tea for the four *preferiti* earlier that afternoon, but that had been hours ago. *Were they ill? Something they ate?* Mortati doubted it. Even on the verge of death the *preferiti* would be here. It was once in a lifetime, usually *never*, that a cardinal had the chance to be elected Supreme Pontiff, and by Vatican Law the cardinal had to be *inside* the Sistine Chapel when the vote took place. Otherwise, he was ineligible.

Although there were four *preferiti*, few cardinals had any doubt who the next Pope would be. The past fifteen days had seen a blizzard of faxes and phone calls discussing potential candidates. As was the custom, four names had been chosen as *preferiti*, each of them fulfilling the unspoken requisites for becoming Pope.

Multilingual in Italian, Spanish, and English.
No skeletons in his closet.
Between sixty-five and eighty years old.

As usual, one of the *preferiti* had risen above the others as the man the college proposed to elect. Tonight that man was Cardinal Aldo Baggia from

Milan. Baggia's untainted record of service, combined with unparalleled language skills and the ability to communicate the essence of spirituality, had made him the clear favorite.

So where the devil is he? Mortati wondered.

Mortati was particularly unnerved by the missing cardinals because the task of supervising this conclave had fallen to him. A week ago, the College of Cardinals had unanimously chosen Mortati for the office known as *The Great Elector* – the conclave's internal master of ceremonies. Even though the camerlengo was the church's ranking official, the camerlengo was only a priest and had little familiarity with the complex election process, so one cardinal was selected to oversee the ceremony from within the Sistine Chapel.

Cardinals often joked that being appointed The Great Elector was the cruelest honor in Christendom. The appointment made one *ineligible* as a candidate during the election, and it also required one spend many days prior to conclave poring over the pages of the *Universi Dominici Gregis* reviewing the subtleties of conclave's arcane rituals to ensure the election was properly administered.

Mortati held no grudge, though. He knew he was the logical choice. Not only was he the senior cardinal, but he had also been a confidant of the late Pope, a fact that elevated his esteem. Although Mortati was technically still within the legal age window for election, he was getting a bit old to be a serious candidate. At seventy-nine years old he had crossed the unspoken threshold beyond which the college no longer trusted one's health to withstand the rigorous schedule of the papacy. A Pope usually worked fourteen-hour days, seven days a week, and died of exhaustion in an average of 6.3 years. The inside joke was that accepting the papacy was a cardinal's 'fastest route to heaven'.

Mortati, many believed, could have been Pope in his younger days had he not been so broad-minded. When it came to pursuing the papacy, there was a Holy Trinity—Conservative. Conservative. Conservative.

Mortati had always found it pleasantly ironic that the late Pope, God rest his soul, had revealed himself as surprisingly liberal once he had taken office. Perhaps sensing the modern world progressing away from the church, the Pope had made overtures, softening the church's position on the sciences, even donating money to selective scientific causes. Sadly, it had been political suicide. Conservative Catholics declared the Pope 'senile', while scientific purists accused him of trying to spread the church's influence where it did not belong.

'So where are they?'

Mortati turned.

One of the cardinals was tapping him nervously on the shoulder. 'You know where they are, don't you?'

Mortati tried not to show too much concern. 'Perhaps still with the camerlengo.'

'At this hour? That would be highly unorthodox!' The cardinal frowned mistrustfully. 'Perhaps the camerlengo lost track of time?'

Mortati sincerely doubted it, but he said nothing. He was well aware that most cardinals did not much care for the camerlengo, feeling he was too young to serve the Pope so closely. Mortati suspected much of the cardinals' dislike was jealousy, and Mortati actually admired the young man, secretly applauding the late Pope's selection for chamberlain. Mortati saw only conviction when he looked in the camerlengo's eyes, and unlike many of the cardinals, the camerlengo put church and faith before petty politics. He was truly a man of God.

Throughout his tenure, the camerlengo's steadfast devotion had become legendary. Many attributed it to the miraculous event in his childhood ... an event that would have left a permanent impression on any man's heart. *The miracle and wonder of it*, Mortati thought, often wishing his own childhood had presented an event that fostered that kind of doubtless faith.

Unfortunately for the church, Mortati knew, the camerlengo would never become Pope in his elder years. Attaining the papacy required a certain amount of political ambition, something the young camerlengo apparently lacked; he had refused his Pope's offers for higher clerical stations many times, saying he preferred to serve the church as a simple man.

'What next?' The cardinal tapped Mortati, waiting.

Mortati looked up. 'I'm sorry?'

'They're late! What shall we do!'

'What *can* we do?' Mortati replied. 'We wait. And have faith.'

Looking entirely unsatisfied with Mortati's response, the cardinal shrunk back into the shadows.

Mortati stood a moment, dabbing his temples and trying to clear his mind. *Indeed, what shall we do?* He gazed past the altar up to Michelangelo's renowned fresco, 'The Last Judgment'. The painting did nothing to soothe his anxiety. It was a horrifying, fifty-foot-tall depiction of Jesus Christ separating mankind into the righteous and sinners, casting the sinners into hell. There was flayed flesh, burning bodies, and even one of Michelangelo's rivals sitting in hell wearing ass's ears. Guy de Maupassant had once written that the

190

painting looked like something painted for a carnival wrestling booth by an ignorant coal heaver.

Cardinal Mortati had to agree.

43

Langdon stood motionless at the Pope's bulletproof window and gazed down at the bustle of media trailers in St Peter's Square. The eerie phone conversation had left him feeling turgid ... distended somehow. Not himself.

The Illuminati, like a serpent from the forgotten depths of history, had risen and wrapped themselves around an ancient foe. No demands. No negotiation. Just retribution. Demonically simple. Squeezing. A revenge 400 years in the making. It seemed that after centuries of persecution, science had bitten back.

The camerlengo stood at his desk, staring blankly at the phone. Olivetti was the first to break the silence. 'Carlo,' he said, using the camerlengo's first name and sounding more like a weary friend than an officer. 'For twenty-six years, I have sworn my life to the protection of this office. It seems tonight I am dishonored.'

The camerlengo shook his head. 'You and I serve God in different capacities, but service always brings honor.'

'These events ... I can't imagine how ... this situation ...' Olivetti looked overwhelmed.

'You realize we have only one possible course of action. I have a responsibility for the safety of the College of Cardinals.'

'I fear that responsibility was mine, signore.'

'Then your men will oversee the immediate evacuation.'

'Signore?'

'Other options can be exercised later – a search for this device, a manhunt for the missing cardinals and their captors. But first the cardinals must be taken to safety. The sanctity of human life weighs above all. Those men are the foundation of this church.'

'You suggest we cancel conclave right now?'

'Do I have a choice?'

'What about your charge to bring a new Pope?'

The young chamberlain sighed and turned to the window, his eyes drifting out onto the sprawl of Rome below. 'His Holiness once told me that a Pope is a man torn between two worlds ... the real world and the divine. He warned that any church that ignored reality would not survive to enjoy the divine.' His voice sounded suddenly wise for its years. 'The real world is upon us tonight. We would be vain to ignore it. Pride and precedent cannot overshadow reason.'

Olivetti nodded, looking impressed. 'I have underestimated you, signore.'

The camerlengo did not seem to hear. His gaze was distant on the window.

'I will speak openly, signore. The real world is *my* world. I immerse myself in its ugliness every day such that others are unencumbered to seek something more pure. Let me advise you on the present situation. It is what I am trained for. Your instincts, though worthy ... could be disastrous.'

The camerlengo turned.

Olivetti sighed. 'The evacuation of the College of

Cardinals from the Sistine Chapel is the worst possible thing you could do right now.'

The camerlengo did not look indignant, only at a loss. 'What do you suggest?'

'Say nothing to the cardinals. Seal conclave. It will buy us time to try other options.'

The camerlengo looked troubled. 'Are you suggesting I lock the entire College of Cardinals on top of a time bomb?'

'Yes, signore. For now. Later, if need be, we can arrange evacuation.'

The camerlengo shook his head. 'Postponing the ceremony *before* it starts is grounds alone for an inquiry, but after the doors are sealed nothing intervenes. Conclave procedure obligates—'

'*Real* world, signore. You're in it tonight. Listen closely.' Olivetti spoke now with the efficient rattle of a field officer. 'Marching one hundred sixty-five cardinals unprepared and unprotected into Rome would be reckless. It would cause confusion and panic in some very old men, and frankly, one fatal stroke this month is enough.'

One fatal stroke. The commander's words recalled the headlines Langdon had read over dinner with some students in the Harvard Commons: POPE SUFFERS STROKE. DIES IN SLEEP.

'In addition,' Olivetti said, 'the Sistine Chapel is a fortress. Although we don't advertise the fact, the structure is heavily reinforced and can repel any attack short of missiles. As preparation we searched every inch of the chapel this afternoon, scanning for bugs and other surveillance equipment. The chapel is clean, a safe haven, and I am confident the antimatter is not inside. There is no safer place those men can be right now. We can always discuss emergency evacuation later if it comes to that.'

Langdon was impressed. Olivetti's cold, smart logic reminded him of Kohler.

'Commander,' Vittoria said, her voice tense, 'there are other concerns. Nobody has ever created this much antimatter. The blast radius, I can only estimate. Some of surrounding Rome may be in danger. If the canister is in one of your central buildings or underground, the effect outside these walls may be minimal, but if the canister is near the perimeter . . . in *this* building for example . . .' She glanced warily out the window at the crowd in St Peter's Square.

'I am well aware of my responsibilities to the outside world,' Olivetti replied, 'and it makes this situation no more grave. The protection of this sanctuary has been my sole charge for over two decades. I have no intention of allowing this weapon to detonate.'

Camerlengo Ventresca looked up. 'You think you can *find* it?'

'Let me discuss our options with some of my surveillance specialists. There is a possibility, if we kill power to Vatican City, that we can eliminate the background RF and create a clean enough environment to get a reading on that canister's magnetic field.'

Vittoria looked surprised, and then impressed. 'You want to *black out* Vatican City?'

'Possibly. I don't yet know if it's possible, but it is one option I want to explore.'

'The cardinals would certainly wonder what happened,' Vittoria remarked.

Olivetti shook his head. 'Conclaves are held by candlelight. The cardinals would never know. After conclave is sealed, I could pull all except a few of my perimeter guards and begin a search. A hundred men could cover a lot of ground in five hours.'

'*Four* hours,' Vittoria corrected. 'I need to fly the canister back to CERN. Detonation is unavoidable without recharging the batteries.'

'There's no way to recharge here?'

Vittoria shook her head. 'The interface is complex. I'd have brought it if I could.'

'*Four* hours then,' Olivetti said, frowning. 'Still time enough. Panic serves no one. Signore, you have ten minutes. Go to the chapel, seal conclave. Give my men some time to do their job. As we get closer to the critical hour, we will make the critical decisions.'

Langdon wondered how close to 'the critical hour' Olivetti would let things get.

The camerlengo looked troubled. 'But the college will ask about the *preferiti* . . . especially about Baggia . . . where they are.'

'Then you will have to think of something, signore. Tell them you served the four cardinals something at tea that disagreed with them.'

The camerlengo looked riled. 'Stand on the altar of the Sistine Chapel and lie to the College of Cardinals?'

'For their own safety. *Una bugia veniale.* A white lie. Your job will be to keep the peace.' Olivetti headed for the door. 'Now if you will excuse me, I need to get started.'

'Commandante,' the camerlengo urged, 'we cannot simply turn our backs on missing cardinals.'

Olivetti stopped in the doorway. 'Baggia and the others are currently outside our sphere of influence. We must let them go . . . for the good of the whole. The military calls it *triage.*'

195

'Don't you mean *abandonment*?'

His voice hardened. 'If there were *any* way, signore . . . any way in heaven to locate those four cardinals, I would lay down my life to do it. And yet . . .' He pointed across the room at the window where the early evening sun glinted off an endless sea of Roman rooftops. 'Searching a city of five million is not within my power. I will not waste precious time to appease my conscience in a futile exercise. I'm sorry.'

Vittoria spoke suddenly. 'But if we *caught* the killer, couldn't you make him talk?'

Olivetti frowned at her. 'Soldiers cannot afford to be saints, Ms Vetra. Believe me, I empathize with your personal incentive to catch this man.'

'It's not only personal,' she said. 'The *killer* knows where the antimatter is . . . *and* the missing cardinals. If we could somehow find him . . .'

'Play into their hands?' Olivetti said. 'Believe me, removing all protection from Vatican City in order to stake out hundreds of churches is what the Illuminati *hope* we will do . . . wasting precious time and man-power when we should be searching . . . or worse yet, leaving the Vatican Bank totally unprotected. Not to mention the remaining cardinals.'

The point hit home.

'How about the Roman Police?' the camerlengo asked. 'We could alert citywide enforcement of the crisis. Enlist their help in finding the cardinals' captor.'

'Another mistake,' Olivetti said. 'You know how the Roman *Carabinieri* feel about us. We'd get a half-hearted effort of a few men in exchange for their selling our crisis to the global media. Exactly what our enemies want. We'll have to deal with the media soon enough as it is.'

I will make your cardinals media luminaries, Langdon

thought, recalling the killer's words. *The first cardinal's body appears at eight o'clock. Then one every hour. The press will love it.*

The camerlengo was talking again, a trace of anger in his voice. 'Commander, we cannot in good conscience do *nothing* about the missing cardinals!'

Olivetti looked the camerlengo dead in the eye. 'The prayer of St Francis, signore. Do you recall it?'

The young priest spoke the single line with pain in his voice. 'God, grant me strength to accept those things I cannot change.'

'Trust me,' Olivetti said. '*This* is one of those things.' Then he was gone.

44

The central office of the British Broadcasting Corporation (BBC) is in London just west of Piccadilly Circus. The switchboard phone rang, and a junior content editor picked up.

'BBC,' she said, stubbing out her Dunhill cigarette.

The voice on the line was raspy, with a Mid-East accent. 'I have a breaking story your network might be interested in.'

The editor took out a pen and a standard Lead Sheet. 'Regarding?'

'The papal election.'

She frowned wearily. The BBC had run a preliminary story yesterday to mediocre response. The public, it seemed, had little interest in Vatican City. 'What's the angle?'

'Do you have a TV reporter in Rome covering the election?'

'I believe so.'

'I need to speak to him directly.'

'I'm sorry, but I cannot give you that number without some idea—'

'There is a threat to the conclave. That is all I can tell you.'

The editor took notes. 'Your name?'

'My name is immaterial.'

The editor was not surprised. 'And you have proof of this claim?'

'I do.'

'I would be happy to take the information, but it is not our policy to give out our reporters' numbers unless—'

'I understand. I will call another network. Thank you for your time. Good-b—'

'Just a moment,' she said. 'Can you hold?'

The editor put the caller on hold and stretched her neck. The art of screening out potential crank calls was by no means a perfect science, but this caller had just passed the BBC's two tacit tests for authenticity of a phone source. He had refused to give his name, and he was eager to get off the phone. Hacks and glory hounds usually whined and pleaded.

Fortunately for her, reporters lived in eternal fear of missing the big story, so they seldom chastised her for passing along the occasional delusional psychotic. Wasting five minutes of a reporter's time was forgivable. Missing a headline was not.

Yawning, she looked at her computer and typed in the keywords 'Vatican City'. When she saw the name of the field reporter covering the papal election, she chuckled to herself. He was a new guy the BBC had just brought up from some trashy London tabloid to handle some of the BBC's more mundane coverage. Editorial had obviously started him at the bottom rung.

He was probably bored out of his mind, waiting all night to record his ten-second video spot. He would most likely be grateful for a break in the monotony.

The BBC content editor copied down the reporter's satellite extension in Vatican City. Then, lighting another cigarette, she gave the anonymous caller the reporter's number.

45

'It won't work,' Vittoria said, pacing the Pope's office. She looked up at the camerlengo. 'Even if a Swiss Guard team can filter electronic interference, they will have to be practically *on top* of the canister before they detect any signal. And that's if the canister is even accessible . . . unenclosed by other barriers. What if it's buried in a metal box somewhere on your grounds? Or up in a metal ventilating duct. There's no way they'll trace it. And what if the Swiss Guards *have* been infiltrated? Who's to say the search will be clean?'

The camerlengo looked drained. 'What are you proposing, Ms Vetra?'

Vittoria felt flustered. *Isn't it obvious!* 'I am proposing, sir, that you take other precautions *immediately*. We can hope against all hope that the commander's search is successful. At the same time, look out the

199

window. Do you see those people? Those buildings across the piazza? Those media vans? The tourists? They are quite possibly within range of the blast. You need to act *now*.'

The camerlengo nodded vacantly.

Vittoria felt frustrated. Olivetti had convinced everyone there was plenty of time. But Vittoria knew if news of the Vatican predicament leaked out, the entire area could fill with onlookers in a matter of minutes. She had seen it once outside the Swiss Parliament building. During a hostage situation involving a bomb, thousands had congregated outside the building to witness the outcome. Despite police warnings that they were in danger, the crowd packed in closer and closer. Nothing captured human interest like human tragedy.

'Signore,' Vittoria urged, 'the man who killed my father is out there somewhere. Every cell in this body wants to run from here and hunt him down. But I am standing in your office . . . because I have a responsibility to you. To you and others. Lives are in danger, signore. Do you hear me?'

The camerlengo did not answer.

Vittoria could hear her own heart racing. *Why couldn't the Swiss Guard trace that damn caller? The Illuminati assassin is the key! He knows where the anti-matter is . . . hell, he knows where the cardinals are! Catch the killer, and everything is solved.*

Vittoria sensed she was starting to come unhinged, an alien distress she recalled only faintly from childhood, the orphanage years, frustration with no tools to handle it. *You have tools,* she told herself, *you always have tools.* But it was no use. Her thoughts intruded, strangling her. She was a researcher and problem solver. But this was a problem with no solution. *What data do you require? What do you want?* She told herself to breathe deeply, but for the first time in her life, she could not. She was suffocating.

Langdon's head ached, and he felt like he was skirting the edges of rationality. He watched Vittoria and the camerlengo, but his vision was blurred by hideous images: explosions, press swarming, cameras rolling, four branded humans.

Shaitan . . . Lucifer . . . Bringer of light . . . Satan . . .

He shook the fiendish images from his mind. *Calculated terrorism*, he reminded himself, grasping at reality. *Planned chaos*. He thought back to a Radcliffe seminar he had once audited while researching praetorian symbolism. He had never seen terrorists the same way since.

'Terrorism,' the professor had lectured, 'has a singular goal. What is it?'

'Killing innocent people?' a student ventured.

'Incorrect. Death is only a *byproduct* of terrorism.'

'A show of strength?'

'No. A weaker persuasion does not exist.'

'To cause terror?'

'Concisely put. Quite simply, the goal of terrorism is to create terror and fear. Fear undermines faith in the establishment. It weakens the enemy from within . . . causing unrest in the masses. Write this down. Terrorism is *not* an expression of rage. Terrorism is a political weapon. Remove a government's façade of infallibility, and you remove its people's faith.'

Loss of faith . . .

Is that what this was all about? Langdon wondered how Christians of the world would react to cardinals being laid out like mutilated dogs. If the faith of a priest did not protect him from the evils of Satan, what hope was there for the rest of us? Langdon's head was pounding louder now ... tiny voices playing tug of war.

Faith does not protect you. Medicine and airbags ... those are things that protect you. God does not protect you. Intelligence protects you. Enlightenment. Put your faith in something with tangible results. How long has it been since someone walked on water? Modern miracles belong to science ... computers, vaccines, space stations ... even the divine miracle of creation. Matter from nothing ... in a lab. Who needs God? No! Science is God.

The killer's voice resonated in Langdon's mind. *Midnight ... mathematical progression of death ... sacrifici vergini nell' altare di scienza.*

Then suddenly, like a crowd dispersed by a single gunshot, the voices were gone.

Robert Langdon bolted to his feet. His chair fell backward and crashed on the marble floor.

Vittoria and the camerlengo jumped.

'I missed it,' Langdon whispered, spellbound. 'It was right in front of me ...'

'Missed what?' Vittoria demanded.

Langdon turned to the priest. 'Father, for three years I have petitioned this office for access to the Vatican Archives. I have been denied seven times.'

'Mr Langdon, I am sorry, but this hardly seems the moment to raise such complaints.'

'I need access immediately. The four missing cardinals. I may be able to figure out where they're going to be killed.'

Vittoria stared, looking certain she had misunderstood.

The camerlengo looked troubled, as if he were the brunt of a cruel joke. 'You expect me to believe this information is in our *archives*?'

'I can't promise I can locate it in time, but if you let me in . . .'

'Mr Langdon, I am due in the Sistine Chapel in four minutes. The archives are across Vatican City.'

'You're serious aren't you?' Vittoria interrupted, staring deep into Langdon's eyes, seeming to sense his earnestness.

'Hardly a joking time,' Langdon said.

'Father,' Vittoria said, turning to the camerlengo, 'if there's a chance . . . any at all of finding where these killings are going to happen, we could stake out the locations and—'

'But the archives?' the camerlengo insisted. 'How could they possibly contain any clue?'

'Explaining it,' Langdon, 'will take longer than you've got. But if I'm right, we can use the information to catch the Hassassin.'

The camerlengo looked as though he wanted to believe but somehow could not. 'Christianity's most sacred codices are in that archive. Treasures I myself am not privileged enough to see.'

'I am aware of that.'

'Access is permitted only by written decree of the curator and the Board of Vatican Librarians.'

'*Or*,' Langdon declared, 'by *papal* mandate. It says so in every rejection letter your curator ever sent me.'

The camerlengo nodded.

'Not to be rude,' Langdon urged, 'but if I'm not mistaken a papal mandate comes from *this* office. As far as I can tell, tonight you hold the trust of his station. Considering the circumstances . . .'

The camerlengo pulled a pocket watch from his cassock and looked at it. 'Mr Langdon, I am prepared to give my life tonight, quite literally, to save this church.'

Langdon sensed nothing but truth in the man's eyes.

'This document,' the camerlengo said, 'do you truly believe it is here? And that it can help us locate these four churches?'

'I would not have made countless solicitations for access if I were not convinced. Italy is a bit far to come on a lark when you make a teacher's salary. The document you have is an ancient—'

'Please,' the camerlengo interrupted. 'Forgive me. My mind cannot process any more details at the moment. Do you know where the secret archives are located?'

Langdon felt a rush of excitement. 'Just behind the Santa Ana Gate.'

'Impressive. Most scholars believe it is through the secret door behind St Peter's Throne.'

'No. That would be the Archivio della Reverenda di Fabbrica di S. Pietro. A common misconception.'

'A librarian docent accompanies every entrant at all times. Tonight, the docents are gone. What you are requesting is carte blanche access. Not even our cardinals enter alone.'

'I will treat your treasures with the utmost respect and care. Your librarians will find not a trace that I was there.'

Overhead the bells of St Peter's began to toll. The camerlengo checked his pocket watch. 'I must go.' He paused a taut moment and looked up at Langdon. 'I will have a Swiss Guard meet you at the archives. I am giving you my trust, Mr Langdon. Go now.'

Langdon was speechless.

The young priest now seemed to possess an eerie poise. Reaching over, he squeezed Langdon's shoulder with surprising strength. 'I want you to find what you are looking for. And find it quickly.'

46

The Secret Vatican Archives are located at the far end of the Belvedere Courtyard directly up a hill from the Gate of Santa Ana. They contain over 20,000 volumes and are rumored to hold such treasures as Leonardo da Vinci's missing diaries and even unpublished books of the Holy Bible.

Langdon strode powerfully up the deserted Via della Fondamenta toward the archives, his mind barely able to accept that he was about to be granted access. Vittoria was at his side, keeping pace effortlessly. Her almond-scented hair tossed lightly in the breeze, and Langdon breathed it in. He felt his thoughts straying and reeled himself back.

Vittoria said, 'You going to tell me what we're looking for?'

'A little book written by a guy named Galileo.'

She sounded surprised. 'You don't mess around. What's in it?'

'It is supposed to contain something called *il segno*.'

'The sign?'

'Sign, clue, signal . . . depends on your translation.'

'Sign to *what*?'

Langdon picked up the pace. 'A secret location.

205

Galileo's Illuminati needed to protect themselves from the Vatican, so they founded an ultrasecret Illuminati meeting place here in Rome. They called it The Church of Illumination.'

'Pretty bold calling a satanic lair a *church*.'

Langdon shook his head. 'Galileo's Illuminati were not the least bit satanic. They were scientists who revered enlightenment. Their meeting place was simply where they could safely congregate and discuss topics forbidden by the Vatican. Although we know the secret lair existed, to this day nobody has ever located it.'

'Sounds like the Illuminati know how to keep a secret.'

'Absolutely. In fact, they never revealed the location of their hideaway to anyone outside the brotherhood. This secrecy protected them, but it also posed a problem when it came to recruiting new members.'

'They couldn't grow if they couldn't advertise,' Vittoria said, her legs and mind keeping perfect pace.

'Exactly. Word of Galileo's brotherhood started to spread in the 1630s, and scientists from around the world made secret pilgrimages to Rome hoping to join the Illuminati ... eager for a chance to look through Galileo's telescope and hear the master's ideas. Unfortunately, though, because of the Illuminati's secrecy, scientists arriving in Rome never knew where to go for the meetings or to whom they could safely speak. The Illuminati wanted new blood, but they could not afford to risk their secrecy by making their whereabouts known.'

Vittoria frowned. 'Sounds like a *situazione senza soluzione*.'

'Exactly. A catch-22, as we would say.'

'So what did they do?'

'They were scientists. They examined the problem and found a solution. A brilliant one, actually. The Illuminati created a kind of ingenious *map* directing scientists to their sanctuary.'

Vittoria looked suddenly skeptical and slowed. 'A map? Sounds careless. If a copy fell into the wrong hands . . .'

'It couldn't,' Langdon said. 'No copies existed anywhere. It was not the kind of map that fit on paper. It was enormous. A blazed trail of sorts across the city.'

Vittoria slowed even further. 'Arrows painted on sidewalks?'

'In a sense, yes, but much more subtle. The map consisted of a series of carefully concealed symbolic markers placed in public locations around the city. One marker led to the next . . . and the next . . . a trail . . . eventually leading to the Illuminati lair.'

Vittoria eyed him askance. 'Sounds like a treasure hunt.'

Langdon chuckled. 'In a manner of speaking, it is. The Illuminati called their string of markers "The Path of Illumination", and anyone who wanted to join the brotherhood had to follow it all the way to the end. A kind of test.'

'But if the Vatican wanted to find the Illuminati,' Vittoria argued, 'couldn't *they* simply follow the markers?'

'No. The path was hidden. A puzzle, constructed in such a way that only certain people would have the ability to track the markers and figure out where the Illuminati church was hidden. The Illuminati intended it as a kind of initiation, functioning not only as a security measure but also as a screening process to ensure that only the brightest scientists arrived at their door.'

'I don't buy it. In the 1600s the clergy were some of the most educated men in the world. If these markers were in public locations, certainly there existed members of the Vatican who could have figured it out.'

'Sure,' Langdon said, 'if they had *known* about the markers. But they didn't. And they never noticed them because the Illuminati designed them in such a way that clerics would never suspect what they were. They used a method known in symbology as *dissimulation*.'

'Camouflage.'

Langdon was impressed. 'You know the term.'

'*Dissimulazione*,' she said. 'Nature's best defense. Try spotting a trumpet fish floating vertically in seagrass.'

'Okay,' Langdon said. 'The Illuminati used the same concept. They created markers that faded into the backdrop of ancient Rome. They couldn't use ambigrams or scientific symbology because it would be far too conspicuous, so they called on an Illuminati artist – the same anonymous prodigy who had created their ambigrammatic symbol "Illuminati" – and they commissioned him to carve four sculptures.'

'Illuminati *sculptures*?'

'Yes, sculptures with two strict guidelines. First, the sculptures had to look like the rest of the artwork in Rome . . . artwork that the Vatican would *never* suspect belonged to the Illuminati.'

'*Religious* art.'

Langdon nodded, feeling a tinge of excitement, talking faster now. 'And the *second* guideline was that the four sculptures had to have very specific themes. Each piece needed to be a subtle tribute to one of the four elements of science.'

'*Four* elements?' Vittoria said. 'There are over a hundred.'

'Not in the 1600s,' Langdon reminded her. 'Early alchemists believed the entire universe was made up of only four substances: Earth, Air, Fire and Water.'

The early cross, Langdon knew, was the most common symbol of the four elements – four arms representing Earth, Air, Fire and Water. Beyond that, though, there existed literally *dozens* of symbolic occurrences of Earth, Air, Fire and Water throughout history – the Pythagorean cycles of life, the Chinese *Hong-Fan*, the Jungian male and female rudiments, the quadrants of the Zodiac, even the Muslims revered the four ancient elements ... although in Islam they were known as 'squares, clouds, lightning, and waves.' For Langdon, though, it was a more modern usage that always gave him chills – the Mason's four mystic grades of Absolute Initiation: Earth, Air, Fire, and Water.

Vittoria seemed mystified. 'So this Illuminati artist created four pieces of art that *looked* religious, but were actually tributes to Earth, Air, Fire, and Water?'

'Exactly,' Langdon said, quickly turning up Via Sentinel toward the archives. 'The pieces blended into the sea of religious artwork all over Rome. By donating the artwork anonymously to specific churches and then using their political influence, the brotherhood facilitated placement of these four pieces in carefully chosen churches in Rome. Each piece of course was a marker ... subtly pointing to the next church ... where the next marker awaited. It functioned as a trail of clues disguised as religious art. If an Illuminati candidate could find the first church and the marker for Earth, he could follow it to Air ... and then to Fire ...

and then to Water ... and finally to the Church of Illumination.'

Vittoria was looking less and less clear. 'And this has something to do with catching the Illuminati assassin?'

Langdon smiled as he played his ace. 'Oh, yes. The Illuminati called these four churches by a very special name. *The Altars of Science.*'

Vittoria frowned. 'I'm sorry, that means noth—' She stopped short. '*L'altare di scienza?*' she exclaimed. 'The Illuminati assassin. He warned that the cardinals would be virgin sacrifices on the altars of science!'

Langdon gave her a smile. 'Four cardinals. Four churches. The four altars of science.'

She looked stunned. 'You're saying the four churches where the cardinals will be sacrificed are the *same* four churches that mark the ancient Path of Illumination?'

'I believe so, yes.'

'But why would the killer have given us that clue?'

'Why not?' Langdon replied. 'Very few historians know about those sculptures. Even fewer believe they exist. And their locations have remained secret for four hundred years. No doubt the Illuminati trusted the secret for another five hours. Besides, the Illuminati don't *need* their Path of Illumination anymore. Their secret lair is probably long gone anyway. They live in the modern world. They meet in bank boardrooms, eating clubs, private golf courses. Tonight they *want* to make their secrets public. This is their moment. Their grand unveiling.'

Langdon feared the Illuminati unveiling would have a special symmetry to it that he had not yet mentioned. *The four brands.* The killer had sworn each cardinal would be branded with a different symbol. *Proof the ancient legends are true,* the killer had said. The legend of the four ambigrammatic brands was as old as the Illuminati itself: earth, air, fire, water – four words crafted in perfect symmetry. Just like the word Illuminati. Each cardinal was to be branded with one of the ancient elements of science. The rumor that the four brands were in *English* rather than Italian remained a point of debate among historians. English seemed a random deviation from their natural tongue . . . and the Illuminati did nothing randomly.

Langdon turned up the brick pathway before the archive building. Ghastly images thrashed in his mind. The overall Illuminati plot was starting to reveal its patient grandeur. The brotherhood had vowed to stay silent as long as it took, amassing enough influence and power that they could resurface without fear, make their stand, fight their cause in broad daylight. The Illuminati were no longer about hiding. They were about flaunting their power, confirming the conspiratorial myths as fact. Tonight was a global publicity stunt.

Vittoria said, 'Here comes our escort.' Langdon looked up to see a Swiss Guard hurrying across an adjacent lawn toward the front door.

When the guard saw them, he stopped in his tracks. He stared at them, as though he thought he was hallucinating. Without a word he turned away and pulled out his walkie-talkie. Apparently incredulous at what he was being asked to do, the guard spoke urgently to the person on the other end. The angry bark coming back was indecipherable to Langdon, but its message was clear. The guard slumped, put away the walkie-talkie, and turned to them with a look of discontent.

Not a word was spoken as the guard guided them into the building. They passed through four steel doors, two passkey entries, down a long stairwell, and into a foyer with two combination keypads. Passing through a high-tech series of electronic gates, they arrived at the end of a long hallway outside a set of wide oak double doors. The guard stopped, looked them over again and, mumbling under his breath, walked to a metal box on the wall. He unlocked it, reached inside, and pressed a code. The doors before them buzzed, and the deadbolt fell open.

The guard turned, speaking to them for the first time. 'The archives are beyond that door. I have been instructed to escort you this far and return for briefing on another matter.'

'You're leaving?' Vittoria demanded.

'Swiss Guards are not cleared for access to the Secret Archives. You are here only because my commander received a direct order from the camerlengo.'

'But how do we get *out*?'

'Monodirectional security. You will have no diffi-culties.' That being the entirety of the conversation, the guard spun on his heel and marched off down the hall.

Vittoria made some comment, but Langdon did not hear. His mind was fixed on the double doors before him, wondering what mysteries lay beyond.

47

Although he knew time was short, Camerlengo Carlo Ventresca walked slowly. He needed the time alone to gather his thoughts before facing opening prayer. So much was happening. As he moved in dim solitude down the Northern Wing, the challenge of the past fifteen days weighed heavy in his bones.

He had followed his holy duties to the letter.

As was Vatican tradition, following the Pope's death the camerlengo had personally confirmed expiration by placing his fingers on the Pope's carotid artery, listening for breath, and then calling the Pope's name three times. By law there was no autopsy. Then he had sealed the Pope's bedroom, destroyed the papal fisherman's ring, shattered the die used to make lead seals, and arranged for the funeral. That done, he began preparations for the conclave.

Conclave, he thought. *The final hurdle.* It was one of the oldest traditions in Christendom. Nowadays, because the outcome of conclave was usually known before it began, the process was criticized as obsolete – more of a burlesque than an election. The camerlengo knew, however, this was only a lack of understanding. Conclave was not an election. It was an ancient, mystic transference of power. The tradition was timeless . . . the secrecy, the folded slips of paper, the burning of the ballots, the mixing of ancient chemicals, the smoke signals.

As the camerlengo approached through the Loggias of Gregory XIII, he wondered if Cardinal Mortati was in a panic yet. Certainly Mortati had noticed the *preferiti* were missing. Without them the voting would go on all night. Mortati's appointment as the Great Elector, the camerlengo assured himself, was a good one. The man was a free-thinker and could speak his mind. The conclave would need a leader tonight more than ever.

As the camerlengo arrived at the top of the Royal Staircase, he felt as though he were standing on the precipice of his life. Even from up here he could hear the rumble of activity in the Sistine Chapel below – the uneasy chatter of 165 cardinals.

One hundred sixty-one cardinals, he corrected.

For an instant the camerlengo was falling, plummeting toward hell, people screaming, flames engulfing him, stones and blood raining from the sky.

And then silence.

When the child awoke, he was in heaven. Everything around him was white. The light was blinding and pure. Although some would say a ten year old could not possibly understand heaven, the young Carlo Ventresca understood heaven very well. He was in heaven right now. Where else would he be? Even in his short decade on earth Carlo had felt the majesty of God – the thundering pipe organs, the towering domes, the voices raised in song, the stained glass, shimmering bronze and gold. Carlo's mother, Maria, brought him to Mass every day. The church was Carlo's home.

'Why do we come to Mass every single day?' Carlo asked, not that he minded at all.

'Because I promised God I would,' she replied. 'And a promise to God is the most important promise of all. Never break a promise to God.'

Carlo promised her he would never break a promise to God. He loved his mother more than anything in the world. She was his holy angel. Sometimes he called her *Maria benedetta* – the Blessed Mary – although she did not like that at all. He knelt with her as she prayed, smelling the sweet scent of her flesh and listening to

214

the murmur of her voice as she counted the rosary. *Hail Mary, Mother of God . . . pray for us sinners . . . now and at the hour of our death.*

'Where is my father?' Carlo asked, already knowing his father had died before he was born.

'God is your father, now,' she would always reply. 'You are a child of the church.'

Carlo loved that.

'Whenever you feel frightened,' she said, 'remember that God is your father now. He will watch over you and protect you forever. God has *big plans* for you, Carlo.' The boy knew she was right. He could already feel God in his blood.

Blood . . .

Blood raining from the sky!

Silence. Then heaven.

His heaven, Carlo learned as the blinding lights were turned off, was actually the Intensive Care Unit in *Santa Clara Hospital* outside of Palermo. Carlo had been the sole survivor of a terrorist bombing that had collapsed a chapel where he and his mother had been attending Mass while on vacation. Thirty-seven people had died, including Carlo's mother. The papers called Carlo's survival *The Miracle of St Francis*. Carlo had, for some unknown reason, only moments before the blast, left his mother's side and ventured into a protected alcove to ponder a tapestry depicting the story of St Francis.

God called me there, he decided. *He wanted to save me.*

Carlo was delirious with pain. He could still see his mother, kneeling at the pew, blowing him a kiss, and then with a concussive roar, her sweet-smelling flesh was torn apart. He could still taste man's *evil*. Blood showered down. His mother's blood! The blessed Maria!

215

God will watch over you and protect you forever, his mother had told him.

But where was God now!

Then, like a worldly manifestation of his mother's truth, a clergyman had come to the hospital. He was not any clergyman. He was a bishop. He prayed over Carlo. The Miracle of St Francis. When Carlo recovered, the bishop arranged for him to live in a small monastery attached to the cathedral over which the bishop presided. Carlo lived and tutored with the monks. He even became an altar boy for his new protector. The bishop suggested Carlo entered public school, but Carlo refused. He could not have been more happy with his new home. He now truly lived in the house of God.

Every night Carlo prayed for his mother.

God saved me for a reason, he thought. *What is the reason?*

When Carlo turned sixteen, he was obliged by Italian law to serve two years of reserve military training. The bishop told Carlo that if he entered seminary he would be exempt from this duty. Carlo told the priest that he planned to enter seminary but that first he needed to understand *evil*.

The bishop did not understand.

Carlo told him that if he was going to spend his life in the church fighting evil, first he had to understand it. He could not think of any better place to understand evil than in the army. The army used guns and bombs. *A bomb killed my Blessed mother!*

The bishop tried to dissuade him, but Carlo's mind was made up.

'Be careful, my son,' the bishop had said. 'And remember the church awaits you when you return.'

216

Carlo's two years of military service had been dreadful. Carlo's youth had been one of silence and reflection. But in the army there was no quiet for reflection. Endless noise. Huge machines everywhere. Not a moment of peace. Although the soldiers went to Mass once a week at the barracks, Carlo did not sense God's presence in any of his fellow soldiers. Their minds were too filled with chaos to see God.

Carlo hated his new life and wanted to go home. But he was determined to stick it out. He had yet to understand evil. He refused to fire a gun, so the military taught him how to fly a medical helicopter. Carlo hated the noise and the smell, but at least it let him fly up in the sky and be closer to his mother in heaven. When he was informed his pilot's training included learning how to parachute, Carlo was terrified. Still, he had no choice.

God will protect me, he told himself.

Carlo's first parachute jump was the most exhilarating physical experience of his life. It was like flying with God. Carlo could not get enough . . . the silence . . . the floating . . . seeing his mother's face in the billowing white clouds as he soared to earth. *God has plans for you, Carlo.* When he returned from the military, Carlo entered the seminary.

That had been twenty-three years ago.

Now, as Camerlengo Carlo Ventresca descended the Royal Staircase, he tried to comprehend the chain of events that had delivered him to this extraordinary crossroads.

Abandon all fear, he told himself, *and give this night over to God.*

He could see the great bronze door of the Sistine

Chapel now, dutifully protected by four Swiss Guards. The guards unbolted the door and pulled it open. Inside, every head turned. The camerlengo gazed out at the black robes and red sashes before him. He understood what God's plans for him were. The fate of the church had been placed in his hands.

The camerlengo crossed himself and stepped over the threshold.

48

BBC journalist Gunther Glick sat sweating in the BBC network van parked on the eastern edge of St Peter's Square and cursed his assignment editor. Although Glick's first monthly review had come back filled with superlatives – resourceful, sharp, dependable – here he was in Vatican City on 'Pope-Watch'. He reminded himself that reporting for the BBC carried a hell of a lot more credibility than fabricating fodder for the *British Tatler*, but still, this was *not* his idea of reporting.

Glick's assignment was simple. Insultingly simple. He was to sit here waiting for a bunch of old farts to elect their next chief old fart, then he was to step outside and record a fifteen-second 'live' spot with the Vatican as a backdrop.

Brilliant.

Glick couldn't believe the BBC still sent reporters into the field to cover this schlock. *You don't see the American networks here tonight. Hell no!* That was because the big boys did it right. They watched CNN, synopsized it, and then filmed their 'live' report in front of a blue screen, superimposing stock video for a realistic backdrop. MSNBC even used in-studio wind and rain machines to give that on-the-scene authenticity. Viewers didn't want truth anymore; they wanted entertainment.

Glick gazed out through the windshield and felt more and more depressed by the minute. The imperial mountain of Vatican City rose before him as a dismal reminder of what men could accomplish when they put their minds to it.

'What have I accomplished in my life?' he wondered aloud. 'Nothing.'

'So give up,' a woman's voice said from behind him.

Glick jumped. He had almost forgotten he was not alone. He turned to the back seat, where his camerawoman, Chinita Macri, sat silently polishing her glasses. She was always polishing her glasses. Chinita was black, although she preferred African American, a little heavy and smart as hell. She wouldn't let you forget it either. She was an odd bird, but Glick liked her. And Glick could sure as hell use the company.

'What's the problem, Gunth?' Chinita asked.

'What are we doing here?'

She kept polishing. 'Witnessing an exciting event.'

'Old men locked in the dark is exciting?'

'You *do* know you're going to hell, don't you?'

'Already there.'

'Talk to me.' She sounded like his mother.

'I just feel like I want to leave my mark.'

'You wrote for the *British Tatler*.'

'Yeah, but nothing with any resonance.'

'Oh, come on, I heard you did a groundbreaking article on the queen's secret sex life with aliens.'

'Thanks.'

219

'Hey, things are looking up. Tonight you make your first fifteen seconds of TV history.'

Glick groaned. He could hear the news anchor already. 'Thanks Gunther, great report.' Then the anchor would roll his eyes and move on to the weather. 'I should have tried for an anchor spot.'

Macri laughed. 'With no experience? And *that* beard? Forget it.'

Glick ran his hands through the reddish gob of hair on his chin. 'I think it makes me look clever.'

The van's cell phone rang, mercifully interrupting yet another one of Glick's failures. 'Maybe that's editorial,' he said, suddenly hopeful. 'You think they want a live update?'

'On *this* story?' Macri laughed. 'You keep dreaming.'

Glick answered the phone in his best anchorman voice. 'Gunther Glick, BBC, Live in Vatican City.'

The man on the line had a thick Arabic accent. 'Listen carefully,' he said. 'I am about to change your life.'

49

Langdon and Vittoria stood alone now outside the double doors that led to the inner sanctum of the Secret Archives. The decor in the colonnade was an incongruous mix of wall-to-wall carpets over marble floors and wireless security cameras gazing down from beside carved cherubs in the ceiling. Langdon dubbed it *Sterile Renaissance*. Beside the arched ingress hung a small bronze plaque.

Curatore, Padre Jaqui Tomaso

Father Jaqui Tomaso. Langdon recognized the
curator's name from the rejection letters at home in his
desk. *Dear Mr Langdon, It is with regret that I am writing
to deny . . .*

Regret. *Bullshit.* Since Jaqui Tomaso's reign had
begun, Langdon had never met a single non-Catholic
American scholar who had been given access to the
Secret Vatican Archives. *Il guardiano*, historians called
him. Jaqui Tomaso was the toughest librarian on earth.

As Langdon pushed the doors open and stepped
through the vaulted portal into the inner sanctum, he
half expected to see Father Jaqui in full military
fatigues and helmet standing guard with a bazooka.
The space, however, was deserted.

Silence. Soft lighting.

Archivio Vaticano. One of his life dreams.

As Langdon's eyes took in the sacred chamber, his
first reaction was one of embarrassment. He realized
what a callow romantic he was. The images he had
held for so many years of this room could not have
been more inaccurate. He had imagined dusty bookshelves piled high with tattered volumes, priests
cataloging by the light of candles and stained-glass
windows, monks poring over scrolls . . .

Not even close.

At first glance the room appeared to be a darkened
airline hangar in which someone had built a dozen
free-standing racquetball courts. Langdon knew of
course what the glass-walled enclosures were. He
was not surprised to see them; humidity and heat
eroded ancient vellums and parchments, and proper

preservation required hermitic vaults like these – air-tight cubicles that kept out humidity and natural acids in the air. Langdon had been inside hermetic vaults many times, but it was always an unsettling experience ... something about entering an airtight container where the oxygen was regulated by a reference librarian.

The vaults were dark, ghostly even, faintly outlined by tiny dome lights at the end of each stack. In the blackness of each cell, Langdon sensed the phantom giants, row upon row of towering stacks, laden with history. This was one hell of a collection.

Vittoria also seemed dazzled. She stood beside him staring mutely at the giant transparent cubes.

Time was short, and Langdon wasted none of it scanning the dimly lit room for a book catalog – a bound encyclopedia that cataloged the library's collection. All he saw was the glow of a handful of computer terminals dotting the room. 'Looks like they've got a Biblion. Their index is computerized.'

Vittoria looked hopeful. 'That should speed things up.'

Langdon wished he shared her enthusiasm, but he sensed this was bad news. He walked to a terminal and began typing. His fears were instantly confirmed. 'The old-fashioned method would have been better.'

'Why?'

He stepped back from the monitor. 'Because *real* books don't have password protection. I don't suppose physicists are natural born hackers?'

Vittoria shook her head. 'I can open oysters, that's about it.'

Langdon took a deep breath and turned to face the eerie collection of diaphanous vaults. He walked to the nearest one and squinted into the dim interior. Inside the glass were amorphous shapes Langdon recognized as the usual bookshelves, parchment bins, and examination tables. He looked up at the indicator tabs glowing at the end of each stack. As in all libraries, the tabs indicated the contents of that row. He read the headings as he moved down the transparent barrier.

PIETRO L'EREMITA ... LE CROCIATE ... URBANO II ... LEVANT ...

'They're labeled,' he said, still walking. 'But it's not alpha-author.' He wasn't surprised. Ancient archives were almost never cataloged alphabetically because so many of the authors were unknown. Titles didn't work either because many historical documents were untitled letters or parchment fragments. Most cataloging was done chronologically. Disconcertingly, however, *this* arrangement did not appear to be chronological.

Langdon felt precious time already slipping away. 'Looks like the Vatican has its own system.'

'What a surprise.'

He examined the labels again. The documents spanned centuries, but all the keywords, he realized, were interrelated. 'I think it's a thematic classification.'

'Thematic?' Vittoria said, sounding like a disapproving scientist. 'Sounds inefficient.'

Actually ... Langdon thought, considering it more closely. *This may be the shrewdest cataloging I've ever seen.* He had always urged his students to understand the overall tones and motifs of an artistic period rather than getting lost in the minutia of dates and specific works. The Vatican Archives, it seemed, were cataloged on a similar philosophy. *Broad strokes ...*

'Everything in this vault,' Langdon said, feeling

223

more confident now, 'centuries of material, has to do with the Crusades. That's this vault's theme.' It was all here, he realized. *Historical accounts, letters, artwork, socio-political data, modern analyses. All in one place ... encouraging a deeper understanding of a topic. Brilliant.*

Vittoria frowned. 'But data can relate to *multiple* themes simultaneously.'

'Which is why they cross-reference with proxy markers.' Langdon pointed through the glass to the colourful plastic tabs inserted among the documents. 'Those indicate secondary documents located elsewhere with their primary themes.'

'Sure,' she said, apparently letting it go. She put her hands on her hips and surveyed the enormous space. Then she looked at Langdon. 'So, Professor, what's the name of this Galileo thing we're looking for?'

Langdon couldn't help but smile. He still couldn't fathom that he was standing in this room. *It's in here,* he thought. *Somewhere in the dark, it's waiting.*

'Follow me,' Langdon said. He started briskly down the first aisle, examining the indicator tabs of each vault. 'Remember how I told you about the Path of Illumination? How the Illuminati recruited new members using an elaborate test?'

'The treasure hunt,' Vittoria said, following closely.

'The challenge the Illuminati had was that after they placed the markers, they needed some way to tell the scientific community the path existed.'

'Logical,' Vittoria said. 'Otherwise nobody would know to look for it.'

'Yes, and even if they *knew* the path existed, scientists would have no way of knowing where the path began. Rome is huge.'

'Okay.'

Langdon proceeded down the next aisle, scanning the tabs as he talked. 'About fifteen years ago, some historians at the Sorbonne and I uncovered a series of Illuminati letters filled with references to the *segno*.'

'The sign. The announcement about the path and where it began.'

'Yes. And since then, plenty of Illuminati academics, myself included, have uncovered other references to the *segno*. It is accepted theory now that the clue exists and that Galileo mass distributed it to the scientific community without the Vatican ever knowing.'

'How?'

'We're not sure, but most likely printed publications. He published many books and newsletters over the years.'

'That the Vatican no doubt saw. Sounds dangerous.'

'True. Nonetheless the *segno* was distributed.'

'But nobody has ever actually found it?'

'No. Oddly though, wherever allusions to the *segno* appear – Masonic diaries, ancient scientific journals, Illuminati letters – it is often referred to by a number.'

'666?'

Langdon smiled. 'Actually it's 503.'

'Meaning?'

'None of us could ever figure it out. I became fascinated with 503, trying everything to find meaning in the number – numerology, map references, latitudes.' Langdon reached the end of the aisle, turned the corner, and hurried to scan the next row of tabs as he spoke. 'For many years the only clue seemed to be that 503 began with the number five . . . one of the sacred Illuminati digits.' He paused.

'Something tells me you recently figured it out, and that's why we're here.'

'Correct,' Langdon said, allowing himself a rare moment of pride in his work. 'Are you familiar with a book by Galileo called *Diàlogo*?'

'Of course. Famous among scientists as the ultimate scientific sellout.'

Sellout wasn't quite the word Langdon would have used, but he knew what Vittoria meant. In the early 1630s, Galileo had wanted to publish a book endorsing the Copernican heliocentric model of the solar system, but the Vatican would not permit the book's release unless Galileo included equally persuasive evidence for the church's *geocentric* model – a model Galileo knew to be dead wrong. Galileo had no choice but to acquiesce to the church's demands and publish a book giving equal time to both the accurate and inaccurate models.

'As you probably know,' Langdon said, 'despite Galileo's compromise, *Diàlogo* was still seen as heretical, and the Vatican placed him under house arrest.'

'No good deed goes unpunished.'

Langdon smiled. 'So true. And yet Galileo was persistent. While under house arrest, he secretly wrote a lesser-known manuscript that scholars often confuse with *Diàlogo*. That book is called *Discorsi*.'

Vittoria nodded. 'I've heard of it. *Discourses on the Tides*.'

Langdon stopped short, amazed she had heard of the obscure publication abut planetary motion and its effect on the tides.

'Hey,' she said, 'you're talking to an Italian marine physicist whose father worshiped Galileo.'

Langdon laughed. *Discorsi* however was not what they were looking for. Langdon explained that *Discorsi* had not been Galileo's only work while under house arrest. Historians believed he had also written an obscure booklet called *Diagramma*.

'*Diagramma della Verità*,' Langdon said. '*Diagram of Truth*.'

'Never heard of it.'

'I'm not surprised. *Diagramma* was Galileo's most secretive work – supposedly some sort of treatise on scientific facts he held to be true but was not allowed to share. Like some of Galileo's previous manuscripts, *Diagramma* was smuggled out of Rome by a friend and quietly published in Holland. The booklet became wildly popular in the European scientific underground. Then the Vatican caught wind of it and went on a book-burning campaign.'

Vittoria now looked intrigued. 'And you think *Diagramma* contained the clue? The *segno*. The information about the Path of Illumination.'

'*Diagramma* is how Galileo got the word out. That I'm sure of.' Langdon entered the third row of vaults and continued surveying the indicator tabs. 'Archivists have been looking for a copy of *Diagramma* for years. But between the Vatican burnings and the booklet's low permanence rating, the booklet has disappeared off the face of the earth.'

'Permanence rating?'

'Durability. Archivists rate documents one through ten for their structural integrity. *Diagramma* was printed on sedge papyrus. It's like tissue paper. Life span of no more than a century.'

'Why not something stronger?'

'Galileo's behest. To protect his followers. This way any scientists caught with a copy could simply drop it in water and the booklet would dissolve. It was great for destruction of evidence, but terrible for archivists.

It is believed that only *one* copy of *Diagramma* survived beyond the eighteenth century.'

'One?' Vittoria looked momentarily starstruck as she glanced around the room. 'And it's *here*?'

'Confiscated from the Netherlands by the Vatican shortly after Galileo's death. I've been petitioning to see it for years now. Ever since I realized what was in it.'

As if reading Langdon's mind, Vittoria moved across the aisle and began scanning the adjacent bay of vaults, doubling their pace.

'Thanks,' he said. 'Look for reference tabs that have anything to do with Galileo, science, scientists. You'll know it when you see it.'

'Okay, but you still haven't told me how you figured out *Diagramma* contained the clue. It had something to do with the number you kept seeing in Illuminati letters? 503?'

Langdon smiled. 'Yes. It took some time, but I finally figured out that 503 is a simple code. It clearly points to *Diagramma*.'

For an instant Langdon relived his moment of unexpected revelation: August 16. Two years ago. He was standing lakeside at the wedding of the son of a colleague. Bagpipes droned on the water as the wedding party made their unique entrance . . . across the lake on a barge. The craft was festooned with flowers and wreaths. It carried a Roman numeral painted proudly on the hull – DCII.

Puzzled by the marking Langdon asked the father of the bride, 'What's with 602?'

'602?'

Langdon pointed to the barge. 'DCII is the Roman numeral for 602.'

The man laughed. 'That's not a Roman numeral.

That's the name of the barge.'

'The DCII?'

The man nodded. '*The Dick and Connie II.*'

Langdon felt sheepish. Dick and Connie were the wedding couple. The barge obviously had been named in their honor. 'What happened to the *DCI*?'

The man groaned. 'It sank yesterday during the rehearsal luncheon.'

Langdon laughed. 'Sorry to hear that.' He looked back out at the barge. *The DCII*, he thought. *Like a miniature QEII.* A second later, it had hit him.

Now Langdon turned to Vittoria. '503,' he said, 'as I mentioned, is a code. It's an Illuminati trick for concealing what was actually intended as a Roman numeral. The number 503 in Roman numerals is—'

'DIII.'

Langdon glanced up. 'That was fast. Please don't tell me you're an Illuminata.'

She laughed. 'I use Roman numerals to codify pelagic strata.'

Of course, Langdon thought. *Don't we all.*

Vittoria looked over. 'So what is the meaning of DIII?'

'DI and DII and DIII are very odd abbreviations. The were used by ancient scientists to distinguish between the three Galilean documents most commonly confused.'

Vittoria drew a quick breath. '*Diàlogo . . . Discorsi . . . Diagramma.*'

'D-one. D-two. D-three. All scientific. All controversial. 503 is DIII. *Diagramma.* The third of his books.'

Vittoria looked troubled. 'But one thing still doesn't make sense. If this *segno*, this clue, this advertisement about the Path of Illumination was really in Galileo's

229

Diagramma, why didn't the Vatican see it when they repossessed all the copies?'

'They may have seen it and not noticed. Remember the Illuminati markers? Hiding things in plain view? Dissimulation? The *segno* apparently was hidden the same way – in plain view. Invisible to those who were not looking for it. And also invisible to those who didn't *understand* it.'

'Meaning?'

'Meaning Galileo hid it well. According to historic record, the *segno* was revealed in a mode the Illuminati called *lingua pura*.'

'The pure language?'

'Yes.'

'Mathematics?'

'That's my guess. Seems pretty obvious. Galileo was a scientist after all, and he was writing *for* scientists. Math would be a logical language in which to lay out the clue. The booklet is called *Diagramma*, so mathematical diagrams may also be part of the code.'

Vittoria sounded only slightly more hopeful. 'I suppose Galileo could have created some sort of mathematical code that went unnoticed by the clergy.'

'You don't sound sold,' Langdon said, moving down the row.

'I'm not. Mainly because *you* aren't. If you were so sure about DIII, why didn't you publish? Then someone who *did* have access to the Vatican Archives could have come in here and checked out *Diagramma* a long time ago.'

'I didn't *want* to publish,' Langdon said. 'I had worked hard to find the information and—' He stopped himself, embarrassed.

'You wanted the *glory*.'

Langdon felt himself flush. 'In a manner of speaking. It's just that—'

'Don't look so embarrassed. You're talking to a scientist. Publish or perish. At CERN we call it "Substantiate or suffocate."'

'It wasn't only wanting to be the first. I was also concerned that if the wrong people found out about the information in *Diagramma*, it might disappear.'

'The wrong people being the Vatican?'

'Not that they are wrong, per se, but the church has always downplayed the Illuminati threat. In the early 1900s the Vatican went so far as to say the Illuminati were a figment of overactive imaginations. The clergy felt, and perhaps rightly so, that the last thing Christians needed to know was that there was a very powerful anti-Christian movement infiltrating their banks, politics and universities.' *Present tense, Robert,* he reminded himself. *There IS a powerful anti-Christian force infiltrating their banks, politics, and universities.*

'So you think the Vatican would have buried any evidence corroborating the Illuminati threat?'

'Quite possibly. Any threat, real or imagined, weakens faith in the church's power.'

'One more question.' Vittoria stopped short and looked at him like he was an alien. 'Are you *serious*?'

Langdon stopped. 'What do you mean?'

'I mean is this *really* your plan to save the day?'

Langdon wasn't sure whether he saw amused pity or sheer terror in her eyes. 'You mean finding *Diagramma*?'

'No, I mean finding *Diagramma*, locating a four-hundred-year-old *segno*, deciphering some mathematical code, and following an ancient trail of art that only the most brilliant scientists in history have ever been able to follow .. all in the next four hours.'

Langdon shrugged. 'I'm open to other suggestions.'

50

Robert Langdon stood outside Archive Vault 9 and read the labels on the stacks.

BRAHE ... CLAVIUS ... COPERNICUS ... KEPLER ... NEWTON ...

As he read the names again, he felt a sudden uneasiness. *Here are the scientists .. but where is Galileo?*

He turned to Vittoria, who was checking the contents of a nearby vault. 'I found the right theme, but Galileo's missing.'

'No he isn't,' she said, frowning as she motioned to the next vault. 'He's over here. But I hope you brought your reading glasses, because this *entire* vault is his.'

Langdon ran over. Vittoria was right. Every indicator tab in Vault 10 carried the same keyword.

IL PROCESSO GALILEANO

Langdon let out a low whistle, now realizing why Galileo had his own vault. 'The Galileo Affair,' he marveled, peering through the glass at the dark outlines of the stacks. 'The longest and most expensive legal proceedings in Vatican history. Fourteen years and six hundred million lire. It's all here.'

'Have a few legal documents.'

'I guess lawyers haven't evolved much over the centuries.'

'Neither have sharks.'

Langdon strode to a large yellow button on the side of the vault. He pressed it, and a bank of overhead lights hummed on inside. The lights were deep red, turning the cube into a glowing crimson cell ... a maze of towering shelves.

'My God,' Vittoria said, looking spooked. 'Are we tanning or working?'

'Parchment and vellum fades, so vault lighting is always done with dark lights.'

'You could go mad in here.'

Or worse, Langdon thought, moving toward the vault's sole entrance. 'A quick word of warning. Oxygen is an oxidant, so hermetic vaults contain very little of it. It's a partial vacuum inside. Your breathing will feel strained.'

'Hey, if old cardinals can survive it.'

True, Langdon thought. *May we be as lucky.*

The vault entrance was a single electronic revolving door. Langdon noted the common arrangement of four access buttons on the door's inner shaft, one accessible from each compartment. When a button was pressed, the motorized door would kick into gear and make the conventional half rotation before grinding to a halt – a standard procedure to preserve the integrity of the inner atmosphere.

'After I'm in,' Langdon said, 'just press the button and follow me through. There's only eight per cent humidity inside, so be prepared to feel some dry mouth.'

Langdon stepped into the rotating compartment and pressed the button. The door buzzed loudly and began to rotate. As he followed its motion, Langdon prepared his body for the physical shock that always accompanied the first few seconds in a hermetic vault. Entering a sealed archive was like going from sea level to 20,000 feet in an instant. Nausea and light-headedness were not uncommon. *Double vision, double over*, he reminded himself, quoting the archivist's mantra. Langdon felt his ears pop. There was a hiss of air, and the door spun to a stop.

He was in.

Langdon's first realization was that the air inside was thinner than he had anticipated. The Vatican, it seemed, took their archives a bit more seriously than most. Langdon fought the gag reflex and relaxed his chest while his pulmonary capillaries dilated. The tightness passed quickly. *Enter the Dolphin*, he mused, gratified his fifty laps a day were good for something. Breathing more normally now, he looked around the vault. Despite the transparent outer walls, he felt a familiar anxiety. *I'm in a box*, he thought. *A blood red box.*

The door buzzed behind him, and Langdon turned to watch Vittoria enter. When she arrived inside, her eyes immediately began watering, and she started breathing heavily.

'Give it a minute,' Langdon said. 'If you get light-headed, bend over.'

'I . . . feel . . .' Vittoria choked, 'like I'm . . . scuba diving . . .with the wrong . . . mixture.'

Langdon waited for her to acclimatize. He knew she would be fine. Vittoria Vetra was obviously in terrific shape, nothing like the doddering ancient Radcliffe alumnae Langdon had once squired through Widener Library's hermetic vault. The tour had ended with

Langdon giving mouth-to-mouth to an old woman who'd almost aspirated her false teeth.

'Feeling better?' he asked.

Vittoria nodded.

'I rode your damn space plane, so I thought I owed you.'

This brought a smile. *'Touché.'*

Langdon reached into the box beside the door and extracted some white cotton gloves.

'Formal affair?' Vittoria asked.

'Finger acid. We can't handle the documents without them. You'll need a pair.'

Vittoria donned some gloves. 'How long do we have?'

Langdon checked his Mickey Mouse watch. 'It's just past seven.'

'We have to find this thing within the hour.'

'Actually,' Langdon said, 'we don't have that kind of time.' He pointed overhead to a filtered cut. 'Normally the curator would turn on a reoxygenation system when someone is inside the vault. Not today. Twenty minutes, we'll both be sucking wind.'

Vittoria blanched noticeably in the reddish glow.

Langdon smiled and smoothed his gloves. 'Substantiate or suffocate, Ms Vetra. Mickey's ticking.'

51

BBC reporter Gunther Glick stared at the cell phone in his hand for ten seconds before he finally hung up.

Chinita Macri studied him from the back of the van. 'What happened? Who was that?'

Glick turned, feeling like a child who had just received a Christmas gift he feared was not really for him. 'I just got a tip. Something's going on inside the Vatican.'

'It's called conclave,' Chinita said. 'Helluva tip.'

'No, something else.' *Something big.* He wondered if the story the caller had just told him could possibly be true. Glick felt ashamed when he realized he was praying it was. 'What if I told you four cardinals have been kidnapped and are going to be murdered at different churches tonight.'

'I'd say you're being hazed by someone at the office with a sick sense of humor.'

'What if I told you we were going to be given the exact location of the first murder?'

'I'd want to know who the hell you just talked to.'

'He didn't say.'

'Perhaps because he's full of shit?'

Glick had come to expect Macri's cynicism, but what she was forgetting was that liars and lunatics had been Glick's business for almost a decade at the *British Tatler*. This caller had been neither. This man had been coldly sane. Logical. *I will call you just before eight,* the man had said, *and tell you where the first killing will occur. The images you record will make you famous.* When Glick had demanded why the caller was giving him this information, the answer had been as icy as the man's Mideastern accent. *The media is the right arm of anarchy.*

'He told me something else too,' Glick said.

'What? That Elvis Presley was just elected Pope?'

'Dial into the BBC database, will you?' Glick's

adrenaline was pumping now. 'I want to see what other stories we've run on these guys.'

'What guys?'

'Indulge me.'

Macri sighed and pulled up the connection to the BBC database. 'This'll take a minute.'

Glick's mind was swimming. 'The caller was very intent to know if I had a cameraman.'

'Videographer.'

'And if we could transmit live.'

'One point five three seven megahertz. What is this about?' The database beeped. 'Okay, we're in. Who is it you're looking for?'

Glick gave her the keyword.

Macri turned and stared. 'I sure as hell hope you're kidding.'

52

The internal organization of Archival Vault 10 was not as intuitive as Langdon had hoped, and the *Diagramma* manuscript did not appear to be located with other similar Galilean publications. Without access to the computerized Biblion and a reference locator, Langdon and Vittoria were stuck.

'You're sure *Diagramma* is in here?' Vittoria asked.

'Positive. It's a confirmed listing in both the *Uficcio della Propaganda delle Fede*—'

'Fine. As long as you're sure.' She headed left, while he went right.

Langdon began his manual search. He needed every

bit of self-restraint not to stop and read every treasure he passed. The collection was staggering. *The Assayer* . . . *The Starry Messenger* . . . *The Sunspot Letters* . . . *Letter to the Grand Duchess Christina* . . . *Apologia pro Galileo* . . . On and on.

It was Vittoria who finally struck gold near the back of the vault. Her throaty voice called out, '*Diagramma della Verità!*'

Langdon dashed through the crimson haze to join her. 'Where?'

Vittoria pointed, and Langdon immediately realized why they had not found it earlier. The manuscript was in a folio bin, not on the shelves. Folio bins were a common means of storing unbound pages. The label on the front of the container left no doubt about the contents.

DIAGRAMMA DELLA VERITA
Galileo Galilei, 1639

Langdon dropped to his knees, his heart pounding, '*Diagramma.*' He gave her a grin. 'Nice work. Help me pull out this bin.'

Vittoria knelt beside him, and they heaved. The metal tray on which the bin was sitting rolled toward them on castors, revealing the top of the container.

'No lock?' Vittoria said, sounding surprised at the simple latch.

'Never. Documents sometimes need to be evacuated quickly. Floods and fires.'

'So open it.'

Langdon didn't need any encouragement. With his academic life's dream right in front of him and the thinning air in the chamber, he was in no mood to

238

dawdle. He unsnapped the latch and lifted the lid. Inside, flat on the floor of the bin, lay a black, duck-cloth pouch. The cloth's breathability was critical to the preservation of its contents. Reaching in with both hands and keeping the pouch horizontal, Langdon lifted it out of the bin.

'I expected a treasure chest,' Vittoria said. 'Looks more like a pillowcase.'

'Follow me,' he said. Holding the bag before him like a sacred offering, Langdon walked to the center of the vault where he found the customary glass-topped archival exam table. Although the central location was intended to minimize in-vault travel of documents, researchers appreciated the privacy the surrounding stacks afforded. Career-making discoveries were uncovered in the top vaults of the world, and most academics did not like rivals peering through the glass as they worked.

Langdon laid the pouch on the table and un-buttoned the opening. Vittoria stood by. Rummaging through a tray of archivist tools, Langdon found the felt-pad pincers archivists called *finger cymbals* – over-sized tweezers with flattened disks on each arm. As his excitement mounted, Langdon feared at any moment he might awake back in Cambridge with a pile of test papers to grade. Inhaling deeply, he opened the bag. Fingers trembling in their cotton gloves, he reached in with his tongs.

'Relax,' Vittoria said. 'It's paper, not plutonium.'

Langdon slid the tongs around the stack of docu-ments inside and was careful to apply even pressure. Then, rather than pulling out the documents, he held them in place while he slid off the bag – an archivist's procedure for minimizing torque on the artifact. Not until the bag was removed and Langdon had turned on the exam darklight beneath the table did he begin breathing again.

Vittoria looked like a specter now, lit from below by the lamp beneath the glass. 'Small sheets,' she said, her voice reverent.

Langdon nodded. The stack of folios before them looked like loose pages from a small paperback novel. Langdon could see that the top sheet was an ornate pen and ink cover sheet with the title, the date, and Galileo's name in his own hand.

In that instant, Langdon forgot the cramped quarters, forgot his exhaustion, forgot the horrifying situation that had brought him here. He simply stared in wonder. Close encounters with history always left Langdon numbed with reverence . . . like seeing the brushstrokes on the Mona Lisa.

The muted, yellow papyrus left no doubt in Langdon's mind as to its age and authenticity, but excluding the inevitable fading, the document was in superb condition. *Slight bleaching of the pigment. Minor sundering and cohesion of the papyrus. But all in all . . . in damn fine condition.* He studied the ornate hand etching of the cover, his vision blurring in the lack of humidity. Vittoria was silent.

'Hand me a spatula, please.' Langdon motioned beside Vittoria to a tray filled with stainless-steel archival tools. She handed it to him. Langdon took the tool in his hand. It was a good one. He ran his fingers across the face to remove any static charge and then, ever so carefully, slid the blade beneath the cover. Then, lifting the spatula, he turned over the cover sheet.

The first page was written in longhand, the tiny,

stylized calligraphy almost impossible to read. Langdon immediately noticed that there were no diagrams or numbers on the page. It was an essay.

'Heliocentricity,' Vittoria said, translating the heading on folio one. She scanned the text. 'Looks like Galileo renouncing the geocentric model once and for all. Ancient Italian, though, so no promises on the translation.'

'Forget it,' Langdon said. 'We're looking for math. The pure language.' He used the spatula tool to flip the next page. Another essay. No math or diagrams. Langdon's hands began to sweat inside his gloves.

'Movement of the Planets,' Vittoria said, translating the title.

Langdon frowned. On any other day, he would have been fascinated to read it; incredibly NASA's current model of planetary orbits, observed through high-powered telescopes, was supposedly almost identical to Galileo's original predictions.

'No math,' Vittoria said. 'He's talking about retrograde motions and elliptical orbits or something.'

Elliptical orbits. Langdon recalled that much of Galileo's legal trouble had begun when he described planetary motion as *elliptical.* The Vatican exalted the perfection of the *circle* and insisted heavenly motion must be only circular. Galileo's Illuminati, however, saw perfection in the ellipse as well, revering the mathematical duality of its twin foci. The Illuminati's ellipse was prominent even today in modern Masonic tracing boards and footing inlays.

'Next,' Vittoria said.

Langdon flipped.

'Lunar phases and tidal moon,' she said. 'No numbers. No diagrams.'

Langdon flipped again. Nothing. He kept flipping through a dozen or so pages. Nothing. Nothing. Nothing.

'I thought this guy was a mathematician,' Vittoria said. 'This is all text.'

Langdon felt the air in his lungs beginning to thin. His hopes were thinning too. The pile was waning.

'Nothing here,' Vittoria said. 'No math. A few dates, a few standard figures, but nothing that looks like it could be a clue.'

Langdon flipped over the last folio and sighed. It, too, was an essay.

'Short book,' Vittoria said, frowning.

Langdon nodded.

'*Merda*, as we say in Rome.'

Shit is right, Langdon thought. His reflection in the glass seemed mocking, like the image staring back at him this morning from his bay window. *An aging ghost.* 'There's *got* to be something,' he said, the hoarse desperation in his voice surprising him. 'The *segno* is here somewhere. I know it!'

'Maybe you were wrong about DIII?'

Langdon turned and stared at her.

'Okay,' she agreed, 'DIII makes perfect sense. But maybe the clue isn't mathematical?'

'*Lingua pura*. What else would it be?'

'Art?'

'Except there are no diagrams or pictures in the book.'

'All I know is that *lingua pura* refers to something other than Italian. Math just seems logical.'

'I agree.'

Langdon refused to accept defeat so quickly. 'The numbers must be written longhand. The math must be in words rather than equations.'

'It'll take some time to read all the pages.'

'Time's something we don't have. We'll have to split the work.' Langdon flipped the stack back over to the beginning. 'I know enough Italian to spot numbers.' Using his spatula, he cut the stack like a deck of cards and laid the first half-dozen pages in front of Vittoria. 'It's in here somewhere. I'm sure.'

Vittoria reached down and flipped her first page by hand.

'Spatula!' Langdon said, grabbing her an extra tool from the tray. 'Use the spatula.'

'I'm wearing gloves,' she grumbled. 'How much damage could I cause?'

'Just use it.'

Vittoria picked up the spatula. 'You feeling what I'm feeling?'

'Tense?'

'No. Short of breath.'

Langdon was definitely starting to feel it too. The air was thinning faster than he had imagined. He knew they had to hurry. Archival conundrums were nothing new for him, but usually he had more than a few minutes to work them out. Without another word, Langdon bowed his head and began translating the first page in his stack.

Show yourself, damn it! Show yourself!

53

Somewhere beneath Rome the dark figure prowled down a stone ramp into the underground tunnel. The

243

ancient passageway was lit only by torches, making the air hot and thick. Up ahead the frightened voices of grown men called out in vain, echoing in the cramped spaces.

As he rounded the corner he saw them, exactly as he had left them – four old men, terrified, sealed behind rusted iron bars in a stone cubicle.

'*Qui êtes-vous?*' one of the men demanded in French. 'What do you want with us?'

'*Hilfe!*' another said in German. 'Let us go!'

'Are you aware who we are?' one asked in English, his accent Spanish.

'Silence,' the raspy voice commanded. There was a finality about the word.

The fourth prisoner, an Italian, quiet and thoughtful, looked into the inky void of his captor's eyes and swore he saw hell itself. *God help us*, he thought.

The killer checked his watch and then returned his gaze to the prisoners. 'Now then,' he said. 'Who will be first?'

54

Inside Archive Vault 10 Robert Langdon recited Italian numbers as he scanned the calligraphy before him. *Mille . . . centi . . . uno, duo, tre . . . cinquanta. I need a numerical reference! Anything, damnit!*

When he reached the end of his current folio, he lifted the spatula to flip the page. As he aligned the blade with the next page, he fumbled, having difficulty holding the tool steady. Minutes later, he looked down and realized he had abandoned his spatula and was turning pages by hand. *Oops*, he thought, feeling vaguely criminal. The lack of oxygen was affecting his inhibitions. *Looks like I'll burn in archivist's hell.*

'About damn time,' Vittoria choked when she saw Langdon turning pages by hand. She dropped her spatula and followed suit.

'Any luck?'

Vittoria shook her head. 'Nothing that looks purely mathematical. I'm skimming . . . but none of this reads like a clue.'

Langdon continued translating his folios with increasing difficulty. His Italian skills were rocky at best, and the tiny penmanship and archaic language were making it slow going. Vittoria reached the end of her stack before Langdon and looked disheartened as she flipped the pages over. She hunkered down for another more intense inspection.

When Langdon finished his final page, he cursed under his breath and looked over at Vittoria. She was scowling, squinting at something on one of her folios. 'What is it?' he asked.

Vittoria did not look up. 'Did you have any footnotes on your pages?'

'Not that I noticed. Why?'

'This page has a footnote. It's obscured in a crease.'

Langdon tried to see what she was looking at, but all he could make out was the page number in the upper right-hand corner of the sheet. Folio 5. It took a moment for the coincidence to register, and even when it did the connection seemed vague. *Folio Five. Five, Pythagoras, pentagrams, Illuminati.* Langdon wondered if the Illuminati would have chosen page five on which to hide their clue. Through the reddish fog surrounding them, Langdon sensed a tiny ray of hope. 'Is the footnote mathematical?'

Vittoria shook her head. 'Text. One line. Very small printing. Almost illegible.'

His hopes faded. 'It's supposed to be math. *Lingua pura.*'

'Yeah, I know.' She hesitated. 'I think you'll want to hear this, though.' Langdon sensed excitement in her voice.

'Go ahead.'

Squinting at the folio, Vittoria read the line. 'The path of light is laid, the sacred test.'

The words were nothing like what Langdon had imagined. 'I'm sorry?'

Vittoria repeated the line. 'The path of light is laid, the sacred test.'

'Path of light?' Langdon felt his posture straightening.

'That's what it says. Path of light.'

As the words sank in, Langdon felt his delirium pierced by an instant of clarity. *The path of light is laid, the sacred test.* He had no idea how it helped them, but the line was as direct a reference to the Path of Illumination as he could imagine. *Path of light. Sacred test.* His head felt like an engine revving on bad fuel. 'Are you sure of the translation?'

Vittoria hesitated. 'Actually . . .' She glanced over at him with a strange look. 'It's not technically a translation. The line is written in *English.*'

For an instant, Langdon thought the acoustics in the chamber had affected his hearing. '*English?*'

Vittoria pushed the document over to him, and Langdon read the minuscule printing at the bottom of the page. '*The path of light is laid, the sacred test.* English? What is *English* doing in an Italian book?'

246

Vittoria shrugged. She too was looking tipsy. 'Maybe English is what they meant by the *lingua pura*? It's considered the international language of science. It's all we speak at CERN.'

'But this was in the 1600s,' Langdon argued. 'Nobody spoke English in Italy, not even—' He stopped short, realizing what he was about to say. 'Not even . . . the *clergy*.' Langdon's academic mind hummed in high gear. 'In the 1600s,' he said, talking faster now, '*English* was one language the Vatican had not yet embraced. They dealt in Italian, Latin, German, even Spanish and French, but English was totally foreign inside the Vatican. They considered English a polluted, free-thinkers language for profane men like Chaucer and Shakespeare.' Langdon flashed suddenly on the Illuminati brands of Earth, Air, Fire, Water. The legend that the brands were in *English* now made a bizarre kind of sense.

'So you're saying maybe Galileo considered English *la lingua pura* because it was the one language the Vatican did not control?'

'Yes. Or maybe by putting the clue in English, Galileo was subtly restricting the readership away from the Vatican.'

'But it's not even a clue,' Vittoria argued. '*The path of light is laid, the sacred test?* What the hell does that mean?'

She's right, Langdon thought. The line didn't help in any way. But as he spoke the phrase again in his mind, a strange fact hit him. *Now that's odd*, he thought. *What are the chances of that?*

'We need to get out of here,' Vittoria said, sounding hoarse.

Langdon wasn't listening. *The path of light is laid, the*

sacred test. 'It's a damn line of iambic pentameter,' he said suddenly, counting the syllables again. 'Five couplets of alternating stressed and unstressed syllables.'

Vittoria looked lost. 'Iambic who?'

For an instant Langdon was back at Phillips Exeter Academy sitting in a Saturday morning English class. *Hell on earth.* The school baseball star, Peter Greer, was having trouble remembering the number of couplets necessary for a line of Shakespearean iambic pentameter. Their professor, an animated schoolmaster named Bissell, leapt onto the table and bellowed, 'Penta-meter, Greer! Think of home plate! A pentagon! Five sides! Penta! Penta! Penta! Jeeeesh!'

Five couplets, Langdon thought. Each couplet, by definition, having *two* syllables. He could not believe in his entire career he had never made the connection. Iambic pentameter was a symmetrical meter based on the sacred Illuminati numbers of 5 and 2!

You're reaching! Langdon told himself, trying to push it from his mind. *A meaningless coincidence!* But the thought stuck. *Five ... for Pythagoras and the pentagram. Two ... for the duality of all things.*

A moment later, another realization sent a numbing sensation down his legs. Iambic pentameter, on account of its simplicity, was often called 'pure verse' or 'pure meter'. *La lingua pura?* Could this have been the pure language the Illuminati had been referring to? *The path of light is laid, the sacred test ...*

'Uh oh,' Vittoria said.

Langdon wheeled to see her rotating the folio upside down. He felt a knot in his gut. *Not again.* 'There's no way that line is an ambigram!'

'No, it's not an ambigram ... but it's ...' She

248

kept turning the document, 90 degrees at every turn.

'It's what?'

Vittoria looked up. 'It's not the *only* line.'

'There's another?'

'There's a different line on every margin. Top, bottom, left, and right. I think it's a poem.'

'Four lines?' Langdon bristled with excitement. *Galileo was a poet?* 'Let me see!'

Vittoria did not relinquish the page. She kept turning the page in quarter turns. 'I didn't see the lines before because they're on the edges.' She cocked her head over the last line. 'Huh. You know what? Galileo didn't even write this.'

'What!'

'The poem is signed John Milton.'

'John *Milton*?' The influential English poet who wrote *Paradise Lost* was a contemporary of Galileo's and a savant who conspiracy buffs put at the top of their list of Illuminati suspects. Milton's alleged affiliation with Galileo's Illuminati was one legend Langdon suspected was true. Not only had Milton made a well-documented 1638 pilgrimage to Rome to 'commune with enlightened men,' but he had held meetings with Galileo during the scientist's house arrest, meetings portrayed in many Renaissance paintings, including Annibale Gatti's famous *Galileo and Milton*, which hung even now in the IMSS Museum in Florence.

'Milton knew Galileo, didn't he?' Vittoria said, finally pushing the folio over to Langdon. 'Maybe he wrote the poem as a favor?'

Langdon clenched his teeth as he took the sheathed document. Leaving it flat on the table, he read the line at the top. Then he rotated the page 90 degrees, reading the line in the right margin. Another twist, and he read the bottom. Another twist, the left. A final twist completed the circle. There were four lines in all. The first line Vittoria had found was actually the third line of the poem. Utterly agape, he read the four lines again, clockwise in sequence: top, right, bottom, left. When he was done, he exhaled. There was no doubt in his mind. 'You found it, Ms Vetra.'

She smiled tightly. 'Good, now can we get the hell out of here?'

'I have to copy these lines down. I need to find a pencil and paper.'

Vittoria shook her head. 'Forget it, professor. No time to play scribe. Mickey's ticking.' She took the page from him and headed for the door.

Langdon stood up. 'You can't take that outside! It's a—'

But Vittoria was already gone.

55

Langdon and Vittoria exploded onto the courtyard outside the Secret Archives. The fresh air felt like a drug as it flowed into Langdon's lungs. The purple spots in his vision quickly faded. The guilt, however, did not. He had just been accomplice to stealing a priceless relic from the world's most private vault. The camerlengo had said, *I am giving you my trust.*

'Hurry,' Vittoria said, still holding the folio in her hand and striding at a half-jog across *Via Belvedere* in the direction of Olivetti's office.

'If any water gets on that papyrus—'

'Calm down. When we decipher this thing, we can return their sacred Folio 5.'

Langdon accelerated to keep up. Beyond feeling like a criminal, he was still dazed over the document's spellbinding implications. *John Milton was an Illuminatus. He composed the poem for Galileo to publish in Folio 5 . . . far from the eyes of the Vatican.*

As they left the courtyard, Vittoria held out the folio for Langdon. 'You think you can decipher this thing? Or did we just kill all those brain cells for kicks?'

Langdon took the document carefully in his hands. Without hesitation he slipped it into one of the breast pockets of his tweed jacket, out of the sunlight and dangers of moisture. 'I deciphered it already.'

Vittoria stopped short. 'You *what*?'

Langdon kept moving.

Vittoria hustled to catch up. 'You read it *once*! I thought it was supposed to be hard!'

Langdon knew she was right, and yet he had deciphered the *segno* in a single reading. A perfect stanza of iambic pentameter, and the first altar of science had revealed itself in pristine clarity. Admittedly, the ease with which he had accomplished the task left him with a nagging disquietude. He was a child of the Puritan work ethic. He could still hear his father speaking the old New England aphorism: *If it wasn't painfully difficult, you did it wrong.* Langdon hoped the saying was false. 'I deciphered it,' he said, moving faster now. 'I know where the first killing is going to happen. We need to warn Olivetti.'

Vittoria closed in on him. 'How could you already know? Let me see that thing again.' With the sleight of a boxer, she slipped a lissome hand into his pocket and pulled out the folio again.

'Careful!' Langdon said. 'You can't—'

Vittoria ignored him. Folio in hand, she floated beside him, holding the document up to the evening light, examining the margins. As she began reading aloud, Langdon moved to retrieve the folio but instead found himself bewitched by Vittoria's accented alto speaking the syllables in perfect rhythm with her gait.

For a moment, hearing the verse aloud, Langdon felt transported in time . . . as though he were one of Galileo's contemporaries, listening to the poem for the first time . . . knowing it was a test, a map, a clue unveiling the four altars of science . . . the four markers that blazed a secret path across Rome. The verse flowed from Vittoria's lips like a song.

> *From Santi's earthly tomb with demon's hole,*
> *'Cross Rome the mystic elements unfold.*
> *The path of light is laid, the sacred test,*
> *Let angels guide you on your lofty quest.*

Vittoria read it twice and then fell silent, as if letting the ancient words resonate on their own.

From Santi's earthly tomb, Langdon repeated in his mind. The poem was crystal clear about that. The Path of Illumination began at Santi's tomb. From there, across Rome, the markers blazed the trail.

> *From Santi's earthly tomb with demon's hole,*
> *'Cross Rome the mystic elements unfold.*

Mystic elements. Also clear. *Earth, Air, Fire, Water.*

Elements of science, the four Illuminati markers disguised as religious sculpture.

'The first marker,' Vittoria said, 'sounds like it's at Santi's tomb.'

Langdon smiled. 'I told you it wasn't that tough.'

'So who is Santi?' she asked, sounding suddenly excited. 'And where's his tomb?'

Langdon chuckled to himself. He was amazed how few people knew *Santi*, the last name of one of the most famous Renaissance artists ever to live. His first name was world renowned ... the child prodigy who at the age of twenty-five was already doing commissions for Pope Julius II, and when he died at only thirty-eight, left behind the greatest collection of frescoes the world had ever seen. Santi was a behemoth in the art world, and being known solely by one's first name was a level of fame achieved only by an elite few ... people like Napoleon, Galileo, and Jesus ... and, of course, the demigods Langdon now heard blaring from Harvard dormitories – Sting, Madonna, Jewel, and the artist formerly known as Prince, who had changed his name to the symbol ⚥, causing Langdon to dub him 'The Tau Cross With Intersecting Hermaphroditic Ankh.'

'Santi,' Langdon said, 'is the last name of the great Renaissance master, Raphael.'

Vittoria looked surprised. 'Raphael? As in *the* Raphael?'

'The one and only.' Langdon pushed on toward the Office of the Swiss Guard.

'So the path starts at Raphael's tomb?'

'It actually makes perfect sense,' Langdon said as they rushed on. 'The Illuminati often considered great artists and sculptors honorary brothers in

253

enlightenment. The Illuminati could have chosen Raphael's tomb as a kind of tribute.' Langdon also knew that Raphael, like many other religious artists, was a suspected closet atheist.

Vittoria slipped the folio carefully back in Langdon's pocket. 'So where is he buried?'

Langdon took a deep breath. 'Believe it or not, Raphael's buried in the Pantheon.'

Vittoria looked skeptical. '*The* Pantheon?'

'*The* Raphael at *the* Pantheon.' Langdon had to admit, the Pantheon was not what he had expected for the placement of the first marker. He would have guessed the first altar of science to be at some quiet, out of the way church, something subtle. Even in the 1600s, the Pantheon, with its tremendous, holed dome, was one of the best known sites in Rome.

'Is the Pantheon even a *church*?' Vittoria asked.

'Oldest Catholic church in Rome.'

Vittoria shook her head. 'But do you really think the first cardinal could be killed at the Pantheon? That's got to be one of the busiest tourist spots in Rome.'

Langdon shrugged. 'The Illuminati said they wanted the whole world watching. Killing a cardinal at the Pantheon would certainly open some eyes.'

'But how does this guy expect to kill someone at the Pantheon and get away unnoticed? It would be impossible.'

'As impossible as kidnapping four cardinals from Vatican City? The poem is precise.'

'And you're *certain* Raphael is buried inside the Pantheon?'

'I've seen his tomb many times.'

Vittoria nodded, still looking troubled. 'What time is it?'

Langdon checked. 'Seven-thirty.'

'Is the Pantheon far?'

'A mile maybe. We've got time.'

'The poem said Santi's *earthly* tomb. Does that mean anything to you?'

Langdon hastened diagonally across the Courtyard of the Sentinel. 'Earthly? Actually, there's probably no more earthly place in Rome than the Pantheon. It got its name from the original religion practiced there – Pantheism – the worship of all gods, specifically the pagan gods of Mother Earth.'

As a student of architecture, Langdon had been amazed to learn that the dimensions of the Pantheon's main chamber were a tribute to Gaea – the goddess of the Earth. The proportions were so exact that a giant spherical globe could fit perfectly inside the building with less than a millimeter to spare.

'Okay,' Vittoria said, sounding more convinced. 'And demon's hole? *From Santi's earthly tomb with demon's hole?*'

Langdon was not quite as sure about this. *'Demon's hole* must mean the *oculus*,' he said, making a logical guess. 'The famous circular opening in the Pantheon's roof.'

'But it's a *church*,' Vittoria said, moving effortlessly beside him. 'Why would they call the opening a *demon's* hole?'

Langdon had actually been wondering that himself. He had never heard the term 'demon's hole', but he did recall a famous sixth-century critique of the Pantheon whose words seemed oddly appropriate now. The Venerable Bede had once written that the hole in the Pantheon's roof had been bored by demons trying to escape the building when it

255

was consecrated by Boniface IV.

'And why,' Vittoria added as they entered a smaller courtyard, 'would the Illuminati use the name Santi if he was really known as *Raphael*?'

'You ask a lot of questions.'

'My dad used to say that.'

'Two possible reasons. One, the word *Raphael* has too many syllables. It would have destroyed the poem's iambic pentameter.'

'Sounds like a stretch.'

Langdon agreed. 'Okay, then maybe using "Santi" was to make the clue more obscure, so only very enlightened men would recognize the reference to Raphael.'

Vittoria didn't appear to buy this either. 'I'm sure Raphael's last name was very well known when he was alive.'

'Surprisingly not. Single name recognition was a status symbol. Raphael shunned his last name much like pop stars do today. Take Madonna, for example. She never uses her surname, Ciccone.'

Victoria looked amused. 'You know Madonna's last name?'

Langdon regretted the example. It was amazing the kind of garbage a mind picked up living with 10,000 adolescents.

As he and Vittoria passed the final gate towards the Office of the Swiss Guard, their progress was halted without warning.

'*Para!*' a voice bellowed behind them.

Langdon and Vittoria wheeled to find themselves looking into the barrel of a rifle.

'*Attento!*' Vittoria exclaimed, jumping back. 'Watch it with—'

'*Non sportarti!*' the guard snapped, cocking the weapon.

'*Soldato!*' a voice commanded from across the courtyard. Olivetti was emerging from the security center. 'Let them go!'

The guard looked bewildered. '*Ma, signore, è una donna—*'

'Inside!' he yelled at the guard.

'*Signore, non posso—*'

'Now! You have new orders. Captain Rocher will be briefing the corps in two minutes. We will be organizing a search.'

Looking bewildered, the guard hurried into the security center. Olivetti marched toward Langdon, rigid and steaming. 'Our most secret archives? I'll want an explanation.'

'We have good news,' Langdon said.

Olivetti's eyes narrowed. 'It better be *damn* good.'

56

The four unmarked Alfa Romeo 155 T-Sparks roared down Via dei Coronari like fighter jets off a runway. The vehicles carried twelve plainclothed Swiss Guards armed with Cherchi-Pardini semiautomatics, local-radius nerve gas canisters, and long-range stun guns. The three sharpshooters carried laser-sighted rifles.

Sitting in the passenger seat of the lead car, Olivetti turned backward toward Langdon and Vittoria. His eyes were filled with rage. 'You assured me a sound explanation, and *this* is what I get?'

Langdon felt cramped in the small car. 'I understand your—'

'No, you don't understand!' Olivetti never raised his voice, but his intensity tripled. 'I have just removed a dozen of my best men from Vatican City on the eve of conclave. And I have done this to stake out the Pantheon based on the testimony of some American I have never met who has just interpreted a four-hundred-year-old poem. I have also just left the search for this antimatter weapon in the hands of secondary officers.'

Langdon resisted the urge to pull Folio 5 from his pocket and wave it in Olivetti's face. 'All I know is that the information we found refers to Raphael's tomb, and Raphael's tomb is inside the Pantheon.'

The officer behind the wheel nodded. 'He's right, commander. My wife and I—'

'Drive,' Olivetti snapped. He turned back to Langdon. 'How could a killer accomplish an assassination in such a crowded place and escape unseen?'

'I don't know,' Langdon said. 'But the Illuminati are obviously highly resourceful. They've broken into both CERN and Vatican City. It's only by luck we know where the first kill zone is. The Pantheon is your one chance to catch this guy.'

'More contradictions,' Olivetti said. '*One* chance? I thought you said there was some sort of pathway. A series of markers. If the Pantheon is the right spot, we can follow the pathway to the other markers. We will have *four* chances to catch this guy.'

'I had hoped so,' Langdon said. 'And we *would* have . . . a century ago.'

Langdon's realization that the Pantheon was the first altar of science had been a bittersweet moment.

History had a way of playing cruel tricks on those who chased it. It was a long shot that the Path of Illumination would be intact after all of these years, with all of its statues in place, but part of Langdon had fantasized about following the path all the way to the end and coming face to face with the sacred Illuminati lair. Alas, he realized, it was not to be. 'The Vatican had all the statues in the Pantheon removed and destroyed in the late 1600s.'

Vittoria looked shocked. 'Why?'

'The statues were pagan Olympian Gods. Unfortunately, that means the first marker is gone . . . and with it—'

'Any hope,' Vittoria said, 'of finding the Path of Illumination and additional markers?'

Langdon shook his head. 'We have *one* shot. The Pantheon. After that, the path disappears.'

Olivetti stared at them both a long moment and then turned and faced front. 'Pull over,' he barked to the driver.

The driver swerved the car toward the curb and put on the brakes. Three other Alfa Romeos skidded in behind them. The Swiss Guard convey screeched to a halt.

'What are you doing!' Vittoria demanded.

'My job,' Olivetti said, turning in his seat, his voice like stone. 'Mr Langdon, when you told me you would explain the situation en route, I assumed I would be approaching the Pantheon with a clear idea of why my men are here. That is not the case. Because I am abandoning critical duties by being here, and because I have found very little that makes sense in this theory of yours about virgin sacrifices and ancient poetry, I cannot in good conscience continue. I am recalling this

259

mission immediately.' He pulled out his walkie-talkie and clicked it on.

Vittoria reached across the seat and grabbed his arm. 'You can't!'

Olivetti slammed down the walkie-talkie and fixed her with a red-hot stare. 'Have you been to the Pantheon, Ms Vetra?'

'No, but I—'

'Let me tell you something about it. The Pantheon is a single room. A circular cell made of stone and cement. It has *one* entrance. No windows. One *narrow* entrance. That entrance is flanked at all times by no less than four armed Roman policemen who protect this shrine from art defacers, anti-Christian terrorists, and gypsy tourist scams.'

'Your point?' she said coolly.

'My point?' Olivetti's knuckles gripped the seat. 'My point is that what you have just told me is going to happen is utterly impossible! Can you give me one plausible scenario of how someone could kill a cardinal *inside* the Pantheon? How does one even get a hostage past the guards *into* the Pantheon in the first place? Much less actually kill him and get away?' Olivetti leaned over the seat, his coffee breath now in Langdon's face. 'How, Mr Langdon? *One* plausible scenario.'

Langdon felt the tiny car shrink around him. *I have no idea! I'm not an assassin! I don't know how he will do it! I only know—*

'*One* scenario?' Vittoria quipped, her voice un-ruffled. 'How about this? The killer flies over in a helicopter and drops a screaming, branded cardinal down through the hole in the roof. The cardinal hits the marble floor and dies.'

Everyone in the car turned and stared at Vittoria. Langdon didn't know what to think. *You've got one sick imagination, lady, but you are quick.*

Olivetti frowned. 'Possible, I admit . . . but hardly—'

'Or the killer drugs the cardinal,' Vittoria said, 'brings him to the Pantheon in a wheelchair like some old tourist. He wheels him inside, quietly slits his throat, and then walks out.'

This seemed to wake up Olivetti a bit.

Not bad! Langdon thought.

'Or,' she said, 'the killer could—'

'I heard you,' Olivetti said. 'Enough.' He took a deep breath and blew it out. Someone rapped sharply on the window, and everyone jumped. It was a soldier from one of the other cars. Olivetti rolled down the window.

'Everything all right, commander?' The soldier was dressed in street clothes. He pulled back the sleeve of his denim shirt to reveal a black chronograph military watch. 'Seven-forty, commander. We'll need time to get in position.'

Olivetti nodded vaguely but said nothing for many moments. He ran a finger back and forth across the dash, making a line in the dust. He studied Langdon in the side-view mirror, and Langdon felt himself being measured and weighed. Finally Olivetti turned back to the guard. There was reluctance in his voice. 'I'll want separate approaches. Cars to Piazza della Rotunda, Via degli Orfani, Piazza Sant'Ignacio, and Sant'Eustachio. No closer than two blocks. Once you're parked, gear up and await my orders. Three minutes.'

'Very good, sir.' The soldier returned to his car.

Langdon gave Vittoria an impressed nod. She

261

smiled back, and for an instant Langdon felt an un-expected connection ... a thread of magnetism between them.

The commander turned in his seat and locked eyes with Langdon. 'Mr Langdon, this had better not blow up in our faces.'

Langdon smiled uneasily. *How could it?*

57

The director of CERN, Maximilian Kohler, opened his eyes to the cool rush of cromolyn and leukotriene in his body, dilating his bronchial tubes and pulmonary capillaries. He was breathing normally again. He found himself lying in a private room in the CERN infirmary, his wheelchair beside the bed.

He took stock, examining the paper robe they had put him in. His clothing was folded on the chair beside the bed. Outside he could hear a nurse making the rounds. He lay there a long minute listening. Then, as quietly as possible, he pulled himself to the edge of the bed and retrieved his clothing. Struggling with his dead legs, he dressed himself. Then he dragged his body onto his wheelchair.

Muffling a cough, he wheeled himself to the door. He moved manually, careful not to engage the motor. When he arrived at the door he peered out. The hall was empty.

Silently, Maximilian Kohler slipped out of the infirmary.

'Seven-forty six and thirty . . . *mark.*' Even speaking into his walkie-talkie, Olivetti's voice never seemed to rise above a whisper.

Langdon felt himself sweating now in his Harris tweed in the backseat of the Alfa Romeo, which was idling in Piazza de la Concorde, three blocks from the Pantheon. Vittoria sat beside him, looking engrossed by Olivetti, who was transmitting his final orders.

'Deployment will be an eight-point hem,' the commander said. 'Full perimeter with a bias on the entry. Target may know you visually, so you will be *pasvisible*. Nonmortal force only. We'll need someone to spot the roof. Target is primary. Asset secondary.'

Jesus, Langdon thought, chilled by the efficiency with which Olivetti had just told his men the cardinal was expendable. *Asset secondary.*

'I repeat. Nonmortal procurement. We need the target alive. Go.' Olivetti snapped off his walkie-talkie.

Vittoria looked stunned, almost angry. 'Commander, isn't anyone going *inside*?'

Olivetti turned. 'Inside?'

'Inside the Pantheon! Where this is supposed to happen?'

'*Attento*,' Olivetti said, his eyes fossilizing. 'If my ranks have been infiltrated, my men may be known by sight. Your colleague has just finished warning me that *this* will be our sole chance to catch the target. I have no intention of scaring anyone off by marching my men inside.'

'But what if the killer is *already* inside?'

Olivetti checked his watch. 'The target was specific.

Eight o'clock. We have fifteen minutes.'

'He said he would *kill* the cardinal at eight o'clock. But he may already have gotten the victim inside somehow. What if your men see the target come out but don't know who he is? Someone needs to make sure the inside is clean.'

'Too risky at this point.'

'Not if the person going in was unrecognizable.'

'Disguising operatives is time consuming and—'

'I meant *me*,' Vittoria said.

Langdon turned and stared at her.

Olivetti shook his head. 'Absolutely not.'

'He killed my father.'

'Exactly, so he may know who you are.'

'You heard him on the phone. He had no idea Leonardo Vetra even *had* a daughter. He sure as hell doesn't know what I look like. I could walk in like a tourist. If I see anything suspicious, I could walk into the square and signal your men to move in.'

'I'm sorry, I cannot allow that.'

'*Comandante?*' Olivetti's receiver crackled. 'We've got a situation from the north point. The fountain is blocking our line of sight. We can't see the entrance unless we move into plain view on the piazza. What's your call? Do you want us blind or vulnerable?'

Vittoria apparently had endured enough. 'That's it. I'm going.' She opened her door and got out.

Olivetti dropped his walkie-talkie and jumped out of the car, circling in front of Vittoria.

Langdon got out too. *What the hell is she doing!*

Olivetti blocked Vittoria's way. 'Ms Vetra, your instincts are good, but I cannot let a civilian interfere.'

'Interfere? You're flying blind. Let me help.'

'I would love to have a recon point inside, but . . .'

'But what?' Vittoria demanded. 'But I'm a *woman*?'

Olivetti said nothing.

'That had better not be what you were going to say, Commander, because you know damn well this is a good idea, and if you let some archaic *macho* bullshit—'

'Let us do our job.'

'Let me help.'

'Too dangerous. We would have no lines of communication with you. I can't let you carry a walkie-talkie, it would give you away.'

Vittoria reached in her shirt pocket and produced her cell phone. 'Plenty of tourists carry phones.'

Olivetti frowned.

Vittoria unsnapped the phone and mimicked a call. 'Hi, honey, I'm standing in the Pantheon. You should see this place!' She snapped the phone shut and glared at Olivetti. 'Who the hell is going to know? It is a no-risk situation. Let me be your eyes!' She motioned to the cell phone on Olivetti's belt. 'What's your number?'

Olivetti did not reply.

The driver had been looking on and seemed to have some thoughts of his own. He got out of the car and took the commander aside. They spoke in hushed tones for ten seconds. Finally Olivetti nodded and returned. 'Program this number.' He began dictating digits.

Vittoria programmed her phone.

'Now call the number.'

Vittoria pressed the auto dial. The phone on Olivetti's belt began ringing. He picked it up and spoke into the receiver. 'Go into the building, Ms Vetra, look around, exit the building, then call and tell me what you see.'

Vittoria snapped the phone shut. 'Thank you, sir.'

Langdon felt a sudden, unexpected surge of protective instinct. 'Wait a minute,' he said to Olivetti. 'You're sending her in there *alone*.'

Vittoria scowled at him. 'Robert, I'll be fine.'

The Swiss Guard driver was talking to Olivetti again.

'It's dangerous,' Langdon said to Vittoria.

'He's right,' Olivetti said. 'Even my best men don't work alone. My lieutenant has just pointed out that the masquerade will be more convincing with both of you anyway.'

Both of us? Langdon hesitated. *Actually, what I meant —*

'Both of you entering together,' Olivetti said, 'will look like a couple on holiday. You can also back each other up. I'm more comfortable with that.'

Vittoria shrugged. 'Fine, but we'll need to go fast.'

Langdon groaned. *Nice move, cowboy.*

Olivetti pointed down the street. 'First street you hit will be Via degli Orfani. Go left. It takes you directly to the Pantheon. Two-minute walk, tops. I'll be here, directing my men and waiting for your call. I'd like you to have protection.' He pulled out his pistol. 'Do either of you know how to use a gun?'

Langdon's heart skipped. *We don't need a gun!*

Vittoria held her hand out. 'I can tag a breaching porpoise from forty meters off the bow of a rocking ship.'

'Good.' Olivetti handed the gun to her. 'You'll have to conceal it.'

Vittoria glanced down at her shorts. Then she looked at Langdon.

Oh no you don't! Langdon thought, but Vittoria was

too fast. She opened his jacket, and inserted the weapon into one of his breast pockets. It felt like a rock dropping into his coat, his only consolation being that *Diagramma* was in the other pocket.

'We look harmless,' Vittoria said. 'We're leaving.' She took Langdon's arm and headed down the street.

The driver called out, 'Arm in arm is good. Remember, you're tourists. *Newlyweds* even. Perhaps if you held hands?'

As they turned the corner Langdon could have sworn he saw on Vittoria's face the hint of a smile.

59

The Swiss Guard 'staging room' is located adjacent to the Corpo di Vigilanza barracks and is used primarily for planning the security surrounding papal appearances and public Vatican events. Today, however, it was being used for something else.

The man addressing the assembled task force was the second-in-command of the Swiss Guard, Captain Elias Rocher. Rocher was a barrel-chested man with soft, puttylike features. He wore the traditional blue captain's uniform with his own personal flair – a red beret cocked sideways on his head. His voice was surprisingly crystalline for such a large man, and when he spoke, his tone had the clarity of a musical instrument. Despite the precision of his inflection, Rocher's eyes were cloudy like those of some nocturnal mammal. His men called him 'orso' – grizzly bear. They sometimes joked that Rocher was 'the bear who walked in the viper's shadow'. Commander Olivetti was the viper. Rocher was just as deadly as the viper, but at least you could see him coming.

Rocher's men stood at sharp attention, nobody moving a muscle, although the information they had just received had increased their aggregate blood pressure by a few thousand points.

Rookie Lieutenant Chartrand stood in the back of the room wishing he had been among the 99 per cent of applicants who had *not* qualified to be here. At twenty years old, Chartrand was the youngest guard on the force. He had been in Vatican City only three months. Like every man there, Chartrand was Swiss Army trained and had endured two years of additional *Ausbildung* in Bern before qualifying for the grueling Vatican *pròva* held in a secret barracks outside of Rome. Nothing in his training, however, had prepared him for a crisis like this.

At first Chartrand thought the briefing was some sort of bizarre training exercise. *Futuristic weapons? Ancient cults? Kidnapped cardinals?* Then Rocher had shown them the live video feed of the weapon in question. Apparently this was no exercise.

'We will be killing power in selected areas,' Rocher was saying, 'to eradicate extraneous magnetic interference. We will move in teams of four. We will wear infrared goggles for vision. Reconnaissance will be done with traditional bug sweepers, recalibrated for sub-three-ohm flux fields. Any questions?'

None.

Chartrand's mind was on overload. 'What if we don't find it in time?' he asked, immediately wishing he had not.

The grizzly bear gazed out at him from beneath his

red beret. Then he dismissed the group with a somber salute. 'Godspeed, men.'

60

Two blocks from the Pantheon, Langdon and Vittoria approached on foot past a line of taxis, their drivers sleeping in the front seats. Nap time was eternal in the Eternal City – the ubiquitous public dozing a perfected extension of the afternoon siestas born of ancient Spain.

Langdon fought to focus his thoughts, but the situation was too bizarre to grasp rationally. Six hours ago he had been sound asleep in Cambridge. Now he was in Europe, caught up in a surreal battle of ancient titans, packing a semiautomatic in his Harris tweed, and holding hands with a woman he had only just met.

He looked at Vittoria. She was focused straight ahead. There was a strength in her grasp – that of an independent and determined woman. Her fingers wrapped around his with the comfort of innate acceptance. No hesitation. Langdon felt a growing attraction. *Get real*, he told himself.

Vittoria seemed to sense his uneasiness. 'Relax,' she said, without turning her head. 'We're supposed to look like newlyweds.'

'I'm relaxed.'

'You're crushing my hand.'

Langdon flushed and loosened up.

'Breathe through your eyes,' she said.

269

'I'm sorry?'

'It relaxes the muscles. It's called *pranayama*.'

'Piranha?'

'Not the fish. *Pranayama*. Never mind.'

As they rounded the corner into Piazza della Rotunda, the Pantheon rose before them. Langdon admired it, as always, with awe. *The Pantheon. Temple to all gods. Pagan gods. Gods of Nature and Earth.* The structure seemed boxier from the outside than he remembered. The vertical pillars and triangular *pronaus* all but obscured the circular dome behind it. Still, the bold and immodest inscription over the entrance assured him they were in the right spot. M AGRIPPA L F COS TERTIUM FECIT. Langdon translated it, as always, with amusement. *Marcus Agrippa, Consul for the third time, built this.*

So much for humility, he thought, turning his eyes to the surrounding area. A scattering of tourists with video cameras wandered the area. Others sat enjoying Rome's best iced coffee at *La Tazza di Oro*'s outdoor café. Outside the entrance to the Pantheon, four armed Roman policemen stood at attention just as Olivetti had predicted.

'Looks pretty quiet,' Vittoria said.

Langdon nodded, but he felt troubled. Now that he was standing here in person, the whole scenario seemed surreal. Despite Vittoria's apparent faith that he was right, Langdon realized he had put everyone on the line here. The Illuminati poem lingered. *From Santi's earthly tomb with demon's hole. YES,* he told himself. This was the spot. Santi's tomb. He had been here many times beneath the Pantheon's *oculus* and stood before the grave of the great Raphael.

'What time is it?' Vittoria asked.

Langdon checked his watch. 'Seven-fifty. Ten minutes till show time.'

'Hope these guys are good,' Vittoria said, eyeing the scattered tourists entering the Pantheon. 'If anything happens inside that dome, we'll all be in the crossfire.'

Langdon exhaled heavily as they moved toward the entrance. The gun felt heavy in his pocket. He wondered what would happen if the policemen frisked him and found the weapon, but the officers did not give them a second look. Apparently the disguise was convincing.

Langdon whispered to Vittoria. 'Ever fire anything other than a tranquilizer gun?'

'Don't you trust me?'

'Trust you? I barely know you.'

Vittoria frowned. 'And here I thought we were newlyweds.'

61

The air inside the Pantheon was cool and damp, heavy with history. The sprawling ceiling hovered overhead as though weightless – the 141-foot unsupported span larger even than the cupola at St Peter's. As always, Langdon felt a chill as he entered the cavernous room. It was a remarkable fusion of engineering and art. Above them the famous circular hole in the roof glowed with a narrow shaft of evening sun. *The oculus*, Langdon thought. *The demon's hole.*

They had arrived.

Langdon's eyes traced the arch of the ceiling sloping

271

outward to the columned walls and finally down to the polished marble floor beneath their feet. The faint echo of footfalls and tourist murmurs reverberated around the dome. Langdon scanned the dozens or so tourists wandering aimlessly in the shadows. *Are you here?*

'Looks pretty quiet,' Vittoria said, still holding his hand.

Langdon nodded.

'Where's Raphael's tomb?'

Langdon thought for a moment, trying to get his bearings. He surveyed the circumference of the room. Tombs. Altars. Pillars. Niches. He motioned to a particularly ornate funerary across the dome and to the left. 'I think that's Raphael's over there.'

Vittoria scanned the rest of the room. 'I don't see anyone who looks like an assassin about to kill a cardinal. Shall we look around?'

Langdon nodded. 'There's only one spot in here where anyone could be hiding. We better check the *rientranze*.'

'The recesses?'

'Yes.' Langdon pointed. 'The recesses in the wall.'

Around the perimeter, interspersed with the tombs, a series of semicircular niches were hewn in the wall. The niches, although not enormous, were big enough to hide someone in the shadows. Sadly, Langdon knew they once contained statues of the Olympian gods, but the pagan sculptures had been destroyed when the Vatican converted the Pantheon to a Christian church. He felt a pang of frustration to know he was standing at the first altar of science, and the marker was gone. He wondered which statue it had been, and where it had pointed. Langdon could imagine no greater thrill

272

than finding an Illuminati marker – a statue that surreptitiously pointed the way down the Path of Illumination. Again he wondered *who* the anonymous Illuminati sculptor had been.

'I'll take the left arc,' Vittoria said, indicating the left half of the circumference. 'You go right. See you in a hundred and eighty degrees.'

Langdon smiled grimly.

As Vittoria moved off, Langdon felt the eerie horror of the situation seeping back into his mind. As he turned and made his way to the right, the killer's voice seemed to whisper in the dead space around him. *Eight o'clock. Virgin sacrifices on the altars of science. A mathematical progression of death. Eight, nine, ten, eleven . . . and at midnight.* Langdon checked his watch: 7.52. Eight minutes.

As Langdon moved toward the first recess, he passed the tomb of one of Italy's Catholic kings. The sarcophagus, like many in Rome, was askew with the wall, positioned awkwardly. A group of visitors seemed confused by this. Langdon did not stop to explain. Formal Christian tombs were often misaligned with the architecture so they could lie facing *east*. It was an ancient superstition that Langdon's Symbology 212 class had discussed just last month.

'That's totally incongruous!' a female student in the front had blurted when Langdon explained the reason for east-facing tombs. 'Why would Christians want their tombs to face the rising *sun*? We're talking about Christianity . . . not *sun* worship!'

Langdon smiled, pacing before the blackboard, chewing an apple. 'Mr Hitzrot!' he shouted.

A young man dozing in back sat up with a start. 'What! Me?'

Langdon pointed to a Renaissance art poster on the wall. 'Who is that man kneeling before God?'

'Um . . . some saint?'

'Brilliant. And how do you *know* he's a saint?'

'He's got a halo?'

'Excellent, and does that golden halo remind you of anything?'

Hitzrot broke into a smile. 'Yeah! Those Egyptian things we studied last term. Those . . . um . . . *sun disks!*'

'Thank you, Hitzrot. Go back to sleep.' Langdon turned back to the class. 'Halos, like much of Christian symbology, were borrowed from the ancient Egyptian religion of *sun* worship. Christianity is filled with examples of sun worship.'

'Excuse me?' the girl in front said. 'I go to church all the time, and I don't see much sun worshiping going on!'

'Really? What do you celebrate on December twenty-fifth?'

'Christmas. The birth of Jesus Christ.'

'And yet according to the Bible, Christ was born in March, so what are we doing celebrating in late December?'

Silence.

Langdon smiled. 'December twenty-fifth, my friends, is the ancient pagan holiday of *sol invictus* – Unconquered Sun – coinciding with the winter solstice. It's that wonderful time of year when the sun returns, and the days start getting longer.'

Langdon took another bite of apple.

'Conquering religions,' he continued, 'often adopt existing holidays to make conversion less shocking. It's called *transmutation*. It helps people acclimatize to the new faith. Worshipers keep the same holy dates, pray in the same sacred locations, use a similar symbology ... and they simply substitute a different god.'

Now the girl in front looked furious. 'You're implying Christianity is just some kind of ... repackaged *sun worship!*'

'Not at all. Christianity did not borrow *only* from sun worship. The ritual of Christian canonization is taken from the ancient "god-making" rite of Euhemerus. The practice of "god-eating" – that is, Holy Communion – was borrowed from the Aztecs. Even the concept of Christ dying for our sins is arguably not exclusively Christian; the self-sacrifice of a young man to absolve the sins of his people appears in the earliest tradition of the Quetzalcoatl.'

The girl glared. 'So, is *anything* in Christianity original?'

'Very little in *any* organized faith is truly original. Religions are not born from scratch. They grow from one another. Modern religion is a collage ... an assimilated historical record of man's quest to understand the divine.'

'Um ... hold on,' Hitzrot ventured, sounding awake now. 'I know something Christian that's original. How about our *image* of God? Christian art never portrays God as the hawk sun god, or as an Aztec, or as anything weird. It always shows God as an old man with a white beard. So our *image* of God is original, right?'

Langdon smiled. 'When the early Christian converts abandoned their former deities – pagan gods, Roman gods, Greek, sun, Mithraic, whatever – they asked the church what their new Christian God looked like.

Wisely, the church chose the most feared, powerful . . . and familiar face in all of recorded.history.'

Hitzrot looked skeptical. 'An old man with a white, flowing beard?'

Langdon pointed to a hierarchy of ancient gods on the wall. At the top sat an old man with a white, flowing beard. 'Does Zeus look familiar?'

The class ended right on cue.

'Good evening,' a man's voice said.

Langdon jumped. He was back in the Pantheon. He turned to face an elderly man in a blue cape with a red cross on the chest. The man gave him a gray-toothed smile.

'You're English, right?' The man's accent was thick Tuscan.

Langdon blinked, confused. 'Actually, no. I'm American.'

The man looked embarrassed. 'Oh heavens, forgive me. You were so nicely dressed, I just figured . . . my apologies.'

'Can I help you?' Langdon asked, his heart beating wildly.

'Actually I thought perhaps I could help *you*. I am the *cicerone* here.' The man pointed proudly to his city-issued badge. 'It is my job to make your visit to Rome more interesting.'

More interesting? Langdon was certain this particular visit to Rome was *plenty* interesting.

'You look like a man of distinction,' the guide fawned, 'no doubt more interested in culture than most. Perhaps I can give you some history on this fascinating building.'

Langdon smiled politely. 'Kind of you, but I'm

actually an art historian myself, and—'

'Superb!' The man's eyes lit up like he'd hit the jack-pot. 'Then you will no doubt find this delightful!'

'I think I'd prefer to—'

'The Pantheon,' the man declared, launching into his memorized spiel, 'was built by Marcus Agrippa in 27 B.C.'

'Yes,' Langdon interjected, 'and rebuilt by Hadrian in 119 A.D.'

'It was the world's largest free-standing dome until 1960 when it was eclipsed by the Superdome in New Orleans!'

Langdon groaned. The man was unstoppable.

'And a fifth-century theologian once called the Pantheon the *House of the Devil*, warning that the hole in the roof was an entrance for demons!'

Langdon blocked him out. His eyes climbed sky-ward to the oculus, and the memory of Vittoria's suggested plot flashed a bone-numbing image in his mind . . . a branded cardinal falling through the hole and hitting the marble floor. *Now* that *would be a media event.* Langdon found himself scanning the Pantheon for reporters. Noné. He inhaled deeply. It was an absurd idea. The logistics of pulling off a stunt like that would be ridiculous.

As Langdon moved off to continue his inspection, the babbling docent followed like a love-starved puppy. *Remind me*, Langdon thought to himself, *there's nothing worse than a gung ho art historian*.

Across the room, Vittoria was immersed in her own search. Standing all alone for the first time since she had heard the news of her father, she felt the stark reality of the last eight hours closing in around her.

277

Her father had been murdered – cruelly and abruptly. Almost equally painful was that her father's creation had been corrupted – now a tool of terrorists. Vittoria was plagued with guilt to think that it was *her* invention that had enabled the antimatter to be transported . . . *her* canister that was now counting down inside the Vatican. In an effort to serve her father's quest for the simplicity of truth . . . she had become a conspirator of chaos.

Oddly, the only thing that felt right in her life at the moment was the presence of a total stranger. Robert Langdon. She found an inexplicable refuge in his eyes . . . like the harmony of the oceans she had left behind early that morning. She was glad he was there. Not only had he been a source of strength and hope for her, Langdon had used his quick mind to render this one chance to catch her father's killer.

Vittoria breathed deeply as she continued her search, moving around the perimeter. She was overwhelmed by the unexpected images of personal revenge that had dominated her thoughts all day. Even as a sworn lover of all life . . . she wanted this executioner *dead*. No amount of good *karma* could make her turn the other cheek today. Alarmed and electrified, she sensed something coursing through her Italian blood that she had never felt before . . . the whispers of Sicilian ancestors defending family honor with brutal justice. *Vendetta*, Vittoria thought, and for the first time in her life understood.

Visions of reprisal spurred her on. She approached the tomb of Raphael Santi. Even from a distance she could tell this guy was special. His casket, unlike the others, was protected by a Plexiglas shield and recessed into the wall. Through the barrier she could see the front of the sarcophagus.

Vittoria studied the grave and then read the one-sentence description plaque beside Raphael's tomb.

Then she read it again.

Then . . . she read it again.

A moment later, she was dashing in horror across the floor. 'Robert! *Robert!*'

62

Langdon's progress around his side of the Pantheon was being hampered somewhat by the guide on his heels, now continuing his tireless narration as Langdon prepared to check the final alcove.

'You certainly seem to be enjoying those niches!' the docent said, looking delighted. 'Were you aware that the tapering thickness of the walls is the reason the dome appears weightless?'

Langdon nodded, not hearing a word as he prepared to examine another niche. Suddenly someone grabbed him from behind. It was Vittoria. She was breathless and tugging at his arm. From the look of terror on her face, Langdon could only imagine one thing. *She found a body.* He felt an upswelling of dread.

'Ah, your wife!' the docent exclaimed, clearly thrilled to have another guest. He motioned to her short pants and hiking boots. 'Now *you* I can tell are American!'

Vittoria's eyes narrowed. 'I'm Italian.'

The guide's smile dimmed. 'Oh, dear.'

'Robert,' Vittoria whispered, trying to turn her back on the guide. 'Galileo's *Diagramma*. I need to see it.'

'*Diagramma?*' the docent said, wheedling back in. 'My! You two certainly know your history! Unfortunately that document is not viewable. It is under secret preservation in the Vatican Arc—'

'Could you excuse us?' Langdon said. He was confused by Vittoria's panic. He took her aside and reached in his pocket, carefully extracting the *Diagramma* folio. 'What's going on?'

'What's the date on this thing?' Vittoria demanded, scanning the sheet.

The docent was on them again, staring at the folio, mouth agape. 'That's not . . . really . . .'

'Tourist reproduction,' Langdon quipped. 'Thank you for your help. Please, my wife and I would like a moment alone.'

The docent backed off, eyes never leaving the paper.

'Date,' Vittoria repeated to Langdon. 'When did Galileo publish . . .'

Langdon pointed to the Roman numeral in the lower line. 'That's the pub date. What's going on?'

Vittoria deciphered the number. '1639?'

'Yes. What's wrong?'

Vittoria's eyes filled with foreboding. 'We're in trouble, Robert. Big trouble. The dates don't match.'

'What dates don't match?'

'Raphael's tomb. He wasn't buried here until 1759. A century *after Diagramma* was published.'

Langdon stared at her, trying to make sense of the words. 'No,' he replied. 'Raphael died in 1520, long *before Diagramma*.'

'Yes, but he wasn't buried *here* until much later.'

Langdon was lost. 'What are you talking about?'

'I just read it. Raphael's body was relocated to the Pantheon in 1758. It was part of some historic tribute to eminent Italians.

As the words settled in, Langdon felt like a rug had just been yanked out from under him.

'When that poem was written,' Vittoria declared, 'Raphael's tomb was somewhere *else*. Back then, the Pantheon had nothing at all to do with Raphael!'

Langdon could not breathe. 'But that . . . means . . .'

'Yes! It means we're in the wrong place!'

Langdon felt himself sway. *Impossible . . . I was certain . . .*

Vittoria ran over and grabbed the docent, pulling him back. 'Signore, excuse us. Where was Raphael's body in the 1600s?'

'Urb . . . Urbino,' he stammered, now looking bewildered. 'His birthplace.'

'Impossible!' Langdon cursed to himself. 'The Illuminati altars of science were here in Rome. I'm certain of it!'

'Illuminati?' The docent gasped, looking again at the document in Langdon's hand. 'Who *are* you people?'

Vittoria took charge. 'We're looking for something called Santi's earthly tomb. In Rome. Can you tell us what that might be?'

The docent looked unsettled. 'This was Raphael's only tomb in Rome.'

Langdon tried to think, but his mind refused to engage. If Raphael's tomb wasn't in Rome in 1655, then what was the poem referring to? *Santi's earthly tomb with demon's hole? What the hell is it? Think!*

'Was there another artist called Santi?' Vittoria asked.

The docent shrugged. 'Not that I know of.'

'How about *anyone* famous at all? Maybe a scientist or a poet or an astronomer named Santi?'

The docent now looked like he wanted to leave. 'No, ma'am. The only Santi I've heard of is Raphael the architect.'

'Architect?' Vittoria said. 'I thought he was a painter!'

'He was both, of course. They all were. Michelangelo, da Vinci, Raphael.'

Langdon didn't know whether it was the docent's words or the ornate tombs around him that brought the revelation to mind, but it didn't matter. The thought occurred. *Santi was an architect.* From there the progression of thoughts fell like dominoes. Renaissance architects lived for only two reasons – to glorify God with big churches, and to glorify dignitaries with lavish tombs. *Santi's tomb. Could it be?* The images came faster now . . .

da Vinci's *Mona Lisa.*

Monet's *Water Lilies.*

Michelangelo's *David.*

Santi's *earthly tomb . . .*

'Santi *designed* the tomb,' Langdon said.

Vittoria turned. 'What?'

'It's not a reference to where Raphael is buried, it's referring to a tomb he *designed*.'

'What are you talking about?'

'I misunderstood the clue. It's not Raphael's burial site we're looking for, it's a tomb Raphael designed for someone *else*. I can't believe I missed it. Half of the sculpting done in Renaissance and Baroque Rome was for the funeraries.' Langdon smiled with the revelation. 'Raphael must have designed hundreds of tombs!'

Vittoria did not look happy. 'Hundreds?'

Langdon's smile faded. 'Oh.'

'Any of them *earthly*, professor?'

Langdon felt suddenly inadequate. He knew embarrassingly little about Raphael's work. Michelangelo he could have helped with, but Raphael's work had never captivated him. Langdon could only name a couple of Raphael's more famous tombs, but he wasn't sure what they looked like.

Apparently sensing Langdon's stymie, Vittoria turned to the docent, who was now inching away. She grabbed his arm and reeled him in. 'I need a tomb. Designed by Raphael. A tomb that could be considered *earthly*.'

The docent now looked distressed. 'A tomb of Raphael's? I don't know. He designed so many. And you probably would mean a *chapel* by Raphael, not a tomb. Architects always designed the chapels in conjunction with the tomb.'

Langdon realized the man was right.

'Are any of Raphael's tombs or chapels considered *earthly*?'

The man shrugged. 'I'm sorry. I don't know what you mean. *Earthly* really doesn't describe anything I know of. I should be going.'

Vittoria held his arm and read from the top line of the folio. 'From Santi's earthly tomb with demon's hole. Does that mean anything to you?'

'Not a thing.'

Langdon looked up suddenly. He had momentarily forgotten the second part of the line. *Demon's hole?* 'Yes!' he said to the docent. 'That's it! Do any of Raphael's chapels have an oculus in them?'

The docent shook his head. 'To my knowledge

the Pantheon is unique.' He paused. 'But . . .'

'But what!' Vittoria and Langdon said in unison.

Now the docent cocked his head, stepping toward them again. 'A demon's hole?' He muttered to himself and picked at his teeth. 'Demon's hole . . . that is . . . *buco diàvolo*?'

Vittoria nodded. 'Literally, yes.'

The docent smiled faintly. 'Now there's a term I have not heard in a while. If I'm not mistaken, a *buco diàvolo* refers to an undercroft.'

'An undercroft?' Langdon asked. 'As in a *crypt*?'

'Yes, but a specific kind of crypt. I believe a demon's hole is an ancient term for a massive burial cavity located in a chapel . . . underneath another tomb.'

'An ossuary annex?' Langdon demanded, immediately recognizing what the man was describing.

The docent looked impressed. 'Yes! That is the term I was looking for!'

Langdon considered it. Ossuary annexes were a cheap ecclesiastic fix to an awkward dilemma. When churches honored their most distinguished members with ornate tombs inside the sanctuary, surviving family members often demanded the family be buried together . . . thus ensuring they too would have a coveted burial spot inside the church. However, if the church did not have space or funds to create tombs for an entire family, they sometimes dug an ossuary annex – a hole in the floor near the tomb where they buried the less worthy family members. The hole was then covered with the Renaissance equivalent of a manhole cover. Although convenient, the ossuary annex went out of style quickly because of the stench that often wafted up into the cathedral. *Demon's hole*, Langdon thought. He had never heard the term. It seemed eerily fitting.

Langdon's heart was now pounding fiercely. *From Santi's earthly tomb with demon's hole*. There seemed to be only one question left to ask. 'Did Raphael design any tombs that had one of these demon's holes?'

The docent scratched his head. 'Actually, I'm sorry . . . I can only think of one.'

Only one? Langdon could not have dreamed of a better response.

'Where!' Vittoria almost shouted.

The docent eyed them strangely. 'It's called the Chigi Chapel. Tomb of Agostino Chigi and his brother, wealthy patrons of the arts and sciences.'

'*Sciences?*' Langdon said, exchanging looks with Vittoria.

'Where?' Vittoria asked again.

The docent ignored the question, seeming enthusiastic again to be of service. 'As for whether or not the tomb is *earthly*, I don't know, but certainly it is . . . shall we say *differénte*.'

'Different?' Langdon said. 'How?'

'Incoherent with the architecture. Raphael was only the architect. Some other sculptor did the interior adornments. I can't remember who.'

Langdon was now all ears. *The anonymous Illuminati master, perhaps?*

'Whoever did the interior monuments lacked taste,' the docent said. '*Dio mio! Atrocità!* Who would want to be buried beneath *pirámides*?'

Langdon could scarcely believe his ears. 'Pyramids? The chapel contains pyramids?'

'I know,' the docent scoffed. 'Terrible, isn't it?'

Vittoria grabbed the docent's arm. 'Signore, *where* is this Chigi Chapel?'

'About a mile north. In the church of Santa Maria del Popolo.'

Vittoria exhaled. 'Thank you. Let's—'

'Hey,' the docent said, 'I just thought of something. What a fool I am.'

Vittoria stopped short. 'Please don't tell me you made a mistake.'

He shook his head. 'No, but it should have dawned on me earlier. The Chigi Chapel was not always known as the Chigi. It used to be called Capella della Terra.'

'Chapel of the Land?' Langdon asked.

'No,' Vittoria said, heading for the door. 'Chapel of the *Earth*.'

Vittoria Vetra whipped out her cell phone as she dashed into Piazza della Rotunda. 'Commander Olivetti,' she said. 'This is the wrong place!'

Olivetti sounded bewildered. 'Wrong? What do you mean?'

'The first altar of science is at the Chigi Chapel!'

'Where?' Now Olivetti sounded angry. 'But Mr Langdon said—'

'Santa Maria del Popolo! One mile north. Get your men over there now! We've got four minutes!'

'But my men are in position *here*! I can't possibly—'

'Move!' Vittoria snapped the phone shut.

Behind her, Langdon emerged from the Panteon, dazed.

She grabbed his hand and pulled him toward the queue of seemingly driverless taxis waiting by the curb. She pounded on the hood of the first car in line. The sleeping driver bolted upright with a startled yelp. Vittoria yanked open the rear door and pushed

286

Langdon inside. Then she jumped in behind him.

'Santa Maria del Popolo,' she ordered. '*Presto!*'

Looking delirious and half terrified, the driver hit the accelerator, peeling out down the street.

63

Gunther Glick had assumed control of the computer from Chinita Macri, who now stood hunched in the back of the cramped BBC van staring in confusion over Glick's shoulder.

'I told you,' Glick said, typing some more keys. 'The *British Tatler* isn't the only paper that runs stories on these guys.'

Macri peered closer. Glick was right. The BBC database showed their distinguished network as having picked up and run six stories in the past ten years on the brotherhood called the Illuminati. *Well, paint me purple*, she thought. 'Who are the journalists who ran the stories,' Macri asked.'Schlock jocks?'

'BBC doesn't hire schlock jocks.'

'They hired *you*.'

Glick scowled. 'I don't know why you're such a skeptic. The Illuminati are well documented throughout history.'

'So are witches, UFOs, and the Loch Ness Monster.'

Glick read the list of stories. 'You ever heard of a guy called Winston Churchill?'

'Rings a bell.'

'BBC did a historical a while back on Churchill's life. Staunch Catholic by the way. Did you know that in

1920 Churchill published a statement condemning the Illuminati and warning Brits of a worldwide conspiracy against morality?'

Macri was dubious. 'Where did it run? In the *British Tatler*?'

Glick smiled. '*London Herald*. February 8, 1920.'

'No way.'

'Feast your eyes.'

Macri looked closer at the clip. *London Herald, Feb. 8, 1920. I had no idea.* 'Well, Churchill was a paranoid.'

'He wasn't alone,' Glick said, reading further. 'Looks like Woodrow Wilson gave three radio broadcasts in 1921 warning of growing Illuminati control over the U.S. banking system. You want a direct quote from the radio transcript?'

'Not really.'

Glick gave her one anyway. 'He said, "There is a power so organized, so subtle, so complete, so pervasive, that none had better speak above their breath when they speak in condemnation of it."'

'I've never heard anything about this.'

'Maybe because in 1921 you were just a kid.'

'Charming.' Macri took the jab in stride. She knew her years were showing. At forty-three, her bushy black curls were streaked with gray. She was too proud for dye. Her mom, a Southern Baptist, had taught Chinita contentedness and self-respect. *When you're a black woman*, her mother said, *ain't no hiding what you are. Day you try, is the day you die. Stand tall, smile bright, and let 'em wonder what secret's making you laugh.*

'Ever heard of Cecil Rhodes?' Glick asked.

Macri looked up. 'The British financier?'

'Yeah. Founded the Rhodes Scholarships.'

'Don't tell me—'

'Illuminatus.'

'BS.'

'BBC, actually. November 16, 1984.'

'*We* wrote that Cecil Rhodes was Illuminati?'

'Sure did. And according to our network, the Rhodes Scholarships were funds set up centuries ago to recruit the world's brightest young minds into the Illuminati.'

'That's ridiculous! My uncle was a Rhodes Scholar!'

Glick winked. 'So was Bill Clinton.'

Macri was getting mad now. She had never had tolerance for shoddy, alarmist reporting. Still, she knew enough about the BBC to know that every story they ran was carefully researched and confirmed.

'Here's one you'll remember,' Glick said. 'BBC, March 5, 1998. Parliament Committee Chair, Chris Mullin, required all members of British Parliament who were Masons to declare their affiliation.'

Macri remembered it. The decree had eventually extended to include policemen and judges as well. 'Why was it again?'

Glick read. '. . . concern that secret factions within the Masons exerted considerable control over political and financial systems.'

'That's right.'

'Caused quite a bustle. The Masons in parliament were furious. Had a right to be. The vast majority turned out to be innocent men who joined the Masons for networking and charity work. They had no clue about the brotherhood's past affiliations.'

'Alleged affiliations.'

'Whatever.' Glick scanned the articles. 'Look at this stuff. Accounts tracing the Illuminati back to Galileo, the *Guerenets* of France, the *Alumbrados* of Spain. Even Karl Marx and the Russian Revolution.'

'History has a way of rewriting itself.'

'Fine, you want something current? Have a look at this. Here's an Illuminati reference from a recent *Wall Street Journal*.'

This caught Macri's ear. 'The *Journal*?'

'Guess what the most popular Internet computer game in America is right now?'

'Pin the tail on Pamela Anderson.'

'Close. It's called, *Illuminati: New World Order*.'

Macri looked over his shoulder at the blurb. '*Steve Jackson Games has a runaway hit . . . a quasi-historical adventure in which an ancient satanic brotherhood from Bavaria sets out to take over the world. You can find them on-line at . . .*' Macri looked up, feeling ill. 'What do these Illuminati guys have against Christianity?'

'Not just Christianity,' Glick said. 'Religion in general.' Glick cocked his head and grinned. 'Although from the phone call we just got, it appears they *do* have a special spot in their hearts for the Vatican.'

'Oh, come on. You don't *really* think that guy who called is who he claims to be, do you?'

'A messenger of the Illuminati? Preparing to kill four cardinals?' Glick smiled. 'I sure hope so.'

64

Langdon and Vittoria's taxi completed the one-mile sprint up the wide Via della Scrofa in just over a minute. They skidded to a stop on the south side of the

Piazza del Popolo just before eight. Not having any lire, Langdon overpaid the driver in U.S. dollars. He and Vittoria jumped out. The piazza was quiet except for the laughter of a handful of locals seated outside the popular Rosati Café – a hot spot of the Italian literati. The breeze smelled of espresso and pastry.

Langdon was still in shock over his mistake at the Pantheon. With a cursory glance at this square, however, his sixth sense was already tingling. The piazza seemed subtly filled with Illuminati significance. Not only was it laid out in a perfectly *elliptical* shape, but dead center stood a towering Egyptian obelisk – a square pillar of stone with a distinctively pyramidal tip. Spoils of Rome's imperial plundering, obelisks were scattered across Rome and referred to by symbologists as 'Lofty Pyramids' – skyward extensions of the sacred pyramidal form.

As Langdon's eyes moved up the monolith, though, his sight was suddenly drawn to something else in the background. Something even more remarkable.

'We're in the right place,' he said quietly, feeling a sudden exposed wariness. 'Have a look at that.' Langdon pointed to the imposing Porta del Popolo – the high stone archway at the far end of the piazza. The vaulted structure had been overlooking the piazza for centuries. Dead center of the archway's highest point was a symbolic engraving. 'Look familiar?'

Vittoria looked up at the huge carving. 'A shining star over a triangular pile of stones?'

Langdon shook his head. 'A source of Illumination over a pyramid.'

Vittoria turned, her eyes suddenly wide. 'Like ... the Great Seal of the United States.'

'Exactly. The Masonic symbol on the one-dollar bill.'

Vittoria took a deep breath and scanned the piazza. 'So where's this damn church?'

The Church of Santa Maria del Popolo stood out like a misplaced battleship, askew at the base of a hill on the southeast corner of the piazza. The eleventh-century stone aerie was made even more clumsy by the tower of scaffolding covering the façade.

Langdon's thoughts were a blur as they raced toward the edifice. He stared up at the church in wonder. Could a murder really be about to take place inside? He wished Olivetti would hurry. The gun felt awkward in his pocket.

The church's front stairs were *ventaglio* – a welcoming, curved fan – ironic in this case because they were blocked with scaffolding, construction equipment, and a sign warning: COSTRUZIONE. NON ENTRARE.

Langdon realized that a church closed for renovation meant total privacy for a killer. Not like the Pantheon. No fancy tricks needed here. Only to find a way in.

Vittoria slipped without hesitation between the sawhorses and headed up the staircase.

'Vittoria,' Langdon cautioned. 'If he's still in there . . .'

Vittoria did not seem to hear. She ascended the main portico to the church's sole wooden door. Langdon hurried up the stairs behind her. Before he could say a word she had grasped the handle and pulled. Langdon held his breath. The door did not budge.

'There must be another entrance,' Vittoria said.

'Probably,' Langdon said, exhaling, 'but Olivetti will be here in a minute. It's too dangerous to go in. We should cover the church from out here until—'

Vittoria turned, here eyes blazing. 'If there's another way *in*, there's another way *out*. If this guy disappears, we're *fungito*.'

Langdon knew enough Italian to know she was right.

The alley on the right side of the church was pinched and dark, with high walls on both sides. It smelled of urine – a common aroma in a city where bars outnumbered public rest rooms twenty to one.

Langdon and Vittoria hurried into the fetid dimness. They had gone about fifteen yards down when Vittoria tugged Langdon's arm and pointed.

Langdon saw it too. Up ahead was an unassuming wooden door with heavy hinges. Langdon recognized it as the standard *porta sacra* – a private entrance for clergy. Most of these entrances had gone out of use years ago as encroaching buildings and limited real estate relegated side entrances to inconvenient alleyways.

Vittoria hurried to the door. She arrived and stared down at the doorknob, apparently perplexed. Langdon arrived behind her and eyed the peculiar donut-shaped hoop hanging where the doorknob should have been.

'An annulus,' he whispered. Langdon reached out and quietly lifted the ring in his hand. He pulled the ring toward him. The fixture clicked. Vittoria shifted, looking suddenly uneasy. Quietly, Langdon twisted the ring clockwise. It spun loosely 360 degrees, not engaging. Langdon frowned and tried the other direction with the same result.

Vittoria looked down the remainder of the alley. 'You think there's another entrance?'

Langdon doubted it. Most Renaissance cathedrals

were designed as makeshift fortresses in the event a city was stormed. They had as few entrances as possible. 'If there *is* another way in,' he said, 'it's probably recessed in the rear bastion – more of an escape route than an entrance.'

Vittoria was already on the move.

Langdon followed deeper into the alley. The walls shot skyward on both sides of him. Somewhere a bell began ringing eight o'clock . . .

Robert Langdon did not hear Vittoria the first time she called to him. He had slowed at a stained-glass window covered with bars and was trying to peer inside the church.

'Robert!' Her voice was a loud whisper.

Langdon looked up. Vittoria was at the end of the alley. She was pointing around the back of the church and waving to him. Langdon jogged reluctantly toward her. At the base of the rear wall, a stone bulwark jutted out concealing a narrow grotto – a kind of compressed passageway cutting directly into the foundation of the church.

'An entrance?' Vittoria asked.

Langdon nodded. *Actually an exit, but we won't get technical.*

Vittoria knelt and peered into the tunnel. 'Let's check the door. See if it's open.'

Langdon opened his mouth to object, but Vittoria took his hand and pulled him into the opening.

'Wait,' Langdon said.

She turned impatiently toward him.

Langdon sighed. 'I'll go first.'

Vittoria looked surprised. 'More chivalry?'

'Age before beauty.'

'Was that a compliment?'

Langdon smiled and moved past her into the dark. 'Careful on the stairs.'

He inched slowly into the darkness, keeping one hand on the wall. The stone felt sharp on his fingertips. For an instant Langdon recalled the ancient myth of Daedelus, how the boy kept one hand on the wall as he moved through the Minotaur's labyrinth, knowing he was guaranteed to find the end if he never broke contact with the wall. Langdon moved forward, not entirely certain he wanted to find the end.

The tunnel narrowed slightly, and Langdon slowed his pace. He sensed Vittoria close behind him. As the wall curved left, the tunnel opened into a semicircular alcove. Oddly, there was faint light here. In the dimness Langdon saw the outline of a heavy wooden door.

'Oh oh,' he said.

'Locked?'

'It *was*.'

'*Was?*' Vittoria arrived at his side.

Langdon pointed. Lit by a shaft of light coming from within, the door hung ajar ... its hinges splintered by a wrecking bar still lodged in the wood.

They stood a moment in silence. Then, in the dark, Langdon felt Vittoria's hands on his chest, groping, sliding beneath his jacket.

'Relax, professor,' she said. 'I'm just getting the gun.'

At that moment, inside the Vatican Museums, a task force of Swiss Guards spread out in all directions. The museum was dark, and the guards wore U.S. Marine issue infrared goggles. The goggles made everything appear an eerie shade of green. Every guard wore headphones connected to an antennalike detector that he waved rhythmically in front of him – the same devices they used twice a week to sweep for electronic bugs inside the Vatican. They moved methodically, checking behind statues, inside niches, closets, under furniture. The antennae would sound if they detected even the tiniest magnetic field.

Tonight, however, they were getting no readings at all.

65

The interior of Santa Maria del Popolo was a murky cave in the dimming light. It looked more like a half-finished subway station than a cathedral. The main sanctuary was an obstacle course of torn-up flooring, brick pallets, mounds of dirt, wheelbarrows, and even a rusty backhoe. Mammoth columns rose through the floor, supporting a vaulted roof. In the air, silt drifted lazily in the muted glow of the stained glass. Langdon stood with Vittoria beneath a sprawling Pinturicchio fresco and scanned the gutted shrine.

Nothing moved. Dead silence.

Vittoria held the gun out in front of her with both hands. Langdon checked his watch: 8.04 p.m. *We're crazy to be in here*, he thought. *It's too dangerous.* Still he knew if the killer were inside, the man could leave through any door he wanted, making a one-gun outside stakeout totally fruitless. Catching him inside was the only way ... that was, if he was even still here. Langdon felt guilt-ridden over the blunder that had cost everyone their chance at the Pantheon. He was in no position to insist on precaution now; *he* was the one who had backed them into this corner.

Vittoria looked harrowed as she scanned the church. 'So,' she whispered. 'Where is this Chigi Chapel?'

Langdon gazed through the dusky ghostliness toward the back of the cathedral and studied the outer walls. Contrary to common perception, Renaissance cathedrals invariably contained *multiple* chapels, huge cathedrals like Notre Dame having dozens. Chapels were less *rooms* than they were *hollows* – semi-circular niches holding tombs around a church's perimeter wall.

Bad news, Langdon thought, seeing the four recesses on each side wall. There were eight chapels in all. Although eight was not a particularly overwhelming number, all eight openings were covered with huge sheets of clear polyurethane due to the construction, the translucent curtains apparently intended to keep dust off the tombs inside the alcoves.

'It could be any of those draped recesses,' Langdon said. 'No way to know which is the Chigi without looking inside every one. Could be a good reason to wait for Oliv—'

'Which is the secondary left apse?' she asked.

Langdon studied her, surprised by her command of architectural terminology. 'Secondary left apse?'

Vittoria pointed at the wall behind him. A decorative tile was embedded in the stone. It was engraved with the same symbol they had seen outside – a pyramid beneath a shining star. The grime-covered plaque beside it read:

COAT OF ARMS OF ALEXANDER CHIGI
WHOSE TOMB IS LOCATED IN THE
SECONDARY LEFT APSE OF THIS CATHEDRAL

Langdon nodded. *Chigi's coat of arms was a pyramid and star?* He suddenly found himself wondering if the wealthy patron Chigi had been an Illuminatus. He nodded to Vittoria. 'Nice work, Nancy Drew.'

'What?'

'Never mind. I—'

A piece of metal clattered to the floor only yards away. The clang echoed through the entire church. Langdon pulled Vittoria behind a pillar as she whipped the gun toward the sound and held it there. Silence. They waited. Again there was a sound, this time a rustling. Langdon held his breath. *I never should have let us come in here!* The sound moved closer, an intermittent scuffling, like a man with a limp. Suddenly around the base of the pillar, an object came into view.

'*Figlio di puttana!*' Vittoria cursed under her breath, jumping back. Langdon fell back with her.

Beside the pillar, dragging a half-eaten sandwich in paper, was an enormous rat. The creature paused when it saw them, staring a long moment down the barrel of Vittoria's weapon, and then, apparently unmoved, continued dragging its prize off to the recesses of the church.

'Son of a . . .' Langdon gasped, his heart racing.

Vittoria lowered the gun, quickly regaining her composure. Langdon peered around the side of the column to see a workman's lunchbox splayed on the floor, apparently knocked off a sawhorse by the resourceful rodent.

Langdon scanned the basilica for movement and whispered, 'If this guy's here, he sure as hell heard *that*. You sure you don't want to wait for Olivetti?'

'Secondary left apse,' Vittoria repeated. 'Where is it?'

Reluctantly Langdon turned and tried to get his bearings. Cathedral terminology was like stage directions – totally counterintuitive. He faced the main altar. *Stage center*. Then he pointed with his thumb backward over his shoulder.

They both turned and looked where he was pointing.

It seemed the Chigi Chapel was located in the third of four recessed alcoves to their right. The good news was that Langdon and Vittoria were on the correct *side* of the church. The bad news was that they were at the wrong *end*. They would have to traverse the length of the cathedral, passing three other chapels, each of them, like the Chigi Chapel, covered with translucent plastic shrouds.

'Wait,' Langdon said. 'I'll go first.'

'Forget it.'

'I'm the one who screwed up at the Pantheon.'

She turned. 'But I'm the one with the gun.'

In her eyes Langdon could see what she was really thinking . . . *I'm the one who lost my father. I'm the one who helped build a weapon of mass destruction. This guy's kneecaps are mine* . . .

Langdon sensed the futility and let her go. He moved beside her, cautiously, down the east side of the basilica. As they passed the first shrouded alcove, Langdon felt taut, like a contestant on some surreal game show. *I'll take curtain number three*, he thought.

The church was quiet, the thick stone walls blocking

out all hints of the outside world. As they hurried past one chapel after the other, pale humanoid forms wavered like ghosts behind the rustling plastic. *Carved marble*, Langdon told himself, hoping he was right. It was 8.06 p.m. Had the killer been punctual and slipped out before Langdon and Vittoria had entered? Or was he still here? Langdon was unsure which scenario he preferred.

They passed the second apse, ominous in the slowly darkening cathedral. Night seemed to be falling quickly now, accentuated by the musty tint of the stained-glass windows. As they pressed on, the plastic curtain beside them billowed suddenly, as if caught in a draft. Langdon wondered if someone somewhere had opened a door.

Vittoria slowed as the third niche loomed before them. She held the gun before her, motioning with her head to the stele beside the apse. Carved in the granite block were two words:

CAPELLA CHIGI

Langdon nodded. Without a sound they moved to the corner of the opening, positioning themselves behind a wide pillar. Vittoria leveled the gun around a corner at the plastic. Then she signaled for Langdon to pull back the shroud.

A good time to start praying, he thought. Reluctantly, he reached over her shoulder. As carefully as possible, he began to pull the plastic aside. It moved an inch and then crinkled loudly. They both froze. Silence. After a moment, moving in slow motion, Vittoria leaned forward and peered through the narrow slit. Langdon looked over her shoulder.

For a moment, neither one of them breathed.

'Empty,' Vittoria finally said, lowering the gun. 'We're too late.'

Langdon did not hear. He was in awe, transported for an instant to another world. In his life, he had never imagined a chapel that looked like this. Finished entirely in chestnut marble, the Chigi Chapel was breathtaking. Langdon's trained eye devoured it in gulps. It was as *earthly* a chapel as Langdon could fathom, almost as if Galileo and the Illuminati had designed it themselves.

Overhead, the domed cupola shone with a field of illuminated stars and the seven astronomical planets. Below that the twelve signs of the zodiac – pagan, earthly symbols rooted in astronomy. The zodiac was also tied directly to Earth, Air, Fire, Water ... the quadrants representing power, intellect, ardor, emotion. *Earth is for power*, Langdon recalled.

Farther down the wall, Langdon saw tributes to the Earth's four temporal seasons – *primavera, estate, autunno, invérno*. But far more incredible than any of this were the two huge structures dominating the room. Langdon stared at them in silent wonder. *It can't be*, he thought. *It just can't be!* But it was. On either side of the chapel, in perfect symmetry, were two ten-foot-high marble pyramids.

'I don't see a cardinal,' Vittoria whispered. 'Or an assassin.' She pulled aside the plastic and stepped in.

Langdon's eyes were transfixed on the pyramids. *What are pyramids doing inside a Christian chapel?* And incredibly, there was more. Dead center of each pyramid, embedded in their anterior façades, were gold medallions ... medallions like few Langdon had ever seen ... perfect *ellipses*. The burnished disks

301

glimmered in the setting sun as it sifted through the cupola. *Galileo's ellipses? Pyramids? A cupola of stars?* The room had more Illuminati significance than any room Langdon could have fabricated in his mind.

'Robert,' Vittoria blurted, her voice cracking. 'Look!'

Langdon wheeled, reality returning as his eyes dropped to where she was pointing. 'Bloody hell!' he shouted, jumping backward.

Sneering up at them from the floor was the image of a skeleton – an intricately detailed, marble mosaic depicting 'death in flight'. The skeleton was carrying a tablet portraying the same pyramid and stars they had seen outside. It was not the image, however, that had turned Langdon's blood cold. It was the fact that the mosaic was mounted on a circular stone – a *cupermento* – that had been lifted out of the floor like a manhole cover and was now sitting off to one side of a dark opening in the floor.

'Demon's hole,' Langdon gasped. He had been so taken with the ceiling he had not even seen it. Tentatively he moved toward the pit. The stench coming up was overwhelming.

Vittoria put a hand over her mouth. '*Che puzza.*'

'Effluvium,' Langdon said. 'Vapors from decaying bone.' He breathed through his sleeve as he leaned out over the hole, peering down. Blackness. 'I can't see a thing.'

'You think anybody's down there?'

'No way to know.'

Vittoria motioned to the far side of the hole where a rotting, wooden ladder descended into the depths.

Langdon shook his head. 'Like hell.'

'Maybe there's a flashlight outside in those tools.'

She sounded eager for an excuse to escape the smell. 'I'll look.'

'Careful!' Langdon warned. 'We don't know for sure that the Hassassin—'

But Vittoria was already gone.

One strong-willed woman, Langdon thought.

As he turned back to the pit, he felt light-headed from the fumes. Holding his breath, he dropped his head below the rim and peered deep into the darkness. Slowly, as his eyes adjusted, he began to see faint shapes below. The pit appeared to open into a small chamber. *Demon's hole.* He wondered how many generations of Chigis had been unceremoniously dumped in. Langdon closed his eyes and waited, forcing his pupils to dilate so he could see better in the dark. When he opened his eyes again, a pale muted figure hovered below in the darkness. Langdon shivered but fought instinct to pull out. *Am I seeing things? Is that a body?* The figure faded. Langdon closed his eyes again and waited, longer this time, so his eyes would pick up the faintest light.

Dizziness started to set in, and his thoughts wandered in the blackness. *Just a few more seconds.* He wasn't sure if it was breathing the fumes or holding his head at a low inclination, but Langdon was definitely starting to feel squeamish. When he finally opened his eyes again, the image before him was totally inexplicable.

He was now staring at a crypt bathed in an eerie bluish light. A faint hissing sound reverberated in his ears. Light flickered on the steep walls of the shaft. Suddenly, a long shadow materialized over him. Startled, Langdon scrambled up.

'Look out!' someone exclaimed behind him.

Before Langdon could turn, he felt a sharp pain on the back of his neck. He spun to see Vittoria twisting a lit blowtorch away from him, the hissing flame throwing blue light around the chapel.

Langdon grabbed his neck. 'What the hell are you doing?'

'I was giving you some light,' she said. 'You backed right into me.'

Langdon glared at the portable blowtorch in her hand.

'Best I could do,' she said. 'No flashlights.'

Langdon rubbed his neck. 'I didn't hear you come in.'

Vittoria handed him the torch, wincing again at the stench of the crypt. 'You think those fumes are combustible?'

'Let's hope not.'

He took the torch and moved slowly toward the hole. Cautiously, he advanced to the rim and pointed the flame down into the hole, lighting the side wall. As he directed the light, his eyes traced the outline of the wall downward. The crypt was circular and about twenty feet across. Thirty feet down, the glow found the floor. The ground was dark and mottled. Earthy. Then Langdon saw the body.

His instinct was to recoil. 'He's here,' Langdon said, forcing himself not to turn away. The figure was a pallid outline against the earthen floor. 'I think he's been stripped naked.' Langdon flashed on the nude corpse.

'Is it one of the cardinals?'

Langdon had no idea, but he couldn't imagine who the hell else it would be. He stared down at the pale blob. Unmoving. Lifeless. *And yet* ... Langdon hesitated. There was something very strange about the way the figure was positioned. He seemed to be . . .

Langdon called out. 'Hello?'

'You think he's alive?'

There was no response from below.

'He's not moving,' Langdon said. 'But he looks . . .' *No, impossible.*

'He looks *what*?' Vittoria was peering over the edge now too.

Langdon squinted into the darkness. 'He looks like he's standing up.'

Vittoria held her breath and lowered her face over the edge for a better look. After a moment, she pulled back. 'You're right. He's standing up! Maybe he's alive and needs help!' She called into the hole. 'Hello?! *Mi puó sentire?*'

There was no echo off the mossy interior. Only silence.

Vittoria headed for the rickety ladder. 'I'm going down.'

Langdon caught her arm. 'No. It's dangerous. I'll go.'

This time Vittoria didn't argue.

66

Chinita Macri was mad. She sat in the passenger's seat of the BBC van as it idled at a corner on Via Tomacelli. Gunther Glick was checking his map of Rome, apparently lost. As she had feared, his mystery caller had phoned back, this time with information.

'Piazza del Popolo,' Glick insisted. 'That's what we're looking for. There's a church there. And inside is proof.'

'Proof.' Chinita stopped polishing the lens in her hand and turned to him. 'Proof that a cardinal has been murdered?'

'That's what he said.'

'You believe everything you hear?' Chinita wished, as she often did, that *she* was the one in charge. Videographers, however, were at the whim of the crazy reporters for whom they shot footage. If Gunther Glick wanted to follow a feeble phone tip, Macri was his dog on a leash.

She looked at him, sitting there in the driver's seat, his jaw set intently. The man's parents, she decided, must have been frustrated comedians to have given him a name like Gunther Glick. No wonder the guy felt like he had something to prove. Nonetheless, despite his unfortunate appellative and annoying eagerness to make a mark, Glick was sweet . . . charming in a pasty, *Briddish*, unstrung sort of way. Like Hugh Grant on lithium.

'Shouldn't we be back at St Peter's?' Macri said as patiently as possible. 'We can check this mystery church out later. Conclave started an hour ago. What if the cardinals come to a decision while we're gone?'

Glick did not seem to hear. 'I think we go to the right, here.' He tilted the map and studied it again. 'Yes, if I take a right . . . and then an immediate left.' He began to pull out onto the narrow street before them.

'Look out!' Macri yelled. She was a video technician, and her eyes were sharp. Fortunately, Glick was pretty fast too. He slammed on the brakes and

306

avoided entering the intersection just as a line of four Alfa Romeos appeared out of nowhere and tore by in a blur. Once past, the cars skidded, decelerating, and cut sharply left one block ahead, taking the exact route Glick had intended to take.

'Maniacs!' Macri shouted.

Glick looked shaken. 'Did you see that?'

'Yeah, I saw that! They almost killed us!'

'No, I mean the cars,' Glick said, his voice suddenly excited. 'They were all the same.'

'So they were maniacs with no imagination.'

'The cars were also full.'

'So what?'

'Four identical cars, *all* with four passengers?'

'You ever heard of carpooling?'

'In Italy?' Glick checked the intersection. 'They haven't even heard of unleaded gas.' He hit the accelerator and peeled out after the cars.

Macri was thrown back in her seat. 'What the hell are you doing?'

Glick accelerated down the street and hung a left after the Alfa Romeos. 'Something tells me you and I are not the only ones going to church right now.'

67

The descent was slow.

Langdon dropped rung by rung down the creaking ladder . . . deeper and deeper beneath the floor of the Chigi Chapel. *Into the Demon's hole*, he thought. He was facing the side wall, his back to the chamber, and he wondered how many more dark, cramped spaces one day could provide. The ladder groaned with every step, and the pungent smell of rotting flesh and dampness was almost asphyxiating. Langdon wondered where the hell Olivetti was.

Vittoria's outline was still visible above, holding the blowtorch inside the hole, lighting Langdon's way. As he lowered himself deeper into the darkness, the bluish glow from above got fainter. The only thing that got stronger was the stench.

Twelve rungs down, it happened. Langdon's foot hit a spot that was slippery with decay, and he faltered. Lunging forward, he caught the ladder with his forearms to avoid plummeting to the bottom. Cursing the bruises now throbbing on his arms, he dragged his body back onto the ladder and began his descent again.

Three rungs deeper, he almost fell again, but this time it was not a rung that caused the mishap. It was a bolt of fear. He had descended past a hollowed niche in the wall before him and suddenly found himself face to face with a collection of skulls. As he caught his breath and looked around him, he realized the wall at this level was honeycombed with shelflike openings – burial niches – all filled with skeletons. In the phosphorescent light, it made for an eerie collection of empty sockets and decaying rib cages flickering around him.

Skeletons by firelight, he grimaced wryly, realizing he had quite coincidentally endured a similar evening just last month. *An evening of bones and flames.* The New York Museum of Archeology's candlelight benefit dinner – salmon flambé in the shadow of a brontosaurus skeleton. He had attended at the invitation of Rebecca Strauss – one-time fashion model now art critic from the *Times*, a whirlwind of black velvet, cigarettes, and not-so-subtly enhanced breasts. She'd called him twice since. Langdon had not returned her calls. *Most ungentlemanly*, he chided, wondering how long Rebecca Strauss would last in a stink-pit like this.

Langdon was relieved to feel the final rung give way to the spongy earth at the bottom. The ground beneath his shoes felt damp. Assuring himself the walls were not going to close in on him, he turned into the crypt. It was circular, about twenty feet across. Breathing through his sleeve again, Langdon turned his eyes to the body. In the gloom, the image was hazy. A white, fleshy outline. Facing the other direction. Motionless. Silent.

Advancing through the murkiness of the crypt, Langdon tried to make sense of what he was looking at. The man had his back to Langdon, and Langdon could not see his face, but he *did* indeed seem to be standing.

'Hello?' Langdon choked through his sleeve. Nothing. As he drew nearer, he realized the man was very short. *Too short . . .*

'What's happening?' Vittoria called from above, shifting the light.

Langdon did not answer. He was now close enough to see it all. With a tremor of repulsion, he understood. The chamber seemed to contract around him. Emerging like a demon from the earthen floor was an old man . . . or at least half of him. He was buried up to his waist in the earth. Standing upright with half of him below ground. Stripped naked. His hands tied behind his back with a red cardinal's sash. He was propped limply upward, spine arched backward like some sort of hideous punching bag. The man's head lay backward, eyes toward the heavens as if pleading for help from God himself.

'Is he dead?' Vittoria called.

Langdon moved toward the body. *I hope so, for his sake.* As he drew to within a few feet, he looked down at the upturned eyes. They bulged outward, blue and bloodshot. Langdon leaned down to listen for breath but immediately recoiled. 'For Christ's sake!'

'What!'

Langdon almost gagged. 'He's dead all right. I just saw the cause of death.' The sight was gruesome. The man's mouth had been jammed open and packed solid with dirt. 'Somebody stuffed a fistful of dirt down his throat. He suffocated.'

'Dirt?' Vittoria said. 'As in . . . *earth*?'

Langdon did a double take. *Earth.* He had almost forgotten. *The brands. Earth, Air, Fire, Water.* The killer had threatened to brand each victim with one of the ancient elements of science. The first element was *Earth. From Santi's earthly tomb.* Dizzy from the fumes, Langdon circled to the front of the body. As he did, the symbologist within him loudly reasserted the artistic challenge of creating the mythical ambigram. *Earth? How?* And yet, an instant later, it was before him. Centuries of Illuminati legend whirled in his mind. The marking on the cardinal's chest was charred and oozing. The flesh was seared black. *La lingua pura . . .*

Langdon stared at the brand as the room began to spin.

'Earth,' he whispered, tilting his head to see the symbol upside down. 'Earth.'

Then, in a wave of horror, he had one final cognition. *There are three more.*

68

Despite the soft glow of candlelight in the Sistine Chapel, Cardinal Mortati was on edge. Conclave had officially begun. And it had begun in a most in-auspicious fashion.

Half an hour ago, at the appointed hour, Camerlengo Carlo Ventresca had entered the chapel. He walked to the front altar and gave opening prayer. Then, he unfolded his hands and spoke to them in a tone as direct as anything Mortati had ever heard from the altar of the Sistine.

'You are well aware,' the camerlengo said, 'that our four *preferiti* are not present in conclave at this moment. I ask, in the name of his late Holiness, that you proceed as you must ... with faith and purpose. May you have only God before your eyes.' Then he turned to go.

'But,' one cardinal blurted out, 'where *are* they?'

The camerlengo paused. 'That I cannot honestly say.'

'When will they return?'

'That I cannot honestly say.'

'Are they okay?'

'That I cannot honestly say.'

'*Will* they return?'

There was a long pause.

'Have faith,' the camerlengo said. Then he walked out of the room.

The doors to the Sistine Chapel had been sealed, as was the custom, with two heavy chains on the outside. Four Swiss Guards stood watch in the hallway beyond. Mortati knew the only way the doors could be opened now, prior to electing a Pope, was if someone inside fell deathly ill, or if the *preferiti* arrived. Mortati prayed it would be the latter, although from the knot in his stomach he was not so sure.

Proceed as we must, Mortati decided, taking his lead from the resolve in the camerlengo's voice. So he had called for a vote. What else could he do?

It had taken thirty minutes to complete the preparatory rituals leading up to this first vote. Mortati had waited patiently at the main altar as each cardinal, in order of seniority, had approached and performed the specific balloting procedure.

Now, at last, the final cardinal had arrived at the altar and was kneeling before him.

'I call as my witness,' the cardinal declared, exactly as those before him, 'Christ the Lord, who will be my judge that my vote is given to the one who before God I think should be elected.'

312

The cardinal stood up. He held his ballot high over his head for everyone to see. Then he lowered the ballot to the altar, where a plate sat atop a large chalice. He placed the ballot on the plate. Next he picked up the plate and used it to drop the ballot into the chalice. Use of the plate was to ensure no one secretly dropped multiple ballots.

After he had submitted his ballot, he replaced the plate over the chalice, bowed to the cross, and returned to his seat.

The final ballot had been cast.

Now it was time for Mortati to go to work.

Leaving the plate on top of the chalice, Mortati shook the ballots to mix them. Then he removed the plate and extracted a ballot at random. He unfolded it. The ballot was exactly two inches wide. He read aloud for everyone to hear.

'Eligo in summum pontificem . . .' he declared, reading the text that was embossed at the top of every ballot. *I elect as Supreme Pontiff . . .* Then he announced the nominee's name that had been written beneath it. After he read the name, he raised a threaded needle and pierced the ballot through the word *Eligo*, carefully sliding the ballot onto the thread. Then he made note of the vote in a logbook.

Next, he repeated the entire procedure. He chose a ballot from the chalice, read it aloud, threaded it onto the line, and made note in his log. Almost immediately, Mortati sensed this first vote would be failed. No consensus. After only seven ballots, already seven different cardinals had been named. As was normal, the handwriting on each ballot was disguised by block printing or flamboyant script. The concealment was ironic in this case because the cardinals were obviously submitting votes for themselves. This apparent conceit, Mortati knew, had nothing to do with self-centered ambition. It was a holding pattern. A defensive maneuver. A stall tactic to ensure no cardinal received enough votes to win ... and another vote would be forced.

The cardinals were waiting for their *preferiti* ...

When the last of the ballots had been tallied, Mortati declared the vote 'failed'.

He took the thread carrying all the ballots and tied the ends together to create a ring. Then he laid the ring of ballots on a silver tray. He added the proper chemicals and carried the tray to a small chimney behind him. Here he lit the ballots. As the ballots burned, the chemicals he'd added created black smoke. The smoke flowed up a pipe to a hole in the roof where it rose above the chapel for all to see. Cardinal Mortati had just sent his first communication to the outside world.

One balloting. No Pope.

69

Nearly asphyxiated by fumes, Langdon struggled up the ladder toward the light at the top of the pit. Above him he heard voices, but nothing making sense. His head was spinning with images of the branded cardinal.

Earth ... Earth ...

As he pushed upward, his vision narrowed and he

feared consciousness would slip away. Two rungs from the top, his balance faltered. He lunged upward trying to find the lip, but it was too far. He lost his grip on the ladder and almost tumbled backward into the dark. There was a sharp pain under his arms, and suddenly Langdon was airborne, legs swinging wildly out over the chasm.

The strong hands of two Swiss Guards hooked him under the armpits and dragged him skyward. A moment later Langdon's head emerged from the Demon's hole, choking and gasping for air. The guards dragged him over the lip of the opening, across the floor, and laid him down, back against the cold marble floor.

For a moment, Langdon was unsure where he was. Overhead he saw stars .. orbiting planets. Hazy figures raced past him. People were shouting. He tried to sit up. He was lying at the base of a stone pyramid. The familiar bite of an angry tongue echoed inside the chapel, and then Langdon knew.

Olivetti was screaming at Vittoria. 'Why the hell didn't you figure that out in the first place?'

Vittoria was trying the explain the situation.

Olivetti cut her off midsentence and turned to bark orders to his men. 'Get that body out of there! Search the rest of the building!'

Langdon tried to sit up. The Chigi Chapel was packed with Swiss Guards. The plastic curtain over the chapel opening had been torn off the entryway, and fresh air filled Langdon's lungs. As his senses slowly returned, Langdon saw Vittoria coming toward him. She knelt down, her face like an angel.

'You okay?' Vittoria took his arm and felt his pulse. Her hands were tender on his skin.

'Thanks.' Langdon sat up fully. 'Olivetti's mad.'

Vittoria nodded. 'He has a right to be. We blew it.'

'You mean *I* blew it.'

'So redeem yourself. Get him next time.'

Next time? Langdon thought it was a cruel comment. *There is no next time! We missed our shot!*

Vittoria checked Langdon's watch. 'Mickey says we've got forty minutes. Get your head together and help me find the next marker.'

'I told you, Vittoria, the sculptures are gone. The Path of Illumination is—' Langdon halted.

Vittoria smiled softly.

Suddenly Langdon was staggering to his feet. He turned dizzying circles, staring at the artwork around him. *Pyramids, stars, planets, ellipses.* Suddenly everything came back. *This is the first altar of science! Not the Pantheon!* It dawned on him now how perfectly Illuminati the chapel was, far more subtle and selective than the world famous Pantheon. The Chigi was an out of the way alcove, a literal hole-in-the-wall, a tribute to a great patron of science, decorated with earthly symbology. *Perfect.*

Langdon steadied himself against the wall and gazed up at the enormous pyramid sculptures. Vittoria was dead right. If *this* chapel was the first altar of science, it might still contain the Illuminati sculpture that served as the first marker. Langdon felt an electrifying rush of hope to realize there was still a chance. If the marker were indeed here, and they could follow it to the next altar of science, they might have another chance to catch the killer.

Vittoria moved closer. 'I found out who the unknown Illuminati sculptor was.'

Langdon's head whipped around. 'You *what*?'

316

'Now we just need to figure out which sculpture in here is the—'

'Wait a minute! You *know* who the Illuminati sculptor was?' He had spent years trying to find that information.

Vittoria smiled. 'It was Bernini.' She paused. '*The* Bernini.'

Langdon immediately knew she was mistaken. Bernini was an impossibility. Gianlorenzo Bernini was the second most famous sculptor of all time, his fame eclipsed only by Michelangelo himself. During the 1600s Bernini created more sculptures than any other artist. Unfortunately, the man they were looking for was supposedly an unknown, a nobody.

Vittoria frowned. 'You don't look excited.'

'Bernini is impossible.'

'Why? Bernini was a contemporary of Galileo. He was a brilliant sculptor.'

'He was a very famous man and a Catholic.'

'Yes,' Vittoria said. 'Exactly like Galileo.'

'No,' Langdon argued. '*Nothing* like Galileo. Galileo was a thorn in the Vatican's side. Bernini was the Vatican's wonder boy. The church *loved* Bernini. He was elected the Vatican's overall artistic authority. He practically lived inside Vatican City his entire life!'

'A perfect cover. Illuminati infiltration.'

Langdon felt flustered. 'Vittoria, the Illuminati members referred to their secret artist as *il maestro ignoto* – the unknown master.'

'Yes, unknown to *them*. Think of the secrecy of the Masons – only the upper-echelon members knew the whole truth. Galileo could have kept Bernini's true identity secret from most members . . . for Bernini's own safety. That way, the Vatican would never find out.'

Langdon was unconvinced but had to admit Vittoria's logic made strange sense. The Illuminati were famous for keeping secret information compartmentalized, only revealing the truth to upper-level members. It was the cornerstone of their ability to stay secret . . . very few knew the whole story.

'And Bernini's affiliation with the Illuminati,' Vittoria added with a smile, 'explains why he designed those two pyramids.'

Langdon turned to the huge sculpted pyramids and shook his head. 'Bernini was a *religious* sculptor. There's no way he carved those pyramids.'

Vittoria shrugged. 'Tell that to the sign behind you.'

Langdon turned to the plaque:

ART OF THE CHIGI CHAPEL
While the architecture is Raphael's,
all interior adornments are those of Gianlorenzo Bernini.

Langdon read the plaque twice, and still he was not convinced. Gianlorenzo Bernini was celebrated for his intricate, holy sculptures of the Virgin Mary, angels, prophets, Popes. What was he doing carving *pyramids*?

Langdon looked up at the towering monuments and felt totally disoriented. Two pyramids, each with a shining, elliptical medallion. They were about as un-Christian as sculpture could get. The pyramids, the stars above, the signs of the Zodiac. *All interior adornments are those of Gianlorenzo Bernini.* If that were true, Langdon realized, it meant Vittoria *had* to be right. By default, Bernini was the Illuminati's unknown master; nobody else had contributed artwork to this chapel! The implications came almost too fast for Langdon to process.

Bernini was an Illuminatus.

Bernini designed the Illuminati ambigrams.

Bernini laid out the path of Illumination.

Langdon could barely speak. Could it be that here in this tiny Chigi Chapel, the world-renowned Bernini had placed a sculpture that pointed across Rome toward the next altar of science?

'Bernini,' he said. 'I never would have guessed.'

'Who other than a famous Vatican artist would have had the clout to put his artwork in specific Catholic chapels around Rome and create the Path of Illumination? Certainly not an unknown.'

Langdon considered it. He looked at the pyramids, wondering if one of them could somehow be the marker. *Maybe both of them?* 'The pyramids face opposite directions,' Langdon said, not sure what to make of them. 'They are also identical, so I don't know which . . .'

'I don't think the pyramids are what we're looking for.'

'But they're the only sculptures here.'

Vittoria cut him off by pointing toward Olivetti and some of his guards who were gathered near the demon's hole.

Langdon followed the line of her hand to the far wall. At first he saw nothing. Then someone moved and he caught a glimpse. White marble. An arm. A torso. And then a sculpted face. Partially hidden in its niche. Two life-size human figures intertwined. Langdon's pulse accelerated. He had been so taken with the pyramids and demon's hole, he had not even seen this sculpture. He moved across the room, through the crowd. As he drew near, Langdon recognized the work was pure Bernini – the intensity of the artistic composition, the intricate faces and flowing clothing, all from the purest white marble Vatican money could buy. It was not until he was almost directly in front of it that Langdon recognized the sculpture itself. He stared up at the two faces and gasped.

'Who are they?' Vittoria urged, arriving behind him.

Langdon stood astonished. '*Habakkuk and the Angel*,' he said, his voice almost inaudible. The piece was a fairly well-known Bernini work that was included in some art history texts. Langdon had forgotten it was here.

'Habakkuk?'

'Yes. The prophet who predicted the annihilation of the earth.'

Vittoria looked uneasy. 'You think this is the marker?'

Langdon nodded in amazement. Never in his life had he been so sure of anything. This was the first Illuminati marker. No doubt. Although Langdon had fully expected the sculpture to somehow 'point' to the next altar of science, he did not expect it to be *literal*. Both the angel and Habakkuk had their arms outstretched and were pointing into the distance.

Langdon found himself suddenly smiling. 'Not too subtle, is it?'

Vittoria looked excited but confused. 'I see them pointing, but they are contradicting each other. The angel is pointing one way, and the prophet the other.'

Langdon chuckled. It was true. Although both figures were pointing into the distance, they were pointing in totally opposite directions. Langdon, however, had already solved that problem. With a burst of energy he headed for the door.

'Where are you going?' Vittoria called.

'Outside the building!' Langdon's legs felt light again as he ran toward the door. 'I need to see what direction that sculpture is pointing!'

'Wait! How do you know *which* finger to follow?'

'The poem,' he called over his shoulder. 'The last line!'

'"Let angels guide you on your lofty quest?"' She gazed upward at the outstretched finger of the angel. Her eyes misted unexpectedly. 'Well I'll be damned!'

70

Gunther Glick and Chinita Macri sat parked in the BBC van in the shadows at the far end of Piazza del Popolo. They had arrived shortly after the four Alfa Romeos, just in time to witness an inconceivable chain of events. Chinita still had no idea what it all meant, but she'd made sure the camera was rolling.

As soon as they'd arrived, Chinita and Glick had seen a veritable army of young men pour out of the Alfa Romeos and surround the church. Some had weapons drawn. One of them, a stiff older man, led a team up the front steps of the church. The soldiers drew guns and blew the locks off the front doors. Macri heard nothing and figured they must have had silencers. Then the soldiers entered.

Chinita had recommended they sit tight and film from the shadows. After all, guns were guns, and they had a clear view of the action from the van. Glick had not argued. Now, across the piazza, men moved in and out of the church. They yelled to each other. Chinita adjusted her camera to follow a team as they searched the surrounding area. All of them, though dressed in civilian clothes, seemed to move with military precision. 'Who do you think they are?' she asked.

'Hell if I know.' Glick looked riveted. 'You getting all this?'

'Every frame.'

Glick sounded smug. 'Still think we should go back to Pope-Watch?'

Chinita wasn't sure what to say. There was obviously something going on here, but she had been in journalism long enough to know that there was often a very dull explanation for interesting events. 'This could be nothing,' she said. 'These guys could have gotten the same tip you got and are just checking it out. Could be a false alarm.'

Glick grabbed her arm. 'Over there! Focus.' He pointed back to the church.

Chinita swung the camera back to the top of the stairs. 'Hello there,' she said, training on the man now emerging from the church.

'Who's the dapper?'

Chinita moved in for a close-up. 'Haven't seen him before.' She tightened in on the man's face and smiled. 'But I wouldn't mind seeing him again.'

Robert Langdon dashed down the stairs outside the church and into the middle of the piazza. It was getting dark now, the springtime sun setting late in southern Rome. The sun had dropped below the surrounding buildings, and shadows streaked the square.

'Okay, Bernini,' he said aloud to himself. 'Where the hell is your angel pointing?'

He turned and examined the orientation of the church from which he had just come. He pictured the Chigi Chapel inside, and the sculpture of the angel inside that. Without hesitation he turned due west, into the glow of the impending sunset. Time was evaporating.

'Southwest,' he said, scowling at the shops and apartments blocking his view. 'The next marker is out there.'

Racking his brain, Langdon pictured page after page of Italian art history. Although very familiar with Bernini's work, Langdon knew the sculptor had been far too prolific for any nonspecialist to know all of it. Still, considering the relative fame of the first marker – *Habakkuk and the Angel* – Langdon hoped the second marker was a work he might know from memory.

Earth, Air, Fire, Water, he thought. *Earth* they had found – inside the Chapel of the Earth – Habakkuk, the prophet who predicted the earth's annihilation.

Air is next. Langdon urged himself to think. *A Bernini sculpture that has something to do with Air!* He was drawing a total blank. Still he felt energized. *I'm on the path of Illumination! It is still intact!*

Looking southwest, Langdon strained to see a spire or cathedral tower jutting up over the obstacles. He saw nothing. He needed a map. If they could figure out what churches were southwest of here, maybe one of them would spark Langdon's memory. *Air,* he pressed. *Air. Bernini. Sculpture. Air. Think!*

Langdon turned and headed back up the cathedral stairs. He was met beneath the scaffolding by Vittoria and Olivetti.

'Southwest,' Langdon said, panting. 'The next church is southwest of here.'

Olivetti's whisper was cold. 'You sure this time?'

Langdon didn't bite. 'We need a map. One that shows all the churches in Rome.'

The commander studied him a moment, his expression never changing.

Langdon checked his watch. 'We only have half an hour.'

Olivetti moved past Langdon down the stairs toward his car, parked directly in front of the cathedral. Langdon hoped he was going for a map.

Vittoria looked excited. 'So the angel's pointing southwest? No idea which churches are southwest?'

'I can't see past the damn buildings.' Langdon turned and faced the square again. 'And I don't know Rome's churches well enou—' He stopped.

Vittoria looked startled. 'What?'

Langdon looked out at the piazza again. Having ascended the church stairs, he was now higher, and his view was better. He still couldn't see anything, but he realized he was moving in the right direction. His eyes climbed the tower of rickety scaffolding above him. It rose six stories, almost to the top of the church's rose window, far higher than the other buildings in the square. He knew in an instant where he was headed.

Across the square, Chinita Macri and Gunther Glick sat glued to the windshield of the BBC van.

'You getting this?' Gunther asked.

Macri tightened her shot on the man now climbing the scaffolding. 'He's a little well dressed to be playing Spiderman if you ask me.'

'And who's Ms Spidey?'

Chinita glanced at the attractive woman beneath the scaffolding. 'Bet you'd like to find out.'

'Think I should call editorial?'

'Not yet. Let's watch. Better to have something in the can before we admit we abandoned conclave.'

'You think somebody really killed one of the old farts in there?'

Chinita clucked. 'You're *definitely* going to hell.'

'And I'll be taking the Pulitzer with me.'

71

The scaffolding seemed less stable the higher Langdon climbed. His view of Rome, however, got better with every step. He continued upward.

He was breathing harder than he expected when he reached the upper tier. He pulled himself onto the last platform, brushed off the plaster, and stood up. The height did not bother him at all. In fact, it was invigorating.

The view was staggering. Like an ocean on fire, the red-tiled rooftops of Rome spread out before him, glowing in the scarlet sunset. From that spot, for the first time in his life, Langdon saw beyond the pollution and traffic of Rome to its ancient roots – *Città di Dio* – The city of God.

Squinting into the sunset, Langdon scanned the rooftops for a church steeple or bell tower. But as he looked farther and farther toward the horizon, he saw nothing. *There are hundreds of churches in Rome*, he thought. *There must be one southwest of here! If the church is even visible*, he reminded himself. *Hell, if the church is even still standing!*

Forcing his eyes to trace the line slowly, he attempted the search again. He knew, of course, that not all churches would have visible spires, especially smaller, out-of-the-way sanctuaries. Not to mention, Rome had changed dramatically since the 1600s when churches were by law the tallest buildings allowed. Now, as Langdon looked out, he saw apartment buildings, high-rises, TV towers.

For the second time, Langdon's eye reached the horizon without seeing anything. Not one single spire. In the distance, on the very edge of Rome, Michelangelo's massive dome blotted the setting sun. St Peter's Basilica. Vatican City. Langdon found himself wondering how the cardinals were faring, and if the Swiss Guards' search had turned up the antimatter. Something told him it hadn't . . . and wouldn't.

The poem was rattling through his head again. He considered it, carefully, line by line. *From Santi's earthly tomb with demon's hole.* They had found Santi's tomb. *'Cross Rome the mystic elements unfold.* The mystic elements were Earth, Air, Fire, Water. *The path of light is laid, the sacred test.* The path of Illumination formed by Bernini's sculptures. *Let angels guide you on your lofty quest.*

The angel was pointing southwest . . .

'Front stairs!' Glick exclaimed, pointing wildly through the windshield of the BBC van. 'Something's going on!'

Macri dropped her shot back down to the main entrance. Something was definitely going on. At the bottom of the stairs, the military-looking man had pulled one of the Alfa Romeos close to the stairs and opened the trunk. Now he was scanning the square as

326

if checking for onlookers. For a moment, Macri thought the man had spotted them, but his eyes kept moving. Apparently satisfied, he pulled out a walkie-talkie and spoke into it.

Almost instantly, it seemed an army emerged from the church. Like an American football team breaking from a huddle, the soldiers formed a straight line across the top of the stairs. Moving like a human wall, they began to descend. Behind them, almost entirely hidden by the wall, four soldiers seemed to be carrying something. Something heavy. Awkward.

Glick leaned forward on the dashboard. 'Are they stealing something from the church?'

Chinita tightened her shot even more, using the telephoto to probe the wall of men, looking for an opening. *One split second*, she willed. *A single frame. That's all I need.* But the men moved as one. *Come on!* Macri stayed with them, and it paid off. When the soldiers tried to lift the object into the trunk, Macri found her opening. Ironically, it was the older man who faltered. Only for an instant, but long enough. Macri had her frame. Actually, it was more like ten frames.

'Call editorial,' Chinita said. 'We've got a dead body.'

Far away, at CERN, Maximilian Kohler maneuvered his wheelchair into Leonardo Vetra's study. With mechanical efficiency, he began sifting through Vetra's files. Not finding what he was after, Kohler moved to Vetra's bedroom. The top drawer of his bedside table was locked. Kohler pried it open with a knife from the kitchen.

Inside Kohler found exactly what he was looking for.

Langdon swung off the scaffolding and dropped back to the ground. He brushed the plaster dust from his clothes. Vittoria was there to greet him.

'No luck?' she said.

He shook his head.

'They put the cardinal in the trunk.'

Langdon looked over to the parked car where Olivetti and a group of soldiers now had a map spread out on the hood. 'Are they looking southwest?'

She nodded. 'No churches. From here the first one you hit is St Peter's.'

Langdon grunted. At least they were in agreement. He moved toward Olivetti. The soldiers parted to let him through.

Olivetti looked up. 'Nothing. But this doesn't show every last church. Just the big ones. About fifty of them.'

'Where are we?' Langdon asked.

Olivetti pointed to Piazza del Popolo and traced a straight line exactly southwest. The line missed, by a substantial margin, the cluster of black squares indicating Rome's major churches. Unfortunately, Rome's major churches were also Rome's older churches ... those that would have been around in the 1600s.

'I've got some decisions to make,' Olivetti said. 'Are you *certain* of the direction?'

Langdon pictured the angel's outstretched finger, the urgency rising in him again. 'Yes, sir. Positive.'

Olivetti shrugged and traced the straight line again. The path intersected the Queen Margherita Bridge, Via Cola di Riezo, and passed through Piazza del Risorgimento, hitting no churches at all until it dead-ended abruptly at the center of St Peter's Square.

'What's wrong with St Peter's?' one of the soldiers said. He had a deep scar under his left eye. 'It's a church.'

Langdon shook his head. 'Needs to be a public place. Hardly seems public at the moment.'

'But the line goes through St Peter's *Square*,' Vittoria added, looking over Langdon's shoulder. 'The square is public.'

Langdon had already considered it. 'No statues, though.'

'Isn't there a monolith in the middle?'

She was right. There was an Egyptian monolith in St Peter's Square. Langdon looked out at the monolith in the piazza in front of them. *The lofty pyramid*. An odd coincidence, he thought. He shook it off. 'The Vatican's monolith is not by Bernini. It was brought in by Caligula. And it has nothing to do with *Air*.' There was another problem as well. 'Besides, the poem says the elements are spread across *Rome*. St Peter's Square is in Vatican City. Not Rome.'

'Depends who you ask,' a guard interjected.

Langdon looked up. 'What?'

'Always a bone of contention. Most maps show St Peter's Square as part of Vatican City, but because it's *outside* the walled city, Roman officials for centuries have claimed it as part of Rome.'

'You're kidding,' Langdon said. He had never known that.

'I only mention it,' the guard continued, 'because Commander Olivetti and Ms Vetra were asking about a sculpture that had to do with Air.'

Langdon was wide-eyed. 'And you know of one in St Peter's Square?'

'Not exactly. It's not really a sculpture. Probably not relevant.'

'Let's hear it,' Olivetti pressed.

The guard shrugged. 'The only reason I know about it is because I'm usually on piazza duty. I know every corner of St Peter's Square.'

'The sculpture,' Langdon urged. 'What does it look like?' Langdon was starting to wonder if the Illuminati could really have been gutsy enough to position their second marker right outside St Peter's Church.

'I patrol past it every day,' the guard said. 'It's in the center, directly where that line is pointing. That's what made me think of it. As I said, it's not really a sculpture. It's more of a . . . block.'

Olivetti looked mad. 'A block?'

'Yes, sir. A marble block embedded in the square. At the base of the monolith. But the block is not a rectangle. It's an ellipse. And the block is carved with the image of a billowing gust of wind.' He paused. '*Air*, I suppose, if you wanted to get scientific about it.'

Langdon stared at the young soldier in amazement. 'A relief!' he exclaimed suddenly.

Everyone looked at him.

'*Relief*,' Langdon said, 'is the other half of sculpture!' *Sculpture is the art of shaping figures in the round and also in relief.* He had written the definition on chalkboards for years. Reliefs were essentially two-dimensional sculptures, like Abraham Lincoln's profile on the penny. Bernini's Chigi Chapel medallions were another perfect example.

'*Bassorelievo?*' the guard asked, using the Italian art term.

'Yes! *Bas-relief!*' Langdon rapped his knuckles on the hood. 'I wasn't thinking in those terms! That tile you're talking about in St Peter's Square is called the *West Ponente* – the West Wind. It's also known as *Respiro di Dio.*'

'Breath of God?'

'Yes! *Air!* And it was carved and put there by the original architect!'

Vittoria looked confused. 'But I thought Michelangelo designed St Peter's.'

'Yes, the *basilica!*' Langdon exclaimed, triumph in his voice. 'But St Peter's *Square* was designed by Bernini!'

As the caravan of Alfa Romeos tore out of Piazza del Popolo, everyone was in too much of a hurry to notice the BBC van pulling out behind them.

73

Gunther Glick floored the BBC van's accelerator and swerved through traffic as he tailed the four speeding Alfa Romeos across the Tiber River on Ponte Margherita. Normally Glick would have made an effort to maintain an inconspicuous distance, but today he could barely keep up. These guys were flying.

Macri sat in her work area in the back of the van finishing a phone call with London. She hung up and yelled to Glick over the sound of the traffic. 'You want the good news or bad news?'

Glick frowned. Nothing was ever simple when dealing with the home office. 'Bad news.'

'Editorial is burned we abandoned our post.'

'Surprise.'

'They also think your tipster is a fraud.'

'Of course.'

'And the boss just warned me that you're a few crumpets short of a proper tea.'

Glick scowled. 'Great. And the good news?'

'They agreed to look at the footage we just shot.'

Glick felt his scowl soften into a grin. *I guess we'll see who's short a few crumpets.* 'So fire it off.'

'Can't transmit until we stop and get a fixed cell read.'

Glick gunned the van onto Via Cola di Rienzo. 'Can't stop now.' He tailed the Alfa Romeos through a hard left swerve around Piazza Risorgimento.

Macri held on to her computer gear in back as everything slid. 'Break my transmitter,' she warned, 'and we'll have to *walk* this footage to London.'

'Sit tight, love. Something tells me we're almost there.'

Macri looked up. 'Where?'

Glick gazed out at the familiar dome now looming directly in front of them. He smiled. 'Right back where we started.'

The four Alfa Romeos slipped deftly into traffic surrounding St Peter's Square. They split up and spread out along the piazza perimeter, quietly unloading men at select points. The debarking guards moved into the throng of tourists and media vans on the edge of the square and instantly became invisible. Some of the guards entered the forest of pillars encompassing the colonnade. They too seemed to evaporate into the surroundings. As Langdon watched through the windshield, he sensed a noose tightening around St Peter's.

In addition to the men Olivetti had just dispatched, the commander had radioed ahead to the Vatican and sent additional undercover guards to the center where Bernini's *West Ponente* was located. As Langdon looked out at the wide-open spaces of St Peter's Square, a familiar question nagged. *How does the Illuminati assassin plan to get away with this? How will he get a cardinal through all these people and kill him in plain view?* Langdon checked his Mickey Mouse watch. It was 8.54 P.M. Six minutes.

In the front seat, Olivetti turned and faced Langdon and Vittoria. 'I want you two right on top of this Bernini brick or block or whatever the hell it is. Same drill. You're tourists. Use the phone if you see anything.'

Before Langdon could respond, Vittoria had his hand and was pulling him out of the car.

The springtime sun was setting behind St Peter's Basilica, and a massive shadow spread, engulfing the piazza. Langdon felt an ominous chill as he and Vittoria moved into the cool, black umbra. Snaking through the crowd, Langdon found himself searching every face they passed, wondering if the killer was among them. Vittoria's hand felt warm.

As they crossed the open expanse of St Peter's Square, Langdon sensed Bernini's sprawling piazza having the exact effect the artist had been commissioned to create – that of 'humbling all those who entered.' Langdon certainly felt humbled at the moment. *Humbled and hungry,* he realized, surprised such a mundane thought could enter his head at a moment like this.

'To the obelisk?' Vittoria asked.

Langdon nodded, arching left across the piazza.

'Time?' Vittoria asked, walking briskly, but casually.
'Five of.'

Vittoria said nothing, but Langdon felt her grip tighten. He was still carrying the gun. He hoped Vittoria would not decide she needed it. He could not imagine her whipping out a weapon in St Peter's Square and blowing away the kneecaps of some killer while the global media looked on. Then again, an incident like that would be nothing compared to the branding and murder of a cardinal out here.

Air, Langdon thought. *The second element of science.* He tried to picture the brand. The method of murder. Again he scanned the sprawling expanse of granite beneath his feet – St Peter's Square – an open desert surrounded by Swiss Guard. If the Hassassin really dared attempt this, Langdon could not imagine how he would escape.

In the center of the piazza rose Caligula's 350-ton Egyptian obelisk. It stretched eighty-one feet skyward to the pyramidal apex onto which was affixed a hollow iron cross. Sufficiently high to catch the last of the evening sun, the cross shone as if magic ... purportedly containing relics of the cross on which Christ was crucified.

Two fountains flanked the obelisk in perfect symmetry. Art historians knew the fountains marked the exact geometric focal points of Bernini's elliptical piazza, but it was an architectural oddity Langdon had never really considered until today. It seemed Rome was suddenly filled with ellipses, pyramids, and startling geometry.

As they neared the obelisk, Vittoria slowed. She exhaled heavily, as if coaxing Langdon to relax along with her. Langdon made the effort, lowering his shoulders and loosening his clenched jaw

Somewhere around the obelisk, boldly positioned outside the largest church in the world, was the second altar of science – Bernini's *West Ponente* – an elliptical block in St Peter's Square.

Gunther Glick watched from the shadows of the pillars surrounding St Peter's Square. On any other day the man in the tweed jacket and the woman in khaki shorts would not have interested him in the least. They appeared to be nothing but tourists enjoying the square. But today was not any other day. Today had been a day of phone tips, corpses, unmarked cars racing through Rome, and men in tweed jackets climbing scaffolding in search of God only knew what. Glick would stay with them.

He looked out across the square and saw Macri. She was exactly where he had told her to go, on the far side of the couple, hovering on their flank. Macri carried her video camera casually, but despite her imitation of a bored member of the press, she stood out more than Glick would have liked. No other reporters were in this far corner of the square, and the acronym 'BBC' stenciled on her camera was drawing some looks from tourists.

The tape Macri had shot earlier of the naked body dumped in the trunk was playing at this very moment on the VCR transmitter back in the van. Glick knew the images were sailing over his head right now en route to London. He wondered what editorial would say.

He wished he and Macri had reached the body sooner, before the army of plainclothed soldiers had intervened. The same army, he knew, had now fanned

335

out and surrounded this piazza. Something big was about to happen.

The media is the right arm of anarchy, the killer had said. Glick wondered if he had missed his chance for a big scoop. He looked out at the other media vans in the distance and watched Macri tailing the mysterious couple across the piazza. Something told Glick he was still in the game . . .

74

Langdon saw what he was looking for a good ten yards before they reached it. Through the scattered tourists, the white marble ellipse of Bernini's *West Ponente* stood out against the gray granite cubes that made up the rest of the piazza. Vittoria apparently saw it too. Her hand tensed.

'Relax,' Langdon whispered. 'Do your piranha thing.'

Vittoria loosened her grip.

As they drew nearer, everything seemed for-biddingly normal. Tourists wandered, nuns chatted along the perimeter of the piazza, a girl fed pigeons at the base of the obelisk.

Langdon refrained from checking his watch. He knew it was almost time.

The elliptical stone arrived beneath their feet, and Langdon and Vittoria slowed to a stop – not over-eagerly – just two tourists pausing dutifully at a point of mild interest.

'*West Ponente*,' Vittoria said, reading the inscription on the stone.

Langdon gazed down at the marble relief and felt suddenly naïve. Not in his art books, not in his numerous trips to Rome, not *ever* had *West Ponente's* significance jumped out at him.

Not until now.

The relief was elliptical, about three feet long, and carved with a rudimentary face – a depiction of the West Wind as an angel-like countenance. Gusting from the angel's mouth, Bernini had drawn a powerful breath of air blowing outward away from the Vatican ... *the breath of God*. This was Bernini's tribute to the second element ... Air ... an ethereal zephyr blown from angel's lips. As Langdon stared, he realized the significance of the relief went deeper still. Bernini had carved the air in *five* distinct gusts. ... five! What was more, flanking the medallion were *two* shining stars. Langdon thought of Galileo. *Two stars, five gusts, ellipses, symmetry* ... He felt hollow. His head hurt.

Vittoria began walking again almost immediately, leading Langdon away from the relief. 'I think someone's following us,' she said.

Langdon looked up. 'Where?'

Vittoria moved a good thirty yards before speaking. She pointed up at the Vatican as if showing Langdon something on the dome. 'The same person has been behind us all the way across the square.' Casually, Vittoria glanced over her shoulder. 'Still on us. Keep moving.'

'You think it's the Hassassin?'

Vittoria shook her head. 'Not unless the Illuminati hires women with BBC cameras.'

When the bells of St Peter's began their deafening clamor, both Langdon and Vittoria jumped. It was time. They had circled away from *West Ponente* in an attempt to lose the reporter but were now moving back toward the relief

Despite the clanging bells, the area seemed perfectly calm. Tourists wandered. A homeless drunk dozed awkwardly at the base of the obelisk. A little girl fed pigeons. Langdon wondered if the reporter had scared the killer off. *Doubtful,* he decided, recalling the killer's promise. *I will make your cardinals media luminaries.*

As the echo of the ninth bell faded away, a peaceful silence descended across the square.

Then . . . the little girl began to scream.

75

Langdon was the first to reach the screaming girl.

The terrified youngster stood frozen, pointing at the base of the obelisk where a shabby, decrepit drunk sat slumped on the stairs. The man was a miserable sight . . . apparently one of Rome's homeless. His gray hair hung in greasy strands in front of his face, and his entire body was wrapped in some sort of dirty cloth. The girl kept screaming as she scampered off into the crowd.

Langdon felt an upsurge of dread as he dashed toward the invalid. There was a dark, widening stain spreading across the man's rags. Fresh, flowing blood.

Then, it was as if everything happened at once.

The old man seemed to crumple in the middle, tottering forward. Langdon lunged, but he was too late. The man pitched forward, toppled off the stairs, and hit the pavement face down. Motionless.

Langdon dropped to his knees. Vittoria arrived beside him. A crowd was gathering.

Vittoria put her fingers on the man's throat from behind. 'There's a pulse,' she declared. 'Roll him.'

Langdon was already in motion. Grasping the man's shoulders, he rolled the body. As he did, the loose rags seemed to slough away like dead flesh. The man flopped limp onto his back. Dead center of his naked chest was a wide area of charred flesh.

Vittoria gasped and pulled back.

Langdon felt paralyzed, pinned somewhere between nausea and awe. The symbol had a terrifying simplicity to it.

'Air,' Vittoria choked. 'It's . . . him.'

Swiss Guards appeared from out of nowhere, shouting orders, racing after an unseen assassin.

Nearby, a tourist explained that only minutes ago, a dark-skinned man had been kind enough to help this poor, wheezing, homeless man across the square . . . even sitting a moment on the stairs with the invalid before disappearing back into the crowd.

Vittoria ripped the rest of the rags off the man's abdomen. He had two deep puncture wounds, one on either side of the brand, just below his rib cage. She cocked the man's head back and began to administer mouth to mouth. Langdon was not prepared for what happened next. As Vittoria blew, the wounds on either side of the man's midsection hissed and sprayed blood into the air like blowholes on a whale. The salty liquid hit Langdon in the face.

Vittoria stopped short, looking horrified. 'His lungs . . .' she stammered. 'They're . . . punctured.'

Langdon wiped his eyes as he looked down at the two perforations. The holes gurgled. The cardinal's lungs were destroyed. He was gone.

Vittoria covered the body as the Swiss Guards moved in.

Langdon stood, disoriented. As he did, he saw her. The woman who had been following them earlier was crouched nearby. Her BBC video camera was shouldered, aimed, and running. She and Langdon locked eyes, and he knew she'd gotten it all. Then, like a cat, she bolted.

76

Chinita Macri was on the run. She had the story of her life.

Her video camera felt like an anchor as she lumbered across St Peter's Square, pushing through the gathering crowd. Everyone seemed to be moving in the opposite direction than her . . . *toward* the commotion. Macri was trying to get as far away as possible. The man in the tweed jacket had seen her, and now she sensed others were after her, men she could not see, closing in from all sides.

Macri was still aghast from the images she had just

recorded. She wondered if the dead man was really who she feared he was. Glick's mysterious phone contact suddenly seemed a little less crazy.

As she hurried in the direction of the BBC van, a young man with a decidedly militaristic air emerged from the crowd before her. Their eyes met, and they both stopped. Like lightning, he raised a walkie-talkie and spoke into it. Then he moved toward her. Macri wheeled and doubled back into the crowd, her heart pounding.

As she stumbled through the mass of arms and legs, she removed the spent video cassette from her camera. *Cellulose gold,* she thought, tucking the tape under her belt flush to her backside and letting her coat tails cover it. For once she was glad she carried some extra weight. *Glick, where the hell are you!*

Another soldier appeared to her left, closing in. Macri knew she had little time. She banked into the crowd again. Yanking a blank cartridge from her case, she slapped it into the camera. Then she prayed.

She was thirty yards from the BBC van when the two men materialized directly in front of her, arms folded. She was going nowhere.

'Film,' one snapped. 'Now'

Macri recoiled, wrapping her arms protectively around her camera. 'No chance.'

One of the men pulled aside his jacket, revealing a sidearm.

'So shoot me,' Macri said, amazed by the boldness of her voice.

'Film,' the first one repeated.

Where the devil is Glick? Macri stamped her foot and yelled as loudly as possible, 'I am a professional video-grapher with the BBC! By Article 12 of the Free Press

Act, this film is property of the British Broadcasting Corporation!'

The men did not flinch. The one with the gun took a step toward her. 'I am a lieutenant with the Swiss Guard, and by the Holy Doctrine governing the property on which you are now standing, you are subject to search and seizure.'

A crowd had started to gather now around them.

Macri yelled, 'I will not under any circumstances give you the film in this camera without speaking to my editor in London. I suggest you—'

The guards ended it. One yanked the camera out of her hands. The other forcibly grabbed her by the arm and twisted her in the direction of the Vatican. '*Grazie,*' he said, leading her through a jostling crowd.

Macri prayed they would not search her and find the tape. If she could somehow protect the film long enough to—

Suddenly, the unthinkable happened. Someone in the crowd was groping under her coat. Macri felt the video yanked away from her. She wheeled, but swallowed her words. Behind her, a breathless Gunther Glick gave her a wink and dissolved back into the crowd.

77

Robert Langdon staggered into the private bathroom adjoining the Office of the Pope. He dabbed the blood from his face and lips. The blood was not his own. It was that of Cardinal Lamassé, who had just died horribly in the crowded square outside the Vatican. *Virgin sacrifices on the altars of science.* So far, the Hassassin had made good on his threat.

Langdon felt powerless as he gazed into the mirror. His eyes were drawn, and stubble had begun to darken his cheeks. The room around him was immaculate and lavish – black marble with gold fixtures, cotton towels, and scented hand soaps.

Langdon tried to rid his mind of the bloody brand he had just seen. *Air.* The image stuck. He had witnessed three ambigrams since waking up this morning . . . and he knew there were two more coming.

Outside the door, it sounded as if Olivetti, the camerlengo, and Captain Rocher were debating what to do next. Apparently, the antimatter search had turned up nothing so far. Either the guards had missed the canister, or the intruder had gotten deeper inside the Vatican than Commander Olivetti had been willing to entertain.

Langdon dried his hands and face. Then he turned and looked for a urinal. No urinal. Just a bowl. He lifted the lid.

As he stood there, tension ebbing from his body, a giddy wave of exhaustion shuddered through his core. The emotions knotting his chest were so many, so incongruous. He was fatigued, running on no food or sleep, walking the Path of Illumination, traumatized by two brutal murders. Langdon felt a deepening horror over the possible outcome of this drama.

Think, he told himself. His mind was blank.

As he flushed, an unexpected realization hit him.

343

This is the Pope's toilet, he thought. *I just took a leak in the Pope's toilet.* He had to chuckle. *The Holy Throne.*

78

In London, a BBC technician ejected a video cassette from a satellite receiver unit and dashed across the control room floor. She burst into the office of the editor-in-chief, slammed the video into his VCR, and pressed play.

As the tape rolled, she told him about the conversation she had just had with Gunther Glick in Vatican City. In addition, BBC photo archives had just given her a positive ID on the victim in St Peter's Square.

When the editor-in-chief emerged from his office, he was ringing a cowbell. Everything in editorial stopped.

'Live in five!' the man boomed. 'On-air talent to prep! Media coordinators, I want your contacts on line! We've got a story we're selling! And we've got film!'

The market coordinators grabbed their Rolodexes.

'Film specs!' one of them yelled.

'Thirty-second trim,' the chief replied.

'Content?'

'Live homicide.'

The coordinators looked encouraged. 'Usage and licensing price?'

'A million U.S. per.'

Heads shot up. 'What!'

'You heard me! I want top of the food chain. CNN,

MSNBC, then the big three! Offer a dial-in preview. Give them five minutes to piggyback before BBC runs it.'

'What the hell happened?' someone demanded. 'The prime minister get skinned alive?'

The chief shook his head. 'Better.'

At that exact instant, somewhere in Rome, the Hassassin enjoyed a fleeting moment of repose in a comfortable chair. He admired the legendary chamber around him. *I am sitting in the Church of Illumination,* he thought. *The Illuminati lair.* He could not believe it was still here after all of these centuries.

Dutifully, he dialed the BBC reporter to whom he had spoken earlier. It was time. The world had yet to hear the most shocking news of all.

79

Vittoria Vetra sipped a glass of water and nibbled absently at some tea scones just set out by one of the Swiss Guards. She knew she should eat, but she had no appetite. The Office of the Pope was bustling now, echoing with tense conversations. Captain Rocher, Commander Olivetti, and half a dozen guards assessed the damage and debated the next move.

Robert Langdon stood nearby staring out at St Peter's Square. He looked dejected. Vittoria walked over. 'Ideas?'

He shook his head.

'Scone?'

His mood seemed to brighten at the sight of food. 'Hell yes. Thanks.' He ate voraciously.

The conversation behind them went quiet suddenly when two Swiss Guards escorted Camerlengo Ventresca through the door. If the chamberlain had looked drained before, Vittoria thought, now he looked empty.

'What happened?' the camerlengo said to Olivetti. From the look on the camerlengo's face, he appeared to have already been told the worst of it.

Olivetti's official update sounded like a battlefield casualty report. He gave the facts with flat efficacy. 'Cardinal Ebner was found dead in the church of Santa Maria del Popolo just after eight o'clock. He had been suffocated and branded with the ambigrammatic word "Earth." Cardinal Lamassé was murdered in St Peter's Square ten minutes ago. He died of perforations to the chest. He was branded with the word "Air", also ambigrammatic. The killer escaped in both instances.'

The camerlengo crossed the room and sat heavily behind the Pope's desk. He bowed his head.

'Cardinals Guidera and Baggia, however, are still alive.'

The camerlengo's head shot up, his expression pained. 'This is our consolation? Two cardinals have been murdered, commander. And the other two will obviously not be alive much longer unless you find them.'

'We will find them,' Olivetti assured. 'I am encouraged.'

'Encouraged? We've had nothing but failure.'

'Untrue. We've lost two battles, signore, but we're winning the war. The Illuminati had intended to turn

346

this evening into a media circus. So far we have thwarted their plan. Both cardinals' bodies have been recovered without incident. In addition,' Olivetti continued, 'Captain Rocher tells me he is making excellent headway on the antimatter search.'

Captain Rocher stepped forward in his red beret. Vittoria thought he looked more human somehow than the other guards – stern but not so rigid. Rocher's voice was emotional and crystalline, like a violin. 'I am hopeful we will have the canister for you within an hour, signore.'

'Captain,' the camerlengo said, 'excuse me if I seem less than hopeful, but I was under the impression that a search of Vatican City would take far more time than we have.'

'A *full* search, yes. However, after assessing the situation, I am confident the antimatter canister is located in one of our white zones – those Vatican sectors accessible to public tours – the museums and St Peter's Basilica, for example. We have already killed power in those zones and are conducting our scan.'

'You intend to search only a small *percentage* of Vatican City?'

'Yes, signore. It is highly unlikely that an intruder gained access to the inner zones of Vatican City. The fact that the missing security camera was stolen from a public access area – a stairwell in one of the museums – clearly implies that the intruder had limited access. Therefore he would only have been able to *relocate* the camera and antimatter in another public access area. It is these areas on which we are focusing our search.'

'But the intruder kidnapped four cardinals. That certainly implies deeper infiltration than we thought.'

'Not necessarily. We must remember that the

cardinals spent much of today in the Vatican museums and St Peter's Basilica, enjoying those areas without the crowds. It is probable that the missing cardinals were taken in one of these areas.'

'But how were they removed from our walls?'

'We are still assessing that.'

'I see.' The camerlengo exhaled and stood up. He walked over to Olivetti. 'Commander, I would like to hear your contingency plan for evacuation.'

'We are still formalizing that, signore. In the meantime, I am faithful Captain Rocher will find the canister.'

Rocher clicked his boots as if in appreciation of the vote of confidence. 'My men have already scanned two-thirds of the white zones. Confidence is high.'

The camerlengo did not appear to share that confidence.

At that moment the guard with a scar beneath one eye came through the door carrying a clipboard and a map. He strode toward Langdon. 'Mr Langdon? I have the information you requested on the *West Ponente*.'

Langdon swallowed his scone. 'Good. Let's have a look.'

The others kept talking while Vittoria joined Robert and the guard as they spread out the map on the Pope's desk.

The soldier pointed to St Peter's Square. 'This is where we are. The central line of *West Ponente's* breath points due east, directly away from Vatican City.' The guard traced a line with his finger from St Peter's Square across the Tiber River and up into the heart of old Rome. 'As you can see, the line passes through almost all of Rome. There are about twenty Catholic churches that fall near this line.'

Langdon slumped. '*Twenty?*'

'Maybe more.'

'Do any of the churches fall *directly* on the line?'

'Some look closer than others,' the guard said, 'but translating the exact bearing of the *West Ponente* onto a map leaves margin for error.'

Langdon looked out at St Peter's Square a moment. Then he scowled, stroking his chin. 'How about *fire*? Any of them have Bernini artwork that has to do with fire?'

Silence.

'How about obelisks?' he demanded. 'Are any of the churches located near obelisks?'

The guard began checking the map.

Vittoria saw a glimmer of hope in Langdon's eyes and realized what he was thinking. *He's right!* The first two markers had been located on or near piazzas that contained obelisks! Maybe obelisks were a theme? Soaring pyramids marking the Illuminati path? The more Vittoria thought about it, the more perfect it seemed . . . four towering beacons rising over Rome to mark the altars of science.

'It's a long shot,' Langdon said, 'but I know that many of Rome's obelisks were erected or moved during Bernini's reign. He was no doubt involved in their placement.'

'Or,' Vittoria added, 'Bernini could have placed his markers *near* existing obelisks.'

Langdon nodded. 'True.'

'Bad news,' the guard said. 'No obelisks on the line.' He traced his finger across the map. 'None even remotely close. Nothing.'

Langdon sighed.

Vittoria's shoulders slumped. She'd thought it was a

promising idea. Apparently, this was not going to be as easy as they'd hoped. She tried to stay positive. 'Robert, think. You must know of a Bernini statue relating to *fire*. Anything at all.'

'Believe me, I've been thinking. Bernini was incredibly prolific. Hundreds of works. I was hoping *West Ponente* would point to a single church. Something that would ring a bell.'

'*Fuòco*,' she pressed. '*Fire*. No Bernini titles jump out?'

Langdon shrugged. 'There's his famous sketches of *Fireworks*, but they're not sculpture, and they're in Leipzig, Germany.'

Vittoria frowned. 'And you're sure the *breath* is what indicates the direction?'

'You saw the relief, Vittoria. The design was totally symmetrical. The only indication of bearing was the breath.'

Vittoria knew he was right.

'Not to mention,' he added, 'because the *West Ponente* signifies *Air*, following the *breath* seems symbolically appropriate.'

Vittoria nodded. *So we follow the breath. But where?*

Olivetti came over. 'What have you got?'

'Too many churches,' the soldier said. 'Two dozen or so. I suppose we could put four men on each church—'

'Forget it,' Olivetti said. 'We missed this guy twice when we knew exactly where he was going to be. A mass stakeout means leaving Vatican City unprotected and canceling the search.'

'We need a reference book,' Vittoria said. 'An index of Bernini's work. If we can scan titles, maybe something will jump out.'

'I don't know,' Langdon said. 'If it's a work Bernini created specifically for the Illuminati, it may be very obscure. It probably won't be listed in a book.'

Vittoria refused to believe it. 'The other two sculptures were fairly well-known. You'd heard of them both.'

Langdon shrugged. 'Yeah.'

'If we scan titles for references to the word "fire", maybe we'll find a statue that's listed as being in the right direction.'

Langdon seemed convinced it was worth a shot. He turned to Olivetti. 'I need a list of all Bernini's work. You guys probably don't have a coffee-table Bernini book around here, do you?'

'Coffee-table book?' Olivetti seemed unfamiliar with the term.

'Never mind. Any list. How about the Vatican Museum? They must have Bernini references.'

The guard with the scar frowned. 'Power in the museum is out, and the records room is enormous. Without the staff there to help—'

'The Bernini work in question,' Olivetti interrupted. 'Would it have been created while Bernini was employed here at the Vatican?'

'Almost definitely,' Langdon said. 'He was here almost his entire career. And certainly during the time period of the Galileo conflict.'

Olivetti nodded. 'Then there's another reference.'

Vittoria felt a flicker of optimism. 'Where?'

The commander did not reply. He took his guard aside and spoke in hushed tones. The guard seemed uncertain but nodded obediently. When Olivetti was finished talking, the guard turned to Langdon.

'This way please, Mr Langdon. It's nine-fifteen. We'll have to hurry.'

Langdon and the guard headed for the door.

Vittoria started after them. 'I'll help.'

Olivetti caught her by the arm. 'No, Ms Vetra. I need a word with you.' His grasp was authoritative.

Langdon and the guard left. Olivetti's face was wooden as he took Vittoria aside. But whatever it was. Olivetti had intended to say to her, he never got the chance. His walkie-talkie crackled loudly. '*Comandante?*'

Everyone in the room turned.

The voice on the transmitter was grim. 'I think you better turn on the television.'

80

When Langdon had left the Vatican Secret Archives only two hours ago, he had never imagined he would see them again. Now, winded from having jogged the entire way with his Swiss Guard escort, Langdon found himself back at the archives once again.

His escort, the guard with the scar, now led Langdon through the rows of translucent cubicles. The silence of the archives felt somehow more forbidding now, and Langdon was thankful when the guard broke it.

'Over here, I think,' he said, escorting Langdon to the back of the chamber where a series of smaller vaults lined the wall. The guard scanned the titles on the vaults and motioned to one of them. 'Yes, here it is. Right where the commander said it would be.'

Langdon read the title. ATTIVI VATICANI. Vatican assets? He scanned the list of contents. Real estate . . . currency . . . Vatican Bank . . . antiquities . . . The list went on.

'Paperwork of all Vatican assets,' the guard said.

Langdon looked at the cubicle. *Jesus*. Even in the dark, he could tell it was packed.

'My commander said that whatever Bernini created while under Vatican patronage would be listed here as an asset.'

Langdon nodded, realizing the commander's instincts just might pay off. In Bernini's day, everything an artist created while under the patronage of the Pope became, by law, property of the Vatican. It was more like feudalism than patronage, but top artists lived well and seldom complained. 'Including works placed in churches *outside* Vatican City?'

The soldier gave him an odd look. 'Of course. All Catholic churches in Rome are property of the Vatican.'

Langdon looked at the list in his hand. It contained the names of the twenty or so churches that were located on a direct line with *West Ponente's* breath. The third altar of science was one of them, and Langdon hoped he had time to figure out which it was. Under other circumstances, he would gladly have explored each church in person. Today, however, he had about twenty minutes to find what he was looking for – the one church containing a Bernini tribute to *fire*.

Langdon walked to the vault's electronic revolving door. The guard did not follow. Langdon sensed an uncertain hesitation. He smiled. 'The air's fine. Thin, but breathable.'

'My orders are to escort you here and then return immediately to the security center.'

'You're *leaving*?'

'Yes. The Swiss Guard are not allowed inside the archives. I am breaching protocol by escorting you this far. The commander reminded me of that.'

'Breaching protocol?' *Do you have any idea what is going on here tonight?* 'Whose side is your damn commander on!'

All friendliness disappeared from the guard's face. The scar under his eye twitched. The guard stared, looking suddenly a lot like Olivetti himself.

'I apologize,' Langdon said, regretting the comment. 'It's just . . . I could use some help.'

The guard did not blink. 'I am trained to follow orders. Not debate them. When you find what you are looking for, contact the commander immediately.'

Langdon was flustered. 'But where will he be?'

The guard removed his walkie-talkie and set it on a nearby table. 'Channel one.' Then he disappeared into the dark.

81

The television in the Office of the Pope was an oversized Hitachi hidden in a recessed cabinet opposite his desk. The doors to the cabinet were now open, and everyone gathered around. Vittoria moved in close. As the screen warmed up, a young female reporter came into view. She was a doe-eyed brunette.

'For MSNBC news,' she announced, 'this is Kelly

Horan-Jones, live from Vatican City.' The image behind her was a night shot of St Peter's Basilica with all its lights blazing.

'You're not *live*,' Rocher snapped. 'That's stock footage! The lights in the basilica are *out*.'

Olivetti silenced him with a hiss.

The reporter continued, sounding tense. 'Shocking developments in the Vatican elections this evening. We have reports that two members of the College of Cardinals have been brutally murdered in Rome.'

Olivetti swore under his breath.

As the reporter continued, a guard appeared at the door, breathless. 'Commander, the central switchboard reports every line lit. They're requesting our official position on—'

'Disconnect it,' Olivetti said, never taking his eyes from the TV.

The guard looked uncertain. 'But, commander—'

'Go!'

The guard ran off.

Vittoria sensed the camerlengo had wanted to say something but had stopped himself. Instead, the man stared long and hard at Olivetti before turning back to the television.

MSNBC was now running tape. The Swiss Guards carried the body of Cardinal Ebner down the stairs outside Santa Maria del Popolo and lifted him into an Alfa Romeo. The tape froze and zoomed in as the cardinal's naked body became visible just before they deposited him in the trunk of the car.

'Who the hell shot this footage?' Olivetti demanded.

The MSNBC reporter kept talking. 'This is believed to be the body of Cardinal Ebner of Frankfurt, Germany. The men removing his body from the church are believed to be Vatican Swiss Guard.' The reporter looked like she was making every effort to appear appropriately moved. They closed in on her face, and she became even more somber. 'At this time, MSNBC would like to issue our viewers a discretionary warning. The images we are about to show are exceptionally vivid and may not be suitable for all audiences.'

Vittoria grunted at the station's feigned concern for viewer sensibility, recognizing the warning as exactly what it was – the ultimate media 'teaser line'. Nobody ever changed channels after a promise like that.

The reporter drove it home. 'Again, this footage may be shocking to some viewers.'

'What footage?' Olivetti demanded. 'You just showed—'

The shot that filled the screen was of a couple in St Peter's Square, moving through the crowd. Vittoria instantly recognized the two people as Robert and herself. In the corner of the screen was a text overlay: COURTESY OF THE BBC. A bell was tolling.

'Oh, no,' Vittoria said aloud. 'Oh . . . no.'

The camerlengo looked confused. He turned to Olivetti. 'I thought you said you confiscated this tape!'

Suddenly, on television, a child was screaming. The image panned to find a little girl pointing at what appeared to be a bloody homeless man. Robert Langdon entered abruptly into the frame, trying to help the little girl. The shot tightened.

Everyone in the Pope's office stared in horrified silence as the drama unfolded before them. The cardinal's body fell face first onto the pavement. Vittoria appeared and called orders. There was blood. A brand. A ghastly, failed attempt to administer CPR.

'This astonishing footage,' the reporter was saying, 'was shot only minutes ago outside the Vatican. Our sources tell us this is the body of Cardinal Lamassé from France. How he came to be dressed this way and why he was not in conclave remain a mystery. So far, the Vatican has refused to comment.' The tape began to roll again.

'Refused comment?' Rocher said. 'Give us a damn minute!'

The reporter was still talking, her eyebrows furrowing with intensity. 'Although MSNBC has yet to confirm a motive for the attack, our sources tell us that responsibility for the murders has been claimed by a group calling themselves the Illuminati.'

Olivetti exploded. *'What!'*

'. . . find out more about the Illuminati by visiting our website at—'

'Non è possibile!' Olivetti declared. He switched channels.

This station had a Hispanic male reporter. '—a satanic cult known as the Illuminati, who some historians believe—'

Olivetti began pressing the remote wildly. Every channel was in the middle of a live update. Most were in English.

'—Swiss Guards removing a body from a church earlier this evening. The body is believed to be that of Cardinal—'

'—lights in the basilica and museums are extinguished leaving speculation—'

'—will be speaking with conspiracy theorist Tyler Tingley, about this shocking resurgence—'

'—rumors of two more assassinations planned for later this evening—'

'—questioning now whether papal hopeful Cardinal Baggia is among the missing—'

Vittoria turned away. Everything was happening so fast. Outside the window, in the settling dark, the raw magnetism of human tragedy seemed to be sucking people toward Vatican City. The crowd in the square thickened almost by the instant. Pedestrians streamed toward them while a new batch of media personnel unloaded vans and staked their claim in St Peter's Square.

Olivetti set down the remote control and turned to the camerlengo. 'Signore, I cannot imagine how this could happen. We took the tape that was in that camera!'

The camerlengo looked momentarily too stunned to speak.

Nobody said a word. The Swiss Guards stood rigid at attention.

'It appears,' the camerlengo said finally, sounding too devastated to be angry, 'that we have not contained this crisis as well as I was led to believe.' He looked out the window at the gathering masses. 'I need to make an address.'

Olivetti shook his head. 'No, signore. That is exactly what the Illuminati want you to do – confirm them, empower them. We must remain silent.'

'And these people?' The camerlengo pointed out the window. 'There will be tens of thousands shortly. Then hundreds of thousands. Continuing this charade only puts them in danger. I need to warn them. Then we need to evacuate our College of Cardinals.'

'There is still time. Let Captain Rocher find the antimatter.'

The camerlengo turned. 'Are you attempting to give me an order?'

'No, I am giving you advice. If you are concerned about the people outside, we can announce a gas leak and clear the area, but admitting we are hostage is dangerous.'

'Commander, I will only say this once. I will not use this office as a pulpit to lie to the world. If I announce anything at all, it will be the truth.'

'The truth? That Vatican City is threatened to be destroyed by satanic terrorists? It only weakens our position.'

The camerlengo glared. 'How much weaker could our position be?'

Rocher shouted suddenly, grabbing the remote and increasing the volume on the television. Everyone turned.

On air, the woman from MSNBC now looked genuinely unnerved. Superimposed beside her was a photo of the late Pope. '. . . breaking information. This just in from the BBC . . .' She glanced off camera as if to confirm she was really supposed to make this announcement. Apparently getting confirmation, she turned and grimly faced the viewers. 'The Illuminati have just claimed responsibility for . . .' She hesitated. 'They have claimed responsibility for the death of the Pope fifteen days ago.'

The camerlengo's jaw fell.

Rocher dropped the remote control.

Vittoria could barely process the information.

'By Vatican law,' the woman continued, 'no formal autopsy is ever performed on a Pope, so the Illuminati claim of murder cannot be confirmed. Nonetheless, the Illuminati hold that the cause of the late Pope's death was not a *stroke* as the Vatican reported, but *poisoning*.'

The room went totally silent again.

Olivetti erupted. 'Madness! A bold-faced lie!'

Rocher began flipping channels again. The bulletin seemed to spread like a plague from station to station. Everyone had the same story. Headlines competed for optimal sensationalism.

MURDER AT THE VATICAN
POPE POISONED
SATAN TOUCHES HOUSE OF GOD

The camerlengo looked away. 'God help us.'

As Rocher flipped, he passed a BBC station. '—tipped me off about the killing at Santa Maria de Popolo—'

'Wait!' the camerlengo said. 'Back.'

Rocher went back. On screen, a prim-looking man sat at a BBC news desk. Superimposed over his shoulder was a still snapshot of an odd-looking man with a red beard. Underneath his photo, it said: GUNTHER GLICK – LIVE IN VATICAN CITY. Reporter Glick was apparently reporting by phone, the connection scratchy '. . . my videographer got the footage of the cardinal being removed from the Chigi Chapel.'

'Let me reiterate for our viewers,' the anchorman in London was saying, 'BBC reporter Gunther Glick is the man who first broke this story. He has been in phone contact twice now with the alleged Illuminati assassin. Gunther, you say the assassin phoned only moments ago to pass along a message from the Illuminati?'

'He did.'

'And their message was that the Illuminati were somehow *responsible* for the Pope's death?' The anchorman sounded incredulous.

'Correct. The caller told me that the Pope's death was *not* a stroke, as the Vatican had thought, but rather that the Pope had been poisoned by the Illuminati.'

Everyone in the Pope's office froze.

'Poisoned?' the anchorman demanded. 'But . . . but *how*!'

'They gave no specifics,' Glick replied, 'except to say that they killed him with a drug known as . . .' – there was a rustling of papers on the line – 'something known as Heparin.'

The camerlengo, Olivetti, and Rocher all exchanged confused looks.

'Heparin?' Rocher demanded, looking unnerved. 'But isn't that . . .?'

The camerlengo blanched. 'The Pope's medication.'

Vittoria was stunned. 'The Pope was on Heparin?'

'He had thrombophlebitis,' the camerlengo said. 'He took an injection once a day.'

Rocher looked flabbergasted. 'But Heparin isn't a *poison*. Why would the Illuminati claim—'

'Heparin is lethal in the wrong dosages,' Vittoria offered. 'It's a powerful anticoagulant. An overdose would cause massive internal bleeding and brain hemorrhages.'

Olivetti eyed her suspiciously. 'How would you know that?'

'Marine biologists use it on sea mammals in captivity to prevent blood clotting from decreased activity. Animals have died from improper administration of the drug.' She paused. 'A Heparin overdose in a human would cause symptoms easily mistaken for a stroke . . . especially in the absence of a proper autopsy.'

The camerlengo now looked deeply troubled.

'Signore,' Olivetti said, 'this is obviously an Illuminati ploy for publicity. Someone overdosing the Pope would be impossible. Nobody had access. And even if we take the bait and try to refute their claim, how could we? Papal law prohibits autopsy. Even *with* an autopsy, we would learn nothing. We would find traces of Heparin in his body from his daily injections.'

'True.' The camerlengo's voice sharpened. 'And yet something else troubles me. No one on the outside *knew* His Holiness was taking this medication.'

There was a silence.

'If he overdosed with Heparin,' Vittoria said, 'his body would show signs.'

Olivetti spun toward her. 'Ms Vetra, in case you didn't hear me, papal autopsies are prohibited by Vatican Law. We are not about to defile His Holiness's body by cutting him open just because an enemy makes a taunting claim!'

Vittoria felt shamed. 'I was not implying . . .' She had not meant to seem disrespectful. 'I certainly was not suggesting you exhume the Pope . . .' She hesitated, though. Something Robert told her in the Chigi passed like a ghost through her mind. He had mentioned that papal sarcophagi were above ground and never cemented shut, a throwback to the days of the pharaohs when sealing and burying a casket was believed to trap the deceased's soul inside. *Gravity* had become the mortar of choice, with coffin lids often weighing hundreds of pounds. *Technically*, she realized, *it would be possible to—*

'What *sort* of signs?' the camerlengo said suddenly.

Vittoria felt her heart flutter with fear. 'Overdoses can cause bleeding of the oral mucosa.'

'Oral what?'

'The victim's gums would bleed. Post mortem, the blood congeals and turns the inside of the mouth black.' Vittoria had once seen a photo taken at an aquarium in London where a pair of killer whales had been mistakenly overdosed by their trainer. The whales floated lifeless in the tank, their mouths hanging open and their tongues black as soot.

The camerlengo made no reply. He turned and stared out the window.

Rocher's voice had lost its optimism. 'Signore, if this claim about poisoning is true . . .'

'It's not true,' Olivetti declared. 'Access to the Pope by an outsider is utterly impossible.'

'*If* this claim is true,' Rocher repeated, 'and our Holy Father *was* poisoned, then that has profound implications for our antimatter search. The alleged assassination implies a much deeper infiltration of Vatican City than we had imagined. Searching the white zones may be inadequate. If we are compromised to such a deep extent, we may not find the canister in time.'

Olivetti leveled his captain with a cold stare. 'Captain, I will tell you what is going to happen.'

'No,' the camerlengo said, turning suddenly. 'I will tell *you* what is going to happen.' He looked directly at Olivetti. 'This has gone far enough. In twenty minutes I will be making a decision whether or not to cancel conclave and evacuate Vatican City. My decision will be final. Is that clear?'

Olivetti did not blink. Nor did he respond.

The camerlengo spoke forcefully now, as though tapping a hidden reserve of power. 'Captain Rocher, you will complete your search of the white zones and report directly to me when you are finished.'

Rocher nodded, throwing Olivetti an uneasy glance.

The camerlengo then singled out two guards. 'I want the BBC reporter, Mr Glick, in this office immediately. If the Illuminati have been communicating with him, he may be able to help us. Go.'

The two soldiers disappeared.

Now the camerlengo turned and addressed the remaining guards. 'Gentlemen, I will not permit any more loss of life this evening. By ten o'clock you will locate the remaining two cardinals and capture the monster responsible for these murders. Do I make myself understood?'

'But, signore,' Olivetti argued, 'we have no idea where—'

'Mr Langdon is working on that. He seems capable. I have faith.'

With that, the camerlengo strode for the door, a new determination in his step. On his way out, he pointed to three guards. 'You three, come with me. Now.'

The guards followed.

In the doorway, the camerlengo stopped. He turned to Vittoria. 'Ms Vetra. You too. Please come with me.'

Vittoria hesitated. 'Where are we going?'

He headed out the door. 'To see an old friend.'

82

At CERN, secretary Sylvie Baudeloque was hungry, wishing she could go home. To her dismay, Kohler had apparently survived his trip to the infirmary; he had phoned and demanded – not asked, *demanded* – that Sylvie stay late this evening. No explanation.

Over the years, Sylvie had programmed herself to ignore Kohler's bizarre mood swings and eccentricities – his silent treatments, his unnerving propensity to secretly film meetings with his wheelchair's porta-video. She secretly hoped one day he would shoot himself during his weekly visit to CERN's recreational pistol range, but apparently he was a pretty good shot.

Now, sitting alone at her desk, Sylvie heard her stomach growling. Kohler had not yet returned, nor had he given her any additional work for the evening. *To hell with sitting here bored and starving*, she decided. She left Kohler a note and headed for the staff dining commons to grab a quick bite.

She never made it.

As she passed CERN's recreational *'suites de loisir'* – a long hallway of lounges with televisions – she noticed the rooms were overflowing with employees who had apparently abandoned dinner to watch the news. Something big was going on. Sylvie entered the first suite. It was packed with byte-heads – wild young computer programmers. When she saw the headlines on the TV, she gasped.

TERROR AT THE VATICAN

Sylvie listened to the report, unable to believe her ears. Some ancient brotherhood killing cardinals? What did that prove? Their hatred? Their dominance? Their ignorance?

And yet, incredibly, the mood in this suite seemed anything but somber.

Two young techies ran by waving T-shirts that bore

a picture of Bill Gates and the message: AND THE GEEK SHALL INHERIT THE EARTH!

'Illuminati!' one shouted. 'I told you these guys were real!'

'Incredible! I thought it was just a game!'

'They killed the Pope, man! The *Pope*!'

'Jeez! I wonder how many points you get for *that*?'

They ran off laughing.

Sylvie stood in stunned amazement. As a Catholic working among scientists, she occasionally endured the antireligious whisperings, but the party these kids seemed to be having was all-out euphoria over the church's loss. How could they be so callous? Why the hatred?

For Sylvie, the church had always been an innocuous entity . . . a place of fellowship and introspection . . . sometimes just a place to sing out loud without people staring at her. The church recorded the benchmarks of her life – funerals, weddings, baptisms, holidays – and it asked for nothing in return. Even the monetary dues were voluntary. Her children emerged from Sunday School every week uplifted, filled with ideas about helping others and being kinder. What could possibly be wrong with *that*?

It never ceased to amaze her that so many of CERN's so-called 'brilliant minds' failed to comprehend the importance of the church. Did they really believe quarks and mesons inspired the average human being? Or that *equations* could replace someone's need for faith in the divine?

Dazed, Sylvie moved down the hallway past the other lounges. All the TV rooms were packed. She began wondering now about the call Kohler had gotten from the Vatican earlier. Coincidence? Perhaps.

The Vatican called CERN from time to time as a 'courtesy' before issuing scathing statements condemning CERN's research – most recently for CERN's breakthroughs in nanotechnology, a field the church denounced because of its implications for genetic engineering. CERN never cared. Invariably, within minutes after a Vatican salvo, Kohler's phone would ring off the hook with tech-investment companies wanting to license the new discovery. 'No such thing as bad press,' Kohler would always say.

Sylvie wondered if she should page Kohler, wherever the hell he was, and tell him to turn on the news. Did he care? Had he heard? Of course, he'd heard. He was probably videotaping the entire report with his freaky little camcorder, smiling for the first time in a year.

As Sylvie continued down the hall, she finally found a lounge where the mood was subdued ... almost melancholy. Here the scientists watching the report were some of CERN's oldest and most respected. They did not even look up as Sylvie slipped in and took a seat.

On the other side of CERN, in Leonardo Vetra's frigid apartment, Maximilian Kohler had finished reading the leather-bound journal he'd taken from Vetra's bedside table. Now he was watching the television reports. After a few minutes, he replaced Vetra's journal, turned off the television, and left the apartment.

Far away, in Vatican City, Cardinal Mortati carried another tray of ballots to the Sistine Chapel chimney. He burned them, and the smoke was black.

Two ballotings. No Pope.

Flashlights were no match for the voluminous blackness of St Peter's Basilica. The void overhead pressed down like a starless night, and Vittoria felt the emptiness spread out around her like a desolate ocean. She stayed close as the Swiss Guards and the camerlengo pushed on. High above, a dove cooed and fluttered away.

As if sensing her discomfort, the camerlengo dropped back and laid a hand on her shoulder. A tangible strength transferred in the touch, as if the man were magically infusing her with the calm she needed to do what they were about to do.

What are we about to do? she thought. *This is madness!*

And yet, Vittoria knew, for all its impiety and inevitable horror, the task at hand was inescapable. The grave decisions facing the camerlengo required information ... information entombed in a sarcophagus in the Vatican Grottoes. She wondered what they would find. *Did the Illuminati murder the Pope? Did their power really reach so far? Am I really about to perform the first papal autopsy?*

Vittoria found it ironic that she felt more apprehensive in this unlit church than she would swimming at night with barracuda. Nature was her refuge. She understood nature. But it was matters of man and spirit that left her mystified. Killer fish gathering in the dark conjured images of the press gathering outside. TV footage of branded bodies reminded her of her father's corpse ... and the killer's harsh laugh. The killer was out there somewhere. Vittoria felt the anger drowning her fear.

As they circled past a pillar – thicker in girth than any redwood she could imagine – Vittoria saw an orange glow up ahead. The light seemed to emanate from beneath the floor in the center of the basilica. As they came closer, she realized what she was seeing. It was the famous sunken sanctuary beneath the main altar – the sumptuous underground chamber that held the Vatican's most sacred relics. As they drew even with the gate surrounding the hollow, Vittoria gazed down at the golden coffer surrounded by scores of glowing oil lamps.

'St Peter's bones?' she asked, knowing full well that they were. Everyone who came to St Peter's knew what was in the golden casket.

'Actually, no,' the camerlengo said. 'A common misconception. That's not a reliquary. The box holds *palliums* – woven sashes that the Pope gives to newly elected cardinals.'

'But I thought—'

'As does everyone. The guidebooks label this as St Peter's tomb, but his true grave is two stories beneath us, buried in the earth. The Vatican excavated it in the forties. Nobody is allowed down there.'

Vittoria was shocked. As they moved away from the glowing recession into the darkness again, she thought of the stories she'd heard of pilgrims traveling thousands of miles to look at that golden box, thinking they were in the presence of St Peter. 'Shouldn't the Vatican tell people?'

'We all benefit from a sense of contact with divinity . . . even if it is only imagined.'

Vittoria, as a scientist, could not argue the logic. She had read countless studies of the placebo effect – aspirins curing cancer in people who *believed* they were using a miracle drug. What was *faith*, after all?

'Change,' the camerlengo said, 'is not something we do well within Vatican City. Admitting our past faults, modernization, are things we historically eschew. His Holiness was trying to change that.' He paused. 'Reaching to the modern world. Searching for new paths to God.'

Vittoria nodded in the dark. 'Like science?'

'To be honest, science seems irrelevant.'

'Irrelevant?' Vittoria could think of a lot of words to describe science, but in the modern world 'irrelevant' did not seem like one of them.

'Science can heal, or science can kill. It depends on the soul of the man using the science. It is the soul that interests me.'

'When did you hear your call?'

'Before I was born.'

Vittoria looked at him.

'I'm sorry, that always seems like a strange question. What I mean is that I've always known I would serve God. From the moment I could first think. It wasn't until I was a young man, though, in the military, that I truly understood my purpose.'

Vittoria was surprised. 'You were in the military?'

'Two years. I refused to fire a weapon, so they made me fly instead. Medevac helicopters. In fact, I still fly from time to time.'

Vittoria tried to picture the young priest flying a helicopter. Oddly, she could see him perfectly behind the controls. Camerlengo Ventresca possessed a grit that seemed to accentuate his conviction rather than cloud it. 'Did you ever fly the Pope?'

'Heavens no. We left that precious cargo to the professionals. His Holiness let me take the helicopter to

370

our retreat in Gandolfo sometimes.' He paused, looking at her. 'Ms Vetra, thank you for your help here today. I am very sorry about your father. Truly.'

'Thank you.'

'I never knew my father. He died before I was born. I lost my mother when I was ten.'

Vittoria looked up. 'You were orphaned?' She felt a sudden kinship.

'I survived an accident. An accident that took my mother.'

'Who took care of you?'

'God,' the camerlengo said. 'He quite literally sent me another father. A bishop from Palermo appeared at my hospital bed and took me in. At the time I was not surprised. I had sensed God's watchful hand over me even as a boy. The bishop's appearance simply confirmed what I had already suspected, that God had somehow chosen me to serve him.'

'You believed God chose you?'

'I did. And I do.' There was no trace of conceit in the camerlengo's voice, only gratitude. 'I worked under the bishop's tutelage for many years. He eventually became a cardinal. Still, he never forgot me. He is the father I remember.' A beam of a flashlight caught the camerlengo's face, and Vittoria sensed a loneliness in his eyes.

The group arrived beneath a towering pillar, and their lights converged on an opening in the floor. Vittoria looked down at the staircase descending into the void and suddenly wanted to turn back. The guards were already helping the camerlengo onto the stairs. They helped her next.

'What became of him?' she asked, descending, trying to keep her voice steady. 'The cardinal who took you in?'

371

'He left the College of Cardinals for another position.'

Vittoria was surprised.

'And then, I'm sorry to say, he passed on.'

'*Le mie condoglianze,*' Vittoria said. 'Recently?'

The camerlengo turned, shadows accentuating the pain on his face. 'Exactly fifteen days ago. We are going to see him right now.'

84

The dark lights glowed hot inside the archival vault. This vault was much smaller than the previous one Langdon had been in. *Less air. Less time.* He wished he'd asked Olivetti to turn on the recirculating fans.

Langdon quickly located the section of assets containing the ledgers cataloging *Belle Arti*. The section was impossible to miss. It occupied almost eight full stacks. The Catholic church owned millions of individual pieces worldwide.

Langdon scanned the shelves searching for Gianlorenzo Bernini. He began his search about midway down the first stack, at about the spot he thought the *B*'s would begin. After a moment of panic fearing the ledger was missing, he realized, to his greater dismay, that the ledgers were not arranged alphabetically. *Why am I not surprised?*

It was not until Langdon circled back to the beginning of the collection and climbed a rolling ladder to the top shelf that he understood the vault's organization. Perched precariously on the upper stacks he found the fattest ledgers of all – those belonging to the masters of the Renaissance – Michelangelo, Raphael, da Vinci, Botticelli. Langdon now realized, appropriate to a vault called 'Vatican Assets,' the ledgers were arranged by the overall monetary *value* of each artist's collection. Sandwiched between Raphael and Michelangelo, Langdon found the ledger marked Bernini. It was over five inches thick.

Already short of breath and struggling with the cumbersome volume, Langdon descended the ladder. Then, like a kid with a comic book, he spread himself out on the floor and opened the cover.

The book was cloth-bound and very solid. The ledger was handwritten in Italian. Each page cataloged a single work, including a short description, date, location, cost of materials, and sometimes a rough sketch of the piece. Langdon fanned through the pages ... over eight hundred in all. Bernini had been a busy man.

As a young student of art, Langdon had wondered how single artists could create so *much* work in their lifetimes. Later he learned, much to his disappointment, that famous artists actually created very little of their own work. They ran studios where they trained young artists to carry out their designs. Sculptors like Bernini created miniatures in clay and hired others to enlarge them into marble. Langdon knew that if Bernini had been required to *personally* complete all of his commissions, he would still be working today.

'Index,' he said aloud, trying to ward off the mental cobwebs. He flipped to the back of the book, intending to look under the letter *F* for titles containing the word *fuòco* – fire – but the *F*'s were not together. Langdon swore under his breath. *What the hell do these people have against alphabetizing?*

The entries had apparently been logged chronologically, one by one, as Bernini created each new work. Everything was listed by date. No help at all.

As Langdon stared at the list, another disheartening thought occurred to him. The title of the sculpture he was looking for might not even contain the word *Fire*. The previous two works – *Habakkuk and the Angel* and *West Ponente* – had not contained specific references to *Earth* or *Air*.

He spent a minute or two flipping randomly through the ledger in hopes that an illustration might jump out at him. Nothing did. He saw dozens of obscure works he had never heard of, but he also saw plenty he recognized . . . *Daniel and the Lion, Apollo and Daphne*, as well as a half dozen fountains. When he saw the fountains, his thoughts skipped momentarily ahead. Water. He wondered if the fourth altar of science was a fountain. A fountain seemed a perfect tribute to water. Langdon hoped they could catch the killer before he had to consider *Water* – Bernini had carved dozens of fountains in Rome, most of them in front of churches.

Langdon turned back to the matter at hand. *Fire*. As he looked through the book, Vittoria's words encouraged him. *You were familiar with the first two sculptures . . . you probably know this one too*. As he turned to the index again, he scanned for titles he knew. Some were familiar, but none jumped out. Langdon now realized he would never complete his search before passing out, so he decided, against his better judgment, that he would have to take the book outside the vault. *It's only a ledger*, he told himself. *It's not like I'm removing an original Galilean folio*. Langdon recalled the folio in his breast pocket and reminded himself to return it before leaving.

Hurrying now, he reached down to lift the volume, but as he did, he saw something that gave him pause. Although there were numerous notations throughout the index, the one that had just caught his eye seemed odd.

The note indicated that the famous Bernini sculpture, *The Ecstasy of St Teresa*, shortly after its unveiling, had been moved from its original location inside the Vatican. This in itself was not what had caught Langdon's eye. He was already familiar with the sculpture's checkered past. Though some thought it a masterpiece, Pope Urban VIII had rejected *The Ecstasy of St Teresa* as too sexually explicit for the Vatican. He had banished it to some obscure chapel across town. What had caught Langdon's eye was that the work had apparently been placed in one of the five churches on his list. What was more, the note indicated it had been moved there *per suggerimento del artista*.

By suggestion of the artist? Langdon was confused. It made no sense that Bernini had suggested his masterpiece be hidden in some obscure location. All artists wanted their work displayed prominently, not in some remote—

Langdon hesitated. *Unless* . . .

He was fearful even to entertain the notion. Was it possible? Had Bernini intentionally created a work so explicit that it forced the Vatican to hide it in some out-of-the-way spot? A location perhaps that Bernini himself could suggest? Maybe a remote church on a direct line with *West Ponente's* breath?

As Langdon's excitement mounted, his vague familiarity with the statue intervened, insisting the work had nothing to do with *fire*. The sculpture, as anyone who had seen it could attest, was anything but scientific – *pornographic* maybe, but certainly not scientific. An English critic had once condemned *The Ecstasy of St Teresa* as 'the most unfit ornament ever to be placed in a Christian Church.' Langdon certainly understood the controversy. Though brilliantly rendered, the statue depicted St Teresa on her back in the throes of a toe-curling orgasm. Hardly Vatican fare.

Langdon hurriedly flipped to the ledger's description of the work. When he saw the sketch, he felt an instantaneous and unexpected tingle of hope. In the sketch, St Teresa did indeed appear to be enjoying herself, but there was another figure in the statue who Langdon had forgotten was there.

An angel.

The sordid legend suddenly came back . . .

St Teresa was a nun sainted after she claimed an angel had paid her a blissful visit in her sleep. Critics later decided her encounter had probably been more sexual than spiritual. Scrawled at the bottom of the ledger, Langdon saw a familiar excerpt. St Teresa's own words left little to the imagination:

> . . . his great golden spear . . . filled with fire . . . plunged into me several times . . . penetrated to my entrails . . . a sweetness so extreme that one could not possibly wish it to stop.

Langdon smiled. *If that's not a metaphor for some serious sex, I don't know what is.* He was smiling also because of the ledger's description of the work.

Although the paragraph was in Italian, the word *fuòco* appeared a half dozen times:

... angel's spear tipped with point of *fire* ...

... angel's head emanating rays of *fire* ...

... woman inflamed by passion's *fire* ..

Langdon was not entirely convinced until he glanced up at the sketch again. The angel's fiery spear was raised like a beacon, pointing the way. *Let angels guide you on your lofty quest.* Even the *type* of angel Bernini had selected seemed significant. *It's a seraph,* Langdon realized. *Seraph literally means 'the fiery one.'*

Robert Langdon was not a man who had ever looked for confirmation from above, but when he read the name of the church where the sculpture now resided, he decided he might become a believer after all.

Santa Maria della Vittoria.

Vittoria, he thought, grinning. *Perfect.*

Staggering to his feet, Langdon felt a rush of dizziness. He glanced up the ladder, wondering if he should replace the book. *The hell with it,* he thought. *Father Jaqui can do it.* He closed the book and left it neatly at the bottom of the shelf

As he made his way toward the glowing button on the vault's electronic exit, he was breathing in shallow gasps. Nonetheless, he felt rejuvenated by his good fortune.

His good fortune, however, ran out before he reached the exit.

Without warning, the vault let out a pained sigh. The lights dimmed, and the exit button went dead. Then, like an enormous expiring beast, the archival complex went totally black. Someone had just killed power.

The Holy Vatican Grottoes are located beneath the main floor of St Peter's Basilica. They are the burial place of deceased Popes.

Vittoria reached the bottom of the spiral staircase and entered the grotto. The darkened tunnel reminded her of CERN's Large Hadron Collider – black and cold. Lit now only by the flashlights of the Swiss Guards, the tunnel carried a distinctly incorporeal feel. On both sides, hollow niches lined the walls. Recessed in the alcoves, as far as the lights let them see, the hulking shadows of sarcophagi loomed.

An iciness raked her flesh. *It's the cold*, she told herself, knowing that was only partially true. She had the sense they were being watched, not by anyone in the flesh, but by specters in the dark. On top of each tomb, in full papal vestments, lay life-sized semblances of each Pope, shown in death, arms folded across their chests. The prostrate bodies seemed to emerge from within the tombs, pressing upward against the marble lids as if trying to escape their mortal restraints. The flashlight procession moved on, and the papal silhouettes rose and fell against the walls, stretching and vanishing in a macabre shadowbox dance.

A silence had fallen across the group, and Vittoria couldn't tell whether it was one of respect or apprehension. She sensed both. The camerlengo moved with his eyes closed, as if he knew every step by heart. Vittoria suspected he had made this eerie promenade many times since the Pope's death . . . perhaps to pray at his tomb for guidance.

I worked under the cardinal's tutelage for many years,

the camerlengo had said. *He was like a father to me.* Vittoria recalled the camerlengo speaking those words in reference to the cardinal who had 'saved' him from the army. Now, however, Vittoria understood the rest of the story. That very cardinal who had taken the camerlengo under his wing had apparently later risen to the papacy and brought with him his young protégé to serve as chamberlain.

That explains a lot, Vittoria thought. She had always possessed a well-tuned perception for others' inner emotions, and something about the camerlengo had been nagging her all day. Since meeting him, she had sensed an anguish more soulful and private than the overwhelming crisis he now faced. Behind his pious calm, she saw a man tormented by personal demons. Now she knew her instincts had been correct. Not only was he facing the most devastating threat in Vatican history, but he was doing it without his mentor and friend . . . flying solo.

The guards slowed now, as if unsure where exactly in the darkness the most recent Pope was buried. The camerlengo continued assuredly and stopped before a marble tomb that seemed to glisten brighter than the others. Lying atop was a carved figure of the late Pope. When Vittoria recognized his face from television, a shot of fear gripped her. *What are we doing?*

'I realize we do not have much time,' the camerlengo said. 'I still ask we take a moment of prayer.'

The Swiss Guard all bowed their heads where they were standing. Vittoria followed suit, her heart pounding in the silence. The camerlengo knelt before the tomb and prayed in Italian. As Vittoria listened to his words, an unexpected grief surfaced as tears . . . tears for her own mentor . . . her own holy father. The camerlengo's words seemed as appropriate for her father as they did for the Pope.

'Supreme father, counselor, friend.' The camerlengo's voice echoed dully around the ring. 'You told me when I was young that the voice in my heart was that of God. You told me I must follow it no matter what painful places it leads. I hear that voice now, asking of me impossible tasks. Give me strength. Bestow on me forgiveness. What I do ... I do in the name of everything you believe. Amen.'

'Amen,' the guards whispered.

Amen, Father. Vittoria wiped her eyes.

The camerlengo stood slowly and stepped away from the tomb. 'Push the covering aside.'

The Swiss Guards hesitated. 'Signore,' one said, 'by law we are at your command.' He paused. 'We will do as you say ...'

The camerlengo seemed to read the young man's mind. 'Someday I will ask your forgiveness for placing you in this position. Today I ask for your obedience. Vatican laws are established to protect this church. It is in that very spirit that I command you to break them now.'

There was a moment of silence and then the lead guard gave the order. The three men set down their flashlights on the floor, and their shadows leapt overhead. Lit now from beneath, the men advanced toward the tomb. Bracing their hands against the marble covering near the head of the tomb, they planted their feet and prepared to push. On signal, they all thrust, straining against the enormous slab. When the lid did not move at all, Vittoria found herself almost hoping it was too heavy She was suddenly fearful of what they would find inside.

The men pushed harder, and still the stone did not move.

'*Ancora*,' the camerlengo said, rolling up the sleeves of his cassock and preparing to push along with them. '*Ora!*' Everyone heaved.

Vittoria was about to offer her own help, but just then, the lid began to slide. The men dug in again, and with an almost primal growl of stone on stone, the lid rotated off the top of the tomb and came to rest at an angle – the Pope's carved head now pushed back into the niche and his feet extended out into the hallway.

Everyone stepped back.

Tentatively, a guard bent and retrieved his flashlight. Then he aimed it into the tomb. The beam seemed to tremble a moment, and then the guard held it steady. The other guards gathered one by one. Even in the darkness Vittoria sensed them recoil. In succession, they crossed themselves.

The camerlengo shuddered when he looked into the tomb, his shoulders dropping like weights. He stood a long moment before turning away.

Vittoria had feared the corpse's mouth might be clenched tight with *rigor mortis* and that she would have to suggest breaking the jaw to see the tongue. She now saw it would be unnecessary. The cheeks had collapsed, and the Pope's mouth gaped wide.

His tongue was black as death.

No light. No sound.

The Secret Archives were black.

Fear, Langdon now realized, was an intense motivator. Short of breath, he fumbled through the blackness toward the revolving door. He found the button on the wall and rammed his palm against it. Nothing happened. He tried again. The door was dead.

Spinning blind, he called out, but his voice emerged strangled. The peril of his predicament suddenly closed in around him. His lungs strained for oxygen as the adrenaline doubled his heart rate. He felt like someone had just punched him in the gut.

When he threw his weight into the door, for an instant he thought he felt the door start to turn. He pushed again, seeing stars. Now he realized it was the entire room turning, not the door. Staggering away, Langdon tripped over the base of a rolling ladder and fell hard. He tore his knee against the edge of a book stack. Swearing, he got up and groped for the ladder.

He found it. He had hoped it would be heavy wood or iron, but it was aluminum. He grabbed the ladder and held it like a battering ram. Then he ran through the dark at the glass wall. It was closer than he thought. The ladder hit head-on, bouncing off. From the feeble sound of the collision, Langdon knew he was going to need a hell of a lot more than an aluminum ladder to break this glass.

When he flashed on the semiautomatic, his hopes surged and then instantly fell. The weapon was gone. Olivetti had relieved him of it in the Pope's office, saying he did not want loaded weapons around with the camerlengo present. It made sense at the time.

Langdon called out again, making less sound than the last time.

Next he remembered the walkie-talkie the guard had left on the table outside the vault. *Why the hell didn't I bring it in!* As the purple stars began to dance before his eyes, Langdon forced himself to think. *You've been trapped before,* he told himself. *You survived worse. You were just a kid and you figured it out.* The crushing darkness came flooding in. *Think!*

Langdon lowered himself onto the floor. He rolled over on his back and laid his hands at his sides. The first step was to gain control.

Relax. Conserve.

No longer fighting gravity to pump blood, Langdon's heart began to slow. It was a trick swimmers used to re-oxygenate their blood between tightly scheduled races.

There is plenty of air in here, he told himself. *Plenty. Now think.* He waited, half-expecting the lights to come back on at any moment. They did not. As he lay there, able to breathe better now, an eerie resignation came across him. He felt peaceful. He fought it.

You will move, damn it! But where . . .

On Langdon's wrist, Mickey Mouse glowed happily as if enjoying the dark: 9.33 p.m. Half an hour until *Fire.* Langdon thought it felt a whole hell of a lot later. His mind, instead of coming up with a plan for escape, was suddenly demanding an explanation. *Who turned off the power? Was Rocher expanding his search? Wouldn't Olivetti have warned Rocher that I'm in here!* Langdon knew at this point it made no difference.

Opening his mouth wide and tipping back his head,

Langdon pulled the deepest breaths he could manage. Each breath burned a little less than the last. His head cleared. He reeled his thoughts in and forced the gears into motion.

Glass walls, he told himself. *But damn thick glass*.

He wondered if any of the books in here were stored in heavy, steel, fireproof file cabinets. Langdon had seen them from time to time in other archives but had seen none here. Besides, finding one in the dark could prove time-consuming. Not that he could lift one anyway, particularly in his present state.

How about the examination table? Langdon knew this vault, like the other, had an examination table in the center of the stacks. *So what!* He knew he couldn't lift it. Not to mention, even if he could drag it, he wouldn't get it far. The stacks were closely packed, the aisles between them far too narrow.

The aisles are too narrow . . .

Suddenly, Langdon knew.

With a burst of confidence, he jumped to his feet far too fast. Swaying in the fog of a head rush, he reached out in the dark for support. His hand found a stack. Waiting a moment, he forced himself to conserve. He would need all of his strength to do this.

Positioning himself against the book stack like a football player against a training sled, he planted his feet and pushed. *If I can somehow tip the shelf.* But it barely moved. He realigned and pushed again. His feet slipped backward on the floor. The stack creaked but did not move.

He needed leverage.

Finding the glass wall again, he placed one hand on it to guide him as he raced in the dark toward the far end of the vault. The back wall loomed suddenly, and he collided with it, crushing his shoulder. Cursing, Langdon circled the shelf and grabbed the stack at about eye level. Then, propping one leg on the glass behind him and another on the lower shelves, he started to climb. Books fell around him, fluttering into the darkness. He didn't care. Instinct for survival had long since overridden archival decorum. He sensed his equilibrium was hampered by the total darkness and closed his eyes, coaxing his brain to ignore visual input. He moved faster now. The air felt leaner the higher he went. He scrambled toward the upper shelves, stepping on books, trying to gain purchase, heaving himself upward. Then, like a rock climber conquering a rock face, Langdon grasped the top shelf. Stretching his legs out behind him, he walked his feet up the glass wall until he was almost horizontal.

Now or never, Robert, a voice urged. *Just like the leg press in the Harvard gym.*

With dizzying exertion, he planted his feet against the wall behind him, braced his arms and chest against the stack, and pushed. Nothing happened.

Fighting for air, he repositioned and tried again, extending his legs. Ever so slightly, the stack moved. He pushed again, and the stack rocked forward an inch or so and then back. Langdon took advantage of the motion, inhaling what felt like an oxygenless breath and heaving again. The shelf rocked farther.

Like a swing set, he told himself. *Keep the rhythm. A little more.*

Langdon rocked the shelf, extending his legs farther with each push. His quadriceps burned now, and he blocked the pain. The pendulum was in motion. *Three more pushes,* he urged himself.

It only took two.

There was an instant of weightless uncertainty. Then, with a thundering of books sliding off the shelves, Langdon and the shelf were falling forward.

Halfway to the ground, the shelf hit the stack next to it. Langdon hung on, throwing his weight forward, urging the second shelf to topple. There was a moment of motionless panic, and then, creaking under the weight, the second stack began to tip. Langdon was falling again.

Like enormous dominoes, the stacks began to topple, one after another. Metal on metal, books tumbling everywhere. Langdon held on as his inclined stack bounced downward like a ratchet on a jack. He wondered how many stacks there were in all. How much would they weigh? The glass at the far end was thick . . .

Langdon's stack had fallen almost to the horizontal when he heard what he was waiting for – a different kind of collision. Far off. At the end of the vault. The sharp smack of metal on glass. The vault around him shook, and Langdon knew the final stack, weighted down by the others, had hit the glass hard. The sound that followed was the most unwelcome sound Langdon had ever heard.

Silence.

There was no crashing of glass, only the resounding thud as the wall accepted the weight of the stacks now propped against it. He lay wide-eyed on the pile of books. Somewhere in the distance there was a creaking. Langdon would have held his breath to listen, but he had none left to hold.

One second. Two . . .

Then, as he teetered on the brink of unconsciousness, Langdon heard a distant yielding . . . a ripple spidering outward through the glass. Suddenly, like a cannon, the glass exploded. The stack beneath Langdon collapsed to the floor.

Like welcome rain on a desert, shards of glass tinkled downward in the dark. With a great sucking hiss, the air gushed in.

Thirty seconds later, in the Vatican Grottoes, Vittoria was standing before a corpse when the electronic squawk of a walkie-talkie broke the silence. The voice blaring out sounded short of breath. 'This is Robert Langdon! Can anyone hear me?'

Vittoria looked up. *Robert!* She could not believe how much she suddenly wished he were there.

The guards exchanged puzzled looks. One took a radio off his belt. 'Mr Langdon? You are on channel three. The commander is waiting to hear from you on channel one.'

'I know he's on channel one, damn it! I don't want to speak to him. I want the camerlengo. Now! Somebody find him for me.'

In the obscurity of the Secret Archives, Langdon stood amidst shattered glass and tried to catch his breath. He felt a warm liquid on his left hand and knew he was bleeding. The camerlengo's voice spoke at once, startling Langdon.

'This is Camerlengo Ventresca. What's going on?'

Langdon pressed the button, his heart still pounding. 'I think somebody just tried to kill me!'

There was a silence on the line.

Langdon tried to calm himself. 'I also know where the next killing is going to be.'

The voice that came back was not the camerlengo's.

387

It was Commander Olivetti's: 'Mr Langdon. Do not speak another word.'

87

Langdon's watch, now smeared with blood, read 9.41 p.m. as he ran across the Courtyard of the Belvedere and approached the fountain outside the Swiss Guard security center. His hand had stopped bleeding and now felt worse than it looked. As he arrived, it seemed everyone convened at once – Olivetti, Rocher, the camerlengo, Vittoria, and a handful of guards.

Vittoria hurried toward him immediately. 'Robert, you're hurt.'

Before Langdon could answer, Olivetti was before him. 'Mr Langdon, I'm relieved you're okay. I'm sorry about the crossed signals in the archives.'

'Crossed signals?' Langdon demanded. 'You knew damn well—'

'It was my fault,' Rocher said, stepping forward, sounding contrite. 'I had no idea you were in the archives. Portions of our white zones are cross-wired with that building. We were extending our search. I'm the one who killed power. If I had known . . '

'Robert,' Vittoria said, taking his wounded hand in hers and looking it over, 'the Pope was poisoned. The Illuminati killed him.'

Langdon heard the words, but they barely registered. He was saturated. All he could feel was the warmth of Vittoria's hands.

The camerlengo pulled a silk handkerchief from his

cassock and handed it to Langdon so he could clean himself. The man said nothing. His green eyes seemed filled with a new fire.

'Robert,' Vittoria pressed, 'you said you found where the next cardinal is going to be killed?'

Langdon felt flighty. 'I do, it's at the—'

'No,' Olivetti interrupted. 'Mr Langdon, when I asked you not to speak another word on the walkie-talkie, it was for a reason.' He turned to the handful of assembled Swiss Guards. 'Excuse us, gentlemen.'

The soldiers disappeared into the security center. No indignity. Only compliance.

Olivetti turned back to the remaining group. 'As much as it pains me to say this, the murder of our Pope is an act that could only have been accomplished with help from within these walls. For the good of all, we can trust no one. Including our guards.' He seemed to be suffering as he spoke the words.

Rocher looked anxious. 'Inside collusion implies—'

'Yes,' Olivetti said. 'The integrity of your search is compromised. And yet it is a gamble we must take. Keep looking.'

Rocher looked like he was about to say something, thought better of it, and left.

The camerlengo inhaled deeply. He had not said a word yet, and Langdon sensed a new rigor in the man, as if a turning point had been reached.

'Commander?' The camerlengo's tone was impermeable. 'I am going to break conclave.'

Olivetti pursed his lips, looking dour. 'I advise against it. We still have two hours and twenty minutes.'

'A heartbeat.'

Olivetti's tone was now challenging. 'What do you

intend to do? Evacuate the cardinals single-handedly?'

'I intend to save this church with whatever power God has given me. How I proceed is no longer your concern.'

Olivetti straightened. 'Whatever you intend to do . . ' He paused. 'I do not have the authority to restrain you. Particularly in light of my apparent failure as head of security. I ask only that you wait. Wait twenty minutes . . . until after ten o'clock. If Mr Langdon's information is correct, I may still have a chance to catch this assassin. There is still a chance to preserve protocol and decorum.'

'Decorum?' The camerlengo let out a choked laugh. 'We have long since passed propriety, commander. In case you hadn't noticed, this is war.'

A guard emerged from the security center and called out to the camerlengo, 'Signore, I just got word we have detained the BBC reporter, Mr Glick.'

The camerlengo nodded. 'Have both he and his camerawoman meet me outside the Sistine Chapel.'

Olivetti's eyes widened. 'What are you doing?'

'Twenty minutes, commander. That's all I'm giving you.' Then he was gone.

When Olivetti's Alfa Romeo tore out of Vatican City, this time there was no line of unmarked cars following him. In the back seat, Vittoria bandaged Langdon's hand with a first-aid kit she'd found in the glove box.

Olivetti stared straight ahead. 'Okay Mr. Langdon. Where are we going?'

Even with its siren now affixed and blaring, Olivetti's Alfa Romeo seemed to go unnoticed as it rocketed across the bridge into the heart of old Rome. All the traffic was moving in the other direction, toward the Vatican, as if the Holy See had suddenly become the hottest entertainment in Rome.

Langdon sat in the backseat, the questions whipping through his mind. He wondered about the killer, if they would catch him this time, if he would tell them what they needed to know, if it was already too late. How long before the camerlengo told the crowd in St Peter's Square they were in danger? The incident in the vault still nagged. *A mistake.*

Olivetti never touched the brakes as he snaked the howling Alfa Romeo toward the Church of Santa Maria della Vittoria. Langdon knew on any other day his knuckles would have been white. At the moment, however, he felt anesthetized. Only the throbbing in his hand reminded him where he was.

Overhead, the siren wailed. *Nothing like telling him we're coming,* Langdon thought. And yet they were making incredible time. He guessed Olivetti would kill the siren as they drew nearer.

Now with a moment to sit and reflect, Langdon felt a tinge of amazement as the news of the Pope's murder finally registered in his mind. The thought was inconceivable, and yet somehow it seemed a perfectly logical event. Infiltration had always been the Illuminati powerbase – rearrangements of power from within. And it was not as if Popes had never been murdered. Countless rumors of treachery abounded, although with no autopsy, none was ever confirmed. Until recently. Academics not long ago had gotten permission to X-ray the tomb of Pope Celestine V, who had allegedly died at the hands of his overeager successor, Boniface VIII. The researchers had hoped the X-ray might reveal some small hint of foul play – a broken bone perhaps. Incredibly, the X-ray had revealed a ten-inch nail driven into the Pope's skull.

Langdon now recalled a series of news clippings fellow Illuminati buffs had sent him years ago. At first he had thought the clippings were a prank, so he'd gone to the Harvard microfiche collection to confirm the articles were authentic. Incredibly, they were. He now kept them on his bulletin board as examples of how even respectable news organizations sometimes got carried away with Illuminati paranoia. Suddenly, the media's suspicions seemed a lot less paranoid. Langdon could see the articles clearly in his mind . . .

THE BRITISH BROADCASTING CORPORATION
June 14,1998

Pope John Paul I, who died in 1978, fell victim to a plot by the P2 Masonic Lodge . . . The secret society P2 decided to murder John Paul I when it saw he was determined to dismiss the American Archbishop Paul Marcinkus as President of the Vatican Bank. The Bank had been implicated in shady financial deals with the Masonic Lodge . . .

THE NEW YORK TIMES
August 24, 1998

Why was the late John Paul I wearing his day shirt in

bed? Why was it torn? The questions don't stop there. No medical investigations were made. Cardinal Villot forbade an autopsy on the grounds that no Pope was ever given a postmortem. And John Paul's medicines mysteriously vanished from his bedside, as did his glasses, slippers and his last will and testament.

LONDON DAILY MAIL
August 27, 1998

... a plot including a powerful, ruthless and illegal Masonic lodge with tentacles stretching into the Vatican.

The cellular in Vittoria's pocket rang, thankfully erasing the memories from Langdon's mind.

Vittoria answered, looking confused as to who might be calling her. Even from a few feet away, Langdon recognized the laserlike voice on the phone.

'Vittoria? This is Maximilian Kohler. Have you found the antimatter yet?'

'Max? You're okay?'

'I saw the news. There was no mention of CERN or the antimatter. This is good. What is happening?'

'We haven't located the canister yet. The situation is complex. Robert Langdon has been quite an asset. We have a lead on catching the man assassinating cardinals. Right now we are headed—'

'Ms Vetra,' Olivetti interrupted. 'You've said enough.'

She covered the receiver, clearly annoyed. 'Commander, this is the president of CERN. Certainly he has a right to—'

'He has a right,' Olivetti snapped, 'to be here handling this situation. You're on an open cellular line. You've said enough.'

Vittoria took a deep breath. 'Max?'

'I may have some information for you,' Max said. 'About your father . . . I may know who he told about the antimatter.'

Vittoria's expression clouded. 'Max, my father said he told no one.'

'I'm afraid, Vittoria, your father *did* tell someone. I need to check some security records. I will be in touch soon.' The line went dead.

Vittoria looked waxen as she returned the phone to her pocket.

'You okay?' Langdon asked.

Vittoria nodded, her trembling fingers revealing the lie.

'The church is near Piazza Barberini,' Olivetti said, killing the siren and checking his watch. 'We have nine minutes.'

When Langdon had first realized the location of the third marker, the position of the church had rung some distant bell for him. *Piazza Barberini*. Something about the name was familiar . . . something he could not place. Now Langdon realized what it was. The piazza was the sight of a controversial subway stop. Twenty years ago, construction of the subway terminal had created a stir among art historians who feared digging beneath Piazza Barberini might topple the multiton obelisk that stood in the center. City planners had removed the obelisk and replaced it with a small fountain called the *Triton*.

In Bernini's day, Langdon now realized, *Piazza Barberini had contained an obelisk!* Whatever doubts Langdon had felt that this was the location of the third marker now totally evaporated.

A block from the piazza, Olivetti turned into an alley, gunned the car halfway down, and skidded to a stop. He pulled off his suit jacket, rolled up his sleeves, and loaded his weapon.

'We can't risk your being recognized,' he said. 'You two were on television. I want you across the piazza, out of sight, watching the front entrance. I'm going in the back.' He produced a familiar pistol and handed it to Langdon. 'Just in case.'

Langdon frowned. It was the second time today he had been handed the gun. He slid it into his breast pocket. As he did, he realized he was still carrying the folio from *Diagramma*. He couldn't believe he had forgotten to leave it behind. He pictured the Vatican Curator collapsing in spasms of outrage at the thought of this priceless artifact being packed around Rome like some tourist map. Then Langdon thought of the mess of shattered glass and strewn documents that he'd left behind in the archives. The curator had other problems. *If the archives even survive the night . . .*

Olivetti got out of the car and motioned back up the alley. 'The piazza is that way. Keep your eyes open and don't let yourselves be seen.' He tapped the phone on his belt. 'Ms Vetra, let's retest our auto dial.'

Vittoria removed her phone and hit the auto dial number she and Olivetti had programmed at the Pantheon. Olivetti's phone vibrated in silent-ring mode on his belt.

The commander nodded. 'Good. If you see anything, I want to know.' He cocked his weapon. 'I'll be inside waiting. This heathen is mine.'

At that moment, very nearby, another cellular phone was ringing.

The Hassassin answered. 'Speak.'

'It is I,' the voice said. 'Janus.'

The Hassassin smiled. 'Hello, master.'

'Your position may be known. Someone is coming to stop you.'

'They are too late. I have already made the arrangements here.'

'Good. Make sure you escape alive. There is work yet to be done.'

'Those who stand in my way will die.'

'Those who stand in your way are knowledgeable.'

'You speak of an American scholar?'

'You are aware of him?'

The Hassassin chuckled. 'Cool-tempered but naïve. He spoke to me on the phone earlier. He is with a female who seems quite the opposite.' The killer felt a stirring of arousal as he recalled the fiery temperament of Leonardo Vetra's daughter.

There was a momentary silence on the line, the first hesitation the Hassassin had ever sensed from his Illuminati master. Finally, Janus spoke. 'Eliminate them if need be.'

The killer smiled. 'Consider it done.' He felt a warm anticipation spreading through his body. *Although the woman I may keep as a prize.*

89

War had broken out in St Peter's Square.

The piazza had exploded into a frenzy of aggression. Media trucks skidded into place like assault vehicles claiming beachheads. Reporters unfurled high-tech electronics like soldiers arming for battle. All around the perimeter of the square, networks jockeyed for position as they raced to erect the newest weapon in media wars – flat-screen displays.

Flat-screen displays were enormous video screens that could be assembled on top of trucks or portable scaffolding. The screens served as a kind of billboard advertisement for the network, broadcasting that network's coverage and corporate logo like a drive-in movie. If a screen were well-situated – in front of the action, for example – a competing network could not shoot the story without including an advertisement for their competitor.

The square was quickly becoming not only a multi-media extravaganza, but a frenzied public vigil. Onlookers poured in from all directions. Open space in the usually limitless square was fast becoming a valuable commodity. People clustered around the towering flat-screen displays, listening to live reports in stunned excitement.

Only a hundred yards away, inside the thick walls of St Peter's Basilica, the world was serene. Lieutenant Chartrand and three other guards moved through the darkness. Wearing their infrared goggles, they fanned out across the nave, swinging their detectors before them. The search of Vatican City's public access areas so far had yielded nothing.

'Better remove your goggles up here,' the senior guard said.

Chartrand was already doing it. They were nearing the Niche of the Palliums – the sunken area in the center of the basilica. It was lit by ninety-nine oil lamps, and the amplified infrared would have seared their eyes.

Chartrand enjoyed being out of the heavy goggles, and he stretched his neck as they descended into the sunken niche to scan the area. The room was beautiful . . . golden and glowing. He had not been down here yet.

It seemed every day since Chartrand had arrived in Vatican City he had learned some new Vatican mystery. These oil lamps were one of them. There were exactly ninety-nine lamps burning at all times. It was tradition. The clergy vigilantly refilled the lamps with sacred oils such that no lamp ever burned out. It was said they would burn until the end of time.

Or at least until midnight, Chartrand thought, feeling his mouth go dry again.

Chartrand swung his detector over the oil lamps. Nothing hidden in here. He was not surprised; the canister, according to the video feed, was hidden in a *dark* area.

As he moved across the niche, he came to a bulkhead grate covering a hole in the floor. The hole led to a steep and narrow stairway that went straight down. He had heard stories about what lay down there. Thankfully they would not have to descend. Rocher's orders were clear. *Search only the public access areas; ignore the white zones.*

'What's that smell?' he asked, turning away from the grate. The niche smelled intoxicatingly sweet.

'Fumes from the lamps,' one of them replied.

Chartrand was surprised. 'Smells more like cologne than kerosene.'

'It's not kerosene. These lamps are close to the papal

altar, so they take a special, ambiental mixture –
ethanol, sugar, butane, and perfume.'

'*Butane?*' Chartrand eyed the lamps uneasily

The guard nodded. 'Don't spill any. Smells like
heaven, but burns like hell.'

The guards had completed searching the Niche of the
Palliums and were moving across the basilica again
when their walkie-talkies went off.

It was an update. The guards listened in shock.

Apparently there were troubling new developments, which could not be shared on-air, but the
camerlengo had decided to break tradition and enter
conclave to address the cardinals. Never before in
history had this been done. Then again, Chartrand
realized, never before in history had the Vatican been
sitting on what amounted to some sort of neoteric
nuclear warhead.

Chartrand felt comforted to know the camerlengo
was taking control. The camerlengo was the person
inside Vatican City for whom Chartrand held the most
respect. Some of the guards thought of the camerlengo
as a *beato* – a religious zealot whose love of God
bordered on obsession – but even they agreed . . .
when it came to fighting the enemies of God, the
camerlengo was the one man who would stand up and
play hardball.

The Swiss Guards had seen a lot of the camerlengo
this week in preparation for conclave, and everyone
had commented that the man seemed a bit rough
around the edges, his verdant eyes a bit more intense
than usual. Not surprisingly, they had all commented;
not only was the camerlengo responsible for planning
the sacred conclave, but he had to do it immediately

on the heels of the loss of his mentor, the Pope.

Chartrand had only been at the Vatican a few months when he heard the story of the bomb that blew up the camerlengo's mother before the kid's very eyes. *A bomb in church . . . and now it's happening all over again.* Sadly, the authorities never caught the bastards who planted the bomb ... probably some anti-Christian hate group they said, and the case faded away. No wonder the camerlengo despised apathy.

A couple months back, on a peaceful afternoon inside Vatican City, Chartrand had bumped into the camerlengo coming across the grounds. The camerlengo had apparently recognized Chartrand as a new guard and invited him to accompany him on a stroll. They had talked about nothing in particular, and the camerlengo made Chartrand feel immediately at home.

'Father,' Chartrand said, 'may I ask you a strange question?'

The camerlengo smiled. 'Only if I may give you a strange answer.'

Chartrand laughed. 'I have asked every priest I know, and I still don't understand.'

'What troubles you?' The camerlengo led the way in short, quick strides, his frock kicking out in front of him as he walked. His black, crepe-sole shoes seemed befitting, Chartrand thought, like reflections of the man's essence ... modern but humble, and showing signs of wear.

Chartrand took a deep breath. 'I don't understand this *omnipotent-benevolent* thing.'

The camerlengo smiled. 'You've been reading Scripture.'

'I try.'

'You are confused because the Bible describes God as an omnipotent and benevolent deity.'

'Exactly.'

'Omnipotent-benevolent simply means that God is all-powerful *and* well-meaning.'

'I understand the concept. It's just . . . there seems to be a contradiction.'

'Yes. The contradiction is pain. Man's starvation, war, sickness . . .'

'Exactly!' Chartrand knew the camerlengo would understand. 'Terrible things happen in this world. Human tragedy seems like proof that God could not possibly be *both* all-powerful and well-meaning. If He *loves* us and has the *power* to change our situation, He would prevent our pain, wouldn't He?'

The camerlengo frowned. 'Would He?'

Chartrand felt uneasy. Had he overstepped his bounds? Was this one of those religious questions you just didn't ask? 'Well . . . if God loves us, and He can protect us, He would *have* to. It seems He is either omnipotent and uncaring, or benevolent and powerless to help.'

'Do you have children, Lieutenant?'

Chartrand flushed. 'No, signore.'

'Imagine you had an eight-year-old son . . . would you love him?'

'Of course.'

'Would you do everything in your power to prevent pain in his life?'

'Of course.'

'Would you let him skateboard?'

Chartrand did a double take. The camerlengo always seemed oddly 'in touch' for a clergyman. 'Yeah, I guess,' Chartrand said. 'Sure, I'd let him skateboard, but I'd tell him to be careful.'

'So as this child's father, you would give him some basic, good advice and then let him go off and make his own mistakes?'

'I wouldn't run behind him and mollycoddle him if that's what you mean.'

'But what if he fell and skinned his knee?'

'He would learn to be more careful.'

The camerlengo smiled. 'So although you have the *power* to interfere and prevent your child's pain, you would *choose* to show your love by letting him learn his own lessons?'

'Of course. Pain is part of growing up. It's how we learn.'

The camerlengo nodded. 'Exactly.'

90

Langdon and Vittoria observed Piazza Barberini from the shadows of a small alleyway on the western corner. The church was opposite them, a hazy cupola emerging from a faint cluster of buildings across the square. The night had brought with it a welcome cool, and Langdon was surprised to find the square deserted. Above them, through open windows, blaring televisions reminded Langdon where everyone had disappeared to.

'. . . no comment yet from the Vatican . . . Illuminati murders of two cardinals . . . satanic presence in Rome . . . speculation about further infiltration . . .'

The news had spread like Nero's fire. Rome sat riveted, as did the rest of the world. Langdon wondered if they would really be able to stop this run-away train. As he scanned the piazza and waited, Langdon realized that despite the encroachment of modern buildings, the piazza still looked remarkably elliptical. High above, like some sort of modern shrine to a bygone hero, an enormous neon sign blinked on the roof of a luxurious hotel. Vittoria had already pointed it out to Langdon. The sign seemed eerily befitting.

HOTEL BERNINI

'Five of ten,' Vittoria said, cat eyes darting around the square. No sooner had she spoken the words than she grabbed Langdon's arm and pulled him back into the shadows. She motioned into the center of the square.

Langdon followed her gaze. When he saw it, he stiffened.

Crossing in front of them, beneath a street lamp, two dark figures appeared. Both were cloaked, their heads covered with dark *mantles*, the traditional black covering of Catholic widows. Langdon would have guessed they were women, but he couldn't be sure in the dark. One looked elderly and moved as if in pain, hunched over. The other, larger and stronger, was helping.

'Give me the gun,' Vittoria said.

'You can't just—'

Fluid as a cat, Vittoria was in and out of his pocket once again. The gun glinted in her hand. Then, in absolute silence, as if her feet never touched the cobblestone, she was circling left in the shadows, arch-ing across the square to approach the couple from the

403

rear. Langdon stood transfixed as Vittoria disappeared. Then, swearing to himself, he hurried after her.

The couple was moving slowly, and it was only a matter of half a minute before Langdon and Vittoria were positioned behind them, closing in from the rear. Vittoria concealed the gun beneath casually crossed arms in front of her, out of sight but accessible in a flash. She seemed to float faster and faster as the gap lessened, and Langdon battled to keep up. When his shoes scuffed a stone and sent it skittering, Vittoria shot him a sideways glare. But the couple did not seem to hear. They were talking.

At thirty feet, Langdon could start to hear voices. No words. Just faint murmurings. Beside him, Vittoria moved faster with every step. Her arms loosened before her, the gun starting to peek out. Twenty feet. The voices were clearer – one much louder than the other. Angry. Ranting. Langdon sensed it was the voice of an old woman. Gruff. Androgynous. He strained to hear what she was saying, but another voice cut the night.

'*Mi scusi!*' Vittoria's friendly tone lit the square like a torch.

Langdon tensed as the cloaked couple stopped short and began to turn. Vittoria kept striding toward them, even faster now, on a collision course. They would have no time to react. Langdon realized his own feet had stopped moving. From behind, he saw Vittoria's arms loosening, her hand coming free, the gun swinging forward. Then, over her shoulder, he saw a face, lit now in the street lamp. The panic surged to his legs, and he lunged forward. 'Vittoria no!'

Vittoria, however, seemed to exist a split second

ahead of him. In a motion as swift as it was casual, Vittoria's arms were raised again, the gun disappearing as she clutched herself like a woman on a chilly night. Langdon stumbled to her side, almost colliding with the cloaked couple before them.

'*Buona sera*,' Vittoria blurted, her voice startled with retreat.

Langdon exhaled in relief. Two elderly women stood before them scowling out from beneath their mantles. One was so old she could barely stand. The other was helping her. Both clutched rosaries. They seemed confused by the sudden interruption.

Vittoria smiled, although she looked shaken. '*Dov'è la chiesa Santa Maria della Vittoria?* Where is the Church of—'

The two women motioned in unison to a bulky silhouette of a building on an inclined street from the direction they had come. '*È là.*'

'*Grazie*,' Langdon said, putting his hands on Vittoria's shoulders and gently pulling her back. He couldn't believe they'd almost attacked a pair of old ladies.

'*Non si puó entrare*,' one woman warned. '*È chiusa temprano.*'

'Closed early?' Vittoria looked surprised. '*Perchè?*'

Both women explained at once. They sounded irate. Langdon understood only parts of the grumbling Italian. Apparently, the women had been inside the church fifteen minutes ago praying for the Vatican in its time of need, when some man had appeared and told them the church was closing early.

'*Hanno conosciuto l'uomo?*' Vittoria demanded, sounding tense. 'Did you know the man?'

The women shook their heads. The man was a

straniero crudo, they explained, and he had forcibly made everyone inside leave, even the young priest and janitor, who said they were calling the police. But the intruder had only laughed, telling them to be sure the police brought cameras.

Cameras? Langdon wondered.

The women clucked angrily and called the man a *bar-àrabo*. Then, grumbling, they continued on their way.

'Bar-àrabo?' Langdon asked Vittoria. 'A barbarian?'

Vittoria looked suddenly taut. 'Not quite. *Bar-àrabo* is derogatory wordplay. It means *Àrabo* . . . Arab.'

Langdon felt a shiver and turned toward the outline of the church. As he did, his eyes glimpsed something in the church's stained-glass windows. The image shot dread through his body.

Unaware, Vittoria removed her cell phone and pressed the auto dial. 'I'm warning Olivetti.'

Speechless, Langdon reached out and touched her arm. With a tremulous hand, he pointed to the church.

Vittoria let out a gasp.

Inside the building, glowing like evil eyes through the stained-glass windows . . . shone the growing flash of flames.

91

Langdon and Vittoria dashed to the main entrance of the church of Santa Maria della Vittoria and found the wooden door locked. Vittoria fired three shots from

Olivetti's semi-automatic into the ancient bolt, and it shattered.

The church had no anteroom, so the entirety of the sanctuary spread out in one gasping sweep as Langdon and Vittoria threw open the main door. The scene before them was so unexpected, so bizarre, that Langdon had to close his eyes and reopen them before his mind could take it all in.

The church was lavish baroque . . . gilded walls and altars. Dead center of the sanctuary, beneath the main cupola, wooden pews had been stacked high and were now ablaze in some sort of epic funeral pyre. A bonfire shooting high into the dome. As Langdon's eyes followed the inferno upward, the true horror of the scene descended like a bird of prey.

High overhead, from the left and right sides of the ceiling, hung two incensor cables – lines used for swinging frankincense vessels above the congregation. These lines, however, carried no incensors now. Nor were they swinging. They had been used for something else . . .

Suspended from the cables was a human being. A naked man. Each wrist had been connected to an opposing cable, and he had been hoisted almost to the point of being torn apart. His arms were outstretched in a spread-eagle as if he were nailed to some sort of invisible crucifix hovering within the house of God.

Langdon felt paralyzed as he stared upward. A moment later, he witnessed the final abomination. The old man was alive, and he raised his head. A pair of terrified eyes gazed down in a silent plea for help. On the man's chest was a scorched emblem. He had been branded. Langdon could not see it clearly, but he had little doubt what the marking said. As the flames climbed higher, lapping at the man's feet, the victim let out a cry of pain, his body trembling.

As if ignited by some unseen force, Langdon felt his body suddenly in motion, dashing down the main aisle toward the conflagration. His lungs filled with smoke as he closed in. Ten feet from the inferno, at a full sprint, Langdon hit a wall of heat. The skin on his face singed, and he fell back, shielding his eyes and landing hard on the marble floor. Staggering upright, he pressed forward again, hands raised in protection.

Instantly he knew. The fire was far too hot.

Moving back again, he scanned the chapel walls. *A heavy tapestry*, he thought. *If I can somehow smother the . . .* But he knew a tapestry was not to be found. *This is a baroque chapel, Robert, not some damn German castle! Think!* He forced his eyes back to the suspended man.

High above, smoke and flames swirled in the cupola. The incensor cables stretched outward from the man's wrists, rising to the ceiling where they passed through pulleys, and descended again to metal cleats on either side of the church. Langdon looked over at one of the cleats. It was high on the wall, but he knew if he could get to it and loosen one of the lines, the tension would slacken and the man would swing wide of the fire.

A sudden surge of flames crackled higher, and Langdon heard a piercing scream from above. The skin on the man's feet was starting to blister. The cardinal was being roasted alive. Langdon fixed his sights on the cleat and ran for it.

In the rear of the church, Vittoria clutched the back of a pew, trying to gather her senses. The image overhead was horrid. She forced her eyes away. *Do something!*

She wondered where Olivetti was. Had he seen the Hassassin? Had he caught him? Where were they now? Vittoria moved forward to help Langdon, but as she did, a sound stopped her.

The crackling of the flames was getting louder by the instant, but a second sound also cut the air. A metallic vibration. Nearby The repetitive pulse seemed to emanate from the end of the pews to her left. It was a stark rattle, like the ringing of a phone, but stony and hard. She clutched the gun firmly and moved down the row of pews. The sound grew louder. On. Off. A recurrent vibration.

As she approached the end of the aisle, she sensed the sound was coming from the floor just around the corner at the end of the pews. As she moved forward, gun outstretched in her right hand, she realized she was also holding something in her left hand – her cell phone. In her panic she had forgotten that outside she had used it to dial the commander ... setting off his phone's silent vibration feature as a warning. Vittoria raised her phone to her ear. It was still ringing. The commander had never answered. Suddenly, with rising fear, Vittoria sensed she knew what was making the sound. She stepped forward, trembling.

The entire church seemed to sink beneath her feet as her eyes met the lifeless form on the floor. No stream of liquid flowed from the body. No signs of violence tattooed the flesh. There was only the fearful geometry of the commander's head ... torqued backward, twisted 180 degrees in the wrong direction. Vittoria fought the images of her own father's mangled body

The phone on the commander's belt lay against the floor, vibrating over and over against the cold marble. Vittoria hung up her own phone, and the ringing stopped. In the silence, Vittoria heard a new sound. A breathing in the dark directly behind her.

She started to spin, gun raised, but she knew she was too late. A laser beam of heat screamed from the top of her skull to the soles of her feet as the killer's elbow crashed down on the back of her neck.

'Now you are mine,' a voice said.

Then, everything went black.

Across the sanctuary, on the left lateral wall, Langdon balanced atop a pew and scraped upward on the wall trying to reach the cleat. The cable was still six feet above his head. Cleats like these were common in churches and were placed high to prevent tampering. Langdon knew priests used wooden ladders called *piuòli* to access the cleats. The killer had obviously used the church's ladder to hoist his victim. *So where the hell is the ladder now!* Langdon looked down, searching the floor around him. He had a faint recollection of seeing a ladder in here somewhere. *But where?* A moment later his heart sank. He realized where he had seen it. He turned toward the raging fire. Sure enough, the ladder was high atop the blaze, engulfed in flames.

Filled now with desperation, Langdon scanned the entire church from his raised platform, looking for anything at all that could help him reach the cleat. As his eyes probed the church, he had a sudden realization.

Where the hell is Vittoria? She had disappeared. *Did she go for help?* Langdon screamed out her name, but there was no response. *And where is Olivetti!*

There was a howl of pain from above, and Langdon sensed he was already too late. As his eyes went skyward again and saw the slowly roasting victim,

Langdon had thoughts for only one thing. *Water. Lots of it. Put out the fire. At least lower the flames.* 'I need water, damn it!' he yelled out loud.

'That's next,' a voice growled from the back of the church.

Langdon wheeled, almost falling off the pews.

Striding up the side aisle directly toward him came a dark monster of a man. Even in the glow of the fire, his eyes burned black. Langdon recognized the gun in his hand as the one from his own jacket pocket . . . the one Vittoria had been carrying when they came in.

The sudden wave of panic that rose in Langdon was a frenzy of disjunct fears. His initial instinct was for Vittoria. What had this animal done to her? Was she hurt? Or *worse*? In the same instant, Langdon realized the man overhead was screaming louder. The cardinal would die. Helping him now was impossible. Then, as the Hassassin leveled the gun at Langdon's chest, Langdon's panic turned inward, his senses on overload. He reacted on instinct as the shot went off. Launching off the bench, Langdon sailed arms first over the sea of church pews.

When he hit the pews, he hit harder than he had imagined, immediately rolling to the floor. The marble cushioned his fall with all the grace of cold steel. Footsteps closed to his right. Langdon turned his body toward the front of the church and began scrambling for his life beneath the pews.

High above the chapel floor, Cardinal Guidera endured his last torturous moments of consciousness. As he looked down the length of his naked body, he saw the skin on his legs begin to blister and peel away. *I am in hell*, he decided. *God, why hast thou forsaken me?*

411

He knew this must be hell because he was looking at the brand on his chest upside down . . . and yet, as if by the devil's magic, the word made perfect sense.

92

Three ballotings. No Pope.

Inside the Sistine Chapel, Cardinal Mortati had begun praying for a miracle. *Send us the candidates!* The delay had gone long enough. A *single* missing candidate, Mortati could understand. But all four? It left no options. Under these conditions, achieving a two-thirds majority would take an act of God Himself.

When the bolts on the outer door began to grind open, Mortati and the entire College of Cardinals wheeled in unison toward the entrance. Mortati knew this unsealing could mean only one thing. By law, the chapel door could only be unsealed for two reasons – to remove the very ill, or to admit late cardinals.

The preferiti are coming!

Mortati's heart soared. Conclave had been saved.

But when the door opened, the gasp that echoed through the chapel was not one of joy. Mortati stared in incredulous shock as the man walked in. For the first time in Vatican history, a *camerlengo* had just crossed the sacred threshold of conclave *after* sealing the doors.

What is he thinking!

The camerlengo strode to the altar and turned to address the thunderstruck audience. 'Signori,' he said, 'I have waited as long as I can. There is something you have a right to know.'

93

Langdon had no idea where he was going. Reflex was his only compass, driving him away from danger. His elbows and knees burned as he clambered beneath the pews. Still he clawed on. Somewhere a voice was telling him to move left. *If you can get to the main aisle, you can dash for the exit.* He knew it was impossible. *There's a wall of flames blocking the main aisle!* His mind hunting for options, Langdon scrambled blindly on. The footsteps closed faster now to his right.

When it happened, Langdon was unprepared. He had guessed he had another ten feet of pews until he reached the front of the church. He had guessed wrong. Without warning, the cover above him ran out. He froze for an instant, half exposed at the front of the church. Rising in the recess to his left, gargantuan from this vantage point, was the very thing that had brought him here. He had entirely forgotten. Bernini's *Ecstasy of St Teresa* rose up like some sort of pornographic still life . . . the saint on her back, arched in pleasure, mouth open in a moan, and over her, an angel pointing his spear of fire.

A bullet exploded in the pew over Langdon's head. He felt his body rise like a sprinter out of a gate. Fueled only by adrenaline, and barely conscious of his actions, he was suddenly running, hunched, head down, pounding across the front of the church to his right. As the bullets erupted behind him, Langdon dove yet again, sliding out of control across the marble floor before crashing in a heap against the railing of a niche on the right-hand wall.

It was then that he saw her. A crumpled heap near the back of the church. *Vittoria!* Her bare legs were twisted beneath her, but Langdon sensed somehow that she was breathing. He had no time to help her.

Immediately, the killer rounded the pews on the far left of the church and bore relentlessly down. Langdon knew in a heartbeat it was over. The killer raised the weapon, and Langdon did the only thing he could do. He rolled his body over the banister into the niche. As he hit the floor on the other side, the marble columns of the balustrade exploded in a storm of bullets.

Langdon felt like a cornered animal as he scrambled deeper into the semicircular niche. Rising before him, the niche's sole contents seemed ironically apropos – a single sarcophagus. *Mine perhaps*, Langdon thought. Even the casket itself seemed fitting. It was a *scàtola* – a small, unadorned, marble box. Burial on a budget. The casket was raised off the floor on two marble blocks, and Langdon eyed the opening beneath it, wondering if he could slide through.

Footsteps echoed behind him.

With no other option in sight, Langdon pressed himself to the floor and slithered toward the casket. Grabbing the two marble supports, one with each hand, he pulled like a breaststroker, dragging his torso

414

into the opening beneath the tomb. The gun went off.

Accompanying the roar of the gun, Langdon felt a sensation he had never felt in his life ... a bullet sailing past his flesh. There was a hiss of wind, like the backlash of a whip, as the bullet just missed him and exploded in the marble with a puff of dust. Blood surging, Langdon heaved his body the rest of the way beneath the casket. Scrambling across the marble floor, he pulled himself out from beneath the casket and to the other side.

Dead end.

Langdon was now face to face with the rear wall of the niche. He had no doubt that this tiny space behind the tomb would become his grave. *And soon*, he realized, as he saw the barrel of the gun appear in the opening beneath the sarcophagus. The Hassassin held the weapon parallel with the floor, pointing directly at Langdon's midsection.

Impossible to miss.

Langdon felt a trace of self-preservation grip his unconscious mind. He twisted his body onto his stomach, parallel with the casket. Face down, he planted his hands flat on the floor, the glass cut from the archives pinching open with a stab. Ignoring the pain, he pushed. Driving his body upward in an awkward push-up, Langdon arched his stomach off the floor just as the gun went off. He could feel the shock wave of the bullets as they sailed beneath him and pulverized the porous travertine behind. Closing his eyes and straining against exhaustion, Langdon prayed for the thunder to stop.

And then it did.

The roar of gunfire was replaced with the cold click of an empty chamber.

Langdon opened his eyes slowly, almost fearful his eyelids would make a sound. Fighting the trembling pain, he held his position, arched like a cat. He didn't even dare breathe. His eardrums numbed by gunfire, Langdon listened for any hint of the killer's departure. Silence. He thought of Vittoria and ached to help her.

The sound that followed was deafening. Barely human. A guttural bellow of exertion.

The sarcophagus over Langdon's head suddenly seemed to rise on its side. Langdon collapsed on the floor as hundreds of pounds teetered toward him. Gravity overcame friction, and the lid was the first to go, sliding off the tomb and crashing to the floor beside him. The casket came next, rolling off its supports and toppling upside down toward Langdon.

As the box rolled, Langdon knew he would either be entombed in the hollow beneath it or crushed by one of the edges. Pulling in his legs and head, Langdon compacted his body and yanked his arms to his sides. Then he closed his eyes and awaited the sickening crush.

When it came, the entire floor shook beneath him. The upper rim landed only millimeters from the top of his head, rattling his teeth in their sockets. His right arm, which Langdon had been certain would be crushed, miraculously still felt intact. He opened his eyes to see a shaft of light. The right rim of the casket had not fallen all the way to the floor and was still propped partially on its supports. Directly overhead, though, Langdon found himself staring quite literally into the face of death.

The original occupant of the tomb was suspended above him, having adhered, as decaying bodies often did, to the bottom of the casket. The skeleton hovered a moment, like a tentative lover, and then with a sticky crackling, it succumbed to gravity and peeled away. The carcass rushed down to embrace him, raining putrid bones and dust into Langdon's eyes and mouth.

Before Langdon could react, a blind arm was slithering through the opening beneath the casket, sifting through the carcass like a hungry python. It groped until it found Langdon's neck and clamped down. Langdon tried to fight back against the iron fist now crushing his larynx, but he found his left sleeve pinched beneath the edge of the coffin. He had only one arm free, and the fight was a losing battle.

Langdon's legs bent in the only open space he had, his feet searching for the casket floor above him. He found it. Coiling, he planted his feet. Then, as the hand around his neck squeezed tighter, Langdon closed his eyes and extended his legs like a ram. The casket shifted, ever so slightly, but enough.

With a raw grinding, the sarcophagus slid off the supports and landed on the floor. The casket rim crashed onto the killer's arm, and there was a muffled scream of pain. The hand released Langdon's neck, twisting and jerking away into the dark. When the killer finally pulled his arm free, the casket fell with a conclusive thud against the flat marble floor.

Complete darkness. Again.

And silence.

There was no frustrated pounding outside the overturned sarcophagus. No prying to get in. Nothing. As Langdon lay in the dark amidst a pile of bones, he fought the closing darkness and turned his thoughts to her.

Vittoria. Are you alive?

417

If Langdon had known the truth – the horror to which Vittoria would soon awake – he would have wished for her sake that she were dead.

94

Sitting in the Sistine Chapel among his stunned colleagues, Cardinal Mortati tried to comprehend the words he was hearing. Before him, lit only by the candlelight, the camerlengo had just told a tale of such hatred and treachery that Mortati found himself trembling. The camerlengo spoke of kidnapped cardinals, branded cardinals, *murdered* cardinals. He spoke of the ancient Illuminati – a name that dredged up forgotten fears – and of their resurgence and vow of revenge against the church. With pain in his voice, the camerlengo spoke of his late Pope . . . the victim of an Illuminati poisoning. And finally, his words almost a whisper, he spoke of a deadly new technology, anti-matter, which in less than two hours threatened to destroy all of Vatican City.

When he was through, it was as if Satan himself had sucked the air from the room. Nobody could move. The camerlengo's words hung in the darkness.

The only sound Mortati could now hear was the anomalous hum of a television camera in back – an electronic presence no conclave in history had ever endured – but a presence demanded by the camerlengo. To the utter astonishment of the cardinals, the camerlengo had entered the Sistine Chapel with two BBC reporters – a man and a woman – and announced that they would be transmitting his solemn statement, *live* to the world.

Now, speaking directly to the camera, the camerlengo stepped forward. 'To the Illuminati,' he said, his voice deepening, 'and to those of science, let me say this.' He paused. 'You have won the war.'

The silence spread now to the deepest corners of the chapel. Mortati could hear the desperate thumping of his own heart.

'The wheels have been in motion for a long time,' the camerlengo said. 'Your victory has been inevitable. Never before has it been as obvious as it is at this moment. Science is the new God.'

What is he saying! Mortati thought. *Has he gone mad? The entire world is hearing this!*

'Medicine, electronic communications, space travel, genetic manipulation . . . these are the miracles about which we now tell our children. These are the miracles we herald as proof that science will bring us the answers. The ancient stories of immaculate conceptions, burning bushes, and parting seas are no longer relevant. God has become obsolete. Science has won the battle. We concede.'

A rustle of confusion and bewilderment swept through the chapel.

'But science's victory,' the camerlengo added, his voice intensifying, 'has cost every one of us. And it has cost us deeply.'

Silence.

'Science may have alleviated the miseries of disease and drudgery and provided an array of gadgetry for our entertainment and convenience, but it has left us in a world without wonder. Our sunsets have been reduced to wavelengths and frequencies. The complexities of the universe have been shredded into mathematical equations. Even our self-worth as human beings has been destroyed. Science proclaims that Planet Earth and its inhabitants are a meaningless speck in the grand scheme. A cosmic accident.' He paused. 'Even the technology that promises to unite us, divides us. Each of us is now electronically connected to the globe, and yet we feel utterly alone. We are bombarded with violence, division, fracture, and betrayal. Skepticism has become a virtue. Cynicism and demand for proof has become enlightened thought. Is it any wonder that humans now feel more depressed and defeated than they have at any point in human history? Does science hold *any-thing* sacred? Science looks for answers by probing our unborn fetuses. Science even presumes to rearrange our own DNA. It shatters God's world into smaller and smaller pieces in quest of meaning . . . and all it finds is more questions.'

Mortati watched in awe. The camerlengo was almost hypnotic now. He had a physical strength in his movements and voice that Mortati had never witnessed on a Vatican altar. The man's voice was wrought with conviction and sadness.

'The ancient war between science and religion is over,' the camerlengo said. 'You have won. But you have not won fairly. You have not won by providing answers. You have won by so radically reorienting our society that the truths we once saw as signposts now seem inapplicable. Religion cannot keep up. Scientific growth is exponential. It feeds on itself like a virus. Every new breakthrough opens doors for new break-throughs. Mankind took thousands of years to progress from the wheel to the car. Yet only decades from the car into space. Now we measure scientific progress in weeks. We are spinning out of control. The rift between us grows deeper and deeper, and as religion is left behind, people find themselves in a spiritual void. We cry out for meaning. And believe me, we *do* cry out. We see UFOs, engage in channeling, spirit contact, out-of-body experiences, mindquests – all these eccentric ideas have a scientific veneer, but they are unashamedly irrational. They are the desperate cry of the modern soul, lonely and tormented, crippled by its own enlightenment and its inability to accept meaning in anything removed from technology.'

Mortati could feel himself leaning forward in his seat. He and the other cardinals and people around the world were hanging on this priest's every utterance. The camerlengo spoke with no rhetoric or vitriol. No references to scripture or Jesus Christ. He spoke in modern terms, unadorned and pure. Somehow, as though the words were flowing from God himself, he spoke the modern language . . . delivering the ancient message. In that moment, Mortati saw one of the reasons the late Pope held this young man so dear. In a world of apathy, cynicism, and technological deification, men like the camerlengo, realists who could speak to our souls like this man just had, were the church's only hope.

The camerlengo was talking more forcefully now. 'Science, you say, will save us. Science, I say, has destroyed us. Since the days of Galileo, the church has tried to slow the relentless march of science, sometimes with misguided means, but always with benevolent intention. Even so, the temptations are too great for man to resist. I warn you, look around yourselves. The promises of science have not been kept. Promises of efficiency and simplicity have bred nothing but pollution and chaos. We are a fractured and frantic species ... moving down a path of destruction.'

The camerlengo paused a long moment and then sharpened his eyes on the camera.

'Who is this God science? Who is the God who offers his people power but no moral framework to tell you how to use that power? What kind of God gives a child *fire* but does not warn the child of its dangers? The language of science comes with no signposts about good and bad. Science textbooks tell us how to create a nuclear reaction, and yet they contain no chapter asking us if it is a good or a bad idea.

'To science, I say this. The church is tired. We are exhausted from trying to be your signposts. Our resources are drying up from our campaign to be the voice of balance as you plow blindly on in your quest for smaller chips and larger profits. We ask not why you will not govern yourselves, but how can you? Your world moves so fast that if you stop even for an instant to consider the implications of your actions, someone more efficient will whip past you in a blur. So you move on. You proliferate weapons of mass destruction, but it is the Pope who travels the world beseeching leaders to use restraint. You clone living creatures, but it is the church reminding us to consider the moral implications of our actions. You encourage people to interact on phones, video screens, and computers, but it is the church who opens its doors and reminds us to commune in person as we were meant to do. You even murder unborn babies in the name of research that will save lives. Again, it is the church who points out the fallacy of this reasoning.

'And all the while, you proclaim the church is ignorant. But who is more ignorant? The man who cannot define lightning, or the man who does not respect its awesome power? This church is reaching out to you. Reaching out to everyone. And yet the more we reach, the more you push us away. Show me *proof* there is a God, you say. I say use your telescopes to look to the heavens, and tell me how there could *not* be a God!' The camerlengo had tears in his eyes now. 'You ask what does God look like. I say, where did that question come from? The answers are one and the same. Do you not see God in your science? How can you miss Him! You proclaim that even the slightest change in the force of gravity or the weight of an atom would have rendered our universe a lifeless mist rather than our magnificent sea of heavenly bodies, and yet you fail to see God's hand in *this*? Is it really so much easier to believe that we simply chose the right card from a deck of billions? Have we become so spiritually bankrupt that we would rather believe in mathematical impossibility than in a power greater than us?

'Whether or not you believe in God,' the camerlengo said, his voice deepening with deliberation, 'you must believe this. When we as a species abandon our trust in the power greater than us, we abandon our sense of accountability. Faith ... *all* faiths ... are admonitions that there is something we cannot understand, something to which we are accountable ... With faith we are accountable to each other, to ourselves, and to a higher truth. Religion is flawed, but only because *man* is flawed. If the outside world could see this church as I do ... looking beyond the ritual of these walls ... they would see a modern miracle ... a brotherhood of imperfect, simple souls wanting only to be a voice of compassion in a world spinning out of control.'

The camerlengo motioned out over the College of Cardinals, and the BBC camerawoman instinctively followed, panning the crowd.

'Are we obsolete?' the camerlengo asked. 'Are these men dinosaurs? Am I? Does the world really need a voice for the poor, the weak, the oppressed, the unborn child? Do we really need souls like these who, though imperfect, spend their lives imploring each of us to read the signposts of morality and not lose our way?'

Mortati now realized that the camerlengo, whether consciously or not, was making a brilliant move. By showing the cardinals, he was personalizing the church. Vatican City was no longer a building, it was *people* – people like the camerlengo who had spent their lives in the service of goodness.

'Tonight we are perched on a precipice,' the camerlengo said. 'None of us can afford to be apathetic. Whether you see this evil as Satan, corruption, or immorality ... the dark force is alive and growing every day. Do not ignore it.' The camerlengo lowered his voice to a whisper, and the camera moved in. 'The force, though mighty, is not invincible. Goodness can prevail. Listen to your hearts. Listen to God. Together we can step back from this abyss.'

Now Mortati understood. This was the reason. Conclave had been violated, but this was the only way. It was a dramatic and desperate plea for help. The camerlengo was speaking to both his enemy and his friends now. He was entreating anyone, friend or foe,

to see the light and stop this madness. Certainly someone listening would realize the insanity of this plot
and come forward.

The camerlengo knelt at the altar. 'Pray with me.'

The College of Cardinals dropped to their knees to
join him in prayer. Outside in St Peter's Square and
around the globe . . . a stunned world knelt with them.

95

The Hassassin arranged his unconscious trophy in the
rear of the van and took a moment to admire her
sprawled body. She was not as beautiful as the women
he bought, and yet she had an animal strength that
excited him. Her body was radiant, dewy with
perspiration. She smelled of musk.

As the Hassassin stood there savoring his prize, he
ignored the throb in his arm. The bruise from the
falling sarcophagus, although painful, was insignificant . . . well worth the compensation that lay before
him. He took consolation in knowing the American
who had done this to him was probably dead by now.

Gazing down at his incapacitated prisoner, the
Hassassin visualized what lay ahead. He ran a palm
up beneath her shirt. Her breasts felt perfect beneath
her bra. *Yes*, he smiled. *You are more than worthy.*
Fighting the urge to take her right there, he closed the
door and drove off into the night.

There was no need to alert the press about *this*
killing . . . the flames would do that for him.

* * *

At CERN, Sylvie sat stunned by the camerlengo's address. Never before had she felt so proud to be a Catholic and so ashamed to work at CERN. As she left the recreational wing, the mood in every single viewing room was dazed and somber. When she got back to Kohler's office, all seven phone lines were ringing. Media inquiries were never routed to Kohler's office, so the incoming calls could only be one thing.

Geld. Money calls.

Antimatter technology already had some takers.

Inside the Vatican, Gunther Glick was walking on air as he followed the camerlengo from the Sistine Chapel. Glick and Macri had just made *the* live transmission of the decade. And what a transmission it had been. The camerlengo had been spellbinding.

Now out in the hallway, the camerlengo turned to Glick and Macri. 'I have asked the Swiss Guard to assemble photos for you – photos of the branded cardinals as well as one of His late Holiness. I must warn you, these are not pleasant pictures. Ghastly burns. Blackened tongues. But I would like you to broadcast them to the world.'

Glick decided it must be perpetual Christmas inside Vatican City. *He wants me to broadcast an exclusive photo of the dead Pope?* 'Are you sure?' Glick asked, trying to keep the excitement from his voice.

The camerlengo nodded. 'The Swiss Guard will also provide you a live video feed of the antimatter canister as it counts down.'

Glick stared. *Christmas. Christmas. Christmas!*

'The Illuminati are about to find out,' the camerlengo declared, 'that they have grossly overplayed their hand.'

Like a recurring theme in some demonic symphony, the suffocating darkness had returned.

No light. No air. No exit.

Langdon lay trapped beneath the overturned sarcophagus and felt his mind careening dangerously close to the brink. Trying to drive his thoughts in any direction other than the crushing space around him, Langdon urged his mind toward some logical process ... mathematics, music, anything. But there was no room for calming thoughts. *I can't move! I can't breathe!*

The pinched sleeve of his jacket had thankfully come free when the casket fell, leaving Langdon now with two mobile arms. Even so, as he pressed upward on the ceiling of his tiny cell, he found it immovable. Oddly, he wished his sleeve were still caught. *At least it might create a crack for some air.*

As Langdon pushed against the roof above, his sleeve fell back to reveal the faint glow of an old friend. Mickey. The greenish cartoon face seemed mocking now.

Langdon probed the blackness for any other sign of light, but the casket rim was flush against the floor. Goddamn Italian perfectionists, he cursed, now imperiled by the same artistic excellence he taught his students to revere ... impeccable edges, faultless parallels, and of course, use only of the most seamless and resilient *Carrara* marble.

Precision can be suffocating.

'Lift the damn thing,' he said aloud, pressing harder through the tangle of bones. The box shifted slightly. Setting his jaw, he heaved again. The box felt like a boulder, but this time it raised a quarter of an inch. A fleeting glimmer of light surrounded him, and then the casket thudded back down. Langdon lay panting in the dark. He tried to use his legs to lift as he had before, but now that the sarcophagus had fallen flat, there was no room even to straighten his knees.

As the claustrophobic panic closed in, Langdon was overcome by images of the sarcophagus shrinking around him. Squeezed by delirium, he fought the illusion with every logical shred of intellect he had.

'Sarcophagus,' he stated aloud, with as much academic sterility as he could muster. But even erudition seemed to be his enemy today. *Sarcophagus is from the Greek 'sarx' meaning 'flesh', and 'phagein' meaning 'to eat'. I'm trapped in a box literally designed to 'eat flesh'.*

Images of flesh eaten from bone only served as a grim reminder that Langdon lay covered in human remains. The notion brought nausea and chills. But it also brought an idea.

Fumbling blindly around the coffin, Langdon found a shard of bone. A rib maybe? He didn't care. All he wanted was a wedge. If he could lift the box, even a crack, and slide the bone fragment beneath the rim, then maybe enough air could . . .

Reaching across his body and wedging the tapered end of the bone into the crack between the floor and the coffin, Langdon reached up with his other hand and heaved skyward. The box did not move. Not even slightly. He tried again. For a moment, it seemed to tremble slightly, but that was all.

With the fetid stench and lack of oxygen choking the strength from his body, Langdon realized he only had time for one more effort. He also knew he would need both arms.

Regrouping, he placed the tapered edge of the bone against the crack, and shifting his body, he wedged the bone against his shoulder, pinning it in place. Careful not to dislodge it, he raised both hands above him. As the stifling confine began to smother him, he felt a welling of intensified panic. It was the second time today he had been trapped with no air. Hollering aloud, Langdon thrust upward in one explosive motion. The casket jostled off the floor for an instant. But long enough. The bone shard he had braced against his shoulder slipped outward into the widening crack. When the casket fell again, the bone shattered. But this time Langdon could see the casket was propped up. A tiny slit of light showed beneath the rim.

Exhausted, Langdon collapsed. Hoping the strangling sensation in his throat would pass, he waited. But it only worsened as the seconds passed. Whatever air was coming through the slit seemed imperceptible. Langdon wondered if it would be enough to keep him alive. And if so, for how long? If he passed out, who would know he was even in there?

With arms like lead, Langdon raised his watch again: 10.12 p.m. Fighting trembling fingers, he fumbled with the watch and made his final play. He twisted one of the tiny dials and pressed a button.

As consciousness faded, and the walls squeezed closer, Langdon felt the old fears sweep over him. He tried to imagine, as he had so many times, that he was in an open field. The image he conjured, however, was no help. The nightmare that had haunted him since his youth came crashing back . . .

* * *

The flowers here are like paintings, *the child thought, laughing as he ran across the meadow. He wished his parents had come along. But his parents were busy pitching camp.*

'Don't explore too far, ' *his mother had said.*

He had pretended not to hear as he bounded off into the woods.

Now, traversing this glorious field, the boy came across a pile of fieldstones. He figured it must be the foundation of an old homestead. He would not go near it. He knew better. Besides, his eyes had been drawn to something else – a brilliant lady's slipper – the rarest and most beautiful flower in New Hampshire. He had only ever seen them in books.

Excited, the boy moved toward the flower. He knelt down. The ground beneath him felt mulchy and hollow. He realized his flower had found an extra fertile spot. It was growing from a patch of rotting wood.

Thrilled by the thought of taking home his prize, the boy reached out . . . fingers extending toward the stem.

He never reached it.

With a sickening crack, the earth gave way.

In the three seconds of dizzying terror as he fell, the boy knew he would die. Plummeting downward, he braced for the bone-crushing collision. When it came, there was no pain. Only softness.

And cold.

He hit the deep liquid face first, plunging into a narrow blackness. Spinning disoriented somersaults, he groped the sheer walls that enclosed him on all sides. Somehow, as if by instinct, he sputtered to the surface.

Light.

Faint. Above him. Miles above him, it seemed.

His arms clawed at the water, searching the walls of the hollow for something to grab onto. Only smooth stone. He had fallen through an abandoned well covering. He screamed for help, but his cries reverberated in the tight shaft. He called out again and again. Above him, the tattered hole grew dim.

Night fell.

Time seemed to contort in the darkness. Numbness set in as he treaded water in the depths of the chasm, calling, crying out. He was tormented by visions of the walls collapsing in, burying him alive. His arms ached with fatigue. A few times he thought he heard voices. He shouted out, but his own voice was muted . . . like a dream.

As the night wore on, the shaft deepened. The walls inched quietly inward. The boy pressed out against the enclosure, pushing it away. Exhausted, he wanted to give up. And yet he felt the water buoy him, cooling his burning fears until he was numb.

When the rescue team arrived, they found the boy barely conscious. He had been treading water for five hours. Two days later, the Boston Globe ran a front-page story called 'The Little Swimmer That Could.'

97

The Hassassin smiled as he pulled his van into the mammoth stone structure overlooking the Tiber River. He carried his prize up and up . . . spiraling higher in the stone tunnel, grateful his load was slender.

He arrived at the door.

The Church of Illumination, he gloated. *The ancient Illuminati meeting room. Who would have imagined it to be here?*

431

Inside, he placed her on a plush divan. Then he expertly bound her arms behind her back and tied her feet. He knew that what he longed for would have to wait until his final task was finished. *Water*.

Still, he thought, he had a moment for indulgence. Kneeling beside her, he ran his hand along her thigh. It was smooth. Higher. His dark fingers snaked beneath the cuff of her shorts. Higher.

He stopped. *Patience*, he told himself, feeling aroused. *There is work to be done.*

He walked for a moment out onto the chamber's high stone balcony. The evening breeze slowly cooled his ardor. Far below the Tiber raged. He raised his eyes to the dome of St Peter's, three quarters of a mile away, naked under the glare of hundreds of press lights.

'Your final hour,' he said aloud, picturing the thousands of Muslims slaughtered during the Crusades. 'At midnight you will meet your God.'

Behind him, the woman stirred. The Hassassin turned. He considered letting her wake up. Seeing terror in a woman's eyes was his ultimate aphrodisiac.

He opted for prudence. It would be better if she remained unconscious while he was gone. Although she was tied and would never escape, the Hassassin did not want to return and find her exhausted from struggling. *I want your strength preserved . . . for me.*

Lifting her head slightly, he placed his palm beneath her neck and found the hollow directly beneath her skull. The crown/meridian pressure point was one he had used countless times. With crushing force, he drove his thumb into the soft cartilage and felt it depress. The woman slumped instantly. *Twenty minutes*, he thought. She would be a tantalizing end to a perfect day. After she had served him and died doing it, he would stand on the balcony and watch the midnight Vatican fireworks.

Leaving his prize unconscious on the couch, the Hassassin went downstairs into a torchlit dungeon. The final task. He walked to the table and revered the sacred, metal forms that had been left there for him.

Water. It was his last.

Removing a torch from the wall as he had done three times already, he began heating the end. When the end of the object was white hot, he carried it to the cell.

Inside, a single man stood in silence. Old and alone.

'Cardinal Baggia,' the killer hissed. 'Have you prayed yet?'

The Italian's eyes were fearless. 'Only for your soul.'

98

The six *pompieri* firemen who responded to the fire at the Church of Santa Maria Della Vittoria extinguished the bonfire with blasts of Halon gas. Water was cheaper, but the steam it created would have ruined the frescoes in the chapel, and the Vatican paid Roman *pompieri* a healthy stipend for swift and prudent service in all Vatican-owned buildings.

Pompieri, by the nature of their work, witnessed tragedy almost daily, but the execution in this church was something none of them would ever forget. Part crucifixion, part hanging, part burning at the stake, the scene was something dredged from a Gothic nightmare.

Unfortunately, the press, as usual, had arrived before the fire department. They'd shot plenty of video before the *pompieri* cleared the church. When the firemen finally cut the victim down and laid him on the floor, there was no doubt who the man was.

'*Cardinale Guidera*,' one whispered. '*Di Barcellona*.'

The victim was nude. The lower half of his body was crimson-black, blood oozing through gaping cracks in his thighs. His shinbones were exposed. One fireman vomited. Another went outside to breathe.

The true horror, though, was the symbol seared on the cardinal's chest. The squad chief circled the corpse in awestruck dread. *Lavoro del diavolo*, he said to himself. *Satan himself did this*. He crossed himself for the first time since childhood.

'*Un' altro corpo!*' someone yelled. One of the firemen had found another body.

The second victim was a man the chief recognized immediately. The austere commander of the Swiss Guard was a man for whom few public law enforcement officials had any affection. The chief called the Vatican, but all the circuits were busy. He knew it didn't matter. The Swiss Guard would hear about this on television in a matter of minutes.

As the chief surveyed the damage, trying to recreate what possibly could have gone on here, he saw a niche riddled with bullet holes. A coffin had been rolled off its supports and fallen upside down in an apparent struggle. It was a mess. *That's for the police and Holy See to deal with*, the chief thought, turning away.

As he turned, though, he stopped. Coming from the coffin he heard a sound. It was not a sound any fireman ever liked to hear.

'*Bomba!*' he cried out. '*Tutti fuori!*'

When the bomb squad rolled the coffin over, they discovered the source of the electronic beeping. They stared, confused.

'*Mèdico!*' one finally screamed. '*Mèdico!*'

99

'Any word from Olivetti?' the camerlengo asked, looking drained as Rocher escorted him back from the Sistine Chapel to the Pope's office.

'No, signore. I am fearing the worst.'

When they reached the Pope's office, the camerlengo's voice was heavy. 'Captain, there is nothing more I can do here tonight. I fear I have done too much already. I am going into this office to pray. I do not wish to be disturbed. The rest is in God's hands.'

'Yes, signore.'

'The hour is late, Captain. Find that canister.'

'Our search continues.' Rocher hesitated. 'The weapon proves to be too well hidden.'

The camerlengo winced, as if he could not think of it. 'Yes. At exactly 11.15 p.m., if the church is still in peril, I want you to evacuate the cardinals. I am putting their safety in your hands. I ask only one thing. Let these men proceed from this place with dignity. Let them exit into St Peter's Square and stand side by side with the rest of the world. I do not want the last image of this church to be frightened old men sneaking out a back door.'

'Very good, signore. And you? Shall I come for you at 11.15 as well?'

'There will be no need.'

'Signore?'

'I will leave when the spirit moves me.'

Rocher wondered if the camerlengo intended to go down with the ship.

The camerlengo opened the door to the Pope's office and entered. 'Actually . . .' he said, turning. 'There is one thing.'

'Signore?'

'There seems to be a chill in this office tonight. I am trembling.'

'The electric heat is out. Let me lay you a fire.'

The camerlengo smiled tiredly. 'Thank you. Thank you, very much.'

Rocher exited the Pope's office where he had left the camerlengo praying by firelight in front of a small statue of the Blessed Mother Mary. It was an eerie sight. A black shadow kneeling in the flickering glow. As Rocher headed down the hall, a guard appeared, running toward him. Even by candlelight Rocher recognized Lieutenant Chartrand. Young, green, and eager.

'Captain,' Chartrand called, holding out a cellular phone. 'I think the camerlengo's address may have worked. We've got a caller here who says he has information that can help us. He phoned on one of the Vatican's private extensions. I have no idea how he got the number.'

Rocher stopped. 'What?'

'He will only speak to the ranking officer.'

'Any word from Olivetti?'

'No, sir.'

He took the receiver. 'This is Captain Rocher. I am ranking officer here.'

'Rocher,' the voice said. 'I will explain to you who I am. Then I will tell you what you are going to do next.'

When the caller stopped talking and hung up, Rocher stood stunned. He now knew from whom he was taking orders.

Back at CERN, Sylvie Baudeloque was frantically trying to keep track of all the licensing inquiries coming in on Kohler's voice mail. When the private line on the director's desk began to ring, Sylvie jumped. Nobody had that number. She answered.

'Yes?'

'Ms Baudeloque? This is Director Kohler. Contact my pilot. My jet is to be ready in five minutes.'

100

Robert Langdon had no idea where he was or how long he had been unconscious when he opened his eyes and found himself staring up at the underside of a baroque, frescoed cupola. Smoke drifted overhead. Something was covering his mouth. An oxygen mask. He pulled it off. There was a terrible smell in the room – like burning flesh.

Langdon winced at the pounding in his head. He tried to sit up. A man in white was kneeling beside him.

'*Riposati!*' the man said, easing Langdon onto his back again. '*Sono il paramédico.*'

Langdon succumbed, his head spiraling like the smoke overhead. *What the hell happened?* Wispy feelings of panic sifted through his mind.

'*Sórcio salvatore*,' the paramedic said. 'Mouse ... savior.'

Langdon felt even more lost. *Mouse savior?*

The man motioned to the Mickey Mouse watch on Langdon's wrist. Langdon's thoughts began to clear. He remembered setting the alarm. As he stared absently at the watch face, Langdon also noted the hour. 10.28 p.m.

He sat bolt upright.

Then, it all came back.

Langdon stood near the main altar with the fire chief and a few of his men. They had been rattling him with questions. Langdon wasn't listening. He had questions of his own. His whole body ached, but he knew he needed to act immediately.

A *pompiero* approached Langdon across the church. 'I checked again, sir. The only bodies we found are Cardinal Guidera and the Swiss Guard commander. There's no sign of a woman here.'

'*Grazie*,' Langdon said, unsure whether he was relieved or horrified. He knew he had seen Vittoria unconscious on the floor. Now she was gone. The only explanation he came up with was not a comforting one. The killer had not been subtle on the phone. *A woman of spirit. I am aroused. Perhaps before this night is over, I will find you. And when I do ...*

Langdon looked around. 'Where is the Swiss Guard?'

'Still no contact. Vatican lines are jammed.'

Langdon felt overwhelmed and alone. Olivetti was dead. The cardinal was dead. Vittoria was missing. A half hour of his life had disappeared in a blink.

Outside, Langdon could hear the press swarming.

He suspected footage of the third cardinal's horrific death would no doubt air soon, if it hadn't already. Langdon hoped the camerlengo had long since assumed the worst and taken action. *Evacuate the damn Vatican! Enough games! We lose!*

Langdon suddenly realized that all of the catalysts that had been driving him – helping to save Vatican City, rescuing the four cardinals, coming face to face with the brotherhood he had studied for years – all of these things had evaporated from his mind. The war was lost. A new compulsion had ignited within him. It was simple. Stark. Primal.

Find Vittoria.

He felt an unexpected emptiness inside. Langdon had often heard that intense situations could unite two people in ways that decades together often did not. He now believed it. In Vittoria's absence he felt something he had not felt in years. Loneliness. The pain gave him strength.

Pushing all else from his mind, Langdon mustered his concentration. He prayed that the Hassassin would take care of business before pleasure. Otherwise, Langdon knew he was already too late. *No*, he told himself, *you have time*. Vittoria's captor still had work to do. He had to surface one last time before disappearing forever.

The last altar of science, Langdon thought. The killer had one final task. *Earth. Air. Fire. Water*.

He looked at his watch. Thirty minutes. Langdon moved past the firemen toward Bernini's *Ecstasy of St Teresa*. This time, as he stared at Bernini's marker, Langdon had no doubt what he was looking for.

Let angels guide you on your lofty quest . . .

Directly over the recumbent saint, against a

backdrop of gilded flame, hovered Bernini's angel. The angel's hand clutched a pointed spear of fire. Langdon's eyes followed the direction of the shaft, arching toward the right side of the church. His eyes hit the wall. He scanned the spot where the spear was pointing. There was nothing there. Langdon knew, of course, the spear was pointing far beyond the wall, into the night, somewhere across Rome.

'What direction is that?' Langdon asked, turning and addressing the chief with a newfound determination.

'Direction?' The chief glanced where Langdon was pointing. He sounded confused. 'I don't know ... west, I think.'

'What churches are in that direction?'

The chief's puzzlement seemed to deepen. 'Dozens. Why?'

Langdon frowned. Of course there were dozens. 'I need a city map. Right away.'

The chief sent someone running out to the fire truck for a map. Langdon turned back to the statue. *Earth ... Air ... Fire ... VITTORIA.*

The final marker is Water, he told himself. *Bernini's Water*. It was in a church out there somewhere. A needle in a haystack. He spurred his mind through all the Bernini works he could recall. *I need a tribute to Water!*

Langdon flashed on Bernini's statue of *Triton* – the Greek God of the sea. Then he realized it was located in the square outside this very church, in entirely the wrong direction. He forced himself to think. *What figure would Bernini have carved as a glorification of water? Neptune and Tritone?* Unfortunately that statue was in London's Victoria & Albert Museum.

'Signore?' A fireman ran in with a map.

Langdon thanked him and spread it out on the altar. He immediately realized he had asked the right people; the fire department's map of Rome was as detailed as any Langdon had ever seen. 'Where are we now?'

The man pointed. 'Next to Piazza Barberini.'

Langdon looked at the angel's spear again to get his bearings. The chief had estimated correctly. According to the map, the spear was pointing west. Langdon traced a line from his current location west across the map. Almost instantly his hopes began to sink. It seemed that with every inch his finger traveled, he passed yet another building marked by a tiny black cross. *Churches.* The city was riddled with them. Finally, Langdon's finger ran out of churches and trailed off into the suburbs of Rome. He exhaled and stepped back from the map. *Damn.*

Surveying the whole of Rome, Langdon's eyes touched down on the three churches where the first three cardinals had been killed. *The Chigi Chapel . . . St Peter's . . . here . . .*

Seeing them all laid out before him now, Langdon noted an oddity in their locations. Somehow he had imagined the churches would be scattered randomly across Rome. But they most definitely were not. Improbably, the three churches seemed to be separated systematically, in an enormous city-wide triangle. Langdon double-checked. He was not imagining things. '*Penna,*' he said suddenly, without looking up.

Someone handed him a ballpoint pen.

Langdon circled the three churches. His pulse quickened. He triple-checked his markings. *A symmetrical triangle!*

441

Langdon's first thought was for the Great Seal on the one-dollar bill – the triangle containing the all-seeing eye. But it didn't make sense. He had marked only *three* points. There were supposed to be four in all.

So where the hell is Water? Langdon knew that anywhere he placed the fourth point, the triangle would be destroyed. The only option to retain the symmetry was to place the fourth marker inside the triangle, at the center. He looked at the spot on the map. Nothing. The idea bothered him anyway. The four elements of science were considered *equal*. Water was not special; Water would not be at the *center* of the others.

Still, his instinct told him the systematic arrangement could not possibly be accidental. *I'm not yet seeing the whole picture.* There was only one alternative. The four points did not make a triangle; they made some other shape.

Langdon looked at the map. *A square, perhaps?* Although a square made no symbolic sense, squares were symmetrical at least. Langdon put his finger on the map at one of the points that would turn the triangle into a square. He saw immediately that a perfect square was impossible. The angles of the original triangle were oblique and created more of a distorted quadrilateral.

As he studied the other possible points around the triangle, something unexpected happened. He noticed that the line he had drawn earlier to indicate the direction of the angel's spear passed perfectly through one of the possibilities. Stupefied, Langdon circled that point. He was now looking at four ink marks on the map, arranged in somewhat of an awkward, kitelike diamond.

He frowned. Diamonds were not an Illuminati symbol either. He paused. *Then again* . . .

For an instant Langdon flashed on the famed Illuminati Diamond. The thought, of course, was ridiculous. He dismissed it. Besides, this diamond was oblong – like a kite – hardly an example of the flawless symmetry for which the Illuminati Diamond was revered.

When he leaned in to examine where he had placed the final mark, Langdon was surprised to find that the fourth point lay dead center of Rome's famed Piazza Navona. He knew the piazza contained a major church, but he had already traced his finger through that piazza and considered the church there. To the best of his knowledge it contained no Bernini works. The church was called Saint Agnes in Agony, named for St Agnes, a ravishing teenage virgin banished to a life of sexual slavery for refusing to renounce her faith.

There must be something in that church! Langdon racked his brain, picturing the inside of the church. He could think of no Bernini works at all inside, much less anything to do with *water*. The arrangement on the map was bothering him too. A diamond. It was far too accurate to be coincidence, but it was not accurate enough to make any sense. *A kite?* Langdon wondered if he had chosen the wrong point. *What am I missing!*

The answer took another thirty seconds to hit him, but when it did, Langdon felt an exhilaration like nothing he had ever experienced in his academic career.

The Illuminati genius, it seemed, would never cease.

The shape he was looking at was not intended as a diamond at all. The four points only formed a diamond because Langdon had connected *adjacent* points. *The Illuminati believe in opposites!* Connecting opposite vertices with his pen, Langdon's fingers were trembling. There before him on the map was a giant cruciform. *It's a cross!* The four elements of science unfolded before his eyes ... sprawled across Rome in an enormous, city-wide cross.

As he stared in wonder, a line of poetry rang in his mind ... like an old friend with a new face.

'Cross Rome the mystic elements unfold ...

'Cross Rome ...

The fog began to clear. Langdon saw that the answer had been in front of him all night! The Illuminati poem had been telling him *how* the altars were laid out. A cross!

'Cross Rome the mystic elements unfold!

It was cunning wordplay. Langdon had originally read the word *'Cross* as an abbreviation of *Across*. He assumed it was poetic license intended to retain the meter of the poem. But it was so much more than that! Another hidden clue.

The cruciform on the map, Langdon realized, was the ultimate Illuminati duality. It was a religious symbol formed by elements of science. Galileo's path of Illumination was a tribute to both science *and* God!

The rest of the puzzle fell into place almost immediately.

Piazza Navona.

Dead center of Piazza Navona, outside the church of St Agnes in Agony, Bernini had forged one of his most celebrated sculptures. Everyone who came to Rome went to see it.

The Fountain of the Four Rivers!

A flawless tribute to water, Bernini's *Fountain of the*

Four Rivers glorified the four major rivers of the Old World – The Nile, Ganges, Danube, and Rio Plata.

Water, Langdon thought. *The final marker*. It was perfect.

And even more perfect, Langdon realized, the cherry on the cake, was that high atop Bernini's fountain stood a towering obelisk.

Leaving confused firemen in his wake, Langdon ran across the church in the direction of Olivetti's lifeless body.

10.31 p.m., he thought. *Plenty of time*. It was the first instant all day that Langdon felt ahead of the game.

Kneeling beside Olivetti, out of sight behind some pews, Langdon discreetly took possession of the commander's semiautomatic and walkie-talkie. Langdon knew he would call for help, but this was not the place to do it. The final altar of science needed to remain a secret for now. The media and fire department racing with sirens blaring to Piazza Navona would be no help at all.

Without a word, Langdon slipped out the door and skirted the press, who were now entering the church in droves. He crossed Piazza Barberini. In the shadows he turned on the walkie-talkie. He tried to hail Vatican City but heard nothing but static. He was either out of range or the transmitter needed some kind of authorization code. Langdon adjusted the complex dials and buttons to no avail. Abruptly, he realized his plan to get help was not going to work. He spun, looking for a pay phone. None. Vatican circuits were jammed anyway.

He was alone.

Feeling his initial surge of confidence decay,

Langdon stood a moment and took stock of his pitiful state – covered in bone dust, cut, deliriously exhausted, and hungry

Langdon glanced back at the church. Smoke spiraled over the cupola, lit by the media lights and fire trucks. He wondered if he should go back and get help. Instinct warned him however that extra help, especially untrained help, would be nothing but a liability. *If the Hassassin sees us coming . . .* He thought of Vittoria and knew this would be his final chance to face her captor.

Piazza Navona, he thought, knowing he could get there in plenty of time and stake it out. He scanned the area for a taxi, but the streets were almost entirely deserted. Even the taxi drivers, it seemed, had dropped everything to find a television. Piazza Navona was only about a mile away but Langdon had no intention of wasting precious energy on foot. He glanced back at the church, wondering if he could borrow a vehicle from someone.

A fire truck? A press van? Be serious.

Sensing options and minutes slipping away, Langdon made his decision. Pulling the gun from his pocket, he committed an act so out of character that he suspected his soul must now be possessed. Running over to a lone Citroën sedan idling at a stoplight, Langdon pointed the weapon through the driver's open window. *'Fuori!'* he yelled.

The trembling man got out.

Langdon jumped behind the wheel and hit the gas.

101

Gunther Glick sat on a bench in a holding tank inside the office of the Swiss Guard. He prayed to every god he could think of. *Please let this NOT be a dream.* It had been the scoop of his life. The scoop of anyone's life. Every reporter on earth wished he were Glick right now. *You are awake,* he told himself *And you are a star. Dan Rather is crying right now.*

Macri was beside him, looking a little bit stunned. Glick didn't blame her. In addition to exclusively broadcasting the camerlengo's address, she and Glick had provided the world with gruesome photos of the cardinals and of the Pope – *that tongue!* – as well as a live video feed of the antimatter canister counting down. *Incredible!*

Of course, all of that had all been at the camerlengo's behest, so that was not the reason Glick and Macri were now locked in a Swiss Guard holding tank. It had been Glick's daring addendum to their coverage that the guards had not appreciated. Glick knew the conversation on which he had just reported was not intended for his ears, but this was his moment in the sun. *Another Glick scoop!*

'The 11th Hour Samaritan?' Macri groaned on the bench beside him, clearly unimpressed.

Glick smiled. 'Brilliant, wasn't it?'

'Brilliantly dumb.'

She's just jealous, Glick knew. Shortly after the camerlengo's address, Glick had again, by chance, been in the right place at the right time. He'd overheard Rocher giving new orders to his men. Apparently Rocher had received a phone call from a mysterious

447

individual who Rocher claimed had critical information regarding the current crisis. Rocher was talking as if this man could help them and was advising his guards to prepare for the guest's arrival.

Although the information was clearly private, Glick had acted as any dedicated reporter would – without honor. He'd found a dark corner, ordered Macri to fire up her remote camera, and he'd reported the news.

'Shocking new developments in God's city,' he had announced, squinting his eyes for added intensity. Then he'd gone on to say that a mystery guest was coming to Vatican City to save the day. *The 11th Hour Samaritan*, Glick had called him – a perfect name for the faceless man appearing at the last moment to do a good deed. The other networks had picked up the catchy sound bite, and Glick was yet again immortalized.

I'm brilliant, he mused. *Peter Jennings just jumped off a bridge.*

Of course Glick had not stopped there. While he had the world's attention, he had thrown in a little of his own conspiracy theory for good measure.

Brilliant. Utterly brilliant.

'You screwed us,' Macri said. 'You totally blew it.'

'What do you mean? I was great!'

Macri stared disbelievingly. 'Former President George Bush? An Illuminatus?'

Glick smiled. How much more obvious could it be? George Bush was a well-documented, 33rd-degree Mason, *and* he was the head of the CIA when the agency closed their Illuminati investigation for lack of evidence. And all those speeches about 'a thousand points of light' and a 'New World Order' . . . Bush was obviously Illuminati.

'And that bit about CERN?' Macri chided. 'You are going to have a very big line of lawyers outside your door tomorrow.'

'CERN? Oh come on! It's so obvious! Think about it! The Illuminati disappear off the face of the earth in the 1950s at about the same time CERN is *founded*. CERN is a haven for the most enlightened people on earth. Tons of private funding. They build a weapon that can destroy the church, and oops! . . . they *lose* it!'

'So you tell the world that CERN is the new home base of the Illuminati?'

'Obviously! Brotherhoods don't just disappear. The Illuminati had to go *somewhere*. CERN is a perfect place for them to hide. I'm not saying everyone at CERN is Illuminati. It's probably like a huge Masonic lodge, where most people are innocent, but the upper echelons—'

'Have you ever heard of slander, Glick? Liability?'

'Have you ever heard of real journalism!'

'Journalism? You were pulling bullshit out of thin air! I should have turned off the camera! And what the hell was that crap about CERN's corporate logo? Satanic symbology? Have you lost your mind?'

Glick smiled. Macri's jealousy was definitely showing. The CERN logo had been the most brilliant coup of all. Ever since the camerlengo's address, all the networks were talking about CERN and anti-matter. Some stations were showing the CERN corporate logo as a backdrop. The logo seemed standard enough – two intersecting circles representing two particle accelerators, and five tangential lines representing particle injection tubes. The whole world was staring at this logo, but it had been Glick, a bit of a symbologist himself, who had first seen the Illuminati symbology hidden in it.

'You're not a symbologist,' Macri chided, 'you're just one lucky-ass reporter. You should have left the symbology to the Harvard guy.'

'The Harvard guy missed it,' Glick said.

The Illuminati significance in this logo is so obvious!

He was beaming inside. Although CERN had lots of accelerators, their logo showed only two. *Two is the Illuminati number of duality.* Although most accelerators had only one injection tube, the logo showed five. *Five is the number of the Illuminati pentagram.* Then had come the coup – the most brilliant point of all. Glick pointed out that the logo contained a large numeral '6' – clearly formed by one of the lines and circles – and when the logo was rotated, another six appeared . . . and then another. The logo contained three sixes! 666! The devil's number! The mark of the beast!

Glick was a genius.

Macri looked ready to slug him.

The jealousy would pass, Glick knew, his mind now wandering to another thought. If CERN was Illuminati headquarters, was CERN where the Illuminati kept their infamous Illuminati Diamond? Glick had read about it on the Internet – '*a flawless diamond, born of the ancient elements with such perfection that all those who saw it could only stand in wonder.*'

Glick wondered if the secret whereabouts of the Illuminati Diamond might be yet another mystery he could unveil tonight.

Piazza Navona. *Fountain of the Four Rivers*.

Nights in Rome, like those in the desert, can be surprisingly cool, even after a warm day. Langdon was huddled now on the fringes of Piazza Navona, pulling his jacket around him. Like the distant white noise of traffic, a cacophony of news reports echoed across the city. He checked his watch. Fifteen minutes. He was grateful for a few moments of rest.

The piazza was deserted. Bernini's masterful fountain sizzled before him with a fearful sorcery. The foaming pool sent a magical mist upward, lit from beneath by underwater floodlights. Langdon sensed a cool electricity in the air.

The fountain's most arresting quality was its height. The central core alone was over twenty feet tall – a rugged mountain of travertine marble riddled with caves and grottoes through which the water churned. The entire mound was draped with pagan figures. Atop this stood an obelisk that climbed another forty feet. Langdon let his eyes climb. On the obelisk's tip, a faint shadow blotted the sky, a lone pigeon perched silently.

A cross, Langdon thought, still amazed by the arrangement of the markers across Rome. Bernini's *Fountain of the Four Rivers* was the last altar of science. Only hours ago Langdon had been standing in the Pantheon convinced the Path of Illumination had been broken and he would never get this far. It had been a foolish blunder. In fact, the entire path was intact. *Earth, Air, Fire, Water*. And Langdon had followed it ... from beginning to end.

Not quite to the end, he reminded himself. The path had *five* stops, not four. This fourth marker fountain somehow pointed to the ultimate destiny – the Illuminati's sacred lair – the Church of Illumination. Langdon wondered if the lair were still standing. He wondered if that was where the Hassassin had taken Vittoria.

Langdon found his eyes probing the figures in the fountain, looking for any clue as to the direction of the lair. *Let angels guide you on your lofty quest.* Almost immediately though, he was overcome by an un-settling awareness. This fountain contained no angels whatsoever. It certainly contained none Langdon could see from where he was standing . . . and none he had ever seen in the past. *The Fountain of the Four Rivers* was a pagan work. The carvings were all profane – humans, animals, even an awkward armadillo. An angel here would stick out like a sore thumb.

Is this the wrong place? He considered the cruciform arrangement of the four obelisks. He clenched his fists. *This fountain is perfect.*

It was only 10.46 p.m. when a black van emerged from the alleyway on the far side of the piazza. Langdon would not have given it a second look except that the van drove with no headlights. Like a shark patrolling a moonlit bay the vehicle circled the perimeter of the piazza.

Langdon hunkered lower, crouched in the shadows beside the huge stairway leading up to the Church of St Agnes in Agony. He gazed out at the piazza, his pulse climbing.

After making two complete circuits, the van banked inward toward Bernini's fountain. It pulled abreast of

452

the basin, moving laterally along the rim until its side was flush with the fountain. Then it parked, its sliding door positioned only inches above the churning water.

Mist billowed.

Langdon felt an uneasy premonition. Had the Hassassin arrived early? Had he come in a van? Langdon had imagined the killer escorting his last victim across the piazza on foot, like he had at St Peter's, giving Langdon an open shot. But if the Hassassin had arrived in a van, the rules had just changed.

Suddenly, the van's side door slid open.

On the floor of the van, contorted in agony, lay a naked man. The man was wrapped in yards of heavy chains. He thrashed against the iron links, but the chains were too heavy. One of the links bisected the man's mouth like a horse's bit, stifling his cries for help. It was then that Langdon saw the second figure, moving around behind the prisoner in the dark, as though making final preparations.

Langdon knew he had only seconds to act.

Taking the gun, he slipped off his jacket and dropped it on the ground. He didn't want the added encumbrance of a tweed jacket, nor did he have any intention of taking Galileo's *Diagramma* anywhere near the water. The document would stay here where it was safe and dry.

Langdon scrambled to his right. Circling the perimeter of the fountain, he positioned himself directly opposite the van. The fountain's massive centerpiece obscured his view. Standing, he ran directly toward the basin. He hoped the thundering water was drowning his footsteps. When he reached the fountain, he climbed over the rim and dropped into the foaming pool.

The water was waist deep and like ice. Langdon grit his teeth and plowed through the water. The bottom was slippery, made doubly treacherous by a stratum of coins thrown for good luck. Langdon sensed he would need more than good luck. As the mist rose all around him, he wondered if it was the cold or the fear that was causing the gun in his hand to shake.

He reached the interior of the fountain and circled back to his left. He waded hard, clinging to the cover of the marble forms. Hiding himself behind the huge carved form of a horse, Langdon peered out. The van was only fifteen feet away. The Hassassin was crouched on the floor of the van, hands planted on the cardinal's chain-clad body, preparing to roll him out the open door into the fountain.

Waist-deep in water, Robert Langdon raised his gun and stepped out of the mist, feeling like some sort of aquatic cowboy making a final stand. 'Don't move.' His voice was steadier than the gun.

The Hassassin looked up. For a moment he seemed confused, as though he had seen a ghost. Then his lips curled into an evil smile. He raised his arms in submission. 'And so it goes.'

'Get out of the van.'

'You look wet.'

'You're early.'

'I am eager to return to my prize.'

Langdon leveled the gun. 'I won't hesitate to shoot.'

'You've already hesitated.'

Langdon felt his finger tighten on the trigger. The cardinal lay motionless now. He looked exhausted, moribund. 'Untie him.'

'Forget him. You've come for the woman. Do not pretend otherwise.'

Langdon fought the urge to end it right there. 'Where is she?'

'Somewhere safe. Awaiting my return.'

She's alive. Langdon felt a ray of hope. 'At the Church of Illumination?'

The killer smiled. 'You will never find its location.'

Langdon was incredulous. *The lair is still standing.* He aimed the gun. 'Where?'

'The location has remained secret for centuries. Even to me it was only revealed recently. I would die before I break that trust.'

'I can find it without you.'

'An arrogant thought.'

Langdon motioned to the fountain. 'I've come this far.'

'So have many. The final step is the hardest.'

Langdon stepped closer, his footing tentative beneath the water. The Hassassin looked remarkably calm, squatting there in the back of the van with his arms raised over his head. Langdon aimed at his chest, wondering if he should simply shoot and be done with it. *No. He knows where Vittoria is. He knows where the antimatter is. I need information!*

From the darkness of the van the Hassassin gazed out at his aggressor and couldn't help but feel an amused pity. The American was brave, that he had proven. But he was also untrained. That he had also proven. Valor without expertise was suicide. There were rules of survival. Ancient rules. And the American was breaking all of them.

You had the advantage – the element of surprise. You squandered it.

The American was indecisive . . . hoping for backup

most likely ... or perhaps a slip of the tongue that would reveal critical information.

Never interrogate before you disable your prey. A cornered enemy is a deadly enemy.

The American was talking again. Probing. Maneuvering.

The killer almost laughed aloud. *This is not one of your Hollywood movies ... there will be no long discussions at gunpoint before the final shoot-out. This is the end. Now.*

Without breaking eye contact, the killer inched his hands across the ceiling of the van until he found what he was looking for. Staring dead ahead, he grasped it.

Then he made his play.

The motion was utterly unexpected. For an instant, Langdon thought the laws of physics had ceased to exist. The killer seemed to hang weightless in the air as his legs shot out from beneath him, his boots driving into the cardinal's side and launching the chain-laden body out the door. The cardinal splashed down, sending up a sheet of spray.

Water dousing his face, Langdon realized too late what had happened. The killer had grasped one of the van's roll bars and used it to swing outward. Now the Hassassin was sailing toward him, feet-first through the spray.

Langdon pulled the trigger, and the silencer spat. The bullet exploded through the toe of the Hassassin's left boot. Instantly Langdon felt the soles of the Hassassin's boots connect with his chest, driving him back with a crushing kick.

The two men splashed down in a spray of blood and water.

As the icy liquid engulfed Langdon's body, his first

cognition was pain. Survival instinct came next. He realized he was no longer holding his weapon. It had been knocked away. Diving deep, he groped along the slimy bottom. His hand gripped metal. A handful of coins. He dropped them. Opening his eyes, Langdon scanned the glowing basin. The water churned around him like a frigid Jacuzzi.

Despite the instinct to breathe, fear kept him on the bottom. Always moving. He did not know from where the next assault would come. He needed to find the gun! His hands groped desperately in front of him.

You have the advantage, he told himself. *You are in your element.* Even in a soaked turtleneck Langdon was an agile swimmer. *Water is your element.*

When Langdon's fingers found metal a second time, he was certain his luck had changed. The object in his hand was no handful of coins. He gripped it and tried to pull it toward him, but when he did, he found himself gliding through the water. The object was stationary.

Langdon realized even before he coasted over the cardinal's writhing body that he had grasped part of the metal chain that was weighing the man down. Langdon hovered a moment, immobilized by the sight of the terrified face staring up at him from the floor of the fountain.

Jolted by the life in the man's eyes, Langdon reached down and grabbed the chains, trying to heave him toward the surface. The body came slowly . . . like an anchor. Langdon pulled harder. When the cardinal's head broke the surface, the old man gasped a few sucking, desperate breaths. Then, violently, his body rolled, causing Langdon to lose his grip on the slippery chains. Like a stone, Baggia went down again and disappeared beneath the foaming water.

Langdon dove, eyes wide in the liquid murkiness. He found the cardinal. This time, when Langdon grabbed on, the chains across Baggia's chest shifted ... parting to reveal a further wickedness ... a word stamped in seared flesh.

An instant later, two boots strode into view. One was gushing blood.

103

As a water polo player, Robert Langdon had endured more than his fair share of underwater battles. The competitive savagery that raged beneath the surface of a water polo pool, away from the eyes of the referees, could rival even the ugliest wrestling match. Langdon had been kicked, scratched, held, and even bitten once by a frustrated defenseman from whom Langdon had continuously twisted away.

Now, though, thrashing in the frigid water of Bernini's fountain, Langdon knew he was a long way from the Harvard pool. He was fighting not for a game, but for his life. This was the second time they had battled. No referees here. No rematches. The arms driving his face toward the bottom of the basin thrust with a force that left no doubt that it intended to kill.

Langdon instinctively spun like a torpedo. *Break the hold!* But the grip torqued him back, his attacker enjoying an advantage no water polo defenseman ever had – two feet on solid ground. Langdon contorted, trying to get his own feet beneath him. The Hassassin seemed to be favoring one arm . . . but nonetheless, his grip held firm.

It was then that Langdon knew he was not coming up. He did the only thing he could think of to do. He stopped trying to surface. *If you can't go north, go east.* Marshalling the last of his strength, Langdon dolphin-kicked his legs and pulled his arms beneath him in an awkward butterfly stroke. His body lurched forward.

The sudden switch in direction seemed to take the Hassassin off guard. Langdon's lateral motion dragged his captor's arms sideways, compromising his balance. The man's grip faltered, and Langdon kicked again. The sensation felt like a towline had snapped. Suddenly Langdon was free. Blowing the stale air from his lungs, Langdon clawed for the surface. A single breath was all he got. With crashing force the Hassassin was on top of him again, palms on his shoulders, all of his weight bearing down. Langdon scrambled to plant his feet beneath him but the Hassassin's leg swung out, cutting Langdon down.

He went under again.

Langdon's muscles burned as he twisted beneath the water. This time his maneuvers were in vain. Through the bubbling water, Langdon scanned the bottom, looking for the gun. Everything was blurred.

The bubbles were denser here. A blinding light flashed in his face as the killer wrestled him deeper, toward a submerged spotlight bolted on the floor of the fountain. Langdon reached out, grabbing the canister. It was hot. Langdon tried to pull himself free, but the contraption was mounted on hinges and pivoted in his hand. His leverage was instantly lost.

The Hassassin drove him deeper still.

It was then Langdon saw it. Poking out from under the coins directly beneath his face. A narrow, black cylinder. *The silencer of Olivetti's gun!* Langdon reached out, but as his fingers wrapped around the cylinder, he did not feel metal, he felt plastic. When he pulled, the flexible rubber hose came flopping toward him like a flimsy snake. It was about two feet long with a jet of bubbles surging from the end. Langdon had not found the gun at all. It was one of the fountain's many harmless *spumanti* . . . bubble makers.

Only a few feet away Cardinal Baggia felt his soul straining to leave his body. Although he had prepared for this moment his entire life, he had never imagined the end would be like this. His physical shell was in agony . . . burned, bruised, and held underwater by an immovable weight. He reminded himself that this suffering was nothing compared to what Jesus had endured.

He died for my sins . . .

Baggia could hear the thrashing of a battle raging nearby. He could not bear the thought of it. His captor was about to extinguish yet another life . . . the man with kind eyes, the man who had tried to help.

As the pain mounted, Baggia lay on his back and stared up through the water at the black sky above him. For a moment he thought he saw stars.

It was time.

Releasing all fear and doubt, Baggia opened his mouth and expelled what he knew would be his final breath. He watched his spirit gurgle heavenward in a burst of transparent bubbles. Then, reflexively, he gasped. The water poured in like icy daggers to his sides. The pain lasted only a few seconds.

Then . . . peace.

The Hassassin ignored the burning in his foot and focused on the drowning American, whom he now held pinned beneath him in the churning water. *Finish it fully.* He tightened his grip, knowing *this* time Robert Langdon would not survive. As he predicted, his victim's struggling became weaker and weaker.

Suddenly Langdon's body went rigid. He began to shake wildly.

Yes, the Hassassin mused. *The rigors. When the water first hits the lungs.* The rigors, he knew, would last about five seconds.

They lasted six.

Then, exactly as the Hassassin expected, his victim went suddenly flaccid. Like a great deflating balloon, Robert Langdon fell limp. It was over. The Hassassin held him down for another thirty seconds to let the water flood all of his pulmonary tissue. Gradually, he felt Langdon's body sink, on its own accord, to the bottom. Finally, the Hassassin let go. The media would find a double surprise in the *Fountain of the Four Rivers*.

'*Tabban!*' the Hassassin swore, clambering out of the fountain and looking at his bleeding toe. The tip of his

461

boot was shredded, and the front of his big toe had been sheared off. Angry at his own carelessness, he tore the cuff from his pant leg and rammed the fabric into the toe of his boot. Pain shot up his leg. *'Ibn al-kalb!'* He clenched his fists and rammed the cloth deeper. The bleeding slowed until it was only a trickle.

Turning his thoughts from pain to pleasure, the Hassassin got into his van. His work in Rome was done. He knew exactly what would soothe his discomfort. Vittoria Vetra was bound and waiting. The Hassassin, even cold and wet, felt himself stiffen.

I have earned my reward.

Across town Vittoria awoke in pain. She was on her back. All of her muscles felt like stone. Tight. Brittle. Her arms hurt. When she tried to move, she felt spasms in her shoulders. It took her a moment to comprehend her hands were tied behind her back. Her initial reaction was confusion. *Am I dreaming?* But when she tried to lift her head, the pain at the base of her skull informed her of her wakefulness.

Confusion transforming to fear, she scanned her surroundings. She was in a crude, stone room – large and well-furnished, lit by torches. Some kind of ancient meeting hall. Old-fashioned benches sat in a circle nearby.

Vittoria felt a breeze, cold now on her skin. Nearby, a set of double doors stood open, beyond them a balcony. Through the slits in the balustrade, Vittoria could have sworn she saw the Vatican.

104

Robert Langdon lay on a bed of coins at the bottom of the *Fountain of the Four Rivers*. His mouth was still wrapped around the plastic hose. The air being pumped through the *spumanti* tube to froth the fountain had been polluted by the pump, and his throat burned. He was not complaining, though. He was alive.

He was not sure how accurate his imitation of a drowning man had been, but having been around water his entire life, Langdon had certainly heard accounts. He had done his best. Near the end, he had even blown all the air from his lungs and stopped breathing so that his muscle mass would carry his body to the floor..

Thankfully, the Hassassin had bought it and let go.

Now, resting on the bottom of the fountain, Langdon had waited as long as he could wait. He was about to start choking. He wondered if the Hassassin was still out there. Taking an acrid breath from the tube, Langdon let go and swam across the bottom of the fountain until he found the smooth swell of the central core. Silently, he followed it upward, surfacing out of sight, in the shadows beneath the huge marble figures.

The van was gone.

That was all Langdon needed to see. Pulling a long breath of fresh air back into his lungs, he scrambled back toward where Cardinal Baggia had gone down. Langdon knew the man would be unconscious now, and chances of revival were slim, but he had to try. When Langdon found the body, he planted his feet on either side, reached down, and grabbed the chains wrapped around the cardinal. Then Langdon pulled. When the cardinal broke water, Langdon could see the eyes were already rolled upward, bulging. Not a good sign. There was no breath or pulse.

Knowing he could never get the body up and over the fountain rim, Langdon lugged Cardinal Baggia through the water and into the hollow beneath the central mound of marble. Here the water became shallow and there was an inclined ledge. Langdon dragged the naked body up onto the ledge as far as he could. Not far.

Then he went to work. Compressing the cardinal's chain-clad chest, Langdon pumped the water from his lungs. Then he began CPR. Counting carefully. Deliberately. Resisting the instinct to blow too hard and too fast. For three minutes Langdon tried to revive the old man. After five minutes, Langdon knew it was over.

Il preferito. The man who would be Pope. Lying dead before him.

Somehow, even now, prostrate in the shadows on the semisubmerged ledge, Cardinal Baggia retained an air of quiet dignity. The water lapped softly across his chest, seeming almost remorseful . . . as if asking forgiveness for being the man's ultimate killer . . . as if trying to cleanse the scalded wound that bore its name.

Gently, Langdon ran a hand across the man's face and closed his upturned eyes. As he did, he felt an exhausted shudder of tears well from within. It startled him. Then, for the first time in years, Langdon cried.

The fog of weary emotion lifted slowly as Langdon waded away from the dead cardinal, back into deep water. Depleted and alone in the fountain, Langdon half-expected to collapse. But instead, he felt a new compulsion rising within him. Undeniable. Frantic. He sensed his muscles hardening with an unexpected grit. His mind, as though ignoring the pain in his heart, forced aside the past and brought into focus the single, desperate task ahead.

Find the Illuminati lair. Help Vittoria.

Turning now to the mountainous core of Bernini's fountain, Langdon summoned hope and launched himself into his quest for the final Illuminati marker. He knew somewhere on this gnarled mass of figures was a clue that pointed to the lair. As Langdon scanned the fountain, though, his hope withered quickly. The words of the *segno* seemed to gurgle mockingly all around him. *Let angels guide you on your lofty quest.* Langdon glared at the carved forms before him. *The fountain is pagan! It has no damn angels anywhere!*

When Langdon completed his fruitless search of the core, his eyes instinctively climbed the towering stone pillar. *Four markers*, he thought, *spread across Rome in a giant cross.*

Scanning the hieroglyphics covering the obelisk, he wondered if perhaps there were a clue hidden in the Egyptian symbology He immediately dismissed the idea. The hieroglyphs predated Bernini by centuries, and hieroglyphs had not even been decipherable until the Rosetta Stone was discovered.

Still, Langdon ventured, maybe Bernini had carved an additional symbol? One that would go unnoticed among all the hieroglyphs?

Feeling a shimmer of hope, Langdon circumnavigated the fountain one more time and studied all four façades of the obelisk. It took him two minutes, and when he reached the end of the final face, his hopes sank. Nothing in the hieroglyphs stood out as any kind of addition. Certainly no angels.

Langdon checked his watch. It was eleven on the dot. He couldn't tell whether time was flying or crawling. Images of Vittoria and the Hassassin started to swirl hauntingly as Langdon clambered his way around the fountain, the frustration mounting as he frantically completed yet another fruitless circle. Beaten and exhausted, Langdon felt ready to collapse. He threw back his head to scream into the night.

The sound jammed in his throat.

Langdon was staring straight up the obelisk. The object perched at the very top was one he had seen earlier and ignored. Now, however, it stopped him short. It was not an angel. Far from it. In fact, he had not even perceived it as *part* of Bernini's fountain. He thought it was a living creature, another one of the city's scavengers perched on a lofty tower.

A pigeon.

Langdon squinted skyward at the object, his vision blurred by the glowing mist around him. It was a pigeon, wasn't it? He could clearly see the head and beak silhouetted against a cluster of stars. And yet the bird had not budged since Langdon's arrival, even with the battle below. The bird sat now exactly as it had been when Langdon entered the square. It was perched high atop the obelisk, gazing calmly westward.

Langdon stared at it a moment and then plunged his hand into the fountain and grabbed a fistful of coins. He hurled the coins skyward. They clattered across the upper levels of the granite obelisk. The bird did not budge. He tried again. This time, one of the coins hit the mark. A faint sound of metal on metal clanged across the square.

The damned pigeon was bronze.

You're looking for an angel, not a pigeon, a voice reminded him. But it was too late. Langdon had made the connection. He realized the bird was not a pigeon at all.

It was a dove.

Barely aware of his own actions, Langdon splashed toward the center of the fountain and began scrambling up the travertine mountain, clambering over huge arms and heads, pulling himself higher. Halfway to the base of the obelisk, he emerged from the mist and could see the head of the bird more clearly.

There was no doubt. It was a dove. The bird's deceptively dark color was the result of Rome's pollution tarnishing the original bronze. Then the significance hit him. He had seen a pair of doves earlier today at the Pantheon. A *pair* of doves carried no meaning. This dove, however, was alone.

The lone dove is the pagan symbol for the Angel of Peace.

The truth almost lifted Langdon the rest of the way to the obelisk. Bernini had chosen the *pagan* symbol for the angel so he could disguise it in a pagan fountain. *Let angels guide you on your lofty quest. The dove is the angel!* Langdon could think of no more lofty perch for the Illuminati's final marker than atop this obelisk.

The bird was looking west. Langdon tried to follow

467

its gaze, but he could not see over the buildings. He climbed higher. A quote from St Gregory of Nyssa emerged from his memory most unexpectedly. *As the soul becomes enlightened . . . it takes the beautiful shape of the dove.*

Langdon rose heavenward. Toward the dove. He was almost flying now. He reached the platform from which the obelisk rose and could climb no higher. With one look around, though, he knew he didn't have to. All of Rome spread out before him. The view was stunning.

To his left, the chaotic media lights surrounding St Peter's. To his right, the smoking cupola of Santa Maria della Vittoria. In front of him in the distance, Piazza del Popolo. Beneath him, the fourth and final point. A giant cross of obelisks.

Trembling, Langdon looked to the dove overhead. He turned and faced the proper direction, and then he lowered his eyes to the skyline.

In an instant he saw it.

So obvious. So clear. So deviously simple.

Staring at it now, Langdon could not believe the Illuminati lair had stayed hidden for so many years. The entire city seemed to fade away as he looked out at the monstrous stone structure across the river in front of him. The building was as famous as any in Rome. It stood on the banks of the Tiber River diagonally adjacent to the Vatican. The building's geometry was stark – a circular castle, within a square fortress, and then, outside its walls, surrounding the entire structure, a park in the shape of a *pentagram*.

The ancient stone ramparts before him were dramatically lit by soft floodlights. High atop the castle stood the mammoth bronze angel. The angel pointed his sword downward at the exact center of the castle. And as if that were not enough, leading solely and directly to the castle's main entrance stood the famous Bridge of Angels . . . a dramatic approachway adorned by twelve towering angels carved by none other than Bernini himself.

In a final breathtaking revelation, Langdon realized Bernini's city-wide cross of obelisks marked the fortress in perfect Illuminati fashion; the cross's central arm passed *directly* through the center of the castle's bridge, dividing it into two equal halves.

Langdon retrieved his tweed coat, holding it away from his dripping body Then he jumped into the stolen sedan and rammed his soggy shoe into the accelerator, speeding off into the night.

106

It was 11.07 p.m. Langdon's car raced through the Roman night. Speeding down Lungotevere Tor Di Nona, parallel with the river, Langdon could now see his destination rising like a mountain to his right.

Castel Sant' Angelo. Castle of the Angel.

Without warning, the turnoff to the narrow Bridge of Angels – Ponte Sant' Angelo – appeared suddenly. Langdon slammed on his brakes and swerved. He turned in time, but the bridge was barricaded. He skidded ten feet and collided with a series of short cement pillars blocking his way. Langdon lurched forward as the vehicle stalled, wheezing and shuddering. He had forgotten the Bridge of Angels, in order to preserve it, was now zoned pedestrians only

Shaken, Langdon staggered from the crumpled car, wishing now he had chosen one of the other routes. He felt chilled, shivering from the fountain. He donned his Harris tweed over his damp shirt, grateful for Harris's trademark double lining. The *Diagramma* folio would remain dry. Before him, across the bridge, the stone fortress rose like a mountain. Aching and depleted, Langdon broke into a loping run.

On both sides of him now, like a gauntlet of escorts, a procession of Bernini angels whipped past, funneling him toward his final destination. *Let angels guide you on your lofty quest.* The castle seemed to rise as he advanced, an unscalable peak, more intimidating to him even than St Peter's. He sprinted toward the bastion, running on fumes, gazing upward at the citadel's circular core as it shot skyward to a gargantuan, sword-wielding angel.

The castle appeared deserted.

Langdon knew through the centuries the building had been used by the Vatican as a tomb, a fortress, a papal hideout, a prison for enemies of the church, and a museum. Apparently, the castle had other tenants as well – the Illuminati. Somehow it made eerie sense. Although the castle was property of the Vatican, it was used only sporadically, and Bernini had made numerous renovations to it over the years. The building was now rumored to be honeycombed with secret entries, passageways, and hidden chambers. Langdon had little doubt that the angel and surrounding pentagonal park were Bernini's doing as well.

Arriving at the castle's elephantine double doors, Langdon shoved them hard. Not surprisingly, they were immovable. Two iron knockers hung at eye level.

Langdon didn't bother. He stepped back, his eyes climbing the sheer outer wall. These ramparts had fended off armies of Berbers, heathens, and Moors. Somehow he sensed his chances of breaking in were slim.

Vittoria, Langdon thought. *Are you in there?*

Langdon hurried around the outer wall. *There must be another entrance!*

Rounding the second bulwark to the west, Langdon arrived breathless in a small parking area off Lungotere Angelo. On this wall he found a second castle entrance, a drawbridge-type ingress, raised and sealed shut. Langdon gazed upward again.

The only lights on the castle were exterior floods illuminating the façade. All the tiny windows inside seemed black. Langdon's eyes climbed higher. At the very peak of the central tower, a hundred feet above, directly beneath the angel's sword, a single balcony protruded. The marble parapet seemed to shimmer slightly, as if the room beyond it were aglow with torchlight. Langdon paused, his soaked body shivering suddenly. A shadow? He waited, straining. Then he saw it again. His spine prickled. *Someone is up there!*

'Vittoria!' he called out, unable to help himself, but his voice was swallowed by the raging Tiber behind him. He wheeled in circles, wondering where the hell the Swiss Guard were. Had they even heard his transmission?

Across the lot a large media truck was parked. Langdon ran toward it. A paunchy man in headphones sat in the cabin adjusting levers. Langdon rapped on the side of the truck. The man jumped, saw Langdon's dripping clothes, and yanked off his headset.

'What's the worry, mate?' His accent was Australian.

'I need your phone.' Langdon was frenzied.

The man shrugged. 'No dial tone. Been trying all night. Circuits are packed.'

Langdon swore aloud. 'Have you seen anyone go in there?' He pointed to the drawbridge.

'Actually, yeah. A black van's been going in and out all night.'

Langdon felt a brick hit the bottom of his stomach.

'Lucky bastard,' the Aussie said, gazing up at the tower, and then frowning at his obstructed view of the Vatican. 'I bet the view from up there is perfect. I couldn't get through the traffic in St Peter's, so I'm shooting from here.'

Langdon wasn't listening. He was looking for options.

'What do you say?' the Australian said. 'This 11th Hour Samaritan for real?'

Langdon turned. 'The what?'

'You didn't hear? The Captain of the Swiss Guard got a call from somebody who claims to have some primo info. The guy's flying in right now. All I know is if he saves the day . . . there go the ratings!' The man laughed.

Langdon was suddenly confused. A good Samaritan flying in to help? Did the person somehow know where the antimatter was? Then why didn't he just *tell* the Swiss Guard? Why was he coming in person? Something was odd, but Langdon didn't have time to figure out what.

'Hey,' the Aussie said, studying Langdon more closely. 'Ain't you that guy I saw on TV? Trying to save that cardinal in St Peter's Square?'

Langdon did not answer. His eyes had suddenly locked on a contraption attached to the top of the truck

– a satellite dish on a collapsible appendage. Langdon looked at the castle again. The outer rampart was fifty feet tall. The inner fortress climbed farther still. A shelled defense. The top was impossibly high from here, but maybe if he could clear the first wall . . .

Langdon spun to the newsman and pointed to the satellite arm. 'How high does that go?'

'Huh?' The man looked confused. 'Fifteen meters. Why?'

'Move the truck. Park next to the wall. I need help.'

'What are you talking about?'

Langdon explained.

The Aussie's eyes went wide. 'Are you insane? That's a two-hundred-thousand-dollar telescoping extension. Not a ladder!'

'You want ratings? I've got information that will make your day.' Langdon was desperate.

'Information worth two hundred grand?'

Langdon told him what he would reveal in exchange for the favor.

Ninety seconds later, Robert Langdon was gripping the top of the satellite arm wavering in the breeze fifty feet off the ground. Leaning out, he grabbed the top of the first bulwark, dragged himself onto the wall, and dropped onto the castle's lower bastion.

'Now keep your bargain!' the Aussie called up. 'Where is he?'

Langdon felt guilt-ridden for revealing this information, but a deal was a deal. Besides, the Hassassin would probably call the press anyway. 'Piazza Navona,' Langdon shouted. 'He's in the fountain.'

The Aussie lowered his satellite dish and peeled out after the scoop of his career.

* * *

In a stone chamber high above the city, the Hassassin removed his soaking boots and bandaged his wounded toe. There was pain, but not so much that he couldn't enjoy himself.

He turned to his prize.

She was in the corner of the room, on her back on a rudimentary divan, hands tied behind her, mouth gagged. The Hassassin moved toward her. She was awake now. This pleased him. Surprisingly, in her eyes, he saw fire instead of fear.

The fear will come.

107

Robert Langdon dashed around the outer bulwark of the castle, grateful for the glow of the floodlights. As he circled the wall, the courtyard beneath him looked like a museum of ancient warfare – catapults, stacks of marble cannonballs, and an arsenal of fearful contraptions. Parts of the castle were open to tourists during the day, and the courtyard had been partially restored to its original state.

Langdon's eyes crossed the courtyard to the central core of the fortress. The circular citadel shot skyward 107 feet to the bronze angel above. The balcony at the top still glowed from within. Langdon wanted to call out but knew better. He would have to find a way in.

He checked his watch.

11.12 p.m.

Dashing down the stone ramp that hugged the inside of the wall, Langdon descended to the courtyard. Back on ground level, he ran through shadows, clockwise around the fort. He passed three porticos, but all of them were permanently sealed. *How did the Hassassin get in?* Langdon pushed on. He passed two modern entrances, but they were pad-locked from the outside. *Not here.* He kept running.

Langdon had circled almost the entire building when he saw a gravel drive cutting across the court-yard in front of him. At one end, on the outer wall of the castle, he saw the back of the gated drawbridge leading back outside. At the other end, the drive dis-appeared into the fortress. The drive seemed to enter a kind of tunnel – a gaping entry in the central core. *Il traforo!* Langdon had read about this castle's *traforo*, a giant spiral ramp that circled up inside the fort, used by commanders on horseback to ride from top to bottom rapidly. *The Hassassin drove up!* The gate block-ing the tunnel was raised, ushering Langdon in. He felt almost exuberant as he ran toward the tunnel. But as he reached the opening, his excitement disappeared.

The tunnel spiraled *down*.

The wrong way. This section of the *traforo* appar-ently descended to the dungeons, not to the top.

Standing at the mouth of a dark bore that seemed to twist endlessly deeper into the earth, Langdon hesitated, looking up again at the balcony. He could swear he saw motion up there. *Decide!* With no other options, he dashed down into the tunnel.

High overhead, the Hassassin stood over his prey. He ran a hand across her arm. Her skin was like cream. The anticipation of exploring her bodily treasures was inebriating. How many ways could he violate her?

The Hassassin knew he deserved this woman. He had served Janus well. She was a spoil of war, and when he was finished with her, he would pull her from the divan and force her to her knees. She would service him again. *The ultimate submission.* Then, at the moment of his own climax, he would slit her throat.

Ghayat assa'adah, they called it. *The ultimate pleasure.*

Afterward, basking in his glory, he would stand on the balcony and savor the culmination of the Illuminati triumph . . . a revenge desired by so many for so long.

The tunnel grew darker. Langdon descended.

After one complete turn into the earth, the light was all but gone. The tunnel leveled out, and Langdon slowed, sensing by the echo of his footfalls that he had just entered a larger chamber. Before him in the murkiness, he thought he saw glimmers of light . . . fuzzy reflections in the ambient gleam. He moved forward, reaching out his hand. He found smooth surfaces. Chrome and glass. It was a vehicle. He groped the surface, found a door, and opened it.

The vehicle's interior dome-light flashed on. He stepped back and recognized the black van immediately. Feeling a surge of loathing, he stared a moment, then he dove in, rooting around in hopes of finding a weapon to replace the one he'd lost in the fountain. He found none. He did, however, find Vittoria's cell phone. It was shattered and useless. The sight of it filled Langdon with fear. He prayed he was not too late.

He reached up and turned on the van's headlights. The room around him blazed into existence, harsh shadows in a simple chamber. Langdon guessed the room was once used for horses and ammunition. It was also a dead end.

No exit. *I came the wrong way!*

At the end of his rope, Langdon jumped from the van and scanned the walls around him. No doorways. No gates. He thought of the angel over the tunnel entrance and wondered if it had been a coincidence. *No!* He thought of the killer's words at the fountain. *She is in the Church of Illumination ... awaiting my return.* Langdon had come too far to fail now. His heart was pounding. Frustration and hatred were starting to cripple his senses.

When he saw the blood on the floor, Langdon's first thought was for Vittoria. But as his eyes followed the stains, he realized they were bloody footprints. The strides were long. The splotches of blood were only on the left foot. *The Hassassin!*

Langdon followed the footprints toward the corner of the room, his sprawling shadow growing fainter. He felt more and more puzzled with every step. The bloody prints looked as though they walked directly into the corner of the room and then disappeared.

When Langdon arrived in the corner, he could not believe his eyes. The granite block in the floor here was not a square like the others. He was looking at another signpost. The block was carved into a perfect pentagram, arranged with the tip pointing into the corner. Ingeniously concealed by overlapping walls, a narrow slit in the stone served as an exit. Langdon slid through. He was in a passage. In front of him were the remains of a wooden barrier that had once been blocking this tunnel.

Beyond it there was light.

Langdon was running now. He clambered over the

wood and headed for the light. The passage quickly opened into another, larger chamber. Here a single torch flickered on the wall. Langdon was in a section of the castle that had no electricity ... a section no tourists would ever see. The room would have been frightful in daylight, but the torch made it even more gruesome.

Il prigione.

There were a dozen tiny jail cells, the iron bars on most eroded away. One of the larger cells, however, remained intact, and on the floor Langdon saw something that almost stopped his heart. Black robes and red sashes on the floor. *This is where he held the cardinals!*

Near the cell was an iron doorway in the wall. The door was ajar and beyond it Langdon could see some sort of passage. He ran toward it. But Langdon stopped before he got there. The trail of blood did not enter the passage. When Langdon saw the words carved over the archway, he knew why.

Il Passetto.

He was stunned. He had heard of this tunnel many times, never knowing where exactly the entrance was. *Il Passetto* – The Little Passage – was a slender, three-quarter-mile tunnel built between Castle St Angelo and the Vatican. It had been used by various Popes to escape to safety during sieges of the Vatican ... as well as by a few less pious Popes to secretly visit mistresses or oversee the torture of their enemies. Nowadays both ends of the tunnel were supposedly sealed with impenetrable locks whose keys were kept in some Vatican vault. Langdon suddenly feared he knew how the Illuminati had been moving in and out of the Vatican. He found himself wondering *who* on the inside had betrayed the church and coughed up the keys. *Olivetti? One of the Swiss Guard?* None of it mattered anymore.

The blood on the floor led to the opposite end of the prison. Langdon followed. Here, a rusty gate hung draped with chains. The lock had been removed and the gate stood ajar. Beyond the gate was a steep ascension of spiral stairs. The floor here was also marked with a pentagramal block. Langdon stared at the block, trembling, wondering if Bernini himself had held the chisel that had shaped these chunks. Overhead, the archway was adorned with a tiny carved cherub. This was it.

The trail of blood curved up the stairs.

Before ascending, Langdon knew he needed a weapon, any weapon. He found a four-foot section of iron bar near one of the cells. It had a sharp, splintered end. Although absurdly heavy, it was the best he could do. He hoped the element of surprise, combined with the Hassassin's wound, would be enough to tip the scales in his advantage. Most of all, though, he hoped he was not too late.

The staircase's spiral treads were worn and twisted steeply upward. Langdon ascended, listening for sounds. None. As he climbed, the light from the prison area faded away. He ascended into the total darkness, keeping one hand on the wall. Higher. In the blackness, Langdon sensed the ghost of Galileo, climbing these very stairs, eager to share his visions of heaven with other men of science and faith.

Langdon was still in a state of shock over the location of the lair. The Illuminati meeting hall was in a building owned by the Vatican. No doubt while the Vatican guards were out searching basements and homes of well-known scientists, the Illuminati were meeting *here* ... right under the Vatican's nose. It suddenly seemed so perfect. Bernini, as head architect of renovations here, would have had unlimited access to this structure ... remodeling it to his own specifications with no questions asked. How many secret entries had Bernini added? How many subtle embellishments pointing the way?

The Church of Illumination. Langdon knew he was close.

As the stairs began narrowing, Langdon felt the passage closing around him. The shadows of history were whispering in the dark, but he moved on. When he saw the horizontal shaft of light before him, he realized he was standing a few steps beneath a landing, where the glow of torchlight spilled out beneath the threshold of a door in front of him. Silently he moved up.

Langdon had no idea where in the castle he was right now, but he knew he had climbed far enough to be near the peak. He pictured the mammoth angel atop the castle and suspected it was directly overhead.

Watch over me, angel, he thought, gripping the bar. Then, silently, he reached for the door.

On the divan, Vittoria's arms ached. When she had first awoken to find them tied behind her back, she'd thought she might be able to relax and work her hands free. But time had run out. The beast had returned. Now he was standing over her, his chest bare and powerful, scarred from battles he had endured. His eyes looked like two black slits as he stared down at her body. Vittoria sensed he was imagining the deeds he was about to perform. Slowly, as if to taunt her, the

Hassassin removed his soaking belt and dropped it on the floor.

Vittoria felt a loathing horror. She closed her eyes. When she opened them again, the Hassassin had produced a switchblade knife. He snapped it open directly in front of her face.

Vittoria saw her own terrified reflection in the steel.

The Hassassin turned the blade over and ran the back of it across her belly. The icy metal gave her chills. With a contemptuous stare, he slipped the blade below the waistline of her shorts. She inhaled. He moved back and forth, slowly, dangerously . . . lower. Then he leaned forward, his hot breath whispering in her ear.

'This blade cut out your father's eye.'

Vittoria knew in that instant that she was capable of killing.

The Hassassin turned the blade again and began sawing upward through the fabric of her khaki shorts. Suddenly, he stopped, looking up. Someone was in the room.

'Get away from her,' a deep voice growled from the doorway.

Vittoria could not see who had spoken, but she recognized the voice. *Robert! He's alive!*

The Hassassin looked as if he had seen a ghost. 'Mr Langdon, you must have a guardian angel.'

108

In the split second it took Langdon to take in his surroundings, he realized he was in a sacred place.

The embellishments in the oblong room, though old and faded, were replete with familiar symbology. Pentagram tiles. Planet frescoes. Doves. Pyramids.

The Church of Illumination. Simple and pure. He had arrived.

Directly in front of him, framed in the opening of the balcony, stood the Hassassin. He was bare chested, standing over Vittoria, who lay bound but very much alive. Langdon felt a wave of relief to see her. For an instant, their eyes met, and a torrent of emotions flowed – gratitude, desperation, and regret.

'So we meet yet again,' the Hassassin said. He looked at the bar in Langdon's hand and laughed out loud. 'And this time you come for me with *that*?'

'Untie her.'

The Hassassin put the knife to Vittoria's throat. 'I will kill her.'

Langdon had no doubt the Hassassin was capable of such an act. He forced a calm into his voice. 'I imagine she would welcome it ... considering the alternative.'

The Hassassin smiled at the insult. 'You're right. She has much to offer. It would be a waste.'

Langdon stepped forward, grasping the rusted bar, and aimed the splintered end directly at the Hassassin. The cut on his hand bit sharply. 'Let her go.'

The Hassassin seemed for a moment to be considering it. Exhaling, he dropped his shoulders. It was a clear motion of surrender, and yet at that exact instant the Hassassin's arm seemed to accelerate unexpectedly. There was a blur of dark muscle, and a blade suddenly came tearing through the air toward Langdon's chest.

Whether it was instinct or exhaustion that buckled

Langdon's knees at that moment, he didn't know, but the knife sailed past his left ear and clattered to the floor behind him. The Hassassin seemed unfazed. He smiled at Langdon, who was kneeling now, holding the metal bar. The killer stepped away from Vittoria and moved toward Langdon like a stalking lion.

As Langdon scrambled to his feet, lifting the bar again, his wet turtleneck and pants felt suddenly more restrictive. The Hassassin, half-clothed, seemed to move much faster, the wound on his foot apparently not slowing him at all. Langdon sensed this was a man accustomed to pain. For the first time in his life, Langdon wished he were holding a very big gun.

The Hassassin circled slowly, as if enjoying himself, always just out of reach, moving toward the knife on the floor. Langdon cut him off. Then the killer moved back toward Vittoria. Again Langdon cut him off.

'There's still time,' Langdon ventured. 'Tell me where the canister is. The Vatican will pay more than the Illuminati ever could.'

'You are naïve.'

Langdon jabbed with the bar. The Hassassin dodged. He navigated around a bench, holding the weapon in front of him, trying to corner the Hassassin in the oval room. *This damn room has no corners!* Oddly, the Hassassin did not seem interested in attacking or fleeing. He was simply playing Langdon's game. Coolly waiting.

Waiting for what? The killer kept circling, a master at positioning himself. It was like an endless game of chess. The weapon in Langdon's hand was getting heavy, and he suddenly sensed he knew what the Hassassin was waiting for. *He's tiring me out.* It was working, too. Langdon was hit by a surge of weariness, the adrenaline alone no longer enough to keep him alert. He knew he had to make a move.

The Hassassin seemed to read Langdon's mind, shifting again, as if intentionally leading Langdon toward a table in the middle of the room. Langdon could tell there was something on the table. Something glinted in the torchlight. *A weapon?* Langdon kept his eyes focused on the Hassassin and maneuvered himself closer to the table. When the Hassassin cast a long, guileless glance at the table, Langdon tried to fight the obvious bait. But instinct overruled. He stole a glance. The damage was done.

It was not a weapon at all. The sight momentarily riveted him.

On the table lay a rudimentary copper chest, crusted with ancient patina. The chest was a pentagon. The lid lay open. Arranged inside in five padded compartments were five brands. The brands were forged of iron – large embossing tools with stout handles of wood. Langdon had no doubt what they said.

ILLUMINATI, EARTH, AIR, FIRE, WATER.

Langdon snapped his head back up, fearing the Hassassin would lunge. He did not. The killer was waiting, almost as if he were refreshed by the game. Langdon fought to recover his focus, locking eyes again with his quarry, thrusting with the pipe. But the image of the box hung in his mind. Although the brands themselves were mesmerizing – artifacts few Illuminati scholars even believed existed – Langdon suddenly realized there had been something *else* about the box that had ignited a wave of foreboding within. As the Hassassin maneuvered again, Langdon stole another glance downward.

My God!

In the chest, the five brands sat in compartments around the outer edge. But in the *center*, there was another compartment. This partition was empty, but it clearly was intended to hold another brand . . . a brand much larger than the others, and perfectly square.

The attack was a blur.

The Hassassin swooped toward him like a bird of prey. Langdon, his concentration having been masterfully diverted, tried to counter, but the pipe felt like a tree trunk in his hands. His parry was too slow. The Hassassin dodged. As Langdon tried to retract the bar, the Hassassin's hands shot out and grabbed it. The man's grip was strong, his injured arm seeming no longer to affect him. Violently, the two men struggled. Langdon felt the bar ripped away, and a searing pain shot through his palm. An instant later, Langdon was staring into the splintered point of the weapon. The hunter had become the hunted.

Langdon felt like he'd been hit by a cyclone. The Hassassin circled, smiling now, backing Langdon against the wall. 'What is your American *adàgio*?' he chided. 'Something about curiosity and the cat?'

Langdon could barely focus. He cursed his carelessness as the Hassassin moved in. Nothing was making sense. *A sixth Illuminati brand?* In frustration he blurted, 'I've never read anything about a *sixth* Illuminati brand!'

'I think you probably have.' The killer chuckled as he herded Langdon around the oval wall.

Langdon was lost. He most certainly had not. There were *five* Illuminati brands. He backed up, searching the room for any weapon at all.

'A perfect union of the ancient elements,' the

485

Hassassin said. 'The final brand is the most brilliant of all. I'm afraid you will never see it, though.'

Langdon sensed he would not be seeing much of anything in a moment. He kept backing up, searching the room for an option. 'And you've seen this final brand?' Langdon demanded, trying to buy time.

'Someday perhaps they will honor me. As I prove myself.' He jabbed at Langdon, as if enjoying a game.

Langdon slid backward again. He had the feeling the Hassassin was directing him around the wall toward some unseen destination. *Where?* Langdon could not afford to look behind him. 'The brand?' he demanded. 'Where is it?'

'Not here. Janus is apparently the only one who holds it.'

'Janus?' Langdon did not recognize the name.

'The Illuminati leader. He is arriving shortly.'

'The Illuminati leader is coming *here*?'

'To perform the final branding.'

Langdon shot a frightened glance to Vittoria. She looked strangely calm, her eyes closed to the world around her, her lungs pulling slowly . . . deeply. Was she the final victim? Was *he*?

'Such conceit,' the Hassassin sneered, watching Langdon's eyes. 'The two of you are nothing. You will die, of course, that is for certain. But the final victim of whom I speak is a truly dangerous enemy.'

Langdon tried to make sense of the Hassassin's words. A dangerous enemy? The top cardinals were all dead. The Pope was dead. The Illuminati had wiped them all out. Langdon found the answer in the vacuum of the Hassassin's eyes.

The camerlengo.

Camerlengo Ventresca was the one man who had

been a beacon of hope for the world through this entire tribulation. The camerlengo had done more to condemn the Illuminati tonight than decades of conspiracy theorists. Apparently he would pay the price. He was the Illuminati's final target.

'You'll never get to him,' Langdon challenged.

'Not I,' the Hassassin replied, forcing Langdon farther back around the wall. 'That honor is reserved for Janus himself.'

'The Illuminati leader *himself* intends to brand the camerlengo?'

'Power has its privileges.'

'But no one could possibly get into Vatican City right now!'

The Hassassin looked smug. 'Not unless he had an appointment.'

Langdon was confused. The only person expected at the Vatican right now was the person the press was calling the 11th Hour Samaritan – the person Rocher said had information that could save—

Langdon stopped short. *Good God!*

The Hassassin smirked, clearly enjoying Langdon's sickening cognition. 'I too wondered how Janus would gain entrance. Then in the van I heard the radio – a report about an 11th hour Samaritan.' He smiled. 'The Vatican will welcome Janus with open arms.'

Langdon almost stumbled backward. *Janus is the Samaritan!* It was an unthinkable deception. The Illuminati leader would get a royal escort directly to the camerlengo's chambers. *But how did Janus fool Rocher? Or was Rocher somehow involved?* Langdon felt a chill. Ever since he had almost suffocated in the secret archives, Langdon had not entirely trusted Rocher.

The Hassassin jabbed suddenly, nicking Langdon in the side.

Langdon jumped back, his temper flaring. 'Janus will never get out alive!'

The Hassassin shrugged. 'Some causes are worth dying for.'

Langdon sensed the killer was serious. Janus coming to Vatican City on a *suicide* mission? A question of honor? For an instant, Langdon's mind took in the entire terrifying cycle. The Illuminati plot had come full circle. The priest whom the Illuminati had inadvertently brought to power by killing the Pope had emerged as a worthy adversary. In a final act of defiance, the Illuminati leader would destroy him.

Suddenly, Langdon felt the wall behind him disappear. There was a rush of cool air, and he staggered backward into the night. *The balcony!* He now realized what the Hassassin had in mind.

Langdon immediately sensed the precipice behind him – a hundred-foot drop to the courtyard below. He had seen it on his way in. The Hassassin wasted no time. With a violent surge, he lunged. The spear sliced toward Langdon's midsection. Langdon skidded back, and the point came up short, catching only his shirt. Again the point came at him. Langdon slid farther back, feeling the banister right behind him. Certain the next jab would kill him, Langdon attempted the absurd. Spinning to one side, he reached out and grabbed the shaft, sending a jolt of pain through his palm. Langdon held on.

The Hassassin seemed unfazed. They strained for a moment against one another, face to face, the Hassassin's breath fetid in Langdon's nostrils. The bar began to slip. The Hassassin was too strong. In a final act of desperation, Langdon stretched out his leg, dangerously off balance as he tried to ram his foot down on the Hassassin's injured toe. But the man was a professional and adjusted to protect his weakness.

Langdon had just played his final card. And he knew he had lost the hand.

The Hassassin's arms exploded upward, driving Langdon back against the railing. Langdon sensed nothing but empty space behind him as the railing hit just beneath his buttocks. The Hassassin held the bar crosswise and drove it into Langdon's chest. Langdon's back arched over the chasm.

'*Ma'assalamah,*' the Hassassin sneered. 'Good-bye.'

With a merciless glare, the Hassassin gave a final shove. Langdon's center of gravity shifted, and his feet swung up off the floor. With only one hope of survival, Langdon grabbed on to the railing as he went over. His left hand slipped, but his right hand held on. He ended up hanging upside down by his legs and one hand . . . straining to hold on.

Looming over him, the Hassassin raised the bar overhead, preparing to bring it crashing down. As the bar began to accelerate, Langdon saw a vision. Perhaps it was the imminence of death or simply blind fear, but in that moment, he sensed a sudden aura surrounding the Hassassin. A glowing effulgence seemed to swell out of nothing behind him . . . like an incoming fireball.

Halfway through his swing, the Hassassin dropped the bar and screamed in agony.

The iron bar clattered past Langdon out into the night. The Hassassin spun away from him, and Langdon saw a blistering torch burn on the killer's back. Langdon pulled himself up to see Vittoria, eyes flaring, now facing the Hassassin.

Vittoria waved a torch in front of her, the vengeance in her face resplendent in the flames. How she had escaped, Langdon did not know or care. He began scrambling back up over the banister.

The battle would be short. The Hassassin was a deadly match. Screaming with rage, the killer lunged for her. She tried to dodge, but the man was on her, holding the torch and about to wrestle it away. Langdon did not wait. Leaping off the banister, Langdon jabbed his clenched fist into the blistered burn on the Hassassin's back.

The scream seemed to echo all the way to the Vatican.

The Hassassin froze a moment, his back arched in anguish. He let go of the torch, and Vittoria thrust it hard into his face. There was a hiss of flesh as his left eye sizzled. He screamed again, raising his hands to his face.

'Eye for an eye,' Vittoria hissed. This time she swung the torch like a bat, and when it connected, the Hassassin stumbled back against the railing. Langdon and Vittoria went for him at the same instant, both heaving and pushing. The Hassassin's body sailed backward over the banister into the night. There was no scream. The only sound was the crack of his spine as he landed spread-eagle on a pile of cannonballs far below.

Langdon turned and stared at Vittoria in bewilderment. Slackened ropes hung off her midsection and shoulders. Her eyes blazed like an inferno.

'Houdini knew yoga.'

109

Meanwhile, in St Peter's Square, the wall of Swiss Guards yelled orders and fanned outward, trying to push the crowds back to a safer distance. It was no use. The crowd was too dense and seemed far more interested in the Vatican's impending doom than in their own safety. The towering media screens in the square were now transmitting a live countdown of the antimatter canister – a direct feed from the Swiss Guard security monitor – compliments of the camerlengo. Unfortunately, the image of the canister counting down was doing nothing to repel the crowds. The people in the square apparently looked at the tiny droplet of liquid suspended in the canister and decided it was not as menacing as they had thought. They could also see the countdown clock now – a little under forty-five minutes until detonation. Plenty of time to stay and watch.

Nonetheless, the Swiss Guards unanimously agreed that the camerlengo's bold decision to address the world with the truth and then provide the media with actual *visuals* of Illuminati treachery had been a savvy maneuver. The Illuminati had no doubt expected the Vatican to be their usual reticent selves in the face of adversity. Not tonight. Camerlengo Carlo Ventresca had proven himself a commanding foe.

Inside the Sistine Chapel, Cardinal Mortati was getting restless. It was past 11.15 p.m. Many of the cardinals were continuing to pray, but others had clustered around the exit, clearly unsettled by the hour. Some of the cardinals began pounding on the door with their fists.

Outside the door Lieutenant Chartrand heard the pounding and didn't know what to do. He checked his watch. It was time. Captain Rocher had given strict orders that the cardinals were not to be let out until he gave the word. The pounding on the door became more intense, and Chartrand felt uneasy. He wondered if the captain had simply forgotten. The captain had been acting very erratic since his mysterious phone call.

Chartrand pulled out his walkie-talkie. 'Captain? Chartrand here. It is past time. Should I open the Sistine?'

'That door stays shut. I believe I already gave you that order.'

'Yes, sir, I just—'

'Our guest is arriving shortly. Take a few men upstairs, and guard the door of the Pope's office. The camerlengo is not to go *anywhere*.'

'I'm sorry, sir?'

'What is it that you don't understand, Lieutenant?'

'Nothing, sir. I am on my way.'

Upstairs in the Office of the Pope, the camerlengo stared in quiet meditation at the fire. *Give me strength, God. Bring us a miracle.* He poked at the coals, wondering if he would survive the night.

110

Eleven-twenty-three p.m.

Vittoria stood trembling on the balcony of Castle St

Angelo, staring out across Rome, her eyes moist with tears. She wanted badly to embrace Robert Langdon, but she could not. Her body felt anesthetized. Readjusting. Taking stock. The man who had killed her father lay far below, dead, and she had almost been a victim as well.

When Langdon's hand touched her shoulder, the infusion of warmth seemed to magically shatter the ice. Her body shuddered back to life. The fog lifted, and she turned. Robert looked like hell – wet and matted – he had obviously been through purgatory to come rescue her.

'Thank you . . .' she whispered.

Langdon gave an exhausted smile and reminded her that it was *she* who deserved thanks – her ability to practically dislocate her shoulders had just saved them both. Vittoria wiped her eyes. She could have stood there forever with him, but the reprieve was short-lived.

'We need to get out of here,' Langdon said.

Vittoria's mind was elsewhere. She was staring out toward the Vatican. The world's smallest country looked unsettlingly close, glowing white under a barrage of media lights. To her shock, much of St Peter's Square was still packed with people! The Swiss Guard had apparently been able to clear only about a hundred and fifty feet back – the area directly in front of the basilica – less than one-third of the square. The shell of congestion encompassing the square was compacted now, those at the safer distances pressing for a closer look, trapping the others inside. *They are too close!* Vittoria thought. *Much too close!*

'I'm going back in,' Langdon said flatly.

Vittoria turned, incredulous. 'Into the *Vatican*?'

Langdon told her about the Samaritan, and how it was a ploy. The Illuminati leader, a man named Janus, was actually coming himself to brand the camerlengo. A final Illuminati act of domination.

'Nobody in Vatican City knows,' Langdon said. 'I have no way to contact them, and this guy is arriving any minute. I have to warn the guards before they let him in.'

'But you'll never get through the crowd!'

Langdon's voice was confident. 'There's a way. Trust me.'

Vittoria sensed once again that the historian knew something she did not. 'I'm coming.'

'No. Why risk both—'

'I have to find a way to get those people out of there! They're in incredible dange—'

Just then, the balcony they were standing on began to shake. A deafening rumble shook the whole castle. Then a white light from the direction of St Peter's blinded them. Vittoria had only one thought. *Oh my God! The antimatter annihilated early!*

But instead of an explosion, a huge cheer went up from the crowd. Vittoria squinted into the light. It was a barrage of media lights from the square, now trained, it seemed, on them! Everyone was turned their way, hollering and pointing. The rumble grew louder. The air in the square seemed suddenly joyous.

Langdon looked baffled. 'What the devil—'

The sky overhead roared.

Emerging from behind the tower, without warning, came the papal helicopter. It thundered fifty feet above them, on a beeline for Vatican City. As it passed overhead, radiant in the media lights, the castle trembled. The lights followed the helicopter as it passed by, and

Langdon and Vittoria were suddenly again in the dark.

Vittoria had the uneasy feeling they were too late as they watched the mammoth machine slow to a stop over St Peter's Square. Kicking up a cloud of dust, the chopper dropped onto the open portion of the square between the crowd and the basilica, touching down at the bottom of the basilica's staircase.

'Talk about an entrance,' Vittoria said. Against the white marble, she could see a tiny speck of a person emerge from the Vatican and move toward the chopper. She would never have recognized the figure except for the bright red beret on his head. 'Red carpet greeting. That's Rocher.'

Langdon pounded his fist on the banister. 'Somebody's got to warn them!' He turned to go.

Vittoria caught his arm. 'Wait!' She had just seen something else, something her eyes refused to believe. Fingers trembling, she pointed toward the chopper. Even from this distance, there was no mistaking. Descending the gangplank was another figure . . . a figure who moved so uniquely that it could only be one man. Although the figure was seated, he accelerated across the open square with effortless control and startling speed.

A king on an electric throne.

It was Maximilian Kohler.

111

Kohler was sickened by the opulence of the Hallway of the Belvedere. The gold leaf in the ceiling alone

495

probably could have funded a year's worth of cancer research. Rocher led Kohler up a handicapped ramp on a circuitous route into the Apostolic Palace.

'No elevator?' Kohler demanded.

'No power.' Rocher motioned to the candles burning around them in the darkened building. 'Part of our search tactic.'

'Tactics which no doubt failed.'

Rocher nodded.

Kohler broke into another coughing fit and knew it might be one of his last. It was not an entirely unwelcome thought.

When they reached the top floor and started down the hallway toward the Pope's office, four Swiss Guards ran toward them, looking troubled. 'Captain, what are you doing up here? I thought this man had information that—'

'He will only speak to the camerlengo.'

The guards recoiled, looking suspicious.

'Tell the camerlengo,' Rocher said forcefully, 'that the director of CERN, Maximilian Kohler, is here to see him. Immediately.'

'Yes, sir!' One of the guards ran off in the direction of the camerlengo's office. The others stood their ground. They studied Rocher, looking uneasy. 'Just one moment, captain. We will announce your guest.'

Kohler, however, did not stop. He turned sharply and maneuvered his chair around the sentinels.

The guards spun and broke into a jog beside him. *'Fermati!* Sir! Stop!'

Kohler felt repugnance for them. Not even the most elite security force in the world was immune to the pity everyone felt for cripples. Had Kohler been a healthy man, the guards would have tackled him.

Cripples are powerless, Kohler thought. *Or so the world believes.*

Kohler knew he had very little time to accomplish what he had come for. He also knew he might die here tonight. He was surprised how little he cared. Death was a price he was ready to pay. He had endured too much in his life to have his work destroyed by someone like Camerlengo Ventresca.

'Signore!' the guards shouted, running ahead and forming a line across the hallway *'You must stop!'* One of them pulled a sidearm and aimed it at Kohler.

Kohler stopped.

Rocher stepped in, looking contrite. 'Mr Kohler, please. It will only be a moment. No one enters the Office of the Pope unannounced.'

Kohler could see in Rocher's eyes that he had no choice but to wait. *Fine*, Kohler thought. *We wait.*

The guards, cruelly it seemed, had stopped Kohler next to a full-length gilded mirror. The sight of his own twisted form repulsed Kohler. The ancient rage brimmed yet again to the surface. It empowered him. He was among the enemy now. *These* were the people who had robbed him of his dignity. These were the people. Because of *them* he had never felt the touch of a woman . . . had never stood tall to accept an award. *What truth do these people possess? What proof damn it! A book of ancient fables? Promises of miracles to come? Science creates miracles every day!*

Kohler stared a moment into his own stony eyes. *Tonight I may die at the hands of religion*, he thought. *But it will not be the first time.*

For a moment, he was eleven years old again, lying in his bed in his parents' Frankfurt mansion. The sheets beneath him were Europe's finest linen, but they were soaked with sweat. Young Max felt like he was on fire, the pain wracking his body unimaginable. Kneeling beside his bed, where they had been for two days, were his mother and father. They were praying.

In the shadows stood three of Frankfurt's best doctors.

'I urge you to reconsider!' one of the doctors said. 'Look at the boy! His fever is increasing. He is in terrible pain. And danger!'

But Max knew his mother's reply before she even said it. '*Gott wird ihn beschuetzen.*'

Yes, Max thought. *God will protect me.* The conviction in his mother's voice gave him strength. *God will protect me.*

An hour later, Max felt like his whole body was being crushed beneath a car. He could not even breathe to cry.

'Your son is in great suffering,' another doctor said. 'Let me at least ease his pain. I have in my bag a simple injection of—'

'*Ruhe, bitte!*' Max's father silenced the doctor without ever opening his eyes. He simply kept praying.

'Father, please!' Max wanted to scream. 'Let them stop the pain!' But his words were lost in a spasm of coughing.

An hour later, the pain had worsened.

'Your son could become paralyzed,' one of the doctors scolded. 'Or even die! We have medicines that will help!'

Frau and Herr Kohler would not allow it. They did not believe in medicine. Who were they to interfere with God's master plan? They prayed harder. After all, God had blessed them with this boy, why would God take the child away? His mother whispered to Max to be strong. She explained that God was testing him . . . like the Bible story of Abraham . . . a test of his faith.

Max tried to have faith, but the pain was excruciating.

'I cannot watch this!' one of the doctors finally said, running from the room.

By dawn, Max was barely conscious. Every muscle in his body spasmed in agony. *Where is Jesus?* he wondered. *Doesn't he love me?* Max felt the life slipping from his body.

His mother had fallen asleep at the bedside, her hands still clasped over him. Max's father stood across the room at the window staring out at the dawn. He seemed to be in a trance. Max could hear the low mumble of his ceaseless prayers for mercy.

It was then that Max sensed the figure hovering over him. *An angel?* Max could barely see. His eyes were swollen shut. The figure whispered in his ear, but it was not the voice of an angel. Max recognized it as one of the doctors . . . the one who had sat in the corner for two days, never leaving, begging Max's parents to let him administer some new drug from England.

'I will never forgive myself,' the doctor whispered, 'if I do not do this.' Then the doctor gently took Max's frail arm. 'I wish I had done it sooner.'

Max felt a tiny prick in his arm – barely discernible through the pain.

Then the doctor quietly packed his things. Before he left, he put a hand on Max's forehead. 'This will save your life. I have great faith in the power of medicine.'

Within minutes, Max felt as if some sort of magic spirit were flowing through his veins. The warmth spread through his body numbing his pain. Finally, for the first time in days, Max slept.

When the fever broke, his mother and father proclaimed a miracle of God. But when it became evident that their son was crippled, they became despondent. They wheeled their son into the church and begged the priest for counseling.

'It was only by the grace of God,' the priest told them, 'that this boy survived.'

Max listened, saying nothing.

'But our son cannot walk!' Frau Kohler was weeping.

The priest nodded sadly 'Yes. It seems God has punished him for not having enough faith.'

'Mr Kohler?' It was the Swiss Guard who had run ahead. 'The camerlengo says he will grant you audience.'

Kohler grunted, accelerating again down the hall.

'He is surprised by your visit,' the guard said.

'I'm sure.' Kohler rolled on. 'I would like to see him alone.'

'Impossible,' the guard said. 'No one—'

'Lieutenant,' Rocher barked. 'The meeting will be as Mr Kohler wishes.'

The guard stared in obvious disbelief.

Outside the door to the Pope's office, Rocher allowed his guards to take standard precautions before letting Kohler in. Their handheld metal detector was rendered worthless by the myriad of electronic devices on Kohler's wheelchair. The guards frisked him but were obviously too ashamed of his disability to do it properly. They never found the revolver affixed beneath his chair. Nor did they relieve him of the other object . . . the one that Kohler knew would bring unforgettable closure to this evening's chain of events.

When Kohler entered the Pope's office, Camerlengo Ventresca was alone, kneeling in prayer beside a dying fire. He did not open his eyes.

'Mr Kohler,' the camerlengo said. 'Have you come to make me a martyr?'

112

All the while, the narrow tunnel called *Il Passetto* stretched out before Langdon and Vittoria as they dashed toward Vatican City. The torch in Langdon's hand threw only enough light to see a few yards ahead. The walls were close on either side, and the ceiling low. The air smelled dank. Langdon raced on into the darkness with Vittoria close at his heels.

The tunnel inclined steeply as it left the Castle St Angelo, proceeding upward into the underside of a stone bastion that looked like a Roman aqueduct. There, the tunnel leveled out and began its secret course toward Vatican City.

As Langdon ran, his thoughts turned over and over in a kaleidoscope of confounding images – Kohler, Janus, the Hassassin, Rocher . . . a sixth brand? *I'm sure you've heard about the sixth brand,* the killer had said. *The most brilliant of all.* Langdon was quite certain he had *not*. Even in conspiracy theory lore, Langdon could think of no references to any sixth brand. Real or imagined. There were rumors of a gold bullion and a flawless Illuminati Diamond but never any mention of a sixth brand.

'Kohler can't be Janus!' Vittoria declared as they ran down the interior of the dike. 'It's impossible!'

Impossible was one word Langdon had stopped using tonight. 'I don't know,' Langdon yelled as they ran. 'Kohler has a serious grudge, and he also has some serious influence.'

'This crisis has made CERN look like monsters! Max would *never* do anything to damage CERN's reputation!'

On one count, Langdon knew CERN had taken a public beating tonight, all because of the Illuminati's insistence on making this a public spectacle. And yet, he wondered how much CERN had *really* been damaged. Criticism from the church was nothing new for CERN. In fact, the more Langdon thought about it, the more he wondered if this crisis might actually *benefit* CERN. If publicity were the game, then antimatter was the jackpot winner tonight. The entire planet was talking about it.

'You know what promoter P. T. Barnum said,' Langdon called over his shoulder. ' "I don't care what you say about me, just spell my name right!" I bet people are already secretly lining up to license antimatter technology. And after they see its true power at midnight tonight . . .'

'Illogical,' Vittoria said. 'Publicizing scientific breakthroughs is not about showing destructive power! This is *terrible* for antimatter, trust me!'

Langdon's torch was fading now. 'Then maybe it's all much simpler than that. Maybe Kohler gambled that the Vatican would keep the antimatter a secret – refusing to empower the Illuminati by confirming the weapon's existence. Kohler expected the Vatican to be their usual tight-lipped selves about the threat, but the camerlengo changed the rules.'

Vittoria was silent as they dashed down the tunnel.

Suddenly the scenario was making more sense to Langdon. 'Yes! Kohler never counted on the camerlengo's reaction. The camerlengo broke the Vatican tradition of secrecy and went public about the crisis. He was dead honest. He put the anti-matter on TV, for God's sake. It was a brilliant response, and Kohler never expected it. And the irony of the whole thing is that the Illuminati attack back-fired. It inadvertently produced a new church leader in the camerlengo. And now Kohler is coming to kill him!'

'Max is a bastard,' Vittoria declared, 'but he is not a murderer. And he would *never* have been involved in my father's assassination.'

In Langdon's mind, it was Kohler's voice that answered. *Leonardo was considered dangerous by many purists at CERN. Fusing science and God is the ultimate scientific blasphemy.* 'Maybe Kohler found out about the antimatter project weeks ago and didn't like the religious implications.'

'So he *killed* my father over it? Ridiculous! Besides, Max Kohler would never have *known* the project existed.'

'While you were gone, maybe your father broke down and consulted Kohler, asking for guidance. You yourself said your father was concerned about the moral implications of creating such a deadly substance.'

'Asking moral guidance from Maximilian Kohler?' Vittoria snorted. 'I don't think so!'

The tunnel banked slightly westward. The faster they ran, the dimmer Langdon's torch became. He began to fear what the place would look like if the light went out. Black.

'Besides,' Vittoria argued, 'why would Kohler have bothered to call you in this morning and ask for help if *he* is behind the whole thing?'

Langdon had already considered it. 'By calling me, Kohler covered his bases. He made sure no one would accuse him of nonaction in the face of crisis. He probably never expected us to get this far.'

The thought of being *used* by Kohler incensed Langdon. Langdon's involvement had given the Illuminati a level of credibility. His credentials and publications had been quoted all night by the media, and as ridiculous as it was, the presence of a Harvard professor in Vatican City had somehow raised the whole emergency beyond the scope of paranoid delusion and convinced skeptics around the world that the Illuminati brotherhood was not only a historical fact, but a force to be reckoned with.

'That BBC reporter,' Langdon said, 'thinks CERN is the new Illuminati lair.'

'What!' Vittoria stumbled behind him. She pulled herself up and ran on. 'He *said* that!?'

'On air. He likened CERN to the Masonic lodges – an innocent organization unknowingly harboring the Illuminati brotherhood within.'

'My God, this is going to destroy CERN.'

Langdon was not so sure. Either way, the theory suddenly seemed less far-fetched. CERN was the ultimate scientific haven. It was home to scientists from over a dozen countries. They seemed to have endless private funding. And Maximilian Kohler was their director.

Kohler is Janus.

'If Kohler's not involved,' Langdon challenged, 'then what is he doing here?'

'Probably trying to stop this madness. Show support. Maybe he really is acting as the Samaritan! He could have found out who knew about the anti-matter project and has come to share information.'

'The killer said he was coming to brand the camerlengo.'

'Listen to yourself! It would be a suicide mission. Max would never get out alive.'

Langdon considered it. *Maybe that was the point.*

The outline of a steel gate loomed ahead, blocking their progress down the tunnel. Langdon's heart almost stopped. When they approached, however, they found the ancient lock hanging open. The gate swung freely.

Langdon breathed a sigh of relief, realizing as he had suspected, that the ancient tunnel was in use. Recently. As in today. He now had little doubt that four terrified cardinals had been secreted through here earlier.

They ran on. Langdon could now hear the sounds of chaos to his left. It was St Peter's Square. They were getting close.

They hit another gate, this one heavier. It too was unlocked. The sound of St Peter's Square faded behind them now, and Langdon sensed they had passed through the outer wall of Vatican City. He wondered where inside the Vatican this ancient passage would conclude. *In the gardens? In the basilica? In the papal residence?*

Then, without warning, the tunnel ended.

The cumbrous door blocking their way was a thick

505

wall of riveted iron. Even by the last flickers of his torch, Langdon could see that the portal was perfectly smooth – no handles, no knobs, no keyholes, no hinges. No entry.

He felt a surge of panic. In architect-speak, this rare kind of door was called a *senza chiave* – a one-way portal, used for security, and only operable from one side – the *other* side. Langdon's hope dimmed to black . . . along with the torch in his hand.

He looked at his watch. Mickey glowed.

11.29 p.m.

With a scream of frustration, Langdon swung the torch and started pounding on the door.

113

Something was wrong.

Lieutenant Chartrand stood outside the Pope's office and sensed in the uneasy stance of the soldier standing with him that they shared the same anxiety. The private meeting they were shielding, Rocher had said, could save the Vatican from destruction. So Chartrand wondered why his protective instincts were tingling. And why was Rocher acting so strangely?

Something definitely was awry.

Captain Rocher stood to Chartrand's right, staring dead ahead, his sharp gaze uncharacteristically distant. Chartrand barely recognized the captain. Rocher had not been himself in the last hour. His decisions made no sense.

Someone should be present inside this meeting!

Chartrand thought. He had heard Maximilian Kohler bolt the door after he entered. *Why had Rocher permitted this?*

But there was so much more bothering Chartrand. *The cardinals.* The cardinals were still locked in the Sistine Chapel. This was absolute insanity. The camerlengo had wanted them evacuated fifteen minutes ago! Rocher had overruled the decision and not informed the camerlengo. Chartrand had expressed concern, and Rocher had almost taken off his head. Chain of command was never questioned in the Swiss Guard, and Rocher was now top dog.

Half an hour, Rocher thought, discreetly checking his Swiss chronometer in the dim light of the candelabra lighting the hall. *Please hurry.*

Chartrand wished he could hear what was happening on the other side of the doors. Still, he knew there was no one he would rather have handling this crisis than the camerlengo. The man had been tested beyond reason tonight, and he had not flinched. He had confronted the problem head-on ... truthful, candid, shining like an example to all. Chartrand felt proud right now to be a Catholic. The Illuminati had made a mistake when they challenged Camerlengo Ventresca.

At that moment, however, Chartrand's thoughts were jolted by an unexpected sound. A banging. It was coming from down the hall. The pounding was distant and muffled, but incessant. Rocher looked up. The captain turned to Chartrand and motioned down the hall. Chartrand understood. He turned on his flashlight and took off to investigate.

The banging was more desperate now. Chartrand ran thirty yards down the corridor to an intersection. The noise seemed to be coming from around the corner, beyond the Sala Clementina. Chartrand felt perplexed. There was only one room back there – the Pope's private library. His Holiness's private library had been locked since the Pope's death. Nobody could possibly be in there!

Chartrand hurried down the second corridor, turned another corner, and rushed to the library door. The wooden portico was diminutive, but it stood in the dark like a dour sentinel. The banging was coming from somewhere inside. Chartrand hesitated. He had never been inside the private library. Few had. No one was allowed in without an escort by the Pope himself.

Tentatively, Chartrand reached for the doorknob and turned. As he had imagined, the door was locked. He put his ear to the door. The banging was louder. Then he heard something else. *Voices! Someone calling out!*

He could not make out the words, but he could hear the panic in their shouts. Was someone trapped in the library? Had the Swiss Guard not properly evacuated the building? Chartrand hesitated, wondering if he should go back and consult Rocher. The hell with that. Chartrand had been trained to make decisions, and he would make one now. He pulled out his side arm and fired a single shot into the door latch. The wood exploded, and the door swung open.

Beyond the threshold Chartrand saw nothing but blackness. He shone his flashlight. The room was rectangular – oriental carpets, high oak shelves packed with books, a stitched leather couch, and a marble fireplace. Chartrand had heard stories of this place – three thousand ancient volumes side by side with hundreds of current magazines and periodicals, anything His Holiness requested. The coffee table was covered with journals of science and politics.

The banging was clearer now. Chartrand shone his light across the room toward the sound. On the far wall, beyond the sitting area, was a huge door made of iron. It looked impenetrable as a vault. It had four mammoth locks. The tiny etched letters dead center of the door took Chartrand's breath away.

IL PASSETTO

Chartrand stared. *The Pope's secret escape route!* Chartrand had certainly heard of *Il Passetto*, and he had even heard rumors that it had once had an entrance here in the library, but the tunnel had not been used in ages! *Who could be banging on the other side?*

Chartrand took his flashlight and rapped on the door. There was a muffled exultation from the other side. The banging stopped, and the voices yelled louder. Chartrand could barely make out their words through the barricade.

'. . . Kohler . . . lie . . . camerlengo . . .'

'Who is that?' Chartrand yelled.

'. . . ert Langdon . . . Vittoria Ve . . .'

Chartrand understood enough to be confused. *I thought you were dead!*

'. . . the door,' the voices yelled. 'Open . . . !'

Chartrand looked at the iron barrier and knew he would need dynamite to get through there. 'Impossible!' he yelled. 'Too thick!'

'. . . meeting . . . stop . . . erlegno . . . danger . . .'

Despite his training on the hazards of panic, Chartrand felt a sudden rush of fear at the last few words. Had he understood correctly? Heart pounding, he turned to run back to the office. As he turned,

509

though, he stalled. His gaze had fallen to something on the door ... something more shocking even than the message coming from beyond it. Emerging from the keyholes of each of the door's massive locks were *keys*. Chartrand stared. The *keys* were here? He blinked in disbelief. The keys to this door were supposed to be in a vault someplace! This passage was never used – not for centuries!

Chartrand dropped his flashlight on the floor. He grabbed the first key and turned. The mechanism was rusted and stiff, but it still worked. Someone had opened it recently. Chartrand worked the next lock. And the next. When the last bolt slid aside, Chartrand pulled. The slab of iron creaked open. He grabbed his light and shone it into the passage.

Robert Langdon and Vittoria Vetra looked like apparitions as they staggered into the library. Both were ragged and tired, but they were very much alive.

'What is this!' Chartrand demanded. 'What's going on! Where did you come from?'

'Where's Max Kohler?' Langdon demanded.

Chartrand pointed. 'In a private meeting with the camer—'

Langdon and Vittoria pushed past him and ran down the darkened hall. Chartrand turned, instinctively raising his gun at their backs. He quickly lowered it and ran after them. Rocher apparently heard them coming, because as they arrived outside the Pope's office, Rocher had spread his legs in a protective stance and was leveling his gun at them. '*Alt!*'

'The camerlengo is in danger!' Langdon yelled, raising his arms in surrender as he slid to a stop. 'Open the door! Max Kohler is going to kill the camerlengo!'

Rocher looked angry.

'Open the door!' Vittoria said. 'Hurry!'

But it was too late.

From inside the Pope's office came a bloodcurdling scream. It was the camerlengo.

114

The confrontation lasted only seconds.

Camerlengo Ventresca was still screaming when Chartrand stepped past Rocher and blew open the door of the Pope's office. The guards dashed in. Langdon and Vittoria ran in behind them.

The scene before them was staggering.

The chamber was lit only by candlelight and a dying fire. Kohler was near the fireplace, standing awkwardly in front of his wheelchair. He brandished a pistol, aimed at the camerlengo, who lay on the floor at his feet, writhing in agony. The camerlengo's cassock was torn open, and his bare chest was seared black. Langdon could not make out the symbol from across the room, but a large, square brand lay on the floor near Kohler. The metal still glowed red.

Two of the Swiss Guards acted without hesitation. They opened fire. The bullets smashed into Kohler's chest, driving him backward. Kohler collapsed into his wheelchair, his chest gurgling blood. His gun went skittering across the floor.

Langdon stood stunned in the doorway.

Vittoria seemed paralyzed. 'Max . . .' she whispered.

The camerlengo, still twisting on the floor, rolled toward Rocher, and with the trancelike terror of the early witch hunts, pointed his index finger at Rocher and yelled a single word. 'ILLUMINATUS!'

'You bastard,' Rocher said, running at him. 'You sanctimonious bas—'

This time it was Chartrand who reacted on instinct, putting three bullets in Rocher's back. The captain fell face first on the tile floor and slid lifeless through his own blood. Chartrand and the guards dashed immediately to the camerlengo, who lay clutching himself, convulsing in pain.

Both guards let out exclamations of horror when they saw the symbol seared on the camerlengo's chest. The second guard saw the brand upside down and immediately staggered backward with fear in his eyes. Chartrand, looking equally overwhelmed by the symbol, pulled the camerlengo's torn cassock up over the burn, shielding it from view.

Langdon felt delirious as he moved across the room. Through a mist of insanity and violence, he tried to make sense of what he was seeing. A crippled scientist, in a final act of symbolic dominance, had flown into Vatican City and branded the church's highest official. *Some things are worth dying for*, the Hassassin had said. Langdon wondered how a handicapped man could possibly have overpowered the camerlengo. Then again, Kohler had a gun. *It doesn't matter how he did it! Kohler accomplished his mission!*

Langdon moved toward the gruesome scene. The camerlengo was being attended, and Langdon felt himself drawn toward the smoking brand on the floor near Kohler's wheelchair. *The sixth brand?* The closer Langdon got, the more confused he became. The brand seemed to be a perfect square, quite large, and had obviously come from the sacred center compartment of the chest in the Illuminati Lair. *A sixth and final brand*, the Hassassin had said. *The most brilliant of all.*

Langdon knelt beside Kohler and reached for the object. The metal still radiated heat. Grasping the wooden handle, Langdon picked it up. He was not sure what he expected to see, but it most certainly was not this.

Langdon stared a long, confused moment. Nothing was making sense. Why had the guards cried out in horror when they saw this? It was a square of meaningless squiggles. *The most brilliant of all?* It was symmetrical, Langdon could tell as he rotated it in his hand, but it was gibberish.

When he felt a hand on his shoulder, Langdon looked up, expecting Vittoria. The hand, however, was covered with blood. It belonged to Maximilian Kohler, who was reaching out from his wheelchair.

Langdon dropped the brand and staggered to his feet. *Kohler's still alive!*

Slumped in his wheelchair, the dying director was still breathing, albeit barely, sucking in sputtering gasps. Kohler's eyes met Langdon's, and it was the same stony gaze that had greeted Langdon at CERN earlier that day. The eyes looked even harder in death, the loathing and enmity rising to the surface.

The scientist's body quivered, and Langdon sensed he was trying to move. Everyone else in the room was focused on the camerlengo, and Langdon wanted to call out, but he could not react. He was transfixed by the intensity radiating from Kohler in these final seconds of his life. The director, with tremulous effort, lifted his arm and pulled a small device off the arm of his wheelchair. It was the size of a matchbox. He held it out, quivering. For an instant, Langdon feared Kohler had a weapon. But it was something else.

'G-give . . .' Kohler's final words were a gurgling whisper. 'G-give this . . . to the m-media.' Kohler collapsed motionless, and the device fell in his lap.

Shocked, Langdon stared at the device. It was electronic. The words SONY RUVI were printed across the front. Langdon recognized it as one of those new ultraminiature, palm-held camcorders. *The balls on this guy!* he thought. Kohler had apparently recorded some sort of final suicide message he wanted the media to broadcast . . . no doubt some sermon about the importance of science and the evils of religion. Langdon decided he had done enough for this man's cause tonight. Before Chartrand saw Kohler's camcorder, Langdon slipped it into his deepest jacket pocket. *Kohler's final message can rot in hell!*

It was the voice of the camerlengo that broke the silence. He was trying to sit up. 'The cardinals,' he gasped to Chartrand.

'Still in the Sistine Chapel!' Chartrand exclaimed. 'Captain Rocher ordered—'

'Evacuate . . . now. Everyone.'

Chartrand sent one of the other guards running off to let the cardinals out.

The camerlengo grimaced in pain. 'Helicopter . . .
out front . . . get me to a hospital.'

115

In St Peter's Square, the Swiss Guard pilot sat in the
cockpit of the parked Vatican helicopter and rubbed
his temples. The chaos in the square around him was
so loud that it drowned out the sound of his idling
rotors. This was no solemn candlelight vigil. He was
amazed a riot had not broken out yet.

With less than twenty-five minutes left until midnight, the people were still packed together, some
praying, some weeping for the church, others screaming obscenities and proclaiming that this was what the
church deserved, still others chanting apocalyptic
Bible verses.

The pilot's head pounded as the media lights
glinted off his windshield. He squinted out at the
clamorous masses. Banners waved over the crowd.

ANTIMATTER IS THE ANTICHRIST!
SCIENTIST=SATANIST
WHERE IS YOUR GOD NOW?

The pilot groaned, his headache worsening. He half
considered grabbing the windshield's vinyl covering
and putting it up so he wouldn't have to watch, but he
knew he would be airborne in a matter of minutes.
Lieutenant Chartrand had just radioed with terrible
news. The camerlengo had been attacked by

Maximilian Kohler and seriously injured. Chartrand, the American, and the woman were carrying the camerlengo out now so he could be evacuated to a hospital.

The pilot felt personally responsible for the attack. He reprimanded himself for not acting on his gut. Earlier, when he had picked up Kohler at the airport, he had sensed something in the scientist's dead eyes. He couldn't place it, but he didn't like it. Not that it mattered. Rocher was running the show, and Rocher insisted *this* was the guy. Rocher had apparently been wrong.

A new clamor arose from the crowd, and the pilot looked over to see a line of cardinals processing solemnly out of the Vatican onto St Peter's Square. The cardinals' relief to be leaving ground zero seemed to be quickly overcome by looks of bewilderment at the spectacle now going on outside the church.

The crowd noise intensified yet again. The pilot's head pounded. He needed an aspirin. Maybe three. He didn't like to fly on medication, but a few aspirin would certainly be less debilitating than this raging headache. He reached for the first-aid kit, kept with assorted maps and manuals in a cargo box bolted between the two front seats. When he tried to open the box, though, he found it locked. He looked around for the key and then finally gave up. Tonight was clearly not his lucky night. He went back to massaging his temples.

Inside the darkened basilica, Langdon, Vittoria, and the two guards strained breathlessly toward the main exit. Unable to find anything more suitable, the four of them were transporting the wounded camerlengo on a narrow table, balancing the inert body between them as though on a stretcher. Outside the doors, the faint roar of human chaos was now audible. The camerlengo teetered on the brink of unconsciousness.

Time was running out.

116

It was 11.39 p.m. when Langdon stepped with the others from St Peter's Basilica. The glare that hit his eyes was searing. The media lights shone off the white marble like sunlight off a snowy tundra. Langdon squinted, trying to find refuge behind the façade's enormous columns, but the light came from all directions. In front of him, a collage of massive video screens rose above the crowd.

Standing there atop the magnificent stairs that spilled down to the piazza below, Langdon felt like a reluctant player on the world's biggest stage. Somewhere beyond the glaring lights, Langdon heard an idling helicopter and the roar of a hundred thousand voices. To their left, a procession of cardinals was now evacuating onto the square. They all stopped in apparent distress to see the scene now unfolding on the staircase.

'Careful now,' Chartrand urged, sounding focused as the group began descending the stairs toward the helicopter.

Langdon felt like they were moving underwater. His arms ached from the weight of the camerlengo and the table. He wondered how the moment could get much less dignified. Then he saw the answer. The two BBC reporters had apparently been crossing the open square on their way back to the press area. But now, with the roar of the crowd, they had turned. Glick and Macri were now running back toward them. Macri's camera was raised and rolling. *Here come the vultures*, Langdon thought.

'*Alt!*' Chartrand yelled. 'Get back!'

But the reporters kept coming. Langdon guessed the other networks would take about six seconds to pick up this live BBC feed again. He was wrong. They took two. As if connected by some sort of universal consciousness, every last media screen in the piazza cut away from their countdown clocks and their Vatican experts and began transmitting the same picture – a jiggling action footage swooping up the Vatican stairs. Now, everywhere Langdon looked, he saw the camerlengo's limp body in a Technicolor close-up.

This is wrong! Langdon thought. He wanted to run down the stairs and interfere, but he could not. It wouldn't have helped anyway. Whether it was the roar of the crowd or the cool night air that caused it, Langdon would never know, but at that moment, the inconceivable occurred.

Like a man awakening from a nightmare, the camerlengo's eyes shot open and he sat bolt upright. Taken entirely by surprise, Langdon and the others fumbled with the shifting weight. The front of the table dipped. The camerlengo began to slide. They tried to recover by setting the table down, but it was too late. The camerlengo slid off the front. Incredibly, he did not fall. His feet hit the marble, and he swayed upright. He stood a moment, looking disoriented, and then, before anyone could stop him, he lurched forward, staggering down the stairs toward Macri.

'*No!*' Langdon screamed.

Chartrand rushed forward, trying to reign in the camerlengo. But the camerlengo turned on him, wild-eyed, crazed. 'Leave me!'

Chartrand jumped back.

The scene went from bad to worse. The camerlengo's torn cassock, having been only laid over his chest by Chartrand, began to slip lower. For a moment, Langdon thought the garment might hold, but that moment passed. The cassock let go, sliding off his shoulders down around his waist.

The gasp that went up from the crowd seemed to travel around the globe and back in an instant. Cameras rolled, flashbulbs exploded. On media screens everywhere, the image of the camerlengo's branded chest was projected, towering and in grisly detail. Some screens were even freezing the image and rotating it 180 degrees.

The ultimate Illuminati victory.

Langdon stared at the brand on the screens. Although it was the imprint of the square brand he had held earlier, the symbol *now* made sense. Perfect sense. The marking's awesome power hit Langdon like a train.

Orientation. Langdon had forgotten the first rule of symbology. *When is a square not a square?* He had also forgotten that iron brands, just like rubber stamps, never looked like their imprints. They were in reverse. Langdon had been looking at the brand's *negative*!

As the chaos grew, an old Illuminati quote echoed with new meaning: 'A flawless diamond, born of the ancient elements with such perfection that all those who saw it could only stare in wonder.'

Langdon knew now the myth was true.

Earth, Air, Fire, Water.

The Illuminati Diamond.

117

Robert Langdon had little doubt that the chaos and hysteria coursing through St Peter's Square at this very instant exceeded anything Vatican Hill had ever witnessed. No battle, no crucifixion, no pilgrimage, no mystical vision ... nothing in the shrine's 2,000-year history could possibly match the scope and drama of this very moment.

As the tragedy unfolded, Langdon felt oddly separate, as if hovering there beside Vittoria at the top of the stairs. The action seemed to distend, as if in a time warp, all the insanity slowing to a crawl ...

The branded camerlengo ... raving for the world to see ...

The Illuminati Diamond ... unveiled in its diabolical genius ...

The countdown clock registering the final twenty minutes of Vatican history ...

The drama, however, had only just begun.

The camerlengo, as if in some sort of post-traumatic trance, seemed suddenly puissant, possessed by demons. He began babbling, whispering to unseen spirits, looking up at the sky and raising his arms to God.

'Speak!' the camerlengo yelled to the heavens. 'Yes, I hear you!'

In that moment, Langdon understood. His heart dropped like a rock.

Vittoria apparently understood too. She went white. 'He's in shock,' she said. 'He's hallucinating. He thinks he's talking to God!'

Somebody's got to stop this, Langdon thought. It was a wretched and embarrassing end. *Get this man to a hospital!*

Below them on the stairs, Chinita Macri was poised and filming, apparently having located her ideal vantage point. The images she filmed appeared instantly across the square behind her on media screens ... like endless drive-in movies all playing the same grisly tragedy.

The whole scene felt epic. The camerlengo, in his torn cassock, with the scorched brand on his chest, looked like some sort of battered champion who had overcome the rings of hell for this one moment of revelation. He bellowed to the heavens.

'Ti sento, Dio! I hear you, God!'

Chartrand backed off, a look of awe on his face.

The hush that fell across the crowd was instant and

absolute. For a moment it was as if the silence had fallen across the entire planet ... everyone in front of their TVs rigid, a communal holding of breath.

The camerlengo stood on the stairs, before the world, and held out his arms. He looked almost Christlike, bare and wounded before the world. He raised his arms to the heavens and, looking up, exclaimed, 'Grazie! Grazie, Dio!'

The silence of the masses never broke.

'Grazie, Dio!' the camerlengo cried out again. Like the sun breaking through a stormy sky, a look of joy spread across his face. 'Grazie, Dio!'

Thank you, God? Langdon stared in wonder.

The camerlengo was radiant now, his eerie transformation complete. He looked up at the sky, still nodding furiously. He shouted to the heavens, 'Upon this rock I will build my church!'

Langdon knew the words, but he had no idea why the camerlengo could possibly be shouting them.

The camerlengo turned back to the crowd and bellowed again into the night. 'Upon this rock I will build my church!' Then he raised his hands to the sky and laughed out loud. 'Grazie, Dio! Grazie!'

The man had clearly gone mad.

The world watched, spellbound.

The culmination, however, was something no one expected.

With a final joyous exultation, the camerlengo turned and dashed back into St Peter's Basilica.

118

Eleven-forty-two p.m.

The frenzied convoy that plunged back into the basilica to retrieve the camerlengo was not one Langdon had ever imagined he would be part of ... much less leading. But he had been closest to the door and had acted on instinct.

He'll die in here, Langdon thought, sprinting over the threshold into the darkened void. 'Camerlengo! Stop!'

The wall of blackness that hit Langdon was absolute. His pupils were contracted from the glare outside, and his field of vision now extended no farther than a few feet before his face. He skidded to a stop. Somewhere in the blackness ahead, he heard the camerlengo's cassock rustle as the priest ran blindly into the abyss.

Vittoria and the guards arrived immediately. Flashlights came on, but the lights were almost dead now and did not even begin to probe the depths of the basilica before them. The beams swept back and forth, revealing only columns and bare floor. The camerlengo was nowhere to be seen.

'Camerlengo!' Chartrand yelled, fear in his voice. 'Wait! Signore!'

A commotion in the doorway behind them caused everyone to turn. Chinita Macri's large frame lurched through the entry. Her camera was shouldered, and the glowing red light on top revealed that it was still transmitting. Glick was running behind her, microphone in hand, yelling for her to slow down.

Langdon could not believe these two. *This is not the time!*

'Out!' Chartrand snapped. 'This is not for your eyes!'

But Macri and Glick kept coming.

'Chinita!' Glick sounded fearful now. 'This is suicide! I'm not coming!'

Macri ignored him. She threw a switch on her camera. The spotlight on top glared to life, blinding everyone.

Langdon shielded his face and turned away in pain. *Damn it!* When he looked up, though, the church around them was illuminated for thirty yards.

At that moment the camerlengo's voice echoed somewhere in the distance. 'Upon this rock I will build my church!'

Macri wheeled her camera toward the sound. Far off, in the grayness at the end of the spotlight's reach, black fabric billowed, revealing a familiar form running down the main aisle of the basilica.

There was a fleeting instant of hesitation as everyone's eyes took in the bizarre image. Then the dam broke. Chartrand pushed past Langdon and sprinted after the camerlengo. Langdon took off next. Then the guards and Vittoria.

Macri brought up the rear, lighting everyone's way and transmitting the sepulchral chase to the world. An unwilling Glick cursed aloud as he tagged along, fumbling through a terrified blow-by-blow commentary.

The main aisle of St Peter's Basilica, Lieutenant Chartrand had once figured out, was longer than an Olympic soccer field. Tonight, however, it felt like twice that. As the guard sprinted after the camerlengo, he wondered where the man was headed. The camerlengo was clearly in shock, delirious no doubt from his physical trauma and bearing witness to the horrific massacre in the Pope's office.

Somewhere up ahead, beyond the reach of the BBC spotlight, the camerlengo's voice rang out joyously. 'Upon this rock I will build my church!'

Chartrand knew the man was shouting Scripture – Matthew 16:18, if Chartrand recalled correctly. *Upon this rock I will build my church.* It was an almost cruelly inapt inspiration – the church was about to be destroyed. Surely the camerlengo had gone mad.

Or had he?

For a fleeting instant, Chartrand's soul fluttered. Holy visions and divine messages had always seemed like wishful delusions to him – the product of over-zealous minds hearing what they wanted to hear – God did not interact *directly*!

A moment later, though, as if the Holy Spirit Himself had descended to persuade Chartrand of His power, Chartrand had a vision.

Fifty yards ahead, in the center of the church, a ghost appeared . . . a diaphanous, glowing outline. The pale shape was that of the half-naked camerlengo. The specter seemed transparent, radiating light. Chartrand staggered to a stop, feeling a knot tighten in his chest. *The camerlengo is glowing!* The body seemed to shine brighter now. Then, it began to sink . . . deeper and deeper, until it disappeared as if by magic into the blackness of the floor.

Langdon had seen the phantom also. For a moment, he too thought he had witnessed a magical vision. But as he passed the stunned Chartrand and ran toward the spot where the camerlengo had disappeared, he realized what had just happened. The camerlengo had arrived at the Niche of the Palliums – the sunken chamber lit by ninety-nine oil lamps. The lamps in the niche shone up from beneath, illuminating him like a ghost. Then, as the camerlengo descended the stairs into the light, he had seemed to disappear beneath the floor.

Langdon arrived breathless at the rim overlooking the sunken room. He peered down the stairs. At the bottom, lit by the golden glow of oil lamps, the camerlengo dashed across the marble chamber toward the set of glass doors that led to the room holding the famous golden box.

What is he doing? Langdon wondered. *Certainly he can't think the golden box—*

The camerlengo yanked open the doors and ran inside. Oddly though, he totally ignored the golden box, rushing right past it. Five feet beyond the box, he dropped to his knees and began struggling to lift an iron grate embedded in the floor.

Langdon watched in horror, now realizing where the camerlengo was headed. *Good God, no!* He dashed down the stairs after him. 'Father! Don't!'

As Langdon opened the glass doors and ran toward the camerlengo, he saw the camerlengo heave on the grate. The hinged, iron bulkhead fell open with a deafening crash, revealing a narrow shaft and a steep stairway that dropped into nothingness. As the camerlengo moved toward the hole, Langdon grabbed his bare shoulders and pulled him back. The man's skin was slippery with sweat, but Langdon held on.

The camerlengo wheeled, obviously startled. 'What are you doing!'

Langdon was surprised when their eyes met. The

camerlengo no longer had the glazed look of a man in a trance. His eyes were keen, glistening with a lucid determination. The brand on his chest looked excruciating.

'Father,' Langdon urged, as calmly as possible, 'you can't go down there. We need to evacuate.'

'My son,' the camerlengo said, his voice eerily sane. 'I have just had a message. I know—'

'Camerlengo!' It was Chartrand and the others. They came dashing down the stairs into the room, lit by Macri's camera.

When Chartrand saw the open grate in the floor, his eyes filled with dread. He crossed himself and shot Langdon a thankful look for having stopped the camerlengo. Langdon understood; he had read enough about Vatican architecture to know what lay beneath that grate. It was the most sacred place in all of Christendom. *Terra Santa.* Holy Ground. Some called it the Necropolis. Some called it the Catacombs. According to accounts from the select few clergy who had descended over the years, the Necropolis was a dark maze of subterranean crypts that could swallow a visitor whole if he lost his way. It was not the kind of place through which they wanted to be chasing the camerlengo.

'Signore,' Chartrand pleaded. 'You're in shock. We need to leave this place. You cannot go down there. It's suicide.'

The camerlengo seemed suddenly stoic. He reached out and put a quiet hand on Chartrand's shoulder. 'Thank you for your concern and service. I cannot tell you how. I cannot tell you I understand. But I have had a revelation. I know where the antimatter is.'

Everyone stared.

The camerlengo turned to the group. 'Upon this rock I will build my church. That was the message. The meaning is clear.'

Langdon was still unable to comprehend the camerlengo's conviction that he had spoken to God, much less that he had deciphered the message. *Upon this rock I will build my church?* They were the words spoken by Jesus when he chose Peter as his first apostle. What did they have to do with anything?

Macri moved in for a closer shot. Glick was mute, as if shell-shocked.

The camerlengo spoke quickly now. 'The Illuminati have placed their tool of destruction on the very cornerstone of this church. At the foundation.' He motioned down the stairs. 'On the very rock upon which this church was built. And I know where that rock is.'

Langdon was certain the time had come to overpower the camerlengo and carry him off. As lucid as he seemed, the priest was talking nonsense. *A rock? The cornerstone in the foundation?* The stairway before them didn't lead to the foundation, it led to the necropolis! 'The quote is a metaphor, Father! There is no actual *rock*!'

The camerlengo looked strangely sad. 'There *is* a rock, my son.' He pointed into the hole. '*Pietro è la pietra.*'

Langdon froze. In an instant it all came clear.

The austere simplicity of it gave him chills. As Langdon stood there with the others, staring down the long staircase, he realized that there was indeed a rock buried in the darkness beneath this church.

Pietro è la pietra. Peter is the rock.

Peter's faith in God was so steadfast that Jesus

called Peter 'the rock' – the unwavering disciple on whose shoulders Jesus would build his church. On this very location, Langdon realized – Vatican Hill – Peter had been crucified and buried. The early Christians built a small shrine over his tomb. As Christianity spread, the shrine got bigger, layer upon layer, culminating in this colossal basilica. The entire Catholic faith had been built, quite literally, upon St Peter. The rock.

'The antimatter is on St Peter's tomb,' the camerlengo said, his voice crystalline.

Despite the seemingly supernatural origin of the information, Langdon sensed a stark logic in it. Placing the antimatter on St Peter's tomb seemed painfully obvious now. The Illuminati, in an act of symbolic defiance, had located the antimatter at the core of Christendom, both literally and figuratively. *The ultimate infiltration.*

'And if you all need worldly proof,' the camerlengo said, sounding impatient now, 'I just found that grate unlocked.' He pointed to the open bulkhead in the floor. 'It is *never* unlocked. Someone has been down there . . . *recently.*'

Everyone stared into the hole.

An instant later, with deceptive agility, the camerlengo spun, grabbed an oil lamp, and headed for the opening.

119

The stone steps declined steeply into the earth.
I'm going to die down here, Vittoria thought, gripping

the heavy rope banister as she bounded down the cramped passageway behind the others. Although Langdon had made a move to stop the camerlengo from entering the shaft, Chartrand had intervened, grabbing Langdon and holding on. Apparently, the young guard was now convinced the camerlengo knew what he was doing.

After a brief scuffle, Langdon had freed himself and pursued the camerlengo with Chartrand close on his heels. Instinctively, Vittoria had dashed after them.

Now she was racing headlong down a precipitous grade where any misplaced step could mean a deadly fall. Far below, she could see the golden glow of the camerlengo's oil lamp. Behind her, Vittoria could hear the BBC reporters hurrying to keep up. The camera spotlight threw gnarled shadows beyond her down the shaft, illuminating Chartrand and Langdon. Vittoria could scarcely believe the world was bearing witness to this insanity. *Turn off the damn camera!* Then again, she knew the light was the only reason any of them could see where they were going.

As the bizarre chase continued, Vittoria's thoughts whipped like a tempest. What could the camerlengo possibly do down here? Even if he found the anti-matter? There was no time!

Vittoria was surprised to find her intuition now telling her the camerlengo was probably right. Placing the antimatter three stories beneath the earth seemed an almost noble and merciful choice. Deep under-ground – much as in Z-lab – an antimatter annihilation would be partially contained. There would be no heat blast, no flying shrapnel to injure onlookers, just a biblical opening of the earth and a towering basilica crumbling into a crater.

Was this Kohler's one act of decency? Sparing lives? Vittoria still could not fathom the director's involvement. She could accept his hatred of religion . . . but this awesome conspiracy seemed beyond him. Was Kohler's loathing really this profound? Destruction of the Vatican? Hiring an assassin? The murders of her father, the Pope, and four cardinals? It seemed unthinkable. And how had Kohler managed all this treachery within the Vatican walls? *Rocher was Kohler's inside man*, Vittoria told herself. *Rocher was an Illuminatus*. No doubt Captain Rocher had keys to everything – the Pope's chambers, *Il Passetto*, the Necropolis, St Peter's tomb, all of it. He could have placed the antimatter on St Peter's tomb – a highly restricted locale – and then commanded his guards not to waste time searching the Vatican's restricted areas. Rocher *knew* nobody would ever find the canister.

But Rocher never counted on the camerlengo's message from above.

The message. This was the leap of faith Vittoria was still struggling to accept. Had God actually *communicated* with the camerlengo? Vittoria's gut said no, and yet hers was the science of entanglement physics – the study of interconnectedness. She witnessed miraculous communications every day – twin sea-turtle eggs separated and placed in labs thousands of miles apart hatching at the same instant . . . acres of jellyfish pulsating in perfect rhythm as if of a single mind. *There are invisible lines of communication everywhere*, she thought.

But between God and man?

Vittoria wished her father were there to give her faith. He had once explained divine communication to her in scientific terms, and he had made her believe.

531

She still remembered the day she had seen him praying and asked him, 'Father, why do you bother to pray? God cannot answer you.'

Leonardo Vetra had looked up from his meditations with a paternal smile. 'My daughter the skeptic. So you don't believe God speaks to man? Let me put it in your language.' He took a model of the human brain down from a shelf and set it in front of her. 'As you probably know, Vittoria, human beings normally use a very small percentage of their brain power. However, if you put them in emotionally charged situations – like physical trauma, extreme joy or fear, deep meditation – all of a sudden their neurons start firing like crazy, resulting in massively enhanced mental clarity.'

'So what?' Vittoria said. 'Just because you think clearly doesn't mean you talk to God.'

'Aha!' Vetra exclaimed. 'And yet remarkable solutions to seemingly impossible problems often occur in these moments of clarity. It's what gurus call higher consciousness. Biologists call it altered states. Psychologists call it super-sentience.' He paused. 'And Christians call it answered prayer.' Smiling broadly, he added, 'Sometimes, divine revelation simply means adjusting your brain to hear what your heart already knows.'

Now, as she dashed down, headlong into the dark, Vittoria sensed perhaps her father was right. Was it so hard to believe that the camerlengo's trauma had put his mind in a state where he had simply 'realized' the antimatter's location?

Each of us is a God, Buddha had said. *Each of us knows all. We need only open our minds to hear our own wisdom.*

It was in that moment of clarity, as Vittoria plunged deeper into the earth, that she felt her own mind open

. . . her own wisdom surface. She sensed now without a doubt what the camerlengo's intentions were. Her awareness brought with it a fear like nothing she had ever known.

'Camerlengo, no!' she shouted down the passage. 'You don't understand!' Vittoria pictured the multitudes of people surrounding Vatican City, and her blood ran cold. 'If you bring the antimatter up . . . everyone will *die*!'

Langdon was leaping three steps at a time now, gaining ground. The passage was cramped, but he felt no claustrophobia. His once debilitating fear was overshadowed by a far deeper dread.

'Camerlengo!' Langdon felt himself closing the gap on the lantern's glow 'You must leave the antimatter where it is! There's no other choice!'

Even as Langdon spoke the words, he could not believe them. Not only had he accepted the camerlengo's divine revelation of the antimatter's location, but he was lobbying for the destruction of St Peter's Basilica – one of the greatest architectural feats on earth . . . as well as all of the art inside.

But the people outside . . . it's the only way.

It seemed a cruel irony that the only way to save the people now was to destroy the church. Langdon figured the Illuminati were amused by the symbolism.

The air coming up from the bottom of the tunnel was cool and dank. Somewhere down here was the sacred *necropolis* . . . burial place of St Peter and countless other early Christians. Langdon felt a chill, hoping this was not a suicide mission.

Suddenly, the camerlengo's lantern seemed to halt. Langdon closed on him fast.

The end of the stairs loomed abruptly from out of the shadows. A wrought-iron gate with three embossed skulls blocked the bottom of the stairs. The camerlengo was there, pulling the gate open. Langdon leapt, pushing the gate shut, blocking the camerlengo's way. The others came thundering down the stairs, everyone ghostly white in the BBC spotlight . . . especially *Glick*, who was looking more pasty with every step.

Chartrand grabbed Langdon. 'Let the camerlengo pass!'

'No!' Vittoria said from above, breathless. 'We must evacuate right now! You *cannot* take the antimatter out of here! If you bring it up, everyone outside will *die!*'

The camerlengo's voice was remarkably calm. 'All of you . . . we must trust. We have little time.'

'You don't understand,' Vittoria said. 'An explosion at ground level will be much worse than one down here!'

The camerlengo looked at her, his green eyes resplendently sane. 'Who said anything about an explosion at ground level?'

Vittoria stared. 'You're *leaving* it down here?'

The camerlengo's certitude was hypnotic. 'There will be no more death tonight.'

'Father, but—'

'Please . . . some *faith*.' The camerlengo's voice plunged to a compelling hush. 'I am not asking anyone to join me. You are all free to go. All I am asking is that you not interfere with His bidding. Let me do what I have been called to do.' The camerlengo's stare intensified. 'I am to save this church. And I *can*. I swear on my life.'

The silence that followed might as well have been thunder.

120

Eleven fifty-one p.m.

Necropolis literally means *City of the Dead.*

Nothing Robert Langdon had ever read about this place prepared him for the sight of it. The colossal subterranean hollow was filled with crumbling mausoleums, like small houses on the floor of a cave. The air smelled lifeless. An awkward grid of narrow walkways wound between the decaying memorials, most of which were fractured brick with marble platings. Like columns of dust, countless pillars of unexcavated earth rose up, supporting a dirt sky, which hung low over the penumbral hamlet.

City of the dead, Langdon thought, feeling trapped between academic wonder and raw fear. He and the others dashed deeper down the winding passages. *Did I make the wrong choice?*

Chartrand had been the first to fall under the camerlengo's spell, yanking open the gate and declaring his faith in the camerlengo. Glick and Macri, at the camerlengo's suggestion, had nobly agreed to provide light to the quest, although considering what accolades awaited them if they got out of here alive, their motivations were certainly suspect. Vittoria had been the least eager of all, and Langdon had seen in her eyes a wariness that looked, unsettlingly, a lot like female intuition.

It's too late now, he thought, he and Vittoria dashing after the others. *We're committed.*

Vittoria was silent, but Langdon knew they were thinking the same thing. *Nine minutes is not enough time to get the hell out of Vatican City if the camerlengo is wrong.*

As they ran on through the mausoleums, Langdon felt his legs tiring, noting to his surprise that the group was ascending a steady incline. The explanation, when it dawned on him, sent shivers to his core. The topography beneath his feet was that of Christ's time. He was running up the original Vatican Hill! Langdon had heard Vatican scholars claim that St Peter's tomb was near the *top* of Vatican Hill, and he had always wondered how they knew. Now he understood. *The damn hill is still here!*

Langdon felt like he was running through the pages of history. Somewhere ahead was St Peter's tomb – *the* Christian relic. It was hard to imagine that the original grave had been marked only with a modest shrine. Not any more. As Peter's eminence spread, new shrines were built on top of the old, and now, the homage stretched 440 feet overhead to the top of Michelangelo's dome, the apex positioned directly over the original tomb within a fraction of an inch.

They continued ascending the sinuous passages. Langdon checked his watch. *Eight minutes.* He was beginning to wonder if he and Vittoria would be joining the deceased here permanently.

'Look out!' Glick yelled from behind them. 'Snake holes!'

Langdon saw it in time. A series of small holes riddled the path before them. He leapt, just clearing them.

Vittoria jumped too, barely avoiding the narrow hollows. She looked uneasy as they ran on. 'Snake holes?'

'Snack holes, actually,' Langdon corrected. 'Trust me, you don't want to know.' The holes, he had just realized, were *libation tubes*. The early Christians had believed in the resurrection of the flesh, and they'd used the holes to literally 'feed the dead' by pouring milk and honey into crypts beneath the floor.

The camerlengo felt weak.

He dashed onward, his legs finding strength in his duty to God and man. *Almost there.* He was in incredible pain. *The mind can bring so much more pain than the body.* Still he felt tired. He knew he had precious little time.

'I will save your church, Father. I swear it.'

Despite the BBC lights behind him, for which he was grateful, the camerlengo carried his oil lamp high. *I am a beacon in the darkness. I am the light.* The lamp sloshed as he ran, and for an instant he feared the flammable oil might spill and burn him. He had experienced enough burned flesh for one evening.

As he approached the top of the hill, he was drenched in sweat, barely able to breathe. But when he emerged over the crest, he felt reborn. He staggered onto the flat piece of earth where he had stood many times. Here the path ended. The necropolis came to an abrupt halt at a wall of earth. A tiny marker read: *Mausoleum S.*

La tomba di San Pietro.

Before him, at waist level, was an opening in the wall. There was no gilded plaque here. No fanfare. Just a simple hole in the wall, beyond which lay a small grotto and a meager, crumbling sarcophagus. The camerlengo gazed into the hole and smiled in exhaustion. He could hear the others coming up the hill behind him. He set down his oil lamp and knelt to pray.

Thank you, God. It is almost over.

Outside in the square, surrounded by astounded cardinals, Cardinal Mortati stared up at the media screen and watched the drama unfold in the crypt below. He no longer knew what to believe. Had the entire world just witnessed what *he* had seen? Had God truly spoken to the camerlengo? Was the antimatter really going to appear on St Peter's—

'Look!' A gasp went up from the throngs.

'There!' Everyone was suddenly pointing at the screen. 'It's a miracle!'

Mortati looked up. The camera angle was unsteady, but it was clear enough. The image was unforgettable.

Filmed from behind, the camerlengo was kneeling in prayer on the earthen floor. In front of him was a rough-hewn hole in the wall. Inside the hollow, among the rubble of ancient stone, was a terra cotta casket. Although Mortati had seen the coffin only once in his life, he knew beyond a doubt what it contained.

San Pietro.

Mortati was not naïve enough to think that the shouts of joy and amazement now thundering through the crowd were exaltations from bearing witness to one of Christianity's most sacred relics. St Peter's tomb was not what had people falling to their knees in spontaneous prayer and thanksgiving. It was the object on *top* of his tomb.

The antimatter canister. It was there . . . where it had

been all day ... hiding in the darkness of the Necropolis. Sleek. Relentless. Deadly. The camerlengo's revelation was correct.

Mortati stared in wonder at the transparent cylinder. The globule of liquid still hovered at its core. The grotto around the canister blinked red as the LED counted down into its final five minutes of life.

Also sitting on the tomb, inches away from the canister, was the wireless Swiss Guard security camera that had been pointed at the canister and transmitting all along.

Mortati crossed himself, certain this was the most frightful image he had seen in his entire life. He realized, a moment later, however, that it was about to get worse.

The camerlengo stood suddenly. He grabbed the antimatter in his hands and wheeled toward the others. His face showing total focus. He pushed past the others and began descending the Necropolis the way he had come, running down the hill.

The camera caught Vittoria Vetra, frozen in terror. 'Where are you going! Camerlengo! I thought you said—'

'Have faith!' he exclaimed as he ran off.

Vittoria spun toward Langdon. 'What do we do?'

Robert Langdon tried to stop the camerlengo, but Chartrand was running interference now, apparently trusting the camerlengo's conviction.

The picture coming from the BBC camera was like a roller coaster ride now, winding, twisting. Fleeting freeze-frames of confusion and terror as the chaotic cortege stumbled through the shadows back toward the Necropolis entrance.

Out in the square, Mortati let out a fearful gasp. 'Is he bringing that up *here*?'

On televisions all over the world, larger than life, the camerlengo raced upward out of the Necropolis with the antimatter before him. 'There will be no more death tonight!'

But the camerlengo was wrong.

121

The camerlengo erupted through the doors of St Peter's Basilica at exactly 11.56 p.m. He staggered into the dazzling glare of the world spotlight, carrying the antimatter before him like some sort of numinous offering. Through burning eyes he could see his own form, half-naked and wounded, towering like a giant on the media screens around the square. The roar that went up from the crowd in St Peter's Square was like none the camerlengo had ever heard– crying, screaming, chanting, praying . . . a mix of veneration and terror.

Deliver us from evil, he whispered.

He felt totally depleted from his race out of the Necropolis. It had almost ended in disaster. Robert Langdon and Vittoria Vetra had wanted to intercept him, to throw the canister back into its subterranean hiding place, to run outside for cover. *Blind fools!*

The camerlengo realized now, with fearful clarity, that on any other night, he would never have won the race. Tonight, however, God again had been with him. Robert Langdon, on the verge of overtaking the camerlengo, had been grabbed by Chartrand, ever trusting and dutiful to the camerlengo's demands for faith. The reporters, of course, were spellbound and lugging too much equipment to interfere.

The Lord works in mysterious ways.

The camerlengo could hear the others behind him now . . . see them on the screens, closing in. Mustering the last of his physical strength, he raised the anti-matter high over his head. Then, throwing back his bare shoulders in an act of defiance to the Illuminati brand on his chest, he dashed down the stairs.

There was one final act.

Godspeed, he thought. *Godspeed.*

Four minutes . . .

Langdon could barely see as he burst out of the basilica. Again the sea of media lights bore into his retinas. All he could make out was the murky outline of the camerlengo, directly ahead of him, running down the stairs. For an instant, refulgent in his halo of media lights, the camerlengo looked celestial, like some kind of modern deity. His cassock was at his waist like a shroud. His body was scarred and wounded by the hands of his enemies, and still he endured. The camerlengo ran on, standing tall, calling out to the world to have faith, running toward the masses carrying this weapon of destruction.

Langdon ran down the stairs after him. *What is he doing? He will kill them all!*

'Satan's work,' the camerlengo screamed, 'has no place in the House of God!' He ran on toward a now terrified crowd.

'Father!' Langdon screamed, behind him. 'There's nowhere to go!'

'Look to the heavens! We forget to look to the heavens!'

In that moment, as Langdon saw where the camerlengo was headed, the glorious truth came flooding all around him. Although Langdon could not see it on account of the lights, he knew their salvation was directly overhead.

A star-filled Italian sky. *The escape route.*

The helicopter the camerlengo had summoned to take him to the hospital sat dead ahead, pilot already in the cockpit, blades already humming in neutral. As the camerlengo ran toward it, Langdon felt a sudden overwhelming exhilaration.

The thoughts that tore through Langdon's mind came as a torrent . . .

First he pictured the wide-open expanse of the Mediterranean Sea. How far was it? Five miles? Ten? He knew the beach at *Fiumocino* was only about seven minutes by train. But by helicopter, 200 miles an hour, no stops . . . If they could fly the canister far enough out to sea, and drop it . . . There were other options too, he realized, feeling almost weightless as he ran. *La Cava Romana!* The marble quarries north of the city were less than three miles away. How large were they? Two square miles? Certainly they were deserted at this hour! Dropping the canister *there* . . .

'Everyone back!' the camerlengo yelled. His chest ached as he ran. 'Get away! Now!'

The Swiss Guard standing around the chopper stood slack-jawed as the camerlengo approached them.

'Back!' the priest screamed.

The guards moved back.

With the entire world watching in wonder, the camerlengo ran around the chopper to the pilot's door and yanked it open. 'Out, son! Now!'

The guard jumped out.

The camerlengo looked at the high cockpit seat and knew that in his exhausted state, he would need both hands to pull himself up. He turned to the pilot, trembling beside him, and thrust the canister into his hands. 'Hold this. Hand it back when I'm in.'

As the camerlengo pulled himself up, he could hear Robert Langdon yelling excitedly, running toward the craft. *Now you understand*, the camerlengo thought. *Now you have faith!*

The camerlengo pulled himself up into the cockpit, adjusted a few familiar levers, and then turned back to his window for the canister.

But the guard to whom he had given the canister stood empty-handed. 'He took it!' the guard yelled.

The camerlengo felt his heart seize. 'Who!'

The guard pointed. 'Him!'

Robert Langdon was surprised by how heavy the canister was. He ran to the other side of the chopper and jumped in the rear compartment where he and Vittoria had sat only hours ago. He left the door open and buckled himself in. Then he yelled to the camerlengo in the front seat.

'Fly, Father!'

The camerlengo craned back at Langdon, his face bloodless with dread. 'What are you doing!'

'*You* fly! I'll throw!' Langdon barked. 'There's no time! Just fly the blessed chopper!'

The camerlengo seemed momentarily paralyzed, the media lights glaring through the cockpit darkening

543

the creases in his face. 'I can do this alone,' he whispered. 'I am *supposed* to do this alone.'

Langdon wasn't listening. *Fly!* he heard himself screaming. *Now! I'm here to help you!* Langdon looked down at the canister and felt his breath catch in his throat when he saw the numbers. '*Three* minutes, Father! *Three!*'

The number seemed to stun the camerlengo back to sobriety. Without hesitation, he turned back to the controls. With a grinding roar, the helicopter lifted off.

Through a swirl of dust, Langdon could see Vittoria running toward the chopper. Their eyes met, and then she dropped away like a sinking stone.

122

Inside the chopper, the whine of the engines and the gale from the open door assaulted Langdon's senses with a deafening chaos. He steadied himself against the magnified drag of gravity as the camerlengo accelerated the craft straight up. The glow of St Peter's Square shrank beneath them until it was an amorphous glowing ellipse radiating in a sea of city lights.

The antimatter canister felt like deadweight in Langdon's hands. He held tighter, his palms slick now with sweat and blood. Inside the trap, the globule of antimatter hovered calmly, pulsing red in the glow of the LED countdown clock.

'Two minutes!' Langdon yelled, wondering where the camerlengo intended to drop the canister.

The city lights beneath them spread out in all directions. In the distance to the west, Langdon could see the twinkling delineation of the Mediterranean coast – a jagged border of luminescence beyond which spread an endless dark expanse of nothingness. The sea looked farther now than Langdon had imagined. Moreover, the concentration of lights at the coast was a stark reminder that even far out at sea an explosion might have devastating effects. Langdon had not even considered the effects of a ten-kiloton tidal wave hitting the coast.

When Langdon turned and looked straight ahead through the cockpit window, he was more hopeful. Directly in front of them, the rolling shadows of the Roman foothills loomed in the night. The hills were spotted with lights – the villas of the very wealthy – but a mile or so north, the hills grew dark. There were no lights at all – just a huge pocket of blackness. Nothing.

The quarries! Langdon thought. *La Cava Romana!*

Staring intently at the barren pocket of land, Langdon sensed that it was plenty large enough. It seemed close, too. Much closer than the ocean. Excitement surged through him. This was obviously where the camerlengo planned to take the antimatter! The chopper was pointing directly toward it! The quarries! Oddly, however, as the engines strained louder and the chopper hurtled through the air, Langdon could see that the quarries were not getting any closer. Bewildered, he shot a glance out the side door to get his bearings. What he saw doused his excitement in a wave of panic. Directly beneath them, thousands of feet straight down, glowed the media lights in St Peter's Square.

We're still over the Vatican!

'Camerlengo!' Langdon choked. 'Go forward! We're high *enough*! You've got to start moving forward! We can't drop the canister back over Vatican City!'

The camerlengo did not reply. He appeared to be concentrating on flying the craft.

'We've got less than *two* minutes!' Langdon shouted, holding up the canister. 'I can see them! *La Cava Romana!* A couple of miles north! We don't have—'

'No,' the camerlengo said. 'It's far too dangerous. I'm sorry.' As the chopper continued to claw heavenward, the camerlengo turned and gave Langdon a mournful smile. 'I wish you had not come, my friend. You have made the ultimate sacrifice.'

Langdon looked in the camerlengo's exhausted eyes and suddenly understood. His blood turned to ice. 'But . . . there must be *somewhere* we can go!'

'*Up*,' the camerlengo replied, his voice resigned. 'It's the only guarantee.'

Langdon could barely think. He had entirely misinterpreted the camerlengo's plan. *Look to the heavens!*

Heaven, Langdon now realized, was literally where he was headed. The camerlengo had never intended to drop the antimatter. He was simply getting it as far away from Vatican City as humanly possible.

This was a one-way trip.

123

In St Peter's Square, Vittoria Vetra stared upward. The helicopter was a speck now, the media lights no longer reaching it. Even the pounding of the rotors had faded to a distant hum. It seemed, in that instant, that the entire world was focused upward, silenced in anticipation, necks craned to the heavens ... all peoples, all faiths ... all hearts beating as one.

Vittoria's emotions were a cyclone of twisting agonies. As the helicopter disappeared from sight, she pictured Robert's face, rising above her. *What had he been thinking? Didn't he understand?*

Around the square, television cameras probed the darkness, waiting. A sea of faces stared heavenward, united in a silent countdown. The media screens all flickered the same tranquil scene ... a Roman sky illuminated with brilliant stars. Vittoria felt the tears begin to well.

Behind her on the marble escarpment, 161 cardinals stared up in silent awe. Some folded their hands in prayer. Most stood motionless, transfixed. Some wept. The seconds ticked past.

In homes, bars, businesses, airports, hospitals around the world, souls were joined in universal witness. Men and women locked hands. Others held their children. Time seemed to hover in limbo, souls suspended in unison.

Then, cruelly, the bells of St Peter's began to toll.

Vittoria let the tears come.

Then ... with the whole world watching ... time ran out.

The dead silence of the event was the most terrifying of all.

High above Vatican City, a pinpoint of light appeared in the sky. For a fleeting instant, a new heavenly body had been born ... a speck of light as pure and white as anyone had ever seen.

Then it happened.

A flash. The point billowed, as if feeding on itself, unraveling across the sky in a dilating radius of blinding white. It shot out in all directions, accelerating with incomprehensible speed, gobbling up the dark. As the sphere of light grew, it intensified, like a burgeoning fiend preparing to consume the entire sky. It raced downward, toward them, picking up speed.

Blinded, the multitudes of starkly lit human faces gasped as one, shielding their eyes, crying out in strangled fear.

As the light roared out in all directions, the unimaginable occurred. As if bound by God's own will, the surging radius seemed to hit a wall. It was as if the explosion were contained somehow in a giant glass sphere. The light rebounded inward, sharpening, rippling across itself. The wave appeared to have reached a predetermined diameter and hovered there. For that instant, a perfect and silent sphere of light glowed over Rome. Night had become day.

Then it hit.

The concussion was deep and hollow – a thunderous shock wave from above. It descended on them like the wrath of hell, shaking the granite foundation of Vatican City, knocking the breath out of people's lungs, sending others stumbling backward. The reverberation circled the colonnade, followed by a sudden torrent of warm air. The wind tore through the square, letting out a sepulchral moan as it whistled through the columns and buffeted the walls. Dust swirled overhead as people huddled . . . witnesses to Armageddon.

Then, as fast as it appeared, the sphere imploded,

sucking back in on itself, crushing inward to the tiny point of light from which it had come.

124

Never before had so many been so silent.

The faces in St Peter's Square, one by one, averted their eyes from the darkening sky and turned downward, each person in his or her own private moment of wonder. The media lights followed suit, dropping their beams back to earth as if out of reverence for the blackness now settling upon them. It seemed for a moment the entire world was bowing its head in unison.

Cardinal Mortati knelt to pray, and the other cardinals joined him. The Swiss Guard lowered their long swords and stood numb. No one spoke. No one moved. Everywhere, hearts shuddered with spontaneous emotion. Bereavement. Fear. Wonder. Belief. And a dread-filled respect for the new and awesome power they had just witnessed.

Vittoria Vetra stood trembling at the foot of the basilica's sweeping stairs. She closed her eyes. Through the tempest of emotions now coursing through her blood, a single word tolled like a distant bell. Pristine. Cruel. She forced it away. And yet the word echoed. Again she drove it back. The pain was too great. She tried to lose herself in the images that blazed in other's minds ... antimatter's mind-boggling power ... the Vatican's deliverance ... the camerlengo ... feats of bravery ... miracles ...

selflessness. And still the word echoed ... tolling through the chaos with a stinging loneliness.

Robert.

He had come for her at Castle St Angelo.

He had saved her.

And now he had been destroyed by *her* creation.

As Cardinal Mortati prayed, he wondered if he too would hear God's voice as the camerlengo had. *Does one need to believe in miracles to experience them?* Mortati was a modern man in an ancient faith. Miracles had never played a part in his belief. Certainly his faith spoke of miracles ... bleeding palms, ascensions from the dead, imprints on shrouds ... and yet, Mortati's rational mind had always justified these accounts as part of the myth. They were simply the result of man's greatest weakness – his *need* for proof. Miracles were nothing but stories we all clung to because we *wished* they were true.

And yet ...

Am I so modern that I cannot accept what my eyes have just witnessed? It was a miracle, was it not? Yes! God, with a few whispered words in the camerlengo's ear, had intervened and saved this church. Why was this so hard to believe? What would it say about God if God had done nothing? That the Almighty did not care? That He was powerless to stop it? *A miracle was the only possible response!*

As Mortati knelt in wonder, he prayed for the camerlengo's soul. He gave thanks to the young chamberlain who, even in his youthful years, had opened this old man's eyes to the miracles of un-questioning faith.

Incredibly, though, Mortati never suspected the

extent to which his faith was about to be tested . . .

The silence of St Peter's Square broke with a ripple at first. The ripple grew to a murmur. And then, suddenly, to a roar. Without warning, the multitudes were crying out as one.

'Look! Look!'

Mortati opened his eyes and turned to the crowd. Everyone was pointing behind him, toward the front of St Peter's Basilica. Their faces were white. Some fell to their knees. Some fainted. Some burst into uncontrollable sobs.

'Look! Look!'

Mortati turned, bewildered, following their outstretched hands. They were pointing to the uppermost level of the basilica, the rooftop terrace, where huge statues of Christ and his apostles watched over the crowd.

There, on the right of Jesus, arms outstretched to the world . . . stood Camerlengo Carlo Ventresca.

125

Robert Langdon was no longer falling.

There was no more terror. No pain. Not even the sound of the racing wind. There was only the soft sound of lapping water, as though he were comfortably asleep on a beach.

In a paradox of self-awareness, Langdon sensed this was death. He felt glad for it. He allowed the drifting numbness to possess him entirely. He let it carry him wherever it was he would go. His pain and fear had been anesthetized, and he did not wish it back at any price. His final memory had been one that could only have been conjured in hell.

Take me. Please . . .

But the lapping that lulled in him a far-off sense of peace was also pulling him back. It was trying to awaken him from a dream. *No! Let me be!* He did not want to awaken. He sensed demons gathering on the perimeter of his bliss, pounding to shatter his rapture. Fuzzy images swirled. Voices yelled. Wind churned. *No, please!* The more he fought, the more the fury filtered through.

Then, harshly, he was living it all again . . .

The helicopter was in a dizzying dead climb. He was trapped inside. Beyond the open door, the lights of Rome looked farther away with every passing second. His survival instinct told him to jettison the canister right now. Langdon knew it would take less than twenty seconds for the canister to fall half a mile. But it would be falling toward a city of people.

Higher! Higher!

Langdon wondered how high they were now. Small prop planes, he knew, flew at altitudes of about four miles. This helicopter *had* to be at a good fraction of that by now. *Two miles up? Three?* There was still a chance. If they timed the drop perfectly, the canister would fall only partway toward earth, exploding a safe distance over the ground and away from the chopper. Langdon looked out at the city sprawling below them.

'And if you calculate incorrectly?' the camerlengo said.

Langdon turned, startled. The camerlengo was not

even looking at him, apparently having read Langdon's thoughts from the ghostly reflection in the windshield. Oddly, the camerlengo was no longer engrossed in his controls. His hands were not even on the throttle. The chopper, it seemed, was now in some sort of autopilot mode, locked in a climb. The camerlengo reached above his head, to the ceiling of the cockpit, fishing behind a cable-housing, where he removed a key, taped there out of view.

Langdon watched in bewilderment as the camerlengo quickly unlocked the metal cargo box bolted between the seats. He removed some sort of large, black, nylon pack. He laid it on the seat next to him. Langdon's thoughts churned. The camerlengo's movements seemed composed, as if he had a solution.

'Give me the canister,' the camerlengo said, his tone serene.

Langdon did not know what to think anymore. He thrust the canister to the camerlengo. 'Ninety seconds!'

What the camerlengo did with the antimatter took Langdon totally by surprise. Holding the canister carefully in his hands, the camerlengo placed it inside the cargo box. Then he closed the heavy lid and used the key to lock it tight.

'What are you doing!' Langdon demanded.

'Leading us from temptation.' The camerlengo threw the key out the open window.

As the key tumbled into the night, Langdon felt his soul falling with it.

The camerlengo then took the nylon pack and slipped his arms through the straps. He fastened a waist clamp around his stomach and cinched it all down like a backpack. He turned to a dumbstruck Robert Langdon.

'I'm sorry,' the camerlengo said. 'It wasn't supposed to happen this way.' Then he opened his door and hurled himself into the night.

The image burned in Langdon's unconscious mind; and with it came the pain. Real pain. Physical pain. Aching. Searing. He begged to be taken, to let it end, but as the water lapped louder in his ears, new images began to flash. His hell had only just begun. He saw bits and pieces. Scattered frames of sheer panic. He lay halfway between death and nightmare, begging for deliverance, but the pictures grew brighter in his mind.

The antimatter canister was locked out of reach. It counted relentlessly downward as the chopper shot upward. *Fifty seconds.* Higher. Higher. Langdon spun wildly in the cabin, trying to make sense of what he had just seen. *Forty-five seconds.* He dug under seats searching for another parachute. *Forty seconds.* There was none! There had to be an option! *Thirty-five seconds.* He raced to the open doorway of the chopper and stood in the raging wind, gazing down at the lights of Rome below. *Thirty-two seconds.*

And then he made the choice.

The unbelievable choice . . .

With no parachute, Robert Langdon had jumped out the door. As the night swallowed his tumbling body, the helicopter seemed to rocket off above him, the sound of its rotors evaporating in the deafening rush of his own free fall.

As he plummeted toward earth, Robert Langdon felt something he had not experienced since his years on the high dive – the inexorable pull of gravity during a dead drop. The faster he fell, the harder the earth seemed to pull, sucking him down. This time, however, the drop was not fifty feet into a pool. The drop was thousands of feet into a city – an endless expanse of pavement and concrete.

Somewhere in the torrent of wind and desperation, Kohler's voice echoed from the grave . . . words he had spoken earlier this morning standing at CERN's free-fall tube. *One square yard of drag will slow a falling body almost twenty per cent.* Twenty per cent, Langdon now realized, was not even close to what one would need to survive a fall like this. Nonetheless, more out of paralysis than hope, he clenched in his hands the sole object he had grabbed from the chopper on his way out the door. It was an odd memento, but it was one that for a fleeting instant had given him hope.

The windshield tarp had been lying in the back of the helicopter. It was a concave rectangle – about four yards by two – like a huge fitted sheet . . . the crudest approximation of a parachute imaginable. It had no harness, only bungie loops at either end for fastening it to the curvature of the windshield. Langdon had grabbed it, slid his hands through the loops, held on, and leapt out into the void.

His last great act of youthful defiance.

No illusions of life beyond this moment.

Langdon fell like a rock. Feet first. Arms raised. His hands gripping the loops. The tarp billowed like a mushroom overhead. The wind tore past him violently.

As he plummeted toward earth, there was a deep explosion somewhere above him. It seemed farther off than he had expected. Almost instantly, the shock wave hit. He felt the breath crushed from his lungs.

There was a sudden warmth in the air all around him. He fought to hold on. A wall of heat raced down from above. The top of the tarp began to smolder . . . but held.

Langdon rocketed downward, on the edge of a billowing shroud of light, feeling like a surfer trying to outrun a thousand-foot tidal wave. Then suddenly, the heat receded.

He was falling again through the dark coolness.

For an instant, Langdon felt hope. A moment later, though, that hope faded like the withdrawing heat above. Despite his straining arms assuring him that the tarp was slowing his fall, the wind still tore past his body with deafening velocity. Langdon had no doubt he was still moving too fast to survive the fall. He would be crushed when he hit the ground.

Mathematical figures tumbled through his brain, but he was too numb to make sense of them . . . *one square yard of drag . . . 20 per cent reduction of speed*. All Langdon could figure was that the tarp over his head was big enough to slow him more than 20 per cent. Unfortunately, though, he could tell from the wind whipping past him that whatever good the tarp was doing was not enough. He was still falling fast . . . there would be no surviving the impact on the waiting sea of concrete.

Beneath him, the lights of Rome spread out in all directions. The city looked like an enormous starlit sky that Langdon was falling into. The perfect expanse of stars was marred only by a dark strip that split the city in two – a wide, unlit ribbon that wound through the dots of light like a fat snake. Langdon stared down at the meandering swatch of black.

Suddenly, like the surging crest of an unexpected wave, hope filled him again.

With almost maniacal vigor, Langdon yanked down hard with his right hand on the canopy. The tarp suddenly flapped louder, billowing, cutting right to find the path of least resistance. Langdon felt himself drifting sideways. He pulled again, harder, ignoring the pain in his palm. The tarp flared, and Langdon sensed his body sliding laterally. Not much. But *some*! He looked beneath him again, to the sinuous serpent of black. It was off to the right, but he was still pretty high. Had he waited too long? He pulled with all his might and accepted somehow that it was now in the hands of God. He focused hard on the widest part of the serpent and . . . for the first time in his life, prayed for a miracle.

The rest was a blur.

The darkness rushing up beneath him . . . the diving instincts coming back . . . the reflexive locking of his spine and pointing of the toes . . . the inflating of his lungs to protect his vital organs . . . the flexing of his legs into a battering ram . . . and finally . . . the thankfulness that the winding Tiber River was raging . . . making its waters frothy and air-filled . . . and three times softer than standing water.

Then there was impact . . . and blackness.

It had been the thundering sound of the flapping canopy that drew the group's eyes away from the fireball in the sky. The sky above Rome had been filled with sights tonight . . . a skyrocketing helicopter, an enormous explosion, and now this strange object that had plummeted into the churning waters of the Tiber River, directly off the shore of the river's tiny island, Isola Tiberina.

Ever since the island had been used to quarantine the sick during the Roman plague of A.D. 1656, it had been thought to have mystic healing properties. For this reason, the island had later become the site for Rome's Hospital Tiberina.

The body was battered when they pulled it onto shore. The man still had a faint pulse, which was amazing, they thought. They wondered if it was Isola Tiberina's mythical reputation for healing that had somehow kept his heart pumping. Minutes later, when the man began coughing and slowly regained consciousness, the group decided the island must indeed be magical.

126

Cardinal Mortati knew there were no words in any language that could have added to the mystery of this moment. The silence of the vision over St Peter's Square sang louder than any chorus of angels.

As he stared up at Camerlengo Ventresca, Mortati felt the paralyzing collision of his heart and mind. The vision seemed real, tangible. And yet . . . how could it be? Everyone had seen the camerlengo get in the helicopter. They had all witnessed the ball of light in the sky. And now, somehow, the camerlengo stood high above them on the rooftop terrace. Transported by angels? Reincarnated by the hand of God?

This is impossible . . .

Mortati's heart wanted nothing more than to believe, but his mind cried out for reason. And yet all around him, the cardinals stared up, obviously seeing what he was seeing, paralyzed with wonder.

It was the camerlengo. There was no doubt. But he looked different somehow. Divine. As if he had been purified. A spirit? A man? His white flesh shone in the spotlights with an incorporeal weightlessness.

In the square there was crying, cheering, spontaneous applause. A group of nuns fell to their knees and wailed *saetas*. A pulsing grew from in the crowd. Suddenly, the entire square was chanting the camerlengo's name. The cardinals, some with tears rolling down their faces, joined in. Mortati looked around him and tried to comprehend. *Is this really happening?*

Camerlengo Carlo Ventresca stood on the rooftop terrace of St Peter's Basilica and looked down over the multitudes of people staring up at him. Was he awake or dreaming? He felt transformed, otherworldly. He wondered if it was his body or just his spirit that had floated down from heaven toward the soft, darkened expanse of the Vatican City Gardens ... alighting like a silent angel on the deserted lawns, his black parachute shrouded from the madness by the towering shadow of St Peter's Basilica. He wondered if it was his body or his spirit that had possessed the strength to climb the ancient Stairway of Medallions to the rooftop terrace where he now stood.

He felt as light as a ghost.

Although the people below were chanting his name, he knew it was not *him* they were cheering. They were cheering from impulsive joy, the same kind of joy he felt every day of his life as he pondered the Almighty. They were experiencing what each of them had always longed for ... an assurance of the beyond ... a substantiation of the power of the Creator.

Camerlengo Ventresca had prayed all his life for this moment, and still, even *he* could not fathom that God had found a way to make it manifest. He wanted to cry out to them. *Your God is a living God! Behold the miracles all around you!*

He stood there a while, numb and yet feeling more than he had ever felt. When, at last, the spirit moved him, he bowed his head and stepped back from the edge.

Alone now, he knelt on the roof, and prayed.

127

The images around him blurred, drifting in and out. Langdon's eyes slowly began to focus. His legs ached, and his body felt like it had been run over by a truck. He was lying on his side on the ground. Something stunk, like bile. He could still hear the incessant sound of lapping water. It no longer sounded peaceful to him. There were other sounds too – talking close around him. He saw blurry white forms. Were they all wearing white? Langdon decided he was either in an asylum or heaven. From the burning in his throat, Langdon decided it could not be heaven.

'He's finished vomiting,' one man said in Italian. *'Turn him.'* The voice was firm and professional.

Langdon felt hands slowly rolling him onto his back. His head swam. He tried to sit up, but the hands gently forced him back down. His body submitted.

Then Langdon felt someone going through his pockets, removing items.

Then he passed out cold.

Dr Jacobus was not a religious man; the science of medicine had bred that from him long ago. And yet, the events in Vatican City tonight had put his systematic logic to the test. *Now bodies are falling from the sky?*

Dr Jacobus felt the pulse of the bedraggled man they had just pulled from the Tiber River. The doctor decided that God himself had hand-delivered this one to safety. The concussion of hitting the water had knocked the victim unconscious, and if it had not been for Jacobus and his crew standing out on the shore watching the spectacle in the sky, this falling soul would surely have gone unnoticed and drowned.

'*É Americano,*' a nurse said, going through the man's wallet after they pulled him to dry land.

American? Romans often joked that Americans had gotten so abundant in Rome that hamburgers should become the official Italian food. *But Americans falling from the sky?* Jacobus flicked a penlight in the man's eyes, testing his dilation. 'Sir? Can you hear me? Do you know where you are?'

The man was unconscious again. Jacobus was not surprised. The man had vomited a lot of water after Jacobus had performed CPR.

'*Si chiama Robert Langdon,*' the nurse said, reading the man's driver's license.

The group assembled on the dock all stopped short.

'*Impossibile!*' Jacobus declared. Robert Langdon was the man from the television – the American professor who had been helping the Vatican. Jacobus had seen Mr Langdon, only minutes ago, getting into a helicopter in St Peter's Square and flying miles up into the air. Jacobus and the others had run out to the dock to witness the antimatter explosion – a tremendous sphere of light like nothing any of them had ever seen. *How could this be the same man!*

'It's him!' the nurse exclaimed, brushing his soaked hair back. 'And I recognize his tweed coat!'

Suddenly someone was yelling from the hospital entryway. It was one of the patients. She was screaming, going mad, holding her portable radio to the sky and praising God. Apparently Camerlengo Ventresca had just miraculously appeared on the roof of the Vatican.

Dr Jacobus decided, when his shift got off at 8 a.m., he was going straight to church.

The lights over Langdon's head were brighter now, sterile. He was on some kind of examination table. He smelled astringents, strange chemicals. Someone had just given him an injection, and they had removed his clothes.

Definitely not gypsies, he decided in his semi-conscious delirium. *Aliens, perhaps?* Yes, he had heard about things like this. Fortunately these beings would not harm him. All they wanted were his—

'Not on your life!' Langdon sat bolt upright, eyes flying open.

'*Attento!*' one of the creatures yelled, steadying him. His badge read Dr Jacobus. He looked remarkably human.

Langdon stammered, 'I . . . thought . . .'

'Easy, Mr Langdon. You're in a hospital.'

The fog began to lift. Langdon felt a wave of relief. He hated hospitals, but they certainly beat aliens harvesting his testicles.

'My name is Dr Jacobus,' the man said. He explained what had just happened. 'You are very lucky to be alive.'

Langdon did not feel lucky. He could barely make sense of his own memories . . . the helicopter . . . the camerlengo. His body ached everywhere. They gave him some water, and he rinsed out his mouth. They placed a new gauze on his palm.

'Where are my clothes?' Langdon asked. He was wearing a paper robe.

One of the nurses motioned to a dripping wad of shredded khaki and tweed on the counter. 'They were soaked. We had to cut them off you.'

Langdon looked at his shredded Harris tweed and frowned.

'You had some Kleenex in your pocket,' the nurse said.

It was then that Langdon saw the ravaged shreds of parchment clinging all over the lining of his jacket. The folio from Galileo's *Diagramma*. The last copy on earth had just dissolved. He was too numb to know how to react. He just stared.

'We saved your personal items.' She held up a plastic bin. 'Wallet, camcorder, and pen. I dried the camcorder off the best I could.'

'I don't own a camcorder.'

The nurse frowned and held out the bin. Langdon looked at the contents. Along with his wallet and pen was a tiny Sony RUVI camcorder. He recalled it now. Kohler had handed it to him and asked him to give it to the media.

'We found it in your pocket. I think you'll need a new one, though.' The nurse flipped open the two-inch screen on the back. 'Your viewer is cracked.' Then

563

she brightened. 'The sound still works, though. Barely.' She held the device up to her ear. 'Keeps playing something over and over.' She listened a moment and then scowled, handing it to Langdon. 'Two guys arguing, I think.'

Puzzled, Langdon took the camcorder and held it to his ear. The voices were pinched and metallic, but they were discernible. One close. One far away. Langdon recognized them both.

Sitting there in his paper gown, Langdon listened in amazement to the conversation. Although he couldn't see what was happening, when he heard the shocking finale, he was thankful he had been spared the visual.

My God!

As the conversation began playing again from the beginning, Langdon lowered the camcorder from his ear and sat in appalled mystification. The antimatter . . . the helicopter . . . Langdon's mind now kicked into gear.

But that means . . .

He wanted to vomit again. With a rising fury of disorientation and rage, Langdon got off the table and stood on shaky legs.

'Mr Langdon!' the doctor said, trying to stop him.

'I need some clothes,' Langdon demanded, feeling the draft on his rear from the backless gown.

'But, you need to rest.'

'I'm checking out. Now. I need some clothes.'

'But, sir, you—'

'Now!'

Everyone exchanged bewildered looks. 'We have no clothes,' the doctor said. 'Perhaps tomorrow a friend could bring you some.'

Langdon drew a slow patient breath and locked

eyes with the doctor. 'Dr Jacobus, I am walking out your door right now. I need clothes. I am going to Vatican City. One does not go to Vatican City with one's ass hanging out. Do I make myself clear?'

Dr Jacobus swallowed hard. 'Get this man something to wear.'

When Langdon limped out of Hospital Tiberina, he felt like an overgrown Cub Scout. He was wearing a blue paramedic's jumpsuit that zipped up the front and was adorned with cloth badges that apparently depicted his numerous qualifications.

The woman accompanying him was heavyset and wore a similar suit. The doctor had assured Langdon she would get him to the Vatican in record time.

'Molto traffico,' Langdon said, reminding her that the area around the Vatican was packed with cars and people.

The woman looked unconcerned. She pointed proudly to one of her patches. *'Sono conducente di ambulanza.'*

'Ambulanza?' That explained it. Langdon felt like he could use an ambulance ride.

The woman led him around the side of the building. On an outcropping over the water was a cement deck where her vehicle sat waiting. When Langdon saw the vehicle he stopped in his tracks. It was an aging medevac chopper. The hull read *Aero-Ambulanza.*

He hung his head.

The woman smiled. 'Fly Vatican City. Very fast.'

The College of Cardinals bristled with ebullience and electricity as they streamed back into the Sistine Chapel. In contrast, Mortati felt in himself a rising confusion he thought might lift him off the floor and carry him away. He believed in the ancient miracles of the Scriptures, and yet what he had just *witnessed* in person was something he could not possibly comprehend. After a lifetime of devotion, seventy-nine years, Mortati knew these events should ignite in him a pious exuberance . . . a fervent and living faith. And yet all he felt was a growing spectral unease. Something did not feel right.

'Signore Mortati!' a Swiss Guard yelled, running down the hall.

'We have gone to the roof as you asked. The camerlengo is . . . *flesh*! He is a true man! He is not a spirit! He is exactly as we knew him!'

'Did he *speak* to you?'

'He kneels in silent prayer! We are afraid to touch him!'

Mortati was at a loss. 'Tell him . . . his cardinals await.'

'Signore, because he is a *man* . . .' the guard hesitated.

'What is it?'

'His chest . . . he is burned. Should we bind his wounds? He must be in pain.'

Mortati considered it. Nothing in his lifetime of service to the church had prepared him for this situation. 'He is a man, so serve him as a man. Bathe him. Bind his wounds. Dress him in fresh robes. We await his arrival in the Sistine Chapel.'

The guard ran off.

Mortati headed for the chapel. The rest of the cardinals were inside now. As he walked down the hall, he saw Vittoria Vetra slumped alone on a bench at the foot of the Royal Staircase. He could see the pain and loneliness of her loss and wanted to go to her, but he knew it would have to wait. He had work to do . . . although he had no idea what that work could possibly be.

Mortati entered the chapel. There was a riotous excitement. He closed the door. *God help me.*

Hospital Tiberina's twin-rotor *Aero-Ambulanza* circled in behind Vatican City, and Langdon clenched his teeth, swearing to God this was the very last helicopter ride of his life.

After convincing the pilot that the rules governing Vatican airspace were the least of the Vatican's concerns right now, he guided her in, unseen, over the rear wall, and landed them on the Vatican's helipad.

'*Grazie*,' he said, lowering himself painfully onto the ground. She blew him a kiss and quickly took off, disappearing back over the wall and into the night.

Langdon exhaled, trying to clear his head, hoping to make sense of what he was about to do. With the camcorder in hand, he boarded the same golf cart he had ridden earlier that day. It had not been charged, and the battery-meter registered close to empty. Langdon drove without headlights to conserve power.

He also preferred no one see him coming.

At the back of the Sistine Chapel, Cardinal Mortati stood in a daze as he watched the pandemonium before him.

'It was a miracle!' one of the cardinals shouted. 'The work of God!'

'Yes!' others exclaimed. 'God has made His will manifest!'

'The camerlengo will be our Pope!' another shouted. 'He is not a cardinal, but God has sent a miraculous sign!'

'Yes!' someone agreed. 'The laws of conclave are *man*'s laws. God's will is before us! I call for a balloting immediately!'

'A balloting?' Mortati demanded, moving toward them. 'I believe that is *my* job.'

Everyone turned.

Mortati could sense the cardinals studying him. They seemed distant, at a loss, offended by his sobriety. Mortati longed to feel his heart swept up in the miraculous exultation he saw in the faces around him. But he was not. He felt an inexplicable pain in his soul ... an aching sadness he could not explain. He had vowed to guide these proceedings with purity of soul, and this hesitancy was something he could not deny.

'My friends,' Mortati said, stepping to the altar. His voice did not seem his own. 'I suspect I will struggle for the rest of my days with the meaning of what I have witnessed tonight. And yet, what you are suggesting regarding the camerlengo ... it cannot possibly be God's will.'

The room fell silent.

'How ... can you say that?' one of the cardinals finally demanded. 'The camerlengo *saved* the church. God spoke to the camerlengo directly! The man survived death itself! What sign do we need!'

'The camerlengo is coming to us now,' Mortati said.

'Let us wait. Let us hear him before we have a balloting. There may be an explanation.'

'An explanation?'

'As your Great Elector, I have vowed to uphold the laws of conclave. You are no doubt aware that by Holy Law the camerlengo is ineligible for election to the papacy. He is not a cardinal. He is a priest ... a chamberlain. There is also the question of his inadequate age.' Mortati felt the stares hardening. 'By even allowing a balloting, I would be requesting that you endorse a man who Vatican Law proclaims ineligible. I would be asking each of you to break a sacred oath.'

'But what happened here tonight,' someone stammered, 'it *certainly* transcends our laws!'

'Does it?' Mortati boomed, not even knowing now where his words were coming from. 'Is it God's will that we discard the rules of the church? Is it God's will that we abandon reason and give ourselves over to frenzy?'

'But did you not see what *we* saw?' another challenged angrily. 'How can you presume to question that kind of power!'

Mortati's voice bellowed now with a resonance he had never known. 'I am not questioning God's power! It is *God* who gave us reason and circumspection! It is God we serve by exercising prudence!'

129

In the hallway outside the Sistine Chapel, Vittoria Vetra sat benumbed on a bench at the foot of the

Royal Staircase. When she saw the figure coming through the rear door, she wondered if she were seeing another spirit. He was bandaged, limping, and wearing some kind of medical suit.

She stood . . . unable to believe the vision. 'Ro . . . bert?'

He never answered. He strode directly to her and wrapped her in his arms. When he pressed his lips to hers, it was an impulsive, longing kiss filled with thankfulness.

Vittoria felt the tears coming. 'Oh, God . . . oh, thank God . . .'

He kissed her again, more passionately, and she pressed against him, losing herself in his embrace. Their bodies locked, as if they had known each other for years. She forgot the fear and pain. She closed her eyes, weightless in the moment.

'It is God's will!' someone was yelling, his voice echoing in the Sistine Chapel. 'Who but the *chosen* one could have survived that diabolical explosion?'

'Me,' a voice reverberated from the back of the chapel.

Mortati and the others turned in wonder at the bedraggled form coming up the center aisle. 'Mr . . . *Langdon*?'

Without a word, Langdon walked slowly to the front of the chapel. Vittoria Vetra entered too. Then two guards hurried in, pushing a cart with a large television on it. Langdon waited while they plugged it in, facing the cardinals. Then Langdon motioned for the guards to leave. They did, closing the door behind them.

Now it was only Langdon, Vittoria, and the

cardinals. Langdon plugged the Sony RUVI's output into the television. Then he pressed PLAY.

The television blared to life.

The scene that materialized before the cardinals revealed the Pope's office. The video had been awkwardly filmed, as if by hidden camera. Off center on the screen the camerlengo stood in the dimness, in front of a fire. Although he appeared to be talking directly to the camera, it quickly became evident that he was speaking to someone else – whoever was making this video. Langdon told them the video was filmed by Maximilian Kohler, the director of CERN. Only an hour ago Kohler had secretly recorded his meeting with the camerlengo by using a tiny camcorder covertly mounted under the arm of his wheelchair.

Mortati and the cardinals watched in bewilderment. Although the conversation was already in progress, Langdon did not bother to rewind. Apparently, whatever Langdon wanted the cardinals to see was coming up ...

'Leonardo Vetra kept diaries?' the camerlengo was saying. 'I suppose that is good news for CERN. If the diaries contain his processes for creating antimatter—'

'They don't,' Kohler said. 'You will be relieved to know those processes died with Leonardo. However, his diaries spoke of something else. *You.*'

The camerlengo looked troubled. 'I don't understand.'

'They described a meeting Leonardo had last month. With *you.*'

The camerlengo hesitated, then looked toward the door. 'Rocher should not have granted you access without consulting me. How did you get in here?'

'Rocher knows the truth. I called earlier and told him what you have done.'

'What *I* have done? Whatever story you told him, Rocher is a Swiss Guard and far too faithful to this church to believe a bitter scientist over his camerlengo.'

'Actually, he is too faithful *not* to believe. He is so faithful that despite the evidence that one of his loyal guards had betrayed the church, he refused to accept it. All day long he has been searching for another explanation.'

'So you gave him one.'

'The truth. Shocking as it was.'

'If Rocher believed you, he would have arrested me.'

'No. I wouldn't let him. I offered him my silence in exchange for this meeting.'

The camerlengo let out an odd laugh. 'You plan to *blackmail* the church with a story that no one will possibly believe?'

'I have no need of blackmail. I simply want to hear the truth from your lips. Leonardo Vetra was a friend.'

The camerlengo said nothing. He simply stared down at Kohler.

'Try this,' Kohler snapped. 'About a month ago, Leonardo Vetra contacted you requesting an urgent audience with the Pope – an audience you granted because the Pope was an admirer of Leonardo's work and because Leonardo said it was an emergency.'

The camerlengo turned to the fire. He said nothing.

'Leonardo came to the Vatican in great secrecy. He was betraying his daughter's confidence by coming here, a fact that troubled him deeply, but he felt he had no choice. His research had left him deeply conflicted and in need of spiritual guidance from the church. In a private meeting, he told you and the Pope that he had made a scientific discovery with profound religious implications. He had *proved* Genesis was physically possible, and that intense sources of energy – what Vetra called *God* – could duplicate the moment of Creation.'

Silence.

'The Pope was stunned,' Kohler continued. 'He wanted Leonardo to go public. His Holiness thought this discovery might begin to bridge the gap between science and religion – one of the Pope's life dreams. Then Leonardo explained to you the downside – the reason he required the church's guidance. It seemed his Creation experiment, exactly as your Bible predicts, produced everything in pairs. Opposites. Light *and* dark. Vetra found himself, in addition to creating matter, creating *antimatter*. Shall I go on?'

The camerlengo was silent. He bent down and stoked the coals.

'After Leonardo Vetra came here,' Kohler said, '*you* came to CERN to see his work. Leonardo's diaries said you made a personal trip to his lab.'

The camerlengo looked up.

Kohler went on. 'The Pope could not travel without attracting media attention, so he sent *you*. Leonardo gave you a secret tour of his lab. He showed you an antimatter annihilation – the Big Bang – the power of Creation. He also showed you a large specimen he kept locked away as proof that his new process could produce antimatter on a large scale. You were in awe. You returned to Vatican City to report to the Pope what you had witnessed.'

The camerlengo sighed. 'And what is it that troubles you? That I would respect Leonardo's confidentiality by pretending before the world tonight that I knew nothing of antimatter?'

'No! It troubles me that Leonardo Vetra practically *proved* the existence of your God, and you had him murdered!'

The camerlengo turned now, his face revealing nothing.

The only sound was the crackle of the fire.

Suddenly, the camera jiggled, and Kohler's arm appeared in the frame. He leaned forward, seeming to struggle with something affixed beneath his wheelchair. When he sat back down, he held a pistol out before him. The camera angle was a chilling one ... looking from behind ... down the length of the outstretched gun ... directly at the camerlengo.

Kohler said, 'Confess your sins, Father. Now.'

The camerlengo looked startled. 'You will never get out of here alive.'

'Death would be a welcome relief from the misery your faith has put me through since I was a boy.' Kohler held the gun with both hands now. 'I am giving you a choice. Confess your sins ... or die right now.'

The camerlengo glanced toward the door.

'Rocher is outside,' Kohler challenged. 'He too is prepared to kill you.'

'Rocher is a sworn protector of th—'

'Rocher let me in here. *Armed*. He is sickened by your lies. You have a single option. Confess to me. I have to hear it from your very lips.'

The camerlengo hesitated.

Kohler cocked his gun. 'Do you really doubt I will kill you?'

'No matter what I tell you,' the camerlengo said, 'a man like you will never understand.'

'Try me.'

The camerlengo stood still for a moment, a dominant silhouette in the dim light of the fire. When he spoke, his words echoed with a dignity more suited to the glorious recounting of altruism than that of a confession.

'Since the beginning of time,' the camerlengo said, 'this church has fought the enemies of God. Sometimes with words. Sometimes with swords. And we have always survived.'

The camerlengo radiated conviction.

'But the demons of the past,' he continued, 'were demons of fire and abomination . . . *they* were enemies we could fight – enemies who inspired *fear*. Yet Satan is shrewd. As time passed, he cast off his diabolical countenance for a new face . . . the face of pure reason. Transparent and insidious, but soulless all the same.' The camerlengo's voice flashed sudden anger – an almost maniacal transition. 'Tell me, Mr Kohler! How can the church condemn that which makes logical sense to our minds! How can we decry that which is now the very foundation of our society! Each time the church raises its voice in warning, *you* shout back, calling us ignorant. Paranoid. Controlling! And so your evil grows. Shrouded in a veil of self-righteous intellectualism. It spreads like a cancer. Sanctified by the miracles of its own technology. Deifying itself! Until we no longer suspect you are anything but pure goodness. Science has come to save us from our sickness, hunger, and pain! Behold science – the new God of endless miracles, omnipotent and benevolent! Ignore the weapons and the chaos. Forget the

575

fractured loneliness and endless peril. Science is here!' The camerlengo stepped toward the gun. 'But I have seen Satan's face lurking ... I have seen the peril ...'

'What are you talking about! Vetra's science practically *proved* the existence of your God! He was your ally!'

'Ally? Science and religion are not in this together! We do not seek the same God, you and I! Who is your God? One of protons, masses, and particle charges? How does your God *inspire*? How does your God reach into the hearts of man and remind him he is accountable to a greater power! Remind him that he is accountable to his fellow man! Vetra was misguided. His work was not religious, it was *sacrilegious*! Man cannot put God's Creation in a test tube and wave it around for the world to see! This does not glorify God, it *demeans* God!' The camerlengo was clawing at his body now, his voice manic.

'And so you had Leonardo Vetra killed!'

'For the church! For all mankind! The madness of it! Man is not ready to hold the power of Creation in his hands. God in a test tube? A droplet of liquid that can vaporize an entire city? He had to be stopped!' The camerlengo fell abruptly silent. He looked away, back toward the fire. He seemed to be contemplating his options.

Kohler's hands leveled the gun. 'You have confessed. You have no escape.'

The camerlengo laughed sadly. 'Don't you see. Confessing your sins *is* the escape.' He looked toward the door. 'When God is on your side, you have options a man like you could never comprehend.' With his words still hanging in the air, the camerlengo grabbed

576

the neck of his cassock and violently tore it open, revealing his bare chest.

Kohler jolted, obviously startled. 'What are you doing!'

The camerlengo did not reply. He stepped backward, toward the fireplace, and removed an object from the glowing embers.

'Stop!' Kohler demanded, his gun still leveled. 'What are you doing!'

When the camerlengo turned, he was holding a red-hot brand. The Illuminati Diamond. The man's eyes looked wild suddenly. 'I had intended to do this all alone.' His voice seethed with a feral intensity. 'But now . . . I see God meant for you to be here. *You* are my salvation.'

Before Kohler could react, the camerlengo closed his eyes, arched his back, and rammed the red hot brand into the center of his own chest. His flesh hissed. '*Mother Mary! Blessed Mother . . . Behold your son!*' He screamed out in agony.

Kohler lurched into the frame now . . . standing awkwardly on his feet, gun wavering wildly before him.

The camerlengo screamed louder, teetering in shock. He threw the brand at Kohler's feet. Then the priest collapsed on the floor, writhing in agony.

What happened next was a blur.

There was a great flurry onscreen as the Swiss Guard burst into the room. The soundtrack exploded with gunfire. Kohler clutched his chest, blown backward, bleeding, falling into his wheelchair.

'No!' Rocher called, trying to stop his guards from firing on Kohler.

The camerlengo, still writhing on the floor, rolled

and pointed frantically at Rocher. *'Illuminatus!'*

'You bastard,' Rocher yelled, running at him. 'You sanctimonious bas—'

Chartrand cut him down with three bullets. Rocher slid dead across the floor.

Then the guards ran to the wounded camerlengo, gathering around him. As they huddled, the video caught the face of a dazed Robert Langdon, kneeling beside the wheelchair, looking at the brand. Then, the entire frame began lurching wildly. Kohler had regained consciousness and was detaching the tiny camcorder from its holder under the arm of the wheelchair. Then he tried to hand the camcorder to Langdon.

'G-give . . .' Kohler gasped. 'G-give this to the m-media.'

Then the screen went blank.

130

The camerlengo began to feel the fog of wonder and adrenaline dissipating. As the Swiss Guard helped him down the Royal Staircase toward the Sistine Chapel, the camerlengo heard singing in St Peter's Square and he knew that mountains had been moved.

Grazie Dio.

He had prayed for strength, and God had given it to him. At moments when he had doubted, God had spoken. *Yours is a Holy mission*, God had said. *I will give you strength*. Even with God's strength, the camerlengo had felt fear, questioning the righteousness of his path.

If not you, God had challenged, *then WHO?*
If not now, then WHEN?
If not this way, then HOW?

Jesus, God reminded him, had saved them all . . . saved them from their own apathy. With two deeds, Jesus had opened their eyes. Horror and Hope. The crucifixion and the resurrection. He had changed the world.

But that was millennia ago. Time had eroded the miracle. People had forgotten. They had turned to false idols – techno-deities and miracles of the mind. *What about miracles of the heart!*

The camerlengo had often prayed to God to show him how to make the people believe again. But God had been silent. It was not until the camerlengo's moment of deepest darkness that God had come to him. *Oh, the horror of that night!*

The camerlengo could still remember lying on the floor in tattered nightclothes, clawing at his own flesh, trying to purge his soul of the pain brought on by a vile truth he had just learned. *It cannot be!* he had screamed. And yet he knew it was. The deception tore at him like the fires of hell. The bishop who had taken him in, the man who had been like a father to him, the clergyman whom the camerlengo had stood beside while he rose to the papacy . . . was a fraud. A common sinner. Lying to the world about a deed so traitorous at its core that the camerlengo doubted even God could forgive it. 'Your *vow!*' the camerlengo had screamed at the Pope. 'You broke your vow to God! *You,* of all men!'

The Pope had tried to explain himself, but the camerlengo could not listen. He had run out, stagger-ing blindly through the hallways, vomiting, tearing at his own skin, until he found himself bloody and alone, lying on the cold earthen floor before St Peter's tomb. *Mother Mary, what do I do?* It was in that moment of pain and betrayal, as the camerlengo lay devastated in the Necropolis, praying for God to take him from this faithless world, that God had come.

The voice in his head resounded like peals of thunder. *'Did you vow to serve your God?'*

'Yes!' the camerlengo cried out.

'Would you die for your God?'

'Yes! Take me now!'

'Would you die for your church?'

'Yes! Please deliver me!'

'But would you die for . . . mankind?'

It was in the silence that followed that the camerlengo felt himself falling into the abyss. He tumbled farther, faster, out of control. And yet he knew the answer. He had always known.

'Yes!' he shouted into the madness. 'I would die for man! Like your son, I would die for them!'

Hours later, the camerlengo still lay shivering on his floor. He saw his mother's face. *God has plans for you,* she was saying. The camerlengo plunged deeper into madness. It was then God had spoken again. This time with silence. But the camerlengo understood. *Restore their faith.*

If not me . . . then who?

If not now . . . then when?

As the guards unbolted the door of the Sistine Chapel, Camerlengo Carlo Ventresca felt the power moving in his veins . . . exactly as it had when he was a boy. God had chosen him. Long ago.

His will be done.

The camerlengo felt reborn. The Swiss Guard had bandaged his chest, bathed him, and dressed him in a fresh white linen robe. They had also given him an injection of morphine for the burn. The camerlengo wished they had not given him painkillers. *Jesus endured his pain for three days before ascending!* He could already feel the drug uprooting his senses . . . a dizzying undertow.

As he walked into the chapel, he was not at all surprised to see the cardinals staring at him in wonder. *They are in awe of God*, he reminded himself. *Not of me, but how God works THROUGH me*. As he moved up the center aisle, he saw bewilderment in every face. And yet, with each new face he passed, he sensed something *else* in their eyes. What was it? The camerlengo had tried to imagine how they would receive him tonight. Joyfully? Reverently? He tried to read their eyes and saw neither emotion.

It was then the camerlengo looked at the altar and saw Robert Langdon.

131

Camerlengo Carlo Ventresca stood in the aisle of the Sistine Chapel. The cardinals were all standing near the front of the church, turned, staring at him. Robert Langdon was on the altar beside a television that was on endless loop, playing a scene the camerlengo recognized but could not imagine how it had come to be. Vittoria Vetra stood beside him, her face drawn.

The camerlengo closed his eyes for a moment,

hoping the morphine was making him hallucinate and that when he opened them the scene might be different. But it was not.

They knew.

Oddly, he felt no fear. *Show me the way, Father. Give me the words that I can make them see Your vision.*

But the camerlengo heard no reply.

Father, We have come too far together to fail now.

Silence.

They do not understand what We have done.

The camerlengo did not know whose voice he heard in his own mind, but the message was stark.

And the truth shall set you free . . .

And so it was that Camerlengo Carlo Ventresca held his head high as he walked toward the front of the Sistine Chapel. As he moved toward the cardinals, not even the diffused light of the candles could soften the eyes boring into him. *Explain yourself*, the faces said. *Make sense of this madness. Tell us our fears are wrong!*

Truth, the camerlengo told himself. *Only truth*. There were too many secrets in these walls . . . one so dark it had driven him to madness. *But from the madness had come the light.*

'If you could give your own soul to save millions,' the camerlengo said, as he moved down the aisle, '*would* you?'

The faces in the chapel simply stared. No one moved. No one spoke. Beyond the walls, the joyous strains of song could be heard in the square.

The camerlengo walked toward them. 'Which is the greater sin? Killing one's enemy? Or standing idle while your true love is strangled?' *They are singing in St Peter's Square!* The camerlengo stopped for a moment and gazed up at the ceiling of the Sistine. Michelangelo's God was staring down from the darkened vault . . . and He seemed pleased.

'I could no longer stand by,' the camerlengo said. Still, as he drew nearer, he saw no flicker of understanding in anyone's eyes. Didn't they see the radiant simplicity of his deeds? Didn't they see the utter necessity!

It had been so pure.

The Illuminati. Science and Satan as one.

Resurrect the ancient fear. Then crush it.

Horror and Hope. Make them believe again.

Tonight, the power of the Illuminati had been unleashed anew . . . and with glorious consequence. The apathy had evaporated. The fear had shot out across the world like a bolt of lightning, uniting the people. And then God's majesty had vanquished the darkness.

I could not stand idly by!

The inspiration had been God's own – appearing like a beacon in the camerlengo's night of agony. *Oh, this faithless world! Someone must deliver them. You. If not you, who? You have been saved for a reason. Show them the old demons. Remind them of their fear. Apathy is death. Without darkness, there is no light. Without evil, there is no good. Make them choose. Dark or light. Where is the fear? Where are the heroes? If not now, when?*

The camerlengo walked up the center aisle directly toward the crowd of standing cardinals. He felt like Moses as the sea of red sashes and caps parted before him, allowing him to pass. On the altar, Robert Langdon switched off the television, took Vittoria's hand, and relinquished the altar. The fact that Robert Langdon had survived, the camerlengo knew, could only have been God's will. God had saved Robert Langdon. The camerlengo wondered why.

The voice that broke the silence was the voice of the only woman in the Sistine Chapel. 'You *killed* my father?' she said, stepping forward.

When the camerlengo turned to Vittoria Vetra, the look on her face was one he could not quite understand – pain yes, but *anger*? Certainly she must understand. Her father's genius was deadly. He had to be stopped. For the good of Mankind.

'He was doing God's work,' Vittoria said.

'God's work is not done in a lab. It is done in the heart.'

'My father's heart was pure! And his research proved—'

'His research proved yet again that man's mind is progressing faster than his soul!' The camerlengo's voice was sharper than he had expected. He lowered his voice. 'If a man as spiritual as your father could create a weapon like the one we saw tonight, imagine what an ordinary man will do with his technology.'

'A man like *you*?'

The camerlengo took a deep breath. Did she not see? Man's morality was not advancing as fast as man's science. Mankind was not spiritually evolved enough for the powers he possessed. *We have never created a weapon we have not used!* And yet he knew that antimatter was nothing – another weapon in man's already burgeoning arsenal. Man could already destroy. Man learned to kill long ago. *And his mother's blood rained down.* Leonardo Vetra's genius was dangerous for another reason.

'For centuries,' the camerlengo said, 'the church has stood by while science picked away at religion bit by bit. Debunking miracles. Training the mind to overcome the heart. Condemning religion as the opiate of the masses. They denounce God as a hallucination – a delusional crutch for those too weak to accept that life is meaningless. I could not stand by while science presumed to harness the power of God himself! *Proof*, you say? Yes, proof of science's ignorance! What is wrong with the admission that something exists beyond our understanding? The day science substantiates God in a lab is the day people stop needing faith!'

'You mean the day they stop needing the *church*,' Vittoria challenged, moving toward him. 'Doubt is your last shred of control. It is *doubt* that brings souls to you. Our need to know that life has meaning. Man's insecurity and need for an enlightened soul assuring him everything is part of a master plan. But the church is not the only enlightened soul on the planet! We all seek God in different ways. What are you afraid of? That God will show himself somewhere *other* than inside these walls? That people will find him in their own lives and leave your antiquated rituals behind? Religions evolve! The mind finds answers, the heart grapples with new truths. My father was on *your* quest! A parallel path! Why couldn't you see that? God is not some omnipotent authority looking down from above, threatening to throw us into a pit of fire if we disobey. God is the energy that flows through the synapses of our nervous system and the chambers of our hearts! God is in all things!'

'*Except* science,' the camerlengo fired back, his eyes showing only pity. 'Science, by definition, is soulless. Divorced from the heart. Intellectual miracles like antimatter arrive in this world with no ethical instructions attached. This in itself is perilous! But when science heralds its Godless pursuits as the enlightened path? Promising answers to questions whose beauty is that they have no answers?' He shook his head. 'No.'

There was a moment of silence. The camerlengo felt suddenly tired as he returned Vittoria's unbending stare. This was not how it was supposed to be. *Is this God's final test?*

It was Mortati who broke the spell. 'The *preferiti*,' he said in a horrified whisper. 'Baggia and the others. Please tell me you did not . . .'

The camerlengo turned to him, surprised by the pain in his voice. Certainly *Mortati* could understand. Headlines carried science's miracles every day. How long had it been for religion? Centuries? Religion needed a miracle! Something to awaken a sleeping world. Bring them back to the path of righteousness. Restore faith. The *preferiti* were not leaders anyway, they were transformers – liberals prepared to embrace the new world and abandon the old ways! This was the only way. A new leader. Young. Powerful. Vibrant. Miraculous. The *preferiti* served the church far more effectively in death than they ever could alive. Horror and Hope. *Offer four souls to save millions.* The world would remember them forever as martyrs. The church would raise glorious tribute to their names. *How many thousands have died for the glory of God? They are only four.*

'The *preferiti*,' Mortati repeated.

'I shared their pain,' the camerlengo defended, motioning to his chest. 'And I too would die for God, but my work is only just begun. They are singing in St Peter's Square!'

The camerlengo saw the horror in Mortati's eyes and again felt confused. Was it the morphine? Mortati was looking at him as if the camerlengo himself had killed these men with his bare hands. *I would do even that for God*, the camerlengo thought, and yet he had not. The deeds had been carried out by the Hassassin – a heathen soul tricked into thinking he was doing the work of the Illuminati. *I am Janus*, the camerlengo had told him. *I will prove my power.* And he had. The Hassassin's hatred had made him God's pawn.

'Listen to the singing,' the camerlengo said, smiling, his own heart rejoicing. 'Nothing unites hearts like the presence of evil. Burn a church and the community rises up, holding hands, singing hymns of defiance as they rebuild. Look how they flock tonight. Fear has brought them home. Forge modern demons for modern man. Apathy is dead. Show them the face of evil – Satanists lurking among us – running our governments, our banks, our schools, threatening to obliterate the very House of God with their misguided science. Depravity runs deep. Man must be vigilant. Seek the goodness. *Become* the goodness!'

In the silence, the camerlengo hoped they now understood. The Illuminati had not resurfaced. The Illuminati were long deceased. Only their myth was alive. The camerlengo had resurrected the Illuminati as a reminder. Those who knew the Illuminati history relived their evil. Those who did not, had learned of it and were amazed how blind they had been. The ancient demons had been resurrected to awaken an indifferent world.

'But . . . the brands?' Mortati's voice was stiff with outrage.

The camerlengo did not answer. Mortati had no way of knowing, but the brands had been confiscated by the Vatican over a century ago. They had been locked away, forgotten and dust covered, in the Papal Vault – the Pope's private reliquary, deep within his Borgia apartments. The Papal Vault contained those items the church deemed too dangerous for anyone's eyes except the Pope's.

Why did they hide that which inspired fear? Fear brought people to God!

The vault's key was passed down from Pope to Pope. Camerlengo Carlo Ventresca had purloined the key and ventured inside; the myth of what the vault contained was bewitching – including the original manuscript for the fourteen unpublished books of the Bible known as the *Apocrypha* and the location of the tomb of the Virgin Mary. In addition to these, the camerlengo had found the Illuminati Collection – all the secrets the church had uncovered after banishing the group from Rome ... their contemptible Path of Illumination ... the cunning deceit of the Vatican's head artist, Bernini ... Europe's top scientists mocking religion as they secretly assembled in the Vatican's own Castle St Angelo. The collection included a pentagon box containing iron brands, one of them the mythical Illuminati Diamond. This was a part of Vatican history the ancients thought best forgotten. The camerlengo, however, had disagreed.

'But the *antimatter* ...' Vittoria demanded. 'You risked destroying the Vatican!'

'There is no risk when God is at your side,' the camerlengo said. 'This cause was His.'

'You're insane!' she seethed.

'Millions were saved.'

'People were *killed*!'

'Souls were saved.'

'Tell that to my father and Max Kohler!'

'CERN's arrogance needed to be revealed. A droplet of liquid that can vaporize a half mile? And you call me mad?' The camerlengo felt a rage rising in him. Did they think his was a simple charge? 'Those who *believe* undergo great tests for God! God asked Abraham to sacrifice his child! God commanded Jesus to endure crucifixion! And so we hang the symbol of the crucifix before our eyes – bloody painful, agonizing – to remind us of evil's power! To keep our hearts vigilant! The scars on Jesus' body are a living reminder of the powers of darkness! My scars are a living reminder! Evil lives, but the power of God will overcome!'

His shouts echoed off the back wall of the Sistine Chapel and then a profound silence fell. Time seemed to stop. Michelangelo's *Last Judgment* rose ominously behind him . . . Jesus casting sinners into hell. Tears brimmed in Mortati's eyes.

'What have you done, Carlo?' Mortati asked in a whisper. He closed his eyes, and a tear rolled. 'His *Holiness*?'

A collective sigh of pain went up, as if everyone in the room had forgotten until that very moment. The Pope. Poisoned.

'A vile liar,' the camerlengo said.

Mortati looked shattered. 'What do you mean? He was honest! He . . . loved you.'

'And I him.' *Oh, how I loved him! But the deceit! The broken vows to God!*

The camerlengo knew they did not understand right now, but they *would*. When he told them, they would see! His Holiness was the most nefarious deceiver the church had ever seen. The camerlengo still remembered that terrible night. He had returned from his trip to CERN with news of Vetra's *Genesis* and

589

of antimatter's horrific power. The camerlengo was certain the Pope would see the perils, but the Holy Father saw only hope in Vetra's breakthrough. He even suggested the Vatican *fund* Vetra's work as a gesture of goodwill toward spiritually based scientific research.

Madness! The church investing in research that threatened to make the church obsolete? Work that spawned weapons of mass destruction? The bomb that had killed his mother . . .

'But . . . you can't!' the camerlengo had exclaimed.

'I owe a deep debt to science,' the Pope had replied. 'Something I have hidden my entire life. Science gave me a gift when I was a young man. A gift I have never forgotten.'

'I don't understand. What does science have to offer a man of *God*?'

'It is complicated,' the Pope had said. 'I will need time to make you understand. But first, there is a simple fact about me that you must know. I have kept it hidden all these years. I believe it is time I told you.'

Then the Pope had told him the astonishing truth.

132

The camerlengo lay curled in a ball on the dirt floor in front of St Peter's tomb. The Necropolis was cold, but it helped clot the blood flowing from the wounds he had torn at his own flesh. His Holiness would not find him here. Nobody would find him here . . .

'It is complicated,' the Pope's voice echoed in his

mind. 'I will need time to make you understand . . .'

But the camerlengo knew no amount of time could make him understand.

Liar! I believed in you! GOD believed in you!

With a single sentence, the Pope had brought the camerlengo's world crashing down around him. Everything the camerlengo had ever believed about his mentor was shattered before his eyes. The truth drilled into the camerlengo's heart with such force that he staggered backward out of the Pope's office and vomited in the hallway.

'Wait!' the Pope had cried, chasing after him. 'Please let me explain!'

But the camerlengo ran off. *How could His Holiness expect him to endure any more?* Oh, the wretched depravity of it! What if someone else found out? Imagine the desecration to the church! Did the Pope's holy vows mean nothing?

The madness came quickly, screaming in his ears, until he awoke before St Peter's tomb. It was then that God came to him with an awesome fierceness.

YOURS IS A VENGEFUL GOD!

Together, they made their plans. Together they would protect the church. Together they would restore faith to this faithless world. Evil was everywhere. And yet the world had become immune! Together they would unveil the darkness for the world to see . . . and God would overcome! Horror and Hope. Then the world would believe!

God's first test had been less horrible than the camerlengo imagined. Sneaking into the Papal bed chambers . . . filling his syringe . . . covering the deceiver's mouth as his body spasmed into death. In the moonlight, the camerlengo could see in the

591

Pope's wild eyes there was something he wanted to say.

But it was too late.

The Pope had said enough.

133

'The Pope fathered a child.'

Inside the Sistine Chapel, the camerlengo stood unwavering as he spoke. Five solitary words of astonishing disclosure. The entire assembly seemed to recoil in unison. The cardinals' accusing miens evaporated into aghast stares, as if every soul in the room were praying the camerlengo was wrong.

The Pope fathered a child.

Langdon felt the shock wave hit him too. Vittoria's hand, tight in his, jolted, while Langdon's mind, already numb with unanswered questions, wrestled to find a center of gravity.

The camerlengo's utterance seemed like it would hang forever in the air above them. Even in the camerlengo's frenzied eyes, Langdon could see pure conviction. Langdon wanted to disengage, tell himself he was lost in some grotesque nightmare, soon to wake up in a world that made sense.

'This must be a lie!' one of the cardinals yelled.

'I will not believe it!' another protested. 'His Holiness was as devout a man as ever lived!'

It was Mortati who spoke next, his voice thin with devastation. 'My friends. What the camerlengo says is true.' Every cardinal in the chapel spun as though

Mortati had just shouted an obscenity. 'The Pope indeed fathered a child.'

The cardinals blanched with dread.

The camerlengo looked stunned. 'You *knew*? But ... how could you possibly know this?'

Mortati sighed. 'When His Holiness was elected ... *I* was the Devil's Advocate.'

There was a communal gasp.

Langdon understood. This meant the information was probably true. The infamous 'Devil's Advocate' was *the* authority when it came to scandalous information inside the Vatican. Skeletons in a Pope's closet were dangerous, and prior to elections, secret inquiries into a candidate's background were carried out by a lone cardinal who served as the 'Devil's Advocate' – that individual responsible for unearthing reasons why the eligible cardinals should *not* become Pope. The Devil's Advocate was appointed in advance by the reigning Pope in preparation for his own death. The Devil's Advocate was never supposed to reveal his identity. *Ever*.

'*I* was the Devil's Advocate,' Mortati repeated. 'That is how I found out.'

Mouths dropped. Apparently tonight was a night when all the rules were going out the window.

The camerlengo felt his heart filling with rage. 'And you ... told *no one*?'

'I confronted His Holiness,' Mortati said. 'And he confessed. He explained the entire story and asked only that I let my heart guide my decision as to whether or not to reveal his secret.'

'And your heart told you to *bury* the information?'

'He was the runaway favorite for the papacy. People

loved him. The scandal would have hurt the church deeply.'

'But he fathered a *child*! He broke his sacred vow of celibacy!' The camerlengo was screaming now. He could hear his mother's voice. *A promise to God is the most important promise of all. Never break a promise to God.* 'The Pope broke his vow!'

Mortati looked delirious with angst. 'Carlo, his love ... was *chaste*. He had broken no vow. He didn't explain it to you?'

'Explain what?' The camerlengo remembered running out of the Pope's office while the Pope was calling to him. *Let me explain!*

Slowly, sadly, Mortati let the tale unfold. Many years ago, the Pope, when he was still just a priest, had fallen in love with a young nun. Both of them had taken vows of celibacy and never even considered breaking their covenant with God. Still, as they fell deeper in love, although they could resist the temptations of the flesh, they both found themselves longing for something they never expected – to participate in God's ultimate miracle of creation – a child. *Their* child. The yearning, especially in her, became overwhelming. Still, God came first. A year later, when the frustration had reached almost unbearable proportions, she came to him in a whirl of excitement. She had just read an article about a new miracle of science – a process by which two people, without ever having sexual relations, could have a child. She sensed this was a sign from God. The priest could see the happiness in her eyes and agreed. A year later she had a child through the miracle of artificial insemination ...

'This cannot ... be true,' the camerlengo said, panicked, hoping it was the morphine washing over his senses. Certainly he was hearing things.

Mortati now had tears in his eyes. 'Carlo, this is why His Holiness has always had an affection for the sciences. He felt he owed a debt to science. Science let him experience the joys of fatherhood without breaking his vow of celibacy. His Holiness told me he had no regrets except one – that his advancing stature in the church prohibited him from being with the woman he loved and seeing his infant grow up.'

Camerlengo Carlo Ventresca felt the madness setting in again. He wanted to claw at his flesh. *How could I have known?*

'The Pope committed no sin, Carlo. He was chaste.'

'But . . .' The camerlengo searched his anguished mind for any kind of rationale. 'Think of the jeopardy . . . of his deeds.' His voice felt weak. 'What if this whore of his came forward? Or, heaven forbid, his *child*? Imagine the shame the church would endure.'

Mortati's voice was tremulous. 'The child has *already* come forward.'

Everything stopped.

'Carlo . . . ?' Mortati crumbled. 'His Holiness's child . . . is *you*.'

At that moment, the camerlengo could feel the fire of faith dim in his heart. He stood trembling on the altar, framed by Michelangelo's towering *Last Judgment*. He knew he had just glimpsed hell itself. He opened his mouth to speak, but his lips wavered, soundless.

'Don't you see?' Mortati choked. '*That* is why His Holiness came to you in the hospital in Palermo when you were a boy. *That* is why he took you in and raised you. The nun he loved was Maria . . . your mother. She left the nunnery to raise you, but she never abandoned her strict devotion to God. When the Pope heard she had died in an explosion and that you, his son, had miraculously survived . . . he swore to God he would never leave you alone again. Carlo, your parents were both virgins. They kept their vows to God. And still they found a way to bring you into the world. You were their miraculous child.'

The camerlengo covered his ears, trying to block out the words. He stood paralyzed on the altar. Then, with his world yanked from beneath him, he fell violently to his knees and let out a wail of anguish.

Seconds. Minutes. Hours.

Time seemed to have lost all meaning inside the four walls of the chapel. Vittoria felt herself slowly breaking free of the paralysis that seemed to have gripped them all. She let go of Langdon's hand and began moving through the crowd of cardinals. The chapel door seemed miles away and she felt like she was moving underwater . . . slow motion.

As she maneuvered through the robes, her motion seemed to pull others from their trance. Some of the cardinals began to pray. Others wept. Some turned to watch her go, their blank expressions turning slowly to a foreboding cognition as she moved toward the door. She had almost reached the back of the crowd when a hand caught her arm. The touch was frail but resolute. She turned, face to face with a wizened cardinal. His visage was clouded by fear.

'No,' the man whispered. 'You cannot.'

Vittoria stared, incredulous.

Another cardinal was at her side now. 'We must think before we act.'

And another. 'The pain this could cause . . .'

Vittoria was surrounded. She looked at them all, stunned. 'But these deeds here today, tonight . . . certainly the world should know the truth.'

'My heart agrees,' the wizened cardinal said, still holding her arm, 'and yet it is a path from which there is no return. We must consider the shattered hopes. The cynicism. How could the people *ever* trust again?'

Suddenly, more cardinals seemed to be blocking her way. There was a wall of black robes before her. 'Listen to the people in the square,' one said. 'What will this do to their hearts? We must exercise prudence.'

'We need time to think and pray,' another said. 'We must act with foresight. The repercussions of this . . .'

'He killed my father!' Vittoria said. 'He killed his *own* father!'

'I'm certain he will pay for his sins,' the cardinal holding her arm said sadly.

Vittoria was certain too, and she intended to *ensure* he paid. She tried to push toward the door again, but the cardinals huddled closer, their faces frightened.

'What are you going to do?' she exclaimed. '*Kill me?*'

The old men blanched, and Vittoria immediately regretted her words. She could see these men were gentle souls. They had seen enough violence tonight. They meant no threat. They were simply trapped. Scared. Trying to get their bearings.

'I want . . .' the wizened cardinal said, '. . . to do what is right.'

'Then you will let her out,' a deep voice declared behind her. The words were calm but absolute. Robert Langdon arrived at her side, and she felt his hand take hers. 'Ms Vetra and I are leaving this chapel. Right now.'

Faltering, hesitant, the cardinals began to step aside.

'Wait!' It was Mortati. He moved toward them now, down the center aisle, leaving the camerlengo alone and defeated on the altar. Mortati looked older all of a sudden, wearied beyond his years. His motion was burdened with shame. He arrived, putting a hand on Langdon's shoulder and one on Vittoria's as well. Vittoria felt sincerity in his touch. The man's eyes were more tearful now.

'*Of course* you are free to go,' Mortati said. 'Of course.' The man paused, his grief almost tangible. 'I ask only this . . .' He stared down at his feet a long moment then back up at Vittoria and Langdon. 'Let *me* do it. I will go into the square right now and find a way. I will tell them. I don't know how . . . but I will find a way. The church's confession should come from within. Our failures should be our own to expose.'

Mortati turned sadly back toward the altar. 'Carlo, you have brought this church to a disastrous juncture.' He paused, looking around. The altar was bare.

There was a rustle of cloth down the side aisle, and the door clicked shut.

The camerlengo was gone.

134

Camerlengo Ventresca's white robe billowed as he moved down the hallway away from the Sistine Chapel. The Swiss Guards had seemed perplexed when he emerged all alone from the chapel and told them he needed a moment of solitude. But they had obeyed, letting him go.

Now as he rounded the corner and left their sight, the camerlengo felt a maelstrom of emotions like nothing he thought possible in human experience. He had poisoned the man he called 'Holy Father,' the man who addressed him as 'my son.' The camerlengo had always believed the words 'father' and 'son' were religious tradition, but now he knew the diabolical truth – the words had been *literal*.

Like that fateful night weeks ago, the camerlengo now felt himself reeling madly through the darkness.

It was raining the morning the Vatican staff banged on the camerlengo's door, awakening him from a fitful sleep. The Pope, they said, was not answering his door or his phone. The clergy were frightened. The camerlengo was the only one who could enter the Pope's chambers unannounced.

The camerlengo entered alone to find the Pope, as he was the night before, twisted and dead in his bed. His Holiness's face looked like that of Satan. His tongue black like death. The Devil himself had been sleeping in the Pope's bed.

The camerlengo felt no remorse. God had spoken.

Nobody would see the treachery . . . not yet. That would come later.

He announced the terrible news – His Holiness was dead of a stroke. Then the camerlengo prepared for conclave.

Mother Maria's voice was whispering in his ear. 'Never break a promise to God.'

'I hear you, Mother,' he replied. 'It is a faithless

world. They need to be brought back to the path of righteousness. Horror and Hope. It is the only way.'

'Yes,' she said. 'If not you ... then who? Who will lead the church out of darkness?'

Certainly not one of the *preferiti*. They were old ... walking death ... liberals who would follow the Pope, endorsing science in his memory, seeking modern followers by abandoning the ancient ways. Old men desperately behind the times, pathetically pretending they were not. They would fail, of course. The church's strength was its tradition, not its transience. The whole world was transitory. The church did not need to change, it simply needed to remind the world it was relevant! Evil lives! God will overcome!

The church needed a leader. Old men do not inspire! Jesus inspired! Young, vibrant, powerful ... *MIRACULOUS*.

'Enjoy your tea,' the camerlengo told the four *preferiti*, leaving them in the Pope's private library before conclave. 'Your guide will be here soon.'

The *preferiti* thanked him, all abuzz that they had been offered a chance to enter the famed Passetto. Most uncommon! The camerlengo, before leaving them, had unlocked the door to the Passetto, and exactly on schedule, the door had opened, and a foreign-looking priest with a torch had ushered the excited *preferiti* in.

The men had never come out.

They will be the Horror. I will be the Hope.

No ... I am the horror.

The camerlengo staggered now through the darkness

of St Peter's Basilica. Somehow, through the insanity and guilt, through the images of his father, through the pain and revelation, even through the pull of the morphine . . . he had found a brilliant clarity. A sense of destiny. *I know my purpose*, he thought, awed by the lucidity of it.

From the beginning, nothing tonight had gone exactly as he had planned. Unforeseen obstacles had presented themselves, but the camerlengo had adapted, making bold adjustments. Still, he had never imagined tonight would end this way, and yet now he saw the preordained majesty of it.

It could end no other way.

Oh, what terror he had felt in the Sistine Chapel, wondering if God had forsaken him! *Oh, what deeds He had ordained!* He had fallen to his knees, awash with doubt, his ears straining for the voice of God but hearing only silence. He had begged for a sign. Guidance. Direction. Was this God's will? The church destroyed by scandal and abomination? No! *God* was the one who had willed the camerlengo to act! *Hadn't He?*

Then he had seen it. Sitting on the altar. A sign. Divine communication – something ordinary seen in an extraordinary light. The crucifix. Humble, wooden. Jesus on the cross. In that moment, it had all come clear . . the camerlengo was not alone. He would never be alone.

This was His will . . . His meaning.

God had always asked great sacrifice of those he loved most. Why had the camerlengo been so slow to understand? Was he too fearful? Too humble? It made no difference. God had found a way. The camerlengo even understood now why Robert Langdon had been saved. It was to bring the truth. To compel this ending.

This was the sole path to the church's salvation!

The camerlengo felt like he was floating as he descended into the Niche of the Palliums. The surge of morphine seemed relentless now, but he knew God was guiding him.

In the distance, he could hear the cardinals clamoring in confusion as they poured from the chapel, yelling commands to the Swiss Guard.

But they would never find him. Not in time.

The camerlengo felt himself drawn ... faster ... descending the stairs into the sunken area where the ninety-nine oil lamps shone brightly. God was returning him to Holy Ground. The camerlengo moved toward the grate covering the hole that led down to the Necropolis. The Necropolis is where this night would end. In the sacred darkness below. He lifted an oil lamp, preparing to descend.

But as he moved across the Niche, the camerlengo paused. Something about this felt wrong. How did this serve God? A solitary and silent end? *Jesus* had suffered before the eyes of the entire world. Surely this could not be God's will! The camerlengo listened for the voice of his God, but heard only the blurring buzz of drugs.

'Carlo.' It was his mother. *'God has plans for you.'*

Bewildered, the camerlengo kept moving.

Then, without warning, God arrived.

The camerlengo stopped short, staring. The light of the ninety-nine oil lanterns had thrown the camerlengo's shadow on the marble wall beside him. Giant and fearful. A hazy form surrounded by golden light. With flames flickering all around him, the camerlengo looked like an angel ascending to heaven. He stood a moment, raising his arms to his sides, watching his own image. Then he turned, looking back up the stairs.

God's meaning was clear.

Three minutes had passed in the chaotic hallways outside the Sistine Chapel, and still nobody could locate the camerlengo. It was as if the man had been swallowed up by the night. Mortati was about to demand a full-scale search of Vatican City when a roar of jubilation erupted outside in St Peter's Square. The spontaneous celebration of the crowd was tumultuous. The cardinals all exchanged startled looks.

Mortati closed his eyes. 'God help us.'

For the second time that evening, the College of Cardinals flooded onto St Peter's Square. Langdon and Vittoria were swept up in the jostling crowd of cardinals, and they too emerged into the night air. The media lights and cameras were all pivoted toward the basilica. And there, having just stepped onto the sacred Papal Balcony located in the exact center of the towering façade, Camerlengo Carlo Ventresca stood with his arms raised to the heavens. Even far away, he looked like purity incarnate. A figurine. Dressed in white. Flooded with light.

The energy in the square seemed to grow like a cresting wave, and all at once the Swiss Guard barriers gave way. The masses streamed toward the basilica in a euphoric torrent of humanity. The onslaught rushed forward – people crying, singing, media cameras flashing. Pandemonium. As the people flooded in around the front of the basilica, the chaos intensified, until it seemed nothing could stop it.

And then something did.

High above, the camerlengo made the smallest of gestures. He folded his hands before him. Then he bowed his head in silent prayer. One by one, then dozens by dozens, then hundreds by hundreds, the people bowed their heads along with him.

The square fell silent . . . as if a spell had been cast.

In his mind, swirling and distant now, the camerlengo's prayers were a torrent of hopes and sorrows . . . *forgive me, Father . . . Mother . . . full of grace . . . you are the church . . . may you understand this sacrifice of your only begotten son.*

Oh, my Jesus . . . save us from the fires of hell . . . take all souls to heaven, especially those most in need of thy mercy . . .

The camerlengo did not open his eyes to see the throngs below him, the television cameras, the whole world watching. He could feel it in his soul. Even in his anguish, the unity of the moment was intoxicating. It was as if a connective web had shot out in all directions around the globe. In front of televisions, at home, and in cars, the world prayed as one. Like synapses of a giant heart all firing in tandem, the people reached for God, in dozens of languages, in hundreds of countries. The words they whispered were newborn and yet as familiar to them as their own voices . . . ancient truths . . . imprinted on the soul.

The consonance felt eternal.

As the silence lifted, the joyous strains of singing began to rise again.

He knew the moment had come.

Most Holy Trinity, I offer Thee the most precious Body, Blood, Soul . . . in reparation for the outrages, sacrileges, and indifferences . . .

The camerlengo already felt the physical pain setting in. It was spreading across his skin like a plague, making him want to claw at his flesh like he had weeks ago when God had first come to him. *Do not forget what pain Jesus endured.* He could taste the fumes now in his throat. Not even the morphine could dull the bite.

My work here is done.

The Horror was his. The Hope was theirs.

In the Niche of the Palliums, the camerlengo had followed God's will and anointed his body. His hair. His face. His linen robe. His flesh. He was soaking now with the sacred, vitreous oils from the lamps. They smelled sweet like his mother, but they burned. *His* would be a merciful ascension. Miraculous and swift. And he would leave behind not scandal . . . but a new strength and wonder.

He slipped his hand into the pocket of his robe and fingered the small, golden lighter he had brought with him from the Pallium *incendiario*.

He whispered a verse from Judgments. *And when the flame went up toward heaven, the angel of the Lord ascended in the flame.*

He positioned his thumb.

They were singing in St Peter's Square . . .

The vision the world witnessed no one would ever forget.

High above on the balcony, like a soul tearing free of its corporeal restrains, a luminous pyre of flame erupted from the camerlengo's center. The fire shot upward, engulfing his entire body instantly. He did not scream. He raised his arms over his head and looked toward heaven. The conflagration roared around him, entirely shrouding his body in a column of light. It raged for what seemed like an eternity, the whole world bearing witness. The light flared brighter and brighter. Then, gradually, the flames dissipated. The camerlengo was gone. Whether he had collapsed behind the balustrade or evaporated into thin air was impossible to tell. All that was left was a cloud of smoke spiraling skyward over Vatican City.

135

Dawn came late to Rome.

An early rainstorm had washed the crowds from St Peter's Square. The media stayed on, huddling under umbrellas and in vans, commentating on the evening's events. Across the world, churches overflowed. It was a time of reflection and discussion ... in all religions. Questions abounded, and yet the answers seemed only to bring deeper questions. Thus far, the Vatican had remained silent, issuing no statement whatsoever.

Deep in the Vatican Grottoes, Cardinal Mortati knelt alone before the open sarcophagus. He reached in and closed the old man's blackened mouth. His Holiness looked peaceful now. In quiet repose for eternity.

At Mortati's feet was a golden urn, heavy with ashes. Mortati had gathered the ashes himself and brought them here. 'A chance for forgiveness,' he said to His Holiness; laying the urn inside the sarcophagus at the Pope's side. 'No love is greater than that of a father for His son.' Mortati tucked the urn out of sight beneath the papal robes. He knew this sacred grotto was reserved exclusively for the relics of Popes, but somehow Mortati sensed this was appropriate.

'Signore?' someone said, entering the grottoes. It was Lieutenant Chartrand. He was accompanied by three Swiss Guards. 'They are ready for you in conclave.'

Mortati nodded. 'In a moment.' He gazed one last time into the sarcophagus before him, and then stood up. He turned to the guards. 'It is time for His Holiness to have the peace he has earned.'

The guards came forward and with enormous effort slid the lid of the Pope's sarcophagus back into place. It thundered shut with finality.

Mortati was alone as he crossed the Borgia Courtyard toward the Sistine Chapel. A damp breeze tossed his robe. A fellow cardinal emerged from the Apostolic Palace and strode beside him.

'May I have the honor of escorting you to conclave, signore?'

'The honor is mine.'

'Signore,' the cardinal said, looking troubled. 'The college owes you an apology for last night. We were blinded by—'

'Please,' Mortati replied. 'Our minds sometimes see what our hearts wish were true.'

The cardinal was silent a long time. Finally he spoke. 'Have you been told? You are no longer our Great Elector.'

Mortati smiled. 'Yes. I thank God for small blessings.'

'The college insisted you be eligible.'

'It seems charity is not dead in the church.'

'You are a wise man. You would lead us well.'

'I am an old man. I would lead you briefly.'

They both laughed.

As they reached the end of the Borgia Courtyard, the cardinal hesitated. He turned to Mortati with a troubled mystification, as if the precarious awe of the night before had slipped back into his heart.

'Were you aware,' the cardinal whispered, 'that we found no remains on the balcony?'

Mortati smiled. 'Perhaps the rain washed them away.'

The man looked to the stormy heavens. 'Yes, perhaps . . .'

136

The midmorning sky still hung heavy with clouds as the Sistine Chapel's chimney gave up its first faint puffs of white smoke. The pearly wisps curled upward toward the firmament and slowly dissipated.

Far below, in St Peter's Square, reporter Gunther Glick watched in reflective silence. The final chapter . . .

Chinita Macri approached him from behind and hoisted her camera onto her shoulder. 'It's time,' she said.

Glick nodded dolefully. He turned toward her, smoothed his hair, and took a deep breath. *My last transmission*, he thought. A small crowd had gathered around them to watch.

'Live in sixty seconds,' Macri announced.

Glick glanced over his shoulder at the roof of the Sistine Chapel behind him. 'Can you get the smoke?'

Macri patiently nodded. 'I know how to frame a shot, Gunther.'

Glick felt dumb. Of course she did. Macri's performance behind the camera last night had probably won her the Pulitzer. *His* performance, on the other hand . . . he didn't want to think about it. He was sure the BBC would let him go; no doubt they would have legal troubles from numerous powerful entities . . . CERN and George Bush among them.

'You look good,' Chinita patronized, looking out from behind her camera now with a hint of concern. 'I wonder if I might offer you . . .' She hesitated, holding her tongue.

'Some *advice*?'

Macri sighed. 'I was only going to say that there's no need to go out with a bang.'

'I know,' he said. 'You want a straight wrap.'

'The straightest in history. I'm trusting you.'

Glick smiled. *A straight wrap? Is she crazy?* A story like last night's deserved so much more. A twist. A final bombshell. An unforeseen revelation of shocking truth.

Fortunately, Glick had just the ticket waiting in the wings . . .

'You're on in . . . five . . . four . . . three . . .'

As Chinita Macri looked through her camera, she sensed a sly glint in Glick's eye. *I was insane to let him do this*, she thought. *What was I thinking?*

But the moment for second thoughts had passed. They were on.

'Live from Vatican City' Glick announced on cue, 'this is Gunther Glick reporting.' He gave the camera a solemn stare as the white smoke rose behind him from the Sistine Chapel. 'Ladies and gentlemen, it is now *official*. Cardinal Saverio Mortati, a seventy-nine-year-old progressive, has just been elected the next Pope of Vatican City. Although an unlikely candidate, Mortati was chosen by an unprecedented *unanimous* vote by the College of Cardinals.'

As Macri watched him, she began to breathe easier. Glick seemed surprisingly professional today. Even austere. For the first time in his life, Glick actually looked and sounded somewhat like a newsman.

'And as we reported earlier,' Glick added, his voice intensifying perfectly, 'the Vatican has yet to offer *any* statement whatsoever regarding the miraculous events of last night.'

Good. Chinita's nervousness waned some more. *So far, so good.*

Glick's expression grew sorrowful now. 'And though last night was a night of wonder, it was also a night of tragedy. Four cardinals perished in yesterday's conflict, along with Commander Olivetti and Captain Rocher of the Swiss Guard, both in the line of duty. Other casualties include Leonardo Vetra, the renowned CERN physicist and pioneer of antimatter technology, as well as Maximilian Kohler, the director of CERN, who apparently came to Vatican City in an effort to help but reportedly passed away in the process. No official report has been issued yet on Mr Kohler's death, but conjecture is that he died due to complications brought on by a long-time illness.'

Macri nodded. The report was going perfectly. Just as they discussed.

'And in the wake of the explosion in the sky over the Vatican last night, CERN's antimatter technology has become *the* hot topic among scientists, sparking excitement and controversy. A statement read by Mr Kohler's assistant in Geneva, Sylvie Baudeloque, announced this morning that CERN's board of directors, although enthusiastic about antimatter's potential, are suspending all research and licensing until further inquiries into its safety can be examined.'

Excellent, Macri thought. *Home stretch.*

'Notably absent from our screens tonight,' Glick reported, 'is the face of Robert Langdon, the Harvard professor who came to Vatican City yesterday to lend his expertise during this Illuminati crisis. Although originally thought to have perished in the antimatter blast, we now have reports that Langdon was spotted in St Peter's Square *after* the explosion. How he got there is still speculation, although a spokesman from Hospital Tiberina claims that Mr Langdon fell out of the sky into the Tiber River shortly after midnight, was treated, and released.' Glick arched his eyebrows at the camera. 'And if *that* is true . . . it was indeed a night of miracles.'

Perfect ending! Macri felt herself smiling broadly. *Flawless wrap! Now sign off!*

But Glick did not sign off. Instead, he paused a moment and then stepped toward the camera. He had a mysterious smile. 'But before we sign off . . .'

No!

'. . . I would like to invite a guest to join me.'

Chinita's hands froze on the camera. *A guest? What the hell is he doing? What guest! Sign off!* But she knew it was too late. Glick had committed.

'The man I am about to introduce,' Glick said, 'is an American . . . a renowned scholar.'

Chinita hesitated. She held her breath as Glick turned to the small crowd around them and motioned for his guest to step forward. Macri said a silent prayer. *Please tell me he somehow located Robert Langdon . . . and not some Illuminati-conspiracy nutcase.*

But as Glick's guest stepped out, Macri's heart sank. It was not Robert Langdon at all. It was a bald man in blue jeans and a flannel shirt. He had a cane and thick glasses. Macri felt terror. *Nutcase!*

'May I introduce,' Glick announced, 'the renowned Vatican scholar from De Paul University in Chicago. Dr Joseph Vanek.'

Macri now hesitated as the man joined Glick on camera. This was no conspiracy buff; Macri had actually *heard* of this guy.

'Dr Vanek,' Glick said. 'You have some rather startling information to share with us regarding last night's conclave.'

'I do indeed,' Vanek said. 'After a night of such surprises, it is hard to imagine there are any surprises left . . . and yet . . .' He paused.

Glick smiled. 'And yet, there is a strange twist to all this.'

Vanek nodded. 'Yes. As perplexing as this will sound, I believe the College of Cardinals unknowingly elected *two* Popes this weekend.'

Macri almost dropped the camera.

Glick gave a shrewd smile. 'Two Popes, you say?'

The scholar nodded. 'Yes. I should first say that I have spent my life studying the laws of papal election. Conclave judicature is extremely complex, and much of it is now forgotten or ignored as obsolete. Even the

612

Great Elector is probably not aware of what I am about to reveal. Nonetheless . . . according to the ancient forgotten laws put forth in the *Romano Pontifici Eligendo, Numero 63* . . . balloting is not the *only* method by which a Pope can be elected. There is another, more *divine* method. It is called "Acclamation by Adoration."' He paused. 'And it happened last night.'

Glick gave his guest a riveted look. 'Please, go on.'

'As you may recall,' the scholar continued, 'last night, when Camerlengo Carlo Ventresca was standing on the roof of the basilica, all of the cardinals below began calling out his name in unison.'

'Yes, I recall.'

'With that image in mind, allow me to read verbatim from the ancient electoral laws.' The man pulled some papers from his pocket, cleared his throat, and began to read. ' "Election by Adoration occurs when . . . all the cardinals, as if by inspiration of the Holy Spirit, freely and spontaneously, unanimously and aloud, proclaim one individual's name." '

Glick smiled. 'So you're saying that last night, when the cardinals chanted Carlo Ventresca's name together, they actually *elected* him Pope?'

'They did indeed. Furthermore, the law states that Election by Adoration supercedes the cardinal eligibility requirement and permits *any* clergyman – ordained priest, bishop, or cardinal – to be elected. So, as you can see, the camerlengo was perfectly qualified for papal election by this procedure.' Dr Vanek looked directly into the camera now 'The facts are these . . . Carlo Ventresca was elected Pope last night. He reigned for just under seventeen minutes. And had he not ascended miraculously into a pillar of fire, he would now be buried in the Vatican Grottoes along with the other Popes.'

'Thank you, doctor.' Glick turned to Macri with a mischievous wink. 'Most illuminating . . .'

137

High atop the steps of the Roman Coliseum, Vittoria laughed and called down to him. 'Robert, hurry up! I knew I should have married a younger man!' Her smile was magic.

He struggled to keep up, but his legs felt like stone. 'Wait,' he begged. 'Please . . .'

There was a pounding in his head.

Robert Langdon awoke with a start.

Darkness.

He lay still for a long time in the foreign softness of the bed, unable to figure out where he was. The pillows were goose down, oversized and wonderful. The air smelled of potpourri. Across the room, two glass doors stood open to a lavish balcony, where a light breeze played beneath a glistening cloud-swept moon. Langdon tried to remember how he had gotten here . . . and where *here* was.

Surreal wisps of memory sifted back into his consciousness . . .

A pyre of mystical fire . . . an angel materializing from out of the crowd . . . her soft hand taking his and leading him into the night . . . guiding his exhausted, battered body through the streets . . . leading him here . . . to this suite . . . propping him half-sleeping in a scalding hot shower . . .

leading him to this bed . . . and watching over him as he fell asleep like the dead.

In the dimness now, Langdon could see a second bed. The sheets were tousled, but the bed was empty. From one of the adjoining rooms, he could hear the faint, steady stream of a shower.

As he gazed at Vittoria's bed, he saw a boldly embroidered seal on her pillowcase. It read: HOTEL BERNINI. Langdon had to smile. Vittoria had chosen well. Old World luxury overlooking Bernini's Triton Fountain . . . there was no more fitting hotel in all of Rome.

As Langdon lay there, he heard a pounding and realized what had awoken him. Someone was knocking at the door. It grew louder.

Confused, Langdon got up. *Nobody knows we're here,* he thought, feeling a trace of uneasiness. Donning a luxuriant Hotel Bernini robe, he walked out of the bedroom into the suite's foyer. He stood a moment at the heavy oak door, and then pulled it open.

A powerful man adorned in lavish purple and yellow regalia stared down at him. 'I am Lieutenant Chartrand,' the man said. 'Vatican Swiss Guard.'

Langdon knew full well who he was. 'How . . . how did you find us?'

'I saw you leave the square last night. I followed you. I'm relieved you're still here.'

Langdon felt a sudden anxiety, wondering if the cardinals had sent Chartrand to escort Langdon and Vittoria back to Vatican City. After all, the two of them were the only two people beyond the College of Cardinals who knew the *truth*. They were a liability.

'His Holiness asked me to give this to you,' Chartrand said, handing over an envelope sealed with the Vatican signet. Langdon opened the envelope and read the handwritten note.

Mr Langdon and Ms Vetra,

Although it is my profound desire to request your discretion in the matters of the past 24 hours, I cannot possibly presume to ask more of you than you have already given. I therefore humbly retreat hoping only that you let your hearts guide you in this matter. The world seems a better place today ... maybe the questions are more powerful than the answers.

My door is always open,

His Holiness, Saverio Mortati

Langdon read the message twice. The College of Cardinals had obviously chosen a noble and munificent leader.

Before Langdon could say anything, Chartrand produced a small package. 'A token of thanks from His Holiness.'

Langdon took the package. It was heavy, wrapped in brown paper.

'By his decree,' Chartrand said, 'this artifact is on indefinite loan to you from the sacred Papal Vault. His Holiness asks only that in your last will and testament you ensure it finds its way home.'

Langdon opened the package and was struck speechless. It was the brand. *The Illuminati Diamond.*

Chartrand smiled. 'May peace be with you.' He turned to go.

'Thank ... you,' Langdon managed, his hands trembling around the precious gift.

The guard hesitated in the hall. 'Mr Langdon, may I ask you something?'

'Of course.'

'My fellow guards and I are curious. Those last few minutes . . . what *happened* up there in the helicopter?'

Langdon felt a rush of anxiety. He knew this moment was coming – the moment of truth. He and Vittoria had talked about it last night as they stole away from St Peter's Square. And they had made their decision. Even before the Pope's note.

Vittoria's father had dreamed his antimatter discovery would bring about a spiritual awakening. Last night's events were no doubt not what he had intended, but the undeniable fact remained . . . at this moment, around the world, people were considering God in ways they never had before. How long the magic would last, Langdon and Vittoria had no idea, but they knew they could never shatter the wonderment with scandal and doubt. *The Lord works in strange ways*, Langdon told himself, wondering wryly if maybe . . . just maybe . . . yesterday had been God's will after all.

'Mr Langdon?' Chartrand repeated. 'I was asking about the helicopter?'

Langdon gave a sad smile. 'Yes, I know . . .' He felt the words flow not from his mind but from his heart. 'Perhaps it was the shock of the fall . . . but my memory . . . it seems . . . it's all a blur . . .'

Chartrand slumped. 'You remember *nothing*?'

Langdon sighed. 'I fear it will remain a mystery forever.'

When Robert Langdon returned to the bedroom, the vision awaiting him stopped him in his tracks. Vittoria stood on the balcony, her back to the railing, her eyes gazing deeply at him. She looked like a heavenly apparition ... a radiant silhouette with the moon behind her. She could have been a Roman goddess, enshrouded in her white terrycloth robe, the drawstring cinched tight, accentuating her slender curves. Behind her, a pale mist hung like a halo over Bernini's Triton Fountain.

Langdon felt wildly drawn to her ... more than to any woman in his life. Quietly, he laid the Illuminati Diamond and the Pope's letter on his bedside table. There would be time to explain all of that later. He went to her on the balcony.

Vittoria looked happy to see him. 'You're awake,' she said, in a coy whisper. '*Finally.*'

Langdon smiled. 'Long day.'

She ran a hand through her luxuriant hair, the neck of her robe falling open slightly 'And now ... I suppose you want your reward.'

The comment took Langdon off guard. 'I'm ... sorry?'

'We're adults, Robert. You can admit it. You feel a longing. I see it in your eyes. A deep, carnal hunger.' She smiled. 'I feel it too. And that craving is about to be satisfied.'

'It is?' He felt emboldened and took a step toward her.

'*Completely.*' She held up a room-service menu. 'I ordered everything they've got.'

The feast was sumptuous. They dined together by moonlight ... sitting on their balcony ... savoring *frisée*, truffles, and risotto. They sipped *Dolcetto* wine and talked late into the night.

Langdon did not need to be a symbologist to read the signs Vittoria was sending him. During dessert of boysenberry cream with *savoiardi* and steaming *Romcaffé*, Vittoria pressed her bare legs against his beneath the table and fixed him with a sultry stare. She seemed to be willing him to set down his fork and carry her off in his arms.

But Langdon did nothing. He remained the perfect gentleman. *Two can play at this game*, he thought, hiding a roguish smile.

When all the food was eaten, Langdon retired to the edge of his bed where he sat alone, turning the Illuminati Diamond over and over in his hands, making repeated comments about the miracle of its symmetry. Vittoria stared at him, her confusion growing to an obvious frustration.

'You find that ambigram terribly interesting, don't you?' she demanded.

Langdon nodded. 'Mesmerizing.'

'Would you say it's the most interesting thing in this room?'

Langdon scratched his head, making a show of pondering it. 'Well, there is *one* thing that interests me more.'

She smiled and took a step toward him. 'That being?'

'How you disproved that Einstein theory using tuna fish.'

Vittoria threw up her hands. '*Dio mio!* Enough with the tuna fish! Don't play with me, I'm warning you.'

Langdon grinned. 'Maybe for your *next* experiment, you could study flounders and prove the earth is flat.'

Vittoria was steaming now, but the first faint hints of an exasperated smile appeared on her lips. 'For your information, professor, my next experiment will make scientific history. I plan to prove neutrinos have mass.'

'Neutrinos have *mass*?' Langdon shot her a stunned look. 'I didn't even know they were Catholic!'

With one fluid motion, she was on him, pinning him down. 'I hope you believe in life after death, Robert Langdon.' Vittoria was laughing as she straddled him, her hands holding him down, her eyes ablaze with a mischievous fire.

'Actually,' he choked, laughing harder now, 'I've always had trouble picturing anything beyond this world.'

'Really? So you've never had a religious experience? A perfect moment of glorious rapture?'

Langdon shook his head. 'No, and I seriously doubt I'm the kind of man who could ever *have* a religious experience.'

Vittoria slipped off her robe. 'You've never been to bed with a yoga master, have you?'

THE END

DAN BROWN
DECEPTION POINT

You may have cracked the code, but can you keep your cool?

When a new NASA satellite detects evidence of an astonishingly rare object buried deep in the Arctic ice, the floundering space agency proclaims a much-needed victory...a victory that has profound implications for U.S. space policy and the impending presidential election.

With the Oval Office in the balance, the President dispatches White House Intelligence analyst Rachel Sexton to the Arctic to verify the authenticity of the find. Accompanied by a team of experts, including the charismatic academic Michael Tolland, Rachel uncovers the unthinkable — evidence of scientific trickery — a bold deception that threatens to plunge the world into controversy.

'An excellent thriller... a big yet believable story unfolding at breakneck pace, with convincing settings and just the right blend of likeable and hateful characters'
Publishers Weekly

'Brown proves once again that he is among the most intelligent and dynamic of authors in the thriller genre'
Library Journal

0552 14919 5

DAN
BROWN

THE
DA VINCI
CODE

'Fascinating and absorbing...
A great, riveting read.
I loved this book'
Harlan Coben

The bestselling
thriller of all time

Harvard professor Robert Langdon receives an urgent late-night phone
call while on business in Paris: the elderly curator of the Louvre has
been brutally murdered inside the museum. Alongside the body, police
have found a series of baffling codes. As Langdon and a gifted French
cryptologist, Sophie Neveu, begin to sort through the bizarre riddles,
they are stunned to find a trail that leads to the works of Leonardo Da
Vinci – and suggests the answer to a mystery that stretches deep into the
vault of history.

Unless Langdon and Neveu can decipher the labyrinthine code and
quickly assemble the pieces of the puzzle, a stunning historical truth will
be lost forever...

0 552 14951 9

Go behind the scenes
of a modern classic

In this exclusive edition Dan Brown allows the reader behind the scenes
of the novel, incorporating over 150 photographs and illustrations
throughout the text, showing the rich historical tapestry from which he
drew his inspiration. The visual sources, which provide both the backdrop
and the stimulus for the novel's action, are revealed for the first time and
uniquely complement the reading experience.

0 593 05425 3

DAN BROWN
DIGITAL
FORTRESS
HIS ACTION-PACKED FIRST NOVEL

Can you crack the code?

When the National Security Agency's invincible code-breaking machine encounters a mysterious code it cannot break, the agency calls in its head cryptographer, Susan Fletcher, a brilliant, beautiful mathematician. What she uncovers sends shock waves through the corridors of power. The NSA is being held hostage – not by guns or bombs, but by a code so complex that if released would cripple U.S. intelligence.

Caught in an accelerating tempest of secrecy and lies, Fletcher battles to save the agency she believes in. Betrayed on all sides, she finds herself fighting not only for her country but for her life, and in the end, for the life of the man she loves...

'Pure genius...
Dan Brown has to be one of the best, smartest,
and most accomplished writers in the country'
Nelson DeMille

0 552 16169 6

Dan Brown is the bestselling author of *Digital Fortress*, *Angels and Demons* and *Deception Point*. He is a graduate of Amherst College and Phillips Exeter Academy, where he has taught English and creative writing. He lives with his wife in New England and can be found on the web at www.danbrown.com

'Far more than the average thriller. Intellectually satisfying . . . page-turning suspense' *Houston Chronicle*

'Brown has assembled a whopper of a plot that will please conspiracy buffs and thriller addicts alike'
Publishers Weekly

A dazzling performance by Brown . . . a delightful display of erudition. Brown delivers a crackling, intricate mystery, complete with breathtaking escapes and several stunning surprises. It's challenging, exciting, and a whole lot more. The race across France and the United Kingdom leads us on a fascinating journey through a covert, enigmatic world revealed through a seemingly endless collection of codes, puzzles, anagrams, cryptograms, and messages hidden not only in Da Vinci's art but in things we think we know well'
Boston Globe

'Brainy stuff. The standard car chases and intrigues are leavened with Crichtonesque discursions on medieval iconography, the formation of the early Christian church, and history's suppression of the "sacred feminine"'
Entertainment Weekly

'A stunning new thriller that will provoke much debate. Dan Brown's extensive research on secret societies and symbology adds intellectual depth to this page-turning thriller. His surprising revelations on Da Vinci's penchant for hiding codes in his paintings will lead the reader to search out such renowned artistic icons as The Mona Lisa, The Madonna of the Rocks and The Last Supper. The Last Supper holds the most astonishing coded secrets of all and, after reading *The Da Vinci Code*, you will never see this famous painting in quite the same way again' Bookreporter.com

'Some readers spurn genre fiction, often due to a misguided belief that mass entertainment is always mindless dribble. For those of you who know better, *The Da Vinci Code* will make you feel justifiably smug. It's that rare book that manages to both entertain and educate simultaneously. Dan Brown has managed to outdo the best of Robert Ludlum in this byzantine . . . and engrossing story. There is enough medieval history to please any historian and enough action to satisfy a hardcore thrill-seeker . . . an early favorite for thriller of the year' *Rocky Mountain News*

'Enthralling ... Dan Brown masterfully concocts an intelligent and lucid thriller that marries the gusto of an international murder mystery with a collection of fascinating esoterica culled from 2,000 years of Western history. Brown's hero and heroine embark on a lofty and intriguing exploration of some of culture's greatest mysteries – from the nature of the Mona Lisa's smile to the secret of the Holy Grail ... rich food for thought' amazon.com

'*The Da Vinci Code* shines – brilliantly – in its exploration of cryptology, particularly the encoding methods developed by Leonardo Da Vinci, whose art and manuscripts are packed with mystifying symbolism and quirky codes'
Wired magazine

'Brown's intricate plot delivers more satisfying twists than a licorice factory' *Booklist*

'A blockbuster with brains. *The Da Vinci Code* is a thrill-a-minute adventure as well as an educational tour of France and England, symbology 101, riddle-breaking for dummies, the magical powers of anagrams, numerical codes to die for and navigational factoids' *The Ottawa Citizen*

'Brown's scholarship never slows down the sizzling action [of this] absorbing new novel ... a labyrinth of intricate schemes, sidetracks, and deceptions' *Bookpage*

'A mystery that challenges our intelligence, and enough believable twists and turns to keep the reader turning the pages. *The Da Vinci Code* by Dan Brown does all this just right. This is how a mystery thriller should be written. So grab this book, sit back, and prepare to be entertained and educated. It's well-written, it's intelligent, and best of all, it's fun' Reviews of Books.com

'Calling Dan Brown's latest novel, *The Da Vinci Code*, simply a "smart suspense novel" is like referring to Harvard as simply a pretty good university. Incorporating massive amounts of historical and academic information is no easy task, but Brown does it in such a seamless fashion that it is almost invisible within the story's natural narrative. Definitely the mark of a master craftsman'
The Mystery Reader

'Narrow escapes, baffling codes ... fascinating discoveries about the Holy Grail, and, yes, a small teaser of budding romance. Brown proves he's one of the new masters of intrigue and suspense' *Philadelphia Inquirer*

'You'll love this. *The Da Vinci Code* has enough twists and turns in a short amount of time to give you over to gasping "More, Dan, more!" It is thrilling that anyone could contrive such an adventure' *Seattle Times*

Also by Dan Brown

DIGITAL FORTRESS
ANGELS AND DEMONS
DECEPTION POINT

THE
DA VINCI
CODE

Dan Brown

CORGI BOOKS

THE DA VINCI CODE
A CORGI BOOK: 0 552 14951 9

Originally published in Great Britain by Bantam Press,
a division of Transworld Publishers

PRINTING HISTORY
Bantam Press edition published 2003
Corgi edition published 2004

41 43 45 47 49 48 46 44 42

Set in 10/11pt Palatino by
Falcon Oast Graphic Art Ltd.

Corgi Books are published by Transworld Publishers,
61–63 Uxbridge Road, London W5 5SA,
a division of The Random House Group Ltd,
in Australia by Random House Australia (Pty) Ltd,
20 Alfred Street, Milsons Point, Sydney, NSW 2061, Australia,
in New Zealand by Random House New Zealand Ltd,
18 Poland Road, Glenfield, Auckland 10, New Zealand
and in South Africa by Random House (Pty) Ltd,
Endulini, 5a Jubilee Road, Parktown 2193, South Africa.

Printed and bound in Great Britain by
Bookmarque Ltd, Croydon, Surrey.

Papers used by Transworld Publishers are natural, recyclable
products made from wood grown in sustainable forests. The
manufacturing processes conform to the environmental
regulations of the country of origin.

For Blythe . . . again.
More than ever.

Acknowledgments

First and foremost, to my friend and editor, Jason Kaufman, for working so hard on this project and for truly understanding what this book is all about. And to the incomparable Heide Lange – tireless champion of The Da Vinci Code, agent extraordinaire and trusted friend.

I cannot fully express my gratitude to the exceptional team at Doubleday, for their generosity, faith and superb guidance. Thank you especially to Bill Thomas and Steve Rubin, who believed in this book from the start. My thanks also to the initial core of early in-house supporters, headed by Michael Palgon, Suzanne Herz, Janelle Moburg, Jackie Everly and Adrienne Sparks, as well as to the talented people of Doubleday's sales force.

My sincere appreciation to the entire team at Transworld Publishers in London, with special thanks to Bill Scott-Kerr and Judith Welsh. My thanks as well to Abner Stein for bringing us all together.

For their generous assistance in the research of the book, I would like to acknowledge the Louvre Museum, the French Ministry of Culture, Project Gutenberg, Bibliothèque Nationale, the Gnostic Society Library, the Department of Paintings Study and Documentation Service at the Louvre, Catholic World News, Royal Observatory Greenwich, London Record Society, the Muniment Collection at Westminster Abbey, John Pike and the Federation of American Scientists, and the five members of Opus Dei (three active, two former) who recounted their stories, both positive and negative, regarding their experiences inside Opus Dei.

My gratitude also to Water Street Bookstore for tracking down so many of my research books, my father Richard Brown for his assistance with Phi and the Divine Proportion, Michael Windsor, Stan Planton, Sylvie Baudeloque, Peter McGuigan, Margie Wachtel, Andre Vernet, Ken Kelleher at Anchorball Web Media, Cara Sottak, Karyn Popham, Esther Sung, Miriam Abramowitz, William Tunstall-Pedoe, Simon Edwards and Griffin Wooden Brown.

And finally, in a novel drawing so heavily on the sacred feminine, I would be remiss if I did not mention the two extraordinary women who have touched my life. First, my mother, Connie Brown – fellow scribe, nurturer, musician and role model. And my wife, Blythe – art historian, painter, front-line editor and without a doubt the most astonishingly talented woman I have ever known.

THE
DA VINCI
CODE

Fact:

The Priory of Sion –
a European secret society founded in
1099 – is a real organization.
In 1975 Paris's Bibliothèque Nationale
discovered parchments known as Les
Dossiers Secrets, identifying numerous
members of the Priory of Sion, including
Sir Isaac Newton, Sandro Botticelli, Victor
Hugo and Leonardo da Vinci.

The Vatican prelature known as Opus
Dei is a deeply devout Catholic
sect that has been the topic of recent
controversy due to reports of brainwashing, coercion and a dangerous
practice known as 'corporal mortification'.
Opus Dei has just completed construction
of a $47 million National Headquarters at
243 Lexington Avenue in New York City.

All descriptions of artwork, architecture,
documents and secret rituals in this novel
are accurate.

Prologue

Renowned curator Jacques Saunière staggered through the vaulted archway of the museum's Grand Gallery. He lunged for the nearest painting he could see, a Caravaggio. Grabbing the gilded frame, the seventy-six-year-old man heaved the masterpiece toward himself until it tore from the wall and Saunière collapsed backward in a heap beneath the canvas.

As he had anticipated, a thundering iron gate fell nearby, barricading the entrance to the suite. The parquet floor shook. Far off, an alarm began to ring.

The curator lay a moment, gasping for breath, taking stock. *I am still alive.* He crawled out from under the canvas and scanned the cavernous space for somewhere to hide.

A voice spoke, chillingly close. 'Do not move.'

On his hands and knees, the curator froze, turning his head slowly.

Only fifteen feet away, outside the sealed gate, the mountainous silhouette of his attacker stared through the iron bars. He was broad and tall, with ghost-pale skin and thinning white hair. His irises were pink with dark red pupils. The albino drew a pistol from his coat

17

and aimed the barrel through the bars, directly at the curator. 'You should not have run.' His accent was not easy to place. 'Now tell me where it is.'

'I told you already,' the curator stammered, kneeling defenceless on the floor of the gallery. 'I have no idea what you are talking about!'

'You are lying.' The man stared at him, perfectly immobile except for the glint in his ghostly eyes. 'You and your brethren possess something that is not yours.'

The curator felt a surge of adrenaline. *How could he possibly know this?*

'Tonight the rightful guardians will be restored. Tell me where it is hidden, and you will live.' The man levelled his gun at the curator's head. 'Is it a secret you will die for?'

Saunière could not breathe.

The man tilted his head, peering down the barrel of his gun.

Saunière held up his hands in defence. 'Wait,' he said slowly. 'I will tell you what you need to know.' The curator spoke his next words carefully. The lie he told was one he had rehearsed many times . . . each time praying he would never have to use it.

When the curator had finished speaking, his assailant smiled smugly. 'Yes. This is exactly what the others told me.'

Saunière recoiled. *The others?*

'I found them, too,' the huge man taunted. 'All three of them. They confirmed what you have just said.'

It cannot be! The curator's true identity, along with the identities of his three *sénéchaux*, was almost as sacred as the ancient secret they protected. Saunière now realized his *sénéchaux*, following strict procedure, had told the same lie before their own deaths. It was part of the protocol.

18

The attacker aimed his gun again. 'When you are gone, I will be the only one who knows the truth.'

The truth. In an instant, the curator grasped the true horror of the situation. *If I die, the truth will be lost for ever.* Instinctively, he tried to scramble for cover.

The gun roared, and the curator felt a searing heat as the bullet lodged in his stomach. He fell forward . . . struggling against the pain. Slowly, Saunière rolled over and stared back through the bars at his attacker.

The man was now taking dead aim at Saunière's head.

Saunière closed his eyes, his thoughts a swirling tempest of fear and regret.

The click of an empty chamber echoed through the corridor.

The curator's eyes flew open.

The man glanced down at his weapon, looking almost amused. He reached for a second clip, but then seemed to reconsider, smirking calmly at Saunière's gut. 'My work here is done.'

The curator looked down and saw the bullet hole in his white linen shirt. It was framed by a small circle of blood a few inches below his breastbone. *My stomach.* Almost cruelly, the bullet had missed his heart. As a veteran of *la Guerre d'Algérie*, the curator had witnessed this horribly drawn-out death before. For fifteen minutes, he would survive as his stomach acids seeped into his chest cavity, slowly poisoning him from within.

'Pain is good, monsieur,' the man said.

Then he was gone.

Alone now, Jacques Saunière turned his gaze again to the iron gate. He was trapped, and the doors could not be reopened for at least twenty minutes. By the time anyone got to him, he would be dead. Even so, the fear that now gripped him was a fear far greater than that of his own death.

I must pass on the secret.

Staggering to his feet, he pictured his three murdered brethren. He thought of the generations who had come before them . . . of the mission with which they had all been entrusted.

An unbroken chain of knowledge.

Suddenly, now, despite all the precautions . . . despite all the fail-safes . . . Jacques Saunière was the only remaining link, the sole guardian of one of the most powerful secrets ever kept.

Shivering, he pulled himself to his feet.

I must find some way . . .

He was trapped inside the Grand Gallery, and there existed only one person on earth to whom he could pass the torch. Saunière gazed up at the walls of his opulent prison. A collection of the world's most famous paintings seemed to smile down on him like old friends.

Wincing in pain, he summoned all of his faculties and strength. The desperate task before him, he knew, would require every remaining second of his life.

Chapter 1

Robert Langdon awoke slowly.

A telephone was ringing in the darkness – a tinny, unfamiliar ring. He fumbled for the bedside lamp and turned it on. Squinting at his surroundings he saw a plush Renaissance bedroom with Louis XVI furniture, hand-frescoed walls, and a colossal mahogany four-poster bed.

Where the hell am I?

The jacquard bathrobe hanging on his bedpost bore the monogram: HOTEL RITZ PARIS.

Slowly, the fog began to lift.

Langdon picked up the receiver. 'Hello?'

'Monsieur Langdon?' a man's voice said. 'I hope I have not awoken you?'

Dazed, Langdon looked at the bedside clock. It was 12:32 A.M. He had been asleep only an hour, but he felt like the dead.

'This is the concierge, monsieur. I apologize for this intrusion, but you have a visitor. He insists it is urgent.'

Langdon still felt fuzzy. *A visitor?* His eyes focused now on a crumpled flyer on his bedside table.

THE AMERICAN UNIVERSITY OF PARIS

proudly presents

AN EVENING WITH ROBERT LANGDON

PROFESSOR OF RELIGIOUS SYMBOLOGY, HARVARD UNIVERSITY

Langdon groaned. Tonight's lecture – a slide show about pagan symbolism hidden in the stones of Chartres Cathedral – had probably ruffled some conservative feathers in the audience. Most likely, some religious scholar had trailed him home to pick a fight.

'I'm sorry,' Langdon said, 'but I'm very tired and—'

'*Mais, monsieur,*' the concierge pressed, lowering his voice to an urgent whisper. 'Your guest is an important man.'

Langdon had little doubt. His books on religious paintings and cult symbology had made him a reluctant celebrity in the art world, and last year Langdon's visibility had increased a hundredfold after his involvement in a widely publicized incident at the Vatican. Since then, the stream of self-important historians and art buffs arriving at his door had seemed never-ending.

'If you would be so kind,' Langdon said, doing his best to remain polite, 'could you take the man's name and number, and tell him I'll try to call him before I leave Paris on Tuesday? Thank you.' He hung up before the concierge could protest.

Sitting up now, Langdon frowned at his bedside *Guest Relations Handbook,* whose cover boasted: SLEEP LIKE A BABY IN THE CITY OF LIGHTS. SLUMBER AT THE PARIS RITZ. He turned and gazed tiredly into the full-length mirror across the room. The man staring back at him was a stranger – tousled and weary.

You need a vacation, Robert.

The past year had taken a heavy toll on him, but he didn't appreciate seeing proof in the mirror. His usually sharp blue eyes looked hazy and drawn tonight. A dark stubble was shrouding his strong jaw and dimpled chin. Around his temples, the grey highlights were advancing, making their way deeper into his thicket of coarse black hair. Although his female colleagues insisted the grey only accentuated his bookish appeal, Langdon knew better.

If Boston Magazine *could see me now.*

Last month, much to Langdon's embarrassment, *Boston Magazine* had listed him as one of that city's top ten most intriguing people – a dubious honour that made him the brunt of endless ribbing by his Harvard colleagues. Tonight, three thousand miles from home, the accolade had resurfaced to haunt him at the lecture he had given.

'Ladies and gentlemen . . .' the hostess had announced to a full house at the American University of Paris's Pavillon Dauphine, 'Our guest tonight needs no introduction. He is the author of numerous books: *The Symbology of Secret Sects, The Art of the Illuminati, The Lost Language of Ideograms,* and when I say he wrote the book on *Religious Iconology,* I mean that quite literally. Many of you use his textbooks in class.'

The students in the crowd nodded enthusiastically.

'I had planned to introduce him tonight by sharing his impressive curriculum vitae. However . . .' She glanced playfully at Langdon, who was seated onstage. 'An audience member has just handed me a far more, shall we say . . . *intriguing* introduction.'

She held up a copy of *Boston Magazine.*

Langdon cringed. *Where the hell did she get that?*

The hostess began reading choice excerpts from the inane article, and Langdon felt himself sinking lower and lower in his chair. Thirty seconds later, the crowd was grinning, and the woman showed no signs of letting up. 'And Mr Langdon's refusal to speak publicly about his unusual role in last year's Vatican conclave certainly wins him points on our intrigue-o-meter.' The hostess goaded the crowd. 'Would you like to hear more?'

The crowd applauded.

Somebody stop her, Langdon pleaded as she dived into the article again.

'Although Professor Langdon might not be considered hunk-handsome like some of our younger awardees, this forty-something academic has more than his share of scholarly allure. His captivating presence is punctuated by an unusually low, baritone speaking voice, which his female students describe as "chocolate for the ears".'

The hall erupted in laughter.

Langdon forced an awkward smile. He knew what came next – some ridiculous line about 'Harrison Ford in Harris tweed' – and because this evening he had figured it was finally safe again to wear his Harris tweed and Burberry turtleneck, he decided to take action.

'Thank you, Monique,' Langdon said, standing prematurely and edging her away from the podium. '*Boston Magazine* clearly has a gift for fiction.' He turned to the audience with an embarrassed sigh. 'And if I find which one of you provided that article, I'll have the consulate deport you.'

The crowd laughed.

'Well, folks, as you all know, I'm here tonight to talk about the power of symbols . . .'

The ringing of Langdon's hotel phone once again broke the silence.

Groaning in disbelief, he picked up. 'Yes?'

As expected, it was the concierge. 'Mr Langdon, again my apologies. I am calling to inform you that your guest is now en route to your room. I thought I should alert you.'

Langdon was wide awake now. 'You sent someone to my *room*?'

'I apologize, monsieur, but a man like this . . . I cannot presume the authority to stop him.'

'Who exactly *is* he?'

But the concierge was gone.

Almost immediately, a heavy fist pounded on Langdon's door.

Uncertain, Langdon slid off the bed, feeling his toes sink deep into the savonnerie carpet. He donned the hotel bathrobe and moved toward the door. 'Who is it?'

'Mr Langdon? I need to speak with you.' The man's English was accented – a sharp, authoritative bark. 'My name is Lieutenant Jérôme Collet. Direction Centrale Police Judiciaire.'

Langdon paused. *The Judicial Police?* The DCPJ was the rough equivalent of the US FBI.

Leaving the security chain in place, Langdon opened the door a few inches. The face staring back at him was thin and washed out. The man was exceptionally lean, dressed in an official-looking blue uniform.

'May I come in?' the agent asked.

Langdon hesitated, feeling uncertain as the stranger's sallow eyes studied him. 'What is this all about?'

'My *capitaine* requires your expertise in a private matter.'

'Now?' Langdon managed. 'It's after midnight.'

'Am I correct that you were scheduled to meet with the curator of the Louvre this evening?'

Langdon felt a sudden surge of uneasiness. He and the revered curator Jacques Saunière had been slated to meet for drinks after Langdon's lecture tonight, but Saunière had never shown up. 'Yes. How did you know that?'

'We found your name in his daily planner.'

'I trust nothing is wrong?'

The agent gave a dire sigh and slid a Polaroid snapshot through the narrow opening in the door.

When Langdon saw the photo, his entire body went rigid.

'This photo was taken less than an hour ago. Inside the Louvre.'

As Langdon stared at the bizarre image, his initial revulsion and shock gave way to a sudden upwelling of anger. 'Who would do this!'

'We had hoped that you might help us answer that very question, considering your knowledge in symbology and your plans to meet him.'

Langdon stared at the picture, his horror now laced with fear. The image was gruesome and profoundly strange, bringing with it an unsettling sense of déjà vu. A little over a year ago, Langdon had received a photograph of a corpse and a similar request for help. Twenty-four hours later, he had almost lost his life inside Vatican City. This photo was entirely different, and yet something about the scenario felt disquietingly familiar.

The agent checked his watch. 'My *capitaine* is waiting, sir.'

Langdon barely heard him. His eyes were still riveted on the picture. 'This symbol here, and the way his body is so oddly . . .'

'Positioned?' the agent offered.

Langdon nodded, feeling a chill as he looked up. 'I can't imagine who would do this to someone.'

The agent looked grim. 'You don't understand, Mr Langdon. What you see in this photograph . . .' He paused. 'Monsieur Saunière did that to himself.'

Chapter 2

One mile away, the hulking albino named Silas limped through the front gate of the luxurious residence on Rue La Bruyère. The spiked *cilice* belt that he wore around his thigh cut into his flesh, and yet his soul sang with satisfaction of service to the Lord.

Pain is good.

His red eyes scanned the lobby as he entered the residence. Empty. He climbed the stairs quietly, not wanting to awaken any of his fellow numeraries. His bedroom door was open; locks were forbidden here. He entered, closing the door behind him.

The room was spartan – hardwood floors, a pine dresser, a canvas mat in the corner that served as his bed. He was a visitor here this week, and yet for many years he had been blessed with a similar sanctuary in New York City.

The Lord has provided me shelter and purpose in my life.

Tonight, at last, Silas felt he had begun to repay his debt. Hurrying to the dresser, he found the cell phone hidden in his bottom drawer and placed a call.

'Yes?' a male voice answered.

'Teacher, I have returned.'

'Speak,' the voice commanded, sounding pleased to hear from him.

'All four are gone. The three *sénéchaux* . . . and the *Grand Master* himself.'

There was a momentary pause, as if for prayer. 'Then I assume you have the information?'

'All four concurred. Independently.'

'And you believed them?'

'Their agreement was too great for coincidence.'

An excited breath. 'Excellent. I had feared the brotherhood's reputation for secrecy might prevail.'

'The prospect of death is strong motivation.'

'So, my pupil, tell me what I must know.'

Silas knew the information he had gleaned from his victims would come as a shock. 'Teacher, all four confirmed the existence of the *clef de voûte* . . . the legendary *keystone*.'

He heard a quick intake of breath over the phone and could feel the Teacher's excitement. 'The *keystone*. Exactly as we suspected.'

According to lore, the brotherhood had created a map of stone – a *clef de voûte* . . . or *keystone* – an engraved tablet that revealed the final resting place of the brotherhood's greatest secret . . . information so powerful that its protection was the reason for the brotherhood's very existence.

'When we possess the keystone,' the Teacher said, 'we will be only one step away.'

'We are closer than you think. The keystone is here in Paris.'

'Paris? Incredible. It is almost too easy.'

Silas relayed the earlier events of the evening . . . how all four of his victims, moments before death, had desperately tried to buy back their godless lives by telling their secret. Each had told Silas the exact same thing – that the keystone was ingeniously hidden at a precise location inside one of Paris's ancient churches – the Eglise de Saint-Sulpice.

'Inside a house of the Lord,' the Teacher exclaimed. 'How they mock us!'

'As they have for centuries.'

The Teacher fell silent, as if letting the triumph of

this moment settle over him. Finally, he spoke. 'You have done a great service to God. We have waited centuries for this. You must retrieve the stone for me. Immediately. Tonight. You understand the stakes.'

Silas knew the stakes were incalculable, and yet what the Teacher was now commanding seemed impossible. 'But the church, it is a fortress. Especially at night. How will I enter?'

With the confident tone of a man of enormous influence, the Teacher explained what was to be done.

When Silas hung up the phone, his skin tingled with anticipation.

One hour, he told himself, grateful that the Teacher had given him time to carry out the necessary penance before entering a house of God. *I must purge my soul of today's sins.* The sins committed today had been holy in purpose. Acts of war against the enemies of God had been committed for centuries. Forgiveness was assured.

Even so, Silas knew, absolution required sacrifice.

Pulling his shades, he stripped naked and knelt in the centre of his room. Looking down, he examined the spiked *cilice* belt clamped around his thigh. All true followers of *The Way* wore this device – a leather strap, studded with sharp metal barbs that cut into the flesh as a perpetual reminder of Christ's suffering. The pain caused by the device also helped counteract the desires of the flesh.

Although Silas already had worn his *cilice* today longer than the requisite two hours, he knew today was no ordinary day. Grasping the buckle, he cinched it one notch tighter, wincing as the barbs dug deeper into his flesh. Exhaling slowly, he savoured the cleansing ritual of his pain.

Pain is good, Silas whispered, repeating the sacred mantra of Father Josemaría Escrivá – the Teacher of all Teachers. Although Escrivá had died in 1975, his wisdom lived on, his words still whispered by thousands of faithful servants around the globe as they knelt on the floor and performed the sacred practice known as 'corporal mortification'.

Silas turned his attention now to a heavy knotted rope coiled neatly on the floor beside him. *The Discipline.* The knots were caked with dried blood. Eager for the purifying effects of his own agony, Silas said a quick prayer. Then, gripping one end of the rope, he closed his eyes and swung it hard over his shoulder, feeling the knots slap against his back. He whipped it over his shoulder again, slashing at his flesh. Again and again, he lashed.

Castigo corpus meum.

Finally, he felt the blood begin to flow.

Chapter 3

The crisp April air whipped through the open window of the Citroën ZX as it skimmed south past the Opera House and crossed Place Vendôme. In the passenger seat, Robert Langdon felt the city tear past him as he tried to clear his thoughts. His quick shower and shave had left him looking reasonably presentable but had done little to ease his anxiety. The frightening image of the curator's body remained locked in his mind.

Jacques Saunière is dead.

Langdon could not help but feel a deep sense of loss at the curator's death. Despite Saunière's reputation for being reclusive, his recognition for dedication to the arts made him an easy man to revere. His books on the secret codes hidden in the paintings of Poussin and Teniers were some of Langdon's favourite classroom texts. Tonight's meeting had been one Langdon was very much looking forward to, and he was disappointed when the curator had not turned up.

Again the image of the curator's body flashed in his mind. *Jacques Saunière did that to himself?* Langdon turned and looked out of the window, forcing the picture from his mind.

Outside, the city was just now winding down – street vendors wheeling carts of candied *amandes*, waiters carrying bags of garbage to the curb, a pair of late-night lovers cuddling to stay warm in a breeze scented with jasmine blossom. The Citroën navigated the chaos with authority, its dissonant two-tone siren parting the traffic like a knife.

'*Le capitaine* was pleased to discover you were still in Paris tonight,' the agent said, speaking for the first time since they'd left the hotel. 'A fortunate coincidence.'

Langdon was feeling anything but fortunate, and coincidence was a concept he did not entirely trust. As someone who had spent his life exploring the hidden interconnectivity of disparate emblems and ideologies, Langdon viewed the world as a web of profoundly intertwined histories and events. *The connections may be invisible,* he often preached to his symbology classes at Harvard, *but they are always there, buried just beneath the surface.*

'I assume,' Langdon said, 'that the American University of Paris told you where I was staying?'

The driver shook his head. 'Interpol.'

Interpol, Langdon thought. *Of course.* He had forgotten that the seemingly innocuous request of all European hotels to see a passport at check-in was more than a quaint formality – it was the law. On any given night, all across Europe, Interpol officials could pinpoint exactly who was sleeping where. Finding Langdon at the Ritz had probably taken all of five seconds.

As the Citroën accelerated southward across the city, the illuminated profile of the Eiffel Tower appeared, shooting skyward in the distance to the right. Seeing it, Langdon thought of Vittoria, recalling their playful promise a year ago that every six months they would meet again at a different romantic spot on the globe. The Eiffel Tower, Langdon suspected, would have made their list. Sadly, he last kissed Vittoria in a noisy airport in Rome more than a year ago.

'Did you mount her?' the agent asked, looking over.

Langdon glanced up, certain he had misunderstood. 'I beg your pardon?'

'She is lovely, no?' The agent motioned through the windshield toward the Eiffel Tower. 'Have you mounted her?'

Langdon rolled his eyes. 'No, I haven't climbed the tower.'

'She is the symbol of France. I think she is perfect.'

Langdon nodded absently. Symbologists often remarked that France – a country renowned for machismo, womanizing and diminutive insecure leaders like Napoleon and Pepin the Short – could not have chosen a more apt national emblem than a thousand-foot phallus.

When they reached the intersection at Rue de Rivoli, the traffic light was red, but the Citroën didn't slow. The agent gunned the sedan across the junction and sped onto a wooded section of Rue Castiglione, which served as the northern entrance to the famed Tuileries Gardens – Paris's own version of Central Park. Most tourists mistranslated Jardins des Tuileries as relating to the thousands of tulips that bloomed here, but *Tuileries* was actually a literal reference to something far less romantic. This park had once been an enormous, polluted excavation pit from which Parisian contractors mined clay to manufacture the city's famous red roofing tiles – or *tuiles*.

As they entered the deserted park, the agent reached under the dash and turned off the blaring siren. Langdon exhaled, savouring the sudden quiet. Outside the car, the pale wash of halogen headlights skimmed over the crushed gravel parkway, the rugged whir of the tyres intoning a hypnotic rhythm. Langdon had always considered the Tuileries to be sacred ground. These were the gardens in which Claude Monet had experimented with form and colour, and literally inspired the birth of the Impressionist movement. Tonight, however, this place held a strange aura of foreboding.

The Citroën swerved left now, angling west down the park's central boulevard. Curling around a circular pond, the driver cut across a desolate avenue out into a wide quadrangle beyond. Langdon could now see the end of the Tuileries Gardens, marked by a giant stone archway.

Arc du Carrousel.

Despite the orgiastic rituals once held at the Arc du Carrousel, art aficionados revered this place for another reason entirely. From the esplanade at the end of the Tuileries, four of the finest art museums in the world could be seen . . . one at each point of the compass.

Out of the right-hand window, south across the Seine and Quai Voltaire, Langdon could see the dramatically lit façade of the old train station – now the esteemed Musée d'Orsay. Glancing left, he could make out the top of the ultramodern Pompidou Centre, which housed the Museum of Modern Art. Behind him to the west, Langdon knew the ancient obelisk of Ramses rose above the trees, marking the Musée du Jeu de Paume.

But it was straight ahead, to the east, through the archway, that Langdon could now see the monolithic Renaissance palace that had become the most famous art museum in the world.

Musée du Louvre.

Langdon felt a familiar tinge of wonder as his eyes made a futile attempt to absorb the entire mass of the edifice. Across a staggeringly expansive plaza, the imposing façade of the Louvre rose like a citadel against the Paris sky. Shaped like an enormous horse-shoe, the Louvre was the longest building in Europe, stretching farther than three Eiffel Towers laid end to end. Not even the million square feet of open plaza between the museum wings could challenge the majesty of the façade's breadth. Langdon had once walked the Louvre's entire perimeter, an astonishing three-mile journey.

Despite the estimated five weeks it would take a visitor to properly appreciate the 65,300 pieces of art in this building, most tourists chose an abbreviated experience Langdon referred to as 'Louvre Lite' – a full sprint through the museum to see the three most famous objects: the *Mona Lisa, Venus de Milo* and *Winged Victory.* Art Buchwald had once boasted he'd seen all three masterpieces in five minutes and fifty-six seconds.

The driver pulled out a handheld walkie-talkie and spoke in rapid-fire French. *'Monsieur Langdon est arrivé. Deux minutes.'*

An indecipherable confirmation came crackling back.

The agent stowed the device, turning now to Langdon. 'You will meet the *capitaine* at the main entrance.'

The driver ignored the signs prohibiting auto traffic on the plaza, revved the engine, and gunned the Citroën up over the curb. The Louvre's main entrance was visible now, rising boldly in the distance, encircled by seven triangular pools from which spouted illuminated fountains.

La Pyramide.

The new entrance to the Paris Louvre had become almost as famous as the museum itself. The controversial, neomodern glass pyramid designed by Chinese-born American architect I. M. Pei still evoked scorn from traditionalists who felt it destroyed the dignity of the Renaissance courtyard. Goethe had described architecture as frozen music, and Pei's critics described this pyramid as fingernails on a chalkboard. Progressive admirers, though, hailed Pei's seventy-one-foot-tall transparent pyramid as a dazzling synergy of ancient structure and modern method – a symbolic link between the old and new – helping usher the Louvre into the next millennium.

'Do you like our pyramid?' the agent asked.

Langdon frowned. The French, it seemed, loved to ask Americans this. It was a loaded question, of course. Admitting you liked the pyramid made you a tasteless American, and expressing dislike was an insult to the French.

'Mitterrand was a bold man,' Langdon replied, splitting the difference. The late French president who had commissioned the pyramid was said to have suffered from a 'Pharaoh complex'. Singlehandedly responsible for filling Paris with Egyptian obelisks, art and artefacts, François Mitterrand had an affinity for Egyptian culture that was so all-consuming that the French still referred to him as the Sphinx.

'What is the captain's name?' Langdon asked, changing topics.

'Bezu Fache,' the driver said, approaching the pyramid's main entrance. 'We call him *le Taureau*.'

Langdon glanced over at him, wondering if every Frenchman had a mysterious animal epithet. 'You call your captain *the Bull?*'

The man arched his eyebrows. 'Your French is better than you admit, Monsieur Langdon.'

My French stinks, Langdon thought, *but my zodiac iconography is pretty good.* Taurus was always the bull. Astrology was a symbolic constant all over the world.

The agent pulled the car to a stop and pointed between two fountains to a large door in the side of the pyramid. 'There is the entrance. Good luck, monsieur.'

'You're not coming?'

'My orders are to leave you here. I have other business to attend to.'

Langdon heaved a sigh and climbed out. *It's your circus.*

The agent revved his engine and sped off.

As Langdon stood alone and watched the departing rearlights, he realized he could easily reconsider, exit the courtyard, grab a taxi, and head home to bed. Something told him it was probably a lousy idea.

As he moved toward the mist of the fountains, Langdon had the uneasy sense he was crossing an imaginary threshold into another world. The dream-like quality of the evening was settling around him again. Twenty minutes ago he had been asleep in his hotel room. Now he was standing in front of a trans-parent pyramid built by the Sphinx, waiting for a policeman they called the Bull.

I'm trapped in a Salvador Dalí painting, he thought.

Langdon strode to the main entrance – an enormous revolving door. The foyer beyond was dimly lit and deserted.

Do I knock?

Langdon wondered if any of Harvard's revered Egyptologists had ever knocked on the front door of a pyramid and expected an answer. He raised his hand to bang on the glass, but out of the darkness below, a figure appeared, striding up the curving staircase. The man was stocky and dark, almost Neanderthal, dressed in a dark double-breasted suit that strained to cover his wide shoulders. He advanced with unmistakable authority on squat, powerful legs. He was speaking on his cell phone but finished the call as he arrived. He motioned for Langdon to enter.

'I am Bezu Fache,' he announced as Langdon pushed through the revolving door. 'Captain of the Central Directorate Judicial Police.' His tone was fitting – a guttural rumble . . . like a gathering storm.

Langdon held out his hand to shake. 'Robert Langdon.'

Fache's enormous palm wrapped around Langdon's with crushing force.

'I saw the photo,' Langdon said. 'Your agent said Jacques Saunière *himself* did—'

'Mr Langdon,' Fache's ebony eyes locked on. 'What you see in the photo is only the beginning of what Saunière did.'

Chapter 4

Captain Bezu Fache carried himself like an angry ox, with his wide shoulders thrown back and his chin tucked hard into his chest. His dark hair was slicked back with oil, accentuating an arrow-like widow's peak that divided his jutting brow and preceded him like the prow of a battleship. As he advanced, his dark eyes seemed to scorch the earth before him, radiating a fiery clarity that forecast his reputation for unblinking severity in all matters.

Langdon followed the captain down the famous marble staircase into the sunken atrium beneath the glass pyramid. As they descended, they passed between two armed Judicial Police guards with machine guns. The message was clear: Nobody goes in or out tonight without the blessing of Captain Fache.

Descending below ground level, Langdon fought a rising trepidation. Fache's presence was anything but welcoming, and the Louvre itself had an almost sepulchral aura at this hour. The staircase, like the aisle of a dark cinema, was illuminated by subtle tread-lighting embedded in each step. Langdon could hear his own footsteps reverberating off the glass overhead. As he glanced up, he could see the faint illuminated wisps of mist from the fountains fading away outside the transparent roof.

'Do you approve?' Fache asked, nodding upward with his broad chin.

Langdon sighed, too tired to play games. 'Yes, your pyramid is magnificent.'

Fache grunted. 'A scar on the face of Paris.'

Strike one. Langdon sensed his host was a hard man to please. He wondered if Fache had any idea that this pyramid, at President Mitterrand's explicit demand, had been constructed of exactly 666 panes of glass – a bizarre request that had always been a hot topic among conspiracy buffs who claimed 666 was the number of Satan.

Langdon decided not to bring it up.

As they dropped farther into the subterranean foyer, the yawning space slowly emerged from the shadows. Built fifty-seven feet beneath ground level, the Louvre's newly constructed 70,000-square-foot lobby spread out like an endless grotto. Constructed in warm ochre marble to be compatible with the honey-coloured stone of the Louvre façade above, the subterranean hall was usually vibrant with sunlight and tourists. Tonight, however, the lobby was barren and dark, giving the entire space a cold and crypt-like atmosphere.

'And the museum's regular security staff?' Langdon asked.

'*En quarantaine,*' Fache replied, sounding as if Langdon were questioning the integrity of Fache's team. 'Obviously, someone gained entry tonight who should not have. All Louvre night wardens are in the Sully Wing being questioned. My own agents have taken over museum security for the evening.'

Langdon nodded, moving quickly to keep pace with Fache.

'How well did you know Jacques Saunière?' the captain asked.

'Actually, not at all. We'd never met.'

Fache looked surprised. 'Your first meeting was to be tonight?'

'Yes. We'd planned to meet at the American

University reception following my lecture, but he never showed up.'

Fache scribbled some notes in a little book. As they walked, Langdon caught a glimpse of the Louvre's lesser-known pyramid – *La Pyramide Inversée* – a huge inverted skylight that hung from the ceiling like a stalactite in an adjoining section of the entresol. Fache guided Langdon up a short set of stairs to the mouth of an arched tunnel, over which a sign read: DENON. The Denon Wing was the most famous of the Louvre's three main sections.

'Who requested tonight's meeting?' Fache asked suddenly. 'You or he?'

The question seemed odd. 'Mr Saunière did,' Langdon replied as they entered the tunnel. 'His secretary contacted me a few weeks ago via e-mail. She said the curator had heard I would be lecturing in Paris this month and wanted to discuss something with me while I was here.'

'Discuss what?'

'I don't know. Art, I imagine. We share similar interests.'

Fache looked sceptical. 'You have *no* idea what your meeting was about?'

Langdon did not. He'd been curious at the time but had not felt comfortable demanding specifics. The venerated Jacques Saunière had a renowned penchant for privacy and granted very few meetings; Langdon was grateful simply for the opportunity to meet him.

'Mr Langdon, can you at least *guess* what our murder victim might have wanted to discuss with you on the night he was killed? It might be helpful.'

The pointedness of the question made Langdon uncomfortable. 'I really can't imagine. I didn't ask. I felt honoured to have been contacted at all. I'm an admirer of Mr Saunière's work. I use his texts often in my classes.'

Fache made note of that fact in his book.

The two men were now halfway up the Denon Wing's entry tunnel, and Langdon could see the twin ascending escalators at the far end, both motionless.

'So you shared interests with him?' Fache asked.

'Yes. In fact, I've spent much of the last year writing the draft for a book that deals with Mr Saunière's primary area of expertise. I was looking forward to picking his brain.'

Fache glanced up. 'Pardon?'

The idiom apparently didn't translate. 'I was looking forward to learning his thoughts on the topic.'

'I see. And what is the topic?'

Langdon hesitated, uncertain exactly how to put it. 'Essentially, the manuscript is about the iconography of goddess worship – the concept of female sanctity and the art and symbols associated with it.'

Fache ran a meaty hand across his hair. 'And Saunière was knowledgeable about this?'

'Nobody more so.'

'I see.'

Langdon sensed Fache did not see at all. Jacques Saunière was considered the premiere goddess iconographer on earth. Not only did Saunière have a personal passion for relics relating to fertility, goddess cults, Wicca and the sacred feminine, but during his twenty-year tenure as curator, Saunière had helped the Louvre amass the largest collection of goddess art on earth – labrys axes from the priestesses' oldest Greek shrine in Delphi, gold caducei wands, hundreds of Tjet ankhs resembling small standing angels, sistrum rattles used in ancient Egypt to dispel evil spirits, and an astonishing array of statues depicting Horus being nursed by the goddess Isis.

'Perhaps Jacques Saunière knew of your manuscript?' Fache offered. 'And he called the meeting to offer his help on your book.'

Langdon shook his head. 'Actually, nobody yet knows about my manuscript. It's still in draft form, and I haven't shown it to anyone except my editor.'

Fache fell silent.

Langdon did not add the *reason* he hadn't yet shown the manuscript to anyone else. The three-hundred-page draft – tentatively titled *Symbols of the Lost Sacred Feminine* – proposed some very unconventional interpretations of established religious iconography which would certainly be controversial.

Now, as Langdon approached the stationary escalators, he paused, realizing Fache was no longer beside him. Turning, Langdon saw Fache standing several yards back at a service elevator.

'We'll take the elevator,' Fache said as the lift doors opened. 'As I'm sure you're aware, the gallery is quite a distance on foot.'

Although Langdon knew the elevator would expedite the long, two-storey climb to the Denon Wing, he remained motionless.

'Is something wrong?' Fache was holding the door, looking impatient.

Langdon exhaled, turning a longing glance back up the open-air escalator. *Nothing's wrong at all*, he lied to himself, trudging back toward the elevator. As a boy, Langdon had fallen down an abandoned well shaft and almost died treading water in the narrow space for hours before being rescued. Since then, he'd suffered a haunting phobia of enclosed spaces – elevators, subways, squash courts. *The elevator is a perfectly safe machine*, Langdon continually told himself, never believing it. *It's a tiny metal box hanging in an enclosed shaft!* Holding his breath, he stepped into the

43

lift, feeling the familiar tingle of adrenaline as the doors slid shut.

Two floors. Ten seconds.

'You and Mr Saunière,' Fache said as the lift began to move, 'you never spoke at all? Never corresponded? Never sent each other anything in the mail?'

Another odd question. Langdon shook his head. 'No. Never.'

Fache cocked his head, as if making a mental note of that fact. Saying nothing, he stared dead ahead at the chrome doors.

As they ascended, Langdon tried to focus on anything other than the four walls around him. In the reflection of the shiny elevator door, he saw the captain's tie clip – a silver crucifix with thirteen embedded pieces of black onyx. Langdon found it vaguely surprising. The symbol was known as a *crux gemmata* – a cross bearing thirteen gems – a Christian ideogram for Christ and His twelve apostles. Somehow Langdon had not expected the captain of the French police to broadcast his religion so openly. Then again, this was France; Christianity was not a religion here so much as a birthright.

'It's a *crux gemmata*,' Fache said suddenly.

Startled, Langdon glanced up to find Fache's eyes on him in the reflection.

The elevator jolted to a stop, and the doors opened.

Langdon stepped quickly out into the hallway, eager for the wide-open space afforded by the famous high ceilings of the Louvre galleries. The world into which he stepped, however, was nothing like he expected.

Surprised, Langdon stopped short.

Fache glanced over. 'I gather, Mr Langdon, you have never seen the Louvre after hours?'

I guess not, Langdon thought, trying to get his bearings.

Usually impeccably illuminated, the Louvre galleries were startlingly dark tonight. Instead of the customary flat-white light flowing down from above, a muted red glow seemed to emanate upward from the baseboards – intermittent patches of red light spilling out onto the tile floors.

As Langdon gazed down the murky corridor, he realized he should have anticipated this scene. Virtually all major galleries employed red service lighting at night – strategically placed, low-level, non-invasive lights that enabled staff members to navigate hallways and yet kept the paintings in relative darkness to slow the fading effects of overexposure to light. Tonight, the museum possessed an almost oppressive quality. Long shadows encroached everywhere, and the usually soaring vaulted ceilings appeared as a low, black void.

'This way,' Fache said, turning sharply right and setting out through a series of interconnected galleries.

Langdon followed, his vision slowly adjusting to the dark. All around, large-format oils began to materialize like photos developing before him in an enormous darkroom . . . their eyes following as he moved through the rooms. He could taste the familiar tang of museum air – an arid, deionized essence that carried a faint hint of carbon – the product of industrial, coal-filter dehumidifiers that ran around the clock to counteract the corrosive carbon dioxide exhaled by visitors.

Mounted high on the walls, the visible security cameras sent a clear message to visitors: *We see you. Do not touch anything.*

'Any of them real?' Langdon asked, motioning to the cameras.

Fache shook his head. 'Of course not.'

Langdon was not surprised. Video surveillance in museums this size was cost-prohibitive and ineffective. With acres of galleries to watch over, the Louvre would require several hundred technicians simply to monitor the feeds. Most large museums now used 'containment security'. *Forget keeping thieves out. Keep them in.* Containment was activated after hours, and if an intruder removed a piece of artwork, compartmentalized exits would seal around that gallery, and the thief would find himself behind bars even before the police arrived.

The sound of voices echoed down the marble corridor up ahead. The noise seemed to be coming from a large recessed alcove that lay ahead on the right. A bright light spilled out into the hallway.

'Office of the curator,' the captain said.

As he and Fache drew nearer the alcove, Langdon peered down a short hallway, into Saunière's luxurious study – warm wood, Old Master paintings and an enormous antique desk on which stood a two-foot-tall model of a knight in full armour. A handful of police agents bustled about the room, talking on phones and taking notes. One of them was seated at Saunière's desk, typing into a laptop. Apparently, the curator's private office had become DCPJ's makeshift command post for the evening.

'*Messieurs,*' Fache called out, and the men turned. '*Ne nous dérangez pas sous aucun prétexte. Entendu?*'

Everyone inside the office nodded their understanding.

Langdon had hung enough NE PAS DERANGER signs on hotel room doors to catch the gist of the captain's orders. Fache and Langdon were not to be disturbed under any circumstances.

Leaving the small congregation of agents behind,

Fache led Langdon farther down the darkened hallway. Thirty yards ahead loomed the gateway to the Louvre's most popular section – *la Grande Galerie* – a seemingly endless corridor that housed the Louvre's most valuable Italian masterpieces. Langdon had already discerned that *this* was where Saunière's body lay; the Grand Gallery's famous parquet floor had been unmistakable in the Polaroid.

As they approached, Langdon saw the entrance was blocked by an enormous steel grate that looked like something used by medieval castles to keep out marauding armies.

'Containment security,' Fache said, as they neared the grate.

Even in the darkness, the barricade looked as if it could have restrained a tank. Arriving outside, Langdon peered through the bars into the dimly lit caverns of the Grand Gallery.

'After you, Mr Langdon,' Fache said.

Langdon turned. *After me, where?*

Fache motioned toward the floor at the base of the grate.

Langdon looked down. In the darkness, he hadn't noticed. The barricade was raised about two feet, providing an awkward clearance underneath.

'This area is still off limits to Louvre security,' Fache said. 'My team from *Police Technique et Scientifique* has just finished their investigation.' He motioned to the opening. 'Please slide under.'

Langdon stared at the narrow crawl space at his feet and then up at the massive iron grate. *He's kidding, right?* The barricade looked like a guillotine waiting to crush intruders.

Fache grumbled something in French and checked his watch. Then he dropped to his knees and slithered his bulky frame underneath the grate. On the other side, he stood up and looked back through the bars at Langdon.

Langdon sighed. Placing his palms flat on the polished parquet, he lay on his stomach and pulled himself forward. As he slid underneath, the nape of his Harris tweed snagged on the bottom of the grate, and he cracked the back of his head on the iron.

Very suave, Robert, he thought, fumbling and then finally pulling himself through. As he stood up, Langdon was beginning to suspect it was going to be a very long night.

Chapter 5

Murray Hill Place – the new Opus Dei World Headquarters and conference centre – is located at 243 Lexington Avenue in New York City. With a price tag of just over $47 million, the 133,000-square-foot tower is clad in red brick and Indiana limestone. Designed by May & Pinska, the building contains over one hundred bedrooms, six dining rooms, libraries, living rooms, meeting rooms and offices. The second, eighth and sixteenth floors contain chapels, ornamented with millwork and marble. The seventeenth floor is entirely residential. Men enter the building through the main doors on Lexington Avenue. Women enter through a side street and are 'acoustically and visually separated' from the men at all times within the building.

Earlier this evening, within the sanctuary of his penthouse apartment, Bishop Manuel Aringarosa had packed a small travel bag and dressed in a traditional black cassock. Normally, he would have wrapped a purple cincture around his waist, but tonight he would be travelling among the public, and he preferred not to draw attention to his high office. Only those with a keen eye would notice his 14-carat gold bishop's ring with purple amethyst, large diamonds and hand-tooled mitre-crozier appliqué. Throwing the travel bag over his shoulder, he said a silent prayer and left his apartment, descending to the lobby where his driver was waiting to take him to the airport.

Now, sitting aboard a commercial airliner bound for Rome, Aringarosa gazed out of the window at the dark Atlantic. The sun had already set, but Aringarosa knew his own star was on the rise. *Tonight the battle will be won*, he thought, amazed that only months ago he had felt powerless against the hands that threatened to destroy his empire.

As president-general of Opus Dei, Bishop Aringarosa had spent the last decade of his life spreading the message of 'God's Work' – literally, *Opus Dei*. The congregation, founded in 1928 by the Spanish priest Josemaría Escrivá, promoted a return to conservative Catholic values and encouraged its members to make sweeping sacrifices in their own lives in order to do the Work of God.

Opus Dei's traditionalist philosophy initially had taken root in Spain before Franco's regime, but with the 1934 publication of Josemaría Escrivá's spiritual book *The Way* – 999 points of meditation for doing God's Work in one's own life – Escrivá's message exploded across the world. Now, with over four million copies of *The Way* in circulation in forty-two languages, Opus Dei was a global force. Its residence halls, teaching centres and even universities could be found in almost every major metropolis on earth. Opus Dei was the fastest-growing and most financially secure Catholic organization in the world. Unfortunately, Aringarosa had learned, in an age of religious cynicism, cults and televangelists, Opus Dei's escalating wealth and power were a magnet for suspicion.

'Many call Opus Dei a brainwashing cult,' reporters often challenged. 'Others call you an ultra-conservative Christian secret society. Which are you?'

'Opus Dei is neither,' the bishop would patiently reply. 'We are a Catholic Church. We are a congregation of Catholics who have chosen as our priority to follow Catholic doctrine as rigorously as we can in our own daily lives.'

'Does God's Work necessarily include vows of chastity, tithing and atonement for sins through self-flagellation and the *cilice?*'

'You are describing only a small portion of the Opus Dei population,' Aringarosa said. 'There are many levels of involvement. Thousands of Opus Dei members are married, have families and do God's Work in their own communities. Others choose lives of asceticism within our cloistered residence halls. These choices are personal, but everyone in Opus Dei shares the goal of bettering the world by doing the Work of God. Surely this is an admirable quest.'

Reason seldom worked, though. The media always gravitated toward scandal, and Opus Dei, like most large organizations, had within its membership a few misguided souls who cast a shadow over the entire group.

Two months ago, an Opus Dei group at a midwestern university had been caught drugging new recruits with mescaline in an effort to induce a euphoric state that neophytes would perceive as a religious experience. Another university student had used his barbed *cilice* belt more often than the recommended two hours a day and had given himself a near lethal infection. In Boston not long ago, a disillusioned young investment banker had signed over his entire life savings to Opus Dei before attempting suicide.

Misguided sheep, Aringarosa thought, his heart going out to them.

Of course, the ultimate embarrassment had been the widely publicized trial of FBI spy Robert Hanssen, who, in addition to being a prominent member of Opus Dei, had turned out to be a sexual deviant, his trial uncovering evidence that he had rigged hidden video cameras in his own bedroom so his friends could watch him having sex with his wife. 'Hardly the pastime of a devout Catholic,' the judge had noted.

Sadly, all of these events had helped spawn the new watch group known as the Opus Dei Awareness Network (ODAN). The group's popular website – *www.odan.org* – relayed frightening stories from former Opus Dei members who warned of the dangers of joining. The media was now referring to Opus Dei as 'God's Mafia' and 'the Cult of Christ'.

We fear what we do not understand, Aringarosa thought, wondering if these critics had any idea how many lives Opus Dei had enriched. The group enjoyed the full endorsement and blessing of the Vatican. *Opus Dei is a personal prelature of the Pope himself.*

Recently, however, Opus Dei had found itself threatened by a force infinitely more powerful than the media . . . an unexpected foe from which Aringarosa could not possibly hide. Five months ago, the kaleidoscope of power had been shaken, and Aringarosa was still reeling from the blow.

'They know not the war they have begun,' Aringarosa whispered to himself, staring out of the plane's window at the darkness of the ocean below. For an instant, his eyes refocused, lingering on the reflection of his awkward face – dark and oblong, dominated by a flat, crooked nose that had been shattered by a fist in Spain when he was a young missionary. The physical flaw barely registered now. Aringarosa's was a world of the soul, not of the flesh.

As the jet passed over the coast of Portugal, the cell phone in Aringarosa's cassock began vibrating in silent ring mode. Despite airline regulations prohibiting the use of cell phones during flights, Aringarosa knew this was a call he could not miss. Only one man possessed this number, the man who had mailed Aringarosa the phone.

Excited, the bishop answered quietly. 'Yes?'

'Silas has located the keystone,' the caller said. 'It is in Paris. Within the Church of Saint-Sulpice.'

Bishop Aringarosa smiled. 'Then we are close.'

'We can obtain it immediately. But we need your influence.'

'Of course. Tell me what to do.'

When Aringarosa switched off the phone, his heart was pounding. He gazed once again into the void of night, feeling dwarfed by the events he had put into motion.

Five hundred miles away, the albino named Silas stood over a small basin of water and dabbed the blood from his back, watching the patterns of red spinning in the water. *Purge me with hyssop and I shall be clean,* he prayed, quoting Psalms. *Wash me, and I shall be whiter than snow.*

Silas was feeling an aroused anticipation that he had not felt since his previous life. It both surprised and electrified him. For the last decade, he had been following *The Way,* cleansing himself of sins . . . rebuilding his life . . . erasing the violence in his past. Tonight, however, it had all come rushing back. The hatred he had fought so hard to bury had been summoned. He had been startled how quickly his past had resurfaced. And with it, of course, had come his skills. Rusty but serviceable.

Jesus' message is one of peace . . . of nonviolence . . . of love. This was the message Silas had been taught from the beginning, and the message he held in his heart. And yet *this* was the message the enemies of Christ now threatened to destroy. *Those who threaten God with force will be met with force. Immovable and steadfast.*

For two millennium, Christian soldiers had

defended their faith against those who tried to displace it. Tonight, Silas had been called to battle.

Drying his wounds, he donned his ankle-length, hooded robe. It was plain, made of dark wool, accentuating the whiteness of his skin and hair. Tightening the rope-tie around his waist, he raised the hood over his head and allowed his red eyes to admire his reflection in the mirror. *The wheels are in motion.*

Chapter 6

Having squeezed beneath the security gate, Robert Langdon now stood just inside the entrance to the Grand Gallery. He was staring into the mouth of a long, deep canyon. On either side of the gallery, stark walls rose thirty feet, evaporating into the darkness above. The reddish glow of the service lighting sifted upward, casting an unnatural smoulder across a staggering collection of Da Vincis, Titians and Caravaggios that hung suspended from ceiling cables. Still lifes, religious scenes and landscapes accompanied portraits of nobility and politicians.

Although the Grand Gallery housed the Louvre's most famous Italian art, many visitors felt the wing's most stunning offering was actually its famous parquet floor. Laid out in a dazzling geometric design of diagonal oak slats, the floor produced an ephemeral optical illusion – a multi-dimensional network that gave visitors the sense they were floating through the gallery on a surface that changed with every step.

As Langdon's gaze began to trace the inlay, his eyes stopped short on an unexpected object lying on the floor just a few yards to his left, surrounded by police tape. He spun toward Fache. 'Is that . . . a *Caravaggio* on the floor?'

Fache nodded without even looking.

The painting, Langdon guessed, was worth upward of two million dollars, and yet it was lying on the floor like a discarded poster. 'What the devil is it doing on the floor!'

Fache glowered, clearly unmoved. 'This is a crime scene, Mr Langdon. We have touched nothing. That canvas was pulled from the wall by the curator. It was how he activated the security system.'

Langdon looked back at the gate, trying to picture what had happened.

'The curator was attacked in his office, fled into the Grand Gallery, and activated the security gate by pulling that painting from the wall. The gate fell immediately, sealing off all access. This is the only door in or out of this gallery.'

Langdon felt confused. 'So the curator actually captured his attacker inside the Grand Gallery?'

Fache shook his head. 'The security gate *separated* Saunière from his attacker. The killer was locked out there in the hallway and shot Saunière through this gate.' Fache pointed toward an orange tag hanging from one of the bars on the gate under which they had just passed. 'The PTS team found flashback residue from a gun. He fired through the bars. Saunière died in here alone.'

Langdon pictured the photograph of Saunière's body. *They said he did that to himself.* Langdon looked out at the enormous corridor before them. 'So where is his body?'

Fache straightened his cruciform tie clip and began to walk. 'As you probably know, the Grand Gallery is quite long.'

The exact length, if Langdon recalled correctly, was around fifteen hundred feet, the length of three Washington Monuments laid end to end. Equally breathtaking was the corridor's width, which easily could have accommodated a pair of side-by-side passenger trains. The centre of the hallway was dotted by the occasional statue or colossal porcelain urn, which served as a tasteful divider and kept the flow of traffic moving down one wall and up the other.

Fache was silent now, striding briskly up the right side of the corridor with his gaze dead ahead. Langdon felt almost disrespectful to be racing past so many masterpieces without pausing for so much as a glance.

Not that I could see anything in this lighting, he thought.

The muted crimson lighting unfortunately conjured memories of Langdon's last experience in noninvasive lighting in the Vatican Secret Archives. This was tonight's second unsettling parallel with his near-death in Rome. He flashed on Vittoria again. She had been absent from his dreams for months. Langdon could not believe Rome had been only a year ago; it felt like decades. *Another life.* His last correspondence from Vittoria had been in December – a postcard saying she was headed to the Java Sea to continue her research in entanglement physics . . . something about using satellites to track manta ray migrations. Langdon had never harboured delusions that a woman like Vittoria Vetra could have been happy living with him on a college campus, but their encounter in Rome had unlocked in him a longing he never imagined he could feel. His lifelong affinity for bachelorhood and the simple freedoms it allowed had been shaken somehow . . . replaced by an unexpected emptiness that seemed to have grown over the past year.

They continued walking briskly, yet Langdon still saw no corpse. 'Jacques Saunière went this *far*?'

'Mr Saunière suffered a bullet wound to his stomach. He died very slowly. Perhaps over fifteen or twenty minutes. He was obviously a man of great personal strength.'

Langdon turned, appalled. 'Security took *fifteen* minutes to get here?'

'Of course not. Louvre security responded immediately to the alarm and found the Grand Gallery sealed. Through the gate, they could hear someone moving around at the far end of the corridor, but they could not see who it was. They shouted, but they got no answer. Assuming it could only be a criminal, they followed protocol and called in the Judicial Police. We took up positions within fifteen minutes. When we arrived, we raised the barricade enough to slip underneath, and I sent a dozen armed agents inside. They swept the length of the gallery to corner the intruder.'

'And?'

'They found no one inside. Except . . .' He pointed farther down the hall. 'Him.'

Langdon lifted his gaze and followed Fache's outstretched finger. At first he thought Fache was pointing to a large marble statue in the middle of the hallway. As they continued, though, Langdon began to see past the statue. Thirty yards down the hall, a single spotlight on a portable pole stand shone down on the floor, creating a stark island of white light in the dark crimson gallery. In the centre of the light, like an insect under a microscope, the corpse of the curator lay naked on the parquet floor.

'You saw the photograph,' Fache said, 'so this should be of no surprise.'

Langdon felt a deep chill as they approached the body. Before him was one of the strangest images he had ever seen.

The pallid corpse of Jacques Saunière lay on the parquet floor exactly as it appeared in the photograph. As Langdon stood over the body and squinted in the harsh light, he reminded himself to his amazement that Saunière had spent his last minutes of life arranging his own body in this strange fashion.

Saunière looked remarkably fit for a man of his years . . . and all of his musculature was in plain view. He had stripped off every shred of clothing, placed it neatly on the floor, and lain down on his back in the centre of the wide corridor, perfectly aligned with the long axis of the room. His arms and legs were sprawled outward in a wide spread-eagle, like those of a child making a snow angel . . . or, perhaps more appropriately, like a man being drawn and quartered by some invisible force.

Just below Saunière's breastbone, a bloody smear marked the spot where the bullet had pierced his flesh. The wound had bled surprisingly little, leaving only a small pool of blackened blood.

Saunière's left index finger was also bloody, apparently having been dipped into the wound to create the most unsettling aspect of his own macabre deathbed; using his own blood as ink, and employing his own naked abdomen as a canvas, Saunière had drawn a simple symbol on his flesh – five straight lines that intersected to form a five-pointed star.

The pentacle.

The bloody star, centred on Saunière's navel, gave his corpse a distinctly ghoulish aura. The photo Langdon had seen was chilling enough, but now, witnessing the scene in person, Langdon felt a deepening uneasiness.

He did this to himself.

'Mr Langdon?' Fache's dark eyes settled on him again.

'It's a pentacle,' Langdon offered, his voice feeling hollow in the huge space. 'One of the oldest symbols on earth. Used over four thousand years before Christ.'

'And what does it mean?'

Langdon always hesitated when he got this question. Telling someone what a symbol 'meant' was like telling them how a song should make them feel – it was different for all people. A white Ku Klux Klan headpiece conjured images of hatred and racism in the United States, and yet the same costume carried a meaning of religious faith in Spain.

'Symbols carry different meanings in different settings,' Langdon said. 'Primarily, the pentacle is a pagan religious symbol.'

Fache nodded. 'Devil worship.'

'No,' Langdon corrected, immediately realizing his choice of vocabulary should have been clearer.

Nowadays, the term *pagan* had become almost synonymous with devil worship – a gross misconception. The word's roots actually reached back to the Latin *paganus*, meaning country-dwellers. 'Pagans' were literally unindoctrinated country-folk who clung to the old, rural religions of Nature worship. In fact, so strong was the Church's fear of those who lived in the rural *villes* that the once innocuous word for 'villager' – *vilain* – came to mean a wicked soul.

'The pentacle,' Langdon clarified, 'is a pre-Christian symbol that relates to Nature worship. The ancients envisioned their world in two halves – masculine and feminine. Their gods and goddesses worked to keep a balance of power. Yin and yang. When male and female were balanced, there was harmony in the world. When they were unbalanced, there was chaos.' Langdon motioned to Saunière's stomach. 'This pentacle is representative of the *female* half of all things – a concept religious historians call the 'sacred feminine' or the 'divine goddess'. Saunière, of all people, would know this.'

'Saunière drew a *goddess* symbol on his stomach?'

Langdon had to admit, it seemed odd. 'In its most specific interpretation, the pentacle symbolizes Venus – the goddess of female sexual love and beauty.'

Fache eyed the naked man, and grunted.

'Early religion was based on the divine order of Nature. The goddess Venus and the planet Venus were one and the same. The goddess had a place in the nighttime sky and was known by many names – Venus, the Eastern Star, Ishtar, Astarte – all of them powerful female concepts with ties to Nature and Mother Earth.'

Fache looked more troubled now, as if he somehow preferred the idea of devil worship.

Langdon decided not to share the pentacle's most astonishing property – the *graphic* origin of its ties to Venus. As a young astronomy student, Langdon had been stunned to learn the planet Venus traced a *perfect* pentacle across the ecliptic sky every eight years. So astonished were the ancients to observe this phenomenon, that Venus and her pentacle became symbols of perfection, beauty, and the cyclic qualities of sexual love. As a tribute to the magic of Venus, the Greeks used her eight-year cycle to organize their Olympic games. Nowadays, few people realized that the four-year schedule of modern Olympics still followed the half-cycles of Venus. Even fewer people knew that the five-pointed star had almost become the official Olympic seal but was modified at the last moment – its five points exchanged for five inter-secting rings to better reflect the games' spirit of inclusion and harmony.

'Mr Langdon,' Fache said abruptly. 'Obviously, the pentacle must *also* relate to the devil. Your American horror films make that point clearly.'

Langdon frowned. *Thank you, Hollywood.* The five-pointed star was now a virtual cliché in Satanic serial killer films, usually scrawled on the wall of some Satanist's apartment along with other alleged demonic symbology. Langdon was always frustrated when he saw the symbol in this context; the pentacle's true origins were actually quite godly.

'I assure you,' Langdon said, 'despite what you see in the movies, the pentacle's demonic interpretation is historically inaccurate. The original feminine meaning is correct, but the symbolism of the pentacle has been distorted over the millennium. In this case, through bloodshed.'

'I'm not sure I follow.'

Langdon glanced at Fache's crucifix, uncertain how to phrase his next point. 'The Church, sir. Symbols are very resilient, but the pentacle was altered by the early Roman Catholic Church. As part of the Vatican's campaign to eradicate pagan religions and convert the masses to Christianity, the Church launched a smear campaign against the pagan gods and goddesses, recasting their divine symbols as evil.'

'Go on.'

'This is very common in times of turmoil,' Langdon continued. 'A newly emerging power will take over the existing symbols and degrade them over time in an attempt to erase their meaning. In the battle between the pagan symbols and Christian symbols, the pagans lost; Poseidon's trident became the devil's pitchfork, the wise crone's pointed hat became the symbol of a witch, and Venus's pentacle became a sign of the devil.' Langdon paused. 'Unfortunately, the United States military has also perverted the pentacle; it's now our foremost symbol of war. We paint it on all our fighter jets and hang it on the shoulders of all our generals.' *So much for the goddess of love and beauty.*

'Interesting.' Fache nodded toward the spread-eagle

corpse. 'And the positioning of the body? What do you make of that?'

Langdon shrugged. 'The position simply reinforces the reference to the pentacle and sacred feminine.'

Fache's expression clouded. 'I beg your pardon?'

'Replication. Repeating a symbol is the simplest way to strengthen its meaning. Jacques Saunière positioned himself in the shape of a five-pointed star.' *If one pentacle is good, two is better.*

Fache's eyes followed the five points of Saunière's arms, legs, and head as he again ran a hand across his slick hair. 'Interesting analysis.' He paused. 'And the *nudity?*' He grumbled as he spoke the word, sounding repulsed by the sight of an aging male body. 'Why did he remove his clothing?'

Damned good question, Langdon thought. He'd been wondering the same thing ever since he first saw the Polaroid. His best guess was that a naked human form was yet another endorsement of Venus – the goddess of human sexuality. Although modern culture had erased much of Venus's association with the male/female physical union, a sharp etymological eye could still spot a vestige of Venus's original meaning in the word 'venereal'. Langdon decided not to go there.

'Mr Fache, I obviously can't tell you why Mr Saunière drew that symbol on himself or placed himself in this way, but I *can* tell you that a man like Jacques Saunière would consider the pentacle a sign of the female deity. The correlation between this symbol and the sacred feminine is widely known by art historians and symbologists.'

'Fine. And the use of his own blood as ink?'

'Obviously he had nothing else to write with.'

Fache was silent a moment. 'Actually, I believe he used blood such that the police would follow certain forensic procedures.'

'I'm sorry?'

'Look at his left hand.'

Langdon's eyes traced the length of the curator's pale arm to his left hand but saw nothing. Uncertain, he circled the corpse and crouched down, now noting with surprise that the curator was clutching a large, felt-tipped marker.

'Saunière was holding it when we found him,' Fache said, leaving Langdon and moving several yards to a portable table covered with investigation tools, cables and assorted electronic gear. 'As I told you,' he said, rummaging around the table, 'we have touched nothing. Are you familiar with this kind of pen?'

Langdon knelt down farther to see the pen's label.

STYLO DE LUMIERE NOIRE.

He glanced up in surprise.

The black-light pen or watermark stylus was a specialized felt-tipped marker originally designed by museums, restorers and forgery police to place invisible marks on items. The stylus wrote in a noncorrosive, alcohol-based fluorescent ink that was visible only under black light. Nowadays, museum maintenance staffs carried these markers on their daily rounds to place invisible 'tick marks' on the frames of paintings that needed restoration.

As Langdon stood up, Fache walked over to the spotlight and turned it off. The gallery plunged into sudden darkness.

Momentarily blinded, Langdon felt a rising uncertainty. Fache's silhouette appeared, illuminated in bright purple. He approached carrying a portable light source, which shrouded him in a violet haze.

'As you may know,' Fache said, his eyes luminescing in the violet glow, 'police use black-light illumination to search crime scenes for blood and other forensic

evidence. So you can imagine our surprise...'
Abruptly, he pointed the light down at the corpse.

Langdon looked down and jumped back in shock.

His heart pounded as he took in the bizarre sight now glowing before him on the parquet floor. Scrawled in luminescent handwriting, the curator's final words glowed purple beside his corpse. As Langdon stared at the shimmering text, he felt the fog that had surrounded this entire night growing thicker.

Langdon read the message again and looked up at Fache. 'What the hell does this mean!'

Fache's eyes shone white. '*That*, monsieur, is precisely the question you are here to answer.'

Not far away, inside Saunière's office, Lieutenant Collet had returned to the Louvre and was huddled over an audio console set up on the curator's enormous desk. With the exception of the eerie, robot-like doll of a medieval knight that seemed to be staring at him from the corner of Saunière's desk, Collet was comfortable. He adjusted his AKG headphones and checked the input levels on the hard-disk recording system. All systems were go. The microphones were functioning flawlessly, and the audio feed was crystal clear.

Le moment de vérité, he mused.

Smiling, he closed his eyes and settled in to enjoy the rest of the conversation now being taped inside the Grand Gallery.

Chapter 7

The modest dwelling within the Church of Saint-Sulpice was located on the second floor of the church itself, to the left of the choir balcony. A two-room suite with a stone floor and minimal furnishings, it had been home to Sister Sandrine Bieil for over a decade. The nearby convent was her formal residence, if anyone asked, but she preferred the quiet of the church and had made herself quite comfortable upstairs with a bed, phone and hot plate.

As the church's *conservatrice d'affaires*, Sister Sandrine was responsible for overseeing all non-religious aspects of church operations – general maintenance, hiring support staff and guides, securing the building after hours, and ordering supplies like communion wine and wafers.

Tonight, asleep in her small bed, she awoke to the shrill of her telephone. Tiredly, she lifted the receiver.

'*Soeur Sandrine. Eglise Saint-Sulpice.*'

'Hello, Sister,' the man said in French.

Sister Sandrine sat up. *What time is it?* Although she recognized her boss's voice, in fifteen years she had never been awoken by him. The abbé was a deeply pious man who went home to bed immediately after mass.

'I apologize if I have awoken you, Sister,' the abbé said, his own voice sounding groggy and on edge. 'I have a favour to ask of you. I just received a call from an influential American bishop. Perhaps you know him? Manuel Aringarosa?'

'The head of Opus Dei?' *Of course I know of him. Who in the Church doesn't?* Aringarosa's conservative prelature had grown powerful in recent years. Their ascension to grace was jump-started in 1982 when Pope John Paul II unexpectedly elevated them to a 'personal prelature of the Pope', officially sanctioning all of their practices. Suspiciously, Opus Dei's elevation occurred the same year the wealthy sect allegedly had transferred almost one billion dollars into the Vatican's Institute for Religious Works – commonly known as the Vatican Bank – bailing it out of an embarrassing bankruptcy. In a second manoeuvre that raised eyebrows, the Pope placed the founder of Opus Dei on the 'fast track' for sainthood, accelerating an often century-long waiting period for canonization to a mere twenty years. Sister Sandrine could not help but feel that Opus Dei's good standing in Rome was suspect, but one did not argue with the Holy See.

'Bishop Aringarosa called to ask me a favour,' the abbé told her, his voice nervous. 'One of his numeraries is in Paris tonight. . . .'

As Sister Sandrine listened to the odd request, she felt a deepening confusion. 'I'm sorry, you say this visiting Opus Dei numerary cannot wait until morning?'

'I'm afraid not. His plane leaves very early. He has always dreamed of seeing Saint-Sulpice.'

'But the church is far more interesting by day. The sun's rays through the oculus, the graduated shadows on the gnomon, *this* is what makes Saint-Sulpice unique.'

'Sister, I agree, and yet I would consider it a personal favour if you could let him in tonight. He can be there at . . . say one o'clock? That's in twenty minutes.'

Sister Sandrine frowned. 'Of course. It would be my pleasure.'

The abbé thanked her and hung up.

Puzzled, Sister Sandrine remained a moment in the warmth of her bed, trying to shake off the cobwebs of sleep. Her sixty-year-old body did not awake as fast as it used to, although tonight's phone call had certainly roused her senses. Opus Dei had always made her uneasy. Beyond the prelature's adherence to the arcane ritual of corporal mortification, their views on women were medieval at best. She had been shocked to learn that female numeraries were forced to clean the men's residence halls for no pay while the men were at mass; women slept on hardwood floors, while the men had straw mats; and women were forced to endure additional requirements of corporal mortification . . . all as added penance for original sin. It seemed Eve's bite from the apple of knowledge was a debt women were doomed to pay for eternity. Sadly, while most of the Catholic Church was gradually moving in the right direction with respect to women's rights, Opus Dei threatened to reverse the progress. Even so, Sister Sandrine had her orders.

Swinging her legs off the bed, she stood slowly, chilled by the cold stone on the soles of her bare feet. As the chill rose through her flesh, she felt an unexpected apprehension.

Women's intuition?

A follower of God, Sister Sandrine had learned to find peace in the calming voices of her own soul. Tonight, however, those voices were as silent as the empty church around her.

Chapter 8

Langdon couldn't tear his eyes from the glowing purple text scrawled across the parquet floor. Jacques Saunière's final communication seemed as unlikely a departing message as any Langdon could imagine.

The message read:

13-3-2-21-1-1-8-5

O, Draconian devil!

Oh, lame saint!

Although Langdon had not the slightest idea what it meant, he did understand Fache's instinct that the pentacle had something to do with devil worship.

O, Draconian devil!

Saunière had left a literal reference to the devil. Equally as bizarre was the series of numbers. 'Part of it looks like a numeric cipher.'

'Yes,' Fache said. 'Our cryptographers are already working on it. We believe these numbers may be the key to who killed him. Maybe a telephone exchange or some kind of social identification. Do the numbers have any symbolic meaning to you?'

Langdon looked again at the digits, sensing it would take him hours to extract any symbolic meaning. *If Saunière had even intended any.* To Langdon, the numbers looked totally random. He was accustomed to symbolic progressions that made some semblance of sense, but everything here – the pentacle, the text, the numbers – seemed disparate at the most fundamental level.

'You alleged earlier,' Fache said, 'that Saunière's actions here were all in an effort to send some sort of message . . . goddess worship or something in that vein? How does this message fit in?'

Langdon knew the question was rhetorical. This bizarre communiqué obviously did not fit Langdon's scenario of goddess worship at all.

O, Draconian devil? Oh, lame saint?

Fache said, 'This text appears to be an accusation of some sort. Wouldn't you agree?'

Langdon tried to imagine the curator's final minutes trapped alone in the Grand Gallery, knowing he was about to die. It seemed logical. 'An accusation against his murderer makes sense, I suppose.'

'My job, of course, is to put a name to that person. Let me ask you this, Mr Langdon. To your eye, beyond the numbers, what about this message is most strange?'

Most strange? A dying man had barricaded himself in the gallery, drawn a pentacle on himself, and scrawled a mysterious accusation on the floor. What about the scenario *wasn't* strange?

'The word "Draconian"?' he ventured, offering the first thing that came to mind. Langdon was fairly certain that a reference to Draco – the ruthless seventh-century BC politician – was an unlikely dying thought. ' "Draconian devil" seems an odd choice of vocabulary.'

'*Draconian?*' Fache's tone came with a tinge of impatience now. 'Saunière's choice of vocabulary hardly seems the primary issue here.'

Langdon wasn't sure what issue Fache had in mind, but he was starting to suspect that Draco and Fache would have got along well.

'Saunière was a Frenchman,' Fache said flatly. 'He

lived in Paris. And yet he chose to write this message . . .'

'In English,' Langdon said, now realizing the captain's meaning.

Fache nodded. '*Précisément*. Any idea why?'

Langdon knew Saunière spoke impeccable English, and yet the reason he had chosen English as the language in which to write his final words escaped Langdon. He shrugged.

Fache motioned back to the pentacle on Saunière's abdomen. 'Nothing to do with devil worship? Are you still certain?'

Langdon was certain of nothing any more. 'The symbology and text don't seem to coincide. I'm sorry I can't be of more help.'

'Perhaps this will clarify.' Fache backed away from the body and raised the black light again, letting the beam spread out in a wider angle. 'And now?'

To Langdon's amazement, a rudimentary circle glowed around the curator's body. Saunière had apparently lain down and swung the pen around himself in several long arcs, essentially inscribing himself inside a circle.

In a flash, the meaning became clear.

'*The Vitruvian Man*,' Langdon gasped. Saunière had created a life-sized replica of Leonardo da Vinci's most famous sketch.

Considered the most anatomically correct drawing of its day, Da Vinci's *The Vitruvian Man* had become a modern-day icon of culture, appearing on posters, mouse pads and T-shirts around the world. The celebrated sketch consisted of a perfect circle in which was inscribed a nude male . . . his arms and legs outstretched in a naked spread-eagle.

Da Vinci. Langdon felt a shiver of amazement. The clarity of Saunière's intentions could not be denied. In

71

his final moments of life, the curator had stripped off his clothing and arranged his body in a clear image of Leonardo da Vinci's *Vitruvian Man*.

The circle had been the missing critical element. A feminine symbol of protection, the circle around the naked man's body completed Da Vinci's intended message – male and female harmony. The question now, though, was *why* Saunière would imitate a famous drawing.

'Mr Langdon,' Fache said, 'certainly a man like yourself is aware that Leonardo da Vinci had a tendency toward the darker arts.'

Langdon was surprised by Fache's knowledge of Da Vinci, and it certainly went a long way toward explaining the captain's suspicions about devil worship. Da Vinci had always been an awkward subject for historians, especially in the Christian tradition. Despite the visionary's genius, he was a flamboyant homosexual and worshipper of Nature's divine order, both of which placed him in a perpetual state of sin against God. Moreover, the artist's eerie eccentricities projected an admittedly demonic aura: Da Vinci exhumed corpses to study human anatomy; he kept mysterious journals in illegible reverse handwriting; he believed he possessed the alchemic power to turn lead into gold and even cheat God by creating an elixir to postpone death; and his inventions included horrific, never-before-imagined weapons of war and torture.

Misunderstanding breeds distrust, Langdon thought.

Even Da Vinci's enormous output of breathtaking Christian art only furthered the artist's reputation for spiritual hypocrisy. Accepting hundreds of lucrative Vatican commissions, Da Vinci painted Christian themes not as an expression of his own beliefs but rather as a commercial venture – a means of funding a lavish lifestyle. Unfortunately, Da Vinci was a prankster who often amused himself by quietly gnawing at the hand that fed him. He incorporated in many of his Christian paintings hidden symbolism that was anything but Christian – tributes to his own beliefs and a subtle thumbing of his nose at the Church. Langdon had even given a lecture once at the National Gallery in London entitled: 'The Secret Life of Leonardo: Pagan Symbolism in Christian Art.'

'I understand your concerns,' Langdon now said, 'but Da Vinci never really practised any dark arts. He was an exceptionally spiritual man, albeit one in constant conflict with the Church.' As Langdon said this, an odd thought popped into his mind. He glanced down at the message on the floor again. *O, Draconian devil! Oh, lame saint!*

'Yes?' Fache said.

Langdon weighed his words carefully. 'I was just thinking that Saunière shared a lot of spiritual ideologies with Da Vinci, including a concern over the Church's elimination of the sacred feminine from modern religion. Maybe, by imitating a famous Da Vinci drawing, Saunière was simply echoing some of their shared frustrations with the modern Church's demonization of the goddess.'

Fache's eyes hardened. 'You think Saunière is calling the Church a lame saint and a Draconian devil?'

Langdon had to admit it seemed far-fetched, and yet the pentacle seemed to endorse the idea on some level. 'All I am saying is that Mr Saunière dedicated his life to studying the history of the goddess, and nothing has done more to erase that history than the Catholic Church. It seems reasonable that Saunière might have chosen to express his disappointment in his final good-bye.'

'Disappointment?' Fache demanded, sounding

hostile now. 'This message sounds more *enraged* than disappointed, wouldn't you say?'

Langdon was reaching the end of his patience. 'Captain, you asked for my instincts as to what Saunière is trying to say here, and that's what I'm giving you.'

'That this is an indictment of the Church?' Fache's jaw tightened as he spoke through clenched teeth. 'Mr Langdon, I have seen a lot of death in my work, and let me tell you something. When a man is murdered by another man, I do not believe his final thoughts are to write an obscure spiritual statement that no one will understand. I believe he is thinking of one thing only.' Fache's whispery voice sliced the air. '*La vengeance*. I believe Saunière wrote this note to tell us who killed him.'

Langdon stared. 'But that makes no sense whatsoever.'

'No?'

'No,' he fired back, tired and frustrated. 'You told me Saunière was attacked in his office by someone he had apparently invited in.'

'Yes.'

'So it seems reasonable to conclude that the curator *knew* his attacker.'

Fache nodded. 'Go on.'

'So if Saunière *knew* the person who killed him, what kind of indictment is this?' He pointed at the floor. 'Numeric codes? Lame saints? Draconian devils? Pentacles on his stomach? It's all too cryptic.'

Fache frowned as if the idea had never occurred to him. 'You have a point.'

'Considering the circumstances,' Langdon said, 'I would assume that if Saunière wanted to tell you who killed him, he would have written down somebody's *name*.'

As Langdon spoke those words, a smug smile crossed Fache's lips for the first time all night. *'Précisément,'* Fache said. *'Précisément.'*

I am witnessing the work of a master, mused Lieutenant Collet as he tweaked his audio gear and listened to Fache's voice coming through the headphones. The *agent supérieur* knew it was moments like these that had lifted the captain to the pinnacle of French law enforcement.

Fache will do what no one else dares.

The delicate art of *cajoler* was a lost skill in modern law enforcement, one that required exceptional poise under pressure. Few men possessed the necessary sangfroid for this kind of operation, but Fache seemed born for it. His restraint and patience bordered on the robotic.

Fache's sole emotion this evening seemed to be one of intense resolve, as if this arrest were somehow personal to him. Fache's briefing of his agents an hour ago had been unusually succinct and assured. *I know who murdered Jacques Saunière,* Fache had said. *You know what to do. No mistakes tonight.*

And so far, no mistakes had been made.

Collet was not yet privy to the evidence that had cemented Fache's certainty of their suspect's guilt, but he knew better than to question the instincts of the Bull. Fache's intuition seemed almost supernatural at times. *God whispers in his ear,* one agent had insisted after a particularly impressive display of Fache's sixth sense. Collet had to admit, if there was a God, Bezu Fache would be on His A-list. The captain attended mass and confession with zealous regularity – far more than the requisite holiday attendance fulfilled by other officials in the name of good public relations. When the Pope visited Paris a few years back, Fache had used all his muscle to obtain the honour of an audience. A photo of Fache with the Pope now hung in his office. *The Papal Bull*, the agents secretly called it.

Collet found it ironic that one of Fache's rare popular public stances in recent years had been his outspoken reaction to the Catholic paedophilia scandal. *These priests should be hanged twice!* Fache had declared. *Once for their crimes against children. And once for shaming the good name of the Catholic Church.* Collet had the odd sense it was the latter that angered Fache more.

Turning now to his laptop computer, Collet attended to the other half of his responsibilities here tonight – the GPS tracking system. The image onscreen revealed a detailed floor plan of the Denon Wing, a structural schematic uploaded from the Louvre Security Office. Letting his eyes trace the maze of galleries and hallways, Collet found what he was looking for.

Deep in the heart of the Grand Gallery blinked a tiny red dot.

La marque.

Fache was keeping his prey on a very tight leash tonight. Wisely so. Robert Langdon had proven himself one cool customer.

Chapter 9

To ensure his conversation with Mr Langdon would not be interrupted, Bezu Fache had turned off his cellular phone. Unfortunately, it was an expensive model equipped with a two-way radio feature, which, contrary to his orders, was now being used by one of his agents to page him.

'Capitaine?' The phone crackled like a walkie-talkie.

Fache felt his teeth clench in rage. He could imagine nothing important enough that Collet would interrupt this *surveillance cachée* – especially at this critical juncture.

He gave Langdon a calm look of apology. 'One moment please.' He pulled the phone from his belt and pressed the radio transmission button. *'Oui?'*

'Capitaine, un agent du Département de Cryptographie est arrivé.'

Fache's anger stalled momentarily. *A cryptographer?* Despite the lousy timing, this was probably good news. Fache, after finding Saunière's cryptic text on the floor, had uploaded photographs of the entire crime scene to the Cryptography Department in hopes someone there could tell him what the hell Saunière was trying to say. If a code breaker had now arrived, it most likely meant someone had decrypted Saunière's message.

'I'm busy at the moment,' Fache radioed back, leaving no doubt in his tone that a line had been crossed. 'Ask the cryptographer to wait at the command post. I'll speak to him when I'm done.'

'*Her,*' the voice corrected. 'It's Agent Neveu.'

Fache was becoming less amused with this call every passing moment. Sophie Neveu was one of DCPJ's biggest mistakes. A young Parisian *déchiffreuse* who had studied cryptography in England at Royal Holloway, Sophie Neveu had been foisted on Fache two years ago as part of the ministry's attempt to incorporate more women into the police force. The ministry's ongoing foray into political correctness, Fache argued, was weakening the department. Women not only lacked the physicality necessary for police work, but their mere presence posed a dangerous distraction to the men in the field. As Fache had feared, Sophie Neveu was proving far more distracting than most.

At thirty-two years old, she had a dogged determination that bordered on obstinate. Her eager espousal of Britain's new cryptologic methodology continually exasperated the veteran French cryptographers above her. And by far the most troubling to Fache was the inescapable universal truth that in an office of middle-aged men, an attractive young woman always drew eyes away from the work at hand.

The man on the radio said, 'Agent Neveu insisted on speaking to you immediately, Captain. I tried to stop her, but she's on her way into the gallery.'

Fache recoiled in disbelief. 'Unacceptable! I made it very clear—'

For a moment, Robert Langdon thought Bezu Fache was suffering a stroke. The captain was mid-sentence when his jaw stopped moving and his eyes bulged. His blistering gaze seemed fixated on something over Langdon's shoulder. Before Langdon could turn to see what it was, he heard a woman's voice chime out behind him.

'*Excusez-moi, messieurs.*'

Langdon turned to see a young woman approaching. She was moving down the corridor toward them with long, fluid strides . . . a haunting certainty to her gait. Dressed casually in a knee-length, cream-coloured Irish sweater over black leggings, she was attractive and looked to be about thirty. Her thick burgundy hair fell unstyled to her shoulders, framing the warmth of her face. Unlike the waifish, cookie-cutter blondes that adorned Harvard dorm room walls, this woman was healthy with an unembellished beauty and genuineness that radiated a striking personal confidence.

To Langdon's surprise, the woman walked directly up to him and extended a polite hand. 'Monsieur Langdon, I am Agent Neveu from DCPJ's Cryptology Department.' Her words curved richly around her muted Anglo-Franco accent. 'It is a pleasure to meet you.'

Langdon took her soft palm in his and felt himself momentarily fixed in her strong gaze. Her eyes were olive-green – incisive and clear.

Fache drew a seething inhalation, clearly preparing to launch into a reprimand.

'Captain,' she said, turning quickly and beating him to the punch, 'please excuse the interruption, but—'

'*Ce n'est pas le moment!*' Fache sputtered.

'I tried to phone you.' Sophie continued in English, as if out of courtesy to Langdon. 'But your cell phone was turned off.'

'I turned it off for a reason,' Fache hissed. 'I am speaking to Mr Langdon.'

'I've deciphered the numeric code,' she said flatly.

Langdon felt a pulse of excitement. *She broke the code?*

Fache looked uncertain how to respond.

'Before I explain,' Sophie said, 'I have an urgent message for Mr Langdon.'

Fache's expression turned to one of deepening concern. 'For Mr Langdon?'

She nodded, turning back to Langdon. 'You need to contact the US Embassy, Mr Langdon. They have a message for you from the States.'

Langdon reacted with surprise, his excitement over the code giving way to a sudden ripple of concern. *A message from the States?* He tried to imagine who could be trying to reach him. Only a few of his colleagues knew he was in Paris.

Fache's broad jaw had tightened with the news. 'The US Embassy?' he demanded, sounding suspicious. 'How would they know to find Mr Langdon *here?*'

Sophie shrugged. 'Apparently they called Mr Langdon's hotel, and the concierge told them Mr Langdon had been collected by a DCPJ agent.'

Fache looked troubled. 'And the embassy contacted DCPJ *Cryptography?*'

'No, sir,' Sophie said, her voice firm. 'When I called the DCPJ switchboard in an attempt to contact you, they had a message waiting for Mr Langdon and asked me to pass it along if I got through to you.'

Fache's brow furrowed in apparent confusion. He opened his mouth to speak, but Sophie had already turned back to Langdon.

'Mr Langdon,' she declared, pulling a small slip of paper from her pocket, 'this is the number for your embassy's messaging service. They asked that you phone in as soon as possible.' She handed him the paper with an intent gaze. 'While I explain the code to Captain Fache, you need to make this call.'

Langdon studied the slip. It had a Paris phone number and extension on it. 'Thank you,' he said, feeling worried now. 'Where do I find a phone?'

Sophie began to pull a cell phone from her sweater pocket, but Fache waved her off. He now looked like Mount Vesuvius about to erupt. Without taking his eyes off Sophie, he produced his own cell phone and held it out. 'This line is secure, Mr Langdon. You may use it.'

Langdon felt mystified by Fache's anger with the young woman. Feeling uneasy, he accepted the captain's phone. Fache immediately marched Sophie several steps away and began chastising her in hushed tones. Disliking the captain more and more, Langdon turned away from the odd confrontation and switched on the cell phone. Checking the slip of paper Sophie had given him, Langdon dialled the number.

The line began to ring.

One ring . . . two rings . . . three rings . . .

Finally the call connected.

Langdon expected to hear an embassy operator, but he found himself instead listening to an answering machine. Oddly, the voice on the tape was familiar. It was that of Sophie Neveu.

'Bonjour, vous êtes bien chez Sophie Neveu,' the woman's voice said. *'Je suis absente pour le moment, mais . . .'*

Confused, Langdon turned back toward Sophie. 'I'm sorry, Ms Neveu? I think you may have given me—'

'No, that's the right number,' Sophie interjected quickly, as if anticipating Langdon's confusion. 'The embassy has an automated message system. You have to dial an access code to pick up your messages.'

Langdon stared. 'But—'

'It's the three-digit code on the paper I gave you.'

Langdon opened his mouth to explain the bizarre error, but Sophie flashed him a silencing glare that lasted only an instant. Her green eyes sent a crystal-clear message.

Don't ask questions. Just do it.

Bewildered, Langdon punched in the extension on the slip of paper: 454.

Sophie's outgoing message immediately cut off, and Langdon heard an electronic voice announce in French: 'You have *one* new message.' Apparently, 454 was Sophie's remote access code for picking up her messages while away from home.

I'm picking up this woman's messages?

Langdon could hear the tape rewinding now. Finally, it stopped, and the machine engaged. Langdon listened as the message began to play. Again, the voice on the line was Sophie's.

'Mr Langdon,' the message began in a fearful whisper. 'Do *not* react to this message. Just listen calmly. You are in danger right now. Follow my directions very closely.'

Chapter 10

Silas sat behind the wheel of the black Audi the Teacher had arranged for him and gazed out at the great Church of Saint-Sulpice. Lit from beneath by banks of floodlights, the church's two bell towers rose like stalwart sentinels above the building's long body. On either flank, a shadowy row of sleek buttresses jutted out like the ribs of a beautiful beast.

The heathens used a house of God to conceal their keystone. Again the brotherhood had confirmed their legendary reputation for illusion and deceit. Silas was looking forward to finding the keystone and giving it to the Teacher so they could recover what the brotherhood had long ago stolen from the faithful.

How powerful that will make Opus Dei.

Parking the Audi on the deserted Place Saint-Sulpice, Silas exhaled, telling himself to clear his mind for the task at hand. His broad back still ached from the corporal mortification he had endured earlier today, and yet the pain was inconsequential compared with the anguish of his life before Opus Dei had saved him.

Still, the memories haunted his soul.

Release your hatred, Silas commanded himself. *Forgive those who trespassed against you.*

Looking up at the stone towers of Saint-Sulpice, Silas fought that familiar undertow . . . that force that often dragged his mind back in time, locking him once again in the prison that had been his world as a young man. The memories of purgatory came as they always did, like a tempest to his senses . . . the reek of rotting cabbage, the stench of death, human urine and faeces. The cries of hopelessness against the howling wind of the Pyrenees and the soft sobs of forgotten men.

Andorra, he thought, feeling his muscles tighten.

Incredibly, it was in that barren and forsaken suzerain between Spain and France, shivering in his stone cell, wanting only to die, that Silas had been saved.

He had not realized it at the time.

The light came long after the thunder.

His name was not Silas then, although he didn't recall the name his parents had given him. He had left home when he was seven. His drunken father, a burly dockworker, enraged by the arrival of an albino son, beat his mother regularly, blaming her for the boy's embarrassing condition. When the boy tried to defend her, he too was badly beaten.

One night, there was a horrific fight, and his mother never got up. The boy stood over his lifeless mother and felt an unbearable upwelling of guilt for permitting it to happen.

This is my fault!

As if some kind of demon were controlling his body, the boy walked to the kitchen and grasped a butcher's knife. Hypnotically, he moved to the bedroom where his father lay on the bed in a drunken stupor. Without a word, the boy stabbed him in the back. His father cried out in pain and tried to roll over, but his son stabbed him again, over and over until the apartment fell quiet.

The boy fled home but found the streets of Marseilles equally unfriendly. His strange appearance made him an outcast among the other young run-aways, and he was forced to live alone in the basement of a dilapidated factory, eating stolen fruit and raw fish from the dock. His only companions were tattered magazines he found in the trash, and he taught himself to read them. Over time, he grew strong. When he was twelve, another drifter – a girl twice his age – mocked him on the streets and attempted to steal his food. The girl found herself pummeled to within inches of her life. When the authorities pulled the boy off her, they gave him an ultimatum – leave Marseilles or go to juvenile prison.

The boy moved down the coast to Toulon. Over time, the looks of pity on the streets turned to looks of fear. The boy had grown to a powerful young man. When people passed by, he could hear them whispering to one another. *A ghost,* they would say, their eyes wide with fright as they stared at his white skin. *A ghost with the eyes of a devil!*

And he felt like a ghost . . . transparent . . . floating from seaport to seaport.

People seemed to look right through him.

At eighteen, in a port town, while attempting to steal a case of cured ham from a cargo ship, he was caught by a pair of crewmen. The two sailors who began to beat him smelled of beer, just as his father had. The memories of fear and hatred surfaced like a monster from the deep. The young man broke the first sailor's neck with his bare hands, and only the arrival of the police saved the second sailor from a similar fate.

Two months later, in shackles, he arrived at a prison in Andorra.

You are as white as a ghost, the inmates ridiculed as the guards marched him in, naked and cold. *Mira el espectro! Perhaps the ghost will pass right through these walls!*

Over the course of twelve years, his flesh and soul withered until he knew he had become transparent.

I am a ghost.

I am weightless.

Yo soy un espectro ... pálido como un fantasma ... caminando este mundo a solas.

One night the ghost awoke to the screams of other inmates. He didn't know what invisible force was shaking the floor on which he slept, nor what mighty hand was trembling the mortar of his stone cell, but as he jumped to his feet, a large boulder toppled onto the very spot where he had been sleeping. Looking up to see where the stone had come from, he saw a hole in the trembling wall, and beyond it, a vision he had not seen in over ten years. The moon.

Even while the earth still shook, the ghost found himself scrambling through a narrow tunnel, staggering out into an expansive vista, and tumbling down a barren mountainside into the woods. He ran all night, always downward, delirious with hunger and exhaustion.

Skirting the edges of consciousness, he found himself at dawn in a clearing where train tracks cut a swath across the forest. Following the rails, he moved on as if dreaming. Seeing an empty freight car, he crawled in for shelter and rest. When he awoke the train was moving. *How long? How far?* A pain was growing in his gut. *Am I dying?* He slept again. This time he awoke to someone yelling, beating him, throwing him out of the freight car. Bloody, he wandered the outskirts of a small village looking in vain for food. Finally, his body too weak to take another step, he lay down by the side of the road and slipped into unconsciousness.

The light came slowly, and the ghost wondered how long he had been dead. *A day? Three days?* It didn't matter. His bed was soft like a cloud, and the air around him smelled sweet with candles. Jesus was there, staring down at him. *I am here,* Jesus said. *The stone has been rolled aside, and you are born again.*

He slept and awoke. Fog shrouded his thoughts. He had never believed in heaven, and yet Jesus was watching over him. Food appeared beside his bed, and the ghost ate it, almost able to feel the flesh materializing on his bones. He slept again. When he awoke, Jesus was still smiling down, speaking. *You are saved, my son. Blessed are those who follow my path.*

Again, he slept.

It was a scream of anguish that startled the ghost from his slumber. His body leapt out of bed, staggered down a hallway toward the sounds of shouting. He entered a kitchen and saw a large man beating a smaller man. Without knowing why, the ghost grabbed the large man and hurled him backward against a wall. The man fled, leaving the ghost standing over the body of a young man in priest's robes. The priest had a badly shattered nose. Lifting the bloody priest, the ghost carried him to a couch.

'Thank you, my friend,' the priest said in awkward French. 'The offertory money is tempting for thieves. You speak French in your sleep. Do you also speak Spanish?'

The ghost shook his head.

'What is your name?' he continued in broken French.

The ghost could not remember the name his parents had given him. All he heard were the taunting gibes of the prison guards.

The priest smiled. '*No hay problema.* My name is Manuel Aringarosa. I am a missionary from Madrid. I was sent here to build a church for the Obra de Dios.'

'Where am I?' His voice sounded hollow.

'Oviedo. In the north of Spain.'

'How did I get here?'

'Someone left you on my doorstep. You were ill. I fed you. You've been here many days.'

The ghost studied his young caretaker. Years had passed since anyone had shown any kindness. 'Thank you, Father.'

The priest touched his bloody lip. 'It is I who am thankful, my friend.'

When the ghost awoke in the morning, his world felt clearer. He gazed up at the crucifix on the wall above his bed. Although it no longer spoke to him, he felt a comforting aura in its presence. Sitting up, he was surprised to find a newspaper clipping on his bedside table. The article was in French, a week old. When he read the story, he was filled with fear. It told of an earthquake in the mountains that had destroyed a prison and freed many dangerous criminals.

His heart began pounding. *The priest knows who I am!* The emotion he felt was one he had not felt for some time. Shame. Guilt. It was accompanied by the fear of being caught. He jumped from his bed. *Where do I run?*

'The Book of Acts,' a voice said from the door.

The ghost turned, frightened.

The young priest was smiling as he entered. His nose was awkwardly bandaged, and he was holding out an old Bible. 'I found one in French for you. The chapter is marked.'

Uncertain, the ghost took the Bible and looked at the chapter the priest had marked.

Acts 16.

The verses told of a prisoner named Silas who lay naked and beaten in his cell, singing hymns to God. When the ghost reached Verse 26, he gasped in shock.

'. . . *And suddenly, there was a great earthquake, so that the foundations of the prison were shaken, and all the doors fell open.*'

His eyes shot up at the priest.

The priest smiled warmly. 'From now on, my friend, if you have no other name, I shall call you Silas.'

The ghost nodded blankly. *Silas*. He had been given flesh. *My name is Silas.*

'It's time for breakfast,' the priest said. 'You will need your strength if you are to help me build this church.'

Twenty thousand feet above the Mediterranean, Alitalia flight 1618 bounced in turbulence, causing passengers to shift nervously. Bishop Aringarosa barely noticed. His thoughts were with the future of Opus Dei. Eager to know how plans in Paris were progressing, he wished he could phone Silas. But he could not. The Teacher had seen to that.

'It is for your own safety,' the Teacher had explained, speaking in English with a French accent. 'I am familiar enough with electronic communications to know they can be intercepted. The results could be disastrous for you.'

Aringarosa knew he was right. The Teacher seemed an exceptionally careful man. He had not revealed his own identity to Aringarosa, and yet he had proven himself a man well worth obeying. After all, he had somehow obtained very secret information. *The names of the brotherhood's four top members!* This had been one of the coups that convinced the bishop the Teacher was truly capable of delivering the astonishing prize he claimed he could unearth.

'Bishop,' the Teacher had told him, 'I have made all the arrangements. For my plan to succeed, you must allow Silas to answer *only* to me for several days. The two of you will not speak. I will communicate with him through secure channels.'

'You will treat him with respect?'

'A man of faith deserves the highest.'

'Excellent. Then I understand. Silas and I shall not speak until this is over.'

'I do this to protect your identity, Silas's identity, and my investment.'

'Your investment?'

'Bishop, if your own eagerness to keep abreast of progress puts you in jail, then you will be unable to pay me my fee.'

The bishop smiled. 'A fine point. Our desires are in accord. Godspeed.'

Twenty million euros, the bishop thought, now gazing out the plane's window. The sum was approximately the same number of US dollars. *A pittance for something so powerful.*

He felt a renewed confidence that the Teacher and Silas would not fail. Money and faith were powerful motivators.

Chapter 11

'Une plaisanterie numérique?' Bezu Fache was livid, glaring at Sophie Neveu in disbelief. *A numeric joke?* 'Your professional assessment of Saunière's code is that it is some kind of mathematical prank?'

Fache was in utter incomprehension of this woman's gall. Not only had she just barged in on Fache without permission, but she was now trying to convince him that Saunière, in his final moments of life, had been inspired to leave a mathematical gag?

'This code,' Sophie explained in rapid French, 'is simplistic to the point of absurdity. Jacques Saunière must have known we would see through it immediately.' She pulled a scrap of paper from her sweater pocket and handed it to Fache. 'Here is the decryption.'

Fache looked at the card.

$$1\text{-}1\text{-}2\text{-}3\text{-}5\text{-}8\text{-}13\text{-}21$$

'This is it?' he snapped. 'All you did was put the numbers in increasing order!'

Sophie actually had the nerve to give a satisfied smile. 'Exactly.'

Fache's tone lowered to a guttural rumble. 'Agent Neveu, I have no idea where the hell you're going with this, but I suggest you get there fast.' He shot an anxious glance at Langdon, who stood nearby with the phone pressed to his ear, apparently still listening to his phone message from the US Embassy. From

91

Langdon's ashen expression, Fache sensed the news was bad.

'Captain,' Sophie said, her tone dangerously defiant, 'the sequence of numbers you have in your hand happens to be one of the most famous mathematical progressions in history.'

Fache was not aware there even existed a mathematical progression that qualified as famous, and he certainly didn't appreciate Sophie's off-hand tone.

'This is the Fibonacci sequence,' she declared, nodding toward the piece of paper in Fache's hand. 'A progression in which each term is equal to the sum of the two preceding terms.'

Fache studied the numbers. Each term was indeed the sum of the two previous, and yet Fache could not imagine what the relevance of all this was to Saunière's death.

'Mathematician Leonardo Fibonacci created this succession of numbers in the thirteenth century. Obviously there can be no coincidence that *all* of the numbers Saunière wrote on the floor belong to Fibonacci's famous sequence.'

Fache stared at the young woman for several moments. 'Fine, if there is no coincidence, would you tell me *why* Jacques Saunière chose to do this. What is he saying? What does this *mean*?'

She shrugged. 'Absolutely nothing. That's the point. It's a simplistic cryptographic joke. Like taking the words of a famous poem and shuffling them at random to see if anyone recognizes what all the words have in common.'

Fache took a menacing step forward, placing his face only inches from Sophie's. 'I certainly hope you have a much more satisfying explanation than *that*.'

Sophie's soft features grew surprisingly stern as she leaned in. 'Captain, considering what you have at stake here tonight, I thought you might appreciate knowing that Jacques Saunière might be playing games with you. Apparently not. I'll inform the director of Cryptography you no longer need our services.'

With that, she turned on her heel, and marched off the way she had come.

Stunned, Fache watched her disappear into the darkness. *Is she out of her mind?* Sophie Neveu had just redefined *le suicide professionnel*.

Fache turned to Langdon, who was still on the phone, looking more concerned than before, listening intently to his phone message. *The US Embassy.* Bezu Fache despised many things . . . but few drew more wrath than the US Embassy.

Fache and the ambassador locked horns regularly over shared affairs of state – their most common battleground being law enforcement for visiting Americans. Almost daily, DCPJ arrested American exchange students in possession of drugs, US businessmen for soliciting underage prostitutes, American tourists for shoplifting or destruction of property. Legally, the US Embassy could intervene and extradite guilty citizens back to the United States, where they received nothing more than a slap on the wrist.

And the embassy invariably did just that.

L'émasculation de la Police Judiciaire, Fache called it. *Paris Match* had run a cartoon recently depicting Fache as a police dog, trying to bite an American criminal, but unable to reach because it was chained to the US Embassy.

Not tonight, Fache told himself. *There is far too much at stake.*

By the time Robert Langdon hung up the phone, he looked ill.

'Is everything all right?' Fache asked.

Weakly, Langdon shook his head.

Bad news from home, Fache sensed, noticing Langdon was sweating slightly as Fache took back his cell phone.

'An accident,' Langdon stammered, looking at Fache with a strange expression. 'A friend . . .' He hesitated. 'I'll need to fly home first thing in the morning.'

Fache had no doubt the shock on Langdon's face was genuine, and yet he sensed another emotion there too, as if a distant fear were suddenly simmering in the American's eyes. 'I'm sorry to hear that,' Fache said, watching Langdon closely. 'Would you like to sit down?' He motioned toward one of the viewing benches in the gallery.

Langdon nodded absently and took a few steps toward the bench. He paused, looking more confused with every moment. 'Actually, I think I'd like to use the toilet.'

Fache frowned inwardly at the delay. 'The toilet. Of course. Let's take a break for a few minutes.' He motioned back down the long hallway in the direction they had come from. 'The toilets are back toward the curator's office.'

Langdon hesitated, pointing in the other direction toward the far end of the Grand Gallery corridor. 'I believe there's a much closer toilet at the end.'

Fache realized Langdon was right. They were two thirds of the way down, and the Grand Gallery dead-ended at a pair of toilets. 'Shall I accompany you?'

Langdon shook his head, already moving deeper into the gallery. 'Not necessary. I think I'd like a few minutes alone.'

Fache was not wild about the idea of Langdon wandering alone down the remaining length of

94

corridor, but he took comfort in knowing the Grand Gallery was a dead end whose only exit was at the other end – the gate under which they had entered. Although French fire regulations required several emergency stairwells for a space this large, those stairwells had been sealed automatically when Saunière tripped the security system. Granted, that system had now been reset, unlocking the stairwells, but it didn't matter – the external doors, if opened, would set off fire alarms and were guarded outside by DCPJ agents. Langdon could not possibly leave without Fache knowing about it.

'I need to return to Mr Saunière's office for a moment,' Fache said. 'Please come and find me directly, Mr Langdon. There is more we need to discuss.'

Langdon gave a quiet wave as he disappeared into the darkness.

Turning, Fache marched angrily in the opposite direction. Arriving at the gate, he slid under, exited the Grand Gallery, marched down the hall, and stormed into the command centre at Saunière's office.

'Who gave the approval to let Sophie Neveu into this building!' Fache bellowed.

Collet was the first to answer. 'She told the guards outside she'd broken the code.'

Fache looked around. 'Is she gone?'

'She's not with you?'

'She left.' Fache glanced out at the darkened hallway. Apparently Sophie had been in no mood to stop by and chat with the other officers on her way out.

For a moment, Fache considered radioing the guards in the entresol and telling them to stop Sophie and drag her back up here before she could leave the premises. He thought better of it. That was only his pride talking . . . wanting the last word. He'd had enough distractions tonight.

Deal with Agent Neveu later, he told himself, already looking forward to firing her.

Pushing Sophie from his mind, Fache stared for a moment at the miniature knight standing on Saunière's desk. Then he turned back to Collet. 'Do you have him?'

Collet gave a curt nod and spun the laptop toward Fache. The red dot was clearly visible on the floor plan overlay, blinking methodically in a room marked TOILETTES PUBLIQUES.

'Good,' Fache said, lighting a cigarette and stalking into the hall. 'I've got a phone call to make. Be damned sure the toilet is the only place Langdon goes.'

Chapter 12

Robert Langdon felt light-headed as he trudged toward the end of the Grand Gallery. Sophie's phone message played over and over in his mind. At the end of the corridor, illuminated signs bearing the international stick-figure symbols for toilets guided him through a maze-like series of dividers displaying Italian drawings and hiding the toilets from sight.

Finding the men's room door, Langdon entered and turned on the lights.

The room was empty.

Walking to the sink, he splashed cold water on his face and tried to wake up. Harsh fluorescent lights glared off the stark tiles, and the room smelled of ammonia. As he towelled off, the door creaked open behind him. He spun.

Sophie Neveu entered, her green eyes flashing fear. 'Thank God you came. We don't have much time.'

Langdon stood beside the sinks, staring in bewilderment at DCPJ cryptographer Sophie Neveu. Only minutes ago, Langdon had listened to her phone message, thinking the newly arrived cryptographer must be insane. And yet, the more he listened, the more he sensed Sophie Neveu was speaking in earnest. *Do not react to this message. Just listen calmly. You are in danger right now. Follow my directions very closely.* Filled with uncertainty, Langdon had decided to do exactly as Sophie advised. He told Fache that the phone message was regarding an injured friend back home. Then he had asked to use the toilet at the end of the Grand Gallery.

Sophie stood before him now, still catching her breath after doubling back to the toilets. In the fluorescent lights, Langdon was surprised to see that her strong air actually radiated from unexpectedly soft features. Only her gaze was sharp, and the juxtaposition conjured images of a multilayered Renoir portrait . . . veiled but distinct, with a boldness that somehow retained its shroud of mystery.

'I wanted to warn you, Mr Langdon . . .' Sophie began, still catching her breath, 'that you are *sous surveillance cachée*. Under a guarded observation.' As she spoke, her accented English resonated off the tiled walls, giving her voice a hollow quality.

'But . . . why?' Langdon demanded. Sophie had already given him an explanation on the phone, but he wanted to hear it from her lips.

'Because,' she said, stepping toward him, 'Fache's primary suspect in this murder is *you*.'

Langdon was braced for the words, and yet they still sounded utterly ridiculous. According to Sophie, Langdon had been called to the Louvre tonight not as a symbologist but rather as a *suspect* and was currently the unwitting target of one of DCPJ's favourite interrogation methods – *surveillance cachée* – a deft deception in which the police calmly invited a suspect to a crime scene and interviewed him in hopes he would get nervous and mistakenly incriminate himself.

'Look in your jacket's left pocket,' Sophie said. 'You'll find proof they are watching you.'

Langdon felt his apprehension rising. *Look in my pocket?* It sounded like some kind of cheap magic trick.

'Just look.'

Bewildered, Langdon reached his hand into his tweed jacket's left pocket – one he never used. Feeling around inside, he found nothing. *What the devil did you expect?* He began wondering if Sophie might just be insane after all. Then his fingers brushed something unexpected. Small and hard. Pinching the tiny object between his fingers, Langdon pulled it out and stared in astonishment. It was a metallic, button-shaped disk, about the size of a watch battery. He had never seen it before. 'What the . . . ?'

'GPS tracking dot,' Sophie said. 'Continuously transmits its location to a Global Positioning System satellite that DCPJ can monitor. We use them to monitor people's locations. It's accurate within two feet anywhere on the globe. They have you on an electronic leash. The agent who picked you up at the hotel slipped it inside your pocket before you left your room.'

Langdon flashed back to the hotel room . . . his quick shower, getting dressed, the DCPJ agent politely holding out Langdon's tweed coat as they left the room. *It's cool outside, Mr Langdon,* the agent had said. *Spring in Paris is not all your song boasts.* Langdon had thanked him and donned the jacket.

Sophie's olive gaze was keen. 'I didn't tell you about the tracking dot earlier because I didn't want you checking your pocket in front of Fache. He can't know you've found it.'

Langdon had no idea how to respond.

'They tagged you with GPS because they thought you might run.' She paused. 'In fact, they *hoped* you would run; it would make their case stronger.'

'Why would I run!' Langdon demanded. 'I'm innocent!'

'Fache feels otherwise.'

Angrily, Langdon stalked toward the trash receptacle to dispose of the tracking dot.

'No!' Sophie grabbed his arm and stopped him. 'Leave it in your pocket. If you throw it out, the signal will stop moving, and they'll know you found the dot. The only reason Fache left you alone is because he can monitor where you are. If he thinks you've discovered what he's doing . . .' Sophie did not finish the thought. Instead, she prised the metallic disc from Langdon's hand and slid it back into the pocket of his tweed coat. 'The dot stays with you. At least for the moment.'

Langdon felt lost. 'How the hell could Fache actually believe I killed Jacques Saunière!'

'He has some fairly persuasive reasons to suspect you.' Sophie's expression was grim. 'There is a piece of evidence here that you have not yet seen. Fache has kept it carefully hidden from you.'

Langdon could only stare.

'Do you recall the three lines of text that Saunière wrote on the floor?'

Langdon nodded. The numbers and words were imprinted on Langdon's mind.

Sophie's voice dropped to a whisper now. 'Unfortunately, what you saw was not the entire message. There was a *fourth* line that Fache photographed and then wiped clean before you arrived.'

Although Langdon knew the soluble ink of a watermark stylus could easily be wiped away, he could not imagine why Fache would erase evidence.

'The last line of the message,' Sophie said, 'was something Fache did not want you to know about.' She paused. 'At least not until he was done with you.'

Sophie produced a computer printout of a photo from her sweater pocket and began unfolding it. 'Fache uploaded images of the crime scene to the Cryptology Department earlier tonight in hopes we could figure out what Saunière's message was trying to say. This is a photo of the complete message.' She handed the page to Langdon.

Bewildered, Langdon looked at the image. The close-up photo revealed the glowing message on the parquet floor. The final line hit Langdon like a kick in the gut.

13-3-2-21-1-1-8-5
O, Draconian devil!
Oh, lame saint!
P.S. Find Robert Langdon

Chapter 13

For several seconds, Langdon stared in wonder at the photograph of Saunière's postscript. *P.S. Find Robert Langdon*. He felt as if the floor were tilting beneath his feet. *Saunière left a postscript with my name on it?* In his wildest dreams, Langdon could not fathom why.

'Now do you understand,' Sophie said, her eyes urgent, 'why Fache ordered you here tonight, and why you are his primary suspect?'

The only thing Langdon understood at the moment was why Fache had looked so smug when Langdon suggested Saunière would have accused his killer by name.

Find Robert Langdon.

'Why would Saunière write this?' Langdon demanded, his confusion now giving way to anger. 'Why would I want to kill Jacques Saunière?'

'Fache has yet to uncover a motive, but he has been recording his entire conversation with you tonight in hopes you might reveal one.'

Langdon opened his mouth, but still no words came.

'He's fitted with a miniature microphone,' Sophie explained. 'It's connected to a transmitter in his pocket that radios the signal back to the command post.'

'This is impossible,' Langdon stammered. 'I have an alibi. I went directly back to my hotel after my lecture. You can ask the hotel desk.'

'Fache already did. His report shows you retrieving

your room key from the concierge at about ten-thirty. Unfortunately, the time of the murder was closer to eleven. You easily could have left your hotel room unseen.'

'This is insanity! Fache has no evidence!'

Sophie's eyes widened as if to say: *No evidence*? 'Mr Langdon, your name is written on the floor beside the body, and Saunière's date book says you were with him at approximately the time of the murder.' She paused. 'Fache has more than enough evidence to take you into custody for questioning.'

Langdon suddenly sensed that he needed a lawyer. 'I didn't do this.'

Sophie sighed. 'This is not American television, Mr Langdon. In France, the laws protect the police, not criminals. Unfortunately, in this case, there is also the media consideration. Jacques Saunière was a very prominent and well-loved figure in Paris, and his murder will be news in the morning. Fache will be under immediate pressure to make a statement, and he looks a lot better having a suspect in custody already. Whether or not you are guilty, you most certainly will be held by DCPJ until they can figure out what really happened.'

Langdon felt like a caged animal. 'Why are you telling me all this?'

'Because, Mr Langdon, I believe you are innocent.' Sophie looked away for a moment and then back into his eyes. 'And also because it is partially *my* fault that you're in trouble.'

'I'm sorry? It's *your* fault Saunière is trying to frame me?'

'Saunière wasn't trying to frame you. It was a mistake. That message on the floor was meant for me.'

Langdon needed a minute to process that one. 'I beg your pardon?'

103

'That message wasn't for the police. He wrote it for *me*. I think he was forced to do everything in such a hurry that he just didn't realize how it would look to the police.' She paused. 'The numbered code is meaningless. Saunière wrote it to make sure the investigation included cryptographers, ensuring that *I* would know as soon as possible what had happened to him.'

Langdon felt himself losing touch fast. Whether or not Sophie Neveu had lost her mind was at this point up for grabs, but at least Langdon now understood why she was trying to help him. *P.S. Find Robert Langdon.* She apparently believed the curator had left her a cryptic postscript telling her to find Langdon. 'But why do you think his message was for you?'

'The Vitruvian Man,' she said flatly. 'That particular sketch has always been my favourite Da Vinci work. Tonight he used it to catch my attention.'

'Hold on. You're saying the curator *knew* your favourite piece of art?'

She nodded. 'I'm sorry. This is all coming out of order. Jacques Saunière and I . . .'

Sophie's voice caught, and Langdon heard a sudden melancholy there, a painful past, simmering just below the surface. Sophie and Jacques Saunière apparently had some kind of special relationship. Langdon studied the beautiful young woman before him, well aware that aging men in France often took young mistresses. Even so, Sophie Neveu as a 'kept woman' somehow didn't seem to fit.

'We had a falling-out ten years ago,' Sophie said, her voice a whisper now. 'We've barely spoken since. Tonight, when Crypto got the call that he had been murdered, and I saw the images of his body and text on the floor, I realized he was trying to send me a message.'

'Because of *The Vitruvian Man*?'

'Yes. And the letters P.S.'

'*Post Script?*'

She shook her head. 'P.S. are my initials.'

'But your name is Sophie Neveu.'

She looked away. 'P.S. is the nickname he called me when I lived with him.' She blushed. 'It stood for *Princesse Sophie.*'

Langdon had no response.

'Silly, I know,' she said. 'But it was years ago. When I was a little girl.'

'You knew him when you were a little *girl?*'

'Quite well,' she said, her eyes welling now with emotion. 'Jacques Saunière was my grandfather.'

Chapter 14

'Where's Langdon?' Fache demanded, exhaling the last of a cigarette as he paced back into the command post.

'Still in the men's room, sir.' Lieutenant Collet had been expecting the question.

Fache grumbled, 'Taking his time, I see.'

The captain eyed the GPS dot over Collet's shoulder, and Collet could almost hear the wheels turning. Fache was fighting the urge to go and check on Langdon. Ideally, the subject of an observation was allowed the most time and freedom possible, lulling him into a false sense of security. Langdon needed to return of his own volition. Still, it had been almost ten minutes.

Too long.

'Any chance Langdon is onto us?' Fache asked.

Collet shook his head. 'We're still seeing small movements inside the men's room, so the GPS dot is obviously still on him. Perhaps he feels ill? If he had found the dot, he would have removed it and tried to run.'

Fache checked his watch. 'Fine.'

Still Fache seemed preoccupied. All evening, Collet had sensed an atypical intensity in his captain. Usually detached and cool under pressure, Fache tonight seemed emotionally engaged, as if this were somehow a personal matter for him.

Not surprising, Collet thought. *Fache needs this arrest desperately*. Recently the Board of Ministers and the media had become more openly critical of Fache's aggressive tactics, his clashes with powerful foreign embassies, and his gross overbudgeting on new technologies. Tonight, a high-tech, high-profile arrest of an American would go a long way to silence Fache's critics, helping him secure the job a few more years until he could retire with the lucrative pension. *God knows he needs the pension,* Collet thought. Fache's zeal for technology had hurt him both professionally and personally. Fache was rumoured to have invested his entire savings in the technology craze a few years back and lost his shirt. *And Fache is a man who wears only the finest shirts.*

Tonight, there was still plenty of time. Sophie Neveu's odd interruption, though unfortunate, had been only a minor wrinkle. She was gone now, and Fache still had cards to play. He had yet to inform Langdon that his name had been scrawled on the floor by the victim. *P.S. Find Robert Langdon.* The American's reaction to that little bit of evidence would be telling indeed.

'Captain?' one of the DCPJ agents now called from across the office. 'I think you had better take this call.' He was holding out a telephone receiver, looking concerned.

'Who is it?' Fache said.

The agent frowned. 'It's the director of our Cryptography Department.'

'And?'

'It's about Sophie Neveu, sir. Something is not quite right.'

Chapter 15

It was time.

Silas felt strong as he stepped from the black Audi, the nighttime breeze rustling his loose-fitting robe. *The winds of change are in the air.* He knew the task before him would require more finesse than force, and he left his handgun in the car. The thirteen-round Heckler and Koch USP 40 had been provided by the Teacher.

A weapon of death has no place in a house of God.

The plaza before the great church was deserted at this hour, the only visible souls on the far side of Place Saint-Sulpice a couple of teenage hookers showing their wares to the late night tourist traffic. Their nubile bodies sent a familiar longing to Silas's loins. His thigh flexed instinctively, causing the barbed *cilice* belt to cut painfully into his flesh.

The lust evaporated instantly. For ten years now, Silas had faithfully denied himself all sexual indulgence, even self-administered. It was *The Way.* He knew he had sacrificed much to follow Opus Dei, but he had received much more in return. A vow of celibacy and the relinquishment of all personal assets hardly seemed a sacrifice. Considering the poverty from which he had come and the sexual horrors he had endured in prison, celibacy was a welcome change.

Now, having returned to France for the first time since being arrested and shipped to prison in Andorra, Silas could feel his homeland testing him, dragging violent memories from his redeemed soul. *You have been reborn,* he reminded himself. His service to God today had required the sin of murder, and it was a sacrifice Silas knew he would have to hold silently in his heart for all eternity.

The measure of your faith is the measure of the pain you can endure, the Teacher had told him. Silas was no stranger to pain and felt eager to prove himself to the Teacher, the one who had assured him his actions were ordained by a higher power.

'*Hago la obra de Dios,*' Silas whispered, moving now toward the church entrance.

Pausing in the shadow of the massive doorway, he took a deep breath. It was not until this instant that he truly realized what he was about to do, and what awaited him inside.

The keystone. It will lead us to our final goal.

He raised his ghost-white fist and banged three times on the door.

Moments later, the bolts of the enormous wooden portal began to move.

Chapter 16

Sophie wondered how long it would take Fache to figure out she had not left the building. Seeing that Langdon was clearly overwhelmed, Sophie questioned whether she had done the right thing by cornering him here in the men's room.

What else was I supposed to do?

She pictured her grandfather's body, naked and spread-eagled on the floor. There was a time when he had meant the world to her, yet tonight, Sophie was surprised to feel almost no sadness for the man. Jacques Saunière was a stranger to her now. Their relationship had evaporated in a single instant one March night when she was twenty-two. *Ten years ago.* Sophie had come home a few days early from graduate university in England and mistakenly witnessed her grandfather engaged in something Sophie was obviously not supposed to see. It was an image she barely could believe to this day.

If I hadn't seen it with my own eyes ...

Too ashamed and stunned to endure her grandfather's pained attempts to explain, Sophie immediately moved out on her own, taking money she had saved, and getting a small flat with some roommates. She vowed never to speak to anyone about what she had seen. Her grandfather tried desperately to reach her, sending cards and letters, begging Sophie to meet him so he could explain. *Explain how!?* Sophie never responded except once – to forbid him ever to call her or try to meet her in public. She was afraid his explanation would be more terrifying than the incident itself.

Incredibly, Saunière had never given up on her, and Sophie now possessed a decade's worth of correspondence unopened in a dresser drawer. To her grandfather's credit, he had never once disobeyed her request and phoned her.

Until this afternoon.

'Sophie?' His voice had sounded startlingly old on her answering machine. 'I have abided by your wishes for so long . . . and it pains me to call, but I must speak to you. Something terrible has happened.'

Standing in the kitchen of her Paris flat, Sophie felt a chill to hear him again after all these years. His gentle voice brought back a flood of fond childhood memories.

'Sophie, please listen.' He was speaking English to her, as he always did when she was a little girl. *Practise French at school. Practise English at home.* 'You cannot be mad for ever. Have you not read the letters that I've sent all these years? Do you not yet understand?' He paused. 'We must speak at once. Please grant your grandfather this one wish. Call me at the Louvre. Right away. I believe you and I are in grave danger.'

Sophie stared at the answering machine. *Danger?* What was he talking about?

'Princess . . .' Her grandfather's voice cracked with an emotion Sophie could not place. 'I know I've kept things from you, and I know it has cost me your love. But it was for your own safety. Now you must know the truth. Please, I must tell you the truth about your family.'

Sophie suddenly could hear her own heart. *My family?* Sophie's parents had died when she was only four. Their car went off a bridge into fast-moving

111

water. Her grandmother and younger brother had also been in the car, and Sophie's entire family had been erased in an instant. She had a box of newspaper clippings to confirm it.

His words had sent an unexpected surge of longing through her bones. *My family!* In that fleeting instant, Sophie saw images from the dream that had awoken her countless times when she was a little girl: *My family is alive! They are coming home!* But, as in her dream, the pictures evaporated into oblivion.

Your family is dead, Sophie. They are not coming home.

'Sophie . . .' her grandfather said on the machine. 'I have been waiting for years to tell you. Waiting for the right moment, but now time has run out. Call me at the Louvre. As soon as you get this. I'll wait here all night. I fear we both may be in danger. There's so much you need to know.'

The message ended.

In the silence, Sophie stood trembling for what felt like minutes. As she considered her grandfather's message, only one possibility made sense, and his true intent dawned.

It was bait.

Obviously, her grandfather wanted desperately to see her. He was trying anything. Her disgust for the man deepened. Sophie wondered if maybe he had fallen terminally ill and had decided to attempt any ploy he could think of to get Sophie to visit him one last time. If so, he had chosen wisely.

My family.

Now, standing in the darkness of the Louvre men's room, Sophie could hear the echoes of this afternoon's phone message. *Sophie, we both may be in danger. Call me.*

She had not called him. Nor had she planned to. Now, however, her scepticism had been deeply challenged. Her grandfather lay murdered inside his own museum. And he had written a code on the floor.

A code for *her*. Of this, she was certain.

Despite not understanding the meaning of his message, Sophie was certain its cryptic nature was additional proof that the words were intended for her. Sophie's passion and aptitude for cryptography were a product of growing up with Jacques Saunière – a fanatic himself for codes, word games and puzzles. *How many Sundays did we spend doing the cryptograms and crosswords in the newspaper?*

At the age of twelve, Sophie could finish the *Le Monde* crossword without any help, and her grandfather graduated her to crosswords in English, mathematical puzzles and substitution ciphers. Sophie devoured them all. Eventually she turned her passion into a profession by becoming a codebreaker for the Judicial Police.

Tonight, the cryptographer in Sophie was forced to respect the efficiency with which her grandfather had used a simple code to unite two total strangers – Sophie Neveu and Robert Langdon.

The question was *why?*

Unfortunately, from the bewildered look in Langdon's eyes, Sophie sensed the American had no more idea than she did why her grandfather had thrown them together.

She pressed again. 'You and my grandfather had planned to meet tonight. What about?'

Langdon looked truly perplexed. 'His secretary set the meeting and didn't offer any specific reason, and I didn't ask. I assumed he'd heard I would be lecturing on the pagan iconography of French cathedrals, was interested in the topic, and thought it would be fun to meet for drinks after the talk.'

Sophie didn't buy it. The connection was flimsy. Her grandfather knew more about pagan iconography than anyone else on earth. Moreover, he was an exceptionally private man, not someone prone to chatting with random American professors unless there were an important reason.

Sophie took a deep breath and probed further. 'My grandfather called me this afternoon and told me he and I were in grave danger. Does *that* mean anything to you?'

Langdon's blue eyes now clouded with concern. 'No, but considering what just happened . . .'

Sophie nodded. Considering tonight's events, she would be a fool not to be frightened. Feeling drained, she walked to the small plate-glass window at the far end of the bathroom and gazed out in silence through the mesh of alarm tape embedded in the glass. They were high up – forty feet at least.

Sighing, she raised her eyes and gazed out at Paris's dazzling landscape. On her left, across the Seine, the illuminated Eiffel Tower. Straight ahead, the Arc de Triomphe. And to the right, high atop the sloping rise of Montmartre, the graceful arabesque dome of Sacré-Coeur, its polished stone glowing white like a resplendent sanctuary.

Here at the westernmost tip of the Denon Wing, the north-south thoroughfare of Place du Carrousel ran almost flush with the building with only a narrow sidewalk separating it from the Louvre's outer wall. Far below, the usual caravan of the city's nighttime delivery trucks sat idling, waiting for the signals to change, their running lights seeming to twinkle mockingly up at Sophie.

'I don't know what to say,' Langdon said, coming up behind her. 'Your grandfather is obviously trying to tell us something. I'm sorry I'm so little help.'

Sophie turned from the window, sensing a sincere regret in Langdon's deep voice. Even with all the trouble around him, he obviously wanted to help her. *The teacher in him*, she thought, having read DCPJ's workup on their suspect. This was an academic who clearly despised not understanding.

We have that in common, she thought.

As a codebreaker, Sophie made her living extracting meaning from seemingly senseless data. Tonight, her best guess was that Robert Langdon, whether he knew it or not, possessed information that she desperately needed. *Princesse Sophie, Find Robert Langdon.* How much clearer could her grandfather's message be? Sophie needed more time with Langdon. Time to think. Time to sort out this mystery together. Unfortunately, time was running out.

Gazing up at Langdon, Sophie made the only play she could think of. 'Bezu Fache will be taking you into custody at any minute. I can get you out of this museum. But we need to act now.'

Langdon's eyes went wide. 'You want me to *run*?'

'It's the smartest thing you could do. If you let Fache take you into custody now, you'll spend weeks in a French jail while DCPJ and the US Embassy fight over which courts try your case. But if we get you out of here, and make it to your embassy, then your government will protect your rights while you and I prove you had nothing to do with this murder.'

Langdon looked not even vaguely convinced. 'Forget it! Fache has armed guards on every single exit! Even if we escape without being shot, running away only makes me look guilty. You need to tell Fache that the message on the floor was for *you*, and that my name is not there as an accusation.'

'I *will* do that,' Sophie said, speaking hurriedly, 'but after you're safely inside the US Embassy. It's only about a mile from here, and my car is parked just out-side the museum. Dealing with Fache from here is too much of a gamble. Don't you see? Fache has made it his mission tonight to prove you are guilty. The only reason he postponed your arrest was to run this observance in hopes you did something that made his case stronger.'

'Exactly. Like *running!*'

The cell phone in Sophie's sweater pocket suddenly began ringing. *Fache probably.* She reached in her sweater and turned off the phone.

'Mr Langdon,' she said hurriedly, 'I need to ask you one last question.' *And your entire future may depend on it.* 'The writing on the floor is obviously not proof of your guilt, and yet Fache told our team he is *certain* you are his man. Can you think of any other reason he might be convinced you're guilty?'

Langdon was silent for several seconds. 'None whatsoever.'

Sophie sighed. *Which means Fache is lying.* Why, Sophie could not begin to imagine, but that was hardly the issue at this point. The fact remained that Bezu Fache was determined to put Robert Langdon behind bars tonight, at any cost. Sophie needed Langdon for herself, and it was this dilemma that left Sophie only one logical conclusion.

I need to get Langdon to the US Embassy.

Turning toward the window, Sophie gazed through the alarm mesh embedded in the plate glass, down the dizzying forty feet to the pavement below. A leap from this height would leave Langdon with a couple of broken legs. At best.

Nonetheless, Sophie made her decision.

Robert Langdon was about to escape the Louvre, whether he wanted to or not.

Chapter 17

'What do you mean she's not answering?' Fache looked incredulous. 'You're calling her cell phone, right? I know she's carrying it.'

Collet had been trying to reach Sophie now for several minutes. 'Maybe her batteries are dead. Or her ringer's off.'

Fache had looked distressed ever since talking to the director of Cryptography on the phone. After hanging up, he had marched over to Collet and demanded he get Agent Neveu on the line. Now Collet had failed, and Fache was pacing like a caged lion.

'Why did Crypto call?' Collet now ventured.

Fache turned. 'To tell us they found no references to Draconian devils and lame saints.'

'That's all?'

'No, also to tell us that they had just identified the numerics as Fibonacci numbers, but they suspected the series was meaningless.'

Collet was confused. 'But they already sent Agent Neveu to tell us that.'

Fache shook his head. 'They didn't send Neveu.'

'What?'

'According to the director, at my orders he paged his entire team to look at the images I'd wired him. When Agent Neveu arrived, she took one look at the photos of Saunière and the code and left the office without a word. The director said he didn't question her behaviour because she was understandably upset by the photos.'

117

'Upset? She's never seen a picture of a dead body?'

Fache was silent a moment. 'I was not aware of this, and it seems neither was the director until a co-worker informed him, but apparently Sophie Neveu is Jacques Saunière's granddaughter.'

Collet was speechless.

'The director said she never once mentioned Saunière to him, and he assumed it was because she probably didn't want preferential treatment for having a famous grandfather.'

No wonder she was upset by the pictures. Collet could barely conceive of the unfortunate coincidence that called in a young woman to decipher a code written by a dead family member. Still, her actions made no sense. 'But she obviously recognized the numbers as Fibonacci numbers because she came here and *told* us. I don't understand why she would leave the office without telling anyone she had figured it out.'

Collet could think of only one scenario to explain the troubling developments: Saunière had written a numeric code on the floor in hopes Fache would involve cryptographers in the investigation, and therefore involve his own granddaughter. As for the rest of the message, was Saunière communicating in some way with his granddaughter? If so, what did the message tell her? And how did Langdon fit in?

Before Collet could ponder it any further, the silence of the deserted museum was shattered by an alarm. The bell sounded like it was coming from inside the Grand Gallery.

'*Alarme!*' one of the agents yelled, eyeing his feed from the Louvre security centre. '*Grande Galerie! Toilettes Messieurs!*'

Fache wheeled to Collet. 'Where's Langdon?'

'Still in the men's room!' Collet pointed to the blinking red dot on his laptop schematic. 'He must have broken the window!' Collet knew Langdon wouldn't get far. Although Paris fire codes required windows above fifteen metres in public buildings be breakable in case of fire, exiting a Louvre second-storey window without the help of a hook and ladder would be suicide. Furthermore, there were no trees or grass on the western end of the Denon Wing to cushion a fall. Directly beneath that toilet window, the two-lane Place du Carrousel ran within a few feet of the outer wall. 'My God,' Collet exclaimed, eyeing the screen. 'Langdon's moving to the window ledge!'

But Fache was already in motion. Yanking his Manurhin MR-93 revolver from his shoulder holster, the captain dashed out of the office.

Collet watched the screen in bewilderment as the blinking dot arrived at the window ledge and then did something utterly unexpected. The dot moved *outside* the perimeter of the building.

What's going on? he wondered. *Is Langdon out on a ledge or—*

'Jesus!' Collet jumped to his feet as the dot shot farther outside the wall. The signal seemed to shudder for a moment, and then the blinking dot came to an abrupt stop about ten yards outside the perimeter of the building.

Fumbling with the controls, Collet called up a Paris street map and recalibrated the GPS. Zooming in, he could now see the exact location of the signal.

It was no longer moving.

It lay at a dead stop in the middle of Place du Carrousel.

Langdon had jumped.

Chapter 18

Fache sprinted down the Grand Gallery as Collet's radio blared over the distant sound of the alarm.

'He jumped!' Collet was yelling. 'I'm showing the signal out on Place du Carrousel! Outside the toilet window! And it's not moving at all! Jesus, I think Langdon has just committed suicide!'

Fache heard the words, but they made no sense. He kept running. The hallway seemed never-ending. As he sprinted past Saunière's body, he set his sights on the partitions at the far end of the Denon Wing. The alarm was getting louder now.

'Wait!' Collet's voice blared again over the radio. 'He's moving! My God, he's alive. Langdon's moving!'

Fache kept running, cursing the length of the hallway with every step.

'Langdon's moving faster!' Collet was still yelling on the radio. 'He's running down Carrousel. Wait . . . he's picking up speed. He's moving too fast!'

Arriving at the partitions, Fache snaked his way through them, saw the toilets door, and ran for it.

The walkie-talkie was barely audible now over the alarm. 'He must be in a car! I think he's in a car! I can't—'

Collet's words were swallowed by the alarm as Fache finally burst into the men's room with his gun drawn. Wincing against the piercing shrill, he scanned the area.

The stalls were empty. The washroom deserted. Fache's eyes moved immediately to the shattered window at the far end of the room. He ran to the opening and looked over the edge. Langdon was nowhere to be seen. Fache could not imagine anyone risking a stunt like this. Certainly if he had dropped that far, he would be badly injured.

The alarm cut off finally, and Collet's voice became audible again over the walkie-talkie.

'. . . moving south . . . faster . . . crossing the Seine on Pont du Carrousel!'

Fache turned to his left. The only vehicle on Pont du Carrousel was an enormous twin-bed Trailor delivery truck moving southward away from the Louvre. The truck's open-air bed was covered with a vinyl tarp, roughly resembling a giant hammock. Fache felt a shiver of apprehension. That truck, only moments ago, had probably been stopped at a red light directly beneath the toilets window.

An insane risk, Fache told himself. Langdon had no way of knowing what the truck was carrying beneath that tarp. What if the truck were carrying steel? Or cement? Or even garbage? A forty-foot leap? It was madness.

'The dot is turning!' Collet called. 'He's turning right on Pont des Saints-Pères!'

Sure enough, the Trailor truck that had crossed the bridge was slowing down and making a right turn onto Pont des Saints-Pères. *So be it,* Fache thought. Amazed, he watched the truck disappear around the corner. Collet was already radioing the agents outside, pulling them off the Louvre perimeter and sending them to their patrol cars in pursuit, all the while broadcasting the truck's changing location like some kind of bizarre play-by-play.

It's over, Fache knew. His men would have the truck surrounded within minutes. Langdon was not going anywhere.

Stowing his weapon, Fache exited the toilets and radioed Collet. 'Bring my car round. I want to be there when we make the arrest.'

As Fache jogged back down the length of the Grand Gallery, he wondered if Langdon had even survived the fall.

Not that it mattered.

Langdon ran. Guilty as charged.

Only fifteen yards from the toilets, Langdon and Sophie stood in the darkness of the Grand Gallery, their backs pressed to one of the large partitions that hid the toilets from the gallery. They had barely managed to hide themselves before Fache had darted past them, gun drawn, and disappeared into the toilets.

The last sixty seconds had been a blur.

Langdon had been standing inside the men's room refusing to run from a crime he didn't commit, when Sophie began eyeing the plate-glass window and examining the alarm mesh running through it. Then she peered downward into the street, as if measuring the drop.

'With a little aim, you can get out of here,' she said.

Aim? Uneasy, he peered out of the window.

Up the street, an enormous twin-bed eighteen-wheeler was headed for the stoplight beneath the window. Stretched across the truck's massive cargo bay was a blue vinyl tarp, loosely covering the truck's load. Langdon hoped Sophie was not thinking what she seemed to be thinking.

'Sophie, there's no way I'm jump—'

'Take out the tracking dot.'

Bewildered, Langdon fumbled in his pocket until he found the tiny metallic disk. Sophie took it from him and strode immediately to the sink. She grabbed a thick bar of soap, placed the tracking dot on top of it, and used her thumb to push the disk down hard into the bar. As the disk sank into the soft surface, she pinched the hole closed, firmly embedding the device in the bar.

Handing the bar to Langdon, Sophie retrieved a heavy, cylindrical trash can from under the sinks. Before Langdon could protest, Sophie ran at the window, holding the can before her like a battering ram. Driving the bottom of the trash can into the centre of the window, she shattered the glass.

Alarms erupted overhead at earsplitting decibel levels.

'Give me the soap!' Sophie yelled, barely audible over the alarm.

Langdon thrust the bar into her hand.

Palming the soap, she peered out of the shattered window at the eighteen-wheeler idling below. The target was very big – an expansive, stationary tarp – and it was less than ten feet from the side of the building. As the traffic lights prepared to change, Sophie took a deep breath and lobbed the bar of soap out into the night.

The soap plummeted downward toward the truck, landing on the edge of the tarp, and sliding downward into the cargo bay just as the traffic light turned green.

'Congratulations,' Sophie said, dragging him toward the door. 'You just escaped from the Louvre.'

Fleeing the men's room, they moved into the shadows just as Fache rushed past.

Now, with the fire alarm silenced, Langdon could hear the sounds of DCPJ sirens tearing away from the

Louvre. *A police exodus.* Fache had hurried off as well, leaving the Grand Gallery deserted.

'There's an emergency stairwell about fifty metres back into the Grand Gallery,' Sophie said. 'Now that the guards are leaving the perimeter, we can get out of here.'

Langdon decided not to say another word all evening. Sophie Neveu was clearly a hell of a lot smarter than he was.

Chapter 19

The Church of Saint-Sulpice, it is said, has the most eccentric history of any building in Paris. Built over the ruins of an ancient temple to the Egyptian goddess Isis, the church possesses an architectural footprint matching that of Notre Dame to within inches. The sanctuary has played host to the baptisms of the Marquis de Sade and Baudelaire, as well as the marriage of Victor Hugo. The attached seminary has a well-documented history of unorthodoxy and was once the clandestine meeting hall for numerous secret societies.

Tonight, the cavernous nave of Saint-Sulpice was as silent as a tomb, the only hint of life the faint smell of incense from mass earlier that evening. Silas sensed an uneasiness in Sister Sandrine's demeanour as she led him into the sanctuary. He was not surprised by this. Silas was accustomed to people being uncomfortable with his appearance.

'You're an American,' she said.

'French by birth,' Silas responded. 'I had my calling in Spain, and I now study in the United States.'

Sister Sandrine nodded. She was a small woman with quiet eyes. 'And you have *never* seen Saint-Sulpice?'

'I realize this is almost a sin in itself.'

'She is more beautiful by day.'

'I am certain. Nonetheless, I am grateful that you would provide me this opportunity tonight.'

'The abbé requested it. You obviously have powerful friends.'

You have no idea, Silas thought.

As he followed Sister Sandrine down the main aisle, Silas was surprised by the austerity of the sanctuary. Unlike Notre Dame with its colourful frescos, gilded altar-work, and warm wood, Saint-Sulpice was stark and cold, conveying an almost barren quality reminiscent of the ascetic cathedrals of Spain. The lack of decor made the interior look even more expansive, and as Silas gazed up into the soaring ribbed vault of the ceiling, he imagined he was standing beneath the hull of an enormous overturned ship.

A fitting image, he thought. The brotherhood's ship was about to be capsized for ever. Feeling eager to get to work, Silas wished Sister Sandrine would leave him. She was a small woman whom Silas could incapacitate easily, but he had vowed not to use force unless absolutely necessary. *She is a woman of the cloth, and it is not her fault the brotherhood chose her church as a hiding place for their keystone. She should not be punished for the sins of others.*

'I am embarrassed, Sister, that you were awoken on my behalf.'

'Not at all. You are in Paris a short time. You should not miss Saint-Sulpice. Are your interests in the church more architectural or historical?'

'Actually, Sister, my interests are spiritual.'

She gave a pleasant laugh. 'That goes without saying. I simply wondered where to begin your tour.'

Silas felt his eyes focus on the altar. 'A tour is unnecessary. You have been more than kind. I can show myself around.'

'It is no trouble,' she said. 'After all, I am awake.'

Silas stopped walking. They had reached the front pew now, and the altar was only fifteen yards away. He turned his massive body fully toward the small woman, and he could sense her recoil as she gazed up into his red eyes. 'If it does not seem too rude, Sister, I am not accustomed to simply walking into a house of God and taking a tour. Would you mind if I took some time alone to pray before I look around?'

Sister Sandrine hesitated. 'Oh, of course. I shall wait in the rear of the church for you.'

Silas put a soft but heavy hand on her shoulder and peered down. 'Sister, I feel guilty already for having awoken you. To ask you to stay awake is too much. Please, you should return to bed. I can enjoy your sanctuary and then let myself out.'

She looked uneasy. 'Are you sure you won't feel abandoned?'

'Not at all. Prayer is a solitary joy.'

'As you wish.'

Silas took his hand from her shoulder. 'Sleep well, Sister. May the peace of the Lord be with you.'

'And also with you.' Sister Sandrine headed for the stairs. 'Please be sure the door closes tightly on your way out.'

'I will be sure of it.' Silas watched her climb out of sight. Then he turned and knelt in the front pew, feeling the *cilice* cut into his leg.

Dear God, I offer up to you this work I do today. . . .

Crouching in the shadows of the choir balcony high above the altar, Sister Sandrine peered silently through the balustrade at the cloaked monk kneeling alone. The sudden dread in her soul made it hard to stay still. For a fleeting instant, she wondered if this mysterious visitor could be the enemy they had warned her about, and if tonight she would have to carry out the orders she had been holding all these years. She decided to stay there in the darkness and watch his every move.

Chapter 20

Emerging from the shadows, Langdon and Sophie moved stealthily up the deserted Grand Gallery corridor toward the emergency exit stairwell.

As he moved, Langdon felt like he was trying to assemble a jigsaw puzzle in the dark. The newest aspect of this mystery was a deeply troubling one: *The captain of the Judicial Police is trying to frame me for murder.*

'Do you think,' he whispered, 'that maybe *Fache* wrote that message on the floor?'

Sophie didn't even turn. 'Impossible.'

Langdon wasn't so sure. 'He seems pretty intent on making me look guilty. Maybe he thought writing my name on the floor would help his case?'

'The Fibonacci sequence? The P.S.? All the Da Vinci and goddess symbolism? That *had* to be my grandfather.'

Langdon knew she was right. The symbolism of the clues meshed too perfectly – the pentacle, *The Vitruvian Man*, Da Vinci, the goddess, and even the Fibonacci sequence. *A coherent symbolic set*, as iconographers would call it. All inextricably tied.

'And his phone call to me this afternoon,' Sophie added. 'He said he had to tell me something. I'm certain his message at the Louvre was his final effort to tell me something important, something he thought you could help me understand.'

Langdon frowned. *O, Draconian devil! Oh, lame saint!* He wished he could comprehend the message, both for Sophie's well-being and for his own. Things had definitely got worse since he first laid eyes on the cryptic words. His fake leap out of the bathroom window was not going to help Langdon's popularity with Fache one bit. Somehow he doubted the captain of the French police would see the humour in chasing down and arresting a bar of soap.

'The doorway isn't much farther,' Sophie said.

'Do you think there's a possibility that the *numbers* in your grandfather's message hold the key to understanding the other lines?' Langdon had once worked on a series of Baconian manuscripts that contained epigraphical ciphers in which certain lines of code were clues as to how to decipher the other lines.

'I've been thinking about the numbers all night. Sums, quotients, products. I don't see anything. Mathematically, they're arranged at random. Cryptographic gibberish.'

'And yet they're all part of the Fibonacci sequence. That can't be coincidence.'

'It's not. Using Fibonacci numbers was my grandfather's way of waving another flag at me – like writing the message in English, or arranging himself like my favourite piece of art, or drawing a pentacle on himself. All of it was to catch my attention.'

'The pentacle has meaning to you?'

'Yes. I didn't get a chance to tell you, but the pentacle was a special symbol between my grandfather and me when I was growing up. We used to play Tarot cards for fun, and my indicator card *always* turned out to be from the suit of pentacles. I'm sure he stacked the deck, but pentacles got to be our little joke.'

Langdon felt a chill. *They played Tarot?* The medieval Italian card game was so replete with hidden heretical symbolism that Langdon had dedicated an entire chapter in his new manuscript to the Tarot. The game's twenty-two cards bore names like *The Female Pope, The*

Empress, and *The Star.* Originally, Tarot had been devised as a secret means to pass along ideologies banned by the Church. Now, Tarot's mystical qualities were passed on by modern fortune-tellers.

The Tarot indicator suit for feminine divinity is pentacles, Langdon thought, realizing that if Saunière had been stacking his granddaughter's deck for fun, pentacles was an apropos inside joke.

They arrived at the emergency stairwell, and Sophie carefully pulled open the door. No alarm sounded. Only the doors to the outside were wired. Sophie led Langdon down a tight set of switchback stairs toward the ground level, picking up speed as they went.

'Your grandfather,' Langdon said, hurrying behind her, 'when he told you about the pentacle, did he mention goddess worship or any resentment of the Catholic Church?'

Sophie shook her head. 'I was more interested in the mathematics of it – the Divine Proportion, PHI, Fibonacci sequences, that sort of thing.'

Langdon was surprised. 'Your grandfather taught you about the number PHI?'

'Of course. The Divine Proportion.' Her expression turned sheepish. 'In fact, he used to joke that I was half divine . . . you know, because of the letters in my name.'

Langdon considered it a moment and then groaned. *s-o-PHI-e.*

Still descending, Langdon refocused on *PHI.* He was starting to realize that Saunière's clues were even more consistent than he had first imagined.

Da Vinci . . . Fibonacci numbers . . . the pentacle.

Incredibly, all of these things were connected by a single concept so fundamental to art history that Langdon often spent several class periods on the topic. *PHI.*

He felt himself suddenly reeling back to Harvard,

standing in front of his 'Symbolism in Art' class, writing his favourite number on the chalkboard.

1.618

Langdon turned to face his sea of eager students. 'Who can tell me what this number is?'

A long-legged maths major at the back raised his hand. 'That's the number PHI.' He pronounced it *fee*.

'Nice job, Stettner,' Langdon said. 'Everyone, meet PHI.'

'Not to be confused with PI,' Stettner added, grinning. 'As we mathematicians like to say: PHI is one *H* of a lot cooler than PI!'

Langdon laughed, but nobody else seemed to get the joke.

Stettner slumped.

'This number PHI,' Langdon continued, 'one-point-six-one-eight, is a very important number in art. Who can tell me why?'

Stettner tried to redeem himself. 'Because it's so pretty?'

Everyone laughed.

'Actually,' Langdon said, 'Stettner's right again. PHI is generally considered the most beautiful number in the universe.'

The laughter abruptly stopped, and Stettner gloated.

As Langdon loaded his slide projector, he explained that the number PHI was derived from the Fibonacci sequence – a progression famous not only because the sum of adjacent terms equalled the next term, but because the *quotients* of adjacent terms possessed the astonishing property of approaching the number 1.618 – PHI!

Despite PHI's seemingly mystical mathematical

origins, Langdon explained, the truly mind-boggling aspect of PHI was its role as a fundamental building block in nature. Plants, animals and even human beings all possessed dimensional properties that adhered with eerie exactitude to the ratio of PHI to 1.

'PHI's ubiquity in nature,' Langdon said, killing the lights, 'clearly exceeds coincidence, and so the ancients assumed the number PHI must have been preordained by the Creator of the universe. Early scientists heralded one-point-six-one-eight as the *Divine Proportion*.'

'Hold on,' said a young woman in the front row. 'I'm a bio major and I've never seen this Divine Proportion in nature.'

'No?' Langdon grinned. 'Ever study the relationship between females and males in a honeybee community?'

'Sure. The female bees always outnumber the male bees.'

'Correct. And did you know that if you divide the number of female bees by the number of male bees in any beehive in the world, you always get the same number?'

'You do?'

'Yup. PHI.'

The girl gaped. 'NO WAY!'

'Way!' Langdon fired back, smiling as he projected a slide of a spiral seashell. 'Recognize this?'

'It's a nautilus,' the bio major said. 'A cephalopod mollusc that pumps gas into its chambered shell to adjust its buoyancy.'

'Correct. And can you guess what the ratio is of each spiral's diameter to the next?'

The girl looked uncertain as she eyed the concentric arcs of the nautilus spiral.

Langdon nodded. 'PHI. The Divine Proportion. One-point-six-one-eight to one.'

The girl looked amazed.

Langdon advanced to the next slide – a close-up of a sunflower's seed head. 'Sunflower seeds grow in opposing spirals. Can you guess the ratio of each rotation's diameter to the next?'

'PHI?' everyone said.

'Bingo.' Langdon began racing through slides now – spiralled pinecone petals, leaf arrangement on plant stalks, insect segmentation – all displaying astonishing obedience to the Divine Proportion.

'This is amazing!' someone cried out.

'Yeah,' someone else said, 'but what does it have to do with *art?*'

'Aha!' Langdon said. 'Glad you asked.' He pulled up another slide – a pale yellow parchment displaying Leonardo da Vinci's famous male nude – *The Vitruvian Man* – named for Marcus Vitruvius, the brilliant Roman architect who praised the Divine Proportion in his text *De Architectura*.

'Nobody understood better than Da Vinci the divine structure of the human body. Da Vinci actually *exhumed* corpses to measure the exact proportions of human bone structure. He was the first to show that the human body is literally made of building blocks whose proportional ratios *always* equal PHI.'

Everyone in class gave him a dubious look.

'Don't believe me?' Langdon challenged. 'Next time you're in the shower, take a tape measure.'

A couple of football players snickered.

'Not just you insecure jocks,' Langdon prompted. '*All* of you. Guys and girls. Try it. Measure the distance from the tip of your head to the floor. Then divide that by the distance from your belly button to the floor. Guess what number you get.'

'Not PHI!' one of the jocks blurted out in disbelief.

'Yes, PHI,' Langdon replied. 'One-point-six-one-eight. Want another example? Measure the distance from your shoulder to your fingertips, and then divide it by the distance from your elbow to your fingertips. PHI again. Another? Hip to floor divided by knee to floor. PHI again. Finger joints. Toes. Spinal divisions. PHI. PHI. PHI. My friends, each of you is a walking tribute to the Divine Proportion.'

Even in the darkness, Langdon could see they were all astounded. He felt a familiar warmth inside. This is why he taught. 'My friends, as you can see, the chaos of the world has an underlying order. When the ancients discovered PHI, they were certain they had stumbled across God's building block for the world, and they worshipped Nature because of that. And one can understand why. God's hand is evident in Nature, and even to this day there exist pagan, Mother Earth-revering religions. Many of us celebrate Nature the way the pagans did, and don't even know it. May Day is a perfect example, the celebration of spring . . . the earth coming back to life to produce her bounty. The mysterious magic inherent in the Divine Proportion was written at the beginning of time. Man is simply playing by Nature's rules, and because *art* is man's attempt to imitate the beauty of the Creator's hand, you can imagine we might be seeing a lot of instances of the Divine Proportion in art this semester.'

Over the next half hour, Langdon showed them slides of artwork by Michelangelo, Albrecht Dürer, Da Vinci, and many others, demonstrating each artist's intentional and rigorous adherence to the Divine Proportion in the layout of his compositions. Langdon unveiled PHI in the architectural dimensions of the Greek Parthenon, the pyramids of Egypt, and even the United Nations Building in New York. PHI appeared in the organizational structures of Mozart's sonatas, Beethoven's Fifth Symphony, as well as the works of Bartók, Debussy, and Schubert. The number PHI, Langdon told them, was even used by Stradivarius to calculate the exact placement of the f-holes in the construction of his famous violins.

'In closing,' Langdon said, walking to the chalk-board, 'we return to *symbols*.' He drew five intersecting lines that formed a five-pointed star. 'This symbol is one of the most powerful images you will see this term. Formally known as a pentagram – or *pentacle*, as the ancients called it – this symbol is considered both divine and magical by many cultures. Can anyone tell me why that might be?'

Stettner, the maths major, raised his hand. 'Because if you draw a pentagram, the lines automatically divide themselves into segments according to the Divine Proportion.'

Langdon gave the kid a proud nod. 'Nice job. Yes, the ratios of line segments in a pentacle *all* equal PHI, making this symbol the *ultimate* expression of the Divine Proportion. For this reason, the five-pointed star has always been the symbol for beauty and perfection associated with the goddess and the sacred feminine.'

The girls in class beamed.

'One note, folks. We've only touched on Da Vinci today, but we'll be seeing a lot more of him this semester. Leonardo was a well-documented devotee of the ancient ways of the goddess. Tomorrow, I'll show you his fresco *The Last Supper*, which is one of the most astonishing tributes to the sacred feminine you will ever see.'

'You're kidding, right?' somebody said. 'I thought *The Last Supper* was about Jesus!'

Langdon winked. 'There are symbols hidden in places you would never imagine.'

* * *

'Come on,' Sophie whispered. 'What's wrong? We're almost there. Hurry!'

Langdon glanced up, feeling himself return from faraway thoughts. He realized he was standing at a dead stop on the stairs, paralysed by sudden revelation.

O, Draconian devil! Oh, lame saint!

Sophie was looking back at him.

It can't be that simple, Langdon thought.

But he knew of course that it was.

There in the bowels of the Louvre . . . with images of PHI and Da Vinci swirling through his mind, Robert Langdon suddenly and unexpectedly deciphered Saunière's code.

'O, Draconian devil!' he said. 'Oh, lame saint! It's the simplest kind of code!'

Sophie was stopped on the stairs below him, staring up in confusion. *A code?* She had been pondering the words all night and had not seen a code. Especially a simple one.

'You said it yourself.' Langdon's voice reverberated with excitement. 'Fibonacci numbers only have meaning in their proper order. Otherwise they're mathematical gibberish.'

Sophie had no idea what he was talking about. *The Fibonacci numbers?* She was certain they had been intended as nothing more than a means to get the Cryptography Department involved tonight. *They have another purpose?* She plunged her hand into her pocket and pulled out the printout, studying her grandfather's message again.

13-3-2-21-1-1-8-5
O, Draconian devil!
Oh, lame saint!

What about the numbers?

'The scrambled Fibonacci sequence is a clue,' Langdon said, taking the printout. 'The numbers are a hint as to how to decipher the rest of the message. He wrote the sequence out of order to tell us to apply the same concept to the text. O, Draconian devil? Oh, lame saint? Those lines mean nothing. They are simply *letters* written out of order.'

Sophie needed only an instant to process Langdon's implication, and it seemed laughably simple. 'You think this message is . . . *une anagramme?*' She stared at him. 'Like a word jumble from a newspaper?'

Langdon could see the scepticism on Sophie's face and certainly understood. Few people realized that anagrams, despite being a trite modern amusement, had a rich history of sacred symbolism.

The mystical teachings of the Kabbala drew heavily on anagrams – rearranging the letters of Hebrew words to derive new meanings. French kings throughout the Renaissance were so convinced that anagrams held magic power that they appointed royal anagrammatists to help them make better decisions by analysing words in important documents. The Romans actually referred to the study of anagrams as *ars magna* – 'the great art'.

Langdon looked up at Sophie, locking eyes with her now. 'Your grandfather's meaning was right in front of us all along, and he left us more than enough clues to see it.'

Without another word, Langdon pulled a pen from his jacket pocket and rearranged the letters in each line.

O, Draconian devil!
Oh, lame saint!

was a perfect anagram of . . .

Leonardo da Vinci!
The Mona Lisa!

Chapter 21

The Mona Lisa.

For an instant, standing in the exit stairwell, Sophie forgot all about trying to leave the Louvre.

Her shock over the anagram was matched only by her embarrassment at not having deciphered the message herself. Sophie's expertise in complex crypt-analysis had caused her to overlook simplistic word games, and yet she knew she should have seen it. After all, she was no stranger to anagrams – especially in English.

When she was young, often her grandfather would use anagram games to hone her English spelling. Once he had written the English word 'planets' and told Sophie that an astonishing ninety-two *other* English words of varying lengths could be formed using those same letters. Sophie had spent three days with an English dictionary until she found them all.

'I can't imagine,' Langdon said, staring at the print-out, 'how your grandfather created such an intricate anagram in the minutes before he died.'

Sophie knew the explanation, and the realization made her feel even worse. *I should have seen this!* She now recalled that her grandfather – a wordplay aficionado and art lover – had entertained himself as a young man by creating anagrams of famous works of art. In fact, one of his anagrams had got him in trouble once when Sophie was a little girl. While being interviewed by an American art magazine, Saunière had expressed his distaste for the modernist Cubist

139

movement by noting that Picasso's masterpiece *Les Demoiselles d'Avignon* was a perfect anagram of *vile meaningless doodles*. Picasso fans were not amused.

'My grandfather probably created this *Mona Lisa* anagram long ago,' Sophie said, glancing up at Langdon. *And tonight he was forced to use it as a makeshift code*. Her grandfather's voice had called out from beyond with chilling precision.

Leonardo da Vinci!

The Mona Lisa!

Why his final words to her referenced the famous painting, Sophie had no idea, but she could think of only one possibility. A disturbing one.

Those were not his final words . . .

Was she supposed to visit the *Mona Lisa*? Had her grandfather left her a message there? The idea seemed perfectly plausible. After all, the famous painting hung in the Salle des Etats – a private viewing chamber accessible only from the Grand Gallery. In fact, Sophie now realized, the doors that opened into the chamber were situated only twenty metres from where her grandfather had been found dead.

He easily could have visited the Mona Lisa *before he died.*

Sophie gazed back up the emergency stairwell and felt torn. She knew she should usher Langdon from the museum immediately, and yet instinct urged her to the contrary. As Sophie recalled her first childhood visit to the Denon Wing, she realized that if her grandfather had a secret to tell her, few places on earth made a more apt rendezvous than Da Vinci's *Mona Lisa*.

'She's just a little bit farther,' her grandfather had whispered, clutching Sophie's tiny hand as he led her

140

through the deserted museum after hours.

Sophie was six years old. She felt small and insignificant as she gazed up at the enormous ceilings and down at the dizzying floor. The empty museum frightened her, although she was not about to let her grandfather know that. She set her jaw firmly and let go of his hand.

'Up ahead is the Salle des Etats,' her grandfather said as they approached the Louvre's most famous room. Despite her grandfather's obvious excitement, Sophie wanted to go home. She had seen pictures of the *Mona Lisa* in books and didn't like it at all. She couldn't understand why everyone made such a fuss.

'*C'est ennuyeux,*' Sophie grumbled.

'Boring,' he corrected. 'French at school. English at home.'

'*Le Louvre, ce n'est pas chez moi!*' she challenged.

He gave her a tired laugh. 'Right you are. Then let's speak English just for fun.'

Sophie pouted and kept walking. As they entered the Salle des Etats, her eyes scanned the narrow room and settled on the obvious spot of honour – the centre of the right-hand wall, where a lone portrait hung behind a protective Plexiglas wall. Her grandfather paused in the doorway and motioned toward the painting.

'Go ahead, Sophie. Not many people get a chance to visit her alone.'

Swallowing her apprehension, Sophie moved slowly across the room. After everything she'd heard about the *Mona Lisa,* she felt as if she were approaching royalty. Arriving in front of the protective Plexiglas, Sophie held her breath and looked up, taking it in all at once.

Sophie was not sure what she had expected to feel, but it most certainly was not this. No jolt of amazement.

No instant of wonder. The famous face looked as it did in books. She stood in silence for what felt like for ever, waiting for something to happen.

'So what do you think?' her grandfather whispered, arriving behind her. 'Beautiful, yes?'

'She's too little.'

Saunière smiled. 'You're little and you're beautiful.'

I am not beautiful, she thought. Sophie hated her red hair and freckles, and she was bigger than all the boys in her class. She looked back at the *Mona Lisa* and shook her head. 'She's even worse than in the books. Her face is . . . *brumeux*.'

'Foggy,' her grandfather tutored.

'Foggy,' Sophie repeated, knowing the conversation would not continue until she repeated her new vocabulary word.

'That's called the *sfumato* style of painting,' he told her, 'and it's very hard to do. Leonardo da Vinci was better at it than anyone.'

Sophie still didn't like the painting. 'She looks like she knows something . . . like when kids at school have a secret.'

Her grandfather laughed. 'That's part of why she is so famous. People like to guess why she is smiling.'

'Do *you* know why she's smiling?'

'Maybe.' Her grandfather winked. 'Someday I'll tell you all about it.'

Sophie stamped her foot. 'I told you I don't like secrets!'

'Princess,' he smiled. 'Life is filled with secrets. You can't learn them all at once.'

'I'm going back up,' Sophie declared, her voice hollow in the stairwell.

'To the *Mona Lisa*?' Langdon recoiled. '*Now?*'

Sophie considered the risk. 'I'm not a murder suspect. I'll take my chances. I need to understand what my grandfather was trying to tell me.'

'What about the embassy?'

Sophie felt guilty turning Langdon into a fugitive only to abandon him, but she saw no other option. She pointed down the stairs to a metal door. 'Go through that door, and follow the illuminated exit signs. My grandfather used to bring me down here. The signs will lead you to a security turnstile. It's mono-directional and opens out.' She handed Langdon her car keys. 'Mine is the red SmartCar in the employee lot. Directly outside this bulkhead. Do you know how to get to the embassy?'

Langdon nodded, eyeing the keys in his hand.

'Listen,' Sophie said, her voice softening. 'I think my grandfather may have left me a message at the *Mona Lisa* – some kind of clue as to who killed him. Or why I'm in danger.' *Or what happened to my family*. 'I have to go and see.'

'But if he wanted to tell you why you were in danger, why wouldn't he simply write it on the floor where he died? Why this complicated word game?'

'Whatever my grandfather was trying to tell me, I don't think he wanted anyone else to hear it. Not even the police.' Clearly, her grandfather had done everything in his power to send a confidential transmission directly to *her*. He had written it in code, included her secret initials, and told her to find Robert Langdon – a wise command, considering the American symbologist had deciphered his code. 'As strange as it may sound,' Sophie said, 'I think he wants me to get to the *Mona Lisa* before anyone else does.'

'I'll come.'

'No! We don't know how long the Grand Gallery will stay empty. *You* have to go.'

143

Langdon seemed hesitant, as if his own academic curiosity were threatening to override sound judgment and drag him back into Fache's hands.

'Go. Now.' Sophie gave him a grateful smile. 'I'll see you at the embassy, Mr Langdon.'

Langdon looked displeased. 'I'll meet you there on *one* condition,' he replied, his voice stern.

She paused, startled. 'What's that?'

'That you stop calling me *Mr* Langdon.'

Sophie detected the faint hint of a lopsided grin growing across Langdon's face, and she felt herself smile back. 'Good luck, Robert.'

When Langdon reached the landing at the bottom of the stairs, the unmistakable smell of linseed oil and plaster dust assaulted his nostrils. Ahead, an illuminated SORTIE/EXIT displayed an arrow pointing down a long corridor.

Langdon stepped into the hallway.

To the right gaped a murky restoration studio out of which peered an army of statues in various states of repair. To the left, Langdon saw a suite of studios that resembled Harvard art classrooms – rows of easels, paintings, palettes, framing tools – an art assembly line.

As he moved down the hallway, Langdon wondered if at any moment he might awake with a start in his bed in Cambridge. The entire evening had felt like a bizarre dream. *I'm about to dash out of the Louvre ... a fugitive.*

Saunière's clever anagrammatic message was still on his mind, and Langdon wondered what Sophie would find at the *Mona Lisa* ... if anything. She had seemed certain her grandfather meant for her to visit the famous painting one more time. As plausible an interpretation as this seemed, Langdon felt haunted now by a troubling paradox.

P.S. Find Robert Langdon.

Saunière had written Langdon's name on the floor, commanding Sophie to find him. But why? Merely so Langdon could help her break an anagram?

It seemed quite unlikely.

After all, Saunière had no reason to think Langdon was especially skilled at anagrams. *We've never even met.* More important, Sophie had stated flat out that *she* should have broken the anagram on her own. It had been Sophie who spotted the Fibonacci sequence, and, no doubt, Sophie who, if given a little more time, would have deciphered the message with no help from Langdon.

Sophie was supposed to break that anagram on her own. Langdon was suddenly feeling more certain about this, and yet the conclusion left an obvious gaping lapse in the logic of Saunière's actions.

Why me? Langdon wondered, heading down the hall. *Why was Saunière's dying wish that his estranged grand-daughter find me? What is it that Saunière thinks I know?*

With an unexpected jolt, Langdon stopped short. Eyes wide, he dug in his pocket and yanked out the computer printout. He stared at the last line of Saunière's message.

P.S. Find Robert Langdon.

He fixated on two letters.

P.S.

In that instant, Langdon felt Saunière's puzzling mix of symbolism fall into stark focus. Like a peal of thunder, a career's worth of symbology and history came crashing down around him. Everything Jacques Saunière had done tonight suddenly made perfect sense.

Langdon's thoughts raced as he tried to assemble

the implications of what this all meant. Wheeling, he stared back in the direction from which he had come.

Is there time?

He knew it didn't matter.

Without hesitation, Langdon broke into a sprint back toward the stairs.

Chapter 22

Kneeling in the first pew, Silas pretended to pray as he scanned the layout of the sanctuary. Saint-Sulpice, like most churches, had been built in the shape of a giant Roman cross. Its long central section – the nave – led directly to the main altar, where it was transversely intersected by a shorter section, known as the transept. The intersection of nave and transept occurred directly beneath the main cupola and was considered the heart of the church . . . her most sacred and mystical point.

Not tonight, Silas thought. *Saint-Sulpice hides her secrets elsewhere.*

Turning his head to the right, he gazed into the south transept, toward the open area of floor beyond the end of the pews, to the object his victims had described.

There it is.

Embedded in the grey granite floor, a thin polished strip of brass glistened in the stone . . . a golden line slanting across the church's floor. The line bore graduated markings, like a ruler. It was a gnomon, Silas had been told, a pagan astronomical device like a sundial. Tourists, scientists, historians and pagans from around the world came to Saint-Sulpice to gaze upon this famous line.

The Rose Line.

Slowly, Silas let his eyes trace the path of the brass strip as it made its way across the floor from his right to left, slanting in front of him at an awkward angle, entirely at odds with the symmetry of the church. Slicing across the main altar itself, the line looked to Silas like a slash wound across a beautiful face. The strip cleaved the communion rail in two and then crossed the entire width of the church, finally reaching the corner of the north transept, where it arrived at the base of a most unexpected structure.

A colossal Egyptian obelisk.

Here, the glistening Rose Line took a ninety-degree *vertical* turn and continued directly up the face of the obelisk itself, ascending thirty-three feet to the very tip of the pyramidical apex, where it finally ceased.

The Rose Line, Silas thought. *The brotherhood hid the keystone at the Rose Line.*

Earlier tonight, when Silas told the Teacher that the Priory keystone was hidden inside Saint-Sulpice, the Teacher had sounded doubtful. But when Silas added that the brothers had all given him a precise location, with relation to a brass line running through Saint-Sulpice, the Teacher had gasped with revelation. 'You speak of the Rose Line!'

The Teacher quickly told Silas of Saint-Sulpice's famed architectural oddity – a strip of brass that segmented the sanctuary on a perfect north-south axis. It was an ancient sundial of sorts, a vestige of the pagan temple that had once stood on this very spot. The sun's rays, shining through the oculus on the south wall, moved farther down the line every day, indicating the passage of time, from solstice to solstice.

The north-south stripe had been known as the Rose Line. For centuries, the symbol of the Rose had been associated with maps and guiding souls in the proper direction. The Compass Rose – drawn on almost every map – indicated North, East, South and West. Originally known as the Wind Rose, it denoted the directions of the thirty-two winds, blowing from the directions of eight major winds, eight half-winds, and sixteen quarter-winds. When diagrammed inside a circle, these thirty-two points of the compass perfectly resembled a traditional thirty-two petal rose bloom. To this day, the fundamental navigational tool was still known as a Compass Rose, its northernmost direction still marked by an arrowhead . . . or, more commonly, the symbol of the fleur-de-lis.

On a globe, a Rose Line – also called a meridian or longitude – was any imaginary line drawn from the North Pole to the South Pole. There were, of course, an infinite number of Rose Lines because every point on the globe could have a longitude drawn through it connecting north and south poles. The question for early navigators was *which* of these lines would be called *the* Rose Line – the zero longitude – the line from which all other longitudes on earth would be measured.

Today that line was in Greenwich, England.

But it had not always been.

Long before the establishment of Greenwich as the prime meridian, the zero longitude of the entire world had passed directly through Paris, and through the Church of Saint-Sulpice. The brass marker in Saint-Sulpice was a memorial to the world's first prime meridian, and although Greenwich had stripped Paris of the honour in 1888, the original Rose Line was still visible today.

'And so the legend is true,' the Teacher had told Silas. 'The Priory keystone has been said to lie "beneath the Sign of the Rose".'

Now, still on his knees in a pew, Silas glanced around the church and listened to make sure no one was there. For a moment, he thought he heard a rustling in the choir balcony. He turned and gazed up for several seconds. Nothing.

I am alone.

Standing now, he faced the altar and genuflected three times. Then he turned left and followed the brass line due north toward the obelisk.

At that moment, at Leonardo da Vinci International Airport in Rome, the jolt of tyres hitting the runway startled Bishop Aringarosa from his slumber.

I drifted off, he thought, impressed he was relaxed enough to sleep.

'*Benvenuto a Roma,*' the intercom announced.

Sitting up, Aringarosa straightened his black cassock and allowed himself a rare smile. This was one trip he had been happy to make. *I have been on the defensive for too long.* Tonight, however, the rules had changed. Only five months ago, Aringarosa had feared for the future of the Faith. Now, as if by the will of God, the solution had presented itself.

Divine intervention.

If all went as planned tonight in Paris, Aringarosa would soon be in possession of something that would make him the most powerful man in Christendom.

Chapter 23

Sophie arrived breathless outside the large wooden doors of the Salle des Etats – the room that housed the *Mona Lisa*. Before entering, she gazed reluctantly farther down the hall, twenty yards or so, to the spot where her grandfather's body still lay under the spotlight.

The remorse that gripped her was powerful and sudden, a deep sadness laced with guilt. The man had reached out to her so many times over the past ten years, and yet Sophie had remained immovable – leaving his letters and packages unopened in a bottom drawer and denying his efforts to see her. *He lied to me! Kept appalling secrets! What was I supposed to do?* And so she had blocked him out. Completely.

Now her grandfather was dead, and he was talking to her from the grave.

The Mona Lisa.

She reached for the huge wooden doors, and pushed. The entryway yawned open. Sophie stood on the threshold a moment, scanning the large rectangular chamber beyond. It too was bathed in a soft red light. The Salle des Etats was one of this museum's rare *culs-de-sac* – a dead end and the only room off the middle of the Grand Gallery. This door, the chamber's sole point of entry, faced a dominating fifteen-foot Botticelli on the far wall. Beneath it, centred on the parquet floor, an immense octagonal viewing divan served as a welcome respite for thousands of visitors to rest their legs while they admired the Louvre's most valuable asset.

Even before Sophie entered, though, she knew she was missing something. *A black light.* She gazed down the hall at her grandfather under the lights in the distance, surrounded by electronic gear. If he had written anything in here, he almost certainly would have written it with the watermark stylus.

Taking a deep breath, Sophie hurried down to the well-lit crime scene. Unable to look at her grandfather, she focused solely on the PTS tools. Finding a small ultraviolet penlight, she slipped it in the pocket of her sweater and hurried back up the hallway toward the open doors of the Salle des Etats.

Sophie turned the corner and stepped over the threshold. Her entrance, however, was met by an unexpected sound of muffled footsteps racing toward her from inside the chamber. *There's someone in here!* A ghostly figure emerged suddenly from out of the reddish haze. Sophie jumped back.

'There you are!' Langdon's hoarse whisper cut the air as his silhouette slid to a stop in front of her.

Her relief was only momentary. 'Robert, I told you to get out of here! If Fache—'

'Where were you?'

'I had to get the black light,' she whispered, holding it up. 'If my grandfather left me a message—'

'Sophie, listen.' Langdon caught his breath as his blue eyes held her firmly. 'The letters P.S. . . . do they mean anything else to you? Anything at all?'

Afraid their voices might echo down the hall, Sophie pulled him into the Salle des Etats and closed the enormous twin doors silently, sealing them inside. 'I told you, the initials mean Princess Sophie.'

'I know, but did you ever see them anywhere *else*? Did your grandfather ever use P.S. in any other way?

As a monogram, or maybe on stationery or a personal item?'

The question startled her. *How would Robert know that?* Sophie had indeed seen the initials P.S. once before, in a kind of monogram. It was the day before her ninth birthday. She was secretly combing the house, searching for hidden birthday presents. Even then, she could not bear secrets kept from her. *What did Grand-père get for me this year?* She dug through cupboards and drawers. *Did he get me the doll I wanted? Where would he hide it?*

Finding nothing in the entire house, Sophie mustered the courage to sneak into her grandfather's bedroom. The room was off-limits to her, but her grandfather was downstairs asleep on the couch.

I'll just take a fast peek!

Tiptoeing across the creaky wood floor to his closet, Sophie peered on the shelves behind his clothing. Nothing. Next she looked under the bed. Still nothing. Moving to his bureau, she opened the drawers and one by one began pawing carefully through them. *There must be something for me here!* As she reached the bottom drawer, she still had not found any hint of a doll. Dejected, she opened the final drawer and pulled aside some black clothes she had never seen him wear. She was about to close the drawer when her eyes caught a glint of gold in the back of the drawer. It looked like a pocket watch chain, but she knew he didn't wear one. Her heart raced as she realized what it must be.

A necklace!

Sophie carefully pulled the chain from the drawer. To her surprise, on the end was a brilliant gold key. Heavy and shimmering. Spellbound, she held it up. It looked like no key she had ever seen. Most keys were flat with jagged teeth, but this one had a triangular column with little pockmarks all over it. Its large golden head was in the shape of a cross, but not a normal cross. This was an even-armed one, like a plus sign. Embossed in the middle of the cross was a strange symbol – two letters intertwined with some kind of flowery design.

'P.S.,' she whispered, scowling as she read the letters. *Whatever could this be?*

'Sophie?' her grandfather spoke from the doorway.

Startled, she spun, dropping the key on the floor with a loud clang. She stared down at the key, afraid to look up at her grandfather's face. 'I . . . was looking for my birthday present,' she said, hanging her head, knowing she had betrayed his trust.

For what seemed like an eternity, her grandfather stood silently in the doorway. Finally, he let out a long troubled breath. 'Pick up the key, Sophie.'

Sophie retrieved the key.

Her grandfather walked in. 'Sophie, you need to respect other people's privacy.' Gently, he knelt down and took the key from her. 'This key is very special. If you had lost it . . .'

Her grandfather's quiet voice made Sophie feel even worse. 'I'm sorry, *Grand-père.* I really am.' She paused. 'I thought it was a necklace for my birthday.'

He gazed at her for several seconds. 'I'll say this once more, Sophie, because it's important. You need to learn to respect other people's privacy.'

'Yes, *Grand-père.*'

'We'll talk about this some other time. Right now, the garden needs to be weeded.'

Sophie hurried outside to do her chores.

The next morning, Sophie received no birthday present from her grandfather. She hadn't expected one, not after what she had done. But he didn't even wish her happy birthday all day. Sadly, she trudged up to bed that night. As she climbed in, though, she found a note card lying on her pillow. On the card was written a simple riddle. Even before she solved the riddle, she was smiling. *I know what this is!* Her grandfather had done this for her last Christmas morning.

A treasure hunt!

Eagerly, she pored over the riddle until she solved it. The solution pointed her to another part of the house, where she found another card and another riddle. She solved this one too, racing on to the next card. Running wildly, she darted back and forth across the house, from clue to clue, until at last she found a clue that directed her back to her own bedroom. Sophie dashed up the stairs, rushed into her room, and stopped in her tracks. There in the middle of the room sat a shining red bicycle with a ribbon tied to the handlebars. Sophie shrieked with delight.

'I know you asked for a doll,' her grandfather said, smiling in the corner. 'I thought you might like this even better.'

The next day, her grandfather taught her to ride, running beside her down the walkway. When Sophie steered out over the thick lawn and lost her balance, they both went tumbling onto the grass, rolling and laughing.

'*Grand-père*,' Sophie said, hugging him. 'I'm really sorry about the key.'

'I know, sweetie. You're forgiven. I can't possibly stay mad at you. Grandfathers and granddaughters always forgive each other.'

Sophie knew she shouldn't ask, but she couldn't help it. 'What does it open? I never saw a key like that. It was very pretty.'

Her grandfather was silent a long moment, and Sophie could see he was uncertain how to answer. *Grand-père never lies.* 'It opens a box,' he finally said. 'Where I keep many secrets.'

Sophie pouted. 'I hate secrets!'

'I know, but these are important secrets. And someday, you'll learn to appreciate them as much as I do.'

'I saw letters on the key, and a flower.'

'Yes, that's my favourite flower. It's called a fleur-de-lis. We have them in the garden. The white ones. In English we call that kind of flower a lily.'

'I know those! They're *my* favourite too!'

'Then I'll make a deal with you.' Her grandfather's eyebrows raised the way they always did when he was about to give her a challenge. 'If you can keep my key a secret, and *never* talk about it ever again, to me or anybody, then someday I will give it to you.'

Sophie couldn't believe her ears. 'You *will?*'

'I promise. When the time comes, the key will be yours. It has your name on it.'

Sophie scowled. 'No it doesn't. It said P.S. My name isn't P.S.!'

Her grandfather lowered his voice and looked around as if to make sure no one was listening. 'Okay, Sophie, if you *must* know, P.S. is a code. It's your secret initials.'

Her eyes went wide. 'I have secret initials?'

'Of course. Granddaughters *always* have secret initials that only their grandfathers know.'

'P.S.?'

He tickled her. '*Princesse Sophie.*'

She giggled. 'I'm not a princess!'

He winked. 'You are to me.'

From that day on, they never again spoke of the key. And she became his Princess Sophie.

Inside the Salle des Etats, Sophie stood in silence and endured the sharp pang of loss.

'The initials,' Langdon whispered, eyeing her strangely. 'Have you seen them?'

Sophie sensed her grandfather's voice whispering in the corridors of the museum. *Never speak of this key, Sophie. To me or to anyone.* She knew she had failed him in forgiveness, and she wondered if she could break his trust again. *P.S. Find Robert Langdon.* Her grandfather wanted Langdon to help. Sophie nodded. 'Yes, I saw the initials P.S. once. When I was very young.'

'Where?'

Sophie hesitated. 'On something very important to him.'

Langdon locked eyes with her. 'Sophie, this is crucial. Can you tell me if the initials appeared with a symbol? A fleur-de-lis?'

Sophie felt herself staggering backward in amazement. 'But . . . how could you possibly know that!'

Langdon exhaled and lowered his voice. 'I'm fairly certain your grandfather was a member of a secret society. A very old covert brotherhood.'

Sophie felt a knot tighten in her stomach. She was certain of it too. For ten years she had tried to forget the incident that had confirmed that horrifying fact for her. She had witnessed something unthinkable. *Unforgivable.*

'The fleur-de-lis,' Langdon said, 'combined with the initials P.S., that is the brotherhood's official device. Their coat of arms. Their logo.'

'How do you know this?' Sophie was praying Langdon was not going to tell her that he *himself* was a member.

'I've written about this group,' he said, his voice tremulous with excitement. 'Researching the symbols of secret societies is a specialty of mine. They call themselves the *Prieuré de Sion* – the Priory of Sion. They're based here in France and attract powerful members from all over Europe. In fact, they are one of the oldest surviving secret societies on earth.'

Sophie had never heard of them.

Langdon was talking in rapid bursts now. 'The Priory's membership has included some of history's most cultured individuals: men like Botticelli, Sir Isaac Newton, Victor Hugo.' He paused, his voice brimming now with academic zeal. 'And, Leonardo da Vinci.'

Sophie stared. 'Da Vinci was in a secret society?'

'Da Vinci presided over the Priory between 1510 and 1519 as the brotherhood's Grand Master, which might help explain your grandfather's passion for Leonardo's work. The two men share a historical fraternal bond. And it all fits perfectly with their fascination for goddess iconology, paganism, feminine deities and contempt for the Church. The Priory has a well-documented history of reverence for the sacred feminine.'

'You're telling me this group is a pagan goddess worship cult?'

'More like *the* pagan goddess worship cult. But more important, they are known as the guardians of an ancient secret. One that made them immeasurably powerful.'

Despite the total conviction in Langdon's eyes, Sophie's gut reaction was one of stark disbelief. *A secret pagan cult? Once headed by Leonardo da Vinci?* It all sounded utterly absurd. And yet, even as she dismissed it, she felt her mind reeling back ten years – to the night she had mistakenly surprised her grandfather and witnessed what she still could not accept. *Could that explain—?*

'The identities of living Priory members are kept

extremely secret,' Langdon said, 'but the P.S. and fleur-de-lis that you saw as a child are proof. It could *only* have been related to the Priory.'

Sophie realized now that Langdon knew far more about her grandfather than she had previously imagined. This American obviously had volumes to share with her, but this was not the place. 'I can't afford to let them catch you, Robert. There's a lot we need to discuss. You need to go!'

Langdon heard only the faint murmur of her voice. He wasn't going anywhere. He was lost in another place now. A place where ancient secrets rose to the surface. A place where forgotten histories emerged from the shadows.

Slowly, as if moving underwater, Langdon turned his head and gazed through the reddish haze toward the *Mona Lisa*.

The fleur-de-lis . . . the flower of Lisa . . . the Mona Lisa.

It was all intertwined, a silent symphony echoing the deepest secrets of the Priory of Sion and Leonardo da Vinci.

A few miles away, on the riverbank beyond Les Invalides, the bewildered driver of a twin-bed Trailor truck stood at gunpoint and watched as the captain of the Judicial Police let out a guttural roar of rage and heaved a bar of soap out into the turgid waters of the Seine.

Chapter 24

Silas gazed upward at the Saint-Sulpice obelisk, taking in the length of the massive marble shaft. His sinews felt taut with exhilaration. He glanced around the church one more time to make sure he was alone. Then he knelt at the base of the structure, not out of reverence, but out of necessity.

The keystone is hidden beneath the Rose Line.

At the base of the Sulpice obelisk.

All the brothers had concurred.

On his knees now, Silas ran his hands across the stone floor. He saw no cracks or markings to indicate a movable tile, so he began rapping softly with his knuckles on the floor. Following the brass line closer to the obelisk, he knocked on each tile adjacent to the brass line. Finally, one of them echoed strangely.

There's a hollow area beneath the floor!

Silas smiled. His victims had spoken the truth.

Standing, he searched the sanctuary for something with which to break the floor tile.

High above Silas, in the balcony, Sister Sandrine stifled a gasp. Her darkest fears had just been confirmed. This visitor was not who he seemed. The mysterious Opus Dei monk had come to Saint-Sulpice for another purpose.

A secret purpose.

You are not the only one with secrets, she thought.

Sister Sandrine Bieil was more than the keeper of this church. She was a sentry. And tonight, the ancient wheels had been set in motion. The arrival of this stranger at the base of the obelisk was a signal from the brotherhood.

It was a silent call of distress.

Chapter 25

The US Embassy in Paris is a compact complex on Avenue Gabriel, just north of the Champs-Elysées. The three-acre compound is considered US soil, meaning all those who stand on it are subject to the same laws and protections as they would encounter standing in the United States.

The embassy's night operator was reading *Time* magazine's International Edition when the sound of her phone interrupted.

'US Embassy,' she answered.

'Good evening.' The caller spoke English accented with French. 'I need some assistance.' Despite the politeness of the man's words, his tone sounded gruff and official. 'I was told you had a phone message for me on your automated system. The name is Langdon. Unfortunately, I have forgotten my three-digit access code. If you could help me, I would be most grateful.'

The operator paused, confused. 'I'm sorry, sir. Your message must be quite old. That system was removed two years ago for security precautions. Moreover, all the access codes were *five*-digit. Who told you we had a message for you?'

'You have *no* automated phone system?'

'No, sir. Any message for you would be hand-written in our services department. What was your name again?'

But the man had hung up.

162

* * *

Bezu Fache felt dumbstruck as he paced the banks of the Seine. He was certain he had seen Langdon dial a local number, enter a three-digit code, and then listen to a recording. *But if Langdon didn't phone the embassy, then who the hell did he call?*

It was at that moment, eyeing his cellular phone, that Fache realized the answers were in the palm of his hand. *Langdon used my phone to place that call.*

Keying into the cell phone's menu, Fache pulled up the list of recently dialled numbers and found the call Langdon had placed.

A Paris exchange, followed by the three-digit code 454.

Redialling the phone number, Fache waited as the line began ringing.

Finally a woman's voice answered. *'Bonjour, vous êtes bien chez Sophie Neveu,'* the recording announced. *'Je suis absente pour le moment, mais . . .'*

Fache's blood was boiling as he typed the numbers 4 . . . 5 . . . 4.

Chapter 26

Despite her monumental reputation, the *Mona Lisa* was a mere thirty-one inches by twenty-one inches – smaller even than the posters of her sold in the Louvre gift shop. She hung on the northwest wall of the Salle des Etats behind a two-inch-thick pane of protective Plexiglas. Painted on a poplar wood panel, her ethereal, mist-filled atmosphere was attributed to Da Vinci's mastery of the *sfumato* style, in which forms appear to evaporate into one another.

Since taking up residence in the Louvre, the *Mona Lisa* – or *La Joconde* as they call her in France – had been stolen twice, most recently in 1911, when she disappeared from the Louvre's *'salle impénétrable'* – Le Salon Carré. Parisians wept in the streets and wrote newspaper articles begging the thieves for the painting's return. Two years later, the *Mona Lisa* was discovered hidden in the false bottom of a trunk in a Florence hotel room.

Langdon, now having made it clear to Sophie that he had no intention of leaving, moved with her across the Salle des Etats. The *Mona Lisa* was still twenty yards ahead when Sophie turned on the black light, and the bluish crescent of penlight fanned out on the floor in front of them. She swung the beam back and forth across the floor like a minesweeper, searching for any hint of luminescent ink.

Walking beside her, Langdon was already feeling the tingle of anticipation that accompanied his face-to-face reunions with great works of art. He strained to see beyond the cocoon of purplish light emanating from the black light in Sophie's hand. To the left, the room's octagonal viewing divan emerged, looking like a dark island on the empty sea of parquet.

Langdon could now begin to see the panel of dark glass on the wall. Behind it, he knew, in the confines of her own private cell, hung the most celebrated painting in the world.

The *Mona Lisa*'s status as the most famous piece of art in the world, Langdon knew, had nothing to do with her enigmatic smile. Nor was it due to the mysterious interpretations attributed her by many art historians and conspiracy buffs. Quite simply, the *Mona Lisa* was famous because Leonardo da Vinci claimed she was his finest accomplishment. He carried the painting with him whenever he travelled and, if asked why, would reply that he found it hard to part with his most sublime expression of female beauty.

Even so, many art historians suspected Da Vinci's reverence for the *Mona Lisa* had nothing to do with its artistic mastery. In actuality, the painting was a surprisingly ordinary *sfumato* portrait. Da Vinci's veneration for this work, many claimed, stemmed from something far deeper: a hidden message in the layers of paint. The *Mona Lisa* was, in fact, one of the world's most documented inside jokes. The painting's well-documented collage of double entendres and playful allusions had been revealed in most art history tomes, and yet, incredibly, the public at large still considered her smile a great mystery.

No mystery at all, Langdon thought, moving forward and watching as the faint outline of the painting began to take shape. *No mystery at all*.

Most recently Langdon had shared the *Mona Lisa*'s secret with a rather unlikely group – a dozen inmates at the Essex County Penitentiary. Langdon's jail seminar was part of a Harvard outreach programme attempting to bring education into the prison system – *Culture for Convicts,* as Langdon's colleagues liked to call it.

Standing at an overhead projector in a darkened penitentiary library, Langdon had shared the *Mona Lisa*'s secret with the prisoners attending class, men whom he found surprisingly engaged – rough, but sharp. 'You may notice,' Langdon told them, walking up to the projected image of the *Mona Lisa* on the library wall, 'that the background behind her face is uneven.' Langdon motioned to the glaring discrepancy. 'Da Vinci painted the horizon line on the left significantly lower than the right.'

'He screwed it up?' one of the inmates asked.

Langdon chuckled. 'No. Da Vinci didn't do that too often. Actually, this is a little trick Da Vinci played. By lowering the countryside on the left, Da Vinci made Mona Lisa look much larger from the left side than from the right side. A little Da Vinci inside joke. Historically, the concepts of male and female have assigned sides – left is female, and right is male. Because Da Vinci was a big fan of feminine principles, he made Mona Lisa look more majestic from the *left* than the right.'

'I heard he was a fag,' said a small man with a goatee.

Langdon winced. 'Historians don't generally put it quite that way, but yes, Da Vinci was a homosexual.'

'Is that why he was into that whole feminine thing?'

'Actually, Da Vinci was in tune with the *balance* between male and female. He believed that a human soul could not be enlightened unless it had both male and female elements.'

'You mean like chicks with dicks?' someone called.

This elicited a hearty round of laughs. Langdon considered offering an etymological sidebar about the word *hermaphrodite* and its ties to Hermes and Aphrodite, but something told him it would be lost on this crowd.

'Hey, Mr Langford,' a muscle-bound man said. 'Is it true that the *Mona Lisa* is a picture of Da Vinci in drag? I heard that was true.'

'It's quite possible,' Langdon said. 'Da Vinci was a prankster, and computerized analysis of the *Mona Lisa* and Da Vinci's self-portraits confirm some startling points of congruency in their faces. Whatever Da Vinci was up to,' Langdon said, 'his Mona Lisa is neither male nor female. It carries a subtle message of androgyny. It is a fusing of both.'

'You sure that's not just some Harvard bullshit way of saying Mona Lisa is one ugly chick.'

Now Langdon laughed. 'You may be right. But actually Da Vinci left a big clue that the painting was supposed to be androgynous. Has anyone here ever heard of an Egyptian god named Amon?'

'Hell yes!' the big guy said. 'God of masculine fertility!'

Langdon was stunned.

'It says so on every box of Amon condoms.' The muscular man gave a wide grin. 'It's got a guy with a ram's head on the front and says he's the Egyptian god of fertility.'

Langdon was not familiar with the brand name, but he was glad to hear the prophylactic manufacturers had got their hieroglyphs right. 'Well done. Amon is indeed represented as a man with a ram's head, and his promiscuity and curved horns are related to our modern sexual slang "horny".'

'No shit!'

'No shit,' Langdon said. 'And do you know who Amon's counterpart was? The Egyptian *goddess* of fertility?'

The question met with several seconds of silence.

'It was Isis,' Langdon told them, grabbing a grease pen. 'So we have the male god, Amon.' He wrote it down. 'And the female goddess, Isis, whose ancient pictogram was once called L'ISA.'

Langdon finished writing and stepped back from the projector.

AMON L'ISA

'Ring any bells?' he asked.

'Mona Lisa . . . holy crap,' somebody gasped.

Langdon nodded. 'Gentlemen, not only does the face of Mona Lisa look androgynous, but her name is an anagram of the divine union of male and female. And *that,* my friends, is Da Vinci's little secret, and the reason for Mona Lisa's knowing smile.'

'My grandfather was here,' Sophie said, dropping suddenly to her knees, now only ten feet from the *Mona Lisa.* She pointed the black light tentatively to a spot on the parquet floor.

At first Langdon saw nothing. Then, as he knelt beside her, he saw a tiny droplet of dried liquid that was luminescing. *Ink?* Suddenly he recalled what black lights were actually used for. *Blood.* His senses tingled. Sophie was right. Jacques Saunière had indeed paid a visit to the *Mona Lisa* before he died.

'He wouldn't have come here without a reason,' Sophie whispered, standing up. 'I know he left a message for me here.' Quickly striding the final few steps to the *Mona Lisa,* she illuminated the floor directly in front of the painting. She waved the light back and forth across the bare parquet.

'There's nothing here!'

At that moment, Langdon saw a faint purple glimmer on the protective glass before the *Mona Lisa*. Reaching down, he took Sophie's wrist and slowly moved the light up to the painting itself.

They both froze.

On the glass, six words glowed in purple, scrawled directly across the *Mona Lisa*'s face.

Chapter 27

Seated at Saunière's desk, Lieutenant Collet pressed the phone to his ear in disbelief. *Did I hear Fache correctly?* 'A bar of soap? But how could Langdon have known about the GPS dot?'

'Sophie Neveu,' Fache replied. 'She told him.'

'What! Why?'

'Damned good question, but I just heard a recording that confirms she tipped him off.'

Collet was speechless. *What was Neveu thinking?* Fache had proof that Sophie had interfered with a DCPJ sting operation? Sophie Neveu was not only going to be fired, she was also going to jail. 'But, Captain . . . then where is Langdon *now*?'

'Have any fire alarms gone off there?'

'No, sir.'

'And no one has come out under the Grand Gallery gate?'

'No. We've got a Louvre security officer on the gate. Just as you requested.'

'Okay, Langdon must still be inside the Grand Gallery.'

'Inside? But what is he doing?'

'Is the Louvre security guard armed?'

'Yes, sir. He's a senior warden.'

'Send him in,' Fache commanded. 'I can't get my men back to the perimeter for a few minutes, and I don't want Langdon breaking for an exit.' Fache paused. 'And you'd better tell the guard Agent Neveu is probably in there with him.'

'Agent Neveu left, I thought.'

'Did you actually *see* her leave?'

'No, sir, but—'

'Well, nobody on the perimeter saw her leave either. They only saw her go in.'

Collet was flabbergasted by Sophie Neveu's bravado. *She's still inside the building?*

'Handle it,' Fache ordered. 'I want Langdon and Neveu at gunpoint by the time I get back.'

As the Trailor truck drove off, Captain Fache rounded up his men. Robert Langdon had proven an elusive quarry tonight, and with Agent Neveu now helping him, he might be far harder to corner than expected.

Fache decided not to take any chances.

Hedging his bets, he ordered half of his men back to the Louvre perimeter. The other half he sent to guard the only location in Paris where Robert Langdon could find safe harbour.

Chapter 28

Inside the Salle des Etats, Langdon stared in astonishment at the six words glowing on the Plexiglas. The text seemed to hover in space, casting a jagged shadow across Mona Lisa's mysterious smile.

'The Priory,' Langdon whispered. 'This proves your grandfather was a member!'

Sophie looked at him in confusion. 'You *understand* this?'

'It's flawless,' Langdon said, nodding as his thoughts churned. 'It's a proclamation of one of the Priory's most fundamental philosophies!'

Sophie looked baffled in the glow of the message scrawled across the *Mona Lisa*'s face.

SO DARK THE CON OF MAN

'Sophie,' Langdon said, 'the Priory's tradition of perpetuating goddess worship is based on a belief that powerful men in the early Christian Church "conned" the world by propagating lies that devalued the female and tipped the scales in favour of the masculine.'

Sophie remained silent, staring at the words.

'The Priory believes that Constantine and his male successors successfully converted the world from matriarchal paganism to patriarchal Christianity by waging a campaign of propaganda that demonized the sacred feminine, obliterating the goddess from modern religion for ever.'

Sophie's expression remained uncertain. 'My grandfather sent me to this spot to find this. He must be trying to tell me more than *that.*'

Langdon understood her meaning. *She thinks this is another code.* Whether a hidden meaning existed here or not, Langdon could not immediately say. His mind was still grappling with the bold clarity of Saunière's outward message.

So dark the con of man, he thought. *So dark indeed.*

Nobody could deny the enormous good the modern Church did in today's troubled world, and yet the Church had a deceitful and violent history. Their brutal crusade to 'reeducate' the pagan and feminine-worshipping religions spanned three centuries, employing methods as inspired as they were horrific.

The Catholic Inquisition published the book that arguably could be called the most blood-soaked publication in human history. *Malleus Maleficarum* – or *The Witches' Hammer* – indoctrinated the world to 'the dangers of freethinking women' and instructed the clergy how to locate, torture and destroy them. Those deemed 'witches' by the Church included all female scholars, priestesses, gypsies, mystics, nature lovers, herb gatherers and any women 'suspiciously attuned to the natural world'. Midwives also were killed for their heretical practice of using medical knowledge to ease the pain of childbirth – a suffering, the Church claimed, that was God's rightful punishment for Eve's partaking of the Apple of Knowledge, thus giving birth to the idea of Original Sin. During three hundred years of witch hunts, the Church burned at the stake an astounding five *million* women.

The propaganda and bloodshed had worked.

Today's world was living proof.

Women, once celebrated as an essential half of

spiritual enlightenment, had been banished from the temples of the world. There were no female Orthodox rabbis, Catholic priests, nor Islamic clerics. The once hallowed act of Hieros Gamos – the natural sexual union between man and woman through which each became spiritually whole – had been recast as a shameful act. Holy men who had once required sexual union with their female counterparts to commune with God now feared their natural sexual urges as the work of the devil, collaborating with his favourite accomplice . . . *woman*.

Not even the feminine association with the *left-hand* side could escape the Church's defamation. In France and Italy, the words for 'left' – *gauche* and *sinistra* – came to have deeply negative overtones, while their right-hand counterparts rang of *right*eousness, dexterity, and correctness. To this day, radical thought was considered *left* wing, irrational thought was *left* brain, and anything evil, *sinister*.

The days of the goddess were over. The pendulum had swung. Mother Earth had become a *man's* world, and the gods of destruction and war were taking their toll. The male ego had spent two millennium running unchecked by its female counterpart. The Priory of Sion believed that it was this obliteration of the sacred feminine in modern life that had caused what the Hopi Native Americans called *koyanisquatsi* – 'life out of balance' – an unstable situation marked by testosterone-fuelled wars, a plethora of misogynistic societies and a growing disrespect for Mother Earth.

'Robert!' Sophie said, her whisper yanking him back. 'Someone's coming!'

He heard the approaching footsteps out in the hallway.

'Over here!' Sophie extinguished the black light and

seemed to evaporate before Langdon's eyes.

For an instant he felt totally blind. *Over where!* As his vision cleared he saw Sophie's silhouette racing toward the centre of the room and ducking out of sight behind the octagonal viewing bench. He was about to dash after her when a booming voice stopped him cold.

'*Arrêtez!*' a man commanded from the doorway.

The Louvre security agent advanced through the entrance to the Salle des Etats, his pistol outstretched, taking deadly aim at Langdon's chest.

Langdon felt his arms raise instinctively for the ceiling.

'*Couchez-vous!*' the guard commanded. '*Lie down!*'

Langdon was face first on the floor in a matter of seconds. The guard hurried over and kicked his legs apart, spreading Langdon out.

'*Mauvaise idée, Monsieur Langdon,*' he said, pressing the gun hard into Langdon's back. '*Mauvaise idée.*'

Face down on the parquet floor with his arms and legs spread wide, Langdon found little humour in the irony of his position. *The Vitruvian Man*, he thought. *Face down.*

Chapter 29

Inside Saint-Sulpice, Silas carried the heavy iron votive candle holder from the altar back toward the obelisk. The shaft would do nicely as a battering ram. Eyeing the grey marble panel that covered the apparent hollow in the floor, he realized he could not possibly shatter the covering without making considerable noise.

Iron on marble. It would echo off the vaulted ceilings.

Would the nun hear him? She should be asleep by now. Even so, it was a chance Silas preferred not to take. Looking around for a cloth to wrap around the tip of the iron pole, he saw nothing except the altar's linen mantle, which he refused to defile. *My cloak*, he thought. Knowing he was alone in the great church, Silas untied his cloak and slipped it off his body. As he removed it, he felt a sting as the wool fibres stuck to the fresh wounds on his back.

Naked now, except for his loin swaddle, Silas wrapped his cloak over the end of the iron rod. Then, aiming at the centre of the floor tile, he drove the tip into it. A muffled thud. The stone did not break. He drove the pole into it again. Again a dull thud, but this time accompanied by a crack. On the third swing, the covering finally shattered, and stone shards fell into a hollow area beneath the floor.

A compartment!

Quickly pulling the remaining pieces from the

opening, Silas gazed into the void. His blood pounded as he knelt down before it. Raising his pale bare arm, he reached inside.

At first he felt nothing. The floor of the compartment was bare, smooth stone. Then, feeling deeper, reaching his arm in under the Rose Line, he touched something! A thick stone tablet. Getting his fingers around the edge, he gripped it and gently lifted the tablet out. As he stood and examined his find, he realized he was holding a rough-hewn stone slab with engraved words. He felt for an instant like a modern-day Moses.

As Silas read the words on the tablet, he felt surprise. He had expected the keystone to be a map, or a complex series of directions, perhaps even encoded. The keystone, however, bore the simplest of inscriptions.

Job 38:11

A Bible verse? Silas was stunned with the devilish simplicity. The secret location of that which they sought was revealed in a Bible verse? The brotherhood stopped at nothing to mock the righteous!

Job. Chapter thirty-eight. Verse eleven.

Although Silas did not recall the exact contents of verse eleven by heart, he knew the Book of Job told the story of a man whose faith in God survived repeated tests. *Appropriate,* he thought, barely able to contain his excitement.

Looking over his shoulder, he gazed down the shimmering Rose Line and couldn't help but smile. There atop the main altar, propped open on a gilded book stand, sat an enormous leather-bound Bible.

Up in the balcony, Sister Sandrine was shaking. Moments ago, she had been about to flee and carry out

177

her orders, when the man below suddenly removed his cloak. When she saw his alabaster-white flesh, she was overcome with a horrified bewilderment. His broad, pale back was soaked with blood-red slashes. Even from here she could see the wounds were fresh.

This man has been mercilessly whipped!

She also saw the bloody *cilice* around his thigh, the wound beneath it dripping. *What kind of God would want a body punished this way?* The rituals of Opus Dei, Sister Sandrine knew, were not something she would ever understand. But that was hardly her concern at this instant. *Opus Dei is searching for the keystone.* How they knew of it, Sister Sandrine could not imagine, although she knew she did not have time to think.

The bloody monk was now quietly donning his cloak again, clutching his prize as he moved toward the altar, toward the Bible.

In breathless silence, Sister Sandrine left the balcony and raced down the hall to her quarters. Getting on her hands and knees, she reached beneath her wooden bed frame and retrieved the sealed envelope she had hidden there years ago.

Tearing it open, she found four Paris phone numbers.

Trembling, she began to dial.

Downstairs, Silas laid the stone tablet on the altar and turned his eager hands to the leather Bible. His long white fingers were sweating now as he turned the pages. Flipping through the Old Testament, he found the Book of Job. He located chapter thirty-eight. As he ran his finger down the column of text, he anticipated the words he was about to read.

They will lead The Way!

Finding verse number eleven, Silas read the text. It was only seven words. Confused, he read it again, sensing something had gone terribly wrong. The verse simply read:

HITHERTO SHALT THOU COME, BUT NO FURTHER.

Chapter 30

Security warden Claude Grouard simmered with rage as he stood over his prostrate captive in front of the *Mona Lisa. This bastard killed Jacques Saunière!* Saunière had been like a well-loved father to Grouard and his security team.

Grouard wanted nothing more than to pull the trigger and bury a bullet in Robert Langdon's back. As senior warden, Grouard was one of the few guards who actually carried a loaded weapon. He reminded himself, however, that killing Langdon would be a generous fate compared to the misery about to be communicated by Bezu Fache and the French prison system.

Grouard yanked his walkie-talkie off his belt and attempted to radio for backup. All he heard was static. The additional electronic security in this chamber always wrought havoc with the guards' communications. *I have to move to the doorway.* Still aiming his weapon at Langdon, Grouard began backing slowly toward the entrance. On his third step, he spied something that made him stop short.

What the hell is that!

An inexplicable mirage was materializing near the centre of the room. A silhouette. There was someone else in the room? A woman was moving through the darkness, walking briskly toward the far left wall. In front of her, a purplish beam of light swung back and forth across the floor, as if she were searching for something with a coloured flashlight.

'*Qui est là?*' Grouard demanded, feeling his adrenaline spike for a second time in the last thirty seconds. He suddenly didn't know where to aim his gun or what direction to move.

'PTS,' the woman replied calmly, still scanning the floor with her light.

Police Technique et Scientifique. Grouard was sweating now. *I thought all the agents were gone!* He now recognized the purple light as ultraviolet, consistent with a PTS team, and yet he could not understand why DCPJ would be looking for evidence in here.

'*Votre nom!*' Grouard yelled, instinct telling him something was amiss. '*Répondez!*'

'*C'est moi,*' the voice responded in calm French. '*Sophie Neveu.*'

Somewhere in the distant recesses of Grouard's mind, the name registered. *Sophie Neveu?* That was the name of Saunière's granddaughter, wasn't it? She used to come in here as a little kid, but that was years ago. *This couldn't possibly be her!* And even if it were Sophie Neveu, that was hardly a reason to trust her; Grouard had heard the rumours of the painful falling-out between Saunière and his granddaughter.

'You know me,' the woman called. 'And Robert Langdon did not kill my grandfather. Believe me.'

Warden Grouard was not about to take *that* on faith. *I need backup!* Trying his walkie-talkie again, he got only static. The entrance was still a good twenty yards behind him, and Grouard began backing up slowly, choosing to leave his gun trained on the man on the floor. As Grouard inched backward, he could see the woman across the room raising her UV light and scrutinizing a large painting that hung on the far side of the Salle des Etats, directly opposite the *Mona Lisa*.

Grouard gasped, realizing which painting it was.

What in the name of God is she doing?

* * *

Across the room, Sophie Neveu felt a cold sweat breaking across her forehead. Langdon was still spread-eagled on the floor. *Hold on, Robert. Almost there.* Knowing the guard would never actually shoot either of them, Sophie now turned her attention back to the matter at hand, scanning the entire area around one masterpiece in particular – another Da Vinci. But the UV light revealed nothing out of the ordinary. Not on the floor, on the walls, or even on the canvas itself.

There must be something here!

Sophie felt totally certain she had deciphered her grandfather's intentions correctly.

What else could he possibly intend?

The masterpiece she was examining was a five-foot-tall canvas. The bizarre scene Da Vinci had painted included an awkwardly posed Virgin Mary sitting with Baby Jesus, John the Baptist and the Angel Uriel on a perilous outcropping of rocks. When Sophie was a little girl, no trip to the *Mona Lisa* had been complete without her grandfather dragging her across the room to see this second painting.

Grand-père, I'm here! But I don't see it!

Behind her, Sophie could hear the guard trying to radio again for help.

Think!

She pictured the message scrawled on the protective glass of the *Mona Lisa. So dark the con of man.* The painting before her had no protective glass on which to write a message, and Sophie knew her grandfather would never have defaced this masterpiece by writing on the painting itself. She paused. *At least not on the front.* Her eyes shot upward, climbing the long cables that dangled from the ceiling to support the canvas.

Could that be it? Grabbing the left side of the carved wood frame, she pulled it toward her. The painting was large and the backing flexed as she swung it away from the wall. Sophie slipped her head and shoulders in behind the painting and raised the black light to inspect the back.

It took only seconds to realize her instinct had been wrong. The back of the painting was pale and blank. There was no purple text here, only the mottled brown backside of aging canvas and—

Wait.

Sophie's eyes locked on an incongruous glint of lustrous metal lodged near the bottom edge of the frame's wooden armature. The object was small, partially wedged in the slit where the canvas met the frame. A shimmering gold chain dangled off it.

To Sophie's utter amazement, the chain was affixed to a familiar gold key. The broad, sculpted head was in the shape of a cross and bore an engraved seal she had not seen since she was nine years old. A fleur-de-lis with the initials P.S. In that instant, Sophie felt the ghost of her grandfather whispering in her ear. *When the time comes, the key will be yours.* A tightness gripped her throat as she realized that her grandfather, even in death, had kept his promise. *This key opens a box,* his voice was saying, *where I keep many secrets.*

Sophie now realized that the entire purpose of tonight's word game had been this key. Her grandfather had it with him when he was killed. Not wanting it to fall into the hands of the police, he hid it behind this painting. Then he devised an ingenious treasure hunt to ensure only Sophie would find it.

'Au secours!' the guard's voice yelled.

Sophie snatched the key from behind the painting and slipped it deep in her pocket along with the UV penlight. Peering out from behind the canvas, she

183

could see the guard was still trying desperately to raise someone on the walkie-talkie. He was backing toward the entrance, still aiming the gun firmly at Langdon.

'*Au secours!*' he shouted again into his radio.

Static.

He can't transmit, Sophie realized, recalling that tourists with cell phones often got frustrated in here when they tried to call home to brag about seeing the *Mona Lisa*. The extra surveillance wiring in the walls made it virtually impossible to get a carrier unless you stepped out into the hall. The guard was backing quickly toward the exit now, and Sophie knew she had to act immediately.

Gazing up at the large painting behind which she was partially ensconced, Sophie realized that Leonardo da Vinci, for the second time tonight, was there to help.

Another few metres, Grouard told himself, keeping his gun levelled.

'*Arrêtez! Ou je la détruis!*' the woman's voice echoed across the room.

Grouard glanced over and stopped in his tracks. '*Mon dieu, non!*'

Through the reddish haze, he could see that the woman had actually lifted the large painting off its cables and propped it on the floor in front of her. At five feet tall, the canvas almost entirely hid her body. Grouard's first thought was to wonder why the painting's trip wires hadn't set off alarms, but of course the artwork cable sensors had yet to be reset tonight. *What is she doing!*

When he saw it, his blood went cold.

The canvas started to bulge in the middle, the

184

fragile outlines of the Virgin Mary, Baby Jesus and John the Baptist beginning to distort.

'*Non!*' Grouard screamed, frozen in horror as he watched the priceless Da Vinci stretching. The woman was pushing her knee into the centre of the canvas from behind! '*NON!*'

Grouard wheeled and aimed his gun at her but instantly realized it was an empty threat. The canvas was only fabric, but it was utterly impenetrable – a six-million-dollar piece of body armour.

I can't put a bullet through a Da Vinci!

'Set down your gun and radio,' the woman said in calm French, 'or I'll put my knee through this painting. I think you know how my grandfather would feel about that.'

Grouard felt dizzy. 'Please . . . no. That's *Madonna of the Rocks*!' He dropped his gun and radio, raising his hands over his head.

'Thank you,' the woman said. 'Now do exactly as I tell you, and everything will work out fine.'

Moments later, Langdon's pulse was still thundering as he ran beside Sophie down the emergency stairwell toward the ground level. Neither of them had said a word since leaving the trembling Louvre guard lying in the Salle des Etats. The guard's pistol was now clutched tightly in Langdon's hands, and he couldn't wait to get rid of it. The weapon felt heavy and dangerously foreign.

Taking the stairs two at a time, Langdon wondered if Sophie had any idea how valuable a painting she had almost ruined. Her choice in art seemed eerily pertinent to tonight's adventure. The Da Vinci she had grabbed, much like the *Mona Lisa*, was notorious among art historians for its plethora of hidden pagan symbolism.

185

'You chose a valuable hostage,' he said as they ran.

'*Madonna of the Rocks,*' she replied. 'But I didn't choose it, my grandfather did. He left me a little something behind the painting.'

Langdon shot her a startled look. 'What!? But how did you know which painting? Why *Madonna of the Rocks?*'

'So dark the con of man.' She flashed a triumphant smile. 'I missed the first two anagrams, Robert. I wasn't about to miss the third.'

Chapter 31

'They're dead!' Sister Sandrine stammered into the telephone in her Saint-Sulpice residence. She was leaving a message on an answering machine. 'Please pick up! They're all dead!'

The first three phone numbers on the list had produced terrifying results – a hysterical widow, a detective working late at a murder scene, and a sombre priest consoling a bereaved family. All three contacts were dead. And now, as she called the fourth and final number – the number she was not supposed to call unless the first three could not be reached – she got an answering machine. The outgoing message offered no name but simply asked the caller to leave a message.

'The floor panel has been broken!' she pleaded as she left the message. 'The other three are dead!'

Sister Sandrine did not know the identities of the four men she protected, but the private phone numbers stashed beneath her bed were for use on only one condition.

If that floor panel is ever broken, the faceless messenger had told her, *it means the upper echelon has been breached. One of us has been mortally threatened and been forced to tell a desperate lie. Call the numbers. Warn the others. Do not fail us in this.*

It was a silent alarm. Foolproof in its simplicity. The plan had amazed her when she first heard it. If the identity of one brother was compromised, he could tell a lie that would start in motion a mechanism

187

to warn the others. Tonight, however, it seemed that more than one had been compromised.

'Please answer,' she whispered in fear. 'Where are you?'

'Hang up the phone,' a deep voice said from the doorway.

Turning in terror, she saw the massive monk. He was clutching the heavy iron candle stand. Shaking, she set the phone back in the cradle.

'They are dead,' the monk said. 'All four of them. And they have played me for a fool. Tell me where the keystone is.'

'I don't know!' Sister Sandrine said truthfully. 'That secret is guarded by others.' *Others who are dead!*

The man advanced, his white fists gripping the iron stand. 'You are a sister of the Church, and yet you serve *them*?'

'Jesus had but one true message,' Sister Sandrine said defiantly. 'I cannot see that message in Opus Dei.'

A sudden explosion of rage erupted behind the monk's eyes. He lunged, lashing out with the candle stand like a club. As Sister Sandrine fell, her last feeling was an overwhelming sense of foreboding.

All four are dead.

The precious truth is lost for ever.

Chapter 32

The security alarm on the west end of the Denon Wing
sent the pigeons in the nearby Tuileries Gardens
scattering as Langdon and Sophie dashed out of the
bulkhead into the Paris night. As they ran across the
plaza to Sophie's car, Langdon could hear police
sirens wailing in the distance.

'That's it there,' Sophie called, pointing to a red
snub-nosed two-seater parked on the plaza.

She's kidding, right? The vehicle was easily the
smallest car Langdon had ever seen.

'SmartCar,' she said. 'A hundred kilometres to the
litre.'

Langdon had barely thrown himself into the
passenger seat before Sophie gunned the SmartCar up
and over a curb onto a gravel divider. He gripped the
dash as the car shot out across a sidewalk and
bounced back down into the small rotary at Carrousel
du Louvre.

For an instant, Sophie seemed to consider taking the
shortcut across the rotary by ploughing straight
ahead, through the median's perimeter hedge, and
bisecting the large circle of grass in the centre.

'No!' Langdon shouted, knowing the hedges
around Carrousel du Louvre were there to hide the
perilous chasm in the centre – *La Pyramide Inversée* –
the upside-down pyramid skylight he had seen earlier
from inside the museum. It was large enough to
swallow their SmartCar in a single gulp. Fortunately,
Sophie decided on the more conventional route,

jamming the wheel hard to the right, circling properly until she exited, cut left, and swung into the northbound lane, accelerating toward Rue de Rivoli.

The two-tone police sirens blared louder behind them, and Langdon could see the lights now in his side view mirror. The SmartCar engine whined in protest as Sophie urged it faster away from the Louvre. Fifty yards ahead, the traffic light at Rivoli turned red. Sophie cursed under her breath and kept racing toward it. Langdon felt his muscles tighten.

'Sophie?'

Slowing only slightly as they reached the intersection, Sophie flicked her headlights and stole a quick glance both ways before flooring the accelerator again and carving a sharp left turn through the empty intersection onto Rivoli.

As they straightened out, Langdon turned in his seat, craning his neck to look out the rear window toward the Louvre. The police did not seem to be chasing them. The sea of blue lights was assembling at the museum.

His heartbeat finally slowing, Langdon turned back round. 'That was interesting.'

Sophie didn't seem to hear. Her eyes remained fixed ahead. The embassy was only about half a mile away, and Langdon settled into his seat.

So dark the con of man.

Sophie's quick thinking had been impressive.

Madonna of the Rocks.

Sophie had said her grandfather left her something behind the painting. *A final message?* Langdon could not help but marvel over Saunière's brilliant hiding place; *Madonna of the Rocks* was yet another fitting link in the evening's chain of interconnected symbolism. Saunière, it seemed, at every turn, was reinforcing his fondness for the dark and mischievous side of Leonardo da Vinci.

Da Vinci's original commission for *Madonna of the Rocks* had come from an organization known as the Confraternity of the Immaculate Conception, which needed a painting for the centrepiece of an altar triptych in their church of San Francesco in Milan. The nuns gave Leonardo specific dimensions, and the desired theme for the painting – the Virgin Mary, baby John the Baptist, Uriel and Baby Jesus sheltering in a cave. Although Da Vinci did as they requested, when he delivered the work, the group reacted with horror. He had filled the painting with explosive and disturbing details.

The painting showed a blue-robed Virgin Mary sitting with her arm around an infant child, presumably Baby Jesus. Opposite Mary sat Uriel, also with an infant, presumably baby John the Baptist. Oddly, though, rather than the usual Jesus-blessing-John scenario, it was baby *John* who was blessing Jesus . . . and Jesus was submitting to his authority! More troubling still, Mary was holding one hand high above the head of infant John and making a decidedly threatening gesture – her fingers looking like eagle's talons, gripping an invisible head. Finally, the most obvious and frightening image: Just below Mary's curled fingers, Uriel was making a cutting gesture with his hand – as if slicing the neck of the invisible head gripped by Mary's claw-like hand.

Langdon's students were always amused to learn that Da Vinci eventually mollified the confraternity by painting them a second, 'watered-down' version of *Madonna of the Rocks* in which everyone was arranged in a more orthodox manner. The second version now hung in London's National Gallery under the name

Virgin of the Rocks, although Langdon still preferred the Louvre's more intriguing original.

As Sophie gunned the car up Champs-Elysées, Langdon said, 'The painting. What was behind it?'

Her eyes remained on the road. 'I'll show you once we're safely inside the embassy.'

'You'll *show* it to me?' Langdon was surprised. 'He left you a physical object?'

Sophie gave a curt nod. 'Embossed with a fleur-de-lis and the initials P.S.'

Langdon couldn't believe his ears.

We're going to make it, Sophie thought as she swung the SmartCar's wheel to the right, cutting sharply past the luxurious Hôtel de Crillon into Paris's tree-lined diplomatic neighbourhood. The embassy was less than a mile away now. She was finally feeling like she could breathe normally again.

Even as she drove, Sophie's mind remained locked on the key in her pocket, her memories of seeing it many years ago, the gold head shaped as an equal-armed cross, the triangular shaft, the indentations, the embossed flowery seal, and the letters P.S.

Although the key barely had entered Sophie's thoughts through the years, her work in the intelligence community had taught her plenty about security, and now the key's peculiar tooling no longer looked so mystifying. *A laser-tooled varying matrix. Impossible to duplicate.* Rather than teeth that moved tumblers, this key's complex series of laser-burned pockmarks was examined by an electric eye. If the eye determined that the hexagonal pockmarks were correctly spaced, arranged, and rotated, then the lock would open.

Sophie could not begin to imagine what a key like this opened, but she sensed Robert would be able to tell her. After all, he had described the key's embossed seal without ever seeing it. The cruciform on top implied the key belonged to some kind of Christian organization, and yet Sophie knew of no churches that used laser-tooled varying matrix keys.

Besides, my grandfather was no Christian....

Sophie had witnessed proof of that ten years ago. Ironically, it had been another *key* – a far more normal one – that had revealed his true nature to her.

The afternoon had been warm when she landed at Charles de Gaulle Airport and hailed a taxi home. *Grand-père will be so surprised to see me,* she thought. Returning from graduate school in Britain for spring break a few days early, Sophie couldn't wait to see him and tell him all about the encryption methods she was studying.

When she arrived at their Paris home, however, her grandfather was not there. Disappointed, she knew he had not been expecting her and was probably working at the Louvre. *But it's Saturday afternoon,* she realized. He seldom worked on weekends. On weekends, he usually—

Grinning, Sophie ran out to the garage. Sure enough, his car was gone. It was the weekend. Jacques Saunière despised city driving and owned a car for one destination only – his vacation château in Normandy, west of Paris. Sophie, after months in the congestion of London, was eager for the smells of nature and to start her vacation right away. It was still early evening, and she decided to leave immediately and surprise him. Borrowing a friend's car, Sophie drove west, winding into the deserted moon-swept hills near Creully. She arrived just after ten o'clock, turning down the long private driveway toward her grandfather's retreat. The access road was over a mile long, and she was halfway down it before she could start to see the house through the trees – a mammoth, old stone château nestled in the woods on the side of a hill.

Sophie had half expected to find her grandfather asleep at this hour and was excited to see the house twinkling with lights. Her delight turned to surprise, however, when she arrived to find the driveway filled with parked cars – Mercedeses, BMWs, Audis and a Rolls-Royce.

Sophie stared a moment and then burst out laughing. *My grand-père, the famous recluse!* Jacques Saunière, it seemed, was far less reclusive than he liked to pretend. Clearly he was hosting a party while Sophie was away at school, and from the looks of the automobiles, some of Paris's most influential people were in attendance.

Eager to surprise him, she hurried to the front door. When she got there, though, she found it locked. She knocked. Nobody answered. Puzzled, she walked around and tried the back door. It too was locked. No answer.

Confused, she stood a moment and listened. The only sound she heard was the cool Normandy air letting out a low moan as it swirled through the valley.

No music.

No voices.

Nothing.

In the silence of the woods, Sophie hurried to the side of the house and clambered up on a woodpile, pressing her face to the living room window. What she saw inside made no sense at all.

'Nobody's here!'

The entire first floor looked deserted.

Where are all the people?

Heart racing, Sophie ran to the woodshed and got the spare key her grandfather kept hidden under the kindling box. She ran to the front door and let herself in. As she stepped into the deserted foyer, the control panel for the security system started blinking red – a warning that the entrant had ten seconds to type the proper code before the security alarms went off.

He has the alarm on during a party?

Sophie quickly typed the code and deactivated the system.

Entering, she found the entire house uninhabited. Upstairs too. As she descended again to the deserted living room, she stood a moment in the silence, wondering what could possibly be happening.

It was then that Sophie heard it.

Muffled voices. And they seemed to be coming from underneath her. Sophie could not imagine. Crouching, she put her ear to the floor and listened. Yes, the sound was definitely coming from below. The voices seemed to be singing, or . . . *chanting*? She was frightened. Almost more eerie than the sound itself was the realization that this house did not even have a basement.

At least none I've ever seen.

Turning now and scanning the living room, Sophie's eyes fell to the only object in the entire house that seemed out of place – her grandfather's favourite antique, a sprawling Aubusson tapestry. It usually hung on the east wall beside the fireplace, but tonight it had been pulled aside on its brass rod, exposing the wall behind it.

Walking toward the bare wooden wall, Sophie sensed the chanting getting louder. Hesitant, she leaned her ear against the wood. The voices were clearer now. People were definitely chanting . . . intoning words Sophie could not discern.

The space behind this wall is hollow!

Feeling around the edge of the panels, Sophie found a recessed fingerhold. It was discreetly crafted. *A sliding door.* Heart pounding, she placed her finger in the slot and pulled it. With noiseless precision, the heavy wall slid sideways. From out of the darkness beyond, the voices echoed up.

Sophie slipped through the door and found herself on a rough-hewn stone staircase that spiralled downward. She'd been coming to this house since she was a child and yet had no idea this staircase even existed!

As she descended, the air grew cooler. The voices clearer. She heard men and women now. Her line of sight was limited by the spiral of the staircase, but the last step was now rounding into view. Beyond it, she could see a small patch of the basement floor – stone, illuminated by the flickering orange blaze of firelight.

Holding her breath, Sophie inched down another few steps and crouched down to look. It took her several seconds to process what she was seeing.

The room was a grotto – a coarse chamber that appeared to have been hollowed from the granite of the hillside. The only light came from torches on the walls. In the glow of the flames, thirty or so people stood in a circle in the centre of the room.

I'm dreaming, Sophie told herself. *A dream. What else could this be?*

Everyone in the room was wearing a mask. The women were dressed in white gossamer gowns and golden shoes. Their masks were white, and in their hands they carried golden orbs. The men wore long black tunics, and their masks were black. They looked like pieces in a giant chess set. Everyone in the circle rocked back and forth and chanted in reverence to something on the floor before them ... something Sophie could not see.

The chanting grew steady again. Accelerating. Thundering now. Faster. The participants took a step inward and knelt. In that instant, Sophie could finally see what they all were witnessing. Even as she staggered back in horror, she felt the image searing itself into her memory for ever. Overtaken by nausea, Sophie spun, clutching at the stone walls as she clambered back up the stairs. Pulling the door closed, she fled the deserted house, and drove in a tearful stupor back to Paris.

That night, with her life shattered by disillusionment and betrayal, she packed her belongings and left her home. On the dining room table, she left a note.

I WAS THERE. DON'T TRY TO FIND ME.

Beside the note, she laid the old spare key from the château's woodshed.

'Sophie!' Langdon's voice intruded. 'Stop! *Stop!*'

Emerging from the memory, Sophie slammed on the brakes, skidding to a halt. 'What? What happened?!'

Langdon pointed down the long street before them.

When she saw it, Sophie's blood went cold. A hundred yards ahead, the intersection was blocked by a couple of DCPJ police cars, parked askew, their purpose obvious. *They've sealed off Avenue Gabriel!*

Langdon gave a grim sigh. 'I take it the embassy is off-limits this evening?'

Down the street, the two DCPJ officers who stood beside their cars were now staring in their direction, apparently curious about the headlights that had halted so abruptly up the street from them.

Okay, Sophie, turn around very slowly.

Putting the SmartCar in reverse, she performed a composed three-point turn and reversed her direction. As she drove away, she heard the sound of squealing tyres behind them. Sirens blared to life.

Cursing, Sophie slammed down the accelerator.

Chapter 33

Sophie's SmartCar tore through the diplomatic quarter, weaving past embassies and consulates, finally racing out a side street and taking a right turn back onto the massive thoroughfare of Champs-Elysées.

Langdon sat white-knuckled in the passenger seat, twisted backward, scanning behind them for any signs of the police. He suddenly wished he had not decided to run. *You didn't,* he reminded himself. Sophie had made the decision for him when she threw the GPS dot out of the men's room window. Now, as they sped away from the embassy, serpentining through sparse traffic on Champs-Elysées, Langdon felt his options deteriorating. Although Sophie seemed to have lost the police, at least for the moment, Langdon doubted their luck would hold for long.

Behind the wheel Sophie was fishing in her sweater pocket. She removed a small metal object and held it out for him. 'Robert, you'd better have a look at this. This is what my grandfather left me behind *Madonna of the Rocks*.'

Feeling a shiver of anticipation, Langdon took the object and examined it. It was heavy and shaped like a cruciform. His first instinct was that he was holding a funeral *pieu* – a miniature version of a memorial spike designed to be stuck into the ground at a gravesite. But then he noted the shaft protruding from the cruciform was prismatic and triangular. The shaft was also pockmarked with hundreds of tiny hexagons that appeared to be finely tooled and scattered at random.

'It's a laser-cut key,' Sophie told him. 'Those hexagons are read by an electric eye.'

A key? Langdon had never seen anything like it.

'Look at the other side,' she said, changing lanes and sailing through an intersection.

When Langdon turned the key, he felt his jaw drop. There, intricately embossed on the centre of the cross, was a stylized fleur-de-lis with the initials P.S.! 'Sophie,' he said, 'this is the seal I told you about! The official device of the Priory of Sion.'

She nodded. 'As I told you, I saw the key a long time ago. He told me never to speak of it again.'

Langdon's eyes were still riveted on the embossed key. Its high-tech tooling and age-old symbolism exuded an eerie fusion of ancient and modern worlds.

'He told me the key opened a box where he kept many secrets.'

Langdon felt a chill to imagine what kind of secrets a man like Jacques Saunière might keep. What an ancient brotherhood was doing with a futuristic key, Langdon had no idea. The Priory existed for the sole purpose of protecting a secret. A secret of incredible power. *Could this key have something to do with it?* The thought was overwhelming. 'Do you know what it opens?'

Sophie looked disappointed. 'I was hoping *you* knew.'

Langdon remained silent as he turned the cruciform in his hand, examining it.

'It looks Christian,' Sophie pressed.

Langdon was not so sure about that. The head of this key was not the traditional long-stemmed Christian cross but rather was a *square* cross – with four arms of equal length – which predated

Christianity by fifteen hundred years. This kind of cross carried none of the Christian connotations of crucifixion associated with the longer-stemmed Latin cross, originated by Romans as a torture device. Langdon was always surprised how few Christians who gazed upon 'the crucifix' realized their symbol's violent history was reflected in its very name: 'cross' and 'crucifix' came from the Latin verb *cruciare* – to torture.

'Sophie,' he said, 'all I can tell you is that equal-armed crosses like this one are considered *peaceful* crosses. Their square configurations make them impractical for use in crucifixion, and their balanced vertical and horizontal elements convey a natural union of male and female, making them symbolically consistent with Priory philosophy.'

She gave him a weary look. 'You have no idea, do you?'

Langdon frowned. 'Not a clue.'

'Okay, we have to get off the road.' Sophie checked her rearview mirror. 'We need a safe place to figure out what that key opens.'

Langdon thought longingly of his comfortable room at the Ritz. Obviously, that was not an option. 'How about my hosts at the American University of Paris?'

'Too obvious. Fache will check with them.'

'You must know people. You live here.'

'Fache will run my phone and e-mail records, talk to my coworkers. My contacts are compromised, and finding a hotel is no good because they all require identification.'

Langdon wondered again if he might have been better off taking his chances letting Fache arrest him at the Louvre. 'Let's call the embassy. I can explain the situation and have the embassy send someone to meet us somewhere.'

'Meet us?' Sophie turned and stared at him as if he were crazy. 'Robert, you're dreaming. Your embassy has no jurisdiction except on their own property. Sending someone to retrieve us would be considered aiding a fugitive of the French government. It won't happen. If you walk into your embassy and request temporary asylum, that's one thing, but asking them to take action against French law enforcement in the field?' She shook her head. 'Call your embassy right now, and they are going to tell you to avoid further damage and turn yourself over to Fache. Then they'll promise to pursue diplomatic channels to get you a fair trial.' She gazed up the line of elegant storefronts on Champs-Elysées. 'How much cash do you have?'

Langdon checked his wallet. 'A hundred dollars. A few euros. Why?'

'Credit cards?'

'Of course.'

As Sophie accelerated, Langdon sensed she was formulating a plan. Dead ahead, at the end of Champs-Elysées, stood the Arc de Triomphe – Napoleon's 164-foot-tall tribute to his own military potency – encircled by France's largest rotary, a nine-lane behemoth.

Sophie's eyes were on the rearview mirror again as they approached the rotary. 'We lost them for the time being,' she said, 'but we won't last another five minutes if we stay in this car.'

So steal a different one, Langdon mused, *now that we're criminals.* 'What are you going to do?'

Sophie gunned the SmartCar into the rotary. 'Trust me.'

Langdon made no response. Trust had not got him very far this evening. Pulling back the sleeve of his jacket, he checked his watch – a vintage, collector's-edition Mickey Mouse wristwatch that had been a gift from his parents on his tenth birthday. Although its juvenile dial often drew odd looks, Langdon had never owned any other watch; Disney animations had been his first introduction to the magic of form and colour, and Mickey now served as Langdon's daily reminder to stay young at heart. At the moment, however, Mickey's arms were skewed at an awkward angle, indicating an equally awkward hour.

2:51 A.M.

'Interesting watch,' Sophie said, glancing at his wrist and manoeuvring the SmartCar around the wide, counterclockwise rotary.

'Long story,' he said, pulling his sleeve back down.

'I imagine it would have to be.' She gave him a quick smile and exited the rotary, heading due north, away from the city centre. Barely making two green lights, she reached the third intersection and took a hard right onto Boulevard Malesherbes. They'd left the rich, tree-lined streets of the diplomatic neighbourhood and plunged into a darker industrial neighbourhood. Sophie took a quick left, and a moment later, Langdon realized where they were.

Gare Saint-Lazare.

Ahead of them, the glass-roofed train terminal resembled the awkward offspring of an airplane hangar and a greenhouse. European train stations never slept. Even at this hour, a half-dozen taxis idled near the main entrance. Vendors manned carts of sandwiches and mineral water while grungy kids in backpacks emerged from the station rubbing their eyes, looking around as if trying to remember what city they were in now. Up ahead on the street, a couple of city policemen stood on the curb giving directions to some confused tourists.

Sophie pulled her SmartCar in behind the line of taxis and parked in a red zone despite plenty of legal parking across the street. Before Langdon could ask what was going on, she was out of the car. She hurried to the window of the taxi in front of them and began speaking to the driver.

As Langdon got out of the SmartCar, he saw Sophie hand the taxi driver a big wad of cash. The taxi driver nodded and then, to Langdon's bewilderment, sped off without them.

'What happened?' Langdon demanded, joining Sophie on the curb as the taxi disappeared.

Sophie was already heading for the train station entrance. 'Come on. We're buying two tickets on the next train out of Paris.'

Langdon hurried along beside her. What had begun as a one-mile dash to the US Embassy had now become a full-fledged evacuation from Paris. Langdon was liking this idea less and less.

Chapter 34

The driver who collected Bishop Aringarosa from Leonardo da Vinci International Airport pulled up in a small, unimpressive black Fiat sedan. Aringarosa recalled a day when all Vatican transports were big luxury cars that sported grille-plate medallions and flags emblazoned with the seal of the Holy See. *Those days are gone.* Vatican cars were now less ostentatious and almost always unmarked. The Vatican claimed this was to cut costs to better serve their dioceses, but Aringarosa suspected it was more of a security measure. The world had gone mad, and in many parts of Europe, advertising your love of Jesus Christ was like painting a bull's-eye on the roof of your car.

Bundling his black cassock around himself, Aringarosa climbed into the back seat and settled in for the long drive to Castel Gandolfo. It would be the same ride he had taken five months ago.

Last year's trip to Rome, he sighed. *The longest night of my life.*

Five months ago, the Vatican had phoned to request Aringarosa's immediate presence in Rome. They offered no explanation. *Your tickets are at the airport.* The Holy See worked hard to retain a veil of mystery, even for its highest clergy.

The mysterious summons, Aringarosa suspected, was probably a photo opportunity for the Pope and other Vatican officials to piggyback on Opus Dei's recent public success – the completion of their World

Headquarters in New York City. *Architectural Digest* had called Opus Dei's building 'a shining beacon of Catholicism sublimely integrated with the modern landscape', and lately the Vatican seemed to be drawn to anything and everything that included the word 'modern'.

Aringarosa had no choice but to accept the invitation, albeit reluctantly. Not a fan of the current papal administration, Aringarosa, like most conservative clergy, had watched with grave concern as the new Pope settled into his first year in office. An unprecedented liberal, His Holiness had secured the papacy through one of the most controversial and unusual conclaves in Vatican history. Now, rather than being humbled by his unexpected rise to power, the Holy Father had wasted no time flexing all the muscle associated with the highest office in Christendom. Drawing on an unsettling tide of liberal support within the College of Cardinals, the Pope was now declaring his papal mission to be 'rejuvenation of Vatican doctrine and updating Catholicism into the third millennium'.

The translation, Aringarosa feared, was that the man was actually arrogant enough to think he could rewrite God's laws and win back the hearts of those who felt the demands of true Catholicism had become too inconvenient in a modern world.

Aringarosa had been using all of his political sway – substantial considering the size of the Opus Dei constituency and their bankroll – to persuade the Pope and his advisers that softening the Church's laws was not only faithless and cowardly, but political suicide. He reminded them that previous tempering of Church law – the Vatican II fiasco – had left a devastating legacy: Church attendance was now lower than ever, donations were drying up, and there were not even enough

Catholic priests to preside over their churches.

People need structure and direction from the Church, Aringarosa insisted, *not coddling and indulgence!*

On that night, months ago, as the Fiat had left the airport, Aringarosa was surprised to find himself heading not toward Vatican City but rather eastward up a sinuous mountain road. 'Where are we going?' he had demanded of his driver.

'Alban Hills,' the man replied. 'Your meeting is at Castel Gandolfo.'

The Pope's summer residence? Aringarosa had never been, nor had he ever desired to see it. In addition to being the Pope's summer vacation home, the sixteenth-century citadel housed the Specula Vaticana – the Vatican Observatory – one of the most advanced astronomical observatories in Europe. Aringarosa had never been comfortable with the Vatican's historical need to dabble in science. What was the rationale for fusing science and faith? Unbiased science could not possibly be performed by a man who possessed faith in God. Nor did faith have any need for physical confirmation of its beliefs.

Nonetheless, there it is, he thought as Castel Gandolfo came into view, rising against a star-filled November sky. From the access road, Gandolfo resembled a great stone monster pondering a suicidal leap. Perched at the very edge of a cliff, the castle leaned out over the cradle of Italian civilization – the valley where the Curiazi and Orazi clans fought long before the founding of Rome.

Even in silhouette, Gandolfo was a sight to behold – an impressive example of tiered, defensive architecture, echoing the potency of this dramatic cliffside setting. Sadly, Aringarosa now saw, the Vatican had ruined the building by constructing two huge aluminium telescope domes atop the roof, leaving this once dignified edifice looking like a proud warrior wearing a couple of party hats.

When Aringarosa got out of the car, a young Jesuit priest hurried out and greeted him. 'Bishop, welcome. I am Father Mangano. An astronomer here.'

Good for you. Aringarosa grumbled his hello and followed his host into the castle's foyer – a wide-open space whose decor was a graceless blend of Renaissance art and astronomy images. Following his escort up the wide travertine marble staircase, Aringarosa saw signs for conference centres, science lecture halls and tourist information services. It amazed him to think the Vatican was failing at every turn to provide coherent, stringent guidelines for spiritual growth and yet somehow still found time to give astrophysics lectures to tourists.

'Tell me,' Aringarosa said to the young priest, 'when did the tail start wagging the dog?'

The priest gave him an odd look. 'Sir?'

Aringarosa waved it off, deciding not to launch into that particular offensive again this evening. *The Vatican has gone mad.* Like a lazy parent who found it easier to acquiesce to the whims of a spoiled child than to stand firm and teach values, the Church just kept softening at every turn, trying to reinvent itself to accommodate a culture gone astray.

The top floor's corridor was wide, lushly appointed, and led in only one direction – toward a huge set of oak doors with a brass sign.

BIBLIOTECA ASTRONOMICA

Aringarosa had heard of this place – the Vatican's Astronomy Library – rumoured to contain more than twenty-five thousand volumes, including rare works of Copernicus, Galileo, Kepler, Newton and Secchi.

Allegedly, it was also the place in which the Pope's highest officers held private meetings . . . those meetings they preferred not to hold within the walls of Vatican City.

Approaching the door, Bishop Aringarosa would never have imagined the shocking news he was about to receive inside, or the deadly chain of events it would put into motion. It was not until an hour later, as he staggered from the meeting, that the devastating implications settled in. *Six months from now!* he had thought. *God help us!*

Now, seated in the Fiat, Bishop Aringarosa realized his fists were clenched just thinking about that first meeting. He released his grip and forced a slow inhalation, relaxing his muscles.

Everything will be fine, he told himself as the Fiat wound higher into the mountains. Still, he wished his cell phone would ring. *Why hasn't the Teacher called me? Silas should have the keystone by now.*

Trying to ease his nerves, the bishop meditated on the purple amethyst in his ring. Feeling the textures of the mitre-crozier appliqué and the facets of the diamonds, he reminded himself that this ring was a symbol of power far less than that which he would soon attain.

Chapter 35

The inside of Gare du Nord looked like every other train station in Europe, a gaping indoor-outdoor cavern dotted with the usual suspects – homeless men holding cardboard signs, collections of bleary-eyed college kids sleeping on backpacks and zoning out to their portable MP3 players, and clusters of blue-clad baggage porters smoking cigarettes.

Sophie raised her eyes to the enormous departure board overhead. The black and white tabs reshuffled, ruffling downward as the information refreshed. When the update was finished, Langdon eyed the offerings. The topmost listing read:

LILLE – RAPIDE – 3:06

'I wish it left sooner,' Sophie said, 'but Lille will have to do.'

Sooner? Langdon checked his watch: 2:59 A.M. The train left in seven minutes and they didn't even have tickets yet.

Sophie guided Langdon toward the ticket window and said, 'Buy us two tickets with your credit card.'

'I thought credit card usage could be traced by—'

'Exactly.'

Langdon decided to stop trying to keep ahead of Sophie Neveu. Using his Visa card, he purchased two tickets to Lille and handed them to Sophie.

Sophie guided him out toward the tracks, where a familiar tone chimed overhead and a P.A. announcer gave the final boarding call for Lille. Sixteen separate tracks spread out before them.

In the distance to the right, at quay three, the train to Lille was belching and wheezing in preparation for departure, but Sophie already had her arm through Langdon's and was guiding him in the exact opposite direction. They hurried through a side lobby, past an all-night café, and finally out a side door onto a quiet street on the west side of the station.

A lone taxi sat idling by the doorway.

The driver saw Sophie and flicked his lights.

Sophie jumped in the back seat. Langdon got in after her.

As the taxi pulled away from the station, Sophie took out their newly purchased train tickets and tore them up.

Langdon sighed. *Seventy dollars well spent.*

It was not until their taxi had settled into a monotonous northbound hum on Rue de Clichy that Langdon felt they'd actually escaped. Out the window to his right, he could see Montmartre and the beautiful dome of Sacré-Coeur. The image was interrupted by the flash of police lights sailing past them in the opposite direction.

Langdon and Sophie ducked down as the sirens faded.

Sophie had told the cab driver simply to head out of the city, and from her firmly set jaw, Langdon sensed she was trying to figure out their next move.

Langdon examined the cruciform key again, holding it to the window, bringing it close to his eyes in an effort to find any markings on it that might indicate where the key had been made. In the intermittent glow of passing streetlights, he saw no markings except the Priory seal.

'It doesn't make sense,' he finally said.

'Which part?'

'That your grandfather would go to so much trouble to give you a key that you wouldn't know what to do with.'

'I agree.'

'Are you sure he didn't write anything else on the back of the painting?'

'I searched the whole area. This is all there was. This key, wedged behind the painting. I saw the Priory seal, stuck the key in my pocket, then we left.'

Langdon frowned, peering now at the blunt end of the triangular shaft. Nothing. Squinting, he brought the key close to his eyes and examined the rim of the head. Nothing there either. 'I think this key was cleaned recently.'

'Why?'

'It smells like rubbing alcohol.'

She turned. 'I'm sorry?'

'It smells like somebody polished it with a cleaner.' Langdon held the key to his nose and sniffed. 'It's stronger on the other side.' He flipped it over. 'Yes, it's alcohol-based, like it's been buffed with a cleaner or—' Langdon stopped.

'What?'

He angled the key to the light and looked at the smooth surface on the broad arm of the cross. It seemed to shimmer in places . . . like it was wet. 'How well did you look at the back of this key before you put it in your pocket?'

'What? Not well. I was in a hurry.'

Langdon turned to her. 'Do you still have the black light?'

Sophie reached in her pocket and produced the UV penlight. Langdon took it and switched it on, shining the beam on the back of the key.

The back luminesced instantly. There was writing there. In penmanship that was hurried but legible.

'Well,' Langdon said, smiling. 'I guess we know what the alcohol smell was.'

Sophie stared in amazement at the purple writing on the back of the key.

24 Rue Haxo

An address! My grandfather wrote down an address!

'Where is this?' Langdon asked.

Sophie had no idea. Facing front again, she leaned forward and excitedly asked the driver, '*Connaissez-vous la Rue Haxo?*'

The driver thought a moment and then nodded. He told Sophie it was out near the tennis stadium on the western outskirts of Paris. She asked him to take them there immediately.

'Fastest route is through Bois de Boulogne,' the driver told her in French. 'Is that okay?'

Sophie frowned. She could think of far less scandalous routes, but tonight she was not going to be picky. '*Oui.*' *We can shock the visiting American.*

Sophie looked back at the key and wondered what they would possibly find at 24 Rue Haxo. *A church? Some kind of Priory headquarters?*

Her mind filled again with images of the secret ritual she had witnessed in the basement grotto ten years ago, and she heaved a long sigh. 'Robert, I have a lot of things to tell you.' She paused, locking eyes with him as the taxi raced westward. 'But first I want you to tell me everything you know about this Priory of Sion.'

Chapter 36

Outside the Salle des Etats, Bezu Fache was fuming as Louvre warden Grouard explained how Sophie and Langdon had disarmed him. *Why didn't you just shoot the blessed painting!*

'Captain?' Lieutenant Collet loped toward them from the direction of the command post. 'Captain, I just heard. They located Agent Neveu's car.'

'Did she make the embassy?'

'No. Train station. Bought two tickets. Train just left.'

Fache waved off warden Grouard and led Collet to a nearby alcove, addressing him in hushed tones. 'What was the destination?'

'Lille.'

'Probably a decoy.' Fache exhaled, formulating a plan. 'Okay, alert the next station, have the train stopped and searched, just in case. Leave her car where it is and put plainclothes on watch in case they try to come back to it. Send men to search the streets around the station in case they fled on foot. Are buses running from the station?'

'Not at this hour, sir. Only the taxi queue.'

'Good. Question the drivers. See if they saw anything. Then contact the taxi company dispatcher with descriptions. I'm calling Interpol.'

Collet looked surprised. 'You're putting this on the *wire*?'

Fache regretted the potential embarrassment, but he saw no other choice.

Close the net fast, and close it tight.

The first hour was critical. Fugitives were predictable the first hour after escape. They always needed the same thing. *Travel. Lodging. Cash.* The Holy Trinity. Interpol had the power to make all three disappear in the blink of an eye. By broadcast-faxing photos of Langdon and Sophie to Paris travel authorities, hotels and banks, Interpol would leave no options – no way to leave the city, no place to hide, and no way to withdraw cash without being recognized. Usually, fugitives panicked on the street and did something stupid. Stole a car. Robbed a store. Used a bank card in desperation. Whatever mistake they committed, they quickly made their whereabouts known to local authorities.

'Only *Langdon*, right?' Collet said. 'You're not flagging Sophie Neveu. She's our own agent.'

'Of course I'm flagging her!' Fache snapped. 'What good is flagging Langdon if she can do all his dirty work? I plan to run Neveu's employment file – friends, family, personal contacts – anyone she might turn to for help. I don't know what she thinks she's doing out there, but it's going to cost her one hell of a lot more than her job!'

'Do you want me on the phones or in the field?'

'Field. Get over to the train station and coordinate the team. You've got the reins, but don't make a move without talking to me.'

'Yes, sir.' Collet ran out.

Fache felt rigid as he stood in the alcove. Outside the window, the glass pyramid shone, its reflection rippling in the windswept pools. *They slipped through my fingers.* He told himself to relax.

Even a trained field agent would be lucky to withstand the pressure that Interpol was about to apply.

A female cryptologist and a schoolteacher?

They wouldn't last till dawn.

215

Chapter 37

The heavily forested park known as the Bois de Boulogne was called many things, but the Parisian cognoscenti knew it as 'the Garden of Earthly Delights'. The epithet, despite sounding flattering, was quite to the contrary. Anyone who had seen the lurid Bosch painting of the same name understood the jab; the painting, like the forest, was dark and twisted, a purgatory for freaks and fetishists. At night, the forest's winding lanes were lined with hundreds of glistening bodies for hire, earthly delights to satisfy one's deepest unspoken desires – male, female, and everything in between.

As Langdon gathered his thoughts to tell Sophie about the Priory of Sion, their taxi passed through the wooded entrance to the park and began heading west on the cobblestone crossfare. Langdon was having trouble concentrating as a scattering of the park's nocturnal residents were already emerging from the shadows and flaunting their wares in the glare of the headlights. Ahead, two topless teenage girls shot smouldering gazes into the taxi. Beyond them, a well-oiled black man in a G-string turned and flexed his buttocks. Beside him, a gorgeous blond woman lifted her miniskirt to reveal that she was not, in fact, a woman.

Heaven help me! Langdon turned his gaze back inside the cab and took a deep breath.

'Tell me about the Priory of Sion,' Sophie said.

Langdon nodded, unable to imagine a less congruous backdrop for the legend he was about to tell. He wondered where to begin. The brotherhood's history spanned more than a millennium . . . an astonishing chronicle of secrets, blackmail, betrayal and even brutal torture at the hands of an angry Pope.

'The Priory of Sion,' he began, 'was founded in Jerusalem in 1099 by a French king named Godefroi de Bouillon, immediately after he had conquered the city.'

Sophie nodded, her eyes riveted on him.

'King Godefroi was allegedly the possessor of a powerful secret – a secret that had been in his family since the time of Christ. Fearing his secret might be lost when he died, he founded a secret brotherhood – the Priory of Sion – and charged them with protecting his secret by quietly passing it on from generation to generation. During their years in Jerusalem, the Priory learned of a stash of hidden documents buried beneath the ruins of Herod's temple, which had been built on top of the earlier ruins of Solomon's temple. These documents, they believed, corroborated Godefroi's powerful secret and were so explosive in nature that the Church would stop at nothing to get them.'

Sophie looked uncertain.

'The Priory vowed that no matter how long it took, these documents must be recovered from the rubble beneath the temple and protected for ever, so the truth would never die. In order to retrieve the documents from within the ruins, the Priory created a military arm – a group of nine knights called the Order of the Poor Knights of Christ and the Temple of Solomon.' Langdon paused. 'More commonly known as the Knights Templar.'

Sophie glanced up with a surprised look of recognition.

Langdon had lectured often enough on the Knights Templar to know that almost everyone on earth had heard of them, at least abstractedly. For academics, the Templars' history was a precarious world where fact, lore and misinformation had become so intertwined that extracting a pristine truth was almost impossible. Nowadays, Langdon hesitated even to mention the Knights Templar while lecturing because it invariably led to a barrage of convoluted inquiries into assorted conspiracy theories.

Sophie already looked troubled. 'You're saying the Knights Templar were founded by the Priory of Sion to retrieve a collection of secret documents? I thought the Templars were created to protect the Holy Land.'

'A common misconception. The idea of protection of pilgrims was the *guise* under which the Templars ran their mission. Their true goal in the Holy Land was to retrieve the documents from beneath the ruins of the temple.'

'And did they find them?'

Langdon grinned. 'Nobody knows for sure, but the one thing on which all academics agree is this: The Knights discovered *something* down there in the ruins . . . something that made them wealthy and powerful beyond anyone's wildest imagination.'

Langdon quickly gave Sophie the standard academic sketch of the accepted Knights Templar history, explaining how the Knights were in the Holy Land during the Second Crusade and told King Baldwin II that they were there to protect Christian pilgrims on the roadways. Although unpaid and sworn to poverty, the Knights told the king they required basic shelter and requested his permission to take up residence in the stables under the ruins of the temple. King Baldwin granted the soldiers' request, and the Knights took up their meagre residence inside the devastated shrine.

The odd choice of lodging, Langdon explained, had been anything but random. The Knights believed the documents the Priory sought were buried deep under the ruins – beneath the Holy of Holies, a sacred chamber where God Himself was believed to reside. Literally, the very centre of the Jewish faith. For almost a decade, the nine Knights lived in the ruins, excavating in total secrecy through solid rock.

Sophie looked over. 'And you said they discovered something?'

'They certainly did,' Langdon said, explaining how it had taken nine years, but the Knights had finally found what they had been searching for. They took the treasure from the temple and travelled to Europe, where their influence seemed to solidify overnight.

Nobody was certain whether the Knights had blackmailed the Vatican or whether the Church simply tried to buy the Knights' silence, but Pope Innocent II immediately issued an unprecedented papal bull that afforded the Knights Templar limitless power and declared them 'a law unto themselves' – an autonomous army independent of all interference from kings and prelates, both religious and political.

With their new carte blanche from the Vatican, the Knights Templar expanded at a staggering rate, both in numbers and political force, amassing vast estates in over a dozen countries. They began extending credit to bankrupt royals and charging interest in return, thereby establishing modern banking and broadening their wealth and influence still further.

By the 1300s, the Vatican sanction had helped the Knights amass so much power that Pope Clement V decided that something had to be done. Working in concert with France's King Philippe IV, the Pope devised an ingeniously planned sting operation to quash the Templars and seize their treasure, thus taking control of the secrets held over the Vatican. In a military manoeuvre worthy of the CIA, Pope Clement issued secret sealed orders to be opened simultaneously by his soldiers all across Europe on Friday, October 13 of 1307.

At dawn on the thirteenth, the documents were unsealed and their appalling contents revealed. Clement's letter claimed that God had visited him in a vision and warned him that the Knights Templar were heretics guilty of devil worship, homosexuality, defiling the cross, sodomy and other blasphemous behaviour. Pope Clement had been asked by God to cleanse the earth by rounding up all the Knights and torturing them until they confessed their crimes against God. Clement's Machiavellian operation came off with clockwork precision. On that day, countless Knights were captured, tortured mercilessly and finally burned at the stake as heretics. Echoes of the tragedy still resonated in modern culture; to this day, Friday the thirteenth was considered unlucky.

Sophie looked confused. 'The Knights Templar were obliterated? I thought fraternities of Templars still exist today?'

'They do, under a variety of names. Despite Clement's false charges and best efforts to eradicate them, the Knights had powerful allies, and some managed to escape the Vatican purges. The Templars' potent treasure trove of documents, which had apparently been their source of power, was Clement's true objective, but it slipped through his fingers. The documents had long since been entrusted to the Templars' shadowy architects, the Priory of Sion, whose veil of secrecy had kept them safely out of range of the Vatican's onslaught. As the Vatican closed in, the Priory smuggled their documents from a Paris preceptory by night onto Templar ships in La Rochelle.'

'Where did the documents go?'

Langdon shrugged. 'That mystery's answer is known only to the Priory of Sion. Because the documents remain the source of constant investigation and speculation even today, they are believed to have been moved and rehidden several times. Current speculation places the documents somewhere in the United Kingdom.'

Sophie looked uneasy.

'For a thousand years,' Langdon continued, 'legends of this secret have been passed on. The entire collection of documents, its power, and the secret it reveals have become known by a single name – Sangreal. Hundreds of books have been written about it, and few mysteries have caused as much interest among historians as the Sangreal.'

'The Sangreal? Does the word have anything to do with the French word *sang* or Spanish *sangre* – meaning "blood"?'

Langdon nodded. Blood was the backbone of the Sangreal, and yet not in the way Sophie probably imagined. 'The legend is complicated, but the important thing to remember is that the Priory guards the proof, and is purportedly awaiting the right moment in history to reveal the truth.'

'What truth? What secret could possibly be that powerful?'

Langdon took a deep breath and gazed out at the underbelly of Paris leering in the shadows. 'Sophie, the word *Sangreal* is an ancient word. It has evolved over the years into another term . . . a more modern name.' He paused. 'When I tell you its modern name, you'll realize you already know a lot about it. In fact, almost everyone on earth has heard the story of the Sangreal.'

Sophie looked sceptical. 'I've never heard of it.'

'Sure you have.' Langdon smiled. 'You're just used to hearing it called by the name "Holy Grail".'

Chapter 38

Sophie scrutinized Langdon in the back of the taxi. *He's joking.* 'The Holy Grail?'

Langdon nodded, his expression serious. 'Holy Grail is the literal meaning of Sangreal. The phrase derives from the French *Sangraal*, which evolved to Sangreal, and was eventually split into two words, *San Greal.*'

Holy Grail. Sophie was surprised she had not spotted the linguistic ties immediately. Even so, Langdon's claim still made no sense to her. 'I thought the Holy Grail was a *cup*. You just told me the Sangreal is a collection of documents that reveals some dark secret.'

'Yes, but the Sangreal documents are only *half* of the Holy Grail treasure. They are buried with the Grail itself . . . and reveal its true meaning. The documents gave the Knights Templar so much power because the pages revealed the true nature of the Grail.'

The true nature of the Grail? Sophie felt even more lost now. The Holy Grail, she had thought, was the cup that Jesus drank from at the Last Supper and with which Joseph of Arimathea later caught His blood at the crucifixion. 'The Holy Grail is the Cup of Christ,' she said. 'How much simpler could it be?'

'Sophie,' Langdon whispered, leaning toward her now, 'according to the Priory of Sion, the Holy Grail is not a cup at all. They claim the Grail legend – that of a *chalice* – is actually an ingeniously conceived allegory. That is, that the Grail story uses the *chalice* as a metaphor for something else, something far more powerful.' He paused. 'Something that fits perfectly with everything your grandfather has been trying to tell us tonight, including all his symbologic references to the sacred feminine.'

Still unsure, Sophie sensed in Langdon's patient smile that he empathized with her confusion, and yet his eyes remained earnest. 'But if the Holy Grail is not a cup,' she asked, 'what is it?'

Langdon had known this question was coming, and yet he still felt uncertain exactly how to tell her. If he did not present the answer in the proper historical background, Sophie would be left with a vacant air of bewilderment – the exact expression Langdon had seen on his own editor's face a few months ago after Langdon handed him a draft of the manuscript he was working on.

'This manuscript claims *what?*' his editor had choked, setting down his wineglass and staring across his half-eaten power lunch. 'You can't be serious.'

'Serious enough to have spent a year researching it.'

Prominent New York editor Jonas Faukman tugged nervously at his goatee. Faukman no doubt had heard some wild book ideas in his illustrious career, but this one seemed to have left the man flabbergasted.

'Robert,' Faukman finally said, 'don't get me wrong. I love your work, and we've had a great run together. But if I agree to publish an idea like this, I'll have people picketing outside my office for months. Besides, it will kill your reputation. You're a Harvard historian, for God's sake, not a pop schlockmeister looking for a quick buck. Where could you possibly find enough credible evidence to support a theory like this?'

With a quiet smile Langdon pulled a piece of paper from the pocket of his tweed coat and handed it to Faukman. The page listed a bibliography of over fifty titles – books by well-known historians, some contemporary, some centuries old – many of them academic bestsellers. All the book titles suggested the same premise Langdon had just proposed. As Faukman read down the list, he looked like a man who had just discovered the earth was actually flat. 'I *know* some of these authors. They're . . . real historians!'

Langdon grinned. 'As you can see, Jonas, this is not only *my* theory. It's been around for a long time. I'm simply building on it. No book has yet explored the legend of the Holy Grail from a symbologic angle. The iconographic evidence I'm finding to support the theory is, well, staggeringly persuasive.'

Faukman was still staring at the list. 'My God, one of these books was written by Sir Leigh Teabing – a British Royal Historian.'

'Teabing has spent much of his life studying the Holy Grail. I've met with him. He was actually a big part of my inspiration. He's a believer, Jonas, along with all of the others on that list.'

'You're telling me all of these historians actually believe . . .' Faukman swallowed, apparently unable to say the words.

Langdon grinned again. 'The Holy Grail is arguably the most sought-after treasure in human history. The Grail has spawned legends, wars and lifelong quests. Does it make sense that it is merely a cup? If so, then certainly *other* relics should generate similar or greater interest – the Crown of Thorns, the True Cross of the Crucifixion, the Titulus – and yet, they do not. Throughout history, the Holy Grail has been the most special.' Langdon grinned. 'Now you know why.'

Faukman was still shaking his head. 'But with all these books written about it, why isn't this theory more widely known?'

'These books can't possibly compete with centuries of established history, especially when that history is endorsed by the ultimate bestseller of all time.'

Faukman's eyes went wide. 'Don't tell me *Harry Potter* is actually about the Holy Grail.'

'I was referring to the Bible.'

Faukman cringed. 'I knew that.'

'*Laissez-le!*' Sophie's shouts cut the air inside the taxi. 'Put it down!'

Langdon jumped as Sophie leaned forward over the seat and yelled at the taxi driver. Langdon could see the driver was clutching his radio mouthpiece and speaking into it.

Sophie turned now and plunged her hand into the pocket of Langdon's tweed jacket. Before Langdon knew what had happened, she had yanked out the pistol, swung it around, and was pressing it to the back of the driver's head. The driver instantly dropped his radio, raising his one free hand overhead.

'Sophie!' Langdon choked. 'What the hell—'

'*Arrêtez!*' Sophie commanded the driver.

Trembling, the driver obeyed, stopping the car.

It was then that Langdon heard the metallic voice of the taxi company's dispatcher coming from the dashboard. '. . . *qui s'appelle Agent Sophie Neveu . . .*' the radio crackled. '*Et un Américain, Robert Langdon . . .*'

Langdon's muscles turned rigid. *They found us already?*

'*Descendez,*' Sophie demanded.

The trembling driver kept his arms over his head as he got out of his taxi and took several steps backward.

Sophie had rolled down her window and now aimed the gun outside at the bewildered cabbie. 'Robert,' she said quietly, 'take the wheel. You're driving.'

Langdon was not about to argue with a woman wielding a gun. He climbed out of the car and jumped back in behind the wheel. The driver was yelling curses, his arms still raised over his head.

'Robert,' Sophie said from the back seat, 'I trust you've seen enough of our magic forest?'

He nodded. *Plenty.*

'Good. Drive us out of here.'

Langdon looked down at the car's controls and hesitated. *Shit.* He groped for the stick shift and clutch. 'Sophie? Maybe you—'

'Go!' she yelled.

Outside, several hookers were walking over to see what was going on. One woman was placing a call on her cell phone. Langdon depressed the clutch and jostled the stick into what he hoped was first gear. He touched the accelerator, testing the gas.

Langdon popped the clutch. The tyres howled as the taxi leapt forward, fishtailing wildly and sending the gathering crowd diving for cover. The woman with the cell phone leapt into the woods, only narrowly avoiding being run down.

'*Doucement!*' Sophie said, as the car lurched down the road. 'What are you doing?'

'I tried to warn you,' he shouted over the sound of gnashing gears. 'I drive an automatic!'

Chapter 39

Although the spartan room in the house on Rue La Bruyère had witnessed a lot of suffering, Silas doubted anything could match the anguish now gripping his pale body. *I was deceived. Everything is lost.*

Silas had been tricked. The brothers had lied, choosing death instead of revealing their true secret. Silas did not have the strength to call the Teacher. Not only had Silas killed the only four people who knew where the keystone was hidden, he had killed a nun inside Saint-Sulpice. *She was working against God! She scorned the work of Opus Dei!*

A crime of impulse, the woman's death complicated matters greatly. Bishop Aringarosa had placed the phone call that got Silas into Saint-Sulpice; what would the abbé think when he discovered the nun was dead? Although Silas had placed her back in her bed, the wound on her head was obvious. Silas had attempted to replace the broken tiles in the floor, but that damage too was obvious. They would know someone had been there.

Silas had planned to hide within Opus Dei when his task here was complete. *Bishop Aringarosa will protect me.* Silas could imagine no more blissful existence than a life of meditation and prayer deep within the walls of Opus Dei's headquarters in New York City. He would never again set foot outside. Everything he needed was within that sanctuary. *Nobody will miss me.* Unfortunately, Silas knew, a prominent man like Bishop Aringarosa could not disappear so easily.

I have endangered the bishop. Silas gazed blankly at the floor and pondered taking his own life. After all, it had been Aringarosa who gave Silas life in the first place . . . in that small rectory in Spain, educating him, giving him purpose.

'My friend,' Aringarosa had told him, 'you were born an albino. Do not let others shame you for this. Do you not understand how special this makes you? Were you not aware that Noah himself was an albino?'

'Noah of the Ark?' Silas had never heard this.

Aringarosa was smiling. 'Indeed, Noah of the Ark. An albino. Like you, he had skin white like an angel. Consider this. Noah saved all of life on the planet. You are destined for great things, Silas. The Lord has freed you for a reason. You have your calling. The Lord needs your help to do His work.'

Over time, Silas learned to see himself in a new light. *I am pure. White. Beautiful. Like an angel.*

At the moment, though, in his room at the residence hall, it was his father's disappointed voice that whispered to him from the past.

Tu es un désastre. Un spectre.

Kneeling on the wooden floor, Silas prayed for forgiveness. Then, stripping off his robe, he reached again for the Discipline.

Chapter 40

Struggling with the gear shift, Langdon managed to manoeuvre the hijacked taxi to the far side of the Bois de Boulogne while stalling only twice. Unfortunately, the inherent humour in the situation was over-shadowed by the taxi dispatcher repeatedly hailing their cab over the radio.

'Voiture cinq-six-trois. Où êtes-vous? Répondez!'

When Langdon reached the exit of the park, he swallowed his machismo and jammed on the brakes. 'You'd better drive.'

Sophie looked relieved as she jumped behind the wheel. Within seconds she had the car humming smoothly westward along Allée de Longchamp, leaving the Garden of Earthly Delights behind.

'Which way is Rue Haxo?' Langdon asked, watching Sophie edge the speedometer over a hundred kilometres an hour.

Sophie's eyes remained focused on the road. 'The cab driver said it's adjacent to the Roland Garros tennis stadium. I know that area.'

Langdon pulled the heavy key from his pocket again, feeling the weight in his palm. He sensed it was an object of enormous consequence. Quite possibly the key to his own freedom.

Earlier, while telling Sophie about the Knights Templar, Langdon had realized that this key, in addition to having the Priory seal embossed on it, possessed a more subtle tie to the Priory of Sion. The equal-armed cruciform was symbolic of balance and harmony but also of the Knights Templar. Everyone had seen the paintings of Knights Templar wearing white tunics emblazoned with red equal-armed crosses. Granted, the arms of the Templar cross were slightly flared at the ends, but they were still of equal length.

A square cross. Just like the one on this key.

Langdon felt his imagination starting to run wild as he fantasized about what they might find. *The Holy Grail.* He almost laughed out loud at the absurdity of it. The Grail was believed to be somewhere in England, buried in a hidden chamber beneath one of the many Templar churches, where it had been hidden since at least 1500.

The era of Grand Master Da Vinci.

The Priory, in order to keep their powerful documents safe, had been forced to move them many times in the early centuries. Historians now suspected as many as six different Grail relocations since its arrival in Europe from Jerusalem. The last Grail 'sighting' had been in 1447 when numerous eyewitnesses described a fire that had broken out and almost engulfed the documents before they were carried to safety in four huge chests that each required six men to carry. After that, nobody claimed to see the Grail ever again. All that remained were occasional whisperings that it was hidden in Great Britain, the land of King Arthur and the Knights of the Round Table.

Wherever it was, two important facts remained:

Leonardo knew where the Grail resided during his lifetime.

That hiding place had probably not changed to this day.

For this reason, Grail enthusiasts still pored over Da Vinci's art and diaries in hopes of unearthing a hidden clue as to the Grail's current location. Some claimed the mountainous backdrop in *Madonna of the Rocks* matched the topography of a series of cave-ridden hills in Scotland. Others insisted that the suspicious placement of disciples in *The Last Supper* was some kind of code. Still others claimed that X-rays of the *Mona Lisa* revealed she originally had been painted wearing a lapis lazuli pendant of Isis – a detail Da Vinci purportedly later decided to paint over. Langdon had never seen any evidence of the pendant, nor could he imagine how it could possibly reveal the Holy Grail, and yet Grail aficionados still discussed it ad nauseam on Internet bulletin boards and world-wide-web chat rooms.

Everyone loves a conspiracy.

And the conspiracies kept coming. Most recent, of course, had been the earthshaking discovery that Da Vinci's famed *Adoration of the Magi* was hiding a dark secret beneath its layers of paint. Italian art diagnostician Maurizio Seracini had unveiled the unsettling truth, which the *New York Times Magazine* carried prominently in a story titled 'The Leonardo Cover-Up'.

Seracini had revealed beyond any doubt that while the *Adoration*'s grey-green sketched underdrawing was indeed Da Vinci's work, the painting itself was not. The truth was that some anonymous painter had filled in Da Vinci's sketch like a paint-by-numbers years after Da Vinci's death. Far more troubling, however, was what lay *beneath* the impostor's paint. Photographs taken with infrared reflectography and X-ray suggested that this rogue painter, while filling in Da Vinci's sketched study, had made suspicious departures from the underdrawing . . . as if to subvert Da Vinci's true intention. Whatever the true nature of the underdrawing, it had yet to be made public. Even so, embarrassed officials at Florence's Uffizi Gallery immediately banished the painting to a warehouse across the street. Visitors at the gallery's Leonardo Room now found a misleading and unapologetic plaque where the *Adoration* once hung.

THIS WORK IS UNDERGOING DIAGNOSTIC TESTS IN PREPARATION FOR RESTORATION.

In the bizarre underworld of modern Grail seekers, Leonardo da Vinci remained the quest's great enigma. His artwork seemed bursting to tell a secret, and yet whatever it was remained hidden, perhaps beneath a layer of paint, perhaps enciphered in plain view, or perhaps nowhere at all. Maybe Da Vinci's plethora of tantalizing clues was nothing but an empty promise left behind to frustrate the curious and bring a smirk to the face of his knowing Mona Lisa.

'Is it possible,' Sophie asked, drawing Langdon back, 'that the key you're holding unlocks the hiding place of the Holy Grail?'

Langdon's laugh sounded forced, even to him. 'I really can't imagine. Besides, the Grail is believed to be hidden in the United Kingdom somewhere, not France.' He gave her the quick history.

'But the Grail seems the only rational conclusion,' she insisted. 'We have an extremely secure key, stamped with the Priory of Sion seal, delivered to us by a member of the Priory of Sion – a brotherhood which, you just told me, are guardians of the Holy Grail.'

Langdon knew her contention was logical, and yet intuitively he could not possibly accept it. Rumours existed that the Priory had vowed someday to bring the Grail back to France to a final resting place, but certainly no historical evidence existed to suggest that this indeed had happened. Even if the Priory had managed to bring the Grail back to France, the address 24 Rue Haxo near a tennis stadium hardly sounded like a noble final resting place. 'Sophie, I really don't see how this key could have anything to do with the Grail.'

'Because the Grail is supposed to be in England?'

'Not only that. The location of the Holy Grail is one of the best kept secrets in history. Priory members wait decades proving themselves trustworthy before being elevated to the highest echelons of the fraternity and learning where the Grail is. That secret is protected by an intricate system of compart-mentalized knowledge, and although the Priory brotherhood is very large, only *four* members at any given time know where the Grail is hidden – the Grand Master and his three *sénéchaux*. The probability of your grandfather being one of those four top people is very slim.'

My grandfather was one of them, Sophie thought, pressing down on the accelerator. She had an image stamped in her memory that confirmed her grand-father's status within the brotherhood beyond any doubt.

'And even if your grandfather *were* in the upper echelon, he would never be allowed to reveal any-thing to anyone outside the brotherhood. It is inconceivable that he would bring you into the inner circle.'

I've already been there, Sophie thought, picturing the ritual in the basement. She wondered if this were the moment to tell Langdon what she had witnessed that night in the Normandy château. For ten years now, simple shame had kept her from telling a soul. Just thinking about it, she shuddered.

Sirens howled somewhere in the distance, and she felt a thickening shroud of fatigue settling over her.

'There!' Langdon said, feeling excited to see the huge complex of the Roland Garros tennis stadium looming ahead.

Sophie snaked her way toward the stadium. After several passes, they located the intersection of Rue Haxo and turned onto it, driving in the direction of the lower numbers. The road became more industrial, lined with businesses.

We need number twenty-four, Langdon told himself, realizing he was secretly scanning the horizon for the spires of a church. *Don't be ridiculous. A forgotten Templar church in this neighborhood?*

'There it is,' Sophie exclaimed, pointing.

Langdon's eyes followed to the structure ahead.

What in the world?

The building was modern. A squat citadel with a giant, neon equal-armed cross emblazoned atop its façade. Beneath the cross were the words:

DEPOSITORY BANK OF ZURICH

Langdon was thankful not to have shared his Templar church hopes with Sophie. A career hazard of symbologists was a tendency to extract hidden meaning from situations that had none. In this case, Langdon had entirely forgotten that the peaceful, equal-armed cross had been adopted as the perfect symbol for the flag of neutral Switzerland.

At least the mystery was solved.

Sophie and Langdon were holding the key to a Swiss bank deposit box.

Chapter 41

Outside Castel Gandolfo, an updraft of mountain air gushed over the top of the cliff and across the high bluff, sending a chill through Bishop Aringarosa as he stepped from the Fiat. *I should have worn more than this cassock*, he thought, fighting the reflex to shiver. The last thing he needed to appear tonight was weak or fearful.

The castle was dark save the windows at the very top of the building, which glowed ominously. *The library*, Aringarosa thought. *They are awake and waiting*. He ducked his head against the wind and continued on without so much as a glance toward the observatory domes.

The priest who greeted him at the door looked sleepy. He was the same priest who had greeted Aringarosa five months ago, albeit tonight he did so with much less hospitality. 'We were worried about you, Bishop,' the priest said, checking his watch and looking more perturbed than worried.

'My apologies. Airlines are so unreliable these days.'

The priest mumbled something inaudible and then said, 'They are waiting upstairs. I will escort you up.'

The library was a vast square room with dark wood from floor to ceiling. On all sides, towering bookcases groaned with volumes. The floor was amber marble with black basalt trim, a handsome reminder that this building had once been a palace.

'Welcome, Bishop,' a man's voice said from across the room.

Aringarosa tried to see who had spoken, but the lights were ridiculously low – much lower than they had been on his first visit, when everything was ablaze. *The night of stark awakening*. Tonight, these men sat in the shadows, as if they were somehow ashamed of what was about to transpire.

Aringarosa entered slowly, regally even. He could see the shapes of three men at a long table on the far side of the room. The silhouette of the man in the middle was immediately recognizable – the obese Secretarius Vaticana, overlord of all legal matters within Vatican City. The other two were high-ranking Italian cardinals.

Aringarosa crossed the library toward them. 'My humble apologies for the hour. We're on different time zones. You must be tired.'

'Not at all,' the secretarius said, his hands folded on his enormous belly. 'We are grateful you have come so far. The least we can do is be awake to meet you. Can we offer you some coffee or refreshments?'

'I'd prefer we don't pretend this is a social visit. I have another plane to catch. Shall we get to business?'

'Of course,' the secretarius said. 'You have acted more quickly than we imagined.'

'Have I?'

'You still have a month.'

'You made your concerns known five months ago,' Aringarosa said. 'Why should I wait?'

'Indeed. We are very pleased with your expediency.'

Aringarosa's eyes travelled the length of the long table to a large black briefcase. 'Is that what I requested?'

'It is.' The secretarius sounded uneasy. 'Although, I must admit, we are concerned with the request. It seems quite . . .'

'Dangerous,' one of the cardinals finished. 'Are you certain we cannot wire it to you somewhere? The sum is exorbitant.'

Freedom is expensive. 'I have no concerns for my own safety. God is with me.'

The men actually looked doubtful.

'The funds are exactly as I requested?'

The secretarius nodded. 'Large-denomination bearer bonds drawn on the Vatican Bank. Negotiable as cash anywhere in the world.'

Aringarosa walked to the end of the table and opened the briefcase. Inside were two thick stacks of bonds, each embossed with the Vatican seal and the title *PORTATORE*, making the bonds redeemable to whoever was holding them.

The secretarius looked tense. 'I must say, Bishop, all of us would feel less apprehensive if these funds were in *cash*.'

I could not lift that much cash, Aringarosa thought, closing the case. 'Bonds are negotiable as cash. You said so yourself.'

The cardinals exchanged uneasy looks, and finally one said, 'Yes, but these bonds are traceable directly to the Vatican Bank.'

Aringarosa smiled inwardly. That was precisely the reason the Teacher suggested Aringarosa get the money in Vatican Bank bonds. It served as insurance. *We are all in this together now.* 'This is a perfectly legal transaction,' Aringarosa defended. 'Opus Dei is a personal prelature of Vatican City, and His Holiness can disperse monies however he sees fit. No law has been broken here.'

'True, and yet . . .' The secretarius leaned forward and his chair creaked under the burden. 'We have no knowledge of what you intend to do with these funds, and if it is in any way illegal . . .'

'Considering what you are asking of me,' Aringarosa countered, 'what I do with this money is not your concern.'

There was a long silence.

They know I'm right, Aringarosa thought. 'Now, I imagine you have something for me to sign?'

They all jumped, eagerly pushing the paper toward him, as if they wished he would simply leave.

Aringarosa eyed the sheet before him. It bore the papal seal. 'This is identical to the copy you sent me?'

'Exactly.'

Aringarosa was surprised how little emotion he felt as he signed the document. The three men present, however, seemed to sigh in relief.

'Thank you, Bishop,' the secretarius said. 'Your service to the Church will never be forgotten.'

Aringarosa picked up the briefcase, sensing promise and authority in its weight. The four men looked at one another for a moment as if there were something more to say, but apparently there was not. Aringarosa turned and headed for the door.

'Bishop?' one of the cardinals called out as Aringarosa reached the threshold.

Aringarosa paused, turning. 'Yes?'

'Where will you go from here?'

Aringarosa sensed the query was more spiritual than geographical, and yet he had no intention of discussing morality at this hour. 'Paris,' he said, and walked out the door.

Chapter 42

The Depository Bank of Zurich was a twenty-four-hour *Geldschrank* bank offering the full modern array of anonymous services in the tradition of the Swiss numbered account. Maintaining offices in Zurich, Kuala Lumpur, New York and Paris, the bank had expanded its services in recent years to offer anonymous computer source code escrow services and faceless digitized backup.

The bread and butter of its operation was by far its oldest and simplest offering – the *anonyme Lager* – blind drop services, otherwise known as anonymous safe-deposit boxes. Clients wishing to store anything from stock certificates to valuable paintings could deposit their belongings anonymously, through a series of high-tech veils of privacy, withdrawing items at any time, also in total anonymity.

As Sophie pulled the taxi to a stop in front of their destination, Langdon gazed out at the building's uncompromising architecture and sensed the Depository Bank of Zurich was a firm with little sense of humour. The building was a windowless rectangle that seemed to be forged entirely of dull steel. Resembling an enormous metal brick, the edifice sat back from the road with a fifteen-foot-tall, neon, equilateral cross glowing over its façade.

Switzerland's reputation for secrecy in banking had become one of the country's most lucrative exports. Facilities like this had become controversial in the art community because they provided a perfect place for art thieves to hide stolen goods, for years if necessary, until the heat was off. Because deposits were protected from police inspection by privacy laws and were attached to numbered accounts rather than people's names, thieves could rest easily knowing their stolen goods were safe and could never be traced to them.

Sophie stopped the taxi at an imposing gate that blocked the bank's driveway – a cement-lined ramp that descended beneath the building. A video camera overhead was aimed directly at them, and Langdon had the feeling that this camera, unlike those at the Louvre, was authentic.

Sophie rolled down the window and surveyed the electronic podium on the driver's side. An LCD screen provided directions in seven languages. Topping the list was English.

```
INSERT KEY.
```

Sophie took the gold laser-pocked key from her pocket and turned her attention back to the podium. Below the screen was a triangular hole.

'Something tells me it will fit,' Langdon said.

Sophie aligned the key's triangular shaft with the hole and inserted it, sliding it in until the entire shaft had disappeared. This key apparently required no turning. Instantly, the gate began to swing open. Sophie took her foot off the brake and coasted down to a second gate and podium. Behind her, the first gate closed, trapping them like a ship in a lock.

Langdon disliked the constricted sensation. *Let's hope this second gate works too.*

This second podium bore familiar directions.

```
INSERT KEY.
```

When Sophie inserted the key, the second gate immediately opened. Moments later they were winding down the ramp into the belly of the structure.

The private garage was small and dim, with spaces for about a dozen cars. At the far end, Langdon spied the building's main entrance. A red carpet stretched across the cement floor, welcoming visitors to a huge door that appeared to be forged of solid metal.

Talk about mixed messages, Langdon thought. *Welcome and keep out.*

Sophie pulled the taxi into a parking space near the entrance and killed the engine. 'You'd better leave the gun here.'

With pleasure, Langdon thought, sliding the pistol under the seat.

Sophie and Langdon got out and walked up the red carpet toward the slab of steel. The door had no handle, but on the wall beside it was another triangular keyhole. No directions were posted this time.

'Keeps out the slow learners,' Langdon said.

Sophie laughed, looking nervous. 'Here we go.' She stuck the key in the hole, and the door swung inward with a low hum. Exchanging glances, Sophie and Langdon entered. The door shut with a thud behind them.

The foyer of the Depository Bank of Zurich employed as imposing a decor as any Langdon had ever seen. Where most banks were content with the usual polished marble and granite, this one had opted for wall-to-wall metal and rivets.

Who's their decorator? Langdon wondered. *Allied Steel?*

Sophie looked equally intimidated as her eyes scanned the lobby.

The grey metal was everywhere – the floor, walls,

counters, doors, even the lobby chairs appeared to be fashioned of moulded iron. Nonetheless, the effect was impressive. The message was clear: You are walking into a vault.

A large man behind the counter glanced up as they entered. He turned off the small television he was watching and greeted them with a pleasant smile. Despite his enormous muscles and visible sidearm, his diction chimed with the polished courtesy of a Swiss bellhop.

'*Bonsoir*,' he said. 'How may I help you?'

The dual-language greeting was the newest hospitality trick of the European host. It presumed nothing and opened the door for the guest to reply in whichever language was more comfortable.

Sophie replied with neither. She simply laid the gold key on the counter in front of the man.

The man glanced down and immediately stood straighter. 'Of course. Your elevator is at the end of the hall. I will alert someone that you are on your way.'

Sophie nodded and took her key back. 'Which floor?'

The man gave her an odd look. 'Your key instructs the elevator which floor.'

She smiled. 'Ah, yes.'

The guard watched as the two newcomers made their way to the elevators, inserted their key, boarded the lift, and disappeared. As soon as the door had closed, he grabbed the phone. He was not calling to alert anyone of their arrival; there was no need for that. A vault greeter already had been alerted automatically when the client's key was inserted outside in the entry gate.

Instead, the guard was calling the bank's night

manager. As the line rang, the guard switched the television back on and stared at it. The news story he had been watching was just ending. It didn't matter. He got another look at the two faces on the television.

The manager answered. '*Oui?*'

'We have a situation down here.'

'What's happening?' the manager demanded.

'The French police are tracking two fugitives tonight.'

'So?'

'Both of them just walked into our bank.'

The manager cursed quietly. 'Okay. I'll contact Monsieur Vernet immediately.'

The guard then hung up and placed a second call. This one to Interpol.

Langdon was surprised to feel the elevator dropping rather than climbing. He had no idea how many floors they had descended beneath the Depository Bank of Zurich before the door finally opened. He didn't care. He was happy to be out of the elevator.

Displaying impressive alacrity, a host was already standing there to greet them. He was elderly and pleasant, wearing a neatly pressed flannel suit that made him look oddly out of place – an old-world banker in a high-tech world.

'*Bonsoir,*' the man said. 'Good evening. Would you be so kind as to follow me, *s'il vous plaît?*' Without waiting for a response, he spun on his heel and strode briskly down a narrow metal corridor.

Langdon walked with Sophie down a series of corridors, past several large rooms filled with blinking mainframe computers.

'*Voici,*' their host said, arriving at a steel door and opening it for them. 'Here you are.'

Langdon and Sophie stepped into another world. The small room before them looked like a lavish sitting room at a fine hotel. Gone were the metal and rivets, replaced with oriental carpets, dark oak furniture, and cushioned chairs. On the broad desk in the middle of the room, two crystal glasses sat beside an opened bottle of Perrier, its bubbles still fizzing. A pewter pot of coffee steamed beside it.

Clockwork, Langdon thought. *Leave it to the Swiss.*

The man gave a perceptive smile. 'I sense this is your first visit to us?'

Sophie hesitated and then nodded.

'Understood. Keys are often passed on as in-heritance, and our first-time users are invariably uncertain of the protocol.' He motioned to the table of drinks. 'This room is yours as long as you care to use it.'

'You say keys are sometimes inherited?' Sophie asked.

'Indeed. Your key is like a Swiss numbered account, which are often willed through generations. On our gold accounts, the shortest safety-deposit box lease is fifty years. Paid in advance. So we see plenty of family turnover.'

Langdon stared. 'Did you say fifty *years*?'

'At a minimum,' their host replied. 'Of course, you can purchase much longer leases, but barring further arrangements, if there is no activity on an account for fifty years, the contents of that safe-deposit box are automatically destroyed. Shall I run through the process of accessing your box?'

Sophie nodded. 'Please.'

Their host swept an arm across the luxurious salon. 'This is your private viewing room. Once I leave the room, you may spend all the time you need in here to review and modify the contents of your safe-deposit box, which arrives . . . over here.' He walked them to the far wall where a wide conveyor belt entered the room in a graceful curve, vaguely resembling a baggage claim carousel. 'You insert your key in that slot there. . . .' The man pointed to a large electronic podium facing the conveyor belt. The podium had a familiar triangular hole. 'Once the computer confirms the markings on your key, you enter your account number, and your safe-deposit box will be retrieved robotically from the vault below for your inspection. When you are finished with your box, you place it back on the conveyor belt, insert your key again, and the process is reversed. Because everything is automated, your privacy is guaranteed, even from the staff of this bank. If you need anything at all, simply press the call button on the table in the centre of the room.'

Sophie was about to ask a question when a telephone rang. The man looked puzzled and embarrassed. 'Excuse me, please.' He walked over to the phone, which was sitting on the table beside the coffee and Perrier.

'*Oui?*' he answered.

His brow furrowed as he listened to the caller. '*Oui . . . oui . . . d'accord.*' He hung up, and gave them an uneasy smile. 'I'm sorry, I must leave you now. Make yourselves at home.' He moved quickly toward the door.

'Excuse me,' Sophie called. 'Could you clarify something before you go? You mentioned that we enter an *account* number?'

The man paused at the door, looking pale. 'But of course. Like most Swiss banks, our safe-deposit boxes are attached to a *number*, not a name. You have a key and a personal account number known only to you. Your key is only half of your identification. Your personal account number is the other half. Otherwise, if you lost your key, anyone could use it.'

246

Sophie hesitated. 'And if my benefactor gave me no account number?'

The banker's heart pounded. *Then you obviously have no business here!* He gave them a calm smile. 'I will ask someone to help you. He will be in shortly.'

Leaving, the banker closed the door behind him and twisted a heavy lock, sealing them inside.

Across town, Collet was standing in the Gare du Nord train terminal when his phone rang.

It was Fache. 'Interpol got a tip,' he said. 'Forget the train. Langdon and Neveu just walked into the Paris branch of the Depository Bank of Zurich. I want your men over there right away.'

'Any leads yet on what Saunière was trying to tell Agent Neveu and Robert Langdon?'

Fache's tone was cold. 'If you arrest them, Lieutenant Collet, then I can ask them personally.'

Collet took the hint. 'Twenty-four Rue Haxo. Right away, Captain.' He hung up and radioed his men.

Chapter 43

André Vernet – president of the Paris branch of the Depository Bank of Zurich – lived in a lavish flat above the bank. Despite his plush accommodation, he had always dreamed of owning a riverside apartment on L'Ile Saint-Louis, where he could rub shoulders with the true *cognoscenti*, rather than here, where he simply met the filthy rich.

When I retire, Vernet told himself, *I will fill my cellar with rare Bordeaux, adorn my salon with a Fragonard and perhaps a Boucher, and spend my days hunting for antique furniture and rare books in the Quartier Latin.*

Tonight, Vernet had been awake only six and a half minutes. Even so, as he hurried through the bank's underground corridor, he looked as if his personal tailor and hairdresser had polished him to a fine sheen. Impeccably dressed in a silk suit, Vernet sprayed some breath spray in his mouth and tightened his tie as he walked. No stranger to being awoken to attend to his international clients arriving from different time zones, Vernet modelled his sleep habits after the Masai warriors – the African tribe famous for their ability to rise from the deepest sleep to a state of total battle readiness in a matter of seconds.

Battle ready, Vernet thought, fearing the comparison might be uncharacteristically apt tonight. The arrival of a gold key client always required an extra flurry of attention, but the arrival of a gold key client who was *wanted* by the Judicial Police would be an extremely delicate matter. The bank had enough battles with law enforcement over the privacy rights of their clients without proof that some of them were criminals.

Five minutes, Vernet told himself. *I need these people out of my bank before the police arrive.*

If he moved quickly, this impending disaster could be deftly sidestepped. Vernet could tell the police that the fugitives in question had indeed walked into his bank as reported, but because they were not clients and had no account number, they were turned away. He wished the damned watchman had not called Interpol. Discretion was apparently not part of the vocabulary of a 15-euro-per-hour watchman.

Stopping at the doorway, he took a deep breath and loosened his muscles. Then, forcing a balmy smile, he unlocked the door and swirled into the room like a warm breeze.

'Good evening,' he said, his eyes finding his clients. 'I am André Vernet. How can I be of serv—' The rest of the sentence lodged somewhere beneath his Adam's apple. The woman before him was as unexpected a visitor as Vernet had ever had.

'I'm sorry, do we know each other?' Sophie asked. She did not recognize the banker, but he for a moment looked as if he'd seen a ghost.

'No . . . ,' the bank president fumbled. 'I don't . . . believe so. Our services are anonymous.' He exhaled and forced a calm smile. 'My assistant tells me you have a gold key but no account number? Might I ask how you came by this key?'

'My grandfather gave it to me,' Sophie replied, watching the man closely. His uneasiness seemed more evident now.

'Really? Your grandfather gave you the key but failed to give you the account number?'

'I don't think he had time,' Sophie said. 'He was murdered tonight.'

Her words sent the man staggering backward. 'Jacques Saunière is dead?' he demanded, his eyes filling with horror. 'But . . . how?!'

Now it was Sophie who reeled, numb with shock. 'You *knew* my grandfather?'

Banker André Vernet looked equally astounded, steadying himself by leaning on an end table. 'Jacques and I were dear friends. When did this happen?'

'Earlier this evening. Inside the Louvre.'

Vernet walked to a deep leather chair and sank into it. 'I need to ask you both a very important question.' He glanced up at Langdon and then back to Sophie. 'Did either of you have anything to do with his death?'

'No!' Sophie declared. 'Absolutely not.'

Vernet's face was grim, and he paused, pondering. 'Your pictures are being circulated by Interpol. This is how I recognized you. You're wanted for a murder.'

Sophie slumped. *Fache ran an Interpol broadcast already?* It seemed the captain was more motivated than Sophie had anticipated. She quickly told Vernet who Langdon was and what had happened inside the Louvre tonight.

Vernet looked amazed. 'And as your grandfather was dying, he left you a message telling you to find Mr Langdon?'

'Yes. And this key.' Sophie laid the gold key on the coffee table in front of Vernet, placing the Priory seal face down.

Vernet glanced at the key but made no move to touch it. 'He left you only this key? Nothing else? No slip of paper?'

Sophie knew she had been in a hurry inside the Louvre, but she was certain she had seen nothing else behind *Madonna of the Rocks*. 'No. Just the key.'

Vernet gave a helpless sigh. 'I'm afraid every key is electronically paired with a ten-digit account number that functions as a password. Without that number, your key is worthless.'

Ten digits. Sophie reluctantly calculated the cryptographic odds. *Ten billion possible choices.* Even if she could bring in DCPJ's most powerful parallel processing computers, she still would need weeks to break the code. 'Certainly, monsieur, considering the circumstances, you can help us.'

'I'm sorry. I truly can do nothing. Clients select their own account numbers via a secure terminal, meaning account numbers are known only to the client and computer. This is one way we ensure anonymity. And the safety of our employees.'

Sophie understood. Convenience stores did the same thing. EMPLOYEES DO NOT HAVE KEYS TO THE SAFE. This bank obviously did not want to risk someone stealing a key and then holding an employee hostage for the account number.

Sophie sat down beside Langdon, glanced down at the key and then up at Vernet. 'Do you have any idea what my grandfather is storing in your bank?'

'None whatsoever. That is the definition of a *Geldschrank* bank.'

'Monsieur Vernet,' she pressed, 'our time tonight is short. I am going to be very direct if I may.' She reached out to the gold key and flipped it over, watching the man's eyes as she revealed the Priory of Sion seal. 'Does the symbol on this key mean anything to you?'

Vernet glanced down at the fleur-de-lis seal and

made no reaction. 'No, but many of our clients emboss corporate logos or initials onto their keys.'

Sophie sighed, still watching him carefully. 'This seal is the symbol of a secret society known as the Priory of Sion.'

Vernet again showed no reaction. 'I know nothing of this. Your grandfather was a friend, but we spoke mostly of business.' The man adjusted his tie, looking nervous now.

'Monsieur Vernet,' Sophie pressed, her tone firm. 'My grandfather called me tonight and told me he and I were in grave danger. He said he had to give me something. He gave me a key to your bank. Now he is dead. Anything you can tell us would be helpful.'

Vernet broke a sweat. 'We need to get out of the building. I'm afraid the police will arrive shortly. My watchman felt obliged to call Interpol.'

Sophie had feared as much. She took one last shot. 'My grandfather said he needed to tell me the truth about my family. Does that mean anything to you?'

'Mademoiselle, your family died in a car accident when you were young. I'm sorry. I know your grandfather loved you very much. He mentioned to me several times how much it pained him that you two had fallen out of touch.'

Sophie was uncertain how to respond.

Langdon asked, 'Do the contents of this account have anything to do with the Sangreal?'

Vernet gave him an odd look. 'I have no idea what that is.' Just then, Vernet's cell phone rang, and he snatched it off his belt. '*Oui?*' He listened a moment, his expression one of surprise and growing concern. '*La police? Si rapidement?*' He cursed, gave some quick directions in French, and said he would be up to the lobby in a minute.

Hanging up the phone, he turned back to Sophie. 'The police have responded far more quickly than usual. They are arriving as we speak.'

Sophie had no intention of leaving empty-handed. 'Tell them we came and went already. If they want to search the bank, demand a search warrant. That will take them time.'

'Listen,' Vernet said, 'Jacques was a friend, and my bank does not need this kind of press, so for those two reasons, I have no intention of allowing this arrest to be made on my premises. Give me a minute and I will see what I can do to help you leave the bank undetected. Beyond that, I cannot get involved.' He stood up and hurried for the door. 'Stay here. I'll make arrangements and be right back.'

'But the safe-deposit box,' Sophie declared. 'We can't just leave.'

'There's nothing I can do,' Vernet said, hurrying out the door. 'I'm sorry.'

Sophie stared after him a moment, wondering if maybe the account number was buried in one of the countless letters and packages her grandfather had sent her over the years and which she had left unopened.

Langdon stood suddenly, and Sophie sensed an unexpected glimmer of contentment in his eyes.

'Robert? You're smiling.'

'Your grandfather was a genius.'

'I'm sorry?'

'Ten digits?'

Sophie had no idea what he was talking about.

'The account number,' he said, a familiar lopsided grin now crossing his face. 'I'm pretty sure he left it for us after all.'

'Where?'

Langdon produced the printout of the crime scene photo and spread it out on the coffee table. Sophie

needed only to read the first line to know Langdon
was correct.

13-3-2-21-1-1-8-5
O, Draconian devil!
Oh, lame saint!
P.S. Find Robert Langdon

Chapter 44

'Ten digits,' Sophie said, her cryptologic senses tingling as she studied the printout.

13-3-2-21-1-1-8-5

Grand-père wrote his account number on the Louvre floor!

When Sophie had first seen the scrambled Fibonacci sequence on the parquet, she had assumed its sole purpose was to encourage DCPJ to call in their cryptographers and get Sophie *involved*. Later, she realized the numbers were also a clue as to how to decipher the other lines – *a sequence out of order . . . a numeric anagram*. Now, utterly amazed, she saw the numbers had a more important meaning still. They were almost certainly the final key to opening her grandfather's mysterious safe-deposit box.

'He was the master of double-entendres,' Sophie said, turning to Langdon. 'He loved anything with multiple layers of meaning. Codes within codes.'

Langdon was already moving toward the electronic podium near the conveyor belt. Sophie grabbed the computer printout and followed.

The podium had a keypad similar to that of a bank ATM terminal. The screen displayed the bank's cruciform logo. Beside the keypad was a triangular hole. Sophie wasted no time inserting the shaft of her key into the hole.

The screen refreshed instantly.

```
ACCOUNT NUMBER:

_ _ _ _ _ _ _ _ _ _
```

The cursor blinked. Waiting.
Ten digits. Sophie read the numbers off the printout, and Langdon typed them in.

```
ACCOUNT NUMBER:
1332211185
```

When he had typed the last digit, the screen refreshed again. A message in several languages appeared. English was on top.

```
CAUTION:
Before you strike the enter key, please
   check the accuracy of your account
               number.
For your own security, if the computer
does not recognize your account number,
   this system will automatically shut
               down.
```

'*Fonction terminer,*' Sophie said, frowning. 'Looks like we only get one try.' Standard ATM machines allowed users *three* attempts to type a PIN before confiscating their bank card. This was obviously no ordinary cash machine.

'The number looks right,' Langdon confirmed, carefully checking what they had typed and comparing it to the printout. He motioned to the ENTER key. 'Fire away.'

Sophie extended her index finger toward the keypad, but hesitated, an odd thought now hitting her.

'Go ahead,' Langdon urged. 'Vernet will be back soon.'

'No.' She pulled her hand away. 'This isn't the right account number.'

'Of course it is! Ten digits. What else would it be?'

'It's too random.'

Too random? Langdon could not have disagreed more. Every bank advised its customers to choose PINs at random so nobody could guess them. Certainly clients *here* would be advised to choose their account numbers at random.

Sophie deleted everything they had just typed in and looked up at Langdon, her gaze self-assured. 'It's far too coincidental that this supposedly *random* account number could be rearranged to form the Fibonacci sequence.'

Langdon realized she had a point. Earlier, Sophie had rearranged this account number into the Fibonacci sequence. What were the odds of being able to do that?

Sophie was at the keypad again, entering a different number, as if from memory. 'Moreover, with my grandfather's love of symbolism and codes, it seems to follow that he would have chosen an account number that had meaning to him, something he could easily remember.' She finished typing the entry and gave a sly smile. 'Something that appeared random . . . but was *not*.'

Langdon looked at the screen.

```
ACCOUNT NUMBER:
1123581321
```

It took him an instant, but when Langdon spotted it, he knew she was right.

The Fibonacci sequence.

1-1-2-3-5-8-13-21

When the Fibonacci sequence was melded into a single ten-digit number, it became virtually unrecognizable. *Easy to remember, and yet seemingly random.* A brilliant ten-digit code that Saunière would never forget. Furthermore, it perfectly explained why the scrambled numbers on the Louvre floor could be rearranged to form the famous progression.

Sophie reached down and pressed the ENTER key.

Nothing happened.

At least nothing they could detect.

At that moment, beneath them, in the bank's cavernous subterranean vault, a robotic claw sprang to life. Sliding on a double-axis transport system attached to the ceiling, the claw headed off in search of the proper coordinates. On the cement floor below, hundreds of identical plastic crates lay aligned on an enormous grid . . . like rows of small coffins in an underground crypt.

Whirring to a stop over the correct spot on the floor, the claw dropped down, an electric eye confirming the bar code on the box. Then, with computer precision, the claw grasped the heavy handle and hoisted the crate vertically. New gears engaged, and the claw transported the box to the far side of the vault, coming to a stop over a stationary conveyor belt.

Gently now, the retrieval arm set down the crate and retracted.

Once the arm was clear, the conveyor belt whirred to life . . .

Upstairs, Sophie and Langdon exhaled in relief to see the conveyor belt move. Standing beside the belt, they felt like weary travellers at baggage claim awaiting a mysterious piece of luggage whose contents were unknown.

The conveyor belt entered the room on their right through a narrow slit beneath a retractable door. The metal door slid up, and a huge plastic box appeared, emerging from the depths on the inclined conveyor belt. The box was black, heavy moulded plastic, and far larger than she imagined. It looked like an air-freight pet transport crate without any airholes.

The box coasted to a stop directly in front of them.

Langdon and Sophie stood there, silent, staring at the mysterious container.

Like everything else about this bank, this crate was industrial – metal clasps, a bar code sticker on top, and moulded heavy-duty handle. Sophie thought it looked like a giant toolbox.

Wasting no time, Sophie unhooked the two buckles facing her. Then she glanced over at Langdon. Together, they raised the heavy lid and let it fall back.

Stepping forward, they peered down into the crate.

At first glance, Sophie thought the crate was empty. Then she saw something. Sitting at the bottom of the crate. A lone item.

The polished wooden box was about the size of a shoebox and had ornate hinges. The wood was a lustrous deep purple with a strong grain. *Rosewood,* Sophie realized. Her grandfather's favourite. The lid bore a beautiful inlaid design of a rose. She and Langdon exchanged puzzled looks. Sophie leaned in and grabbed the box, lifting it out.

My God, it's heavy!

She carried it gingerly to a large receiving table and set it down. Langdon stood beside her, both of them staring at the small treasure chest her grandfather apparently had sent them to retrieve.

Langdon stared in wonderment at the lid's hand-carved inlay – a five-petal rose. He had seen this type of rose many times. 'The five-petal rose,' he whispered, 'is a Priory symbol for the Holy Grail.'

Sophie turned and looked at him. Langdon could see what she was thinking, and he was thinking it too. The dimensions of the box, the apparent weight of its contents, and a Priory symbol for the Grail all seemed to imply one unfathomable conclusion. *The Cup of Christ is in this wooden box.* Langdon again told himself it was impossible.

'It's a perfect size,' Sophie whispered, 'to hold . . . a chalice.'

It can't be a chalice.

Sophie pulled the box toward her across the table, preparing to open it. As she moved it, though, something unexpected happened. The box let out an odd gurgling sound.

Langdon did a double take. *There's liquid inside?*

Sophie looked equally confused. 'Did you just hear . . . ?'

Langdon nodded, lost. 'Liquid.'

Reaching forward, Sophie slowly unhooked the clasp and raised the lid.

The object inside was unlike anything Langdon had ever seen. One thing was immediately clear to both of them, however. This was definitely *not* the Cup of Christ.

Chapter 45

'The police are blocking the street,' André Vernet said, walking into the waiting room. 'Getting you out will be difficult.' As he closed the door behind him, Vernet saw the heavy-duty plastic case on the conveyor belt and halted in his tracks. *My God! They accessed Saunière's account?*

Sophie and Langdon were at the table, huddling over what looked to be a large wooden jewellery box. Sophie immediately closed the lid and looked up. 'We had the account number after all,' she said.

Vernet was speechless. This changed everything. He respectfully diverted his eyes from the box and tried to figure out his next move. *I have to get them out of the bank!* But with the police already having set up a roadblock, Vernet could imagine only one way to do that. 'Mademoiselle Neveu, if I can get you safely out of the bank, will you be taking the item with you or returning it to the vault before you leave?'

Sophie glanced at Langdon and then back to Vernet. 'We need to take it.'

Vernet nodded. 'Very well. Then whatever the item is, I suggest you wrap it in your jacket as we move through the hallways. I would prefer nobody else see it.'

As Langdon shed his jacket, Vernet hurried over to the conveyor belt, closed the now empty crate, and typed a series of simple commands. The conveyor belt began moving again, carrying the plastic container back down to the vault. Pulling the gold key from the podium, he handed it to Sophie.

'This way please. Hurry.'

When they reached the rear loading dock, Vernet could see the flash of police lights filtering through the underground garage. He frowned. They were probably blocking the ramp. *Am I really going to try to pull this off?* He was sweating now.

Vernet motioned to one of the bank's small armoured trucks. *Transport sûr* was another service offered by the Depository Bank of Zurich. 'Get in the cargo hold,' he said, heaving open the massive rear door and motioning to the glistening steel compartment. 'I'll be right back.'

As Sophie and Langdon climbed in, Vernet hurried across the loading dock to the dock overseer's office, let himself in, collected the keys for the truck, and found a driver's uniform jacket and cap. Shedding his own suit coat and tie, he began to put on the driver's jacket. Reconsidering, he donned a shoulder holster beneath the uniform. On his way out, he grabbed a driver's pistol from the rack, put in a clip, and stuffed it in the holster, buttoning his uniform over it. Returning to the truck, Vernet pulled the driver's cap down low and peered in at Sophie and Langdon, who were standing inside the empty steel box.

'You'll want this on,' Vernet said, reaching inside and flicking a wall switch to illuminate the lone courtesy bulb on the hold's ceiling. 'And you'd better sit down. Not a sound on our way out the gate.'

Sophie and Langdon sat down on the metal floor. Langdon cradled the treasure wadded in his tweed jacket. Swinging the heavy doors closed, Vernet locked them inside. Then he got in behind the wheel and revved the engine.

As the armoured truck lumbered toward the top of

the ramp, Vernet could feel the sweat already collecting beneath his driver's cap. He could see there were far more police lights in front than he had imagined. As the truck powered up the ramp, the interior gate swung inward to let him pass. Vernet advanced and waited while the gate behind him closed before pulling forward and tripping the next sensor. The second gate opened, and the exit beckoned.

Except for the police car blocking the top of the ramp.

Vernet dabbed his brow and pulled forward.

A lanky officer stepped out and waved him to a stop a few metres from the roadblock. Four patrol cars were parked out front.

Vernet stopped. Pulling his driver's cap down farther, he effected as rough a façade as his cultured upbringing would allow. Not budging from behind the wheel, he opened the door and gazed down at the agent, whose face was stern and sallow.

'*Qu'est-ce qui se passe?*' Vernet asked, his tone rough.

'*Je suis Jérôme Collet,*' the agent said. '*Lieutenant Police Judiciaire.*' He motioned to the truck's cargo hold. '*Qu'est-ce qu'il y a là ô dedans?*'

'Hell if I know,' Vernet replied in crude French. 'I'm only a driver.'

Collet looked unimpressed. 'We're looking for two criminals.'

Vernet laughed. 'Then you came to the right spot. Some of these bastards I drive for have so much money they must be criminals.'

The agent held up a passport picture of Robert Langdon. 'Was this man in your bank tonight?'

Vernet shrugged. 'No clue. I'm a dock rat. They don't let us anywhere near the clients. You need to go in and ask the front desk.'

'Your bank is demanding a search warrant before we can enter.'

Vernet put on a disgusted look. 'Administrators. Don't get me started.'

'Open your truck, please.' Collet motioned toward the cargo hold.

Vernet stared at the agent and forced an obnoxious laugh. 'Open the truck? You think I have keys? You think they trust us? You should see the crap wages I get paid.'

The agent's head tilted to one side, his scepticism evident. 'You're telling me you don't have keys to your own truck?'

Vernet shook his head. 'Not the cargo area. Ignition only. These trucks get sealed by overseers on the loading dock. Then the truck sits in dock while someone drives the cargo keys to the drop-off. Once we get the call that the cargo keys are with the recipient, then I get the okay to drive. Not a second before. I never know what the hell I'm lugging.'

'When was *this* truck sealed?'

'Must have been hours ago. I'm driving all the way up to St Thurial tonight. Cargo keys are already up there.'

The agent made no response, his eyes probing as if trying to read Vernet's mind.

A drop of sweat was preparing to slide down Vernet's nose. 'You mind?' he said, wiping his nose with his sleeve and motioning to the police car blocking his way. 'I'm on a tight schedule.'

'Do all the drivers wear Rolexes?' the agent asked, pointing to Vernet's wrist.

Vernet glanced down and saw the glistening band of his absurdly expensive watch peeking out from beneath the sleeve of his jacket. *Merde.* 'This piece of shit? Bought it for twenty euro from a Taiwanese street vendor in St Germain des Prés. I'll sell it to you for forty.'

The agent paused and finally stepped aside. 'No thanks. Have a safe trip.'

Vernet did not breathe again until the truck was a good fifty metres down the street. And now he had another problem. His cargo. *Where do I take them?*

Chapter 46

Silas lay prone on the canvas mat in his room, allowing the lash wounds on his back to clot in the air. Tonight's second session with the Discipline had left him dizzy and weak. He had yet to remove the *cilice* belt, and he could feel the blood trickling down his inner thigh. Still, he could not justify removing the strap.

I have failed the Church.

Far worse, I have failed the bishop.

Tonight was supposed to be Bishop Aringarosa's salvation. Five months ago, the bishop had returned from a meeting at the Vatican Observatory, where he had learned something that left him deeply changed. Depressed for weeks, Aringarosa had finally shared the news with Silas.

'But this is impossible!' Silas had cried out. 'I cannot accept it!'

'It is true,' Aringarosa said. 'Unthinkable, but true. In only six months.'

The bishop's words terrified Silas. He prayed for deliverance, and even in those dark days, his trust in God and *The Way* never wavered. It was only a month later that the clouds parted miraculously and the light of possibility shone through.

Divine intervention, Aringarosa had called it.

The bishop had seemed hopeful for the first time. 'Silas,' he whispered, 'God has bestowed upon us an opportunity to protect *The Way*. Our battle, like all battles, will take sacrifice. Will you be a soldier of God?'

Silas fell to his knees before Bishop Aringarosa – the man who had given him a new life – and he said, 'I am a lamb of God. Shepherd me as your heart commands.'

When Aringarosa described the opportunity that had presented itself, Silas knew it could only be the hand of God at work. *Miraculous fate!* Aringarosa put Silas in contact with the man who had proposed the plan – a man who called himself the Teacher. Although the Teacher and Silas never met face-to-face, each time they spoke by phone, Silas was awed, both by the profundity of the Teacher's faith and by the scope of his power. The Teacher seemed to be a man who knew all, a man with eyes and ears in all places. How the Teacher gathered his information, Silas did not know, but Aringarosa had placed enormous trust in the Teacher, and he had told Silas to do the same. 'Do as the Teacher commands you,' the bishop told Silas. 'And we will be victorious.'

Victorious. Silas now gazed at the bare floor and feared victory had eluded them. The Teacher had been tricked. The keystone was a devious dead end. And with the deception, all hope had vanished.

Silas wished he could call Bishop Aringarosa and warn him, but the Teacher had removed all their lines of direct communication tonight. *For our safety.*

Finally, overcoming enormous trepidation, Silas crawled to his feet and found his robe, which lay on the floor. He dug his cell phone from the pocket. Hanging his head in shame, he dialled.

'Teacher,' he whispered, 'all is lost.' Silas truthfully told the man how he had been tricked.

'You lose your faith too quickly,' the Teacher replied. 'I have just received news. Most unexpected and welcome. The secret lives. Jacques Saunière transferred information before he died. I will call you soon. Our work tonight is not yet done.'

Chapter 47

Riding inside the dimly lit cargo hold of the armoured truck was like being transported inside a cell for solitary confinement. Langdon fought the all too familiar anxiety that haunted him in confined spaces. *Vernet said he would take us a safe distance out of the city. Where? How far?*

Langdon's legs had got stiff from sitting cross-legged on the metal floor, and he shifted his position, wincing to feel the blood pouring back into his lower body. In his arms, he still clutched the bizarre treasure they had extricated from the bank.

'I think we're on the highway now,' Sophie whispered.

Langdon sensed the same thing. The truck, after an unnerving pause atop the bank ramp, had moved on, snaking left and right for a minute or two, and was now accelerating to what felt like top speed. Beneath them, the bulletproof tyres hummed on smooth pavement. Forcing his attention to the rosewood box in his arms, Langdon laid the precious bundle on the floor, unwrapped his jacket, and extracted the box, pulling it toward him. Sophie shifted her position so they were sitting side by side. Langdon suddenly felt like they were two kids huddled over a Christmas present.

In contrast to the warm colours of the rosewood box, the inlaid rose had been crafted of a pale wood, probably ash, which shone clearly in the dim light. *The Rose.* Entire armies and religions had been built on this symbol, as had secret societies. *The Rosicrucians.*

The Knights of the Rosy Cross.

'Go ahead,' Sophie said. 'Open it.'

Langdon took a deep breath. Reaching for the lid, he stole one more admiring glance at the intricate woodwork and then, unhooking the clasp, he opened the lid, revealing the object within.

Langdon had harboured several fantasies about what they might find inside this box, but clearly he had been wrong on every account. Nestled snugly inside the box's heavily padded interior of crimson silk lay an object Langdon could not even begin to comprehend.

Crafted of polished white marble, it was a stone cylinder approximately the dimensions of a tennis ball can. More complicated than a simple column of stone, however, the cylinder appeared to have been assembled in many pieces. Five doughnut-sized discs of marble had been stacked and affixed to one another within a delicate brass framework. It looked like some kind of tubular, multiwheeled kaleidoscope. Each end of the cylinder was affixed with an end cap, also marble, making it impossible to see inside. Having heard liquid within, Langdon assumed the cylinder was hollow.

As mystifying as the construction of the cylinder was, however, it was the engravings around the tube's circumference that drew Langdon's primary focus. Each of the five discs had been carefully carved with the same unlikely series of letters – the entire alphabet. The lettered cylinder reminded Langdon of one of his childhood toys – a rod threaded with lettered tumblers that could be rotated to spell different words.

'Amazing, isn't it?' Sophie whispered.

Langdon glanced up. 'I don't know. What the hell is it?'

Now there was a glint in Sophie's eye. 'My grandfather used to craft these as a hobby. They were invented by Leonardo da Vinci.'

Even in the diffuse light, Sophie could see Langdon's surprise.

'Da Vinci?' he muttered, looking again at the canister.

'Yes. It's called a *cryptex*. According to my grandfather, the blueprints come from one of Da Vinci's secret diaries.'

'What is it for?'

Considering tonight's events, Sophie knew the answer might have some interesting implications. 'It's a vault,' she said. 'For storing secret information.'

Langdon's eyes widened further.

Sophie explained that creating models of Da Vinci's inventions was one of her grandfather's best-loved hobbies. A talented craftsman who spent hours in his wood and metal shop, Jacques Saunière enjoyed imitating master craftsmen – Fabergé, assorted cloisonné artisans, and the less artistic, but far more practical, Leonardo da Vinci.

Even a cursory glance through Da Vinci's journals revealed why the luminary was as notorious for his lack of follow-through as he was famous for his brilliance. Da Vinci had drawn up blueprints for hundreds of inventions he had never built. One of Jacques Saunière's favourite pastimes was bringing Da Vinci's more obscure brainstorms to life – timepieces, water pumps, cryptexes, and even a fully articulated model of a medieval French knight, which now stood proudly on the desk in his office. Designed by Da Vinci in 1495 as an outgrowth of his earliest anatomy and kinesiology studies, the internal mechanism of the robot knight possessed accurate joints and tendons, and was designed to sit up, wave its arms, and move its head via a flexible neck while opening and closing an anatomically correct jaw. This armour-clad knight, Sophie had always believed, was the most beautiful object her grandfather had ever built . . . that was, until she had seen the cryptex in this rosewood box.

'He made me one of these when I was little,' Sophie said. 'But I've never seen one so ornate and large.'

Langdon's eyes had never left the box. 'I've never heard of a cryptex.'

Sophie was not surprised. Most of Leonardo's unbuilt inventions had never been studied or even named. The term *cryptex* possibly had been her grandfather's creation, an apt title for this device that used the science of *cryptology* to protect information written on the contained scroll or *codex*.

Da Vinci had been a cryptology pioneer, Sophie knew, although he was seldom given credit. Sophie's university instructors, while presenting computer encryption methods for securing data, praised modern cryptologists like Zimmerman and Schneier but failed to mention that it was Leonardo who had invented one of the first rudimentary forms of public key encryption centuries ago. Sophie's grandfather, of course, had been the one to tell her all about that.

As their armoured truck roared down the highway, Sophie explained to Langdon that the cryptex had been Da Vinci's solution to the dilemma of sending secure messages over long distances. In an era without telephones or e-mail, anyone wanting to convey private information to someone far away had no option but to write it down and then trust a messenger to carry the letter. Unfortunately, if a messenger suspected the letter might contain valuable information, he could make far more money

271

selling the information to adversaries than he could delivering the letter properly.

Many great minds in history had invented crypto-logic solutions to the challenge of data protection: Julius Caesar devised a code-writing scheme called the Caesar Box; Mary, Queen of Scots created a substitution cipher and sent secret communiqués from prison; and the brilliant Arab scientist Abu Yusuf Ismail al-Kindi protected his secrets with an ingeniously conceived polyalphabetic substitution cipher.

Da Vinci, however, eschewed mathematics and cryptology for a *mechanical* solution. The cryptex. A portable container that could safeguard letters, maps, diagrams, anything at all. Once information was sealed inside the cryptex, only the individual with the proper password could access it.

'We require a password,' Sophie said, pointing out the lettered dials. 'A cryptex works much like a bicycle's combination lock. If you align the dials in the proper position, the lock slides open. This cryptex has five lettered dials. When you rotate them to their proper sequence, the tumblers inside align, and the entire cylinder slides apart.'

'And inside?'

'Once the cylinder slides apart, you have access to a hollow central compartment, which can hold a scroll of paper on which is the information you want to keep private.'

Langdon looked incredulous. 'And you say your grandfather built these for you when you were younger?'

'Some smaller ones, yes. A couple of times for my birthday, he gave me a cryptex and told me a riddle. The answer to the riddle was the password to the cryptex, and once I figured it out, I could open it up and find my birthday card.'

'A lot of work for a card.'

'No, the cards always contained another riddle or clue. My grandfather loved creating elaborate treasure hunts around our house, a string of clues that eventually led to my real gift. Each treasure hunt was a test of character and merit, to ensure I earned my rewards. And the tests were never simple.'

Langdon eyed the device again, still looking sceptical. 'But why not just pry it apart? Or smash it? The metal looks delicate, and marble is a soft rock.'

Sophie smiled. 'Because Da Vinci is too smart for that. He designed the cryptex so that if you try to force it open in any way, the information self-destructs. Watch.' Sophie reached into the box and carefully lifted out the cylinder. 'Any information to be inserted is first written on a papyrus scroll.'

'Not vellum?'

Sophie shook her head. 'Papyrus. I know sheep's vellum was more durable and more common in those days, but it had to be papyrus. The thinner the better.'

'Okay.'

'Before the papyrus was inserted into the cryptex's compartment, it was rolled around a delicate glass vial.' She tipped the cryptex, and the liquid inside gurgled. 'A vial of liquid.'

'Liquid *what?*'

Sophie smiled. 'Vinegar.'

Langdon hesitated a moment and then began nodding. 'Brilliant.'

Vinegar and papyrus, Sophie thought. If someone attempted to force open the cryptex, the glass vial would break, and the vinegar would quickly dissolve the papyrus. By the time anyone extracted the secret message, it would be a glob of meaningless pulp.

'As you can see,' Sophie told him, 'the only way to

273

access the information inside is to know the proper five-letter password. And with five dials, each with twenty-six letters, that's twenty-six to the fifth power.' She quickly estimated the permutations. 'Approximately twelve million possibilities.'

'If you say so,' Langdon said, looking like he had approximately twelve million questions running through his head. 'What information do you think is inside?'

'Whatever it is, my grandfather obviously wanted very badly to keep it secret.' She paused, closing the box lid and eyeing the five-petal Rose inlaid on it. Something was bothering her. 'Did you say earlier that the Rose is a symbol for the Grail?'

'Exactly. In Priory symbolism, the Rose and the Grail are synonymous.'

Sophie furrowed her brow. 'That's strange, because my grandfather always told me the Rose meant *secrecy*. He used to hang a rose on his office door at home when he was having a confidential phone call and didn't want me to disturb him. He encouraged me to do the same.' *Sweetie*, her grandfather said, *rather than lock each other out, we can each hang a rose – la fleur des secrets – on our door when we need privacy. This way we learn to respect and trust each other. Hanging a rose is an ancient Roman custom.*

'*Sub rosa*,' Langdon said. 'The Romans hung a rose over meetings to indicate the meeting was confidential. Attendees understood that whatever was said *under the rose* – or *sub rosa* – had to remain a secret.'

Langdon quickly explained that the Rose's overtone of secrecy was not the only reason the Priory used it as a symbol for the Grail. *Rosa rugosa*, one of the oldest species of rose, had five petals and pentagonal symmetry, just like the guiding star of Venus, giving the Rose strong iconographic ties to *womanhood*. In addition, the Rose had close ties to the concept of 'true direction' and navigating one's way. The Compass Rose helped travellers navigate, as did Rose Lines, the longitudinal lines on maps. For this reason, the Rose was a symbol that spoke of the Grail on many levels – secrecy, womanhood and guidance – the feminine chalice and guiding star that led to secret truth.

As Langdon finished his explanation, his expression seemed to tighten suddenly.

'Robert? Are you okay?'

His eyes were riveted to the rosewood box. '*Sub . . . rosa,*' he choked, a fearful bewilderment sweeping across his face. 'It can't be.'

'What?'

Langdon slowly raised his eyes. 'Under the sign of the Rose,' he whispered. 'This cryptex . . . I think I know what it is.'

Chapter 48

Langdon could scarcely believe his own supposition, and yet, considering *who* had given this stone cylinder to them, *how* he had given it to them, and now, the inlaid Rose on the container, Langdon could formulate only one conclusion.

I am holding the Priory keystone.

The legend was specific.

The keystone is an encoded stone that lies beneath the sign of the Rose.

'Robert?' Sophie was watching him. 'What's going on?'

Langdon needed a moment to gather his thoughts. 'Did your grandfather ever speak to you of something called *la clef de voûte*?'

'The key to the vault?' Sophie translated.

'No, that's the literal translation. *Clef de voûte* is a common architectural term. *Voûte* refers not to a bank vault, but to a *vault* in an archway. Like a *vaulted* ceiling.'

'But vaulted ceilings don't have keys.'

'Actually they do. Every stone archway requires a central, wedge-shaped stone at the top which locks the pieces together and carries all the weight. This stone is, in an architectural sense, the key to the vault. In English we call it a *keystone*.' Langdon watched her eyes for any spark of recognition.

Sophie shrugged, glancing down at the cryptex. 'But this obviously is not a keystone.'

Langdon didn't know where to begin. Keystones as a masonry technique for building stone archways had been one of the best-kept secrets of the early Masonic brotherhood. *The Royal Arch Degree. Architecture. Keystones.* It was all interconnected. The secret knowledge of how to use a wedged keystone to build a vaulted archway was part of the wisdom that had made the Masons such wealthy craftsmen, and it was a secret they guarded carefully. Keystones had always had a tradition of secrecy. And yet, the stone cylinder in the rosewood box was obviously something quite different. The Priory keystone – if this was indeed what they were holding – was not at all what Langdon had imagined.

'The Priory keystone is not my speciality,' Langdon admitted. 'My interest in the Holy Grail is primarily symbologic, so I tend to ignore the plethora of lore regarding how to actually find it.'

Sophie's eyebrows arched. '*Find* the Holy Grail?'

Langdon gave an uneasy nod, speaking his next words carefully. 'Sophie, according to Priory lore, the keystone is an encoded map . . . a map that reveals the hiding place of the Holy Grail.'

Sophie's face went blank. 'And you think this is it?'

Langdon didn't know what to say. Even to him it sounded unbelievable, and yet the keystone was the only logical conclusion he could muster. *An encrypted stone, hidden beneath the sign of the Rose.*

The idea that the cryptex had been designed by Leonardo da Vinci – former Grand Master of the Priory of Sion – shone as another tantalizing indicator that this was indeed the Priory keystone. *A former Grand Master's blueprint . . . brought to life centuries later by another Priory member.* The bond was too palpable to dismiss.

For the last decade, historians had been searching for the keystone in French churches. Grail seekers, familiar with the Priory's history of cryptic double-talk, had concluded *la clef de voûte* was a literal keystone – an architectural wedge – an engraved, encrypted stone, inserted into a vaulted archway in a church. *Beneath the sign of the Rose.* In architecture, there was no shortage of roses. *Rose windows. Rosette reliefs.* And, of course, an abundance of *cinquefoils* – the five-petalled decorative flowers often found at the top of archways, directly over the keystone. The hiding place seemed diabolically simple. The map to the Holy Grail was incorporated high in an archway of some forgotten church, mocking the blind church-goers who wandered beneath it.

'This cryptex *can't* be the keystone,' Sophie argued. 'It's not old enough. I'm certain my grandfather made this. It can't be part of any ancient Grail legend.'

'Actually,' Langdon replied, feeling a tingle of excitement ripple through him, 'the keystone is believed to have been created by the Priory sometime in the past couple of decades.'

Sophie's eyes flashed disbelief. 'But if this cryptex reveals the hiding place of the Holy Grail, why would my grandfather give it to *me*? I have no idea how to open it or what to do with it. I don't even know what the Holy Grail *is*!'

Langdon realized to his surprise that she was right. He had not yet had a chance to explain to Sophie the true nature of the Holy Grail. That story would have to wait. At the moment, they were focused on the keystone.

If that is indeed what this is . . .

Against the hum of the bulletproof wheels beneath them, Langdon quickly explained to Sophie everything he had heard about the keystone. Allegedly, for centuries, the Priory's biggest secret – the location of the Holy Grail – was never written down. For security's sake, it was verbally transferred to each new rising *sénéchal* at a clandestine ceremony.

However, at some point during the last century, whisperings began to surface that the Priory policy had changed. Perhaps it was on account of new electronic eavesdropping capabilities, but the Priory vowed never again even to *speak* the location of the sacred hiding place.

'But then how could they pass on the secret?' Sophie asked.

'That's where the keystone comes in,' Langdon explained. 'When one of the top four members died, the remaining three would choose from the lower echelons the next candidate to ascend as *sénéchal*. Rather than *telling* the new *sénéchal* where the Grail was hidden, they gave him a test through which he could prove he was worthy.'

Sophie looked unsettled by this, and Langdon suddenly recalled her mentioning how her grandfather used to make treasure hunts for her – *preuves de mérite*. Admittedly, the keystone was a similar concept. Then again, tests like this were extremely common in secret societies. The best known was the Masons', wherein members ascended to higher degrees by proving they could keep a secret and by performing rituals and various tests of merit over many years. The tasks became progressively harder until they culminated in a successful candidate's induction as thirty-second-degree Mason.

'So the keystone is a *preuve de mérite*,' Sophie said. 'If a rising Priory *sénéchal* can open it, he proves himself worthy of the information it holds.'

Langdon nodded. 'I forgot you'd had experience with this sort of thing.'

'Not only with my grandfather. In cryptology, that's called a "self-authorizing language". That is, if you're smart enough to read it, you're permitted to know what is being said.'

Langdon hesitated a moment. 'Sophie, you realize that if this is indeed the keystone, your grandfather's access to it implies he was exceptionally powerful within the Priory of Sion. He would have to have been one of the highest four members.'

Sophie sighed. 'He was powerful in a secret society. I'm certain of it. I can only assume it was the Priory.'

Langdon did a double take. 'You *knew* he was in a secret society?'

'I saw some things I wasn't supposed to see ten years ago. We haven't spoken since.' She paused. 'My grandfather was not only a ranking top member of the group . . . I believe he was *the* top member.'

Langdon could not believe what she had just said. 'Grand Master? But . . . there's no way you could know that!'

'I'd rather not talk about it.' Sophie looked away, her expression as determined as it was pained.

Langdon sat in stunned silence. *Jacques Saunière? Grand Master?* Despite the astonishing repercussions if it were true, Langdon had the eerie sensation it almost made perfect sense. After all, previous Priory Grand Masters had *also* been distinguished public figures with artistic souls. Proof of that fact had been uncovered years ago in Paris's Bibliothèque Nationale in papers that became known as *Les Dossiers Secrets*.

Every Priory historian and Grail buff had read the *Dossiers*. Catalogued under Number 4° lm¹ 249, the *Dossiers Secrets* had been authenticated by many specialists and incontrovertibly confirmed what historians had suspected for a long time: Priory Grand Masters included Leonardo da Vinci, Botticelli, Sir Isaac Newton, Victor Hugo, and, more recently, Jean Cocteau, the famous Parisian artist.

Why not Jacques Saunière?

Langdon's incredulity intensified with the realization that he had been slated to *meet* Saunière tonight. *The Priory Grand Master called a meeting with me. Why? To make artistic small talk?* It suddenly seemed unlikely. After all, if Langdon's instincts were correct, the Grand Master of the Priory of Sion had just transferred the brotherhood's legendary keystone to his granddaughter and simultaneously commanded her to find Robert Langdon.

Inconceivable!

Langdon's imagination could conjure no set of circumstances that would explain Saunière's behaviour. Even if Saunière feared his own death, there were three *sénéchaux* who also possessed the secret and therefore guaranteed the Priory's security. Why would Saunière take such an enormous risk giving his granddaughter the keystone, especially when the two of them didn't get along? And why involve Langdon . . . a total stranger?

A piece of this puzzle is missing, Langdon thought.

The answers were apparently going to have to wait. The sound of the slowing engine caused them both to look up. Gravel crunched beneath the tyres. *Why is he pulling over already?* Langdon wondered. Vernet had told them he would take them well outside the city to safety. The truck decelerated to a crawl and made its way over unexpectedly rough terrain. Sophie shot Langdon an uneasy look, hastily closing the cryptex box and latching it. Langdon slipped his jacket back on.

When the truck came to a stop, the engine remained idling as the locks on the rear doors began to turn. When the doors swung open, Langdon was surprised to see they were parked in a wooded area, well off the road. Vernet stepped into view, a strained look in his eye. In his hand, he held a pistol.

'I'm sorry about this,' he said. 'I really have no choice.'

Chapter 49

André Vernet looked awkward with a pistol, but his eyes shone with a determination that Langdon sensed would be unwise to test.

'I'm afraid I must insist,' Vernet said, training the weapon on the two of them in the back of the idling truck. 'Set the box down.'

Sophie clutched the box to her chest. 'You said you and my grandfather were friends.'

'I have a duty to protect your grandfather's assets,' Vernet replied. 'And that is exactly what I am doing. Now set the box on the floor.'

'My grandfather entrusted this to me!' Sophie declared.

'Do it,' Vernet commanded, raising the gun.

Sophie set the box at her feet.

Langdon watched the gun barrel swing now in his direction.

'Mr Langdon,' Vernet said, 'you will bring the box over to me. And be aware that I'm asking you because *you* I would not hesitate to shoot.'

Langdon stared at the banker in disbelief. 'Why are you doing this?'

'Why do you imagine?' Vernet snapped, his accented English terse now. 'To protect my client's assets.'

'*We* are your clients now,' Sophie said.

Vernet's visage turned ice-cold, an eerie transformation. 'Mademoiselle Neveu, I don't know *how* you got that key and account number tonight, but it seems obvious that foul play was involved. Had I known the extent of your crimes, I would never have helped you leave the bank.'

'I told you,' Sophie said, 'we had nothing to do with my grandfather's death!'

Vernet looked at Langdon. 'And yet the radio claims you are wanted not only for the murder of Jacques Saunière but for those of three *other* men as well?'

'What!' Langdon was thunderstruck. *Three more murders?* The coincidental number hit him harder than the fact that he was the prime suspect. It seemed too unlikely to be a coincidence. *The three sénéchaux?* Langdon's eyes dropped to the rosewood box. *If the sénéchaux were murdered, Saunière had no options. He had to transfer the keystone to someone.*

'The police can sort that out when I turn you in,' Vernet said. 'I have got my bank involved too far already.'

Sophie glared at Vernet. 'You obviously have no intention of turning us in. You would have driven us back to the bank. And instead you bring us out here and hold us at gunpoint?'

'Your grandfather hired me for one reason – to keep his possessions both safe and private. Whatever this box contains, I have no intention of letting it become a piece of catalogued evidence in a police investigation. Mr Langdon, bring me the box.'

Sophie shook her head. 'Don't do it.'

A gunshot roared, and a bullet tore into the wall above him. The reverberation shook the back of the truck as a spent shell clinked onto the cargo floor.

Shit! Langdon froze.

Vernet spoke more confidently now. 'Mr Langdon, pick up the box.'

Langdon lifted the box.

'Now bring it over to me.' Vernet was taking dead

aim, standing on the ground behind the rear bumper, his gun outstretched into the cargo hold now.

Box in hand, Langdon moved across the hold toward the open door.

I've got to do something! Langdon thought. *I'm about to hand over the Priory keystone!* As Langdon moved toward the doorway, his position of higher ground became more pronounced, and he began wondering if he could somehow use it to his advantage. Vernet's gun, though raised, was at Langdon's knee level. *A well-placed kick perhaps?* Unfortunately, as Langdon neared, Vernet seemed to sense the dangerous dynamic developing, and he took several steps back, repositioning himself six feet away. Well out of reach.

Vernet commanded, 'Place the box beside the door.'

Seeing no options, Langdon knelt down and set the rosewood box at the edge of the cargo hold, directly in front of the open doors.

'Now stand up.'

Langdon began to stand up but paused, spying the small, spent pistol shell on the floor beside the truck's precision-crafted doorsill.

'Stand up, and step away from the box.'

Langdon paused a moment longer, eyeing the metal threshold. Then he stood. As he did, he discreetly brushed the shell over the edge onto the narrow ledge that was the door's lower sill. Fully upright now, Langdon stepped backward.

'Return to the back wall and turn around.'

Langdon obeyed.

Vernet could feel his own heart pounding. Aiming the gun with his right hand, he reached now with his left for the wooden box. He discovered that it was far too heavy. *I need two hands.* Turning his eyes back to his captives, he calculated the risk. Both were a good fifteen feet away, at the far end of the cargo hold, facing away from him. Vernet made up his mind. Quickly, he laid down the gun on the bumper, lifted the box with two hands, and set it on the ground, immediately grabbing the gun again and aiming it back into the hold. Neither of his prisoners had moved.

Perfect. Now all that remained was to close and lock the door. Leaving the box on the ground for the moment, he grabbed the metal door and began to heave it closed. As the door swung past him, Vernet reached up to grab the single bolt that needed to be slid into place. The door closed with a thud, and Vernet quickly grabbed the bolt, pulling it to the left. The bolt slid a few inches and crunched to an unexpected halt, not lining up with its sleeve. *What's going on?* Vernet pulled again, but the bolt wouldn't lock. The mechanism was not properly aligned. *The door isn't fully closed!* Feeling a surge of panic, Vernet shoved hard against the outside of the door, but it refused to budge. *Something is blocking it!* Vernet turned to throw his full shoulder into the door, but this time the door exploded outward, striking Vernet in the face and sending him reeling backward onto the ground, his nose shattering in pain. The gun flew as Vernet reached for his face and felt the warm blood running from his nose.

Robert Langdon hit the ground somewhere nearby, and Vernet tried to get up, but he couldn't see. His vision blurred and he fell backward again. Sophie Neveu was shouting. Moments later, Vernet felt a cloud of dirt and exhaust billowing over him. He heard the crunching of tyres on gravel and sat up just in time to see the truck's wide wheelbase fail to navigate a turn. There was a crash as the front bumper clipped a tree. The engine roared, and the tree bent. Finally, it was the bumper that gave, tearing half off. The armoured car lurched away, its front bumper dragging. When the truck reached the paved access road, a shower of sparks lit up the night, trailing the truck as it sped away.

Vernet turned his eyes back to the ground where the truck had been parked. Even in the faint moonlight he could see there was nothing there.

The wooden box was gone.

Chapter 50

The unmarked Fiat sedan departing from Castel Gandolfo snaked downward through the Alban Hills into the valley below. In the back seat, Bishop Aringarosa smiled, feeling the weight of the bearer bonds in the briefcase on his lap and wondering how long it would be before he and the Teacher could make the exchange.

Twenty million euros.

The sum would buy Aringarosa power far more valuable than that.

As his car sped back toward Rome, Aringarosa again found himself wondering why the Teacher had not yet contacted him. Pulling his cell phone from his cassock pocket, he checked the carrier signal. Extremely faint.

'Cell service is intermittent up here,' the driver said, glancing at him in the rearview mirror. 'In about five minutes, we'll be out of the mountains, and service improves.'

'Thank you.' Aringarosa felt a sudden surge of concern. *No service in the mountains?* Maybe the Teacher had been trying to reach him all this time. Maybe something had gone terribly wrong.

Quickly, Aringarosa checked the phone's voice mail. Nothing. Then again, he realized, the Teacher never would have left a recorded message; he was a man who took enormous care with his communications. Nobody understood better than the Teacher the perils of speaking openly in this modern world.

Electronic eavesdropping had played a major role in how he had gathered his astonishing array of secret knowledge.

For this reason, he takes extra precautions.

Unfortunately, the Teacher's protocols for caution included a refusal to give Aringarosa any kind of contact number. *I alone will initiate contact,* the Teacher had informed him. *So keep your phone close.* Now that Aringarosa realized his phone might not have been working properly, he feared what the Teacher might think if he had been repeatedly phoning with no answer.

He'll think something is wrong.

Or that I failed to get the bonds.

The bishop broke a light sweat.

Or worse . . . that I took the money and ran!

Chapter 51

Even at a modest sixty kilometres an hour, the dangling front bumper of the armoured truck grated against the deserted suburban road with a grinding roar, spraying sparks up onto the hood.

We've got to get off the road, Langdon thought.

He could barely even see where they were headed. The truck's lone working headlight had been knocked off-centre and was casting a skewed sidelong beam into the woods beside the country highway. Apparently the *armour* in this 'armoured truck' referred only to the cargo hold and not the front end.

Sophie sat in the passenger seat, staring blankly at the rosewood box on her lap.

'Are you okay?' Langdon asked.

Sophie looked shaken. 'Do you believe him?'

'About the three additional murders? Absolutely. It answers a lot of questions – the issue of your grandfather's desperation to pass on the keystone, as well as the intensity with which Fache is hunting me.'

'No, I meant about Vernet trying to protect his bank.'

Langdon glanced over. 'As opposed to?'

'Taking the keystone for himself.'

Langdon had not even considered it. 'How would he even know what this box contains?'

'His bank stored it. He knew my grandfather. Maybe he knew things. He might have decided he wanted the Grail for himself.'

Langdon shook his head. Vernet hardly seemed the type. 'In my experience, there are only two reasons

289

people seek the Grail. Either they are naive and believe they are searching for the long-lost Cup of Christ . . .'

'Or?'

'Or they know the truth and are threatened by it. Many groups throughout history have sought to destroy the Grail.'

The silence between them accentuated the sound of the scraping bumper. They had driven a few kilometres now, and as Langdon watched the cascade of sparks coming off the front of the truck, he wondered if it was dangerous. Either way, if they passed another car, it would certainly draw attention. Langdon made up his mind.

'I'm going to see if I can bend this bumper back.'

Pulling onto the shoulder, he brought the truck to a stop.

Silence at last.

As Langdon walked toward the front of the truck, he felt surprisingly alert. Staring into the barrel of yet another gun tonight had given him a second wind. He took a deep breath of nighttime air and tried to get his wits about him. Accompanying the gravity of being a hunted man, Langdon was starting to feel the ponderous weight of responsibility, the prospect that he and Sophie might actually be holding an encrypted set of directions to one of the most enduring mysteries of all time.

As if this burden were not great enough, Langdon now realized that any possibility of finding a way to return the keystone to the Priory had just evaporated. News of the three additional murders had dire implications. *The Priory has been infiltrated. They are compromised.* The brotherhood was obviously being watched, or there was a mole within the ranks. It seemed to explain why Saunière might have transferred the keystone to Sophie and Langdon –

people *outside* the brotherhood, people he knew were not compromised. *We can't very well give the keystone back to the brotherhood.* Even if Langdon had any idea how to find a Priory member, chances were good that whoever stepped forward to take the keystone could be the enemy himself. For the moment, at least, it seemed the keystone was in Sophie and Langdon's hands, whether they wanted it or not.

The truck's front end looked worse than Langdon had imagined. The left headlight was gone, and the right one looked like an eyeball dangling from its socket. Langdon straightened it, and it dislodged again. The only good news was that the front bumper had been torn almost clean off. Langdon gave it a hard kick and sensed he might be able to break it off entirely.

As he repeatedly kicked the twisted metal, Langdon recalled his earlier conversation with Sophie. *My grandfather left me a phone message*, Sophie had told him. *He said he needed to tell me the truth about my family.* At the time it had meant nothing, but now, knowing the Priory of Sion was involved, Langdon felt a startling new possibility emerge.

The bumper broke off suddenly with a crash. Langdon paused to catch his breath. At least the truck would no longer look like a Fourth of July sparkler. He grabbed the bumper and began dragging it out of sight into the woods, wondering where they should go next. They had no idea how to open the cryptex, or why Saunière had given it to them. Unfortunately, their survival tonight seemed to depend on getting answers to those very questions.

We need help, Langdon decided. *Professional help.*

In the world of the Holy Grail and the Priory of Sion, that meant only one man. The challenge, of course, would be selling the idea to Sophie.

* * *

Inside the armoured car, while Sophie waited for Langdon to return, she could feel the weight of the rosewood box on her lap and resented it. *Why did my grandfather give this to me?* She had not the slightest idea what to do with it.

Think, Sophie! Use your head. Grand-père is trying to tell you something!

Opening the box, she eyed the cryptex's dials. *A proof of merit.* She could feel her grandfather's hand at work. *The keystone is a map that can be followed only by the worthy.* It sounded like her grandfather to the core.

Lifting the cryptex out of the box, Sophie ran her fingers over the dials. *Five letters.* She rotated the dials one by one. The mechanism moved smoothly. She aligned the discs such that her chosen letters lined up between the cryptex's two brass alignment arrows on either end of the cylinder. The dials now spelled a five-letter word that Sophie knew was absurdly obvious.

G-R-A-I-L

Gently, she held the two ends of the cylinder and pulled, applying pressure slowly. The cryptex didn't budge. She heard the vinegar inside gurgle and stopped pulling. Then she tried again.

V-I-N-C-I

Again, no movement.

V-O-U-T-E

Nothing. The cryptex remained locked solid.

Frowning, she replaced it in the rosewood box and closed the lid. Looking outside at Langdon, Sophie felt grateful he was with her tonight. *P.S. Find Robert Langdon.* Her grandfather's rationale for including him was now clear. Sophie was not equipped to understand her grandfather's intentions, and so he had assigned Robert Langdon as her guide. A tutor to oversee her education. Unfortunately for Langdon, he had turned out to be far more than a tutor tonight. He had become the target of Bezu Fache . . . and some unseen force intent on possessing the Holy Grail.

Whatever the Grail turns out to be.

Sophie wondered if finding out was worth her life.

As the armoured truck accelerated again, Langdon was pleased how much more smoothly it drove. 'Do you know how to get to Versailles?'

Sophie eyed him. 'Sightseeing?'

'No, I have a plan. There's a religious historian I know who lives near Versailles. I can't remember exactly where, but we can look it up. I've been to his estate a few times. His name is Leigh Teabing. He's a former British Royal Historian.'

'And he lives in Paris?'

'Teabing's life passion is the Grail. When whisperings of the Priory keystone surfaced about fifteen years ago, he moved to France to search churches in hopes of finding it. He's written some books on the keystone and the Grail. He may be able to help us figure out how to open it and what to do with it.'

Sophie's eyes were wary. 'Can you trust him?'

'Trust him to what? Not steal the information?'

'And not to turn us in.'

'I don't intend to tell him we're wanted by the police. I'm hoping he'll take us in until we can sort all this out.'

'Robert, has it occurred to you that every television in France is probably getting ready to broadcast our pictures? Bezu Fache always uses the media to his advantage. He'll make it impossible for us to move around without being recognized.'

Terrific, Langdon thought. *My French TV debut will be on 'Paris's Most Wanted.'* At least Jonas Faukman would be pleased; every time Langdon made the news, his book sales jumped.

'Is this man a good enough friend?' Sophie asked.

Langdon doubted Teabing was someone who watched television, especially at this hour, but still the question deserved consideration. Instinct told Langdon that Teabing would be totally trustworthy. An ideal safe harbour. Considering the circumstances, Teabing would probably trip over himself to help them as much as possible. Not only did he owe Langdon a favour, but Teabing was a Grail researcher, and Sophie claimed her grandfather was the actual *Grand Master* of the Priory of Sion. If Teabing heard *that,* he would salivate at the thought of helping them figure this out.

'Teabing could be a powerful ally,' Langdon said. *Depending on how much you want to tell him.*

'Fache probably will be offering a monetary reward.'

Langdon laughed. 'Believe me, money is the last thing this guy needs.' Leigh Teabing was wealthy in the way small countries were wealthy. A descendant of Britain's first Duke of Lancaster, Teabing had got his money the old-fashioned way – he'd inherited it. His estate outside Paris was a seventeenth-century palace with two private lakes.

Langdon had first met Teabing several years ago through the British Broadcasting Corporation. Teabing had approached the BBC with a proposal for a historical documentary in which he would expose the explosive history of the Holy Grail to a mainstream television audience. The BBC producers loved Teabing's hot premise, his research, and his credentials, but they had concerns that the concept was so shocking and hard to swallow that the net-work might end up tarnishing its reputation for quality journalism. At Teabing's suggestion, the BBC solved its credibility fears by soliciting three cameos from respected historians from around the world, all of whom corroborated the stunning nature of the Holy Grail secret with their own research.

Langdon had been among those chosen.

The BBC had flown Langdon to Teabing's Paris estate for the filming. He sat before cameras in Teabing's opulent drawing room and shared his story, admitting his initial scepticism on hearing of the alter-native Holy Grail story, then describing how years of research had persuaded him that the story was true. Finally, Langdon offered some of his own research – a series of symbologic connections that strongly supported the seemingly controversial claims.

When the programme aired in Britain, despite its ensemble cast and well-documented evidence, the premise rubbed so hard against the grain of popular Christian thought that it instantly confronted a firestorm of hostility. It never aired in the States, but the repercussions echoed across the Atlantic. Shortly afterward, Langdon received a postcard from an old friend – the Catholic Bishop of Philadelphia. The card simply read: *Et tu, Robert?*

'Robert,' Sophie asked, 'you're *certain* we can trust this man?'

'Absolutely. We're colleagues, he doesn't need money, and I happen to know he despises the French authorities. The French government taxes him at absurd rates because he bought a historic landmark. He'll be in no hurry to cooperate with Fache.'

Sophie stared out at the dark roadway. 'If we go to him, how much do you want to tell him?'

Langdon looked unconcerned. 'Believe me, Leigh Teabing knows more about the Priory of Sion and the Holy Grail than anyone on earth.'

Sophie eyed him. 'More than my grandfather?'

'I meant more than anyone *outside* the brotherhood.'

'How do you know Teabing isn't a member of the brotherhood?'

'Teabing has spent his life trying to broadcast the truth about the Holy Grail. The Priory's oath is to keep its true nature hidden.'

'Sounds to me like a conflict of interest.'

Langdon understood her concerns. Saunière had given the cryptex directly to Sophie, and although she didn't know what it contained or what she was supposed to do with it, she was hesitant to involve a total stranger. Considering the information potentially enclosed, the instinct was probably a good one. 'We don't need to tell Teabing about the keystone immediately. Or at all, even. His house will give us a place to hide and think, and maybe when we talk to him about the Grail, you'll start to have an idea why your grandfather gave this to you.'

'*Us*,' Sophie reminded.

Langdon felt a humble pride and wondered yet again why Saunière had included him.

'Do you know more or less where Mr Teabing lives?' Sophie asked.

'His estate is called Château Villette.'

Sophie turned with an incredulous look. '*The* Château Villette?'

'That's the one.'

'Nice friends.'

'You know the estate?'

'I've passed it. It's in the castle district. Twenty minutes from here.'

Langdon frowned. 'That far?'

'Yes, which will give you enough time to tell me what the Holy Grail *really* is.'

Langdon paused. 'I'll tell you at Teabing's. He and I specialize in different areas of the legend, so between the two of us, you'll get the full story.' Langdon smiled. 'Besides, the Grail has been Teabing's life, and hearing the story of the Holy Grail from Leigh Teabing will be like hearing the theory of relativity from Einstein himself.'

'Let's hope Leigh doesn't mind late-night visitors.'

'For the record, it's *Sir* Leigh.' Langdon had made that mistake only once. 'Teabing is quite a character. He was knighted by the Queen several years back after composing an extensive history of the House of York.'

Sophie looked over. 'You're kidding, right? We're going to visit a *knight*?'

Langdon gave an awkward smile. 'We're on a Grail quest, Sophie. Who better to help us than a knight?'

Chapter 52

The sprawling 185-acre estate of Château Villette was located twenty-five minutes northwest of Paris in the environs of Versailles. Designed by François Mansart in 1668 for the Count of Aufflay, it was one of Paris's most significant historical châteaux. Complete with two rectangular lakes and gardens designed by Le Nôtre, Château Villette was more of a modest castle than a mansion. The estate had fondly become known as *la Petite Versailles*.

Langdon brought the armoured truck to a shuddering stop at the foot of the mile-long driveway. Beyond the imposing security gate, Sir Leigh Teabing's residence rose on a meadow in the distance. The sign on the gate was in English: PRIVATE PROPERTY. NO TRESPASSING.

As if to proclaim his home a British Isle unto itself, Teabing had not only posted his signs in English, but he had installed his gate's intercom entry system on the *right-hand* side of the truck – the passenger's side everywhere in Europe except England.

Sophie gave the misplaced intercom an odd look. 'And if someone arrives without a passenger?'

'Don't ask.' Langdon had already been through that with Teabing. 'He prefers things the way they are at home.'

Sophie rolled down her window. 'Robert, you'd better do the talking.'

Langdon shifted his position, leaning out across Sophie to press the intercom button. As he did, an

298

alluring whiff of Sophie's perfume filled his nostrils, and he realized how close they were. He waited there, awkwardly prone, while a telephone began ringing over the small speaker.

Finally, the intercom crackled and an irritated French accent spoke. 'Château Villette. Who is calling?'

'This is Robert Langdon,' Langdon called out, sprawled across Sophie's lap. 'I'm a friend of Sir Leigh Teabing. I need his help.'

'My master is sleeping. As was I. What is your business with him?'

'It is a private matter. One of great interest to him.'

'Then I'm sure he will be pleased to receive you in the morning.'

Langdon shifted his weight. 'It's quite important.'

'As is Sir Leigh's sleep. If you are a friend, then you are aware he is in poor health.'

Sir Leigh Teabing had suffered from polio as a child and now wore leg braces and walked with crutches, but Langdon had found him such a lively and colourful man on his last visit that it hardly seemed an infirmity. 'If you would, please tell him I have uncovered new information about the Grail. Information that cannot wait until morning.'

There was a long pause.

Langdon and Sophie waited, the truck idling loudly.

A full minute passed.

Finally, someone spoke. 'My good man, I daresay you are still on Harvard Standard Time.' The voice was crisp and light.

Langdon grinned, recognizing the thick English accent. 'Leigh, my apologies for waking you at this obscene hour.'

'My manservant tells me that not only are you in

299

Paris, but you speak of the Grail.'

'I thought that might get you out of bed.'

'And so it has.'

'Any chance you'd open the gate for an old friend?'

'Those who seek the truth are more than friends. They are brothers.'

Langdon rolled his eyes at Sophie, well accustomed to Teabing's predilection for dramatic antics.

'Indeed I will open the gate,' Teabing proclaimed, 'but first I must confirm your heart is true. A test of your honour. You will answer three questions.'

Langdon groaned, whispering at Sophie. 'Bear with me here. As I mentioned, he's something of a character.'

'Your first question,' Teabing declared, his tone Herculean. 'Shall I serve you coffee, or tea?'

Langdon knew Teabing's feelings about the American phenomenon of coffee. 'Tea,' he replied. 'Earl Grey.'

'Excellent. Your second question. Milk or sugar?'

Langdon hesitated.

'*Milk,*' Sophie whispered in his ear. 'I think the English take milk.'

'Milk,' Langdon said.

Silence.

'Sugar?'

Teabing made no reply.

Wait! Langdon now recalled the bitter beverage he had been served on his last visit and realized this question was a trick. '*Lemon!*' he declared. 'Earl Grey with *lemon.*'

'Indeed.' Teabing sounded deeply amused now. 'And finally, I must make the most grave of inquiries.' Teabing paused and then spoke in a solemn tone. 'In which year did a Harvard sculler last outrow an Oxford man at Henley?'

Langdon had no idea, but he could imagine only one reason the question had been asked. 'Surely such a travesty has never occurred.'

The gate clicked open. 'Your heart is true, my friend. You may pass.'

Chapter 53

'Monsieur Vernet!' The night manager of the Depository Bank of Zurich felt relieved to hear the bank president's voice on the phone. 'Where did you go, sir? The police are here, everyone is waiting for you!'

'I have a little problem,' the bank president said, sounding distressed. 'I need your help right away.'

You have more than a little problem, the manager thought. The police had entirely surrounded the bank and were threatening to have the DCPJ captain himself show up with the warrant the bank had demanded. 'How can I help you, sir?'

'Armored truck number three. I need to find it.'

Puzzled, the manager checked his delivery schedule. 'It's here. Downstairs at the loading dock.'

'Actually, no. The truck was stolen by the two individuals the police are tracking.'

'What? How did they drive out?'

'I can't go into the specifics on the phone, but we have a situation here that could potentially be extremely unfortunate for the bank.'

'What do you need me to do, sir?'

'I'd like you to activate the truck's emergency transponder.'

The night manager's eyes moved to the LoJack control box across the room. Like many armoured cars, each of the bank's trucks had been equipped with a radio-controlled homing device, which could be activated remotely from the bank. The manager had only used the emergency system once, after a hijacking, and it had worked flawlessly – locating the truck and transmitting the coordinates to the authorities automatically. Tonight, however, the manager had the impression the president was hoping for a bit more prudence. 'Sir, you are aware that if I activate the LoJack system, the transponder will simultaneously inform the authorities that we have a problem.'

Vernet was silent for several seconds. 'Yes, I know. Do it anyway. Truck number three. I'll hold. I need the exact location of that truck the instant you have it.'

'Right away, sir.'

Thirty seconds later, forty kilometres away, hidden in the undercarriage of the armoured truck, a tiny transponder blinked to life.

Chapter 54

As Langdon and Sophie drove the armoured truck up the winding, poplar-lined driveway toward the house, Sophie could already feel her muscles relaxing. It was a relief to be off the road, and she could think of few safer places to get their feet under them than this private, gated estate owned by a good-natured foreigner.

They turned into the sweeping circular driveway, and Château Villette came into view on their right. Three storeys tall and at least sixty metres long, the edifice had grey stone facing illuminated by outside spotlights. The coarse façade stood in stark juxta-position to the immaculately landscaped gardens and glassy pond.

The inside lights were just now coming on.

Rather than driving to the front door, Langdon pulled into a parking area nestled in the evergreens. 'No reason to risk being spotted from the road,' he said. 'Or having Leigh wonder why we arrived in a wrecked armoured truck.'

Sophie nodded. 'What do we do with the cryptex? We probably shouldn't leave it out here, but if Leigh sees it, he'll certainly want to know what it is.'

'Not to worry,' Langdon said, removing his jacket as he stepped out of the car. He wrapped the tweed coat around the box and held the bundle in his arms like a baby.

Sophie looked dubious. 'Subtle.'

'Teabing never answers his own door; he prefers to make an entrance. I'll find somewhere inside to stash this before he joins us.' Langdon paused. 'Actually, I should probably warn you before you meet him. Sir Leigh has a sense of humour that people often find a bit . . . strange.'

Sophie doubted anything tonight would strike her as strange anymore.

The pathway to the main entrance was hand-laid cobblestone. It curved to a door of carved oak and cherry with a brass knocker the size of a grapefruit. Before Sophie could grasp the knocker, the door swung open from within.

A prim and elegant butler stood before them, making final adjustments on the white tie and tuxedo he had apparently just donned. He looked to be about fifty, with refined features and an austere expression that left little doubt he was unamused by their presence here.

'Sir Leigh will be down presently,' he declared, his accent thick French. 'He is dressing. He prefers not to greet visitors while wearing only a nightshirt. May I take your coat?' He scowled at the bunched-up tweed in Langdon's arms.

'Thank you, I'm fine.'

'Of course you are. Right this way, please.'

The butler guided them through a lush marble foyer into an exquisitely adorned drawing room, softly lit by tassel-draped Victorian lamps. The air inside smelled antediluvian, regal somehow, with traces of pipe tobacco, tea leaves, cooking sherry, and the earthen aroma of stone architecture. Against the far wall, flanked between two glistening suits of chain mail armour, was a rough-hewn fireplace large enough to roast an ox. Walking to the hearth, the butler knelt and touched a match to a pre-laid arrangement of oak logs and kindling. A fire quickly crackled to life.

The man stood, straightening his jacket. 'His master requests that you make yourselves at home.' With that, he departed, leaving Langdon and Sophie alone.

Sophie wondered which of the fireside antiques she was supposed to sit on – the Renaissance velvet divan, the rustic eagle-claw rocker, or the pair of stone pews that looked like they'd been lifted from some Byzantine temple.

Langdon unwrapped the cryptex from his coat, walked to the velvet divan and slid the wooden box deep underneath it, well out of sight. Then, shaking out his jacket, he put it back on, smoothed the lapels, and smiled at Sophie as he sat down directly over the stashed treasure.

The divan it is, Sophie thought, taking a seat beside him.

As she stared into the growing fire, enjoying the warmth, Sophie had the sensation that her grandfather would have loved this room. The dark wood panelling was bedecked with Old Master paintings, one of which Sophie recognized as a Poussin, her grandfather's second-favourite painter. On the mantel above the fireplace, an alabaster bust of Isis watched over the room.

Beneath the Egyptian goddess, inside the fireplace, two stone gargoyles served as andirons, their mouths gaping to reveal their menacing hollow throats. Gargoyles had always terrified Sophie as a child; that was, until her grandfather cured her of the fear by taking her atop Notre Dame Cathedral in a rainstorm. 'Princess, look at these silly creatures,' he had told her, pointing to the gargoyle rainspouts with their mouths gushing water. 'Do you hear that funny sound in their throats?' Sophie nodded, having to smile at the burping sound of the water gurgling through their throats. 'They're *gargling*,' her grandfather told her. '*Gargariser!* And that's where they get the silly name "gargoyles".' Sophie had never again been afraid.

The fond memory caused Sophie a pang of sadness as the harsh reality of the murder gripped her again. *Grand-père is gone.* She pictured the cryptex under the divan and wondered if Leigh Teabing would have any idea how to open it. *Or if we even should ask him.* Sophie's grandfather's final words had instructed her to find Robert Langdon. He had said nothing about involving anyone else. *We needed somewhere to hide,* Sophie said, deciding to trust Robert's judgment.

'Sir Robert!' a voice bellowed somewhere behind them. 'I see you travel with a maiden.'

Langdon stood up. Sophie jumped to her feet as well. The voice had come from the top of a curled staircase that snaked up to the shadows of the second floor. At the top of the stairs, a form moved in the shadows, only his silhouette visible.

'Good evening,' Langdon called up. 'Sir Leigh, may I present Sophie Neveu.'

'An honour.' Teabing moved into the light.

'Thank you for having us,' Sophie said, now seeing the man wore metal leg braces and used crutches. He was coming down one stair at a time. 'I realize it's quite late.'

'It is so late, my dear, it's early.' He laughed. '*Vous n'êtes pas Américaine?*'

Sophie shook her head. '*Parisienne.*'

'Your English is superb.'

'Thank you. I studied at Royal Holloway.'

'So then, that explains it.' Teabing hobbled lower through the shadows. 'Perhaps Robert told you I schooled just down the road at Oxford.' Teabing fixed

Langdon with a devilish smile. 'Of course, I also applied to Harvard as my safety school.'

Their host arrived at the bottom of the stairs, appearing to Sophie no more like a knight than Sir Elton John. Portly and ruby-faced, Sir Leigh Teabing had bushy red hair and jovial hazel eyes that seemed to twinkle as he spoke. He wore pleated trousers and a roomy silk shirt under a paisley waistcoat. Despite the aluminium braces on his legs, he carried himself with a resilient, vertical dignity that seemed more a by-product of noble ancestry than any kind of conscious effort.

Teabing arrived and extended a hand to Langdon. 'Robert, you've lost weight.'

Langdon grinned. 'And you've found some.'

Teabing laughed heartily, patting his rotund belly. 'Touché. My only carnal pleasures these days seem to be culinary.' Turning now to Sophie, he gently took her hand, bowing his head slightly, breathing lightly on her fingers and diverting his eyes. 'M'lady.'

Sophie glanced at Langdon, uncertain whether she'd stepped back in time or into a nuthouse.

The butler who had answered the door now entered carrying a tea service, which he arranged on a table in front of the fireplace.

'This is Rémy Legaludec,' Teabing said, 'my manservant.'

The slender butler gave a stiff nod and disappeared yet again.

'Rémy is *Lyonnais*,' Teabing whispered, as if it were an unfortunate disease. 'But he does sauces quite nicely.'

Langdon looked amused. 'I would have thought you'd import an English staff?'

'Good heavens, no! I would not wish an English chef on anyone except the French tax collectors.' He glanced over at Sophie. '*Pardonnez-moi*, Mademoiselle Neveu. Please be assured that my distaste for the French extends only to politics and the soccer pitch. Your government steals my money, and your football squad recently humiliated us.'

Sophie offered an easy smile.

Teabing eyed her a moment and then looked at Langdon. 'Something has happened. You both look shaken.'

Langdon nodded. 'We've had an interesting night, Leigh.'

'No doubt. You arrive on my doorstep un-announced in the middle of the night speaking of the Grail. Tell me, is this indeed about the Grail, or did you simply say that because you know it is the one topic for which I would rouse myself in the middle of the night?'

A little of both, Sophie thought, picturing the cryptex hidden beneath the couch.

'Leigh,' Langdon said, 'we'd like to talk to you about the Priory of Sion.'

Teabing's bushy eyebrows arched with intrigue. 'The keepers. So this is indeed about the Grail. You say you come with information? Something new, Robert?'

'Perhaps. We're not quite sure. We might have a better idea if we could get some information from you first.'

Teabing wagged his finger. 'Ever the wily American. A game of quid pro quo. Very well. I am at your service. What is it I can tell you?'

Langdon sighed. 'I was hoping you would be kind enough to explain to Ms Neveu the true nature of the Holy Grail.'

Teabing looked stunned. 'She doesn't *know*?'

Langdon shook his head.

The smile that grew on Teabing's face was almost obscene. 'Robert, you've brought me a *virgin*?'

Langdon winced, glancing at Sophie. '*Virgin* is the term Grail enthusiasts use to describe anyone who has never heard the true Grail story.'

Teabing turned eagerly to Sophie. 'How much do you know, my dear?'

Sophie quickly outlined what Langdon had explained earlier – the Priory of Sion, the Knights Templar, the Sangreal documents, and the Holy Grail, which many claimed was not a cup . . . but rather something far more powerful.

'That's *all*?' Teabing fired Langdon a scandalous look. 'Robert, I thought you were a gentleman. You've robbed her of the climax!'

'I know, I thought perhaps you and I could . . .' Langdon apparently decided the unseemly metaphor had gone far enough.

Teabing already had Sophie locked in his twinkling gaze. 'You are a Grail virgin, my dear. And trust me, you will never forget your first time.'

Chapter 55

Seated on the divan beside Langdon, Sophie drank her tea and ate a scone, feeling the welcome effects of caffeine and food. Sir Leigh Teabing was beaming as he awkwardly paced before the open fire, his leg braces clicking on the stone hearth.

'The Holy Grail,' Teabing said, his voice sermonic. 'Most people ask me only *where* it is. I fear that is a question I may never answer.' He turned and looked directly at Sophie. 'However . . . the far more relevant question is this: *What* is the Holy Grail?'

Sophie sensed a rising air of academic anticipation now in both of her male companions.

'To fully understand the Grail,' Teabing continued, 'we must first understand the Bible. How well do you know the New Testament?'

Sophie shrugged. 'Not at all, really. I was brought up by a man who worshipped Leonardo da Vinci.'

Teabing looked both startled and pleased. 'An enlightened soul. Superb! Then you must be aware that Leonardo was one of the keepers of the secret of the Holy Grail. And he hid clues in his art.'

'Robert told me as much, yes.'

'And Da Vinci's views on the New Testament?'

'I have no idea.'

Teabing's eyes turned mirthful as he motioned to the bookshelf across the room. 'Robert, would you mind? On the bottom shelf. *La Storia di Leonardo*.'

Langdon went across the room, found a large art book, and brought it back, setting it down on the table between them. Twisting the book to face Sophie, Teabing flipped open the heavy cover and pointed inside the rear cover to a series of quotations. 'From Da Vinci's notebook on polemics and speculation,' Teabing said, indicating one quote in particular. 'I think you'll find this relevant to our discussion.'

Sophie read the words.

Many have made a trade of delusions
and false miracles, deceiving the stupid multitude.
— LEONARDO DA VINCI

'Here's another,' Teabing said, pointing to a different quote.

Blinding ignorance does mislead us.
O! Wretched mortals, open your eyes!
— LEONARDO DA VINCI

Sophie felt a little chill. 'Da Vinci is talking about the Bible?'

Teabing nodded. 'Leonardo's feelings about the Bible relate directly to the Holy Grail. In fact, Da Vinci painted the true Grail, which I will show you in a moment, but first we must speak of the Bible.' Teabing smiled. 'And everything you need to know about the Bible can be summed up by the great canon doctor Martyn Percy.' Teabing cleared his throat and declared, 'The Bible did not arrive by fax from heaven.'

'I beg your pardon?'

'The Bible is a product of *man*, my dear. Not of God. The Bible did not fall magically from the clouds. Man created it as a historical record of tumultuous times, and it has evolved through countless translations,

312

additions and revisions. History has never had a definitive version of the book.'

'Okay.'

'Jesus Christ was a historical figure of staggering influence, perhaps the most enigmatic and inspirational leader the world has ever seen. As the prophesied Messiah, Jesus toppled kings, inspired millions and founded new philosophies. As a descendant of the lines of King Solomon and King David, Jesus possessed a rightful claim to the throne of the King of the Jews. Understandably, His life was recorded by thousands of followers across the land.' Teabing paused to sip his tea and then placed the cup back on the mantel. 'More than *eighty* gospels were considered for the New Testament, and yet only a relative few were chosen for inclusion – Matthew, Mark, Luke and John among them.'

'Who chose which gospels to include?' Sophie asked.

'Aha!' Teabing burst in with enthusiasm. 'The fundamental irony of Christianity! The Bible, as we know it today, was collated by the pagan Roman emperor Constantine the Great.'

'I thought Constantine was a Christian,' Sophie said.

'Hardly,' Teabing scoffed. 'He was a lifelong pagan who was baptized on his deathbed, too weak to protest. In Constantine's day, Rome's official religion was sun worship – the cult of *Sol Invictus*, or the Invincible Sun – and Constantine was its head priest. Unfortunately for him, a growing religious turmoil was gripping Rome. Three centuries after the crucifixion of Jesus Christ, Christ's followers had multiplied exponentially. Christians and pagans began warring, and the conflict grew to such proportions that it threatened to rend Rome in two. Constantine decided something had to be done. In

325 AD, he decided to unify Rome under a single religion. Christianity.'

Sophie was surprised. 'Why would a pagan emperor choose *Christianity* as the official religion?'

Teabing chuckled. 'Constantine was a very good businessman. He could see that Christianity was on the rise, and he simply backed the winning horse. Historians still marvel at the brilliance with which Constantine converted the sun-worshipping pagans to Christianity. By fusing pagan symbols, dates and rituals into the growing Christian tradition, he created a kind of hybrid religion that was acceptable to both parties.'

'Transmogrification,' Langdon said. 'The vestiges of pagan religion in Christian symbology are undeniable. Egyptian sun disks became the halos of Catholic saints. Pictograms of Isis nursing her miraculously conceived son Horus became the blueprint for our modern images of the Virgin Mary nursing Baby Jesus. And virtually all the elements of the Catholic ritual – the mitre, the altar, the doxology and communion, the act of "God-eating" – were taken directly from earlier pagan mystery religions.'

Teabing groaned. 'Don't get a symbologist started on Christian icons. Nothing in Christianity is original. The pre-Christian God Mithras – called *the Son of God* and *the Light of the World* – was born on December 25, died, was buried in a rock tomb, and then resurrected in three days. By the way, December 25 is also the birthday of Osiris, Adonis and Dionysus. The newborn Krishna was presented with gold, frankincense, and myrrh. Even Christianity's weekly holy day was stolen from the pagans.'

'What do you mean?'

'Originally,' Langdon said, 'Christianity honoured the Jewish Sabbath of Saturday, but Constantine shifted it to coincide with the pagan's veneration day of the sun.' He paused, grinning. 'To this day, most churchgoers attend services on Sunday morning with no idea that they are there on account of the pagan sun god's weekly tribute – *Sun*day.'

Sophie's head was spinning. 'And all of this relates to the Grail?'

'Indeed,' Teabing said. 'Stay with me. During this fusion of religions, Constantine needed to strengthen the new Christian tradition, and held a famous ecumenical gathering known as the Council of Nicaea.'

Sophie had heard of it only insofar as its being the birthplace of the Nicene Creed.

'At this gathering,' Teabing said, 'many aspects of Christianity were debated and voted upon – the date of Easter, the role of the bishops, the administration of sacraments, and, of course, the *divinity* of Jesus.'

'I don't follow. His divinity?'

'My dear,' Teabing declared, 'until *that* moment in history, Jesus was viewed by His followers as a mortal prophet . . . a great and powerful man, but a *man* nonetheless. A mortal.'

'Not the Son of God?'

'Right,' Teabing said. 'Jesus' establishment as "the Son of God" was officially proposed and voted on by the Council of Nicaea.'

'Hold on. You're saying Jesus' divinity was the result of a *vote*?'

'A relatively close vote at that,' Teabing added. 'Nonetheless, establishing Christ's divinity was critical to the further unification of the Roman empire and to the new Vatican power base. By officially endorsing Jesus as the Son of God, Constantine turned Jesus into a deity who existed beyond the scope of the human world, an entity whose power was unchallengeable. This not only precluded further pagan challenges to Christianity, but now the followers of Christ were able to redeem themselves *only* via the established sacred channel – the Roman Catholic Church.'

Sophie glanced at Langdon, and he gave her a soft nod of concurrence.

'It was all about power,' Teabing continued. 'Christ as Messiah was critical to the functioning of Church and state. Many scholars claim that the early Church literally *stole* Jesus from His original followers, hijacking His human message, shrouding it in an impenetrable cloak of divinity, and using it to expand their own power. I've written several books on the topic.'

'And I assume devout Christians send you hate mail on a daily basis?'

'Why would they?' Teabing countered. 'The vast majority of educated Christians know the history of their faith. Jesus was indeed a great and powerful man. Constantine's underhanded political manoeuvres don't diminish the majesty of Christ's life. Nobody is saying Christ was a fraud, or denying that He walked the earth and inspired millions to better lives. All we are saying is that Constantine took advantage of Christ's substantial influence and importance. And in doing so, he shaped the face of Christianity as we know it today.'

Sophie glanced at the art book before her, eager to move on and see the Da Vinci painting of the Holy Grail.

'The twist is this,' Teabing said, talking faster now. 'Because Constantine upgraded Jesus' status almost four centuries *after* Jesus' death, thousands of documents already existed chronicling His life as a *mortal* man. To rewrite the history books, Constantine knew he would need a bold stroke. From this sprang the most profound moment in Christian history.' Teabing paused, eyeing Sophie. 'Constantine commissioned and financed a new Bible, which omitted those gospels that spoke of Christ's *human* traits and embellished those gospels that made Him godlike. The earlier gospels were outlawed, gathered up, and burned.'

'An interesting note,' Langdon added. 'Anyone who chose the forbidden gospels over Constantine's version was deemed a heretic. The word *heretic* derives from that moment in history. The Latin word *haereticus* means "choice". Those who "chose" the original history of Christ were the world's first *heretics*.'

'Fortunately for historians,' Teabing said, 'some of the gospels that Constantine attempted to eradicate managed to survive. The Dead Sea Scrolls were found in the 1950s hidden in a cave near Qumran in the Judaean desert. And, of course, the Coptic Scrolls in 1945 at Nag Hammadi. In addition to telling the true Grail story, these documents speak of Christ's ministry in very human terms. Of course, the Vatican, in keeping with their tradition of misinformation, tried very hard to suppress the release of these scrolls. And why wouldn't they? The scrolls highlight glaring historical discrepancies and fabrications, clearly confirming that the modern Bible was compiled and edited by men who possessed a political agenda – to promote the divinity of the man Jesus Christ and use His influence to solidify their own power base.'

'And yet,' Langdon countered, 'it's important to remember that the modern Church's desire to suppress these documents comes from a sincere belief in their established view of Christ. The Vatican is made up of deeply pious men who truly believe these contrary documents could only be false testimony.'

Teabing chuckled as he eased himself into a chair opposite Sophie. 'As you can see, our professor has a far softer heart for Rome than I do. Nonetheless, he is correct about the modern clergy believing these opposing documents are false testimony. That's understandable. Constantine's Bible has been their truth for ages. Nobody is more indoctrinated than the indoctrinator.'

'What he means,' Langdon said, 'is that we worship the gods of our fathers.'

'What I mean,' Teabing countered, 'is that almost everything our fathers taught us about Christ is *false*. As are the stories about the Holy Grail.'

Sophie looked again at the Da Vinci quote before her. *Blinding ignorance does mislead us. O! Wretched mortals, open your eyes!*

Teabing reached for the book and flipped toward the centre. 'And finally, before I show you Da Vinci's paintings of the Holy Grail, I'd like you to take a quick look at this.' He opened the book to a colourful graphic that spanned both full pages. 'I assume you recognize this fresco?'

He's kidding, right? Sophie was staring at the most famous fresco of all time – *The Last Supper* – Da Vinci's legendary painting on the wall of Santa Maria delle Grazie in Milan. The decaying fresco portrayed Jesus and His disciples at the moment that Jesus announced one of them would betray Him. 'I know the fresco, yes.'

'Then perhaps you would indulge me this little game? Close your eyes if you would.'

Uncertain, Sophie closed her eyes.

'Where is Jesus sitting?' Teabing asked.

'In the centre.'

'Good. And what food are He and His disciples breaking and eating?'

'Bread.' *Obviously.*

'Superb. And what drink?'

'Wine. They drank wine.'

'Great. And one final question. How many wine-glasses are on the table?'

Sophie paused, realizing it was the trick question. *And after dinner, Jesus took the cup of wine, sharing it with His disciples.* 'One cup,' she said. 'The chalice.' *The Cup of Christ. The Holy Grail.* 'Jesus passed a single chalice of wine, just as modern Christians do at communion.'

Teabing sighed. 'Open your eyes.'

She did. Teabing was grinning smugly. Sophie looked down at the painting, seeing to her astonishment that *everyone* at the table had a glass of wine, including Christ. Thirteen cups. Moreover, the cups were tiny, stemless, and made of glass. There was no chalice in the painting. No Holy Grail.

Teabing's eyes twinkled. 'A bit strange, don't you think, considering that both the Bible and our standard Grail legend celebrate this moment as the definitive arrival of the Holy Grail. Oddly, Da Vinci appears to have forgotten to paint the Cup of Christ.'

'Surely art scholars must have noted that.'

'You will be shocked to learn what anomalies Da Vinci included here that most scholars either do not see or simply choose to ignore. This fresco, in fact, is the entire key to the Holy Grail mystery. Da Vinci lays it all out in the open in *The Last Supper.*'

Sophie scanned the work eagerly. 'Does this fresco tell us *what* the Grail really is?'

'Not *what* it is,' Teabing whispered. 'But rather *who* it is. The Holy Grail is not a thing. It is, in fact, . . . a *person.*'

Chapter 56

Sophie stared at Teabing a long moment and then turned to Langdon. 'The Holy Grail is a person?'

Langdon nodded. 'A woman, in fact.' From the blank look on Sophie's face, Langdon could tell they had already lost her. He recalled having a similar reaction the first time he heard the statement. It was not until he understood the *symbology* behind the Grail that the feminine connection became clear.

Teabing apparently had a similar thought. 'Robert, perhaps this is the moment for the symbologist to clarify?' He went to a nearby end table, found a piece of paper, and laid it in front of Langdon.

Langdon pulled a pen from his pocket. 'Sophie, are you familiar with the modern icons for male and female?' He drew the common male symbol ♂ and female symbol ♀.

'Of course,' she said.

'These,' he said quietly, 'are not the original symbols for male and female. Many people incorrectly assume the male symbol is derived from a shield and spear, while the female symbol represents a mirror reflecting beauty. In fact, the symbols originated as ancient astronomical symbols for the planet-god Mars and planet-goddess Venus. The original symbols are far simpler.' Langdon drew another icon on the paper.

'This symbol is the original icon for *male*,' he told her. 'A rudimentary phallus.'

'Quite to the point,' Sophie said.

'As it were,' Teabing added.

Langdon went on. 'This icon is formally known as the *blade*, and it represents aggression and manhood. In fact, this exact phallus symbol is still used today on modern military uniforms to denote rank.'

'Indeed.' Teabing grinned. 'The more penises you have, the higher your rank. Boys will be boys.'

Langdon winced. 'Moving on, the female symbol, as you might imagine, is the exact opposite.' He drew another symbol on the page. 'This is called the *chalice*.'

Sophie glanced up, looking surprised.

Langdon could see she had made the connection. 'The chalice,' he said, 'resembles a cup or vessel, and more important, it resembles the shape of a woman's womb. This symbol communicates femininity, womanhood and fertility.' Langdon looked directly at her now. 'Sophie, legend tells us the Holy Grail is a chalice – a cup. But the Grail's description as a *chalice* is actually an allegory to protect the true nature of the Holy Grail. That is to say, the legend uses the chalice as a *metaphor* for something far more important.'

'A woman,' Sophie said.

'Exactly.' Langdon smiled. 'The Grail is literally the ancient symbol for womanhood, and the *Holy* Grail represents the sacred feminine and the goddess, which of course has now been lost, virtually eliminated by the Church. The power of the female and her ability to produce life was once very sacred, but it posed a threat to the rise of the predominantly male Church, and so the sacred feminine was demonized and called unclean. It was *man*, not God, who created the concept of "original sin", whereby Eve tasted of the apple and caused the downfall of the human race. Woman, once the sacred giver of life, was now the enemy.'

'I should add,' Teabing chimed, 'that this concept of woman as life-bringer was the foundation of ancient religion. Childbirth was mystical and powerful. Sadly, Christian philosophy decided to embezzle the female's creative power by ignoring biological truth and making *man* the Creator. Genesis tells us that Eve was created from Adam's rib. Woman became an off-shoot of man. And a sinful one at that. Genesis was the beginning of the end for the goddess.'

'The Grail,' Langdon said, 'is symbolic of the lost goddess. When Christianity came along, the old pagan religions did not die easily. Legends of chivalric quests for the lost Grail were in fact stories of forbidden quests to find the lost sacred feminine. Knights who claimed to be "searching for the chalice" were speaking in code as a way to protect themselves from a Church that had subjugated women, banished the Goddess, burned nonbelievers and forbidden the pagan reverence for the sacred feminine.'

Sophie shook her head. 'I'm sorry, when you said the Holy Grail was a person, I thought you meant it was an actual person.'

'It is,' Langdon said.

'And not just *any* person,' Teabing blurted, clambering excitedly to his feet. 'A woman who carried with her a secret so powerful that, if revealed, it threatened to devastate the very foundation of Christianity!'

Sophie looked overwhelmed. 'Is this woman well known in history?'

'Quite.' Teabing collected his crutches and motioned down the hall. 'And if we adjourn to the study, my friends, it would be my honour to show you Da Vinci's painting of her.'

Two rooms away, in the kitchen, manservant Rémy Legaludec stood in silence before a television. The news station was broadcasting photos of a man and woman . . . the same two individuals to whom Rémy had just served tea.

Chapter 57

Standing at the roadblock outside the Depository Bank of Zurich, Lieutenant Collet wondered what was taking Fache so long to come up with the search warrant. The bankers were obviously hiding something. They claimed Langdon and Neveu had arrived earlier and were turned away from the bank because they did not have proper account identification.

So why won't they let us inside for a look?

Finally, Collet's cellular phone rang. It was the command post at the Louvre. 'Do we have a search warrant yet?' Collet demanded.

'Forget about the bank, Lieutenant,' the agent told him. 'We just got a tip. We have the exact location where Langdon and Neveu are hiding.'

Collet sat down hard on the hood of his car. 'You're kidding.'

'I have an address in the suburbs. Somewhere near Versailles.'

'Does Captain Fache know?'

'Not yet. He's busy on an important call.'

'I'm on my way. Have him call as soon as he's free.' Collet took down the address and jumped in his car. As he peeled away from the bank, Collet realized he had forgotten to ask *who* had tipped DCPJ off to Langdon's location. Not that it mattered. Collet had been blessed with a chance to redeem his scepticism and earlier blunders. He was about to make the most high-profile arrest of his career.

Collet radioed the five cars accompanying him. 'No sirens, men. Langdon can't know we're coming.'

Forty kilometres away, a black Audi pulled off a rural road and parked in the shadows on the edge of a field. Silas got out and peered through the rungs of the wrought-iron fence that encircled the vast compound before him. He gazed up the long moonlit slope to the château in the distance.

The downstairs lights were all ablaze. *Odd for this hour*, Silas thought, smiling. The information the Teacher had given him was obviously accurate. *I will not leave this house without the keystone*, he vowed. *I will not fail the bishop and the Teacher.*

Checking the thirteen-round clip in his Heckler Koch, Silas pushed it through the bars and let it fall onto the mossy ground inside the compound. Then, gripping the top of the fence, he heaved himself up and over, dropping to the ground on the other side. Ignoring the slash of pain from his *cilice*, Silas retrieved his gun and began the long trek up the grassy slope.

Chapter 58

Teabing's 'study' was like no study Sophie had ever seen. Six or seven times larger than even the most luxurious of office spaces, the knight's *cabinet de travail* resembled an ungainly hybrid of science laboratory, archival library and indoor flea market. Lit by three overhead chandeliers, the boundless tile floor was dotted with clustered islands of worktables buried beneath books, artwork, artefacts and a surprising amount of electronic gear – computers, projectors, microscopes, copy machines and flatbed scanners.

'I converted the ballroom,' Teabing said, looking sheepish as he shuffled into the room. 'I have little occasion to dance.'

Sophie felt as if the entire night had become some kind of twilight zone where nothing was as she expected. 'This is all for your work?'

'Learning the truth has become my life's love,' Teabing said. 'And the Sangreal is my favourite mistress.'

The Holy Grail is a woman, Sophie thought, her mind a collage of interrelated ideas that seemed to make no sense. 'You said you have a *picture* of this woman who you claim is the Holy Grail.'

'Yes, but it is not I who *claim* she is the Grail. Christ Himself made that claim.'

'Which one is the painting?' Sophie asked, scanning the walls.

'Hmmm . . .' Teabing made a show of seeming to have forgotten. 'The Holy Grail. The Sangreal. The

Chalice.' He wheeled suddenly and pointed to the far wall. On it hung an eight-foot-long print of *The Last Supper*, the same exact image Sophie had just been looking at. 'There she is!'

Sophie was certain she had missed something. 'That's the same painting you just showed me.'

He winked. 'I know, but the enlargement is so much more exciting. Don't you think?'

Sophie turned to Langdon for help. 'I'm lost.'

Langdon smiled. 'As it turns out, the Holy Grail *does* indeed make an appearance in *The Last Supper*. Leonardo included her prominently.'

'Hold on,' Sophie said. 'You told me the Holy Grail is a *woman*. *The Last Supper* is a painting of thirteen men.'

'Is it?' Teabing arched his eyebrows. 'Take a closer look.'

Uncertain, Sophie made her way closer to the painting, scanning the thirteen figures – Jesus Christ in the middle, six disciples on His left, and six on His right. 'They're all men,' she confirmed.

'Oh?' Teabing said. 'How about the one seated in the place of honour, at the right hand of the Lord?'

Sophie examined the figure to Jesus' immediate right, focusing in. As she studied the person's face and body, a wave of astonishment rose within her. The individual had flowing red hair, delicate folded hands, and the hint of a bosom. It was, without a doubt . . . female.

'That's a woman!' Sophie exclaimed.

Teabing was laughing. 'Surprise, surprise. Believe me, it's no mistake. Leonardo was skilled at painting the difference between the sexes.'

Sophie could not take her eyes from the woman beside Christ. *The Last Supper is supposed to be thirteen men. Who is this woman?* Although Sophie had seen this classic image many times, she had not once noticed this glaring discrepancy.

'Everyone misses it,' Teabing said. 'Our preconceived notions of this scene are so powerful that our mind blocks out the incongruity and overrides our eyes.'

'It's known as *scotoma*,' Langdon added. 'The brain does it sometimes with powerful symbols.'

'Another reason you might have missed the woman,' Teabing said, 'is that many of the photographs in art books were taken before 1954, when the details were still hidden beneath layers of grime and several restorative repaintings done by clumsy hands in the eighteenth century. Now, at last, the fresco has been cleaned down to Da Vinci's original layer of paint.' He motioned to the photograph. '*Et voilà!*'

Sophie moved closer to the image. The woman to Jesus' right was young and pious-looking, with a demure face, beautiful red hair and hands folded quietly. *This is the woman who singlehandedly could crumble the Church?*

'Who is she?' Sophie asked.

'That, my dear,' Teabing replied, 'is Mary Magdalene.'

Sophie turned. 'The prostitute?'

Teabing drew a short breath, as if the word had injured him personally. 'Magdalene was no such thing. That unfortunate misconception is the legacy of a smear campaign launched by the early Church. The Church needed to defame Mary Magdalene in order to cover up her dangerous secret – her role as the Holy Grail.'

'Her *role*?'

'As I mentioned,' Teabing clarified, 'the early Church needed to convince the world that the mortal prophet Jesus was a *divine* being. Therefore, any gospels that described *earthly* aspects of Jesus' life had to be omitted from the Bible. Unfortunately for the early editors, one particularly troubling earthly theme kept recurring in the gospels. Mary Magdalene.' He paused. 'More specifically, her marriage to Jesus Christ.'

'I beg your pardon?' Sophie's eyes moved to Langdon and then back to Teabing.

'It's a matter of historical record,' Teabing said, 'and Da Vinci was certainly aware of that fact. *The Last Supper* practically shouts at the viewer that Jesus and Magdalene were a pair.'

Sophie glanced back to the fresco.

'Notice that Jesus and Magdalene are clothed as mirror images of one another.' Teabing pointed to the two individuals in the centre of the fresco.

Sophie was mesmerized. Sure enough, their clothes were inverse colours. Jesus wore a red robe and blue cloak; Mary Magdalene wore a blue robe and red cloak. *Yin and yang.*

'Venturing into the more bizarre,' Teabing said, 'note that Jesus and His bride appear to be joined at the hip and are leaning away from one another as if to create this clearly delineated negative space between them.'

Even before Teabing traced the contour for her, Sophie saw it – the indisputable $\vee$ shape at the focal point of the painting. It was the same symbol Langdon had drawn earlier for the Grail, the chalice and the female womb.

'Finally,' Teabing said, 'if you view Jesus and Magdalene as compositional elements rather than as people, you will see another obvious shape leap out at you.' He paused. 'A *letter* of the alphabet.'

Sophie saw it at once. To say the letter leapt out at her was an understatement. The letter was suddenly all Sophie could see. Glaring in the centre of the painting was the unquestionable outline of an enormous, flawlessly formed letter M.

'A bit too perfect for coincidence, wouldn't you say?' Teabing asked.

Sophie was amazed. 'Why is it there?'

Teabing shrugged. 'Conspiracy theorists will tell you it stands for *Matrimonio* or *Mary Magdalene*. To be honest, nobody is certain. The only certainty is that the hidden M is no mistake. Countless Grail-related works contain the hidden letter M – whether as watermarks, underpaintings, or compositional allusions. The most blatant M, of course, is emblazoned on the altar at Our Lady of Paris in London, which was designed by a former Grand Master of the Priory of Sion, Jean Cocteau.'

Sophie weighed the information. 'I'll admit, the hidden M's are intriguing, although I assume nobody is claiming they are proof of Jesus' marriage to Magdalene.'

'No, no,' Teabing said, going to a nearby table of books. 'As I said earlier, the marriage of Jesus and Mary Magdalene is part of the historical record.' He began pawing through his book collection. 'Moreover, Jesus as a married man makes infinitely more sense than our standard biblical view of Jesus as a bachelor.'

'Why?' Sophie asked.

'Because Jesus was a Jew,' Langdon said, taking over while Teabing searched for his book, 'and the social decorum during that time virtually forbade a Jewish man to be unmarried. According to Jewish custom, celibacy was condemned, and the obligation for a Jewish father was to find a suitable wife for his son. If Jesus were not married, at least one of the Bible's gospels would have mentioned it and offered some explanation for His unnatural state of bachelorhood.'

Teabing located a huge book and pulled it toward

him across the table. The leather-bound edition was poster-sized, like a huge atlas. The cover read: *The Gnostic Gospels.* Teabing heaved it open, and Langdon and Sophie joined him. Sophie could see it contained photographs of what appeared to be magnified passages of ancient documents – tattered papyrus with handwritten text. She did not recognize the ancient language, but the facing pages bore typed translations.

'These are photocopies of the Nag Hammadi and Dead Sea scrolls, which I mentioned earlier,' Teabing said. 'The earliest Christian records. Troublingly, they do not match up with the gospels in the Bible.' Flipping toward the middle of the book, Teabing pointed to a passage. 'The Gospel of Philip is always a good place to start.'

Sophie read the passage:

And the companion of the Saviour is Mary Magdalene. Christ loved her more than all the disciples and used to kiss her often on her mouth. The rest of the disciples were offended by it and expressed disapproval. They said to him, 'Why do you love her more than all of us?'

The words surprised Sophie, and yet they hardly seemed conclusive. 'It says nothing of marriage.'

'*Au contraire.*' Teabing smiled, pointing to the first line. 'As any Aramaic scholar will tell you, the word companion, in those days, literally meant spouse.'

Langdon concurred with a nod.

Sophie read the first line again. *And the companion of the Saviour is Mary Magdalene.*

Teabing flipped through the book and pointed out several other passages that, to Sophie's surprise, clearly suggested Magdalene and Jesus had a romantic relationship. As she read the passages, Sophie recalled an angry priest who had banged on her grandfather's door when she was a schoolgirl.

'Is this the home of Jacques Saunière?' the priest had demanded, glaring down at young Sophie when she pulled open the door. 'I want to talk to him about this editorial he wrote.' The priest held up a newspaper.

Sophie summoned her grandfather, and the two men disappeared into his study and closed the door. *My grandfather wrote something in the paper?* Sophie immediately ran to the kitchen and flipped through that morning's paper. She found her grandfather's name on an article on the second page. She read it. Sophie didn't understand all of what was said, but it sounded like the French government, under pressure from priests, had agreed to ban an American film called *The Last Temptation of Christ*, which was about Jesus having sex with a lady called Mary Magdalene. Her grandfather's article said the Church was arrogant and wrong to ban it.

No wonder the priest is mad, Sophie thought.

'It's pornography! Sacrilege!' the priest yelled, emerging from the study and storming to the front door. 'How can you possibly endorse that! This American Martin Scorsese is a blasphemer, and the Church will permit him no pulpit in France!' The priest slammed the door on his way out.

When her grandfather came into the kitchen, he saw Sophie with the paper and frowned. 'You're quick.'

Sophie said, 'You think Jesus Christ had a girlfriend?'

'No, dear, I said the Church should not be allowed to tell us what notions we can and can't entertain.'

'Did Jesus have a girlfriend?'

332

Her grandfather was silent for several moments. 'Would it be so bad if He did?'

Sophie considered it and then shrugged. 'I wouldn't mind.'

Sir Leigh Teabing was still talking. 'I shan't bore you with the countless references to Jesus and Magdalene's union. That has been explored ad nauseam by modern historians. I would, however, like to point out the following.' He motioned to another passage. 'This is from the Gospel of Mary Magdalene.'

Sophie had not known a gospel existed in Magdalene's words. She read the text:

> And Peter said, 'Did the Saviour really speak with a woman without our knowledge? Are we to turn about and all listen to her? Did he prefer her to us?'
>
> And Levi answered, 'Peter, you have always been hot-tempered. Now I see you contending against the woman like an adversary. If the Saviour made her worthy, who are you indeed to reject her? Surely the Saviour knows her very well. That is why he loved her more than us.'

'The woman they are speaking of,' Teabing explained, 'is Mary Magdalene. Peter is jealous of her.'

'Because Jesus preferred Mary?'

'Not only that. The stakes were far greater than mere affection. At this point in the gospels, Jesus suspects He will soon be captured and crucified. So He gives Mary Magdalene instructions on how to carry on His Church after He is gone. As a result, Peter expresses his discontent over playing second fiddle to a woman. I daresay Peter was something of a sexist.'

Sophie was trying to keep up. 'This is Saint Peter. The rock on which Jesus built His Church.'

'The same, except for one catch. According to these unaltered gospels, it was not *Peter* to whom Christ gave directions with which to establish the Christian Church. It was *Mary Magdalene*.'

Sophie looked at him. 'You're saying the Christian Church was to be carried on by a *woman*?'

'That was the plan. Jesus was the original feminist. He intended for the future of His Church to be in the hands of Mary Magdalene.'

'And Peter had a problem with that,' Langdon said, pointing to *The Last Supper*. 'That's Peter there. You can see that Da Vinci was well aware of how Peter felt about Mary Magdalene.'

Again, Sophie was speechless. In the painting, Peter was leaning menacingly toward Mary Magdalene and slicing his blade-like hand across her neck. The same threatening gesture as in *Madonna of the Rocks*!

'And here too,' Langdon said, pointing now to the crowd of disciples near Peter. 'A bit ominous, no?'

Sophie squinted and saw a hand emerging from the crowd of disciples. 'Is that hand wielding a *dagger*?'

'Yes. Stranger still, if you count the arms, you'll see that this hand belongs to . . . no one at all. It's dis-embodied. Anonymous.'

Sophie was starting to feel overwhelmed. 'I'm sorry, I still don't understand how all of this makes Mary Magdalene the Holy Grail.'

'Aha!' Teabing exclaimed again. 'Therein lies the rub!' He turned once more to the table and pulled out a large chart, spreading it out for her. It was an elaborate genealogy. 'Few people realize that Mary Magdalene, in addition to being Christ's right hand, was a powerful woman already.'

Sophie could now see the title of the family tree.

THE TRIBE OF BENJAMIN

'Mary Magdalene is here,' Teabing said, pointing near the top of the genealogy.

Sophie was surprised. 'She was of the House of Benjamin?'

'Indeed,' Teabing said. 'Mary Magdalene was of royal descent.'

'But I was under the impression Magdalene was poor.'

Teabing shook his head. 'Magdalene was recast as a whore in order to erase evidence of her powerful family ties.'

Sophie found herself again glancing at Langdon, who again nodded. She turned back to Teabing. 'But why would the early Church *care* if Magdalene had royal blood?'

The Briton smiled. 'My dear child, it was not Mary Magdalene's royal blood that concerned the Church so much as it was her consorting with Christ, who *also* had royal blood. As you know, the Book of Matthew tells us that Jesus was of the House of David. A descendant of King Solomon – King of the Jews. By marrying into the powerful House of Benjamin, Jesus fused two royal bloodlines, creating a potent political union with the potential of making a legitimate claim to the throne and restoring the line of kings as it was under Solomon.'

Sophie sensed he was at last coming to his point.

Teabing looked excited now. 'The legend of the Holy Grail is a legend about royal blood. When Grail legend speaks of "the chalice that held the blood of Christ" . . . it speaks, in fact, of Mary Magdalene – the female womb that carried Jesus' royal bloodline.'

The words seemed to echo across the ballroom and back before they fully registered in Sophie's mind. *Mary Magdalene carried the royal bloodline of Jesus Christ?* 'But how could Christ have a bloodline unless . . . ?' She paused and looked at Langdon.

Langdon smiled softly. 'Unless they had a child.'

Sophie stood transfixed.

'Behold,' Teabing proclaimed, 'the greatest cover-up in human history. Not only was Jesus Christ married, but He was a father. My dear, Mary Magdalene was the Holy Vessel. She was the chalice that bore the royal bloodline of Jesus Christ. She was the womb that bore the lineage, and the vine from which the sacred fruit sprang forth!'

Sophie felt the hairs stand up on her arms. 'But how could a secret *that* big be kept quiet all of these years?'

'Heavens!' Teabing said. 'It has been anything but *quiet*! The royal bloodline of Jesus Christ is the source of the most enduring legend of all time – the Holy Grail. Magdalene's story has been shouted from the rooftops for centuries in all kinds of metaphors and languages. Her story is everywhere once you open your eyes.'

'And the Sangreal documents?' Sophie said. 'They allegedly contain proof that Jesus had a royal bloodline?'

'They do.'

'So the entire Holy Grail legend is all about royal blood?'

'Quite literally,' Teabing said. 'The word *Sangreal* derives from *San Greal* – or Holy Grail. But in its most ancient form, the word *Sangreal* was divided in a different spot.' Teabing wrote on a piece of scrap paper and handed it to her.

She read what he had written.

Sang Real

Instantly, Sophie recognized the translation.
Sang Real literally meant *Royal Blood*.

Chapter 59

The male receptionist in the lobby of the Opus Dei headquarters on Lexington Avenue in New York City was surprised to hear Bishop Aringarosa's voice on the line. 'Good evening, sir.'

'Have I had any messages?' the bishop demanded, sounding unusually anxious.

'Yes, sir. I'm very glad you called in. I couldn't reach you in your apartment. You had an urgent phone message about half an hour ago.'

'Yes?' He sounded relieved by the news. 'Did the caller leave a name?'

'No, sir, just a number.' The operator relayed the number.

'Prefix thirty-three? That's France, am I right?'

'Yes, sir. Paris. The caller said it was critical you contact him immediately.'

'Thank you. I have been waiting for that call.' Aringarosa quickly severed the connection.

As the receptionist hung up the receiver, he wondered why Aringarosa's phone connection sounded so crackly. The bishop's daily schedule showed him in New York this weekend, and yet he sounded a world away. The receptionist shrugged it off. Bishop Aringarosa had been acting very strangely the last few months.

My cellular phone must not have been receiving, Aringarosa thought as the Fiat approached the exit for Rome's

Ciampino Charter Airport. *The Teacher was trying to reach me.* Despite Aringarosa's concern at having missed the call, he felt encouraged that the Teacher felt confident enough to call Opus Dei headquarters directly.

Things must have gone well in Paris tonight.

As Aringarosa began dialling the number, he felt excited to know he would soon be in Paris. *I'll be on the ground before dawn.* Aringarosa had a chartered turbo prop awaiting him here for the short flight to France. Commercial carriers were not an option at this hour, especially considering the contents of his briefcase.

The line began to ring.

A female voice answered. *'Direction Centrale Police Judiciaire.'*

Aringarosa felt himself hesitate. This was unexpected. 'Ah, yes . . . I was asked to call this number?'

'Qui êtes-vous?' the woman said. 'Your name?'

Aringarosa was uncertain if he should reveal it. *The French Judicial Police?*

'Your *name*, monsieur?' the woman pressed.

'Bishop Manuel Aringarosa.'

'Un moment.' There was a click on the line.

After a long wait, another man came on, his tone gruff and concerned. 'Bishop, I am glad I finally reached you. You and I have much to discuss.'

338

Chapter 60

Sangreal . . . *Sang Real . . . San Greal . . . Royal Blood . . . Holy Grail.*

It was all intertwined.

The Holy Grail is Mary Magdalene . . . the mother of the royal bloodline of Jesus Christ. Sophie felt a new wave of disorientation as she stood in the silence of the ballroom and stared at Robert Langdon. The more pieces Langdon and Teabing laid on the table tonight, the more unpredictable this puzzle became.

'As you can see, my dear,' Teabing said, hobbling toward a bookshelf, 'Leonardo is not the only one who has been trying to tell the world the truth about the Holy Grail. The royal bloodline of Jesus Christ has been chronicled in exhaustive detail by scores of historians.' He ran a finger down a row of several dozen books.

Sophie tilted her head and scanned the list of titles:

THE TEMPLAR REVELATION:
Secret Guardians of the True Identity of Christ

THE WOMAN WITH THE ALABASTER JAR:
Mary Magdalene and the Holy Grail

THE GODDESS IN THE GOSPELS
Reclaiming the Sacred Feminine

'Here is perhaps the best-known tome,' Teabing said, pulling a tattered hardcover from the stack and handing it to her.

The cover read:

HOLY BLOOD, HOLY GRAIL
The Acclaimed International Bestseller

Sophie glanced up. 'An international bestseller? I've never heard of it.'

'You were young. This caused quite a stir back in the nineteen eighties. To my taste, the authors made some dubious leaps of faith in their analysis, but their fundamental premise is sound, and to their credit, they finally brought the idea of Christ's bloodline into the mainstream.'

'What was the Church's reaction to the book?'

'Outrage, of course. But that was to be expected. After all, this was a secret the Vatican had tried to bury in the fourth century. That's part of what the Crusades were about. Gathering and destroying information. The threat Mary Magdalene posed to the men of the early Church was potentially ruinous. Not only was she the woman to whom Jesus had assigned the task of founding the Church, but she also had physical proof that the Church's newly proclaimed *deity* had spawned a mortal bloodline. The Church, in order to defend itself against the Magdalene's power, perpetuated her image as a whore and buried evidence of Christ's marriage to her, thereby defusing any potential claims that Christ had a surviving bloodline and was a mortal prophet.'

Sophie glanced at Langdon, who nodded. 'Sophie, the historical evidence supporting this is substantial.'

'I admit,' Teabing said, 'the assertions are dire, but you must understand the Church's powerful motivations to conduct such a cover-up. They could never have survived public knowledge of a bloodline. A child of Jesus would undermine the critical notion of Christ's divinity and therefore the Christian Church, which declared itself the sole vessel through which humanity could access the divine and gain entrance to the kingdom of heaven.'

'The five-petal rose,' Sophie said, pointing suddenly to the spine of one of Teabing's books. *The same exact design inlaid on the rosewood box.*

Teabing glanced at Langdon and grinned. 'She has a good eye.' He turned back to Sophie. 'That is the Priory symbol for the Grail. Mary Magdalene. Because her name was forbidden by the Church, Mary Magdalene became secretly known by many pseudo-nyms – the Chalice, the Holy Grail, and the Rose.' He paused. 'The Rose has ties to the five-pointed pentacle of Venus and the guiding Compass Rose. By the way, the word *rose* is identical in English, French, German, and many other languages.'

'Rose,' Langdon added, 'is also an anagram of Eros, the Greek god of sexual love.'

Sophie gave him a surprised look as Teabing ploughed on.

'The Rose has always been the premiere symbol of female sexuality. In primitive goddess cults, the five petals represented the five stations of female life – birth, menstruation, motherhood, menopause, and death. And in modern times, the flowering rose's ties to womanhood are considered more visual.' He glanced at Robert. 'Perhaps the symbologist could explain?'

Robert hesitated. A moment too long.

'Oh, heavens!' Teabing huffed. 'You Americans are such prudes.' He looked back at Sophie. 'What Robert is fumbling with is the fact that the blossoming flower resembles the female genitalia, the sublime blossom from which all mankind enters the world. And if you've ever seen any paintings by Georgia O'Keeffe, you'll know exactly what I mean.'

'The point here,' Langdon said, motioning back

to the bookshelf, 'is that all of these books substantiate the same historical claim.'

'That Jesus was a father.' Sophie was still uncertain.

'Yes,' Teabing said. 'And that Mary Magdalene was the womb that carried His royal lineage. The Priory of Sion, to this day, still worships Mary Magdalene as the Goddess, the Holy Grail, the Rose and the Divine Mother.'

Sophie again flashed on the ritual in the basement.

'According to the Priory,' Teabing continued, 'Mary Magdalene was pregnant at the time of the crucifixion. For the safety of Christ's unborn child, she had no choice but to flee the Holy Land. With the help of Jesus' trusted uncle, Joseph of Arimathea, Mary Magdalene secretly traveled to France, then known as Gaul. There she found safe refuge in the Jewish community. It was here in France that she gave birth to a daughter. Her name was Sarah.'

Sophie glanced up. 'They actually know the child's *name*?'

'Far more than that. Magdalene's and Sarah's lives were scrupulously chronicled by their Jewish protectors. Remember that Magdalene's child belonged to the lineage of Jewish kings – David and Solomon. For this reason, the Jews in France considered Magdalene sacred royalty and revered her as the progenitor of the royal line of kings. Countless scholars of that era chronicled Mary Magdalene's days in France, including the birth of Sarah and the subsequent family tree.'

Sophie was startled. 'There exists a *family tree* of Jesus Christ?'

'Indeed. And it is purportedly one of the cornerstones of the Sangreal documents. A complete genealogy of the early descendants of Christ.'

'But what good is a documented genealogy of

Christ's bloodline?' Sophie asked. 'It's not proof. Historians could not possibly confirm its authenticity.'

Teabing chuckled. 'No more so than they can confirm the authenticity of the Bible.'

'Meaning?'

'Meaning that history is always written by the winners. When two cultures clash, the loser is obliterated, and the winner writes the history books – books which glorify their own cause and disparage the conquered foe. As Napoleon once said, "What is history, but a fable agreed upon?" ' He smiled. 'By its very nature, history is always a one-sided account.'

Sophie had never thought of it that way.

'The Sangreal documents simply tell the *other* side of the Christ story. In the end, which side of the story you believe becomes a matter of faith and personal exploration, but at least the information has survived. The Sangreal documents include tens of thousands of pages of information. Eyewitness accounts of the Sangreal treasure describe it as being carried in four enormous trunks. In those trunks are reputed to be the *Purist Documents* – thousands of pages of unaltered, pre-Constantine documents, written by the early followers of Jesus, revering Him as a wholly human teacher and prophet. Also rumoured to be part of the treasure is the legendary "Q" *Document* – a manuscript that even the Vatican admit they believe exists. Allegedly, it is a book of Jesus' teachings, possibly written in His own hand.'

'Writings by Christ Himself?'

'Of course,' Teabing said. 'Why wouldn't Jesus have kept a chronicle of His ministry? Most people did in those days. Another explosive document believed to be in the treasure is a manuscript called *The Magdalene Diaries* – Mary Magdalene's personal account of her relationship with Christ, His crucifixion and her time in France.'

Sophie was silent for a long moment. 'And these four chests of documents were the treasure that the Knights Templar found under Solomon's Temple?'

'Exactly. The documents that made the Knights so powerful. The documents that have been the object of countless Grail quests throughout history.'

'But you said the Holy Grail was *Mary Magdalene*. If people are searching for documents, why would you call it a search for the Holy Grail?'

Teabing eyed her, his expression softening. 'Because the hiding place of the Holy Grail includes a sarcophagus.'

Outside, the wind howled in the trees.

Teabing spoke more quietly now. 'The quest for the Holy Grail is literally the quest to kneel before the bones of Mary Magdalene. A journey to pray at the feet of the outcast one, the lost sacred feminine.'

Sophie felt an unexpected wonder. 'The hiding place of the Holy Grail is actually . . . a *tomb*?'

Teabing's hazel eyes got misty. 'It is. A tomb containing the body of Mary Magdalene and the documents that tell the true story of her life. At its heart, the quest for the Holy Grail has always been a quest for the Magdalene – the wronged Queen, entombed with proof of her family's rightful claim to power.'

Sophie waited a moment as Teabing gathered himself. So much about her grandfather was still not making sense. 'Members of the Priory,' she finally said, 'all these years have answered the charge of protecting the Sangreal documents and the tomb of Mary Magdalene?'

'Yes, but the brotherhood had another, more important duty as well – to protect the *bloodline* itself. Christ's lineage was in perpetual danger. The early Church feared that if the lineage were permitted to grow, the secret of Jesus and Magdalene would eventually surface and challenge the fundamental Catholic doctrine – that of a divine Messiah who did not consort with women or engage in sexual union.' He paused. 'Nonetheless, Christ's line grew quietly under cover in France until making a bold move in the fifth century, when it intermarried with French royal blood and created a lineage known as the Merovingian bloodline.'

This news surprised Sophie. Merovingian was a term learned by every student in France. 'The Merovingians founded Paris.'

'Yes. That's one of the reasons the Grail legend is so rich in France. Many of the Vatican's Grail quests here were in fact stealth missions to erase members of the royal bloodline. Have you heard of King Dagobert?'

Sophie vaguely recalled the name from a grisly tale in history class. 'Dagobert was a Merovingian king, wasn't he? Stabbed in the eye while sleeping?'

'Exactly. Assassinated by the Vatican in collusion with Pepin d'Heristal. Late seventh century. With Dagobert's murder, the Merovingian bloodline was almost exterminated. Fortunately, Dagobert's son, Sigisbert, secretly escaped the attack and carried on the lineage, which later included Godefroi de Bouillon – founder of the Priory of Sion.'

'The same man,' Langdon said, 'who ordered the Knights Templar to recover the Sangreal documents from beneath Solomon's Temple and thus provide the Merovingians proof of their hereditary ties to Jesus Christ.'

Teabing nodded, heaving a ponderous sigh. 'The modern Priory of Sion has a momentous duty. Theirs is a threefold charge. The brotherhood must protect the Sangreal documents. They must protect the tomb of Mary Magdalene. And, of course, they must nurture and protect the bloodline of Christ – those few members of the royal Merovingian bloodline who have survived into modern times.'

The words hung in the huge space, and Sophie felt an odd vibration, as if her bones were reverberating with some new kind of truth. *Descendants of Jesus who survived into modern times.* Her grandfather's voice again was whispering in her ear. *Princess, I must tell you the truth about your family.*

A chill raked her flesh.

Royal blood.

She could not imagine.

Princess Sophie.

'Sir Leigh?' The manservant's words crackled through the intercom on the wall, and Sophie jumped. 'If you could join me in the kitchen a moment?'

Teabing scowled at the ill-timed intrusion. He went over to the intercom and pressed the button. 'Rémy, as you know, I am busy with my guests. If we need anything else from the kitchen tonight, we will help ourselves. Thank you and good night.'

'A word with you before I retire, sir. If you would.'

Teabing grunted and pressed the button. 'Make it quick, Rémy.'

'It is a household matter, sir, hardly fare for guests to endure.'

Teabing looked incredulous. 'And it cannot wait until morning?'

'No, sir. My question won't take a minute.'

Teabing rolled his eyes and looked at Langdon and Sophie. 'Sometimes I wonder who is serving whom?' He pressed the button again. 'I'll be right there, Rémy. Can I bring you anything when I come?'

'Only freedom from oppression, sir.'

'Rémy, you realize your *steak au poivre* is the only reason you still work for me.'

'So you tell me, sir. So you tell me.'

Chapter 61

Princess Sophie.

Sophie felt hollow as she listened to the clicking of Teabing's crutches fade down the hallway. Numb, she turned and faced Langdon in the deserted ballroom. He was already shaking his head as if reading her mind.

'No, Sophie,' he whispered, his eyes reassuring. 'The same thought crossed my mind as soon as you told me your grandfather was in the Priory, and when I realized you said he wanted to tell you a secret about your family. But it's impossible.' Langdon paused. 'Saunière is not a Merovingian name.'

Sophie wasn't sure whether to feel relieved or disappointed. Earlier, Langdon had asked an unusual passing question about Sophie's mother's maiden name. Chauvel. The question now made sense. 'And Chauvel?' she asked, anxious.

Again he shook his head. 'I'm sorry. I know that would have answered some questions for you. Only two direct lines of Merovingians remain. Their family names are Plantard and Saint-Clair. Both families live in hiding, probably protected by the Priory.'

Sophie repeated the names silently in her mind and then shook her head. There was no one in her family named Plantard or Saint-Clair. A weary undertow was pulling at her now. She realized she was no closer than she had been at the Louvre to understanding what truth her grandfather had wanted to reveal to her. Sophie wished her grandfather had never mentioned her family this afternoon. He had torn open old wounds that felt as painful now as ever. *They are dead, Sophie. They are not coming back.* She thought of her mother singing her to sleep at night, of her father giving her rides on his shoulders, and of her grandmother and younger brother smiling at her with their fervent green eyes. All that was stolen. And all she had left was her grandfather.

And now he is gone too. I am alone.

Sophie turned quietly back to *The Last Supper* and gazed at Mary Magdalene's long red hair and quiet eyes. There was something in the woman's expression that echoed the loss of a loved one. Sophie could feel it too.

'Robert?' she said softly.

He stepped closer.

'I know Leigh said the Grail story is all around us, but tonight is the first time I've ever heard any of this.'

Langdon looked as if he wanted to put a comforting hand on her shoulder, but he refrained. 'You've heard her story before, Sophie. Everyone has. We just don't realize it when we hear it.'

'I don't understand.'

'The Grail story is everywhere, but it is hidden. When the Church outlawed speaking of the shunned Mary Magdalene, her story and importance had to be passed on through more discreet channels . . . channels that supported metaphor and symbolism.'

'Of course. The arts.'

Langdon motioned to *The Last Supper*. 'A perfect example. Some of today's most enduring art, literature and music secretly tell the history of Mary Magdalene and Jesus.'

Langdon quickly told her about works by Da Vinci, Botticelli, Poussin, Bernini, Mozart and Victor Hugo that all whispered of the quest to restore the banished sacred feminine. Enduring legends like Sir Gawain

348

and the Green Knight, King Arthur and Sleeping Beauty were Grail allegories. Victor Hugo's *Hunchback of Notre Dame* and Mozart's *Magic Flute* were filled with Masonic symbolism and Grail secrets.

'Once you open your eyes to the Holy Grail,' Langdon said, 'you see her everywhere. Paintings. Music. Books. Even in cartoons, theme parks, and popular movies.'

Langdon held up his Mickey Mouse watch and told her that Walt Disney had made it his quiet life's work to pass on the Grail story to future generations. Throughout his entire life, Disney had been hailed as 'the Modern-Day Leonardo da Vinci'. Both men were generations ahead of their times, uniquely gifted artists, members of secret societies and, most notably, avid pranksters. Like Leonardo, Walt Disney loved implanting hidden messages and symbolism in his art. For the trained symbologist, watching an early Disney movie was like being barraged by an avalanche of allusion and metaphor.

Most of Disney's hidden messages dealt with religion, pagan myth and stories of the subjugated goddess. It was no mistake that Disney retold tales like *Cinderella*, *Sleeping Beauty* and *Snow White* – all of which dealt with the incarceration of the sacred feminine. Nor did one need a background in symbolism to understand that Snow White – a princess who fell from grace after partaking of a poisoned apple – was a clear allusion to the downfall of Eve in the Garden of Eden. Or that *Sleeping Beauty*'s Princess Aurora – code-named 'Rose' and hidden deep in the forest to protect her from the clutches of the evil witch – was the Grail story for children.

Despite its corporate image, Disney still had a savvy, playful element among its employees, and their artists still amused themselves by inserting hidden symbolism in Disney products. Langdon would never forget one of his students bringing in a DVD of *The Lion King* and pausing the film to reveal a freeze-frame in which the word SEX was clearly visible, spelled out by floating dust particles over Simba's head. Although Langdon suspected this was more of a cartoonist's sophomoric prank than any kind of enlightened allusion to pagan human sexuality, he had learned not to underestimate Disney's grasp of symbolism. *The Little Mermaid* was a spellbinding tapestry of spiritual symbols so specifically goddess-related that they could not be coincidence.

When Langdon had first seen *The Little Mermaid*, he had actually gasped aloud when he noticed that the painting in Ariel's underwater home was none other than seventeenth-century artist Georges de la Tour's *The Penitent Magdalene* – a famous homage to the banished Mary Magdalene – fitting decor considering the movie turned out to be a ninety-minute collage of blatant symbolic references to the lost sanctity of Isis, Eve, Pisces the fish goddess and, repeatedly, Mary Magdalene. The Little Mermaid's name, Ariel, possessed powerful ties to the sacred feminine and, in the Book of Isaiah, was synonymous with 'the Holy City besieged'. Of course, the Little Mermaid's flowing red hair was certainly no coincidence either.

The clicking of Teabing's crutches approached in the hallway, his pace unusually brisk. When their host entered the study, his expression was stern.

'You'd better explain yourself, Robert,' he said coldly. 'You have not been honest with me.'

Chapter 62

'I'm being framed, Leigh,' Langdon said, trying to stay calm. *You know me. I wouldn't kill anyone.*

Teabing's tone did not soften. 'Robert, you're on television, for Christ's sake. Did you know you were wanted by the authorities?'

'Yes.'

'Then you abused my trust. I'm astonished you would put me at risk by coming here and asking me to ramble on about the Grail so you could hide out in my home.'

'I didn't kill anyone.'

'Jacques Saunière is dead, and the police say you did it.' Teabing looked saddened. 'Such a contributor to the arts . . .'

'Sir?' The manservant had appeared now, standing behind Teabing in the study doorway, his arms crossed. 'Shall I show them out?'

'Allow me.' Teabing hobbled across the study, unlocked a set of wide glass doors, and swung them open onto a side lawn. 'Please find your car, and leave.'

Sophie did not move. 'We have information about *the clef de voûte. The Priory keystone.*'

Teabing stared at her for several seconds and scoffed derisively. 'A desperate ploy. Robert knows how I've sought it.'

'She's telling the truth,' Langdon said. 'That's why we came to you tonight. To talk to you about the keystone.'

The manservant intervened now. 'Leave, or I shall call the authorities.'

'Leigh,' Langdon whispered, 'we know where it is.'

Teabing's balance seemed to falter a bit.

Rémy now marched stiffly across the room. 'Leave at once! Or I will forcibly—'

'Rémy!' Teabing spun, snapping at his servant. 'Excuse us for a moment.'

The servant's jaw dropped. 'Sir? I must protest. These people are—'

'I'll handle this.' Teabing pointed to the hallway.

After a moment of stunned silence, Rémy skulked out like a banished dog.

In the cool night breeze coming through the open doors, Teabing turned back to Sophie and Langdon, his expression still wary. 'This had better be good. What do you know of the keystone?'

In the thick brush outside Teabing's study, Silas clutched his pistol and gazed through the glass doors. Only moments ago, he had circled the house and seen Langdon and the woman talking in the large study. Before he could move in, a man on crutches entered, yelled at Langdon, threw open the doors, and demanded his guests leave. *Then the woman mentioned the keystone, and everything changed.* Shouts turned to whispers. Moods softened. And the glass doors were quickly closed.

Now, as he huddled in the shadows, Silas peered through the glass. *The keystone is somewhere inside the house.* Silas could feel it.

Staying in the shadows, he inched closer to the glass, eager to hear what was being said. He would give them five minutes. If they did not reveal where they had placed the keystone, Silas would have to enter and persuade them with force.

Inside the study, Langdon could sense their host's bewilderment.

'Grand Master?' Teabing choked, eyeing Sophie. 'Jacques Saunière?'

Sophie nodded, seeing the shock in his eyes.

'But you could not possibly know that!'

'Jacques Saunière was my grandfather.'

Teabing staggered back on his crutches, shooting a glance at Langdon, who nodded. Teabing turned back to Sophie. 'Miss Neveu, I am speechless. If this is true, then I am truly sorry for your loss. I should admit, for my research, I have kept lists of men in Paris whom I thought might be good candidates for involvement in the Priory. Jacques Saunière was on that list along with many others. But Grand Master, you say? It's hard to fathom.' Teabing was silent a moment and then shook his head. 'But it still makes no sense. Even if your grandfather were the Priory Grand Master and created the keystone himself, he would never tell you how to find it. The keystone reveals the pathway to the brotherhood's ultimate treasure. Granddaughter or not, you are not eligible to receive such knowledge.'

'Mr Saunière was dying when he passed on the information,' Langdon said. 'He had limited options.'

'He didn't *need* options,' Teabing argued. 'There exist three *sénéchaux* who also know the secret. That is the beauty of their system. One will rise to Grand Master and they will induct a new *sénéchal* and share the secret of the keystone.'

'I presume you didn't see the entire news broadcast,' Sophie said. 'In addition to my grandfather, *three* other prominent Parisians were murdered today. All in similar ways. All looked like they had been interrogated.'

Teabing's jaw fell. 'And you think they were . . .'

'The *sénéchaux*,' Langdon said.

'But how? A murderer could not possibly learn the identities of *all* four top members of the Priory of Sion! Look at *me*, I have been researching them for decades, and I can't even name *one* Priory member. It seems inconceivable that all three *sénéchaux* and the Grand Master could be discovered and killed in one day.'

'I doubt the information was gathered in a single day,' Sophie said. 'It sounds like a well-planned *décapiter*. It's a technique we use to fight organized crime syndicates. If DCPJ wants to move on a certain group, they will silently listen and watch for months, identify all the main players, and then move in and take them all at the same moment. Decapitation. With no leadership, the group falls into chaos and divulges other information. It's possible someone patiently watched the Priory and then attacked, hoping the top people would reveal the location of the keystone.'

Teabing looked unconvinced. 'But the brothers would never talk. They are sworn to secrecy. Even in the face of death.'

'Exactly,' Langdon said. 'Meaning, if they never divulged the secret, *and* they were killed . . .'

Teabing gasped. 'Then the location of the keystone would be lost for ever!'

'And with it,' Langdon said, 'the location of the Holy Grail.'

Teabing's body seemed to sway with the weight of Langdon's words. Then, as if too tired to stand another moment, he flopped in a chair and stared out the window.

Sophie walked over, her voice soft. 'Considering my grandfather's predicament, it seems possible that in total desperation he tried to pass the secret on to someone outside the brotherhood. Someone he thought he could trust. Someone in his family.'

Teabing was pale. 'But someone capable of such an attack . . . of discovering so much about the brotherhood . . .' He paused, radiating a new fear. 'It could only be one force. This kind of infiltration could only have come from the Priory's oldest enemy.'

Langdon glanced up. 'The Church.'

'Who else? Rome has been seeking the Grail for centuries.'

Sophie was sceptical. 'You think the *Church* killed my grandfather?'

Teabing replied, 'It would not be the first time in history the Church has killed to protect itself. The documents that accompany the Holy Grail are explosive, and the Church has wanted to destroy them for years.'

Langdon was having trouble buying Teabing's premise that the Church would blatantly murder people to obtain these documents. Having met the new Pope and many of the cardinals, Langdon knew they were deeply spiritual men who would never condone assassination. *Regardless of the stakes.*

Sophie seemed to be having similar thoughts. 'Isn't it possible that these Priory members were murdered by someone *outside* the Church? Someone who didn't understand what the Grail really is? The Cup of Christ, after all, would be quite an enticing treasure. Certainly treasure hunters have killed for less.'

'In my experience,' Teabing said, 'men go to far greater lengths to avoid what they fear than to obtain what they desire. I sense a desperation in this assault on the Priory.'

'Leigh,' Langdon said, 'the argument is paradoxical. Why would members of the Catholic clergy *murder*

Priory members in an effort to find and destroy documents they believe are false testimony anyway?'

Teabing chuckled. 'The ivory towers of Harvard have made you soft, Robert. Yes, the clergy in Rome are blessed with potent faith, and because of this, their beliefs can weather any storm, including documents that contradict everything they hold dear. But what about the rest of the world? What about those who are not blessed with absolute certainty? What about those who look at the cruelty in the world and say, where is God today? Those who look at Church scandals and ask, who are these men who claim to speak the truth about Christ and yet lie to cover up the sexual abuse of children by their own priests?' Teabing paused. 'What happens to those people, Robert, if persuasive scientific evidence comes out that the Church's version of the Christ story is inaccurate, and that the greatest story ever told is, in fact, the greatest story ever *sold*?'

Langdon did not respond.

'I'll tell you what happens if the documents get out,' Teabing said. 'The Vatican faces a crisis of faith unprecedented in its two-millennium history.'

After a long silence, Sophie said, 'But if it is the Church who is responsible for this attack, why would they act now? After all these years? The Priory keeps the Sangreal documents hidden. They pose no immediate threat to the Church.'

Teabing heaved an ominous sigh and glanced at Langdon. 'Robert, I assume you are familiar with the Priory's final charge?'

Langdon felt his breath catch at the thought. 'I am.'

'Miss Neveu,' Teabing said, 'the Church and the Priory have had a tacit understanding for years. That is, the Church does not attack the Priory, and the Priory keeps the Sangreal documents hidden.' He paused.

'However, part of the Priory history has always included a plan to unveil the secret. With the arrival of a specific date in history, the brotherhood plans to break the silence and carry out its ultimate triumph by unveiling the Sangreal documents to the world and shouting the true story of Jesus Christ from the mountaintops.'

Sophie stared at Teabing in silence. Finally, she too sat down. 'And you think that date is approaching? And the Church knows it?'

'A speculation,' Teabing said, 'but it would certainly provide the Church motivation for an all-out attack to find the documents before it was too late.'

Langdon had the uneasy feeling that Teabing was making good sense. 'Do you think the Church would actually be capable of uncovering hard evidence of the Priory's date?'

'Why not – if we're assuming the Church was able to uncover the identities of the Priory members, then certainly they could have learned of their plans. And even if they don't have the exact date, their superstitions may be getting the better of them.'

'Superstitions?' Sophie asked.

'In terms of prophecy,' Teabing said, 'we are currently in an epoch of enormous change. The millennium has recently passed, and with it has ended the two-thousand-year-long astrological Age of Pisces – the fish, which is also the sign of Jesus. As any astrological symbologist will tell you, the Piscean ideal believes that man must be *told* what to do by higher powers because man is incapable of thinking for himself. Hence it has been a time of fervent religion. Now, however, we are entering the Age of Aquarius – the water bearer – whose ideals claim that man will learn the *truth* and be able to think for himself. The ideological shift is enormous, and it is occurring right now.'

Langdon felt a shiver. Astrological prophecy never held much interest or credibility for him, but he knew there were those in the Church who followed it very closely. 'The Church calls this transitional period the End of Days.'

Sophie looked sceptical. 'As in the end of the world? The Apocalypse?'

'No.' Langdon replied. 'That's a common misconception. Many religions speak of the End of Days. It refers not to the end of the world, but rather the end of our current age – Pisces, which began at the time of Christ's birth, spanned two thousand years, and waned with the passing of the millennium. Now that we've passed into the Age of Aquarius, the End of Days has arrived.'

'Many Grail historians,' Teabing added, 'believe that *if* the Priory is indeed planning to release this truth, *this* point in history would be a symbolically apt time. Most Priory academics, myself included, anticipated the brotherhood's release would coincide precisely with the millennium. Obviously, it did not. Admittedly, the Roman calendar does not mesh perfectly with astrological markers, so there is some grey area in the prediction. Whether the Church now has inside information that an exact date is looming, or whether they are just getting nervous on account of astrological prophecy, I don't know. Anyway, it's immaterial. Either scenario explains how the Church might be motivated to launch a preemptive attack against the Priory.' Teabing frowned. 'And believe me, if the Church finds the Holy Grail, they will destroy it. The documents and the relics of the blessed Mary Magdalene as well.' His eyes grew heavy. 'Then, my dear, with the Sangreal documents gone, all evidence will be lost. The Church will have won their age-old war to rewrite history. The past will be erased for ever.'

Slowly, Sophie pulled the cruciform key from her sweater pocket and held it out to Teabing.

Teabing took the key and studied it. 'My goodness. The Priory seal. Where did you get this?'

'My grandfather gave it to me tonight before he died.'

Teabing ran his fingers across the cruciform. 'A key to a church?'

She drew a deep breath. 'This key provides access to the keystone.'

Teabing's head snapped up, his face wild with disbelief. 'Impossible! What church did I miss? I've searched every church in France!'

'It's not in a church,' Sophie said. 'It's in a Swiss depository bank.'

Teabing's look of excitement waned. 'The keystone is in a bank?'

'A vault,' Langdon offered.

'A *bank* vault?' Teabing shook his head violently. 'That's impossible. The keystone is supposed to be hidden beneath the sign of the Rose.'

'It is,' Langdon said. 'It was stored in a rosewood box inlaid with a five-petal Rose.'

Teabing looked thunderstruck. 'You've seen the keystone?'

Sophie nodded. 'We visited the bank.'

Teabing came over to them, his eyes wild with fear. 'My friends, we must do something. The keystone is in danger! We have a duty to protect it. What if there are other keys? Perhaps stolen from the murdered *sénéchaux*? If the Church can gain access to the bank as you have—'

'Then they will be too late,' Sophie said. 'We removed the keystone.'

'What! You removed the keystone from its hiding place?'

'Don't worry,' Langdon said. 'The keystone is well hidden.'

'*Extremely* well hidden, I hope!'

'Actually,' Langdon said, unable to hide his grin, 'that depends on how often you dust under your couch.'

The wind outside Château Villette had picked up, and Silas's robe danced in the breeze as he crouched near the window. Although he had been unable to hear much of the conversation, the word *keystone* had sifted through the glass on numerous occasions.

It is inside.

The Teacher's words were fresh in his mind. *Enter Château Villette. Take the keystone. Hurt no one.*

Now, Langdon and the others had adjourned suddenly to another room, extinguishing the study lights as they went. Feeling like a panther stalking prey, Silas crept to the glass doors. Finding them unlocked, he slipped inside and closed the doors silently behind him. He could hear muffled voices from another room. Silas pulled the pistol from his pocket, turned off the safety and inched down the hallway.

Chapter 63

Lieutenant Collet stood alone at the foot of Leigh Teabing's driveway and gazed up at the massive house. *Isolated. Dark. Good ground cover.* Collet watched his half-dozen agents spreading silently out along the length of the fence. They could be over it and have the house surrounded in a matter of minutes. Langdon could not have chosen a more ideal spot for Collet's men to make a surprise assault.

Collet was about to call Fache himself when at last his phone rang.

Fache sounded not nearly as pleased with the developments as Collet would have imagined. 'Why didn't someone tell me we had a lead on Langdon?'

'You were on a phone call and—'

'Where exactly are you, Lieutenant Collet?'

Collet gave him the address. 'The estate belongs to a British national named Teabing. Langdon drove a fair distance to get here, and the vehicle is inside the security gate, with no signs of forced entry, so chances are good that Langdon knows the occupant.'

'I'm coming out,' Fache said. 'Don't make a move. I'll handle this personally.'

Collet's jaw dropped. 'But Captain, you're twenty minutes away! We should act immediately. I have him staked out. I'm with eight men total. Four of us have field rifles and the others have sidearms.'

'Wait for me.'

'Captain, what if Langdon has a hostage in there? What if he sees us and decides to leave on foot? We need to move *now*! My men are in position and ready to go.'

'Lieutenant Collet, you will wait for me to arrive before taking action. That is an order.' Fache hung up.

Stunned, Lieutenant Collet switched off his phone. *Why the hell is Fache asking me to wait?* Collet knew the answer. Fache, though famous for his instinct, was notorious for his pride. *Fache wants credit for the arrest.* After putting the American's face all over the television, Fache wanted to be sure his own face got equal time. Collet's job was simply to hold down the fort until the boss showed up to save the day.

As he stood there, Collet flashed on a second possible explanation for this delay. *Damage control.* In law enforcement, hesitating to arrest a fugitive only occurred when uncertainty had arisen regarding the suspect's guilt. *Is Fache having second thoughts that Langdon is the right man?* The thought was frightening. Captain Fache had gone out on a limb tonight to arrest Robert Langdon – *surveillance cachée*, Interpol, and now television. Not even the great Bezu Fache would survive the political fallout if he had mistakenly splashed a prominent American's face all over French television, claiming he was a murderer. If Fache now realized he'd made a mistake, then it made perfect sense that he would tell Collet not to make a move. The last thing Fache needed was for Collet to storm an innocent Brit's private estate and take Langdon at gunpoint.

Moreover, Collet realized, if Langdon were innocent, it explained one of this case's strangest paradoxes: Why had Sophie Neveu, the *granddaughter* of the victim, helped the alleged killer escape? Unless Sophie knew Langdon was falsely charged. Fache had posited all kinds of explanations tonight to explain Sophie's odd behaviour, including that Sophie, as

Saunière's sole heir, had persuaded her secret lover Robert Langdon to kill off Saunière for the inheritance money. Saunière, if he had suspected this, might have left the police the message *P.S. Find Robert Langdon*. Collet was fairly certain something else was going on here. Sophie Neveu seemed of far too solid a character to be mixed up in something that sordid.

'Lieutenant?' One of the field agents came running over. 'We found a car.'

Collet followed the agent about fifty yards past the driveway. The agent pointed to a wide shoulder on the opposite side of the road. There, parked in the brush, almost out of sight, was a black Audi. It had rental plates. Collet felt the hood. Still warm. Hot even.

'That must be how Langdon got here,' Collet said. 'Call the rental company. Find out if it's stolen.'

'Yes, sir.'

Another agent waved Collet back over in the direction of the fence. 'Lieutenant, have a look at this.' He handed Collet a pair of night vision binoculars. 'The grove of trees near the top of the driveway.'

Collet aimed the binoculars up the hill and adjusted the image intensifier dials. Slowly, the greenish shapes came into focus. He located the curve of the driveway and slowly followed it up, reaching the grove of trees. All he could do was stare. There, shrouded in the greenery, was an armoured truck. A truck identical to the one Collet had permitted to leave the Depository Bank of Zurich earlier tonight. He prayed this was some kind of bizarre coincidence, but he knew it could not be.

'It seems obvious,' the agent said, 'that this truck is how Langdon and Neveu got away from the bank.'

Collet was speechless. He thought of the armoured

truck driver he had stopped at the roadblock. The Rolex. His impatience to leave. *I never checked the cargo hold.*

Incredulous, Collet realized that someone in the bank had actually lied to DCPJ about Langdon and Sophie's whereabouts and then helped them escape. *But who? And why?* Collet wondered if maybe *this* were the reason Fache had told him not to take action yet. Maybe Fache realized there were more people involved tonight than just Langdon and Sophie. *And if Langdon and Neveu arrived in the armoured truck, then who drove the Audi?*

Hundreds of miles to the south, a chartered Beechcraft Baron 58 raced northward over the Tyrrhenian Sea. Despite calm skies, Bishop Aringarosa clutched an airsickness bag, certain he could be ill at any moment. His conversation with Paris had not at all been what he had imagined.

Alone in the small cabin, Aringarosa twisted the gold ring on his finger and tried to ease his overwhelming sense of fear and desperation. *Everything in Paris has gone terribly wrong.* Closing his eyes, Aringarosa said a prayer that Bezu Fache would have the means to fix it.

Chapter 64

Teabing sat on the divan, cradling the wooden box on his lap and admiring the lid's intricate inlaid Rose. *Tonight has become the strangest and most magical night of my life.*

'Lift the lid,' Sophie whispered, standing over him, beside Langdon.

Teabing smiled. *Do not rush me.* Having spent over a decade searching for this keystone, he wanted to savour every millisecond of this moment. He ran a palm across the wooden lid, feeling the texture of the inlaid flower.

'The Rose,' he whispered. *The Rose is Magdalene is the Holy Grail. The Rose is the compass that guides the way.* Teabing felt foolish. For years he had travelled to cathedrals and churches all over France, paying for special access, examining hundreds of archways beneath rose windows, searching for an encrypted keystone. *La clef de voûte – a stone key beneath the sign of the Rose.*

Teabing slowly unlatched the lid and raised it.

As his eyes finally gazed upon the contents, he knew in an instant it could only be the keystone. He was staring at a stone cylinder, crafted of inter-connecting lettered dials. The device seemed surprisingly familiar to him.

'Designed from Da Vinci's diaries,' Sophie said. 'My grandfather made them as a hobby.'

Of course, Teabing realized. He had seen the sketches and blueprints. *The key to finding the Holy Grail lies inside this stone.* Teabing lifted the heavy cryptex from the box, holding it gently. Although he had no idea how to open the cylinder, he sensed his own destiny lay inside. In moments of failure, Teabing had questioned whether his life's quest would ever be rewarded. Now those doubts were gone for ever. He could hear the ancient words . . . the foundation of the Grail legend:

Vous ne trouvez pas le Saint-Graal, c'est le Saint-Graal qui vous trouve.

You do not find the Grail, the Grail finds you.

And tonight, incredibly, the key to finding the Holy Grail had walked right through his front door.

While Sophie and Teabing sat with the cryptex and talked about the vinegar, the dials and what the password might be, Langdon carried the rosewood box across the room to a well-lit table to get a better look at it. Something Teabing had just said was now running through Langdon's mind.

The key to the Grail is hidden beneath the sign of the Rose.

Langdon held the wooden box up to the light and examined the inlaid symbol of the Rose. Although his familiarity with art did not include woodworking or inlaid furniture, he had just recalled the famous tiled ceiling of the Spanish monastery outside of Madrid, where, three centuries after its construction, the ceiling tiles began to fall out, revealing sacred texts scrawled by monks on the plaster beneath.

Langdon looked again at the Rose.

Beneath the Rose.

Sub Rosa.

Secret.

A bump in the hallway behind him made Langdon turn. He saw nothing but shadows. Teabing's manservant most likely had passed through. Langdon turned back to the box. He ran his finger over the smooth edge of the inlay, wondering if he could pry the Rose out, but the craftsmanship was perfect. He doubted even a razor blade could fit in between the inlaid Rose and the carefully carved depression into which it was seated.

Opening the box, he examined the inside of the lid. It was smooth. As he shifted its position, though, the light caught what appeared to be a small hole on the underside of the lid, positioned in the exact centre. Langdon closed the lid and examined the inlaid symbol from the top. No hole.

It doesn't pass through.

Setting the box on the table, he looked around the room and spied a stack of papers with a paper clip on it. Borrowing the clip, he returned to the box, opened it, and studied the hole again. Carefully, he unbent the paper clip and inserted one end into the hole. He gave a gentle push. It took almost no effort. He heard something clatter quietly onto the table. Langdon closed the lid to look. It was a small piece of wood, like a puzzle piece. The wooden Rose had popped out of the lid and fallen onto the desk.

Speechless, Langdon stared at the bare spot on the lid where the Rose had been. There, engraved in the wood, written in an immaculate hand, were four lines of text in a language he had never seen.

The characters look vaguely Semitic, Langdon thought to himself, *and yet I don't recognize the language!*

A sudden movement behind him caught his attention. Out of nowhere, a crushing blow to the head knocked Langdon to his knees.

As he fell, he thought for a moment he saw a pale ghost hovering over him, clutching a gun. Then everything went black.

Chapter 65

Sophie Neveu, despite working in law enforcement, had never found herself at gunpoint until tonight. Almost inconceivably, the gun into which she was now staring was clutched in the pale hand of an enormous albino with long white hair. He looked at her with red eyes that radiated a frightening, disembodied quality. Dressed in a wool robe with a rope tie, he resembled a medieval cleric. Sophie could not imagine who he was, and yet she was feeling a sudden newfound respect for Teabing's suspicions that the Church was behind this.

'You know what I have come for,' the monk said, his voice hollow.

Sophie and Teabing were seated on the divan, arms raised as their attacker had commanded. Langdon lay groaning on the floor. The monk's eyes fell immediately to the keystone on Teabing's lap.

Teabing's tone was defiant. 'You will not be able to open it.'

'My Teacher is very wise,' the monk replied, inching closer, the gun shifting between Teabing and Sophie.

Sophie wondered where Teabing's manservant was. *Didn't he hear Robert fall?*

'Who is your teacher?' Teabing asked. 'Perhaps we can make a financial arrangement.'

'The Grail is priceless.' He moved closer.

'You're bleeding,' Teabing noted calmly, nodding to the monk's right ankle where a trickle of blood had run down his leg. 'And you're limping.'

'As do you,' the monk replied, motioning to the metal crutches propped beside Teabing. 'Now, hand me the keystone.'

'You know of the keystone?' Teabing said, sounding surprised.

'Never mind what I know. Stand up slowly, and give it to me.'

'Standing is difficult for me.'

'Precisely. I would prefer nobody attempt any quick moves.'

Teabing slipped his right hand through one of his crutches and grasped the keystone in his left. Lurching to his feet, he stood erect, palming the heavy cylinder in his left hand and leaning unsteadily on his crutch with his right.

The monk closed to within a few feet, keeping the gun aimed directly at Teabing's head. Sophie watched, feeling helpless as the monk reached out to take the cylinder.

'You will not succeed,' Teabing said. 'Only the worthy can unlock this stone.'

God alone judges the worthy, Silas thought.

'It's quite heavy,' the man on crutches said, his arm wavering now. 'If you don't take it soon, I'm afraid I shall drop it!' He swayed perilously.

Silas stepped quickly forward to take the stone, and as he did, the man on crutches lost his balance. The crutch slid out from under him, and he began to topple sideways to his right. *No!* Silas lunged to save the stone, lowering his weapon in the process. But the keystone was moving away from him now. As the man fell to his right, his left hand swung backward, and the cylinder tumbled from his palm onto the couch. At the same instant, the metal crutch that had been sliding out from under the man seemed to accelerate, cutting a wide arc through the air toward Silas's leg.

Splinters of pain tore up Silas's body as the crutch made perfect contact with his *cilice*, crushing the barbs into his already raw flesh. Buckling, Silas crumpled to his knees, causing the belt to cut deeper still. The pistol discharged with a deafening roar, the bullet burying itself harmlessly in the floorboards as Silas fell. Before he could raise the gun and fire again, the woman's foot caught him square beneath the jaw.

At the bottom of the driveway, Collet heard the gunshot. The muffled pop sent panic through his veins. With Fache on the way, Collet had already relinquished any hopes of claiming personal credit for finding Langdon tonight. But Collet would be damned if Fache's ego landed him in front of a Ministerial Review Board for negligent police procedure.

A weapon was discharged inside a private home! And you waited at the bottom of the driveway?

Collet knew the opportunity for a stealth approach had long since passed. He also knew if he stood idly by for another second, his entire career would be history by morning. Eyeing the estate's iron gate, he made his decision.

'Tie on, and pull it down.'

In the distant recesses of his groggy mind, Robert Langdon had heard the gunshot. He'd also heard a scream of pain. His own? A jackhammer was boring a hole into the back of his cranium. Somewhere nearby, people were talking.

'Where the devil were you?' Teabing was yelling.

The manservant hurried in. 'What happened? Oh my God! Who is that? I'll call the police!'

'Bloody hell! Don't call the police. Make yourself useful and get us something with which to restrain this monster.'

'And some ice!' Sophie called after him.

Langdon drifted out again. More voices. Movement. Now he was seated on the divan. Sophie was holding an ice pack to his head. His skull ached. As Langdon's vision finally began to clear, he found himself staring at a body on the floor. *Am I hallucinating?* The massive body of an albino monk lay bound and gagged with duct tape. His chin was split open, and the robe over his right thigh was soaked with blood. He too appeared to be just now coming to.

Langdon turned to Sophie. 'Who is that? What . . . happened?'

Teabing hobbled over. 'You were rescued by a knight brandishing an Excalibur made by Acme Orthopaedic.'

Huh? Langdon tried to sit up.

Sophie's touch was shaken but tender. 'Just give yourself a minute, Robert.'

'I fear,' Teabing said, 'that I've just demonstrated for your lady friend the unfortunate benefit of my condition. It seems everyone underestimates you.'

From his seat on the divan, Langdon gazed down at the monk and tried to imagine what had happened.

'He was wearing a *cilice*,' Teabing explained.

'A what?'

Teabing pointed to a bloody strip of barbed leather that lay on the floor. 'A discipline belt. He wore it on his thigh. I took careful aim.'

Langdon rubbed his head. He knew of discipline belts. 'But how . . . did you know?'

Teabing grinned. 'Christianity is my field of study, Robert, and there are certain sects who wear their hearts on their sleeves.' He pointed his crutch at the blood soaking through the monk's cloak. 'As it were.'

'Opus Dei,' Langdon whispered, recalling recent media coverage of several prominent Boston businessmen who were members of Opus Dei. Apprehensive coworkers had falsely and publicly accused the men of wearing *cilice* belts beneath their three-piece suits. In fact, the three men did no such thing. Like many members of Opus Dei, these businessmen were at the 'supernumerary' stage and practised no corporal mortification at all. They were devout Catholics, caring fathers to their children, and deeply dedicated members of the community. Not surprisingly, the media spotlighted their spiritual commitment only briefly before moving on to the shock value of the sect's more stringent 'numerary' members . . . members like the monk now lying on the floor before Langdon.

Teabing was looking closely at the bloody belt. 'But why would Opus Dei be trying to find the Holy Grail?'

Langdon was too groggy to consider it.

'Robert,' Sophie said, walking to the wooden box. 'What's this?' She was holding the small Rose inlay he had removed from the lid.

'It covered an engraving on the box. I think the text might tell us how to open the keystone.'

Before Sophie and Teabing could respond, a sea of blue police lights and sirens erupted at the bottom of the hill and began snaking up the half-mile driveway.

Teabing frowned. 'My friends, it seems we have a decision to make. And we'd better make it fast.'

Chapter 66

Collet and his agents burst through the front door of Sir Leigh Teabing's estate with their guns drawn. Fanning out, they began searching all the rooms on the first level. They found a bullet hole in the drawing room floor, signs of a struggle, a small amount of blood, a strange, barbed leather belt and a partially used roll of duct tape. The entire level seemed deserted.

Just as Collet was about to divide his men to search the basement and grounds behind the house, he heard voices on the level above them.

'They're upstairs!'

Rushing up the wide staircase, Collet and his men moved room by room through the huge home, securing darkened bedrooms and hallways as they closed in on the sounds of voices. The sound seemed to be coming from the last bedroom on an exceptionally long hallway. The agents inched down the corridor, sealing off alternate exits.

As they neared the final bedroom, Collet could see the door was wide open. The voices had stopped suddenly, and had been replaced by an odd rumbling, like an engine.

Sidearm raised, Collet gave the signal. Reaching silently around the door frame, he found the light switch and flicked it on. Spinning into the room with men pouring in after him, Collet shouted and aimed his weapon at . . . nothing.

An empty guest bedroom. Pristine.

The rumbling sounds of an automobile engine poured from a black electronic panel on the wall beside the bed. Collet had seen these elsewhere in the house. Some kind of intercom system. He raced over. The panel had about a dozen labelled buttons:

STUDY . . . KITCHEN . . . LAUNDRY . . .
CELLAR . . .

So where the hell do I hear a car?

MASTER BEDROOM . . . SUN ROOM . . . BARN . . .
LIBRARY . . .

Barn! Collet was downstairs in seconds, running toward the back door, grabbing one of his agents on the way. The men crossed the rear lawn and arrived breathless at the front of a weathered grey barn. Even before they entered, Collet could hear the fading sounds of a car engine. He drew his weapon, rushed in, and flicked on the lights.

The right side of the barn was a rudimentary workshop – lawnmowers, automotive tools, gardening supplies. A familiar intercom panel hung on the wall nearby. One of its buttons was flipped down, transmitting.

GUEST BEDROOM II.

Collet wheeled, anger brimming. *They lured us upstairs with the intercom!* Searching the other side of the barn, he found a long line of horse stalls. No horses. Apparently the owner preferred a different kind of horsepower; the stalls had been converted into an impressive automotive parking facility. The collection was astonishing – a black Ferrari, a pristine

374

Rolls-Royce, an antique Aston Martin sports coupé, a vintage Porsche 356.

The last stall was empty.

Collet ran over and saw oil stains on the stall floor. *They can't get off the compound.* The driveway and gate were barricaded with two patrol cars to prevent this very situation.

'Sir?' The agent pointed down the length of the stalls.

The barn's rear slider was wide open, giving way to a dark, muddy slope of rugged fields that stretched out into the night behind the barn. Collet ran to the door, trying to see out into the darkness. All he could make out was the faint shadow of a forest in the distance. No headlights. This wooded valley was probably crisscrossed by dozens of unmapped fire roads and hunting trails, but Collet was confident his quarry would never make the woods. 'Get some men spread out down there. They're probably already stuck somewhere nearby. These fancy sports cars can't handle terrain.'

'Um, sir?' The agent pointed to a nearby pegboard on which hung several sets of keys. The labels above the keys bore familiar names.

DAIMLER . . . ROLLS-ROYCE . . . ASTON MARTIN
. . . PORSCHE . . .

The last peg was empty.

When Collet read the label above the empty peg, he knew he was in trouble.

Chapter 67

The Range Rover was Java Black Pearl, four-wheel drive, standard transmission, with high-strength polypropylene lamps, rear light cluster fittings and the steering wheel on the right.

Langdon was pleased he was not driving.

Teabing's manservant Rémy, on orders from his master, was doing an impressive job of manoeuvring the vehicle across the moonlit fields behind Château Villette. With no headlights, he had crossed an open knoll and was now descending a long slope, moving farther away from the estate. He seemed to be heading toward a jagged silhouette of wooded land in the distance.

Langdon, cradling the keystone, turned in the passenger seat and eyed Teabing and Sophie in the back seat.

'How's your head, Robert?' Sophie asked, sounding concerned.

Langdon forced a pained smile. 'Better, thanks.' It was killing him.

Beside her, Teabing glanced over his shoulder at the bound and gagged monk lying in the cramped luggage area behind the back seat. Teabing had the monk's gun on his lap and looked like an old photo of a British safari chap posing over his kill.

'So glad you popped in this evening, Robert,' Teabing said, grinning as if he were having fun for the first time in years.

'Sorry to get you involved in this, Leigh.'

'Oh, please, I've waited my entire life to be involved.' Teabing looked past Langdon out the windshield at the shadow of a long hedgerow. He tapped Rémy on the shoulder from behind. 'Remember, no brake lights. Use the emergency brake if you need it. I want to get into the woods a bit. No reason to risk them seeing us from the house.'

Rémy coasted to a crawl and guided the Range Rover through an opening in the hedge. As the vehicle lurched onto an overgrown pathway, almost immediately the trees overhead blotted out the moonlight.

I can't see a thing, Langdon thought, straining to distinguish any shapes at all in front of them. It was pitch black. Branches rubbed against the left side of the vehicle, and Rémy corrected in the other direction. Keeping the wheel more or less straight now, he inched ahead about thirty yards.

'You're doing beautifully, Rémy,' Teabing said. 'That should be far enough. Robert, if you could press that little blue button just below the vent there. See it?'

Langdon found the button and pressed it.

A muted yellow glow fanned out across the path in front of them, revealing thick underbrush on either side of the pathway. *Fog lights*, Langdon realized. They gave off just enough light to keep them on the path, and yet they were deep enough into the woods now that the lights would not give them away.

'Well, Rémy,' Teabing chimed happily. 'The lights are on. Our lives are in your hands.'

'Where are we going?' Sophie asked.

'This trail continues about three kilometres into the forest,' Teabing said. 'Cutting across the estate and then arching north. Provided we don't hit any standing water or fallen trees, we shall emerge unscathed on the shoulder of highway five.'

Unscathed. Langdon's head begged to differ. He

turned his eyes down to his own lap, where the keystone was safely stowed in its wooden box. The inlaid Rose on the lid was back in place, and although his head felt muddled, Langdon was eager to remove the inlay again and examine the engraving beneath more closely. He unlatched the lid and began to raise it when Teabing laid a hand on his shoulder from behind.

'Patience, Robert,' Teabing said. 'It's bumpy and dark. God save us if we break anything. If you didn't recognize the language in the light, you won't do any better in the dark. Let's focus on getting away in one piece, shall we? There will be time for that very soon.'

Langdon knew Teabing was right. With a nod, he relatched the box.

The monk in the back was moaning now, struggling against his trusses. Suddenly, he began kicking wildly.

Teabing spun around and aimed the pistol over the seat. 'I can't imagine your complaint, sir. You trespassed in my home and planted a nasty welt on the skull of a dear friend. I would be well within my rights to shoot you right now and leave you to rot in the woods.'

The monk fell silent.

'Are you sure we should have brought him?' Langdon asked.

'Bloody well positive!' Teabing exclaimed. 'You're wanted for murder, Robert. This scoundrel is your ticket to freedom. The police apparently want you badly enough to have tailed you to my home.'

'My fault,' Sophie said. 'The armoured car probably had a transmitter.'

'Not the point,' Teabing said. 'I'm not surprised the *police* found you, but I *am* surprised that this Opus Dei character found you. From all you've told me, I can't imagine how this man could have tailed you to my home unless he had a contact either within the Judicial Police or within the Zurich Depository.'

Langdon considered it. Bezu Fache certainly seemed intent on finding a scapegoat for tonight's murders. And Vernet had turned on them rather suddenly, although considering Langdon was being charged with four murders, the banker's change of heart seemed understandable.

'This monk is not working alone, Robert,' Teabing said, 'and until you learn *who* is behind all this, you both are in danger. The good news, my friend, is that you are now in the position of power. This monster behind me holds that information, and whoever is pulling his strings has got to be quite nervous right now.'

Rémy was picking up speed, getting comfortable with the trail. They splashed through some water, climbed a small rise, and began descending again.

'Robert, could you be so kind as to hand me that phone?' Teabing pointed to the car phone on the dash. Langdon handed it back, and Teabing dialled a number. He waited for a very long time before someone answered. 'Richard? Did I wake you? Of course, I did. Silly question. I'm sorry. I have a small problem. I'm feeling a bit off. Rémy and I need to pop up to the Isles for my treatments. Well, right away, actually. Sorry for the short notice. Can you have Elizabeth ready in about twenty minutes? I know, do the best you can. See you shortly.' He hung up.

'Elizabeth?' Langdon said.

'My plane. She cost me a Queen's ransom.'

Langdon turned full around and looked at him.

'What?' Teabing demanded. 'You two can't expect to stay in France with the entire Judicial Police after you. London will be much safer.'

Sophie had turned to Teabing as well. 'You think we should leave the country?'

'My friends, I am far more influential in the civilized world than here in France. Furthermore, the Grail is believed to be in Great Britain. If we unlock the keystone, I am certain we will discover a map that indicates we have moved in the proper direction.'

'You're running a big risk,' Sophie said, 'by helping us. You won't make any friends with the French police.'

Teabing gave a wave of disgust. 'I am finished with France. I moved here to find the keystone. That work is now done. I shan't care if I ever again see Château Villette.'

Sophie sounded uncertain. 'How will we get through airport security?'

Teabing chuckled. 'I fly from Le Bourget – an executive airfield not far from here. French doctors make me nervous, so every fortnight, I fly north to take my treatments in England. I pay for certain special privileges at both ends. Once we're airborne, you can make a decision as to whether or not you'd like someone from the US Embassy to meet us.'

Langdon suddenly didn't want anything to do with the embassy. All he could think of was the keystone, the inscription and whether it would all lead to the Grail. He wondered if Teabing was right about Britain. Admittedly most modern legends placed the Grail somewhere in the United Kingdom. Even King Arthur's mythical, Grail-rich Isle of Avalon was now believed to be none other than Glastonbury, England. Wherever the Grail lay, Langdon never imagined he would actually be looking for it. *The Sangreal documents. The true history of Jesus Christ. The tomb of Mary Magdalene.* He suddenly felt as if he were living in some kind of limbo tonight . . . a bubble where the real world could not reach him.

'Sir?' Rémy said. 'Are you truly thinking of returning to England for good?'

'Rémy, you needn't worry,' Teabing assured. 'Just because I am returning to the Queen's realm does not mean I intend to subject my palate to bangers and mash for the rest of my days. I expect you will join me there permanently. I'm planning to buy a splendid villa in Devon, and we'll have all your things shipped out immediately. An adventure, Rémy. I say, an adventure!'

Langdon had to smile. As Teabing railed on about his plans for a triumphant return to Britain, Langdon felt himself caught up in the man's infectious enthusiasm.

Gazing absently out the window, Langdon watched the woods passing by, ghostly pale in the yellow blush of the fog lights. The side mirror was tipped inward, brushed askew by branches, and Langdon saw the reflection of Sophie sitting quietly in the back seat. He watched her for a long while and felt an unexpected upwelling of contentment. Despite his troubles tonight, Langdon was thankful to have landed in such good company.

After several minutes, as if suddenly sensing his eyes on her, Sophie leaned forward and put her hands on his shoulders, giving him a quick rub. 'You okay?'

'Yeah,' Langdon said. 'Somehow.'

Sophie sat back in her seat, and Langdon saw a quiet smile cross her lips. He realized that he too was now grinning.

Wedged in the back of the Range Rover, Silas could barely breathe. His arms were wrenched backward and heavily lashed to his ankles with kitchen twine and duct tape. Every bump in the road sent pain shooting through his twisted shoulders. At least his captors had removed the *cilice*. Unable to inhale through the strip of tape over his mouth, he could only breathe through his nostrils, which were slowly clogging up due to the dusty rear cargo area into which he had been crammed. He began coughing.

'I think he's choking,' the French driver said, sounding concerned.

The British man who had struck Silas with his crutch now turned and peered over the seat, frowning coldly at Silas. 'Fortunately for you, we British judge man's civility not by his compassion for his friends, but by his compassion for his enemies.' The Brit reached down and grabbed the duct tape on Silas's mouth. In one fast motion, he tore it off.

Silas felt as if his lips had just caught fire, but the air pouring into his lungs was sent from God.

'Whom do you work for?' the British man demanded.

'I do the work of God,' Silas spat back through the pain in his jaw where the woman had kicked him.

'You belong to Opus Dei,' the man said. It was not a question.

'You know nothing of who I am.'

'Why does Opus Dei want the keystone?'

Silas had no intention of answering. The keystone was the link to the Holy Grail, and the Holy Grail was the key to protecting the faith.

I do the work of God. The Way is in peril.

Now, in the Range Rover, struggling against his bonds, Silas feared he had failed the Teacher and the bishop for ever. He had no way even to contact them and tell them the terrible turn of events. *My captors have the keystone! They will reach the Grail before we do!* In the stifling darkness, Silas prayed. He let the pain of his body fuel his supplications.

A miracle, Lord. I need a miracle. Silas had no way of knowing that hours from now, he would get one.

'Robert?' Sophie was still watching him. 'A funny look just crossed your face.'

Langdon glanced back at her, realizing his jaw was firmly set and his heart was racing. An incredible notion had just occurred to him. *Could it really be that simple an explanation?* 'I need to use your cell phone, Sophie.'

'Now?'

'I think I just figured something out.'

'What?'

'I'll tell you in a minute. I need your phone.'

Sophie looked wary. 'I doubt Fache is tracing, but keep it under a minute just in case.' She gave him her phone.

'How do I dial the States?'

'You need to reverse the charges. My service doesn't cover transatlantic.'

Langdon dialled zero, knowing that the next sixty seconds might answer a question that had been puzzling him all night.

Chapter 68

New York editor Jonas Faukman had just climbed into bed for the night when the telephone rang. *A little late for callers*, he grumbled, picking up the receiver.

An operator's voice asked him, 'Will you accept charges for a collect call from Robert Langdon?'

Puzzled, Jonas turned on the light. 'Uh . . . sure, okay.'

The line clicked. 'Jonas?'

'Robert? You wake me up *and* you charge me for it?'

'Jonas, forgive me,' Langdon said. 'I'll keep this very short. I really need to know. The manuscript I gave you. Have you—'

'Robert, I'm sorry, I know I said I'd send the edits out to you this week, but I'm swamped. Next Monday. I promise.'

'I'm not worried about the edits. I need to know if you sent any copies out for blurbs without telling me?'

Faukman hesitated. Langdon's newest manuscript – an exploration of the history of goddess worship – included several sections about Mary Magdalene that were going to raise some eyebrows. Although the material was well documented and had been covered by others, Faukman had no intention of printing Advance Reading Copies of Langdon's book without at least a few endorsements from serious historians and art luminaries. Jonas had chosen ten big names in the art world and sent them all sections of the manuscript along with a polite letter asking if they would be willing to write a short endorsement for the jacket. In Faukman's experience, most people jumped at the opportunity to see their name in print.

'Jonas?' Langdon pressed. 'You sent out my manuscript, didn't you?'

Faukman frowned, sensing Langdon was not happy about it. 'The manuscript was clean, Robert, and I wanted to surprise you with some terrific blurbs.'

A pause. 'Did you send one to the curator of the Paris Louvre?'

'What do you think? Your manuscript referenced his Louvre collection several times, his books are in your bibliography, and the guy has some serious clout for foreign sales. Saunière was a no-brainer.'

The silence on the other end lasted a long time. 'When did you send it?'

'About a month ago. I also mentioned you would be in Paris soon and suggested you two chat. Did he ever call you to meet?' Faukman paused, rubbing his eyes. 'Hold on, aren't you supposed to *be* in Paris this week?'

'I *am* in Paris.'

Faukman sat upright. 'You called me collect from *Paris*?'

'Take it out of my royalties, Jonas. Did you ever hear back from Saunière? Did he like the manuscript?'

'I don't know. I haven't yet heard from him.'

'Well, don't hold your breath. I've got to run, but this explains a lot. Thanks.'

'Robert—'

But Langdon was gone.

Faukman hung up the phone, shaking his head in disbelief. *Authors*, he thought. *Even the sane ones are nuts.*

* * *

Inside the Range Rover, Leigh Teabing let out a guffaw. 'Robert, you're saying you wrote a manuscript that delves into a secret society, and your editor *sent* a copy to that secret society?'

Langdon slumped. 'Evidently.'

'A cruel coincidence, my friend.'

Coincidence has nothing to do with it, Langdon knew. Asking Jacques Saunière to endorse a manuscript on goddess worship was as obvious as asking Tiger Woods to endorse a book on golf. Moreover, it was virtually guaranteed that any book on goddess worship would have to mention the Priory of Sion.

'Here's the million-dollar question,' Teabing said, still chuckling. 'Was your position on the Priory favourable or unfavourable?'

Langdon could hear Teabing's true meaning loud and clear. Many historians questioned why the Priory was still keeping the Sangreal documents hidden. Some felt the information should have been shared with the world long ago. 'I took no position on the Priory's actions.'

'You mean lack thereof.'

Langdon shrugged. Teabing was apparently on the side of making the documents public. 'I simply provided history on the brotherhood and described them as a modern goddess worship society, keepers of the Grail and guardians of ancient documents.'

Sophie looked at him. 'Did you mention the keystone?'

Langdon winced. He had. Numerous times. 'I talked about the supposed keystone as an example of the lengths to which the Priory would go to protect the Sangreal documents.'

Sophie looked amazed. 'I guess that explains *P.S. Find Robert Langdon.*'

Langdon sensed it was actually something *else* in the manuscript that had piqued Saunière's interest, but that topic was something he would discuss with Sophie when they were alone.

'So,' Sophie said, 'you lied to Captain Fache.'

'What?' Langdon demanded.

'You told him you had never corresponded with my grandfather.'

'I didn't! My editor sent him a manuscript.'

'Think about it, Robert. If Captain Fache didn't find the envelope in which your editor sent the manuscript, he would have to conclude that *you* sent it.' She paused. 'Or worse, that you hand-delivered it and lied about it.'

When the Range Rover arrived at Le Bourget Airfield, Rémy drove to a small hangar at the far end of the airstrip. As they approached, a tousled man in wrinkled khakis hurried from the hangar, waved, and slid open the enormous corrugated metal door to reveal a sleek white jet within.

Langdon stared at the glistening fuselage. '*That's* Elizabeth?'

Teabing grinned. 'Beats the bloody Chunnel.'

The man in khakis hurried toward them, squinting into the headlights. 'Almost ready, sir,' he called in a British accent. 'My apologies for the delay, but you took me by surprise and–' He stopped short as the group unloaded. He looked at Sophie and Langdon, and then Teabing.

Teabing said, 'My associates and I have urgent business in London. We've no time to waste. Please prepare to depart immediately.' As he spoke, Teabing took the pistol out of the vehicle and handed it to Langdon.

The pilot's eyes bulged at the sight of the weapon. He walked over to Teabing and whispered, 'Sir, my humble apologies, but my diplomatic flight allowance provides only for you and your manservant. I cannot take your guests.'

'Richard,' Teabing said, smiling warmly, 'two thousand pounds sterling and that loaded gun say you *can* take my guests.' He motioned to the Range Rover. 'And the unfortunate fellow in the back.'

Chapter 69

The Hawker 731's twin Garrett TFE-731 engines thundered, powering the plane skyward with gut-wrenching force. Outside the window, Le Bourget Airfield dropped away with startling speed.

I'm fleeing the country, Sophie thought, her body forced back into the leather seat. Until this moment, she had believed her game of cat and mouse with Fache would be somehow justifiable to the Ministry of Defence. *I was attempting to protect an innocent man. I was trying to fulfil my grandfather's dying wishes.* That window of opportunity, Sophie knew, had just closed. She was leaving the country, without documentation, accompanying a wanted man and transporting a bound hostage. If a 'line of reason' had ever existed, she had just crossed it. *At almost the speed of sound.*

Sophie was seated with Langdon and Teabing near the front of the cabin – the *Fan Jet Executive Elite Design*, according to the gold medallion on the door. Their plush swivel chairs were bolted to tracks on the floor and could be repositioned and locked around a rectangular hardwood table. A mini-boardroom. The dignified surroundings, however, did little to camouflage the less than dignified state of affairs in the rear of the plane where, in a separate seating area near the toilet, Teabing's manservant Rémy sat with the pistol in hand, begrudgingly carrying out Teabing's orders to stand guard over the bloody monk who lay trussed at his feet like a piece of luggage.

'Before we turn our attention to the keystone,'

Teabing said, 'I was wondering if you would permit me a few words.' He sounded apprehensive, like a father about to give the birds-and-the-bees lecture to his children. 'My friends, I realize I am but a guest on this journey, and I am honoured as such. And yet, as someone who has spent his life in search of the Grail, I feel it is my duty to warn you that you are about to step onto a path from which there is no return, regardless of the dangers involved.' He turned to Sophie. 'Miss Neveu, your grandfather gave you this cryptex in hopes you would keep the secret of the Holy Grail alive.'

'Yes.'

'Understandably, you feel obliged to follow the trail wherever it leads.'

Sophie nodded, although she felt a second motivation still burning within her. *The truth about my family.* Despite Langdon's assurances that the keystone had nothing to do with her past, Sophie still sensed something deeply personal entwined within this mystery, as if this cryptex, forged by her grandfather's own hands, were trying to speak to her and offer some kind of resolution to the emptiness that had haunted her all these years.

'Your grandfather and three others died tonight,' Teabing continued, 'and they did so to keep this keystone away from the Church. Opus Dei came within inches tonight of possessing it. You understand, I hope, that this puts you in a position of exceptional responsibility. You have been handed a torch. A two-thousand-year-old flame that cannot be allowed to go out. This torch cannot fall into the wrong hands.' He paused, glancing at the rosewood box. 'I realize you have been given no choice in this matter, Miss Neveu, but considering what is at stake here, you must either fully embrace this responsibility . . . or you must pass that responsibility to someone else.'

'My grandfather gave the cryptex to me. I'm sure he thought I could handle the responsibility.'

Teabing looked encouraged but unconvinced. 'Good. A strong will is necessary. And yet, I am curious if you understand that successfully unlocking the keystone will bring with it a far greater trial.'

'How so?'

'My dear, imagine that you are suddenly holding a map that reveals the location of the Holy Grail. In that moment, you will be in possession of a truth capable of altering history for ever. You will be the keeper of a truth that man has sought for centuries. You will be faced with the responsibility of revealing that truth to the world. The individual who does so will be revered by many and despised by many. The question is whether you will have the necessary strength to carry out that task.'

Sophie paused. 'I'm not sure that is *my* decision to make.'

Teabing's eyebrows arched. 'No? If not the possessor of the keystone, then who?'

'The brotherhood who has successfully protected the secret for so long.'

'The Priory?' Teabing looked sceptical. 'But how? The brotherhood was shattered tonight. *Decapitated*, as you so aptly put it. Whether they were infiltrated by some kind of eavesdropping or by a spy within their ranks, we will never know, but the fact remains that someone got to them and uncovered the identities of their four top members. I would not trust anyone who stepped forward from the brotherhood at this point.'

'So what do you suggest?' Langdon asked.

'Robert, you know as well as I do that the Priory has not protected the truth all these years to have it gather dust until eternity. They have been waiting for the right moment in history to share their secret. A time when the world is ready to handle the truth.'

'And you believe that moment has arrived?' Langdon asked.

'Absolutely. It could not be more obvious. All the historical signs are in place, and if the Priory did not intend to make their secret known very soon, why has the Church now attacked?'

Sophie argued, 'The monk has not yet told us his purpose.'

'The monk's purpose is the Church's purpose,' Teabing replied, 'to destroy the documents that reveal the great deception. The Church came closer tonight than they have ever come, and the Priory has put its trust in you, Miss Neveu. The task of saving the Holy Grail clearly includes carrying out the Priory's final wishes of sharing the truth with the world.'

Langdon intervened. 'Leigh, asking Sophie to make that decision is quite a load to drop on someone who only an hour ago learned the Sangreal documents exist.'

Teabing sighed. 'I apologize if I am pressing, Miss Neveu. Clearly I have always believed these documents should be made public, but in the end the decision belongs to you. I simply feel it is important that you begin to think about what happens should we succeed in opening the keystone.'

'Gentlemen,' Sophie said, her voice firm, 'to quote your words, "You do not find the Grail, the Grail finds you." I am going to trust that the Grail has found me for a reason, and when the time comes, I will know what to do.'

Both of them looked startled.

'So then,' she said, motioning to the rosewood box. 'Let's move on.'

Chapter 70

Standing in the drawing room of Château Villette, Lieutenant Collet watched the dying fire and felt despondent. Captain Fache had arrived moments earlier and was now in the next room, yelling into the phone, trying to coordinate the failed attempt to locate the missing Range Rover.

It could be anywhere by now, Collet thought.

Having disobeyed Fache's direct orders and lost Langdon for a second time, Collet was grateful that PTS had located a bullet hole in the floor, which at least corroborated Collet's claims that a shot had been fired. Still, Fache's mood was sour, and Collet sensed there would be dire repercussions when the dust settled.

Unfortunately, the clues they were turning up here seemed to shed no light at all on what was going on or who was involved. The black Audi outside had been rented in a false name with false credit card numbers, and the prints in the car matched nothing in the Interpol database.

Another agent hurried into the living room, his eyes urgent. 'Where's Captain Fache?'

Collet barely looked up from the burning embers. 'He's on the phone.'

'I'm off the phone,' Fache snapped, stalking into the room. 'What have you got?'

The second agent said, 'Sir, Central just heard from André Vernet at the Depository Bank of Zurich. He wants to talk to you privately. He is changing his story.'

'Oh?' Fache said.

Now Collet looked up.

'Vernet is admitting that Langdon and Neveu spent time inside his bank tonight.'

'We figured that out,' Fache said. 'Why did Vernet lie about it?'

'He said he'll talk only to you, but he's agreed to cooperate fully.'

'In exchange for what?'

'For our keeping his bank's name out of the news and also for helping him recover some stolen property. It sounds like Langdon and Neveu stole something from Saunière's account.'

'What?' Collet blurted. 'How?'

Fache never flinched, his eyes riveted on the second agent. 'What did they steal?'

'Vernet didn't elaborate, but he sounds like he's willing to do anything to get it back.'

Collet tried to imagine how this could happen. Maybe Langdon and Neveu had held a bank employee at gunpoint? Maybe they forced Vernet to open Saunière's account and facilitate an escape in the armoured truck. As feasible as it was, Collet was having trouble believing Sophie Neveu could be involved in anything like that.

From the kitchen, another agent yelled to Fache. 'Captain? I'm going through Mr Teabing's speed dial numbers, and I'm on the phone with Le Bourget Airfield. I've got some bad news.'

Thirty seconds later, Fache was packing up and preparing to leave Château Villette. He had just learned that Teabing kept a private jet nearby at Le Bourget Airfield and that the plane had taken off about a half hour ago.

The Bourget representative on the phone had claimed not to know who was on the plane or where it was headed. The takeoff had been unscheduled, and no flight plan had been logged. Highly illegal, even for a small airfield. Fache was certain that by applying the right pressure, he could get the answers he was looking for.

'Lieutenant Collet,' Fache barked, heading for the door, 'I have no choice but to leave you in charge of the PTS investigation here. Try to do something right for a change.'

Chapter 71

As the Hawker levelled off, with its nose aimed for England, Langdon carefully lifted the rosewood box from his lap, where he had been protecting it during takeoff. Now, as he set the box on the table, he could sense Sophie and Teabing leaning forward with anticipation.

Unlatching the lid and opening the box, Langdon turned his attention not to the lettered dials of the cryptex, but rather to the tiny hole on the underside of the box lid. Using the tip of a pen, he carefully removed the inlaid Rose on top and revealed the text beneath it. *Sub Rosa*, he mused, hoping a fresh look at the text would bring clarity. Focusing all his energies, Langdon studied the strange text.

After several seconds, he began to feel the initial frustration resurfacing. 'Leigh, I just can't seem to place it.'

* * *

From where Sophie was seated across the table, she could not yet see the text, but Langdon's inability to immediately identify the language surprised her. *My grandfather spoke a language so obscure that even a symbologist can't identify it?* She quickly realized she should not find this surprising. This would not be the first secret Jacques Saunière had kept from his granddaughter.

Opposite Sophie, Leigh Teabing felt ready to burst. Eager for his chance to see the text, he quivered with excitement, leaning in, trying to see around Langdon, who was still hunched over the box.

'I don't know,' Langdon whispered intently. 'My first guess is a Semitic, but now I'm not so sure. Most primary Semitics include *nikkudim*. This has none.'

'Probably ancient,' Teabing offered.

'*Nikkudim?*' Sophie inquired.

Teabing never took his eyes from the box. 'Most modern Semitic alphabets have no vowels and use *nikkudim* – tiny dots and dashes written either below or within the consonants – to indicate what vowel sound accompanies them. Historically speaking, *nikkudim* are a relatively modern addition to language.'

Langdon was still hovering over the script. 'A Sephardic transliteration, perhaps . . .?'

Teabing could bear it no longer. 'Perhaps if I just . . .' Reaching over, he edged the box away from Langdon and pulled it toward himself. No doubt Langdon had a solid familiarity with the standard ancients – Greek, Latin, the Romances – but from the fleeting glance Teabing had of *this* language, he thought it looked more specialized, possibly a Rashi script or a STA'M with crowns.

Taking a deep breath, Teabing feasted his eyes upon the engraving. He said nothing for a very long time. With each passing second, Teabing felt his confidence deflating. 'I'm astonished,' he said. 'This language looks like nothing I've ever seen!'

Langdon slumped.

'Might I see it?' Sophie asked.

Teabing pretended not to hear her. 'Robert, you said earlier that you thought you'd *seen* something like this before?'

Langdon looked vexed. 'I thought so. I'm not sure. The script looks familiar somehow.'

'Leigh?' Sophie repeated, clearly not appreciating being left out of the discussion. 'Might I have a look at the box my grandfather made?'

'Of course, dear,' Teabing said, pushing it over to her. He hadn't meant to sound belittling, and yet Sophie Neveu was light-years out of her league. If a British Royal Historian and a Harvard symbologist could not even identify the language—

'Aah,' Sophie said, seconds after examining the box. 'I should have guessed.'

Teabing and Langdon turned in unison, staring at her.

'Guessed *what*?' Teabing demanded.

Sophie shrugged. 'Guessed that *this* would be the language my grandfather would have used.'

'You're saying you can *read* this text?' Teabing exclaimed.

'Quite easily,' Sophie chimed, obviously enjoying herself now. 'My grandfather taught me this language when I was only six years old. I'm fluent.' She leaned across the table and fixed Teabing with an admonishing glare. 'And frankly, sir, considering your allegiance to the Crown, I'm a little surprised you didn't recognize it.'

In a flash, Langdon knew.

No wonder the script looks so damned familiar!

Several years ago, Langdon had attended an event at Harvard's Fogg Museum. Harvard dropout Bill Gates had returned to his alma mater to lend to the museum one of his priceless acquisitions – eighteen sheets of paper he had recently purchased at auction from the Armand Hammar Estate.

His winning bid – a cool $30.8 million.

The author of the pages – Leonardo da Vinci.

The eighteen folios – now known as Leonardo's *Codex Leicester* after their famous owner, the Earl of Leicester – were all that remained of one of Leonardo's most fascinating notebooks: essays and drawings outlining Da Vinci's progressive theories on astronomy, geology, archaeology and hydrology.

Langdon would never forget his reaction after waiting in line and finally viewing the priceless parchment. Utter letdown. The pages were unintelligible. Despite being beautifully preserved and written in an impeccably neat penmanship – crimson ink on cream paper – the codex looked like gibberish. At first Langdon thought he could not read them because Da Vinci wrote his notebooks in an archaic Italian. But after studying them more closely, he realized he could not identify a single Italian word, or even one letter.

'Try this, sir,' whispered the female docent at the display case. She motioned to a hand mirror affixed to the display on a chain. Langdon picked it up and examined the text in the mirror's surface.

Instantly it was clear.

Langdon had been so eager to peruse some of the great thinker's ideas that he had forgotten one of the man's numerous artistic talents was an ability to write in a mirrored script that was virtually illegible to anyone other than himself. Historians still debated whether Da Vinci wrote this way simply to amuse himself or to keep people from peering over his shoulder and stealing his ideas, but the point was moot. Da Vinci did as he pleased.

Sophie smiled inwardly to see that Robert understood her meaning. 'I can read the first few words,' she said. 'It's English.'

Teabing was still sputtering. 'What's going on?'

'Reverse text,' Langdon said. 'We need a mirror.'

'No we don't,' Sophie said. 'I bet this veneer is thin enough.' She lifted the rosewood box up to a canister light on the wall and began examining the underside of the lid. Her grandfather couldn't actually write in reverse, so he always cheated by writing *normally* and then flipping the paper over and tracing the reversed impression. Sophie's guess was that he had wood-burned *normal* text into a block of wood and then run the back of the block through a sander until the wood was paper thin and the wood-burning could be seen *through* the wood. Then he'd simply flipped the piece over, and laid it in.

As Sophie moved the lid closer to the light, she saw she was right. The bright beam sifted through the thin layer of wood, and the script appeared in reverse on the underside of the lid.

Instantly legible.

'English,' Teabing croaked, hanging his head in shame. 'My native tongue.'

At the rear of the plane, Rémy Legaludec strained to hear beyond the rumbling engines, but the conversation up front was inaudible. Rémy did not like the way the night was progressing. Not at all. He looked down at the bound monk at his feet. The man lay perfectly still now, as if in a trance of acceptance or, perhaps, in silent prayer for deliverance.

Chapter 72

Fifteen thousand feet in the air, Robert Langdon felt the physical world fade away as all of his thoughts converged on Saunière's mirror-image poem, which was illuminated through the lid of the box.

Sophie quickly found some paper and copied it down longhand. When she was done, the three of them took turns reading the text. It was like some kind of archaeological crossword . . . a riddle that promised to reveal how to open the cryptex. Langdon read the verse slowly.

An ancient word of wisdom frees this scroll . . . and helps us keep her scatter'd family whole . . . a headstone praised by templars is the key . . . and atbash will reveal the truth to thee.

Before Langdon could even ponder what ancient password the verse was trying to reveal, he felt something far more fundamental resonate within him – the metre of the poem. *Iambic pentameter.*

Langdon had come across this metre often over the years while researching secret societies across Europe, including just last year in the Vatican Secret Archives. For centuries, iambic pentameter had been a preferred poetic metre of outspoken literati across the globe, from the ancient Greek writer Archilochus to Shakespeare, Milton, Chaucer and Voltaire – bold souls who chose to write their social commentaries in a metre that many of the day believed had mystical properties. The roots of iambic pentameter were deeply pagan.

Iambs. Two syllables with opposite emphasis. Stressed and unstressed. Yin yang. A balanced pair. Arranged in strings of five. Pentameter. Five for the pentacle of Venus and the sacred feminine.

'It's pentameter!' Teabing blurted, turning to Langdon. 'And the verse is in English! *La lingua pura!*'

Langdon nodded. The Priory, like many European secret societies at odds with the Church, had considered English the only European *pure* language for centuries. Unlike French, Spanish and Italian, which were rooted in Latin – *the tongue of the Vatican* – English was linguistically removed from Rome's propaganda machine, and therefore became a sacred, secret tongue for those brotherhoods educated enough to learn it.

'This poem,' Teabing gushed, 'references not only the Grail, but the Knights Templar and the scattered family of Mary Magdalene! What more could we ask for?'

'The password,' Sophie said, looking again at the poem. 'It sounds like we need some kind of ancient word of wisdom?'

'Abracadabra?' Teabing ventured, his eyes twinkling.

A word of five letters, Langdon thought, pondering the staggering number of ancient words that might be considered *words of wisdom* – selections from mystic chants, astrological prophecies, secret society inductions, Wicca incantations, Egyptian magic spells, pagan mantras – the list was endless.

'The password,' Sophie said, 'appears to have something to do with the Templars.' She read the text aloud. '"A headstone praised by Templars is the key."'

'Leigh,' Langdon said, 'you're the Templar specialist. Any ideas?'

Teabing was silent for several seconds and then sighed. 'Well, a headstone is obviously a grave marker of some sort. It's possible the poem is referencing a gravestone the Templars praised at the tomb of Magdalene, but that doesn't help us much because we have no idea where her tomb is.'

'The last line,' Sophie said, 'says that *Atbash* will reveal the truth. I've heard that word. Atbash.'

'I'm not surprised,' Langdon replied. 'You probably heard it in Cryptology 101. The Atbash Cipher is one of the oldest codes known to man.'

Of course! Sophie thought. *The famous Hebrew encoding system.*

The Atbash Cipher had indeed been part of Sophie's early cryptology training. The cipher dated back to 500 BC and was now used as a classroom example of a basic rotational substitution scheme. A common form of Jewish cryptogram, the Atbash Cipher was a simple substitution code based on the twenty-two-letter Hebrew alphabet. In Atbash, the first letter was substituted by the last letter, the second letter by the next to last letter, and so on.

'Atbash is sublimely appropriate,' Teabing said. 'Text encrypted with Atbash is found throughout the Kabbala, the Dead Sea Scrolls and even the Old Testament. Jewish scholars and mystics are *still* finding hidden meanings using Atbash. The Priory certainly would include the Atbash Cipher as part of their teachings.'

'The only problem,' Langdon said, 'is that we don't have anything on which to apply the cipher.'

Teabing sighed. 'There must be a code word on the headstone. We must find this headstone praised by Templars.'

Sophie sensed from the grim look on Langdon's face that finding the Templar headstone would be no small feat.

Atbash is the key, Sophie thought. *But we don't have a door*.

It was three minutes later that Teabing heaved a frustrated sigh and shook his head. 'My friends, I'm stymied. Let me ponder this while I get us some nibbles and check on Rémy and our guest.' He stood up and headed for the back of the plane.

Sophie felt tired as she watched him go.

Outside the window, the blackness of the predawn was absolute. Sophie felt as if she were being hurtled through space with no idea where she would land. Having grown up solving her grandfather's riddles, she had the uneasy sense right now that this poem before them contained information they still had not seen.

There is more there, she told herself. *Ingeniously hidden . . . but present nonetheless*.

Also plaguing her thoughts was a fear that what they eventually found inside this cryptex would not be as simple as 'a map to the Holy Grail'. Despite Teabing's and Langdon's confidence that the truth lay just within the marble cylinder, Sophie had solved enough of her grandfather's treasure hunts to know that Jacques Saunière did not give up his secrets easily.

Chapter 73

Bourget Airfield's night shift air traffic controller had been dozing before a blank radar screen when the captain of the Judicial Police practically broke down his door.

'Teabing's jet,' Bezu Fache blared, marching into the small tower, 'where did it go?'

The controller's initial response was a babbling, lame attempt to protect the privacy of their British client – one of the airfield's most respected customers. It failed miserably.

'Okay,' Fache said, 'I am placing you under arrest for permitting a private plane to take off without registering a flight plan.' Fache motioned to another officer, who approached with handcuffs, and the traffic controller felt a surge of terror. He thought of the newspaper articles debating whether the nation's police captain was a hero or a menace. That question had just been answered.

'Wait!' the controller heard himself whimper at the sight of the handcuffs. 'I can tell you this much. Sir Leigh Teabing makes frequent trips to London for medical treatments. He has a hangar at Biggin Hill Executive Airport in Kent. On the outskirts of London.'

Fache waved off the man with the cuffs. 'Is Biggin Hill his destination tonight?'

'I don't know,' the controller said honestly. 'The plane left on its usual tack, and his last radar contact suggested the United Kingdom. Biggin Hill is an extremely likely guess.'

'Did he have others onboard?'

'I swear, sir, there is no way for me to know that. Our clients can drive directly to their hangars, and load as they please. Who is onboard is the responsibility of the customs officials at the receiving airport.'

Fache checked his watch and gazed out at the scattering of jets parked in front of the terminal. 'If they're going to Biggin Hill, how long until they land?'

The controller fumbled through his records. 'It's a short flight. His plane could be on the ground by . . . around six-thirty. Fifteen minutes from now.'

Fache frowned and turned to one of his men. 'Get a transport up here. I'm going to London. And get me the Kent local police. Not British MI5. I want this quiet. Kent *local*. Tell them I want Teabing's plane to be permitted to land. Then I want it surrounded on the tarmac. Nobody deplanes until I get there.'

Chapter 74

'You're quiet,' Langdon said, gazing across the Hawker's cabin at Sophie.

'Just tired,' she replied. 'And the poem. I don't know.'

Langdon was feeling the same way. The hum of the engines and the gentle rocking of the plane were hypnotic, and his head still throbbed where he'd been hit by the monk. Teabing was still in the back of the plane, and Langdon decided to take advantage of the moment alone with Sophie to tell her something that had been on his mind. 'I think I know part of the reason why your grandfather conspired to put us together. I think there's something he wanted me to explain to you.'

'The history of the Holy Grail and Mary Magdalene isn't enough?'

Langdon felt uncertain how to proceed. 'The rift between you. The reason you haven't spoken to him in ten years. I think maybe he was hoping I could somehow make that right by explaining what drove you apart.'

Sophie squirmed in her seat. 'I haven't told you what drove us apart.'

Langdon eyed her carefully. 'You witnessed a sex rite. Didn't you?'

Sophie recoiled. 'How do you know that?'

'Sophie, you told me you witnessed something that convinced you your grandfather was in a secret society. And whatever you saw upset you enough that you haven't spoken to him since. I know a fair amount about secret societies. It doesn't take the brains of Da Vinci to guess what you saw.'

Sophie stared.

'Was it in the spring?' Langdon asked. 'Sometime around the equinox? Mid-March?'

Sophie looked out the window. 'I was on spring break from university. I came home a few days early.'

'You want to tell me about it?'

'I'd rather not.' She turned suddenly back to Langdon, her eyes welling with emotion. 'I don't know what I saw.'

'Were both men and women present?'

After a beat, she nodded.

'Dressed in white and black?'

She wiped her eyes and then nodded, seeming to open up a little. 'The women were in white gossamer gowns . . . with golden shoes. They held golden orbs. The men wore black tunics and black shoes.'

Langdon strained to hide his emotion, and yet he could not believe what he was hearing. Sophie Neveu had unwittingly witnessed a two-thousand-year-old sacred ceremony. 'Masks?' he asked, keeping his voice calm. 'Androgynous masks?'

'Yes. Everyone. Identical masks. White on the women. Black on the men.'

Langdon had read descriptions of this ceremony and understood its mystic roots. 'It's called Hieros Gamos,' he said softly. 'It dates back more than two thousand years. Egyptian priests and priestesses performed it regularly to celebrate the reproductive power of the female.' He paused, leaning toward her. 'And if you witnessed Hieros Gamos without being properly prepared to understand its meaning, I imagine it would be pretty shocking.'

Sophie said nothing.

'Hieros Gamos is Greek,' he continued. 'It means

sacred marriage.'

'The ritual I saw was no marriage.'

'Marriage as in *union,* Sophie.'

'You mean as in sex.'

'No.'

'No?' she said, her olive eyes testing him.

Langdon backpedalled. 'Well . . . yes, in a manner of speaking, but not as we understand it today.' He explained that although what she saw probably *looked* like a sex ritual, Hieros Gamos had nothing to do with eroticism. It was a spiritual act. Historically, intercourse was the act through which male and female experienced God. The ancients believed that the male was spiritually incomplete until he had carnal knowledge of the sacred feminine. Physical union with the female remained the sole means through which man could become spiritually complete and ultimately achieve *gnosis* – knowledge of the divine. Since the days of Isis, sex rites had been considered man's only bridge from earth to heaven. 'By communing with woman,' Langdon said, 'man could achieve a climactic instant when his mind went totally blank and he could see God.'

Sophie looked sceptical. 'Orgasm as prayer?'

Langdon gave a noncommittal shrug, although Sophie was essentially correct. Physiologically speaking, the male climax was accompanied by a split second entirely devoid of thought. A brief mental vacuum. A moment of clarity during which God could be glimpsed. Meditation gurus achieved similar states of thoughtlessness without sex and often described Nirvana as a never-ending spiritual orgasm.

'Sophie,' Langdon said quietly, 'it's important to remember that the ancients' view of sex was entirely opposite from ours today. Sex begot new life – the ultimate miracle – and miracles could be performed only by a god. The ability of the woman to produce life from her womb made her sacred. A god. Intercourse was the revered union of the two halves of the human spirit – male and female – through which the male could find spiritual wholeness and communion with God. What you saw was not about sex, it was about spirituality. The Hieros Gamos ritual is not a perversion. It's a deeply sacrosanct ceremony.'

His words seemed to strike a nerve. Sophie had been remarkably poised all evening, but now, for the first time, Langdon saw the aura of composure beginning to crack. Tears materialized in her eyes again, and she dabbed them away with her sleeve.

He gave her a moment. Admittedly, the concept of sex as a pathway to God was mind-boggling at first. Langdon's Jewish students always looked flabbergasted when he first told them that the early Jewish tradition involved ritualistic sex. *In the Temple, no less.* Early Jews believed that the Holy of Holies in Solomon's Temple housed not only God but also His powerful female equal, Shekinah. Men seeking spiritual wholeness came to the Temple to visit priestesses – or *hierodules* – with whom they made love and experienced the divine through physical union. The Jewish tetragrammaton YHWH – the sacred name of God – in fact derived from Jehovah, an androgynous physical union between the masculine *Jah* and the pre-Hebraic name for Eve, *Havah.*

'For the early Church,' Langdon explained in a soft voice, 'mankind's use of sex to commune directly with God posed a serious threat to the Catholic power base. It left the Church out of the loop, undermining their self-proclaimed status as the *sole* conduit to God. For obvious reasons, they worked hard to demonize sex and recast it as a disgusting and sinful act. Other major religions did the same.'

411

Sophie was silent, but Langdon sensed she was starting to understand her grandfather better. Ironically, Langdon had made this same point in a class lecture earlier this semester. 'Is it surprising we feel conflicted about sex?' he asked his students. 'Our ancient heritage and our very physiologies tell us sex is natural – a cherished route to spiritual fulfilment – and yet modern religion decries it as shameful, teaching us to fear our sexual desire as the hand of the devil.'

Langdon decided not to shock his students with the fact that more than a dozen secret societies around the world – many of them quite influential – still practised sex rites and kept the ancient traditions alive. Tom Cruise's character in the film *Eyes Wide Shut* discovered this the hard way when he sneaked into a private gathering of ultra-elite Manhattanites only to find himself witnessing Hieros Gamos. Sadly, the filmmakers had got most of the specifics wrong, but the basic gist was there – a secret society communing to celebrate the magic of sexual union.

'Professor Langdon?' A male student at the back raised his hand, sounding hopeful. 'Are you saying that instead of going to chapel, we should have more sex?'

Langdon chuckled, not about to take the bait. From what he'd heard about Harvard parties, these kids were having more than enough sex. 'Gentlemen,' he said, knowing he was on tender ground, 'might I offer a suggestion for all of you. Without being so bold as to condone premarital sex, and without being so naive as to think you're all chaste angels, I will give you this bit of advice about your sex lives.'

All the men in the audience leaned forward, listening intently.

'The next time you find yourself with a woman, look in your heart and see if you cannot approach sex as a mystical, spiritual act. Challenge yourself to find that spark of divinity that man can only achieve through union with the sacred feminine.'

The women smiled knowingly, nodding.

The men exchanged dubious giggles and off-colour jokes.

Langdon sighed. College men were still boys.

Sophie's forehead felt cold as she pressed it against the plane's window and stared blankly into the void, trying to process what Langdon had just told her. She felt a new regret well within her. *Ten years.* She pictured the stacks of unopened letters her grandfather had sent her. *I will tell Robert everything.* Without turning from the window, Sophie began to speak. Quietly. Fearfully.

As she began to recount what had happened that night, she felt herself drifting back . . . alighting in the woods outside her grandfather's Normandy château . . . searching the deserted house in confusion . . . hearing the voices below her . . . and then finding the hidden door. She inched down the stone staircase, one step at a time, into that basement grotto. She could taste the earthy air. Cool and light. It was March. In the shadows of her hiding place on the staircase, she watched as the strangers swayed and chanted by flickering orange candles.

I'm dreaming, Sophie told herself. *This is a dream. What else could this be?*

The women and men were staggered, black, white, black, white. The women's beautiful gossamer gowns billowed as they raised in their right hands golden orbs and called out in unison, '*I was with you in the beginning, in the dawn of all that is holy, I bore you from the womb before the start of day.*'

The women lowered their orbs, and everyone rocked back and forth as if in a trance. They were revering something in the centre of the circle.

What are they looking at?

The voices accelerated now. Louder. Faster.

'The woman whom you behold is love!' The women called, raising their orbs again.

The men responded, *'She has her dwelling in eternity!'*

The chanting grew steady again. Accelerating. Thundering now. Faster. The participants stepped inward and knelt.

In that instant, Sophie could finally see what they were all watching.

On a low, ornate altar in the centre of the circle lay a man. He was naked, positioned on his back, and wearing a black mask. Sophie instantly recognized his body and the birthmark on his shoulder. She almost cried out. *Grand-père!* This image alone would have shocked Sophie beyond belief, and yet there was more.

Straddling her grandfather was a naked woman wearing a white mask, her luxuriant silver hair flowing out behind it. Her body was plump, far from perfect, and she was gyrating in rhythm to the chanting – making love to Sophie's grandfather.

Sophie wanted to turn and run, but she couldn't. The stone walls of the grotto imprisoned her as the chanting rose to a fever pitch. The circle of participants seemed almost to be singing now, the noise rising in crescendo to a frenzy. With a sudden roar, the entire room seemed to erupt in climax. Sophie could not breathe. She suddenly realized she was quietly sobbing. She turned and staggered silently up the stairs, out of the house, and drove trembling back to Paris.

Chapter 75

The chartered turboprop was just passing over the twinkling lights of Monaco when Aringarosa hung up on Fache for the second time. He reached for the air-sickness bag again but felt too drained even to be sick. *Just let it be over!*

Fache's newest update seemed unfathomable, and yet almost nothing tonight made sense anymore. *What is going on?* Everything had spiralled wildly out of control. *What have I got Silas into? What have I got myself into!*

On shaky legs, Aringarosa walked to the cockpit. 'I need to change destinations.'

The pilot glanced over his shoulder and laughed. 'You're joking, right?'

'No. I have to get to London immediately.'

'Father, this is a charter flight, not a taxi.'

'I will pay you extra, of course. How much? London is only one hour farther north and requires almost no change of direction, so—'

'It's not a question of money, Father, there are other issues.'

'Ten thousand euros. Right now.'

The pilot turned, his eyes wide with shock. 'How much? What kind of priest carries that kind of cash?'

Aringarosa walked back to his black briefcase, opened it, and removed one of the bearer bonds. He handed it to the pilot.

'What is this?' the pilot demanded.

'A ten-thousand-euro bearer bond drawn on the Vatican Bank.'

The pilot looked dubious.

'It's the same as cash.'

'Only cash is cash,' the pilot said, handing the bond back.

Aringarosa felt weak as he steadied himself against the cockpit door. 'This is a matter of life or death. You must help me. I need to get to London.'

The pilot eyed the bishop's gold ring. 'Real diamonds?'

Aringarosa looked at the ring. 'I could not possibly part with this.'

The pilot shrugged, turning and focusing back out of the windshield.

Aringarosa felt a deepening sadness. He looked at the ring. Everything it represented was about to be lost to the bishop anyway. After a long moment, he slid the ring from his finger and placed it gently on the instrument panel.

Aringarosa slunk out of the cockpit and sat back down. Fifteen seconds later, he could feel the pilot banking a few more degrees to the north.

Even so, Aringarosa's moment of glory was in shambles.

It had all begun as a holy cause. A brilliantly crafted scheme. Now, like a house of cards, it was collapsing in on itself . . . and the end was nowhere in sight.

Chapter 76

Langdon could see Sophie was still shaken from recounting her experience of Hieros Gamos. For his part, Langdon was amazed to have heard it. Not only had Sophie witnessed the full-blown ritual, but her own grandfather had been the celebrant . . . the Grand Master of the Priory of Sion. It was heady company. *Da Vinci, Botticelli, Isaac Newton, Victor Hugo, Jean Cocteau . . . Jacques Saunière.*

'I don't know what else I can tell you,' Langdon said softly.

Sophie's eyes were a deep green now, tearful. 'He raised me like his own daughter.'

Langdon now recognized the emotion that had been growing in her eyes as they spoke. It was remorse. Distant and deep. Sophie Neveu had shunned her grandfather and was now seeing him in an entirely different light.

Outside, the dawn was coming fast, its crimson aura gathering off the starboard. The earth was still black beneath them.

'Victuals, my dears?' Teabing rejoined them with a flourish, presenting several cans of Coke and a box of old crackers. He apologized profusely for the limited fare as he doled out the goods. 'Our friend the monk isn't talking yet,' he chimed, 'but give him time.' He bit into a cracker and eyed the poem. 'So, my lovely, any headway?' He looked at Sophie. 'What is your grandfather trying to tell us here? Where the devil is this headstone? This headstone praised by Templars.'

Sophie shook her head and remained silent.

While Teabing again dug into the verse, Langdon popped a Coke and turned to the window, his thoughts awash with images of secret rituals and unbroken codes. *A headstone praised by Templars is the key.* He took a long sip from the can. *A headstone praised by Templars.* The cola was warm.

The dissolving veil of night seemed to evaporate quickly, and as Langdon watched the transformation, he saw a shimmering ocean stretch out beneath them. *The English Channel.* It wouldn't be long now.

Langdon willed the light of day to bring with it a second kind of illumination, but the lighter it became outside, the further he felt from the truth. He heard the rhythms of iambic pentameter and chanting, Hieros Gamos and sacred rites, resonating with the rumble of the jet.

A headstone praised by Templars.

The plane was over land again when a flash of enlightenment struck him. Langdon set down his empty can of Coke hard. 'You won't believe this,' he said, turning to the others. 'The Templar headstone – I figured it out.'

Teabing's eyes turned to saucers. 'You *know* where the headstone is?'

Langdon smiled. 'Not *where* it is. *What* it is.'

Sophie leaned in to hear.

'I think the headstone references a literal *stone head*,' Langdon explained, savouring the familiar excitement of academic breakthrough. 'Not a grave marker.'

'A stone head?' Teabing demanded.

Sophie looked equally confused.

'Leigh,' Langdon said, turning, 'during the Inquisition, the Church accused the Knights Templar of all kinds of heresies, right?'

'Correct. They fabricated all kinds of charges.

Sodomy, urination on the cross, devil worship, quite a list.'

'And on that list was the worship of *false idols*, right? Specifically, the Church accused the Templars of secretly performing rituals in which they prayed to a carved stone head . . . the pagan god—'

'Baphomet!' Teabing blurted. 'My heavens, Robert, you're right! A headstone praised by Templars!'

Langdon quickly explained to Sophie that Baphomet was a pagan fertility god associated with the creative force of reproduction. Baphomet's head was represented as that of a ram or goat, a common symbol of procreation and fecundity. The Templars honoured Baphomet by encircling a stone replica of his head and chanting prayers.

'Baphomet,' Teabing tittered. 'The ceremony honoured the creative magic of sexual union, but Pope Clement convinced everyone that Baphomet's head was in fact that of the devil. The Pope used the head of Baphomet as the linchpin in his case against the Templars.'

Langdon concurred. The modern belief in a *horned* devil known as Satan could be traced back to Baphomet and the Church's attempts to recast the horned fertility god as a symbol of evil. The Church had obviously succeeded, although not entirely. Traditional American Thanksgiving tables still bore pagan, horned fertility symbols. The cornucopia or 'horn of plenty' was a tribute to Baphomet's fertility and dated back to Zeus being suckled by a goat whose horn broke off and magically filled with fruit. Baphomet also appeared in group photographs when some joker raised two fingers behind a friend's head in the V-symbol of horns; certainly few of the pranksters realized their mocking gesture was in fact advertising their victim's robust sperm count.

'Yes, yes,' Teabing was saying excitedly. 'Baphomet must be what the poem is referring to. A headstone praised by Templars.'

'Okay,' Sophie said, 'but if Baphomet is the headstone praised by Templars, then we have a new dilemma.' She pointed to the dials on the cryptex. 'Baphomet has eight letters. We only have room for five.'

Teabing grinned broadly. 'My dear, this is where the Atbash Cipher comes into play.'

Chapter 77

Langdon was impressed. Teabing had just finished writing out the entire twenty-two-letter Hebrew alphabet – *alef-beit* – from memory. Granted, he'd used Roman equivalents rather than Hebrew characters, but even so, he was now reading through them with flawless pronunciation.

A B G D H V Z Ch T Y K L M N S O P Tz Q R Sh Th

'*Alef, Beit, Gimel, Dalet, Hei, Vav, Zayin, Chet, Tet, Yud, Kaf, Lamed, Mem, Nun, Samech, Ayin, Pei, Tzadik, Kuf, Reish, Shin and Tav.*' Teabing dramatically mopped his brow and ploughed on. 'In formal Hebrew spelling, the vowel sounds are not written. Therefore, when we write the word *Baphomet* using the Hebrew alphabet, it will lose its three vowels in translation, leaving us—'

'Five letters,' Sophie blurted.

Teabing nodded and began writing again. 'Okay, here is the proper spelling of Baphomet in Hebrew letters. I'll sketch in the missing vowels for clarity's sake.

B a P V o M e Th

'Remember, of course,' he added, 'that Hebrew is normally written in the opposite direction, but we can just as easily use Atbash this way. Next, all we have to do is create our substitution scheme by rewriting the entire alphabet in reverse order opposite the original alphabet.'

'There's an easier way,' Sophie said, taking the pen from Teabing. 'It works for all reflectional substitution ciphers, including the Atbash. A little trick I learned at Royal Holloway.' Sophie wrote the first half of the alphabet from left to right, and then, beneath it, wrote the second half, right to left. 'Cryptanalysts call it the fold-over. Half as complicated. Twice as clean.'

A	B	G	D	H	V	Z	Ch	T	Y	K
Th	Sh	R	Q	Tz	P	O	S	N	M	L

Teabing eyed her handiwork and chuckled. 'Right you are. Glad to see those boys at the Holloway are doing their job.'

Looking at Sophie's substitution matrix, Langdon felt a rising thrill that he imagined must have rivalled the thrill felt by early scholars when they first used the Atbash Cipher to decrypt the now famous *Mystery of Sheshach*. For years, religious scholars had been baffled by biblical references to a city called *Sheshach*. The city did not appear on any map nor in any other documents, and yet it was mentioned repeatedly in the Book of Jeremiah – the king of Sheshach, the city of Sheshach, the people of Sheshach. Finally, a scholar applied the Atbash Cipher to the word, and his results were mind-numbing. The cipher revealed that Sheshach was in fact a *code word* for another very well-known city. The decryption process was simple.

Sheshach, in Hebrew, was spelled: Sh-Sh-K.

Sh-Sh-K, when placed in the substitution matrix, became B-B-L.

B-B-L, in Hebrew, spelled *Babel*.

The mysterious city of Sheshach was revealed as the city of Babel, and a frenzy of biblical examination ensued. Within weeks, several more Atbash code words were uncovered in the Old Testament, unveiling myriad hidden meanings that scholars had no idea were there.

'We're getting close,' Langdon whispered, unable to control his excitement.

'Inches, Robert,' Teabing said. He glanced over at Sophie and smiled. 'You ready?'

She nodded.

'Okay, Baphomet in Hebrew without the vowels reads: *B-P-V-M-Th*. Now we simply apply your Atbash substitution matrix to translate the letters into our five-letter password.'

Langdon's heart pounded. *B-P-V-M-Th*. The sun was pouring through the windows now. He looked at Sophie's substitution matrix and slowly began to make the conversion. *B is Sh . . . P is V . . .*

Teabing was grinning like a schoolboy at Christmas. 'And the Atbash Cipher reveals . . .' He stopped short. 'Good God!' His face went white.

Langdon's head snapped up.

'What's wrong?' Sophie demanded.

'You won't believe this.' Teabing glanced at Sophie. 'Especially you.'

'What do you mean?' she said.

'This is . . . ingenious,' he whispered. 'Utterly ingenious!' Teabing wrote again on the paper. 'Drumroll, please. Here is your password.' He showed them what he had written.

Sh-V-P-Y-A

Sophie scowled. 'What is it?'

Langdon didn't recognize it either.

Teabing's voice seemed to tremble with awe. 'This, my friend, is actually an ancient word of wisdom.'

Langdon read the letters again. *An ancient word of*

wisdom frees this scroll. An instant later he got it. He had never seen this coming. 'An ancient word of wisdom!'

Teabing was laughing. 'Quite literally!'

Sophie looked at the word and then at the dial. Immediately she realized Langdon and Teabing had failed to see a serious glitch. 'Hold on! This can't be the password,' she argued. 'The cryptex doesn't have an Sh on the dial. It uses a traditional Roman alphabet.'

'*Read* the word,' Langdon urged. 'Keep in mind two things. In Hebrew, the symbol for the sound Sh can also be pronounced as S, depending on the accent. Just as the letter P can be pronounced F.'

SVFYA? she thought, puzzled.

'Genius!' Teabing added. 'The letter Vav is often a placeholder for the vowel sound O!'

Sophie again looked at the letters, attempting to sound them out.

'*S . . . o . . . f . . . y . . . a.*'

She heard the sound of her voice, and could not believe what she had just said. 'Sophia? This spells Sophia?'

Langdon was nodding enthusiastically. 'Yes! *Sophia* literally means *wisdom* in Greek. The root of your name, Sophie, is literally a "word of wisdom".'

Sophie suddenly missed her grandfather immensely. *He encrypted the Priory keystone with my name.* A knot caught in her throat. It all seemed so perfect. But as she turned her gaze to the five lettered dials on the cryptex, she realized a problem still existed. 'But wait . . . the word Sophia has *six* letters.'

Teabing's smile never faded. 'Look at the poem again. Your grandfather wrote, '"An *ancient* word of wisdom." '

'Yes?'

Teabing winked. 'In ancient Greek, wisdom is spelled S-O-F-I-A.'

Chapter 78

Sophie felt a wild excitement as she cradled the cryptex and began dialling in the letters. *An ancient word of wisdom frees this scroll*. Langdon and Teabing seemed to have stopped breathing as they looked on.

S . . . O . . . F . . .

'Carefully,' Teabing urged. 'Ever so carefully.'

. . . I . . . A.

Sophie aligned the final dial. 'Okay,' she whispered, glancing up at the others. 'I'm going to pull it apart.'

'Remember the vinegar,' Langdon whispered with fearful exhilaration. 'Be careful.'

Sophie knew that if this cryptex were like those she had opened in her youth, all she would need to do is grip the cylinder at both ends, just beyond the dials, and pull, applying slow, steady pressure in opposite directions. If the dials were properly aligned with the password, then one of the ends would slide off, much like a lens cap, and she could reach inside and remove the rolled papyrus document, which would be wrapped around the vial of vinegar. However, if the password they had entered were *incorrect*, Sophie's outward force on the ends would be transferred to a hinged lever inside, which would pivot downward into the cavity and apply pressure to the glass vial, eventually shattering it if she pulled too hard.

Pull gently, she told herself.

Teabing and Langdon both leaned in as Sophie

wrapped her palms around the ends of the cylinder. In the excitement of deciphering the code word, Sophie had almost forgotten what they expected to find inside. *This is the Priory keystone.* According to Teabing, it contained a map to the Holy Grail, unveiling the tomb of Mary Magdalene and the Sangreal treasure . . . the ultimate treasure trove of secret truth.

Now gripping the stone tube, Sophie double-checked that all of the letters were properly aligned with the indicator. Then, slowly, she pulled. Nothing happened. She applied a little more force. Suddenly, the stone slid apart like a well-crafted telescope. The heavy end piece detached in her hand. Langdon and Teabing almost jumped to their feet. Sophie's heart rate climbed as she set the end cap on the table and tipped the cylinder to peer inside.

A scroll!

Peering down the hollow of the rolled paper, Sophie could see it had been wrapped around a cylindrical object – the vial of vinegar, she assumed. Strangely, though, the paper around the vinegar was not the customary delicate papyrus but rather, vellum. *That's odd,* she thought, *vinegar can't dissolve a lambskin vellum.* She looked again down the hollow of the scroll and realized the object in the centre was not a vial of vinegar after all. It was something else entirely.

'What's wrong?' Teabing asked. 'Pull out the scroll.'

Frowning, Sophie grabbed the rolled vellum and the object around which it was wrapped, pulling them both out of the container.

'That's not papyrus,' Teabing said. 'It's too heavy.'

'I know. It's padding.'

'For what? The vial of vinegar?'

'No.' Sophie unrolled the scroll and revealed what was wrapped inside. 'For *this*.'

When Langdon saw the object inside the sheet of vellum, his heart sank.

'God help us,' Teabing said, slumping. 'Your grandfather was a pitiless architect.'

Langdon stared in amazement. *I see Saunière has no intention of making this easy.*

On the table sat a second cryptex. Smaller. Made of black onyx. It had been nested within the first. Saunière's passion for dualism. *Two cryptexes. Everything in pairs. Double entendres. Male female. Black nested within white.* Langdon felt the web of symbolism stretching onward. *White gives birth to black.*

Every man sprang from woman.

White – female.

Black – male.

Reaching over, Langdon lifted the smaller cryptex. It looked identical to the first, except half the size and black. He heard the familiar gurgle. Apparently, the vial of vinegar they had heard earlier was inside this smaller cryptex.

'Well, Robert,' Teabing said, sliding the page of vellum over to him. 'You'll be pleased to hear that at least we're flying in the right direction.'

Langdon examined the thick vellum sheet. Written in ornate penmanship was another four-line verse. Again, in iambic pentameter. The verse was cryptic, but Langdon needed to read only as far as the first line to realize that Teabing's plan to come to Britain was going to pay off.

IN LONDON LIES A KNIGHT A POPE INTERRED.

The remainder of the poem clearly implied that the password for opening the second cryptex could be found by visiting this knight's tomb, somewhere in the city.

Langdon turned excitedly to Teabing. 'Do you have any idea what knight this poem is referring to?'

Teabing grinned. 'Not the foggiest. But I know in precisely which crypt we should look.'

At that moment, fifteen miles ahead of them, six Kent police cars streaked down rain-soaked streets toward Biggin Hill Executive Airport.

Chapter 79

Lieutenant Collet helped himself to a Perrier from Teabing's refrigerator and strode back out through the drawing room. Rather than accompanying Fache to London where the action was, he was now baby-sitting the PTS team that had spread out through Château Villette.

So far, the evidence they had uncovered was unhelpful: a single bullet buried in the floor; a paper with several symbols scrawled on it along with the words *blade* and *chalice*; and a bloody spiked belt that PTS had told Collet was associated with the conser-vative Catholic group Opus Dei, which had caused a stir recently when a news programme exposed their aggressive recruiting practices in Paris.

Collet sighed. *Good luck making sense of this unlikely mélange.*

Moving down a lavish hallway, Collet entered the vast ballroom study, where the chief PTS examiner was busy dusting for fingerprints. He was a corpulent man in braces.

'Anything?' Collet asked, entering.

The examiner shook his head. 'Nothing new. Multiple sets matching those in the rest of the house.'

'How about the prints on the *cilice* belt?'

'Interpol is still working. I uploaded everything we found.'

Collet motioned to two sealed evidence bags on the desk. 'And this?'

The man shrugged. 'Force of habit. I bag anything peculiar.'

Collet walked over. *Peculiar?*

'This Brit's a strange one,' the examiner said. 'Have a look at this.' He sifted through the evidence bags and selected one, handing it to Collet.

The photo showed the main entrance of a Gothic cathedral – the traditional, recessed archway, narrowing through multiple, ribbed layers to a small doorway.

Collet studied the photo and turned. 'This is peculiar?'

'Turn it over.'

On the back, Collet found notations scrawled in English, describing a cathedral's long hollow nave as a secret pagan tribute to a woman's womb. This was strange. The notation describing the cathedral's doorway, however, was what startled him. 'Hold on! He thinks a cathedral's entrance represents a woman's . . .'

The examiner nodded. 'Complete with receding labial ridges and a nice little cinquefoil clitoris above the doorway.' He sighed. 'Kind of makes you want to go back to church.'

Collet picked up the second evidence bag. Through the plastic, he could see a large glossy photograph of what appeared to be an old document. The heading at the top read:

Les Dossiers Secrets – Number 4° lm¹ 249

'What's this?' Collet asked.

'No idea. He's got copies of it all over the place, so I bagged it.'

Collet studied the document.

PRIEURE DE SION – LES NAUTONIERS/ GRAND MASTERS

JEAN DE GISORS	*1188–1220*
MARIE DE SAINT-CLAIR	*1220–1266*
GUILLAUME DE GISORS	*1266–1307*
EDOUARD DE BAR	*1307–1336*
JEANNE DE BAR	*1336–1351*
JEAN DE SAINT-CLAIR	*1351–1366*
BLANCE D'EVREUX	*1366–1398*
NICOLAS FLAMEL	*1398–1418*
RENE D'ANJOU	*1418–1480*
IOLANDE DE BAR	*1480–1483*
SANDRO BOTTICELLI	*1483–1510*
LEONARDO DA VINCI	*1510–1519*
CONNETABLE DE BOURBON	*1519–1527*
FERDINAND DE GONZAQUE	*1527–1575*
LOUIS DE NEVERS	*1575–1595*
ROBERT FLUDD	*1595–1637*
J. VALENTIN ANDREA	*1637–1654*
ROBERT BOYLE	*1654–1691*
ISAAC NEWTON	*1691–1727*
CHARLES RADCLYFFE	*1727–1746*
CHARLES DE LORRAINE	*1746–1780*
MAXIMILIAN DE LORRAINE	*1780–1801*
CHARLES NODIER	*1801–1844*
VICTOR HUGO	*1844–1885*
CLAUDE DEBUSSY	*1885–1918*
JEAN COCTEAU	*1918–1963*

Prieuré de Sion? Collet wondered.

'Lieutenant?' Another agent stuck his head in. 'The switchboard has an urgent call for Captain Fache, but they can't reach him. Will you take it?'

Collet returned to the kitchen and took the call.

It was André Vernet.

The banker's refined accent did little to mask the tension in his voice. 'I thought Captain Fache said he would call me, but I have not yet heard from him.'

'The captain is quite busy,' Collet replied. 'May I help you?'

'I was assured I would be kept abreast of your progress tonight.'

For a moment, Collet thought he recognized the timbre of the man's voice, but he couldn't quite place it. 'Monsieur Vernet, I am currently in charge of the Paris investigation. My name is Lieutenant Collet.'

There was a long pause on the line. 'Lieutenant, I have another call coming in. Please excuse me. I will call you later.' He hung up.

For several seconds, Collet held the receiver. Then it dawned on him. *I knew I recognized that voice!* The revelation made him gasp.

The armoured truck driver.

With the fake Rolex.

Collet now understood why the banker had hung up so quickly. Vernet had remembered the name Lieutenant Collet – the officer he blatantly lied to earlier tonight.

Collet pondered the implications of this bizarre development. *Vernet is involved.* Instinctively, he knew he should call Fache. Emotionally, he knew this lucky break was going to be his moment to shine.

He immediately called Interpol and requested every shred of information they could find on the Depository Bank of Zurich and its president, André Vernet.

Chapter 80

'Seat belts, please,' Teabing's pilot announced as the Hawker 731 descended into a gloomy morning drizzle. 'We'll be landing in five minutes.'

Teabing felt a joyous sense of homecoming when he saw the misty hills of Kent spreading wide beneath the descending plane. England was less than an hour from Paris, and yet a world away. This morning, the damp, spring green of his homeland looked particularly welcoming. *My time in France is over. I am returning to England victorious. The keystone has been found.* The question remained, of course, as to *where* the keystone would ultimately lead. *Somewhere in the United Kingdom.* Where exactly, Teabing had no idea, but he was already tasting the glory.

As Langdon and Sophie looked on, Teabing got up and went to the far side of the cabin, then slid aside a wall panel to reveal a discreetly hidden wall safe. He dialled in the combination, opened the safe, and extracted two passports. 'Documentation for Rémy and myself.' He then removed a thick stack of fifty-pound notes. 'And documentation for you two.'

Sophie looked leery. 'A bribe?'

'Creative diplomacy. Executive airfields make certain allowances. A British customs official will greet us at my hangar and ask to board the plane. Rather than permitting him to come on, I'll tell him I'm travelling with a French celebrity who prefers that nobody knows she is in England – press considerations, you know – and I'll offer the official this generous tip as gratitude for his discretion.'

Langdon looked amazed. 'And the official will *accept*?'

'Not from *anyone*, they won't, but these people all know me. I'm not an arms dealer, for heaven's sake. I was knighted.' Teabing smiled. 'Membership has its privileges.'

Rémy approached up the aisle now, the Heckler Koch pistol cradled in his hand. 'Sir, my agenda?'

Teabing glanced at his servant. 'I'm going to have you stay onboard with our guest until we return. We can't very well drag him all over London with us.'

Sophie looked wary. 'Leigh, I was serious about the French police finding your plane before we return.'

Teabing laughed. 'Yes, imagine their surprise if they board and find Rémy.'

Sophie looked surprised by his cavalier attitude. 'Leigh, you transported a bound hostage across international borders. This is serious.'

'So are my lawyers.' He scowled toward the monk in the rear of the plane. 'That animal broke into my home and almost killed me. That is a fact, and Rémy will corroborate.'

'But you tied him up and flew him to London!' Langdon said.

Teabing held up his right hand and feigned a courtroom oath. 'Your honour, forgive an eccentric old knight his foolish prejudice for the British court system. I realize I should have called the French authorities, but I'm a snob and do not trust those *laissez-faire* French to prosecute properly. This man almost murdered me. Yes, I made a rash decision forcing my manservant to help me bring him to England, but I was under great stress. Mea culpa. Mea culpa.'

Langdon looked incredulous. 'Coming from you, Leigh, that just might fly.'

'Sir?' the pilot called back. 'The tower just radioed. They've got some kind of maintenance problem out near your hangar, and they're asking me to bring the plane directly to the terminal instead.'

Teabing had been flying to Biggin Hill for over a decade, and this was a first. 'Did they mention what the problem is?'

'The controller was vague. Something about a petrol leak at the pumping station? They asked me to park in front of the terminal and keep everyone onboard until further notice. Safety precaution. We're not supposed to deplane until we get the all clear from airport authorities.'

Teabing was sceptical. *Must be one hell of a petrol leak.* The pumping station was a good half mile from his hangar.

Rémy also looked concerned. 'Sir, this sounds highly irregular.'

Teabing turned to Sophie and Langdon. 'My friends, I have an unpleasant suspicion that we are about to be met by a welcoming committee.'

Langdon gave a bleak sigh. 'I guess Fache still thinks I'm his man.'

'Either that,' Sophie said, 'or he is too deep into this to admit his error.'

Teabing was not listening. Regardless of Fache's mind-set, action needed to be taken fast. *Don't lose sight of the ultimate goal. The Grail. We're so close.* Below them, the landing gear descended with a clunk.

'Leigh,' Langdon said, sounding deeply remorseful, 'I should turn myself in and sort this out legally. Leave you all out of it.'

'Oh, heavens, Robert!' Teabing waved it off. 'Do

you really think they're going to let the rest of us go? I just transported you illegally. Miss Neveu assisted in your escape from the Louvre, and we have a man tied up in the back of the plane. Really now! We're all in this together.'

'Maybe a different airport?' Sophie said.

Teabing shook his head. 'If we pull up now, by the time we get clearance anywhere else, our welcoming party will include army tanks.'

Sophie slumped.

Teabing sensed that if they were to have any chance of postponing confrontation with the British authorities long enough to find the Grail, bold action had to be taken. 'Give me a minute,' he said, hobbling toward the cockpit.

'What are you doing?' Langdon asked.

'Sales meeting,' Teabing said, wondering how much it would cost him to persuade his pilot to perform one highly irregular manoeuvre.

Chapter 81

The Hawker *is on final approach.*

Simon Edwards – Executive Services Officer at Biggin Hill Airport – paced the control tower, squinting nervously at the rain-drenched runway. He never appreciated being awoken early on a Saturday morning, but it was particularly distasteful that he had been called in to oversee the arrest of one of his most lucrative clients. Sir Leigh Teabing paid Biggin Hill not only for a private hangar but a 'per landing fee' for his frequent arrivals and departures. Usually, the airfield had advance warning of his schedule and was able to follow a strict protocol for his arrival. Teabing liked things just so. The custom-built Jaguar stretch limousine that he kept in his hangar was to be fully tanked, polished, and the day's *Times* laid out on the back seat. A customs official was to be waiting for the plane at the hangar to expedite the mandatory documentation and luggage check. Occasionally, customs agents accepted large tips from Teabing in exchange for turning a blind eye to the transport of harmless organics – mostly luxury foods – French escargots, a particularly ripe unprocessed Roquefort, certain fruits. Many customs laws were absurd, anyway, and if Biggin Hill didn't accommodate its clients, certainly competing airfields would. Teabing was provided with what he wanted here at Biggin Hill, and the employees reaped the benefits.

Edwards's nerves felt frayed now as he watched the jet coming in. He wondered if Teabing's penchant for spreading the wealth had got him in trouble somehow; the French authorities seemed very intent on containing him. Edwards had not yet been told what the charges were, but they were obviously serious. At the French authorities' request, Kent police had ordered the Biggin Hill air traffic controller to radio the Hawker's pilot and order him directly to the terminal rather than to the client's hangar. The pilot had agreed, apparently believing the far-fetched story of a petrol leak.

Though the British police did not generally carry weapons, the gravity of the situation had brought out an armed response team. Now, eight policemen with handguns stood just inside the terminal building, awaiting the moment when the plane's engines powered down. The instant this happened, a runway attendant would place safety wedges under the tyres so the plane could no longer move. Then the police would step into view and hold the occupants at bay until the French police arrived to handle the situation.

The Hawker was low in the sky now, skimming the treetops to their right. Simon Edwards went downstairs to watch the landing from tarmac level. The Kent police were poised, just out of sight, and the maintenance man waited with his wedges. Out on the runway, the Hawker's nose tipped up, and the tyres touched down in a puff of smoke. The plane settled in for deceleration, streaking from right to left in front of the terminal, its white hull glistening in the wet weather. But rather than braking and turning into the terminal, the jet coasted calmly past the access lane and continued on toward Teabing's hangar in the distance.

All the police spun and stared at Edwards. 'I thought you said the pilot agreed to come to the terminal!'

Edwards was bewildered. 'He *did*!'

Seconds later, Edwards found himself wedged in a police car racing across the tarmac toward the distant hangar. The convoy of police was still a good five hundred yards away as Teabing's Hawker taxied calmly into the private hangar and disappeared. When the cars finally arrived and skidded to a stop outside the gaping hangar door, the police poured out, guns drawn.

Edwards jumped out too.

The noise was deafening.

The Hawker's engines were still roaring as the jet finished its usual rotation inside the hangar, positioning itself nose-out in preparation for later departure. As the plane completed its 180-degree turn and rolled toward the front of the hangar, Edwards could see the pilot's face, which understandably looked surprised and fearful to see the barricade of police cars.

The pilot brought the plane to a final stop, and powered down the engines. The police streamed in, taking up positions around the jet. Edwards joined the Kent chief inspector, who moved warily toward the hatch. After several seconds, the fuselage door popped open.

Leigh Teabing appeared in the doorway as the plane's electronic stairs smoothly dropped down. As he gazed out at the sea of weapons aimed at him, he propped himself on his crutches and scratched his head. 'Simon, did I win the policemen's lottery while I was away?' He sounded more bewildered than concerned.

Simon Edwards stepped forward, swallowing the frog in his throat. 'Good morning, sir. I apologize for the confusion. We've had a petrol leak and your pilot said he was coming to the terminal.'

'Yes, yes, well, I told him to come here instead. I'm late for an appointment. I pay for this hangar, and this rubbish about avoiding a petrol leak sounded overcautious.'

'I'm afraid your arrival has taken us a bit off guard, sir.'

'I know. I'm off my schedule, I am. Between you and me, the new medication gives me the tinkles. Thought I'd come over for a tune-up.'

The policemen all exchanged looks. Edwards winced. 'Very good, sir.'

'Sir,' the Kent chief inspector said, stepping forward. 'I need to ask you to stay onboard for another half hour or so.'

Teabing looked unamused as he hobbled down the stairs. 'I'm afraid that is impossible. I have a medical appointment.' He reached the tarmac. 'I cannot afford to miss it.'

The chief inspector repositioned himself to block Teabing's progress away from the plane. 'I am here at the orders of the French Judicial Police. They claim you are transporting fugitives from the law on this plane.'

Teabing stared at the chief inspector a long moment, and then burst out laughing. 'Is this one of those hidden camera programmes? Jolly good!'

The chief inspector never flinched. 'This is serious, sir. The French police claim you also may have a hostage onboard.'

Teabing's manservant Rémy appeared in the doorway at the top of the stairs. 'I *feel* like a hostage working for Sir Leigh, but he assures me I am free to go.' Rémy checked his watch. 'Master, we really are running late.' He nodded toward the Jaguar stretch limousine in the far corner of the hangar. The enormous automobile was ebony with smoked glass and whitewall tyres. 'I'll bring the car.' Rémy started down the stairs.

'I'm afraid we cannot let you leave,' the chief

inspector said. 'Please return to your aircraft. Both of you. Representatives from the French police will be landing shortly.'

Teabing looked now toward Simon Edwards. 'Simon, for heaven's sake, this is ridiculous! We don't have anyone else on board. Just the usual – Rémy, our pilot, and myself. Perhaps you could act as an intermediary? Go and have a look onboard, and verify that the plane is empty.'

Edwards knew he was trapped. 'Yes, sir. I can have a look.'

'The devil you will!' the Kent chief inspector declared, apparently knowing enough about executive airfields to suspect Simon Edwards might well lie about the plane's occupants in an effort to keep Teabing's business at Biggin Hill. 'I will look myself.'

Teabing shook his head. 'No you won't, Inspector. This is private property and until you have a search warrant, you will stay off my plane. I am offering you a reasonable option here. Mr Edwards can perform the inspection.'

'No deal.'

Teabing's demeanour turned frosty. 'Inspector, I'm afraid I don't have time to indulge in your games. I'm late, and I'm leaving. If it is that important to you to stop me, you'll just have to shoot me.' With that, Teabing and Rémy walked around the chief inspector and headed across the hangar toward the parked limousine.

The Kent chief inspector felt only distaste for Leigh Teabing as the man hobbled around him in defiance. Men of privilege always felt like they were above the law.

They are not. The chief inspector turned and aimed at Teabing's back. 'Stop! I will fire!'

'Go ahead,' Teabing said without breaking stride or glancing back. 'My lawyers will fricassee your testicles for breakfast. And if you dare board my plane without a warrant, your spleen will follow.'

No stranger to power plays, the chief inspector was unimpressed. Technically, Teabing was correct and the police needed a warrant to board his jet, but because the flight had originated in France, and because the powerful Bezu Fache had given his authority, the Kent chief inspector felt certain his career would be far better served by finding out what it was on this plane that Teabing seemed so intent on hiding.

'Stop them,' the inspector ordered. 'I'm searching the plane.'

His men raced over, guns levelled, and physically blocked Teabing and his servant from reaching the limousine.

Now Teabing turned. 'Inspector, this is your last warning. Do not even think of boarding that plane. You will regret it.'

Ignoring the threat, the chief inspector gripped his sidearm and marched up the plane's gangway. Arriving at the hatch, he peered inside. After a moment, he stepped into the cabin. *What the devil?*

With the exception of the frightened-looking pilot in the cockpit, the aircraft was empty. Entirely devoid of human life. Quickly checking the bathroom, the chairs, and the luggage areas, the inspector found no traces of anyone hiding . . . much less multiple individuals.

What the hell was Bezu Fache thinking? It seemed Leigh Teabing had been telling the truth.

The Kent chief inspector stood alone in the deserted cabin and swallowed hard. *Shit.* His face flushed, he stepped back onto the gangway, gazing across the hangar at Leigh Teabing and his servant, who were now under gunpoint near the limousine. 'Let them go,' the inspector ordered. 'We received a bad tip.'

Teabing's eyes were menacing even across the hangar. 'You can expect a call from my lawyers. And for future reference, the French police cannot be trusted.'

With that, Teabing's manservant opened the door at the rear of the stretch limousine and helped his crippled master into the back seat. Then the servant walked the length of the car, climbed in behind the wheel, and gunned the engine. Policemen scattered as the Jaguar peeled out of the hangar.

'Well played, my good man,' Teabing chimed from the rear seat as the limousine accelerated out of the airport. He turned his eyes now to the dimly lit front recesses of the spacious interior. 'Everyone comfy?'

Langdon gave a weak nod. He and Sophie were still crouched on the floor beside the bound and gagged albino.

Moments earlier, as the Hawker taxied into the deserted hangar, Rémy had popped the hatch as the plane jolted to a stop halfway through its turn. With the police closing in fast, Langdon and Sophie dragged the monk down the gangway to ground level and out of sight behind the limousine. Then the jet engines had roared again, rotating the plane and completing its turn as the police cars came skidding into the hangar.

Now, as the limousine raced toward Kent, Langdon and Sophie clambered toward the rear of the limo's long interior, leaving the monk bound on the floor. They settled onto the long seat facing Teabing. The

Englishman gave them both a roguish smile and opened the cabinet on the limo's bar. 'Could I offer you a drink? Some nibbles? Crisps? Nuts? Seltzer?'

Sophie and Langdon both shook their heads.

Teabing grinned and closed the bar. 'So then, about this knight's tomb . . .'

Chapter 82

'Fleet Street?' Langdon asked, eyeing Teabing in the back of the limo. *There's a crypt on Fleet Street?* So far, Leigh was being playfully cagey about where he thought they would find the 'knight's tomb', which, according to the poem, would provide the password for opening the smaller cryptex.

Teabing grinned and turned to Sophie. 'Miss Neveu, give the Harvard boy one more shot at the verse, will you?'

Sophie fished in her pocket and pulled out the black cryptex, which was wrapped in the vellum. Everyone had decided to leave the rosewood box and larger cryptex behind in the plane's strongbox, carrying with them only what they needed, the far more portable and discreet black cryptex. Sophie unwrapped the vellum and handed the sheet to Langdon.

Although Langdon had read the poem several times onboard the jet, he had been unable to extract any specific location. Now, as he read the words again, he processed them slowly and carefully, hoping the pentametric rhythms would reveal a clearer meaning now that he was on the ground.

In London lies a knight a Pope interred.
His labour's fruit a Holy wrath incurred.
You seek the orb that ought be on his tomb.
It speaks of Rosy flesh and seeded womb.

The language seemed simple enough. There was a

knight buried in London. A knight who laboured at something that angered the Church. A knight whose tomb was missing an orb that *should* be present. The poem's final reference – *Rosy flesh and seeded womb* – was a clear allusion to Mary Magdalene, the Rose who bore the seed of Jesus.

Despite the apparent straightforwardness of the verse, Langdon still had no idea *who* this knight was or where he was buried. Moreover, once they located the tomb, it sounded as if they would be searching for something that was absent. *The orb that ought be on his tomb?*

'No thoughts?' Teabing clucked in disappointment, although Langdon sensed the Royal Historian was enjoying being one up. 'Miss Neveu?'

She shook her head.

'What would you two do without me?' Teabing said. 'Very well, I will walk you through it. It's quite simple really. The first line is the key. Would you read it please?'

Langdon read aloud. '"In London lies a knight a Pope interred."'

'Precisely. A knight a *Pope* interred.' He eyed Langdon. 'What does that mean to you?'

Langdon shrugged. 'A knight buried by a Pope? A knight whose funeral was presided over by a Pope?'

Teabing laughed loudly. 'Oh, that's rich. Always the optimist, Robert. Look at the second line. This knight obviously did something that incurred the holy wrath of the Church. Think again. Consider the dynamic between the Church and the Knights Templar. A knight a Pope interred?'

'A knight a Pope *killed*?' Sophie asked.

Teabing smiled and patted her knee. 'Well done, my dear. A knight a Pope *buried*. Or killed.'

Langdon thought of the notorious Templar

round-up in 1307 – unlucky Friday the thirteenth – when Pope Clement killed and interred hundreds of Knights Templar. 'But there must be endless graves of "knights killed by Popes".'

'Aha, not so!' Teabing said. 'Many of them were burned at the stake and tossed unceremoniously into the Tiber River. But this poem refers to a *tomb*. A tomb in London. And there are few knights buried in London.' He paused, eyeing Langdon as if waiting for light to dawn. Finally he huffed. 'Robert, for heaven's sake! The church built in London by the Priory's military arm – the Knights Templar themselves!'

'The Temple Church?' Langdon drew a startled breath. 'It has a crypt?'

'Ten of the most frightening tombs you will ever see.'

Langdon had never actually visited the Temple Church, although he'd come across numerous references in his Priory research. Once the epicentre of all Templar/Priory activities in the United Kingdom, the Temple Church had been so named in honour of Solomon's Temple, from which the Knights Templar had extracted their own title, as well as the Sangreal documents that gave them all their influence in Rome. Tales abounded of knights performing strange, secretive rituals within the Temple Church's unusual sanctuary. 'The Temple Church is on Fleet Street?'

'Actually, it's just off Fleet Street on Inner Temple Lane.' Teabing looked mischievous. 'I wanted to see you sweat a little more before I gave it away.'

'Thanks.'

'Neither of you has ever been there?'

Sophie and Langdon shook their heads.

'I'm not surprised,' Teabing said. 'The church is hidden now behind much larger buildings. Few people even know it's there. Eerie old place. The architecture is pagan to the core.'

Sophie looked surprised. 'Pagan?'

'Pantheonically pagan!' Teabing exclaimed. 'The church is *round*. The Templars ignored the traditional Christian cruciform layout and built a perfectly circular church in honour of the sun.' His eyebrows did a devilish dance. 'A not so subtle howdy-do to the boys in Rome. They might as well have resurrected Stonehenge in central London.'

Sophie eyed Teabing. 'What about the rest of the poem?'

The historian's mirthful air faded. 'I'm not sure. It's puzzling. We will need to examine each of the ten tombs carefully. With luck, one of them will have a conspicuously absent orb.'

Langdon realized how close they really were. If the missing orb revealed the password, they would be able to open the second cryptex. He had a hard time imagining what they might find inside.

Langdon eyed the poem again. It was like some kind of primordial crossword puzzle. *A five-letter word that speaks of the Grail?* On the plane, they had already tried all the obvious passwords – GRAIL, GRAAL, GREAL, VENUS, MARIA, JESUS, SARAH – but the cylinder had not budged. *Far too obvious.* Apparently there existed some other five-letter reference to the Rose's seeded womb. The fact that the word was eluding a specialist like Leigh Teabing signified to Langdon that it was no ordinary Grail reference.

'Sir Leigh?' Rémy called over his shoulder. He was watching them in the rearview mirror through the open divider. 'You said Fleet Street is near Blackfriars Bridge?'

'Yes, take Victoria Embankment.'

'I'm sorry. I'm not sure where that is. We usually go only to the hospital.'

Teabing rolled his eyes at Langdon and Sophie and grumbled, 'I swear, sometimes it's like baby-sitting a child. One moment, please. Help yourself to a drink and savoury snacks.' He left them, clambering awkwardly toward the open divider to talk to Rémy.

Sophie turned to Langdon now, her voice quiet. 'Robert, nobody knows you and I are in England.'

Langdon realized she was right. The Kent police would tell Fache the plane was empty, and Fache would have to assume they were still in France. *We are invisible.* Leigh's little stunt had just bought them a lot of time.

'Fache will not give up easily,' Sophie said. 'He has too much riding on this arrest now.'

Langdon had been trying not to think about Fache. Sophie had promised she would do everything in her power to exonerate Langdon once this was over, but Langdon was starting to fear it might not matter. *Fache could easily be part of this plot.* Although Langdon could not imagine the Judicial Police tangled up in the Holy Grail, he sensed too much coincidence tonight to disregard Fache as a possible accomplice. *Fache is religious, and he is intent on pinning these murders on me.* Then again, Sophie had argued that Fache might simply be overzealous to make the arrest. After all, the evidence against Langdon was substantial. In addition to Langdon's name scrawled on the Louvre floor and in Saunière's date book, Langdon now appeared to have lied about his manuscript and then run away. *At Sophie's suggestion.*

'Robert, I'm sorry you're so deeply involved,' Sophie said, placing her hand on his knee. 'But I'm very glad you're here.'

The comment sounded more pragmatic than romantic, and yet Langdon felt an unexpected flicker of attraction between them. He gave her a tired smile. 'I'm a lot more fun when I've slept.'

Sophie was silent for several seconds. 'My grandfather asked me to trust you. I'm glad I listened to him for once.'

'Your grandfather didn't even know me.'

'Even so, I can't help but think you've done everything he would have wanted. You helped me find the keystone, explained the Sangreal, told me about the ritual in the basement.' She paused. 'Somehow I feel closer to my grandfather tonight than I have for years. I know he would be happy about that.'

In the distance, now, the skyline of London began to materialize through the dawn drizzle. Once dominated by Big Ben and Tower Bridge, the horizon now bowed to the Millennium Eye – a colossal, ultramodern Ferris wheel that climbed five hundred feet and afforded breathtaking views of the city. Langdon had attempted to board it once, but the 'viewing capsules' reminded him of sealed sarcophagi, and he opted to keep his feet on the ground and enjoy the view from the airy banks of the Thames.

Langdon felt a squeeze on his knee, pulling him back, and Sophie's green eyes were on him. He realized she had been speaking to him. 'What do *you* think we should do with the Sangreal documents if we ever find them?' she whispered.

'What I think is immaterial,' Langdon said. 'Your grandfather gave the cryptex to you, and you should do with it what your instinct tells you he would want done.'

'I'm asking for your opinion. You obviously wrote something in that manuscript that made my grandfather trust your judgment. He scheduled a private meeting with you. That's rare.'

'Maybe he wanted to tell me I have it all wrong.'

'Why would he tell me to find you unless he liked your ideas? In your manuscript, did you support the idea that the Sangreal documents should be revealed or stay buried?'

'Neither. I made no judgment either way. The manuscript deals with the symbology of the sacred feminine – tracing her iconography throughout history. I certainly didn't presume to know where the Grail is hidden or whether it should ever be revealed.'

'And yet you're writing a book about it, so you obviously feel the information should be shared.'

'There's an enormous difference between hypothetically discussing an alternative history of Christ, and . . .' He paused.

'And what?'

'And presenting to the world thousands of ancient documents as scientific evidence that the New Testament is false testimony.'

'But you told me the New Testament is based on fabrications.'

Langdon smiled. 'Sophie, *every* faith in the world is based on fabrication. That is the definition of *faith* – acceptance of that which we imagine to be true, that which we cannot prove. Every religion describes God through metaphor, allegory and exaggeration, from the early Egyptians through modern Sunday school. Metaphors are a way to help our minds process the unprocessible. The problems arise when we begin to believe literally in our own metaphors.'

'So you are in favour of the Sangreal documents staying buried for ever?'

'I'm a historian. I'm opposed to the destruction of documents, and I would love to see religious scholars have more information to ponder the exceptional life of Jesus Christ.'

'You're arguing both sides of my question.'

'Am I? The Bible represents a fundamental guidepost

for millions of people on the planet, in much the same way the Koran, Torah and Pali Canon offer guidance to people of other religions. If you and I could dig up documentation that contradicted the holy stories of Islamic belief, Judaic belief, Buddhist belief, pagan belief, should we do that? Should we wave a flag and tell the Buddhists that we have proof the Buddha did not come from a lotus blossom? Or that Jesus was not born of a *literal* virgin birth? Those who truly understand their faiths understand the stories are metaphorical.'

Sophie looked sceptical. 'My friends who are devout Christians definitely believe that Christ *literally* walked on water, *literally* turned water into wine and was born of a *literal* virgin birth.'

'My point exactly,' Langdon said. 'Religious allegory has become a part of the fabric of reality. And living in that reality helps millions of people cope and be better people.'

'But it appears their reality is false.'

Langdon chuckled. 'No more false than that of a mathematical cryptographer who believes in the imaginary number '*i*' because it helps her break codes.'

Sophie frowned. 'That's not fair.'

A moment passed.

'What was your question again?' Langdon asked.

'I can't remember.'

He smiled. 'Works every time.'

Chapter 83

Langdon's Mickey Mouse wristwatch read almost seven-thirty when he emerged from the Jaguar limousine onto Inner Temple Lane with Sophie and Teabing. The threesome wound through a maze of buildings to a small courtyard outside the Temple Church. The rough-hewn stone shimmered in the rain, and doves cooed in the architecture overhead.

London's ancient Temple Church was constructed entirely of Caen stone. A dramatic, circular edifice with a daunting façade, a central turret and a protruding nave off one side, the church looked more like a military stronghold than a place of worship. Consecrated on the tenth of February in 1185 by Heraclius, Patriarch of Jerusalem, the Temple Church survived eight centuries of political turmoil, the Great Fire of London and the First World War, only to be heavily damaged by Luftwaffe incendiary bombs in 1940. After the war, it was restored to its original, stark grandeur.

The simplicity of the circle, Langdon thought, admiring the building for the first time. The architecture was coarse and simple, more reminiscent of Rome's rugged Castel Sant'Angelo than the refined Pantheon. The boxy annex jutting out to the right was an unfortunate eyesore, although it did little to shroud the original pagan shape of the primary structure.

'It's early on a Saturday,' Teabing said, hobbling toward the entrance, 'so I'm assuming we won't have services to deal with.'

The church's entryway was a recessed stone niche

inside which stood a large wooden door. To the left of the door, looking entirely out of place, hung a bulletin board covered with concert schedules and religious service announcements.

Teabing frowned as he read the board. 'They don't open to sightseers for another couple of hours.' He moved to the door and tried it. The door didn't budge. Putting his ear to the wood, he listened. After a moment, he pulled back, a scheming look on his face as he pointed to the bulletin board. 'Robert, check the service schedule, will you? Who is presiding this week?'

Inside the church, an altar boy was almost finished vacuuming the communion kneelers when he heard a knocking on the sanctuary door. He ignored it. The Reverend Harvey Knowles had his own keys and was not due for another couple of hours. The knocking was probably a curious tourist or indigent. The altar boy kept vacuuming, but the knocking continued. *Can't you read?* The sign on the door clearly stated that the church did not open until nine-thirty on Saturday. The altar boy remained with his chores.

Suddenly, the knocking turned to a forceful banging, as if someone were hitting the door with a metal rod. The young man switched off his vacuum cleaner and marched angrily toward the door. Unlatching it from within, he swung it open. Three people stood in the entryway. Tourists, he grumbled. 'We open at nine-thirty.'

The heavyset man, apparently the leader, stepped forward using metal crutches. 'I am Sir Leigh Teabing,' he said, his accent highbrow British. 'As you are no doubt aware, I am escorting Mr and Mrs Christopher Wren the Fourth.' He stepped aside, flourishing his arm toward the attractive couple behind them. The woman was soft-featured, with lush burgundy hair. The man was tall, dark-haired and looked vaguely familiar.

The altar boy had no idea how to respond. Sir Christopher Wren was the Temple Church's most famous benefactor. He had made possible all the restorations following damage caused by the Great Fire. He had also been dead since the early eighteenth century. 'Um . . . an honour to meet you?'

The man on crutches frowned. 'Good thing you're not in sales, young man, you're not very convincing. Where is the Reverend Knowles?'

'It's Saturday. He's not due in until later.'

The crippled man's scowl deepened. 'There's gratitude. He assured us he would be here, but it looks as though we'll do it without him. It won't take long.'

The altar boy remained blocking the doorway. 'I'm sorry, *what* won't take long?'

The visitor's eyes sharpened now, and he leaned forward whispering as if to save everyone some embarrassment. 'Young man, apparently you are new here. Every year Sir Christopher Wren's descendants bring a pinch of the old man's ashes to scatter in the Temple sanctuary. It is part of his last will and testament. Nobody is particularly happy about making the trip, but what can we do?'

The altar boy had been here a couple of years but had never heard of this custom. 'It would be better if you waited until nine-thirty. The church isn't open yet, and I'm not finished hoovering.'

The man on crutches glared angrily. 'Young man, the only reason there's anything left of this building for you to hoover is on account of the gentleman in that woman's pocket.'

'I'm sorry?'

'Mrs Wren,' the man on crutches said, 'would you be so kind as to show this impertinent young man the reliquary of ashes?'

The woman hesitated a moment and then, as if awaking from a trance, reached in her sweater pocket and pulled out a small cylinder wrapped in protective fabric.

'There, you see?' the man on crutches snapped. 'Now, you can either grant his dying wish and let us sprinkle his ashes in the sanctuary, or I tell Mr Knowles how we've been treated.'

The altar boy hesitated, well acquainted with Mr Knowles' deep observance of church tradition . . . and, more important, with his foul temper when anything cast this time-honoured shrine in anything but favourable light. Maybe Mr Knowles had simply forgotten these family members were coming. If so, then there was far more risk in turning them away than in letting them in. *After all, they said it would only take a minute. What harm could it do?*

When the altar boy stepped aside to let the three people pass, he could have sworn Mr and Mrs Wren looked just as bewildered by all of this as he was. Uncertain, the boy returned to his chores, watching them out of the corner of his eye.

Langdon had to smile as the threesome moved deeper into the church. 'Leigh,' he whispered, 'you lie entirely too well.'

Teabing's eyes twinkled. 'Oxford Theatre Club. They still talk of my Julius Caesar. I'm certain nobody has ever performed the first scene of Act Three with more dedication.'

Langdon glanced over. 'I thought Caesar was *dead* in that scene.'

Teabing smirked. 'Yes, but my toga tore open when I fell, and I had to lie on stage for half an hour with my todger hanging out. Even so, I never moved a muscle. I was brilliant, I tell you.'

Langdon cringed. *Sorry I missed it.*

As the group moved through the rectangular annex toward the archway leading into the main church, Langdon was surprised by the barren austerity. Although the altar layout resembled that of a linear Christian chapel, the furnishings were stark and cold, bearing none of the traditional ornamentation. 'Bleak,' he whispered.

Teabing chuckled. 'Church of England. Anglicans drink their religion straight. Nothing to distract from their misery.'

Sophie motioned through the vast opening that gave way to the circular section of the church. 'It looks like a fortress in there,' she whispered.

Langdon agreed. Even from here, the walls looked unusually robust.

'The Knights Templar were warriors,' Teabing reminded, the sound of his aluminium crutches echoing in this reverberant space. 'A religio-military society. Their churches were their strongholds and their banks.'

'Banks?' Sophie asked, glancing at Leigh.

'Heavens, yes. The Templars *invented* the concept of modern banking. For European nobility, travelling with gold was perilous, so the Templars allowed nobles to deposit gold in their nearest Temple Church and then draw it from any *other* Temple Church across Europe. All they needed was proper documentation.' He winked. 'And a small commission. They were the original ATMs.' Teabing pointed toward a stained-glass window where the breaking sun was refracting through a white-clad knight riding a rose-coloured horse. 'Alanus Marcel,' Teabing said, 'Master of the Temple in the early twelve hundreds. He and his successors actually held the Parliamentary chair of Primus Baro Angiae.'

Langdon was surprised. 'First Baron of the Realm?'

Teabing nodded. 'The Master of the Temple, some claim, held more influence than the king himself.' As they arrived outside the circular chamber, Teabing shot a glance over his shoulder at the altar boy, who was vacuuming in the distance. 'You know,' Teabing whispered to Sophie, 'the Holy Grail is said to once have been stored in this church overnight while the Templars moved it from one hiding place to another. Can you imagine the four chests of Sangreal documents sitting right here with Mary Magdalene's sarcophagus? It gives me gooseflesh.'

Langdon was feeling gooseflesh too as they stepped into the circular chamber. His eye traced the curvature of the chamber's pale stone perimeter, taking in the carvings of gargoyles, demons, monsters and pained human faces, all staring inward. Beneath the carvings, a single stone pew curled around the entire circumference of the room.

'Theatre in the round,' Langdon whispered.

Teabing raised a crutch, pointing toward the far left of the room and then to the far right. Langdon had already seen them.

Ten stone knights.

Five on the left. Five on the right.

Lying supine on the floor, the carved, life-sized figures rested in peaceful poses. The knights were depicted wearing full armour, shields, and swords, and the tombs gave Langdon the uneasy sensation that someone had sneaked in and poured plaster over the knights while they were sleeping. All of the figures were deeply weathered, and yet each was clearly unique – different armoury pieces, distinct leg and arm positions, facial features, and markings on their shields.

In London lies a knight a Pope interred.

Langdon felt shaky as he inched deeper into the circular room.

This had to be the place.

Chapter 84

In a rubbish-strewn alley very close to Temple Church, Rémy Legaludec pulled the Jaguar limousine to a stop behind a row of industrial waste bins. Killing the engine, he checked the area. Deserted. He got out of the car, walked toward the rear, and climbed back into the limousine's main cabin where the monk was.

Sensing Rémy's presence, the monk in the back emerged from a prayer-like trance, his red eyes looking more curious than fearful. All evening Rémy had been impressed with this trussed man's ability to stay calm. After some initial struggles in the Range Rover, the monk seemed to have accepted his plight and given over his fate to a higher power.

Loosening his bow tie, Rémy unbuttoned his high, starched, wing-tipped collar and felt as if he could breathe for the first time in years. He went to the limousine's wet bar, where he poured himself a Smirnoff vodka. He drank it in a single swallow and followed it with a second.

Soon I will be a man of leisure.

Searching the bar, Rémy found a standard service wine-opener and flicked open the sharp blade. The knife was usually employed to slice the lead foil from corks on fine bottles of wine, but it would serve a far more dramatic purpose this morning. Rémy turned and faced Silas, holding up the glimmering blade.

Now those red eyes flashed fear.

Rémy smiled and moved toward the back of the

limousine. The monk recoiled, struggling against his bonds.

'Be still,' Rémy whispered, raising the blade.

Silas could not believe that God had forsaken him. Even the physical pain of being bound Silas had turned into a spiritual exercise, asking the throb of his blood-starved muscles to remind him of the pain Christ endured. *I have been praying all night for liberation.* Now, as the knife descended, Silas clenched his eyes shut.

A slash of pain tore through his shoulder blades. He cried out, unable to believe he was going to die here in the back of this limousine, unable to defend himself. *I was doing God's work. The Teacher said he would protect me.*

Silas felt the biting warmth spreading across his back and shoulders and could picture his own blood, spilling out over his flesh. A piercing pain cut through his thighs now, and he felt the onset of that familiar undertow of disorientation – the body's defence mechanism against the pain.

As the biting heat tore through all of his muscles now, Silas clenched his eyes tighter, determined that the final image of his life would not be of his own killer. Instead he pictured a younger Bishop Aringarosa, standing before the small church in Spain . . . the church that he and Silas had built with their own hands. *The beginning of my life.*

Silas felt as if his body were on fire.

'Take a drink,' the tuxedoed man whispered, his accent French. 'It will help with your circulation.'

Silas's eyes flew open in surprise. A blurry image was leaning over him, offering a glass of liquid. A mound of shredded duct tape lay on the floor beside the bloodless knife.

'Drink this,' he repeated. 'The pain you feel is the blood rushing into your muscles.'

Silas felt the fiery throb transforming now to a prickling sting. The vodka tasted terrible, but he drank it, feeling grateful. Fate had dealt Silas a healthy share of bad luck tonight, but God had solved it all with one miraculous twist.

God has not forsaken me.

Silas knew what Bishop Aringarosa would call it.

Divine intervention.

'I had wanted to free you earlier,' the servant apologized, 'but it was impossible. With the police arriving at Château Villette, and then at Biggin Hill airport, this was the first possible moment. You understand, don't you, Silas?'

Silas recoiled, startled. 'You know my name?'

The servant smiled.

Silas sat up now, rubbing his stiff muscles, his emotions a torrent of incredulity, appreciation and confusion. 'Are you . . . the Teacher?'

Rémy shook his head, laughing at the proposition. 'I wish I had that kind of power. No, I am not the Teacher. Like you, I serve him. But the Teacher speaks highly of you. My name is Rémy.'

Silas was amazed. 'I don't understand. If you work for the Teacher, why did Langdon bring the keystone to *your* home?'

'Not my home. The home of the world's foremost Grail historian, Sir Leigh Teabing.'

'But *you* live there. The odds . . .'

Rémy smiled, seeming to have no trouble with the apparent coincidence of Langdon's chosen refuge. 'It was all utterly predictable. Robert Langdon was in possession of the keystone, and he needed help. What more logical place to run than to the home of Leigh Teabing? That I happen to live there is why the Teacher approached me in the first place.' He paused. 'How do you think the Teacher knows so much about the Grail?'

Now it dawned, and Silas was stunned. The Teacher had recruited a servant who had access to all of Sir Leigh Teabing's research. It was brilliant.

'There is much I have to tell you,' Rémy said, handing Silas the loaded Heckler Koch pistol. Then he reached through the open partition and retrieved a small, palm-sized revolver from the glove box. 'But first, you and I have a job to do.'

Captain Fache descended from his transport plane at Biggin Hill and listened in disbelief to the Kent chief inspector's account of what had happened in Teabing's hangar.

'I searched the plane myself,' the inspector insisted, 'and there was no one inside.' His tone turned haughty. 'And I should add that if Sir Leigh Teabing presses charges against me, I will—'

'Did you interrogate the pilot?'

'Of course not. He is French, and our jurisdiction requires—'

'Take me to the plane.'

Arriving at the hangar, Fache needed only sixty seconds to locate an anomalous smear of blood on the pavement near where the limousine had been parked. Fache walked up to the plane and rapped loudly on the fuselage.

'This is the captain of the French Judicial Police. Open the door!'

The terrified pilot opened the hatch and lowered the stairs.

Fache ascended. Three minutes later, with the help of his sidearm, he had a full confession, including a description of the bound albino monk. In addition, he learned that the pilot saw Langdon and Sophie leave something behind in Teabing's safe, a wooden box of some sort. Although the pilot denied knowing what was in the box, he admitted it had been the focus of Langdon's full attention during the flight to London.

'Open the safe,' Fache demanded.

The pilot looked terrified. 'I don't know the combination!'

'That's too bad. I was going to offer to let you keep your pilot's licence.'

The pilot wrung his hands. 'I know some men in maintenance here. Maybe they could drill it?'

'You have half an hour.'

The pilot leapt for his radio.

Fache strode to the back of the plane and poured himself a hard drink. It was early, but he had not yet slept, so this hardly counted as drinking before noon. Sitting in a plush bucket seat, he closed his eyes, trying to sort out what was going on. *The Kent police's blunder could cost me dearly.* Everyone was now on the lookout for a black Jaguar limousine.

Fache's phone rang, and he wished for a moment's peace. '*Allo?*'

'I'm en route to London.' It was Bishop Aringarosa. 'I'll be arriving in an hour.'

Fache sat up. 'I thought you were going to Paris.'

'I am deeply concerned. I have changed my plans.'

'You should not have.'

'Do you have Silas?'

'No. His captors eluded the local police before I landed.'

Aringarosa's anger rang sharply. 'You assured me you would stop that plane!'

Fache lowered his voice. 'Bishop, considering your situation, I recommend you not test my patience today. I will find Silas and the others as soon as possible. Where are you landing?'

'One moment.' Aringarosa covered the receiver and then came back. 'The pilot is trying to get clearance at Heathrow. I'm his only passenger, but our redirect was unscheduled.'

'Tell him to come to Biggin Hill Executive Airport in Kent. I'll get him clearance. If I'm not here when you land, I'll have a car waiting for you.'

'Thank you.'

'As I expressed when we first spoke, Bishop, you would do well to remember that you are not the only man on the verge of losing everything.'

Chapter 85

You seek the orb that ought be on his tomb.

Each of the carved knights within the Temple Church lay on his back with his head resting on a rectangular stone pillow. Sophie felt a chill. The poem's reference to an 'orb' conjured images of the night in her grandfather's basement.

Hieros Gamos. The orbs.

Sophie wondered if the ritual had been performed in this very sanctuary. The circular room seemed custom-built for such a pagan rite. A stone pew encircled a bare expanse of floor in the middle. *A theatre in the round*, as Robert had called it. She imagined this chamber at night, filled with masked people, chanting by torchlight, all witnessing a 'sacred communion' in the centre of the room.

Forcing the image from her mind, she advanced with Langdon and Teabing toward the first group of knights. Despite Teabing's insistence that their investigation should be conducted meticulously, Sophie felt eager and pushed ahead of them, making a cursory walk-through of the five knights on the left.

Scrutinizing these first tombs, Sophie noted the similarities and differences between them. Every knight was on his back, but three of the knights had their legs extended straight out while two had their legs crossed. The oddity seemed to have no relevance to the missing orb. Examining their clothing, Sophie noted that two of the knights wore tunics over their armour, while the other three wore ankle-length robes. Again, utterly unhelpful. Sophie turned her attention to the only other obvious difference – their hand positions. Two knights clutched swords, two prayed,. and one had his arms at his sides. After a long moment looking at the hands, Sophie shrugged, having seen no hint anywhere of a conspicuously absent orb.

Feeling the weight of the cryptex in her sweater pocket, she glanced back at Langdon and Teabing. The men were moving slowly, still only at the third knight, apparently having no luck either. In no mood to wait, she turned away from them toward the second group of knights. As she crossed the open space, she quietly recited the poem she had read so many times now that it was committed to memory.

In London lies a knight a Pope interred.
His labour's fruit a Holy wrath incurred.
You seek the orb that ought be on his tomb.
It speaks of Rosy flesh and seeded womb.

When Sophie arrived at the second group of knights, she found that this second group was similar to the first. All lay with varied body positions, wearing armour and swords.

That was, all except the tenth and final tomb.

Hurrying over to it, she stared down.

No pillow. No armour. No tunic. No sword.

'Robert? Leigh?' she called, her voice echoing around the chamber. 'There's something missing over here.'

Both men looked up and immediately began to cross the room toward her.

'An orb?' Teabing called excitedly. His crutches clicked out a rapid staccato as he hurried across the room. 'Are we missing an orb?'

'Not exactly,' Sophie said, frowning at the tenth tomb. 'We seem to be missing an entire knight.'

Arriving beside her, both men gazed down in confusion at the tenth tomb. Rather than a knight lying in the open air, this tomb was a sealed stone coffin. The coffin was trapezoidal, tapered at the feet, widening toward the top, with a peaked lid.

'Why isn't this knight shown?' Langdon asked.

'Fascinating,' Teabing said, stroking his chin. 'I had forgotten about this oddity. It's been years since I was here.'

'This coffin,' Sophie said, 'looks like it was carved at the same time and by the same sculptor as the other nine tombs. So why is this knight in a coffin rather than in the open?'

Teabing shook his head. 'One of this church's mysteries. To the best of my knowledge, nobody has ever found any explanation for it.'

'Hello?' the altar boy said, arriving with a perturbed look on his face. 'Forgive me if this seems rude, but you told me you wanted to spread ashes, and yet you seem to be sightseeing.'

Teabing scowled at the boy and turned to Langdon. 'Mr Wren, apparently your family's philanthropy does not buy you the time it used to, so perhaps we should take out the ashes and get on with it.' Teabing turned to Sophie. 'Mrs Wren?'

Sophie played along, pulling the vellum-wrapped cryptex from her pocket.

'Now then,' Teabing snapped at the boy, 'if you would give us some privacy?'

The altar boy did not move. He was eyeing Langdon closely now. 'You look familiar.'

Teabing huffed. 'Perhaps that is because Mr Wren comes here every year!'

Or perhaps, Sophie now feared, *because he saw*

Langdon on television at the Vatican last year.

'I have never met Mr Wren,' the altar boy declared.

'You're mistaken,' Langdon said politely. 'I believe you and I met in passing last year. Mr Knowles failed to formally introduce us, but I recognized your face as we came in. Now, I realize this is an intrusion, but if you could afford me a few more minutes, I have travelled a great distance to scatter ashes amonst these tombs.' Langdon spoke his lines with Teabing-esque believability.

The altar boy's expression turned even more sceptical. 'These are not *tombs*.'

'I'm sorry?' Langdon said.

'Of course they are tombs,' Teabing declared. 'What are you talking about?'

The altar boy shook his head. 'Tombs contain bodies. These are effigies. Stone tributes to real men. There are no bodies beneath these figures.'

'This is a crypt!' Teabing said.

'Only in outdated history books. This was believed to be a crypt but was revealed as nothing of the sort during the 1950 renovation.' He turned back to Langdon. 'And I imagine Mr Wren would *know* that. Considering it was his family that uncovered that fact.'

An uneasy silence fell.

It was broken by the sound of a door slamming out in the annex.

'That must be Mr Knowles,' Teabing said. 'Perhaps you should go and see?'

The altar boy looked doubtful but stalked back toward the annex, leaving Langdon, Sophie and Teabing to eye one another gloomily.

'Leigh,' Langdon whispered. 'No bodies? What is he talking about?'

Teabing looked distraught. 'I don't know. I always

469

thought . . . certainly, this *must* be the place. I can't imagine he knows what he is talking about. It makes no sense!'

'Can I see the poem again?' Langdon said.

Sophie pulled the cryptex from her pocket and carefully handed it to him.

Langdon unwrapped the vellum, holding the cryptex in his hand while he examined the poem. 'Yes, the poem definitely references a *tomb*. Not an effigy.'

'Could the poem be wrong?' Teabing asked. 'Could Jacques Saunière have made the same mistake I just did?'

Langdon considered it and shook his head. 'Leigh, you said it yourself. This church was built by Templars, the military arm of the Priory. Something tells me the Grand Master of the Priory would have a pretty good idea if there were knights buried here.'

Teabing looked flabbergasted. 'But this place is perfect.' He wheeled back toward the knights. 'We must be missing something!'

Entering the annex, the altar boy was surprised to find it deserted. 'Mr Knowles?' *I know I heard the door*, he thought, moving forward until he could see the entryway.

A thin man in a tuxedo stood near the doorway, scratching his head and looking lost. The altar boy gave an irritated huff, realizing he had forgotten to relock the door when he let the others in. Now some pathetic sod had wandered in off the street, looking for directions to some wedding from the looks of it. 'I'm sorry,' he called out, passing a large pillar, 'we're closed.'

A flurry of cloth ruffled behind him, and before the

altar boy could turn, his head snapped backward, a powerful hand clamping hard over his mouth from behind, muffling his scream. The hand over the boy's mouth was snow-white, and he smelled alcohol.

The prim man in the tuxedo calmly produced a very small revolver, which he aimed directly at the boy's forehead.

The altar boy felt his groin grow hot and realized he had wet himself.

'Listen carefully,' the tuxedoed man whispered. 'You will exit this church silently, and you will run. You will not stop. Is that clear?'

The boy nodded as best he could with the hand over his mouth.

'If you call the police . . .' The tuxedoed man pressed the gun to his skin. 'I will find you.'

The next thing the boy knew, he was sprinting across the outside courtyard with no plans of stopping until his legs gave out.

Chapter 86

Like a ghost, Silas drifted silently behind his target. Sophie Neveu sensed him too late. Before she could turn, Silas pressed the gun barrel into her spine and wrapped a powerful arm across her chest, pulling her back against his hulking body. She yelled in surprise. Teabing and Langdon both turned now, their expressions astonished and fearful.

'What . . . ?' Teabing choked out. 'What did you do to Rémy!'

'Your only concern,' Silas said calmly, 'is that I leave here with the keystone.' This recovery mission, as Rémy had described it, was to be clean and simple: *Enter the church, take the keystone, and walk out; no killing, no struggle.*

Holding Sophie firm, Silas dropped his hand from her chest, down to her waist, slipping it inside her deep sweater pockets, searching. He could smell the soft fragrance of her hair through his own alcohol-laced breath. 'Where is it?' he whispered. *The keystone was in her sweater pocket earlier. So where is it now?*

'It's over here,' Langdon's deep voice resonated from across the room.

Silas turned to see Langdon holding the black cryptex before him, waving it back and forth like a matador tempting a dumb animal.

'Set it down,' Silas demanded.

'Let Sophie and Leigh leave the church,' Langdon replied. 'You and I can settle this.'

Silas pushed Sophie away from him and aimed the gun at Langdon, moving toward him.

'Not a step closer,' Langdon said. 'Not until they leave the building.'

'You are in no position to make demands.'

'I disagree.' Langdon raised the cryptex high over his head. 'I will not hesitate to smash this on the floor and break the vial inside.'

Although Silas sneered outwardly at the threat, he felt a flash of fear. This was unexpected. He aimed the gun at Langdon's head and kept his voice as steady as his hand. 'You would never break the keystone. You want to find the Grail as much as I do.'

'You're wrong. You want it much more. You've proven you're willing to kill for it.'

Forty feet away, peering out from the annex pews near the archway, Rémy Legaludec felt a rising alarm. The manoeuvre had not gone as planned, and even from here, he could see Silas was uncertain how to handle the situation. At the Teacher's orders, Rémy had forbidden Silas to fire his gun.

'Let them go,' Langdon again demanded, holding the cryptex high over his head and staring into Silas's gun.

The monk's red eyes filled with anger and frustration, and Rémy tightened with fear that Silas might actually shoot Langdon while he was holding the cryptex. *The cryptex cannot fall!*

The cryptex was to be Rémy's ticket to freedom and wealth. A little over a year ago, he was simply a fifty-five-year-old manservant living within the walls of Château Villette, catering to the whims of the insufferable cripple Sir Leigh Teabing. Then he was approached with an extraordinary proposition. Rémy's association with Sir Leigh Teabing – the pre-eminent Grail historian on earth – was going to bring Rémy everything he had ever dreamed of in life. Since then, every moment he had spent inside Château Villette had been leading him to this very instant.

I am so close, Rémy told himself, gazing into the sanctuary of the Temple Church and the keystone in Robert Langdon's hand. If Langdon dropped it, all would be lost.

Am I willing to show my face? It was something the Teacher had strictly forbidden. Rémy was the only one who knew the Teacher's identity.

'Are you certain you want *Silas* to carry out this task?' Rémy had asked the Teacher less than half an hour ago, upon getting orders to steal the keystone. 'I myself am capable.'

The Teacher was resolute. 'Silas served us well with the four Priory members. He will recover the keystone. *You* must remain anonymous. If others see you, they will need to be eliminated, and there has been enough killing already. Do not reveal your face.'

My face will change, Rémy thought. *With what you've promised to pay me, I will become an entirely new man.* Surgery could even change his fingerprints, the Teacher had told him. Soon he would be free – another unrecognizable, beautiful face soaking up the sun on the beach. 'Understood,' Rémy said. 'I will assist Silas from the shadows.'

'For your own knowledge, Rémy,' the Teacher had told him, 'the tomb in question is not in the Temple Church. So have no fear. They are looking in the wrong place.'

Rémy was stunned. 'And you know where the tomb is?'

'Of course. Later, I will tell you. For the moment,

you must act quickly. If the others figure out the true location of the tomb and leave the church before you take the cryptex, we could lose the Grail for ever.'

Rémy didn't give a damn about the Grail, except that the Teacher refused to pay him until it was found. Rémy felt giddy every time he thought of the money he soon would have. *One third of twenty million euros. Plenty to disappear for ever.* Rémy had pictured the beach towns on the Côte d'Azur, where he planned to live out his days basking in the sun and letting others serve him for a change.

Now, however, here in the Temple Church, with Langdon threatening to break the keystone, Rémy's future was at risk. Unable to bear the thought of coming this close only to lose it all, Rémy made the decision to take bold action. The gun in his hand was a concealable, small-calibre, J-frame Medusa, but it would be very deadly at close range.

Stepping from the shadows, Rémy marched into the circular chamber and aimed the gun directly at Teabing's head. 'Old man, I've been waiting a long time to do this.'

Sir Leigh Teabing's heart practically stalled to see Rémy aiming a gun at him. *What is he doing!* Teabing recognized the tiny Medusa revolver as his own, the one he kept locked in the limousine glove box for safety.

'Rémy?' Teabing sputtered in shock. 'What is going on?'

Langdon and Sophie looked equally dumbstruck.

Rémy circled behind Teabing and rammed the pistol barrel into his back, high and on the left, directly behind his heart.

Teabing felt his muscles seize with terror. 'Rémy, I

don't—'

'I'll make it simple,' Rémy snapped, eyeing Langdon over Teabing's shoulder. 'Set down the keystone, or I pull the trigger.'

Langdon seemed momentarily paralysed. 'The keystone is worthless to you,' he stammered. 'You cannot possibly open it.'

'Arrogant fools,' Rémy sneered. 'Have you not noticed that I have been listening tonight as you discussed these poems? Everything I heard, I have shared with others. Others who know more than you. You are not even looking in the right place. The tomb you seek is in another location entirely!'

Teabing felt panicked. *What is he saying!*

'Why do you want the Grail?' Langdon demanded. 'To destroy it? Before the End of Days?'

Rémy called to the monk. 'Silas, take the keystone from Mr Langdon.'

As the monk advanced, Langdon stepped back, raising the keystone high, looking fully prepared to hurl it at the floor.

'I would rather break it,' Langdon said, 'than see it in the wrong hands.'

Teabing now felt a wave of horror. He could see his life's work evaporating before his eyes. All his dreams about to be shattered.

'Robert, no!' Teabing exclaimed. 'Don't! That's the Grail you're holding! Rémy would *never* shoot me. We've known each other for ten—'

Rémy aimed at the ceiling and fired the Medusa. The blast was enormous for such a small weapon, the gunshot echoing like thunder inside the stone chamber.

Everyone froze.

'I am not playing games,' Rémy said. 'The next one is in his back. Hand the keystone to Silas.'

Langdon reluctantly held out the cryptex. Silas

stepped forward and took it, his red eyes gleaming with the self-satisfaction of vengeance. Slipping the keystone in the pocket of his robe, Silas backed off, still holding Langdon and Sophie at gunpoint.

Teabing felt Rémy's arm clamp hard around his neck as the servant began backing out of the building, dragging Teabing with him, the gun still pressed in his back.

'Let him go,' Langdon demanded.

'We're taking Mr Teabing for a drive,' Rémy said, still backing up. 'If you call the police, he will die. If you do anything to interfere, he will die. Is that clear?'

'Take me,' Langdon demanded, his voice cracking with emotion. 'Let Leigh go.'

Rémy laughed. 'I don't think so. He and I have such a nice history. Besides, he still might prove useful.'

Silas was backing up now, keeping Langdon and Sophie at gunpoint as Rémy pulled Leigh toward the exit, his crutches dragging behind him.

Sophie's voice was unwavering. 'Who are you working for?'

The question brought a smirk to the departing Rémy's face. 'You would be surprised, Mademoiselle Neveu.'

Chapter 87

The fireplace in Château Villette's drawing room was cold, but Collet paced before it nonetheless as he read the faxes from Interpol.

Not at all what he expected.

André Vernet, according to official records, was a model citizen. No police record – not even a parking ticket. Educated at a good lycée and the Sorbonne, he had a *cum laude* degree in international finance. Interpol said Vernet's name appeared in the newspapers from time to time, but always in a positive light. Apparently the man had helped design the security parameters that kept the Depository Bank of Zurich a leader in the ultramodern world of electronic security. Vernet's credit card records showed a penchant for art books, expensive wine and classical CDs – mostly Brahms – which he apparently enjoyed on an exceptionally high-end stereo system he had purchased several years ago.

Zero, Collet sighed.

The only red flag tonight from Interpol had been a set of fingerprints that apparently belonged to Teabing's servant. The chief PTS examiner was reading the report in a comfortable chair across the room.

Collet looked over. 'Anything?'

The examiner shrugged. 'Prints belong to Rémy Legaludec. Wanted for petty crime. Nothing serious. Looks like he got kicked out of university for rewiring phone jacks to get free service . . . later did some petty theft. Breaking and entering. Skipped out on a hospital bill once for an emergency tracheotomy.' He glanced up, chuckling. 'Peanut allergy.'

Collet nodded, recalling a police investigation into a restaurant that had failed to note on its menu that the chili recipe contained peanut oil. An unsuspecting patron had died of anaphylactic shock at the table after a single bite.

'Legaludec is probably a live-in here to avoid getting picked up.' The examiner looked amused. 'His lucky night.'

Collet sighed. 'All right, you better forward this info to Captain Fache.'

The examiner headed off just as another PTS agent burst into the living room. 'Lieutenant! We found something in the barn.'

From the anxious look on the agent's face, Collet could only guess. 'A body.'

'No, sir. Something more...' He hesitated. 'Unexpected.'

Rubbing his eyes, Collet followed the agent out to the barn. As they entered the musty, cavernous space, the agent motioned toward the centre of the room, where a wooden ladder now ascended high into the rafters, propped against the ledge of a hayloft suspended high above them.

'That ladder wasn't there earlier,' Collet said.

'No, sir. I set that up. We were dusting for prints near the Rolls when I saw the ladder lying on the floor. I wouldn't have given it a second thought except the rungs were worn and muddy. This ladder gets regular use. The height of the hayloft matched the ladder, so I raised it and climbed up to have a look.'

Collet's eyes climbed the ladder's steep incline to the soaring hayloft. *Someone goes up there regularly?* From down here, the loft appeared to be a deserted platform, and yet admittedly most of it was invisible from this line of sight.

A senior PTS agent appeared at the top of the ladder, looking down. 'You'll definitely want to see this, Lieutenant,' he said, waving Collet up with a latex-gloved hand.

Nodding tiredly, Collet walked over to the base of the old ladder and grasped the bottom rungs. The ladder was an antique tapered design and narrowed as Collet ascended. As he neared the top, Collet almost lost his footing on a thin rung. The barn below him spun. Alert now, he moved on, finally reaching the top. The agent above him reached out, offering his wrist. Collet grabbed it and made the awkward transition onto the platform.

'It's over there,' the PTS agent said, pointing deep into the immaculately clean loft. 'Only one set of prints up here. We'll have an ID shortly.'

Collet squinted through the dim light toward the far wall. *What the hell?* Nestled against the far wall sat an elaborate computer workstation – two tower CPUs, a flat-screen video monitor with speakers, an array of hard drives, and a multichannel audio console that appeared to have its own filtered power supply.

Why in the world would anyone work all the way up here? Collet moved toward the gear. 'Have you examined the system?'

'It's a listening post.'

Collet spun. 'Surveillance?'

The agent nodded. 'Very advanced surveillance.' He motioned to a long project table strewn with electronic parts, manuals, tools, wires, soldering irons and other electronic components. 'Someone clearly knows what he's doing. A lot of this gear is as sophisticated as our own equipment. Miniature microphones, photoelectric recharging cells, high-capacity RAM chips. He's even got some of those new nano drives.'

Collet was impressed.

'Here's a complete system,' the agent said, handing Collet an assembly not much larger than a pocket calculator. Dangling off the contraption was a foot-long wire with a stamp-sized piece of wafer-thin foil stuck on the end. 'The base is a high-capacity hard disk audio recording system with rechargeable battery. That strip of foil at the end of the wire is a combination microphone and photoelectric recharging cell.'

Collet knew them well. These foil-like, photocell microphones had been an enormous breakthrough a few years back. Now, a hard disk recorder could be affixed behind a lamp, for example, with its foil microphone moulded into the contour of the base and dyed to match. As long as the microphone was positioned such that it received a few hours of sunlight per day, the photo cells would keep recharging the system. Bugs like this one could listen indefinitely.

'Reception method?' Collet asked.

The agent signalled to an insulated wire that ran out of the back of the computer, up the wall, through a hole in the barn roof. 'Simple radio wave. Small antenna on the roof.'

Collet knew these recording systems were generally placed in offices, were voice-activated to save hard disk space, and recorded snippets of conversation during the day, transmitting compressed audio files at night to avoid detection. After transmitting, the hard drive erased itself and prepared to do it all over again the next day.

Collet's gaze moved now to a shelf on which were stacked several hundred audio cassettes, all labelled with dates and numbers. *Someone has been very busy.*

He turned back to the agent. 'Do you have any idea what target is being bugged?'

'Well, Lieutenant,' the agent said, walking to the computer and launching a piece of software. 'It's the strangest thing. . . .'

Chapter 88

Langdon felt utterly spent as he and Sophie hurdled a turnstile at the Temple tube station and dashed deep into the grimy labyrinth of tunnels and platforms. The guilt ripped through him.

I involved Leigh, and now he's in enormous danger.

Rémy's involvement had been a shock, and yet it made sense. Whoever was pursuing the Grail had recruited someone on the inside. *They went to Teabing's for the same reason I did.* Throughout history, those who held knowledge of the Grail had always been magnets for thieves and scholars alike. The fact that Teabing had been a target all along should have made Langdon feel less guilty about involving him. It did not. *We need to find Leigh and help him. Immediately.*

Langdon followed Sophie to the westbound District and Circle Line platform, where she hurried to a pay phone to call the police, despite Rémy's warning to the contrary. Langdon sat on a grungy bench nearby, feeling remorseful.

'The best way to help Leigh,' Sophie reiterated as she dialled, 'is to involve the London authorities immediately. Trust me.'

Langdon had not initially agreed with this idea, but as they had hatched their plan, Sophie's logic began to make sense. Teabing was safe at the moment. Even if Rémy and the others knew where the knight's tomb was located, they still might need Teabing's help deciphering the orb reference. What worried Langdon was what would happen *after* the Grail map had been found. *Leigh will become a huge liability.*

If Langdon were to have any chance of helping Leigh, or of ever seeing the keystone again, it was essential that he find the tomb first. *Unfortunately, Rémy has a big head start.*

Slowing Rémy down had become Sophie's task.

Finding the right tomb had become Langdon's.

Sophie would make Rémy and Silas fugitives of the London police, forcing them into hiding or, better yet, catching them. Langdon's plan was less certain – to take the tube to nearby King's College, which was renowned for its electronic theological database. *The ultimate research tool*, Langdon had heard. *Instant answers to any religious historical question.* He wondered what the database would have to say about 'a knight a Pope interred'.

He stood up and paced, wishing the train would hurry.

At the pay phone, Sophie's call finally connected to the London police.

'Snow Hill Division,' the dispatcher said. 'How may I direct your call?'

'I'm reporting a kidnapping.' Sophie knew to be concise.

'Name please?'

Sophie paused. 'Agent Sophie Neveu with the French Judicial Police.'

The title had the desired effect. 'Right away, ma'am. Let me get a detective on the line for you.'

As the call went through, Sophie began wondering if the police would even believe her description of Teabing's captors. *A man in a tuxedo.* How much easier to identify could a suspect be? Even if Rémy changed clothes, he was partnered with an albino monk. *Impossible to miss.* Moreover, they had a hostage and could not take public transportation. She wondered how many Jaguar stretch limos there could be in London.

Sophie's connection to the detective seemed to be taking for ever. *Come on!* She could hear the line clicking and buzzing, as if she was being transferred.

Fifteen seconds passed.

Finally a man came on the line. 'Agent Neveu?'

Stunned, Sophie registered the gruff tone immediately.

'Agent Neveu,' Bezu Fache demanded. 'Where the hell are you?'

Sophie was speechless. Captain Fache had apparently requested the London police dispatcher alert him if Sophie called in.

'Listen,' Fache said, speaking to her in terse French. 'I made a terrible mistake tonight. Robert Langdon is innocent. All charges against him have been dropped. Even so, both of you are in danger. You need to come in.'

Sophie's jaw fell slack. She had no idea how to respond. Fache was not a man who apologized for anything.

'You did not tell me,' Fache continued, 'that Jacques Saunière was your grandfather. I fully intend to overlook your insubordination last night on account of the emotional stress you must be under. At the moment, however, you and Langdon need to go to the nearest London police headquarters for refuge.'

He knows I'm in London? What else does Fache know? Sophie heard what sounded like drilling or machinery in the background. She also heard an odd clicking on the line. 'Are you tracing this call, Captain?'

Fache's voice was firm now. 'You and I need to cooperate, Agent Neveu. We both have a lot to lose here. This is damage control. I made errors in judgment last night, and if those errors result in the deaths of an American professor and a DCPJ cryptologist, my career will be over. I've been trying to pull you back into safety for the last several hours.'

A warm wind was now pushing through the station as a train approached with a low rumble. Sophie had every intention of being on it. Langdon apparently had the same idea; he was gathering himself together and moving toward her now.

'The man you want is Rémy Legaludec,' Sophie said. 'He is Teabing's servant. He just kidnapped Teabing inside the Temple Church and—'

'Agent Neveu!' Fache bellowed as the train thundered into the station. 'This is not something to discuss on an open line. You and Langdon will come in now. For your own well-being! That is a direct order!'

Sophie hung up and dashed with Langdon onto the train.

Chapter 89

The immaculate cabin of Teabing's Hawker was now covered with steel shavings and smelled of compressed air and propane. Bezu Fache had sent everyone away and sat alone with his drink and the heavy wooden box found in Teabing's safe.

Running his finger across the inlaid Rose, he lifted the ornate lid. Inside he found a stone cylinder with lettered dials. The five dials were arranged to spell SOFIA. Fache stared at the word a long moment and then lifted the cylinder from its padded resting place and examined every inch. Then, pulling slowly on the ends, Fache slid off one of the end caps. The cylinder was empty.

Fache set it back in the box and gazed absently out the jet's window at the hangar, pondering his brief conversation with Sophie, as well as the information he'd received from PTS in Château Villette. The sound of his phone shook him from his daydream.

It was the DCPJ switchboard. The dispatcher was apologetic. The president of the Depository Bank of Zurich had been calling repeatedly, and although he had been told several times that the captain was in London on business, he just kept calling. Begrudgingly Fache told the operator to forward the call.

'Monsieur Vernet,' Fache said, before the man could even speak, 'I am sorry I did not call you earlier. I have been busy. As promised, the name of your bank has not appeared in the media. So what precisely is your concern?'

Vernet's voice was anxious as he told Fache how Langdon and Sophie had extracted a small wooden box from the bank and then persuaded Vernet to help them escape. 'Then when I heard on the radio that they were criminals,' Vernet said, 'I pulled over and demanded the box back, but they attacked me and stole the truck.'

'You are concerned for a wooden box,' Fache said, eyeing the Rose inlay on the cover and again gently opening the lid to reveal the white cylinder. 'Can you tell me what was in the box?'

'The contents are immaterial,' Vernet fired back. 'I am concerned with the reputation of my bank. We have never had a robbery. *Ever*. It will ruin us if I cannot recover this property on behalf of my client.'

'You said Agent Neveu and Robert Langdon had a password and a key. What makes you say they stole the box?'

'They *murdered* people tonight. Including Sophie Neveu's grandfather. The key and password were obviously ill-gotten.'

'Mr Vernet, my men have done some checking into your background and your interests. You are obviously a man of great culture and refinement. I would imagine you are a man of honour, as well. As am I. That said, I give you my word as commanding officer of the *Police Judiciaire* that your box, along with your bank's reputation, is in the safest of hands.'

Chapter 90

High in the hayloft at Château Villette, Collet stared at the computer monitor in amazement. 'This system is eavesdropping on *all* these locations?'

'Yes,' the agent said. 'It looks like data has been collected for over a year now.'

Collet read the list again, speechless.

COLBERT SOSTAQUE – Chairman of the Conseil Constitutionnel
JEAN CHAFFÉE – Curator, Musée du Jeu de Paume
EDOUARD DESROCHERS – Senior Archivist, Mitterrand Library
JACQUES SAUNIÈRE – Curator, Musée du Louvre
MICHEL BRETON – Head of DAS (French Intelligence)

The agent pointed to the screen. 'Number four is of obvious concern.'

Collet nodded blankly. He had noticed it immediately. *Jacques Saunière was being bugged.* He looked at the rest of the list again. *How could anyone possibly manage to bug these prominent people?* 'Have you heard any of the audio files?'

'A few. Here's one of the most recent.' The agent clicked a few computer keys. The speakers crackled to life. *'Capitaine, un agent du Département de Cryptographie est arrivé.'*

Collet could not believe his ears. 'That's me! That's my voice!' He recalled sitting at Saunière's desk and radioing Fache in the Grand Gallery to alert him of Sophie Neveu's arrival.

The agent nodded. 'A lot of our Louvre investigation tonight would have been audible if someone had been interested.'

'Have you sent anyone in to sweep for the bug?'

'No need. I know exactly where it is.' The agent went to a pile of old notes and blueprints on the work-table. He selected a page and handed it to Collet. 'Look familiar?'

Collet was amazed. He was holding a photocopy of an ancient schematic diagram, which depicted a rudimentary machine. He was unable to read the handwritten Italian labels, and yet he knew what he was looking at. A model for a fully articulated medieval French knight.

The knight sitting on Saunière's desk!

Collet's eyes moved to the margins, where someone had scribbled notes on the photocopy in red felt-tipped marker. The notes were in French and appeared to be ideas outlining how best to insert a listening device into the knight.

Chapter 91

Silas sat in the passenger seat of the parked Jaguar limousine near the Temple Church. His hands felt damp on the keystone as he waited for Rémy to finish tying and gagging Teabing in the back with the rope they had found in the trunk.

Finally, Rémy climbed out of the rear of the limo, walked around, and slid into the driver's seat beside Silas.

'Secure?' Silas asked.

Rémy chuckled, shaking off the rain and glancing over his shoulder through the open partition at the crumpled form of Leigh Teabing, who was barely visible in the shadows in the rear. 'He's not going anywhere.'

Silas could hear Teabing's muffled cries and realized Rémy had used some of the old duct tape to gag him.

'*Ferme ta gueule!*' Rémy shouted over his shoulder at Teabing. Reaching to a control panel on the elaborate dash, Rémy pressed a button. An opaque partition raised behind them, sealing off the back. Teabing disappeared, and his voice was silenced. Rémy glanced at Silas. 'I've been listening to his miserable whimpering long enough.'

Minutes later, as the Jaguar stretch limo powered through the streets, Silas's cell phone rang. *The Teacher*. He answered excitedly. 'Hello?'

491

'Silas,' the Teacher's familiar French accent said, 'I am relieved to hear your voice. This means you are safe.'

Silas was equally comforted to hear the Teacher. It had been hours, and the operation had veered wildly off course. Now, at last, it seemed to be back on track. 'I have the keystone.'

'This is superb news,' the Teacher told him. 'Is Rémy with you?'

Silas was surprised to hear the Teacher use Rémy's name. 'Yes. Rémy freed me.'

'As I ordered him to do. I am only sorry you had to endure captivity for so long.'

'Physical discomfort has no meaning. The important thing is that the keystone is ours.'

'Yes. I need it delivered to me at once. Time is of the essence.'

Silas was eager to meet the Teacher face-to-face at last. 'Yes, sir, I would be honoured.'

'Silas, I would like *Rémy* to bring it to me.'

Rémy? Silas was crestfallen. After everything Silas had done for the Teacher, he had believed he would be the one to hand over the prize. *The Teacher favours Rémy?*

'I sense your disappointment,' the Teacher said, 'which tells me you do not understand my meaning.' He lowered his voice to a whisper. 'You must believe that I would much prefer to receive the keystone from *you* – a man of God rather than a criminal – but Rémy must be dealt with. He disobeyed my orders and made a grave mistake that has put our entire mission at risk.'

Silas felt a chill and glanced over at Rémy. Kidnapping Teabing had not been part of the plan, and deciding what to do with him posed a new problem.

'You and I are men of God,' the Teacher whispered.

'We cannot be deterred from our goal.' There was an ominous pause on the line. 'For this reason alone, I will ask Rémy to bring me the keystone. Do you understand?'

Silas sensed anger in the Teacher's voice and was surprised the man was not more understanding. *Showing his face could not be avoided*, Silas thought. *Rémy did what he had to do. He saved the keystone.* 'I understand,' Silas managed.

'Good. For your own safety, you need to get off the street immediately. The police will be looking for the limousine soon, and I do not want you caught. Opus Dei has a residence in London, no?'

'Of course.'

'And you are welcome there?'

'As a brother.'

'Then go there and stay out of sight. I will call you the moment I am in possession of the keystone and have attended to my current problem.'

'You are in London?'

'Do as I say, and everything will be fine.'

'Yes, sir.'

The Teacher heaved a sigh, as if what he now had to do was profoundly regrettable. 'It's time I speak to Rémy.'

Silas handed Rémy the phone, sensing it might be the last call Rémy Legaludec ever took.

As Rémy took the phone, he knew this poor, twisted monk had no idea what fate awaited him now that he had served his purpose.

The Teacher used you, Silas.

And your bishop is a pawn.

Rémy still marvelled at the Teacher's powers of persuasion. Bishop Aringarosa had trusted everything.

He had been blinded by his own desperation. *Aringarosa was far too eager to believe.* Although Rémy did not particularly like the Teacher, he felt pride at having gained the man's trust and helped him so substantially. *I have earned my payday.*

'Listen carefully,' the Teacher said. 'Take Silas to the Opus Dei residence hall and drop him off a few streets away. Then drive to St. James's Park. It is adjacent to The Mall. You can park the limousine on Horse Guards Parade. We'll talk there.'

With that, the connection went dead.

Chapter 92

King's College, established by King George IV in 1829, houses its Department of Theology and Religious Studies adjacent to Parliament on property granted by the Crown. King's College Religion Department boasts not only 150 years' experience in teaching and research, but the 1982 establishment of the Research Institute in Systematic Theology, which possesses one of the most complete and electronically advanced religious research libraries in the world.

Langdon still felt shaky as he and Sophie came in from the rain and entered the library. The primary research room was as Teabing had described it – a dramatic octagonal chamber dominated by an enormous round table around which King Arthur and his knights might have been comfortable were it not for the presence of twelve flat-screen computer work-stations. On the far side of the room, a reference librarian was just pouring a pot of tea and settling in for her day of work.

'Lovely morning,' she said cheerfully, leaving the tea and walking over. 'May I help you?'

'Thank you, yes,' Langdon replied. 'My name is—'

'Robert Langdon.' She gave a pleasant smile. 'I know who you are.'

For an instant, he feared Fache had put him on English television as well, but the librarian's smile suggested otherwise. Langdon still had not got used to these moments of unexpected celebrity. Then again, if anyone on earth were going to recognize his face, it would be a librarian in a Religious Studies reference facility.

'Pamela Gettum,' the librarian said, offering her hand. She had a genial, erudite face and a pleasingly fluid voice. The horn-rimmed glasses hanging around her neck were thick.

'A pleasure,' Langdon said. 'This is my friend Sophie Neveu.'

The two women greeted one another, and Gettum turned immediately back to Langdon. 'I didn't know you were coming.'

'Neither did we. If it's not too much trouble, we could really use your help finding some information.'

Gettum shifted, looking uncertain. 'Normally our services are by petition and appointment only, unless of course you're the guest of someone at the college?'

Langdon shook his head. 'I'm afraid we've come unannounced. A friend of mine speaks very highly of you. Sir Leigh Teabing?' Langdon felt a pang of gloom as he said the name. 'The British Royal Historian.'

Gettum brightened now, laughing. 'Heavens, yes. What a character. Fanatical! Every time he comes in, it's always the same search strings. Grail. Grail. Grail. I swear that man will die before he gives up on that quest.' She winked. 'Time and money afford one such lovely luxuries, wouldn't you say? A regular Don Quixote, that one.'

'Is there any chance you can help us?' Sophie asked. 'It's quite important.'

Gettum glanced around the deserted library and then winked at them both. 'Well, I can't very well claim I'm too busy, now can I? As long as you sign in, I can't imagine anyone being too upset. What did you have in mind?'

'We're trying to find a tomb in London.'

Gettum looked dubious. 'We've got about twenty

thousand of them. Can you be a little more specific?'

'It's the tomb of a *knight*. We don't have a name.'

'A knight. That tightens the net substantially. Much less common.'

'We don't have much information about the knight we're looking for,' Sophie said, 'but this is what we know.' She produced a slip of paper on which she had written only the first two lines of the poem.

Hesitant to show the entire poem to an outsider, Langdon and Sophie had decided to share just the first two lines, those that identified the knight. *Compartmentalized cryptography*, Sophie had called it. When an intelligence agency intercepted a code containing sensitive data, cryptographers each worked on a discrete section of the code. This way, when they broke it, no single cryptographer possessed the entire deciphered message.

In this case, the precaution was probably excessive; even if this librarian saw the entire poem, identified the knight's tomb and knew what orb was missing, the information was useless without the cryptex.

Gettum sensed an urgency in the eyes of this famed American scholar, almost as if his finding this tomb quickly were a matter of critical importance. The green-eyed woman accompanying him also seemed anxious.

Puzzled, Gettum put on her glasses and examined the paper they had just handed her.

In London lies a knight a Pope interred.
His labour's fruit a Holy wrath incurred.

She glanced at her guests. 'What is this? Some kind of Harvard treasure hunt?'

497

Langdon's laugh sounded forced. 'Yeah, something like that.'

Gettum paused, feeling she was not getting the whole story. Nonetheless, she felt intrigued and found herself pondering the verse carefully. 'According to this rhyme, a knight did something that incurred displeasure with God, and yet a Pope was kind enough to bury him in London.'

Langdon nodded. 'Does it ring any bells?'

Gettum moved toward one of the workstations. 'Not offhand, but let's see what we can pull up in the database.'

Over the past two decades, King's College Research Institute in Systematic Theology had used optical character recognition software in unison with linguistic translation devices to digitize and catalogue an enormous collection of texts – encyclopedias of religion, religious biographies, sacred scriptures in dozens of languages, histories, Vatican letters, diaries of clerics, anything at all that qualified as writings on human spirituality. Because the massive collection was now in the form of bits and bytes rather than physical pages, the data were infinitely more accessible.

Settling into one of the workstations, Gettum eyed the slip of paper and began typing. 'To begin, we'll run a straight Boolean with a few obvious keywords and see what happens.'

'Thank you.'

Gettum typed in a few words:

LONDON, KNIGHT, POPE

As she clicked the SEARCH button, she could feel the hum of the massive mainframe downstairs scanning data at a rate of 500 MB/sec. 'I'm asking the system to show us any documents whose complete text contains all three of these keywords. We'll get more hits than we want, but it's a good place to start.'

The screen was already showing the first of the hits now.

```
Painting the Pope. The Collected
Portraits of Sir Joshua Reynolds.
London University Press.
```

Gettum shook her head. 'Obviously not what you're looking for.'

She scrolled to the next hit.

```
The London Writings of Alexander Pope
            by G. Wilson Knight.
```

Again she shook her head.

As the system churned on, the hits came up more quickly than usual. Dozens of texts appeared, many of them referencing the eighteenth-century English writer Alexander Pope, whose counterreligious, mock-epic poetry apparently contained plenty of references to knights and London.

Gettum shot a quick glance to the numeric field at the bottom of the screen. This computer, by calculating the current number of hits and multiplying by the percentage of the database left to search, provided a rough guess of how much information would be found. This particular search looked like it was going to return an obscenely large amount of data.

```
Estimated number of total hits: 2,692
```

'We need to refine the parameters further,' Gettum said, stopping the search. 'Is this all the information you have regarding the tomb? There's nothing else to go on?'

Langdon glanced at Sophie Neveu, looking uncertain.

This is no treasure hunt, Gettum sensed. She had heard the whisperings of Robert Langdon's experience in Rome last year. This American had been granted access to the most secure library on earth – the Vatican Secret Archives. She wondered what kinds of secrets Langdon might have learned inside and if his current desperate hunt for a mysterious London tomb might relate to information he had gained within the Vatican. Gettum had been a librarian long enough to know the most common reason people came to London to look for knights. *The Grail.*

Gettum smiled and adjusted her glasses. 'You are friends with Leigh Teabing, you are in England, and you are looking for a knight.' She folded her hands. 'I can only assume you are on a Grail quest.'

Langdon and Sophie exchanged startled looks.

Gettum laughed. 'My friends, this library is a base camp for Grail seekers. Leigh Teabing among them. I wish I had a shilling for every time I'd run searches for the Rose, Mary Magdalene, Sangreal, Merovingian, Priory of Sion, et cetera, et cetera. Everyone loves a conspiracy.' She took off her glasses and eyed them. 'I need more information.'

In the silence, Gettum sensed her guests' desire for discretion was quickly being outweighed by their eagerness for a fast result.

'Here,' Sophie Neveu blurted. 'This is everything we know.' Borrowing a pen from Langdon, she wrote two more lines on the slip of paper and handed it to Gettum.

You seek the orb that ought be on his tomb.
It speaks of Rosy flesh and seeded womb.

Gettum gave an inward smile. *The Grail indeed,* she thought, noting the references to the Rose and her seeded womb. 'I can help you,' she said, looking up from the slip of paper. 'Might I ask where this verse came from? And why you are seeking an orb?'

'You might ask,' Langdon said, with a friendly smile, 'but it's a long story and we have very little time.'

'Sounds like a polite way of saying "mind your own business".'

'We would be for ever in your debt, Pamela,' Langdon said, 'if you could find out who this knight is and where he is buried.'

'Very well,' Gettum said, typing again. 'I'll play along. If this is a Grail-related issue, we should cross-reference against Grail keywords. I'll add a proximity parameter and remove the title weighting. That will limit our hits only to those instances of textual keywords that occur near a Grail-related word.'

Search for:
KNIGHT, LONDON, POPE, TOMB

Within 100 word proximity of:
GRAIL, ROSE, SANGREAL, CHALICE

'How long will this take?' Sophie asked.

'A few hundred terabytes with multiple cross-referencing fields?' Gettum's eyes glimmered as she clicked the SEARCH key. 'A mere fifteen minutes.'

Langdon and Sophie said nothing, but Gettum sensed this sounded like an eternity to them.

'Tea?' Gettum asked, standing and walking toward the pot she had made earlier. 'Leigh always loves my tea.'

Chapter 93

London's Opus Dei Centre is a modest brick building at 5 Orme Court, overlooking the North Walk at Kensington Gardens. Silas had never been here, but he felt a rising sense of refuge and asylum as he approached the building on foot. Despite the rain, Rémy had dropped him off a short distance away in order to keep the limousine off the main streets. Silas didn't mind the walk. The rain was cleansing.

At Rémy's suggestion, Silas had wiped down his gun and disposed of it through a sewer grate. He was glad to get rid of it. He felt lighter. His legs still ached from being bound all that time, but Silas had endured far greater pain. He wondered, though, about Teabing, whom Rémy had left bound in the back of the limousine. The Briton certainly had to be feeling the pain by now.

'What will you do with him?' Silas had asked Rémy as they drove over here.

Rémy had shrugged. 'That is a decision for the Teacher.' There was an odd finality in his tone.

Now, as Silas approached the Opus Dei building, the rain began to fall harder, soaking his heavy robe, stinging the wounds of the day before. He was ready to leave behind the sins of the last twenty-four hours and purge his soul. His work was done.

Moving across a small courtyard to the front door, Silas was not surprised to find the door unlocked. He opened it and stepped into the minimalist foyer. A muted electronic chime sounded upstairs as Silas stepped onto the carpet. The bell was a common feature in these halls where the residents spent most of the day in their rooms in prayer. Silas could hear movement above on the creaky wood floors.

A man in a cloak came downstairs. 'May I help you?' He had kind eyes that seemed not even to register Silas's startling physical appearance.

'Thank you. My name is Silas. I am an Opus Dei numerary.'

'American?'

Silas nodded. 'I am in town only for the day. Might I rest here?'

'You need not even ask. There are two empty rooms on the third floor. Shall I bring you some tea and bread?'

'Thank you.' Silas was famished.

Silas went upstairs to a modest room with a window, where he took off his wet robe and knelt down to pray in his undergarments. He heard his host come up and lay a tray outside his door. Silas finished his prayers, ate his food and lay down to sleep.

Three stories below, a phone was ringing. The Opus Dei numerary who had welcomed Silas answered the line.

'This is the London police,' the caller said. 'We are trying to find an albino monk. We've had a tip-off that he might be there. Have you seen him?'

The numerary was startled. 'Yes, he is here. Is something wrong?'

'He is there *now*?'

'Yes, upstairs praying. What is going on?'

'Leave him precisely where he is,' the officer commanded. 'Don't say a word to anyone. I'm sending officers over right away.'

Chapter 94

St James's Park is a sea of green in the middle of London, a public park bordering the palaces of Westminster, Buckingham and St James's. Once enclosed by King Henry VIII and stocked with deer for the hunt, St James's Park is now open to the public. On sunny afternoons, Londoners picnic beneath the willows and feed the pond's resident pelicans, whose ancestors were a gift to Charles II from the Russian ambassador.

The Teacher saw no pelicans today. The stormy weather had brought instead seagulls from the ocean. The lawns were covered with them – hundreds of white bodies all facing the same direction, patiently riding out the damp wind. Despite the morning fog, the park afforded splendid views of the Houses of Parliament and Big Ben. Gazing across the sloping lawns, past the duck pond and the delicate silhouettes of the weeping willows, the Teacher could see the spires of the building that housed the knight's tomb – the real reason he had told Rémy to come to this spot.

As the Teacher approached the front passenger door of the parked limousine, Rémy leaned across and opened the door. The Teacher paused outside, taking a pull from the flask of cognac he was carrying. Then, dabbing his mouth, he slid in beside Rémy and closed the door.

Rémy held up the keystone like a trophy. 'It was almost lost.'

'You have done well,' the Teacher said.

'*We* have done well,' Rémy replied, laying the keystone in the Teacher's eager hands.

The Teacher admired it a long moment, smiling. 'And the gun? You wiped it down?'

'Back in the glove box where I found it.'

'Excellent.' The Teacher took another drink of cognac and handed the flask to Rémy. 'Let's toast our success. The end is near.'

Rémy accepted the bottle gratefully. The cognac tasted salty, but Rémy didn't care. He and the Teacher were truly partners now. He could feel himself ascending to a higher station in life. *I will never be a servant again.* As Rémy gazed down the embankment at the duck pond below, Château Villette seemed miles away.

Taking another swig from the flask, Rémy could feel the cognac warming his blood. The warmth in Rémy's throat, however, mutated quickly to an uncomfortable heat. Loosening his bow tie, Rémy tasted an unpleasant grittiness and handed the flask back to the Teacher. 'I've probably had enough,' he managed, weakly.

Taking the flask, the Teacher said, 'Rémy, as you are aware, you are the only one who knows my face. I placed enormous trust in you.'

'Yes,' he said, feeling feverish as he loosened his tie further. 'And your identity shall go with me to the grave.'

The Teacher was silent a long moment. 'I believe you.' Pocketing the flask and the keystone, the Teacher reached for the glove box and pulled out the tiny Medusa revolver. For an instant, Rémy felt a surge of fear, but the Teacher simply slipped it in his trousers pocket.

What is he doing? Rémy felt himself sweating suddenly.

505

'I know I promised you freedom,' the Teacher said, his voice now sounding regretful. 'But considering your circumstances, this is the best I can do.'

The swelling in Rémy's throat came on like an earthquake, and he lurched against the steering column, grabbing his throat and tasting vomit in his narrowing trachea. He let out a muted croak of a scream, not even loud enough to be heard outside the car. The saltiness in the cognac now registered.

I'm being murdered!

Incredulous, Rémy turned to see the Teacher sitting calmly beside him, staring straight ahead through the windshield. Rémy's eyesight blurred, and he gasped for breath. *I made everything possible for him! How could he do this!* Whether the Teacher had intended to kill Rémy all along or whether it had been Rémy's actions in the Temple Church that had made the Teacher lose faith, Rémy would never know. Terror and rage coursed through him now. Rémy tried to lunge for the Teacher, but his stiffening body could barely move. *I trusted you with everything!*

Rémy tried to lift his clenched fists to blow the horn, but instead he slipped sideways, rolling onto the seat, lying on his side beside the Teacher, clutching at his throat. The rain fell harder now. Rémy could no longer see, but he could sense his oxygen-deprived brain straining to cling to his last faint shreds of lucidity. As his world slowly went black, Rémy Legaludec could have sworn he heard the sounds of the soft Riviera surf.

The Teacher stepped from the limousine, pleased to see that nobody was looking in his direction. *I had no choice*, he told himself, surprised how little remorse he felt for what he had just done. *Rémy sealed his own fate.*

The Teacher had feared all along that Rémy might need to be eliminated when the mission was complete, but by brazenly showing himself in the Temple Church, Rémy had accelerated the necessity dramatically. Robert Langdon's unexpected visit to Château Villette had brought the Teacher both a fortuitous windfall and an intricate dilemma. Langdon had delivered the keystone directly to the heart of the operation, which was a pleasant surprise, and yet he had brought the police on his tail. Rémy's prints were all over Château Villette, as well as in the barn's listening post, where Rémy had carried out the surveillance. The Teacher was grateful he had taken so much care in preventing any ties between Rémy's activities and his own. Nobody could implicate the Teacher unless Rémy talked, and that was no longer a concern.

One more loose end to tie up here, the Teacher thought, moving now toward the rear door of the limousine. *The police will have no idea what happened . . . and no living witness left to tell them.* Glancing around to ensure nobody was watching, he pulled open the door and climbed into the spacious rear compartment.

Minutes later, the Teacher was crossing St James's Park. *Only two people now remain. Langdon and Neveu.* They were more complicated. But manageable. At the moment, however, the Teacher had the cryptex to attend to.

Gazing triumphantly across the park, he could see his destination. *In London lies a knight a Pope interred.* As soon as the Teacher had heard the poem, he had known the answer. Even so, that the others had not figured it out was not surprising. *I have an unfair advantage.* Having listened to Saunière's conversations

507

for months now, the Teacher had heard the Grand Master mention this famous knight on occasion, expressing esteem almost matching that he held for Da Vinci. The poem's reference to the knight was brutally simple once one saw it – a credit to Saunière's wit – and yet how this tomb would reveal the final password was still a mystery.

You seek the orb that ought be on his tomb.

The Teacher vaguely recalled photos of the famous tomb and, in particular, its most distinguishing feature. *A magnificent orb.* The huge sphere mounted atop the tomb was almost as large as the tomb itself. The presence of the orb seemed both encouraging and troubling to the Teacher. On one hand, it felt like a signpost, and yet, according to the poem, the missing piece of the puzzle was an orb that *ought* to be on his tomb . . . not one that was already there. He was counting on his closer inspection of the tomb to unveil the answer.

The rain was getting heavier now, and he tucked the cryptex deep in his right-hand pocket to protect it from the dampness. He kept the tiny Medusa revolver in his left, out of sight. Within minutes, he was stepping into the quiet sanctuary of London's grandest nine-hundred-year-old building.

Just as the Teacher was stepping out of the rain, Bishop Aringarosa was stepping into it. On the rainy tarmac at Biggin Hill Executive Airport, Aringarosa emerged from his cramped plane, bundling his cassock against the cold damp. He had hoped to be greeted by Captain Fache. Instead a young British police officer approached with an umbrella.

'Bishop Aringarosa? Captain Fache had to leave. He asked me to look after you. He suggested I take you to Scotland Yard. He thought it would be safest.'

Safest? Aringarosa looked down at the heavy briefcase of Vatican bonds clutched in his hand. He had almost forgotten. 'Yes, thank you.'

Aringarosa climbed into the police car, wondering where Silas could be. Minutes later, the police scanner crackled with the answer.

5 Orme Court.

Aringarosa recognized the address instantly.

The Opus Dei Centre in London.

He spun to the driver. 'Take me there at once!'

Chapter 95

Langdon's eyes had not left the computer screen since the search began.

Five minutes. Only two hits. Both irrelevant.

He was starting to get worried.

Pamela Gettum was in the adjoining room, preparing hot drinks. Langdon and Sophie had inquired unwisely if there might be some *coffee* brewing alongside the tea Gettum had offered, and from the sound of the microwave beeps in the next room, Langdon suspected their request was about to be rewarded with instant Nescafé.

Finally, the computer pinged happily.

'Sounds like you got another,' Gettum called from the next room. 'What's the title?'

Langdon eyed the screen.

```
Grail Allegory in Medieval Literature:
A Treatise on Sir Gawain and the Green
               Knight.
```

'Allegory of the Green Knight,' he called back.

'No good,' Gettum said. 'Not many mythological green giants buried in London.'

Langdon and Sophie sat patiently in front of the screen and waited through two more dubious returns. When the computer pinged again, though, the offering was unexpected.

DIE OPERN VON RICHARD WAGNER

'The operas of Wagner?' Sophie asked.

Gettum peeked back in the doorway, holding a packet of instant coffee. 'That seems like a strange match. Was Wagner a knight?'

'No,' Langdon said, feeling a sudden intrigue. 'But he was a well-known Freemason.' *Along with Mozart, Beethoven, Shakespeare, Gershwin, Houdini and Disney.* Volumes had been written about the ties between the Masons and the Knights Templar, the Priory of Sion, and the Holy Grail. 'I want to look at this one. How do I see the full text?'

'You don't want the full text,' Gettum called. 'Click on the hypertext title. The computer will display your keyword hits along with mono prelogs and triple postlogs for context.'

Langdon had no idea what she had just said, but he clicked anyway.

A new window popped up.

```
 . . . mythological knight named Parsifal
                who . . .
      . . . metaphorical Grail quest that
               arguably . . .
 . . . the London Philharmonic in 1855 . . .
Rebecca Pope's opera anthology 'Diva's . . .
 . . . Wagner's tomb in Bayreuth, Germany . . .
```

'Wrong Pope,' Langdon said, disappointed. Even so, he was amazed by the system's ease of use. The keywords with context were enough to remind him that Wagner's opera *Parsifal* was a tribute to Mary Magdalene and the bloodline of Jesus Christ, told through the story of a young knight on a quest for truth.

'Just be patient,' Gettum urged. 'It's a numbers game. Let the machine run.'

Over the next few minutes, the computer returned several more Grail references, including a text about *troubadours* – France's famous wandering minstrels. Langdon knew it was no coincidence that the word *minstrel* and *minister* shared an etymological root. The troubadours were the travelling servants or 'ministers' of the Church of Mary Magdalene, using music to disseminate the story of the sacred feminine among the common folk. To this day, the troubadours sang songs extolling the virtues of 'our Lady' – a mysterious and beautiful woman to whom they pledged themselves for ever.

Eagerly, he checked the hypertext but found nothing.

The computer pinged again.

KNIGHTS, KNAVES, POPES, AND PENTACLES:
THE HISTORY OF THE HOLY GRAIL THROUGH TAROT

'Not surprising,' Langdon said to Sophie. 'Some of our keywords have the same names as individual cards.' He reached for the mouse to click on a hyperlink. 'I'm not sure if your grandfather ever mentioned it when you played Tarot with him, Sophie, but this game is a 'flash-card catechism' into the story of the Lost Bride and her subjugation by the evil Church.'

Sophie eyed him, looking incredulous. 'I had no idea.'

'That's the point. By teaching through a metaphorical game, the followers of the Grail disguised their message from the watchful eye of the Church.' Langdon often wondered how many modern card players had any clue that their four suits – spades, hearts, clubs, diamonds – were Grail-related symbols that came directly from Tarot's four suits of swords, cups, sceptres and pentacles.

Spades were Swords – The blade. Male.

Hearts were Cups – The chalice. Feminine.

Clubs were Sceptres – The Royal Line. The flowering staff.

Diamonds were Pentacles – The goddess. The sacred feminine.

Four minutes later, as Langdon began feeling fearful they would not find what they had come for, the computer produced another hit.

> **The Gravity of Genius:**
> Biography of a Modern Knight.

'Gravity of Genius?' Langdon called out to Gettum. 'Bio of a modern knight?'

Gettum stuck her head around the corner. 'How modern? Please don't tell me it's your Sir Rudy Giuliani. Personally, I found that one a bit off the mark.'

Langdon had his own qualms about the newly knighted Sir Mick Jagger, but this hardly seemed the moment to debate the politics of modern British knighthood. 'Let's have a look.' Langdon summoned up the hypertext keywords.

> . . . honourable **knight**, Sir Isaac Newton . . .
> . . . in **London** in 1727 and . . .
> . . . his **tomb** in Westminster Abbey . . .
> . . . Alexander **Pope**, friend and colleague . . .

'I suppose 'modern' is a relative term,' Sophie called to Gettum. 'It's an old book. About Sir Isaac Newton.'

Gettum shook her head in the doorway. 'No good. Newton was buried in Westminster Abbey, the seat of English Protestantism. There's no way a Catholic Pope was present. Cream and sugar?'

Sophie nodded.

Gettum waited. 'Robert?'

Langdon's heart was hammering. He pulled his eyes from the screen and stood up. 'Sir Isaac Newton is our knight.'

Sophie remained seated. 'What are you talking about?'

'Newton is buried in London,' Langdon said. 'His labours produced new sciences that incurred the wrath of the Church. And he was a Grand Master of the Priory of Sion. What more could we want?'

'What more?' Sophie pointed to the poem. 'How about a knight a Pope interred? You heard Ms Gettum. Newton was not buried by a Catholic Pope.'

Langdon reached for the mouse. 'Who said anything about a *Catholic* Pope?' He clicked on the 'Pope' hyperlink, and the complete sentence appeared.

```
Sir Isaac Newton's burial, attended by
  kings and nobles, was presided over by
Alexander Pope, friend and colleague, who
 gave a stirring eulogy before sprinkling
              dirt on the tomb.
```

Langdon looked at Sophie. 'We had the correct Pope on our second hit. Alexander.' He paused. 'A. Pope.'

In London lies a knight A. Pope interred.

Sophie stood up, looking stunned.

Jacques Saunière, the master of double-entendres, had proven once again that he was a frighteningly clever man.

Chapter 96

Silas awoke with a start.

He had no idea what had awoken him or how long he had been asleep. *Was I dreaming?* Sitting up now on his straw mat, he listened to the quiet breathing of the Opus Dei residence hall, the stillness textured only by the soft murmurs of someone praying aloud in a room below him. These were familiar sounds and should have comforted him.

And yet he felt a sudden and unexpected wariness.

Standing, wearing only his undergarments, Silas walked to the window. *Was I followed?* The courtyard below was deserted, exactly as he had seen it when he entered. He listened. Silence. *So why am I uneasy?* Long ago Silas had learned to trust his intuition. Intuition had kept him alive as a child on the streets of Marseilles long before prison . . . long before he was born again by the hand of Bishop Aringarosa. Peering out the window, he now saw the faint outline of a car through the hedge. On the car's roof was a police siren. A floorboard creaked in the hallway. A door latch moved.

Silas reacted on instinct, surging across the room and sliding to a stop just behind the door as it crashed open. The first police officer stormed through, swinging his gun left then right at what appeared an empty room. Before he realized where Silas was, Silas had thrown his shoulder into the door, crushing a second officer as he came through. As the first officer wheeled to shoot, Silas dove for his legs. The gun went off, the bullet sailing above Silas's head, just as he connected with the officer's shins, driving his legs out from under him, and sending the man down, his head hitting the floor. The second officer staggered to his feet in the doorway, and Silas drove a knee into his groin, then went clambering over the writhing body into the hall.

Almost naked, Silas hurled his pale body down the staircase. He knew he had been betrayed, but by whom? When he reached the foyer, more officers were surging through the front door. Silas turned the other way and dashed deeper into the residence hall. *The women's entrance. Every Opus Dei building has one.* Winding down narrow hallways, Silas snaked through a kitchen, past terrified workers, who left to avoid the naked albino as he knocked over bowls and silverware, bursting into a dark hallway near the boiler room. He now saw the door he sought, an exit light gleaming at the end.

Running full speed through the door out into the rain, Silas leapt off the low landing, not seeing the officer coming the other way until it was too late. The two men collided, Silas's broad, naked shoulder grinding into the man's sternum with crushing force. He drove the officer backward onto the pavement, landing hard on top of him. The officer's gun clattered away. Silas could hear men running down the hall shouting. Rolling, he grabbed the loose gun just as the officers emerged. A shot rang out on the stairs, and Silas felt a searing pain below his ribs. Filled with rage, he opened fire at all three officers, their blood spraying.

A dark shadow loomed behind, coming out of nowhere. The angry hands that grabbed at his bare shoulders felt as if they were infused with the power of the devil himself. The man roared in his ear. *SILAS, NO!*

Silas spun and fired. Their eyes met. Silas was already screaming in horror as Bishop Aringarosa fell.

Chapter 97

More than three thousand people are entombed or enshrined within Westminster Abbey. The colossal stone interior burgeons with the remains of kings, statesmen, scientists, poets and musicians. Their tombs, packed into every last niche and alcove, range in grandeur from the most regal of mausoleums – that of Queen Elizabeth I, whose canopied sarcophagus inhabits its own private, apsidal chapel – down to the most modest etched floor tiles whose inscriptions have worn away with centuries of foot traffic, leaving it to one's imagination whose relics might lie below the tile in the undercroft.

Designed in the style of the great cathedrals of Amiens, Chartres and Canterbury, Westminster Abbey is considered neither cathedral nor parish church. It bears the classification of *royal peculiar*, subject only to the Sovereign. Since hosting the coronation of William the Conqueror on Christmas Day in 1066, the dazzling sanctuary has witnessed an endless procession of royal ceremonies and affairs of state – from the canonization of Edward the Confessor to the marriage of Prince Andrew and Sarah Ferguson to the funerals of Henry V, Queen Elizabeth I and Princess Diana.

Even so, Robert Langdon currently felt no interest in any of the abbey's ancient history, save one event – the funeral of the British knight Sir Isaac Newton.

In London lies a knight a Pope interred.

Hurrying through the grand portico on the north

transept, Langdon and Sophie were met by guards who politely ushered them through the abbey's newest addition – a large walk-through metal detector – now present in most historic buildings in London. They both passed through without setting off the alarm and continued to the abbey entrance.

Stepping across the threshold into Westminster Abbey, Langdon felt the outside world evaporate with a sudden hush. No rumble of traffic. No hiss of rain. Just a deafening silence, which seemed to reverberate back and forth as if the building were whispering to itself.

Langdon's and Sophie's eyes, like those of almost every visitor, shifted immediately skyward, where the abbey's great abyss seemed to explode overhead. Grey stone columns ascended like redwoods into the shadows, arching gracefully over dizzying expanses, and then shooting back down to the stone floor. Before them, the wide alley of the north transept stretched out like a deep canyon, flanked by sheer cliffs of stained glass. On sunny days, the abbey floor was a prismatic patchwork of light. Today, the rain and darkness gave this massive hollow a wraithlike aura . . . more like that of the crypt it truly was.

'It's practically empty,' Sophie whispered.

Langdon felt disappointed. He had hoped for a lot more people. *A more public place.* Their earlier experience in the deserted Temple Church was not one Langdon wanted to repeat. He had been anticipating a certain feeling of security in the popular tourist destination, but Langdon's recollections of bustling throngs in a well-lit abbey had been formed during the peak summer tourist season. Today was a rainy April morning. Rather than crowds and shimmering stained glass, all Langdon saw was acres of desolate floor and shadowy, empty alcoves.

'We passed through metal detectors,' Sophie reminded, apparently sensing Langdon's apprehension. 'If anyone is in here, they can't be armed.'

Langdon nodded but still felt circumspect. He had wanted to bring the London police with them, but Sophie's fears of who might be involved put a damper on any contact with the authorities. *We need to recover the cryptex*, Sophie had insisted. *It is the key to everything.*

She was right, of course.

The key to getting Leigh back alive.

The key to finding the Holy Grail.

The key to learning who is behind this.

Unfortunately, their only chance to recover the keystone seemed to be here and now . . . at the tomb of Isaac Newton. Whoever held the cryptex would have to pay a visit to the tomb to decipher the final clue, and if they had not already come and gone, Sophie and Langdon intended to intercept them.

Striding toward the left wall to get out of the open, they moved into an obscure side aisle behind a row of pilasters. Langdon couldn't shake the image of Leigh Teabing being held captive, probably tied up in the back of his own limousine. Whoever had ordered the top Priory members killed would not hesitate to eliminate others who stood in the way. It seemed a cruel irony that Teabing – a modern British knight – was a hostage in the search for his own countryman, Sir Isaac Newton.

'Which way is it?' Sophie asked, looking around.

The tomb. Langdon had no idea. 'We should find a docent and ask.'

Langdon knew better than to wander aimlessly in here. Westminster Abbey was a tangled warren of mausoleums, perimeter chambers and walk-in burial niches. Like the Louvre's Grand Gallery, it had a lone point of entry – the door through which they had just passed – easy to find your way in, but impossible to find your way out. *A literal tourist trap*, one of Langdon's befuddled colleagues had called it. Keeping architectural tradition, the abbey was laid out in the shape of a giant crucifix. Unlike most churches, however, it had its entrance on the *side*, rather than the standard rear of the church via the narthex at the bottom of the nave. Moreover, the abbey had a series of sprawling cloisters attached. One false step through the wrong archway, and a visitor was lost in a labyrinth of outdoor passageways surrounded by high walls.

'Docents wear crimson robes,' Langdon said, approaching the centre of the church. Peering obliquely across the towering gilded altar to the far end of the south transept, Langdon saw several people crawling on their hands and knees. This prostrate pilgrimage was a common occurrence in Poets' Corner, although it was far less holy than it appeared. *Tourists doing grave rubbings.*

'I don't see any docents,' Sophie said. 'Maybe we can find the tomb on our own?'

Without a word, Langdon led her another few steps to the centre of the abbey and pointed to the right.

Sophie drew a startled breath as she looked down the length of the abbey's nave, the full magnitude of the building now visible. 'Aah,' she said. 'Let's find a docent.'

At that moment, a hundred yards down the nave, out of sight behind the choir screen, the stately tomb of Sir Isaac Newton had a lone visitor. The Teacher had been scrutinizing the monument for ten minutes now.

Newton's tomb consisted of a massive black-marble

sarcophagus on which reclined the sculpted form of Sir Isaac Newton, wearing classical costume, and leaning proudly against a stack of his own books – *Divinity, Chronology, Opticks* and *Philosophiae Naturalis Principia Mathematica*. At Newton's feet stood two winged boys holding a scroll. Behind Newton's recumbent body rose an austere pyramid. Although the pyramid itself seemed an oddity, it was the giant shape mounted halfway *up* the pyramid that most intrigued the Teacher.

An orb.

The Teacher pondered Saunière's beguiling riddle. *You seek the orb that ought be on his tomb.* The massive orb protruding from the face of the pyramid was carved in basso-relievo and depicted all kinds of heavenly bodies – constellations, signs of the zodiac, comets, stars and planets. Above it, the image of the Goddess of Astronomy beneath a field of stars.

Countless orbs.

The Teacher had been convinced that once he found the tomb, discerning the missing orb would be easy. Now he was not so sure. He was gazing at a complicated map of the heavens. Was there a missing planet? Had some astronomical orb been omitted from a constellation? He had no idea. Even so, the Teacher could not help but suspect that the solution would be ingeniously clean and simple – 'a knight a pope interred.' *What orb am I looking for?* Certainly, an advanced knowledge of astrophysics was not a prerequisite for finding the Holy Grail, was it?

It speaks of Rosy flesh and seeded womb.

The Teacher's concentration was broken by several approaching tourists. He slipped the cryptex back in his pocket and watched warily as the visitors went to a nearby table, left a donation in the cup and restocked on the complimentary grave-rubbing supplies set out by the abbey. Armed with fresh charcoal pencils and large sheets of heavy paper, they headed off toward the front of the abbey, probably to the popular Poets' Corner to pay their respects to Chaucer, Tennyson and Dickens by rubbing furiously on their graves.

Alone again, he stepped closer to the tomb, scanning it from bottom to top. He began with the clawed feet beneath the sarcophagus, moved upward past Newton, past his books on science, past the two boys with their mathematical scroll, up the face of the pyramid to the giant orb with its constellations, and finally up to the niche's star-filled canopy.

What orb ought to be here . . . and yet is missing? He touched the cryptex in his pocket as if he could somehow divine the answer from Saunière's crafted marble. *Only five letters separate me from the Grail.*

Pacing now near the corner of the choir screen, he took a deep breath and glanced up the long nave toward the main altar in the distance. His gaze dropped from the gilded altar down to the bright crimson robe of an abbey docent who was being waved over by two very familiar individuals.

Langdon and Neveu.

Calmly, the Teacher moved two steps back behind the choir screen. *That was fast.* He had anticipated Langdon and Sophie would eventually decipher the poem's meaning and come to Newton's tomb, but this was sooner than he had imagined. Taking a deep breath, the Teacher considered his options. He had grown accustomed to dealing with surprises.

I am holding the cryptex.

Reaching down to his pocket, he touched the second object that gave him his confidence: the Medusa revolver. As expected, the abbey's metal detectors had blared as the Teacher passed through with the concealed gun. Also as expected, the guards had backed off at once when the Teacher glared indignantly and flashed his identification card. Official rank always commanded the proper respect.

Although initially the Teacher had hoped to solve the cryptex alone and avoid any further complications, he now sensed that the arrival of Langdon and Neveu was actually a welcome development. Considering the lack of success he was having with the 'orb' reference, he might be able to use their expertise. After all, if Langdon had deciphered the poem to find the tomb, there was a reasonable chance he also knew something about the orb. And if Langdon knew the password, then it was just a matter of applying the right pressure.

Not here, of course.

Somewhere private.

The Teacher recalled a small announcement sign he had seen on his way into the abbey. Immediately he knew the perfect place to lure them.

The only question now . . . what to use as bait.

Chapter 98

Langdon and Sophie moved slowly down the north aisle, keeping to the shadows behind the ample pillars that separated it from the open nave. Despite having travelled more than halfway down the nave, they still had no clear view of Newton's tomb. The sarcophagus was recessed in a niche, obscured from this oblique angle.

'At least there's nobody over there,' Sophie whispered.

Langdon nodded, relieved. The entire section of the nave near Newton's tomb was deserted. 'I'll go over,' he whispered. 'You should stay hidden just in case someone—'

Sophie had already stepped from the shadows and was headed across the open floor.

'—is watching,' Langdon sighed, hurrying to join her.

Crossing the massive nave on a diagonal, Langdon and Sophie remained silent as the elaborate sepulchre revealed itself in tantalizing increments . . . a black-marble sarcophagus . . . a reclining statue of Newton . . . two winged boys . . . a huge pyramid . . . and . . . *an enormous orb*.

'Did you know about that?' Sophie said, sounding startled.

Langdon shook his head, also surprised.

'Those look like constellations carved on it,' Sophie said.

As they approached the niche, Langdon felt a slow

sinking sensation. Newton's tomb was covered with orbs – stars, comets, planets. *You seek the orb that ought be on his tomb?* It could turn out to be like trying to find a missing blade of grass on a golf course.

'Astronomical bodies,' Sophie said, looking concerned. 'And a lot of them.'

Langdon frowned. The only link between the planets and the Grail that Langdon could imagine was the pentacle of Venus, and he had already tried the password 'Venus' en route to the Temple Church.

Sophie moved directly to the sarcophagus, but Langdon hung back a few feet, keeping an eye on the abbey around them.

'*Divinity*,' Sophie said, tilting her head and reading the titles of the books on which Newton was leaning. '*Chronology. Opticks. Philosophiae Naturalis Principia Mathematica*?' She turned to him. 'Ring any bells?'

Langdon stepped closer, considering it. '*Principia Mathematica*, as I remember, has something to do with the gravitation pull of planets . . . which admittedly are orbs, but it seems a little far-fetched.'

'How about the signs of the zodiac?' Sophie asked, pointing to the constellations on the orb. 'You were talking about Pisces and Aquarius earlier, weren't you?'

The End of Days, Langdon thought. 'The end of Pisces and the beginning of Aquarius was allegedly the historical marker at which the Priory planned to release the Sangreal documents to the world.' *But the millennium came and went without incident, leaving historians uncertain when the truth was coming*.

'It seems possible,' Sophie said, 'that the Priory's plans to reveal the truth might be related to the last line of the poem.'

It speaks of Rosy flesh and seeded womb. Langdon felt a shiver of potential. He had not considered the line that way before.

'You told me earlier,' she said, 'that the timing of the Priory's plans to unveil the truth about "the Rose" and her fertile womb was linked directly to the position of planets – orbs.'

Langdon nodded, feeling the first faint wisps of possibility materializing. Even so, his intuition told him astronomy was not the key. The Grand Master's previous solutions had all possessed an eloquent, symbolic significance – the *Mona Lisa*, *Madonna of the Rocks*, SOFIA. This eloquence was definitely lacking in the concept of planetary orbs and the zodiac. Thus far, Jacques Saunière had proven himself a meticulous code writer, and Langdon had to believe that his final password – those five letters that unlocked the Priory's ultimate secret – would prove to be not only symbolically fitting but also crystal clear. If this solution were anything like the others, it would be painfully obvious once it dawned.

'Look!' Sophie gasped, jarring his thoughts as she grabbed his arm. From the fear in her touch Langdon sensed someone must be approaching, but when he turned to her, she was staring aghast at the top of the black marble sarcophagus. 'Someone was here,' she whispered, pointing to a spot on the sarcophagus near Newton's outstretched right foot.

Langdon did not understand her concern. A careless tourist had left a charcoal, grave-rubbing pencil on the sarcophagus lid near Newton's foot. *It's nothing*. Langdon reached out to pick it up, but as he leaned toward the sarcophagus, the light shifted on the polished black-marble slab, and Langdon froze. Suddenly, he saw why Sophie was afraid.

Scrawled on the sarcophagus lid, at Newton's feet, shimmered a barely visible charcoal-pencil message:

I have Teabing.
Go through Chapter House,
out south exit, to public garden.

Langdon read the words twice, his heart pounding wildly.

Sophie turned and scanned the nave.

Despite the pall of trepidation that settled over him upon seeing the words, Langdon told himself this was good news. *Leigh is still alive.* There was another implication here too. 'They don't know the password either,' he whispered.

Sophie nodded. Otherwise why make their presence known?

'They may want to trade Leigh for the password.'

'Or it's a trap.'

Langdon shook his head. 'I don't think so. The garden is *outside* the abbey walls. A very public place.' Langdon had once visited the abbey's famous College Garden – a small fruit orchard and herb garden – left over from the days when monks grew natural pharmacological remedies here. Boasting the oldest living fruit trees in Great Britain, College Garden was a popular spot for tourists to visit without having to enter the abbey. 'I think sending us outside is a show of faith. So we feel safe.'

Sophie looked dubious. 'You mean outside, where there are no metal detectors?'

Langdon scowled. She had a point.

Gazing back at the orb-filled tomb, Langdon wished he had some idea about the cryptex password . . . something with which to negotiate. *I got Leigh involved in this, and I'll do whatever it takes if there is a chance to help him.*

'The note says to go through the Chapter House to the south exit,' Sophie said. 'Maybe from the exit we would have a view of the garden? That way we could assess the situation before we walked out there and exposed ourselves to any danger?'

The idea was a good one. Langdon vaguely recalled the Chapter House as a huge octagonal hall where the original British Parliament convened in the days before the modern Parliament building existed. It had been years since he had been there, but he remembered it being out through the cloister somewhere. Taking several steps back from the tomb, Langdon peered around the choir screen to his right, across the nave to the side opposite that which they had descended.

A gaping vaulted passageway stood nearby, with a large sign.

THIS WAY TO:

CLOISTERS
DEANERY
COLLEGE HALL
MUSEUM
PYX CHAMBER
ST FAITH'S CHAPEL
CHAPTER HOUSE

Langdon and Sophie were jogging as they passed beneath the sign, moving too quickly to notice the small announcement apologizing that certain areas were closed for renovations.

They emerged immediately into a high-walled, open-roof courtyard through which morning rain was falling. Above them, the wind howled across the opening with a low drone, like someone blowing over the mouth of a bottle. Entering the narrow, low-hanging walkways that bordered the courtyard perimeter, Langdon felt the familiar uneasiness he always felt in enclosed spaces. These walkways were called *cloisters*, and Langdon noted with uneasiness that these particular *cloisters* lived up to their Latin ties to the word *claustrophobic*.

Focusing his mind straight ahead toward the end of the tunnel, Langdon followed the signs for the Chapter House. The rain was spitting now, and the walkway was cold and damp with gusts of rain that blew through the lone pillared wall that was the cloister's only source of light. Another couple scurried past them the other way, hurrying to get out of the worsening weather. The cloisters looked deserted now, admittedly the abbey's least enticing section in the wind and rain.

Forty yards down the east cloister, an archway materialized on their left, giving way to another hallway. Although this was the entrance they were looking for, the opening was cordoned off by a swag and an official-looking sign.

CLOSED FOR RENOVATION

PYX CHAMBER
ST FAITH'S CHAPEL
CHAPTER HOUSE

The long, deserted corridor beyond the swag was littered with scaffolding and drop cloths. Immediately beyond the swag, Langdon could see the entrances to the Pyx Chamber and St Faith's Chapel on the right and left. The entrance to the Chapter House, however, was much farther away, at the far end of the long hallway. Even from here, Langdon could see that its heavy wooden door was wide open, and the spacious octagonal interior was bathed in a greyish natural light from the room's enormous windows that looked out on College Garden. *Go through Chapter House, out south exit, to public garden.*

'We just left the east cloister,' Langdon said, 'so the south exit to the garden must be through there and to the right.'

Sophie was already stepping over the swag and moving forward.

As they hurried down the dark corridor, the sounds of the wind and rain from the open cloister faded behind them. The Chapter House was a kind of satellite structure – a freestanding annex at the end of the long hallway to ensure the privacy of the Parliament proceedings housed there.

'It looks huge,' Sophie whispered as they approached.

Langdon had forgotten just how large this room was. Even from outside the entrance, he could gaze across the vast expanse of floor to the breathtaking windows on the far side of the octagon, which rose five stories to a vaulted ceiling. They would certainly have a clear view of the garden from in here.

Crossing the threshold, both Langdon and Sophie found themselves having to squint. After the gloomy cloisters, the Chapter House felt like a solarium. They were a good ten feet into the room, searching the south wall, when they realized the door they had been promised was not there.

They were standing in an enormous dead end.

The creaking of a heavy door behind them made them turn, just as the door closed with a resounding thud and the latch fell into place. The lone man who had been standing behind the door looked calm as he aimed a small revolver at them. He was portly and was propped on a pair of aluminium crutches.

For a moment Langdon thought he must be dreaming.

It was Leigh Teabing.

Chapter 99

Sir Leigh Teabing felt rueful as he gazed out over the barrel of his Medusa revolver at Robert Langdon and Sophie Neveu. 'My friends,' he said, 'since the moment you walked into my home last night, I have done everything in my power to keep you out of harm's way. But your persistence has now put me in a difficult position.'

He could see the expressions of shock and betrayal on Sophie's and Langdon's faces, and yet he was confident that soon they would both understand the chain of events that had guided the three of them to this unlikely crossroads.

There is so much I have to tell you both . . . so much you do not yet understand.

'Please believe,' Teabing said, 'I never had any intention of your being involved. *You* came to my home. You came searching for me.'

'Leigh?' Langdon finally managed. 'What the hell are you doing? We thought you were in trouble. We came here to help you!'

'As I trusted you would,' he said. 'We have much to discuss.'

Langdon and Sophie seemed unable to tear their stunned gazes from the revolver aimed at them.

'It is simply to ensure your full attention,' Teabing said. 'If I had wanted to harm you, you would be dead by now. When you walked into my home last night, I risked everything to spare your lives. I am a man of honour, and I vowed in my deepest conscience only to sacrifice those who had betrayed the Sangreal.'

'What are you talking about?' Langdon said. 'Betrayed the Sangreal?'

'I discovered a terrible truth,' Teabing said, sighing. 'I learned *why* the Sangreal documents were never revealed to the world. I learned that the Priory had decided not to release the truth after all. That's why the millennium passed without any revelation, why nothing happened as we entered the End of Days.'

Langdon drew a breath, about to protest.

'The Priory,' Teabing continued, 'was given a sacred charge to share the truth. To release the Sangreal documents when the End of Days arrived. For centuries, men like Da Vinci, Botticelli and Newton risked everything to protect the documents and carry out that charge. And now, at the ultimate moment of truth, Jacques Saunière changed his mind. The man honoured with the greatest responsibility in Christian history eschewed his duty. He decided the time was not right.' Teabing turned to Sophie. 'He failed the Grail. He failed the Priory. And he failed the memory of all the generations that had worked to make that moment possible.'

'You?' Sophie declared, glancing up now, her green eyes boring into him with rage and realization. '*You* are the one responsible for my grandfather's murder?'

Teabing scoffed. 'Your grandfather and his *sénéchaux* were traitors to the Grail.'

Sophie felt a fury rising from deep within. *He's lying!*

Teabing's voice was relentless. 'Your grandfather sold out to the Church. It is obvious they pressured him to keep the truth quiet.'

Sophie shook her head. 'The Church had no influence on my grandfather!'

Teabing laughed coldly. 'My dear, the Church has

two thousand years of experience pressuring those who threaten to unveil its lies. Since the days of Constantine, the Church has successfully hidden the truth about Mary Magdalene and Jesus. We should not be surprised that now, once again, they have found a way to keep the world in the dark. The Church may no longer employ crusaders to slaughter nonbelievers, but their influence is no less persuasive. No less insidious.' He paused, as if to punctuate his next point. 'Miss Neveu, for some time now your grandfather has wanted to tell you the truth about your family.'

Sophie was stunned. 'How could you know that?'

'My methods are immaterial. The important thing for you to grasp right now is this.' He took a deep breath. 'The deaths of your mother, father, grand-mother and brother were *not* accidental.'

The words sent Sophie's emotions reeling. She opened her mouth to speak but was unable.

Langdon shook his head. 'What are you saying?'

'Robert, it explains everything. All the pieces fit. History repeats itself. The Church has a precedent of murder when it comes to silencing the Sangreal. With the End of Days imminent, killing the Grand Master's loved ones sent a very clear message. Be quiet, or you and Sophie are next.'

'It was a car accident,' Sophie stammered, feeling the childhood pain welling inside her. 'An *accident*!'

'Bedtime stories to protect your innocence,' Teabing said. 'Consider that only two family members went untouched – the Priory's Grand Master and his lone granddaughter – the perfect pair to provide the Church with control over the brotherhood. I can only imagine the terror the Church wielded over your grandfather these past years, threatening to kill you if he dared release the Sangreal secret, threatening to finish the job they started unless Saunière influenced the Priory to reconsider its ancient vow.'

'Leigh,' Langdon argued, now visibly riled, 'certainly you have no proof that the Church had anything to do with those deaths, or that it influenced the Priory's decision to remain silent.'

'Proof?' Teabing fired back. 'You want proof the Priory was influenced? The new millennium has arrived, and yet the world remains ignorant! Is that not proof enough?'

In the echoes of Teabing's words, Sophie heard another voice speaking. *Sophie, I must tell you the truth about your family.* She realized she was trembling. Could *this* possibly be that truth her grandfather had wanted to tell her? That her family had been *murdered*? What did she truly know about the crash that took her family? Only sketchy details. Even the stories in the newspaper had been vague. An accident? Bedtime stories? Sophie flashed suddenly on her grandfather's overprotectiveness, how he never liked to leave her alone when she was young. Even when Sophie was grown and away at university, she had the sense her grandfather was watching over. She wondered if there had been Priory members in the shadows throughout her entire life, looking after her.

'You suspected he was being manipulated,' Langdon said, glaring with disbelief at Teabing. 'So you *murdered* him?'

'I did not pull the trigger,' Teabing said. 'Saunière was dead years ago, when the Church stole his family from him. He was compromised. Now he is free of that pain, released from the shame caused by his inability to carry out his sacred duty. Consider the alternative. Something had to be done. Shall the world be ignorant for ever? Shall the Church be allowed to cement its lies into our history books for all eternity? Shall the Church be permitted to influence indefinitely with murder and extortion? No, something needed to be done! And now we are poised to carry out Saunière's legacy and right a terrible wrong.' He paused. 'The three of us. Together.'

Sophie felt only incredulity. 'How could you *possibly* believe that we would help you?'

'Because, my dear, *you* are the reason the Priory failed to release the documents. Your grandfather's love for you prevented him from challenging the Church. His fear of reprisal against his only remaining family crippled him. He never had a chance to explain the truth because you rejected him, tying his hands, making him wait. Now you owe the world the truth. You owe it to the memory of your grandfather.'

Robert Langdon had given up trying to get his bearings. Despite the torrent of questions running through his mind, he knew only one thing mattered now – getting Sophie out of here alive. All the guilt Langdon had mistakenly felt earlier for involving Teabing had now been transferred to Sophie.

I took her to Château Villette. I am responsible.

Langdon could not fathom that Leigh Teabing would be capable of killing them in cold blood here in the Chapter House, and yet Teabing certainly had been involved in killing others during his misguided quest. Langdon had the uneasy feeling that gunshots in this secluded, thick-walled chamber would go unheard, especially in this rain. *And Leigh just admitted his guilt to us.*

Langdon glanced at Sophie, who looked shaken. *The Church murdered Sophie's family to silence the Priory?* Langdon felt certain the modern Church did not murder people. There had to be some other explanation.

'Let Sophie leave,' Langdon declared, staring at Leigh. 'You and I should discuss this alone.'

Teabing gave an unnatural laugh. 'I'm afraid that is one show of faith I cannot afford. I can, however, offer you *this*.' He propped himself fully on his crutches, gracelessly keeping the gun aimed at Sophie, and removed the keystone from his pocket. He swayed a bit as he held it out for Langdon. 'A token of trust, Robert.'

Robert felt wary and didn't move. *Leigh is giving the keystone back to us?*

'Take it,' Teabing said, thrusting it awkwardly toward Langdon.

Langdon could imagine only one reason Teabing would give it back. 'You opened it already. You removed the map.'

Teabing was shaking his head. 'Robert, if I had solved the keystone, I would have disappeared to find the Grail myself and kept you uninvolved. No, I do not know the answer. And I can admit that freely. A true knight learns humility in the face of the Grail. He learns to obey the signs placed before him. When I saw you enter the abbey, I understood. You were here for a reason. To help. I am not looking for singular glory here. I serve a far greater master than my own pride. The Truth. Mankind deserves to know that truth. The Grail found us all, and now she is begging to be revealed. We must work together.'

Despite Teabing's pleas for cooperation and trust, his gun remained trained on Sophie as Langdon stepped forward and accepted the cold marble cylinder. The vinegar inside gurgled as Langdon grasped it and stepped backward. The dials were still in random order, and the cryptex remained locked.

Langdon eyed Teabing. 'How do you know I won't smash it right now?'

Teabing's laugh was an eerie chortle. 'I should have realized your threat to break it in the Temple Church was an empty one. Robert Langdon would never break the keystone. You are an historian, Robert. You are holding the key to two thousand years of history – the lost key to the Sangreal. You can feel the souls of all the knights burned at the stake to protect her secret. Would you have them die in vain? No, you will vindicate them. You will join the ranks of the great men you admire – Da Vinci, Botticelli, Newton – each of whom would have been honoured to be in your shoes right now. The contents of the keystone are crying out to us. Longing to be set free. The time has come. Destiny has led us to this moment.'

'I cannot help you, Leigh. I have no idea how to open this. I only saw Newton's tomb for a moment. And even if I knew the password . . .' Langdon paused, realizing he had said too much.

'You would not tell me?' Teabing sighed. 'I am disappointed and surprised, Robert, that you do not appreciate the extent to which you are in my debt. My task would have been far simpler had Rémy and I eliminated you both when you walked into Château Villette. Instead I risked everything to take the nobler course.'

'This is *noble*?' Langdon demanded, eyeing the gun.

'Saunière's fault,' Teabing said. 'He and his *sénéchaux* lied to Silas. Otherwise, I would have obtained the keystone without complication. How was I to imagine the Grand Master would go to such ends to deceive me and bequeath the keystone to an estranged granddaughter?' Teabing looked at Sophie with disdain. 'Someone so unqualified to hold this knowledge that she required a symbologist baby-sitter.' Teabing glanced back at Langdon. 'Fortunately, Robert, your involvement turned out to be my saving grace. Rather than the keystone remaining locked in the depository bank for ever, you extracted it and walked into my home.'

Where else would I run? Langdon thought. *The community of Grail historians is small, and Teabing and I have a history together.*

Teabing now looked smug. 'When I learned Saunière left you a dying message, I had a pretty good idea you were holding valuable Priory information. Whether it was the keystone itself, or information on where to find it, I was not sure. But with the police on your heels, I had a sneaking suspicion you might arrive on my doorstep.'

Langdon glared. 'And if we had not?'

'I was formulating a plan to extend you a helping hand. One way or another, the keystone was coming to Château Villette. The fact that you delivered it into my waiting hands only serves as proof that my cause is just.'

'What!' Langdon was appalled.

'Silas was supposed to break in and steal the keystone from you in Château Villette – thus removing you from the equation without hurting you, and exonerating me from any suspicion of complicity. However, when I saw the intricacy of Saunière's codes, I decided to include you both in my quest a bit longer. I could have Silas steal the keystone later, once I knew enough to carry on alone.'

'The Temple Church,' Sophie said, her tone awash with betrayal.

Light begins to dawn, Teabing thought. The Temple Church was the perfect location to steal the keystone from Robert and Sophie, and its apparent relevance to the poem made it a plausible decoy. Rémy's orders had been clear – stay out of sight while Silas recovers the keystone. Unfortunately, Langdon's threat to smash the keystone on the chapel floor had caused Rémy to panic. *If only Rémy had not revealed himself*, Teabing thought ruefully, recalling his own mock kidnapping. *Rémy was the sole link to me, and he showed his face!*

Fortunately, Silas remained unaware of Teabing's true identity and was easily fooled into taking him from the church and then watching naively as Rémy pretended to tie their hostage in the back of the limousine. With the soundproof divider raised, Teabing was able to phone Silas in the front seat, use the fake French accent of the Teacher, and direct Silas to go straight to Opus Dei. A simple anonymous tip to the police was all it would take to remove Silas from the picture.

One loose end tied up.

The other loose end was harder. *Rémy.*

Teabing struggled deeply with the decision, but in the end Rémy had proven himself a liability. *Every Grail quest requires sacrifice.* The cleanest solution had been staring Teabing in the face from the limousine's wet bar – a flask, some cognac, and a can of peanuts. The powder at the bottom of the can would be more than enough to trigger Rémy's deadly allergy. When Rémy parked the limo on Horse Guards Parade, Teabing climbed out of the back, walked to the side passenger door, and sat in the front next to Rémy. Minutes later, Teabing got out of the car, climbed into the rear again, cleaned up the evidence, and finally emerged to carry out the final phase of his mission.

Westminster Abbey had been a short walk, and although Teabing's leg braces, crutches and gun had set off the metal detector, the rent-a-cops never knew what to do. *Do we ask him to remove his braces and crawl through? Do we frisk his deformed body?* Teabing presented the flustered guards a far easier solution – an embossed card identifying him as Knight of the Realm. The poor fellows practically tripped over one another ushering him in.

Now, eyeing the bewildered Langdon and Neveu, Teabing resisted the urge to reveal how he had brilliantly implicated Opus Dei in the plot that would soon bring about the demise of the entire Church. That would have to wait. Right now there was work to do.

'Mes amis,' Teabing declared in flawless French, *'vous ne trouvez pas le Saint-Graal, c'est le Saint-Graal qui vous trouve.'* He smiled. 'Our paths together could not be more clear. The Grail has found us.'

Silence.

He spoke to them in a whisper now. 'Listen. Can you hear it? The Grail is speaking to us across the centuries. She is begging to be saved from the Priory's folly. I implore you both to recognize this opportunity. There could not possibly be three more capable people assembled at this moment to break the final code and open the cryptex.' Teabing paused, his eyes alight. 'We need to swear an oath together. A pledge of faith to one another. A knight's allegiance to uncover the truth and make it known.'

Sophie stared deep into Teabing's eyes and spoke in a steely tone. 'I will never swear an oath with my grandfather's murderer. Except an oath that I will see you go to prison.'

Teabing's heart turned grave, then resolute. 'I am sorry you feel that way, mademoiselle.' He turned and aimed the gun at Langdon. 'And you, Robert? Are you with me, or against me?'

Chapter 100

Bishop Manuel Aringarosa's body had endured many kinds of pain, and yet the searing heat of the bullet wound in his chest felt profoundly foreign to him. Deep and grave. Not a wound of the flesh . . . but closer to the soul.

He opened his eyes, trying to see, but the rain on his face blurred his vision. *Where am I?* He could feel powerful arms holding him, carrying his limp body like a rag doll, his black cassock flapping.

Lifting a weary arm, he mopped his eyes and saw the man holding him was Silas. The great albino was struggling down a misty sidewalk, shouting for a hospital, his voice a heartrending wail of agony. His red eyes were focused dead ahead, tears streaming down his pale, blood-spattered face.

'My son,' Aringarosa whispered, 'you're hurt.'

Silas glanced down, his visage contorted in anguish. 'I am so very sorry, Father.' He seemed almost too pained to speak.

'No, Silas,' Aringarosa replied. 'It is I who am sorry. This is my fault.' *The Teacher promised me there would be no killing, and I told you to obey him fully.* 'I was too eager. Too fearful. You and I were deceived.' *The Teacher was never going to deliver us the Holy Grail.*

Cradled in the arms of the man he had taken in all those years ago, Bishop Aringarosa felt himself reel back in time. To Spain. To his modest beginnings, building a small Catholic church in Oviedo with Silas. And later, to New York City, where he had proclaimed the glory of God with the towering Opus Dei Center on Lexington Avenue.

Five months ago, Aringarosa had received devastating news. His life's work was in jeopardy. He recalled, with vivid detail, the meeting inside Castel Gandolfo that had changed his life . . . the news that had set this entire calamity into motion.

Aringarosa had entered Gandolfo's Astronomy Library with his head held high, fully expecting to be lauded by throngs of welcoming hands, all eager to pat him on the back for his superior work representing Catholicism in America.

But only three people were present.

The Vatican secretarius. Obese. Dour.

Two high-ranking Italian cardinals. Sanctimonious. Smug.

'Secretarius?' Aringarosa said, puzzled.

The rotund overseer of legal affairs shook Aringarosa's hand and motioned to the chair opposite him. 'Please, make yourself comfortable.'

Aringarosa sat, sensing something was wrong.

'I am not skilled in small talk, Bishop,' the secretarius said, 'so let me be direct about the reason for your visit.'

'Please. Speak openly.' Aringarosa glanced at the two cardinals, who seemed to be measuring him with self-righteous anticipation.

'As you are well aware,' the secretarius said, 'His Holiness and others in Rome have been concerned lately with the political fallout from Opus Dei's more controversial practices.'

Aringarosa felt himself bristle instantly. He already had been through this on numerous occasions with the new pontiff, who, to Aringarosa's great dismay, had turned out to be a distressingly fervent voice for liberal change in the Church.

'I want to assure you,' the secretarius added quickly, 'that His Holiness does not seek to change anything about the way you run your ministry.'

I should hope not! 'Then why am I here?'

The enormous man sighed. 'Bishop, I am not sure how to say this delicately, so I will state it directly. Two days ago, the Secretariat Council voted unanimously to revoke the Vatican's sanction of Opus Dei.'

Aringarosa was certain he had heard incorrectly. 'I beg your pardon?'

'Plainly stated, six months from today, Opus Dei will no longer be considered a prelature of the Vatican. You will be a church unto yourself. The Holy See will be disassociating itself from you. His Holiness agrees and we are already drawing up the legal papers.'

'But . . . that is impossible!'

'On the contrary, it is quite possible. And necessary. His Holiness has become uneasy with your aggressive recruiting policies and your practices of corporal mortification.' He paused. 'Also your policies regarding women. Quite frankly, Opus Dei has become a liability and an embarrassment.'

Bishop Aringarosa was stupefied. 'An embarrassment?'

'Certainly you cannot be surprised it has come to this.'

'Opus Dei is the only Catholic organization whose numbers are growing! We now have over eleven hundred priests!'

'True. A troubling issue for us all.'

Aringarosa shot to his feet. 'Ask His Holiness if Opus Dei was an embarrassment in 1982 when we helped the Vatican Bank!'

'The Vatican will always be grateful for that,' the secretarius said, his tone appeasing, 'and yet there are those who still believe your financial munificence in

1982 is the only reason you were granted prelature status in the first place.'

'That is not true!' The insinuation offended Aringarosa deeply.

'Whatever the case, we plan to act in good faith. We are drawing up severance terms that will include a reimbursement of those monies. It will be paid in five instalments.'

'You are buying me off?' Aringarosa demanded. 'Paying me to go quietly? When Opus Dei is the only remaining voice of reason!'

One of the cardinals glanced up. 'I'm sorry, did you say *reason*?'

Aringarosa leaned across the table, sharpening his tone to a point. 'Do you really wonder why Catholics are leaving the Church? Look around you, Cardinal. People have lost respect. The rigours of faith are gone. The doctrine has become a buffet table. Abstinence, confession, communion, baptism, mass – take your pick – choose whatever combination pleases you and ignore the rest. What kind of spiritual guidance is the Church offering?'

'Third-century laws,' the second cardinal said, 'cannot be applied to the modern followers of Christ. The rules are not workable in today's society.'

'Well, they seem to be working for Opus Dei!'

'Bishop Aringarosa,' the secretarius said, his voice conclusive. 'Out of respect for your organization's relationship with the previous Pope, His Holiness will be giving Opus Dei six months to *voluntarily* break away from the Vatican. I suggest you cite your differences of opinion with the Holy See and establish yourself as your own Christian organization.'

'I refuse!' Aringarosa declared. 'And I'll tell him that in person!'

'I'm afraid His Holiness no longer cares to meet you.'

545

Aringarosa stood up. 'He would not *dare* abolish a personal prelature established by a previous Pope!'

'I'm sorry.' The secretarius's eyes did not flinch. 'The Lord giveth and the Lord taketh away.'

Aringarosa had staggered from that meeting in bewilderment and panic. Returning to New York, he stared out at the skyline in disillusionment for days, overwhelmed with sadness for the future of Christianity.

It was several weeks later that he received the phone call that changed all that. The caller sounded French and identified himself as *the Teacher* – a title common in the prelature. He said he knew of the Vatican's plans to pull support from Opus Dei.

How could he know that? Aringarosa wondered. He had hoped only a handful of Vatican power brokers knew of Opus Dei's impending annulment. Apparently the word was out. When it came to containing gossip, no walls in the world were as porous as those surrounding Vatican City.

'I have ears everywhere, Bishop,' the Teacher whispered, 'and with these ears I have gained certain knowledge. With your help, I can uncover the hiding place of a sacred relic that will bring you enormous power . . . enough power to make the Vatican bow before you. Enough power to save the Faith.' He paused. 'Not just for Opus Dei. But for all of us.'

The Lord taketh away . . . and the Lord giveth. Aringarosa felt a glorious ray of hope. 'Tell me your plan.'

Bishop Aringarosa was unconscious when the doors of St Mary's Hospital hissed open. Silas lurched into the entryway delirious with exhaustion. Dropping to his knees on the tile floor, he cried out for help. Everyone in the reception area gaped in wonderment at the half-naked albino offering forth a bleeding clergyman.

The doctor who helped Silas heave the delirious bishop onto a trolley looked gloomy as he felt Aringarosa's pulse. 'He's lost a lot of blood. I am not hopeful.'

Aringarosa's eyes flickered, and he returned for a moment, his gaze locating Silas. 'My child . . .'

Silas's soul thundered with remorse and rage. 'Father, if it takes my lifetime, I will find the one who deceived us, and I will kill him.'

Aringarosa shook his head, looking sad as they prepared to wheel him away. 'Silas . . . if you have learned nothing from me, please . . . learn this.' He took Silas's hand and gave it a firm squeeze. 'Forgiveness is God's greatest gift.'

'But Father . . .'

Aringarosa closed his eyes. 'Silas, you must pray.'

Chapter 101

Robert Langdon stood beneath the lofty cupola of the deserted Chapter House and stared into the barrel of Leigh Teabing's gun.

Robert, are you with me, or against me? The Royal Historian's words echoed in the silence of Langdon's mind.

There was no viable response, Langdon knew. Answer yes, and he would be selling out Sophie. Answer no, and Teabing would have no choice but to kill them both.

Langdon's years in the classroom had not imbued him with any skills relevant to handling confrontations at gunpoint, but the classroom *had* taught him something about answering paradoxical questions. *When a question has no correct answer, there is only one honest response.*

The grey area between yes and no.

Silence.

Staring at the cryptex in his hands, Langdon chose simply to walk away.

Without ever lifting his eyes, he stepped backward, out into the room's vast empty spaces. *Neutral ground.* He hoped his focus on the cryptex signalled to Teabing that collaboration might be an option, and that his silence signalled to Sophie he had not abandoned her.

All the while buying time to think.

The act of thinking, Langdon suspected, was exactly what Teabing wanted him to do. *That's why he handed me the cryptex. So I could feel the weight of my decision.* The British historian hoped the touch of the Grand Master's cryptex would make Langdon fully grasp the magnitude of its contents, coaxing his academic curiosity to overwhelm all else, forcing him to realize that failure to unlock the keystone would mean the loss of history itself.

With Sophie at gunpoint across the room, Langdon feared that discovering the cryptex's elusive password would be his only remaining hope of bartering for her release. *If I can free the map, Teabing will negotiate.* Forcing his mind to this critical task, Langdon moved slowly toward the far windows ... allowing his mind to fill with the numerous astronomical images on Newton's tomb.

> You seek the orb that ought be on his tomb.
> It speaks of Rosy flesh and seeded womb.

Turning his back to the others, he walked toward the towering windows, searching for any inspiration in their stained-glass mosaics. There was none.

Place yourself in Saunière's mind, he urged, gazing outward now into College Garden. *What would he believe is the orb that ought be on Newton's tomb?* Images of stars, comets and planets twinkled in the falling rain, but Langdon ignored them. Saunière was not a man of science. He was a man of humanity, of art, of history. *The sacred feminine ... the chalice ... the Rose ... the banished Mary Magdalene ... the decline of the goddess ... the Holy Grail.*

Legend had always portrayed the Grail as a cruel mistress, dancing in the shadows just out of sight, whispering in your ear, luring you one more step and then evaporating into the mist.

Gazing out at the rustling trees of College Garden, Langdon sensed her playful presence. The signs were everywhere. Like a taunting silhouette emerging from the fog, the branches of Britain's oldest apple tree burgeoned with five-petalled blossoms, all glistening like Venus. The goddess was in the garden now. She was dancing in the rain, singing songs of the ages, peeking out from behind the bud-filled branches as if to remind Langdon that the fruit of knowledge was growing just beyond his reach.

Across the room, Sir Leigh Teabing watched with confidence as Langdon gazed out the window as if under a spell.

Exactly as I hoped, Teabing thought. *He will come round.*

For some time now, Teabing had suspected Langdon might hold the key to the Grail. It was no coincidence that Teabing launched his plan into action on the same night Langdon was scheduled to meet Jacques Saunière. Listening in on the curator, Teabing was certain the man's eagerness to meet Langdon privately could mean only one thing. *Langdon's mysterious manuscript has touched a nerve with the Priory. Langdon has stumbled onto a truth, and Saunière fears its release.* Teabing felt certain the Grand Master was summoning Langdon to silence him.

The Truth has been silenced long enough!

Teabing knew he had to act quickly. Silas's attack would accomplish two goals. It would prevent Saunière from persuading Langdon to keep quiet, and it would ensure that once the keystone was in Teabing's hands, Langdon would be in Paris for recruitment should Teabing need him.

Arranging the fatal meeting between Saunière and Silas had been almost too easy. *I had inside information about Saunière's deepest fears.* Yesterday afternoon, Silas had phoned the curator and posed as a distraught priest. 'Monsieur Saunière, forgive me, I must speak to you at once. I should never breach the sanctity of the confessional, but in this case, I feel I must. I just took confession from a man who claimed to have murdered members of your family.'

Saunière's response was startled but wary. 'My family died in an accident. The police report was conclusive.'

'Yes, a *car* accident,' Silas said, baiting the hook. 'The man I spoke to said he forced their car off the road into a river.'

Saunière fell silent.

'Monsieur Saunière, I would never have phoned you directly except this man made a comment which makes me now fear for *your* safety.' He paused. 'The man also mentioned your granddaughter, Sophie.'

The mention of Sophie's name had been the catalyst. The curator leapt into action. He ordered Silas to come and see him immediately in the safest location Saunière knew – his Louvre office. Then he phoned Sophie to warn her she might be in danger. Drinks with Robert Langdon were instantly abandoned.

Now, with Langdon separated from Sophie on the far side of the room, Teabing sensed he had success-fully alienated the two companions from one another. Sophie Neveu remained defiant, but Langdon clearly saw the larger picture. He was trying to figure out the password. *He understands the importance of finding the Grail and releasing her from bondage.*

'He won't open it for you,' Sophie said coldly. 'Even if he can.'

Teabing was glancing at Langdon as he held the gun on Sophie. He was fairly certain now he was going to have to use the weapon. Although the idea troubled him, he knew he would not hesitate if it came to that. *I have given her every opportunity to do the right thing. The Grail is bigger than any one of us.*

At that moment, Langdon turned from the window. 'The tomb . . .' he said suddenly, facing them with a faint glimmer of hope in his eyes. 'I know where to look on Newton's tomb. Yes, I think I can find the password!'

Teabing's heart soared. 'Where, Robert? Tell me!'

Sophie sounded horrified. 'Robert, no! You're not going to help him, *are* you?'

Langdon approached with a resolute stride, holding the cryptex before him. 'No,' he said, his eyes hardening as he turned to Leigh. 'Not until he lets you go.'

Teabing's optimism darkened. 'We are so close, Robert. Don't you dare start playing games with me!'

'No games,' Langdon said. 'Let her go. Then I'll take you to Newton's tomb. We'll open the cryptex together.'

'I'm not going anywhere,' Sophie declared, her eyes narrowing with rage. 'That cryptex was given to me by my grandfather. It is not *yours* to open.'

Langdon wheeled, looking fearful. 'Sophie, please! You're in danger. I'm trying to help you!'

'How? By unveiling the secret my grandfather died trying to protect? He trusted you, Robert. *I* trusted you!'

Langdon's blue eyes showed panic now, and Teabing could not help but smile to see the two of them working against one another. Langdon's attempts to be gallant were more pathetic than anything. *On the verge of unveiling one of history's greatest secrets, and he troubles himself with a woman who has proven herself unworthy of the quest.*

'Sophie,' Langdon pleaded. 'Please . . . you must leave.'

She shook her head. 'Not unless you either hand me the cryptex or smash it on the floor.'

'What?' Langdon gasped.

'Robert, my grandfather would prefer his secret lost

for ever than see it in the hands of his murderer.'
Sophie's eyes looked as if they would well with tears,
but they did not. She stared directly back at Teabing.
'Shoot me if you have to. I am not leaving my grandfather's legacy in your hands.'

Very well. Teabing aimed the weapon.

'No!' Langdon shouted, raising his arm and suspending the cryptex precariously over the hard stone
floor. 'Leigh, if you even think about it, I will drop this.'

Teabing laughed. 'That bluff worked on Rémy. Not
on me. I know you better than that.'

'Do you, Leigh?'

*Yes I do. Your poker face needs work, my friend. It took
me several seconds, but I can see now that you are lying.
You have no idea where on Newton's tomb the answer lies.*
'Truly, Robert? You know where on the tomb to look?'

'I do.'

The falter in Langdon's eyes was fleeting but Leigh
caught it. There was a lie there. A desperate, pathetic
ploy to save Sophie. Teabing felt a profound disappointment in Robert Langdon.

*I am a lone knight, surrounded by unworthy souls. And
I will have to decipher the keystone on my own.*

Langdon and Neveu were nothing but a threat to
Teabing now . . . and to the Grail. As painful as the
solution was going to be, he knew he could carry it
out with a clean conscience. The only challenge would
be to persuade Langdon to set down the keystone so
Teabing could safely end this charade.

'A show of faith,' Teabing said, lowering the gun
from Sophie. 'Set down the keystone, and we'll talk.'

Langdon knew his lie had failed.

He could see the dark resolve in Teabing's face and
knew the moment was upon them. *When I set this*

down, he will kill us both. Even without looking at Sophie, he could hear her heart beseeching him in silent desperation. *Robert, this man is not worthy of the Grail. Please do not place it in his hands. No matter what the cost.*

Langdon had already made his decision several minutes ago, while standing alone at the window overlooking College Garden.

Protect Sophie.

Protect the Grail.

Langdon had almost shouted out in desperation. *But I cannot see how!*

The stark moments of disillusionment had brought with them a clarity unlike any he had ever felt. *The Truth is right before your eyes, Robert.* He knew not from where the epiphany came. *The Grail is not mocking you, she is calling out to a worthy soul.*

Now, bowing down like a subject several yards in front of Leigh Teabing, Langdon lowered the cryptex to within inches of the stone floor.

'Yes, Robert,' Teabing whispered, aiming the gun at him. 'Set it down.'

Langdon's eyes moved heavenward, up into the gaping void of the Chapter House cupola. Crouching lower, Langdon lowered his gaze to Teabing's gun, aimed directly at him.

'I'm sorry, Leigh.'

In one fluid motion, Langdon leapt up, swinging his arm skyward, launching the cryptex straight up toward the dome above.

Leigh Teabing did not feel his finger pull the trigger, but the Medusa discharged with a thundering crash. Langdon's crouched form was now vertical, almost airborne, and the bullet exploded in the floor near

554

Langdon's feet. Half of Teabing's brain attempted to adjust his aim and fire again in rage, but the more powerful half dragged his eyes upward into the cupola.

The keystone!

Time seemed to freeze, morphing into a slow-motion dream as Teabing's entire world became the airborne keystone. He watched it rise to the apex of its climb . . . hovering for a moment in the void . . . and then tumbling downward, end over end, back toward the stone floor.

All of Teabing's hopes and dreams were plummeting toward earth. *It cannot strike the floor! I can reach it!* Teabing's body reacted on instinct. He released the gun and heaved himself forward, dropping his crutches as he reached out with his soft, manicured hands. Stretching his arms and fingers, he snatched the keystone from midair.

Falling forward with the keystone victoriously clutched in his hand, Teabing knew he was falling too fast. With nothing to break his fall, his outstretched arms hit first, and the cryptex collided hard with the floor.

There was a sickening crunch of glass within.

For a full second, Teabing did not breathe. Lying there outstretched on the cold floor, staring the length of his outstretched arms at the marble cylinder in his bare palms, he implored the glass vial inside to hold. Then the acrid tang of vinegar cut the air, and Teabing felt the cool liquid flowing out through the dials onto his palm.

Wild panic gripped him. *NO!* The vinegar was streaming now, and Teabing pictured the papyrus dissolving within. *Robert, you fool! The secret is lost!*

Teabing felt himself sobbing uncontrollably. *The Grail is gone. Everything destroyed.* Shuddering in disbelief over Langdon's actions, Teabing tried to force the cylinder apart, longing to catch a fleeting glimpse of history before it dissolved for ever. To his shock, as he pulled the ends of the keystone, the cylinder separated.

He gasped and peered inside. It was empty except for shards of wet glass. No dissolving papyrus. Teabing rolled over and looked up at Langdon. Sophie stood beside him, aiming the gun down at Teabing.

Bewildered, Teabing looked back at the keystone and saw it. The dials were no longer at random. They spelled a five-letter word: APPLE.

'The orb from which Eve partook,' Langdon said coolly, 'incurring the Holy wrath of God. Original sin. The symbol of the fall of the sacred feminine.'

Teabing felt the truth come crashing down on him in excruciating austerity. The orb that ought be on Newton's tomb could be none other than the Rosy apple that fell from heaven, struck Newton on the head, and inspired his life's work. *His labour's fruit! The Rosy flesh with a seeded womb!*

'Robert,' Teabing stammered, overwhelmed. 'You opened it. Where . . . is the map?'

Without blinking, Langdon reached into the breast pocket of his tweed coat and carefully extracted a delicate rolled papyrus. Only a few yards from where Teabing lay, Langdon unrolled the scroll and looked at it. After a long moment, a knowing smile crossed Langdon's face.

He knows! Teabing's heart craved that knowledge. His life's dream was right in front of him. 'Tell me!' Teabing demanded. 'Please! Oh God, please! It's not too late!'

As the sound of heavy footsteps thundered down the hall toward the Chapter House, Langdon quietly rolled the papyrus and slipped it back in his pocket.

'No!' Teabing cried out, trying in vain to stand.

When the doors burst open, Bezu Fache entered like a bull into a ring, his feral eyes scanning, finding his target – Leigh Teabing – helpless on the floor. Exhaling in relief, Fache holstered his Manurhin sidearm and turned to Sophie. 'Agent Neveu, I am relieved you and Mr. Langdon are safe. You should have come in when I asked.'

The British police entered on Fache's heels, seizing the anguished prisoner and placing him in handcuffs.

Sophie seemed stunned to see Fache. 'How did you find us?'

Fache pointed to Teabing. 'He made the mistake of showing his ID when he entered the abbey. The guards heard a police broadcast about our search for him.'

'It's in Langdon's pocket!' Teabing was screaming like a madman. 'The map to the Holy Grail!'

As they hoisted Teabing and carried him out, he threw back his head and howled. 'Robert! Tell me where it's hidden!'

As Teabing passed, Langdon looked him in the eye. 'Only the worthy find the Grail, Leigh. You taught me that.'

Chapter 102

The mist had settled low on Kensington Gardens as Silas limped into a quiet hollow out of sight. Kneeling on the wet grass, he could feel a warm stream of blood flowing from the bullet wound below his ribs. Still, he stared straight ahead.

The fog made it look like heaven here.

Raising his bloody hands to pray, he watched the raindrops caress his fingers, turning them white again. As the droplets fell harder across his back and shoulders, he could feel his body disappearing bit by bit into the mist.

I am a ghost.

A breeze rustled past him, carrying the damp, earthy scent of new life. With every living cell in his broken body, Silas prayed. He prayed for forgiveness. He prayed for mercy. And, above all, he prayed for his mentor . . . Bishop Aringarosa . . . that the Lord would not take him before his time. *He has so much work left to do.*

The fog was swirling around him now, and Silas felt so light that he was sure the wisps would carry him away. Closing his eyes, he said a final prayer.

From somewhere in the mist, the voice of Manuel Aringarosa whispered to him.

Our Lord is a good and merciful God.

Silas's pain at last began to fade, and he knew the bishop was right.

Chapter 103

It was late afternoon when the London sun broke through and the city began to dry. Bezu Fache felt weary as he emerged from the interrogation room and hailed a cab. Sir Leigh Teabing had vociferously proclaimed his innocence, and yet from his incoherent rantings about the Holy Grail, secret documents, and mysterious brotherhoods, Fache suspected the wily historian was setting the stage for his lawyers to plead an insanity defence.

Sure, Fache thought. *Insane*. Teabing had displayed ingenious precision in formulating a plan that protected his innocence at every turn. He had exploited both the Vatican and Opus Dei, two groups that turned out to be completely innocent. His dirty work had been carried out unknowingly by a fanatical monk and a desperate bishop. More clever still, Teabing had situated his electronic listening post in the *one* place a man with polio could not possibly reach. The actual surveillance had been carried out by his manservant, Rémy – the lone person privy to Teabing's true identity – now conveniently dead of an allergic reaction.

Hardly the handiwork of someone lacking mental faculties, Fache thought.

The information coming from Collet out of Château Villette suggested that Teabing's cunning ran so deep that Fache himself might even learn from it. To successfully hide bugs in some of Paris's most powerful offices, the British historian had turned to the

Greeks. *Trojan horses.* Some of Teabing's intended targets received lavish gifts of artwork, others unwittingly bid at auctions in which Teabing had placed specific lots. In Saunière's case, the curator had received a dinner invitation to Château Villette to discuss the possibility of Teabing's funding a new Da Vinci Wing at the Louvre. Saunière's invitation had contained an innocuous postscript expressing fascination with a robotic knight that Saunière was rumoured to have built. *Bring him to dinner,* Teabing had suggested. Saunière apparently had done just that and left the knight unattended long enough for Rémy Legaludec to make one inconspicuous addition.

Now, sitting in the back of the cab, Fache closed his eyes. *One more thing to attend to before I return to Paris.*

The St Mary's Hospital recovery room was sunny.

'You've impressed us all,' the nurse said, smiling down at him. 'Nothing short of miraculous.'

Bishop Aringarosa gave a weak smile. 'I have always been blessed.'

The nurse finished puttering, leaving the bishop alone. The sunlight felt welcome and warm on his face. Last night had been the darkest night of his life.

Despondently, he thought of Silas, whose body had been found in the park.

Please forgive me, my son.

Aringarosa had longed for Silas to be part of his glorious plan. Last night, however, Aringarosa had received a call from Bezu Fache, questioning the bishop about his apparent connection to a nun who had been murdered in Saint-Sulpice. Aringarosa realized the evening had taken a horrifying turn. News of the four additional murders transformed his horror to anguish. *Silas, what have you done!* Unable to reach the Teacher, the bishop knew he had been cut loose. *Used.* The only way to stop the horrific chain of events he had helped put in motion was to confess everything to Fache, and from that moment on, Aringarosa and Fache had been racing to catch up with Silas before the Teacher persuaded him to kill again.

Feeling bone weary, Aringarosa closed his eyes and listened to the television coverage of the arrest of a prominent British knight, Sir Leigh Teabing. *The Teacher laid bare for all to see.* Teabing had caught wind of the Vatican's plans to disassociate itself from Opus Dei. He had chosen Aringarosa as the perfect pawn in his plan. *After all, who more likely to leap blindly after the Holy Grail than a man like myself with everything to lose? The Grail would have brought enormous power to anyone who possessed it.*

Leigh Teabing had protected his identity shrewdly – feigning a French accent and a pious heart, and demanding as payment the one thing he did not need – money. Aringarosa had been far too eager to be suspicious. The price tag of twenty million euros was paltry when compared with the prize of obtaining the Grail, and with the Vatican's separation payment to Opus Dei, the finances had worked nicely. *The blind see what they want to see.* Teabing's ultimate insult, of course, had been to demand payment in Vatican bonds, so that if anything went wrong, the investigation would lead to Rome.

'I am glad to see you're well, My Lord.'

Aringarosa recognized the gruff voice in the doorway, but the face was unexpected – stern, powerful features, slicked-back hair and a broad neck that strained against his dark suit. 'Captain Fache?' Aringarosa asked. The compassion and concern the captain had shown for Aringarosa's plight last night had conjured images of a far gentler physique.

The captain approached the bed and hoisted a familiar, heavy black briefcase onto a chair. 'I believe this belongs to you.'

Aringarosa looked at the briefcase filled with bonds and immediately looked away, feeling only shame. 'Yes ... thank you.' He paused while working his fingers across the seam of his bedsheet, then continued. 'Captain, I have been giving this deep thought, and I need to ask a favour of you.'

'Of course.'

'The families of those in Paris who Silas ...' He paused, swallowing the emotion. 'I realize no sum could possibly serve as sufficient restitution, and yet, if you could be kind enough to divide the contents of this briefcase among them ... the families of the deceased.'

Fache's dark eyes studied him a long moment. 'A virtuous gesture, My Lord. I will see to it your wishes are carried out.'

A heavy silence fell between them.

On the television, a lean French police officer was giving a press conference in front of a sprawling mansion. Fache saw who it was and turned his attention to the screen.

'Lieutenant Collet,' a BBC reporter said, her voice accusing. 'Last night, your captain publicly charged two innocent people with murder. Will Robert Langdon and Sophie Neveu be seeking accountability from your department? Will this cost Captain Fache his job?'

Lieutenant Collet's smile was tired but calm. 'It is my experience that Captain Bezu Fache seldom makes mistakes. I have not yet spoken to him on this matter, but knowing how he operates, I suspect his public manhunt for Agent Neveu and Mr Langdon was part of a ruse to lure out the real killer.'

The reporters exchanged surprised looks.

Collet continued. 'Whether or not Mr Langdon and Agent Neveu were willing participants in the sting, I do not know. Captain Fache tends to keep his more creative methods to himself. All I can confirm at this point is that the captain has successfully arrested the man responsible, and that Mr Langdon and Agent Neveu are both innocent and safe.'

Fache had a faint smile on his lips as he turned back to Aringarosa. 'A good man, that Collet.'

Several moments passed. Finally, Fache ran his hand over his forehead, slicking back his hair as he gazed down at Aringarosa. 'My Lord, before I return to Paris, there is one final matter I'd like to discuss – your impromptu flight to London. You bribed a pilot to change course. In doing so, you broke a number of international laws.'

Aringarosa slumped. 'I was desperate.'

'Yes. As was the pilot when my men interrogated him.' Fache reached in his pocket and produced a purple amethyst ring with a familiar hand-tooled mitre-crozier appliqué.

Aringarosa felt tears welling as he accepted the ring and slipped it back on his finger. 'You've been so kind.' He held out his hand and clasped Fache's. 'Thank you.'

Fache waved off the gesture, walking to the window and gazing out at the city, his thoughts obviously far away. When he turned, there was an uncertainty about him. 'My Lord, where do you go from here?'

Aringarosa had been asked the exact same question as he left Castel Gandolfo the night before. 'I suspect my path is as uncertain as yours.'

'Yes.' Fache paused. 'I suspect I will be retiring early.'

Aringarosa smiled. 'A little faith can do wonders, Captain. A little faith.'

Chapter 104

Rosslyn Chapel – often called the Cathedral of Codes – stands seven miles south of Edinburgh, on the site of an ancient Mithraic temple. Built by the Knights Templar in 1446, the chapel is engraved with a mind-boggling array of symbols from the Jewish, Christian, Egyptian, Masonic and pagan traditions.

The chapel's geographic coordinates fall precisely on the north-south meridian that runs through Glastonbury. This longitudinal Rose Line is the traditional marker of King Arthur's Isle of Avalon and is considered the central pillar of Britain's sacred geometry. It is from this hallowed Rose Line that Rosslyn – originally spelled Roslin – takes its name.

Rosslyn's rugged spires were casting long evening shadows as Robert Langdon and Sophie Neveu pulled their rental car into the grassy parking area at the foot of the bluff on which the chapel stood. Their short flight from London to Edinburgh had been restful, although neither of them had slept for the anticipation of what lay ahead. Gazing up at the stark edifice framed against a cloud-swept sky, Langdon felt like Alice falling headlong into the rabbit hole. *This must be a dream.* And yet he knew the text of Saunière's final message could not have been more specific.

The Holy Grail 'neath ancient Roslin waits.

Langdon had fantasized that Saunière's 'Grail map' would be a diagram – a drawing with an X-marks-the-spot – and yet the Priory's final secret had been unveiled in the same way Saunière had spoken to them from the beginning. *Simple verse.* Four explicit lines that pointed without a doubt to this very spot. In addition to identifying Rosslyn by name, the verse made reference to several of the chapel's renowned architectural features.

Despite the clarity of Saunière's final revelation, Langdon had been left feeling more off balance than enlightened. To him, Rosslyn Chapel seemed far too obvious a location. For centuries, this stone chapel had echoed with whispers of the Holy Grail's presence. The whispers had turned to shouts in recent decades when ground-penetrating radar revealed the presence of an astonishing structure *beneath* the chapel – a massive subterranean chamber. Not only did this deep vault dwarf the chapel atop it, but it appeared to have no entrance or exit. Archaeologists petitioned to begin blasting through the bedrock to reach the mysterious chamber, but the Rosslyn Trust expressly forbade any excavation of the sacred site. Of course, this only fuelled the fires of speculation. What was the Rosslyn Trust trying to hide?

Rosslyn had now become a pilgrimage site for mystery seekers. Some claimed they were drawn here by the powerful magnetic field that emanated in-explicably from these coordinates, some claimed they came to search the hillside for a hidden entrance to the vault, but most admitted they had come simply to wander the grounds and absorb the lore of the Holy Grail.

Although Langdon had never been to Rosslyn before now, he always chuckled when he heard the chapel described as the current home of the Holy Grail. Admittedly, Rosslyn *once* might have been home to the Grail, long ago . . . but certainly no longer.

Far too much attention had been drawn to Rosslyn in past decades, and sooner or later someone would find a way to break into the vault.

True Grail academics agreed that Rosslyn was a decoy – one of the devious dead ends the Priory crafted so convincingly. Tonight, however, with the Priory's keystone offering a verse that pointed directly to this spot, Langdon no longer felt so smug. A perplexing question had been running through his mind all day:

Why would Saunière go to such effort to guide us to so obvious a location?

There seemed only one logical answer.

There is something about Rosslyn we have yet to understand.

'Robert?' Sophie was standing outside the car, looking back at him. 'Are you coming?' She was holding the rosewood box, which Captain Fache had returned to them. Inside, both cryptexes had been reassembled and nested as they had been found. The papyrus verse was locked safely at its core – minus the shattered vial of vinegar.

Making their way up the long gravel path, Langdon and Sophie passed the famous west wall of the chapel. Casual visitors assumed this oddly protruding wall was a section of the chapel that had not been finished. The truth, Langdon recalled, was far more intriguing.

The west wall of Solomon's Temple.

The Knights Templar had designed Rosslyn Chapel as an exact architectural blueprint of Solomon's Temple in Jerusalem – complete with a west wall, a narrow rectangular sanctuary, and a subterranean vault like the Holy of Holies, in which the original nine knights had first unearthed their priceless treasure. Langdon had to admit, there existed an intriguing symmetry in the idea of the Templars building a modern Grail repository that echoed the Grail's original hiding place.

Rosslyn Chapel's entrance was more modest than Langdon expected. The small wooden door had two iron hinges and a simple, oak sign.

ROSLIN

This ancient spelling, Langdon explained to Sophie, derived from the Rose Line meridian on which the chapel sat; or, as Grail academics preferred to believe, from the 'Line of Rose' – the ancestral lineage of Mary Magdalene.

The chapel would be closing soon, and as Langdon pulled open the door, a warm puff of air escaped, as if the ancient edifice were heaving a weary sigh at the end of a long day. Her entry arches burgeoned with carved cinquefoils.

Roses. The womb of the goddess.

Entering with Sophie, Langdon felt his eyes reaching across the famous sanctuary and taking it all in. Although he had read accounts of Rosslyn's arrestingly intricate stonework, seeing it in person was an overwhelming encounter.

Symbology heaven, one of Langdon's colleagues had called it.

Every surface in the chapel had been carved with symbols – Christian cruciforms, Jewish stars, Masonic seals, Templar crosses, cornucopias, pyramids, astrological signs, plants, vegetables, pentacles and roses. The Knights Templar had been master stonemasons, erecting Templar churches all over Europe, but Rosslyn was considered their most sublime labour of love and veneration. The master masons had left no stone uncarved. Rosslyn Chapel was a shrine to all faiths . . . to all traditions . . . and, above all, to nature and the goddess.

The sanctuary was empty except for a handful of visitors listening to a young man giving the day's last tour. He was leading them in a single-file line along a well-known route on the floor – an invisible pathway linking six key architectural points within the sanctuary. Generations of visitors had walked these straight lines, connecting the points, and their countless footsteps had engraved an enormous symbol on the floor.

The Star of David, Langdon thought. *No coincidence there*. Also known as Solomon's Seal, this hexagram had once been the secret symbol of the stargazing priests and was later adopted by the Israelite kings – David and Solomon.

The guide had seen Langdon and Sophie enter, and although it was closing time, offered a pleasant smile and motioned for them to feel free to look around.

Langdon nodded his thanks and began to move deeper into the sanctuary. Sophie, however, stood riveted in the entryway, a puzzled look on her face.

'What is it?' Langdon asked.

Sophie stared out at the chapel. 'I think . . . I've been here.'

Langdon was surprised. 'But you said you hadn't even *heard* of Rosslyn.'

'I hadn't . . .' She scanned the sanctuary, looking uncertain. 'My grandfather must have brought me here when I was very young. I don't know. It feels familiar.' As her eyes scanned the room, she began nodding with more certainty. 'Yes.' She pointed to the front of the sanctuary. 'Those two pillars . . . I've seen them.'

Langdon looked at the pair of intricately sculpted columns at the far end of the sanctuary. Their white lacework carvings seemed to smoulder with a ruddy glow as the last of the day's sunlight streamed in through the west window. The pillars – positioned where the altar would normally stand – were an oddly matched pair. The pillar on the left was carved with simple, vertical lines, while the pillar on the right was embellished with an ornate, flowering spiral.

Sophie was already moving toward them. Langdon hurried after her, and as they reached the pillars, Sophie was nodding with incredulity. 'Yes, I'm positive I have seen these!'

'I don't doubt you've seen them,' Langdon said, 'but it wasn't necessarily *here*.'

She turned. 'What do you mean?'

'These two pillars are the most duplicated architectural structures in history. Replicas exist all over the world.'

'Replicas of Rosslyn?' She looked sceptical.

'No. Of the pillars. Do you remember earlier that I mentioned Rosslyn *itself* is a copy of Solomon's Temple? Those two pillars are exact replicas of the two pillars that stood at the head of Solomon's Temple.' Langdon pointed to the pillar on the left. 'That's called *Boaz* – or the Mason's Pillar. The other is called *Jachin* – or the Apprentice Pillar.' He paused. 'In fact, virtually every Masonic temple in the world has two pillars like these.'

Langdon had already explained to her about the Templars' powerful historic ties to the modern Masonic secret societies, whose primary degrees – Apprentice Freemason, Fellowcraft Freemason and Master Mason – harked back to early Templar days. Sophie's grandfather's final verse made direct reference to the Master Masons who adorned Rosslyn with their carved artistic offerings. It also noted Rosslyn's central ceiling, which was covered with carvings of stars and planets.

'I've never been in a Masonic temple,' Sophie said, still eyeing the pillars. 'I am almost positive I saw these *here*.' She turned back into the chapel, as if looking for something else to jog her memory.

The rest of the visitors were now leaving, and the young verger made his way across the chapel to them with a pleasant smile. He was a handsome young man in his late twenties, with a Scottish brogue and strawberry blond hair. 'I'm about to close up for the day. May I help you find anything?'

How about the Holy Grail? Langdon wanted to say.

'The code,' Sophie blurted, in sudden revelation. 'There's a code here!'

The verger looked pleased by her enthusiasm. 'Yes, there is, ma'am.'

'It's on the ceiling,' she said, turning to the right-hand wall. 'Somewhere over . . . there.'

He smiled. 'Not your first visit to Rosslyn, I see.'

The code, Langdon thought. He had forgotten that little bit of lore. Among Rosslyn's numerous mysteries was a vaulted archway from which hundreds of stone blocks protruded, jutting down to form a bizarre multifaceted surface. Each block was carved with a symbol, seemingly at random, creating a cipher of unfathomable proportion. Some people believed the code revealed the entrance to the vault beneath the chapel. Others believed it told the true Grail legend. Not that it mattered – cryptographers had been trying for centuries to decipher its meaning. To this day the Rosslyn Trust offered a generous reward to anyone who could unveil the secret meaning, but the code remained a mystery.

'I'd be happy to show . . .'

* * *

The verger's voice trailed off.

My first code, Sophie thought, moving alone, in a trance, toward the encoded archway. Having handed the rosewood box to Langdon, she could feel herself momentarily forgetting all about the Holy Grail, the Priory of Sion, and all the mysteries of the past day. When she arrived beneath the encoded ceiling and saw the symbols above her, the memories came flooding back. She was recalling her first visit here, and strangely, the memories conjured an unexpected sadness.

She was a little girl . . . a year or so after her family's death. Her grandfather had brought her to Scotland on a short vacation. They had come to see Rosslyn Chapel before going back to Paris. It was late evening, and the chapel was closed. But they were still inside.

'Can we go home, *Grand-père*?' Sophie begged, feeling tired.

'Soon, dear, very soon.' His voice was melancholy. 'I have one last thing I need to do here. How about if you wait in the car?'

'You're doing another big person thing?'

He nodded. 'I'll be fast. I promise.'

'Can I do the archway code again? That was fun.'

'I don't know. I have to step outside. You won't be frightened in here alone?'

'Of course not!' she said in a huff. 'It's not even dark yet!'

He smiled. 'Very well then.' He led her over to the elaborate archway he had shown her earlier.

Sophie immediately plopped down on the stone floor, lying on her back and staring up at the collage of puzzle pieces overhead. 'I'm going to break this code before you get back!'

'It's a race then.' He bent over, kissed her forehead, and walked to the nearby side door. 'I'll be right outside. I'll leave the door open. If you need me, just call.' He exited into the soft evening light.

Sophie lay there on the floor, gazing up at the code. Her eyes felt sleepy. After a few minutes, the symbols got fuzzy. And then they disappeared.

When Sophie awoke, the floor felt cold.

'*Grand-père?*'

There was no answer. Standing up, she brushed herself off. The side door was still open. The evening was getting darker. She walked outside and could see her grandfather standing on the porch of a nearby stone house directly behind the church. Her grandfather was talking quietly to a person barely visible inside the screened door.

'*Grand-père?*' she called.

Her grandfather turned and waved, motioning for her to wait just a moment. Then, slowly, he said some final words to the person inside and blew a kiss toward the screened door. He came to her with tearful eyes.

'Why are you crying, *Grand-père?*'

He picked her up and held her close. 'Oh, Sophie, you and I have said good-bye to a lot of people this year. It's hard.'

Sophie thought of the accident, of saying good-bye to her mother and father, her grandmother and baby brother. 'Were you saying good-bye to *another* person?'

'To a dear friend whom I love very much,' he replied, his voice heavy with emotion. 'And I fear I will not see her again for a very long time.'

Standing with the verger, Langdon had been scanning the chapel walls and feeling a rising wariness that a dead end might be looming. Sophie had wandered off to look at the code and left Langdon holding the rosewood box, which contained a Grail map that now appeared to be no help at all. Although Saunière's poem clearly indicated Rosslyn, Langdon was not sure what to do now that they had arrived. The poem made reference to a 'blade and chalice', which Langdon saw nowhere.

The Holy Grail 'neath ancient Roslin waits.
The blade and chalice guarding o'er Her
gates.

Again Langdon sensed there remained some facet of this mystery yet to reveal itself.

'I hate to pry,' the verger said, eyeing the rosewood box in Langdon's hands. 'But this box . . . might I ask where you got it?'

Langdon gave a weary laugh. 'That's an exceptionally long story.'

The young man hesitated, his eyes on the box again. 'It's the strangest thing – my grandmother has a box *exactly* like that – a jewellery box. Identical polished rosewood, same inlaid rose, even the hinges look the same.'

Langdon knew the young man must be mistaken. If ever a box had been one of a kind, it was *this* one – the box custom-made for the Priory keystone. 'The two boxes may be similar but—'

The side door closed loudly, drawing both of their gazes. Sophie had exited without a word and was now wandering down the bluff toward a fieldstone house nearby. Langdon stared after her. *Where is she going?* She had been acting strangely ever since they entered the building. He turned to the guide. 'Do you know what that house is?'

He nodded, also looking puzzled that Sophie was going down there. 'That's the chapel rectory. The chapel curator lives there. She also happens to be the head of the Rosslyn Trust.' He paused. 'And my grandmother.'

'Your grandmother heads the Rosslyn Trust?'

The young man nodded. 'I live with her in the rectory and help keep up the chapel and give tours.' He shrugged. 'I've lived here my whole life. My grandmother brought me up in that house.'

Concerned for Sophie, Langdon moved across the chapel toward the door to call out to her. He was only halfway there when he stopped short. Something the young man said just registered.

My grandmother brought me up.

Langdon looked out at Sophie on the bluff, then down at the rosewood box in his hand. *Impossible.* Slowly, Langdon turned back to the young man. 'You said your grandmother has a box like this one?'

'Almost identical.'

'Where did she get it?'

'My grandfather made it for her. He died when I was a baby, but my grandmother still talks about him. She says he was a genius with his hands. He made all kinds of things.'

Langdon glimpsed an unimaginable web of connections emerging. 'You said your grandmother brought you up. Do you mind my asking what happened to your parents?'

The young man looked surprised. 'They died when I was young.' He paused. 'The same day as my grandfather.'

Langdon's heart pounded. 'In a car accident?'

The guide recoiled, a look of bewilderment in his olive-green eyes. 'Yes. In a car accident. My entire family died that day. I lost my grandfather, my parents, and . . .' He hesitated, glancing down at the floor.

'And your sister,' Langdon said.

Out on the bluff, the fieldstone house was exactly as Sophie remembered it. Night was falling now, and the house exuded a warm and inviting aura. The smell of bread wafted through the open screened door, and a golden light shone in the windows. As Sophie approached, she could hear the quiet sounds of sobbing from within.

Through the screened door, Sophie saw an elderly woman in the hallway. Her back was to the door, but Sophie could see she was crying. The woman had long, luxuriant, silver hair that conjured an un-expected wisp of memory. Feeling herself drawn closer, Sophie stepped onto the porch stairs. The woman was clutching a framed photograph of a man and touching her fingertips to his face with loving sadness.

It was a face Sophie knew well.

Grand-père.

The woman had obviously heard the sad news of his death last night.

A board squeaked beneath Sophie's feet, and the woman turned slowly, her sad eyes finding Sophie's. Sophie wanted to run, but she stood transfixed. The woman's fervent gaze never wavered as she set down the photo and approached the screened door. An eternity seemed to pass as the two women stared at one another through the thin mesh. Then, like the slowly gathering swell of an ocean wave, the woman's visage transformed from one of uncertainty . . . to disbelief . . . to hope . . . and finally, to cresting joy.

Throwing open the door, she came out, reaching with soft hands, cradling Sophie's thunderstruck face. 'Oh, dear child . . . look at you!'

Although Sophie did not recognize her, she knew who this woman was. She tried to speak but found she could not even breathe.

'Sophie,' the woman sobbed, kissing her forehead.

Sophie's words were a choked whisper. 'But . . . *Grand-père* said you were . . .'

'I know.' The woman placed her tender hands on Sophie's shoulders and gazed at her with familiar eyes. 'Your grandfather and I were forced to say so many things. We did what we thought was right. I'm so sorry. It was for your own safety, princess.'

Sophie heard her final word, and immediately thought of her grandfather, who had called her princess for so many years. The sound of his voice seemed to echo now in the ancient stones of Rosslyn, settling through the earth and reverberating in the unknown hollows below.

The woman threw her arms around Sophie, the tears flowing faster. 'Your grandfather wanted so badly to tell you everything. But things were difficult between you two. He tried so hard. There's so much to explain. So very much to explain.' She kissed Sophie's forehead once again, then whispered in her ear. 'No more secrets, princess. It's time you learn the truth about our family.'

Sophie and her grandmother were seated on the porch stairs in a tearful hug when the young guide dashed across the lawn, his eyes shining with hope and disbelief.

'Sophie?'

Through her tears, Sophie nodded, standing. She

did not know the young man's face, but as they embraced, she could feel the power of the blood coursing through his veins . . . the blood she now understood they shared.

When Langdon walked across the lawn to join them, Sophie could not imagine that only yesterday she had felt so alone in the world. And now, somehow, in this foreign place, in the company of three people she barely knew, she felt at last that she was home.

Chapter 105

Night had fallen over Rosslyn.

Robert Langdon stood alone on the porch of the fieldstone house enjoying the sounds of laughter and reunion drifting through the screened door behind him. The mug of potent Brazilian coffee in his hand had granted him a hazy reprieve from his mounting exhaustion, and yet he sensed the reprieve would be fleeting. The fatigue in his body went to the core.

'You slipped out quietly,' a voice behind him said.

He turned. Sophie's grandmother emerged, her silver hair shimmering in the night. Her name, for the last twenty-eight years at least, was Marie Chauvel.

Langdon gave a tired smile. 'I thought I'd give your family some time together.' Through the window, he could see Sophie talking with her brother.

Marie came over and stood beside him. 'Mr Langdon, when I first heard of Jacques's murder, I was terrified for Sophie's safety. Seeing her standing in my doorway tonight was the greatest relief of my life. I cannot thank you enough.'

Langdon had no idea how to respond. Although he had offered to give Sophie and her grandmother time to talk in private, Marie had asked him to stay and listen. *My husband obviously trusted you, Mr Langdon, so I do as well.*

And so Langdon had remained, standing beside Sophie and listening in mute astonishment while Marie told the story of Sophie's late parents.

Incredibly, both had been from Merovingian families – direct descendants of Mary Magdalene and Jesus Christ. Sophie's parents and ancestors, for protection, had changed their family names of Plantard and Saint-Clair. Their children represented the most direct surviving royal bloodline and therefore were carefully guarded by the Priory. When Sophie's parents were killed in a car accident whose cause could not be determined, the Priory feared the identity of the royal line had been discovered.

'Your grandfather and I,' Marie had explained in a voice choked with pain, 'had to make a grave decision the instant we received the phone call. Your parents' car had just been found in the river.' She dabbed at the tears in her eyes. 'All six of us – including you two grandchildren – were supposed to be travelling together in that car that very night. Fortunately we changed our plans at the last moment, and your parents were alone. Hearing of the accident, Jacques and I had no way to know what had really happened ... or if this was truly an *accident*.' Marie looked at Sophie. 'We knew we had to protect our grandchildren, and we did what we thought was best. Jacques reported to the police that your brother and I had been in the car ... our two bodies apparently washed off in the current. Then your brother and I went underground with the Priory. Jacques, being a man of prominence, did not have the luxury of disappearing. It only made sense that Sophie, being the eldest, would stay in Paris to be taught and raised by Jacques, close to the heart and protection of the Priory.' Her voice fell to a whisper. 'Separating the family was the hardest thing we ever had to do. Jacques and I saw each other only very infrequently, and always in the most secret of settings ... under the protection of the Priory. There are certain ceremonies to which the brotherhood always stays faithful.'

Langdon had sensed the story went far deeper, but he also sensed it was not for him to hear. So he had stepped outside. Now, gazing up at the spires of Rosslyn, Langdon could not escape the hollow gnaw of Rosslyn's unsolved mystery. *Is the Grail really here at Rosslyn? And if so, where are the blade and chalice that Saunière mentioned in his poem?*

'I'll take that,' Marie said, motioning to Langdon's hand.

'Oh, thank you.' Langdon held out his empty coffee cup.

She stared at him. 'I was referring to your *other* hand, Mr Langdon.'

Langdon looked down and realized he was holding Saunière's papyrus. He had taken it from the cryptex once again in hopes of seeing something he had missed earlier. 'Of course, I'm sorry.'

Marie looked amused as she took the paper. 'I know of a man at a bank in Paris who is probably very eager to see the return of this rosewood box. André Vernet was a dear friend of Jacques, and Jacques trusted him explicitly. André would have done anything to honour Jacques's requests for the care of this box.'

Including shooting me, Langdon recalled, deciding not to mention that he had probably broken the poor man's nose. Thinking of Paris, Langdon flashed on the three *sénéchaux* who had been killed the night before. 'And the Priory? What happens now?'

'The wheels are already in motion, Mr Langdon. The brotherhood has endured for centuries, and it will endure this. There are always those waiting to move up and rebuild.'

All evening Langdon had suspected that Sophie's grandmother was closely tied to the operations of the

Priory. After all, the Priory had always had women members. Four Grand Masters had been women. The *sénéchaux* were traditionally men – the guardians – and yet women held far more honoured status within the Priory and could ascend to the highest post from virtually any rank.

Langdon thought of Leigh Teabing and Westminster Abbey. It seemed a lifetime ago. 'Was the Church pressuring your husband not to release the Sangreal documents at the End of Days?'

'Heavens no. The End of Days is a legend of paranoid minds. There is nothing in the Priory doctrine that identifies a date at which the Grail should be unveiled. In fact the Priory has always maintained that the Grail should *never* be unveiled.'

'Never?' Langdon was stunned.

'It is the mystery and wonderment that serve our souls, not the Grail itself. The beauty of the Grail lies in her ethereal nature.' Marie Chauvel gazed up at Rosslyn now. 'For some, the Grail is a chalice that will bring them everlasting life. For others, it is the quest for lost documents and secret history. And for most, I suspect the Holy Grail is simply a grand idea . . . a glorious unattainable treasure that somehow, even in today's world of chaos, inspires us.'

'But if the Sangreal documents remain hidden, the story of Mary Magdalene will be lost for ever,' Langdon said.

'Will it? Look around you. Her story is being told in art, music and books. More so every day. The pendulum is swinging. We are starting to sense the dangers of our history . . . and of our destructive paths. We are beginning to sense the need to restore the sacred feminine.' She paused. 'You mentioned you are writing a manuscript about the symbols of the sacred feminine, are you not?'

'I am.'

She smiled. 'Finish it, Mr Langdon. Sing her song. The world needs modern troubadours.'

Langdon fell silent, feeling the weight of her message upon him. Across the open spaces, a new moon was rising above the tree line. Turning his eyes toward Rosslyn, Langdon felt a boyish craving to know her secrets. *Don't ask*, he told himself. *This is not the moment.* He glanced at the papyrus in Marie's hand, and then back at Rosslyn.

'Ask the question, Mr Langdon,' Marie said, looking amused. 'You have earned the right.'

Langdon felt himself flush.

'You want to know if the Grail is here at Rosslyn.'

'Can you tell me?'

She sighed in mock exasperation. 'Why is it that men simply *cannot* let the Grail rest?' She laughed, obviously enjoying herself. 'Why do you think it's here?'

Langdon motioned to the papyrus in her hand. 'Your husband's poem speaks specifically of Rosslyn, except it also mentions a blade and chalice watching over the Grail. I didn't see any symbols of the blade and chalice up there.'

'The blade and chalice?' Marie asked. 'What exactly do they look like?'

Langdon sensed she was toying with him, but he played along, quickly describing the symbols.

A look of vague recollection crossed her face. 'Ah, yes, of course. The blade represents all that is masculine. I believe it is drawn like this, no?' Using her index finger, she traced a shape on her palm.

'Yes,' Langdon said. Marie had drawn the less common 'closed' form of the blade, although Langdon had seen the symbol portrayed both ways.

'And the inverse,' she said, drawing again on her palm, 'is the chalice, which represents the feminine.'

'Correct,' Langdon said.

'And you are saying that in all the hundreds of symbols we have here in Rosslyn Chapel, these two shapes appear nowhere?'

'I didn't see them.'

'And if I show them to you, will you get some sleep?'

Before Langdon could answer, Marie Chauvel had stepped off the porch and was heading toward the chapel. Langdon hurried after her. Entering the ancient building, Marie turned on the lights and pointed to the centre of the sanctuary floor. 'There you are, Mr Langdon. The blade and chalice.'

Langdon stared at the scuffed stone floor. It was blank. 'There's nothing here. . . .'

Marie sighed and began to walk along the famous path worn into the chapel floor, the same path Langdon had seen the visitors walking earlier this evening. As his eyes adjusted to see the giant symbol, he still felt lost. 'But that's the Star of Dav—'

Langdon stopped short, mute with amazement as it dawned on him.

The blade and chalice.
Fused as one.

The Star of David ... the perfect union of male and female ... Solomon's Seal ... marking the Holy of Holies, where the male and female deities – Yahweh and Shekinah – were thought to dwell.

Langdon needed a minute to find his words. 'The verse does point here to Rosslyn. Completely. Perfectly.'

Marie smiled. 'Apparently.'

The implications chilled him. 'So the Holy Grail is in the vault beneath us?'

She laughed. 'Only in spirit. One of the Priory's most ancient charges was one day to return the Grail to her homeland of France where she could rest for eternity. For centuries, she was dragged across the countryside to keep her safe. Most undignified. Jacques's charge when he became Grand Master was to restore her honour by returning her to France and building her a resting place fit for a queen.'

'And he succeeded?'

Now her face grew serious. 'Mr Langdon, considering what you've done for me tonight, and as curator of the Rosslyn Trust, I can tell you for certain that the Grail is no longer here.'

Langdon decided to press. 'But the keystone is supposed to point to the place where the Holy Grail is hidden *now*. Why does it point to Rosslyn?'

'Maybe you're misreading its meaning. Remember, the Grail can be deceptive. As could my late husband.'

'But how much clearer could he be?' he asked. 'We are standing over an underground vault marked by the blade and chalice, underneath a ceiling of stars, surrounded by the art of Master Masons. Everything speaks of Rosslyn.'

'Very well, let me see this mysterious verse.' She unrolled the papyrus and read the poem aloud in a deliberate tone.

584

The Holy Grail 'neath ancient Roslin waits.
The blade and chalice guarding o'er Her gates.
Adorned in masters' loving art, She lies.
She rests at last beneath the starry skies.

When she finished, she was still for several seconds, until a knowing smile crossed her lips. 'Aah, Jacques.'

Langdon watched her expectantly. 'You *understand* this?'

'As you have witnessed on the chapel floor, Mr Langdon, there are many ways to see simple things.'

Langdon strained to understand. Everything about Jacques Saunière seemed to have double meanings, and yet Langdon could see no further.

Marie gave a tired yawn. 'Mr Langdon, I will make a confession to you. I have never officially been privy to the present location of the Grail. But, of course, I was married to a person of enormous influence . . . and my woman's intuition is strong.' Langdon started to speak but Marie continued. 'I am sorry that after all your hard work, you will be leaving Rosslyn without any real answers. And yet, something tells me you will eventually find what you seek. One day it will dawn on you.' She smiled. 'And when it does, I trust that you, of all people, can keep a secret.'

There was a sound of someone arriving in the doorway. 'Both of you disappeared,' Sophie said, entering.

'I was just leaving,' her grandmother replied, walking over to Sophie at the door. 'Good night, princess.' She kissed Sophie's forehead. 'Don't keep Mr Langdon out too late.'

Langdon and Sophie watched her grandmother walk back toward the fieldstone house. When Sophie turned to him, her eyes were awash in deep emotion. 'Not exactly the ending I expected.'

That makes two of us, he thought. Langdon could see she was overwhelmed. The news she had received tonight had changed everything in her life. 'Are you okay? It's a lot to take in.'

She smiled quietly. 'I have a family. That's where I'm going to start. Who we are and where we came from will take some time.'

Langdon remained silent.

'Beyond tonight, will you stay with us?' Sophie asked. 'At least for a few days?'

Langdon sighed, wanting nothing more. 'You need some time here with your family, Sophie. I'm going back to Paris in the morning.'

She looked disappointed but seemed to know it was the right thing to do. Neither of them spoke for a long time. Finally Sophie reached over and, taking his hand, led him out of the chapel. They walked to a small rise on the bluff. From here, the Scottish countryside spread out before them, suffused in a pale moonlight that sifted through the departing clouds. They stood in silence, holding hands, both of them fighting the descending shroud of exhaustion.

The stars were just now appearing, but to the west, a single point of light glowed brighter than any other. Langdon smiled when he saw it. It was Venus. The ancient Goddess shining down with her steady and patient light.

The night was growing cooler, a crisp breeze rolling up from the lowlands. After a while, Langdon looked over at Sophie. Her eyes were closed, her lips relaxed in a contented smile. Langdon could feel his own eyes growing heavy. Reluctantly, he squeezed her hand. 'Sophie?'

Slowly, she opened her eyes and turned to him. Her face was beautiful in the moonlight. She gave him a sleepy smile. 'Hi.'

Langdon felt an unexpected sadness to realize he would be returning to Paris without her. 'I may be gone before you wake up.' He paused, a knot growing in his throat. 'I'm sorry, I'm not very good at—'

Sophie reached out and placed her soft hand on the side of his face. Then, leaning forward, she kissed him tenderly on the cheek. 'When can I see you again?'

Langdon reeled momentarily, lost in her eyes. 'When?' He paused, curious if she had any idea how much he had been wondering the same thing. 'Well, actually, next month I'm lecturing at a conference in Florence. I'll be there a week without much to do.'

'Is that an invitation?'

'We'd be living in luxury. They're giving me a room at the Brunelleschi.'

Sophie smiled playfully. 'You presume a lot, Mr Langdon.'

He cringed at how it had sounded. 'What I meant—'

'I would love nothing more than to meet you in Florence, Robert. But on *one* condition.' Her tone turned serious. 'No museums, no churches, no tombs, no art, no relics.'

'In Florence? For a week? There's nothing else to do.'

Sophie leaned forward and kissed him again, now on the lips. Their bodies came together, softly at first, and then completely. When she pulled away, her eyes were full of promise.

'Right,' Langdon managed. 'It's a date.'

Epilogue

Robert Langdon awoke with a start. He had been dreaming. The bathrobe beside his bed bore the monogram HOTEL RITZ PARIS. He saw a dim light filtering through the blinds. *Is it dusk or dawn?* he wondered.

Langdon's body felt warm and deeply contented. He had slept the better part of the last two days. Sitting up slowly in bed, he now realized what had awoken him . . . the strangest thought. For days he had been trying to sort through a barrage of information, but now Langdon found himself fixed on something he'd not considered before.

Could it be?

He remained motionless a long moment.

Getting out of bed, he walked to the marble shower. Stepping inside, he let the powerful jets massage his shoulders. Still, the thought enthralled him.

Impossible.

Twenty minutes later, Langdon stepped out of the Hotel Ritz into Place Vendôme. Night was falling. The days of sleep had left him disoriented . . . and yet his mind felt oddly lucid. He had promised himself he would stop in the hotel lobby for a café au lait to clear his thoughts, but instead his legs carried him directly out of the front door into the gathering Paris night.

Walking east on Rue des Petits Champs, Langdon felt a growing excitement. He turned south onto Rue Richelieu, where the air grew sweet with the scent of blossoming jasmine from the stately gardens of the Palais Royal.

He continued south until he saw what he was looking for – the famous royal arcade – a glistening expanse of polished black marble. Moving onto it, Langdon scanned the surface beneath his feet. Within seconds, he found what he knew was there – several bronze medallions embedded in the ground in a perfectly straight line. Each disk was five inches in diameter and embossed with the letters N and S.

Nord. Sud.

He turned due south, letting his eye trace the extended line formed by the medallions. He began moving again, following the trail, watching the pavement as he walked. As he cut across the corner of the Comédie-Française, another bronze medallion passed beneath his feet. *Yes!*

The streets of Paris, Langdon had learned years ago, were adorned with 135 of these bronze markers, embedded in sidewalks, courtyards, and streets, on a north-south axis across the city. He had once followed the line from Sacré-Coeur, north across the Seine, and finally to the ancient Paris Observatory. There he discovered the significance of the sacred path it traced.

The earth's original prime meridian.
The first zero longitude of the world.
Paris's ancient Rose Line.

Now, as Langdon hurried across Rue de Rivoli, he could feel his destination within reach. Less than a block away.

The Holy Grail 'neath ancient Roslin waits.

The revelations were coming now in waves. Saunière's ancient spelling of Roslin . . . the blade

589

and chalice . . . the tomb adorned with masters' art.

Is that why Saunière needed to talk with me? Had I unknowingly guessed the truth?

He broke into a jog, feeling the Rose Line beneath his feet, guiding him, pulling him toward his destination. As he entered the long tunnel of Passage Richelieu, the hairs on his neck began to bristle with anticipation. He knew that at the end of this tunnel stood the most mysterious of Parisian monuments – conceived and commissioned in the 1980s by the Sphinx himself, François Mitterrand, a man rumoured to move in secret circles, a man whose final legacy to Paris was a place Langdon had visited only days before.

Another lifetime.

With a final surge of energy, Langdon burst from the passageway into the familiar courtyard and came to a stop. Breathless, he raised his eyes, slowly, disbelieving, to the glistening structure in front of him.

The Louvre Pyramid.

Gleaming in the darkness.

He admired it only a moment. He was more interested in what lay to his right. Turning, he felt his feet again tracing the invisible path of the ancient Rose Line, carrying him across the courtyard to the Carrousel du Louvre – the enormous circle of grass surrounded by a perimeter of neatly trimmed hedges – once the site of Paris's primeval nature-worshipping festivals . . . joyous rites to celebrate fertility and the Goddess.

Langdon felt as if he were crossing into another world as he stepped over the bushes to the grassy area within. This hallowed ground was now marked by one of the city's most unusual monuments. There in the centre, plunging into the earth like a crystal chasm, gaped the giant inverted pyramid of glass that he had seen a few nights ago when he entered the Louvre's subterranean entresol.

La Pyramide Inversée.

Tremulous, Langdon walked to the edge and peered down into the Louvre's sprawling underground complex, aglow with amber light. His eye was trained not just on the massive inverted pyramid, but on what lay directly beneath it. There, on the floor of the chamber below, stood the tiniest of structures . . . a structure Langdon had mentioned in his manuscript.

Langdon felt himself awaken fully now to the thrill of unthinkable possibility. Raising his eyes again to the Louvre, he sensed the huge wings of the museum enveloping him . . . hallways that burgeoned with the world's finest art.

Da Vinci . . . Botticelli . . .

Adorned in masters' loving art, She lies.

Alive with wonder, he stared once again downward through the glass at the tiny structure below.

I must go down there!

Stepping out of the circle, he hurried across the courtyard back toward the towering pyramid entrance of the Louvre. The day's last visitors were trickling out of the museum.

Pushing through the revolving door, Langdon descended the curved staircase into the pyramid. He could feel the air grow cooler. When he reached the bottom, he entered the long tunnel that stretched beneath the Louvre's courtyard, back toward *La Pyramide Inversée*.

At the end of the tunnel, he emerged into a large chamber. Directly before him, hanging down from above, gleamed the inverted pyramid – a breathtaking V-shaped contour of glass.

The Chalice.

Langdon's eyes traced its narrowing form downward to its tip, suspended only six feet above the floor. There, directly beneath it, stood the tiny structure.

A miniature pyramid. Only three feet tall. The only structure in this colossal complex that had been built on a small scale.

Langdon's manuscript, while discussing the Louvre's elaborate collection of goddess art, had made passing note of this modest pyramid. '*The miniature structure itself protrudes up through the floor as though it were the tip of an iceberg – the apex of an enormous, pyramidical vault, submerged below like a hidden chamber.*'

Illuminated in the soft lights of the deserted entresol, the two pyramids pointed at one another, their bodies perfectly aligned, their tips almost touching.

The Chalice above. The Blade below.

The blade and chalice guarding o'er Her gates.

Langdon heard Marie Chauvel's words. *One day it will dawn on you.*

He was standing beneath the ancient Rose Line, surrounded by the work of masters. *What better place for Saunière to keep watch?* Now at last, he sensed he understood the true meaning of the Grand Master's verse. Raising his eyes to heaven, he gazed upward through the glass to a glorious, star-filled night.

She rests at last beneath the starry skies.

Like the murmurs of spirits in the darkness, forgotten words echoed. *The quest for the Holy Grail is the quest to kneel before the bones of Mary Magdalene. A journey to pray at the feet of the outcast one.*

With a sudden upwelling of reverence, Robert Langdon fell to his knees.

For a moment, he thought he heard a woman's voice . . . the wisdom of the ages . . . whispering up from the chasms of the earth.

THE END

Robert Langdon's first adventure was described in

Angels and Demons

Read the first few thrilling pages now . . .

PROLOGUE

Physicist Leonardo Vetra smelled burning flesh, and he knew it was his own. He stared up in terror at the dark figure looming over him. 'What do you want!'

'*La chiave*,' the raspy voice replied. 'The password.'

'But . . . I don't—'

The intruder pressed down again, grinding the white hot object deeper into Vetra's chest. There was the hiss of broiling flesh.

Vetra cried out in agony. 'There *is* no password!' He felt himself drifting toward unconsciousness.

The figure glared. '*Ne avevo paura*. I was afraid of that.'

Vetra fought to keep his senses, but the darkness was closing in. His only solace was in knowing his attacker would never obtain what he had come for. A moment later, however, the figure produced a blade and brought it to Vetra's face. The blade hovered. Carefully. Surgically.

'For the love of God!' Vetra screamed. But it was too late.

1

High atop the steps of the Great Pyramid of Giza, a young woman laughed and called down to him. 'Robert, hurry up! I knew I should have married a younger man!' Her smile was magic.

He struggled to keep up, but his legs felt like stone. 'Wait,' he begged. 'Please . . .'

As he climbed, his vision began to blur. There was a thundering in his ears. *I must reach her!* But when he looked up again, the woman had disappeared. In her place stood an old man with rotting teeth. The man stared down, curling his lips into a lonely grimace. Then he let out a scream of anguish that resounded across the desert.

Robert Langdon awoke with a start from his nightmare. The phone beside his bed was ringing. Dazed, he picked up the receiver.

'Hello?'

'I'm looking for Robert Langdon,' a man's voice said.

Langdon sat up in his empty bed and tried to clear his mind. 'This . . . is Robert Langdon.' He squinted at his digital clock. It was 5.18 a.m.

'I must see you immediately.'

'Who is this?'

'My name is Maximilian Kohler. I'm a discrete particle physicist.'

'A *what*?' Langdon could barely focus. 'Are you sure you've got the right Langdon?'

'You're a professor of religious iconology at Harvard University. You've written three books on symbology and—'

'Do you know what time it is?'

'I apologize. I have something you need to see. I can't discuss it on the phone.'

A knowing groan escaped Langdon's lips. This had happened before. One of the perils of writing books about religious symbology was the calls from religious zealots who wanted him to confirm their latest sign from God. Last month, a stripper from Oklahoma had promised Langdon the best sex of his life if he would fly down and verify the authenticity of a cruciform that had magically appeared on her bed sheets. *The Shroud of Tulsa*, Langdon had called it.

'How did you get my number?' Langdon tried to be polite, despite the hour.

'On the Worldwide Web. The site for your book.'

Langdon frowned. He was damn sure his book's site did not include his home phone number. The man was obviously lying.

'I need to see you,' the caller insisted. 'I'll pay you well.'

Now Langdon was getting mad. 'I'm sorry, but I really—'

'If you leave immediately, you can be here by—'

'I'm not going anywhere! It's five o'clock in the morning!' Langdon hung up and collapsed back in bed. He closed his eyes and tried to fall back asleep. It was no use. The dream was emblazoned in his mind. Reluctantly, he put on his robe and went downstairs.

* * *

Robert Langdon wandered barefoot through his deserted Massachusetts Victorian home and nursed his ritual insomnia remedy – a mug of steaming Nestlé's Quik. The April moon filtered through the bay windows and played on the oriental carpets. Langdon's colleagues often joked that his place looked more like an anthropology museum than a home. His shelves were packed with religious artefacts from around the world – an *ekuaba* from Ghana, a gold cross from Spain, a cycladic idol from the Aegean, and even a rare woven *boccus* from Borneo, a young warrior's symbol of perpetual youth.

As Langdon sat on his brass Maharishi's chest and savoured the warmth of the chocolate, the bay window caught his reflection. The image was distorted and pale . . . like a ghost. *An aging ghost*, he thought, cruelly reminded that his youthful spirit was living in a mortal shell.

Although not overly handsome in a classical sense, the forty-five-year-old Langdon had what his female colleagues referred to as an 'erudite' appeal – wisps of grey in his thick brown hair, probing blue eyes, an arrestingly deep voice, and the strong, carefree smile of a collegiate athlete. A varsity diver in prep school and college, Langdon still had the body of a swimmer, a toned, six-foot physique that he vigilantly maintained with fifty laps a day in the university pool.

Langdon's friends had always viewed him as a bit of an enigma – a man caught between centuries. On weekends he could be seen lounging on the quad in blue jeans, discussing computer graphics or religious history with students; other times he could be spotted in his Harris tweed and paisley vest, photographed in the pages of upscale art magazines at museum openings where he had been asked to lecture.

Although a tough teacher and strict disciplinarian,

Langdon was the first to embrace what he hailed as the 'lost art of good clean fun.' He relished recreation with an infectious fanaticism that had earned him a fraternal acceptance among his students. His campus nickname – 'The Dolphin' – was a reference both to his affable nature and his legendary ability to dive into a pool and outmanoeuvre the entire opposing squad in a water polo match.

As Langdon sat alone, absently gazing into the darkness, the silence of his home was shattered again, this time by the ring of his fax machine. Too exhausted to be annoyed, Langdon forced a tired chuckle.

God's people, he thought. *Two thousand years of waiting for their Messiah, and they're still persistent as hell.*

Wearily, he returned his empty mug to the kitchen and walked slowly to his oak-paneled study. The incoming fax lay in the tray. Sighing, he scooped up the paper and looked at it.

Instantly, a wave of nausea hit him.

The image on the page was that of a human corpse. The body had been stripped naked, and its head had been twisted, facing completely backward. On the victim's chest was a terrible burn. The man had been branded . . . imprinted with a single word. It was a word Langdon knew well. Very well. He stared at the ornate lettering in disbelief.

'Illuminati,' he stammered, his heart pounding. *It can't be . . .*

In slow motion, afraid of what he was about to

witness, Langdon rotated the fax 180 degrees. He looked at the word upside down.

Instantly, the breath went out of him. It was like he had been hit by a truck. Barely able to believe his eyes, he rotated the fax again, reading the brand right-side up and then upside down.

'Illuminati,' he whispered.

Stunned, Langdon collapsed in a chair. He sat a moment in utter bewilderment. Gradually, his eyes were drawn to the blinking red light on his fax machine. Whoever had sent this fax was still on the line . . . waiting to talk. Langdon gazed at the blinking light a long time.

Then, trembling, he picked up the receiver.

2

'Do I have your attention now?' the man's voice said when Langdon finally answered the line.

'Yes, sir, you damn well do. You want to explain yourself?'

'I tried to tell you before.' The voice was rigid, mechanical. 'I'm a physicist. I run a research facility. We've had a murder. You saw the body.'

'How did you find me?' Langdon could barely focus. His mind was racing from the image on the fax.

'I already told you. The Worldwide Web. The site for your book, *The Art of the Illuminati*.'

Langdon tried to gather his thoughts. His book was virtually unknown in mainstream literary circles, but it had developed quite a following on-line. Nonetheless, the caller's claim still made no sense.

'That page has no contact information,' Langdon challenged. 'I'm certain of it.'

'I have people here at the lab very adept at extracting user information from the Web.'

Langdon was sceptical. 'Sounds like your lab knows *a lot* about the Web.'

'We should,' the man fired back. 'We *invented* it.'

Something in the man's voice told Langdon he was not joking.

'I must see you,' the caller insisted. 'This is not a matter we can discuss on the phone. My lab is only an hour's flight from Boston.'

Langdon stood in the dim light of his study and analysed the fax in his hand. The image was overpowering, possibly representing the epigraphical find of the century, a decade of his research confirmed in a single symbol.

'It's urgent,' the voice pressured.

Langdon's eyes were locked on the brand. *Illuminati*, he read over and over. His work had always been based on the symbolic equivalent of fossils – ancient documents and historical hearsay – but this image before him was today. Present tense. He felt like a paleontologist coming face to face with a living dinosaur.

'I've taken the liberty of sending a plane for you,' the voice said. 'It will be in Boston in twenty minutes.'

Langdon felt his mouth go dry. *An hour's flight . . .*

'Please forgive my presumption,' the voice said. 'I need you here.'

Langdon looked again at the fax – an ancient myth confirmed in black and white. The implications were frightening. He gazed absently through the bay window. The first hint of dawn was sifting through the birch trees in his backyard, but the view looked somehow different this morning. As an odd combination of fear and exhilaration settled over him, Langdon knew he had no choice.

'You win,' he said. 'Tell me where to meet the plane.'

3

Thousands of miles away, two men were meeting. The chamber was dark. Medieval. Stone.

'*Benvenuto,*' the man in charge said. He was seated in the shadows, out of sight. 'Were you successful?'

'*Si,*' the dark figure replied. '*Perfettamente.*' His words were as hard as the rock walls.

'And there will be no doubt who is responsible?'

'None.'

'Superb. Do you have what I asked for?'

The killer's eyes glistened, black like oil. He produced a heavy electronic device and set it on the table.

The man in the shadows seemed pleased. 'You have done well.'

'Serving the brotherhood is an honour,' the killer replied.

'Phase two begins shortly. Get some rest. Tonight we change the world.'

Read the complete book – available from
Corgi Books

DAN
BROWN

ANGELS
AND
DEMONS

*'A breathless,
real-time adventure...
Exciting, fast-paced,
with an unusually high IQ'*
San Francisco Chronicle

The gripping prequel
to *The Da Vinci Code*

When a world renowned scientist is found brutally murdered, a Harvard professor, Robert Langdon, is summoned to identify the mysterious symbol seared onto the dead man's chest. His conclusion: it is the work of the Illuminati, a secret brotherhood presumed extinct for nearly four hundred years – now reborn to continue their bitter vendetta against their sworn enemy, the Catholic church.

In Rome, the college of cardinals assembles to elect a new pope. Yet somewhere within the walls of the Vatican, an unstoppable bomb of terrifying power relentlessly counts down to oblivion. While the minutes tick away, Langdon joins forces with Vittoria Vetra, a beautiful and mysterious Italian scientist, to decipher the labyrinthine trail of ancient symbols that snakes across Rome to the long-forgotten Illuminati lair – a secret refuge wherein lies the only hope for the Vatican.

But, with each revelation comes another twist, another turn in the plot, which leaves Langdon and Vetra reeling and at the mercy of a seemingly invincible enemy...

0 552 15073 8

SPECIAL ILLUSTRATED COLLECTOR'S EDITION ALSO AVAILABLE
Experience the inspiration
for this brilliant thriller

Go behind the scenes of the novel to explore over 150 photographs and illustrations throughout the text, showing the rich historical tapestry from which Dan Brown drew his inspiration. The visual sources that provide both the backdrop and the stimulus for the novel's action are revealed for the first time and uniquely complement the reading experience.

0 593 05486 5

DAN BROWN

THE
DA VINCI CODE

SPECIAL ILLUSTRATED COLLECTOR'S EDITION

Go behind the scenes of the bestselling thriller of all time

Breaking the mould of traditional suspense novels, *The Da Vinci Code* is simultaneously lightning-paced, intelligent and intricately layered with remarkable research and detail. And in this exclusive edition Dan Brown allows the reader behind the scenes of the novel, which now incorporates over 150 photographs and illustrations throughout the text, showing the rich historical tapestry from which he drew his inspiration. The visual sources, which provide both the backdrop and the stimulus for the novel's action, are revealed for the first time and uniquely complement the reading experience.

'Wow... Blockbuster perfection...
An exhilaratingly brainy thriller'
New York Times

'Fascinating and absorbing...
A great, riveting read. I loved this book'
Harlan Coben

'Intrigue and menace mingle in
one of the finest mysteries I've ever read'
Clive Cussler

'Dan Brown has built a world that is rich in
fascinating detail, and I could not get enough of it'
Robert Crais

0 593 05425 3

Dan Brown is the bestselling author of *Digital Fortress*, *Deception Point*, *Angels and Demons* and *The Da Vinci Code*. He is a graduate of Amherst College and Phillips Exeter Academy, where he teaches English and creative writing. He lives in New England with his wife. Visit the author's website at *www.danbrown.com*

Also by Dan Brown

DIGITAL FORTRESS
ANGELS AND DEMONS
THE DA VINCI CODE

DECEPTION POINT

Dan Brown

CORGI BOOKS

DECEPTION POINT
A CORGI BOOK : 0 552 15176 9

First publication in Great Britain

PRINTING HISTORY
Corgi edition published 2002
Corgi edition reissued 2004

35 37 38 36

Set in 10/12pt Palatino by
Kestrel Data, Exeter, Devon.

Corgi Books are published by Transworld Publishers,
61–63 Uxbridge Road, London W5 5SA,
a division of The Random House Group Ltd,
in Australia by Random House Australia (Pty) Ltd,
20 Alfred Street, Milsons Point, Sydney, NSW 2061, Australia,
in New Zealand by Random House New Zealand Ltd,
18 Poland Road, Glenfield, Auckland 10, New Zealand
and in South Africa by Random House (Pty) Ltd,
Endulini, 5a Jubilee Road, Parktown 2193, South Africa.

Printed and bound in Germany by
GGP Media GmbH, Poessneck

Papers used by Transworld Publishers are natural, recyclable
products made from wood grown in sustainable forests.
The manufacturing processes conform to the environmental
regulations of the country of origin.

ACKNOWLEDGEMENTS

With warm thanks to Jason Kaufman for his superb guidance and insightful editorial skills; Blythe Brown for her tireless research and creative input; Bill Scott-Kerr for his enthusiasm for my work and for navigating it so expertly across the Atlantic; my good friend Jake Elwell at Wieser & Wieser; the National Security Archive; the NASA Public Affairs Office; Stan Planton, who continues to be a source for information on all things; the National Security Agency; glaciologist Martin O. Jeffries; and the superb minds of Brett Trotter, Thomas D. Nadeau, and Jim Barrington. Thanks also to Connie and Dick Brown, the U.S. Intelligence Policy Documentation Project, Suzanne O'Neill, Margie Wachtel, Morey Stettner, Owen King, Alison McKinnell, Mary and Stephen Gorman, Dr Karl Singer, Dr Michael I. Latz of Scripps Institute of Oceanography, April at Micron Electronics, Esther Sung, the National Air and Space Museum, Dr Gene Allmendinger, the incomparable Heide Lange at Sanford J. Greenburger Associates, and John Pike at the Federation of American Scientists.

AUTHOR'S NOTE

The Delta Force, the National Reconnaissance Office, and the Space Frontier Foundation are real organizations. All technologies described in this novel exist.

If this discovery is confirmed, it will surely be one of the most stunning insights into our universe that science has ever uncovered. Its implications are as far-reaching and awe-inspiring as can be imagined. Even as it promises answers to some of our oldest questions, it poses still others even more fundamental.

> President Bill Clinton, in a press conference
> following a discovery known as ALH84001
> on August 7, 1996

DECEPTION POINT

PROLOGUE

Death, in this forsaken place, could come in countless forms. Geologist Charles Brophy had endured the
savage splendor of this terrain for years, and yet
nothing could prepare him for a fate as barbarous and
unnatural as the one about to befall him.

As Brophy's four huskies pulled his sled of geologic
sensing equipment across the tundra, the dogs suddenly slowed, looking skyward.

'What is it, girls?' Brophy asked, stepping off the sled.

Beyond the gathering storm clouds, a twin-rotor
transport helicopter arched in low, hugging the glacial
peaks with military dexterity.

That's odd, he thought. He never saw helicopters this
far north. The aircraft landed fifty yards away, kicking
up a stinging spray of granulated snow. His dogs
whined, looking wary.

When the chopper doors slid open, two men
descended. They were dressed in full-weather whites,
armed with rifles, and moved toward Brophy with
urgent intent.

'Dr Brophy?' one called.

The geologist was baffled. 'How did you know my
name? Who are you?'

13

'Take out your radio, please.'

'I'm sorry?'

'Just do it.'

Bewildered, Brophy pulled his radio from his parka.

'We need you to transmit an emergency communiqué. Decrease your radio frequency to one hundred kilohertz.'

One hundred kilohertz? Brophy felt utterly lost. *Nobody can receive anything that low.* 'Has there been an accident?'

The second man raised his rifle and pointed it at Brophy's head. 'There's no time to explain. Just do it.'

Trembling, Brophy adjusted his transmission frequency.

The first man now handed him a note card with a few lines typed on it. 'Transmit this message. Now.'

Brophy looked at the card. 'I don't understand. This information is incorrect. I didn't—'

The man pressed his rifle hard against the geologist's temple.

Brophy's voice was shaking as he transmitted the bizarre message.

'Good,' the first man said. 'Now get yourself and your dogs into the chopper.'

At gunpoint, Brophy maneuvered his reluctant dogs and sled up a skid ramp into the cargo bay. As soon as they were settled, the chopper lifted off, turning westward.

'Who the hell are you?' Brophy demanded, breaking a sweat inside his parka. *And what was the meaning of that message?*

The men said nothing.

As the chopper gained altitude, the wind tore

14

through the open door. Brophy's four huskies, still rigged to the loaded sled, were whimpering now.

'At least close the door,' Brophy demanded. 'Can't you see my dogs are frightened!'

The men did not respond.

As the chopper rose to 4,000 feet, it banked steeply out over a series of ice chasms and crevasses. Suddenly, the men stood. Without a word, they gripped the heavily laden sled and pushed it out the open door. Brophy watched in horror as his dogs scrambled in vain against the enormous weight. In an instant the animals disappeared, dragged howling out of the chopper.

Brophy was already on his feet screaming when the men grabbed him. They hauled him to the door. Numb with fear, Brophy swung his fists, trying to fend off the powerful hands pushing him outward.

It was no use. Moments later he was tumbling toward the chasms below.

1

Toulos Restaurant, adjacent to Capitol Hill, boasts a politically incorrect menu of baby veal and horse carpaccio, making it an ironic hotspot for the quintessential Washingtonian power breakfast. This morning Toulos was busy – a cacophony of clanking silverware, espresso machines, and cellphone conversations.

The maitre d' was sneaking a sip of his morning Bloody Mary when the woman entered. He turned with a practiced smile.

'Good morning,' he said. 'May I help you?'

The woman was attractive, in her mid-thirties, wearing gray, pleated flannel pants, conservative flats, and an ivory Laura Ashley blouse. Her posture was straight – chin raised ever so slightly – not arrogant, just strong. The woman's hair was light brown and fashioned in Washington's most popular style – the 'anchorwoman' – a lush feathering, curled under at the shoulders . . . long enough to be sexy, but short enough to remind you she was probably smarter than you.

'I'm a little late,' the woman said, her voice unassuming. 'I have a breakfast meeting with Senator Sexton.'

The maitre d' felt an unexpected tingle of nerves. *Senator Sedgewick Sexton.* The senator was a regular here and currently one of the country's most famous men. Last week, having swept all twelve Republican primaries on Super Tuesday, the senator was virtually guaranteed his party's nomination for President of the United States. Many believed the senator had a superb chance of stealing the White House from the embattled President next fall. Lately Sexton's face seemed to be on every national magazine, his campaign slogan plastered all across America: 'Stop spending. Start mending.'

'Senator Sexton is in his booth,' the maitre d' said. 'And you are?'

'Rachel Sexton. His daughter.'

How foolish of me, he thought. The resemblance was quite apparent. The woman had the senator's penetrating eyes and refined carriage – that polished air of resilient nobility. Clearly the senator's classic good looks had not skipped generations, although Rachel Sexton seemed to carry her blessings with a grace and humility her father could learn from.

'A pleasure to have you, Ms Sexton.'

As the maitre d' led the senator's daughter across the dining area, he was embarrassed by the gauntlet of male eyes following her . . . some discreet, others less so. Few women dined at Toulos and even fewer who looked like Rachel Sexton.

'Nice body,' one diner whispered. 'Sexton already find himself a new wife?'

'That's his daughter, you idiot,' another replied.

The man chuckled. 'Knowing Sexton, he'd probably screw her anyway.'

*   *   *

When Rachel arrived at her father's table, the senator was on his cellphone talking loudly about one of his recent successes. He glanced up at Rachel only long enough to tap his Cartier and remind her she was late.

I missed you, too, Rachel thought.

Her father's first name was Thomas, although he'd adopted his middle name long ago. Rachel suspected it was because he liked the alliteration. Senator Sedgewick Sexton. The man was a silver-haired, silver-tongued political animal who had been anointed with the slick look of a soap opera doctor, which seemed appropriate considering his talents of impersonation.

'Rachel!' Her father clicked off his phone and stood to kiss her cheek.

'Hi, Dad.' She did not kiss him back.

'You look exhausted.'

And so it begins, she thought. 'I got your message. What's up?'

'I can't ask my daughter out for breakfast?'

Rachel had learned long ago her father seldom requested her company unless he had some ulterior motive.

Sexton took a sip of coffee. 'So, how are things with you?'

'Busy. I see your campaign's going well.'

'Oh, let's not talk business.' Sexton leaned across the table, lowering his voice. 'How's that guy at the State Department I set you up with?'

Rachel exhaled, already fighting the urge to check her watch. 'Dad, I really haven't had time to call him. And I wish you'd stop trying to—'

'You've got to make time for the important things, Rachel. Without love, everything else is meaningless.'

A number of comebacks came to mind, but Rachel

chose silence. Being the bigger person was not difficult when it came to her father. 'Dad, you wanted to see me? You said this was important.'

'It is.' Her father's eyes studied her closely.

Rachel felt part of her defenses melt away under his gaze, and she cursed the man's power. The senator's eyes were his gift – a gift Rachel suspected would probably carry him to the White House. On cue, his eyes would well with tears, and then, an instant later, they would clear, opening a window to an impassioned soul, extending a bond of trust to all. *It's all about trust*, her father always said. The senator had lost Rachel's years ago, but he was quickly gaining the country's.

'I have a proposition for you,' Senator Sexton said.

'Let me guess,' Rachel replied, attempting to refortify her position. 'Some prominent divorcé looking for a young wife?'

'Don't kid yourself, honey. You're not that young anymore.'

Rachel felt the familiar shrinking sensation that so often accompanied meetings with her father.

'I want to throw you a life raft,' he said.

'I wasn't aware I was drowning.'

'You're not. The President is. You should jump ship before it's too late.'

'Haven't we had this conversation?'

'Think about your future, Rachel. You can come work for me.'

'I hope that's not why you asked me to breakfast.'

The senator's veneer of calm broke ever so slightly. 'Rachel, can't you see that your working for him reflects badly on me? And on my campaign.'

Rachel sighed. She and her father had been through this. 'Dad, I don't work for the President. I haven't

20

even *met* the President. I work in Fairfax, for God's sake!'

'Politics is perception, Rachel. It *appears* you work for the President.'

Rachel exhaled, trying to keep her cool. 'I worked too hard to get this job, Dad. I'm not quitting.'

The senator's eyes narrowed. 'You know, sometimes your selfish attitude really—'

'Senator Sexton?' A reporter materialized beside the table.

Sexton's demeanor thawed instantly. Rachel groaned and took a croissant from the basket on the table.

'Ralph Sneeden,' the reporter said. '*Washington Post*. May I ask you a few questions?'

The senator smiled, dabbing his mouth with a napkin. 'My pleasure, Ralph. Just make it quick. I don't want my coffee getting cold.'

The reporter laughed on cue. 'Of course, sir.' He pulled out a minirecorder and turned it on. 'Senator, your television ads call for legislation ensuring equal salaries for women in the workplace . . . as well as for tax cuts for new families. Can you comment on your rationale?'

'Sure. I'm simply a huge fan of strong women and strong families.'

Rachel practically choked on her croissant.

'And on the subject of families,' the reporter followed up, 'you talk a lot about education. You've proposed some highly controversial budget cuts in an effort to allocate more funds to our nation's schools.'

'I believe the children are our future.'

Rachel could not believe her father had sunk to quoting pop songs.

'Finally, sir,' the reporter said, 'you've taken an

enormous jump in the polls these past few weeks. The President has got to be worried. Any thoughts on your recent success?'

'I think it has to do with trust. Americans are starting to see that the President cannot be trusted to make the tough decisions facing this nation. Runaway government spending is putting this country deeper in debt every day, and Americans are starting to realize that it's time to stop spending and start mending.'

Like a stay of execution from her father's rhetoric, the pager in Rachel's handbag went off. Normally the harsh electronic beeping was an unwelcome interruption, but at the moment, it sounded almost melodious.

The senator glared indignantly at having been interrupted.

Rachel fished the pager from her handbag and pressed a preset sequence of five buttons, confirming that she was indeed the person holding the pager. The beeping stopped, and the LCD began blinking. In fifteen seconds she would receive a secure text message.

Sneeden grinned at the senator. 'Your daughter is obviously a busy woman. It's refreshing to see you two still find time in your schedules to dine together.'

'As I said, family comes first.'

Sneeden nodded, and then his gaze hardened. 'Might I ask, sir, how you and your daughter manage your conflicts of interest?'

'Conflicts?' Senator Sexton cocked his head with an innocent look of confusion. 'What conflicts do you mean?'

Rachel glanced up, grimacing at her father's act. She knew exactly where this was headed. *Damn reporters*, she thought. Half of them were on political payrolls.

The reporter's question was what journalists called a *grapefruit* – a question that was supposed to look like a tough inquiry but was in fact a scripted favor to the senator – a slow lob pitch that her father could line up and smash out of the park, clearing the air about a few things.

'Well, sir . . .' The reporter coughed, feigning uneasiness over the question. 'The conflict is that your daughter works for your opponent.'

Senator Sexton exploded in laughter, defusing the question instantly. 'Ralph, first of all, the President and I are not *opponents*. We are simply two patriots who have different ideas about how to run the country we love.'

The reporter beamed. He had his sound bite. 'And second?'

'Second, my daughter is not employed by the President; she is employed by the intelligence community. She compiles intel reports and sends them to the White House. It's a fairly low-level position.' He paused and looked at Rachel. 'In fact, dear, I'm not sure you've even *met* the President, have you?'

Rachel stared, her eyes smoldering.

The beeper chirped, drawing Rachel's gaze to the incoming message on the LCD screen.

– RPRT DIRNRO STAT –

She deciphered the shorthand instantly and frowned. The message was unexpected, and most certainly bad news. At least she had her exit cue.

'Gentlemen,' she said. 'It breaks my heart, but I have to go. I'm late for work.'

'Ms Sexton,' the reporter said quickly, 'before you go, I was wondering if you could comment on the rumors that you called this breakfast meeting to discuss the possibility of leaving your current post to work for your father's campaign?'

Rachel felt like someone had thrown hot coffee in her face. The question took her totally off guard. She looked at her father and sensed in his smirk that the question had been prepped. She wanted to climb across the table and stab him with a fork.

The reporter shoved the recorder into her face. 'Miss Sexton?'

Rachel locked eyes with the reporter. 'Ralph, or whoever the hell you are, get this straight: I have no intention of abandoning my job to work for Senator Sexton, and if you print anything to the contrary, you'll need a shoehorn to get that recorder out of your ass.'

The reporter's eyes widened. He clicked off his recorder, hiding a grin. 'Thank you both.' He disappeared.

Rachel immediately regretted the outburst. She had inherited her father's temper, and she hated him for it. *Smooth, Rachel, Very smooth.*

Her father glared disapprovingly. 'You'd do well to learn some poise.'

Rachel began collecting her things. 'This meeting is over.'

The senator was apparently done with her anyway. He pulled out his cellphone to make a call. ''Bye, sweetie. Stop by the office one of these days and say hello. And get married, for God's sake. You're thirty-three years old.'

'Thirty-*four*,' she snapped. 'Your secretary sent a card.'

He clucked ruefully. 'Thirty-four. Almost an old maid. You know by the time I was thirty-four, I'd already—'

24

'Married Mom and screwed the neighbor?' The words came out louder than Rachel had intended, her voice hanging naked in an ill-timed lull. Diners nearby glanced over.

Senator Sexton's eyes flash-froze, two ice-crystals boring into her. 'You watch yourself, young lady.'

Rachel headed for the door. *No, you watch yourself, Senator.*

2

The three men sat in silence inside their ThermaTech storm tent. Outside, an icy wind buffeted the shelter, threatening to tear it from its moorings. None of the men took notice; each had seen situations far more threatening than this one.

Their tent was stark white, pitched in a shallow depression, out of sight. Their communication devices, transport, and weapons were all state-of-the-art. The group leader was code-named Delta-One. He was muscular and lithe with eyes as desolate as the topography on which he was stationed.

The military chronograph on Delta-One's wrist emitted a sharp beep. The sound coincided in perfect unison with beeps emitted from the chronographs worn by the other two men.

Another thirty minutes had passed.

It was time. Again.

Reflexively, Delta-One left his two partners and stepped outside into the darkness and pounding wind. He scanned the moonlit horizon with infrared binoculars. As always, he focused on the structure. It was 1,000 meters away – an enormous and unlikely edifice rising from the barren terrain. He and his team had been watching it for ten days now, since its construction. Delta-One had no doubt that the information inside would change the world. Lives already had been lost to protect it.

At the moment, everything looked quiet outside the structure.

The true test, however, was what was happening *inside*.

Delta-One reentered the tent and addressed his two fellow soldiers. 'Time for a flyby.'

Both men nodded. The taller of them, Delta-Two, opened a laptop computer and turned it on. Positioning himself in front of the screen, Delta-Two placed his hand on a mechanical joystick and gave it a short jerk. A thousand meters away, hidden deep within the building, a surveillance robot the size of a mosquito received his transmission and sprang to life.

3

Rachel Sexton was still steaming as she drove her white Integra up Leesburg Highway. The bare maples of the Falls Church foothills rose stark against a crisp March sky, but the peaceful setting did little to calm her anger. Her father's recent surge in the polls should have endowed him with a modicum of confident grace, and yet it seemed only to fuel his self-importance.

The man's deceit was doubly painful because he was

the only immediate family Rachel had left. Rachel's mother had died three years ago, a devastating loss whose emotional scars still raked at Rachel's heart. Rachel's only solace was knowing that the death, with ironic compassion, had liberated her mother from a deep despair over a miserable marriage to the senator.

Rachel's pager beeped again, pulling her thoughts back to the road in front of her. The incoming message was the same.

– RPRT DIRNRO STAT –

Report to the director of NRO stat. She sighed. *I'm coming, for God's sake!*

With rising uncertainty, Rachel drove to her usual exit, turned onto the private access road, and rolled to a stop at the heavily armed sentry booth. This was 14225 Leesburg Highway, one of the most secretive addresses in the country.

While the guard scanned her car for bugs, Rachel gazed out at the mammoth structure in the distance. The 1,000,000-square-foot complex sat majestically on 68 forested acres just outside D.C. in Fairfax, Virginia. The building's facade was a bastion of one-way glass that reflected the army of satellite dishes, antennas, and rayodomes on the surrounding grounds, doubling their already awe-inspiring numbers.

Two minutes later, Rachel had parked and crossed the manicured grounds to the main entrance, where a carved granite sign announced

NATIONAL RECONNAISSANCE OFFICE (NRO)

The two armed Marines flanking the bulletproof revolving door stared straight ahead as Rachel passed between them. She felt the same sensation she always felt as she pushed through these doors . . . that she was entering the belly of a sleeping giant.

Inside the vaulted lobby, Rachel sensed the faint echoes of hushed conversations all around her, as if the words were sifting down from the offices above. An enormous tiled mosaic proclaimed the NRO directive:

ENABLING U.S. GLOBAL INFORMATION SUPERIORITY,
DURING PEACE AND THROUGH WAR.

The walls here were lined with massive photographs – rocket launches, submarine christenings, intercept installations – towering achievements that could be celebrated only within these walls.

Now, as always, Rachel felt the problems of the outside world fading behind her. She was entering the shadow world. A world where the problems thundered in like freight trains, and the solutions were meted out with barely a whisper.

As Rachel approached the final checkpoint, she wondered what kind of problem had caused her pager to ring twice in the last thirty minutes.

'Good morning, Ms Sexton.' The guard smiled as she approached the steel doorway.

Rachel returned the smile as the guard held out a tiny swab for Rachel to take.

'You know the drill,' he said.

Rachel took the hermetically sealed cotton swab and removed the plastic covering. Then she placed it in her mouth like a thermometer. She held it under her tongue for two seconds. Then, leaning forward, she allowed the guard to remove it. The guard inserted the moistened swab into a slit in a machine behind him. The machine took four seconds to confirm the DNA sequences in Rachel's saliva. Then a monitor flickered on, displaying Rachel's photo and security clearance.

The guard winked. 'Looks like you're still you.' He pulled the used swab from the machine and dropped it through an opening, where it was instantly incinerated. 'Have a good one.' He pressed a button and the huge steel doors swung open.

As Rachel made her way into the maze of bustling corridors beyond, she was amazed that even after six years here she was still daunted by the colossal scope of this operation. The agency encompassed six other U.S. installations, employed over ten thousand agents, and had operating costs of over $10 billion per year.

In total secrecy, the NRO built and maintained an astonishing arsenal of cutting-edge spy technologies: worldwide electronic intercepts; spy satellites; silent, embedded relay chips in telecomm products; even a global naval-recon network known as Classic Wizard, a secret web of 1,456 hydrophones mounted on sea-floors around the world, capable of monitoring ship movements anywhere on the globe.

NRO technologies not only helped the United States win military conflicts, but they provided an endless stream of peacetime data to agencies such as the CIA, NSA, and Department of Defense, helping them thwart terrorism, locate crimes against the environment, and give policymakers the data needed to make informed decisions on an enormous array of topics.

Rachel worked here as a 'gister.' Gisting, or data reduction, required analyzing complex reports and distilling their essence or 'gist' into concise, single-page briefs. Rachel had proven herself a natural. *All those years of cutting through my father's bullshit*, she thought.

Rachel now held the NRO's premiere gisting post –

intelligence liaison to the White House. She was responsible for sifting through the NRO's daily intelligence reports, deciding which stories were relevant to the President, distilling those reports into single-page briefs, and then forwarding the synopsized material to the President's National Security Adviser. In NRO-speak, Rachel Sexton 'manufactured finished product and serviced *the* customer.'

Although the job was difficult and required long hours, the position was a badge of honor for her, a way to assert her independence from her father. Senator Sexton had offered countless times to support Rachel if she would quit the post, but Rachel had no intention of becoming financially beholden to a man like Sedgewick Sexton. Her mother was testimony to what could happen when a man like that held too many cards.

The sound of Rachel's pager echoed in the marble hall.

Again? She didn't even bother to check the message.

Wondering what the hell was going on, she boarded the elevator, skipped her own floor, and went straight to the top.

4

To call the NRO director a plain man was in itself an overstatement. NRO Director William Pickering was diminutive, with pale skin, a forgettable face, a bald head, and hazel eyes, which despite having gazed upon the country's deepest secrets, appeared as two shallow pools. Nonetheless, to those who worked under him, Pickering towered. His subdued personality and unadorned philosophies were legendary at the NRO. The man's quiet diligence, combined with his wardrobe of plain black suits, had earned him the nickname the 'Quaker.' A brilliant strategist and the model of efficiency, the Quaker ran his world with an unrivaled clarity. His mantra: 'Find the truth. Act on it.'

When Rachel arrived in the director's office, he was on the phone. Rachel was always surprised by the sight of him: William Pickering looked nothing like a man who wielded enough power to wake the President at any hour.

Pickering hung up and waved her in. 'Agent Sexton, have a seat.' His voice had a lucid rawness to it.

'Thank you, sir.' Rachel sat.

Despite most people's discomfort around William Pickering's blunt demeanor, Rachel had always liked the man. He was the exact antithesis of her father . . . physically unimposing, anything but charismatic, and he did his duty with a selfless patriotism, shunning the spotlight her father loved so much.

Pickering removed his glasses and gazed at her. 'Agent Sexton, the President called me about a half hour ago. In direct reference to you.'

Rachel shifted in her seat. Pickering was known for getting to the point. *One hell of an opening*, she thought. 'Not a problem with one of my gists, I hope.'

'On the contrary. He says the White House is impressed with your work.'

Rachel exhaled silently. 'So what did he want?'

'A meeting with you. In person. Immediately.'

Rachel's unease sharpened. 'A personal meeting? About *what*?'

'Damn good question. He wouldn't tell me.'

Now Rachel was lost. Keeping information from the director of the NRO was like keeping Vatican secrets from the Pope. The standing joke in the intelligence community was that if William Pickering didn't know about it, it hadn't happened.

Pickering stood, pacing now in front of his window. 'He asked that I contact you immediately and send you to meet with him.'

'Right now?'

'He sent transportation. It's waiting outside.'

Rachel frowned. The President's request was unnerving on its own account, but it was the look of concern on Pickering's face that really worried her. 'You obviously have reservations.'

'I sure as hell do!' Pickering showed a rare flash of emotion. 'The President's timing seems almost callow in its transparency. You are the daughter of the man who is currently challenging him in the polls, and he demands a private meeting with you? I find this highly inappropriate. Your father no doubt would agree.'

Rachel knew Pickering was right – not that she gave a damn what her father thought. 'Do you not trust the President's motives?'

'My oath is to provide intel support to the current White House administration, not pass judgment on their politics.'

Typical Pickering response, Rachel realized. William Pickering made no bones about his view of politicians as transitory figureheads who passed fleetingly across a chessboard whose real players were men like Pickering himself – seasoned 'lifers' who had been around long enough to understand the game with some perspective. Two full terms in the White House, Pickering often said, was not nearly enough to comprehend the true complexities of the global political landscape.

'Maybe it's an innocent request,' Rachel offered, hoping the President was above trying some sort of cheap campaign stunt. 'Maybe he needs a reduction of some sensitive data.'

'Not to sound belittling, Agent Sexton, but the White House has access to plenty of qualified gisting personnel if they need it. If it's an internal White House job, the President should know better than to contact you. And if not, then he sure as hell should know better than to request an NRO asset and then refuse to tell me what he wants it for.'

Pickering always referred to his employees as assets, a manner of speech many found disconcertingly cold.

'Your father is gaining political momentum,' Pickering said. 'A *lot* of it. The White House has got to be getting nervous.' He sighed. 'Politics is a desperate business. When the President calls a secret meeting with his challenger's daughter, I'd guess there's more on his mind than intelligence gists.'

Rachel felt a distant chill. Pickering's hunches had an uncanny tendency to be dead on. 'And you're afraid the White House feels desperate enough to introduce *me* into the political mix?'

Pickering paused a moment. 'You are not exactly silent about your feelings for your father, and I have little doubt the President's campaign staff is aware of the rift. It occurs to me that they may want to use you against him somehow.'

'Where do I sign up?' Rachel said, only half joking.

Pickering looked unimpressed. He gave her a stern stare. 'A word of warning, Agent Sexton. If you feel that your personal issues with your father are going to cloud your judgment in dealing with the President, I strongly advise that you decline the President's request for a meeting.'

'Decline?' Rachel gave a nervous chuckle. 'I obviously can't refuse the President.'

'No,' the director said, 'but I can.'

His words rumbled a bit, reminding Rachel of the other reason Pickering was called the 'Quaker.' Despite being a small man, William Pickering could cause political earthquakes if he were crossed.

'My concerns here are simple,' Pickering said. 'I have a responsibility to protect the people who work for me, and I don't appreciate even the vague implication that one of them might be used as a pawn in a political game.'

'What do you recommend I do?'

Pickering sighed. 'My suggestion is that you meet with him. Commit to nothing. Once the President tells you what the hell is on his mind, call me. If I think he's playing political hardball with you, trust me, I'll pull you out so fast the man won't know what hit him.'

'Thank you, sir.' Rachel sensed a protective aura from the director that she often longed for in her own father. 'And you said the President already sent a car?'

'Not exactly.' Pickering frowned and pointed out the window.

Uncertain, Rachel went over and gazed out in the direction of Pickering's outstretched finger.

A snub-nosed MH-60G PaveHawk helicopter sat idling on the lawn. One of the fastest choppers ever made, this PaveHawk was emblazoned with the White House insignia. The pilot stood nearby, checking his watch.

Rachel turned to Pickering in disbelief. 'The White

House sent a *PaveHawk* to take me fifteen miles into D.C.?'

'Apparently the President hopes you are either impressed or intimidated.' Pickering eyed her. 'I suggest you are neither.'

Rachel nodded. She was both.

Four minutes later, Rachel Sexton exited the NRO and climbed into the waiting helicopter. Before she had even buckled herself in, the craft was airborne, banking hard across the Virginia woods. Rachel gazed out at the blur of trees beneath her and felt her pulse rising. It would have risen faster had she known this chopper would never reach the White House.

5

The frigid wind battered the fabric of the ThermaTech tent, but Delta-One hardly noticed. He and Delta-Three were focused on their comrade, who was manipulating the joystick in his hand with surgical dexterity. The screen before them displayed a live video transmission from a pinpoint camera mounted aboard the microrobot.

The ultimate surveillance tool, Delta-One thought, still amazed every time they powered it up. Lately, in the world of micromechanics, fact seemed to be outpacing fiction.

Micro Electro Mechanical Systems (MEMS) – microbots – were the newest tool in high-tech surveillance – 'fly on the wall technology,' they called it.

Literally.

Although microscopic, remote-controlled robots sounded like science fiction, in fact they had been around since the 1990s. *Discovery* magazine had run a cover story in May 1997 on microbots, featuring both 'flying' and 'swimming' models. The swimmers – nanosubs the size of salt grains – could be injected into the human bloodstream *à la* the movie *Fantastic Voyage*. They were now being used by advanced medical facilities to help doctors navigate arteries by remote control, observe live intravenous video transmissions, and locate arterial blockages without ever lifting a scalpel.

Contrary to intuition, building a *flying* microbot was an even simpler business. The aerodynamics technology for getting a machine to fly had been around since Kittyhawk, and all that remained had been the issue of miniaturization. The first flying microbots, designed by NASA as unmanned exploration tools for future Mars missions, had been several inches long. Now, however, advances in nanotechnology, lightweight energy-absorbent materials, and micromechanics had made the flying microbots a reality.

The true breakthrough had come from the new field biomimics – copying Mother Nature. Miniature dragon-flies, as it turned out, were the ideal prototype for these agile and efficient flying microbots. The PH2 model Delta-Two was currently flying was only one centimeter long – the size of a *mosquito* – and employed a dual pair of transparent, hinged, silicon-leaf wings, giving it unparalleled mobility and efficiency in the air.

The microbot's refueling mechanism had been another breakthrough. The first microbot prototypes could only recharge their energy cells by hovering

36

directly beneath a bright light source, not ideal for stealth or use in dark locales. The newer prototypes, however, could recharge simply by parking within a few inches of a magnetic field. Conveniently, in modern society, magnetic fields were ubiquitous and discreetly placed – power outlets, computer monitors, electric motors, audio speakers, cellphones – it seemed there was never any shortage of obscure recharging stations. Once a microbot had been introduced successfully into a locale, it could transmit audio and video almost indefinitely. The Delta Force's PH2 had been transmitting for over a week now with no trouble whatsoever.

Now, like an insect hovering inside a cavernous barn, the airborne microbot hung silently in the still air of the structure's massive central room. With a bird's-eye view of the space below, the microbot circled silently above unsuspecting occupants – technicians, scientists, specialists in countless fields of study. As the PH2 circled, Delta-One spotted two familiar faces engaged in conversation. They would be a telling mark. He told Delta-Two to drop down and have a listen.

Manipulating the controls, Delta-Two switched on the robot's sound sensors, oriented the microbot's parabolic amplifier, and decreased the robot's elevation until it was ten feet over the scientists' heads. The transmission was faint, but discernible.

'I still can't believe it,' one scientist was saying. The excitement in his voice had not diminished since his arrival here forty-eight hours ago.

The man with whom he was talking obviously shared the enthusiasm. 'In your lifetime . . . did you ever think you would witness anything like this?'

'Never,' the scientist replied, beaming. 'It's all a magnificent dream.'

Delta-One had heard enough. Clearly everything inside was proceeding as expected. Delta-Two maneuvered the microbot away from the conversation and flew it back to its hiding place. He parked the tiny device undetected near the cylinder of an electric generator. The PH2's power cells immediately began recharging for the next mission.

6

Rachel Sexton's thoughts were lost in the morning's bizarre developments as her PaveHawk transport tore across the morning sky, and it was not until the helicopter rocketed out across Chesapeake Bay that she realized they were heading in entirely the wrong direction. The initial flash of confusion instantly gave way to trepidation.

'Hey!' she yelled to the pilot. 'What are you doing?' Her voice was barely audible over the rotors. 'You're supposed to be taking me to the White House!'

The pilot shook his head. 'Sorry, ma'am. The President is not at the White House this morning.'

Rachel tried to remember if Pickering had specifically mentioned the White House or whether she had simply assumed. 'So where is the President?'

'Your meeting with him is elsewhere.'

No shit. 'Where elsewhere?'

'Not far now.'

'That's not what I asked.'

'Sixteen more miles.'

Rachel scowled at him. *This guy should be a politician.* 'Do you dodge bullets as well as you dodge questions?'

The pilot did not answer.

It took less than seven minutes for the chopper to cross the Chesapeake. When land was in sight again, the pilot banked north and skirted a narrow peninsula, where Rachel saw a series of runways and military-looking buildings. The pilot dropped down toward them, and Rachel then realized what this place was. The six launchpads and charred rocket towers were a good clue, but if that was not enough, the roof of one of the buildings had been painted with two enormous words: WALLOPS ISLAND.

Wallops Island was one of NASA's oldest launch sites. Still used today for satellite launches and testing of experimental aircraft, Wallops was NASA's base away from the spotlight.

The President is at Wallops Island? It made no sense.

The chopper pilot aligned his trajectory with a series of three runways that ran the length of the narrow peninsula. They seemed to be heading for the far end of the center runway.

The pilot began to slow. 'You will be meeting the President in his office.'

Rachel turned, wondering if the guy was joking. 'The President of the United States has an office on Wallops Island?'

The pilot looked dead serious. 'The President of the United States has an office wherever he likes, ma'am.'

He pointed toward the end of the runway. Rachel saw the mammoth shape glistening in the distance, and her heart almost stopped. Even at 300 yards,

39

she recognized the light blue hull of the modified 747.

'I'm meeting him aboard the . . .'

'Yes, ma'am. His home away from home.'

Rachel stared out at the massive aircraft. The military's cryptic designation for this prestigious plane was VC-25-A, although the rest of the world knew it by another name: Air Force One.

'Looks like you're in the *new* one this morning,' the pilot said, motioning to the numbers on the plane's tail fin.

Rachel nodded blankly. Few Americans knew that there were actually two Air Force Ones in service – a pair of identical, specially configured 747-200-Bs, one with the tail number 28000 and the other 29000. Both planes had cruising speeds of 600 mph and had been modified for in-flight refueling, giving them virtually unlimited range.

As the PaveHawk settled onto the runway beside the President's plane, Rachel now understood the references to Air Force One being the commander-in-chief's 'portable home court advantage.' The machine was an intimidating sight.

When the President flew to other countries to meet heads of state, he often requested – for security purposes – that the meeting take place on the runway aboard his jet. Although some of the motives were security, certainly another incentive was to gain a negotiating edge through raw intimidation. A visit to Air Force One was far more intimidating than any trip to the White House. The six-foot-high letters along the fuselage trumpeted 'UNITED STATES OF AMERICA.' A female English cabinet member had once accused President Nixon of 'waving his manhood in her face'

40

when he asked her to join him aboard Air Force One. Later the crew jokingly nicknamed the plane 'Big Dick.'

'Ms Sexton?' A blazer-clad Secret Serviceman materialized outside the chopper and opened the door for her. 'The President is waiting for you.'

Rachel got out of the chopper and gazed up the steep gangway at the bulging hull. *Into the flying phallus*. She had once heard the flying 'Oval Office' had over four thousand square feet of interior floor space, including four separate private sleeping quarters, berths for a twenty-six-member flight crew, and two galleys capable of providing food for fifty people.

Climbing the stairway, Rachel felt the Secret Service-man on her heels, urging her upward. High above, the cabin door stood open like a tiny puncture wound on the side of a gargantuan silver whale. She moved toward the darkened entryway and felt her confidence starting to ebb.

Easy, Rachel. It's just a plane.

On the landing, the Secret Serviceman politely took her arm and guided her into a surprisingly narrow corridor. They turned right, walked a short distance, and emerged into a luxurious and spacious cabin. Rachel immediately recognized it from photographs.

'Wait here,' the serviceman said, and he disappeared.

Rachel stood alone in Air Force One's famous wood-paneled fore cabin. This was the room used for meetings, entertaining dignitaries, and, apparently, for scaring the hell out of first-time passengers. The room spanned the entire width of the plane, as did its thick tan carpeting. The furnishings were impeccable – cordovan leather armchairs around a bird's-eye maple meeting table, burnished brass floor lamps beside a continental sofa, and hand-etched crystal glassware on a mahogany wet bar.

Supposedly, Boeing designers had carefully laid out this fore cabin to provide passengers with 'a sense of order mixed with tranquility.' Tranquility, however, was the last thing Rachel Sexton was feeling at the moment. The only thing she could think of was the number of world leaders who had sat in this very room and made decisions that shaped the world.

Everything about this room said power, from the faint aroma of fine pipe tobacco to the ubiquitous presidential seal. The eagle clasping the arrows and olive branches was embroidered on throw pillows, carved into the ice bucket, and even printed on the cork coasters on the bar. Rachel picked up a coaster and examined it.

'Stealing souvenirs already?' a deep voice asked behind her.

Startled, Rachel wheeled, dropping the coaster on the floor. She knelt awkwardly to retrieve it. As she grasped the coaster, she turned to see the President of the United States gazing down at her with an amused grin.

'I'm not royalty, Ms Sexton. There's really no need to kneel.'

7

Senator Sedgewick Sexton savored the privacy of his Lincoln stretch limousine as it snaked through Washington's morning traffic toward his office. Across from him, Gabrielle Ashe, his twenty-four-year-old personal assistant, read him his daily schedule. Sexton was barely listening.

I love Washington, he thought, admiring the assistant's perfect shape beneath her cashmere sweater. *Power is the greatest aphrodisiac of all . . . and it brings women like this to D.C. in droves.*

Gabrielle was a New York Ivy Leaguer with dreams of being a senator herself one day. *She'll make it too*, Sexton thought. She was incredible-looking and sharp as a whip. Above all, she understood the rules of the game.

Gabrielle Ashe was black, but her tawny coloring was more of a deep cinnamon or mahogany, the kind of comfortable in-between that Sexton knew bleeding heart 'whites' could endorse without feeling like they were giving away the farm. Sexton described Gabrielle to his cronies as Halle Berry's looks with Hillary Clinton's brains and ambition, although sometimes he thought even that was an understatement.

Gabrielle had been a tremendous asset to his campaign since he'd promoted her to his personal campaign assistant three months ago. And to top it all off, she was working for free. Her compensation for a sixteen-hour workday was learning the ropes in the trenches with a seasoned politician.

Of course, Sexton gloated, *I've persuaded her to do a bit more than just work.* After promoting Gabrielle, Sexton had invited her to a late night 'orientation session' in his private office. As expected, his young assistant arrived starstruck and eager to please. With a slow-moving patience mastered over decades, Sexton worked his magic . . . building up Gabrielle's trust, carefully stripping away her inhibitions, exhibiting

43

tantalizing control, and finally seducing her right there in his office.

Sexton had little doubt the encounter had been one of the most sexually gratifying experiences of the young woman's life, and yet, in the light of the day, Gabrielle clearly regretted the indiscretion. Embarrassed, she offered to resign. Sexton refused. Gabrielle stayed on, but she made her intentions very clear. The relationship had been strictly business ever since.

Gabrielle's pouty lips were still moving. '. . . don't want you to be lackadaisical going into this CNN debate this afternoon. We still don't know who the White House is sending as opposition. You'll want to peruse these notes I typed.' She handed him a folder.

Sexton took the folder, savoring the scent of her perfume mixed with the plush leather seats.

'You aren't listening,' she said.

'Certainly am.' He grinned. 'Forget about this CNN debate. Worse case scenario, the White House snubs me by sending some low-level campaign intern. Best case scenario, they send a bigwig, and I eat him for lunch.'

Gabrielle frowned. 'Fine. I've included a list of the most probable hostile topics in your notes.'

'The usual suspects no doubt.'

'With one new entry. I think you might face some hostile backlash from the gay community for your comments last night on *Larry King*.'

Sexton shrugged, barely listening. 'Right. The same-sex marriage thing.'

Gabrielle gave him a disapproving look. 'You *did* come out against it pretty strongly.'

Same-sex marriages, Sexton thought in disgust. *If it were up to me, the faggots wouldn't even have the right to vote*. 'Okay, I'll turn it down a notch.'

'Good. You've been pushing the envelope a bit on some of these hot topics lately. Don't get cocky. The public can turn in an instant. You're gaining now, and you have momentum. Just ride it out. There's no need to hit the ball out of the park today. Just keep it in play.'

'Any news from the White House?'

Gabrielle looked pleasantly baffled. 'Continued silence. It's official; your opponent has become the "Invisible Man."'

Sexton could barely believe his good fortune lately. For months, the President had been working hard on the campaign trail. Then suddenly, a week ago, he had locked himself in the Oval Office, and nobody had seen or heard from him since. It was as if the President simply could not face Sexton's groundswell of voter support.

Gabrielle ran a hand through her straightened black hair. 'I hear the White House campaign staff is as confused as we are. The President is offering no explanation for his vanishing act, and everyone over there is furious.'

'Any theories?' Sexton asked.

Gabrielle gazed at him over her scholarly glasses. 'As it turns out, I got some interesting data this morning from a contact of mine in the White House.'

Sexton recognized the look in her eyes. Gabrielle Ashe had scored some insider information again. Sexton wondered if she were giving some presidential aide backseat blow jobs in exchange for campaign secrets. Sexton didn't care . . . so long as the information kept coming.

'Rumor has it,' his assistant said, lowering her voice, 'the President's strange behavior all started last week after an emergency private briefing with the administrator of NASA. Apparently the President emerged from the meeting looking dazed. He immediately cleared his schedule, and he's been in close contact with NASA ever since.'

Sexton certainly liked the sound of that. 'You think maybe NASA delivered some more bad news?'

'Seems a logical explanation,' she said hopefully. 'Although it would have to be pretty critical to make the President drop everything.'

Sexton considered it. Obviously, whatever was going on with NASA had to be bad news. *Otherwise the President would throw it in my face.* Sexton had been pounding the President pretty hard on NASA funding lately. The space agency's recent string of failed missions and gargantuan budget overruns had earned NASA the dubious honor of becoming Sexton's unofficial poster child against big government overspending and inefficiency. Admittedly, attacking NASA – one of the most prominent symbols of American pride – was not the way most politicians would think of winning votes, but Sexton had a weapon few other politicians had – Gabrielle Ashe. And her impeccable instincts.

The savvy young woman had come to Sexton's attention several months ago when she was working as a coordinator in Sexton's Washington campaign office. With Sexton trailing badly in the primary polls and his message of government overspending falling on deaf ears, Gabrielle Ashe wrote him a note suggesting a radical new campaign angle. She told the senator he should attack NASA's huge budget overruns and continued White House bailouts as the quintessential example of President Herney's careless overspending.

'NASA is costing Americans a fortune,' Gabrielle

wrote, including a list of financial figures, failures, and bailouts. 'Voters have no idea. They would be horrified. I think you should make NASA a political issue.'

Sexton groaned at her naïveté. 'Yeah, and while I'm at it, I'll rail against singing the national anthem at baseball games.'

In the weeks that followed, Gabrielle continued to send information about NASA across the senator's desk. The more Sexton read, the more he realized this young Gabrielle Ashe had a point. Even by government agency standards, NASA was an astounding money pit – expensive, inefficient, and in recent years, grossly incompetent.

One afternoon Sexton was doing an on-air interview about education. The host was pressing Sexton about where he would find funding for his promised over-haul of public schools. In response, Sexton decided to test Gabrielle's NASA theory with a half-joking response. 'Money for education?' he said. 'Well, maybe I'll cut the space program in half. I figure if NASA can spend fifteen billion a year in space, I should be able to spend seven and a half billion on the kids here on earth.'

In the transmission booth, Sexton's campaign managers gasped in horror at the careless remark. After all, entire campaigns had been sunk by far less than taking a potshot at NASA. Instantly, the phone lines at the radio station lit up. Sexton's campaign managers cringed; the space patriots were circling for the kill.

Then something unexpected happened.

'Fifteen billion a year?' the first caller said, sounding shocked. 'With a *B*? Are you telling me that my son's math class is overcrowded because schools can't afford enough teachers, and NASA is spending fifteen billion dollars a year taking pictures of space dust?'

'Um . . . that's right,' Sexton said warily.

'Absurd! Does the President have the power to do something about that?'

'Absolutely,' Sexton replied, gaining confidence. 'A President can veto the budget request of any agency he or she deems overfunded.'

'Then you have my vote, Senator Sexton. Fifteen billion for space research, and our kids don't have teachers. It's outrageous! Good luck, sir. I hope you go all the way.'

The next caller came on the line. 'Senator, I just read that NASA's International Space Station is way overbudget and the President is thinking of giving NASA emergency funding to keep the project going. Is that true?'

Sexton jumped at this one. 'True!' He explained that the space station was originally proposed as a joint venture, with twelve countries sharing the costs. But after construction began, the station's budget spiraled wildly out of control, and many countries dropped out in disgust. Rather than scrapping the project, the President decided to cover everyone's expenses. 'Our cost for the ISS project,' Sexton announced, 'has risen from the proposed eight billion to a staggering *one hundred* billion dollars!'

The caller sounded furious. 'Why the hell doesn't the President pull the plug?'

Sexton could have kissed the guy. 'Damn good question. Unfortunately, one third of the building supplies are already in orbit, and the President spent *your* tax dollars putting them there, so pulling the plug would be admitting he made a multibillion-dollar blunder with *your* money.'

The calls kept coming. For the first time, it seemed Americans were waking up to the idea that NASA was an option – not a national fixture.

When the show was over, with the exception of a few NASA diehards calling in with poignant overtures about man's eternal quest for knowledge, the consensus was in: Sexton's campaign had stumbled onto the holy grail of campaigning – a new 'hot button' – a yet untapped controversial issue that struck a nerve with voters.

In the weeks that followed, Sexton trounced his opponents in five crucial primaries. He announced Gabrielle Ashe as his new personal campaign assistant, praising her for her work in bringing the NASA issue to the voters. With the wave of a hand, Sexton had made a young African-American woman a rising political star, and the issue of his racist and sexist voting record disappeared overnight.

Now, as they sat together in the limousine, Sexton knew Gabrielle had yet again proven her worth. Her new information about last week's secret meeting between the NASA administrator and the President certainly suggested more NASA troubles were brewing – perhaps another country pulling funding from the space station.

As the limousine passed the Washington Monument, Senator Sexton could not help but feel he had been anointed by destiny.

Despite having ascended to the most powerful political office in the world, President Zachary Herney was average in height, with a slender build and narrow shoulders. He had a freckled face, bifocals, and thinning black hair. His unimposing physique, however, stood in stark contrast to the almost princely love the man commanded from those who knew him. It was said that if you met Zach Herney once, you would walk to the ends of the earth for him.

'So glad you could make it,' President Herney said, reaching out to shake Rachel's hand. His grasp was warm and sincere.

Rachel fought the frog in her throat. 'Of . . . course, Mr President. An honor to meet you.'

The President gave her a comforting grin, and Rachel sensed firsthand the legendary Herney affability. The man possessed an easygoing countenance political cartoonists loved because no matter how skewed a rendition they drew, no one ever mistook the man's effortless warmth and amiable smile. His eyes mirrored sincerity and dignity at all times.

'If you follow me,' he said in a cheery voice, 'I've got a cup of coffee with your name on it.'

'Thank you, sir.'

The President pressed the intercom and called for some coffee in his office.

As Rachel followed the President through the plane, she could not help but notice that he looked extremely happy and well rested for a man who was down in the polls. He was also very casually dressed – blue jeans, a polo shirt, and L.L. Bean hiking boots.

Rachel tried to make conversation. 'Doing . . . some hiking, Mr President?'

'Not at all. My campaign advisers have decided this should be my new look. What do you think?'

Rachel hoped for his sake that he wasn't serious. 'It's very . . . um . . . *manly*, sir.'

Herney was deadpan. 'Good. We're thinking it will help me win back some of the women's vote from your father.' After a beat, the President broke into a broad smile. 'Ms Sexton, that was a *joke*. I think we both know I'll need more than a polo shirt and blue jeans to win this election.'

The President's openness and good humor were quickly evaporating any tension Rachel felt about being there. What this President lacked in physical brawn, he more than made up for in diplomatic rapport. Diplomacy was about people skills, and Zach Herney had the gift.

Rachel followed the President toward the back of the plane. The deeper they went, the less the interior resembled a plane – curved hallways, wallpapered walls, even an exercise room complete with StairMaster and rowing machine. Oddly, the plane seemed almost entirely deserted.

'Traveling alone, Mr President?'

He shook his head. 'Just landed, actually.'

Rachel was surprised. *Landed from where?* Her intel briefs this week had included nothing about presidential travel plans. Apparently he was using Wallops Island to travel quietly.

'My staff deplaned right before you arrived,' the

President said. 'I'm headed back to the White House shortly to meet them, but I wanted to meet you here instead of my office.'

'Trying to intimidate me?'

'On the contrary. Trying to respect you, Ms Sexton. The White House is anything but private, and news of a meeting between the two of us would put you in an awkward position with your father.'

'I appreciate that, sir.'

'It seems you're managing a delicate balancing act quite gracefully, and I see no reason to disrupt that.'

Rachel flashed on her breakfast meeting with her father and doubted that it qualified as 'graceful.' Nonetheless, Zach Herney was going out of his way to be decent, and he certainly didn't have to.

'May I call you Rachel?' Herney asked.

'Of course.' *May I call you Zach?*

'My office,' the President said, ushering her through a carved maple door.

The office aboard Air Force One certainly was cozier than its White House counterpart, but its furnishings still carried an air of austerity. The desk was mounded with papers, and behind it hung an imposing oil painting of a classic, three-masted schooner under full sail trying to outrun a raging storm. It seemed a perfect metaphor for Zach Herney's presidency at the moment.

The President offered Rachel one of the three executive chairs facing his desk. She sat. Rachel expected him to sit behind his desk, but instead he pulled one of the chairs up and sat next to her.

Equal footing, she realized. *The master of rapport*.

'Well, Rachel,' Herney said, sighing tiredly as he settled into his chair. 'I imagine you've got to be pretty damned confused to be sitting here right now, am I right?'

Whatever was left of Rachel's guard crumbled away with the candor in the man's voice. 'Actually, sir, I'm baffled.'

Herney laughed out loud. 'Terrific. It's not every day I can baffle someone from the NRO.'

'It's not every day someone from the NRO is invited aboard Air Force One by a President in hiking boots.'

The President laughed again.

A quiet rap on the office door announced the arrival of coffee. One of the flight crew entered with a steaming pewter pot and two pewter mugs on a tray. At the President's bidding, she laid the tray on the desk and disappeared.

'Cream and sugar?' the President asked, standing up to pour.

'Cream, please.' Rachel savored the rich aroma. *The President of the United States is personally serving me coffee?*

Zach Herney handed her a heavy pewter mug. 'Authentic Paul Revere,' he said. 'One of the little luxuries.'

Rachel sipped the coffee. It was the best she had ever tasted.

'Anyhow,' the President said, pouring himself a cup and sitting back down, 'I've got limited time here, so let's get to business.' The President plopped a sugar cube in his coffee and gazed up at her. 'I imagine Bill Pickering warned you that the only reason I would want to see you would be to use you to my political advantage?'

'Actually, sir, that's *exactly* what he said.'

The President chuckled. 'Always the cynic.'

'So he's wrong?'

'Are you kidding?' the President laughed. 'Bill Pickering is never wrong. He's dead-on as usual.'

9

Gabrielle Ashe gazed absently out the window of Senator Sexton's limousine as it moved through the morning traffic toward Sexton's office building. She wondered how the hell she had arrived at this point in her life. Personal assistant to Senator Sedgewick Sexton. This was exactly what she had wanted, wasn't it?

I'm sitting in a limousine with the next President of the United States.

Gabrielle stared across the car's plush interior at the senator, who seemed to be far away in his own thoughts. She admired his handsome features and perfect attire. He looked presidential.

Gabrielle had first seen Sexton speak when she was a poli-sci major at Cornell University three years ago. She would never forget how his eyes probed the audience, as if sending a message directly to her – *trust me*. After Sexton's speech, Gabrielle waited in line to meet him.

'Gabrielle Ashe,' the senator said, reading her name tag. 'A lovely name for a lovely young woman.' His eyes were reassuring.

'Thank you, sir,' Gabrielle replied, feeling the man's strength as she shook his hand. 'I was really impressed by your message.'

'Glad to hear it!' Sexton thrust a business card into her hand. 'I'm always looking for bright young minds

54

who share my vision. When you get out of school, track me down. My people may have a job for you.'

Gabrielle opened her mouth to thank him, but the senator was already on to the next person in line. Nonetheless, in the months that followed, Gabrielle found herself following Sexton's career on television. She watched with admiration as he spoke out against big government spending – spearheading budget cuts, streamlining the IRS to work more effectively, trimming fat at the DEA, and even abolishing redundant civil service programs. Then, when the senator's wife died suddenly in a car crash, Gabrielle watched in awe as Sexton somehow turned the negative into a positive. Sexton rose above his personal pain and declared to the world that he would be running for the presidency and dedicating the remainder of his public service to his wife's memory. Gabrielle decided right then and there that she wanted to work closely with Senator Sexton's presidential campaign.

Now she had gotten as close as anyone could get.

Gabrielle recalled the night she had spent with Sexton in his plush office, and she cringed, trying to block out the embarrassing images in her mind. *What was I thinking?* She knew she should have resisted, but somehow she'd found herself unable. Sedgewick Sexton had been an idol of hers for so long . . . and to think he wanted *her*.

The limousine hit a bump, jarring her thoughts back to the present.

'You okay?' Sexton was watching her now.

Gabrielle flashed a hurried smile. 'Fine.'

'You aren't still thinking about that drudge, are you?'

She shrugged. 'I'm still a little worried, yeah.'

'Forget it. The drudge was the best thing that ever happened to my campaign.'

A drudge, Gabrielle had learned the hard way, was the political equivalent of leaking information that your rival used a penis enlarger or subscribed to *Stud Muffin* magazine. Drudging wasn't a glamorous tactic, but when it paid off, it paid off big.

Of course, when it backfired . . .

And backfire it had. For the White House. About a month ago, the President's campaign staff, unsettled by the slipping polls, had decided to get aggressive and leak a story they suspected to be true – that Senator Sexton had engaged in an affair with his personal assistant, Gabrielle Ashe. Unfortunately for the White House, there was no hard evidence. Senator Sexton, a firm believer in the best defense is a strong offense, seized the moment for attack. He called a national press conference to proclaim his innocence and outrage. *I cannot believe*, he said, gazing into the cameras with pain in his eyes, *that the President would dishonor my wife's memory with these malicious lies.*

Senator Sexton's performance on TV was so convincing that Gabrielle herself practically believed they had not slept together. Seeing how effortlessly he lied, Gabrielle realized that Senator Sexton was indeed a dangerous man.

Lately, although Gabrielle was certain she was backing the *strongest* horse in this presidential race, she had begun to question whether she was backing the *best* horse. Working closely with Sexton had been an eye-opening experience – akin to a behind-the-scenes tour of Universal Studios, where one's childlike awe over the movies is sullied by the realization that Hollywood isn't magic after all.

Although Gabrielle's faith in Sexton's message remained intact, she was beginning to question the messenger.

10

'What I am about to tell you, Rachel,' the President said, 'is classified "UMBRA." Well beyond your current security clearance.'

Rachel felt the walls of Air Force One closing in around her. The President had flown her to Wallops Island, invited her onboard his plane, poured her coffee, told her flat out that he intended to use her to political advantage against her own father, and now he was announcing he intended to give her classified information illegally. However affable Zach Herney appeared on the surface, Rachel Sexton had just learned something important about him. This man took control in a hurry.

'Two weeks ago,' the President said, locking eyes with her, 'NASA made a discovery.'

The words hung a moment in the air before Rachel could process them. *A NASA discovery?* Recent intelligence updates had suggested nothing out of the ordinary going on with the space agency. Of course, these days a 'NASA discovery' usually meant realizing they'd grossly underbudgeted some new project.

'Before we talk further,' the President said, 'I'd like to know if you share your father's cynicism over space exploration.'

Rachel resented the comment. 'I certainly hope you

didn't call me here to ask me to control my father's rants against NASA.'

He laughed. 'Hell, no. I've been around the Senate long enough to know that *nobody* controls Sedgewick Sexton.'

'My father is an opportunist, sir. Most successful politicians are. And unfortunately NASA has made itself an opportunity.' The recent string of NASA errors had been so unbearable that one either had to laugh or cry – satellites that disintegrated in orbit, space probes that never called home, the International Space Station budget rising tenfold and member countries bailing out like rats from a sinking ship. Billions were being lost, and Senator Sexton was riding it like a wave – a wave that seemed destined to carry him to the shores of 1600 Pennsylvania Avenue.

'I will admit,' the President continued, 'NASA has been a walking disaster area lately. Every time I turn around, they give me yet another reason to slash their funding.'

Rachel saw her opening for a foothold and took it. 'And yet, sir, didn't I just read that you bailed them out last week with another three million in emergency funding to keep them solvent?'

The President chuckled. 'Your father was pleased with that one, wasn't he?'

'Nothing like sending ammunition to your executioner.'

'Did you hear him on *Nightline?* "Zach Herney is a space addict, and the taxpayers are funding his habit." '

'But you keep proving him right, sir.'

Herney nodded. 'I make it no secret that I'm an enormous fan of NASA. I always have been. I was a child of the space race – Sputnik, John Glenn, Apollo 11

– and I have never hesitated to express my feelings of admiration and national pride for our space program. In my mind, the men and women of NASA are history's modern pioneers. They attempt the impossible, accept failure, and then go back to the drawing board while the rest of us stand back and criticize.'

Rachel remained silent, sensing that just below the President's calm exterior was an indignant rage over her father's endless anti-NASA rhetoric. Rachel found herself wondering what the hell NASA had found. The President was certainly taking his time coming to the point.

'Today,' Herney said, his voice intensifying, 'I intend to change your entire opinion of NASA.'

Rachel eyed him with uncertainty. 'You have my vote already, sir. You may want to concentrate on the rest of the country.'

'I intend to.' He took a sip of coffee and smiled. 'And I'm going to ask you to help me.' Pausing, he leaned toward her. 'In a most unusual way.'

Rachel could now feel Zach Herney scrutinizing her every move, like a hunter trying to gauge if his prey intended to run or fight. Unfortunately, Rachel saw nowhere to run.

'I assume,' the President said, pouring them both more coffee, 'that you're aware of a NASA project called EOS?'

Rachel nodded. 'Earth Observation System. I believe my father has mentioned EOS once or twice.'

The weak attempt at sarcasm drew a frown from the President. The truth was that Rachel's father mentioned the Earth Observation System every chance he got. It was one of NASA's most controversial big-ticket ventures – a constellation of five satellites designed to look down from space and analyze the planet's environment: ozone depletion, polar ice melt, global warming, rainforest defoliation. The intent was to provide environmentalists with never before seen macroscopic data so that they could plan better for earth's future.

Unfortunately, the EOS project had been wrought with failure. Like so many NASA projects of late, it had been plagued with costly overruns right from the start. And Zach Herney was the one taking the heat. He had used the support of the environmental lobby to push the $1.4 billion EOS project through Congress. But rather than delivering the promised contributions to global earth science, EOS had spiraled quickly into a costly nightmare of failed launches, computer malfunctions, and somber NASA press conferences. The only smiling face lately was that of Senator Sexton, who was smugly reminding voters just how much of *their* money the President had spent on EOS and just how lukewarm the returns had been.

The President dropped a sugar cube into his mug. 'As surprising as this may sound, the NASA discovery I'm referring to was *made* by EOS.'

Now Rachel felt lost. If EOS had enjoyed a recent success, NASA certainly would have announced it, wouldn't they? Her father had been crucifying EOS in the media, and the space agency could use any good news they could find.

'I've heard nothing,' Rachel said, 'about any EOS discovery.'

'I know. NASA prefers to keep the good news to themselves for a while.'

Rachel doubted it. 'In my experience, sir, when it comes to NASA, no news is generally bad news.'

60

Restraint was not a forte of the NASA public relations department. The standing joke at the NRO was that NASA held a press conference every time one of their scientists so much as farted.

The President frowned. 'Ah, yes. I forget I'm talking to one of Pickering's NRO security disciples. Is he still moaning and groaning about NASA's loose lips?'

'Security is his business, sir. He takes it very seriously.'

'He damn well better. I just find it hard to believe that two agencies with so much in common constantly find something to fight about.'

Rachel had learned early in her tenure under William Pickering that although both NASA and the NRO were space-related agencies, they had philosophies that were polar opposites. The NRO was a defense agency and kept all of its space activities classified, while NASA was academic and excitedly publicized all of its break-throughs around the globe – often, William Pickering argued, at the risk of national security. Some of NASA's finest technologies – high-resolution lenses for satellite telescopes, long-range communications systems, and radio imaging devices – had a nasty habit of appearing in the intelligence arsenal of hostile countries and being used to spy against us. Bill Pickering often grumbled that NASA scientists had big brains . . . and even bigger mouths.

A more pointed issue between the agencies, however, was the fact that because NASA handled the NRO's satellite launches, many of NASA's recent failures directly affected the NRO. No failure had been more dramatic than that of 12 August 1998, when a NASA/Air Force Titan 4 rocket blew up forty seconds into launch and obliterated its payload – a *$1.2 billion*

NRO satellite code-named Vortex 2. Pickering seemed particularly unwilling to forget that one.

'So why hasn't NASA gone public about this recent success?' Rachel challenged. 'They certainly could use some good news right now.'

'NASA is being silent,' the President declared, 'because I *ordered* them to be.'

Rachel wondered if she had heard him correctly. If so, the President was committing some kind of political hara-kiri that she did not understand.

'This discovery,' the President said, 'is . . . shall we say . . . nothing short of astounding in its ramifications.'

Rachel felt an uneasy chill. In the world of intelligence, 'astounding ramifications' seldom meant good news. She now wondered if all the EOS secrecy was on account of the satellite system having spotted some impending environmental disaster. 'Is there a problem?'

'No problem at all. What EOS discovered is quite wonderful.'

Rachel fell silent.

'Suppose, Rachel, that I told you NASA has just made a discovery of such scientific importance . . . such earth-shattering significance . . . that it validated every dollar Americans have ever spent in space?'

Rachel could not imagine.

The President stood up. 'Let's take a walk, shall we?'

11

Rachel followed President Herney out onto the glistening gangway of Air Force One. As they descended the stairs, Rachel felt the bleak March air clearing her mind. Unfortunately, clarity only made the President's claims seem more outlandish than before.

NASA made a discovery of such scientific importance that it validates every dollar Americans have ever spent in space?

Rachel could only imagine that a discovery of that magnitude would only center on one thing – the holy grail of NASA – contact with extraterrestrial life. Unfortunately, Rachel knew enough about *that* particular holy grail to know it was utterly implausible.

As an intelligence analyst, Rachel constantly fielded questions from friends who wanted to know about the alleged government cover-ups of alien contact. She was consistently appalled by the theories her 'educated' friends bought into – crashed alien saucers hidden in secret government bunkers, extraterrestrial corpses kept on ice, even unsuspecting civilians being abducted and surgically probed.

It was all absurd, of course. There were no aliens. No cover-ups.

Everyone in the intelligence community understood that the vast majority of sightings and alien abductions were simply the product of active imaginations or moneymaking hoaxes. When authentic photographic UFO evidence *did* exist, it had a strange habit of occurring near U.S. military airbases that were testing advanced classified aircraft. When Lockheed began air-testing a radical new jet called the Stealth Bomber, UFO sightings around Edwards Air Force Base increased fifteenfold.

'You have a skeptical look on your face,' the President said, eying her askance.

The sound of his voice startled Rachel. She glanced over, unsure how to respond. 'Well . . . ' She hesitated.

'May I assume, sir, that we are not talking about alien spacecrafts or little green men?'

The President looked quietly amused. 'Rachel, I think you'll find this discovery far more intriguing than science fiction.'

Rachel was relieved to hear NASA had not been so desperate as to try selling the President on an alien story. Nonetheless, his comment served only to deepen the mystery. 'Well,' she said, 'whatever NASA found, I must say the timing is exceptionally convenient.'

Herney paused on the gangway. 'Convenient? How so?'

How so? Rachel stopped and stared. 'Mr President, NASA is currently in a life or death battle to justify its very existence, and you are under attack for continuing to fund it. A major NASA breakthrough right now would be a panacea for both NASA and your campaign. Your critics will obviously find the timing highly suspect.'

'So . . . are you calling me a liar or a fool?'

Rachel felt a knot rise in her throat. 'I meant no disrespect, sir. I simply—'

'Relax.' A faint grin grew on Herney's lips, and he started to descend again. 'When the NASA administrator first told me about this discovery, I flat out rejected it as absurd. I accused him of masterminding the most transparent political sham in history.'

Rachel felt the knot in her throat dissolve somewhat.

At the bottom of the ramp, Herney stopped and looked at her. 'One reason I've asked NASA to keep their discovery under wraps is to protect them. The magnitude of this find is well beyond anything NASA has ever announced. It will make landing men on the moon seem insignificant. Because everyone, myself included, has so much to gain – and lose – I thought it prudent for someone to double-check the NASA data before we step into the world spotlight with a formal announcement.'

Rachel was startled. 'Certainly you can't mean *me*, sir?'

The President laughed. 'No, this is not your area of expertise. Besides, I've already achieved verification through extragovernmental channels.'

Rachel's relief gave way to a new mystification. 'Extragovernmental, sir? You mean you used the *private* sector? On something this classified?'

The President nodded with conviction. 'I put together an external confirmation team – four civilian scientists – non-NASA personnel with big names and serious reputations to protect. They used their own equipment to make observations and come to their own conclusions. Over the past forty-eight hours, these civilian scientists have confirmed the NASA discovery beyond the shadow of a doubt.'

Now Rachel was impressed. The President had protected himself with typical Herney aplomb. By hiring the ultimate team of skeptics – outsiders who had nothing to gain by confirming the NASA discovery – Herney had immunized himself against suspicions that this might be a desperate NASA ploy to justify its budget, reelect their NASA-friendly President, and ward off Senator Sexton's attacks.

'Tonight at eight P.M.,' Herney said, 'I will be calling a press conference at the White House to announce this discovery to the world.'

Rachel felt frustrated. Herney had essentially told her nothing. 'And this discovery is *what*, precisely?'

The President smiled. 'You will find patience a virtue

today. This discovery is something you need to see for yourself. I need you to understand this situation fully before we proceed. The administrator of NASA is waiting to brief you. He will tell you everything you need to know. Afterward, you and I will further discuss your role.'

Rachel sensed an impending drama in the President's eyes and recalled Pickering's hunch that the White House had something up its sleeve. Pickering, it appeared, was right, as usual.

Herney motioned to a nearby airplane hangar. 'Follow me,' he said, walking toward it.

Rachel followed, confused. The building before them had no windows, and its towering bay doors were sealed. The only access seemed to be a small entryway on the side. The door was ajar. The President guided Rachel to within a few feet of the door and stopped.

'End of the line for me,' he said, motioning to the door. 'You go through there.'

Rachel hesitated. 'You're not coming?'

'I need to return to the White House. I'll speak to you shortly. Do you have a cellphone?'

'Of course, sir.'

'Give it to me.'

Rachel produced her phone and handed it to him, assuming he intended to program a private contact number into it. Instead, he slipped her phone into his pocket.

'You're now off-the-grid,' the President said. 'All your responsibilities at work have been covered. You will not speak to anyone else today without express permission from myself or the NASA administrator. Do you understand?'

Rachel stared. *Did the President just steal my cellphone?*

'After the administrator briefs you on the discovery, he will put you in contact with me via secure channels. I'll talk to you soon. Good luck.'

Rachel looked at the hangar door and felt a growing uneasiness.

President Herney put a reassuring hand on her shoulder and nodded toward the door. 'I assure you, Rachel, you will not regret assisting me in this matter.'

Without another word, the President strode toward the PaveHawk that had brought Rachel in. He climbed aboard, and took off. He never once looked back.

12

Rachel Sexton stood alone on the threshold of the isolated Wallops hangar and peered into the blackness beyond. She felt like she was on the cusp of another world. A cool and musty breeze flowed outward from the cavernous interior, as if the building were breathing.

'Hello?' she called out, her voice wavering slightly.

Silence.

With rising trepidation, she stepped over the threshold. Her vision went blank for an instant as her eyes became accustomed to the dimness.

'Ms Sexton, I presume?' a man's voice said, only yards away.

Rachel jumped, wheeling toward the sound. 'Yes, sir.'

The hazy shape of a man approached.

As Rachel's vision cleared, she found herself standing face to face with a young, stone-jawed buck in a NASA flight suit. His body was fit and muscle-bound, his chest bedecked with countless patches.

'Commander Wayne Loosigian,' the man said. 'Sorry if I startled you, ma'am. It's pretty dark in here. I haven't had a chance to open the bay doors yet.' Before Rachel could respond, the man added, 'It will be my honor to be your pilot this morning.'

'Pilot?' Rachel stared at the man. *I just had a pilot.* 'I'm here to see the administrator.'

'Yes, ma'am. My orders are to transport you to him immediately.'

It took a moment for the statement to sink in. When it hit her, she felt a stab of deceit. Apparently, her travels were not over. 'Where *is* the administrator?' Rachel demanded, wary now.

'I do not have that information,' the pilot replied. 'I will receive his coordinates after we are airborne.'

Rachel sensed that the man was telling the truth. Apparently she and Director Pickering were not the only two people being kept in the dark this morning. The President was taking the issue of security very seriously, and Rachel felt embarrassed by how quickly and effortlessly the President had taken her 'off-the-grid.' *Half an hour in the field, and I'm already stripped of all communication, and my director has no idea where I am.*

Standing now before her stiff-backed NASA pilot, Rachel had little doubt her morning plans were cast in stone. This carnival ride was leaving with Rachel onboard whether she liked it or not. The only question was where it was headed.

The pilot strode over to the wall and pressed a button. The far side of the hangar began sliding loudly to one side. Light poured in from the outside, silhouetting a large object in the center of the hangar.

Rachel's mouth fell open. *God help me.*

There in the middle of the hangar stood a ferocious-looking black fighter jet. It was the most streamlined aircraft Rachel had ever seen.

'You *are* joking,' she said.

'Common first reaction, ma'am, but the F-14 Tomcat Split-tail is a highly proven craft.'

It's a missile with wings.

The pilot led Rachel toward his craft. He motioned to the dual cockpit. 'You'll be riding in back.'

'Really?' She gave him a tight smile. 'And here I thought you wanted me to drive.'

After donning a thermal flight suit over her clothes, Rachel found herself climbing into the cockpit. Awkwardly, she wedged her hips into the narrow seat.

'NASA obviously has no fat-assed pilots,' she said.

The pilot gave a grin as he helped Rachel buckle herself in. Then he slid a helmet over her head.

'We'll be flying pretty high,' he said. 'You'll want oxygen.' He pulled an oxygen mask from the side dash and began snapping it onto her helmet.

'I can manage,' Rachel said, reaching up and taking over.

'Of course, ma'am.'

Rachel fumbled with the molded mouthpiece and then finally snapped it onto her helmet. The mask's fit was surprisingly awkward and uncomfortable.

The commander stared at her for a long moment, looking vaguely amused.

'Is something wrong?' she demanded.

'Not at all, ma'am.' He seemed to be hiding a smirk. 'Hack sacks are under your seat. Most people get sick their first time in a split-tail.'

'I should be fine,' Rachel assured him, her voice muffled by the smothering fit of the mask. 'I'm not prone to motion sickness.'

The pilot shrugged. 'A lot of Navy Seals say the same thing, and I've cleaned plenty of Seal puke out of my cockpit.'

She nodded weakly. *Lovely*.

'Any questions before we go?'

Rachel hesitated a moment and then tapped on the mouthpiece cutting into her chin. 'It's cutting off my circulation. How do you wear these things on long flights?'

The pilot smiled patiently. 'Well, ma'am, we don't usually wear them upside down.'

Poised at the end of the runway, engines throbbing beneath her, Rachel felt like a bullet in a gun waiting for someone to pull the trigger. When the pilot pushed the throttle forward, the Tomcat's twin Lockheed 345 engines roared to life, and the entire world shook. The brakes released, and Rachel slammed backward in her seat. The jet tore down the runway and lifted off within a matter of seconds. Outside, the earth dropped away at a dizzying rate.

Rachel closed her eyes as the plane rocketed skyward. She wondered where she had gone wrong this morning. She was supposed to be at a desk writing gists. Now she was straddling a testosterone-fueled torpedo and breathing through an oxygen mask.

By the time the Tomcat leveled out at 45,000 feet, Rachel was feeling queasy. She willed herself to focus her thoughts elsewhere. Gazing down at the ocean nine miles below, Rachel felt suddenly far from home.

Up front, the pilot was talking to someone on the

radio. When the conversation ended, the pilot hung up the radio, and immediately banked the Tomcat sharply left. The plane tipped almost to the vertical, and Rachel felt her stomach do a somersault. Finally, the plane leveled out again.

Rachel groaned. 'Thanks for the warning, hotshot.'

'I'm sorry, ma'am, but I've just been given the classified coordinates of your meeting with the administrator.'

'Let me guess,' Rachel said. 'Due north?'

The pilot seemed confused. 'How did you know that?'

Rachel sighed. *You gotta love these computer-trained pilots.* 'It's nine A.M., sport, and the sun is on our right. We're flying north.'

There was a moment of silence from the cockpit. 'Yes, ma'am, we'll be traveling north this morning.'

'And how *far* north are we going?'

The pilot checked the coordinates. 'Approximately three thousand miles.'

Rachel sat bolt upright. 'What?' She tried to picture a map, unable even to imagine what was *that* far north. 'That's a four-hour flight!'

'At our current speed, yes,' the pilot said. 'Hold on, please.'

Before Rachel could respond, the man retracted the F-14's wings into low-drag position. An instant later, Rachel felt herself slammed into her seat yet again as the plane shot forward as though it had been standing still. Within a minute they were cruising at almost 1,500 miles per hour.

Rachel was feeling dizzy now. As the sky tore by with blinding speed, she felt an uncontrollable wave of nausea hit her. The President's voice echoed faintly. *I assure you, Rachel, you will not regret assisting me in this matter.*

Groaning, Rachel reached for her hack sack. *Never trust a politician.*

13

Although he disliked the menial filth of public taxis, Senator Sedgewick Sexton had learned to endure the occasional demeaning moment along his road to glory. The grungy Mayflower cab that had just deposited him in the lower parking garage of the Purdue Hotel afforded Sexton something his stretch limousine could not – anonymity.

He was pleased to find this lower level deserted, only a few dusty cars dotting a forest of cement pillars. As he made his way diagonally across the garage on foot, Sexton glanced at his watch.

11:15 A.M. Perfect.

The man with whom Sexton was meeting was always touchy about punctuality. Then again, Sexton reminded himself, considering who the man represented, he could be touchy about any damned thing he wanted.

Sexton saw the white Ford Windstar minivan parked in exactly the same spot as it had been for every one of their meetings – in the eastern corner of the garage, behind a row of trash bins. Sexton would have preferred to meet this man in a suite upstairs, but he certainly understood the precautions. This man's friends had not gotten to where they were by being careless.

As Sexton moved toward the van, he felt the familiar edginess that he always experienced before these encounters. Forcing himself to relax his shoulders, he climbed into the passenger's seat with a cheery wave. The dark-haired gentleman in the driver's seat did not smile. The man was almost seventy years old, but his leathery complexion exuded a toughness appropriate to his post as figurehead of an army of brazen visionaries and ruthless entrepreneurs.

'Close the door,' the man said, his voice callous.

Sexton obeyed, tolerating the man's gruffness graciously. After all, this man represented men who controlled enormous sums of money, much of which had been pooled recently to poise Sedgewick Sexton on the threshold of the most powerful office in the world. These meetings, Sexton had come to understand, were less strategy sessions than they were monthly reminders of just how beholden the senator had become to his benefactors. These men were expecting a serious return on their investment. The 'return,' Sexton had to admit, was a shockingly bold demand; and yet, almost more incredibly, it was something that would be within Sexton's sphere of influence once he took the Oval Office.

'I assume,' Sexton said, having learned how this man liked to get down to business, 'that another installment has been made?'

'It has. And as usual, you are to use these funds solely for your campaign. We have been pleased to see the polls shifting consistently in your favor, and it appears your campaign managers have been spending our money effectively.'

'We're gaining fast.'

'As I mentioned to you on the phone,' the old man said, 'I have persuaded six more to meet with you tonight.'

'Excellent.' Sexton had blocked off the time already.

The old man handed Sexton a folder. 'Here is their information. Study it. They want to know you understand their concerns specifically. They want to know you are sympathetic. I suggest you meet them at your residence.'

'My home? But I usually meet—'

'Senator, these six men run companies that possess resources well in excess of the others you have met. These men are the big fish, and they are wary. They have more to gain and therefore more to lose. I've worked hard to persuade them to meet with you. They will require special handling. A personal touch.'

Sexton gave a quick nod. 'Absolutely. I can arrange a meeting at my home.'

'Of course, they will want total privacy.'

'As will I.'

'Good luck,' the old man said. 'If tonight goes well, it could be your last meeting. These men alone can provide what is needed to push the Sexton campaign over the top.'

Sexton liked the sound of that. He gave the old man a confident smile. 'With luck, my friend, come election time, we will all claim victory.'

'Victory?' The old man scowled, leaning toward Sexton with ominous eyes. 'Putting you in the White House is only the *first step* toward victory, Senator. I assume you have not forgotten that.'

14

The White House is one of the smallest presidential mansions in the world, measuring only 170 feet in length, 85 feet in depth, and sitting on a mere 18 acres of landscaped grounds. Architect James Hoban's plan for a boxlike stone structure with a hipped roof, balustrade, and columnar entrance, though clearly un-original, was selected from the open design contest by judges who praised it as 'attractive, dignified, and flexible.'

President Zach Herney, even after three and a half years in the White House, seldom felt at home here among the maze of chandeliers, antiques, and armed Marines. At the moment, however, as he strode toward the West Wing, he felt invigorated and oddly at ease, his feet almost weightless on the plush carpeting.

Several members of the White House staff looked up as the President approached. Herney waved and greeted each by name. Their responses, though polite, were subdued and accompanied by forced smiles.

'Good morning, Mr President.'

'Nice to see you, Mr President.'

'Good day, sir.'

As the President made his way toward his office, he sensed whisperings in his wake. There was an insurrec-tion afoot inside the White House. For the past couple of weeks, the disillusionment at 1600 Pennsylvania Avenue had been growing to a point where Herney was starting to feel like Captain Bligh – commanding a struggling ship whose crew was preparing for mutiny.

The President didn't blame them. His staff had worked grueling hours to support him in the upcoming election, and now, all of a sudden, it seemed the President was fumbling the ball.

Soon they will understand, Herney told himself. *Soon I'll be the hero again.*

He regretted having to keep his staff in the dark for so long, but secrecy was absolutely critical. And when it came to keeping secrets, the White House was known as the leakiest ship in Washington.

Herney arrived in the waiting room outside the Oval Office and gave his secretary a cheery wave. 'You look nice this morning, Dolores.'

'You too, sir,' she said, eyeing his casual attire with unveiled disapproval.

Herney lowered his voice. 'I'd like you to organize a meeting for me.'

'With whom, sir?'

'The entire White House staff.'

His secretary glanced up. 'Your *entire* staff, sir? All one hundred and forty-five of them?'

'Exactly.'

She looked uneasy. 'Okay. Shall I set it up in . . . the Briefing Room?'

Herney shook his head. 'No. Let's set it up in my office.'

Now she stared. 'You want to see your *entire* staff inside the Oval Office?'

'Exactly.'

'All at once, sir?'

'Why not? Set it up for four P.M.'

The secretary nodded as though humoring a mental

76

patient. 'Very well, sir. And the meeting is regarding . . . ?'

'I have an important announcement to make to the American people tonight. I want my staff to hear it first.'

A sudden dejected look swept across his secretary's face, almost as if she had secretly been dreading this moment. She lowered her voice. 'Sir, are you pulling out of the race?'

Herney burst out laughing. 'Hell no, Dolores! I'm gearing up to fight!'

She looked doubtful. The media reports had all been saying President Herney was throwing the election.

He gave her a reassuring wink. 'Dolores, you've done a terrific job for me these past few years, and you'll do a terrific job for me for another four. We're *keeping* the White House. I swear it.'

His secretary looked like she wanted to believe it. 'Very well, sir. I'll alert the staff. Four P.M.'

As Zach Herney entered the Oval Office, he couldn't help but smile at the image of his entire staff crammed into the deceptively small chamber.

Although this great office had enjoyed many nicknames over the years – the Loo, Dick's Den, the Clinton Bedroom – Herney's favorite was 'the Lobster Trap.' It seemed most fitting. Each time a newcomer entered the Oval Office, disorientation set in immediately. The symmetry of the room, the gently curving walls, the discreetly disguised doorways in and out, all gave visitors the dizzying sense they'd been blindfolded and spun around. Often, after a meeting in the Oval Office, a visiting dignitary would stand up, shake hands with the President, and march straight into a storage closet. Depending on how the meeting had gone, Herney would either stop the guest in time or watch in amusement as the visitor embarrassed himself.

Herney had always believed the most dominating aspect of the Oval Office was the colorful American eagle emblazoned on the room's oval carpet. The eagle's left talon clutched an olive branch and his right a bundle of arrows. Few outsiders knew that during times of peace, the eagle faced left – toward the olive branch. But in times of war, the eagle mysteriously faced right – toward the arrows. The mechanism behind this little parlor trick was the source of quiet speculation among White House staff because it was traditionally known only by the President and the head of housekeeping. The truth behind the enigmatic eagle, Herney had found to be disappointingly mundane. A storage room in the basement contained the second oval carpet, and housekeeping simply swapped the carpets in the dead of night.

Now, as Herney gazed down at the peaceful, left-gazing eagle, he smiled to think that perhaps he should swap carpets in honor of the little war he was about to launch against Senator Sedgewick Sexton.

15

The U.S. Delta Force is the sole fighting squad whose actions are granted complete presidential immunity from the law.

Presidential Decision Directive 25 (PDD 25) grants

Delta Force soldiers 'freedom from all legal account-ability,' including exception from the 1876 Posse Comitatus Act, a statute imposing criminal penalties for anyone using the military for personal gain, domestic law enforcement, or unsanctioned covert operations. Delta Force members are handpicked from the Combat Applications Group (CAG), a classified organization within the Special Operations Command in Fort Bragg, North Carolina. Delta Force soldiers are trained killers – experts in SWAT operations, rescuing hostages, surprise raids, and elimination of covert enemy forces.

Because Delta Force missions usually involve high levels of secrecy, the traditional multitiered chain of command is often circumvented in favor of 'mono-caput' management – a single controller who holds authority to control the unit as he or she sees fit. The controller tends to be a military government powerbroker with sufficient rank or influence to run the mission. Regardless of the identity of their controller, Delta Force missions are classified at the highest level, and once a mission is completed, Delta Force soldiers never speak of it again – not to one another, and not to their commanding officers within Special Ops.

Fly. Fight. Forget.

The Delta team currently stationed above the 82nd Parallel was doing no flying or fighting. They were simply watching.

Delta-One had to admit that this had been a most unusual mission so far, but he had learned long ago never to be surprised by what he was asked to do. In the past five years he had been involved in Middle East hostage rescues, tracking and exterminating terrorist cells working inside the United States, and even the discreet elimination of several dangerous men and women around the globe.

Just last month his Delta team had used a flying microbot to induce a lethal heart attack in a particularly malicious South American drug lord. Using a microbot equipped with a hairline titanium needle containing a potent vasoconstrictor, Delta-Two had flown the device into the man's house through an open second-story window, found the man's bedroom, and then pricked him on the shoulder while he was sleeping. The microbot was back out the window and 'feet dry' before the man woke up with chest pain. The Delta team was already flying home by the time his victim's wife was calling the paramedics.

No breaking and entering.

Death by natural causes.

It had been a thing of beauty.

More recently, another microbot stationed inside a prominent senator's office to monitor his personal meetings had captured images of a lurid sexual encounter. The Delta team jokingly referred to that mission as 'insertion behind enemy lines.'

Now, after being trapped on surveillance duty inside this tent for the last ten days, Delta-One was ready for this mission to be over.

Remain in hiding.

Monitor the structure – inside and out.

Report to your controller any unexpected developments.

Delta-One had been trained never to feel any emotion regarding his assignments. This mission, however, had certainly raised his heart rate when he and his team were first briefed. The briefing had been 'faceless' – every phase explained via secure electronic channels.

Delta-One had never met the controller responsible for this mission.

Delta-One was preparing a dehydrated protein meal when his watch beeped in unison with the others. Within seconds the CrypTalk communications device beside him blinked on alert. He stopped what he was doing and picked up the handheld communicator. The other two men watched in silence.

'Delta-One,' he said, speaking into the transmitter.

The two words were instantly identified by the voice recognition software inside the device. Each word was then assigned a reference number, which was encrypted and sent via satellite to the caller. On the caller's end, at a similar device, the numbers were decrypted, translated back into words using a predetermined, self-randomizing dictionary. Then the words were spoken aloud by a synthetic voice. Total delay, eighty milliseconds.

'Controller here,' said the person overseeing the operation. The robotic tone of the CrypTalk was eerie – inorganic and androgynous. 'What is your op status?'

'Everything proceeding as planned,' Delta-One replied.

'Excellent. I have an update on the time frame. The information goes public tonight at eight P.M. Eastern.'

Delta-One checked his chronograph. *Only eight more hours.* His job here would be finished soon. That was encouraging.

'There is another development,' the controller said. 'A new player has entered the arena.'

'What new player?'

Delta-One listened. *An interesting gamble.* Someone out there was playing for keeps. 'Do you think she can be trusted?'

'She needs to be watched very closely.'

'And if there is trouble?'

There was no hesitation on the line. 'Your orders stand.'

16

Rachel Sexton had been flying due north for over an hour. Other than a fleeting glimpse of Newfoundland, she had seen nothing but water beneath the F-14 for the entire journey.

Why did it have to be water? she thought, grimacing. Rachel had plunged through the ice on a frozen pond while ice-skating when she was seven. Trapped beneath the surface, she was certain she would die. It had been her mother's powerful grasp that finally yanked Rachel's waterlogged body to safety. Ever since that harrowing ordeal, Rachel had battled a persistent case of hydrophobia – a distinct wariness of open water, especially cold water. Today, with nothing but the North Atlantic as far as Rachel could see, her old fears had come creeping back.

Not until the pilot checked his bearings with Thule airbase in northern Greenland did Rachel realize how far they had traveled. *I'm above the Arctic Circle?* The revelation intensified her uneasiness. *Where are they taking me? What has NASA found?* Soon the blue-gray expanse below her became speckled with thousands of stark white dots.

Icebergs.

Rachel had seen icebergs only once before in her life,

six years ago when her mother persuaded Rachel to join her on an Alaskan mother-daughter cruise. Rachel had suggested countless alternative *land*-based vacations, but her mother was insistent. 'Rachel, honey,' her mother had said, 'two thirds of this planet is covered with water, and sooner or later, you've got to learn to deal with it.' Mrs Sexton was a resilient New Englander intent on raising a strong daughter.

The cruise had been the last trip Rachel and her mother ever took.

Katherine Wentworth Sexton. Rachel felt a distant pang of loneliness. Like the howling wind outside the plane, the memories came tearing back, pulling at her the way they always did. Their final conversation had been by phone. Thanksgiving morning.

'I'm so sorry, Mom,' Rachel said, phoning home from a snowbound O'Hare Airport. 'I know our family has never spent Thanksgiving Day apart. It looks like today will be our first.'

Rachel's mom sounded crushed. 'I was so looking forward to seeing you.'

'Me too, Mom. Think of me eating airport food while you and Dad feast on turkey.'

There was a pause on the line. 'Rachel, I wasn't going to tell you until you got here, but your father says he has too much work to make it home this year. He'll be staying at his D.C. suite for the long weekend.'

'What?' Rachel's surprise gave way immediately to anger. 'But, it's Thanksgiving. The Senate isn't in session! He's less than two hours away. He should be with you!'

'I know. He says he's exhausted – far too tired to drive. He's decided he needs to spend this weekend curled up with his backlog of work.'

Work? Rachel was skeptical. A more likely guess was that Senator Sexton would be curled up with another woman. His infidelities, though discreet, had been going on for years. Mrs Sexton was no fool, but her husband's affairs were always accompanied by persuasive alibis and pained indignity at the mere suggestion he could be unfaithful. Finally, Mrs Sexton saw no alternative but to bury her pain by turning a blind eye. Although Rachel had urged her mother to consider divorce, Katherine Wentworth Sexton was a woman of her word. *Till death do us part,* she told Rachel. *Your father blessed me with you – a beautiful daughter – and for that I thank him. He will have to answer for his actions to a higher power someday.*

Now, standing in the airport, Rachel's anger was simmering. 'But, this means you'll be alone for Thanksgiving!' She felt sick to her stomach. The senator deserting his family on Thanksgiving Day was a new low, even for him.

'Well . . .' Mrs Sexton said, her voice disappointed but decisive. 'I obviously can't let all this food go to waste. I'll drive it up to Aunt Ann's. She's always invited us up for Thanksgiving. I'll give her a call right now.'

Rachel felt only marginally less guilty. 'Okay. I'll be home as soon as I can. I love you, Mom.'

'Safe flight, sweetheart.'

It was 10:30 that night when Rachel's taxi finally pulled up the winding driveway of the Sextons' luxurious estate. Rachel immediately knew something was wrong. Three police cars sat in the driveway. Several news vans too. All the house lights were on. Rachel dashed in, her heart racing.

A Virginia State policeman met her at the doorway.

His face was grim. He didn't have to say a word. Rachel knew. There had been an accident.

'Route Twenty-five was slick with freezing rain,' the officer said. 'Your mother went off the road into a wooded ravine. I'm sorry. She died on impact.'

Rachel's body went numb. Her father, having returned immediately when he got the news, was now in the living room holding a small press conference, stoically announcing to the world that his wife had passed away in a crash on her way back from Thanksgiving dinner with family.

Rachel stood in the wings, sobbing through the entire event.

'I only wish,' her father told the media, his eyes tearful, 'that I had been home for her this weekend. This never would have happened.'

You should have thought of that years ago, Rachel cried, her loathing for her father deepening with every passing instant.

From that moment on, Rachel divorced herself from her father in the way Mrs Sexton never had. The senator barely seemed to notice. He suddenly had gotten very busy using his late wife's fortunes to begin courting his party's nomination for president. The sympathy vote didn't hurt either.

Cruelly now, three years later, even at a distance the senator was making Rachel's life lonely. Her father's run for the White House had put Rachel's dreams of meeting a man and starting a family on indefinite hold. For Rachel it had become far easier to take herself completely out of the social game than to deal with the endless stream of power-hungry Washingtonian suitors hoping to snag a grieving, potential 'first daughter' while she was still in their league.

*   *   *

Outside the F-14, the daylight had started to fade. It was late winter in the Arctic – a time of perpetual darkness. Rachel realized she was flying into a land of permanent night.

As the minutes passed, the sun faded entirely, dropping below the horizon. They continued north, and a brilliant three-quarter moon appeared, hanging white in the crystalline glacial air. Far below, the ocean waves shimmered, the icebergs looking like diamonds sewn into a dark sequin mesh.

Finally, Rachel spotted the hazy outline of land. But it was not what she had expected. Looming out of the ocean before the plane was an enormous snowcapped mountain range.

'Mountains?' Rachel asked, confused. 'There are mountains *north* of Greenland?'

'Apparently,' the pilot said, sounding equally surprised.

As the nose of the F-14 tipped downward, Rachel felt an eerie weightlessness. Through the ringing in her ears she could hear a repeated electronic ping in the cockpit. The pilot had apparently locked on to some kind of directional beacon and was following it in.

As they passed below 3,000 feet, Rachel stared out at the dramatic moonlit terrain beneath them. At the base of the mountains, an expansive, snowy plain swept wide. The plateau spread gracefully seaward about ten miles until it ended abruptly at a sheer cliff of solid ice that dropped vertically into the ocean.

It was then that Rachel saw it. A sight like nothing she had ever seen anywhere on earth. At first she thought the moonlight must be playing tricks on her. She squinted down at the snowfields, unable to comprehend what she was looking at. The lower the plane descended, the clearer the image became.

What in the name of God?

The plateau beneath them was striped . . . as if someone had painted the snow with three huge striations of silver paint. The glistening strips ran parallel to the coastal cliff. Not until the plane dropped past 500 feet did the optical illusion reveal itself. The three silver stripes were deep troughs, each one over thirty yards wide. The troughs had filled with water and frozen into broad, silvery channels that stretched in parallel across the plateau. The white berms between them were mounded dikes of snow.

As they dropped toward the plateau, the plane started bucking and bouncing in heavy turbulence. Rachel heard the landing gear engage with a heavy clunk, but she still saw no landing strip. As the pilot struggled to keep the plane under control, Rachel peered out and spotted two lines of blinking strobes straddling the outermost ice trough. She realized to her horror what the pilot was about to do.

'We're landing on *ice*?' she demanded.

The pilot did not respond. He was concentrating on the buffeting wind. Rachel felt a drag in her gut as the craft decelerated and dropped toward the ice channel. High snow berms rose on either side of the aircraft, and Rachel held her breath, knowing the slightest miscalculation in the narrow channel would mean certain death. The wavering plane dropped lower between the berms, and the turbulence suddenly disappeared. Sheltered there from the wind, the plane touched down perfectly on the ice.

The Tomcat's rear thrusters roared, slowing the plane. Rachel exhaled. The jet taxied about a hundred yards farther and rolled to a stop at a red line spray-painted boldly across the ice.

The view to the right was nothing but a wall of snow in the moonlight – the side of an ice berm. The view on the left was identical. Only through the windshield ahead of them did Rachel have any visibility . . . an endless expanse of ice. She felt like she had landed on a dead planet. Aside from the line on the ice, there were no signs of life.

Then Rachel heard it. In the distance, another engine was approaching. Higher pitched. The sound grew louder until a machine came into view. It was a large, multitreaded snow tractor churning toward them up the ice trough. Tall and spindly, it looked like a towering futuristic insect grinding toward them on voracious spinning feet. Mounted high on the chassis was an enclosed Plexiglas cabin with a rack of flood-lights illuminating its way.

The machine shuddered to a halt directly beside the F-14. The door on the Plexiglas cabin opened, and a figure climbed down a ladder onto the ice. He was bundled from head to foot in a puffy white jumpsuit that gave the impression he had been inflated.

Mad Max meets the Pillsbury Dough Boy, Rachel thought, relieved at least to see this strange planet was inhabited.

The man signaled for the F-14 pilot to pop the hatch. The pilot obeyed.

When the cockpit opened, the gust of air that tore through Rachel's body chilled her instantly to the core.

Close the damn lid!

'Ms Sexton?' the figure called up to her. His accent was American. 'On behalf of NASA, I welcome you.'

88

Rachel was shivering. *Thanks a million*.

'Please unhook your flight harness, leave your helmet in the craft, and deplane by using the fuselage toeholds. Do you have any questions?'

'Yes,' Rachel shouted back. 'Where the hell am I?'

17

Marjorie Tench – senior adviser to the President – was a loping skeleton of a creature. Her gaunt six-foot frame resembled an Erector Set construction of joints and limbs. Overhanging her precarious body was a jaundiced face whose skin resembled a sheet of parchment paper punctured by two emotionless eyes. At fifty-one, she looked seventy.

Tench was revered in Washington as a goddess in the political arena. She was said to possess analytical skills that bordered on the clairvoyant. Her decade running the State Department's Bureau of Intelligence and Research had helped hone a lethally sharp, critical mind. Unfortunately, accompanying Tench's political savvy came an icy temperament that few could endure for more than a few minutes. Marjorie Tench had been blessed with all the brains of a supercomputer – and the warmth of one, too. Nonetheless, President Zach Herney had little trouble tolerating the woman's idiosyncrasies; her intellect and hard work were almost single-handedly responsible for putting Herney in office in the first place.

'Marjorie,' the President said, standing to welcome her into the Oval Office. 'What can I do for you?' He did not offer her a seat. The typical social graces did not apply to women like Marjorie Tench. If Tench wanted a seat, she would damn well take one.

'I see you set the staff briefing for four o'clock this afternoon.' Her voice was raspy from cigarettes. 'Excellent.'

Tench paced a moment, and Herney sensed the intricate cogs of her mind turning over and over. He was grateful. Marjorie Tench was one of the select few on the President's staff who was fully aware of the NASA discovery, and her political savvy was helping the President plan his strategy.

'This CNN debate today at one o'clock,' Tench said, coughing. 'Who are we sending to spar with Sexton?'

Herney smiled. 'A junior campaign spokesperson.' The political tactic of frustrating the 'hunter' by never sending him any big game was as old as debates themselves.

'I have a better idea,' Tench said, her barren eyes finding his. 'Let me take the spot myself.'

Zach Herney's head shot up. 'You?' *What the hell is she thinking?* 'Marjorie, you don't do media spots. Besides, it's a midday cable show. If I send my senior adviser, what kind of message does that send? It makes us look like we're panicking.'

'Exactly.'

Herney studied her. Whatever convoluted scheme Tench was hatching, there was no way in hell Herney would permit her to appear on CNN. Anyone who had ever laid eyes on Marjorie Tench knew there was a reason she worked *behind* the scenes. Tench was a frightful-looking woman – not the kind of face a President wanted delivering the White House message.

'I am taking this CNN debate,' she repeated. This time she was not asking.

'Marjorie,' the President maneuvered, feeling uneasy now, 'Sexton's campaign will obviously claim your presence on CNN is proof the White House is running scared. Sending out our big guns early makes us look desperate.'

The woman gave a quiet nod and lit a cigarette. 'The more desperate we look, the better.'

For the next sixty seconds, Marjorie Tench outlined why the President would be sending her to the CNN debate instead of some lowly campaign staffer. When Tench was finished, the President could only stare in amazement.

Once again, Marjorie Tench had proven herself a political genius.

18

The Milne Ice Shelf is the largest solid ice floe in the Northern Hemisphere. Located above the 82nd Parallel on the northernmost coast of Ellesmere Island in the high Arctic, the Milne Ice Shelf is 4 miles wide and reaches thicknesses of over three hundred feet.

Now, as Rachel climbed into the Plexiglas enclosure atop the ice tractor, she was grateful for the extra parka and gloves waiting for her on her seat, as well as the heat pouring out of the tractor's vents. Outside, on the ice runway, the F-14's engines roared, and the plane began taxiing away.

Rachel looked up in alarm. 'He's leaving?'

Her new host climbed into the tractor, nodding. 'Only science personnel and immediate NASA support team members are allowed on-site.'

As the F-14 tore off into the sunless sky, Rachel felt suddenly marooned.

'We'll be taking the IceRover from here,' the man said. 'The administrator is waiting.'

Rachel gazed out at the silvery path of ice before them and tried to imagine what the hell the administrator of NASA was doing up here.

'Hold on,' the NASA man shouted, working some levers. With a grinding growl, the machine rotated ninety degrees in place like a treaded army tank. It was now facing the high wall of a snow berm.

Rachel looked at the steep incline and felt a ripple of fear. *Surely he doesn't intend to—*

'Rock and roll!' The driver popped the clutch, and the craft accelerated directly toward the slope. Rachel let out a muffled cry and held on. As they hit the incline, the spiked treads tore into the snow, and the contraption began to climb. Rachel was certain they would tip over backward, but the cabin remained surprisingly horizontal as the treads clawed up the slope. When the huge machine heaved up onto the crest of the berm, the driver brought it to a stop and beamed at his white-knuckled passenger. 'Try *that* in an SUV! We took the shock-system design from the Mars Pathfinder and popped it on this baby! Worked like a charm.'

Rachel gave a wan nod. 'Neat.'

Sitting now atop the snow berm, Rachel looked out at the inconceivable view. One more large berm stood before them, and then the undulations stopped abruptly. Beyond, the ice smoothed into a glistening expanse that was inclined ever so slightly. The moonlit sheet of ice stretched out into the distance, where it eventually narrowed and snaked up into the mountains.

'That's the Milne Glacier,' the driver said, pointing up into the mountains. 'Starts up there and flows down into this wide delta that we're sitting on now.'

The driver gunned the engine again, and Rachel held on as the craft accelerated down the steep face. At the bottom, they clawed across another ice river and rocketed up the next berm. Mounting the crest and quickly skimming down the far side, they slid out onto a smooth sheet of ice and started crunching across the glacier.

'How far?' Rachel saw nothing but ice in front of them.

'About two miles ahead.'

Rachel thought it seemed far. The wind outside pounded the IceRover in relentless gusts, rattling the Plexiglas as if trying to hurl them back toward the sea.

'That's the katabatic wind,' the driver yelled. 'Get used to it!' He explained that this area had a permanent offshore gale called the katabatic – Greek for flowing downhill. The relentless wind was apparently the product of heavy, cold air 'flowing' down the glacial face like a raging river downhill. 'This is the only place on earth,' the driver added, laughing, 'where hell actually freezes over!'

Several minutes later, Rachel began to see a hazy shape in the distance in front of them – the silhouette of an enormous white dome emerging from the ice. Rachel rubbed her eyes. *What in the world . . . ?*

'*Big* Eskimos up here, eh?' the man joked.

Rachel tried to make sense of the structure. It looked like a scaled-down Houston Astrodome.

'NASA put it up a week and a half ago,' he said. 'Multistage inflatable plexipolysorbate. Inflate the pieces, affix them to one another, connect the whole thing to the ice with pitons and wires. Looks like an enclosed big top tent, but it's actually the NASA proto-type for the portable habitat we hope to use on Mars someday. We call it a "habisphere." '

'Habisphere?'

'Yeah, get it? Because it's not a *whole* sphere, it's only *habi*-sphere.'

Rachel smiled and stared out at the bizarre building now looming closer on the glacial plain. 'And because NASA hasn't gone to Mars yet, you guys decided to have a big sleepover out here instead?'

The man laughed. 'Actually, I would have preferred Tahiti, but fate pretty much decided the location.'

Rachel gazed uncertainly up at the edifice. The off-white shell was a ghostly contour against a dark sky. As the IceRover neared the structure, it ground to a stop at a small door on the side of the dome, which was now opening. Light from inside spilled out onto the snow. A figure stepped out. He was a bulky giant wearing a black fleece pullover that amplified his size and made him look like a bear. He moved toward the IceRover.

Rachel had no doubt who the huge man was: Lawrence Ekstrom, administrator of NASA.

The driver gave a solacing grin. 'Don't let his size fool you. The guy's a pussycat.'

More like a tiger, Rachel thought, well acquainted with Ekstrom's reputation for biting the heads off those who stood in the way of his dreams.

When Rachel climbed down from the IceRover, the

wind almost blew her over. She wrapped the coat around herself and moved toward the dome.

The NASA administrator met her halfway, extending a huge gloved paw. 'Ms Sexton. Thank you for coming.'

Rachel nodded uncertainly and shouted over the howling wind, 'Frankly, sir, I'm not sure I had much choice.'

A thousand meters farther up the glacier, Delta-One gazed through infrared binoculars and watched as the administrator of NASA ushered Rachel Sexton into the dome.

19

NASA administrator Lawrence Ekstrom was a giant of a man, ruddy and gruff, like an angry Norse god. His prickly blond hair was cropped military short above a furrowed brow, and his bulbous nose was spidered with veins. At the moment, his stony eyes drooped with the weight of countless sleepless nights. An influential aerospace strategist and operations adviser at the Pentagon before his appointment to NASA, Ekstrom had a reputation for surliness matched only by his incontestable dedication to whatever mission was at hand.

As Rachel Sexton followed Lawrence Ekstrom into the habisphere, she found herself walking through an eerie, translucent maze of hallways. The labyrinthine network appeared to have been fashioned by hanging sheets of opaque plastic across tautly strung wires. The floor of the maze was nonexistent – a sheet of solid ice, carpeted with strips of rubber matting for traction. They passed a rudimentary living area lined with cots and chemical toilets.

Thankfully, the air in the habisphere was warm, albeit heavy with the mingled potpourri of indistinguishable smells that accompany humans in tight quarters. Somewhere a generator droned, apparently the source of the electricity that powered the bare bulbs hanging from draped extension cords in the hallway.

'Ms Sexton,' Ekstrom grunted, guiding her briskly toward some unknown destination. 'Let me be candid with you right from the start.' His tone conveyed anything but pleasure to have Rachel as his guest. 'You are here because the *President* wants you here. Zach Herney is a personal friend of mine and a faithful NASA supporter. I respect him. I owe him. And I trust him. I do not question his direct orders, even when I resent them. Just so there is no confusion, be aware that I do not share the President's enthusiasm for involving you in this matter.'

Rachel could only stare. *I traveled 3,000 miles for this kind of hospitality?* This guy was no Martha Stewart. 'With all due respect,' she fired back, 'I am *also* under presidential orders. I have not been told my purpose here. I made this trip on good faith.'

'Fine,' Ekstrom said. 'Then I will speak bluntly.'

'You've made a damn good start.'

Rachel's tough response seemed to jolt the administrator. His stride slowed a moment, his eyes clearing as he studied her. Then, like a snake uncoiling, he heaved a long sigh and picked up the pace.

'Understand,' Ekstrom began, 'that you are here on a classified NASA project against my better judgment.

Not only are you a representative of the NRO, whose director enjoys dishonoring NASA personnel as loose-lipped children, but you are the daughter of the man who has made it his personal mission to destroy my agency. This should be NASA's hour in the sun; my men and women have endured a lot of criticism lately and deserve this moment of glory. However, due to a torrent of skepticism spearheaded by *your* father, NASA finds itself in a political situation where my hard-working personnel are forced to share the spotlight with a handful of random civilian scientists and the daughter of the man who is trying to destroy us.'

I am not my father, Rachel wanted to shout, but this was hardly the moment to debate politics with the head of NASA. 'I did not come here for the spotlight, sir.'

Ekstrom glared. 'You may find you have no alternative.'

The comment took her by surprise. Although President Herney had said nothing specific about her assisting him in any sort of 'public' way, William Pickering had certainly aired his suspicions that Rachel might become a political pawn. 'I'd like to know what I'm doing here,' Rachel demanded.

'You and me both. I do not have that information.'

'I'm sorry?'

'The President asked me to brief you fully on our discovery the moment you arrived. Whatever role he wants you to play in this circus is between you and him.'

'He told me your Earth Observation System had made a discovery.'

Ekstrom glanced sidelong at her. 'How familiar are you with the EOS project?'

'EOS is a constellation of five NASA satellites which

97

scrutinize the earth in different ways – ocean mapping, geologic fault analyses, polar ice-melt observation, location of fossil fuel reserves—'

'Fine,' Ekstrom said, sounding unimpressed. 'So you're aware of the newest addition to the EOS constellation? It's called PODS.'

Rachel nodded. The Polar Orbiting Density Scanner (PODS) was designed to help measure the effects of global warming. 'As I understand it, PODS measures the thickness and hardness of the polar ice cap?'

'In effect, yes. It uses spectral band technology to take composite density scans of large regions and find softness anomalies in the ice – slush spots, internal melting, large fissures – indicators of global warming.'

Rachel was familiar with composite density scanning. It was like a subterranean ultrasound. NRO satellites had used similar technology to search for subsurface density variants in Eastern Europe and locate mass burial sites, which confirmed for the President that ethnic cleansing was indeed going on.

'Two weeks ago,' Ekstrom said, 'PODS passed over this ice shelf and spotted a density anomaly that looked nothing like anything we'd expected to see. Two hundred feet beneath the surface, perfectly embedded in a matrix of solid ice, PODS saw what looked like an amorphous globule about ten feet in diameter.'

'A water pocket?' Rachel asked.

'No. Not liquid. Strangely, this anomaly was *harder* than the ice surrounding it.'

Rachel paused. 'So . . . it's a boulder or something?'

Ekstrom nodded. 'Essentially.'

Rachel waited for the punch line. It never came. *I'm here because NASA found a big rock in the ice?*

'Not until PODS calculated the density of this rock

did we get excited. We immediately flew a team up here to analyze it. As it turns out, the rock in the ice beneath us is significantly *more* dense than any type of rock found here on Ellesmere Island. More dense, in fact, than any type of rock found within a four-hundred-mile radius.'

Rachel gazed down at the ice beneath her feet, picturing the huge rock down there somewhere. 'You're saying someone *moved* it here?'

Ekstrom looked vaguely amused. 'The stone weighs more than eight tons. It is embedded under two *hundred* feet of solid ice, meaning it has been there untouched for over three hundred years.'

Rachel felt tired as she followed the administrator into the mouth of a long, narrow corridor, passing between two armed NASA workers who stood guard. Rachel glanced at Ekstrom. 'I assume there's a logical explanation for the stone's presence here . . . and for all this secrecy?'

'There most certainly is,' Ekstrom said, deadpan. 'The rock PODS found is a meteorite.'

Rachel stopped dead in the passageway and stared at the administrator. 'A *meteorite?*' A surge of disappointment washed over her. A meteorite seemed utterly anticlimactic after the President's big buildup. *This discovery will single-handedly justify all of NASA's past expenditures and blunders?* What was Herney thinking? Meteorites were admittedly one of the rarest rocks on earth, but NASA discovered meteorites all the time.

'This meteorite is one of the largest ever found,' Ekstrom said, standing rigid before her. 'We believe it is a fragment of a larger meteorite documented to have hit the Arctic Ocean in the seventeen hundreds. Most likely, this rock was thrown as ejecta from that ocean impact, landed on the Milne Glacier, and was slowly buried by snow over the past three hundred years.'

Rachel scowled. This discovery changed nothing. She felt a growing suspicion that she was witnessing an overblown publicity stunt by a desperate NASA and White House – two struggling entities attempting to elevate a propitious find to the level of earth-shattering NASA victory.

'You don't look too impressed,' Ekstrom said.

'I guess I was just expecting something . . . else.'

Ekstrom's eyes narrowed. 'A meteorite of this size is a very rare find, Ms Sexton. There are only a few larger in the world.'

'I realize—'

'But the *size* of the meteorite is not what excites us.'

Rachel glanced up.

'If you would permit me to finish,' Ekstrom said, 'you will learn that *this* meteorite displays some rather astonishing characteristics never before seen in any meteorite. Large or small.' He motioned down the passageway. 'Now, if you would follow me, I'll introduce you to someone more qualified than I am to discuss this find.'

Rachel was confused. 'Someone more qualified than the administrator of NASA?'

Ekstrom's Nordic eyes locked in on hers. 'More qualified, Ms Sexton, insofar as he is a civilian. I had assumed because you are a professional data analyst that you would prefer to get your data from an *unbiased* source.'

Touché. Rachel backed off.

She followed the administrator down the narrow corridor, where they dead-ended at a heavy, black drapery. Beyond the drape, Rachel could hear the reverberant murmur of countless voices rumbling on the other side, echoing as if in a giant open space.

Without a word, the administrator reached up and pulled aside the curtain. Rachel was blinded by a dazzling brightness. Hesitant, she stepped forward, squinting into the glistening space. As her eyes adjusted, she gazed out at the massive room before her and drew an awestruck breath.

'My God,' she whispered. *What is this place?*

20

The CNN production facility outside of Washington, D.C., is one of 212 studios worldwide that link via satellite to the global headquarters of Turner Broadcasting System in Atlanta.

It was 1:45 P.M. when Senator Sedgewick Sexton's limousine pulled into the parking lot. Sexton was feeling smug as he got out and strode toward the entrance. He and Gabrielle were greeted inside by a pot-bellied CNN producer who wore an effusive smile.

'Senator Sexton,' the producer said. 'Welcome. Great news. We just found out who the White House sent as a sparring partner for you.' The producer gave a foreboding grin. 'I hope you brought your game face.' He motioned through the production glass out into the studio.

Sexton looked through the glass and almost fell over. Staring back at him, through the smoky haze of her cigarette, was the ugliest face in politics.

'Marjorie Tench?' Gabrielle blurted. 'What the hell is *she* doing here?'

Sexton had no idea, but whatever the reason, her presence here was fantastic news – a clear sign that the President was in desperation mode. Why else would he send his senior adviser to the front lines? President Zach Herney was rolling out the big guns, and Sexton welcomed the opportunity.

The bigger the foe, the harder they fall.

The senator had no doubt that Tench would be a sly opponent, but gazing now at the woman, Sexton could not help but think that the President had made a serious error in judgment. Marjorie Tench was hideous-looking. At the moment, she sat slouched in her chair, smoking a cigarette, her right arm moving in languid rhythm back and forth to her thin lips like a giant praying mantis feeding.

Jesus, Sexton thought, *if there was ever a face that should stick to radio.*

The few times Sedgewick Sexton had seen the White House senior adviser's jaundiced mug in a magazine, he could not believe he was looking at one of the most powerful faces in Washington.

'I don't like this,' Gabrielle whispered.

Sexton barely heard her. The more he considered the opportunity, the more he liked it. Even more fortuitous than Tench's media-unfriendly face was Tench's reputation on one key issue: Marjorie Tench was extremely vocal that America's leadership role in the future could only be secured through technological superiority. She was an avid supporter of high-tech government R&D programs, and, most important – NASA. Many believed it was Tench's behind-the-scenes pressure that kept the President positioned so staunchly behind the failing space agency.

Sexton wondered if perhaps the President was now punishing Tench for all the bad advice about supporting NASA. *Is he throwing his senior adviser to the wolves?*

Gabrielle Ashe gazed through the glass at Marjorie Tench and felt a growing uneasiness. This woman was smart as hell *and* she was an unexpected twist. Those two facts had her instincts tingling. Considering the woman's stance on NASA, the President sending her to face-off against Senator Sexton seemed ill-advised. But the President was certainly no fool. Something told Gabrielle this interview was bad news.

Gabrielle already sensed the senator salivating over his odds, which did little to curb her concern. Sexton had a habit of going overboard when he got cocky. The NASA issue had been a welcome boost in the polls, but Sexton had been pushing very hard lately, she thought. Plenty of campaigns had been lost by candidates who went for the knockout when all they needed was to finish the round.

The producer looked eager for the impending blood match. 'Let's get you set up, Senator.'

As Sexton headed for the studio, Gabrielle caught his sleeve. 'I know what you're thinking,' she whispered. 'But just be smart. Don't go overboard.'

'Overboard? Me?' Sexton grinned.

'Remember this woman is very good at what she does.'

Sexton gave her a suggestive smirk. 'So am I.'

The cavernous main chamber of NASA's habisphere would have been a strange sight anywhere on earth, but the fact that it existed on an Arctic ice shelf made it that much more difficult for Rachel Sexton to assimilate.

Staring upward into a futuristic dome crafted of white interlocking triangular pads, Rachel felt like she had entered a colossal sanatorium. The walls sloped downward to a floor of solid ice, where an army of halogen lamps stood like sentinels around the perimeter, casting stark light skyward and giving the whole chamber an ephemeral luminosity.

Snaking across the ice floor, black foam carpet-runners wound like boardwalks through a maze of portable scientific work stations. Amid the electronics, thirty or forty white-clad NASA personnel were hard at work, conferring happily and talking in excited tones. Rachel immediately recognized the electricity in the room.

It was the thrill of new discovery.

As Rachel and the administrator circled the outer edge of the dome, she noted the surprised looks of displeasure from those who recognized her. Their whispers carried clearly in the reverberant space.

Isn't that Senator Sexton's daughter?

What the hell is SHE doing here?

I can't believe the administrator is even speaking to her!

Rachel half expected to see voodoo dolls of her father dangling everywhere. The animosity around her, though, was not the only emotion in the air; Rachel also sensed a distinct smugness – as if NASA clearly knew who would be having the last laugh.

The administrator led Rachel toward a series of tables where a lone man sat at a computer work station. He was dressed in a black turtleneck, wide-whale corduroys, and heavy boat shoes, rather than the matching NASA weather gear everyone else seemed to be wearing. He had his back to them.

The administrator asked Rachel to wait as he went over and spoke to the stranger. After a moment, the man in the turtleneck gave him a congenial nod and started shutting down his computer. The administrator returned.

'Mr Tolland will take it from here,' he said. 'He's another one of the President's recruits, so you two should get along fine. I'll join you later.'

'Thank you.'

'I assume you've heard of Michael Tolland?'

Rachel shrugged, her brain still taking in the incredible surroundings. 'Name doesn't ring a bell.'

The man in the turtleneck arrived, grinning. 'Doesn't ring a bell?' His voice was resonant and friendly. 'Best news I've heard all day. Seems I never get a chance to make a first impression anymore.'

When Rachel glanced up at the newcomer, her feet froze in place. She knew the man's handsome face in an instant. Everyone in America did.

'Oh,' she said, blushing as the man shook her hand. 'You're *that* Michael Tolland.'

When the President had told Rachel he had recruited top-notch civilian scientists to authenticate NASA's discovery, Rachel had imagined a group of wizened nerds with monogrammed calculators. Michael Tolland was the antithesis. One of the best known 'science celebrities' in America today, Tolland hosted a weekly documentary called *Amazing Seas*, during which he brought viewers face-to-face with spellbinding oceanic phenomena – underwater volcanoes, ten-foot sea worms, killer tidal waves. The media hailed Tolland as a cross between Jacques Cousteau and Carl Sagan, crediting his knowledge, unpretentious enthusiasm, and lust for adventure as the formula that had rocketed *Amazing Seas* to the top of the ratings. Of course, most critics admitted, Tolland's rugged good looks and self-effacing charisma probably didn't hurt his popularity with the female audience.

'Mr Tolland . . .' Rachel said, fumbling the words a bit. 'I'm Rachel Sexton.'

Tolland smiled a pleasant, crooked smile. 'Hi, Rachel. Call me Mike.'

Rachel found herself uncharacteristically tongue-tied. Sensory overload was setting in . . . the habisphere, the meteorite, the secrets, finding herself unexpectedly face-to-face with a television star. 'I'm surprised to see you here,' she said, attempting to recover. 'When the President told me he'd recruited civilian scientists for authentication of a NASA find, I guess I expected . . .' She hesitated.

'*Real* scientists?' Tolland grinned.

Rachel flushed, mortified. 'That's not what I meant.'

'Don't worry about it,' Tolland said. 'That's all I've heard since I got here.'

The administrator excused himself, promising to catch up with them later. Tolland turned now to Rachel with a curious look. 'The administrator tells me your father is Senator Sexton?'

Rachel nodded. *Unfortunately.*

'A Sexton spy behind enemy lines?'

'Battle lines are not always drawn where you might think.'

An awkward silence.

'So tell me,' Rachel said quickly, 'what's a world-famous oceanographer doing on a glacier with a bunch of NASA rocket scientists?'

Tolland chuckled. 'Actually, some guy who looked a lot like the President asked me to do him a favor. I opened my mouth to say "Go to hell," but somehow I blurted, "Yes, sir."'

Rachel laughed for the first time all morning. 'Join the club.'

Although most celebrities seemed smaller in person, Rachel thought Michael Tolland appeared taller. His brown eyes were just as vigilant and passionate as they were on television, and his voice carried the same modest warmth and enthusiasm. Looking to be a weathered and athletic forty-five, Michael Tolland had coarse black hair that fell in a permanent windswept tuft across his forehead. He had a strong chin and a carefree mannerism that exuded confidence. When he'd shaken Rachel's hand, the callused roughness of his palms reminded her he was not a typical 'soft' television personality but rather an accomplished seaman and hands-on researcher.

'To be honest,' Tolland admitted, sounding sheepish, 'I think I was recruited more for my PR value than for my scientific knowledge. The President asked me to come up and make a documentary for him.'

'A documentary? About a *meteorite*? But you're an oceanographer.'

'That's exactly what I told him! But he said he didn't know of any meteorite documentarians. He told me my involvement would help bring mainstream credibility to this find. Apparently he plans to broadcast my documentary as part of tonight's big press conference when he announces the discovery.'

A celebrity spokesman. Rachel sensed the savvy political maneuverings of Zach Herney at work. NASA was often accused of talking over the public's head. Not this time. They'd pulled in the master scientific communicator, a face Americans already knew and trusted when it came to science.

Tolland pointed kitty-corner across the dome to a far wall where a press area was being set up. There was a blue carpet on the ice, television cameras, media lights, a long table with several microphones. Someone was hanging a backdrop of a huge American flag.

'That's for tonight,' he explained. 'The NASA administrator and some of his top scientists will be connected live via satellite to the White House so they can participate in the President's eight o'clock broadcast.'

Appropriate, Rachel thought, pleased to know Zach Herney didn't plan to cut NASA out of the announcement entirely.

'So,' Rachel said with a sigh, 'is someone finally going to tell me what's so special about this meteorite?'

Tolland arched his eyebrows and gave her a mysterious grin. 'Actually, what's so special about this meteorite is best *seen*, not explained.' He motioned for Rachel to follow him toward the neighboring work area. 'The guy stationed over here has plenty of samples he can show you.'

'Samples? You actually have *samples* of the meteorite?'

'Absolutely. We've drilled quite a few. In fact, it was

the initial core samples that alerted NASA to the importance of the find.'

Unsure of what to expect, Rachel followed Tolland into the work area. It appeared deserted. A cup of coffee sat on a desk scattered with rock samples, calipers, and other diagnostic gear. The coffee was steaming.

'Marlinson!' Tolland yelled, looking around. No answer. He gave a frustrated sigh and turned to Rachel. 'He probably got lost trying to find cream for his coffee. I'm telling you, I went to Princeton postgrad with this guy, and he used to get lost in his own dorm. Now he's a National Medal of Science recipient in astrophysics. Go figure.'

Rachel did a double take. 'Marlinson? You don't by any chance mean the famous Corky Marlinson, do you?'

Tolland laughed. 'One and the same.'

Rachel was stunned. 'Corky Marlinson is *here*?' Marlinson's ideas on gravitational fields were legendary among NRO satellite engineers. 'Marlinson is one of the President's civilian recruits?'

'Yeah, one of the *real* scientists.'

Real is right, Rachel thought. Corky Marlinson was as brilliant and respected as they came.

'The incredible paradox about Corky,' Tolland said, 'is that he can quote you the distance to Alpha Centauri in millimeters, but he can't tie his own necktie.'

'I wear clip-ons!' a nasal, good-natured voice barked nearby. 'Efficiency over style, Mike. You Hollywood types don't understand that!'

Rachel and Tolland turned to the man now emerging from behind a large stack of electronic gear. He was squat and rotund, resembling a pug dog with bubble eyes and a thinning, comb-over haircut. When the man saw Tolland standing with Rachel, he stopped in his tracks.

'Jesus Christ, Mike! We're at the friggin' North Pole and you still manage to meet gorgeous women. I knew I should have gone into television!'

Michael Tolland was visibly embarrassed. 'Ms Sexton, please excuse Mr Marlinson. What he lacks in tact, he more than makes up for in random bits of totally useless knowledge about our universe.'

Corky approached. 'A true pleasure, ma'am. I didn't catch your name.'

'Rachel,' she said. 'Rachel Sexton.'

'Sexton?' Corky let out a playful gasp. 'No relation to that shortsighted, depraved senator, I hope!'

Tolland winced. 'Actually, Corky, Senator Sexton is Rachel's father.'

Corky stopped laughing and slumped. 'You know, Mike, it's really no wonder I've never had any luck with the ladies.'

22

Prize-winning astrophysicist Corky Marlinson ushered Rachel and Tolland into his work area and began sifting through his tools and rock samples. The man moved like a tightly wound spring about to explode.

'All right,' he said, quivering excitedly, 'Ms Sexton, you're about to get the Corky Marlinson thirty-second meteorite primer.'

Tolland gave Rachel a be-patient wink. 'Bear with him. The man really wanted to be an actor.'

'Yeah, and Mike wanted to be a respected scientist.' Corky rooted around in a shoebox and produced three small rock samples and aligned them on his desk. 'These are the three main classes of meteorites in the world.'

Rachel looked at the three samples. All appeared as awkward spheroids about the size of golf balls. Each had been sliced in half to reveal its cross section.

'All meteorites,' Corky said, 'consist of varying amounts of nickel-iron alloys, silicates, and sulfides. We classify them on the basis of their metal-to-silicate ratios.'

Rachel already had the feeling Corky Marlinson's meteorite 'primer' was going to be more than thirty seconds.

'This first sample here,' Corky said, pointing to a shiny, jet-black stone, 'is an iron-core meteorite. Very heavy. This little guy landed in Antarctica a few years back.'

Rachel studied the meteorite. It most certainly looked otherworldly – a blob of heavy grayish iron whose outer crust was burned and blackened.

'That charred outer layer is called a fusion crust,' Corky said. 'It's the result of extreme heating as the meteor falls through our atmosphere. All meteorites exhibit that charring.' Corky moved quickly to the next sample. 'This next one is what we call a stony-iron meteorite.'

Rachel studied the sample, noting that it too was charred on the outside. This sample, however, had a light-greenish tint, and the cross section looked like a collage of colorful angular fragments resembling a kaleidoscopic puzzle.

'Pretty,' Rachel said.

'Are you kidding, it's *gorgeous*!' Corky talked for a minute about the high olivine content causing the green luster, and then he reached dramatically for the third and final sample, handing it to Rachel.

Rachel held the final meteorite in her palm. This one was grayish brown in color, resembling granite. It felt heavier than a terrestrial stone, but not substantially. The only indication suggesting it was anything other than a normal rock was its fusion crust – the scorched outer surface.

'This,' Corky said with finality, 'is called a stony meteorite. It's the most common class of meteorite. More than ninety percent of meteorites found on earth are of this category.'

Rachel was surprised. She had always pictured meteorites more like the first sample – metallic, alien-looking blobs. The meteorite in her hand looked anything but extraterrestrial. Aside from the charred exterior, it looked like something she might step over on the beach.

Corky's eyes were bulging now with excitement. 'The meteorite buried in the ice here at Milne is a stony meteorite – a lot like the one in your hand. Stony meteorites appear almost identical to our terrestrial igneous rocks, which makes them tough to spot. Usually a blend of lightweight silicates – feldspar, olivine, pyroxene. Nothing too exciting.'

I'll say, Rachel thought, handing the sample back to him. 'This one looks like a rock someone left in a fireplace and burned.'

Corky burst out laughing. 'One *hell* of a fireplace! The meanest blast furnace ever built doesn't come close to reproducing the heat a meteoroid feels when it hits our atmosphere. They get ravaged!'

Tolland gave Rachel an empathetic smile. 'This is the good part.'

'Picture this,' Corky said, taking the meteorite sample from Rachel. 'Let's imagine this little fella is the size of a house.' He held the sample high over his head. 'Okay . . . it's in space . . . floating across our solar system . . . cold-soaked from the temperature of space to minus one hundred degrees Celsius.'

Tolland was chuckling to himself, apparently already having seen Corky's reenactment of the meteorite's arrival on Ellesmere Island.

Corky began lowering the sample. 'Our meteorite is moving toward earth . . . and as it's getting very close, our gravity locks on . . . accelerating . . . accelerating . . .'

Rachel watched as Corky sped up the sample's trajectory, mimicking the acceleration of gravity.

'Now it's moving fast,' Corky exclaimed. 'Over ten miles per second – thirty-six thousand miles per hour! At one hundred and thirty-five kilometers above the earth's surface, the meteorite begins to encounter friction with the atmosphere.' Corky shook the sample violently as he lowered it toward the ice. 'Falling below one hundred kilometers, it's starting to glow! Now the atmospheric density is increasing, and the friction is incredible! The air around the meteoroid is becoming incandescent as the surface material melts from the heat.' Corky started making burning and sizzling sound effects. 'Now it's falling past the eighty-kilometer mark, and the exterior becomes heated to over eighteen hundred degrees Celsius!'

Rachel watched in disbelief as the presidential award-winning astrophysicist shook the meteorite more fiercely, sputtering out juvenile sound effects.

'Sixty kilometers!' Corky was shouting now. 'Our

meteoroid encounters the atmospheric wall. The air is too dense! It violently decelerates at more than three hundred times the force of gravity!' Corky made a screeching braking sound and slowed his descent dramatically. 'Instantly, the meteorite cools and stops glowing. We've hit dark flight! The meteoroid's surface hardens from its molten stage to a charred fusion crust.'

Rachel heard Tolland groan as Corky knelt on the ice to perform the coup de grâce – earth impact.

'Now,' Corky said, 'our huge meteorite is skipping across our lower atmosphere . . .' On his knees, he arched the meteorite toward the ground on a shallow slant. 'It's headed toward the Arctic Ocean . . . on an oblique angle . . . falling . . . looking almost like it will skip off the ocean . . . falling . . . and . . .' He touched the sample to the ice. 'BAM!'

Rachel jumped.

'The impact is cataclysmic! The meteorite explodes. Fragments fly off, skipping and spinning across the ocean.' Corky went into slow motion now, rolling and tumbling the sample across the invisible ocean toward Rachel's feet. 'One piece keeps skimming, tumbling toward Ellesmere Island . . .' He brought it right up to her toe. 'It skips off the ocean, bouncing up onto land . . .' He moved it up and over the tongue of her shoe and rolled it to a stop on top of her foot near her ankle. 'And finally comes to rest high on the Milne Glacier, where snow and ice quickly cover it, protecting it from atmospheric erosion.' Corky stood up with a smile.

Rachel's mouth fell slack. She gave an impressed laugh. 'Well, Dr Marlinson, that explanation was exceptionally . . .'

'Lucid?' Corky offered.

Rachel smiled. 'In a word.'

114

Corky handed the sample back to her. 'Look at the cross section.'

Rachel studied the rock's interior a moment, seeing nothing.

'Tilt it into the light,' Tolland prompted, his voice warm and kind. 'And look closely.'

Rachel brought the rock close to her eyes and tilted it against the dazzling halogens reflecting overhead. Now she saw it – tiny metallic globules glistening in the stone. Dozens of them were peppered throughout the cross section like minuscule droplets of mercury, each only about a millimeter across.

'Those little bubbles are called "chondrules," ' Corky said. 'And they occur *only* in meteorites.'

Rachel squinted at the droplets. 'Granted, I've never seen anything like this in an earth rock.'

'Nor will you!' Corky declared. 'Chondrules are one geologic structure we simply do not have on earth. Some chondrules are exceptionally old – perhaps made up of the earliest materials in the universe. Other chondrules are much younger, like the ones in your hand. The chondrules in that meteorite date only about one hundred and ninety million years old.'

'One hundred ninety million years is *young*?'

'Heck, yes! In cosmological terms, that's yesterday. The point here, though, is that this sample contains *chondrules* – conclusive meteoric evidence.'

'Okay,' Rachel said. 'Chondrules are conclusive. Got it.'

'And finally,' Corky said, heaving a sigh, 'if the fusion crust and chondrules don't convince you, we astronomers have a foolproof method to confirm meteoric origin.'

'Being?'

Corky gave a casual shrug. 'We simply use a petro-graphic polarizing microscope, an X-ray fluorescence spectrometer, a neutron activation analyzer, or an induction-coupled plasma spectrometer to measure ferromagnetic ratios.'

Tolland groaned. 'Now he's showing off. What Corky means is that we can prove a rock is a meteorite simply by measuring its chemical content.'

'Hey, ocean boy!' Corky chided. 'Let's leave the science to the scientists, shall we?' He immediately turned back to Rachel. 'In earth rocks, the mineral nickel occurs in either extremely high percentages or extremely low; nothing in the middle. In meteorites, though, the nickel content falls within a midrange set of values. Therefore, if we analyze a sample and find the nickel content reflects a midrange value, we can guarantee beyond the shadow of a doubt that the sample is a meteorite.'

Rachel felt exasperated. 'Okay, gentlemen, fusion crusts, chondrules, midrange nickel contents, all of which prove it's from space. I get the picture.' She laid the sample back on Corky's table. 'But why am I here?'

Corky heaved a portentous sigh. 'You want to see a sample of the meteorite NASA found in the ice under-neath us?'

Before I die here, please.

This time Corky reached in his breast pocket and produced a small, disk-shaped piece of stone. The slice of rock was shaped like an audio CD, about half an inch thick, and appeared to be similar in composition to the stony meteorite she had just seen.

'This is a slice of a core sample that we drilled yesterday.' Corky handed the disk to Rachel.

The appearance certainly was not earth-shattering.

Like the sample she had seen earlier, it was an orangish-white, heavy rock. Part of the rim was charred and black, apparently a segment of the meteorite's outer skin. 'I see the fusion crust,' she said.

Corky nodded. 'Yeah, this sample was taken from near the outside of the meteorite, so it still has some crust on it.'

Rachel tilted the disk in the light and spotted the tiny metallic globules. 'And I see the chondrules.'

'Good,' Corky said, his voice tense with excitement. 'And I can tell you from having run this thing through a petrographic polarizing microscope that its nickel content is midrange – nothing like a terrestrial rock. Congratulations, you've now successfully confirmed the rock in your hand came from space.'

Rachel looked up, confused. 'Dr Marlinson, it's a meteorite. It's *supposed* to come from space. Am I missing something here?'

Corky and Tolland exchanged knowing looks. Tolland put a hand on Rachel's shoulder and whispered, 'Flip it over.'

Rachel turned the disk over so she could see the other side. It took only an instant for her brain to process what she was looking at.

Then the truth hit her like a truck.

Impossible! she gasped, and yet as she stared at the rock she realized her definition of 'impossible' had just changed forever. Embedded in the stone was a form that in an earth specimen might be considered commonplace, and yet in a meteorite was utterly inconceivable.

'It's . . .' Rachel stammered, almost unable to speak the word. 'It's . . . a *bug*! This meteorite contains the fossil of a bug!'

117

Both Tolland and Corky were beaming. 'Welcome aboard,' Corky said.

The torrent of emotions that gripped Rachel left her momentarily mute, and yet even in her bewilderment, she could clearly see that this fossil, beyond question, had once been a living biological organism. The petrified impression was about three inches long and looked to be the underside of some kind of huge beetle or crawling insect. Seven pairs of hinged legs were clustered beneath a protective outer shell, which seemed to be segmented in plates like that of an armadillo.

Rachel felt dizzy. 'An insect from space . . .'

'It's an isopod,' Corky said. 'Insects have three pairs of legs, not seven.'

Rachel did not even hear him. Her head was spinning as she studied the fossil before her.

'You can clearly see,' Corky said, 'that the dorsal shell is segmented in plates like a terrestrial pill bug, and yet the two prominent tail-like appendages differentiate it as something closer to a louse.'

Rachel's mind had already tuned Corky out. The classification of the species was totally irrelevant. The puzzle pieces now came crashing into place – the President's secrecy, the NASA excitement . . .

There is a fossil in this meteorite! Not just a speck of bacteria or microbes, but an advanced life-form! Proof of life elsewhere in the universe!

Ten minutes into the CNN debate, Senator Sexton wondered how he could have been worried at all. Marjorie Tench was grossly overestimated as an opponent. Despite the senior adviser's reputation for ruthless sagacity, she was turning out to be more of a sacrificial lamb than a worthy opponent.

Granted, early in the conversation Tench had grabbed the upper hand by hammering the senator's prolife platform as biased against women, but then, just as it seemed Tench was tightening her grip, she'd made a careless mistake. While questioning how the senator expected to fund educational improvements without raising taxes, Tench made a snide allusion to Sexton's constant scapegoating of NASA.

Although NASA was a topic Sexton definitely intended to address toward the end of the discussion, Marjorie Tench had opened the door early. *Idiot!*

'Speaking of NASA,' Sexton segued casually. 'Can you comment on the rumors I keep hearing that NASA has suffered another recent failure?'

Marjorie Tench did not flinch. 'I'm afraid I have not heard that rumor.' Her cigarette voice was like sandpaper.

'So, no comment?'

'I'm afraid not.'

Sexton gloated. In the world of media sound bites, 'no comment' translated loosely to 'guilty as charged.'

'I see,' Sexton said. 'And how about the rumors of a

secret, emergency meeting between the President and the administrator of NASA?'

This time Tench looked surprised. 'I'm not sure what meeting you're referring to. The President takes many meetings.'

'Of course, he does.' Sexton decided to go straight at her. 'Ms Tench, you are a great supporter of the space agency, is that right?'

Tench sighed, sounding tired of Sexton's pet issue. 'I believe in the importance of preserving America's technological edge – be that military, industry, intelligence, telecommunications. NASA is certainly part of that vision. Yes.'

In the production booth, Sexton could see Gabrielle's eyes telling him to back off, but Sexton could taste blood. 'I'm curious, ma'am, is it *your* influence behind the President's continued support of this obviously ailing agency?'

Tench shook her head. 'No. The President is also a staunch believer in NASA. He makes his own decisions.'

Sexton could not believe his ears. He had just given Marjorie Tench a chance to partially exonerate the President by personally accepting some of the blame for NASA funding. Instead, Tench had thrown it right back at the President. *The President makes his own decisions.* It seemed Tench was already trying to distance herself from a campaign in trouble. No big surprise. After all, when the dust settled, Marjorie Tench would be looking for a job.

Over the next few minutes, Sexton and Tench parried. Tench made some weak attempts to change the subject, while Sexton kept pressing her on the NASA budget.

'Senator,' Tench argued, 'you want to cut NASA's budget, but do you have any idea how many high-tech jobs will be lost?'

Sexton almost laughed in the woman's face. *This gal is considered the smartest mind in Washington?* Tench obviously had something to learn about the demographics of this country. High-tech jobs were inconsequential in comparison to the huge numbers of hardworking blue-collar Americans.

Sexton pounced. 'We're talking about *billions* in savings here, Marjorie, and if the result is that a bunch of NASA scientists have to get in their BMWs and take their marketable skills elsewhere, then so be it. I'm committed to being tough on spending.'

Marjorie Tench fell silent, as if reeling from that last punch.

The CNN host prompted, 'Ms Tench? A reaction?'

The woman finally cleared her throat and spoke. 'I guess I'm just surprised to hear that Mr Sexton is willing to establish himself as so staunchly anti-NASA.'

Sexton's eyes narrowed. *Nice try, lady.* 'I am not anti-NASA, and I resent the accusation. I am simply saying that NASA's budget is indicative of the kind of runaway spending that your President endorses. NASA said they could build the shuttle for five billion; it cost twelve billion. They said they could build the space station for eight billion; now it's one hundred billion.'

'Americans are leaders,' Tench countered, 'because we set lofty goals and stick to them through the tough times.'

'That national pride speech doesn't work on me, Marge. NASA has overspent its allowance three times in the past two years and crawled back to the President with its tail between its legs and asked for more money to fix its mistakes. Is that national pride? If you want to talk about national pride, talk about strong schools. Talk about universal health care. Talk about smart kids growing up in a country of opportunity. *That's* national pride!'

Tench glared. 'May I ask you a direct question, Senator?'

Sexton did not respond. He simply waited.

The woman's words came out deliberately, with a sudden infusion of grit. 'Senator, if I told you that we could not explore space for less than NASA is currently spending, would you act to abolish the space agency altogether?'

The question felt like a boulder landing in Sexton's lap. Maybe Tench wasn't so stupid after all. She had just blindsided Sexton with a 'fence-buster' – a carefully crafted yes/no question designed to force a fence-straddling opponent to choose clear sides and clarify his position once and for all.

Instinctively Sexton tried sidestepping. 'I have no doubt that with proper management NASA can explore space for a lot less than we are currently—'

'Senator Sexton, answer the question. Exploring space is a dangerous and costly business. It's much like building a passenger jet. We should either do it *right* – or not at all. The risks are too great. My question remains: If you become president, and you are faced with the decision to continue NASA funding at its current level or entirely scrap the U.S. space program, which would you choose?'

Shit. Sexton glanced up at Gabrielle through the glass. Her expression echoed what Sexton already knew. *You're committed. Be direct. No waffling.* Sexton held his chin high. 'Yes. I would transfer NASA's current budget directly into our school systems if faced with that decision. I would vote for our children over space.'

The look on Marjorie Tench's face was one of absolute shock. 'I'm stunned. Did I hear you correctly? As president, you would act to *abolish* this nation's space program?'

Sexton felt an anger simmering. Now Tench was putting words in his mouth. He tried to counter, but Tench was already talking.

'So you're saying, Senator, for the record, that you would do away with the agency that put men on the moon?'

'I am saying that the space race is over! Times have changed. NASA no longer plays a critical role in the lives of everyday Americans and yet we continue to fund them as though they do.'

'So you don't think space is the future?'

'Obviously space is the future, but NASA is a dinosaur! Let the private sector explore space. American taxpayers shouldn't have to open their wallets every time some Washington engineer wants to take a billion-dollar photograph of Jupiter. Americans are tired of selling out their children's future to fund an outdated agency that provides so little in return for its gargantuan costs!'

Tench sighed dramatically. 'So little in return? With the exception perhaps of the SETI program, NASA has had enormous returns.'

Sexton was shocked that the mention of SETI had even escaped Tench's lips. Major blunder. *Thanks for reminding me.* The Search for Extraterrestrial Intelligence was NASA's most abysmal money pit ever. Although NASA had tried to give the project a facelift by renaming it 'Origins' and shuffling some of its objectives, it was still the same losing gamble.

'Marjorie,' Sexton said, taking his opening, 'I'll address SETI only because you mention it.'

Oddly, Tench looked almost eager to hear this.

Sexton cleared his throat. 'Most people are not aware that NASA has been looking for ET for thirty-five years now. And it's a pricey treasure hunt – satellite dish arrays, huge transceivers, millions in salaries to scientists who sit in the dark and listen to blank tape. It's an embarrassing waste of resources.'

'You're saying there's nothing up there?'

'I'm saying that if any other government agency had spent forty-five million over thirty-five years and had not produced *one* single result, they would have been axed a long time ago.' Sexton paused to let the gravity of the statement settle in. 'After thirty-five years, I think it's pretty obvious we're not going to find extraterrestrial life.'

'And if you're wrong?'

Sexton rolled his eyes. 'Oh, for heaven's sake, Ms Tench, if I'm wrong I'll eat my hat.'

Marjorie Tench locked her jaundiced eyes on Senator Sexton. 'I'll remember you said that, Senator.' She smiled for the first time. 'I think we *all* will.'

Six miles away, inside the Oval Office, President Zach Herney turned off the television and poured himself a drink. As Marjorie Tench had promised, Senator Sexton had taken the bait – hook, line, and sinker.

Michael Tolland felt himself beaming empathetically as Rachel Sexton gaped in silence at the fossilized meteorite in her hand. The refined beauty of the woman's face now seemed to dissolve into the expression of innocent wonder – a young girl who had just seen Santa Claus for the first time.

I know just how you feel, he thought.

Tolland had been struck the same way only forty-eight hours ago. He too had been stunned into silence. Even now, the scientific and philosophical implications of the meteorite astounded him, forcing him to rethink everything he had ever believed about nature.

Tolland's oceanographic discoveries included several previously unknown deepwater species, and yet this 'space bug' was another level of breakthrough altogether. Despite Hollywood's propensity for casting extraterrestrials as little green men, astrobiologists and science buffs all agreed that given the sheer numbers and adaptability of earth's insects, extraterrestrial life would in all probability be buglike if it were ever discovered.

Insects were members of the phylum Arthropoda – creatures having hard outer skeletons and jointed legs. With over 1.25 million known species and an estimated five hundred thousand still to be classified, earth's 'bugs' outnumbered all of the other animals combined. They made up 95 percent of all the planet's species and an astounding 40 percent of the planet's biomass.

It was not so much the bugs' abundance that impressed as it was their resilience. From the Antarctic ice beetle to Death Valley's sun scorpion, bugs happily inhabited deadly ranges in temperature, dryness, and even pressure. They also had mastered exposure to the most deadly force known in the universe – radiation. Following a nuclear test in 1945, air force officers had donned radiation suits and examined ground zero, only to discover cockroaches and ants happily carrying on as if nothing had happened. Astronomers realized that an arthropod's protective exoskeleton made it a perfectly viable candidate to inhabit the countless radiation-saturated planets where nothing else could live.

It appeared the astrobiologists had been right, Tolland thought. *ET is a bug.*

Rachel's legs felt weak beneath her. 'I can't . . . believe it,' she said, turning the fossil in her hands. 'I never thought . . .'

'Give it some time to sink in,' Tolland said, grinning. 'Took me twenty-four hours to get my feet back under me.'

'I see we have a newcomer,' said an uncharacteristically tall Asian man, walking over to join them.

Corky and Tolland seemed to deflate instantly with the man's arrival. Apparently the moment of magic had been shattered.

'Dr Wailee Ming,' the man said, introducing himself. 'Chairman of paleontology at UCLA.'

The man carried himself with the pompous rigidity of renaissance aristocracy, continuously stroking the out-of-place bow tie that he wore beneath his knee-length camel-hair coat. Wailee Ming was apparently not one to let a remote setting come in the way of his prim appearance.

'I'm Rachel Sexton.' Her hand was still trembling as she shook Ming's smooth palm. Ming was obviously another of the President's civilian recruits.

'It would be my pleasure, Ms Sexton,' the paleontologist said, 'to tell you anything you want to know about these fossils.'

'And plenty you *don't* want to know,' Corky grumbled.

Ming fingered his bow tie. 'My paleontologic specialty is extinct Arthropoda and Mygalomorphae. Obviously the most impressive characteristic of this organism is—'

'—is that it's from another friggin' planet!' Corky interjected.

Ming scowled and cleared his throat. 'The most impressive characteristic of this organism is that it fits *perfectly* into our Darwinian system of terrestrial taxonomy and classification.'

Rachel glanced up. *They can classify this thing?* 'You mean kingdom, phylum, species, that sort of thing?'

'Exactly,' Ming said. 'This species, if found on earth, would be classified as the order Isopoda and would fall into a class with about two thousand species of lice.'

'Lice?' she said. 'But it's huge.'

'Taxonomy is not size specific. House cats and tigers are related. Classification is about physiology. This species is clearly a louse: it has a flattened body, seven pairs of legs, and a reproductive pouch identical in structure to wood lice, pill bugs, beach hoppers, sow bugs, and gribbles. The other fossils clearly reveal more specialized—'

'Other fossils?'

Ming glanced at Corky and Tolland. 'She doesn't know?'

Tolland shook his head.

Ming's face brightened instantly. 'Ms Sexton, you haven't heard the good part yet.'

'There are more fossils,' Corky interjected, clearly trying to steal Ming's thunder. '*Lots* more.' Corky scurried over to a large manila envelope and retrieved a folded sheet of oversized paper. He spread it out on the desk in front of Rachel. 'After we drilled some cores, we dropped an X-ray camera down. This is a graphic rendering of the cross section.'

Rachel looked at the X-ray printout on the table, and immediately had to sit down. The three-dimensional cross section of the meteorite was packed with dozens of these bugs.

'Paleolithic records,' Ming said, 'are usually found in heavy concentrations. Often times, mud slides trap organisms en masse, covering nests or entire communities.'

Corky grinned. 'We think the collection in the meteorite represents a nest.' He pointed to one of the bugs on the printout. 'And there's mommy.'

Rachel looked at the specimen in question, and her jaw dropped. The bug looked to be about two feet long.

'Big-ass louse, eh?' Corky said.

Rachel nodded, dumbstruck, as she pictured lice the size of bread loaves wandering around on some distant planet.

'On earth,' Ming said, 'our bugs stay relatively small because gravity keeps them in check. They can't grow larger than their exoskeletons can support. However, on a planet with diminished gravity, insects could evolve to much greater dimensions.'

128

'Imagine swatting mosquitoes the size of condors,' Corky joked, taking the core sample from Rachel and slipping it into his pocket.

Ming scowled. 'You had better not be stealing that!'

'Relax,' Corky said. 'We've got eight tons more where this came from.'

Rachel's analytical mind churned through the data before her. 'But how can life from space be so similar to life on earth? I mean, you're saying this bug *fits* in our Darwinian classification?'

'Perfectly,' Corky said. 'And believe it or not, a lot of astronomers have predicted that extraterrestrial life would be very similar to life on earth.'

'But why?' she demanded. 'This species came from an entirely different environment.'

'Panspermia.' Corky smiled broadly.

'I beg your pardon?'

'Panspermia is the theory that life was *seeded* here from another planet.'

Rachel stood up. 'You're losing me '

Corky turned to Tolland. 'Mike, you're the primordial seas guy.'

Tolland looked happy to take over. 'Earth was once a lifeless planet, Rachel. Then suddenly, as if overnight, life exploded. Many biologists think the explosion of life was the magical result of an ideal mixture of elements in the primordial seas. But we've never been able to reproduce that in a lab, so religious scholars have seized that failure as proof of God, meaning life could not exist unless God touched the primordial seas and infused them with life.'

'But we astronomers,' Corky declared, 'came up with another explanation for the overnight explosion of life on earth.'

'Panspermia,' Rachel said, now understanding what they were talking about. She had heard the panspermia theory before but didn't know its name. 'The theory that a meteorite splashed into the primordial soup, bringing the first seeds of microbial life to earth.'

'Bingo,' Corky said. 'Where they percolated and sprang to life.'

'And if *that's* true,' Rachel said, 'then the underlying ancestry of earth's life-forms and extraterrestrial life-forms would be identical.'

'Double bingo.'

Panspermia, Rachel thought, still barely able to grasp the implications. 'So, not only does this fossil confirm that life exists elsewhere in the universe, but it practically *proves* panspermia . . . that life on earth was seeded from elsewhere in the universe.'

'Triple bingo.' Corky flashed her an enthusiastic nod. 'Technically, we may *all* be extraterrestrials.' He put his fingers over his head like two antennas, crossed his eyes, and wagged his tongue like some kind of insect.

Tolland looked at Rachel with a pathetic grin. 'And this guy's the pinnacle of our evolution.'

25

Rachel Sexton felt a dreamlike mist swirling around her as she walked across the habisphere, flanked by Michael Tolland. Corky and Ming followed close behind.

'You okay?' Tolland asked, watching her.

Rachel glanced over, giving a weak smile. 'Thanks. It's just . . . so much.'

Her mind reeled back to the infamous 1997 NASA discovery – ALH84001 – a Mars meteorite that NASA claimed contained fossil traces of bacterial life. Sadly, only weeks after NASA's triumphant press conference, several civilian scientists stepped forward with proof that the rock's 'signs of life' were really nothing more than kerogen produced by terrestrial contamination. NASA's credibility had taken a huge hit over that gaffe. The *New York Times* took the opportunity to sarcastically redefine the agency's acronym: NASA – NOT ALWAYS SCIENTIFICALLY ACCURATE.

In that same edition, paleobiologist Stephen Jay Gould summed up the problems with ALH84001 by pointing out that the evidence in it was chemical and inferential, rather than 'solid,' like an unambiguous bone or shell.

Now, however, Rachel realized NASA had found irrefutable proof. No skeptical scientist could possibly step forward and question *these* fossils. NASA was no longer touting blurry, enlarged photos of alleged microscopic bacteria – they were offering up real meteorite samples where bio-organisms visible to the naked eye had been embedded in the stone. *Foot-long lice!*

Rachel had to laugh when she realized she'd been a childhood fan of a song by David Bowie that referred to 'spiders from Mars.' Few would have guessed how close the androgynous British pop star would come to foreseeing astrobiology's greatest moment.

As the distant strains of the song ran through Rachel's mind, Corky hurried up behind her. 'Has Mike bragged about his documentary yet?'

Rachel replied, 'No, but I'd love to hear about it.'

Corky slapped Tolland on the back. 'Go for it, big boy. Tell her why the President decided that the most important moment in science history should be handed over to a snorkeling TV star.'

Tolland groaned. 'Corky, if you don't mind?'

'Fine, I'll explain,' Corky said, prying his way in between them. 'As you probably know, Ms Sexton, the President will be giving a press conference tonight to tell the world about the meteorite. Because the vast majority of the world is made up of half-wits, the President asked Mike to come onboard and dumb everything down for them.'

'Thanks, Corky,' Tolland said. 'Very nice.' He looked at Rachel. 'What Corky's trying to say is that because there's so much scientific data to convey, the President thought a short visual documentary about the meteorite might help make the information more accessible to mainstream America, many of whom, oddly, don't have advanced degrees in astrophysics.'

'Did you know,' Corky said to Rachel, 'that I've just learned our nation's President is a closet fan of *Amazing Seas*?' He shook his head in mock disgust. 'Zach Herney – the ruler of the free world – has his secretary tape Mike's program so he can decompress after a long day.'

Tolland shrugged. 'The man's got taste, what can I say?'

Rachel was now starting to realize just how masterful the President's plan was. Politics was a media game, and Rachel could already imagine the enthusiasm and scientific credibility the face of Michael Tolland on-screen would bring to the press conference. Zach Herney had recruited the ideal man to endorse his little NASA coup. Skeptics would be hard-pressed to challenge the President's data if it came from the nation's top television science personality as well as several respected civilian scientists.

Corky said, 'Mike's already taken video depositions from all of us civilians for his documentary, as well as from most of the top NASA specialists. And I'll bet my National Medal that *you're* next on his list.'

Rachel turned and eyed him. 'Me? What are you talking about? I have no credentials. I'm an intelligence liaison.'

'Then why did the President send you up here?'

'He hasn't told me yet.'

An amused grin crossed Corky's lips. 'You're a White House intelligence liaison who deals in clarification and authentication of data, right?'

'Yes, but nothing scientific.'

'*And* you're the daughter of the man who built a campaign around criticizing the money NASA has wasted in space?'

Rachel could hear it coming.

'You have to admit, Ms Sexton,' Ming chimed in, 'a deposition from you would give this documentary a whole new dimension of credibility. If the President sent you up here, he must want you to participate somehow.'

Rachel again flashed on William Pickering's concern that she was being used.

Tolland checked his watch. 'We should probably head over,' he said, motioning toward the center of the habisphere. 'They should be getting close.'

'Close to what?' Rachel asked.

'Extraction time. NASA is bringing the meteorite to the surface. It should be up any time now.'

Rachel was stunned. 'You guys are actually *removing* an eight-ton rock from under two hundred feet of solid ice?'

Corky looked gleeful. 'You didn't think NASA was going to leave a discovery like this buried in the ice, did you?'

'No, but . . .' Rachel had seen no signs of large-scale excavation equipment anywhere inside the habisphere. 'How the heck is NASA planning on getting the meteorite out?'

Corky puffed up. 'No problem. You're in a room full of rocket scientists!'

'Blather,' Ming scoffed, looking at Rachel. 'Dr Marlinson enjoys flexing other people's muscles. The truth is that everyone here was stumped about how to get the meteorite out. It was *Dr Mangor* who proposed a viable solution.'

'I haven't met Dr Mangor.'

'Glaciologist from the University of New Hampshire,' Tolland said. 'The fourth and final civilian scientist recruited by the President. And Ming here is correct, it was Mangor who figured it out.'

'Okay,' Rachel said. 'So what did this guy propose?'

'Gal,' Ming corrected, sounding smitten. 'Dr Mangor is a *woman*.'

'Debatable,' Corky grumbled. He looked over at Rachel. 'And by the way, Dr Mangor is going to hate *you*.'

Tolland shot Corky an angry look.

'Well, she will!' Corky defended. 'She'll hate the competition.'

Rachel felt lost. 'I'm sorry? Competition?'

'Ignore him,' Tolland said. 'Unfortunately, the fact that Corky is a total moron somehow escaped the National Science Committee. You and Dr Mangor will get along fine. She is a professional. She's considered one of the world's top glaciologists. She actually moved to Antarctica for a few years to study glacial movement.'

'Odd,' Corky said, 'I heard UNH took up a donation and sent her there so they could get some peace and quiet on campus.'

'Are you aware,' Ming snapped, seeming to have taken the comment personally, 'that Dr Mangor almost died down there! She got lost in a storm and lived on seal blubber for five weeks before anyone found her.'

Corky whispered to Rachel, 'I heard no one was looking.'

26

The limousine ride back from the CNN studio to Sexton's office felt long for Gabrielle Ashe. The senator sat across from her, gazing out the window, obviously gloating over the debate.

'They sent Tench to an afternoon cable show,' he said, turning with a handsome smile. 'The White House is getting frantic.'

Gabrielle nodded, noncommittal. She'd sensed a look of smug satisfaction on Marjorie Tench's face as the woman drove off. It made her nervous.

Sexton's personal cellphone rang, and he fished in his pocket to grab it. The senator, like most politicians, had a hierarchy of phone numbers at which his contacts could reach him, depending on how important they were. Whoever was calling him now was at the top of the list; the call was coming in on Sexton's private line, a number even Gabrielle was discouraged to call.

'Senator Sedgewick Sexton,' he chimed, accentuating the musical quality of his name.

Gabrielle couldn't hear the caller over the sound of the limo, but Sexton listened intently, replying with enthusiasm. 'Fantastic. I'm so pleased you called. I'm thinking six o'clock? Super. I have an apartment here in D.C. Private. Comfortable. You have the address, right? Okay. Looking forward to meeting you. See you tonight then.'

Sexton hung up, looking pleased with himself.

'New Sexton fan?' Gabrielle asked.

'They're multiplying,' he said. 'This guy's a heavy hitter.'

'Must be. Meeting him in your apartment?' Sexton usually defended the sanctified privacy of his apartment like a lion protecting its only remaining hiding place.

Sexton shrugged. 'Yeah. Thought I'd give him the personal touch. This guy might have some pull in the home stretch. Got to keep making those personal connections, you know. It's all about trust.'

Gabrielle nodded, pulling out Sexton's daily planner. 'You want me to put him in your calendar?'

'No need. I'd planned to take a night at home anyway.'

Gabrielle found tonight's page and noticed it was already shaded out in Sexton's handwriting with the bold letters 'P.E.' – Sexton shorthand for either personal event, private evening, or piss-off everyone; nobody was quite sure which. From time to time, the senator scheduled himself a 'P.E.' night so he could hole up in his apartment, take his phones off the hook, and do what he enjoyed most – sip brandy with old cronies and pretend he'd forgotten about politics for the evening.

Gabrielle gave him a surprised look. 'So you're actually letting business intrude on prescheduled P.E. time? I'm impressed.'

'This guy happened to catch me on a night when I've got some time. I'll talk to him for a little while. See what he has to say.'

Gabrielle wanted to ask who this mystery caller was, but Sexton clearly was being intentionally vague. Gabrielle had learned when not to pry.

As they turned off the beltway and headed back toward Sexton's office building, Gabrielle glanced down again at the P.E. time blocked out in Sexton's planner and had the strange sensation Sexton knew this call was coming.

27

The ice at the center of the NASA habisphere was dominated by an eighteen-foot tripod structure of composite scaffolding, which looked like a cross between an oil rig and an awkward model of the Eiffel Tower. Rachel studied the device, unable to fathom how it could be used to extract the enormous meteorite.

Beneath the tower, several winches had been screwed into steel plates affixed to the ice with heavy bolts. Threaded through the winches, iron cables banked upward over a series of pulleys atop the tower. From there, the cables plunged vertically downward into narrow bore holes drilled in the ice. Several large

NASA men took turns tightening the winches. With each new tightening, the cables slithered a few inches upward through the bore holes, as if the men were raising an anchor.

I'm clearly missing something, Rachel thought, as she and the others moved closer to the extraction site. The men seemed to be hoisting the meteorite directly *through* the ice.

'EVEN TENSION! DAMN IT!' a woman's voice screamed nearby, with all the grace of a chain saw.

Rachel looked over to see a small woman in a bright yellow snowsuit smeared with grease. She had her back to Rachel, but even so, Rachel had no trouble guessing that she was in charge of this operation. Making notations on a clipboard, the woman stalked back and forth like a disgusted drillmaster.

'Don't tell me you ladies are tired!'

Corky called out, 'Hey, Norah, quit bossing those poor NASA boys and come flirt with me.'

The woman did not even turn around. 'Is that you, Marlinson? I'd know that weenie little voice anywhere. Come back when you reach puberty.'

Corky turned to Rachel. 'Norah keeps us warm with her charm.'

'I heard that, space boy,' Dr Mangor fired back, still making notes. 'And if you're checking out my ass, these snow pants add thirty pounds.'

'No worries,' Corky called. 'It's not your woolly-mammoth butt that drives me wild, it's your winning personality.'

'Bite me.'

Corky laughed again. 'I have great news, Norah. Looks like you're not the only woman the President recruited.'

'No shit. He recruited *you.*'

Tolland took over. 'Norah? Have you got a minute to meet someone?'

At the sound of Tolland's voice, Norah immediately stopped what she was doing and turned around. Her hardened demeanor dissolved instantly. 'Mike!' She rushed over, beaming. 'Haven't seen you in a few hours.'

'I've been editing the documentary.'

'How's my segment?'

'You look brilliant and lovely.'

'He used special effects,' Corky said.

Norah ignored the remark, glancing now at Rachel with a polite but standoffish smile. She looked back at Tolland. 'I hope you're not cheating on me, Mike.'

Tolland's rugged face flushed slightly as he made introductions. 'Norah, I'd like you to meet Rachel Sexton. Ms Sexton works in the intelligence community and is here at the request of the President. Her father is Senator Sedgewick Sexton.'

The introduction brought a confused look to Norah's face. 'I won't even pretend to understand that one.' Norah did not remove her gloves as she gave Rachel's hand a half-hearted shake. 'Welcome to the top of the world.'

Rachel smiled. 'Thanks.' She was surprised to see that Norah Mangor, despite the toughness of her voice, had a pleasant and impish countenance. Her pixie haircut was brown with streaks of gray, and her eyes were keen and sharp – two ice crystals. There was a steely confidence about her that Rachel liked.

'Norah,' Tolland said. 'Have you got a minute to share what you're doing with Rachel?'

Norah arched her eyebrows. 'You two on a first-name basis already? My, my.'

Corky groaned. 'I told you, Mike.'

Norah Mangor showed Rachel around the base of the tower while Tolland and the others trailed behind, talking among themselves.

'See those bore holes in the ice under the tripod?' Norah asked, pointing, her initial put-out tone softening now to one of rapt fervor for her work.

Rachel nodded, gazing down at the holes in the ice. Each was about a foot in diameter and had a steel cable inserted into it.

'Those holes are left over from when we drilled core samples and took X-rays of the meteorite. Now we're using them as entry points to lower heavy-duty screw eyes down the empty shafts and screw them into the meteorite. After that, we dropped a couple hundred feet of braided cable down each hole, snagged the screw eyes with industrial hooks, and now we're simply winching it up. It's taking these ladies several hours to get it to the surface, but it's coming.'

'I'm not sure I follow,' Rachel said. 'The meteorite is under thousands of tons of ice. How are you lifting it?'

Norah pointed to the top of the scaffolding where a narrow beam of pristine red light shone vertically downward toward the ice beneath the tripod. Rachel had seen it earlier and assumed it was simply some sort of visual indicator – a pointer demarking the spot where the object was buried.

'That's a gallium arsennide semiconductor laser,' Norah said.

Rachel looked more closely at the beam of light and

now saw that it had actually melted a tiny hole in the ice and shone down into the depths.

'Very hot beam,' Norah said. 'We're heating the meteorite as we lift.'

When Rachel grasped the simple brilliance of the woman's plan, she was impressed. Norah had simply aimed the laser beam downward, melting through the ice until the beam hit the meteorite. The stone, being too dense to be melted by a laser, began absorbing the laser's heat, eventually getting warm enough to melt the ice around it. As the NASA men hoisted the hot meteorite, the heated rock, combined with the upward pressure, melted the surrounding ice, clearing a pathway to raise it to the surface. The melt water accumulating over the meteorite simply seeped back down around the edges of the stone to refill the shaft.

Like a hot knife through a frozen stick of butter.

Norah motioned to the NASA men on the winches. 'The generators can't handle this kind of strain, so I'm using manpower to lift.'

'That's crap!' one of the workers interjected. 'She's using manpower because she likes to see us sweat!'

'Relax,' Norah fired back. 'You girls have been bitching for two days that you're cold. I cured that. Now keep pulling.'

The workers laughed.

'What are the pylons for?' Rachel asked, pointing to several orange highway cones positioned around the tower at what appeared to be random locations. Rachel had seen similar cones dispersed around the dome.

'Critical glaciology tool,' Norah said. 'We call them SHABAs. That's short for "step here and break ankle." ' She picked up one of the pylons to reveal a circular bore hole that plunged like a bottomless well into the depths of the glacier. 'Bad place to step.' She replaced the pylon. 'We drilled holes all over the glacier for a structural continuity check. As in normal archeology, the number of years an object has been buried is indicated by how *deep* beneath the surface it's found. The farther down one finds it, the longer it's been there. So when an object is discovered under the ice, we can date that object's arrival by how much ice has accumulated on top of it. To make sure our core dating measurements are accurate, we check multiple areas of the ice sheet to confirm that the area is one solid slab and hasn't been disrupted by earthquake, fissuring, avalanche, what have you.'

'So how does this glacier look?'

'Flawless,' Norah said. 'A perfect, solid slab. No fault lines or glacial turnover. This meteorite is what we call a "static fall." It's been in the ice untouched and un-affected since it landed in 1716.'

Rachel did a double take. 'You know the exact *year* it fell?'

Norah looked surprised by the question. 'Hell, yes. That's why they called me in. I read ice.' She motioned to a nearby pile of cylindrical tubes of ice. Each looked like a translucent telephone pole and was marked with a bright orange tag. 'Those ice cores are a frozen geologic record.' She led Rachel over to the tubes. 'If you look closely you can see individual layers in the ice.'

Rachel crouched down and could indeed see that the tube was made up of what appeared to be countless strata of ice with subtle differences in luminosity and clarity. The layers varied between paper thin to about a quarter of an inch thick.

'Each winter brings a heavy snowfall to the ice shelf,' Norah said, 'and each spring brings a partial thaw. So we see a new compression layer every season. We simply start at the top – the most recent winter – and count backward.'

'Like counting rings on a tree.'

'It's not quite that simple, Ms Sexton. Remember, we're measuring *hundreds* of feet of layerings. We need to read climatological markers to benchmark our work – precipitation records, airborne pollutants, that sort of thing.'

Tolland and the others joined them now. Tolland smiled at Rachel. 'She knows a lot about ice, doesn't she?'

Rachel felt oddly happy to see him. 'Yeah, she's amazing.'

'And for the record,' Tolland nodded, 'Dr Mangor's 1716 date is right on. NASA came up with the exact same year of impact well before we even got here. Dr Mangor drilled her own cores, ran her own tests, and confirmed NASA's work.'

Rachel was impressed.

'And coincidentally,' Norah said, '1716 is the exact year early explorers claimed to have seen a bright fireball in the sky over northern Canada. The meteor became known as the Jungersol Fall, after the name of the exploration's leader.'

'So,' Corky added, 'the fact that the core dates *and* the historic record match is virtual proof that we're looking at a fragment of the same meteorite that Jungersol recorded seeing in 1716.'

'Dr Mangor!' one of the NASA workers called out. 'Leader hasps are starting to show!'

'Tour's over, folks,' Norah said. 'Moment of truth.'

She grabbed a folding chair, climbed up onto it, and shouted out at the top of her lungs. *'Surfacing in five minutes, everyone!'*

All around the dome, like Pavlovian dogs responding to a dinner bell, the scientists dropped what they were doing and hurried toward the extraction zone.

Norah Mangor put her hands on her hips and surveyed her domain. 'Okay, let's raise the *Titanic*.'

28

'Step aside!' Norah hollered, moving through the growing crowd. The workers scattered. Norah took control, making a show of checking the cable tensions and alignments.

'Heave!' one of the NASA men yelled. The men tightened their winches, and the cables ascended another six inches out of the hole.

As the cables continued to move upward, Rachel felt the crowd inching forward in anticipation. Corky and Tolland were nearby, looking like kids at Christmas. On the far side of the hole, the hulking frame of NASA administrator Lawrence Ekstrom arrived, taking a position to watch the extraction.

'Hasps!' one of the NASA men yelled. 'Leaders are showing!'

The steel cables rising through the boreholes changed from silver braid to yellow leader chains.

'Six more feet! Keep it steady!'

The group around the scaffolding fell into a rapt silence, like onlookers at a séance awaiting the appearance of some divine specter – everyone straining for the first glimpse.

Then Rachel saw it.

Emerging from the thinning layer of ice, the hazy form of the meteorite began to show itself. The shadow was oblong and dark, blurry at first, but getting clearer every moment as it melted its way upward.

'Tighter!' a technician yelled. The men tightened the winches, and the scaffolding creaked.

'Five more feet! Keep the tension even!'

Rachel could now see the ice above the stone beginning to bulge upward like a pregnant beast about to give birth. Atop the hump, surrounding the laser's point of entry, a small circle of surface ice began to give way, melting, dissolving into a widening hole.

'Cervix is dilated!' someone shouted. 'Nine hundred centimeters!'

A tense laughter broke the silence.

'Okay, kill the laser!'

Someone threw a switch, and the beam disappeared.

And then it happened.

Like the fiery arrival of some paleolithic god, the huge rock broke the surface with a hiss of steam. Through the swirling fog, the hulking shape rose out of the ice. The men manning the winches strained harder until finally the entire stone broke free of the frozen restraints and swung, hot and dripping, over an open shaft of simmering water.

Rachel felt mesmerized.

Dangling there on its cables, dripping wet, the meteorite's rugged surface glistened in the fluorescent lights, charred and rippled with the appearance of an enormous petrified prune. The rock was smooth and rounded on one end, this section apparently blasted away by friction as it streaked through the atmosphere.

Looking at the charred fusion crust, Rachel could almost see the meteor rocketing earthward in a furious ball of flames. Incredibly, that was centuries ago. Now, the captured beast hung there on its cables, water dripping from its body.

The hunt was over.

Not until this moment had the drama of this event truly struck Rachel. The object hanging before her was from another world, millions of miles away. And trapped within it was evidence – no, *proof* – that man was not alone in the universe.

The euphoria of the moment seemed to grip everyone at the same instant, and the crowd broke into spontaneous hoots and applause. Even the administrator seemed caught up in it. He clapped his men and women on the back, congratulating them. Looking on, Rachel felt a sudden joy for NASA. They'd had some tough luck in the past. Finally things were changing. They deserved this moment.

The gaping hole in the ice now looked like a small swimming pool in the middle of the habisphere. The surface of the 200-foot-deep pool of melted water sloshed for a while against the icy walls of the shaft and then finally grew calm. The waterline in the shaft was a good four feet beneath the glacier's surface, the discrepancy caused by both the removal of the meteorite's mass and ice's property of shrinking as it melts.

Norah Mangor immediately set up SHABA pylons all around the hole. Although the hole was clearly visible, any curious soul who ventured too close and accidentally slipped in would be in dire jeopardy. The walls of the shaft were solid ice, with no footholds, and climbing out unassisted would be impossible.

Lawrence Ekstrom came padding across the ice toward them. He moved directly to Norah Mangor and shook her hand firmly. 'Well done, Dr Mangor.'

'I'll expect lots of praise in print,' Norah replied.

'You'll get it.' The administrator turned now to Rachel. He looked happier, relieved. 'So, Ms Sexton, is the professional skeptic convinced?'

Rachel couldn't help but smile. 'Stunned is more like it.'

'Good. Then follow me.'

Rachel followed the administrator across the habisphere to a large metal box that resembled an industrial shipping container. The box was painted with military camouflage patterns and stenciled letters: P-S-C.

'You'll call the President from in here,' Ekstrom said.

Portable Secure Comm, Rachel thought. These mobile communications booths were standard battlefield installations, although Rachel had never expected to see one used as part of a peacetime NASA mission. Then again, Administrator Ekstrom's background was the Pentagon, so he certainly had access to toys like this. From the stern faces on the two armed guards watching over the PSC, Rachel got the distinct impression that contact with the outside world was made only with express consent from Administrator Ekstrom.

Looks like I'm not the only one who is off-the-grid.

Ekstrom spoke briefly with one of the guards outside the trailer and then returned to Rachel. 'Good luck,' he said. Then he left.

A guard rapped on the trailer door, and it opened

from within. A technician emerged and motioned for Rachel to enter. She followed him in.

The inside of the PSC was dark and stuffy. In the bluish glow of the lone computer monitor, Rachel could make out racks of telephone gear, radios, and satellite telecommunications devices. She already felt claustrophobic. The air inside was bitter, like a basement in winter.

'Sit here, please, Ms Sexton.' The technician produced a rolling stool and positioned Rachel in front of a flat-screen monitor. He arranged a microphone in front of her and placed a bulky pair of AKG headphones on her head. Checking a logbook of encryption passwords, the technician typed a long series of keys on a nearby device. A timer materialized on the screen in front of Rachel.

00:60 SECONDS

The technician gave a satisfied nod as the timer began to count down. 'One minute until connection.' He turned and left, slamming the door behind him. Rachel could hear the bolt lock outside.

Great.

As she waited in the dark, watching the sixty-second clock slowly count down, she realized that this was the first moment of privacy she'd had since early that morning. She'd woken up today without the slightest inkling of what lay ahead. *Extraterrestrial life.* As of today, the most popular modern myth of all time was no longer a myth.

Rachel was just now starting to sense how truly devastating this meteorite would be to her father's campaign. Although NASA funding had no business being on a political par with abortion rights, welfare, and health care, her father had *made* it an issue. Now it was going to blow up in his face.

Within hours, Americans would feel the thrill of a NASA triumph all over again. There would be teary-eyed dreamers. Slack-jawed scientists. Children's imaginations running free. Issues of dollars and cents would fade away as petty, overshadowed by this monumental moment. The President would emerge like a phoenix, transforming himself into a hero, while in the midst of the celebration, the businesslike senator would suddenly appear small-minded, a penny-pinching scrooge with no American sense of adventure.

The computer beeped, and Rachel glanced up.

00:05 SECONDS

The screen in front of her flickered suddenly, and a blurry image of the White House seal materialized on-screen. After a moment, the image dissolved into the face of President Herney.

'Hello, Rachel,' he said, a mischievous glint in his eye. 'I trust you've had an interesting afternoon?'

29

The office of Senator Sedgewick Sexton was located in the Philip A. Hart Senate Office Building on C Street to the northeast of the Capitol. The building was a neomodern grid of white rectangles that critics claimed looked more like a prison than an office building. Many who worked there felt the same.

On the third floor, Gabrielle Ashe's long legs paced briskly back and forth in front of her computer terminal. On the screen was a new e-mail message. She was not sure what to make of it.

The first two lines read:

Gabrielle had been receiving messages like this
for the last couple of weeks. The return address
was bogus, although she'd been able to track it to a
'whitehouse.gov' domain. It seemed her mysterious
informant was a White House insider, and whoever
it was had become Gabrielle's source for all kinds
of valuable political information recently, including
the news of a covert meeting between the NASA
administrator and the President.

Gabrielle had been leery of the e-mails at first, but
when she checked out the tips, she was amazed to find
the information consistently accurate and helpful
– classified information on NASA overexpenditures,
costly upcoming missions, data showing that NASA's
search for extraterrestrial life was grossly overfunded
and pathetically unproductive, even internal opinion
polls warning that NASA was the issue turning voters
away from the President.

To enhance her perceived value to the senator,
Gabrielle had not informed him she was receiving unsolicited e-mail help from inside the White House.
Instead, she simply passed the information to him as
coming from 'one of her sources.' Sexton was always
appreciative and seemed to know better than to ask *who*
her source was. She could tell he suspected Gabrielle
was doing sexual favors. Troublingly, it didn't seem to
bother him in the least.

Gabrielle stopped pacing and looked again at the
newly arrived message. The connotations of all the

e-mails were clear: someone inside the White House wanted Senator Sexton to win this election and was helping him do it by aiding his attack against NASA.

But who? And why?

A rat from a sinking ship, Gabrielle decided. In Washington it was not at all uncommon for a White House employee, fearing his President was about to be ousted from office, to offer quiet favors to the apparent successor in hopes of securing power or another position after the changeover. It seemed someone smelled Sexton victory and was buying stock early.

The message currently on Gabrielle's screen made her nervous. It was like none other she had ever received. The first two lines didn't bother her so much. It was the last two:

EAST APPOINTMENT GATE, 4:30 P.M.
COME ALONE.

Her informant had never before asked to meet in person. Even so, Gabrielle would have expected a more subtle location for a face-to-face meeting. *East Appointment Gate?* Only one East Appointment Gate existed in Washington, as far as she knew. *Outside the White House? Is this some kind of joke?*

Gabrielle knew she could not respond via e-mail; her messages were always bounced back as undeliverable. Her correspondent's account was anonymous. Not surprising.

Should I consult Sexton? She quickly decided against it. He was in a meeting. Besides, if she told him about this e-mail, she'd have to tell him about the others. She decided her informant's offer to meet in public in broad daylight must be to make Gabrielle feel safe. After all, this person had done nothing but help her for the last two weeks. He or she was obviously a friend.

Reading the e-mail one last time, Gabrielle checked the clock. She had an hour.

The NASA administrator was feeling less edgy now that the meteorite was successfully out of the ice. *Everything is falling into place*, he told himself as he headed across the dome to the work area of Michael Tolland. *Nothing can stop us now.*

'How's it coming?' Ekstrom asked, striding up behind the television scientist.

Tolland glanced up from his computer, looking tired but enthusiastic. 'Editing is almost done. I'm just overlaying some of the extraction footage your people shot. Should be done momentarily.'

'Good.' The President had asked Ekstrom to upload Tolland's documentary to the White House as soon as possible.

Although Ekstrom had been cynical about the President's desire to use Michael Tolland on this project, seeing the rough cuts of Tolland's documentary had changed Ekstrom's mind. The television star's spirited narrative, combined with his interviews of the civilian scientists, had been brilliantly fused into a thrilling and comprehensible fifteen minutes of scientific programming. Tolland had achieved effortlessly what NASA so often failed to do – describe a scientific discovery at the level of the average American intellect without being patronizing.

'When you're done editing,' Ekstrom said, 'bring the finished product over to the press area. I'll have someone upload a digital copy to the White House.'

'Yes, sir.' Tolland went back to work.

Ekstrom moved on. When he arrived at the north wall, he was encouraged to find the habisphere's 'press area' had come together nicely. A large blue carpet had been rolled out on the ice. Centered on the rug sat a long symposium table with several microphones, a NASA drape, and an enormous American flag as a backdrop. To complete the visual drama, the meteorite had been transported on a palette sled to its position of honor, directly in front of the symposium table.

Ekstrom was pleased to see the mood in the press area was one of celebration. Much of his staff was now crowded around the meteorite, holding their hands out over its still-warm mass like campers around a campfire.

Ekstrom decided that this was the moment. He walked over to several cardboard boxes sitting on the ice behind the press area. He'd had the boxes flown in from Greenland this morning.

'Drinks are on me!' he yelled, handing out cans of beer to his cavorting staff.

'Hey, boss!' someone yelled. 'Thanks! It's even cold!'

Ekstrom gave a rare smile. 'I've been keeping it on ice.'

Everyone laughed.

'Wait a minute!' someone else yelled, scowling good-naturedly at his can. 'This stuff's Canadian! Where's your patriotism?'

'We're on a budget, here, folks. Cheapest stuff I could find.'

More laughter.

'*Attention shoppers,*' one of the NASA television crew yelled into a megaphone. '*We're about to switch to media lighting. You may experience temporary blindness.*'

'And no kissing in the dark,' someone yelled. 'This is a family program!'

Ekstrom chuckled, enjoying the raillery as his crew made final adjustments to the spotlights and accent lighting.

'Switching to media lighting in five, four, three, two . . .'

The dome's interior dimmed rapidly as the halogen lamps shut down. Within seconds, all the lights were off. An impenetrable darkness engulfed the dome.

Someone let out a mock scream.

'Who pinched my ass?' someone yelled, laughing.

The blackness lasted only a moment before it was pierced by the intense glare of media spotlights. Everyone squinted. The transformation was now complete; the north quadrant of the NASA habisphere had become a television studio. The remainder of the dome now looked like a gaping barn at night. The only light in the other sections was the muted reflection of the media lights reflecting off the arched ceiling and throwing long shadows across the now deserted work stations.

Ekstrom stepped back into the shadows, gratified to see his team carousing around the illuminated meteorite. He felt like a father at Christmas, watching his kids enjoy themselves around the tree.

God knows they deserve it, Ekstrom thought, never suspecting what calamity lay ahead.

The weather was changing.

Like a mournful harbinger of impending conflict, the katabatic wind let out a plaintive howl and gusted hard against the Delta Force's shelter. Delta-One finished battening down the storm coverings and went back inside to his two partners. They'd been through this before. It would soon pass.

Delta-Two was staring at the live video feed from the microbot. 'You better look at this,' he said.

Delta-One came over. The inside of the habisphere was in total darkness except for the bright lighting on the north side of the dome near the stage. The remainder of the habisphere appeared only as a dim outline. 'It's nothing,' he said. 'They're just testing their television lighting for tonight.'

'The lighting's not the problem.' Delta-Two pointed to the dark blob in the middle of the ice – the water-filled hole from which the meteorite had been extracted. '*That's* the problem.'

Delta-One looked at the hole. It was still surrounded by pylons, and the surface of the water appeared calm. 'I don't see anything.'

'Look again.' He maneuvered the joystick, spiraling the microbot down toward the surface of the hole.

As Delta-One studied the darkened pool of melted water more closely, he saw something that caused him to recoil in shock. 'What the . . . ?'

Delta-Three came over and looked. He too looked

stunned. 'My God. Is that the extraction pit? Is the water supposed to be doing that?'

'No,' Delta-One said. 'It sure as hell isn't.'

32

Although Rachel Sexton was currently sitting inside a large metal box situated 3,000 miles from Washington, D.C., she felt the same pressure as if she'd been summoned to the White House. The videophone monitor before her displayed a crystal clear image of President Zach Herney seated in the White House communications room before the presidential seal. The digital audio connection was flawless, and with the exception of an almost imperceptible delay, the man could have been in the next room.

Their conversation was upbeat and direct. The President seemed pleased, though not at all surprised, by Rachel's favorable assessment of NASA's find and of his choice to use Michael Tolland's captivating persona as a spokesman. The President's mood was good-natured and jocular.

'As I'm sure you will agree,' Herney said, his voice growing more serious now, 'in a perfect world, the ramifications of this discovery would be purely scientific in nature.' He paused, leaning forward, his face filling the screen. 'Unfortunately, we don't live in a perfect world, and this NASA triumph is going to be a political football the moment I announce it.'

'Considering the conclusive proof and who you've recruited for endorsements, I can't imagine how the public or any of your opposition will be able to do anything other than accept this discovery as confirmed fact.'

Herney gave an almost sad chuckle. 'My political opponents will *believe* what they see, Rachel. My concerns are that they won't *like* what they see.'

Rachel noted how careful the President was being not to mention her father. He spoke only in terms of 'the opposition' or 'political opponents.' 'And you think your opposition will cry conspiracy simply for political reasons?' she asked.

'That is the nature of the game. All anyone needs to do is cast a faint doubt, saying that this discovery is some kind of political fraud concocted by NASA and the White House, and all of a sudden, I'm facing an inquiry. The newspapers forget NASA has found proof of extraterrestrial life, and the media starts focusing on uncovering evidence of a conspiracy. Sadly, any innuendo of conspiracy with respect to this discovery will be bad for science, bad for the White House, bad for NASA, and, quite frankly, bad for the country.'

'Which is why you postponed announcing until you had full confirmation and some reputable civilian endorsements.'

'My goal is to present this data in so incontrovertible a way that any cynicism is nipped in the bud. I want this discovery celebrated with the untainted dignity it deserves. NASA merits no less.'

Rachel's intuition was tingling now. *What does he want from me?*

'Obviously,' he continued, 'you're in a unique position to help me. Your experience as an analyst as well as your obvious ties to my opponent give you enormous credibility with respect to this discovery.'

Rachel felt a growing disillusionment. *He wants to use me . . . just like Pickering said he would!*

'That said,' Herney continued, 'I would like to ask that you endorse this discovery *personally*, for the record, as my White House intelligence liaison . . . and as the daughter of my opponent.'

There it was. On the table.

Herney wants me to endorse.

Rachel really had thought Zach Herney was above this kind of spiteful politics. A public endorsement from Rachel would immediately make the meteorite a *personal* issue for her father, leaving the senator unable to attack the discovery's credibility without attacking the credibility of his own daughter – a death sentence for a 'families first' candidate.

'Frankly, sir,' Rachel said, looking into the monitor, 'I'm stunned you would ask me to do that.'

The President looked taken aback. 'I thought you would be excited to help out.'

'Excited? Sir, my differences with my father aside, this request puts me in an impossible position. I have enough problems with my father without going head-to-head with him in some kind of public death match. Despite my admitted dislike of the man, he *is* my father, and pitting me against him in a public forum frankly seems beneath you.'

'Hold on!' Herney waved his hands in surrender. 'Who said anything about a public forum?'

Rachel paused. 'I assume you'd like me to join the administrator of NASA on the podium for the eight o'clock press conference.'

Herney's guffaw boomed in the audio speakers. 'Rachel, what kind of man do you think I am? Do you really imagine I'd ask someone to stab her father in the back on national television?'

'But, you said—'

'And do you think I would make the NASA administrator share the limelight with the daughter of his arch enemy? Not to burst your bubble, Rachel, but this press conference is a *scientific* presentation. I'm not sure your knowledge of meteorites, fossils, or ice structures would lend the event much credibility.'

Rachel felt herself flush. 'But then . . . what endorsement did you have in mind?'

'One more appropriate to your position.'

'Sir?'

'You are my White House intelligence liaison. You brief my staff on issues of national importance.'

'You want me to endorse this for your *staff*?'

Herney still looked amused by the misunderstanding. 'Yes, I do. The skepticism I'll face *outside* the White House is nothing compared to what I'm facing from my staff right now. We're in the midst of a full-scale mutiny here. My credibility in-house is shot. My staff has begged me to cut back NASA funding. I've ignored them, and it's been political suicide.'

'Until now.'

'Exactly. As we discussed this morning, this discovery's timing will seem suspect to political cynics, and nobody's as cynical as my staff is at the moment. Therefore, when they hear this information for the first time, I want it to come from—'

'You haven't told your *staff* about the meteorite?'

'Only a few top advisers. Keeping this discovery a secret has been a top priority.'

Rachel was stunned. *No wonder he's facing a mutiny.* 'But this is not my usual area. A meteorite could hardly be considered an *intelligence*-related gist.'

'Not in the traditional sense, but it certainly has all the elements of your usual work – complex data that needs to be distilled, substantial political ramifications—'

'I am not a meteorite specialist, sir. Shouldn't your staff be briefed by the administrator of NASA?'

'Are you kidding? Everyone here hates him. As far as my staff is concerned, Ekstrom is the snake-oil salesman who has lured me into bad deal after bad deal.'

Rachel could see the point. 'How about Corky Marlinson? The National Medal in Astrophysics? He's got far more credibility than I do.'

'My staff is made up of politicians, Rachel, not scientists. You've met Dr Marlinson. I think he's terrific, but if I let an astrophysicist loose on my team of left-brain, think-inside-the-box intellectuals, I'll end up with a herd of deer in the headlights. I need someone accessible. You're the one, Rachel. My staff knows your work, and considering your family name, you're about as unbiased a spokesperson as my staff could hope to hear from.'

Rachel felt herself being pulled in by the President's affable style. 'At least you admit my being the daughter of your opponent has something to do with your request.'

The President gave a sheepish chuckle. 'Of course it does. But, as you can imagine, my staff will be briefed one way or another, no matter what you decide. You are not the cake, Rachel, you are simply the icing. You are the individual most qualified to do this briefing, and you also happen to be a close relative of the man who wants to kick my staff out of the White House next term. You've got credibility on two accounts.'

'You should be in sales.'

'As a matter of fact, I am. As is your father. And to be honest, I'd like to close a deal for a change.' The President removed his glasses and looked into Rachel's eyes. She felt a touch of her father's power in him. 'I am asking you as a favor, Rachel, and also because I believe it is part of your job. So which is it? Yes or no? Will you brief my staff on this matter?'

Rachel felt trapped inside the tiny PSC trailer. *Nothing like the hard sell.* Even from 3,000 miles away, Rachel could feel the strength of his will pressing through the video screen. She also knew this was a perfectly reasonable request, whether she liked it or not.

'I'd have conditions,' Rachel said.

Herney arched his eyebrows. 'Being?'

'I meet your staff in private. No reporters. This is a private briefing, not a public endorsement.'

'You have my word. Your meeting is already slated for a very private location.'

Rachel sighed. 'All right then.'

The President beamed. 'Excellent.'

Rachel checked her watch, surprised to see it was already a little past four o'clock. 'Hold on,' she said, puzzled, 'if you're going live at eight P.M., we don't have time. Even in that vile contraption you sent me up here in, I couldn't get back to the White House for another couple of hours at the very fastest. I'd have to prepare my remarks and—'

The President shook his head. 'I'm afraid I didn't make myself clear. You'll be doing the briefing from where you are via video conference.'

'Oh.' Rachel hesitated. 'What time did you have in mind?'

'Actually,' Herney said, grinning. 'How about right now? Everyone is already assembled, and they're staring at a big blank television set. They're waiting for you.'

Rachel's body tensed. 'Sir, I'm totally unprepared. I can't possibly—'

'Just tell them the truth. How hard is that?'

'But—'

'Rachel,' the President said, leaning toward the screen. 'Remember, you compile and relay data for a living. It's what you do. Just talk about what's going on up there.' He reached up to flick a switch on his video transmission gear, but paused. 'And I think you'll be pleased to find I've set you up in a position of power.'

Rachel didn't understand what he meant, but it was too late to ask. The President threw the switch.

The screen in front of Rachel went blank for a moment. When it refreshed, Rachel was staring at one of the most unnerving images she had ever seen. Directly in front of her was the White House Oval Office. It was packed. Standing room only. The entire White House staff appeared to be there. And every one of them was staring at her. Rachel now realized her view was from atop the President's desk.

Speaking from a position of power. Rachel was sweating already.

From the looks on the faces of the White House staffers, they were as surprised to see Rachel as she was to see them.

'Ms Sexton?' a raspy voice called out.

Rachel searched the sea of faces and found who had spoken. It was a lanky woman just now taking a seat in the front row. Marjorie Tench. The woman's distinctive appearance was unmistakable, even in a crowd.

162

'Thank you for joining us, Ms Sexton,' Marjorie Tench said, sounding smug. 'The President tells us you have some news?'

Enjoying the darkness, paleontologist Wailee Ming sat alone in quiet reflection at his private work area. His senses were alive with anticipation for tonight's event. *Soon I will be the most famous paleontologist in the world.* He hoped Michael Tolland had been generous and featured Ming's comments in the documentary.

As Ming savored his impending fame, a faint vibration shuddered through the ice beneath his feet, causing him to jump up. His earthquake instinct from living in Los Angeles made him hypersensitive to even the faintest palpitations of the ground. At the moment, though, Ming felt foolish to realize the vibration was perfectly normal. *It's just ice calving*, he reminded himself, exhaling. He still hadn't gotten used to it. Every few hours, a distant explosion rumbled through the night as somewhere along the glacial frontier a huge block of ice cracked off and fell into the sea. Norah Mangor had a nice way of putting it. *New icebergs being born . . .*

On his feet now, Ming stretched his arms. He looked across the habisphere, and off in the distance beneath the blaze of television spotlights, he could see a celebration was getting underway. Ming was not much for parties and headed in the opposite direction across the habisphere.

The labyrinth of deserted work areas now felt like a ghost town, the entire dome taking on an almost sepulchral feel. A chill seemed to have settled inside, and Ming buttoned up his long, camel-hair coat.

Up ahead he saw the extraction shaft – the point from which the most magnificent fossils in all of human history had been taken. The giant metal tripod had now been stowed and the pool sat alone, surrounded by pylons like some kind of shunned pothole on a vast parking lot of ice. Ming wandered over to the pit, standing a safe distance back, peering into the 200-foot-deep pool of frigid water. Soon it would refreeze, erasing all traces that anyone had ever been here.

The pool of water was a beautiful sight, Ming thought. Even in the dark.

Especially in the dark.

Ming hesitated at the thought. Then it registered.

There's something wrong.

As Ming focused more closely on the water, he felt his previous contentedness give way to a sudden whirlwind of confusion. He blinked his eyes, stared again, and then quickly turned his gaze across the dome . . . fifty yards away toward the mass of people celebrating in the press area. He knew they could not see him way over here in the dark.

I should tell someone about this, shouldn't I?

Ming looked again at the water, wondering what he would tell them. Was he seeing an optical illusion? Some kind of strange reflection?

Uncertain, Ming stepped beyond the pylons and squatted down at the edge of the pit. The water level was four feet below the ice level, and he leaned down to get a better look. Yes, something was definitely strange. It was impossible to miss, and yet it had not

164

become visible until the lights in the dome had gone out.

Ming stood up. Somebody definitely needed to hear about this. He started off at a hurried pace toward the press area. Completing only a few steps, Ming slammed on the brakes. *Good God!* He spun back toward the hole, his eyes going wide with realization. It had just dawned on him.

'Impossible!' he blurted aloud.

And yet Ming knew that was the only explanation. *Think carefully*, he cautioned. *There must be a more reasonable rationale.* But the harder Ming thought, the more convinced he was of what he was seeing. *There is no other explanation!* He could not believe that NASA and Corky Marlinson had somehow missed something this incredible, but Ming wasn't complaining.

This is Wailee Ming's discovery now!

Trembling with excitement, Ming ran to a nearby work area and found a beaker. All he needed was a little water sample. Nobody was going to believe this!

34

'As intelligence liaison to the White House,' Rachel Sexton was saying, trying to keep her voice from shaking as she addressed the crowd on the screen before her, 'my duties include traveling to political hot spots around the globe, analyzing volatile situations, and reporting to the President and White House staff.'

A bead of sweat formed just below her hairline and

Rachel dabbed it away, silently cursing the President for dropping this briefing into her lap with zero warning.

'Never before have my travels taken me to quite this exotic a spot.' Rachel motioned stiffly to the cramped trailer around her. 'Believe it or not, I am addressing you right now from above the Arctic Circle on a sheet of ice that is over three hundred feet thick.'

Rachel sensed a bewildered anticipation in the faces on the screen before her. They obviously knew they had been packed into the Oval Office for a reason, but certainly none of them imagined it would have anything to do with a development above the Arctic Circle.

The sweat was beading again. *Get it together, Rachel. This is what you do.* 'I sit before you tonight with great honor, pride, and . . . above all, excitement.'

Blank looks.

Screw it, she thought, angrily wiping the sweat away. *I didn't sign up for this.* Rachel knew what her mother would say if she were here now: *When in doubt, just spit it out!* The old Yankee proverb embodied one of her mom's basic beliefs – that all challenges can be overcome by speaking the truth, no matter how it comes out.

Taking a deep breath, Rachel sat up tall and looked straight into the camera. 'Sorry, folks, if you're wondering how I could be sweating my butt off above the Arctic Circle . . . I'm a little nervous.'

The faces before her seemed to jolt back a moment. Some uneasy laughter.

'In addition,' Rachel said, 'your boss gave me about ten seconds' warning before telling me I would be facing his entire staff. This baptism by fire is not exactly what I had in mind for my first visit to the Oval Office.'

More laughter this time.

'And,' she said, glancing down at the bottom of the screen, 'I had certainly not imagined I would be sitting at the President's desk . . . much less *on* it!'

This brought a hearty laugh and some broad smiles. Rachel felt her muscles starting to relax. *Just give it to them straight.*

'Here's the situation.' Rachel's voice now sounded like her own. Easy and clear. 'President Herney has been absent from the media spotlight this past week not because of his lack of interest in his campaign, but rather because he has been engrossed in another matter. One he felt was far more important.'

Rachel paused, her eyes making contact now with her audience.

'There has been a scientific discovery made in a location called the Milne Ice Shelf in the high Arctic. The President will be informing the world about it in a press conference tonight at eight o'clock. The find was made by a group of hardworking Americans who have endured a string of tough luck lately and deserve a break. I'm talking about NASA. You can be proud to know that your President, with apparent clairvoyant confidence, has made a point of standing beside NASA lately through thick and thin. Now, it appears his loyalty is going to be rewarded.'

It was not until that very instant that Rachel realized how historically momentous this was. A tightness rose in her throat, and she fought it off, plowing onward.

'As an intelligence officer who specializes in the analysis and verification of data, I am one of several people the President has called upon to examine the NASA data. I have examined it personally as well as

167

conferring with several specialists – both government and civilian – men and women whose credentials are beyond reproach and whose stature is beyond political influence. It is my professional opinion that the data I am about to present to you is factual in its origins and unbiased in its presentation. Moreover, it is my personal opinion that the President, in good faith to his office and the American people, has shown admirable care and restraint in delaying an announcement I know he would have loved to have made last week.'

Rachel watched the crowd before her exchanging puzzled looks. They all returned their gaze to her, and she knew she had their undivided attention.

'Ladies and gentlemen, you are about to hear what I'm sure you will agree is one of the most exciting pieces of information ever revealed in this office.'

35

The aerial view currently being transmitted to the Delta Force by the microbot circling inside the habisphere looked like something that would win an avant-garde film contest – the dim lighting, the glistening extraction hole, and the well-dressed Asian lying on the ice, his camel-hair coat splayed around him like enormous wings. He was obviously trying to extract a water sample.

'We've got to stop him,' said Delta-Three.

Delta-One agreed. The Milne Ice Shelf held secrets his team was authorized to protect with force.

'How do we stop him?' Delta-Two challenged,

still gripping the joystick. 'These microbots are not equipped.'

Delta-One scowled. The microbot currently hovering inside the habisphere was a recon model, stripped down for longer flight. It was about as lethal as a housefly.

'We should call the controller,' Delta-Three stated.

Delta-One stared intently at the image of the solitary Wailee Ming, perched precariously on the rim of the extraction pit. Nobody was anywhere near him – and ice cold water had a way of muffling one's ability to scream. 'Give me the controls.'

'What are you doing?' the soldier on the joystick demanded.

'What we were *trained* to do,' Delta-One snapped, taking over. 'Improvise.'

36

Wailee Ming lay on his stomach beside the extraction hole, his right arm extended over the rim trying to extract a water sample. His eyes were definitely not playing tricks on him; his face, now only a yard or so from the water, could see everything perfectly.

This is incredible!

Straining harder, Ming maneuvered the beaker in his fingers, trying to reach down to the surface of the water. All he needed was another few inches.

Unable to extend his arm any farther, Ming repositioned himself closer to the hole. He pressed the toes of his boots against the ice and firmly replanted his left hand on the rim. Again, he extended his right arm as far as he could. *Almost.* He shifted a little closer. *Yes!* The edge of the beaker broke the surface of the water. As the liquid flowed into the container, Ming stared in disbelief.

Then, without warning, something utterly inexplicable occurred. Out of the darkness, like a bullet from a gun, flew a tiny speck of metal. Ming only saw it for a fraction of a second before it smashed into his right eye.

The human instinct to protect one's eyes was so innately ingrained, that despite Ming's brain telling him that any sudden movements risked his balance, he recoiled. It was a jolting reaction more out of surprise than pain. Ming's left hand, closest to his face, shot up reflexively to protect the assaulted eyeball. Even as his hand was in motion, Ming knew he had made a mistake. With all of his weight leaning forward, and his only means of support suddenly gone, Wailee Ming teetered. He recovered too late. Dropping the beaker and trying to grab on to the slick ice to stop his fall, he slipped – plummeting forward into the darkened hole.

The fall was only four feet, and yet as Ming hit the icy water head first he felt like his face had hit pavement at fifty miles an hour. The liquid that engulfed his face was so cold it felt like burning acid. It brought an instantaneous spike of panic.

Upside down and in the darkness, Ming was momentarily disoriented, not knowing which way to turn toward the surface. His heavy camel-hair coat kept the icy blast from his body – but only for a second or two. Finally righting himself, Ming came sputtering up for air, just as the water found its way to his back and chest, engulfing his body in a lung-crushing vise of cold.

'Hee . . . lp,' he gasped, but Ming could barely pull in enough air to let out a whimper. He felt like the wind had been knocked out of him.

'Heee . . . lp!' His cries were inaudible even to himself. Ming clambered toward the side of the extraction pit and tried to pull himself out. The wall before him was vertical ice. Nothing to grab. Underwater, his boots kicked the side of the wall, searching for a foothold. Nothing. He strained upward, reaching for the rim. It was only a foot out of reach.

Ming's muscles were already having trouble responding. He kicked his legs harder, trying to propel himself high enough up the wall to grab the rim. His body felt like lead, and his lungs seemed to have shrunk to nothing, as if they were being crushed by a python. His water-laden coat was getting heavier by the second, pulling him downward. Ming tried to pull it off his body, but the heavy fabric stuck.

'Help . . . me!'

The fear came on in torrents now.

Drowning, Ming had once read, was the most horrific death imaginable. He had never dreamed he would find himself on the verge of experiencing it. His muscles refused to cooperate with his mind, and already he was fighting just to keep his head above water. His soggy clothing pulled him downward as his numb fingers scratched the sides of the pit.

His screams were only in his mind now.

And then it happened.

Ming went under. The sheer terror of being conscious of his own impending death was something he never imagined he would experience. And yet here he was . . . sinking slowly down the sheer ice wall of a 200-foot-deep hole in the ice. Multitudes of thoughts flashed before his eyes. Moments from his childhood. His career. He wondered if anyone would find him down here. Or would he simply sink to the bottom and freeze there . . . entombed in the glacier for all time.

Ming's lungs were screaming for oxygen. He held his breath, still trying to kick toward the surface. *Breathe!* He fought the reflex, clamping his insensate lips together. *Breathe!* He tried in vain to swim upward. *Breathe!* At that instant, in a deadly battle of human reflex against reason, Ming's breathing instinct overcame his ability to keep his mouth closed.

Wailee Ming inhaled.

The water crashing into his lungs felt like scalding oil on his sensitive pulmonary tissue. He felt like he was burning from the inside out. Cruelly, water does not kill immediately. Ming spent seven horrifying seconds inhaling in the icy water, each breath more painful than the last, each inhalation offering none of what his body so desperately craved.

Finally, as Ming slid downward into the icy darkness, he felt himself going unconscious. He welcomed the escape. All around him in the water Ming saw tiny glowing specks of light. It was the most beautiful thing he had ever seen.

37

The East Appointment Gate of the White House is located on East Executive Avenue between the Treasury Department and the East Lawn. The reinforced perimeter fence and cement bollards installed after the attack on the Marine barracks in Beirut give this entry an air that is anything but welcoming.

Outside the gate, Gabrielle Ashe checked her watch, feeling a growing nervousness. It was 4:45 P.M., and still nobody had made contact.

EAST APPOINTMENT GATE, 4:30 P.M. COME ALONE.

Here I am, she thought. *Where are you?*

Gabrielle scanned the faces of the tourists milling about, waiting for someone to catch her eye. A few men looked her over and moved on. Gabrielle was beginning to wonder if this had been such a good idea. She sensed the Secret Serviceman in the sentry shack had his eye on her now. Gabrielle decided her informant had gotten cold feet. Gazing one last time through the heavy fence toward the White House, Gabrielle sighed and turned to go.

'Gabrielle Ashe?' the Secret Serviceman called out behind her.

Gabrielle wheeled, her heart catching in her throat. *Yes?*

The man in the guard shack waved her over. He was lean with a humorless face. 'Your party is ready to see you now.' He unlocked the main gate and motioned for her to enter.

Gabrielle's feet refused to move. 'I'm coming inside?'

The guard nodded. 'I was asked to apologize for keeping you waiting.'

Gabrielle looked at the open doorway and still could not move. *What's going on?* This was not at all what she had expected.

'You are Gabrielle Ashe, are you not?' the guard demanded, looking impatient now.

173

'Yes, sir, but—'

'Then I strongly suggest you follow me.'

Gabrielle's feet jolted into motion. As she stepped tentatively over the threshold, the gate slammed shut behind her.

38

Two days without sunlight had rearranged Michael Tolland's biological clock. Although his watch said it was late afternoon, Tolland's body insisted it was the middle of the night. Now, having put the finishing touches on his documentary, Michael Tolland had downloaded the entire video file onto a digital video disk and was making his way across the darkened dome. Arriving at the illuminated press area, he delivered the disk to the NASA media technician in charge of overseeing the presentation.

'Thanks, Mike,' the technician said, winking as he held up the video disk. 'Kind of redefines "must-see TV," eh?'

Tolland gave a tired chuckle. 'I hope the President likes it.'

'No doubt. Anyhow, your work is done. Sit back and enjoy the show.'

'Thanks.' Tolland stood in the brightly lit press area and surveyed the convivial NASA personnel toasting the meteorite with cans of Canadian beer. Even though Tolland wanted to celebrate, he felt exhausted, emotionally drained. He glanced around for Rachel Sexton, but apparently she was still talking to the President.

He wants to put her on-air, Tolland thought. Not that he blamed him; Rachel would be a perfect addition to the cast of meteorite spokespeople. In addition to her good looks, Rachel exuded an accessible poise and self-confidence that Tolland seldom saw in the women he met. Then again, most of the women Tolland met were in television – either ruthless power women or gorgeous on-air 'personalities' who lacked exactly that.

Now, slipping quietly away from the crowd of bustling NASA employees, Tolland navigated the web of pathways across the dome, wondering where the other civilian scientists had disappeared to. If they felt half as drained as he did, they should be in the bunking area grabbing a catnap before the big moment. Ahead of him in the distance, Tolland could see the circle of SHABA pylons around the deserted extraction pit. The empty dome overhead seemed to echo with the hollow voices of distant memories. Tolland tried to block them out.

Forget the ghosts, he willed himself. They often haunted him at times like these, when he was tired or alone – times of personal triumph or celebration. *She should be with you right now*, the voice whispered. Alone in the darkness, he felt himself reeling backward into oblivion.

Celia Birch had been his sweetheart in graduate school. One Valentine's Day, Tolland took her to her favorite restaurant. When the waiter brought Celia's dessert, it was a single rose and a diamond ring. Celia understood immediately. With tears in her eyes, she spoke a single word that made Michael Tolland as happy as he'd ever been.

'Yes.'

Filled with anticipation, they bought a small house

near Pasadena, where Celia got a job as a science teacher. Although the pay was modest, it was a start, and it was also close to Scripps Institute of Oceanography in San Diego, where Tolland had landed his dream job aboard a geologic research ship. Tolland's work meant he was away for three or four days at a time, but his reunions with Celia were always passionate and exciting.

While at sea, Tolland began videotaping some of his adventures for Celia, making minidocumentaries of his work onboard the ship. After one trip, he returned with a grainy home video that he'd shot out of the window of a deepwater submersible – the first footage ever shot of a bizarre chemotropic cuttlefish that nobody even knew existed. On camera, as he narrated the video, Tolland was practically bursting out of the submarine with enthusiasm.

Literally thousands of undiscovered species, he gushed, *live in these depths! We've barely scratched the surface! There are mysteries down here that none of us can imagine!*

Celia was enthralled with her husband's ebullience and concise scientific explanation. On a whim, she showed the tape to her science class, and it became an instant hit. Other teachers wanted to borrow it. Parents wanted to make copies. It seemed everyone was eagerly awaiting Michael's next installment. Celia suddenly had an idea. She called a college friend of hers who worked for NBC and sent her a videotape.

Two months later, Michael Tolland came to Celia and asked her to take a walk with him on Kingman Beach. It was their special place, where they always went to share their hopes and dreams.

'I have something I want to tell you,' Tolland said.

Celia stopped, taking her husband's hands as the water lapped around their feet. 'What is it?'

Tolland was bursting. 'Last week, I got a call from NBC television. They think I should host an oceanic documentary series. It's perfect. They want to make a pilot next year! Can you believe it?'

Celia kissed him, beaming. 'I believe it. You'll be great.'

Six months later, Celia and Tolland were sailing near Catalina when Celia began complaining of pain in her side. They ignored it for a few weeks, but finally it got too much. Celia went in to have it checked out.

In an instant, Tolland's dream life shattered into a hellish nightmare. Celia was ill. Very ill.

'Advanced stages of lymphoma,' the doctors explained. 'Rare in people her age, but certainly not unheard of.'

Celia and Tolland visited countless clinics and hospitals, consulting with specialists. The answer was always the same. Incurable.

I will not accept that! Tolland immediately quit his job at Scripps Institute, forgot all about the NBC documentary, and focused all of his energy and love on helping Celia get well. She fought hard too, bearing the pain with a grace that only made him love her more. He took her for long walks on Kingman Beach, made her healthy meals, and told her stories of the things they would do when she got better.

But it was not to be.

Only seven months had passed when Michael Tolland found himself sitting beside his dying wife in a stark hospital ward. He no longer recognized her face. The savageness of the cancer was rivaled only by the brutality of the chemotherapy. She was left a ravaged skeleton. The final hours were the hardest.

'Michael,' she said, her voice raspy. 'It's time to let go.'

'I can't.' Tolland's eyes welled.

'You're a survivor,' Celia said. 'You have to be. Promise me you'll find another love.'

'I'll never want another.' Tolland meant it.

'You'll have to learn.'

Celia died on a crystal clear Sunday morning in June. Michael Tolland felt like a ship torn from its moorings and thrown adrift in a raging sea, his compass smashed. For weeks he spun out of control. Friends tried to help, but his pride could not bear their pity.

You have a choice to make, he finally realized. *Work or die.*

Hardening his resolve, Tolland threw himself back into *Amazing Seas*. The program quite literally saved his life. In the four years that followed, Tolland's show took off. Despite the matchmaking efforts of his friends, Tolland endured only a handful of dates. All were fiascos or mutual disappointments, so Tolland finally gave up and blamed his busy travel schedule for his lack of social life. His best friends knew better, though; Michael Tolland simply was not ready.

The meteorite extraction pit loomed before Tolland now, pulling him from his painful reverie. He shook off the chill of his memories and approached the opening. In the darkened dome, the melt water in the hole had taken on an almost surreal and magical beauty. The surface of the pool was shimmering like a moonlit pond. Tolland's eyes were drawn to specks of light on the top layer of the water, as if someone had sprinkled blue-green sparkles onto the surface. He stared a long moment at the shimmering.

Something about it seemed peculiar.

At first glance, he thought the gleaming water was simply reflecting the glow of the spotlights from across the dome. Now he saw this was not the case at all. The shimmers possessed a greenish tint and seemed to pulse in a rhythm, as if the surface of the water were alive, illuminating itself from within.

Unsettled, Tolland stepped beyond the pylons for a closer look.

Across the habisphere, Rachel Sexton exited the PSC trailer into darkness. She paused a moment, disoriented by the shadowy vault around her. The habisphere was now a gaping cavern, lit only by incidental effulgence radiating out from the stark media lights against the north wall. Unnerved by the darkness around her, she headed instinctively for the illuminated press area.

Rachel felt pleased with the outcome of her briefing of the White House staff. Once she'd recovered from the President's little stunt, she'd smoothly conveyed everything she knew about the meteorite. As she spoke, she watched the expressions on the faces of the President's staff go from incredulous shock, to hopeful belief, and finally to awestruck acceptance.

'Extraterrestrial life?' she had heard one of them exclaim. 'Do you know what that means?'

'Yes,' another replied. 'It means we're going to win this election.'

As Rachel approached the dramatic press area, she imagined the impending announcement and couldn't help but wonder if her father really deserved the presidential steamroller that was about to blindside him, crushing his campaign in a single blow.

The answer, of course, was yes.

Whenever Rachel Sexton felt any soft spot for her father, all she had to do was remember her mother.

Katherine Sexton. The pain and shame Sedgewick Sexton had brought on her was reprehensible . . . coming home late every night, looking smug and smelling of perfume. The feigned religious zeal her father hid behind – all the while lying and cheating, knowing Katherine would never leave him.

Yes, she decided, *Senator Sexton was about to get exactly what he deserved.*

The crowd in the press area was jovial. Everyone held beers. Rachel moved through the crowd feeling like a coed at a frat party. She wondered where Michael Tolland had gone.

Corky Marlinson materialized beside her. 'Looking for Mike?'

Rachel startled. 'Well . . . no . . . sort of.'

Corky shook his head in disgust. 'I knew it. Mike just left. I think he was headed back to go grab a few winks.' Corky squinted across the dusky dome. 'Although it looks like you can still catch him.' He gave her a puggish smile and pointed. 'Mike becomes mesmerized every time he sees water.'

Rachel followed Corky's outstretched finger toward the center of the dome, where the silhouette of Michael Tolland stood, gazing down into the water in the extraction pit.

'What's he doing?' she asked. 'That's kind of dangerous over there.'

Corky grinned. 'Probably taking a leak. Let's go push him.'

Rachel and Corky crossed the darkened dome toward the extraction pit. As they drew close to Michael Tolland, Corky called out.

'Hey, aqua man! Forget your swimsuit?'

Tolland turned. Even in the dimness, Rachel could

see his expression was uncharacteristically grave. His face looked oddly illuminated, as if he were being lit from below.

'Everything okay, Mike?' she asked.

'Not exactly.' Tolland pointed into the water.

Corky stepped over the pylons and joined Tolland at the edge of the shaft. Corky's mood seemed to cool instantly when he looked in the water. Rachel joined them, stepping past the pylons to the edge of the pit. When she peered into the hole, she was surprised to see specks of blue-green light shimmering on the surface. Like neon dust particles floating in the water. They seemed to be pulsating green. The effect was beautiful.

Tolland picked up a shard of ice off the glacial floor and tossed it into the water. The water phosphoresced at the point of impact, glowing with a sudden green splash.

'Mike,' Corky said, looking uneasy, 'please tell me you know what that is.'

Tolland frowned. 'I know exactly what this is. My question is, what the hell is it doing *here*?'

39

'We've got flagellates,' Tolland said, staring into the luminescent water.

'Flatulence?' Corky scowled. 'Speak for yourself.'

Rachel sensed Michael Tolland was in no joking mood.

'I don't know how it could have happened,' Tolland said, 'but somehow this water contains bioluminescent dinoflagellates.'

'Bioluminescent what?' Rachel said. *Speak English.*

'Monocelled plankton capable of oxidizing a luminescent catalyst called luceferin.'

That was English?

Tolland exhaled and turned to his friend. 'Corky, there any chance the meteorite we pulled out of that hole had living organisms on it?'

Corky burst out laughing. 'Mike, be serious!'

'I am serious.'

'No chance, Mike! Believe me, if NASA had any inkling whatsoever that there were extraterrestrial organisms living on that rock, you can be damn sure they never would have extracted it into the open air.'

Tolland looked only partially comforted, his relief apparently clouded by a deeper mystery. 'I can't be for sure without a microscope,' Tolland said, 'but it looks to me like this is a bioluminescent plankton from the phylum Pyrrophyta. Its name means fire plant. The Arctic Ocean is filled with it.'

Corky shrugged. 'So why'd you ask if they were from space?'

'Because,' Tolland said, 'the meteorite was buried in glacial ice – *fresh*water from snowfalls. The water in that hole is glacial melt and has been frozen for three centuries. How could ocean creatures get in there?'

Tolland's point brought a long silence.

Rachel stood at the edge of the pool and tried to get her mind around what she was looking at. *Bioluminescent plankton in the extraction shaft. What does it mean?*

'There's got to be a crack somewhere down there,' Tolland said. 'It's the only explanation. The plankton must have entered the shaft through a fissure in the ice that allowed ocean water to seep in.'

Rachel didn't understand. 'Seep in? From where?' She recalled her long IceRover ride in from the ocean. 'The coast is a good two miles from here.'

Both Corky and Tolland gave Rachel an odd look. 'Actually,' Corky said, 'the ocean is directly *underneath* us. This slab of ice is floating.'

Rachel stared at the two men, feeling utterly perplexed. 'Floating? But . . . we're on a glacier.'

'Yes, we're on a glacier,' Tolland said, 'but we're not over land. Glaciers sometimes flow off a landmass and fan out over water. Because ice is lighter than water, the glacier simply continues to flow, floating out over the ocean like an enormous ice raft. That's the definition of an ice *shelf* . . . the floating section of a glacier.' He paused. 'We're actually almost a mile out to sea at the moment.'

Shocked, Rachel instantly became wary. As she adjusted her mental picture of her surroundings, the thought of standing over the Arctic Ocean brought with it a sense of fear.

Tolland seemed to sense her uneasiness. He stamped his foot reassuringly on the ice. 'Don't worry. This ice is three hundred feet thick, with two hundred of those feet floating below the water like an ice cube in a glass. Makes the shelf very stable. You could build a skyscraper on this thing.'

Rachel gave a wan nod, not entirely convinced. The misgivings aside, she now understood Tolland's theory about the origins of the plankton. *He thinks there's a crack that goes all the way down to the ocean, allowing plankton to come up through it into the hole.* It was feasible, Rachel decided, and yet it involved a paradox that bothered her. Norah Mangor had been very clear about the integrity of the glacier, having drilled countless test cores to confirm its solidity.

Rachel looked at Tolland. 'I thought the glacier's perfection was the cornerstone of all the strata-dating records. Didn't Dr Mangor say the glacier had *no* cracks or fissures?'

Corky frowned. 'Looks like the ice queen muffed it.'

Don't say that too loudly, Rachel thought, *or you'll get an ice pick in the back.*

Tolland stroked his chin as he watched the phosphorescing creatures. 'There's literally no other explanation. There *must* be a crack. The weight of the ice shelf on top of the ocean must be pushing plankton-rich seawater up into the hole.'

One hell of a crack, Rachel thought. If the ice here was 300 feet thick and the hole was 200 feet deep, then this hypothetical crack had to pass through 100 feet of solid ice. *Norah Mangor's test cores showed no cracks.*

'Do me a favor,' Tolland said to Corky. 'Go find Norah. Let's hope to God she knows something about this glacier that she's not telling us. And find Ming, too, maybe he can tell us what these little glow-beasties are.'

Corky headed off.

'Better hurry,' Tolland called after him, glancing back into the hole. 'I could swear this bioluminescence is fading.'

Rachel looked at the hole. Sure enough, the green was not so brilliant now.

Tolland removed his parka and lay down on the ice next to the hole.

Rachel watched, confused. 'Mike?'

'I want to find out if there's any saltwater flowing in.'

'By lying on the ice without a coat?'

'Yup.' Tolland crawled on his belly to the edge of the

hole. Holding one sleeve of the coat over the edge, he let the other sleeve dangle down the shaft until the cuff skimmed the water. 'This is a highly accurate salinity test used by world-class oceanographers. It's called "licking a wet jacket."'

Out on the ice shelf, Delta-One struggled with the controls, trying to keep the damaged microbot in flight over the group now assembled around the excavation pit. From the sounds of the conversation beneath, he knew things were unraveling fast.

'Call the controller,' he said. 'We've got a serious problem.'

40

Gabrielle Ashe had taken the White House public tour countless times in her youth, secretly dreaming of someday working inside the presidential mansion, and becoming part of the elite team that charted the country's future. At the moment, however, she would have preferred to be anywhere else in the world.

As the Secret Serviceman from the East Gate led Gabrielle into an ornate foyer, she wondered what in the world her anonymous informant was trying to prove. Inviting Gabrielle into the White House was insane. *What if I'm seen?* Gabrielle had become quite visible lately in the media as Senator Sexton's right-hand aide. Certainly someone would recognize her.

'Ms Ashe?'

Gabrielle looked up. A kind-faced sentry in the foyer

gave her a welcoming smile. 'Look over there, please.'
He pointed.

Gabrielle looked where he was pointing and was blinded by a flashbulb.

'Thank you, ma'am.' The sentry led her to a desk and handed her a pen. 'Please sign the entry log.' He pushed a heavy leather binder in front of her.

Gabrielle looked at the log. The page before her was blank. She recalled hearing once that all White House visitors sign on their own blank page to preserve the privacy of their visit. She signed her name.

So much for a secret meeting.

Gabrielle walked through a metal detector, and was then given a cursory pat down.

The sentry smiled. 'Enjoy your visit, Ms Ashe.'

Gabrielle followed the Secret Serviceman fifty feet down a tiled hallway to a second security desk. Here, another sentry was assembling a guest pass that was just rolling out of a lamination machine. He punched a hole in it, affixed a neck cord, and slipped it over Gabrielle's head. The plastic was still warm. The photo on the ID was the snapshot they had taken fifteen seconds earlier down the hall.

Gabrielle was impressed. *Who says government is inefficient?*

They continued, the Secret Serviceman leading her deeper into the White House complex. Gabrielle was feeling more uneasy with every step. Whoever had extended the mysterious invitation certainly was not concerned about keeping the meeting private. Gabrielle had been issued an official pass, signed the guest log, and was now being marched in plain view through the first floor of the White House where public tours were gathered.

186

'And this is the China Room,' a tour guide was saying to a group of tourists, 'home of Nancy Reagan's $952 per setting red-rimmed china that sparked a debate over conspicuous consumption back in 1981.'

The Secret Serviceman led Gabrielle past the tour toward a huge marble staircase, where another tour was ascending. 'You are about to enter the thirty-two-hundred-square-foot East Room,' the guide was narrating, 'where Abigail Adams once hung John Adams's laundry. Then we will pass to the Red Room, where Dolley Madison liquored up visiting heads of state before James Madison negotiated with them.'

The tourists laughed.

Gabrielle followed past the stairway through a series of ropes and barricades into a more private section of the building. Here they entered a room Gabrielle had only seen in books and on television. Her breath grew short.

My God, this is the Map Room!

No tour ever came in here. The room's paneled walls could swing outward to reveal layer upon layer of world maps. This was the place where Roosevelt had charted the course of World War II. Unsettlingly, it was also the room from which Clinton had admitted his affair with Monica Lewinsky. Gabrielle pushed that particular thought from her mind. Most important, the Map Room was a passageway into the West Wing – the area inside the White House where the true power-brokers worked. This was the last place Gabrielle Ashe had expected to be going. She had imagined her e-mail was coming from some enterprising young intern or secretary working in one of the complex's more mundane offices. Apparently not.

I'm going into the West Wing . . .

The Secret Serviceman marched her to the very end of a carpeted hallway and stopped at an unmarked door. He knocked. Gabrielle's heart was pounding.

'It's open,' someone called from inside.

The man opened the door and motioned for Gabrielle to enter.

Gabrielle stepped in. The shades were down, and the room was dim. She could see the faint outline of a person sitting at a desk in the darkness.

'Ms Ashe?' The voice came from behind a cloud of cigarette smoke. 'Welcome.'

As Gabrielle's eyes accustomed to the dark, she began to make out an unsettlingly familiar face, and her muscles went taut with surprise. *THIS is who has been sending me e-mail?*

'Thank you for coming,' Marjorie Tench said, her voice cold.

'Ms . . . Tench?' Gabrielle stammered, suddenly unable to breathe.

'Call me Marjorie.' The hideous woman stood up, blowing smoke out of her nose like a dragon. 'You and I are about to become best friends.'

41

Norah Mangor stood at the extraction shaft beside Tolland, Rachel, and Corky and stared into the pitch-black meteorite hole. 'Mike,' she said, 'you're cute, but you're insane. There's no bioluminescence here.'

Tolland now wished he'd thought to take some video; while Corky had gone to find Norah and Ming, the bioluminescence had begun fading rapidly. Within a couple of minutes, all the twinkling had simply stopped.

Tolland threw another piece of ice into the water, but nothing happened. No green splash.

'Where did they go?' Corky asked.

Tolland had a fairly good idea. Bioluminescence – one of nature's most ingenious defense mechanisms – was a natural response for plankton in distress. A plankton sensing it was about to be consumed by larger organisms would begin flashing in hopes of attracting much larger predators that would scare off the original attackers. In this case, the plankton, having entered the shaft through a crack, suddenly found themselves in a primarily freshwater environment and bioluminesced in panic as the freshwater slowly killed them. 'I think they died.'

'They were murdered,' Norah scoffed. 'The Easter Bunny swam in and ate them.'

Corky glared at her. 'I saw the luminescence too, Norah.'

'Was it before or after you took LSD?'

'Why would we lie about this?' Corky demanded.

'Men lie.'

'Yeah, about sleeping with other women, but never about bioluminescent plankton.'

Tolland sighed. 'Norah, certainly you're aware that plankton *do* live in the oceans beneath the ice.'

'Mike,' she replied with a glare, 'please don't tell me my business. For the record, there are over two hundred species of diatoms that thrive under Arctic ice shelves. Fourteen species of autotrophic nanno-flagellates, twenty heterotrophic flagellates, forty heterotrophic dinoflagellates, and several metazoans, including polychaetes, amphipods, copepods, euphausids, and fish. Any questions?'

Tolland frowned. 'Clearly you know more about Arctic fauna than I do, and you agree there's plenty of life underneath us. So why are you so skeptical that we saw bioluminescent plankton?'

'Because, Mike, this shaft is *sealed*. It's a closed, freshwater environment. No ocean plankton could possibly get in here!'

'I tasted salt in the water,' Tolland insisted. 'Very faint, but present. Saltwater is getting in here somehow.'

'Right,' Norah said skeptically. 'You tasted salt. You licked the sleeve of an old sweaty parka, and now you've decided that the PODS density scans and fifteen separate core samples are inaccurate.'

Tolland held out the wet sleeve of his parka as proof.

'Mike, I'm not licking your damn jacket.' She looked into the hole. 'Might I ask why droves of alleged plankton decided to swim into this alleged crack?'

'Heat?' Tolland ventured. 'A lot of sea creatures are attracted by heat. When we extracted the meteorite, we heated it. The plankton may have been drawn instinctively toward the temporarily warmer environment in the shaft.'

Corky nodded. 'Sounds logical.'

'Logical?' Norah rolled her eyes. 'You know, for a prize-winning physicist and a world-famous oceanographer, you're a couple of pretty dense specimens. Has it occurred to you that even if there is a crack – which I can assure you there is not – it is physically impossible for any seawater to be flowing *into* this shaft.' She stared at both of them with pathetic disdain.

'But, Norah . . .' Corky began.

'Gentlemen! We're standing *above* sea level here.' She stamped her foot on the ice. 'Hello? This ice sheet rises a hundred feet above the sea. You might recall the big cliff at the end of this shelf? We're higher than the ocean. If there were a fissure into this shaft, the water would be flowing *out* of this shaft, not into it. It's called gravity.'

Tolland and Corky looked at each other.

'Shit,' Corky said. 'I didn't think of that.'

Norah pointed into the water-filled shaft. 'You may also have noticed that the water level isn't changing?'

Tolland felt like an idiot. Norah was absolutely right. If there had been a crack, the water would be flowing *out*, not in. Tolland stood in silence a long moment, wondering what to do next.

'Okay,' Tolland sighed. 'Apparently, the fissure theory makes no sense. But we saw bioluminescence in the water. The only conclusion is that this is not a closed environment after all. I realize much of your ice-dating data is built on the premise that the glacier is a solid block, but—'

'Premise?' Norah was obviously getting agitated. 'Remember, this was not just *my* data, Mike. NASA made the same findings. We *all* confirmed this glacier is solid. No cracks.'

Tolland glanced across the dome toward the crowd gathered around the press conference area. 'Whatever is going on, I think, in good faith, we need to inform the administrator and—'

'This is bullshit!' Norah hissed. 'I'm telling you this glacial matrix is pristine. I'm not about to have my core data questioned by a salt lick and some absurd hallucinations.' She stormed over to a nearby supply area and began collecting some tools. 'I'll take a proper

191

water sample, and show you this water contains no saltwater plankton – living or dead!'

Rachel and the others looked on as Norah used a sterile pipette on a string to harvest a water sample from the melt pool. Norah placed several drops in a tiny device that resembled a miniature telescope. Then she peered through the oculus, pointing the device toward the light emanating from the other side of the dome. Within seconds she was cursing.

'Jesus Christ!' Norah shook the device and looked again. 'Damn it! Something's got to be wrong with this refractometer!'

'Saltwater?' Corky gloated.

Norah frowned. 'Partial. It's registering three percent brine – which is totally impossible. This glacier is a snow pack. Pure freshwater. There should be no salt.' Norah carried the sample to a nearby microscope and examined it. She groaned.

'Plankton?' Tolland asked.

'*G. polyhedra*,' she replied, her voice now sedate. 'It's one of the planktons we glaciologists commonly see in the oceans under ice shelves.' She glanced over at Tolland. 'They're dead now. Obviously they didn't survive long in a three percent saltwater environment.'

The four of them stood in silence a moment beside the deep shaft.

Rachel wondered what the ramifications of this paradox were for the overall discovery. The dilemma appeared minor when compared to the overall scope of the meteorite, and yet, as an intel analyst, Rachel had witnessed the collapse of entire theories based on smaller snags than this.

'What's going on over here?' The voice was a low rumble.

Everyone looked up. The bearish frame of the NASA administrator emerged from the dark.

'Minor quandary with the water in the shaft,' Tolland said. 'We're trying to sort it out.'

Corky sounded almost gleeful. 'Norah's ice data is screwed.'

'Bite me twice,' Norah whispered.

The administrator approached, his furry eyebrows lowering. 'What's wrong with the ice data?'

Tolland heaved an uncertain sigh. 'We're showing a three percent saltwater mix in the meteorite shaft, which contradicts the glaciology report that the meteorite was encased in a pristine freshwater glacier.' He paused. 'There's also plankton present.'

Ekstrom looked almost angry. 'Obviously that's impossible. There are no fissures in this glacier. The PODS scans confirmed that. This meteorite was sealed in a solid matrix of ice.'

Rachel knew Ekstrom was correct. According to NASA's density scans, the ice sheet was rock solid. Hundreds of feet of frozen glacier on all sides of the meteorite. No cracks. And yet as Rachel imagined how density scans were taken, a strange thought occurred to her . . .

'In addition,' Ekstrom was saying, 'Dr Mangor's core samples confirmed the solidity of the glacier.'

'Exactly!' Norah said, tossing the refractometer on a desk. 'Double corroboration. No fault lines in the ice. Which leaves us no explanation whatsoever for the salt and plankton.'

'Actually,' Rachel said, the boldness of her voice surprising even herself. 'There *is* another possibility.'

The brainstorm had hit her from the most unlikely of memories.

Everyone was looking at her now, their skepticism obvious.

Rachel smiled. 'There's a perfectly sound rationale for the presence of salt and plankton.' She gave Tolland a wry look. 'And frankly, Mike, I'm surprised it didn't occur to you.'

42

'Plankton *frozen* in the glacier?' Corky Marlinson sounded not at all sold on Rachel's explanation. 'Not to rain on your parade, but usually when things freeze they die. These little buggers were flashing us, remember?'

'Actually,' Tolland said, giving Rachel an impressed look, 'she may have a point. There are a number of species that enter suspended animation when their environment requires it. I did an episode on that phenomenon once.'

Rachel nodded. 'You showed northern pike that got frozen in lakes and had to wait until the thaw to swim away. You also talked about microorganisms called "waterbears" that became totally dehydrated in the desert, remained that way for decades, and then re-inflated when rains returned.'

Tolland chuckled. 'So you really *do* watch my show?'

Rachel gave a slightly embarrassed shrug.

'What's your point, Ms Sexton?' Norah demanded.

'Her point,' Tolland said, 'which should have dawned

on me earlier, is that one of the species I mentioned on that program was a kind of plankton that gets frozen in the polar ice cap every winter, hibernates inside the ice, and then swims away every summer when the ice cap thins.' Tolland paused. 'Granted the species I featured on the show was not the bioluminescent species we saw here, but maybe the same thing happened.'

'Frozen plankton,' Rachel continued, excited to have Michael Tolland so enthusiastic about her idea, 'could explain everything we're seeing here. At some point in the past, fissures could have opened in this glacier, filled with plankton-rich saltwater, and then refroze. What if there were *frozen* pockets of saltwater in this glacier? Frozen saltwater containing frozen plankton? Imagine if while you were raising the heated meteorite through the ice, it passed through a frozen saltwater pocket. The saltwater ice would have melted, releasing the plankton from hibernation, and giving us a small percentage of salt mixed in the freshwater.'

'Oh, for the love of God!' Norah exclaimed with a hostile groan. 'Suddenly *everyone's* a glaciologist!'

Corky also looked skeptical. 'But wouldn't PODS have spotted any brine ice pockets when it did its density scans? After all, brine ice and freshwater ice have different densities.'

'*Barely* different,' Rachel said.

'Four percent is a substantial difference,' Norah challenged.

'Yes, in a *lab*,' Rachel replied. 'But PODS takes its measurements from 120 miles up in space. Its computers were designed to differentiate between the obvious – ice and slush, granite and limestone.' She turned to the administrator. 'Am I right to assume that when PODS measures densities from space, it probably lacks the resolution to distinguish brine ice from fresh ice?'

The administrator nodded. 'Correct. A four percent differential is below PODS's tolerance threshold. The satellite would see brine ice and fresh ice as identical.'

Tolland now looked intrigued. 'This would also explain the static water level in the shaft.' He looked at Norah. 'You said the plankton species you saw in the extraction shaft was called—'

'*G. polyhedra*,' Norah declared. 'And now you're wondering if *G. polyhedra* is capable of hibernating inside the ice? You'll be pleased to know the answer is *yes*. Absolutely. *G. polyhedra* is found in droves around ice shelves, it bioluminesces, and it can hibernate inside the ice. Any other questions?'

Everyone exchanged looks. From Norah's tone, there was obviously some sort of 'but' – and yet it seemed she had just confirmed Rachel's theory.

'So,' Tolland ventured, 'you're saying it's possible, right? This theory makes sense?'

'Sure,' Norah said, 'if you're totally retarded.'

Rachel glared. 'I *beg* your pardon?'

Norah Mangor locked stares with Rachel. 'I imagine in your business, a little bit of knowledge is a dangerous thing? Well, trust me when I tell you that the same holds true for glaciology.' Norah's eyes shifted now, looking at each of the four people around her. 'Let me clarify this for everyone once and for all. The frozen brine pockets that Ms Sexton has proposed do occur. They are what glaciologists call interstices. Interstices, however, form not as pockets of saltwater but rather as highly branched networks of brine ice whose tendrils are as wide as a human hair. That meteorite would have had to pass through one hell of a dense series of interstices to release enough saltwater to create a three percent mixture in a pool that deep.'

Ekstrom scowled. 'So is it possible or not?'

'Not on your life,' Norah said flatly. 'Totally imposs-ible. I would have hit pockets of brine ice in my core samples.'

'Core samples are drilled essentially in random spots, right?' Rachel asked. 'Is there any chance the cores' placements, simply by bad luck, could have missed a pocket of sea ice?'

'I drilled directly down *over* the meteorite. Then I drilled multiple cores only a few yards on either side. You can't get any closer.'

'Just asking.'

'The point is moot,' Norah said. 'Brine interstices occur only in *seasonal* ice – ice that forms and melts every season. The Milne Ice Shelf is *fast* ice – ice that forms in the mountains and holds fast until it migrates to the calving zone and falls into the sea. As convenient as frozen plankton would be for explaining this mysterious little phenomenon, I can guarantee there are no hidden networks of frozen plankton in this glacier.'

The group fell silent again.

Despite the stark rebuttal of the frozen plankton theory, Rachel's systematic analysis of the data refused to accept the rejection. Instinctively, Rachel knew that the presence of frozen plankton in the glacier beneath them was the simplest solution to the riddle. *The Law of Parsimony,* she thought. Her NRO instructors had driven it into her subconscious. *When multiple explanations exist, the simplest is usually correct.*

Norah Mangor obviously had a lot to lose if her ice-core data was wrong, and Rachel wondered if maybe Norah had seen the plankton, realized she'd made a mistake in claiming the glacier was solid, and was now simply trying to cover her tracks.

'All I know,' Rachel said, 'is that I just briefed the entire White House staff and told them this meteorite was discovered in a pristine matrix of ice and had been sealed there, untouched by outside influence since 1716, when it broke off of a famous meteorite called the Jungersol. This fact now appears to be in some question.'

The NASA administrator was silent, his expression grave.

Tolland cleared his throat. 'I have to agree with Rachel. There was saltwater and plankton in the pool. No matter what the explanation is, that shaft is obviously not a closed environment. We can't say it is.'

Corky was looking uncomfortable. 'Um, folks, not to sound like the astrophysicist here, but in my field when we make mistakes, we're usually off by *billions* of years. Is this little plankton/saltwater mix-up really all that important? I mean, the perfection of the ice surrounding the meteorite in no way affects the meteorite itself, right? We still have the fossils. Nobody is questioning *their* authenticity. If it turns out we've made a mistake with the ice-core data, nobody will really care. All they'll care about is that we found proof of life on another planet.'

'I'm sorry, Dr Marlinson,' Rachel said, 'as someone who analyzes data for a living, I have to disagree. Any tiny flaw in the data NASA presents tonight has the potential to cast doubt over the credibility of the entire discovery. Including the authenticity of the fossils.'

Corky's jaw fell open. 'What are you talking about? Those fossils are irrefutable!'

'I know that. You know that. But if the public catches wind that NASA knowingly presented ice-core data that was in question, trust me, they will immediately start wondering what else NASA lied about.'

Norah stepped forward, eyes flashing. 'My ice-core data is *not* in question.' She turned to the administrator. 'I can *prove* to you, categorically, that there is no brine ice trapped anywhere in this ice shelf!'

The administrator eyed her a long moment. 'How?'

Norah outlined her plan. When she was done, Rachel had to admit, the idea sounded like a reasonable one.

The administrator did not look so sure. 'And the results will be definitive?'

'One hundred percent confirmation,' Norah assured him. 'If there's one goddamn ounce of frozen saltwater anywhere near that meteorite shaft, you will see it. Even a few droplets will light up on my gear like Times Square.'

The administrator's brow furrowed beneath his military buzz cut. 'There's not much time. The press conference is in a couple of hours.'

'I can be back in twenty minutes.'

'How far out on the glacier did you say you have to go?'

'Not far. Two hundred yards should do it.'

Ekstrom nodded. 'Are you certain it's safe?'

'I'll take flares,' Norah replied. 'And Mike will go with me.'

Tolland's head shot up. 'I will?'

'You sure as hell will, Mike! We'll be tethered. I'd appreciate a strong set of arms out there if the wind whips up.'

'But—'

'She's right,' the administrator said, turning to

Tolland. 'If she goes, she can't go alone. I'd send some of my men with her, but frankly, I'd rather keep this plankton issue to ourselves until we figure out if it's a problem or not.'

Tolland gave a reluctant nod.

'I'd like to go too,' Rachel said.

Norah spun like a cobra. 'The hell you will.'

'Actually,' the administrator said, as if an idea had just occurred to him, 'I think I'd feel safer if we used the standard quad tether configuration. If you go dual, and Mike slips, you'll never hold him. Four people are a lot safer than two.' He paused glancing at Corky. 'That would mean either you or Dr Ming.' Ekstrom glanced around the habisphere. 'Where is Dr Ming, anyway?'

'I haven't seen him in a while,' Tolland said. 'He might be catching a nap.'

Ekstrom turned to Corky. 'Dr Marlinson, I cannot require that you go out with them, and yet—'

'What the hell?' Corky said. 'Seeing as everyone is getting along so well.'

'No!' Norah exclaimed. 'Four people will slow us down. Mike and I are going alone.'

'You are *not* going alone.' The administrator's tone was final. 'There's a reason tethers are built as quads, and we're going to do this as safely as possible. The last thing I need is an accident a couple hours before the biggest press conference in NASA's history.'

Gabrielle Ashe felt a precarious uncertainty as she sat in the heavy air of Marjorie Tench's office. *What could this woman possibly want with me?* Behind the room's sole desk, Tench leaned back in her chair, her hard features seeming to radiate pleasure with Gabrielle's discomfort.

'Does the smoke bother you?' Tench asked, tapping a fresh cigarette from her pack.

'No,' Gabrielle lied.

Tench was already lighting up anyway. 'You and your candidate have taken quite an interest in NASA during this campaign.'

'True,' Gabrielle snapped, making no effort to hide her anger, 'thanks to some creative encouragement. I'd like an explanation.'

Tench gave an innocent pout. 'You want to know why I've been sending you e-mail fodder for your attack on NASA?'

'The information you sent me hurt your President.'

'In the short run, yes.'

The ominous tone in Tench's voice made Gabrielle uneasy. 'What's that supposed to mean?'

'Relax, Gabrielle. My e-mails didn't change things much. Senator Sexton was NASA-bashing long before I stepped in. I simply helped him clarify his message. Solidify his position.'

'Solidify his position?'

'Exactly.' Tench smiled, revealing stained teeth.

'Which, I must say, he did quite effectively this afternoon on CNN.'

Gabrielle recalled the senator's reaction to Tench's fence-buster question. *Yes, I would act to abolish NASA.* Sexton had gotten himself cornered, but he'd played out of the rough with a strong drive. It was the right move. Wasn't it? From Tench's contented look, Gabrielle sensed there was information missing.

Tench stood suddenly, her lanky frame dominating the cramped space. With the cigarette dangling from her lips, she walked over to a wall safe, removed a thick manila envelope, returned to the desk, and sat back down.

Gabrielle eyed the burgeoning envelope.

Tench smiled, cradling the envelope in her lap like a poker player holding a royal flush. Her yellowed fingertips flicked at the corner, making an annoying repetitive scratch, as if savoring the anticipation.

Gabrielle knew it was just her own guilty conscience, but her first fears were that the envelope contained some kind of proof of her sexual indiscretion with the senator. *Ridiculous*, she thought. The encounter had occurred after hours in Sexton's locked senatorial office. Not to mention, if the White House actually had any evidence, they would have gone public with it already.

They may be suspicious, Gabrielle thought, *but they don't have proof.*

Tench crushed out her cigarette. 'Ms Ashe, whether or not you are aware, you are caught in the middle of a battle that has been raging behind the scenes in Washington since 1996.'

This opening gambit was not at all what Gabrielle expected. 'I beg your pardon?'

Tench lit another cigarette. Her spindly lips curled

around it, and the tip glowed red. 'What do you know about a bill called the Space Commercialization Promotions Act?'

Gabrielle had never heard of it. She shrugged, lost.

'Really?' Tench said. 'That surprises me. Considering your candidate's platform. The Space Commercialization Promotions Act was proposed back in 1996 by Senator Walker. The bill, in essence, cites the failure of NASA to do anything worthwhile since putting a man on the moon. It calls for the privatization of NASA by immediately selling off NASA assets to private aerospace companies and allowing the free-market system to explore space more efficiently, thus relieving the burden NASA now places on taxpayers.'

Gabrielle had heard NASA critics suggest privatization as a solution to NASA's woes, but she was not aware the idea had actually taken the form of an official bill.

'This commercialization bill,' Tench said, 'has been presented to Congress four times now. It is similar to bills that have successfully privatized government industries like uranium production. Congress has passed the space commercialization bill all four times it has seen it. Thankfully, the White House vetoed it on all occasions. Zachary Herney has had to veto it twice.'

'Your point?'

'My point is that this bill is one Senator Sexton will certainly support if he becomes President. I have reason to believe Sexton will have no qualms about selling off NASA assets to commercial bidders the first chance he gets. In short, your candidate would support privatization over having American tax dollars fund space exploration.'

'To my knowledge, the senator has never commented

publicly about his stance on any Space Commercialization Promotions Act.'

'True. And yet knowing his politics, I assume you would not be surprised if he supported it.'

'Free-market systems tend to breed efficiency.'

'I'll take that as a "yes." ' Tench stared. 'Sadly, privatizing NASA is an abominable idea, and there are countless reasons why every White House administration since the bill's inception has shot it down.'

'I've heard the arguments against privatizing space,' Gabrielle said, 'and I understand your concerns.'

'Do you?' Tench leaned toward her. 'Which arguments have you heard?'

Gabrielle shifted uneasily. 'Well, the standard academic fears mostly – the most common being that if we privatize NASA, our current pursuit of scientific space knowledge would be quickly abandoned in favor of profitable ventures.'

'True. Space science would die in a heartbeat. Instead of spending money to study our universe, private space companies would strip-mine asteroids, build tourist hotels in space, offer commercial satellite launch services. Why would private companies bother studying the origins of our universe when it would cost them billions and show no financial return?'

'They wouldn't,' Gabrielle countered. 'But certainly a National Endowment for Space Science could be founded to fund academic missions.'

'We already have that system in place. It's called NASA.'

Gabrielle fell silent.

'The abandonment of science in favor of profits is a side issue,' Tench said. 'Hardly relevant compared to the utter chaos that would result by permitting the private sector to run free in space. We would have the wild west all over again. We would see pioneers staking claims on the moon and on asteroids and protecting those claims with force. I've heard petitions from companies who want to build neon billboards that blink advertisements in the nighttime sky. I've seen petitions from space hotels and tourist attractions whose proposed operations include ejecting their trash into the void of space and creating orbiting trash heaps. In fact, I just read a proposal yesterday from a company that wants to turn space into a mausoleum by launching the deceased into orbit. Can you imagine our telecommunications satellites colliding with dead bodies? Last week, I had a billionaire CEO in my office who was petitioning to launch a mission to a near-field asteroid, drag it closer to earth, and mine it for precious minerals. I actually had to remind this guy that dragging asteroids into near earth orbit posed potential risks of global catastrophe! Ms Ashe, I can assure you, if this bill passes, the throngs of entrepreneurs rushing into space will not be rocket scientists. They will be entrepreneurs with deep pockets and shallow minds.'

'Persuasive arguments,' Gabrielle said, 'and I'm sure the senator would weigh those issues carefully if he ever found himself in a position to vote on the bill. Might I ask what any of this has to do with me?'

Tench's gaze narrowed over her cigarette. 'A lot of people stand to make a lot of money in space, and the political lobby is mounting to remove all restrictions and open the floodgates. The veto power of the office of the President is the only remaining barrier against privatization . . . against complete anarchy in space.'

'Then I commend Zach Herney for vetoing the bill.'

'My fear is that your candidate would not be so prudent if elected.'

'Again, I assume the senator would carefully weigh all the issues if he were ever in a position to pass judgment on the bill.'

Tench did not look entirely convinced. 'Do you know how much Senator Sexton spends on media advertising?'

The question came out of left field. 'Those figures are public domain.'

'More than three million a month.'

Gabrielle shrugged. 'If you say so.' The figure was close.

'That's a lot of money to spend.'

'He's *got* a lot of money to spend.'

'Yes, he planned well. Or rather, *married* well.' Tench paused to blow smoke. 'It's sad about his wife, Katherine. Her death hit him hard.' A tragic sigh followed, clearly feigned. 'Her death was not all that long ago, was it?'

'Come to your point, or I'm leaving.'

Tench let out a lung-shaking cough and reached for the burgeoning manila folder. She pulled out a small stack of stapled papers and handed them to Gabrielle. 'Sexton's financial records.'

Gabrielle studied the documents in astonishment. The records went back several years. Although Gabrielle was not privy to the internal workings of Sexton's finances, she sensed this data was authentic – banking accounts, credit card accounts, loans, stock assets, real estate assets, debts, capital gains and losses. 'This is private data. Where did you get this?'

'My source is not your concern. But if you spend some time studying these figures, you will clearly see

206

that Senator Sexton does not have the kind of money he is currently spending. After Katherine died, he squandered the vast majority of her legacy on bad investments, personal comforts, and buying himself what appears to be certain victory in the primaries. As of six months ago, your candidate was broke.'

Gabrielle sensed this had to be a bluff. If Sexton were broke, he sure wasn't acting it. He was buying advertising time in bigger and bigger blocks every week.

'Your candidate,' Tench continued, 'is currently out-spending the President four to one. And he has no personal money.'

'We get a lot of donations.'

'Yes, some of them legal.'

Gabrielle's head shot up. 'I *beg* your pardon?'

Tench leaned across the desk, and Gabrielle could smell her nicotine breath. 'Gabrielle Ashe, I am going to ask you a question, and I suggest you think very carefully before you answer. It could affect whether you spend the next few years in jail or not. Are you aware that Senator Sexton is accepting enormous illegal campaign bribes from aerospace companies who have billions to gain from the privatization of NASA?'

Gabrielle stared. 'That's an absurd allegation!'

'Are you saying you are unaware of this activity?'

'I think I would *know* if the senator were accepting bribes of the magnitude you are suggesting.'

Tench smiled coldly. 'Gabrielle, I understand that Senator Sexton has shared *a lot* of himself with you, but I assure you there is plenty you do not know about the man.'

Gabrielle stood up. 'This meeting is over.'

'On the contrary,' Tench said, removing the remaining

contents of the folder and spreading it on the desk. 'This meeting is just beginning.'

44

Inside the habisphere's 'staging room,' Rachel Sexton felt like an astronaut as she slid into one of NASA's Mark IX microclimate survival suits. The black, one-piece, hooded jumpsuit resembled an inflatable scuba suit. Its two-ply, memory-foam fabric was fitted with hollow channels through which a dense gel was pumped to help the wearer regulate body temperature in both hot and cold environments.

Now, as Rachel pulled the tight-fitting hood over her head, her eyes fell on the NASA administrator. He appeared as a silent sentinel at the door, clearly displeased with the necessity for this little mission.

Norah Mangor was muttering obscenities as she got everyone outfitted. 'Here's an extra pudgy,' she said, tossing Corky his suit.

Tolland was already half into his.

Once Rachel was fully zipped up, Norah found the stopcock on Rachel's side and connected her to an infusion tube that coiled out of a silver canister resembling a large scuba tank.

'Inhale,' Norah said, opening the valve.

Rachel heard a hiss and felt gel being injected into the suit. The memory foam expanded, and the suit compressed around her, pressing down on her inner layer of clothing. The sensation reminded her of sticking her hand underwater while wearing a rubber glove.

As the hood inflated around her head, it pressed in on her ears, making everything sound muffled. *I'm in a cocoon.*

'Best thing about the Mark IX,' Norah said, 'is the padding. You can fall on your ass and not feel a thing.'

Rachel believed it. She felt like she was trapped inside a mattress.

Norah handed Rachel a series of tools – an ice ax, tether snaps, and carabiners, which she affixed to the belt harnessed on Rachel's waist.

'All this?' Rachel asked, eyeing the gear. 'To go two hundred yards?'

Norah's eyes narrowed. 'You want to come or not?'

Tolland gave Rachel a reassuring nod. 'Norah's just being careful.'

Corky connected to the infusion tank and inflated his suit, looking amused. 'I feel like I'm wearing a giant condom.'

Norah gave a disgusted groan. 'Like you'd know, virgin boy.'

Tolland sat down next to Rachel. He gave her a weak smile as she donned her heavy boots and crampons. 'You sure you want to come?' His eyes had a protective concern that drew her in.

Rachel hoped her confident nod belied her growing trepidation. *Two hundred yards . . . not far at all.* 'And you thought you could find excitement only on the high seas.'

Tolland chuckled, talking as he attached his own crampons. 'I've decided I like liquid water much better than this frozen stuff.'

'I've never been a big fan of either,' Rachel said. 'I fell through the ice as a kid. Water's made me nervous ever since.'

Tolland glanced over, his eyes sympathetic. 'Sorry to hear that. When this is over, you'll have to come out and visit me on the *Goya*. I'll change your mind about water. Promise.'

The invitation surprised her. The *Goya* was Tolland's research ship – well known both from its role in *Amazing Seas* as well as its reputation as one of the strangest-looking ships on the ocean. Although a visit to the *Goya* would be unnerving for Rachel, she knew it would be hard to pass up.

'She's anchored twelve miles off the coast of New Jersey at the moment,' Tolland said, struggling with his crampon latches.

'Sounds like an unlikely spot.'

'Not at all. The Atlantic seaboard is an incredible place. We were gearing up to shoot a new documentary when I was so rudely interrupted by the President.'

Rachel laughed. 'Shooting a documentary on what?'

'*Sphyrna mokarran* and megaplumes.'

Rachel frowned. 'Glad I asked.'

Tolland finished attaching his crampons and looked up. 'Seriously, I'll be filming out there for a couple weeks. Washington's not that far from the Jersey coast. Come out when you get back home. No reason to spend your life afraid of the water. My crew would roll out the red carpet for you.'

Norah Mangor's voice blared. 'Are we going outside, or should I get you two some candles and champagne?'

Gabrielle Ashe had no idea what to make of the documents now spread out before her on Marjorie Tench's desk. The pile included photocopied letters, faxes, transcripts of phone conversations, and they all seemed to support the allegation that Senator Sexton was in covert dialogue with private space companies.

Tench pushed a couple of grainy black-and-white photographs toward Gabrielle. 'I assume this is news to you?'

Gabrielle looked at the photos. The first candid shot showed Senator Sexton getting out of a taxi in some kind of underground garage. *Sexton never takes taxis.* Gabrielle looked at the second shot – a telephoto of Sexton climbing into a parked white minivan. An old man appeared to be in the van waiting for him.

'Who is that?' Gabrielle said, suspicious the photos might be faked.

'A big shot from the SFF.'

Gabrielle was doubtful. 'The Space Frontier Foundation?'

The SFF was like a 'union' for private space companies. It represented aerospace contractors, entrepreneurs, venture capitalists – any private entity that wanted to go into space. They tended to be critical of NASA, arguing that the U.S. space program employed unfair business practices to prevent private companies from launching missions into space.

'The SFF,' Tench said, 'now represents over a

hundred major corporations, some very wealthy enterprises who are waiting eagerly for the Space Commercialization Promotions Act to be ratified.'

Gabrielle considered it. For obvious reasons the SFF was a vocal supporter of Sexton's campaign, although the senator had been careful not to get too close to them because of their controversial lobbying tactics. Recently the SFF had published an explosive rant charging that NASA was in fact an 'illegal monopoly' whose ability to operate at a loss and still stay in business represented unfair competition to private firms. According to the SFF, whenever AT&T needed a telecomm satellite launched, several private space companies offered to do the job at a reasonable $50 million. Unfortunately, NASA always stepped in and offered to launch AT&T's satellites for a mere $25 million, even though it cost NASA five times that to do the job! *Operating at a loss is one way NASA keeps its grip on space*, the SFF lawyers accused. *And taxpayers pick up the tab.*

'This photo reveals,' Tench said, 'that your candidate is holding secret meetings with an organization that represents private space enterprises.' Tench motioned to several other documents on the table. 'We also have internal SFF memos calling for huge sums of money to be collected from SFF member companies – in amounts commensurate with their net worth – and transferred to accounts controlled by Senator Sexton. In effect, these private space agencies are anteing up to put Sexton in office. I can only assume he has agreed to pass the commercialization bill and privatize NASA if elected.'

Gabrielle looked at the pile of papers, unconvinced. 'Do you expect me to believe that the White House has evidence that its opponent is engaged in profoundly illegal campaign finance – and yet, for some reason, you are keeping it secret?'

'What would you believe?'

Gabrielle glared. 'Frankly, considering your skills for manipulation, a more logical solution seems that you are plying me somehow with phony documents and photos produced by some enterprising White House staffer and his desktop publishing computer.'

'Possible, I admit. But not true.'

'No? Then how did you get all these internal documents from corporations? The resources required to steal all of this evidence from so many companies certainly exceeds the grasp of the White House.'

'You're right. This information arrived here as an unsolicited gift.'

Gabrielle was now lost.

'Oh yes,' Tench said, 'we get a lot of it. The President has many powerful political allies who would like to see him stay in office. Remember, your candidate is suggesting cuts all over the place – a lot of them right here in Washington. Senator Sexton certainly has no qualms about citing the FBI's bloated budget as an example of government overspending. He's taken some potshots at the IRS, too. Maybe someone at the bureau or at the service got a little annoyed.'

Gabrielle got the implication. People at the FBI and IRS would have ways of getting this kind of information. They might then send it to the White House as an unsolicited favor to help the President's election. But what Gabrielle could not make herself believe was that Senator Sexton would ever be engaged in illegal campaign funding. 'If this data is accurate,' Gabrielle challenged, 'which I strongly doubt it is, why haven't you gone public?'

'Why do you think?'

'Because it was gathered illegally.'

'How we got it makes no difference.'

'Of course it makes a difference. It's inadmissible in a hearing.'

'What hearing? We'd simply leak this to a newspaper, and they'd run it as a "credible-source" story with photos and documentation. Sexton would be guilty until proven innocent. His vocal anti-NASA stance would be virtual proof that he is taking bribes.'

Gabrielle knew it was true. 'Fine,' she challenged, 'then why haven't you leaked the information?'

'Because it's a negative. The President promised not to go negative in the campaign and he wants to stick to that promise as long as he can.'

Yeah, right! 'You're telling me the President is so upstanding that he refuses to go public with this because people might consider it a negative?'

'It's a negative for the country. It implicates dozens of private companies, many of which are made up of honest people. It besmirches the office of the U.S. Senate and is bad for the country's morale. Dishonest politicians hurt *all* politicians. Americans need to trust their leaders. This would be an ugly investigation and would most likely send a U.S. senator and numerous prominent aerospace executives to jail.'

Although Tench's logic did make sense, Gabrielle still doubted the allegations. 'What does any of this have to do with me?'

'Simply put, Ms Ashe, if we release these documents, your candidate will be indicted for illegal campaign financing, lose his Senate seat, and most likely do prison time.' Tench paused. 'Unless . . .'

Gabrielle saw a snakelike glint in the senior adviser's eyes. 'Unless *what*?'

Tench took a long drag on her cigarette. 'Unless you decide to help us avoid all that.'

A murky silence settled over the room.

Tench coughed roughly. 'Gabrielle, listen, I decided to share this unfortunate information with you for three reasons. First, to show you Zach Herney is a decent man who considers the government's well-being before his personal gain. Second, to inform you that your candidate is not as trustworthy as you might think. And third, to persuade you to accept the offer I am about to make.'

'That offer being?'

'I'd like to offer you a chance to do the right thing. The *patriotic* thing. Whether you know it or not, you're in a unique position to spare Washington all kinds of unpleasant scandal. If you can do what I am about to ask, perhaps you could even earn yourself a place on the President's team.'

A place on the President's team? Gabrielle couldn't believe what she was hearing. 'Ms Tench, whatever you have in mind, I do not appreciate being blackmailed, coerced, or talked down to. I work for the senator's campaign because I believe in his politics. And if *this* is any indication of the way Zach Herney exerts political influence, I have no interest in being associated with him! If you've got something on Senator Sexton, then I suggest you leak it to the press. Frankly, I think this whole thing's a sham.'

Tench gave a dreary sigh. 'Gabrielle, your candidate's illegal funding is a fact. I'm sorry. I know you trust him.' She lowered her voice. 'Look, here's the point. The President and I will go public with the funding issue if we must, but it will get ugly on a grand scale. This scandal involves several major U.S. corporations breaking the law. A lot of innocent people will pay the price.' She took a long drag and exhaled. 'What the President and I are hoping for here . . . is some *other* way to discredit the senator's ethics. A way that is more contained . . . one in which no innocent parties get hurt.' Tench set down her cigarette and folded her hands. 'Simply put, we would like you to publicly admit that you had an affair with the senator.'

Gabrielle's entire body went rigid. Tench sounded utterly certain of herself. *Impossible*, Gabrielle knew. There was no proof. The sex had happened only once, behind locked doors in Sexton's senatorial office. *Tench has nothing. She's fishing.* Gabrielle fought to retain her steady tone. 'You assume a lot, Ms Tench.'

'Which? That you had an affair? Or that you would abandon your candidate?'

'Both.'

Tench gave a curt smile and stood up. 'Well, let's put one of those facts to rest right now, shall we?' She walked to her wall safe again and returned with a red manila folder. It was stamped with the White House seal. She unhooked the clasp, tipped the envelope over, and dumped the contents out on the desk in front of Gabrielle.

As dozens of color photographs spilled out onto the desk, Gabrielle saw her entire career come crashing down before her.

Outisde the habisphere, the katabatic wind roaring down off the glacier was nothing like the ocean winds Tolland was accustomed to. On the ocean, wind was a function of tides and pressure fronts and came in gusting ebbs and flows. The katabatic, however, was a slave to simple physics – heavy cold air rushing down a glacial incline like a tidal wave. It was the most resolute gale force Tolland had ever experienced. Had it been coming at twenty knots, the katabatic would have been a sailor's dream, but at its current eighty knots it could quickly become a nightmare even for those on solid ground. Tolland found that if he paused and leaned backward, the stalwart squall could easily prop him up.

Making the raging river of air even more unnerving to Tolland was the slight downwind grade of the ice shelf. The ice was sloped ever so slightly toward the ocean, two miles away. Despite the sharp spikes on the Pitbull Rapido crampons attached to his boots, Tolland had the uneasy feeling that any misstep might leave him caught up in a gale and sliding down the endless icy slope. Norah Mangor's two-minute course in glacier safety now seemed dangerously inadequate.

Piranha Ice ax, Norah had said, fastening a lightweight T-shaped tool to each of their belts as they suited up in the habisphere. *Standard blade, banana blade, semitubular blade, hammer, and adze. All you need to remember is, if anyone slips or gets caught up in a gust, grab your ax with one hand on the head and one on the shaft, ram the banana blade into the ice, and fall on it, planting your crampons.*

With those words of assurance, Norah Mangor had affixed YAK belay harnesses to each of them, they all donned goggles, and headed out into the afternoon darkness.

Now, the four figures made their way down the glacier in a straight line with ten yards of belay rope separating each of them. Norah was in the lead position, followed by Corky, then Rachel, and Tolland as anchor.

As they moved farther away from the habisphere, Tolland felt a growing uneasiness. In his inflated suit, although warm, he felt like some kind of uncoordinated space traveler trekking across a distant planet. The moon had disappeared behind thick, billowing storm clouds, plunging the ice sheet into an impenetrable blackness. The katabatic wind seemed to be getting stronger by the minute, applying a constant pressure to Tolland's back. As his eyes strained through his goggles to make out the expansive emptiness around them, he began to perceive a true danger in this place. Redundant NASA safety precautions or not, Tolland was surprised the administrator had been willing to risk four lives out here instead of two. Especially when the additional two lives were that of a senator's daughter and a famous astrophysicist. Tolland was not surprised to feel a protective concern for Rachel and Corky. As someone who had captained a ship, he was used to feeling responsible for those around him.

'Stay behind me,' Norah shouted, her voice swallowed by the wind. 'Let the sled lead the way.'

The aluminum sled on which Norah was transporting her testing gear resembled an oversized Flexible Flyer. The craft was prepacked with diagnostic gear and safety accessories she'd been using on the glacier over the past few days. All of her gear – including a battery pack, safety flares, and a powerful front-mounted spotlight – was bound under a secured, plastic tarp. Despite the heavy load, the sled glided effortlessly on long, straight runners. Even on the almost imperceptible incline, the sled moved downhill on its own accord, and Norah applied a gentle restraint, almost as if allowing the sled to lead the way.

Sensing the distance growing between the group and the habisphere, Tolland looked over his shoulder. Only fifty yards away, the pale curvature of the dome had all but disappeared in the blustery blackness.

'You at all worried about finding our way back?' Tolland yelled. 'The habisphere is almost invisi—' His words were cut short by the loud hiss of a flare igniting in Norah's hand. The sudden red-white glow illuminated the ice shelf in a ten-yard radius all around them. Norah used her heel to dig a small impression in the surface snow, piling up a protective ridge on the upwind side of the hole. Then she rammed the flare into the indentation.

'High-tech bread crumbs,' Norah shouted.

'Bread crumbs?' Rachel asked, shielding her eyes from the sudden light.

'Hansel and Gretel,' Norah shouted. 'These flares will last an hour – plenty of time to find our way back.'

With that, Norah headed out again, leading them down the glacier – into the darkness once again.

Gabrielle Ashe stormed out of Marjorie Tench's office and practically knocked over a secretary in doing so. Mortified, all Gabrielle could see were the photographs – images – arms and legs intertwined. Faces filled with ecstasy.

Gabrielle had no idea how the photos had been taken, but she knew damn well they were real. They had been taken in Senator Sexton's office and seemed to have been shot from above as if by hidden camera. *God help me.* One of the photos showed Gabrielle and Sexton having sex directly on top of the senator's desk, their bodies sprawled across a scatter of official-looking documents.

Marjorie Tench caught up with Gabrielle outside the Map Room. Tench was carrying the red envelope of photos. 'I assume from your reaction that you believe these photos are authentic?' The President's senior adviser actually looked like she was having a good time. 'I'm hoping they persuade you that our other data is accurate as well. They came from the same source.'

Gabrielle felt her entire body flushing as she marched down the hall. *Where the hell is the exit?*

Tench's gangly legs had no trouble keeping up. 'Senator Sexton swore to the world that you two are platonic associates. His televised statement was actually quite convincing.' Tench motioned smugly over her shoulder. 'In fact, I have a tape in my office if you'd like to refresh your memory?'

Gabrielle needed no refresher. She remembered the

press conference all too well. Sexton's denial was as adamant as it was heartfelt.

'It's unfortunate,' Tench said, sounding not at all disappointed, 'but Senator Sexton looked the American people in the eye and told a bald-faced lie. The public has a right to know. And they *will* know. I'll see to it personally. The only question now is how the public finds out. We believe it's best coming from you.'

Gabrielle was stunned. 'You really think I'm going to help lynch my own candidate?'

Tench's face hardened. 'I am trying to take the high ground here, Gabrielle. I'm giving you a chance to save everyone a lot of embarrassment by holding your head high and telling the truth. All I need is a signed statement admitting your affair.'

Gabrielle stopped short. 'What?'

'Of course. A signed statement gives us the leverage we need to deal with the senator *quietly*, sparing the country this ugly mess. My offer is simple: sign a statement for me, and these photos never need to see the light of day.'

'You want a statement?'

'Technically, I would need an affidavit, but we have a notary here in the building who could—'

'You're crazy.' Gabrielle was walking again.

Tench stayed at her side, sounding more angry now. 'Senator Sexton is going down one way or another, Gabrielle, and I'm offering you a chance to get out of this without seeing your own naked ass in the morning paper! The President is a decent man and doesn't *want* these photos publicized. If you just give me an affidavit and confess to the affair on your own terms, then all of us can retain a little dignity.'

'I'm not for sale.'

'Well, your candidate certainly is. He's a dangerous man, and he's breaking the law.'

'*He's* breaking the law? You're the ones breaking into offices and taking illegal surveillance pictures! Ever heard of Watergate?'

'We had nothing to do with gathering this dirt. These photos came from the same source as the SFF campaign-funding information. Someone's been watching you two very closely.'

Gabrielle tore past the security desk where she had gotten her security badge. She ripped off the badge and tossed it to the wide-eyed guard. Tench was still on her tail.

'You'll need to decide fast, Ms Ashe,' Tench said as they neared the exit. 'Either bring me an affidavit admitting you slept with the senator, or at eight o'clock tonight, the President will be forced to go public with everything – Sexton's financial dealings, the photos of you, the works. And believe me, when the public sees that you stood idly by and let Sexton lie about your relationship, you'll go down in flames right beside him.'

Gabrielle saw the door and headed for it.

'On my desk by eight o'clock tonight, Gabrielle. Be smart.' Tench tossed her the folder of photographs on her way out. 'Keep them, sweetie. We've got plenty more.'

48

Rachel Sexton felt a growing chill inside as she moved down the ice sheet into a deepening night. Disquieting images swirled in her mind – the meteorite, the phos-phorescent plankton, the implications if Norah Mangor had made a mistake with the ice cores.

A solid matrix of freshwater ice, Norah had argued, reminding them all that she had drilled cores all around the area as well as directly over the meteorite. If the glacier contained saltwater interstices filled with plankton, she would have seen them. Wouldn't she? Nonetheless, Rachel's intuition kept returning to the simplest solution.

There are plankton frozen in this glacier.

Ten minutes and four flares later, Rachel and the others were approximately 250 yards from the habi-sphere. Without warning, Norah stopped short. 'This is the spot,' she said, sounding like a water-witch diviner who had mystically sensed the perfect spot to drill a well.

Rachel turned and glanced up the slope behind them. The habisphere had long since disappeared into the dim, moonlit night, but the line of flares was clearly visible, the farthest one twinkling reassuringly like a faint star. The flares were in a perfectly straight line, like a carefully calculated runway. Rachel was impressed with Norah's skills.

'Another reason we let the sled go first,' Norah called out when she saw Rachel admiring the line of flares. 'The runners are straight. If we let gravity lead the sled and we don't interfere, we're guaranteed to travel in a straight line.'

'Neat trick,' Tolland yelled. 'Wish there were some-thing like that for the open sea.'

This IS the open sea, Rachel thought, picturing the ocean beneath them. For a split second, the most distant flame caught her attention. It had disappeared, as if the light had been blotted out by a passing form. A moment later, though, the light reappeared. Rachel felt a sudden uneasiness. 'Norah,' she yelled over the wind, 'did you say there were polar bears up here?'

The glaciologist was preparing a final flare and either did not hear or was ignoring her.

'Polar bears,' Tolland yelled, 'eat seals. They only attack humans when we invade their space.'

'But this *is* polar bear country, right?' Rachel could never remember which pole had bears and which had penguins.

'Yeah,' Tolland shouted back. 'Polar bears actually give the Arctic its name. *Arktos* is Greek for bear.'

Terrific. Rachel gazed nervously into the dark.

'Antarctica has *no* polar bears,' Tolland said. 'So they call it *Anti-arktos.*'

'Thanks, Mike,' Rachel yelled. 'Enough talk of polar bears.'

He laughed. 'Right. Sorry.'

Norah pressed a final flare into the snow. As before, the four of them were engulfed in a reddish glow, looking bloated in their black weather suits. Beyond the circle of light emanating from the flare, the rest of the world became totally invisible, a circular shroud of blackness engulfing them.

As Rachel and the others looked on, Norah planted her feet and used careful overhand motions to reel the sled several yards back up the slope to where they were standing. Then, keeping the rope taut, she crouched and manually activated the sled's talon brakes – four angled spikes that dug into the ice to keep the sled stationary. That done, she stood up and brushed herself off, the rope around her waist falling slack.

'All right,' Norah shouted. 'Time to go to work.'

The glaciologist circled to the downwind end of the sled and began unfastening the butterfly eyelets holding the protective canvas over the gear. Rachel, feeling like she had been a little hard on Norah, moved to help by unfastening the rear of the flap.

'Jesus, NO!' Norah yelled, her head snapping up. 'Don't *ever* do that!'

Rachel recoiled, confused.

'Never unfasten the upwind side!' Norah said. 'You'll create a wind sock! This sled would have taken off like an umbrella in a wind tunnel!'

Rachel backed off. 'I'm sorry. I . . .'

Norah glared. 'You and space boy shouldn't be out here.'

None of us should, Rachel thought.

Amateurs, Norah seethed, cursing the administrator's insistence on sending Corky and Sexton along. *These clowns are going to get someone killed out here.* The last thing Norah wanted right now was to play baby-sitter.

'Mike,' she said, 'I need help lifting the GPR off the sled.'

Tolland helped her unpack the Ground Penetrating Radar and position it on the ice. The instrument looked like three miniature snowplow blades that had been affixed in parallel to an aluminum frame. The entire device was no more than a yard long and was connected by cables to a current attenuator and a marine battery on the sled.

'That's radar?' Corky asked, yelling over the wind.

Norah nodded in silence. Ground Penetrating Radar was far more equipped to see brine ice than PODS was. The GPR transmitter sent pulses of electromagnetic energy through the ice, and the pulses bounced differently off substances of differing crystal structure. Pure freshwater froze in a flat, shingled lattice. However, seawater froze in more of a meshed or forked lattice on account of its sodium content, causing the GPR pulses to bounce back erratically, greatly diminishing the number of reflections.

Norah powered up the machine. 'I'll be taking a kind of echo-location cross-sectional image of the ice sheet around the extraction pit,' she yelled. 'The machine's internal software will render a cross section of the glacier and then print it out. Any sea ice will register as a shadow.'

'Printout?' Tolland looked surprised. 'You can *print* out here?'

Norah pointed to a cable from the GPR leading to a device still protected under the canopy. 'No choice but to print. Computer screens use too much valuable battery power, so field glaciologists print data to heat-transfer printers. Colors aren't brilliant, but laser toner clumps below neg twenty. Learned that the hard way in Alaska.'

Norah asked everyone to stand on the downhill side of the GPR as she prepared to align the transmitter such that it would scan the area of the meteorite hole, almost three football fields away. But as Norah looked back through the night in the general direction from which they had come, she couldn't see a damn thing. 'Mike, I need to align the GPR transmitter with the meteorite site, but this flare has me blinded. I'm going back up the slope just enough to get out of the light. I'll hold my arms in line with the flares, and you adjust the alignment on the GPR.'

Tolland nodded, kneeling down beside the radar device.

Norah stamped her crampons into the ice and leaned forward against the wind as she moved up the incline toward the habisphere. The katabatic today was much stronger than she'd imagined, and she sensed a storm coming in. It didn't matter. They would be done here in a matter of minutes. *They'll see I'm right.* Norah clomped twenty yards back toward the habisphere. She reached the edge of the darkness just as the belay rope went taut.

Norah looked back up the glacier. As her eyes adjusted to the dark, the line of flares slowly came into view several degrees to her left. She shifted her position until she was perfectly lined up with them. Then she held her arms out like a compass, turning her body, indicating the exact vector. 'I'm in line with them now!' she yelled.

Tolland adjusted the GPR device and waved. 'All set!'

Norah took a final look up the incline, grateful for the illuminated pathway home. As she looked out, though, something odd occurred. For an instant, one of the nearest flares entirely disappeared from view. Before Norah could worry that it was dying out, the flare reappeared. If Norah didn't know better, she would assume something had passed between the flare and her location. Certainly nobody else was out here . . . unless of course the administrator had started to feel guilty and sent a NASA team out after them. Somehow Norah doubted it. Probably nothing, she decided. A gust of wind had momentarily killed the flame.

Norah returned to the GPR. 'All lined up?'

Tolland shrugged. 'I think so.'

Norah went over to the control device on the sled and pressed a button. A sharp buzz emanated from the GPR and then stopped. 'Okay,' she said. 'Done.'

'That's it?' Corky said.

'All the work is in setup. The actual shot takes only a second.'

Onboard the sled, the heat-transfer printer had already begun to hum and click. The printer was enclosed in a clear plastic covering and was slowly ejecting a heavy, curled paper. Norah waited until the device had completed printing, and then she reached up under the plastic and removed the printout. *They'll see*, she thought, carrying the printout over to the flare so that everyone could see it. *There won't be any saltwater*.

Everyone gathered around as Norah stood over the flare, clutching the printout tightly in her gloves. She took a deep breath and uncurled the paper to examine the data. The image on the paper made her recoil in horror.

'Oh, God!' Norah stared, unable to believe what she was looking at. As expected, the printout revealed a clear cross section of the water-filled meteorite shaft. But what Norah had never expected to see was the hazy grayish outline of a humanoid form floating halfway down the shaft. Her blood turned to ice. 'Oh God . . . there's a body in the extraction pit.'

Everyone stared in stunned silence.

The ghostlike body was floating head down in the narrow shaft. Billowing around the corpse like some sort of cape was an eerie shroudlike aura. Norah now realized what the aura was. The GPR had captured a faint trace of the victim's heavy coat, what could only be a familiar, long, dense camel hair.

'It's . . . Ming,' she said in a whisper. 'He must have slipped . . .'

Norah Mangor never imagined that seeing Ming's

body in the extraction pit would be the lesser of the two shocks the printout would reveal, but as her eyes traced downward in the shaft, she saw something else.

The ice beneath the extraction shaft . . .

Norah stared. Her first thought was that something had gone wrong with the scan. Then, as she studied the image more closely, an unsettling realization began to grow, like the storm gathering around them. The paper's edges flapped wildly in the wind as she turned and looked more intently at the printout.

But . . . that's impossible!

Suddenly, the truth came crashing down. The realization felt like it was going to bury her. She forgot all about Ming.

Norah now understood. *The saltwater in the shaft!* She fell to her knees in the snow beside the flare. She could barely breathe. Still clutching the paper in her hands, she began trembling.

My God . . . it didn't even occur to me.

Then, with a sudden eruption of rage, she spun her head in the direction of the NASA habisphere. 'You bastards!' she screamed, her voice trailing off in the wind. 'You goddamned *bastards!*'

In the darkness, only fifty yards away, Delta-One held his CrypTalk device to his mouth and spoke only two words to his controller. 'They know.'

Norah Mangor was still kneeling on the ice when the bewildered Michael Tolland pulled the Ground Penetrating Radar's printout from her trembling hands. Shaken from seeing the floating body of Ming, Tolland tried to gather his thoughts and decipher the image before him.

He saw the cross section of the meteorite shaft descending from the surface down to 200 feet into the ice. He saw Ming's body floating in the shaft. Tolland's eyes drifted lower now, and he sensed something was amiss. Directly *beneath* the extraction shaft, a dark column of sea ice extended downward to the open ocean below. The vertical pillar of saltwater ice was massive – the same diameter as the shaft.

'My God!' Rachel yelled, looking over Tolland's shoulder. 'It looks like the meteorite shaft continues all the way *through* the ice shelf into the ocean!'

Tolland stood transfixed, his brain unable to accept what he knew to be the only logical explanation. Corky looked equally alarmed.

Norah shouted, 'Someone drilled up under the shelf!' Her eyes were wild with rage. 'Someone intentionally *inserted* that rock from underneath the ice!'

Although the idealist in Tolland wanted to reject Norah's words, the scientist in him knew she could easily be right. The Milne Ice Shelf was floating over the ocean with plenty of clearance for a submersible. Because everything weighed significantly less underwater, even a small submersible not much bigger than Tolland's one-man research Triton easily could have transported the meteorite in its payload arms. The sub could have approached from the ocean, submerged beneath the ice shelf, and drilled upward into the ice. Then, it could have used an extending payload arm or inflatable balloons to push the meteorite up into the shaft. Once the meteorite was in place, the ocean water that had risen into the shaft behind the meteorite would begin to freeze. As soon as the shaft closed enough to hold the meteorite in place, the sub could retract its arm and disappear, leaving Mother Nature to seal the remainder of the tunnel and erase all traces of the deception.

'But *why*?' Rachel demanded, taking the printout from Tolland and studying it. 'Why would someone do that? Are you sure your GPR is working?'

'Of course, I'm sure! And the printout perfectly explains the presence of phosphorescent bacteria in the water!'

Tolland had to admit, Norah's logic was chillingly sound. Phosphorescent dinoflagellates would have followed instinct and swum upward into the meteorite shaft, becoming trapped just beneath the meteorite and freezing into the ice. Later, when Norah heated the meteorite, the ice directly beneath would have melted, releasing the plankton. Again, they would swim upward, this time reaching the surface inside the habisphere, where they would eventually die for lack of saltwater.

'This is crazy!' Corky yelled. 'NASA has a meteorite with extraterrestrial fossils in it. Why would they care *where* it's found? Why would they go to the trouble to bury it under an ice shelf?'

'Who the hell knows,' Norah fired back, 'but GPR printouts don't lie. We were tricked. That meteorite isn't part of the Jungersol Fall. It was inserted in the ice *recently*. Within the last year, or the plankton would be dead!' She was already packing up her GPR gear on the sled and fastening it down. 'We've got to get back and tell someone! The President is about to go public with all the wrong data! NASA tricked him!'

'Wait a minute!' Rachel yelled. 'We should at least run another scan to make sure. None of this makes sense. Who will believe it?'

'Everyone,' Norah said, preparing her sled. 'When I march into the habisphere and drill another core sample out of the bottom of the meteorite shaft and it comes up as saltwater ice, I guarantee you *everyone* will believe this!'

Norah disengaged the brakes on the equipment sled, redirected it toward the habisphere, and started back up the slope, digging her crampons into the ice and pulling the sled behind her with surprising ease. She was a woman on a mission.

'Let's go!' Norah shouted, pulling the tethered group along as she headed toward the perimeter of the illuminated circle. 'I don't know what NASA's up to here, but I sure as hell don't appreciate being used as a pawn for their—'

Norah Mangor's neck snapped back as if she'd been rammed in the forehead by some invisible force. She let out a guttural gasp of pain, wavered, and collapsed backward onto the ice. Almost instantly, Corky let out a cry and spun around as if his shoulder had been propelled backward. He fell to the ice, writhing in pain.

*　　*　　*

232

Rachel immediately forgot all about the printout in her hand, Ming, the meteorite, and the bizarre tunnel beneath the ice. She had just felt a small projectile graze her ear, barely missing her temple. Instinctively, she dropped to her knees, yanking Tolland down with her.

'What's going on?' Tolland screamed.

A hailstorm was all Rachel could imagine – balls of ice blowing down off the glacier – and yet from the force with which Corky and Norah had just been hit, Rachel knew the hailstones would have to be moving at hundreds of miles an hour. Eerily, the sudden barrage of marble-sized objects seemed now to focus on Rachel and Tolland, pelting all around them, sending up plumes of exploding ice. Rachel rolled onto her stomach, dug her crampon's toe spikes into the ice, and launched toward the only cover available. The sled. Tolland arrived a moment later, scrambling and hunkering down beside her.

Tolland looked out at Norah and Corky unprotected on the ice. 'Pull them in with the tether!' he yelled, grabbing the rope and trying to pull.

But the tether was wrapped around the sled.

Rachel stuffed the printout in the Velcro pocket of her Mark IX suit, and scrambled on all fours toward the sled, trying to untangle the rope from the sled runners. Tolland was right behind her.

The hailstones suddenly rained down in a barrage against the sled, as if Mother Nature had abandoned Corky and Norah and was taking direct aim at Rachel and Tolland. One of the projectiles slammed into the top of the sled tarp, partially embedding itself, and then bounced over, landing on the sleeve of Rachel's coat.

When Rachel saw it, she froze. In an instant, the bewilderment she had been feeling turned to terror.

These 'hailstones' were man-made. The ball of ice on her sleeve was a flawlessly shaped spheroid the size of a large cherry. The surface was polished and smooth, marred only by a linear seam around the circumference, like an old-fashioned lead musket ball, machined in a press. The globular pellets were, without a doubt, man-made.

Ice bullets . . .

As someone with miltary clearance, Rachel was well acquainted with the new experimental 'IM' weaponry – Improvised Munitions – snow rifles that compacted snow into ice pellets, desert rifles that melted sand into glass projectiles, water-based firearms that shot pulses of liquid water with such force that they could break bones. Improvised Munitions weaponry had an enormous advantage over conventional weapons because IM weapons used available resources and literally manufactured munitions on the spot, providing soldiers unlimited rounds without their having to carry heavy conventional bullets. The ice balls being fired at them now, Rachel knew, were being compressed 'on demand' from snow fed into the butt of the rifle.

As was often the case in the intelligence world, the more one knew, the more frightening a scenario became. This moment was no exception. Rachel would have preferred blissful ignorance, but her knowledge of IM weaponry instantly led her to a sole chilling conclusion: they were being attacked by some kind of U.S. Special Ops force, the only forces in the country currently cleared to use these experimental IM weapons in the field.

The presence of a military covert operations unit brought with it a second, even more terrifying realization: the probability of surviving this attack was close to zero.

The morbid thought was terminated as one of the ice pellets found an opening and came screaming through the wall of gear on the sled, colliding with her stomach. Even in her padded Mark IX suit, Rachel felt like an invisible prizefighter had just gut-punched her. Stars began to dance around the periphery of her vision, and she teetered backward, grabbing gear on the sled for balance. Michael Tolland dropped Norah's tether and lunged to support Rachel, but he arrived too late. Rachel fell backward, pulling a pile of equipment with her. She and Tolland tumbled to the ice in a pile of electronic apparatus.

'They're . . . bullets . . .' she gasped, the air momentarily crushed from her lungs. 'Run!'

50

The Washington MetroRail subway now leaving Federal Triangle station could not speed away from the White House fast enough for Gabrielle Ashe. She sat rigid in a deserted corner of the train as darkened shapes tore past outside in a blur. Marjorie Tench's big red envelope lay in Gabrielle's lap, pressing down like a ten-ton weight.

I've got to talk to Sexton! she thought, the train accelerating now in the direction of Sexton's office building. *Immediately!*

Now, in the dim, shifting light of the train, Gabrielle felt like she was enduring some kind of hallucinogenic drug trip. Muted lights whipped by overhead like slow-motion discotheque strobes. The ponderous tunnel rose on all sides like a deepening canyon.

Tell me this is not happening.

She gazed down at the envelope on her lap. Unclasping the flap, she reached inside and pulled out one of the photos. The internal lights of the train flickered for a moment, the harsh glare illuminating a shocking image – Sedgewick Sexton lying naked in his office, his gratified face turned perfectly toward the camera while Gabrielle's dark form lay nude beside him.

She shivered, rammed the photo back inside, and fumbled to reclasp the envelope.

It's over.

As soon as the train exited the tunnel and climbed onto the above-ground tracks near L'Enfant Plaza, Gabrielle dug out her cellphone and called the senator's private cellular number. His voice mail answered. Puzzled, she phoned the senator's office. The secretary answered.

'It's Gabrielle. Is he in?'

The secretary sounded peeved. 'Where have you been? He was looking for you.'

'I had a meeting that ran long. I need to talk to him right away.'

'You'll have to wait till morning. He's at Westbrooke.'

Westbrooke Place Luxury Apartments was the building where Sexton kept his D.C. residence. 'He's not picking up his private line,' Gabrielle said.

'He blocked off tonight as a P.E.,' the secretary reminded. 'He left early.'

Gabrielle scowled. *Personal Event.* In all the excitement, she'd forgotten Sexton had scheduled himself a night alone at home. He was very particular about not being disturbed during his P.E. blocks. *Bang on my door only if the building is on fire,* he would say. *Other than that, it can wait until morning.* Gabrielle decided Sexton's building was definitely on fire. 'I need you to reach him for me.'

'Impossible.'

'This is serious, I really—'

'No, I mean *literally* impossible. He left his pager on my desk on his way out and told me he was not to be disturbed all night. He was adamant.' She paused. 'More so than usual.'

Shit. 'Okay, thanks.' Gabrielle hung up.

'*L'Enfant Plaza*,' a recording announced in the subway car. '*Connection all stations.*'

Closing her eyes, Gabrielle tried to clear her mind, but devastating images rushed in . . . the lurid photos of herself and the senator . . . the pile of documents alleging Sexton was taking bribes. Gabrielle could still hear Tench's raspy demands. *Do the right thing. Sign the affidavit. Admit the affair.*

As the train screeched into the station, Gabrielle forced herself to imagine what the senator would do if the photos hit the presses. The first thing to pop in her mind both shocked and shamed her.

Sexton would lie.

Was this truly her first instinct regarding her candidate?

Yes. He would lie . . . brilliantly.

If these photos hit the media without Gabrielle's having admitted the affair, the senator would simply claim the photos were a cruel forgery. This was the age of digital photo editing; anyone who had ever been on-line had seen the flawlessly retouched spoof photographs of celebrities' heads digitally melded onto other people's bodies, often those of porn stars engaged in lewd acts. Gabrielle had already witnessed the senator's ability to look into a television camera and lie convincingly about their affair; she had no doubt he could persuade the world these photos were a lame attempt to derail his career. Sexton would lash out with indignant outrage, perhaps even insinuate that the President himself had ordered the forgery.

No wonder the White House hasn't gone public. The photos, Gabrielle realized, could backfire just like the initial drudge. As vivid as the pictures seemed, they were totally inconclusive.

Gabrielle felt a sudden surge of hope.

The White House can't prove any of this is real!

Tench's powerplay on Gabrielle had been ruthless in its simplicity: admit your affair or watch Sexton go to jail. Suddenly it made perfect sense. The White House *needed* Gabrielle to admit the affair, or the photos were worthless. A sudden glimmer of confidence brightened her mood.

As the train sat idling and the doors slid open, another distant door seemed to open in Gabrielle's mind, revealing an abrupt and heartening possibility.

Maybe everything Tench told me about the bribery was a lie.

After all, what had Gabrielle really seen? Yet again, nothing conclusive – some Xeroxed bank documents, a grainy photo of Sexton in a garage. All of it potentially counterfeit. Tench cunningly could have showed Gabrielle bogus financial records in the same sitting as the genuine sex photos, hoping Gabrielle would accept the *entire* package as true. It was called 'authentication by association,' and politicians used it all the time to sell dubious concepts.

Sexton is innocent, Gabrielle told herself. The White House was desperate, and they had decided to take a wild gamble on scaring Gabrielle into going public about the affair. They needed Gabrielle to desert Sexton publicly – scandalously. *Get out while you can*, Tench had told her. *You have until eight o'clock tonight*. The ultimate pressure sales job. *All of it fits*, she thought.

Except one thing . . .

The only confusing piece of the puzzle was that Tench had been sending Gabrielle anti-NASA e-mails. This certainly suggested NASA really *did* want Sexton to solidify his anti-NASA stance so they could use it against him. Or did it? Gabrielle realized that even the e-mails had a perfectly logical explanation.

What if the e-mails were not really from Tench?

It was possible Tench caught a traitor on staff sending Gabrielle data, fired that person, and then stepped in and e-mailed the final message herself, calling Gabrielle in for a meeting. *Tench could have pretended she leaked all the NASA data on purpose – to set Gabrielle up.*

The subway hydraulics hissed now in L'Enfant Plaza, the doors preparing to close.

Gabrielle stared out at the platform, her mind racing. She had no idea if her suspicions were making any sense or if they were just wishful thinking, but whatever the hell was going on, she knew she had to talk to the senator right away – P.E. night or not.

Clutching the envelope of photographs, Gabrielle hurried off the train just as the doors hissed shut. She had a new destination.

Westbrooke Place Apartments.

239

Fight or flight.

As a biologist, Tolland knew that vast physiological changes occurred when an organism sensed danger. Adrenaline flooded the cerebral cortex, jolting the heart rate and commanding the brain to make the oldest and most intuitive of all biological decisions – whether to do battle or flee.

Tolland's instinct told him to flee, and yet reason reminded him he was still tethered to Norah Mangor. There was nowhere to flee anyway. The only cover for miles was the habisphere, and the attackers, whoever the hell they were, had positioned themselves high on the glacier and cut off that option. Behind him, the wide open sheet of ice fanned out into a two-mile-long plain that terminated in a sheer drop to a frigid sea. Flight in that direction meant death by exposure. The practical barriers to fleeing notwithstanding, Tolland knew he could not possibly leave the others. Norah and Corky were still out in the open, tethered to Rachel and Tolland.

Tolland stayed down near Rachel as the ice pellets continued to slam into the side of the toppled equipment sled. He pillaged the strewn contents, searching for a weapon, a flare gun, a radio . . . anything.

'Run!' Rachel yelled, her breathing still strained.

Then, oddly, the hailstorm of ice bullets abruptly stopped. Even in the pounding wind, the night felt suddenly calm . . . as if a storm had let up unexpectedly.

It was then, peering cautiously around the sled, that Tolland witnessed one of the most chilling sights he had ever seen.

Gliding effortlessly out of the darkened perimeter into the light, three ghostly figures emerged, coasting silently in on skis. The figures wore full white weather suits. They carried no ski poles but rather large rifles that looked like no guns Tolland had ever seen. Their skis were bizarre as well, futuristic and short, more like elongated Rollerblades than skis.

Calmly, as if knowing they had already won this battle, the figures coasted to a stop beside their closest victim – the unconscious Norah Mangor. Tolland rose shakily to his knees and peered over the sled at the attackers. The visitors stared back at him through eerie electronic goggles. They were apparently uninterested. At least for the moment.

Delta-One felt no remorse as he stared down at the woman lying unconscious on the ice before him. He had been trained to carry out orders, not to question motives.

The woman was wearing a thick, black, thermal suit and had a welt on the side of her face. Her breathing was short and labored. One of the IM ice rifles had found its mark and knocked her unconscious.

Now it was time to finish the job.

As Delta-One knelt down beside the oblivious woman, his teammates trained their rifles on the other targets – one on the small, unconscious man lying on the ice nearby, and one on the overturned sled where the two other victims were hiding. Although his men easily could have moved in to finish the job, the remaining three victims were unarmed and had nowhere to run. Rushing to finish them all off at once was careless. *Never disperse your focus unless absolutely necessary. Face one adversary at a time.* Exactly as they had been trained, the Delta Force would kill these people one at a time. The magic, however, was that they would leave no trace to suggest how they had died.

Crouched beside the unconscious woman, Delta-One removed his thermal gloves and scooped up a handful of snow. Packing the snow, he opened the woman's mouth and began stuffing it down her throat. He filled her entire mouth, ramming the snow as deep as he could down her windpipe. She would be dead within three minutes.

This technique, invented by the Russian mafia, was called the *byelaya smert* – white death. This victim would suffocate long before the snow in her throat melted. Once dead, however, her body would stay warm long enough to dissolve the blockage. Even if foul play were suspected, no murder weapon or evidence of violence would be apparent immediately. Eventually someone might figure it out, but it would buy them time. The ice bullets would fade into the environment, buried in the snow, and the welt on this woman's head would look like she'd taken a nasty spill on the ice – not surprising in these gale force winds.

The other three people would be incapacitated and killed in much the same way. Then Delta-One would load all of them on the sled, drag them several hundred yards off course, reattach their belay lines and arrange the bodies. Hours from now, the four of them would be found frozen in the snow, apparent victims of over-exposure and hypothermia. Those who discovered them would be puzzled what they were doing off course, but nobody would be surprised that they were dead. After all, their flares had burned out, the weather was perilous, and getting lost on the Milne Ice Shelf could bring death in a hurry.

Delta-One had now finished packing snow down the woman's throat. Before turning his attention to the others, Delta-One unhooked the woman's belay harness. He could reconnect it later, but at the moment, he did not want the two people behind the sled getting ideas about pulling his victim to safety.

Michael Tolland had just witnessed a murderous act more bizarre than his darkest mind could imagine. Having cut Norah Mangor free, the three attackers were turning their attention to Corky.

I've got to do something!

Corky had come to and was moaning, trying to sit up, but one of the soldiers pushed him back down on his back, straddled him, and pinned Corky's arms to the ice by kneeling on them. Corky let out a cry of pain that was instantly swallowed up by the raging wind.

In a kind of demented terror, Tolland tore through the scattered contents of the overturned sled. *There must be something here! A weapon! Something!* All he saw was diagnostic ice gear, most of it smashed beyond recognition by the ice pellets. Beside him, Rachel groggily tried to sit up, using her ice ax to prop herself up. 'Run . . . Mike . . .'

Tolland eyed the ax that was strapped to Rachel's wrist. It could be a weapon. Sort of. Tolland wondered what his chances were attacking three armed men with a tiny ax.

Suicide.

As Rachel rolled and sat up, Tolland spied something behind her. A bulky vinyl bag. Praying against

243

fate that it contained a flare gun or radio, he clambered past her and grabbed the bag. Inside he found a large, neatly folded sheet of Mylar fabric. Worthless. Tolland had something similar on his research ship. It was a small weather balloon, designed to carry payloads of observational weather gear not much heavier than a personal computer. Norah's balloon would be no help here, particularly without a helium tank.

With the growing sounds of Corky's struggle, Tolland felt a helpless sensation he had not felt in years. Total despair. Total loss. Like the cliché of one's life passing before one's eyes before death, Tolland's mind flashed unexpectedly through long forgotten childhood images. For an instant he was sailing in San Pedro, learning the age-old sailor's pastime of spinnaker-flying – hanging on a knotted rope, suspended over the ocean, plunging laughing into the water, rising and falling like a kid hanging on a belfry rope, his fate determined by a billowing spinnaker sail and the whim of the ocean breeze.

Tolland's eyes instantly snapped back to the Mylar balloon in his hand, realizing that his mind had not been surrendering, but rather it had been trying to remind him of a solution! *Spinnaker flying.*

Corky was still struggling against his captor as Tolland yanked open the protective bag around the balloon. Tolland had no illusions that this plan was anything other than a long shot, but he knew remaining here was certain death for all of them. He clutched the folded mass of Mylar. The payload clip warned: CAUTION: NOT FOR USE IN WINDS OVER 10 KNOTS.

The hell with that! Gripping it hard to keep it from unfurling, Tolland clambered over to Rachel, who was

244

propped on her side. He could see the confusion in her eyes as he nestled close, yelling, 'Hold this!'

Tolland handed Rachel the folded pad of fabric and then used his free hands to slip the balloon's payload clasp through one of the carabiners on his harness. Then, rolling on his side, he slipped the clasp through one of Rachel's carabiners as well.

Tolland and Rachel were now one.

Joined at the hip.

From between them, the loose tether trailed off across the snow to the struggling Corky . . . and ten yards farther to the empty clip beside Norah Mangor.

Norah is already gone, Tolland told himself. *Nothing you can do.*

The attackers were crouched over Corky's writhing body now, packing a handful of snow, and preparing to stuff it down Corky's throat. Tolland knew they were almost out of time.

Tolland grabbed the folded balloon from Rachel. The fabric was as light as tissue paper – and virtually indestructible. *Here goes nothing.* 'Hold on!'

'Mike?' Rachel said. 'What—'

Tolland hurled the pad of wadded Mylar into the air over their heads. The howling wind snatched it up and spread it out like a parachute in a hurricane. The sheath filled instantly, billowing open with a loud snap.

Tolland felt a wrenching yank on his harness, and he knew in an instant he had grossly underestimated the power of the katabatic wind. Within a fraction of a second, he and Rachel were half airborne, being dragged down the glacier. A moment later, Tolland felt a jerk as his tether drew taut on Corky Marlinson. Twenty yards back, his terrified friend was yanked out from under his stunned attackers, sending one of them tumbling backward. Corky let out a blood-curdling scream as he too accelerated across the ice, barely missing the overturned sled, then fishtailing inward. A second rope trailed limp beside Corky . . . the rope that had been connected to Norah Mangor.

Nothing you can do, Tolland told himself.

Like a tangled mass of human marionettes, the three bodies skimmed down the glacier. Ice pellets went sailing by, but Tolland knew the attackers had missed their chance. Behind him, the white-clad soldiers faded away, shrinking to illuminated specks in the glow of the flares.

Tolland now felt the ice ripping beneath his padded suit with relentless acceleration, and the relief at having escaped faded fast. Less than two miles directly ahead of them, the Milne Ice Shelf came to an abrupt end at a precipitous cliff – and beyond it . . . a 100-foot drop to the lethal pounding surf of the Arctic Ocean.

52

Marjorie Tench was smiling as she made her way downstairs toward the White House Communications Office, the computerized broadcast facility that disseminated press releases formulated upstairs in the Communications Bullpen. The meeting with Gabrielle Ashe had gone well. Whether or not Gabrielle was scared enough to turn over an affidavit admitting the affair was uncertain, but it sure as hell was worth a try.

Gabrielle would be smart to bail out on him, Tench

thought. The poor girl had no idea just how hard Sexton was about to fall.

In a few hours, the President's meteoric press conference was going to cut Sexton down at the knees. That was in the bank. Gabrielle Ashe, if she cooperated, would be the death blow that sent Sexton crawling off in shame. In the morning, Tench could release Gabrielle's affidavit to the press along with footage of Sexton denying it.

One-two punch.

After all, politics was not just about winning the election, it was about winning decisively – having the momentum to carry out one's vision. Historically, any president who squeaked into office on a narrow margin accomplished much less; he was weakened right out of the gate, and Congress never seemed to let him forget it.

Ideally, the destruction of Senator Sexton's campaign would be comprehensive – a two-pronged attack sacking *both* his politics and his ethics. This strategy, known in Washington as the 'high-low,' was stolen from the art of military warfare. *Force the enemy to battle on two fronts.* When a candidate possessed a piece of negative information about his opponent, he often waited until he had a second piece and went public with both simultaneously. A double-edged attack was always more effective than a single shot, particularly when the dual attack incorporated separate aspects of his campaign – the first against his politics, the second against his character. Rebuttal of a *political* attack took logic, while rebuttal of a *character* attack took passion; disputing both simultaneously was an almost impossible balancing act.

Tonight, Senator Sexton would find himself

scrambling to extract himself from the political nightmare of an astounding NASA triumph, and yet his plight would deepen considerably if he were forced to defend his NASA position while being called a liar by a prominent female member of his staff.

Arriving now at the doorway of the Communications Office, Tench felt alive with the thrill of the fight. Politics was war. She took a deep breath and checked her watch. 6.15 P.M. The first shot was about to be fired.

She entered.

The Communications Office was small not for lack of room, but for lack of necessity. It was one of the most efficient mass communications stations in the world and employed a staff of only five people. At the moment, all five employees stood over their banks of electronic gear looking like swimmers poised for the starting gun.

They are ready, Tench saw in their eager gazes.

It always amazed her that this tiny office, given only two hours' head start, could contact more than *one third* of the world's civilized population. With electronic connections to literally tens of thousands of global news sources – from the largest television conglomerates to the smallest home-town newspapers – the White House Communications Office could, at the touch of a few buttons, reach out and touch the world.

Fax-broadcast computers churned press releases into the in-boxes of radio, television, print, and Internet media outlets from Maine to Moscow. Bulk e-mail programs blanketed on-line news wires. Telephone autodialers phoned thousands of media content managers and played recorded voice announcements. A breaking news web page provided constant updates and preformatted content. The 'live-feed-capable' news sources – CNN, NBC, ABC, CBS, foreign syndicates – would be assaulted from all angles and promised free, live television feeds. Whatever else these networks were airing would come to a screeching halt for an emergency presidential address.

Full penetration.

Like a general inspecting her troops, Tench strode in silence over to the copy desk and picked up the print-out of the 'flash release' that now sat loaded in all the transmission machines like cartridges in a shotgun.

When Tench read it, she had to laugh quietly to herself. By usual standards, the release loaded for broadcast was heavy-handed – more of an advertise-ment than an announcement – but the President had ordered the Communications Office to pull out all the stops. And that they had. This text was perfect – keyword-rich and content light. A deadly combination. Even the news wires that used automated 'keyword-sniffer' programs to sort their incoming mail would see multiple flags on this one:

From: White House Communications Office
Subject: Urgent Presidential Address

The *President of the United States* will be holding an *urgent* press conference tonight at 8:00 P.M. Eastern Standard Time from the White House briefing room. The topic of his announcement is currently *classified*. Live A/V feeds will be available via customary outlets.

Laying the paper back down on the desk, Marjorie Tench looked around the Communications Office and gave the staff an impressed nod. They looked eager.

Lighting a cigarette, she puffed a moment, letting the

anticipation build. Finally, she grinned. 'Ladies and gentlemen. Start your engines.'

53

All logical reasoning had evaporated from Rachel Sexton's mind. She held no thoughts for the meteorite, the mysterious GPR printout in her pocket, Ming, the horrific attack on the ice sheet. There was one matter at hand.

Survival.

The ice skimmed by in a blur beneath her like an endless, sleek highway. Whether her body was numb with fear or simply cocooned by her protective suit, Rachel did not know, but she felt no pain. She felt nothing.

Yet.

Lying on her side, attached to Tolland at the waist, Rachel lay face-to-face with him in an awkward embrace. Somewhere ahead of them, the balloon billowed, fat with wind, like a parachute on the back of a dragster. Corky trailed behind, swerving wildly like a tractor trailer out of control. The flare marking the spot where they had been attacked had all but disappeared in the distance.

The hissing of their nylon Mark IX suits on the ice grew higher and higher in pitch as they continued to accelerate. She had no idea how fast they were going now, but the wind was at least sixty miles an hour, and the frictionless runway beneath them seemed to be racing by faster and faster with every passing second.

The impervious Mylar balloon apparently had no intentions of tearing or relinquishing its hold.

We need to release, she thought. They were racing away from one deadly force – directly toward another. *The ocean is probably less than a mile ahead now!* The thought of icy water brought back terrifying memories.

The wind gusted harder, and their speed increased. Somewhere behind them Corky let out a scream of terror. At this speed, Rachel knew they had only a few minutes before they were dragged out over the cliff into the frigid ocean.

Tolland was apparently having similar thoughts because he was now fighting with the payload clasp attached to their bodies.

'I can't unhook us!' he yelled. 'There's too much tension!'

Rachel hoped a momentary lull in the wind might give Tolland some slack, but the katabatic pulled on with relentless uniformity. Trying to help, Rachel twisted her body and rammed the toe cleat of one of her crampons into the ice, sending a rooster tail of ice shards into the air. Their velocity slowed ever so slightly.

'Now!' she yelled, lifting her foot.

For an instant the payload line on the balloon slackened slightly. Tolland yanked down, trying to take advantage of the loose line to maneuver the payload clip out of their carabiners. Not even close.

'Again!' he yelled.

This time they both twisted against one another and rammed their toe prongs into the ice, sending a double plume of ice into the air. This slowed the contraption more perceptibly.

'Now!'

On Tolland's cue, they both let up. As the balloon surged forward again, Tolland rammed his thumb into the carabiner latch and twisted the hook, trying to release the clasp. Although closer this time, he still needed more slack. The carabiners, Norah had bragged, were first-rate, Joker safety clips, specifically crafted with an extra loop in the metal so they would never release if there were any tension on them at all.

Killed by safety clips, Rachel thought, not finding the irony the least bit amusing.

'One more time!' Tolland yelled.

Mustering all her energy and hope, Rachel twisted as far as she could and rammed both of her toes into the ice. Arching her back, she tried to lift all her weight onto her toes. Tolland followed her lead until they were both angled roughly on their stomachs, the connection at their belts straining their harnesses. Tolland rammed his toes down and Rachel arched farther. The vibrations sent shock waves up her legs. She felt like her ankles were going to break.

'Hold it . . . hold it . . .' Tolland contorted himself to release the Joker clip as their speed decreased. 'Almost . . .'

Rachel's crampons snapped. The metal cleats tore off of her boots and went tumbling backward into the night, bouncing over Corky. The balloon immediately lurched forward, sending Rachel and Tolland fishtailing to one side. Tolland lost his grasp on the clip.

'Shit!'

The Mylar balloon, as if angered at having been momentarily restrained, lurched forward now, pulling even harder, dragging them down the glacier toward the sea. Rachel knew they were closing fast on the cliff, although they faced danger even before the hundred-foot drop into the Arctic Ocean. Three huge snow berms stood in their path. Even protected by the padding in the Mark IX suits, the experience of launching at high speed up and over the snow mounds filled her with terror.

Fighting in desperation with their harnesses, Rachel tried to find a way to release the balloon. It was then that she heard the rhythmic ticking on the ice – the rapid-fire staccato of lightweight metal on the sheet of bare ice. The ax.

In her fear, she had entirely forgotten the ice ax attached to the rip cord on her belt. The lightweight aluminum tool was bouncing along beside her leg. She looked up at the payload cable on the balloon. Thick, heavy-duty braided nylon. Reaching down, she fumbled for the bouncing ax. She grasped the handle and pulled it toward her, stretching the elastic rip cord. Still on her side, Rachel struggled to raise her arms over her head, placing the ax's serrated edge against the thick cord. Awkwardly, she began sawing the taut cable.

'Yes!' Tolland yelled, fumbling now for his own ax.

Sliding on her side, Rachel was stretched out, her arms above her, sawing at the taut cable. The line was strong, and the individual nylon strands were fraying slowly. Tolland gripped his own ax, twisted, raised his arms over his head, and tried to saw from underneath in the same spot. Their banana blades clicked together as they worked in tandem like lumberjacks. The rope began fraying on both sides now.

We're going to do it, Rachel thought. *This thing is going to break!*

Suddenly, the silver bubble of Mylar before them swooped upward as if it had hit an updraft. Rachel realized to her horror that it was simply following the contour of the land.

They had arrived.

The berms.

The wall of white loomed only an instant before they were on it. The blow to Rachel's side as they hit the incline drove the wind from her lungs and wrenched the ax from her hand. Like a tangled water-skier being dragged up over a jump, Rachel felt her body dragged up the face of the berm and launched. She and Tolland were suddenly catapulted in a dizzying upward snarl. The trough between the berms spread out far beneath them, but the frayed payload cable held fast, lifting their accelerated bodies upward, carrying them clear out over the first trough. For an instant, she glimpsed what lay ahead. Two more berms – a short plateau – and then the drop-off to the sea.

As if to give a voice to Rachel's own dumbstruck terror, the high-pitched scream of Corky Marlinson cut through the air. Somewhere behind them, he sailed up over the first berm. All three of them went airborne, the balloon clawing upward like a wild animal trying to break its captor's chains.

Suddenly, like a gunshot in the night, a sudden snap echoed overhead. The frayed rope gave way, and the tattered end recoiled in Rachel's face. Instantly, they were falling. Somewhere overhead the Mylar balloon billowed out of control . . . spiraling out to sea.

Tangled in carabiners and harnesses, Rachel and Tolland tumbled back toward earth. As the white mound of the second berm rose up toward them, Rachel braced for impact. Barely clearing the top of the second berm, they crashed down the far side, the blow partially cushioned by their suits and the descending contour of the berm. As the world around her turned into a blur of arms and legs and ice, Rachel felt herself rocketing down the incline out onto the central ice trough. Instinctively she spread her arms and legs, trying to slow down before they hit the next berm. She felt them slowing, but only slightly, and it seemed only seconds before she and Tolland were sliding back up an incline. At the top, there was another instant of weightlessness as they cleared the crest. Then, filled with terror, Rachel felt them begin their dead slide down the other side and out onto the final plateau . . . the last eighty feet of the Milne Glacier.

As they skidded toward the cliff, Rachel could feel the drag of Corky on the tether, and she knew they were all slowing down. She knew it was too little too late. The end of the glacier raced toward them, and Rachel let out a helpless scream.

Then it happened.

The edge of the ice slid out from underneath them. The last thing Rachel remembered was falling.

54

The Westbrooke Place Apartments are located at 2201 N Street NW and promote themselves as one of the few un-questionably correct addresses in Washington. Gabrielle hurried through the gilded revolving door into the marble lobby, where a deafening waterfall reverberated.

The doorman at the front desk looked surprised to see her. 'Ms Ashe? I didn't know you were stopping by tonight.'

'I'm running late.' Gabrielle quickly signed in. The clock overhead read 6:22 P.M.

The doorman scratched his head. 'The senator gave me a list, but you weren't—'

'They always forget the people who help them most.' She gave a harried smile and strode past him toward the elevator.

Now the doorman looked uneasy. 'I better call up.'

'Thanks,' Gabrielle said, as she boarded the elevator and headed up. *The senator's phone is off the hook.*

Riding the elevator to the ninth floor, Gabrielle exited and made her way down the elegant hallway. At the end, outside Sexton's doorway, she could see one of his bulky personal safety escorts – glorified bodyguards – sitting in the hall. He looked bored. Gabrielle was surprised to see security on duty, although apparently not as surprised as the guard was to see her. He jumped to his feet as she approached.

'I know,' Gabrielle called out, still halfway down the hall. 'It's a P.E. night. He doesn't want to be disturbed.'

The guard nodded emphatically. 'He gave me very strict orders that no visitors—'

'It's an emergency.'

The guard physically blocked the doorway. 'He's in a private meeting.'

'Really?' Gabrielle pulled the red envelope from under her arm. She flashed the White House seal in the man's face. 'I was just in the Oval Office. I need to give the senator this information. Whatever old pals he's schmoozing tonight are going to have to do without him for a few minutes. Now, let me in.'

The guard withered slightly at the sight of the White House seal on the envelope.

Don't make me open this, Gabrielle thought.

'Leave the folder,' he said. 'I'll take it in to him.'

'The hell you will. I have direct orders from the White House to hand-deliver this. If I don't talk to him immediately, we can all start looking for jobs tomorrow morning. Do you understand?'

The guard looked deeply conflicted, and Gabrielle sensed the senator had indeed been unusually adamant tonight about having no visitors. She moved in for the kill. Holding the White House envelope directly in his face, Gabrielle lowered her voice to a whisper and uttered the six words all Washington security personnel feared most.

'You do *not* understand the situation.'

Security personnel for politicians *never* understood the situation, and they hated that fact. They were hired guns, kept in the dark, never sure whether to stand firm in their orders or risk losing their jobs by mule-headedly ignoring some obvious crisis.

The guard swallowed hard, eyeing the White House envelope again. 'Okay, but I'm telling the senator you *demanded* to be let in.'

He unlocked the door, and Gabrielle pushed past him before he changed his mind. She entered the apartment and quietly closed the door behind her, relocking it.

Now inside the foyer, Gabrielle, could hear muffled voices in Sexton's den down the hall – men's voices. Tonight's P.E. was obviously not the private meeting implied by Sexton's earlier call.

As Gabrielle moved down the hall toward the den, she passed an open closet where a half dozen expensive men's coats hung inside – distinctive wool and tweed. Several briefcases sat on the floor. Apparently work stayed in the hall tonight. Gabrielle would have walked right past the cases except that one of the briefcases caught her eye. The nameplate bore a distinctive company logo. A bright red rocket.

She paused, kneeling down to read it:

SPACE AMERICA, INC.

Puzzled, she examined the other briefcases.

BEAL AEROSPACE. MICROCOSM, INC. ROTARY ROCKET COMPANY. KISTLER AEROSPACE.

Marjorie Tench's raspy voice echoed in her mind. *Are you aware that Sexton is accepting bribes from private aerospace companies?*

Gabrielle's pulse began racing as she gazed down the darkened hallway toward the archway that led into the senator's den. She knew she should speak up, announce her presence, and yet she felt herself inching quietly forward. She moved to within a few feet of the archway and stood soundlessly in the shadows . . . listening to the conversation beyond.

55

While Delta-Three stayed behind to collect Norah Mangor's body and the sled, the other two soldiers accelerated down the glacier after their quarry.

On their feet they wore ElektroTread-powered skis. Modeled after the consumer Fast Trax motorized skis, the classified ElektroTreads were essentially snow skis with miniaturized tank treads affixed – like snowmobiles worn on the feet. Speed was controlled by pushing the tips of the index finger and thumb together, compressing two pressure plates inside the right-hand glove. A powerful gel battery was molded around the foot, doubling as insulation and allowing the skis to run silently. Ingeniously, the kinetic energy generated by gravity and the spinning treads as the wearer glided *down* a hill was automatically harvested to recharge the batteries for the next incline.

Keeping the wind at his back, Delta-One crouched low, skimming seaward as he surveyed the glacier before him. His night vision system was a far cry from the Patriot model used by the Marines. Delta-One was looking through a hands-free face mount with a 40 x 90 mm six-element lens, three-element Magnification Doubler, and Super Long Range IR. The world outside appeared in a translucent tint of cool blue, rather than the usual green – the color scheme especially designed for highly reflective terrains like the Arctic.

As he approached the first berm, Delta-One's goggles revealed several bright stripes of freshly disturbed snow, rising up and over the berm like a neon arrow in the night. Apparently the three escapees had either not thought to unhook their makeshift sail or had been unable to. Either way, if they had not released by the final berm, they were now somewhere out in the ocean. Delta-One knew his quarry's protective clothing would lengthen the usual life expectancy in the water, but the relentless offshore currents would drag them out to sea. Drowning would be inevitable.

Despite his confidence, Delta-One had been trained never to assume. He needed to see bodies. Crouching low, he pressed his fingers together and accelerated up the first incline.

Michael Tolland lay motionless, taking stock of his bruises. He was battered, but he sensed no broken bones. He had little doubt the gel-filled Mark IX had saved him any substantial trauma. As he opened his eyes, his thoughts were slow to focus. Everything seemed softer here . . . quieter. The wind still howled, but with less ferocity.

We went over the edge – didn't we?

Focusing, Tolland found he was lying on ice, draped across Rachel Sexton, almost at right angles, their locked carabiners twisted. He could feel her breathing beneath him, but he could not see her face. He rolled off her, his muscles barely responding.

'Rachel . . . ?' Tolland wasn't sure if his lips were making sound or not.

Tolland recalled the final seconds of their harrowing ride – the upward drag of the balloon, the payload cable snapping, their bodies plummeting down the far side of the berm, sliding up and over the final mound, skimming toward the edge – the ice running out. Tolland and Rachel had fallen, but the fall had been oddly short. Rather than the expected plunge to the sea, they had fallen only ten feet or so before hitting another slab of ice and sliding to a stop with the dead weight of Corky in tow.

Now, raising his head, Tolland looked toward the sea. Not far away, the ice ended in a sheer cliff, beyond which he could hear the sounds of the ocean. Looking back up the glacier, Tolland strained to see into the night. Twenty yards back, his eyes met a high wall of ice, which seemed to hang above them. It was then that he realized what had happened. Somehow they had slid off the main glacier onto a lower terrace of ice. This section was flat, as large as a hockey rink, and had partially collapsed – preparing to cleave off into the ocean at any moment.

Ice calving, Tolland thought, eyeing the precarious platform of ice on which he was now lying. It was a broad square slab that hung off the glacier like a colossal balcony, surrounded on three sides by precipices to the ocean. The sheet of ice was attached to the glacier only at its back, and Tolland could see the connection was anything but permanent. The boundary where the lower terrace clung to the Milne Ice Shelf was marked by a gaping pressure fissure almost four feet across. Gravity was well on its way to winning this battle.

Almost more frightening than seeing the fissure was Tolland's seeing the motionless body of Corky Marlinson crumpled on the ice. Corky lay ten yards away at the end of a taut tether attached to them.

Tolland tried to stand up, but he was still attached to Rachel. Repositioning himself, he began detaching their interlocking carabiners.

Rachel looked weak as she tried to sit up. 'We didn't . . . go over?' Her voice was bewildered.

'We fell onto a lower block of ice,' Tolland said, finally unfastening himself from her. 'I've got to help Corky.'

Painfully, Tolland attempted to stand, but his legs felt feeble. He grabbed the tether and heaved. Corky began sliding toward them across the ice. After a dozen or so pulls, Corky was lying on the ice a few feet away.

Corky Marlinson looked beaten. He'd lost his goggles, suffered a bad cut on his cheek, and his nose was bleeding. Tolland's worries that Corky might be dead were quickly allayed when Corky rolled over and looked at Tolland with an angry glare.

'Jesus,' he stammered. 'What the hell was *that* little trick?'

Tolland felt a wave of relief.

Rachel sat up now, wincing. She looked around. 'We need to . . . get off of here. This block of ice looks like it's about to fall.'

Tolland couldn't have agreed more. The only question was how.

They had no time to consider a solution. A familiar high-pitched whir became audible above them on the glacier. Tolland's gaze shot up to see two white-clad figures ski effortlessly up onto the edge and stop in unison. The two men stood there a moment, peering down at their battered prey like chess masters savoring checkmate before the final kill.

Delta-One was surprised to see the three escapees alive. He knew, however, this was a temporary condition. They had fallen onto a section of the glacier that had already begun its inevitable plunge to the sea. This quarry could be disabled and killed in the same manner as the other woman, but a far cleaner solution had just presented itself. A way in which no bodies would ever be found.

Gazing downward over the lip, Delta-One focused on the gaping crevasse that had begun to spread like a wedge between the ice shelf and the clinging block of ice. The section of ice on which the three fugitives sat was dangerously perched . . . ready to break away and fall into the ocean any day now.

Why not today . . .

Here on the ice shelf, the night was rocked every few hours by deafening booms – the sound of ice cracking off parts of the glacier and plummeting into the ocean. Who would take notice?

Feeling the familiar warm rush of adrenaline that

accompanied the preparation for a kill, Delta-One reached in his supply pack and pulled out a heavy, lemon-shaped object. Standard issue for military assault teams, the object was called a flash-bang – a 'nonlethal' concussion grenade that temporarily disoriented an enemy by generating a blinding flash and deafening concussion wave. Tonight, however, Delta-One knew this flash-bang would most certainly be lethal.

He positioned himself near the edge and wondered how far the crevasse descended before tapering to a close. Twenty feet? Fifty feet? He knew it didn't matter. His plan would be effective regardless.

With calm bred from the performance of countless executions, Delta-One dialed a ten-second delay into the grenade's screw-dial, slid out the pin, and threw the grenade down into the chasm. The bomb plummeted into the darkness and disappeared.

Then Delta-One and his partner cleared back up onto the top of the berm and waited. This would be a sight to behold.

Even in her delirious state of mind, Rachel Sexton had a very good idea what the attackers had just dropped into the crevasse. Whether Michael Tolland also knew or whether he was reading the fear in her eyes was unclear, but she saw him go pale, shooting a horrified glance down at the mammoth slab of ice on which they were stranded, clearly realizing the inevitable.

Like a storm cloud lit by an internal flash of lightning, the ice beneath Rachel illuminated from within. The eerie white translucence shot out in all directions. For a hundred yards around them, the glacier flashed white. The concussion came next. Not a rumble like an earthquake, but a deafening shock wave of gut-churning force. Rachel felt the impact tearing up through the ice into her body.

Instantly, as if a wedge had been driven between the ice shelf and the block of ice supporting them, the cliff began to shear off with a sickening crack. Rachel's eyes locked with Tolland's in a freeze-frame of terror. Corky let out a scream nearby.

The bottom dropped out.

Rachel felt weightless for an instant, hovering over the multimillion-pound block of ice. Then they were riding the iceberg down – plummeting into the frigid sea.

56

The deafening grating of ice against ice assaulted Rachel's ears as the massive slab slid down the face of the Milne Ice Shelf, sending towering plumes of spray into the air. As the slab splashed downward, it slowed, and Rachel's previously weightless body crashed down onto the top of the ice. Tolland and Corky landed hard nearby.

As the block's downward momentum plunged it deeper into the sea, Rachel could see the foaming surface of the ocean racing upward with a kind of taunting deceleration, like the ground beneath a bungee-jumper whose cord was a few feet too long. Rising . . . rising . . . and then it was there. Her childhood nightmare was back. *The ice . . . the water . . . the darkness.* The dread was almost primal.

The top of the slab slipped below the waterline, and the frigid Arctic Ocean poured over the edges in a torrent. As the ocean rushed in all around her, Rachel felt herself sucked under. The bare skin on her face tightened and burned as the saltwater hit. The flooring of ice disappeared beneath her, and Rachel fought her way back to the surface, buoyed by the gel in her suit. She took in a mouthful of saltwater, sputtering to the surface. She could see the others floundering nearby, all of them tangled in tethers. Just as Rachel righted herself, Tolland yelled out.

'It's coming back up!'

As his words echoed above the tumult, Rachel felt an eerie upwelling in the water beneath her. Like a massive locomotive straining to reverse direction, the slab of ice had groaned to a stop underwater and was now beginning its ascent directly beneath them. Fathoms below, a sickening low frequency rumble resonated upward through the water as the gigantic submerged sheet began scraping its way back up the face of the glacier.

The slab rose fast, accelerating as it came, swooping up from the darkness. Rachel felt herself rising. The ocean roiled all around as the ice met her body. She scrambled in vain, trying to find her balance as the ice propelled her skyward along with millions of gallons of seawater. Buoying upward, the giant sheet bobbed above the surface, heaving and teetering, looking for its center of gravity. Rachel found herself scrambling in waist-deep water across the enormous, flat expanse. As the water began pouring off the surface, the current swallowed Rachel and dragged her toward the edge. Sliding, splayed flat on her stomach, Rachel could see the edge looming fast.

Hold on! Rachel's mother's voice was calling the same way it had when Rachel was just a child floundering beneath the icy pond. *Hold on! Don't go under!*

The wrenching yank on her harness expelled what little air Rachel had left in her lungs. She jerked to a dead stop only yards from the edge. The motion spun her in space. Ten yards away, she could see Corky's limp body, still tethered to her, also jolting to a stop. They had been flowing off the sheet in opposite directions and his momentum had stopped her. As the water ran off and grew more shallow, another dark form appeared over near Corky. He was on his hands and knees, grasping Corky's tether and vomiting saltwater.

Michael Tolland.

As the last of the wake drained past her and flowed off the iceberg, Rachel lay in terrified silence, listening to the sounds of the ocean. Then, feeling the onset of deadly cold, she dragged herself onto her hands and knees. The 'berg was still bobbing back and forth, like a giant ice cube. Delirious and in pain, she crawled back toward the others.

High above on the glacier, Delta-One peered through his night-vision goggles at the water churning around the Arctic Ocean's newest tabular iceberg. Although he saw no bodies in the water, he was not surprised. The ocean was dark, and his quarry's weather suits and skullcaps were black.

As he passed his gaze across the surface of the enormous floating sheet of ice, he had a hard time keeping it in focus. It was receding quickly, already heading out to sea in the strong offshore currents. He was about to turn his gaze back to the sea when he saw something unexpected. Three specks of black on the ice. *Are those bodies?* Delta-One tried to bring them into focus.

'See something?' Delta-Two asked.

Delta-One said nothing, focusing in with his magnifier. In the pale tint of the iceberg, he was stunned to see three human forms huddled motionless on the island of ice. Whether they were alive or dead, Delta-One had no idea. It hardly mattered. If they were alive, even in weather suits, they'd be dead within the hour; they were wet, a storm was coming in, and they were drifting seaward into one of the most deadly oceans on the planet. Their bodies would never be found.

'Just shadows,' Delta-One said, turning from the cliff. 'Let's get back to base.'

57

Senator Sedgewick Sexton set his snifter of Courvoisier on the mantelpiece of his Westbrooke apartment and stoked the fire for several moments, gathering his thoughts. The six men in the den with him sat in silence now ... waiting. The small talk was over. It was time for Senator Sexton to make his pitch. They knew it. He knew it.

Politics was sales.

Establish trust. Let them know you understand their problems.

'As you may know,' Sexton said, turning toward them, 'over the past months, I have met with many men in your same position.' He smiled and sat down, joining them on their level. 'You are the only ones I have ever brought into my home. You are extraordinary men, and I am honored to meet you.'

Sexton folded his hands and let his eyes circle the room, making personal contact with each of his guests. Then he focused in on his first mark – the heavyset man in the cowboy hat.

'Space Industries of Houston,' Sexton said. 'I'm glad you came.'

The Texan grunted. 'I hate this town.'

'I don't blame you. Washington has been unfair to you.'

The Texan stared out from beneath the rim of his hat but said nothing.

'Twelve years back,' Sexton began, 'you made an offer to the U.S. government. You proposed to build them a U.S. space station for a mere five billion dollars.'

'Yeah, I did. I still have the blueprints.'

'And yet NASA convinced the government that a U.S. space station should be a *NASA* project.'

'Right. NASA started building almost a decade ago.'

'A decade. And not only is the NASA space station not yet fully operational, but the project so far has cost *twenty* times your bid. As an American taxpayer, I am sickened.'

A grumble of agreement circled the room. Sexton let his eyes move, reconnecting with the group.

'I am well aware,' the senator said, addressing everyone now, 'that several of your companies have offered to launch private space shuttles for as little as fifty million dollars per flight.'

More nods.

'And yet NASA undercuts you by charging only thirty-eight million dollars per flight . . . even though their *actual* per flight cost is over one hundred and fifty million dollars!'

'It's how they keep us out of space,' one of the men

said. 'The private sector cannot possibly compete with a company that can afford to run shuttle flights at a four hundred percent loss and still stay in business.'

'Nor should you *have* to,' Sexton said.

Nods all around.

Sexton turned now to the austere entrepreneur beside him, a man whose file Sexton had read with interest. Like many of the entrepreneurs funding Sexton's campaign, this man was a former military engineer who had become disillusioned with low wages and government bureaucracy and had abandoned his military post to seek his fortune in aerospace.

'Kistler Aerospace,' Sexton said, shaking his head in despair. 'Your company has designed and manufactured a rocket that can launch payloads for as little as two thousand dollars per pound compared to NASA's costs of *ten thousand dollars* per pound.' Sexton paused for effect. 'And yet you have no clients.'

'Why *would* I have any clients?' the man replied. 'Last week NASA undercut us by charging Motorola only eight hundred and twelve dollars per pound to launch a telecomm satellite. The government launched that satellite at a nine hundred percent loss!'

Sexton nodded. Taxpayers were unwittingly subsidizing an agency that was ten times less efficient than its competition. 'It has become painfully clear,' he said, his voice darkening, 'that NASA is working very hard to stifle competition in space. They crowd out private aerospace businesses by pricing services below market value.'

'It's the Wal-Marting of space,' the Texan said.

Damn good analogy, Sexton thought. *I'll have to remember that.* Wal-Mart was notorious for moving into a new territory, selling products below market value, and driving all local competition out of business.

'I'm goddamned sick and tired,' the Texan said, 'of having to pay millions in business taxes so Uncle Sam can use that money to steal my clients!'

'I hear you,' Sexton said. 'I understand.'

'It's the lack of corporate sponsorships that's killing Rotary Rocket,' a sharply dressed man said. 'The laws against sponsorship are criminal!'

'I couldn't agree more.' Sexton had been shocked to learn that another way NASA entrenched its monopoly of space was by passing federal mandates banning advertisements on space vehicles. Instead of allowing private companies to secure funding through corporate sponsorships and advertising logos – the way, for example, professional race car drivers did – space vehicles could only display the words USA and the company name. In a country that spent $185 billion a year on advertising, not one advertising dollar ever found its way into the coffers of private space companies.

'It's robbery,' one of the men snapped. 'My company hopes to stay in business long enough to launch the country's first tourist-shuttle prototype next May. We expect enormous press coverage. The Nike Corporation just offered us seven million in sponsorship dollars to paint the Nike swoosh and "Just do it!" on the side of the shuttle. Pepsi offered us twice that for "Pepsi: The choice of a new generation." But according to federal law, if our shuttle displays advertising, we are prohibited from launching it!'

'That's right,' Senator Sexton said. 'And if elected, I will work to abolish that antisponsorship legislation. That is a promise. Space should be open for advertising the way every square inch of earth is open to advertising.'

Sexton gazed out now at his audience, his eyes locking in, his voice growing solemn. 'We all need to be aware, however, that the biggest obstacle to privatization of NASA is not laws, but rather, it is public perception. Most Americans still hold a romanticized view of the American space program. They still believe NASA is a *necessary* government agency.'

'It's those goddamned Hollywood movies!' one man said. 'How many NASA-saves-the-world-from-a-killer-asteroid movies can Hollywood make, for Christ's sake? It's propaganda!'

The plethora of NASA movies coming out of Hollywood, Sexton knew, was simply a matter of economics. Following the wildly popular movie *Top Gun* – a Tom Cruise jet pilot blockbuster that played like a two-hour advertisement for the U.S. Navy – NASA realized the true potential of Hollywood as a public relations powerhouse. NASA quietly began offering film companies *free* filming access to all of NASA's dramatic facilities – launchpads, mission control, training facilities. Producers, who were accustomed to paying enormous on-site licensing fees when they filmed anywhere else, jumped at the opportunity to save millions in budget costs by making NASA thrillers on 'free' sets. Of course, Hollywood only got access if NASA approved the script.

'Public brainwashing,' a Hispanic grunted. 'The movies aren't half as bad as the publicity stunts. Sending a senior citizen into space? And now NASA is planning an all-female shuttle crew? All for publicity!'

Sexton sighed, his tone turning tragic. 'True, and I know I don't have to remind you what happened back in the Eighties when the Department of Education was bankrupt and cited NASA as wasting millions that could be spent on education. NASA devised a PR stunt to prove NASA was education-friendly. They sent a public school teacher into space.' Sexton paused. 'You all remember Christa McAuliffe.'

The room fell silent.

'Gentlemen,' Sexton said, stopping dramatically in front of the fire. 'I believe it is time Americans understood the truth, for the good of all of our futures. It's time Americans understand that NASA is not leading us skyward, but rather is stifling space exploration. Space is no different than any other industry, and keeping the private sector grounded verges on a criminal act. Consider the computer industry, in which we see such an explosion of progress that we can barely keep up from week to week! Why? Because the computer industry is a free-market system: it rewards efficiency and vision with *profits*. Imagine if the computer industry were government-run? We would still be in the Dark Ages. We're stagnating in space. We should put space exploration into the hands of the private sector where it belongs. Americans would be stunned by the growth, jobs, and realized dreams. I believe we should let the free-market system spur us to new heights in space. If elected, I will make it my personal mission to unlock the doors to the final frontier and let them swing wide open.'

Sexton lifted his snifter of cognac.

'My friends, you came here tonight to decide if I am someone worthy of your trust. I hope I am on the way to earning it. In the same way it takes investors to build a company, it takes investors to build a presidency. In the same way corporate stockholders expect returns,

272

you as political investors expect returns. My message to you tonight is simple: invest in me, and I will never forget you. Ever. Our missions are one and the same.'

Sexton extended his glass toward them in a toast.

'With your help, my friends, soon I will be in the White House . . . and you will all be launching your dreams.'

Only fifteen feet away, Gabrielle Ashe stood in the shadows, rigid. From the den came the harmonious clink of crystal snifters and the crackle of the fire.

58

In a panic, the young NASA technician dashed through the habisphere. *Something terrible has happened!* He found Administrator Ekstrom alone near the press area.

'Sir,' the technician gasped, running up. 'There's been an accident!'

Ekstrom turned, looking distant, as if his thoughts were already deeply troubled with other matters. 'What did you say? An accident? Where?'

'In the extraction pit. A body just floated up. Dr Wailee Ming.'

Ekstrom's face was blank. 'Dr Ming? But . . .'

'We pulled him out, but it was too late. He's dead.'

'For Christ's sake. How long has he been in there?'

'We think about an hour. It looks like he fell in, sank to the bottom, but when his body bloated, he floated up again.'

Ekstrom's reddish skin turned crimson. 'Goddamn it! Who else knows about this?'

'Nobody, sir. Only two of us. We fished him out, but we thought we better tell you before—'

'You did the right thing.' Ekstrom exhaled a weighty sigh. 'Stow Dr Ming's body immediately. Say nothing.'

The technician felt perplexed. 'But, sir, I—'

Ekstrom put a large hand on the man's shoulder. 'Listen to me carefully. This is a tragic accident, one I deeply regret. Of course I will deal with it appropriately when the time comes. Now, however, is not the time.'

'You want me to *hide* his body?'

Ekstrom's cold Nordic eyes bore down. 'Think about it. We could tell everyone, but what would that accomplish? We're about an hour off from this press conference. Announcing that we've had a fatal accident would overshadow the discovery and have a devastating effect on morale. Dr Ming made a careless mistake; I have no intention of making NASA pay for it. These civilian scientists have taken enough of the spotlight without my letting one of their slipshod errors cast a shadow over our public moment of glory. Dr Ming's accident remains a secret until after the press conference. Do you understand?'

The man nodded, pale. 'I'll stow his body.'

59

Michael Tolland had been at sea enough times to know the ocean took victims without remorse or hesitation. As he lay in exhaustion on the expansive sheet of ice, he could just make out the ghostly outline of the towering Milne Ice Shelf receding in the distance. He knew the powerful Arctic current flowing off the Elizabethan Islands spiraled in an enormous loop around the polar ice cap and would eventually skirt land in northern Russia. Not that it mattered. That would be months from now.

We've got maybe thirty minutes . . . forty-five at the most.

Without the protective insulation of their gel-filled suits, Tolland knew they would be dead already. Thankfully, the Mark IXs had kept them dry – the most critical aspect of surviving cold weather. The thermal gel around their bodies had not only cushioned their fall, but it was now helping their bodies retain what little heat they had left.

Soon hypothermia would set in. It would start with a vague numbness in limbs as the blood retreated to the body's core to protect the critical internal organs. Delirious hallucinations would come next, as the pulse and respiration slowed, cheating the brain of oxygen. Then, the body would make a final effort to conserve its remaining heat by shutting down all operations except the heart and respiration. Unconsciousness would follow. In the end, heart and respiration centers in the brain would stop functioning altogether.

Tolland turned his gaze toward Rachel, wishing he could do something to save her.

The numbness spreading through Rachel Sexton's body was less painful than she would have imagined. Almost a welcome anesthetic. *Nature's morphine.* She had lost her goggles in the collapse, and she could barely open her eyes against the cold.

She could see Tolland and Corky on the ice nearby. Tolland was looking at her, eyes filled with regret. Corky was moving but obviously in pain. His right cheekbone was smashed and bloody.

Rachel's body trembled wildly as her mind searched for answers. *Who? Why?* Her thoughts were muddled by a growing heaviness inside her. Nothing was making sense. She felt like her body was slowly shutting down, lulled by an invisible force pulling her to sleep. She fought it. A fiery anger ignited within her now, and she tried to fan the flames.

They tried to kill us! She peered out at the threatening sea and sensed their attackers had succeeded. *We're already dead.* Even now, knowing she would probably not live to learn the whole truth about the deadly game being played out on the Milne Ice Shelf, Rachel suspected she already knew who to blame.

Administrator Ekstrom had the most to gain. He was the one who sent them out on the ice. He had ties to the Pentagon and Special Ops. *But what did Ekstrom have to gain by inserting the meteorite beneath the ice? What did anyone have to gain?*

Rachel flashed on Zach Herney, wondering if the President was a coconspirator or an unknowing pawn? *Herney knows nothing. He's innocent.* The President obviously had been duped by NASA. Now Herney was only about an hour away from making NASA's announcement. And he would do so armed with a video documentary containing endorsements from four civilian scientists.

Four *dead* civilian scientists.

Rachel could do nothing to stop the press conference now, but she vowed that whoever was responsible for this attack would not get away with it.

Summoning her strength, Rachel tried to sit up. Her limbs felt like granite, all her joints screaming in pain as she bent her legs and arms. Slowly, she pulled herself to her knees, steadying herself on the flat ice. Her head spun. All around her the ocean churned. Tolland lay nearby, gazing up at her with inquisitive eyes. Rachel sensed he probably thought she was kneeling in prayer. She was not, of course, although prayer probably had as good a chance of saving them as what she was about to attempt.

Rachel's right hand fumbled across her waist and found the ice ax still bungeed to her belt. Her stiff fingers gripped the handle. She inverted the ax, positioning it like an upside down T. Then, with all her energy, she drove the butt downward into the ice. *Thud*. Again. *Thud*. The blood felt like cold molasses in her veins. *Thud*. Tolland looked on in obvious confusion. Rachel drove the ax down again. *Thud*.

Tolland tried to lift himself onto his elbow. 'Ra . . . chel?'

She did not answer. She needed all her energy. *Thud*. *Thud*.

'I don't think . . .' Tolland said, 'this far north . . . that the SAA . . . could hear . . .'

Rachel turned, surprised. She had forgotten Tolland was an oceanographer and might have some idea what she was up to. *Right idea . . . but I'm not calling the SAA*.

She kept pounding.

The SAA stood for a Suboceanic Acoustic Array, a relic of the Cold War now used by oceanographers worldwide to listen for whales. Because underwater sounds carried for hundreds of miles, the SAA network of fifty-nine underwater microphones around the world could listen to a surprisingly large percentage of

277

the planet's oceans. Unfortunately, this remote section of the Arctic was not part of that percentage, but Rachel knew there were others out there listening to the ocean floor – others that few on earth knew existed. She kept pounding. Her message was simple and clear.

THUD. THUD. THUD.

THUD . . . THUD . . . THUD . . .

THUD. THUD. THUD.

Rachel had no delusions that her actions would save their lives; she could already feel a frosty tightness gripping her body. She doubted she had a half hour of life left in her. Rescue was beyond the realm of possibility now. But this was not about rescue.

THUD. THUD. THUD.

THUD . . . THUD . . . THUD . . .

THUD. THUD. THUD.

'There's . . . no time . . .' Tolland said.

It's not . . . about us, she thought. *It's about the information in my pocket*. Rachel pictured the incriminating GPR printout inside the Velcro pocket of her Mark IX suit. *I need to get the GPR printout into the hands of the NRO . . . and soon*.

Even in her delirious state, Rachel was certain her message would be received. In the mid-Eighties, the NRO had replaced the SAA with an array thirty times as powerful. Total global coverage: Classic Wizard, the NRO's $12 million ear to the ocean floor. In the next few hours the Cray supercomputers at the NRO/NSA listening post in Menwith Hill, England, would flag an anomalous sequence in one of the Arctic's hydrophones, decipher the pounding as an SOS, triangulate the coordinates, and dispatch a rescue plane from Thule Air Force Base in Greenland. The plane would find three bodies on an iceberg. Frozen. Dead. One would be an NRO employee . . . and she would be carrying a strange piece of thermal paper in her pocket.

A GPR printout.

Norah Mangor's final legacy.

When the rescuers studied the printout, the mysterious insertion tunnel beneath the meteorite would be revealed. From there, Rachel had no idea what would happen, but at least the secret would not die with them here on the ice.

60

Every president's transition into the White House involves a private tour of three heavily guarded warehouses containing priceless collections of past White House furniture: desks, silverware, bureaus, beds, and other items used by past presidents as far back as George Washington. During the tour, the transitioning president is invited to select any heirlooms he likes and use them as furnishings inside the White House during his term. Only the bed in the Lincoln Bedroom is a permanent White House fixture. Ironically, Lincoln never slept in it.

The desk at which Zach Herney was currently sitting inside the Oval Office had once belonged to his idol, Harry Truman. The desk, though small by modern standards, served as a daily reminder to Zach Herney that the 'buck' did indeed stop here, and that Herney was ultimately responsible for any shortcomings of his administration. Herney accepted the responsibility as an honor and did his best to instill in his staff the motivations to do whatever it took to get the job done.

'Mr President?' his secretary called out, peering into the office. 'Your call just went through.'

Herney waved. 'Thank you.'

He reached for his phone. He would have preferred some privacy for this call, but he sure as hell was not going to get any of that right now. Two makeup specialists hovered like gnats, poking and primping at his face and hair. Directly in front of his desk, a television crew was setting up, and an endless swarm of advisers and PR people scurried around the office, excitedly discussing strategy.

T minus one hour . . .

Herney pressed the illuminated button on his private phone. 'Lawrence? You there?'

'I'm here.' The NASA administrator's voice sounded consumed, distant.

'Everything okay up there?'

'Storm's still moving in, but my people tell me the satellite link will not be affected. We're good to go. One hour and counting.'

'Excellent. Spirits high, I hope.'

'Very high. My staff's excited. In fact, we just shared some beers.'

Herney laughed. 'Glad to hear it. Look, I wanted to call and thank you before we do this thing. Tonight's going to be one hell of a night.'

The administrator paused, sounding uncharacteristically uncertain. 'That it will, sir. We've been waiting a long time for this.'

Herney hesitated. 'You sound exhausted.'

'I need some sunlight and a real bed.'

'One more hour. Smile for the cameras, enjoy the

moment, and then we'll get a plane up there to bring you back to D.C.'

'Looking forward to it.' The man fell silent again.

As a skilled negotiator, Herney was trained to listen, to hear what was being said between the lines. Something in the administrator's voice sounded off somehow. 'You sure everything's okay up there?'

'Absolutely. All systems go.' The administrator seemed eager to change the subject. 'Did you see the final cut of Michael Tolland's documentary?'

'Just watched it,' Herney said. 'He did a fantastic job.'

'Yes. You made a good call bringing him in.'

'Still mad at me for involving civilians?'

'Hell, yes,' the administrator growled good-naturedly, his voice with the usual strength to it.

It made Herney feel better. *Ekstrom's fine*, Herney thought. *Just a little tired.* 'Okay, I'll see you in an hour via satellite. We'll give 'em something to talk about.'

'Right.'

'Hey, Lawrence?' Herney's voice grew low and solemn now. 'You've done a hell of thing up there. I won't ever forget it.'

Outside the habisphere, buffeted by wind, Delta-Three struggled to right and repack Norah Mangor's toppled equipment sled. Once all the equipment was back on-board, he battened down the vinyl top and draped Mangor's dead body across the top, tying her down. As he was preparing to drag the sled off course, his two partners came skimming up the glacier toward him.

'Change of plans,' Delta-One called out above the wind. 'The other three went over the edge.'

Delta-Three was not surprised. He also knew what it

meant. The Delta Force's plan to stage an accident by arranging four dead bodies on the ice shelf was no longer a viable option. Leaving a lone body would pose more questions than answers. 'Sweep?' he asked.

Delta-One nodded. 'I'll recover the flares and you two get rid of the sled.'

While Delta-One carefully retraced the scientists' path, collecting every last clue that anyone had been there at all, Delta-Three and his partner moved down the glacier with the laden equipment sled. After struggling over the berms, they finally reached the precipice at the end of the Milne Ice Shelf. They gave a push, and Norah Mangor and her sled slipped silently over the edge, plummeting into the Arctic Ocean.

Clean sweep, Delta-Three thought.

As they headed back to base, he was pleased to see the wind obliterating the tracks made by their skis.

61

The nuclear submarine *Charlotte* had been stationed in the Arctic Ocean for five days now. Its presence here was highly classified.

A Los Angeles-class sub, the *Charlotte* was designed to 'listen and not be heard.' Its 42 tons of turbine engines were suspended on springs to dampen any vibration they might cause. Despite its requirement for stealth, the LA-class sub had one of the largest footprints of any reconnaissance sub in the water. Stretching more than 360 feet from nose to stern, the hull, if placed on an NFL football field, would crush both goalposts and then some. Seven times the length of the U.S. Navy's first Holland-class submarine, the *Charlotte* displaced 6,927 tons of water when fully submerged and could cruise at an astounding 35 knots.

The vessel's normal cruising depth was just below the thermocline, a natural temperature gradient that distorted sonar reflections from above and made the sub invisible to surface radar. With a crew of 158 and max dive depth of over 1,500 feet, the vessel represented the state-of-the-art submersible and was the oceanic workhorse of the United States Navy. Its evaporative electrolysis oxygenation system, two nuclear reactors, and engineered provisions gave it the ability to circumnavigate the globe twenty-one times without surfacing. Human waste from the crew, as on most cruise ships, was compressed into sixty-pound blocks and ejected into the ocean – the huge bricks of feces jokingly referred to as 'whale turds.'

The technician sitting at the oscillator screen in the sonar room was one of the best in the world. His mind was a dictionary of sounds and waveforms. He could distinguish between the sounds of several dozen Russian submarine propellers, hundreds of marine animals, and even pinpoint underwater volcanoes as far away as Japan.

At the moment, however, he was listening to a dull, repetitive echo. The sound, although easily distinguishable, was most unexpected.

'You aren't going to believe what's coming through my listening cans,' he said to his catalog assistant, handing over the headphones.

His assistant donned the headphones, an incredulous look crossing his face. 'My God. It's clear as day. What do we do?'

The sonar man was already on the phone to the captain.

When the submarine's captain arrived in the sonar room, the technician piped a live sonar feed over a small set of speakers. The captain listened, expressionless.

THUD. THUD. THUD.

THUD . . . THUD . . . THUD . . .

Slower. Slower. The pattern was becoming looser. More and more faint.

'What are the coordinates?' the captain demanded.

The technician cleared his throat. 'Actually, sir, it's coming from the surface, about three miles to our starboard.'

62

In the darkened hallway outside Senator Sexton's den, Gabrielle Ashe's legs were trembling. Not so much out of exhaustion from standing motionless, but from disillusionment over what she was listening to. The meeting in the next room was still going, but Gabrielle didn't have to hear another word. The truth seemed painfully obvious.

Senator Sexton is taking bribes from private space agencies. Marjorie Tench had been telling the truth.

The revulsion Gabrielle felt spreading through her now was one of betrayal. She had believed in Sexton. She'd fought for him. *How can he do this?* Gabrielle had seen the senator lie publicly from time to time to protect his private life, but that was politics. *This* was breaking the law.

He's not even elected yet, and he's already selling out the White House!

Gabrielle knew she could no longer support the senator. Promising to deliver the NASA privatization bill could be done only with a contemptuous disregard for both the law and the democratic system. Even if the senator *believed* it would be in everyone's best interest, to sell that decision flat out, in advance, slammed the door on the checks and balances of government, ignoring potentially persuasive arguments from Congress, advisers, voters, and lobbyists. Most important, guaranteeing the privatization of NASA, Sexton had paved the way for endless abuses of that advanced knowledge – insider trading the most common – blatantly favoring the wealthy inside cadre at the expense of honest public investors.

Feeling sick to her stomach, Gabrielle wondered what she should do.

A telephone rang sharply behind her, shattering the silence of the hallway. Startled, Gabrielle turned. The sound was coming from the closet in the foyer – a cellphone in the pocket of one of the visitor's coats.

''Scuse me, friends,' a Texas drawl said in the den. 'That's me.'

Gabrielle could hear the man get up. *He's coming this way!* Wheeling, she dashed back up the carpet the way she'd come. Halfway up the hall, she cut left, ducking into the darkened kitchen just as the Texan exited the den and turned up the hall. Gabrielle froze, motionless in the shadows.

The Texan strode by without noticing.

Over the sound of her pounding heart, Gabrielle could hear him rustling in the closet. Finally, he answered the ringing phone.

'Yeah? . . . When? . . . Really? We'll switch it on. Thanks.' The man hung up and headed back toward the den, calling out as he went, 'Hey! Turn on the television. Sounds like Zach Herney's giving an urgent press conference tonight. Eight o'clock. All channels. Either we're declaring war on China, or the International Space Station just fell into the ocean.'

'Now wouldn't *that* be something to toast!' someone called out.

Everyone laughed.

Gabrielle felt the kitchen spinning around her now. *An eight P.M. press conference?* Tench, it seemed, had not been bluffing after all. She had given Gabrielle until 8:00 P.M. to give her an affidavit admitting the affair. *Distance yourself from the senator before it's too late*, Tench had told her. Gabrielle had assumed the deadline was so the White House could leak the information to tomorrow's papers, but now it seemed the White House intended to go public with the allegations themselves.

An urgent press conference? The more Gabrielle considered it, though, the stranger it seemed. *Herney is going live with this mess? Personally?*

The television came on in the den. Blaring. The news announcer's voice was bursting with excitement. 'The White House has offered no clues as to the topic of tonight's surprise presidential address, and speculation abounds. Some political analysts now think that following the President's recent absence on the campaign trail, Zach Herney may be preparing to announce he will not be running for a second term.'

A hopeful cheer arose in the den.

Absurd, Gabrielle thought. With all the dirt the White House had on Sexton right now, there was no way in hell the President was throwing in the towel tonight. *This press conference is about something else.* Gabrielle had a sinking feeling she'd already been warned what it was.

With rising urgency, she checked her watch. Less than an hour. She had a decision to make, and she knew exactly to whom she needed to talk. Clutching the envelope of photos under her arm, she quietly exited the apartment.

In the hallway, the bodyguard looked relieved. 'I heard some cheering inside. Sounds like you were a hit.'

She smiled curtly and headed for the elevator.

Outside in the street, the settling night felt unusually bitter. Flagging a cab, she climbed in and tried to reassure herself she knew exactly what she was doing.

'ABC television studios,' she told the driver. 'And hurry.'

63

As Michael Tolland lay on his side on the ice, he rested his head on an outstretched arm, which he could no longer feel. Although his eyelids felt heavy, he fought to keep them open. From this odd vantage point, Tolland took in the final images of his world – now just sea and ice – in a strange sideways tilt. It seemed a fitting end to a day in which nothing had been what it seemed.

An eerie calm had begun to settle over the floating raft of ice. Rachel and Corky had both fallen silent, and the pounding had stopped. The farther from the glacier they floated, the calmer the wind became. Tolland heard his own body getting quieter too. With the tight skullcap over his ears, he could hear his own breathing amplified in his head. It was getting slower . . . shallower. His body was no longer able to fight off the compressing sensation that accompanied his own blood racing from his extremities like a crew abandoning ship, flowing instinctively to his vital organs in a last-ditch effort to keep him conscious.

A losing battle, he knew.

Strangely, there was no pain anymore. He had passed through that stage. The sensation now was that of having been inflated. Numbness. Floating. As the first of his reflexive operations – blinking – began to shut down, Tolland's vision blurred. The aqueous humor that circulated between his cornea and lens was freezing repeatedly. Tolland gazed back toward the blur of the Milne Ice Shelf, now only a faint white form in the hazy moonlight.

He felt his soul admitting defeat. Teetering on the brink between presence and absence, he stared out at the ocean waves in the distance. The wind howled all around him.

It was then that Tolland began hallucinating. Strangely, in the final seconds before unconsciousness, he did not hallucinate rescue. He did not hallucinate warm and comforting thoughts. His final delusion was a terrifying one.

A leviathan was rising from the water beside the iceberg, breaching the surface with an ominous hiss. Like some mythical sea monster, it came – sleek, black, and lethal, with water foaming around it. Tolland forced himself to blink his eyes. His vision cleared slightly. The beast was close, bumping up against the ice like a huge shark butting a small boat. Massive, it towered before him, its skin shimmering and wet.

As the hazy image went black, all that was left were the sounds. Metal on metal. Teeth gnashing at the ice. Coming closer. Dragging bodies away.

Rachel . . .

Tolland felt himself being grabbed roughly.

And then everything went blank.

64

Gabrielle Ashe was at a full jog when she entered the third-floor production room of ABC News. Even so, she was moving slower than everyone else in the room. The intensity in production was at a fever pitch twenty-four hours a day, but at the moment the cubicle grid in front of her looked like the stock exchange on speed. Wild-eyed editors screamed to one another over the tops of their compartments, fax-waving reporters darted from cubicle to cubicle comparing notes, and frantic interns inhaled Snickers and Mountain Dew between errands.

Gabrielle had come to ABC to see Yolanda Cole.

Usually Yolanda could be found in production's high-rent district – the glass-walled private offices reserved for the decision makers who actually required some quiet to think. Tonight, however, Yolanda was out on the floor, in the thick of it. When she saw Gabrielle, she let out her usual shriek of exuberance.

'Gabs!' Yolanda was wearing a batik body-wrap and tortoiseshell glasses. As always, several pounds of garish costume jewelry were draped off her like tinsel. Yolanda waddled over, waving. 'Hug!'

Yolanda Cole had been a content editor with ABC News in Washington for sixteen years. A freckle-faced Pole, Yolanda was a squat, balding woman whom everyone affectionately called 'Mother.' Her matronly presence and good humor disguised a street-savvy ruthlessness for getting the story. Gabrielle had met Yolanda at a Women in Politics mentoring seminar she'd attended shortly after her arrival in Washington. They'd chatted about Gabrielle's background, the challenges of being a woman in D.C., and finally about Elvis Presley – a passion they were surprised to discover they shared. Yolanda had taken Gabrielle under her wing and helped her make connections. Gabrielle still stopped by every month or so to say hello.

Gabrielle gave her a big hug, Yolanda's enthusiasm already lifting her spirits.

Yolanda stepped back and looked Gabrielle over. 'You look like you aged a hundred years, girl! What happened to you?'

Gabrielle lowered her voice. 'I'm in trouble, Yolanda.'

'That's not the word on the street. Sounds like your man is on the rise.'

'Is there some place we can talk in private?'

'Bad timing, honey. The President is holding a press conference in about half an hour, and we still haven't a clue what it's all about. I've got to line up expert commentary, and I'm flying blind.'

'I know what the press conference is about.'

Yolanda lowered her glasses, looking skeptical. 'Gabrielle, our correspondent *inside* the White House is in the dark on this one. You say Sexton's campaign has advance knowledge?'

'No, I'm saying *I* have advance knowledge. Give me five minutes. I'll tell you everything.'

Yolanda glanced down at the red White House envelope in Gabrielle's hand. 'That's a White House internal. Where'd you get that?'

'In a private meeting with Marjorie Tench this afternoon.'

Yolanda stared a long moment. 'Follow me.'

Inside the privacy of Yolanda's glass-walled cubicle, Gabrielle confided in her trusted friend, confessing to a one-night affair with Sexton and the fact that Tench had photographic evidence.

Yolanda smiled broadly and shook her head laughing. Apparently she had been in Washington journalism so long that nothing shocked her. 'Oh, Gabs, I had a hunch you and Sexton had probably hooked up. Not surprising. He's got a reputation, and you're a pretty girl. Too bad about the photos. I wouldn't worry about it, though.'

Don't worry about it?

Gabrielle explained that Tench had accused Sexton of taking illegal bribes from space companies and that Gabrielle had just overheard a secret SFF meeting confirming that fact. Again Yolanda's expression conveyed little surprise or concern – until Gabrielle told her what she was thinking of doing about it.

Yolanda now looked troubled. 'Gabrielle, if you want to hand over a legal document saying you slept with a U.S. senator and stood by while he lied about it, that's your business. But I'm telling you, it's a very bad move for you. You need to think long and hard about what it could mean for you.'

'You're not listening. I don't have that kind of time!'

'I *am* listening, and sweetheart, whether or not the

clock is ticking, there are certain things you just do not do. You do *not* sell out a U.S. senator in a sex scandal. It's suicide. I'm telling you, girl, if you take down a presidential candidate, you better get in your car and drive as far from D.C. as possible. You'll be a marked woman. A lot of people spend a lot of money to put candidates at the top. There's big finances and power at stake here – the kind of power people kill for.'

Gabrielle fell silent now.

'Personally,' Yolanda said, 'I think Tench was leaning on you in hopes you'd panic and do something dumb – like bail out and confess to the affair.' Yolanda pointed to the red envelope in Gabrielle's hands. 'Those shots of you and Sexton don't mean squat unless you or Sexton admit they're accurate. The White House knows if they leak those photos, Sexton will just claim they're phony and throw them back in the President's face.'

'I thought of that, but still the campaign finance bribery issue is—'

'Honey, think about it. If the White House hasn't gone public yet with bribery allegations, they probably don't intend to. The President is pretty serious about no negative campaigning. My guess is he decided to save an aerospace industry scandal and sent Tench after you with a bluff in hopes he might scare you out of hiding on the sex thing. Make you stab your candidate in the back.'

Gabrielle considered it. Yolanda was making sense, and yet something still felt odd. Gabrielle pointed through the glass at the bustling news room. 'Yolanda, you guys are gearing up for a big presidential press conference. If the President is not going public about bribery or sex, what's it all about?'

Yolanda looked stunned. 'Hold on. You think this press conference is about you and Sexton?'

'Or the bribery. Or both. Tench told me I had until eight tonight to sign a confession or else the President was going to announce—'

Yolanda's laughter shook the entire glass cubicle. 'Oh please! Wait! You're killing me!'

Gabrielle was in no mood for joking. 'What?'

'Gabs, listen,' Yolanda managed, between laughs, 'trust me on this. I've been dealing with the White House for sixteen years, and there's no way Zach Herney has called together the *global* media to tell them he suspects Senator Sexton is accepting shady campaign financing or sleeping with you. That's the kind of information you *leak*. Presidents don't gain popularity by interrupting regularly scheduled programming to bitch and moan about sex or alleged infractions of cloudy campaign finance laws.'

'Cloudy?' Gabrielle snapped. 'Flat out selling your decision on a space bill for millions in ad money is hardly a cloudy issue!'

'Are you *sure* that's what he is doing?' Yolanda's tone hardened now. 'Are you sure enough to drop your skirt on national TV? Think about it. It takes a lot of alliances to get anything done these days, and campaign finance is complex stuff. Maybe Sexton's meeting was perfectly legal.'

'He's breaking the law,' Gabrielle said. *Isn't he?*

'Or so Marjorie Tench would have you believe. Candidates accept behind-the-scenes donations all the time from big corporations. It may not be pretty, but it's not necessarily illegal. In fact, most legal issues deal not with where the money comes from but *how* the candidate chooses to spend it.'

Gabrielle hesitated, feeling uncertain now.

'Gabs, the White House played you this afternoon. They tried to turn you against your candidate, and so far you've called their bluff. If I were looking for someone to trust, I think I'd stick with Sexton before jumping ship to someone like Marjorie Tench.'

Yolanda's phone rang. She answered, nodding, uh-huh-ing, taking notes. 'Interesting,' she finally said. 'I'll be right there. Thanks.'

Yolanda hung up and turned with an arched brow. 'Gabs, sounds like you're off the hook. Just as I predicted.'

'What's going on?'

'I don't have a specific yet, but I can tell you this much – the President's press conference has nothing to do with sex scandals or campaign finance.'

Gabrielle felt a flash of hope and wanted badly to believe her. 'How do you know that?'

'Someone on the inside just leaked that the press conference is NASA-related.'

Gabrielle sat up suddenly. 'NASA?'

Yolanda winked. 'This could be your lucky night. My bet is President Herney is feeling so much pressure from Senator Sexton that he's decided the White House has no choice but to pull the plug on the International Space Station. That explains all the global media coverage.'

A press conference killing the space station? Gabrielle could not imagine.

Yolanda stood up. 'That Tench attack this afternoon? It was probably just a last-ditch effort to get a foothold over Sexton before the President had to go public with the bad news. Nothing like a sex scandal to take the attention away from another presidential flop.

Anyhow, Gabs, I've got work to do. My advice to you –
get yourself a cup of coffee, sit right here, turn on my
television, and ride this out like the rest of us. We've got
twenty minutes until show time, and I'm telling you,
there is no way the President is going Dumpster-diving
tonight. He's got the whole world watching. Whatever
he has to say carries some serious weight.' She gave a
reassuring wink. 'Now give me the envelope.'

'What?'

Yolanda held out a demanding hand. 'These pictures
are getting locked in my desk until this is over. I want
to be sure you don't do something idiotic.'

Reluctantly, Gabrielle handed over the envelope.

Yolanda locked the photos carefully in a desk drawer
and pocketed the keys. 'You'll thank me, Gabs. I swear
it.' She playfully ruffled Gabrielle's hair on her way out.
'Sit tight. I think good news is on the way.'

Gabrielle sat alone in the glass cubicle and tried to let
Yolanda's upbeat attitude lift her mood. All Gabrielle
could think of, though, was the self-satisfied smirk on
the face of Marjorie Tench this afternoon. Gabrielle
could not imagine what the President was about to tell
the world, but it was definitely not going to be good
news for Senator Sexton.

65

Rachel Sexton felt like she was being burned alive.

It's raining fire!

She tried to open her eyes, but all she could make
out were foggy shapes and blinding lights. It was

raining all around her. Scalding hot rain. Pounding down on her bare skin. She was lying on her side and could feel hot tiles beneath her body. She curled more tightly into the fetal position, trying to protect herself from the scalding liquid falling from above. She smelled chemicals. Chlorine, maybe. She tried to crawl away, but she could not. Powerful hands pressed down on her shoulders, holding her down.

Let me go! I'm burning!

Instinctively, she again fought to escape, and again she was rebuffed, the strong hands clamping down. 'Stay where you are,' a man's voice said, the accent was American. Professional. 'It will be over soon.'

What will be over? Rachel wondered. *The pain? My life?* She tried to focus her vision. The lights in this place were harsh. She sensed the room was small. Cramped. Low ceilings.

'I'm burning!' Rachel's scream was a whisper.

'You're fine,' the voice said. 'This water is lukewarm. Trust me.'

Rachel realized she was mostly undressed, wearing only her soaked underwear. No embarrassment registered; her mind was filled with too many other questions.

The memories were coming back now in a torrent. The ice shelf. The GPR. The attack. *Who? Where am I?* She tried to put the pieces together, but her mind felt torpid, like a set of clogged gears. From out of the muddled confusion came a single thought: *Michael and Corky . . . where are they?*

Rachel tried to focus her bleary vision but saw only the men standing over her. They were all dressed in the same blue jumpsuits. She wanted to speak, but her mouth refused to formulate a single word. The burning sensation in her skin was now giving way to sudden deep waves of aching that rolled through the muscles like seismic tremors.

'Let it happen,' the man over her said. 'The blood needs to flow back into your musculature.' He spoke like a doctor. 'Try to move your limbs as much as you can.'

The pain racking Rachel's body felt as if every muscle was being beaten with a hammer. She lay there on the tile, her chest contracting, and she could barely breathe.

'Move your legs and arms,' the man insisted. 'No matter what it feels like.'

Rachel tried. Each movement felt like a knife being thrust into her joints. The jets of water grew hotter again. The scalding was back. The crushing pain went on. At the precise instant she thought she could not withstand another moment, Rachel felt someone giving her an injection. The pain seemed to subside quickly, less and less violent, releasing. The tremors slowed. She felt herself breathing again.

A new sensation was spreading through her body now, the eerie bite of pins and needles. Everywhere – stabbing – sharper and sharper. Millions of tiny needle-point jabs, intensifying whenever she moved. She tried to hold motionless, but the water jets continued to buffet her. The man above her was holding her arms, moving them.

God that hurts! Rachel was too weak to fight. Tears of exhaustion and pain poured down her face. She shut her eyes hard, blocking out the world.

Finally, the pins and needles began to dissipate. The rain from above stopped. When Rachel opened her eyes, her vision was clearer.

It was then that she saw them.

Corky and Tolland lay nearby, quivering, half-naked and soaked. From the looks of anguish on their faces, Rachel sensed that they had just endured similar experiences. Michael Tolland's brown eyes were blood-shot and glassy. When he saw Rachel, he managed a weak smile, his blue lips trembling.

Rachel tried to sit up, to take in their bizarre surroundings. The three of them were lying in a trembling twist of half-naked limbs on the floor of a tiny shower room.

66

Strong arms lifted her.

Rachel felt the powerful strangers drying her body and wrapping her in blankets. She was being placed on a medical bed of some sort and vigorously massaged on her arms, legs, and feet. Another injection in her arm.

'Adrenaline,' someone said.

Rachel felt the drug coursing through her veins like a life force, invigorating her muscles. Although she still felt an icy hollowness tight like a drum in her gut, Rachel sensed the blood slowly returning to her limbs.

Back from the dead.

She tried to focus her vision. Tolland and Corky were lying nearby, shivering in blankets as the men mas-saged their bodies and gave them injections as well. Rachel had no doubt that this mysterious assemblage of men had just saved their lives. Many of them were soaking wet, apparently having jumped into the showers fully clothed to help. Who they were or how they had gotten to Rachel and the others in time was beyond her. It made no difference at the moment. *We're alive.*

'Where . . . are we?' Rachel managed, the simple act of trying to speak bringing on a crashing headache.

The man massaging her replied, 'You're on the medical deck of a Los Angeles class—'

'*On deck!*' someone called out.

Rachel sensed a sudden commotion all around her, and she tried to sit up. One of the men in blue helped, propping her up, and pulling the blankets up around her. Rachel rubbed her eyes and saw someone striding into the room.

The newcomer was a powerful African-American man. Handsome and authoritative. His uniform was khaki. 'At ease,' he declared, moving toward Rachel, stopping over her and gazing down at her with strong black eyes. 'Harold Brown,' he said, his voice deep and commanding. 'Captain of the U.S.S. *Charlotte*. And you are?'

U.S.S. Charlotte, Rachel thought. The name seemed vaguely familiar. 'Sexton . . .' she replied. 'I'm Rachel Sexton.'

The man looked puzzled. He stepped closer, studying her more carefully. 'I'll be damned. So you are.'

Rachel felt lost. *He knows me?* Rachel was certain she did not recognize the man, although as her eyes dropped from his face to the patch on his chest, she saw the familiar emblem of an eagle clutching an anchor surrounded by the words U.S. NAVY.

It now registered why she knew the name *Charlotte*.

'Welcome aboard, Ms Sexton,' the captain said.

'You've gisted a number of this ship's recon reports. I know who you are.'

'But what are you doing in these waters?' she stammered.

His face hardened somewhat. 'Frankly, Ms Sexton, I was about to ask you the same question.'

Tolland sat up slowly now, opening his mouth to speak. Rachel silenced him with a firm shake of her head. *Not here. Not now.* She had no doubt the first thing Tolland and Corky would want to talk about was the meteorite and the attack, but this was certainly not a topic to discuss in front of a Navy submarine crew. In the world of intelligence, regardless of crisis, CLEARANCE remained king; the meteorite situation remained highly classified.

'I need to speak to NRO director William Pickering,' she told the captain. 'In private, and immediately.'

The captain arched his eyebrows, apparently un-accustomed to taking orders on his own ship.

'I have classified information I need to share.'

The captain studied her a long moment. 'Let's get your body temperature back, and then I'll put you in contact with the NRO director.'

'It's urgent, sir. I—' Rachel stopped short. Her eyes had just seen a clock on the wall over the pharma-ceutical closet.

19:51 HOURS.

Rachel blinked, staring. 'Is . . . is that clock *right?*'

'You're on a navy vessel, ma'am. Our clocks are accurate.'

'And is that . . *Eastern* time?'

'7:51 P.M. Eastern Standard. We're out of Norfolk.'

My God! she thought, stunned. *It's only 7:51 P.M.?* Rachel had the impression hours had passed since she passed out. It was not even past eight o'clock? *The President has not yet gone public about the meteorite! I still have time to stop him!* She immediately slid down off the bed, wrapping the blanket around her. Her legs felt shaky. 'I need to speak to the President right away.'

The captain looked confused. 'The president of what?'

'Of the United States!'

'I thought you wanted William Pickering.'

'I don't have time. I need the President.'

The captain did not move, his huge frame blocking her way. 'My understanding is that the President is about to give a very important live press conference. I doubt he's taking personal phone calls.'

Rachel stood as straight as she could on her wobbly legs and fixed her eyes on the captain. 'Sir, you do not have the clearance for me to explain the situation, but the President is about to make a terrible mistake. I have information he desperately needs to hear. Now. You need to trust me.'

The captain stared at her a long moment. Frowning, he checked the clock again. 'Nine minutes? I can't get you a secure connection to the White House in that short a time. All I could offer is a radiophone. Unsecured. And we'd have to go to antenna depth, which will take a few—'

'Do it! Now!'

The White House telephone switchboard was located on the lower level of the East Wing. Three switchboard operators were always on duty. At the moment, only two were seated at the controls. The third operator was at a full sprint toward the Briefing Room. In her hand, she carried a cordless phone. She'd tried to patch the call through to the Oval Office, but the President was already en route to the press conference. She'd tried to call his aides on their cellulars, but before televised briefings, all cellular phones in and around the Briefing Room were turned off so as not to interrupt the proceedings.

Running a cordless phone directly to the President at a time like this seemed questionable at best, and yet when the White House's NRO liaison called claiming she had emergency information that the President must get before going live, the operator had little doubt she needed to jump. The question now was whether she would get there in time.

In a small medical office onboard the U.S.S. *Charlotte*, Rachel Sexton clutched a phone receiver to her ear and waited to talk to the President. Tolland and Corky sat nearby, still looking shaken. Corky had five stitches and a deep bruise on his cheekbone. All three of them had been helped into Thinsulate thermal underwear, heavy navy flight suits, oversized wool socks, and deck boots. With a hot cup of stale coffee in her hand, Rachel was starting to feel almost human again.

'What's the holdup?' Tolland pressed. 'It's seven fifty-six!'

Rachel could not imagine. She had successfully reached one of the White House operators, explained who she was and that this was an emergency. The operator seemed sympathetic, had placed Rachel on hold, and was now, supposedly, making it her top priority to patch Rachel through to the President.

Four minutes, Rachel thought. *Hurry up!*

Closing her eyes, Rachel tried to gather her thoughts. It had been one hell of a day. *I'm on a nuclear submarine*, she said to herself, knowing she was damned lucky to be anywhere at all. According to the submarine captain, the *Charlotte* had been on a routine patrol in the Bering Sea two days ago and had picked up anomalous underwater sounds coming from the Milne Ice Shelf – drilling, jet noise, lots of encrypted radio traffic. They had been redirected and told to lie quietly and listen. An hour or so ago, they'd heard an explosion in the ice shelf and moved in to check it out. That was when they heard Rachel's SOS call.

'Three minutes left!' Tolland sounded anxious now as he monitored the clock.

Rachel was definitely getting nervous now. What was taking so long? Why hadn't the President taken her call? If Zach Herney went public with the data as it stood—

Rachel forced the thought from her mind and shook the receiver. *Pick up!*

As the White House operator dashed toward the stage entrance of the Briefing Room, she was met with a gathering throng of staff members. Everyone here was talking excitedly, making final preparations. She could see the President twenty yards away waiting at the entrance. The makeup people were still primping.

'Coming through!' the operator said, trying to get through the crowd. 'Call for the President. Excuse me. Coming through!'

'*Live in two minutes!*' a media coordinator called out.

Clutching the phone, the operator shoved her way toward the President. 'Call for the President!' she panted. 'Coming through!'

A towering roadblock stepped into her path. Marjorie Tench. The senior adviser's long face grimaced down in disapproval. 'What's going on?'

'I have an emergency!' The operator was breathless. '. . . phone call for the President.'

Tench looked incredulous. 'Not now, you don't!'

'It's from Rachel Sexton. She says it's urgent.'

The scowl that darkened Tench's face appeared to be more one of puzzlement than anger. Tench eyed the cordless phone. 'That's a house line. That's not secure.'

'No, ma'am. But the incoming call is open anyway. She's on a radiophone. She needs to speak to the President right away.'

'*Live in ninety seconds!*'

Tench's cold eyes stared, and she held out a spider-like hand. 'Give me the phone.'

The operator's heart was pounding now. 'Ms Sexton wants to speak to President Herney directly. She told me to postpone the press conference until she'd talked to him. I assured—'

Tench stepped toward the operator now, her voice a seething whisper. 'Let me tell you how this works. You do not take orders from the daughter of the President's opponent, you take them from me. I can assure you, this is as close as you are getting to the President until I find out what the hell is going on.'

The operator looked toward the President, who was now surrounded by microphone technicians, stylists, and several staff members talking him through final revisions of his speech.

'*Sixty seconds!*' the television supervisor yelled.

Onboard the *Charlotte*, Rachel Sexton was pacing wildly in the tight space when she finally heard a click on the telephone line.

A raspy voice came on. 'Hello?'

'President Herney?' Rachel blurted.

'Marjorie Tench,' the voice corrected. 'I am the President's senior adviser. Whoever this is, I must warn you that prank calls against the White House are in violation of—'

For Christ's sake! 'This is not a prank! This is Rachel Sexton. I'm your NRO liaison and—'

'I am aware of who Rachel Sexton is, ma'am. And I am doubtful that you are she. You've called the White House on an unsecured line telling me to interrupt a major presidential broadcast. That is hardly proper MO for someone with—'

'Listen,' Rachel fumed, 'I briefed your whole staff a couple of hours ago on a meteorite. You sat in the front row. You watched my briefing on a television sitting on the President's desk! Any questions?'

Tench fell silent a moment. 'Ms Sexton, what is the meaning of this?'

'The meaning is that you have to stop the President! His meteorite data is all wrong! We've just learned the meteorite was inserted from *beneath* the ice shelf. I don't know by whom, and I don't know why! But things are not what they seem up here! The President is about to endorse some seriously errant data, and I strongly advise—'

'Wait one goddamned minute!' Tench lowered her voice. 'Do you realize what you are saying?'

'Yes! I suspect the NASA administrator has orchestrated some kind of large-scale fraud, and President Herney is about to get caught in the middle. You've at least got to postpone ten minutes so I can explain to him what's been going on up here. Someone tried to kill me, for God's sake!'

Tench's voice turned to ice. 'Ms Sexton, let me give you a word of warning. If you are having second thoughts about your role in helping the White House in this campaign, you should have thought of that long before you personally endorsed that meteorite data for the President.'

'What?' *Is she even listening?*

'I'm revolted by your display. Using an unsecured line is a cheap stunt. Implying the meteorite data has been faked? What kind of intelligence official uses a radiophone to call the White House and talk about classified information? Obviously you are *hoping* someone intercepts this message.'

'Norah Mangor was killed over this! Dr Ming is also dead. You've got to warn—'

'Stop right there! I don't know what you're playing at, but I will remind you – and anyone *else* who happens to be intercepting this phone call – that the White House possesses videotaped depositions from NASA's top scientists, several renowned civilian scientists, and *yourself*, Ms Sexton, all endorsing the meteorite data as accurate. Why you are suddenly changing your story, I can only imagine. Whatever the reason, consider yourself relieved of your White House post as of this instant, and if you try to taint this discovery with any more absurd allegations of foul play, I assure you the White House and NASA will sue you for defamation so fast you won't have a chance to pack a suitcase before you go to jail.'

Rachel opened her mouth to speak, but no words came.

'Zach Herney has been generous to you,' Tench snapped, 'and frankly this smacks of a cheap Sexton publicity stunt. Drop it right now, or we'll press charges. I swear it.'

The line went dead.

Rachel's mouth was still hanging open when the captain knocked on the door.

'Ms Sexton?' the captain said, peering in. 'We're picking up a faint signal from Canadian National Radio. President Zach Herney has just begun his press conference.'

68

Standing at the podium in the White House Briefing Room, Zach Herney felt the heat of the media lights and knew the world was watching. The targeted blitz performed by the White House Press Office had created a contagion of media buzz. Those who did not hear about the address via television, radio, or on-line news, invariably heard about it from neighbors, coworkers, and family. By 8:00 P.M., anyone not living in a cave was speculating about the topic of the President's address. In bars and living rooms over the globe, millions leaned toward their televisions in apprehensive wonder.

It was during moments like these – facing the world – that Zach Herney truly felt the weight of his office. Anyone who said power was not addictive had never really experienced it. As he began his address, however, Herney sensed something was amiss. He was not a man prone to stage fright, and so the tingle of apprehension now tightening in his core startled him.

It's the magnitude of the audience, he told himself. And yet he knew something else. Instinct. Something he had seen.

It had been such a little thing, and yet . . .

He told himself to forget it. It was nothing. And yet it stuck.

Tench.

Moments ago, as Herney was preparing to take the stage, he had seen Marjorie Tench in the yellow hallway, talking on a cordless phone. This was strange in itself, but it was made more so by the White House operator standing beside her, her face white with apprehension. Herney could not hear Tench's phone conversation, but he could see it was contentious. Tench was arguing with a vehemence and anger the President had seldom seen – even from Tench. He paused a moment and caught her eye, inquisitive.

Tench gave him the thumbs-up. Herney had never seen Tench give *anyone* the thumbs-up. It was the last image in Herney's mind as he was cued onto the stage.

On the blue rug in the press area inside the NASA habisphere on Ellesmere Island, Administrator Lawrence Ekstrom was seated at the center of the long symposium table, flanked by top NASA officials and scientists. On a large monitor facing them the President's opening statement was being piped in live. The remainder of the NASA crew was huddled around other monitors, teeming with excitement as their commander-in-chief launched into his press conference.

'Good evening,' Herney was saying, sounding uncharacteristically stiff. 'To my fellow countrymen, and to our friends around the world . . .'

Ekstrom gazed at the huge charred mass of rock displayed prominently in front of him. His eyes moved to a standby monitor, where he watched himself, flanked by his most austere personnel, against a backdrop of a huge American flag and NASA logo. The dramatic lighting made the setting look like some kind of neomodern painting – the twelve apostles at the last supper. Zach Herney had turned this whole thing into a political sideshow. *Herney had no choice.* Ekstrom still felt like a televangelist, packaging God for the masses.

In about five minutes the President would introduce Ekstrom and his NASA staff. Then, in a dramatic satellite linkup from the top of the world, NASA would join the President in sharing this news with the world. After a brief account of how the discovery was made, what it meant for space science, and some mutual backpatting, NASA and the President would hand duty off to celebrity scientist, Michael Tolland, whose documentary would roll for just under fifteen minutes. Afterward, with credibility and enthusiasm at its peak, Ekstrom and the President would say their goodnights, promising more information to come in the days ahead via endless NASA press conferences.

As Ekstrom sat and waited for his cue, he felt a

cavernous shame settling inside him. He'd known he would feel it. He'd been expecting it.

He'd told lies . . . endorsed untruths.

Somehow, though, the lies seemed inconsequential now. Ekstrom had a bigger weight on his mind.

In the chaos of the ABC production room, Gabrielle Ashe stood shoulder to shoulder with dozens of strangers, all necks craned toward the bank of television monitors suspended from the ceiling. A hush fell as the moment arrived. Gabrielle closed her eyes, praying that when she opened them she would not be looking at images of her own naked body.

The air inside Senator Sexton's den was alive with excitement. All of his visitors were standing now, their eyes glued to the large-screen television.

Zach Herney stood before the world, and incredibly, his greeting had been awkward. He seemed momentarily uncertain.

He looks shaky, Sexton thought. *He never looks shaky.*

'Look at him,' somebody whispered. 'It has to be bad news.'

The space station? Sexton wondered.

Herney looked directly into the camera and took a deep breath. 'My friends, I have puzzled for many days now over how best to make this announcement . . .'

Three easy words, Senator Sexton willed him. *We blew it.*

Herney spoke for a moment about how unfortunate it was that NASA had become such an issue in this election and how, that being the case, he felt he needed to preface the timing of his impending statement with an apology.

'I would have preferred any other moment in history to make this announcement,' he said. 'The political charge in the air tends to make doubters out of dreamers, and yet as your President, I have no choice but to share with you what I have recently learned.' He smiled. 'It seems the magic of the cosmos is something which does not work on any human schedule . . . not even that of a president.'

Everyone in Sexton's den seemed to recoil in unison. *What?*

'Two weeks ago,' Herney said, 'NASA's new Polar Orbiting Density Scanner passed over the Milne Ice Shelf on Ellesmere Island, a remote landmass located above the Eightieth Parallel in the high Arctic Ocean.'

Sexton and the others exchanged confused looks.

'This NASA satellite,' Herney continued, 'detected a large, high-density rock buried two hundred feet under the ice.' Herney smiled now for the first time, finding his stride. 'On receiving the data, NASA immediately suspected PODS had found a meteorite.'

'A meteorite?' Sexton sputtered, standing. 'This is news?'

'NASA sent a team up to the ice shelf to take core samples. It was then that NASA made . . .' He paused. 'Frankly, they made the scientific discovery of the century.'

Sexton took an incredulous step toward the television. *No* . . . His guests shifted uneasily.

'Ladies and gentlemen,' Herney announced, 'several hours ago, NASA pulled from the Arctic ice an eight-ton meteorite, which contains . . .' The President paused again, giving the whole world time to lean forward. 'A meteorite which contains *fossils* of a life-form. Dozens of them. Unequivocal proof of extraterrestrial life.'

On cue, a brilliant image illuminated on the screen behind the President – a perfectly delineated fossil of an enormous buglike creature embedded in a charred rock.

In Sexton's den, six entrepreneurs jumped up in wide-eyed horror. Sexton stood frozen in place.

'My friends,' the President said, 'the fossil behind me is one hundred and ninety million years old. It was discovered in a fragment of a meteorite called the Jungersol Fall which hit the Arctic Ocean almost three centuries ago. NASA's exciting new PODS satellite discovered this meteorite fragment buried in an ice shelf. NASA and this administration have taken enormous care over the past two weeks to confirm every aspect of this momentous discovery before making it public. In the next half hour you will be hearing from numerous NASA and civilian scientists, as well as viewing a short documentary prepared by a familiar face whom I'm sure you all will recognize. Before I go any further, though, I absolutely must welcome, live via satellite from above the Arctic Circle, the man whose leadership, vision, and hard work is solely responsible for this historic moment. It is with great honor that I present NASA administrator Lawrence Ekstrom.'

Herney turned to the screen on perfect cue.

The image of the meteorite dramatically dissolved into a regal-looking panel of NASA scientists seated at a long table, flanked by the dominant frame of Lawrence Ekstrom.

'Thank you, Mr President.' Ekstrom's air was stern and proud as he stood up and looked directly into the camera. 'It gives me great pride to share with all of you, this – NASA's finest hour.'

Ekstrom spoke passionately about NASA and the

discovery. With a fanfare of patriotism and triumph, he segued flawlessly to a documentary hosted by civilian science-celebrity Michael Tolland.

As he watched, Senator Sexton fell to his knees in front of the television, his fingers clutching at his silver mane. *No! God, no!*

Marjorie Tench was livid as she broke away from the jovial chaos outside the Briefing Room and marched back to her private corner in the West Wing. She was in no mood for celebration. The phone call from Rachel Sexton had been most unexpected.

Most disappointing.

Tench slammed her office door, stalked to her desk, and dialed the White House operator. 'William Pickering. NRO.'

Tench lit a cigarette and paced the room as she waited for the operator to track down Pickering. Normally, he might have gone home for the night, but with the White House's big windup into tonight's press conference, Tench guessed Pickering had been in his office all evening, glued to his television screen, wondering what could possibly be going on in the world about which the NRO director did not have prior knowledge.

Tench cursed herself for not trusting her instincts when the President said he wanted to send Rachel Sexton to Milne. Tench had been wary, feeling it was an unnecessary risk. But the President had been convincing, persuading Tench that the White House staff had grown cynical over the past weeks and would be suspect of the NASA discovery if the news came from in-house. As Herney had promised, Rachel Sexton's endorsement had squelched suspicions, prevented any skeptical in-house debate, and forced the White House staff to move forward with a unified front. Invaluable, Tench had to admit. And yet now Rachel Sexton had changed her tune.

The bitch called me on an unsecured line.

Rachel Sexton was obviously intent on destroying the credibility of this discovery, and Tench's only solace was knowing the President had captured Rachel's earlier briefing on videotape. *Thank God.* At least Herney had thought to obtain that small insurance. Tench was starting to fear they were going to need it.

At the moment, however, Tench was trying to stem the bleeding in other ways. Rachel Sexton was a smart woman, and if she truly intended to go head-to-head with the White House and NASA, she would need to recruit some powerful allies. Her first logical choice would be William Pickering. Tench already knew how Pickering felt about NASA. She needed to get to Pickering before Rachel did.

'Ms Tench?' the transparent voice on the line said. 'William Pickering here. To what do I owe this honor?'

Tench could hear the television in the background – NASA commentary. She could already sense in his tone that he was still reeling from the press conference. 'Do you have a minute, Director?'

'I expected you'd be busy celebrating. Quite a night for you. Looks like NASA and the President are back in the fight.'

Tench heard stark amazement in his voice, combined

314

with a tinge of acrimony – the latter no doubt on account of the man's legendary distaste for hearing breaking news at the same time as the rest of the world.

'I apologize,' Tench said, trying to build an immediate bridge, 'that the White House and NASA were forced to keep you unapprised.'

'You are aware,' Pickering said, 'that the NRO detected NASA activity up there a couple weeks ago and ran an inquiry?'

Tench frowned. *He's pissed.* 'Yes, I know. And yet—'

'NASA told us it was nothing. They said they were running some kind of extreme environment training exercises. Testing equipment, that sort of thing.' Pickering paused. 'We bought the lie.'

'Let's not call it a *lie*,' Tench said. 'More of a necessary misdirection. Considering the magnitude of the discovery, I trust you understand NASA's need to keep this quiet.'

'From the public, perhaps.'

Pouting was not in the repertoire of men like William Pickering, and Tench sensed this was as close as he would get. 'I only have a minute,' Tench said, working to retain her dominant position, 'but I thought I should call and warn you.'

'Warn me?' Pickering waxed wry momentarily. 'Has Zach Herney decided to appoint a new, NASA-friendly NRO director?'

'Of course not. The President understands your criticisms of NASA are simply issues of security, and he is working to plug those holes. I'm actually calling about one of your employees.' She paused. 'Rachel Sexton. Have you heard from her this evening?'

'No. I sent her to the White House this morning

at the President's request. You've obviously kept her busy. She has yet to check in.'

Tench was relieved to have gotten to Pickering first. She took a drag on her cigarette and spoke as calmly as possible. 'I suspect you may be getting a call from Ms Sexton sometime soon.'

'Good. I've been expecting one. I've got to tell you, when the President's press conference began, I was concerned Zach Herney might have convinced Ms Sexton to participate publicly. I'm pleased to see he resisted.'

'Zach Herney is a decent person,' Tench said, 'which is more than I can say for Rachel Sexton.'

There was a long pause on the line. 'I hope I misunderstood that.'

Tench sighed heavily. 'No, sir, I'm afraid you did not. I'd prefer not to talk specifics on the phone, but Rachel Sexton, it seems, has decided she wants to undermine the credibility of this NASA announcement. I have no idea why, but after she reviewed and endorsed NASA's data earlier this afternoon, she has suddenly pulled an about-face and is spouting some of the most improbable allegations imaginable of NASA treachery and fraud.'

Pickering sounded intense now. 'Excuse me?'

'Troubling, yes. I hate to be the one to tell you this, but Ms Sexton contacted me two minutes before the press conference and warned me to cancel the whole thing.'

'On what grounds?'

'Absurd ones, frankly. She said she'd found serious flaws in the data.'

Pickering's long silence was more wary than Tench would have liked. 'Flaws?' he finally said.

'Ridiculous, really, after two full weeks of NASA experimentation and—'

'I find it very hard to believe someone like Rachel Sexton would have told you to postpone the President's press conference unless she had a damn good reason.' Pickering sounded troubled. 'Maybe you should have listened to her.'

'Oh, please!' Tench blurted, coughing. 'You saw the press conference. The meteorite data was confirmed and reconfirmed by countless specialists. Including civilians. Doesn't it seem suspicious to you that Rachel Sexton – the daughter of the only man whom this announcement hurts – is suddenly changing her tune?'

'It seems suspicious, Ms Tench, only because I happen to know that Ms Sexton and her father are barely civil to one another. I cannot imagine why Rachel Sexton would, after years of service to the President, suddenly decide to switch camps and tell lies to support her father.'

'Ambition, perhaps? I really don't know. Maybe the opportunity to be first daughter . . .' Tench let it hang.

Pickering's tone hardened instantly. 'Thin ice, Ms Tench. Very thin.'

Tench scowled. What the hell did she expect? She was accusing a prominent member of Pickering's staff of treason against the President. The man was going to be defensive.

'Put her on,' Pickering demanded. 'I'd like to speak to Ms Sexton myself.'

'I'm afraid that's impossible,' Tench replied. 'She's not at the White House.'

'Where is she?'

'The President sent her to Milne this morning to examine the data firsthand. She has yet to return.'

Pickering sounded livid now. 'I was never informed—'

'I do not have time for hurt pride, Director. I have simply called as a courtesy. I wanted to warn you that Rachel Sexton has decided to pursue her own agenda with respect to tonight's announcement. She will be looking for allies. If she contacts you, you would be wise to know that the White House is in possession of a video taken earlier today in which she endorsed this meteorite data in its entirety in front of the President, his cabinet, and his entire staff. If now, for whatever motives she might have, Rachel Sexton attempts to besmirch the good name of Zach Herney or of NASA, then I swear to you the White House will see to it she falls hard and far.' Tench waited a moment, to be sure her meaning had settled in. 'I expect you to repay the courtesy of this call by informing me immediately if Rachel Sexton contacts you. She is attacking the President directly, and the White House intends to detain her for questioning before she does any serious damage. I will be waiting for your call, Director. That's all. Good night.'

Marjorie Tench hung up, certain that William Pickering had never been talked to like that in his life. At least now he knew she was serious.

On the top floor of the NRO, William Pickering stood at his window and stared into the Virginia night. The call from Marjorie Tench had been deeply troubling. He chewed at his lip as he tried to assemble the pieces in his mind.

'Director?' his secretary said, knocking quietly. 'You have another phone call.'

'Not now,' Pickering said absently.

'It's Rachel Sexton.'

Pickering wheeled. Tench was apparently a fortune-teller. 'Okay. Patch her through, right away.'

'Actually, sir, it's an encrypted AV stream. Do you want to take it in the conference room?'

An AV stream? 'Where is she calling from?'

The secretary told him.

Pickering stared. Bewildered, he hurried down the hall toward the conference room. This was something he had to see.

The *Charlotte*'s 'dead room' – designed after a similar structure at Bell Laboratories – was what was formally known as an anechoic chamber. An acoustical clean room containing no parallel or reflective surfaces, it absorbed sound with 99.4 percent efficiency. Because of the acoustically conductive nature of metal and water, conversations onboard submarines were always vulnerable to interception by nearby eavesdroppers or parasitic suction mics attached to the outer hull. The dead room was, in effect, a tiny chamber inside the submarine from which absolutely no sound could escape. All conversations inside this insulated box were entirely secure.

The chamber looked like a walk-in closet whose ceiling, walls, and floor had been completely covered with foam spires jutting inward from all directions. It reminded Rachel of a cramped underwater cave where stalagmites had run wild, growing off every surface.

Most unsettling, however, was the apparent lack of a floor.

The floor was a taut, meshed chicken-wire grid strung horizontally across the room like a fishing net, giving the inhabitants the feeling that they were suspended midway up the wall. The mesh was rubberized and stiff beneath the feet. As Rachel gazed down through the webbed flooring, she felt like she was crossing a string bridge suspended over a surrealistic fractalized landscape. Three feet below, a forest of foam needles pointed ominously upward.

Instantly upon entering Rachel had sensed the disorientating lifelessness to the air, as if every bit of energy had been sucked out. Her ears felt as if they'd been stuffed with cotton. Only her breath was audible inside her head. She called out, and the effect was that of speaking into a pillow. The walls absorbed every reverberation, making the only perceivable vibrations those inside her head.

Now the captain had departed, closing the padded door behind him. Rachel, Corky, and Tolland were seated in the center of the room at a small U-shaped table that stood on long metal stilts that descended through the mesh. On the table were affixed several gooseneck microphones, headphones, and a video console with a fish-eye camera on top. It looked like a mini-United Nations symposium.

As someone who worked in the U.S. intelligence community – the world's foremost manufacturers of hard laser microphones, underwater parabolic eavesdroppers, and other hypersensitive listening devices – Rachel was well aware there were few places on earth where one could have a truly secure conversation. The dead room was apparently one of those places. The mics and headphones on the table enabled a face-to-face 'conference call' in which people could speak freely, knowing the vibrations of their words could not escape the room. Their voices, upon entering the microphones, would be heavily encrypted for their long journey through the atmosphere.

'Level check.' The voice materialized suddenly inside their headphones, causing Rachel, Tolland, and Corky to jump. 'Do you read me, Ms Sexton?'

Rachel leaned into the microphone. 'Yes. Thank you.' *Whoever you are.*

'I have Director Pickering on the line for you. He's accepting AV. I am signing off now. You will have your data stream momentarily.'

Rachel heard the line go dead. There was a distant whirr of static and then a rapid series of beeps and clicks in the headphones. With startling clarity, the video screen in front of them sprang to life, and Rachel saw Director Pickering in the NRO conference room. He was alone. His head snapped up and he looked into Rachel's eyes.

She felt oddly relieved to see him.

'Ms Sexton,' he said, his expression perplexed and troubled. 'What in the world is going on?'

'The meteorite, sir,' Rachel said. 'I think we may have a serious problem.'

Inside the *Charlotte*'s dead room, Rachel Sexton introduced Michael Tolland and Corky Marlinson to

Pickering. Then she took charge and launched into a quick account of the day's incredible chain of events.

The NRO director sat motionless as he listened.

Rachel told him about the bioluminescent plankton in the extraction pit, their journey onto the ice shelf and discovery of an insertion shaft beneath the meteorite, and finally of their sudden attack by a military team she suspected was Special Ops.

William Pickering was known for his ability to listen to disturbing information without so much as flinching an eye, and yet his gaze grew more and more troubled with each progression in Rachel's story. She sensed disbelief and then rage when she talked about Norah Mangor's murder and their own near-death escape. Although Rachel wanted to voice her suspicions of the NASA administrator's involvement, she knew Pickering well enough not to point fingers without evidence. She gave Pickering the story as cold hard facts. When she was finished, Pickering did not respond for several seconds.

'Ms Sexton,' he finally said, 'all of you . . .' He moved his gaze to each of them. 'If what you're saying is true, and I cannot imagine why three of you would lie about this, you are all very lucky to be alive.'

They all nodded in silence. The President had called in four civilian scientists . . . and two of them were now dead.

Pickering heaved a disconsolate sigh, as if he had no idea what to say next. The events clearly made little sense. 'Is there any way,' Pickering asked, 'that this insertion shaft you're seeing in that GPR printout is a natural phenomenon?'

Rachel shook her head. 'It's too perfect.' She unfolded the soggy GPR printout and held it up in front of the camera. 'Flawless.'

Pickering studied the image, scowling in agreement. 'Don't let that out of your hands.'

'I called Marjorie Tench to warn her to stop the President,' Rachel said. 'But she shut me down.'

'I know. She told me.'

Rachel looked up, stunned. 'Marjorie Tench called you?' *That was fast.*

'Just now. She's very concerned. She feels you are attempting some kind of stunt to discredit the President and NASA. Perhaps to help your father.'

Rachel stood up. She waved the GPR printout and motioned to her two companions. 'We were almost killed! Does this look like some kind of stunt? And why would I—'

Pickering held up his hands. 'Easy. What Ms Tench failed to tell me was that there were three of you.'

Rachel could not recall if Tench had even given her time to mention Corky and Tolland.

'Nor did she tell me you had physical evidence,' Pickering said. 'I was skeptical of her claims before I spoke to you, and now I am convinced she is mistaken. I do not doubt your claims. The question at this point is what it all means.'

There was a long silence.

William Pickering rarely looked confused, but he shook his head, seeming lost. 'Let's assume for the moment that someone *did* insert this meteorite beneath the ice. That begs the obvious issue of *why*. If NASA has a meteorite with fossils in it, why would they, or anyone else for that matter, care where it is found?'

'It appears,' Rachel said, 'that the insertion was performed such that PODS would make the discovery, and the meteorite would appear to be a fragment from a known impact.'

'The Jungersol Fall,' Corky prompted.

'But of what *value* is the meteorite's association with a known impact?' Pickering demanded, sounding almost mad. 'Aren't these fossils an astounding discovery any-where and anytime? No matter what meteoritic event they are associated with?'

All three nodded.

Pickering hesitated, looking displeased. 'Unless . . . of course . . .'

Rachel saw the wheels turning behind the director's eyes. He had found the simplest explanation for placing the meteorite concurrent with the Jungersol strata, but the simplest explanation was also the most troubling.

'Unless,' Pickering continued, 'the careful placement was intended to lend credibility to totally false data.' He sighed, turning to Corky. 'Dr Marlinson, what is the possibility that this meteorite is a counterfeit.'

'Counterfeit, sir?'

'Yes. A fake. Manufactured.'

'A *fake* meteorite?' Corky gave an awkward laugh. 'Utterly impossible! That meteorite was examined by countless professionals. *Myself* included. Chemical scans, spectrograph, rubidium-strontium dating. It is unlike any kind of rock ever seen on earth. The meteorite is authentic. Any astrogeologist would agree.'

Pickering seemed to consider this a long time, gently stroking his tie. 'And yet taking into account the amount NASA has to gain from this discovery right now, the apparent signs of tampering with evidence, and your being attacked . . . the first and only logical conclusion I can draw is that this meteorite is a well-executed fraud.'

'Impossible!' Corky sounded angry now. 'With all respect, sir, meteorites are not some Hollywood special

324

effect that can be conjured up in a lab to fool a bunch of unsuspecting astrophysicists. They are chemically complex objects with unique crystalline structures and element ratios!'

'I am not challenging you, Dr Marlinson. I am simply following a logical chain of analysis. Considering someone wanted to kill you to keep you from revealing it was inserted under the ice, I'm inclined to entertain all kinds of wild scenarios here. What specifically makes you certain this rock is indeed a meteorite?'

'Specifically?' Corky's voice cracked in the headphones. 'A flawless fusion crust, the presence of chondrules, a nickel ratio unlike anything ever found on earth. If you're suggesting that someone tricked us by manufacturing this rock in a lab, then all I can say is that the lab was about one hundred and ninety million years old.' Corky dug in his pocket and pulled out a stone shaped like a CD. He held it in front of the camera. 'We chemically dated samples like this with numerous methods. Rubidium-strontium dating is *not* something you can fake!'

Pickering looked surprised. 'You have a sample?'

Corky shrugged. 'NASA had dozens of them floating around.'

'You mean to tell me,' Pickering said, looking at Rachel now, 'that NASA discovered a meteorite they think contains life, and they're letting people walk off with samples?'

'The point,' Corky said, 'is that the sample in my hands is genuine.' He held the rock close to the camera. 'You could give this to any petrologist or geologist or astronomer on earth, they would run tests, and they would tell you two things: one, it is one hundred and ninety million years old; and two, it is chemically dissimilar from the kind of rock we have here on earth.'

Pickering leaned forward, studying the fossil embedded in the rock. He seemed momentarily transfixed. Finally, he sighed. 'I am not a scientist. All I can say is that if that meteorite is genuine, which it appears it is, I would like to know why NASA didn't present it to the world at face value? Why has someone carefully placed it under the ice as if to *persuade* us of its authenticity?'

At that moment, inside the White House, a security officer was dialing Marjorie Tench.

The senior adviser answered on the first ring. 'Yeah?'

'Ms Tench,' the officer said, 'I have the information you requested earlier. The radiophone call that Rachel Sexton placed to you earlier this evening. We have the trace.'

'Tell me.'

'Secret Service ops says the signal originated aboard the naval submarine U.S.S. *Charlotte*.'

'What?'

'They don't have coordinates, ma'am, but they are certain of the vessel code.'

'Oh, for Christ's sake!' Tench slammed down the receiver without another word.

72

The muted acoustics of the *Charlotte*'s dead room were starting to make Rachel feel mildly nauseated. On-screen, William Pickering's troubled gaze moved now to Michael Tolland. 'You're quiet, Mr Tolland.'

Tolland glanced up like a student who had been called on unexpectedly. 'Sir?'

'You just gave quite a convincing documentary on television,' Pickering said. 'What's your take on the meteorite now?'

'Well, sir,' Tolland said, his discomfort obvious, 'I have to agree with Dr Marlinson. I believe the fossils and meteorite are authentic. I'm fairly well versed in dating techniques, and the age of that stone was confirmed by multiple tests. The nickel content as well. These data cannot be forged. There exists no doubt the rock, formed one hundred and ninety million years ago, exhibits nonterrestrial nickel ratios and contains dozens of confirmed fossils whose formation is also dated at one hundred and ninety million years. I can think of no other possible explanation than that NASA has found an authentic meteorite.'

Pickering fell silent now. His expression was one of quandary, a look Rachel had never before seen on William Pickering.

'What should we do, sir?' Rachel asked. 'Obviously we need to alert the President there are problems with the data.'

Pickering frowned. 'Let's hope the President doesn't *already* know.'

Rachel felt a knot rise in her throat. Pickering's implication was clear. *President Herney could be involved.* Rachel strongly doubted it, and yet both the President and NASA had plenty to gain here.

'Unfortunately,' Pickering said, 'with the exception of this GPR printout revealing an insertion shaft, all of the scientific data points to a credible NASA discovery.' He paused, dire. 'And this issue of your being attacked . . .' He looked up at Rachel. 'You mentioned Special Ops.'

327

'Yes, sir.' She told him again about the Improvised Munitions and tactics.

Pickering looked more and more unhappy by the moment. Rachel sensed her boss was contemplating the number of people who might have access to a small military kill force. Certainly the President had access. Probably Marjorie Tench too, as senior adviser. Quite possibly NASA administrator Lawrence Ekstrom with his ties to the Pentagon. Unfortunately, as Rachel considered the myriad of possibilities, she realized the controlling force behind the attack could have been almost anyone with high-level political clout and the right connections.

'I could phone the President right now,' Pickering said, 'but I don't think that's wise, at least until we know who's involved. My ability to protect you becomes limited once we involve the White House. In addition, I'm not sure what I would tell him. If the meteorite is real, which you all feel it is, then your allegation of an insertion shaft and attack doesn't make sense; the President would have every right to question the validity of my claim.' He paused as if calculating the options. 'Regardless . . . whatever the truth is or who the players are, some very powerful people will take hits if this information goes public. I suggest we get you to safety right away, before we start rocking any boats.'

Get us to safety? The comment surprised Rachel. 'I think we're fairly safe on a nuclear submarine, sir.'

Pickering looked skeptical. 'Your presence on that submarine won't stay secret long. I'm pulling you out immediately. Frankly, I'll feel better when the three of you are sitting in my office.'

Senator Sexton huddled alone on his couch feeling like a refugee. His Westbrooke Place apartment that had only an hour ago been filled with new friends and supporters now looked forsaken, scattered with the rubble of snifters and business cards, abandoned by men who had quite literally dashed out the door.

Now Sexton crouched in solitude before his television, wanting more than anything to turn it off and yet being unable to pull himself from the endless media analyses. This was Washington, and it didn't take long for the analysts to rush through their pseudoscientific and philosophical hyperbole and lock in on the ugly stuff – the politics. Like torture masters rubbing acid in Sexton's wounds, the newscasters were stating and restating the obvious.

'Hours ago, Sexton's campaign was soaring,' one analyst said. 'Now, with NASA's discovery, the senator's campaign has crashed back to earth.'

Sexton winced, reaching for the Courvoisier and taking a hit right out of the bottle. Tonight, he knew, would be the longest and loneliest night of his life. He despised Marjorie Tench for setting him up. He despised Gabrielle Ashe for ever mentioning NASA in the first place. He despised the President for being so goddamned lucky. And he despised the world for laughing at him.

'Obviously, this is devastating for the senator,' the analyst was saying. 'The President and NASA have claimed an incalculable triumph with this discovery. News like this would revitalize the President's campaign regardless of Sexton's position on NASA, but with Sexton's admission today that he would go so far as to abolish NASA funding outright if need be . . . well, this presidential announcement is a one-two punch from which the senator will not recover.'

I was tricked, Sexton said. *The White House fucking set me up.*

The analyst was smiling now. 'All of the credibility NASA has lost with Americans recently has just been restored in spades. There's a real feeling of national pride out there on the streets right now.'

'As there should be. They love Zach Herney, and they were losing faith. You've got to admit, the President was lying down and taking some pretty big hits recently, but he's come out of it smelling like a rose.'

Sexton thought of the CNN debate that afternoon and hung his head, thinking he might be sick to his stomach. All of the NASA inertia he had so carefully built up over the last months had not only come to a screeching halt, but it had become an anchor around his neck. He looked like a fool. He'd been brazenly played by the White House. He was already dreading all the cartoons in tomorrow's paper. His name would be the punch line to every joke in the country. Obviously, there would be no more quiet SFF campaign funding. Everything had changed. All of the men who had been in his apartment had just seen their dreams go down the toilet. The privatization of space had just struck a brick wall.

Taking another hit of cognac, the senator stood up and walked unevenly to his desk. He gazed down at the unhooked phone receiver. Knowing it was an act of masochistic self-flagellation, he slowly replaced the phone receiver in its cradle and began counting the seconds.

One . . . two . . . The phone rang. He let the machine pick up.

'Senator Sexton, Judy Oliver from CNN. I'd like to give you an opportunity to react to the NASA discovery this evening. Please call me.' She hung up.

Sexton started counting again. *One . . .* The phone started ringing. He ignored it, letting the machine get it. Another reporter.

Holding his bottle of Courvoisier, Sexton wandered toward the sliding door of his balcony. He pulled it aside and stepped out into the cool air. Leaning against the railing, he gazed out across town to the illuminated facade of the White House in the distance. The lights seemed to twinkle gleefully in the wind.

Bastards, he thought. *For centuries we've been looking for proof of life in the heavens. Now we find it in the same fucking year as my election? This wasn't propitious, this was goddamned clairvoyant.* Every apartment window, for as far as Sexton could see, had a television on. Sexton wondered where Gabrielle Ashe was tonight. This was all her fault. She'd fed him NASA failure after NASA failure.

He raised the bottle to take another swig.

Goddamned Gabrielle . . . she's the reason I'm in this so deep.

Across town, standing amid the chaos of the ABC production room, Gabrielle Ashe felt numb. The President's announcement had come out of left field, leaving her suspended in a semicatatonic haze. She stood, lock-kneed in the center of the production room floor, staring up at one of the television monitors while pandemonium raged around her.

The initial seconds of the announcement had brought dead silence to the newsroom floor. It had lasted only moments before the place erupted into a deafening carnival of scrambling reporters. These people were professionals. They had no time for personal reflection. There would be time for that after the work was done. At the moment, the world wanted to know more, and ABC had to provide it. This story had everything – science, history, political drama – an emotional mother lode. Nobody in the media was sleeping tonight.

'Gabs?' Yolanda's voice was sympathetic. 'Let's get you back into my office before someone realizes who you are and starts grilling you on what this means for Sexton's campaign.'

Gabrielle felt herself guided through a haze into Yolanda's glass-walled office. Yolanda sat her down and handed her a glass of water. She tried to force a smile. 'Look on the bright side, Gabs. Your candidate's campaign is fucked, but at least you're not.'

'Thanks. Terrific.'

Yolanda's tone turned serious. 'Gabrielle, I know you feel like shit. Your candidate just got hit by a Mack truck, and if you ask me, he's not getting up. At least not in time to turn this thing around. But at least nobody's splashing your picture all over the television. Seriously. This is good news. Herney won't need a sex scandal now. He's looking far too presidential right now to talk sex.'

It seemed a small consolation to Gabrielle.

'As for Tench's allegations of Sexton's illegal

campaign finance . . .' Yolanda shook her head. 'I have my doubts. Granted, Herney is serious about no negative campaigning. And granted, a bribery investigation would be bad for the country. But is Herney really so patriotic that he would forgo a chance to crush his opposition, simply to protect national morale? My guess is Tench stretched the truth about Sexton's finances in an effort to scare. She gambled, hoping you'd jump ship and give the President a free sex scandal. And you've got to admit, Gabs, *tonight* would have been a hell of a night for Sexton's morals to come into question!'

Gabrielle nodded vaguely. A sex scandal would have been a one-two punch from which Sexton's career never would have recovered . . . ever.

'You outlasted her, Gabs. Marjorie Tench went fishing, but you didn't bite. You're home free. There'll be other elections.'

Gabrielle nodded vaguely, unsure what to believe anymore.

'You've got to admit,' Yolanda said, 'the White House played Sexton brilliantly – hurling him down the NASA path, getting him to commit, coaxing him to put all his eggs in the NASA basket.'

Totally my fault, Gabrielle thought.

'And this announcement we just watched, my God, it was genius! The importance of the discovery entirely aside, the production values were brilliant. Live feeds from the Arctic? A Michael Tolland documentary? Good God, how can you compete? Zach Herney nailed it tonight. There's a reason the guy is President.'

And will be for another four years . . .

'I've got to get back to work, Gabs,' Yolanda said. 'You sit right there as long as you want. Get your feet under you.' Yolanda headed out the door. 'Hon, I'll check back in a few minutes.'

Alone now, Gabrielle sipped her water, but it tasted foul. Everything did. *It's all my fault*, she thought, trying to ease her conscience by reminding herself of all the glum NASA press conferences of the past year – the space station setbacks, the postponement of the X-33, all the failed Mars probes, continuous budget bailouts. Gabrielle wondered what she could have done differently.

Nothing, she told herself. *You did everything right*.

It had simply backfired.

74

The thundering navy SeaHawk chopper had been scrambled under a covert operation status out of Thule Air Force Base in northern Greenland. It stayed low, out of radar range, as it shot through the gale winds across seventy miles of open sea. Then, executing the bizarre orders they had been given, the pilots fought the wind and brought the craft to a hover above a preordained set of coordinates on the empty ocean.

'Where's the rendezvous?' the copilot yelled, confused. They had been told to bring a chopper with a rescue winch, so he anticipated a search-and-retrieve operation. 'You sure these are the right coordinates?' He scanned the choppy seas with a search light, but there was nothing below them except—

'Holy shit!' The pilot pulled back on the stick, jolting upward.

The black mountain of steel rose before them out of the waves without warning. A gargantuan unmarked submarine blew its ballast and rose on a cloud of bubbles.

The pilots exchanged uneasy laughs. 'Guess that's them.'

As ordered, the transaction proceeded under complete radio silence. The doublewide portal on the peak of the sail opened and a seaman flashed them signals with a strobe light. The chopper then moved over the sub and dropped a three-man rescue harness, essentially three rubberized loops on a retractable cable. Within sixty seconds, the three unknown 'danglers' were swinging beneath the chopper, ascending slowly against the downdraft of the rotors.

When the copilot hauled them aboard – two men and a woman – the pilot flashed the sub the 'all clear.' Within seconds, the enormous vessel disappeared beneath the windswept sea, leaving no trace it had ever been there.

With the passengers safely aboard, the chopper pilot faced front, dipped the nose of the chopper, and accelerated south to complete his mission. The storm was closing fast, and these three strangers were to be brought safely back to Thule AFB for further jet transport. Where they were headed, the pilot had no idea. All he knew was that his orders had been from high up, and he was transporting very precious cargo.

When the Milne storm finally exploded, unleashing its full force on the NASA habisphere, the dome shuddered as if ready to lift off the ice and launch out to sea. The steel stabilizing cables pulled taut against their stakes, vibrating like huge guitar strings and letting out a doleful drone. The generators outside stuttered, causing the lights to flicker, threatening to plunge the huge room into total blackness.

NASA administrator Lawrence Ekstrom strode across the interior of the dome. He wished he were getting the hell out of here tonight, but that was not to be. He would remain another day, giving additional on-site press conferences in the morning and over-seeing preparations to transport the meteorite back to Washington. He wanted nothing more at the moment than to get some sleep; the day's unexpected problems had taken a lot out of him.

Ekstrom's thoughts turned yet again to Wailee Ming, Rachel Sexton, Norah Mangor, Michael Tolland, and Corky Marlinson. Some of the NASA staff had begun noticing the civilians were missing.

Relax, Ekstrom told himself. *Everything is under control.*

He breathed deeply, reminding himself that every-one on the planet was excited about NASA and space right now. Extraterrestrial life hadn't been this exciting a topic since the famous 'Roswell incident' back in 1947 – the alleged crash of an alien spaceship in Roswell,

New Mexico, which was now the shrine to millions of UFO-conspiracy theorists even today.

During Ekstrom's years working at the Pentagon, he had learned that the Roswell incident had been nothing more than a military accident during a classified operation called Project Mogul – the flight test of a spy balloon being designed to listen in on Russian atomic tests. A prototype, while being tested, had drifted off course and crashed in the New Mexico desert. Unfortunately, a civilian found the wreckage before the military did.

Unsuspecting rancher William Brazel had stumbled across a debris field of radical synthesized neoprene and lightweight metals unlike anything he'd ever seen, and he immediately called in the sheriff. Newspapers carried the story of the bizarre wreckage, and public interest grew fast. Fueled by the military's denial that the wreckage was theirs, reporters launched investigations, and the covert status of Project Mogul came into serious jeopardy. Just as it seemed the sensitive issue of a spy balloon was about to be revealed, something wonderful happened.

The media drew an unexpected conclusion. They decided the scraps of futuristic substance could only have come from an extraterrestrial source – creatures more scientifically advanced than humans. The military's denial of the incident obviously had to be one thing only – a cover-up of contact with aliens! Although baffled by this new hypothesis, the air force was not about to look a gift horse in the mouth. They grabbed the alien story and ran with it; the world's suspicion that aliens were visiting New Mexico was far less a threat to national security than that of the Russians catching wind of Project Mogul.

To fuel the alien cover story, the intelligence community shrouded the Roswell incident in secrecy and began orchestrating 'security leaks' – quiet murmurings of alien contacts, recovered spaceships, and even a mysterious 'Hangar 18' at Dayton's Wright-Patterson Air Force Base where the government was keeping alien bodies on ice. The world bought the story, and Roswell fever swept the globe. From that moment on, whenever a civilian mistakenly spotted an advanced U.S. military aircraft, the intelligence community simply dusted off the old conspiracy.

That's not an aircraft, that's an alien spaceship!

Ekstrom was amazed to think this simple deception was still working today. Every time the media reported a sudden flurry of UFO sightings, Ekstrom had to laugh. Chances were some lucky civilian had caught a glimpse of one of the NRO's fifty-seven fast-moving, unmanned reconnaissance aircraft known as Global Hawks – oblong, remote-controlled aircraft that looked like nothing else in the sky.

Ekstrom found it pathetic that countless tourists still made pilgrimages to the New Mexico desert to scan the night skies with their video cameras. Occasionally one got lucky and captured 'hard evidence' of a UFO – bright lights flitting around the sky with more maneuverability and speed than any aircraft humans had ever built. What these people failed to realize, of course, was that there existed a twelve-year lag between what the government could build and what the public knew about. These UFO-gazers were simply catching a glimpse of the next generation of U.S. aircraft being developed out at Area 51 – many of which were the brainstorms of NASA engineers. Of course, intelligence officials never corrected the misconception;

it was obviously preferable that the world read about another UFO sighting than to have people learn the U.S. military's true flight capabilities.

But everything has changed now, Ekstrom thought. In a few hours, the extraterrestrial myth would become a confirmed reality, forever.

'Administrator?' A NASA technician hurried across the ice behind him. 'You have an emergency secure call in the PSC.'

Ekstrom sighed, turning. *What the hell could it be now?* He headed for the communications trailer.

The technician hurried along beside him. 'The guys manning the radar in the PSC were curious, sir . . .'

'Yeah?' Ekstrom's thoughts were still far away.

'The fat-body sub stationed off the coast here? We were wondering why you didn't mention it to us.'

Ekstrom glanced up. 'I'm sorry?'

'The submarine, sir? You could have at least told the guys on radar. Additional seaboard security is understandable, but it took our radar team off guard.'

Ekstrom stopped short. *'What* submarine?'

The technician stopped now too, clearly not expecting the administrator's surprise. 'She's not part of our operation?'

'No! Where is it?'

The technician swallowed hard. 'About three miles out. We caught her on radar by chance. Only surfaced for a couple minutes. Pretty big blip. Had to be a fat-body. We figured you'd asked the navy to stand watch over this op without telling any of us.'

Ekstrom stared. 'I most certainly did not!'

Now the technician's voice wavered. 'Well, sir, then I guess I should inform you that a sub just rendezvoused with an aircraft right off the coast here. Looked like a

personnel change. Actually, we were all pretty impressed anyone would attempt a wet-dry vertical in
this kind of wind.'

Ekstrom felt his muscles stiffen. *What the hell is a
submarine doing directly off the coast of Ellesmere Island
without my knowledge?* 'Did you see what direction the
aircraft flew after rendezvous?'

'Back toward Thule air base. For connecting transport
to the mainland, I assume.'

Ekstrom said nothing the rest of the way to the PSC.
When he entered the cramped darkness, the hoarse
voice on the line had a familiar rasp.

'We've got a problem,' Tench said, coughing as she
spoke. 'It's about Rachel Sexton.'

76

Senator Sexton was not sure how long he had been
staring into space when he heard the pounding. When
he realized the throbbing in his ears was not from
the alcohol but rather from someone at his apartment
door, he got up from the couch, stowed the bottle of
Courvoisier, and made his way to the foyer.

'Who is it?' Sexton yelled, in no mood for visitors.

His bodyguard's voice called in with the identity of
Sexton's unexpected guest. Sexton sobered instantly.
That was fast. Sexton had hoped not to have to have this
conversation until morning.

Taking a deep breath and straightening his hair,
Sexton opened the door. The face before him was all
too familiar – tough and leathery despite the man's

seventy-something years. Sexton had met with him only this morning in the white Ford Windstar minivan in a hotel parking garage. *Was it only this morning?* Sexton wondered. God, how things had changed since then.

'May I come in?' the dark-haired man asked.

Sexton stepped aside, allowing the head of the Space Frontier Foundation to pass.

'Did the meeting go well?' the man asked, as Sexton closed the door.

Did it go well? Sexton wondered if the man lived in a cocoon. 'Things were terrific until the President came on television.'

The old man nodded, looking displeased. 'Yes. An incredible victory. It will hurt our cause greatly.'

Hurt our cause? Here was an optimist. With NASA's triumph tonight, this guy would be dead and buried before the Space Frontier Foundation attained their goals of privatization.

'For years I have suspected proof was forthcoming,' the old man said. 'I did not know how or when, but sooner or later we had to know for sure.'

Sexton was stunned. 'You're not surprised?'

'The mathematics of the cosmos virtually requires other life-forms,' the man said, moving toward Sexton's den. 'I am not surprised that this discovery has been made. Intellectually, I am thrilled. Spiritually, I am in awe. Politically, I am deeply disturbed. The timing could not be worse.'

Sexton wondered why the man had come. It sure as hell wasn't to cheer him up.

'As you know,' the man said, 'SFF member companies have spent millions trying to open the frontier of space to private citizens. Recently, much of that money has gone to your campaign.'

Sexton felt suddenly defensive. 'I had no control over tonight's fiasco. The White House baited me to attack NASA!'

'Yes. The President played the game well. And yet, all may not be lost.' There was an odd glint of hope in the old man's eyes.

He's senile, Sexton decided. All was definitely lost. Every station on television right now was talking about the destruction of the Sexton campaign.

The old man showed himself into the den, sat on the couch, and fixed his tired eyes on the senator. 'Do you recall,' the man said, 'the problems NASA initially had with the anomaly software onboard the PODS satellite?'

Sexton could not imagine where this was headed. *What the hell difference does that make now? PODS found a goddamned meteorite with fossils!*

'If you remember,' the man said, 'the onboard software did not function properly at first. You made a big deal of it in the press.'

'As I should have!' Sexton said, sitting down opposite the man. 'It was another NASA failure!'

The man nodded. 'I agree. But shortly after that, NASA held a press conference announcing they had come up with a work-around – some sort of patch for the software.'

Sexton hadn't actually seen the press conference, but he'd heard it was short, flat, and hardly newsworthy – the PODS project leader giving a dull technical description of how NASA had overcome a minor glitch in PODS's anomaly-detection software and gotten everything up and running.

'I have been watching PODS with interest ever since it failed,' the man said. He produced a videocassette and walked to Sexton's television, putting the video in the VCR. 'This should interest you.'

The video began to play. It showed the NASA press room at headquarters in Washington. A well-dressed man was taking the podium and greeting the audience. The subtitle beneath the podium read:

CHRIS HARPER, Section Manager
Polar Orbiting Density Scanner Satellite (PODS)

Chris Harper was tall, refined, and spoke with the quiet dignity of a European American who still clung proudly to his roots. His accent was erudite and polished. He was addressing the press with confidence, giving them some bad news about PODS.

'Although the PODS satellite is in orbit and functioning well, we have a minor setback with the onboard computers. A minor programming error for which I take full responsibility. Specifically, the FIR filter has a faulty voxel index, which means the PODS's anomaly-detection software is not functioning properly. We're working on a fix.'

The crowd sighed, apparently accustomed to NASA letdowns. 'What does that mean for the current effectiveness of the satellite?' someone asked.

Harper took it like a pro. Confident and matter-of-fact. 'Imagine a perfect set of eyes without a functioning brain. Essentially the PODS satellite is seeing twenty-twenty, but it has no idea what it's looking at. The purpose of the PODS mission is to look for melt pockets in the polar ice cap, but without the computer to analyze the density data PODS receives from its scanners, PODS cannot discern where the points of interest are. We should have the situation remedied after the next shuttle mission can make an adjustment to the onboard computer.'

A groan of disappointment rose in the room.

The old man glanced over at Sexton. 'He presents bad news pretty well, doesn't he?'

'He's from NASA,' Sexton grumbled. 'That's what they do.'

The VCR tape went blank for an instant and then switched to another NASA press conference.

'This second press conference,' the old man said to Sexton, 'was given only a few weeks ago. Quite late at night. Few people saw it. This time Dr Harper is announcing *good* news.'

The footage launched. This time Chris Harper looked disheveled and uneasy. 'I am pleased to announce,' Harper said, sounding anything but pleased, 'that NASA has found a work-around for the PODS satellite's software problem.' He fumbled through an explanation of the work-around – something about redirecting the raw data from PODS and sending it through computers here on earth rather than relying on the onboard PODS computer. Everyone seemed impressed. It all sounded quite feasible and exciting. When Harper was done, the room gave him an enthusiastic round of applause.

'So we can expect data soon?' someone in the audience asked.

Harper nodded, sweating. 'A couple of weeks.'

More applause. Hands shot up around the room.

'That's all I have for you now,' Harper said, looking ill as he packed up his papers. 'PODS is up and running. We'll have data soon.' He practically ran off the stage.

Sexton scowled. He had to admit, this was odd. Why did Chris Harper look so comfortable giving bad news and so uncomfortable giving good news? It should have been in reverse. Sexton hadn't actually seen this press conference when it aired, although he'd read about the software fix. The fix, at the time, seemed an inconsequential NASA salvage; the public perception remained unimpressed – PODS was just another NASA project that had malfunctioned and was being awkwardly patched together with a less than ideal solution.

The old man turned off the television. 'NASA claimed Dr Harper was not feeling well that night.' He paused. 'I happen to think Harper was lying.'

Lying? Sexton stared, his fuzzy thoughts unable to piece together any logical rationale for why Harper would have lied about the software. Still, Sexton had told enough lies in his life to recognize a poor liar when he saw one. He had to admit, Dr Harper sure looked suspicious.

'Perhaps you don't realize?' the old man said. 'This little announcement you just heard Chris Harper give is the single most important press conference in NASA history.' He paused. 'That convenient software fix he just described is what allowed PODS to find the meteorite.'

Sexton puzzled. *And you think he was lying about it?* 'But, if Harper was lying, and the PODS software isn't really working, then how the hell did NASA find the meteorite?'

The old man smiled. 'Exactly.'

The U.S. military's fleet of 'repo' aircraft repossessed during drug-trade arrests consisted of over a dozen private jets, including three reconditioned G4s used for transporting military VIPs. A half hour ago, one of those G4s had lifted off the Thule runway, fought its way above the storm, and was now pounding southward into the Canadian night en route to Washington. Onboard, Rachel Sexton, Michael Tolland, and Corky Marlinson had the eight-seat cabin to themselves, looking like some kind of disheveled sports team in their matching blue U.S.S. *Charlotte* jumpsuits and caps.

Despite the roar of the Grumman engines, Corky Marlinson was asleep in the rear. Tolland sat near the front, looking exhausted as he gazed out the window at the sea. Rachel was beside him, knowing she could not sleep even if she'd been sedated. Her mind churned through the mystery of the meteorite, and, most recently, the dead room conversation with Pickering. Before signing off, Pickering had given Rachel two additional pieces of disturbing information.

First, Marjorie Tench claimed to possess a video recording of Rachel's private deposition to the White House staff. Tench was now threatening to use the video as evidence if Rachel tried to go back on her confirmation of the meteorite data. The news was particularly unsettling because Rachel had specifically told Zach Herney that her remarks to the staff were for in-house use only. Apparently Zach Herney had ignored that request.

The second bit of troubling news dealt with a CNN debate her father had attended earlier in the afternoon. Apparently, Marjorie Tench had made a rare appearance and deftly baited Rachel's father into crystallizing his position against NASA. More specifically, Tench had cajoled him into crudely proclaiming his skepticism that extraterrestrial life would ever be found.

Eat his hat? That's what Pickering said her father had offered to do if NASA ever found extraterrestrial life. Rachel wondered how Tench had managed to coax out that propitious little sound bite. Clearly, the White House had been setting the stage carefully – ruthlessly lining up all the dominoes, preparing for the big Sexton collapse. The President and Marjorie Tench, like some sort of political tag team wrestling duo, had maneuvered for the kill. While the President remained dignified outside the ring, Tench had moved in, circling, cunningly lining up the senator for the presidential body slam.

The President had told Rachel he'd asked NASA to delay announcing the discovery in order to provide time to confirm the accuracy of the data. Rachel now realized there were other advantages to waiting. The extra time had given the White House time to dole out the rope with which the senator would hang himself.

Rachel felt no sympathy for her father, and yet she now realized that beneath the warm and fuzzy exterior of President Zach Herney, a shrewd shark lurked. You did not become the most powerful man in the world without a killer instinct. The question now was whether this shark was an innocent bystander – or a player.

Rachel stood, stretching her legs. As she paced the

aisle of the plane, she felt frustrated that the pieces to this puzzle seemed so contradictory. Pickering, with his trademark chaste logic, had concluded the meteorite must be fake. Corky and Tolland, with scientific assurance, insisted the meteorite was authentic. Rachel only knew what she had seen – a charred, fossilized rock being pulled from the ice.

Now, as she passed beside Corky, she gazed down at the astrophysicist, battered from his ordeal on the ice. The swelling on his cheek was going down now, and the stitches looked good. He was asleep, snoring, his pudgy hands clutching the disk-shaped meteorite sample like some kind of security blanket.

Rachel reached down and gently slipped the meteorite sample away from him. She held it up, studying the fossils again. *Remove all assumptions*, she told herself, forcing herself to reorganize her thoughts. *Reestablish the chain of substantiation*. It was an old NRO trick. Rebuilding a proof from scratch was a process known as a 'null start' – something all data analysts practiced when the pieces didn't quite fit.

Reassemble the proof.

She began pacing again.

Does this stone represent proof of extraterrestrial life?

Proof, she knew, was a conclusion built on a pyramid of facts, a broad base of accepted information on which more specific assertions were made.

Remove all the base assumptions. Start again.

What do we have?

A rock.

She pondered that for a moment. *A rock. A rock with fossilized creatures.* Walking back toward the front of the plane, she took her seat beside Michael Tolland.

'Mike, let's play a game.'

Tolland turned from the window, looking distant, apparently deep in his own thoughts. 'A game?'

She handed him the meteorite sample. 'Let's pretend you're seeing this fossilized rock for the first time. I've told you nothing about where it came from or how it was found. What would you tell me it is?'

Tolland heaved a disconsolate sigh. 'Funny you should ask. I just had the strangest thought . . .'

Hundreds of miles behind Rachel and Tolland, a strange-looking aircraft stayed low as it tore south above a deserted ocean. Onboard, the Delta Force was silent. They had been pulled out of locations in a hurry, but never like this.

Their controller was furious.

Earlier, Delta-One had informed the controller that unexpected events on the ice shelf had left his team with no option but to exercise force – force that had included killing four civilians, including Rachel Sexton and Michael Tolland.

The controller reacted with shock. Killing, although an authorized last resort, obviously never had been part of the controller's plan.

Later, the controller's displeasure over the killings turned to outright rage when he learned the assassinations had not gone as planned.

'Your team failed!' the controller seethed, the androgynous tone hardly masking the person's rage. 'Three of your four targets are still alive!'

Impossible! Delta-One had thought. 'But we witnessed—'

'They made contact with a submarine and are now en route to Washington.'

'What?'

The controller's tone turned lethal. 'Listen carefully. I am about to give you new orders. And this time you will not fail.'

78

Senator Sexton was actually feeling a flicker of hope as he walked his unexpected visitor back out to the elevator. The head of the SFF, as it turned out, had not come to chastise Sexton, but rather to give him a pep talk and tell him the battle was not yet over.

A possible chink in NASA's armor.

The videotape of the bizarre NASA press conference had convinced Sexton that the old man was right – PODS mission director Chris Harper was lying. *But why? And if NASA never fixed the PODS software, how did NASA find the meteorite?*

As they walked to the elevator, the old man said, 'Sometimes all it takes to unravel something is a single strand. Perhaps we can find a way to eat away at NASA's victory from within. Cast a shadow of distrust. Who knows where it will lead?' The old man locked his tired eyes on Sexton. 'I am not ready to lay down and die, Senator. And I trust nor are you.'

'Of course not,' Sexton said, mustering resolve in his voice. 'We've come too far.'

'Chris Harper lied about fixing PODS,' the man said as he boarded the elevator. 'And we need to know why.'

'I will get that information as fast as I can,' Sexton replied. *I have just the person.*

'Good. Your future depends on it.'

As Sexton headed back toward his apartment, his step was a little lighter, his head a little clearer. *NASA lied about PODS*. The only question was how Sexton could prove it.

His thoughts had already turned to Gabrielle Ashe. Wherever she was at the moment, she had to be feeling like shit. Gabrielle had no doubt seen the press conference and was now standing on a ledge somewhere getting ready to jump. Her proposition of making NASA a major issue in Sexton's campaign had turned out to be the biggest mistake of Sexton's career.

She owes me, Sexton thought. *And she knows it*.

Gabrielle already had proven she had a knack for obtaining NASA secrets. *She has a contact*, Sexton thought. She'd been scoring insider information for weeks now. Gabrielle had connections she was not sharing. Connections she could pump for information on PODS. Moreover, tonight Gabrielle would be motivated. She had a debt to repay, and Sexton suspected she would do anything to regain his favor.

As Sexton arrived back at his apartment door, his bodyguard nodded. 'Evening, Senator. I trust I did the right thing by letting Gabrielle in earlier? She said it was critical she talk to you.'

Sexton paused. 'I'm sorry?'

'Ms Ashe? She had important information for you earlier tonight. That's why I let her in.'

Sexton felt his body stiffen. He looked at his apartment door. *What the hell is this guy talking about?*

The guard's expression changed to one of confusion and concern. 'Senator, are you okay? You remember, right? Gabrielle arrived during your meeting. She talked to you, right? She *must* have. She was in there quite a while.'

Sexton stared a long moment, feeling his pulse sky-rocket. *This moron let Gabrielle into my apartment during a private SFF meeting?* She stuck around inside and then departed without a word? Sexton could only imagine what Gabrielle might have overheard. Swallowing his anger, he forced a smile to his guard. 'Oh, yes! I'm sorry. I'm exhausted. Had a couple of drinks, too. Ms Ashe and I did indeed speak. You did the right thing.'

The guard looked relieved.

'Did she say where she went when she left?'

The guard shook his head. 'She was in a big hurry.'

'Okay, thanks.'

Sexton entered his apartment fuming. *How complicated were my goddamn directions? No visitors!* He had to assume if Gabrielle had been inside for any length of time and then snuck out without a word, she must have heard things she was not meant to hear. *Tonight of all nights.*

Senator Sexton knew above all he could not afford to lose Gabrielle Ashe's trust; women could become vengeful and stupid when they felt deceived. Sexton needed to bring her back. Tonight more than ever, he needed her in his camp.

79

On the fourth floor of the ABC television studios, Gabrielle Ashe sat alone in Yolanda's glass-walled office and stared at the fraying carpet. She had always prided herself on good instincts and knowing whom she could trust. Now, for the first time in years, Gabrielle felt alone, uncertain which way to turn.

The sound of her cellphone lifted her gaze from the carpet. Reluctant, she picked up. 'Gabrielle Ashe.'

'Gabrielle, it's me.'

She recognized the timbre of Senator Sexton's voice immediately, although he sounded surprisingly calm considering what had just transpired.

'It's been one hell of a night over here,' he said, 'so just let me talk. I'm sure you saw the President's conference. Christ, did we play the wrong cards. I'm sick over it. You're probably blaming yourself. Don't. Who the hell would have guessed? Not your fault. Anyhow, listen up. I think there may be a way to get our feet back under us.'

Gabrielle stood up, unable to imagine what Sexton could be talking about. This is hardly the reaction she had expected.

'I had a meeting tonight,' Sexton said, 'with representatives from private space industries, and—'

'You did?' Gabrielle blurted, stunned to hear him admit it. 'I mean . . . I had no idea.'

'Yeah, nothing major. I would have asked you to sit in, but these guys are touchy about privacy. Some of them are donating money to my campaign. It's not something they like to advertise.'

Gabrielle felt totally disarmed. 'But . . . isn't that illegal?'

'Illegal? Hell no! All the donations are under the two-thousand-dollar cap. Small potatoes. These guys barely make a dent, but I listen to their gripes anyway. Call it an investment in the future. I'm quiet about it because, frankly, the appearances aren't so great. If the White House caught wind, they'd spin the hell out of it.

Anyhow, look, that's not the point. I called to tell you that after tonight's meeting, I was talking to the head of the SFF . . .'

For several seconds, although Sexton was still talking, all Gabrielle could hear was the blood rushing in shame to her face. Without the slightest challenge from her, the senator had calmly admitted tonight's meeting with private space companies. *Perfectly legal.* And to think what Gabrielle had almost considered doing! Thank God Yolanda had stopped her. *I almost jumped ship to Marjorie Tench!*

'. . . and so I told the head of the SFF,' the senator was saying, 'that you might be able to get that information for us.'

Gabrielle tuned back in. 'Okay.'

'The contact from whom you've been getting all your inside NASA information these past few months? I assume you still have access?'

Marjorie Tench. Gabrielle cringed, knowing she could never tell the senator that the informant had been manipulating her all along. 'Um . . . I think so,' Gabrielle lied.

'Good. There's some information I need from you. Right away.'

As she listened, Gabrielle realized just how badly she had been underestimating Senator Sedgewick Sexton lately. Some of the man's luster had worn off since she'd first begun following his career. But tonight, it was back. In the face of what appeared to be the ultimate death blow to his campaign, Sexton was plotting a counterattack. And although it had been Gabrielle who led him down this inauspicious path, he was not punishing her. Instead, he was giving her a chance to redeem herself.

And redeem herself she would.
Whatever it took.

William Pickering gazed out his office window at the distant line of headlights on Leesburg Highway. He often thought about her when he stood up here alone at the top of the world.

All this power . . . and I couldn't save her.

Pickering's daughter, Diana, had died in the Red Sea while stationed aboard a small navy escort ship, training to become a navigator. Her ship had been anchored in safe harbor on a sunny afternoon when a handmade dory loaded with explosives and powered by two suicide terrorists motored slowly across the harbor and exploded on contact with the hull. Diana Pickering and thirteen other young American soldiers had been killed that day.

William Pickering had been devastated. The anguish overwhelmed him for weeks. When the terrorist attack was traced to a known cell whom the CIA had been tracking unsuccessfully for years, Pickering's sadness turned into rage. He had marched into CIA headquarters and demanded answers.

The answers he got were hard to swallow.

Apparently the CIA had been prepared to move on this cell months before and was simply waiting for the high-res satellite photos so that they could plan a pinpoint attack on the terrorists' mountain hideout in Afghanistan. Those photos were scheduled to be taken by the $1.2 billion NRO satellite code-named Vortex 2, the same satellite that had been blown up on the launchpad by its NASA launch vehicle. Because of the NASA accident, the CIA strike had been postponed, and now Diana Pickering had died.

Pickering's mind told him that NASA had not been directly responsible, but his heart found it hard to forgive. The investigation of the rocket explosion revealed that the NASA engineers responsible for the fuel injection system had been forced to use second-rate materials in an effort to stay on budget.

'For nonmanned flights,' Lawrence Ekstrom explained in a press conference, 'NASA strives for cost-effectiveness above all. In this case, the results were admittedly not optimal. We will be looking into it.'

Not optimal. Diana Pickering was dead.

Furthermore, because the spy satellite was classified, the public never learned that NASA had disintegrated a $1.2 billion NRO project, and along with it, indirectly, numerous American lives.

'Sir?' Pickering's secretary's voice came over his intercom, startling him. 'Line one. It's Marjorie Tench.'

Pickering shook himself out of his daze and looked at his telephone. *Again?* The blinking light on line one seemed to pulse with an irate urgency. Pickering frowned and took the call.

'Pickering here.'

Tench's voice was seething mad. 'What did she tell you?'

'I'm sorry?'

'Rachel Sexton contacted you. What did she tell you? She was on a submarine, for God's sake! Explain that!'

Pickering could tell immediately that denying the

fact was not an option; Tench had been doing her homework. Pickering was surprised she'd found out about the *Charlotte*, but she'd apparently thrown her weight around until she got some answers. 'Ms Sexton contacted me, yes.'

'You arranged a pickup. And you didn't contact me?'

'I arranged transport. That is correct.' Two hours remained until Rachel Sexton, Michael Tolland, and Corky Marlinson were scheduled to arrive at the nearby Bollings Air Force Base.

'And yet you chose not to inform me?'

'Rachel Sexton has made some very disturbing accusations.'

'Regarding the authenticity of the meteorite . . . and some kind of attack on her life?'

'Among other things.'

'Obviously, she is lying.'

'You are aware she is with two others who corroborate her story?'

Tench paused. 'Yes. Most disturbing. The White House is very concerned by their claims.'

'The White House? Or you personally?'

Her tone turned razor sharp. 'As far as you are concerned, Director, there is no difference tonight.'

Pickering was unimpressed. He was no stranger to blustering politicians and support staff trying to establish footholds over the intel community. Few put up as strong a front as Marjorie Tench. 'Does the President know you're calling me?'

'Frankly, Director, I'm shocked that you would even entertain these lunatic ravings.'

You didn't answer my question. 'I see no logical reason for these people to lie. I have to assume they are either telling the truth, or they have made an honest mistake.'

'Mistake? Claims of attacks? Flaws in the meteorite data that NASA never saw? Please! This is an obvious political ploy.'

'If so, the motives escape me.'

Tench sighed heavily and lowered her voice. 'Director, there are forces at work here of which you might not be aware. We can speak about that at length later, but at the moment I need to know where Ms Sexton and the others are. I need to get to the bottom of this before they do any lasting damage. Where are they?'

'That is not information I am comfortable sharing. I will contact you after they arrive.'

'Wrong. I will be there to greet them when they arrive.'

You and how many Secret Service agents? Pickering wondered. 'If I inform you of their arrival time and location, will we all have a chance to chat like friends, or do you intend to have a private army take them into custody?'

'These people pose a direct threat to the President. The White House has every right to detain and question them.'

Pickering knew she was right. Under Title 18, Section 3056 of the United States Code, agents of the U.S. Secret Service can carry firearms, use deadly force, and make 'un-warranted' arrests simply on suspicion that a person has committed or is intending to commit a felony or any act of aggression against the President. The service possessed carte blanche. Regular detainees included unsavory loiterers outside the White House and school kids who sent threatening e-mail pranks.

Pickering had no doubt the service could justify dragging Rachel Sexton and the others into the basement of the White House and keeping them there indefinitely. It would be a dangerous play, but Tench clearly realized the stakes were huge. The question was what would happen next if Pickering allowed Tench to take control. He had no intention of finding out.

'I will do whatever necessary,' Tench declared, 'to protect the President from false accusations. The mere implication of foul play will cast a heavy shadow on the White House and NASA. Rachel Sexton has abused the trust the President gave her, and I have no intention of seeing the President pay the price.'

'And if I request that Ms Sexton be permitted to present her case to an official panel of inquiry?'

'Then you would be disregarding a direct presidential order and giving her a platform from which to make a goddamn political mess! I will ask you one more time, Director. Where are you flying them?'

Pickering exhaled a long breath. Whether or not he told Marjorie Tench that the plane was coming into Bollings Air Force Base, he knew she had the means to find out. The question was whether or not she would do it. He sensed from the determination in her voice that she would not rest. Marjorie Tench was scared.

'Marjorie,' Pickering said, with unmistakable clarity of tone. 'Someone is lying to me. Of this I am certain. Either it is Rachel Sexton and two civilian scientists – or it is you. I believe it is you.'

Tench exploded. 'How dare—'

'Your indignity has no resonance with me, so save it. You would be wise to know that I have absolute proof NASA and the White House broadcast untruths tonight.'

Tench fell suddenly silent.

Pickering let her reel a moment. 'I'm not looking for a

political meltdown any more than you are. But there have been lies. Lies that cannot stand. If you want me to help you, you've got to start by being honest with me.'

Tench sounded tempted but wary. 'If you're so certain there were lies, why haven't you stepped forward?'

'I don't interfere in political matters.'

Tench muttered something that sounded a lot like 'bullshit.'

'Are you trying to tell me, Marjorie, that the President's announcement tonight was entirely accurate?'

There was a long silence on the line.

Pickering knew he had her. 'Listen, we both know this is a time bomb waiting to explode. But it's not too late. There are compromises we can make.'

Tench said nothing for several seconds. Finally she sighed. 'We should meet.'

Touchdown, Pickering thought.

'I have something to show you,' Tench said. 'And I believe it will shed some light on this matter.'

'I'll come to your office.'

'No,' she said hurriedly. 'It's late. Your presence here would raise concerns. I'd prefer to keep this matter between us.'

Pickering read between the lines. *The President knows nothing about this.* 'You're welcome to come here,' he said.

Tench sounded distrusting. 'Let's meet somewhere discreet.'

Pickering had expected as much.

'The FDR Memorial is convenient to the White House,' Tench said. 'It will be empty at this time of night.'

Pickering considered it. The FDR Memorial sat

midway between the Jefferson and Lincoln memorials, in an extremely safe part of town. After a long beat, Pickering agreed.

'One hour,' Tench said, signing off. 'And come alone.'

Immediately upon hanging up, Marjorie Tench phoned NASA Administrator Ekstrom. Her voice was tight as she relayed the bad news.

'Pickering could be a problem.'

81

Gabrielle Ashe was brimming with new hope as she stood at Yolanda Cole's desk in the ABC production room and dialed directory assistance.

The allegations Sexton had just conveyed to her, if confirmed, had shocking potential. *NASA lied about PODS?* Gabrielle had seen the press conference in question and recalled thinking it was odd, and yet she'd forgotten all about it; PODS was not a critical issue a few weeks ago. Tonight, however, PODS had become *the* issue.

Now Sexton needed inside information, and he needed it fast. He was relying on Gabrielle's 'informant' to get the information. Gabrielle had assured the senator she would do her best. The problem, of course, was that her informant was Marjorie Tench, who would be no help at all. So Gabrielle would have to get the information another way.

'Directory assistance,' the voice on the phone said.

361

Gabrielle told them what she needed. The operator came back with three listings for a Chris Harper in Washington. Gabrielle tried them all.

The first number was a law firm. The second had no answer. The third was now ringing.

A woman answered on the first ring. 'Harper residence.'

'Mrs Harper?' Gabrielle said as politely as possible. 'I hope I haven't woken you?'

'Heavens no! I don't think anyone's asleep tonight.' She sounded excited. Gabrielle could hear the television in the background. Meteorite coverage. 'You're calling for Chris, I assume?'

Gabrielle's pulse quickened. 'Yes, ma'am.'

'I'm afraid Chris isn't here. He raced off to work as soon as the President's address was over.' The woman chuckled to herself. 'Of course, I doubt there's any work going on. Most likely a party. The announcement came as quite a surprise to him, you know. To everyone. Our phone's been ringing all night. I bet the whole NASA crew's over there by now.'

'E Street complex?' Gabrielle asked, assuming the woman meant NASA headquarters.

'Righto. Take a party hat.'

'Thanks. I'll track him down over there.'

Gabrielle hung up. She hurried out onto the production room floor and found Yolanda, who was just finishing prepping a group of space experts who were about to give enthusiastic commentary on the meteorite.

Yolanda smiled when she saw Gabrielle coming. 'You look better,' she said. 'Starting to see the silver lining here?'

'I just talked to the senator. His meeting tonight wasn't what I thought.'

'I told you Tench was playing you. How's the senator taking the meteorite news?'

'Better than expected.'

Yolanda looked surprised. 'I figured he'd jumped in front of a bus by now.'

'He thinks there may be a snag in the NASA data.'

Yolanda let out a dubious snort. 'Did he see the same press conference I just saw? How much more confirmation and reconfirmation can anyone need?'

'I'm going over to NASA to check on something.'

Yolanda's penciled eyebrows raised in cautionary arches. 'Senator Sexton's right-hand aide is going to march into NASA headquarters? Tonight? Can you say "public stoning"?'

Gabrielle told Yolanda about Sexton's suspicion that the PODS section manager Chris Harper had lied about fixing the anomaly software.

Yolanda clearly wasn't buying it. 'We covered that press conference, Gabs, and I'll admit, Harper was not himself that night, but NASA said he was sick as a dog.'

'Senator Sexton is convinced he lied. Others are convinced too. Powerful people.'

'If the PODS anomaly-detection software wasn't fixed, how did PODS spot the meteorite?'

Sexton's point exactly, Gabrielle thought. 'I don't know. But the senator wants me to get him some answers.'

Yolanda shook her head. 'Sexton is sending you into a hornets' nest on a desperate pipe dream. Don't go. You don't owe him a thing.'

'I totally screwed up his campaign.'

'Rotten luck screwed up his campaign.'

'But if the senator is right and the PODS section manager actually lied—'

'Honey, if the PODS section manager lied to the world, what makes you think he'll tell *you* the truth?'

Gabrielle had considered that and was already formulating her plan. 'If I find a story over there, I'll call you.'

Yolanda gave a skeptical laugh. 'If you find a story over there, I'll eat my hat.'

82

Erase everything you know about this rock sample.

Michael Tolland had been struggling with his own disquieting ruminations about the meteorite, but now, with Rachel's probing questions, he was feeling an added unease over the issue. He looked down at the rock slice in his hand.

Pretend someone handed it to you with no explanation of where it was found or what it is. What would your analysis be?

Rachel's question, Tolland knew, was loaded, and yet as an analytical exercise, it proved powerful. By discarding all the data he had been given on his arrival at the habisphere, Tolland had to admit that his analysis of the fossils was profoundly biased by a singular premise – that the rock in which the fossils were found was a meteorite.

What if I had NOT been told about the meteorite? he asked himself. Although still unable to fathom any other explanation, Tolland allowed himself the leeway of hypothetically removing 'the meteorite' as a presupposition, and when he did, the results were somewhat unsettling. Now Tolland and Rachel, joined by a groggy Corky Marlinson, were discussing the ideas.

'So,' Rachel repeated, her voice intense, 'Mike, you're saying that if someone handed you this fossilized rock with *no* explanation whatsoever, you would have to conclude it was from earth.'

'Of course,' Tolland replied. 'What else could I conclude? It's a far greater leap to assert you've found extraterrestrial life than it is to assert you've found a fossil of some previously undiscovered terrestrial species. Scientists discover dozens of new species every year.'

'Two-foot-long lice?' Corky demanded, sounding incredulous. 'You would assume a bug that big is from *earth*?'

'Not *now*, maybe,' Tolland replied, 'but the species doesn't necessarily have to be currently living. It's a fossil. It's one hundred and seventy million years old. About the same age as our Jurassic. A lot of prehistoric fossils are over-sized creatures that look shocking when we discover their fossilized remains – enormous winged reptiles, dinosaurs, birds.'

'Not to be the physicist here, Mike,' Corky said, 'but there's a serious flaw in your argument. The prehistoric creatures you just named – dinosaurs, reptiles, birds – they all have internal *skeletons*, which gives them the capability to grow to large sizes despite the earth's gravity. But this fossil . . .' He took the sample and held it up. 'These guys have *exo*skeletons. They're arthropods. Bugs. You yourself said that any bug this big could only have evolved in a low-gravity environment. Otherwise its outer skeleton would have collapsed under its own weight.'

'Correct,' Tolland said. 'This species would have collapsed under its own weight if it walked around on earth.'

Corky's brow furrowed with annoyance. 'Well, Mike, unless some caveman was running an antigravity louse farm, I don't see how you could possibly conclude a two-foot-long bug is *earthly* in origin.'

Tolland smiled inwardly to think Corky was missing such a simple point. 'Actually, there is another possibility.' He focused closely on his friend. 'Corky, you're used to looking *up*. Look *down*. There's an abundant antigravity environment right here on earth. And it's been here since prehistoric times.'

Corky stared. 'What the hell are you talking about?'

Rachel also looked surprised.

Tolland pointed out the window at the moonlit sea glistening beneath the plane. 'The ocean.'

Rachel let out a low whistle. 'Of course.'

'Water is a low-gravity environment,' Tolland explained. 'Everything weighs less underwater. The ocean supports enormous fragile structures that could never exist on land – jellyfish, giant squid, ribbon eels.'

Corky acquiesced, but only slightly. 'Fine, but the prehistoric ocean never had giant bugs?'

'Sure, it did. And it still does, in fact. People eat them every day. They're a delicacy in most countries.'

'Mike, who the hell eats giant sea bugs?'

'Anyone who eats lobsters, crabs, and shrimp.'

Corky stared.

'Crustaceans are essentially giant sea bugs,' Tolland explained. 'They're a suborder of the phylum Arthropoda – lice, crabs, spiders, insects, grasshoppers, scorpions, lobsters – they're all related. They're all species with jointed appendages and external skeletons.'

366

Corky suddenly looked ill.

'From a classification standpoint, they look a lot like bugs,' Tolland explained. 'Horseshoe crabs resemble giant trilobites. And the claws of a lobster resemble those of a large scorpion.'

Corky turned green. 'Okay, I've eaten my last lobster roll.'

Rachel looked fascinated. 'So arthropods on land stay small because the gravity selects naturally for smallness. But in the water, their bodies are buoyed up, so they can grow very large.'

'Exactly,' Tolland said. 'An Alaskan king crab could be wrongly classified as a giant spider if we had limited fossil evidence.'

Rachel's excitement seemed to fade now to concern. 'Mike, again barring the issue of the meteorite's apparent authenticity, tell me this: do you think the fossils we saw at Milne could possibly have come from the ocean? *Earth's* ocean?'

Tolland felt the directness of her gaze and sensed the true weight of her question. 'Hypothetically, I would have to say yes. The ocean floor has sections that are one hundred and ninety million years old. The same age as the fossils. And theoretically the oceans could have sustained life-forms that looked like this.'

'Oh please!' Corky scoffed. 'I can't believe what I'm hearing here. *Barring* the issue of the meteorite's authenticity? The meteorite is irrefutable. Even if earth has ocean floor the same age as that meteorite, we sure as hell don't have ocean floor that has fusion crust, anomalous nickel content, and chondrules. You're grasping at straws.'

Tolland knew Corky was right, and yet imagining the fossils as sea creatures had robbed Tolland of some of his awe over them. They seemed somehow more familiar now.

'Mike,' Rachel said, 'why didn't any of the NASA scientists consider that these fossils might be ocean creatures? Even from an ocean on another planet?'

'Two reasons, really. Pelagic fossil samples – those from the ocean floor – tend to exhibit a plethora of intermingled species. Anything living in the millions of cubic feet of life above the ocean floor will eventually die and sink to the bottom. This means the ocean floor becomes a graveyard for species from every depth, pressure, and temperature environment. But the sample at Milne was clean – a single species. It looked more like something we might find in the desert. A brood of similar animals getting buried in a sandstorm, for example.'

Rachel nodded. 'And the second reason you guessed land rather than sea?'

Tolland shrugged. 'Gut instinct. Scientists have always believed space, if it were populated, would be populated by *insects*. And from what we've observed of space, there's a lot more dirt and rock out there than water.'

Rachel fell silent.

'Although . . .' Tolland added. Rachel had him thinking now. 'I'll admit there are very deep parts of the ocean floor that oceanographers call dead zones. We don't really understand them, but they are areas in which the current and food sources are such that almost nothing lives there. Just a few species of bottom-dwelling scavengers. So from that standpoint, I suppose a single-species fossil is not entirely out of the question.'

'Hello?' Corky grumbled. 'Remember the fusion

crust? The mid-level nickel content? The chondrules? Why are we even talking about this?'

Tolland did not reply.

'This issue of the nickel content,' Rachel said to Corky. 'Explain this to me again. The nickel content in earth rocks is either very high or very low, but in meteorites the nickel content is within a specific mid-range window?'

Corky bobbed his head. 'Precisely.'

'And so the nickel content in this sample falls precisely within the expected range of values?'

'Very close, yes.'

Rachel looked surprised. 'Hold on. *Close?* What's that supposed to mean?'

Corky looked exasperated. 'As I explained earlier, all meteorite mineralogies are different. As scientists find new meteorites, we constantly need to update our calculations as to what we consider an acceptable nickel content for meteorites.'

Rachel looked stunned as she held up the sample. 'So, *this* meteorite forced you to reevaluate what you consider acceptable nickel content in a meteorite? It fell outside the established midrange nickel window?'

'Only slightly,' Corky fired back.

'Why didn't anyone mention this?'

'It's a nonissue. Astrophysics is a dynamic science which is constantly being updated.'

'*During* an incredibly important analysis?'

'Look,' Corky said with a huff, 'I can assure you the nickel content in that sample is a helluva lot closer to other meteorites than it is to any earth rock.'

Rachel turned to Tolland. 'Did you know about this?'

Tolland gave a reluctant nod. It hadn't seemed

a major issue at the time. 'I was told this meteorite exhibited slightly higher nickel content than seen in other meteorites, but the NASA specialists seemed unconcerned.'

'For good reason!' Corky interjected. 'The mineralogical proof here is *not* that the nickel content is conclusively meteoritelike, but rather that it is conclusively non-earth-like.'

Rachel shook her head. 'Sorry, but in my business that's the kind of faulty logic that gets people killed. Saying a rock is non-earth-like doesn't prove it's a meteorite. It simply proves that it's not like anything we've ever seen on earth.'

'What the hell's the difference?'

'Nothing,' Rachel said. 'If you've seen every rock on earth.'

Corky fell silent a moment. 'Okay,' he finally said, 'ignore the nickel content if it makes you nervous. We still have a flawless fusion crust and chondrules.'

'Sure,' Rachel said, sounding unimpressed. 'Two out of three ain't bad.'

83

The structure housing the NASA central headquarters was a mammoth glass rectangle located at 300 E Street in Washington, D.C. The building was spidered with over 200 miles of data cabling and thousands of tons of computer processors. It was home to 1,134 civil servants who oversee NASA's $15 billion annual budget and the daily operations of the 12 NASA bases nationwide.

Despite the late hour, Gabrielle was not at all surprised to see the building's foyer filling with people, an apparent convergence of excited media crews and even more excited NASA personnel. Gabrielle hurried inside. The entryway resembled a museum, dominated dramatically by fullsize replicas of famous mission capsules and satellites suspended overhead. Television crews were staking claims on the expensive marble floor, seizing wide-eyed NASA employees who came through the door.

Gabrielle scanned the crowd, but did not see anyone who looked like PODS mission director Chris Harper. Half the people in the lobby had press passes and half had NASA photo IDs around their necks. Gabrielle had neither. She spotted a young woman with a NASA ID and hurried over to her.

'Hi. I'm looking for Chris Harper?'

The woman eyed Gabrielle strangely, as if she recognized her from somewhere and couldn't quite place it. 'I saw Dr Harper go through a while ago. I think he headed upstairs. Do I know you?'

'I don't think so,' Gabrielle said, turning away. 'How do I get upstairs?'

'Do you work for NASA?'

'No, I don't.'

'Then you can't get upstairs.'

'Oh. Is there a phone I might use to—'

'Hey,' the woman said, looking suddenly angry. 'I know who you are. I've seen you on television with Senator Sexton. I can't believe you would have the nerve—'

Gabrielle was already gone, disappearing into the crowd. Behind her, she could hear the woman angrily telling others Gabrielle was here.

Terrific. Two seconds through the door, and I'm already on the Most Wanted List.

Gabrielle kept her head down as she hurried to the far side of the lobby. A building directory was mounted on the wall. She scanned the listings, looking for Chris Harper. Nothing. The directory showed no names at all. It was arranged by department.

PODS? she wondered, scanning the list for anything that had to do with the Polar Orbiting Density Scanner. She saw nothing. She was afraid to glance over her shoulder, half expecting to see a crew of angry NASA employees coming to stone her. All she saw on the list that looked even remotely promising was on the fourth floor:

EARTH SCIENCE ENTERPRISE, PHASE II
Earth Observing System (EOS)

Keeping her head turned away from the crowd, Gabrielle made her way toward an alcove that housed a bank of elevators and a water fountain. She searched for the elevator call buttons, but saw only slits. *Damn.* The elevators were security controlled – key card ID access for employees only.

A group of young men came hurrying toward the elevators, talking exuberantly. They wore NASA photo IDs around their necks. Gabrielle quickly bent over the fountain, watching behind her. A pimple-faced man inserted his ID into the slot and opened the elevator. He was laughing, shaking his head in amazement.

'The guys in SETI must be going nuts!' he said as everyone boarded the elevator. 'Their horn carts traced drift fields under two hundred milliJanskys for twenty years, and the physical proof was buried in the ice here on earth the whole time!'

The elevator doors closed, and the men disappeared.

Gabrielle stood up, wiping her mouth, wondering what to do. She looked around for an interoffice phone. Nothing. She wondered if she could somehow steal a key card, but something told her that was probably unwise. Whatever she did, she knew she had to do it fast. She could now see the woman she'd first spoken to out in the lobby, moving through the crowd with a NASA security officer.

A trim, bald man came around the corner, hustling toward the elevators. Gabrielle again bent over the fountain. The man did not seem to notice her. Gabrielle watched in silence as the man leaned forward and inserted his ID card into the slit. Another set of elevator doors slid open, and the man stepped on.

Screw it, Gabrielle thought, making up her mind. *Now or never.*

As the elevator slid closed, Gabrielle spun from the fountain and ran over, sticking her hand out and catching the door. The doors bounced back open, and she stepped in, her face bright with excitement. 'You ever seen it like this?' she gushed to the startled bald man. 'My God. It's crazy!'

The man gave her an odd look.

'The guys at SETI must be going nuts!' Gabrielle said. 'Their horn carts traced drift fields under two hundred milliJanskys for twenty years, and the physical proof was buried in the ice here on earth the whole time!'

The man looked surprised. 'Well . . . yes, it's quite . . .' He glanced at her neck, apparently troubled not to see an ID. 'I'm sorry, do you—'

'Fourth floor please. Came in such a hurry I barely

remembered to put on my underwear!' She laughed, stealing a quick look at the guy's ID: JAMES THEISEN, *Finance Administration.*

'Do you work here?' The man looked uncomfortable. 'Miss . . . ?'

Gabrielle let her mouth fall slack. 'Jim! I'm hurt! Nothing like making a woman feel unmemorable!'

The man went pale for a moment, looking uneasy, and running an embarrassed hand across his head. 'I'm sorry. All this excitement, you know. I admit, you *do* look very familiar. What program are you working on?'

Shit. Gabrielle flashed a confident smile. 'EOS.'

The man pointed to the illuminated fourth floor button. 'Obviously. I mean specifically, which *project*?'

Gabrielle felt her pulse quicken. She could only think of one. 'PODS.'

The man looked surprised. 'Really? I thought I'd met everyone on Dr Harper's team.'

She gave an embarrassed nod. 'Chris keeps me hidden away. I'm the idiot programmer who screwed up voxel index on the anomaly software.'

Now it was the bald man whose jaw dropped. 'That was *you*?'

Gabrielle frowned. 'I haven't slept in weeks.'

'But Dr *Harper* took all the heat for that!'

'I know. Chris is that kind of guy. At least he got it straightened out. What an announcement tonight, though, isn't it? This meteorite. I'm just in shock!'

The elevator stopped on the fourth floor. Gabrielle jumped out. 'Great seeing you, Jim. Give my best to the boys in budgeting!'

'Sure,' the man stammered as the doors slid shut. 'Nice seeing you again.'

Zach Herney, like most presidents before him, survived on four or five hours of sleep a night. Over the last few weeks, however, he had survived on far less. As the excitement of the evening's events slowly began to ebb, Herney felt the late hour settling in his limbs.

He and some of his upper level staff were in the Roosevelt Room enjoying celebratory champagne and watching the endless loop of press conference replays, Tolland documentary excerpts, and pundit recaps on network television. On-screen at the moment, an exuberant network correspondent stood in front of the White House gripping her microphone.

'Beyond the mind-numbing repercussions for mankind as a species,' she announced, 'this NASA discovery has some harsh political repercussions here in Washington. The unearthing of these meteoric fossils could not have come at a better time for the embattled President.' Her voice grew somber. 'Nor at a worse time for Senator Sexton.' The broadcast cut to a replay of the now infamous CNN debate from earlier in the day.

'After thirty-five years,' Sexton declared, 'I think it's pretty obvious we're not going to find extraterrestrial life!'

'And if you're wrong?' Marjorie Tench replied.

Sexton rolled his eyes. 'Oh, for heaven's sake, Ms Tench, if I'm wrong I'll eat my hat.'

Everyone in the Roosevelt Room laughed. Tench's

cornering of the senator could have played as cruel and heavy-handed in retrospect, and yet viewers didn't seem to notice; the haughty tone of the senator's response was so smug that Sexton appeared to be getting exactly what he deserved.

The President looked around the room for Tench. He had not seen her since before his press conference, and she was not here now. *Odd*, he thought. *This is her celebration as much as it is mine.*

The news report on television was wrapping up, outlining yet again the White House's quantum political leap forward and Senator Sexton's disastrous slide.

What a difference a day makes, the President thought. *In politics, your world can change in an instant.*

By dawn he would realize just how true those words could be.

85

Pickering could be a problem, Tench had said.

Administrator Ekstrom was too preoccupied with this new information to notice that the storm outside the habisphere was raging harder now. The howling cables had increased in pitch, and the NASA staff was nervously milling and chatting rather than going to sleep. Ekstrom's thoughts were lost in a different storm – an explosive tempest brewing back in Washington. The last few hours had brought countless problems, all of which Ekstrom was trying to deal with. And yet one problem now loomed larger than all the others combined.

Pickering could be a problem.

Ekstrom could think of no one on earth against whom he'd less rather match wits than William Pickering. Pickering had ridden Ekstrom and NASA for years now, trying to control privacy policy, lobbying for different mission priorities, and railing against NASA's escalating failure ratio.

Pickering's disgust with NASA, Ekstrom knew, went far deeper than the recent loss of his billion-dollar NRO SIGINT satellite in a NASA launchpad explosion, or the NASA security leaks, or the battle over recruiting key aerospace personnel. Pickering's grievances against NASA were an ongoing drama of disillusionment and resentment.

NASA's X-33 space plane, which was supposed to be the shuttle replacement, had run five years overdue, meaning dozens of NRO satellite maintenance and launch programs were scrapped or put on hold. Recently, Pickering's rage over the X-33 reached a fever pitch when he discovered NASA had canceled the project entirely, swallowing an estimated $900 million loss.

Ekstrom arrived at his office, pulled the curtain aside, and entered. Sitting down at his desk he put his head in his hands. He had some decisions to make. What had started as a wonderful day was becoming a nightmare unraveling around him. He tried to put himself in the mindset of William Pickering. What would the man do next? Someone as intelligent as Pickering *had* to see the importance of this NASA discovery. He had to forgive certain choices made in desperation. He had to see the irreversible damage that would be done by polluting this moment of triumph.

What would Pickering do with the information he had? Would he let it ride, or would he make NASA pay for their shortcomings?

Ekstrom scowled, having little doubt which it would be.

After all, William Pickering had deeper issues with NASA . . . an ancient personal bitterness that went far deeper than politics.

86

Rachel was quiet now, staring blankly at the cabin of the G4 as the plane headed south along the Canadian coastline of the Gulf of St Lawrence. Tolland sat nearby, talking to Corky. Despite the majority of evidence suggesting the meteorite was authentic, Corky's admission that the nickel content was 'outside the pre-established midrange values' had served to rekindle Rachel's initial suspicion. Secretly planting a meteorite beneath the ice only made sense as part of a brilliantly conceived fraud.

Nonetheless, the remaining scientific evidence pointed toward the meteorite's validity.

Rachel turned from the window, glancing down at the disk-shaped meteorite sample in her hand. The tiny chondrules shimmered. Tolland and Corky had been discussing these metallic chondrules for some time now, talking in scientific terms well over Rachel's head – equilibrated olivine levels, metastable glass matrices, and metamorphic rehomogenation. Nonetheless, the upshot was clear: Corky and Tolland were in agree-

378

ment that the chondrules were *decidedly* meteoric. No fudging of that data.

Rachel rotated the disk-shaped specimen in her hand, running a finger over the rim where part of the fusion crust was visible. The charring looked relatively fresh – certainly not 300 years old – although Corky had explained that the meteorite had been hermetically sealed in ice and avoided atmospheric erosion. This seemed logical. Rachel had seen programs on television where human remains were dug from the ice after 4,000 years and the person's skin looked almost perfect.

As she studied the fusion crust, an odd thought occurred to her – an obvious piece of data had been omitted. Rachel wondered if it had simply been an oversight in all the data that was thrown at her or did someone simply forget to mention it.

She turned suddenly to Corky. 'Did anyone date the fusion crust?'

Corky glanced over, looking confused. 'What?'

'Did anyone date the burn? That is, do we know for a fact that the burn on the rock occurred at exactly the time of the Jungersol Fall?'

'Sorry,' Corky said, 'that's impossible to date. Oxidation resets all the necessary isotopic markers. Besides, radioisotope decay rates are too slow to measure anything under five hundred years.'

Rachel considered that a moment, understanding now why the burn date was not part of the data. 'So, as far as we know, this rock could have been burned in the Middle Ages or last weekend, right?'

Tolland chuckled. 'Nobody said science had all the answers.'

Rachel let her mind wander aloud. 'A fusion crust is essentially just a severe burn. Technically speaking, the

379

burn on this rock could have happened at any time in the past half century, in any number of different ways.'

'Wrong,' Corky said. 'Burned in any number of different ways? No. Burned in *one* way. Falling through the atmosphere.'

'There's no other possibility? How about in a furnace?'

'A furnace?' Corky said. 'These samples were examined under an electron microscope. Even the cleanest furnace on earth would have left fuel residue all over the stone – nuclear, chemical, fossil fuel. Forget it. And how about the striations from streaking through the atmosphere? You wouldn't get those in a furnace.'

Rachel had forgotten about the orientation striations on the meteorite. It did indeed appear to have fallen through the air. 'How about a volcano?' she ventured. 'Ejecta thrown violently from an eruption?'

Corky shook his head. 'The burn is far too clean.'

Rachel glanced at Tolland.

The oceanographer nodded. 'Sorry, I've had some experience with volcanoes, both above and below water. Corky's right. Volcanic ejecta is penetrated by dozens of toxins – carbon dioxide, sulfur dioxide, hydrogen sulfide, hydrochloric acid – all of which would have been detected in our electronic scans. That fusion crust, whether we like it or not, is the result of a clean atmospheric friction burn.'

Rachel sighed, looking back out the window. *A clean burn*. The phrase stuck with her. She turned back to Tolland. 'What do you mean by a clean burn?'

He shrugged. 'Simply that under an electron microscope, we see no remnants of fuel elements, so we know heating was caused by kinetic energy and friction, rather than chemical or nuclear ingredients.'

'If you didn't find any foreign fuel elements, what did you find? Specifically, what was the composition of the fusion crust?'

'We found,' Corky said, 'exactly what we *expected* to find. Pure atmospheric elements. Nitrogen, oxygen, hydrogen. No petroleums. No sulfurs. No volcanic acids. Nothing peculiar. All the stuff we see when meteorites fall through the atmosphere.'

Rachel leaned back in her seat, her thoughts focusing now.

Corky leaned forward to look at her. 'Please don't tell me your new theory is that NASA took a fossilized rock up in the space shuttle and sent it hurtling toward earth hoping nobody would notice the fireball, the massive crater, or the explosion?'

Rachel had not thought of that, although it was an interesting premise. Not feasible, but interesting all the same. Her thoughts were actually closer to home. *All natural atmospheric elements. Clean burn. Striations from racing through the air.* A faint light had gone off in a distant corner of her mind. 'The ratios of the atmospheric elements you saw,' she said. 'Were they *exactly* the same ratios you see on every other meteorite with a fusion crust?'

Corky seemed to hedge slightly at the question. 'Why do you ask?'

Rachel saw him hesitate and felt her pulse quicken. 'The ratios were off, weren't they?'

'There is a scientific explanation.'

Rachel's heart was suddenly pounding. 'Did you by any chance see an unusually high content of *one* element in particular?'

Tolland and Corky exchanged startled looks. 'Yes,' Corky said, 'but—'

'Was it ionized hydrogen?'

The astrophysicist's eyes turned to saucers. 'How could you possibly know that?'

Tolland also looked utterly amazed.

Rachel stared at them both. 'Why didn't anyone mention this to me?'

'Because there's a perfectly sound scientific explanation!' Corky declared.

'I'm all ears,' Rachel said.

'There was surplus ionized hydrogen,' Corky said, 'because the meteorite passed through the atmosphere near the North Pole, where the earth's magnetic field causes an abnormally high concentration of hydrogen ions.'

Rachel frowned. 'Unfortunately, I have another explanation.'

87

The fourth floor of NASA headquarters was less impressive than the lobby – long sterile corridors with office doors equally spaced along the walls. The corridor was deserted. Laminated signs pointed in all directions.

← LANDSAT 7

TERRA →

← ACRIMSAT

← JASON 1

AQUA →

PODS →

Gabrielle followed the signs for PODS. Winding her way down a series of long corridors and inter-sections, she came to a set of heavy steel doors. The stencil read:

POLAR ORBITING DENSITY SCANNER (PODS)
Section Manager, Chris Harper

The doors were locked, secured both by key card and a PIN pad access. Gabrielle put her ear to the cold metal door. For a moment, she thought she heard talking. Arguing. Maybe not. She wondered if she should just bang on the door until someone inside let her in. Unfortunately, her plan for dealing with Chris Harper required a bit more subtlety than banging on doors. She looked around for another entrance but saw none. A custodial alcove stood adjacent to the door, and Gabrielle stepped in, searching the dimly lit niche for a janitor's key ring or key card. Nothing. Just brooms and mops.

Returning to the door, she put her ear to the metal again. This time she definitely heard voices. Getting louder. And footsteps. The latch engaged from inside.

Gabrielle had no time to hide as the metal door burst open. She jumped to the side, plastering herself against the wall behind the door as a group of people hurried through, talking loudly. They sounded angry.

'What the hell is Harper's problem? I thought he'd be on cloud nine!'

'On a night like tonight,' another said as the group passed by, 'he wants to be alone? He should be cel-ebrating!'

As the group moved away from Gabrielle, the heavy door started swinging closed on pneumatic hinges, revealing her location. She remained rigid as the men continued down the hall. Waiting as long as she possibly could, until the door was only inches from closing, Gabrielle lunged forward and caught the door handle with just inches to spare. She stood motionless as the men turned the corner down the hall, too engaged in their conversation to look back.

Heart pounding, Gabrielle pulled open the door and stepped into the dimly lit area beyond. She quietly closed the door.

The space was a wide open work area that reminded her of a college physics laboratory: computers, work islands, electronic gear. As her eyes became accustomed to the darkness, Gabrielle could see blueprints and sheets of calculations scattered around. The entire area was dark except for an office on the far side of the lab, where a light shone under the door. Gabrielle walked over quietly. The door was closed, but through the window she could see a man sitting at a computer. She recognized the man from the NASA press conference. The nameplate on the door read:

Chris Harper
Section Manager, PODS

Having come this far, Gabrielle suddenly felt apprehensive, wondering if she could actually pull this off. She reminded herself how certain Sexton was that Chris Harper had lied. *I would bet my campaign on it*, Sexton had said. Apparently there were others who felt the same, others who were waiting for Gabrielle to uncover the truth so they could close in on NASA, attempting to gain even a tiny foothold after tonight's devastating developments. After the way Tench and the Herney administration had played Gabrielle this afternoon, she was eager to help.

Gabrielle raised her hand to knock on the door but paused, Yolanda's voice running through her mind. *If Chris Harper lied to the world about PODS, what makes you think he'll tell YOU the truth?*

Fear, Gabrielle told herself, having almost fallen victim to it herself today. She had a plan. It involved a tactic she'd seen the senator use on occasion to scare information out of political opponents. Gabrielle had absorbed a lot under Sexton's tutelage, and not all of it attractive or ethical. But tonight she needed every advantage. If she could persuade Chris Harper to admit he had lied – for whatever reason – Gabrielle would open a small door of opportunity for the senator's campaign. Beyond that, Sexton was a man whom, if given an inch to maneuver, could wriggle his way out of almost any jam.

Gabrielle's plan for dealing with Harper was something Sexton called 'overshooting' – an interrogation technique invented by the early Roman authorities to coax confessions from criminals they suspected were lying. The method was deceptively simple:

Assert the information you want confessed.

Then allege something far worse.

The object was to give the opponent a chance to choose the lesser of two evils – in this case, the truth.

The trick was exuding confidence, something Gabrielle was not feeling at the moment. Taking a deep breath, Gabrielle ran through the script in her mind, and then knocked firmly on the office door.

'I told you I'm busy!' Harper called out, his English accent familiar.

She knocked again. Louder.

'I told you I'm not interested in coming down!'

This time she banged on the door with her fist.

Chris Harper came over and yanked open the door. 'Bloody hell, do you—' He stopped short, clearly surprised to see Gabrielle.

'Dr Harper,' she said, infusing her voice with intensity.

'How did you get up here?'

Gabrielle's face was stern. 'Do you know who I am?'

'Of course. Your boss has been slamming my project for months. How did you get in?'

'Senator Sexton sent me.'

Harper's eyes scanned the lab behind Gabrielle. 'Where is your staff escort?'

'That's not your concern. The senator has influential connections.'

'In this building?' Harper looked dubious.

'You've been dishonest, Dr Harper. And I'm afraid the senator has called a special senatorial justice board to look into your lies.'

A pall crossed Harper's face. 'What are you talking about?'

'Smart people like yourself don't have the luxury of playing stupid, Dr Harper. You're in trouble, and the senator sent me up here to offer you a deal. The senator's campaign took a huge hit tonight. He's got nothing left to lose, and he's ready to take you down with him if he needs to.'

'What the devil are you talking about?'

Gabrielle took a deep breath and made her play. 'You lied in your press conference about the PODS anomaly-detection software. We know that. A lot of people know that. That's not the issue.' Before Harper could open his mouth to argue, Gabrielle steamed onward. 'The senator could blow the whistle on your lies right now, but he's not interested. He's interested in the bigger story. I think you know what I'm talking about.'

'No, I—'

'Here's the senator's offer. He'll keep his mouth shut about your software lies if you give him the name of the top NASA executive with whom you're embezzling funds.'

Chris Harper's eyes seemed to cross for a moment. 'What? I'm not embezzling!'

'I suggest you watch what you say, sir. The senatorial committee has been collecting documentation for months now. Did you really think you two would slip by undetected? Doctoring PODS paperwork and redirecting allocated NASA funds to private accounts? Lying and embezzling can put you in jail, Dr Harper.'

'I did no such thing!'

'You're saying you didn't lie about PODS?'

'No, I'm saying I bloody well didn't embezzle money!'

'So, you're saying you *did* lie about PODS.'

Harper stared, clearly at a loss for words.

'Forget about the lying,' Gabrielle said, waving it off. 'Senator Sexton is not interested in the issue of your lying in a press conference. We're used to that. You guys found a meteorite, nobody cares how you did it. The issue for him is the embezzlement. He needs to take down someone high in NASA. Just tell him who you're working with, and he'll steer the investigation clear of you entirely. You can make it easy and tell us who the other person is, or the senator will make it ugly and start talking about anomaly-detection software and phony work-arounds.'

'You're bluffing. There are no embezzled funds.'

'You're an awful liar, Dr Harper. I've seen the documentation. Your name is on all the incriminating paperwork. Over and over.'

'I swear I know nothing about any embezzlement!'

Gabrielle let out a disappointed sigh. 'Put yourself in my position, Dr Harper. I can only draw two conclusions here. Either you're lying to me, the same way you lied in that press conference. Or you're telling the truth, and someone powerful in the agency is setting you up as a fall guy for his own misdealings.'

The proposition seemed to give Harper pause.

Gabrielle checked her watch. 'The senator's deal is on the table for an hour. You can save yourself by giving him the name of the NASA exec with whom you're embezzling taxpayers' money. He doesn't care about you. He wants the big fish. Obviously the individual in question has some power here at NASA; he or she has managed to keep his or her identity off the paper trail, allowing you to be the fall guy.'

Harper shook his head. 'You're lying.'

'Would you like to tell that to a court?'

'Sure. I'll deny the whole thing.'

'Under oath?' Gabrielle grunted in disgust. 'Suppose you'll also deny you lied about fixing the PODS software?' Gabrielle's heart was pounding as she stared straight into the man's eyes. 'Think carefully about your options here, Dr Harper. American prisons can be most unpleasant.'

Harper glared back, and Gabrielle willed him to fold. For a moment she thought she saw a glimmer of surrender, but when Harper spoke, his voice was like steel.

'Ms Ashe,' he declared, anger simmering in his eyes,

'you are clutching at thin air. You and I both know there is no embezzlement going on at NASA. The only liar in this room is *you*.'

Gabrielle felt her muscles go rigid. The man's gaze was angry and sharp. She wanted to turn and run. *You tried to bluff a rocket scientist. What the hell did you expect?* She forced herself to hold her head high. 'All I know,' she said, feigning utter confidence and indifference to his position, 'is the incriminating documents I've seen – conclusive evidence that you and another are embezzling NASA funds. The senator simply asked me to come here tonight and offer you the option of giving up your partner instead of facing the inquiry alone. I will tell the senator you prefer to take your chances with a judge. You can tell the court what you told me – you're not embezzling funds and you didn't lie about the PODS software.' She gave a grim smile. 'But after that lame press conference you gave two weeks ago, somehow I doubt it.' Gabrielle spun on her heel and strode across the darkened PODS laboratory. She wondered if maybe *she'd* be seeing the inside of a prison instead of Harper.

Gabrielle held her head high as she walked off, waiting for Harper to call her back. Silence. She pushed her way through the metal doors and strode out into the hallway, hoping the elevators up here were not key-card operated like the lobby. She'd lost. Despite her best efforts, Harper wasn't biting. *Maybe he was telling the truth in his PODS press conference*, Gabrielle thought.

A crash resounded down the hall as the metal doors behind her burst open. 'Ms Ashe,' Harper's voice called out. 'I swear I know nothing about any embezzlement. I'm an honest man!'

Gabrielle felt her heart skip a beat. She forced herself

to keep walking. She gave a casual shrug and called out over her shoulder, 'And yet you lied in your press conference.'

Silence. Gabrielle kept moving down the hallway.

'Hold on!' Harper yelled. He came jogging up beside her, his face pale. 'This embezzlement thing,' he said, lowering his voice. 'I think I know who set me up.'

Gabrielle stopped dead in her tracks, wondering if she had heard him correctly. She turned as slowly and casually as she could. 'You expect me to believe someone is setting you up?'

Harper sighed. 'I swear I know nothing about embezzlement. But if there's evidence against me . . .'

'Mounds of it.'

Harper sighed. 'Then it's all been planted. To discredit me if need be. And there's only one person who would have done that.'

'Who?'

Harper looked her in the eye. 'Lawrence Ekstrom hates me.'

Gabrielle was stunned. 'The *administrator* of NASA?'

Harper gave a grim nod. 'He's the one who forced me to lie in that press conference.'

88

Even with the Aurora aircraft's misted-methane propulsion system at half power, the Delta Force was hurtling through the night at three times the speed of sound – over two thousand miles an hour. The repetitive throb of the Pulse Detonation Wave Engines behind them gave the ride a hypnotic rhythm. A hundred feet below, the ocean churned wildly, whipped up by the Aurora's vacuum wake, which sucked fifty-foot rooster tails skyward in long parallel sheets behind the plane.

This is the reason the SR-71 Blackbird was retired, Delta-One thought.

The Aurora was one of those secret aircraft that nobody was supposed to know existed, but everyone did. Even the Discovery channel had covered Aurora and its testing out at Groom Lake in Nevada. Whether the security leaks had come from the repeated 'skyquakes' heard as far away as Los Angeles, or the fortunate eyewitness sighting by a North Sea oil-rig driller, or the administrative gaffe that left a description of Aurora in a public copy of the Pentagon budget, nobody would ever know. It hardly mattered. The word was out: the U.S. military had a plane capable of Mach 6 flight, and it was no longer on the drawing board. It was in the skies overhead.

Built by Lockheed, the Aurora looked like a flattened American football. It was 110 feet long, 60 feet wide, smoothly contoured with a crystalline patina of thermal tiles much like the space shuttle. The speed was primarily the result of an exotic new propulsion system known as a Pulse Detonation Wave Engine, which burned a clean, misted, liquid hydrogen and left a tell-tale pulse contrail in the sky. For this reason, it only flew at night.

Tonight, with the luxury of enormous speed, the Delta Force was taking the long way home, out across the open ocean. Even so, they were overtaking their quarry. At this rate, the Delta Force would be arriving on the eastern seaboard in under an hour, a good two hours before its prey. There had been discussion of tracking and shooting down the plane in question, but the controller rightly feared a radar capture of the incident or the burned wreckage might bring on a massive investigation. It was best to let the plane land as scheduled, the controller had decided. Once it became clear where their quarry intended to land, the Delta Force would move in.

Now, as Aurora streaked over the desolate Labrador Sea, Delta-One's CrypTalk indicated an incoming call. He answered.

'The situation has changed,' the electronic voice informed them. 'You have another mark before Rachel Sexton and the scientists land.'

Another mark. Delta-One could feel it. Things were unraveling. The controller's ship had sprung another leak, and the controller needed them to patch it as fast as possible. *The ship would not be leaking,* Delta-One reminded himself, *if we had hit our marks successfully on the Milne Ice Shelf.* Delta-One knew damn well he was cleaning up his own mess.

'A fourth party has become involved,' the controller said.

'Who?'

The controller paused a moment – and then gave them a name.

The three men exchanged startled looks. It was a name they knew well.

No wonder the controller sounded reluctant! Delta-One thought. For an operation conceived as a 'zero-casualty' venture, the body count and target profile was climbing fast. He felt his sinews tighten as the controller prepared to inform them exactly how and where they would eliminate this new individual.

'The stakes have increased considerably,' the controller said. 'Listen closely. I will give you these instructions only once.'

High above northern Maine, a G4 jet continued speeding toward Washington. Onboard, Michael Tolland and Corky Marlinson looked on as Rachel Sexton began to explain her theory for why there might be increased hydrogen ions in the fusion crust of the meteorite.

'NASA has a private test facility called Plum Brook Station,' Rachel explained, hardly able to believe she was going to talk about this. Sharing classified information out of protocol was not something she had ever done, but considering the circumstances, Tolland and Corky had a right to know this. 'Plum Brook is essentially a test chamber for NASA's most radical new engine systems. Two years ago I wrote a gist about a new design NASA was testing there – something called an expander cycle engine.'

Corky eyed her suspiciously. 'Expander cycle engines are still in the theoretical stage. On paper. Nobody's actually testing. That's decades away.'

Rachel shook her head. 'Sorry, Corky. NASA has prototypes. They're testing.'

'What?' Corky looked skeptical. 'ECE's run on liquid oxygen-hydrogen, which freezes in space, making the engine worthless to NASA. They said they were not even going to try to build an ECE until they overcame the freezing fuel problem.'

'They overcame it. They got rid of the oxygen and turned the fuel into a "slush-hydrogen" mixture, which is some kind of cryogenic fuel consisting of pure hydrogen in a semifrozen state. It's very powerful and very clean burning. It's also a contender for the propulsion system if NASA runs missions to Mars.'

Corky looked amazed. 'This can't be true.'

'It *better* be true,' Rachel said. 'I wrote a brief about it for the President. My boss was up in arms because NASA wanted to publicly announce slush-hydrogen as a big success, and Pickering wanted the White House to force NASA to keep slush-hydrogen classified.'

'Why?'

'Not important,' Rachel said, having no intention of sharing more secrets than she had to. The truth was that Pickering's desire to classify slush-hydrogen's success was to fight a growing national security concern few knew existed – the alarming expansion of China's space technology. The Chinese were currently developing a deadly 'for-hire' launch platform, which they intended to rent out to high bidders, most of whom would be U.S. enemies. The implications for U.S. security were devastating. Fortunately, the NRO knew China was pursuing a doomed propulsion-fuel model for their launch platform, and Pickering saw no reason to tip them off about NASA's more promising slush-hydrogen propellant.

'So,' Tolland said, looking uneasy, 'you're saying NASA has a clean-burning propulsion system that runs on pure hydrogen?'

Rachel nodded. 'I don't have figures, but the exhaust temperatures of these engines are apparently several times hotter than anything ever before developed. They're requiring NASA to develop all kinds of new nozzle materials.' She paused. 'A large rock, placed behind one of these slush-hydrogen engines, would be scalded by a hydrogen-rich blast of exhaust fire coming out at an unprecedented temperature. You'd get quite a fusion crust.'

'Come on now!' Corky said. 'Are we back to the fake meteorite scenario?'

Tolland seemed suddenly intrigued. 'Actually, that's quite an idea. The setup would be more or less like leaving a boulder on the launchpad under the space shuttle during liftoff.'

'God save me,' Corky muttered. 'I'm airborne with idiots.'

'Corky,' Tolland said. 'Hypothetically speaking, a rock placed in an exhaust field would exhibit similar burn features to one that fell through the atmosphere, wouldn't it? You'd have the same directional striations and backflow of the melting material.'

Corky grunted. 'I suppose.'

'And Rachel's clean-burning hydrogen fuel would leave no chemical residue. Only hydrogen. Increased levels of hydrogen ions in the fusion pocking.'

Corky rolled his eyes. 'Look, if one of these ECE engines actually exists, and runs on slush-hydrogen, I suppose what you're talking about is possible. But it's extremely far-fetched.'

'Why?' Tolland asked. 'The process seems fairly simple.'

Rachel nodded. 'All you need is a one-hundred-and-ninety-million-year-old fossilized rock. Blast it in a slush-hydrogen-engine exhaust fire, and bury it in the ice. Instant meteorite.'

'To a tourist, maybe,' Corky said, 'but not to a NASA scientist! You still haven't explained the chondrules!'

Rachel tried to recall Corky's explanation of how chondrules formed. 'You said chondrules are caused by rapid heating and cooling events in space, right?'

Corky sighed. 'Chondrules form when a rock, chilled in space, suddenly becomes superheated to a partial-melt stage – somewhere near 1,550 Celsius. Then the rock must cool again, extremely rapidly, hardening the liquid pockets into chondrules.'

Tolland studied his friend. 'And this process can't happen on earth?'

'Impossible,' Corky said. 'This planet does not have the temperature variance to cause that kind of rapid shift. You're talking here about nuclear heat and the absolute zero of space. Those extremes simply don't exist on earth.'

Rachel considered it. 'At least not *naturally*.'

Corky turned. 'What's that supposed to mean?'

'Why couldn't the heating and cooling event have occurred here on earth artificially?' Rachel asked. 'The rock could have been blasted by a slush-hydrogen engine and then rapidly cooled in a cryogenic freezer.'

Corky stared. 'Manufactured chondrules?'

'It's an idea.'

'A ridiculous one,' Corky replied, flashing his meteorite sample. 'Perhaps you forget? These chondrules were irrefutably dated at one hundred and ninety million years.' His tone grew patronizing. 'To the best of my knowledge, Ms Sexton, one hundred and ninety million years ago, nobody was running slush-hydrogen engines and cryogenic coolers.'

Chondrules or not, Tolland thought, *the evidence is piling up*. He had been silent now for several minutes, deeply troubled by Rachel's newest revelation about the fusion crust. Her hypothesis, though staggeringly bold, had opened all kinds of new doors and gotten Tolland thinking in new directions. *If the fusion crust is explainable . . . what other possibilities does that present?*

'You're quiet,' Rachel said, beside him.

Tolland glanced over. For an instant, in the muted lighting of the plane, he saw a softness in Rachel's eyes that reminded him of Celia. Shaking off the memories, he gave her a tired sigh. 'Oh, I was just thinking . . .'

She smiled. 'About meteorites?'

'What else?'

'Running through all the evidence, trying to figure out what's left?'

'Something like that.'

'Any thoughts?'

'Not really. I'm troubled by how much of the data has collapsed in light of discovering that insertion shaft beneath the ice.'

'Hierarchical evidence is a house of cards,' Rachel said. 'Pull out your primary assumption, and everything gets shaky. The *location* of the meteorite find was a primary assumption.'

I'll say. 'When I arrived at Milne, the administrator told me the meteorite had been found inside a pristine matrix of three-hundred-year-old ice and was more dense than any rock found anywhere in the area, which I took as logical proof that the rock had to fall from space.'

'You and the rest of us.'

'The midrange nickel content, though persuasive, is apparently not conclusive.'

'It's *close*,' Corky said nearby, apparently listening in. 'But not exact.'

Corky acquiesced with a reluctant nod.

'And,' Tolland said, 'this never before seen species of space bug, though shockingly bizarre, in reality could be nothing more than a very old, deepwater crustacean.'

Rachel nodded. 'And now the fusion crust . . .'

'I hate to say it,' Tolland said, glancing at Corky, 'but it's starting to feel like there's more negative evidence than positive.'

'Science is not about hunches,' Corky said. 'It's about evidence. The chondrules in this rock are decidedly meteoric. I agree with you both that everything we've seen is deeply disturbing, but we cannot ignore these chondrules. The evidence in favor is conclusive, while the evidence against is circumstantial.'

Rachel frowned. 'So where does that leave us?'

'Nowhere,' Corky said. 'The chondrules prove we are dealing with a meteorite. The only question is why someone stuck it under the ice.'

Tolland wanted to believe his friend's sound logic, but something just felt wrong.

'You don't look convinced, Mike,' Corky said.

Tolland gave his friend a bewildered sigh. 'I don't know. Two out of three wasn't bad, Corky. But we're down to one out of three. I just feel like we're missing something.'

90

I got caught, Chris Harper thought, feeling a chill as he pictured an American prison cell. *Senator Sexton knows I lied about the PODS software.*

As the PODS section manager escorted Gabrielle

Ashe back into his office and closed the door, he felt his hatred of the NASA administrator grow deeper by the instant. Tonight Harper had learned just how deep the administrator's lies truly ran. In addition to forcing Harper to lie about having fixed PODS's software, the administrator had apparently set up some insurance just in case Harper got cold feet and decided not to be a team player.

Evidence of embezzlement, Harper thought. *Blackmail. Very sly.* After all, who would believe an embezzler trying to discredit the single greatest moment in American space history? Harper had already witnessed to what lengths the NASA administrator would go to save America's space agency, and now with the announcement of a meteorite with fossils, the stakes had skyrocketed.

Harper paced for several seconds around the wide table on which sat a scale model of the PODS satellite – a cylindrical prism with multiple antennae and lenses behind reflective shields. Gabrielle sat down, her dark eyes watching, waiting. The nausea in Harper's gut reminded him of how he had felt during the infamous press conference. He'd put on a lousy show that night, and everyone had questioned him about it. He'd had to lie again and say he was feeling ill that night and was not himself. His colleagues and the press shrugged off his lackluster performance and quickly forgot about it.

Now the lie had come back to haunt him.

Gabrielle Ashe's expression softened. 'Mr Harper, with the administrator as an enemy, you will need a powerful ally. Senator Sexton could well be your only friend at this point. Let's start with the PODS software lie. Tell me what happened.'

Harper sighed. He knew it was time to tell the

truth. *I bloody well should have told the truth in the first place!* 'The PODS launch went smoothly,' he began. 'The satellite settled into a perfect polar orbit just as planned.'

Gabrielle Ashe looked bored. She apparently knew all this. 'Go on.'

'Then came the trouble. When we geared up to start searching the ice for density anomalies, the onboard anomaly-detection software failed.'

'Uh . . . huh.'

Harper's words came faster now. 'The software was supposed to be able to rapidly examine thousands of acres of data and find parts of the ice that fell outside the range of normal ice density. Primarily the software was looking for soft spots in the ice – global warming indicators – but if it stumbled across other density incongruities, it was programmed to flag those as well. The plan was for PODS to scan the Arctic Circle over several weeks and identify any anomalies that we could use to measure global warming.'

'But without functioning software,' Gabrielle said, 'PODS was no good. NASA would have had to examine images of every square inch of the Arctic by hand, looking for trouble spots.'

Harper nodded, reliving the nightmare of his programming gaffe. 'It would take decades. The situation was terrible. Because of a flaw in my programming, PODS was essentially worthless. With the election coming up and Senator Sexton being so critical of NASA . . .' He sighed.

'Your mistake was devastating to NASA and the President.'

'It couldn't have come at a worse time. The administrator was livid. I promised him I could fix the problem

400

during the next shuttle mission – a simple matter of swapping out the chip that held the PODS software system. But it was too little too late. He sent me home on leave – but essentially I was fired. That was a month ago.'

'And yet you were back on television two weeks ago announcing you'd found a work-around.'

Harper slumped. 'A terrible mistake. That was the day I got a desperate call from the administrator. He told me something had come up, a possible way to redeem myself. I came into the office immediately and met with him. He asked me to hold a press conference and tell everyone I'd found a work-around for the PODS software and that we would have data in a few weeks. He said he'd explain it to me later.'

'And you agreed.'

'No, I refused! But an hour later, the administrator was back in my office – with the White House senior adviser!'

'What?' Gabrielle looked astounded by this. 'Marjorie Tench?'

An awful creature, Harper thought, nodding. 'She and the administrator sat me down and told me *my* mistake had quite literally put NASA and the President on the brink of total collapse. Ms Tench told me about the senator's plans to privatize NASA. She told me I owed it to the President and space agency to make it all right. Then she told me how.'

Gabrielle leaned forward. 'Go on.'

'Marjorie Tench informed me that the White House, by sheer good fortune, had intercepted strong geologic evidence that an enormous meteorite was buried in the Milne Ice Shelf. One of the biggest ever. A meteorite of that size would be a major find for NASA.'

Gabrielle looked stunned. 'Hold on, so you're saying someone already *knew* the meteorite was there before PODS discovered it?'

'Yes. PODS had nothing to do with the discovery. The administrator knew the meteorite existed. He simply gave me the coordinates and told me to reposition PODS over the ice shelf and *pretend* PODS made the discovery.'

'You're kidding me.'

'That was my reaction when they asked me to participate in the sham. They refused to tell me how they'd found out the meteorite was there, but Ms Tench insisted it didn't matter and that this was the ideal opportunity to salvage my PODS fiasco. If I could pretend the PODS satellite located the meteorite, then NASA could praise PODS as a much needed success and boost the President before the election.'

Gabrielle was awestruck. 'And of course you couldn't claim PODS had detected a meteorite until you'd announced that the PODS anomaly-detection software was up and running.'

Harper nodded. 'Hence the press conference lie. I was forced into it. Tench and the administrator were ruthless. They reminded me I'd let everyone down – the President had funded my PODS project, NASA had spent years on it, and now I'd ruined the whole thing with a programming blunder.'

'So you agreed to help.'

'I didn't have a choice. My career was essentially over if I didn't. And the reality was that if I hadn't muffed the software, PODS *would have* found that meteorite on its own. So, it seemed a small lie at the time. I rationalized it by telling myself that the software would be fixed in a few months when the space shuttle went up, so I would simply be announcing the fix a little early.'

Gabrielle let out a whistle. 'A tiny lie to take advantage of a meteoric opportunity.'

Harper was feeling ill just talking about it. 'So . . . I did it. Following the administrator's orders, I held a press conference announcing that I'd found a workaround for my anomaly-detection software, I waited a few days, and then I repositioned PODS over the administrator's meteorite coordinates. Then, following the proper chain of command, I phoned the EOS director and reported that PODS had located a hard density anomaly in the Milne Ice Shelf. I gave him the coordinates and told him the anomaly appeared to be dense enough to be a meteorite. Excitedly, NASA sent a small team up to Milne to take some drill cores. That's when the operation got very hush-hush.'

'So, you had no idea the meteorite had *fossils* until tonight?'

'Nobody here did. We're all in shock. Now everyone is calling me a hero for finding proof of extraterrestrial bioforms, and I don't know what to say.'

Gabrielle was silent a long moment, studying Harper with firm black eyes. 'But if PODS didn't locate the meteorite in the ice, how did the administrator know the meteorite was there?'

'Someone else found it first.'

'Someone *else*? Who?'

Harper sighed. 'A Canadian geologist named Charles Brophy – a researcher on Ellesmere Island. Apparently he was doing geologic ice soundings on the Milne Ice Shelf when he by chance discovered the presence of what appeared to be a huge meteorite in the ice. He

403

radioed it in, and NASA happened to intercept the transmission.'

Gabrielle stared. 'But isn't this Canadian furious that NASA is taking all the credit for the find?'

'No,' Harper said, feeling a chill. 'Conveniently, he's dead.'

91

Michael Tolland closed his eyes and listened to the drone of the G4 jet engine. He had given up trying to think anymore about the meteorite until they got back to Washington. The chondrules, according to Corky, were conclusive; the rock in the Milne Ice Shelf could only be a meteorite. Rachel had hoped to have a conclusive answer for William Pickering by the time they landed, but her thought experiments had run into a dead end with the chondrules. As suspicious as the meteorite evidence was, the meteorite appeared to be authentic.

So be it.

Rachel had obviously been shaken by the trauma in the ocean. Tolland was amazed, though, by her resilience. She was focused now on the issue at hand – trying to find a way to debunk or authenticate the meteorite, and trying to assess who had tried to kill them.

For most of the trip, Rachel had been in the seat beside Tolland. He'd enjoyed talking to her, despite the trying circumstances. Several minutes ago, she'd headed back to the restroom, and now Tolland was surprised to find himself missing her beside him. He wondered how long it had been since he'd missed a woman's presence – a woman other than Celia.

'Mr Tolland?'

Tolland glanced up.

The pilot was sticking his head into the cabin. 'You asked me to tell you when we were in telephone range of your ship? I can get you that connection if you want.'

'Thanks.' Tolland made his way up the aisle.

Inside the cockpit, Tolland placed a call to his crew. He wanted to let them know he would not be back for another day or two. Of course, he had no intention of telling them what trouble he'd run into.

The phone rang several times, and Tolland was surprised to hear the ship's SHINCOM 2100 communications system pick up. The outgoing message was not the usual professional-sounding greeting but rather the rowdy voice of one of Tolland's crew, the onboard joker.

'Hiya, hiya, this is the *Goya*,' the voice announced. 'We're sorry nobody's here right now, but we've all been abducted by very large lice! Actually, we've taken temporary shore leave to celebrate Mike's huge night. Gosh, are we proud! You can leave your name and number, and maybe we'll be back tomorrow when we're sober. Ciao! Go ET!'

Tolland laughed, missing his crew already. Obviously they'd seen the press conference. He was glad they'd gone ashore; he'd abandoned them rather abruptly when the President called, and their sitting idle at sea was crazy. Although the message said everyone had gone ashore, Tolland had to assume they would not have left his ship unattended, particularly in the strong currents where it was now anchored.

Tolland pressed the numeric code to play any internal voice mail messages they'd left for him. The line beeped once. One message. The voice was the same rowdy crewmember.

'Hi, Mike, hell of a show! If you're hearing this, you're probably checking your messages from some swanky White House party and wondering where the hell we are. Sorry we abandoned ship, buddy, but this was not a dry-celebration kind of night. Don't worry, we anchored her really good and left the porch light on. We're secretly hoping she gets pirated so you'll let NBC buy you that new boat! Just kidding, man. Don't worry, Xavia agreed to stay onboard and mind the fort. She said she preferred time alone to partying with a bunch of drunken fishmongers. Can you believe that?'

Tolland chuckled, relieved to hear someone was aboard watching the ship. Xavia was responsible, definitely not the partying type. A respected marine geologist, Xavia had the reputation for speaking her mind with a caustic honesty.

'Anyhow, Mike,' the message went on, 'tonight was incredible. Kind of makes you proud to be a scientist, doesn't it? Everyone's talking about how good this looks for NASA. Screw NASA, I say! This looks even better for *us*! *Amazing Seas* ratings must have gone up a few million points tonight. You're a star, man. A real one. Congrats. Excellent job.'

There was hushed talking on the line, and the voice came back. 'Oh, yeah, and speaking of Xavia, just so you don't get too big a head, she wants to razz you about something. Here she is.'

Xavia's razor voice came on the machine. 'Mike, Xavia, you're a God, yada yada. And because I love you so much, I've agreed to baby-sit this antediluvian wreck of yours. Frankly, it will be nice to be away from these hoodlums you call scientists. Anyhow, in addition to baby-sitting the ship, the crew has asked me, in my role as onboard bitch, to do everything in my power to keep you from turning into a conceited bastard, which after tonight I realize is going to be difficult, but I had to be the first to tell you that you made a boo-boo in your documentary. Yes, you heard me. A rare Michael Tolland brain fart. Don't worry, there are only about three people on earth who will notice, and they're all anal-retentive marine geologists with no sense of humor. A lot like me. But you know what they say about us geologists – always looking for *faults*!' She laughed. 'Anyhow, it's nothing, a minuscule point about meteorite petrology. I only mention it to ruin your night. You might get a call or two about it, so I thought I'd give you the heads-up so you don't end up sounding like the moron we all know you really are.' She laughed again. 'Anyhow, I'm not much of a party animal, so I'm staying onboard. Don't bother calling me; I had to turn on the machine because the goddamned press have been calling all night. You're a real star tonight, despite your screwup. Anyhow, I'll fill you in on it when you get back. Ciao.'

The line went dead.

Michael Tolland frowned. *A mistake in my documentary?*

Rachel Sexton stood in the restroom of the G4 and looked at herself in the mirror. She looked pale, she thought, and more frail than she'd imagined. Tonight's scare had taken a lot out of her. She wondered how long it would be before she would stop shivering, or before she would go near an ocean. Removing her

U.S.S. *Charlotte* cap, she let her hair down. *Better*, she thought, feeling more like herself.

Looking into her eyes, Rachel sensed a deep weariness. Beneath it, though, she saw the resolve. She knew that was her mother's gift. *Nobody tells you what you can and can't do.* Rachel wondered if her mother had seen what happened tonight. *Someone tried to kill me, Mom. Someone tried to kill all of us . . .*

Rachel's mind, as it had for several hours now, scrolled through the list of names.

Lawrence Ekstrom . . . Marjorie Tench . . . President Zach Herney. All had motives. And, more chillingly, all had means. *The President is not involved*, Rachel told herself, clinging to her hope that the President she respected so much more than her own father was an innocent bystander in this mysterious incident.

We still know nothing.

Not who . . . not if . . . not why.

Rachel had wanted to have answers for William Pickering but, so far, all she'd managed to do was raise more questions.

When Rachel left the restroom, she was surprised to see Michael Tolland was not in his seat. Corky was dozing nearby. As Rachel looked around, Mike stepped out of the cockpit as the pilot hung up a radiophone. His eyes were wide with concern.

'What is it?' Rachel asked.

Tolland's voice was heavy as he told her about the phone message.

A mistake in his presentation? Rachel thought Tolland was overreacting. 'It's probably nothing. She didn't tell you specifically what the error was?'

'Something to do with meteorite petrology.'

'Rock structure?'

'Yeah. She said the only people who would notice the mistake were a few other geologists. It sounds like whatever error I made was relating to the composition of the meteorite itself.'

Rachel drew a quick breath, understanding now. 'Chondrules?'

'I don't know, but it seems pretty coincidental.'

Rachel agreed. The chondrules were the one remaining shred of evidence that categorically supported NASA's claim that this was indeed a meteorite.

Corky came over, rubbing his eyes. 'What's going on?'

Tolland filled him in.

Corky scowled, shaking his head. 'It's not a problem with the chondrules, Mike. No way. All of your data came from NASA. And from *me*. It was flawless.'

'What other petrologic error could I have made?'

'Who the hell knows? Besides, what do marine geologists know about chondrules?'

'I have no idea, but she's damned sharp.'

'Considering the circumstances,' Rachel said, 'I think we should talk to this woman before we talk to Director Pickering.'

Tolland shrugged. 'I called her four times and got the machine. She's probably in the hydrolab and can't hear a damn thing anyway. She won't get my messages until morning at the earliest.' Tolland paused, checking his watch. 'Although . . .'

'Although what?'

Tolland eyed her intensely. 'How important do you think it is that we talk to Xavia before we talk to your boss?'

'If she has something to say about chondrules? I'd say it's critical. Mike,' Rachel said, 'at the moment, we've got all kinds of contradictory data. William Pickering is a man accustomed to having clear answers. When we meet him, I'd love to have something substantial for him to act on.'

'Then we should make a stop.'

Rachel did a double take. 'On your ship?'

'It's off the coast of New Jersey. Almost directly on our way to Washington. We can talk to Xavia, find out what she knows. Corky still has the meteorite sample, and if Xavia wants to run some geologic tests on it, the ship has a fairly well-equipped lab. I can't imagine it would take us more than an hour to get some conclusive answers.'

Rachel felt a pulse of anxiety. The thought of having to face the ocean again so soon was unnerving. *Conclusive answers*, she told herself, tempted by the possibility. *Pickering will definitely want answers.*

92

Delta-One was glad to be back on solid ground.

The Aurora aircraft, despite running at only one-half power and taking a circuitous ocean route, had completed its journey in under two hours and afforded the Delta Force a healthy head start to take up position and prepare themselves for the additional kill the controller had requested.

Now, on a private military runway outside D.C., the Delta Force left the Aurora behind and boarded their new transport – a waiting OH-58D Kiowa Warrior helicopter.

Yet again, the controller has arranged for the best, Delta-One thought.

The Kiowa Warrior, originally designed as a light observation helicopter, had been 'expanded and improved' to create the military's newest breed of attack helicopter. The Kiowa boasted infrared thermal imaging capability enabling its designator/laser range finder to provide autonomous designation for laser-guided precision weapons like Air-to-Air Stinger missiles and the AGM-1148 Hellfire Missile System. A high-speed digital signal processor provided simultaneous multitarget tracking of up to six targets. Few enemies had ever seen a Kiowa up close and survived to tell the tale.

Delta-One felt a familiar rush of power as he climbed into the Kiowa pilot's seat and strapped himself in. He had trained on this craft and flown it in covert ops three times. Of course, never before had he been gunning for a prominent *American* official. The Kiowa, he had to admit, was the perfect aircraft for the job. Its Rolls-Royce Allison engine and twin semirigid blades were 'silent running,' which essentially meant targets on the ground could not hear the chopper until it was directly over them. And because the aircraft was capable of flying blind without lights and was painted flat black with no reflective tail numbers, it was essentially invisible unless the target had radar.

Silent black helicopters.

The conspiracy theorists were going nuts over these. Some claimed the invasion of silent black helicopters was proof of 'New World Order storm troopers' under the authority of the United Nations. Others claimed the choppers were silent alien probes. Still others who saw the Kiowas in tight formation at night were deceived into thinking they were looking at fixed running lights on a much larger craft – a single flying saucer that was apparently capable of vertical flight.

Wrong again. But the military loved the diversion.

During a recent covert mission, Delta-One had flown a Kiowa armed with the most secretive new U.S. military technology – an ingenious holographic weapon nicknamed S&M. Despite conjuring associations with sadomasochism, S&M stood for 'smoke and mirrors' – holographic images 'projected' into the sky over enemy territory. The Kiowa had used S&M technology to project holograms of U.S. aircraft over an enemy anti-aircraft installation. The panicked anti-aircraft gunners fired maniacally at the circling ghosts. When all of their ammunition was gone, the United States sent in the real thing.

As Delta-One and his men lifted off the runway, Delta-One could still hear the words of his controller. *You have another mark.* It seemed an egregious understatement considering their new target's identity. Delta-One reminded himself, however, that it was not his place to question. His team had been given an order, and they would carry it out in the exact method instructed – as shocking as that method was.

I hope to hell the controller is certain this is the right move.

As the Kiowa lifted off the runway, Delta-One headed southwest. He had seen the FDR Memorial twice, but tonight would be his first time from the air.

'This meteorite was originally discovered by a Canadian geologist?' Gabrielle Ashe stared in astonishment at the young programmer, Chris Harper. 'And this Canadian is now *dead*?'

Harper gave a grim nod.

'How long have you known this?' she demanded.

'A couple of weeks. After the administrator and Marjorie Tench forced me to perjure myself in the press conference, they knew I couldn't go back on my word. They told me the truth about how the meteorite was really discovered.'

PODS is not responsible for finding the meteorite! Gabrielle had no idea where all of this information would lead, but clearly it was scandalous. Bad news for Tench. Great news for the senator.

'As I mentioned,' Harper said, looking somber now, 'the true way the meteorite was discovered was through an intercepted radio transmission. Are you familiar with a program called INSPIRE? The Interactive NASA Space Physics Ionosphere Radio Experiment.'

Gabrielle had heard of it only vaguely.

'Essentially,' Harper said, 'it's a series of very low frequency radio receivers near the North Pole that listen to the sounds of the earth – plasma wave emissions from the northern lights, broadband pulses from lightning storms, that sort of thing.'

'Okay.'

'A few weeks ago, one of INSPIRE's radio receivers

picked up a stray transmission from Ellesmere Island. A Canadian geologist was calling for help at an exceptionally low frequency.' Harper paused. 'In fact, the frequency was *so* low that nobody other than NASA's VLF receivers could possibly have heard it. We assumed the Canadian was long-waving.'

'I'm sorry?'

'Broadcasting at the lowest possible frequency to get maximum distance on his transmission. He was in the middle of nowhere, remember; a standard frequency transmission probably would not have made it far enough to be heard.'

'What did his message say?'

'The transmission was short. The Canadian said he had been out doing ice soundings on the Milne Ice Shelf, had detected an ultradense anomaly buried in the ice, suspected it was a giant meteorite, and while taking measurements had become trapped in a storm. He gave his coordinates, asked for rescue from the storm, and signed off. The NASA listening post sent a plane from Thule to rescue him. They searched for hours and finally discovered him, miles off course, dead at the bottom of a crevasse with his sled and dogs. Apparently he tried to outrun the storm, got blinded, went off course, and fell into a crevasse.'

Gabrielle considered the information, intrigued. 'So suddenly NASA knew about a meteorite that nobody else knew about?'

'Exactly. And ironically, if my software had been working properly, the PODS satellite would have spotted that same meteorite – a week before the Canadian did.'

The coincidence gave Gabrielle pause. 'A meteorite

'buried for three hundred years was almost discovered *twice* in the same week?'

'I know. A little bizarre, but science can be like that. Feast or famine. The point is that the administrator felt like the meteorite *should* have been our discovery anyway – if I had done my job correctly. He told me that because the Canadian was dead, nobody would be the wiser if I simply redirected PODS to the coordinates the Canadian had transmitted in his SOS. Then I could pretend to discover the meteorite from scratch, and we could salvage some respect from an embarrassing failure.'

'And that's what you did.'

'As I said, I had no choice. I had let down the mission.' He paused. 'Tonight, though, when I heard the President's press conference and found out the meteorite I'd pretended to discover contained *fossils* . . .'

'You were stunned.'

'Bloody well floored, I'd say!'

'Do you think the administrator knew the meteorite contained fossils before he asked you to pretend PODS found it?'

'I can't imagine how. That meteorite was buried and untouched until the first NASA team got there. My best guess is that NASA had no idea what they'd really found until they got a team up there to drill cores and X-ray. They asked me to lie about PODS, thinking they'd have a moderate victory with a big meteorite. Then when they got there, they realized just how big a find it really was.'

Gabrielle's breath was shallow with excitement. 'Dr Harper, will you testify that NASA and the White House forced you to lie about the PODS software?'

'I don't know.' Harper looked frightened. 'I can't

imagine what kind of damage that would do to the agency . . . to this discovery.'

'Dr Harper, you and I both know this meteorite remains a *wonderful* discovery, regardless of how it came about. The point here is that you lied to the American people. They have a right to know that PODS is not everything NASA says it is.'

'I don't know. I despise the administrator, but my *coworkers* . . . they are good people.'

'And they deserve to know they are being deceived.'

'And this evidence against me of embezzlement?'

'You can erase that from your mind,' Gabrielle said, having almost forgotten her con. 'I will tell the senator you know nothing of the embezzlement. It is simply a frame job – insurance set up by the administrator to keep you quiet about PODS.'

'Can the senator protect me?'

'Fully. You've done nothing wrong. You were simply following orders. Besides, with the information you've just given me about this Canadian geologist, I can't imagine the senator will even need to raise the issue of embezzlement at all. We can focus entirely on NASA's misinformation regarding PODS and the meteorite. Once the senator breaks the information about the Canadian, the administrator won't be able to risk trying to discredit you with lies.'

Harper still looked worried. He fell silent, somber as he pondered his options. Gabrielle gave him a moment. She'd realized earlier that there was another troubling coincidence to this story. She wasn't going to mention it, but she could see Dr Harper needed a final push.

'Do you have dogs, Dr Harper?'

He glanced up. 'I'm sorry?'

'I just thought it was odd. You told me that shortly

after this Canadian geologist radioed in the meteorite coordinates, his sled dogs ran blindly into a crevasse?'

'There was a storm. They were off course.'

Gabrielle shrugged, letting her skepticism show. 'Yeah . . . okay.'

Harper clearly sensed her hesitation. 'What are you saying?'

'I don't know. There's just a lot of coincidence surrounding this discovery. A Canadian geologist transmits meteorite coordinates on a frequency that *only* NASA can hear? And then his sled dogs run blindly off a cliff?' She paused. 'You obviously understand that this geologist's death paved the way for this entire NASA triumph.'

The color drained from Harper's face. 'You think the administrator would *kill* over this meteorite.'

Big politics. Big money, Gabrielle thought. 'Let me talk to the senator and we'll be in touch. Is there a back way out of here?'

Gabrielle Ashe left a pale Chris Harper and descended a fire stairwell into a deserted alley behind NASA. She flagged down a taxi that had just dropped off more NASA celebrators.

'Westbrooke Place Luxury Apartments,' she told the driver. She was about to make Senator Sexton a much happier man.

Wondering what she had agreed to, Rachel stood near the entrance of the G4 cockpit, stretching a radio transceiver cable into the cabin so she could place her call out of earshot of the pilot. Corky and Tolland looked on. Although Rachel and NRO director William Pickering had planned to maintain radio silence until her arrival at Bollings Air Force Base outside of D.C., Rachel now had information she was certain Pickering would want to hear immediately. She had phoned his secure cellular, which he carried at all times.

When William Pickering came on the line, he was all business. 'Speak with care, please. I cannot guarantee this connection.'

Rachel understood. Pickering's cellular, like most NRO field phones, had an indicator that detected unsecured incoming calls. Because Rachel was on a radiophone, one of the least secure communication modes available, Pickering's phone had warned him. This conversation would need to be vague. No names. No locations.

'My voice is my identity,' Rachel said, using the standard field greeting in this situation. She had expected the director's response would be displeasure that she had risked contacting him, but Pickering's reaction sounded positive.

'Yes, I was about to make contact with you myself. We need to redirect. I'm concerned you may have a welcoming party.'

Rachel felt a sudden trepidation. *Someone is watching us.* She could hear the danger in Pickering's tone. *Redirect.* He would be pleased to know she had called to make that exact request, albeit for entirely different reasons.

'The issue of authenticity,' Rachel said. 'We've been discussing it. We may have a way to confirm or deny categorically.'

'Excellent. There have been developments, and at least then I would have solid ground on which to proceed.'

'The proof involves our making a quick stop. One of us has access to a laboratory facility—'

'No exact locations, please. For your own safety.'

Rachel had no intention of broadcasting her plans over this line. 'Can you get us clearance to land at GAS-AC?'

Pickering was silent a moment. Rachel sensed he was trying to process the word. GAS-AC was an obscure NRO gisting shorthand for the Coast Guard's Group Air Station Atlantic City. Rachel hoped the director would know it.

'Yes,' he finally said. 'I can arrange that. Is that your final destination?'

'No. We will require further helicopter transport.'

'An aircraft will be waiting.'

'Thank you.'

'I recommend you exercise extreme caution until we know more. Speak to no one. Your suspicions have drawn deep concern among powerful parties.'

Tench, Rachel thought, wishing she had managed to make contact with the President directly.

'I am currently in my car, en route to meet the woman in question. She has requested a private meeting in a neutral location. It should reveal much.'

Pickering is driving somewhere to meet Tench? Whatever Tench was going to tell him must be important if she refused to tell him on the phone.

Pickering said, 'Do not discuss your final coordinates with anyone. And no more radio contact. Is that clear?'

'Yes, sir. We'll be at GAS-AC in an hour.'

'Transport will be arranged. When you reach your ultimate destination, you can call me via more secure channels.' He paused. 'I cannot overstate the importance of secrecy to your safety. You have made powerful enemies tonight. Take appropriate caution.' Pickering was gone.

Rachel felt tense as she closed the connection and turned to Tolland and Corky.

'Change of destination?' Tolland said, looking eager for answers.

Rachel nodded, feeling reluctant. 'The *Goya.*'

Corky sighed, glancing down at the meteorite sample in his hand. 'I still can't imagine NASA could possibly have . . .' He faded off, looking more worried with every passing minute.

We'll know soon enough, Rachel thought.

She went into the cockpit and returned the radio transceiver. Glancing out the windscreen at the rolling plateau of moonlit clouds racing beneath them, she had the unsettling feeling they were not going to like what they found onboard Tolland's ship.

William Pickering felt an unusual solitude as he drove his sedan down the Leesburg Highway. It was almost 2:00 A.M., and the road was empty. It had been years since he'd been driving this late.

Marjorie Tench's raspy voice still grated on his mind. *Meet me at the FDR Memorial.*

Pickering tried to recall the last time he had seen Marjorie Tench face-to-face – never a pleasant experience. It had been two months ago. At the White House. Tench was seated opposite Pickering at a long oak table surrounded by members of the National Security Council, Joint Chiefs, CIA, President Herney, and the administrator of NASA.

'Gentlemen,' the head of the CIA had said, looking directly at Marjorie Tench. 'Yet again, I am before you to urge this administration to confront the ongoing security crisis of NASA.'

The declaration took no one in the room by surprise. NASA's security woes had become a tired issue in the intelligence community. Two days previously, more than three hundred high-resolution satellite photos from one of NASA's earth-observing satellites had been stolen by hackers out of a NASA database. The photos – inadvertently revealing a classified U.S. military training facility in North Africa – had turned up on the black market, where they had been purchased by hostile intelligence agencies in the Middle East.

'Despite the best of intentions,' the CIA director said

with a weary voice, 'NASA continues to be a threat to national security. Simply put, our space agency is not equipped to protect the data and technologies they develop.'

'I realize,' the President replied, 'that there have been indiscretions. Damaging leaks. And it troubles me deeply.' He motioned across the table to the stern face of NASA administrator Lawrence Ekstrom. 'We are yet again looking into ways to tighten NASA's security.'

'With due respect,' the CIA director said, 'whatever security changes NASA implements will be ineffective as long as NASA operations remain outside the umbrella of the United States intelligence community.'

The statement brought an uneasy rustle from those assembled. Everyone knew where this was headed.

'As you know,' the CIA director went on, his tone sharpening, 'all U.S. government entities who deal with sensitive intelligence information are governed by strict rules of secrecy – military, CIA, NSA, NRO – all of them must abide by stringent laws regarding the conceal-ment of the data they glean and the technologies they develop. I ask you all, yet again, why NASA – the agency currently producing the largest portion of cutting-edge aerospace, imaging, flight, software, reconnaissance, and telecomm technologies used by the military and intelligence community – exists *outside* this umbrella of secrecy.'

The President heaved a weighty sigh. The proposal was clear. *Restructure NASA to become part of the U.S. military intelligence community.* Although similar re-structurings had happened with other agencies in the past, Herney refused to entertain the idea of placing NASA under the auspices of the Pentagon, the CIA, the NRO, or any other military directive. The National

Security Council was starting to splinter on the issue, many siding with the intelligence community.

Lawrence Ekstrom never looked pleased at these meetings, and this was no exception. He shot an acrimonious glare toward the CIA director. 'At the risk of repeating myself, sir, the technologies NASA develops are for nonmilitary, academic applications. If your intelligence community wants to turn one of our space telescopes around and look at China, that's your choice.'

The CIA director looked like he was about to boil over.

Pickering caught his eye and stepped in. 'Larry,' he said, careful to keep an even tone, 'every year NASA kneels before Congress and begs for money. You're running operations with too little funding, and you're paying the price in failed missions. If we incorporate NASA into the intelligence community, NASA will no longer need to ask Congress for help. You would be funded by the black budget at significantly higher levels. It's a win-win. NASA will have the money it needs to run itself properly, and the intelligence community will have peace of mind that NASA technologies are protected.'

Ekstrom shook his head. 'On principle, I cannot endorse painting NASA with that brush. NASA is about space science; we have nothing to do with national security.'

The CIA director stood up, something never done when the President was seated. Nobody stopped him. He glared down at the administrator of NASA. 'Are you telling me you think science has *nothing* to do with national security? Larry, they are synonymous, for God's sake! It is only this country's scientific and technological edge that keeps us secure, and whether we like it or not, NASA is playing a bigger and bigger part in developing those technologies. Unfortunately, your agency leaks like a sieve and has proven time and again that its security is a liability!'

The room fell silent.

Now the administrator of NASA stood up and locked eyes with his attacker. 'So you suggest locking twenty thousand NASA scientists in airtight military labs and making them work for you? Do you really think NASA's newest space telescopes would have been conceived had it not been for our scientists' *personal* desire to see deeper into space? NASA makes astonishing breakthroughs for one reason only – our employees want to understand the cosmos more deeply. They are a community of dreamers who grew up staring at starry skies and asking themselves what was up there. Passion and curiosity are what drive NASA's innovation, not the promise of military superiority.'

Pickering cleared his throat, speaking softly, trying to lower the temperatures around the table. 'Larry, I'm certain the director is not talking about recruiting NASA scientists to build military satellites. Your NASA mission statement would not change. NASA would carry on business as usual, except you would have increased funding and increased security.' Pickering turned now to the President. 'Security is expensive. Everyone in this room certainly realizes that NASA's security leaks are a result of underfunding. NASA has to toot its own horn, cut corners on security measures, run joint projects with other countries so they can share the price tag. I am proposing that NASA remain the superb, scientific, nonmilitary entity it currently is, but with a bigger budget, and some discretion.'

Several members of the security council nodded in quiet agreement.

President Herney stood slowly, staring directly at William Pickering, clearly not at all amused with the way Pickering had just taken over. 'Bill, let me ask you this: NASA is hoping to go to Mars in the next decade. How will the intelligence community feel about spending a hefty portion of the black budget running a mission to Mars – a mission that has no immediate national security benefits?'

'NASA will be able to do as they please.'

'Bullshit,' Herney replied flatly.

Everyone's eyes shot up. President Herney seldom used profanity.

'If there is one thing I've learned as president,' Herney declared, 'it's that those who control the dollars control the direction. I refuse to put NASA's purse strings in the hands of those who do not share the objectives for which the agency was founded. I can only imagine how much pure science would get done with the *military* deciding which NASA missions are viable.'

Herney's eyes scanned the room. Slowly, purposefully, he returned his rigid gaze to William Pickering.

'Bill,' Herney sighed, 'your displeasure that NASA is engaged in joint projects with foreign space agencies is painfully shortsighted. At least *someone* is working constructively with the Chinese and Russians. Peace on this planet will not be forged by military strength. It will be forged by those who come together *despite* their governments' differences. If you ask me, NASA's joint missions do more to promote national security than any billion-dollar spy satellite, and with a hell of a lot better hope for the future.'

Pickering felt an anger welling deep within him. *How dare a politician talk down to me this way!* Herney's idealism played fine in a boardroom, but in the real world, it got people killed.

'Bill,' Marjorie Tench interrupted, as if sensing Pickering was about to explode, 'we know you lost a child. We know this is a personal issue for you.'

Pickering heard nothing but condescension in her tone.

'But please remember,' Tench said, 'that the White House is currently holding back a floodgate of investors who want us to open space to the private sector. If you ask me, for all its mistakes, NASA has been one hell of a friend to the intel community. You all might just want to count your blessings.'

A rumble strip on the shoulder of the highway jolted Pickering's mind back to the present. His exit was coming up. As he approached the exit for D.C., he passed a bloody deer lying dead by the side of the road. He felt an odd hesitation . . . but he kept driving.

He had a rendezvous to keep.

96

The Franklin Delano Roosevelt Memorial is one of the largest memorials in the nation. With a park, waterfalls, statuary, alcoves, and basin, the memorial is divided into four outdoor galleries, one for each of FDR's terms in office.

A mile from the memorial, a lone Kiowa Warrior

coasted in, high over the city, its running lights dimmed. In a town boasting as many VIPs and media crews as D.C., helicopters in the skies were as common as birds flying south. Delta-One knew that as long as he stayed well outside what was known as 'the dome' – a bubble of protected airspace around the White House – he should draw little attention. They would not be here long.

The Kiowa was at 2,100 feet when it slowed adjacent to, but not directly over, the darkened FDR Memorial. Delta-One hovered, checking his position. He looked to his left, where Delta-Two was manning the night vision telescopic viewing system. The video feed showed a greenish image of the entry drive of the memorial. The area was deserted.

Now they would wait.

This would not be a quiet kill. There were some people you simply did not kill quietly. Regardless of the method, there would be repercussions. Investigations. Inquiries. In these cases, the best cover was to make a lot of noise. Explosions, fire, and smoke made it appear you were making a statement, and the first thought would be foreign terrorism. Especially when the target was a high-profile official.

Delta-One scanned the night-vision transmission of the tree-shrouded memorial below. The parking lot and entry road were empty. *Soon*, he thought. The location of this private meeting, though in an urban area, was fortuitously desolate at this hour. Delta-One turned his eyes from the screen to his own weapons controls.

The Hellfire system would be the weapon of choice tonight. A laser-guided, anti-armor missile, the Hellfire provided fire-and-forget capability. The projectile could home in on a laser spot that was projected from ground

427

observers, other aircraft, or the launching aircraft itself. Tonight, the missile would be guided autonomously through the laser designator in a mast-mounted sight. Once the Kiowa's designator had 'painted' the target with a laser beam, the Hellfire missile would be self-directing. Because the Hellfire could be fired either from the air or ground, its employment here tonight would not necessarily imply an aircraft's involvement. In addition, the Hellfire was a popular munition among black-market arms dealers, so terrorist activity could certainly be blamed.

'Sedan,' Delta-Two said.

Delta-One glanced at the transmission screen. A nondescript, black luxury sedan was approaching on the access road exactly on schedule. This was the typical motor pool car of large government agencies. The driver dimmed the car's headlights on entering the memorial. The car circled several times and then parked near a grove of trees. Delta-One watched the screen as his partner trained the telescopic night vision on the driver's side window. After a moment, the person's face came into view.

Delta-One drew a quick breath.

'Target confirmed,' his partner said.

Delta-One looked at the night-vision screen – with its deadly crucifix of cross-hairs – and he felt like a sniper aiming at royalty. *Target confirmed*.

Delta-Two turned to the left side avionics compartment and activated the laser designator. He aimed, and 2,000 feet below, a pinpoint of light appeared on the roof of the sedan, invisible to the occupant. 'Target painted,' he said.

Delta-One took a deep breath. He fired.

A sharp hissing sound sizzled beneath the fuselage,

followed by a remarkably dim trail of light streaking toward the earth. One second later, the car in the parking lot blew apart in a blinding eruption of flames. Twisted metal flew everywhere. Burning tires rolled into the woods.

'Kill complete,' Delta-One said, already accelerating the helicopter away from the area. 'Call the controller.'

Less than two miles away, President Zach Herney was preparing for bed. The Lexan bullet-proof windows of 'the residence' were an inch thick. Herney never heard the blast.

The Coast Guard Group Air Station Atlantic City is located in a secure section of William J. Hughes Federal Aviation Administration Technical Center at the Atlantic City International Airport. The group's area of responsibility includes the Atlantic seaboard from Asbury Park to Cape May.

Rachel Sexton jolted awake as the plane's tires screeched down on the tarmac of the lone runway nestled between two enormous cargo buildings. Surprised to find she had fallen asleep, Rachel groggily checked her watch.

2:13 A.M. She felt like she'd been asleep for days.

A warm onboard blanket was tucked carefully around her, and Michael Tolland was also just waking up beside her. He gave her a weary smile.

Corky staggered up the aisle and frowned when he

saw them. 'Shit, you guys are still here? I woke up hoping tonight had been a bad dream.'

Rachel knew exactly how he felt. *I'm headed back out to sea.*

The plane taxied to a stop, and Rachel and the others climbed out onto a barren runway. The night was overcast, but the coastal air felt heavy and warm. In comparison to Ellesmere, New Jersey felt like the tropics.

'Over here!' a voice called out.

Rachel and the others turned to see one of the Coast Guard's classic, crimson-colored HH-65 Dolphin helicopters waiting nearby. Framed by the brilliant white stripe on the chopper's tail, a fully suited pilot waved them over.

Tolland gave Rachel an impressed nod. 'Your boss certainly gets things done.'

You have no idea, she thought.

Corky slumped. 'Already? No dinner stop?'

The pilot welcomed them over and helped them aboard. Never asking their names, he spoke exclusively in pleasantries and safety precautions. Pickering had apparently made it clear to the Coast Guard that this flight was not an advertised mission. Nonetheless, despite Pickering's discretion, Rachel could see that their identities had remained a secret for only a matter of seconds; the pilot failed to hide his wide-eyed double take upon seeing television celebrity Michael Tolland.

Rachel was already feeling tense as she buckled herself in beside Tolland. The Aerospatiale engine overhead shrieked to life, and the Dolphin's sagging 39-foot rotors began to flatten out into a silver blur. The whine turned to a roar, and it lifted off the runway, climbing into the night.

The pilot turned in the cockpit and called out, 'I was informed you would tell me your destination once we were airborne.'

Tolland gave the pilot the coordinates of an offshore location about thirty miles southeast of their current position.

His ship is twelve miles off the coast, Rachel thought, feeling a shiver.

The pilot typed the coordinates into his navigation system. Then he settled in and gunned the engines. The chopper tipped forward and banked southeast.

As the dark dunes of the New Jersey coast slipped away beneath the aircraft, Rachel turned her eyes away from the blackness of the ocean spreading out beneath her. Despite the wariness of being back over the water again, she tried to take comfort in knowing she was accompanied by a man who had made the ocean a lifetime friend. Tolland was pressed close beside her in the narrow fuselage, his hips and shoulders touching hers. Neither made any attempt to shift positions.

'I know I shouldn't say this,' the pilot sputtered suddenly, as if ready to burst with excitement, 'but you're obviously Michael Tolland, and I've got to say, well, we've been watching you on TV all night! The *meteorite!* It's absolutely incredible! You must be in awe!'

Tolland nodded patiently. 'Speechless.'

'The documentary was fantastic! You know, the networks keep playing it over and over. None of tonight's duty pilots wanted this gig because everyone wanted to keep watching television, but I drew short straw. Can you believe it? Short straw! And here I am! If the boys had any idea I'd be flying the actual—'

'We appreciate the ride,' Rachel interrupted, 'and

we need you to keep our presence here to yourself. Nobody's supposed to know we're here.'

'Absolutely, ma'am. My orders were very clear.' The pilot hesitated, and then his expression brightened. 'Hey, we aren't by any chance heading for the *Goya*, are we?'

Tolland gave a reluctant nod. 'We are.'

'Holy shit!' the pilot exclaimed. 'Excuse me. Sorry, but I've seen her on your show. The twin-hull, right? Strange-looking beast! I've never actually been on a SWATH design. I never dreamed *yours* would be the first!'

Rachel tuned the man out, feeling a rising uneasiness to be heading out to sea.

Tolland turned to her. 'You okay? You could have stayed onshore. I told you that.'

I should have stayed onshore, Rachel thought, knowing pride would never have let her. 'No thanks, I'm fine.'

Tolland smiled. 'I'll keep an eye on you.'

'Thanks.' Rachel was surprised how the warmth in his voice made her feel more secure.

'You've seen the *Goya* on television, right?'

She nodded. 'It's a . . . um . . . an *interesting*-looking ship.'

Tolland laughed. 'Yeah. She was an extremely progressive prototype in her day, but the design never quite caught on.'

'Can't imagine why,' Rachel joked, picturing the ship's bizarre profile.

'Now NBC is pressuring me to use a newer ship. Something . . . I don't know, flashier, sexier. Another season or two, and they'll make me part with her.' Tolland sounded melancholy at the thought.

'You wouldn't love a brand-new ship?'

'I don't know . . . a lot of memories onboard the *Goya*.'

Rachel smiled softly. 'Well, as my mom used to say, sooner or later we've all got to let go of our past.'

Tolland's eyes held hers for a long moment. 'Yeah, I know.'

98

'Shit,' the taxi driver said, looking over his shoulder at Gabrielle. 'Looks like an accident up ahead. We ain't going nowhere. Not for a while.'

Gabrielle glanced out the window and saw the spinning lights of emergency vehicles piercing the night. Several policemen stood in the road ahead, halting traffic around the Mall.

'Must be a hell of an accident,' the driver said, motioning toward some flames near the FDR Memorial.

Gabrielle frowned at the flickering glow. *Now, of all times.* She needed to get to Senator Sexton with this new information about PODS and the Canadian geologist. She wondered if NASA's lies about how they found the meteorite would be a big enough scandal to breathe life back into Sexton's campaign. *Maybe not for most politicians*, she thought, but this was Sedgewick Sexton, a man who had built his campaign on amplifying the failures of others.

Gabrielle was not always proud of the senator's ability to put negative ethical spin on opponents' political misfortunes, but it was effective. Sexton's mastery of innuendo and indignity could probably turn

433

this one compartmentalized NASA fib into a sweeping question of character that infected the entire space agency – and by association, the President.

Outside the window, the flames at the FDR Memorial seemed to climb higher. Some nearby trees had caught fire, and the fire trucks were now hosing them down. The taxi driver turned on the car radio and began channel-surfing.

Sighing, Gabrielle closed her eyes and felt the exhaustion roll over her in waves. When she'd first come to Washington, she'd dreamed of working in politics forever, maybe someday in the White House. At the moment, however, she felt like she'd had enough politics for a lifetime – the duel with Marjorie Tench, the lewd photographs of herself and the senator, all of NASA's lies . . .

A newscaster on the radio was saying something about a car bomb and possible terrorism.

I've got to get out of this town, Gabrielle thought for the first time since coming to the nation's capital.

99

The controller seldom felt weary, but today had taken its toll. Nothing had gone as anticipated – the tragic discovery of the insertion shaft in the ice, the diffi-culties of keeping the information a secret, and now the growing list of victims.

Nobody was supposed to die . . . except the Canadian.

It seemed ironic that the most technically difficult part of the plan had turned out to be the least problematic.

The insertion, completed months ago, had come off without a hitch. Once the anomaly was in place, all that remained was to wait for the Polar Orbiting Density Scanner (PODS) satellite to launch. PODS was slated to scan enormous sections of the Arctic Circle, and sooner or later the anomaly software onboard would detect the meteorite and give NASA a major find.

But the damned software didn't work.

When the controller learned that the anomaly software had failed and had no chance of being fixed until after the election, the entire plan was in jeopardy. Without PODS, the meteorite would go undetected. The controller had to come up with some way to surreptitiously alert someone in NASA to the meteorite's existence. The solution involved orchestrating an emergency radio transmission from a Canadian geologist in the general vicinity of the insertion. The geologist, for obvious reasons, had to be killed immediately and his death made to look accidental. Throwing an innocent geologist from a helicopter had been the beginning. Now things were unraveling fast.

Wailee Ming. Norah Mangor. Both dead.

The bold kill that had just taken place at the FDR Memorial.

Soon to be added to the list were Rachel Sexton, Michael Tolland, and Dr Marlinson.

There is no other way, the controller thought, fighting the growing remorse. *Far too much is at stake.*

The Coast Guard Dolphin was still two miles from the *Goya*'s coordinates and flying at 3,000 feet when Tolland yelled up to the pilot.

'Do you have NightSight onboard this thing?'

The pilot nodded. 'I'm a rescue unit.'

Tolland had expected as much. NightSight was Raytheon's marine thermal imaging system, capable of locating wreck survivors in the dark. The heat given off by a swimmer's head would appear as a red speck on an ocean of black.

'Switch it on,' Tolland said.

The pilot looked confused. 'Why? You missing someone?'

'No. I want everyone to see something.'

'We won't see a thing on thermal from this high up unless there's a burning oil slick.'

'Just switch it on,' Tolland said.

The pilot gave Tolland an odd look and then adjusted some dials, commanding the thermal lens beneath the chopper to survey a three-mile swatch of ocean in front of them. An LCD screen on his dashboard lit up. The image came into focus.

'Holy shit!' The helicopter lurched momentarily as the pilot recoiled in surprise and then recovered, staring at the screen.

Rachel and Corky leaned forward, looking at the image with equal surprise. The black background of the ocean was illuminated by an enormous swirling spiral of pulsating red.

Rachel turned to Tolland with trepidation. 'It looks like a cyclone.'

'It is,' Tolland said. 'A cyclone of warm currents. About a half mile across.'

The Coast Guard pilot chuckled in amazement. 'That's a big one. We see these now and then, but I hadn't heard about this one yet.'

'Just surfaced last week,' Tolland said. 'Probably won't last more than another few days.'

'What causes it?' Rachel asked, understandably perplexed by the huge vortex of swirling water in the middle of the ocean.

'Magma dome,' the pilot said.

Rachel turned to Tolland, looking wary. 'A volcano?'

'No,' Tolland said. 'The East Coast typically doesn't have active volcanoes, but occasionally we get rogue pockets of magma that well up under the seafloor and cause hot spots. The hot spot causes a reverse temperature gradient – hot water on the bottom and cooler water on top. It results in these giant spiral currents. They're called megaplumes. They spin for a couple of weeks and then dissipate.'

The pilot looked at the pulsating spiral on his LCD screen. 'Looks like this one's still going strong.' He paused, checking the coordinates of Tolland's ship and then looked over his shoulder in surprise. 'Mr Tolland, it looks like you're parked fairly near the middle of it.'

Tolland nodded. 'Currents are a little slower near the eye. Eighteen knots. Like anchoring in a fast-moving river. Our chain's been getting a real workout this week.'

'Jesus,' the pilot said. 'Eighteen-knot current? Don't fall overboard!' He laughed.

Rachel did not laugh. 'Mike, you didn't mention this megaplume, magma dome, hot-current situation.'

He put a reassuring hand on her knee. 'It's perfectly safe, trust me.'

Rachel frowned. 'So this documentary you were making out here was about this magma dome phenomenon?'

'Megaplumes and *Sphyrna mokarran*.'

'That's right. You mentioned that earlier.'

Tolland gave a coy smile. '*Sphyrna mokarran* love warm water, and right now, every last one for a hundred miles is congregating in this milewide circle of heated ocean.'

'Neat.' Rachel gave an uneasy nod. 'And what, pray tell, are *Sphyrna mokarran*?'

'Ugliest fish in the sea.'

'Flounder?'

Tolland laughed. 'Great hammerhead shark.'

Rachel stiffened beside him. 'You've got hammer-head *sharks* around your boat?'

Tolland winked. 'Relax, they're not dangerous.'

'You wouldn't say that unless they were dangerous.'

Tolland chuckled. 'I guess you're right.' He called playfully up to the pilot. 'Hey, how long has it been since you guys saved anyone from an attack by a hammerhead?'

The pilot shrugged. 'Gosh. We haven't saved anyone from a hammerhead in decades.'

Tolland turned to Rachel. 'See. *Decades*. No worries.'

'Just last month,' the pilot added, 'we had an attack where some idiot skin diver was chumming—'

'Hold on!' Rachel said. 'You said you hadn't saved anyone in *decades*!'

'Yeah,' the pilot replied. '*Saved* anyone. Usually, we're too late. Those bastards kill in a hurry.'

From the air, the flickering outline of the *Goya* loomed on the horizon. At half a mile, Tolland could make out the brilliant deck lights that his crewmember Xavia had wisely left glowing. When he saw the lights, he felt like a weary traveler pulling into his driveway.

'I thought you said only one person was onboard,' Rachel said, looking surprised to see all the lights.

'Don't you leave a light on when you're home alone?'

'One light. Not the entire house.'

Tolland smiled. Despite Rachel's attempts to be light-hearted, he could tell she was extremely apprehensive about being out here. He wanted to put an arm around her and reassure her, but he knew there was nothing he could say. 'The lights are on for security. Makes the ship look active.'

Corky chuckled. 'Afraid of pirates, Mike?'

'Nope. Biggest danger out here is the idiots who don't know how to read radar. Best defense against getting rammed is to make sure everyone can see you.'

Corky squinted down at the glowing vessel. '*See* you? It looks like a Carnival Cruise line on New Year's Eve. Obviously, NBC pays your electric.'

The Coast Guard chopper slowed and banked around the huge illuminated ship, and the pilot began maneuvering toward the helipad on the stern deck. Even from the air, Tolland could make out the raging current pulling at the ship's hull struts. Anchored from its bow, the *Goya* was aimed into the current, straining at its massive anchor line like a chained beast.

'She really is a beauty,' the pilot said, laughing.

Tolland knew the comment was sarcastic. The *Goya* was ugly. 'Butt-ugly' according to one television reviewer. One of only seventeen SWATH ships ever built, the *Goya*'s Small-Waterplane-Area Twin-Hull was anything but attractive.

The vessel was essentially a massive horizontal platform floating thirty feet above the ocean on four huge struts affixed to pontoons. From a distance, the ship looked like a low-slung drilling platform. Up close, it resembled a deck barge on stilts. The crew quarters, research labs, and navigation bridge were housed in a series of tiered structures on top, giving one the rough impression of a giant floating coffee table supporting a hodgepodge of multistaged buildings.

Despite its less than streamlined appearance, the *Goya*'s design enjoyed significantly less water-plane area, resulting in increased stability. The suspended platform enabled better filming, easier lab work, and fewer seasick scientists. Although NBC was pressuring Tolland to let them buy him something newer, Tolland had refused. Granted, there were better ships out there now, even more stable ones, but the *Goya* had been his home for almost a decade now – the ship on which he had fought his way back after Celia's death. Some nights he still heard her voice in the wind out on deck. If and when the ghosts ever disappeared, Tolland would consider another ship.

Not yet.

*   *   *

When the chopper finally set down on the *Goya*'s stern deck, Rachel Sexton felt only half relieved. The good news was that she was no longer flying over the ocean. The bad news was that she was now standing on it. She fought off the shaky sensation in her legs as she climbed onto the deck and looked around. The deck was surprisingly cramped, particularly with the helicopter on its pad. Moving her eyes toward the bow, Rachel gazed at the ungainly, stacked edifice that made up the bulk of the ship.

Tolland stood close beside her. 'I know,' he said, talking loudly over the sound of the raging current. 'It looks bigger on television.'

Rachel nodded. 'And more stable.'

'This is one of the safest ships on the sea. I promise.' Tolland put a hand on her shoulder and guided her across the deck.

The warmth of his hand did more to calm Rachel's nerves than anything he could have said. Nonetheless, as she looked toward the rear of the ship, she saw the roiling current streaming out behind them as though the ship was at full throttle. *We're sitting on a megaplume*, she thought.

Centered on the foremost section of rear deck, Rachel spied a familiar, one-man Triton submersible hanging on a giant winch. The Triton – named for the Greek god of the sea – looked nothing like its predecessor, the steel-encased Alvin. The Triton had a hemispherical acrylic dome in front, making it look more like a giant fishbowl than a sub. Rachel could think of few things more terrifying than submerging hundreds of feet into the ocean with nothing between her face and the ocean but a sheet of clear acrylic. Of course, according to Tolland, the only unpleasant part of riding in the Triton was the initial deployment – being slowly winched down through the trap door in the *Goya*'s deck, hanging like a pendulum thirty feet above the sea.

'Xavia is probably in the hydrolab,' Tolland said, moving across the deck. 'This way.'

Rachel and Corky followed Tolland across the stern deck. The Coast Guard pilot remained in his chopper with strict instructions not to use the radio.

'Have a look at this,' Tolland said, pausing at the stern railing of the ship.

Hesitantly, Rachel neared the railing. They were very high up. The water was a good thirty feet below them, and yet Rachel could still feel the heat rising off the water.

'It's about the temperature of a warm bath,' Tolland said over the sound of the current. He reached toward a switch-box on the railing. 'Watch this.' He flipped a switch.

A wide arc of light spread through the water behind the ship, illuminating it from within like a lit swimming pool. Rachel and Corky gasped in unison.

The water around the ship was filled with dozens of ghostly shadows. Hovering only feet below the illuminated surface, armies of sleek, dark forms swam in parallel against the current, their unmistakable hammer-shaped skulls wagging back and forth as if to the beat of some prehistoric rhythm.

'Christ, Mike,' Corky stammered. 'So glad you shared this with us.'

Rachel's body went rigid. She wanted to step back from the railing, but she could not move. She was transfixed by the petrifying vista.

'Incredible, aren't they?' Tolland said. His hand was on her shoulder again, comforting. 'They'll tread water in the warm spots for weeks. These guys have the best noses in the sea – enhanced telencephalon olfactory lobes. They can smell blood up to a mile away.'

Corky looked skeptical. 'Enhanced telencephalon olfactory lobes?'

'Don't believe me?' Tolland began rooting around in an aluminum cabinet adjacent to where they were standing. After a moment, he pulled out a small, dead fish. 'Perfect.' He took a knife from the cooler and cut the limp fish in several places. It started to drip blood.

'Mike, for God's sake,' Corky said. 'That's disgusting.'

Tolland tossed the bloody fish overboard and it fell thirty feet. The instant it hit the water, six or seven sharks darted in a tumbling ferocious brawl, their rows of silvery teeth gnashed wildly at the bloody fish. In an instant, the fish was gone.

Aghast, Rachel turned and stared at Tolland, who was already holding another fish. Same kind. Same size.

'This time, no blood,' Tolland said. Without cutting the fish, he threw it in the water. The fish splashed down, but nothing happened. The hammerheads seemed not to notice. The bait carried away on the current, having drawn no interest whatsoever.

'They attack *only* on sense of smell,' Tolland said, leading them away from the railing. 'In fact, you could swim out here in total safety – provided you didn't have any open wounds.'

Corky pointed to the stitches on his cheek.

Tolland frowned. 'Right. No swimming for you.'

Gabrielle Ashe's taxi was not moving.

Sitting at a roadblock near the FDR Memorial, Gabrielle looked out at the emergency vehicles in the distance and felt as if a surrealistic fog bank had settled over the city. Radio reports were coming in now that the exploded car might have contained a high-level government official.

Pulling out her cellphone, she dialed the senator. He was no doubt starting to wonder what was taking Gabrielle so long.

The line was busy.

Gabrielle looked at the taxi's clicking meter and frowned. Some of the other cars stuck here were pulling up onto the curbs and turning around to find alternative routes.

The driver looked over his shoulder. 'You wanna wait? Your dime.'

Gabrielle saw more official vehicles arriving now. 'No. Let's go around.'

The driver grunted in the affirmative and began maneuvering the awkward multipoint turn. As they bounced over the curbs, Gabrielle tried Sexton again.

Still busy.

Several minutes later, having made a wide loop, the taxi was traveling up C Street. Gabrielle saw the Philip A. Hart Office Building looming. She had intended to go straight to the senator's apartment, but with her office this close . . .

'Pull over,' she blurted to the driver. 'Right there. Thanks.' She pointed.

The cab stopped.

Gabrielle paid the amount on the meter and added $10. 'Can you wait ten minutes?'

The cabbie looked at the money and then at his watch. 'Not a minute longer.'

Gabrielle hurried off. *I'll be out in five.*

The deserted marble corridors of the Senate office building felt almost sepulchral at this hour. Gabrielle's muscles were tense as she hurried through the gauntlet of austere statues lining the third-floor entryway. Their stony eyes seemed to follow her like silent sentinels.

Arriving at the main door of Senator Sexton's five-room office suite, Gabrielle used her key card to enter. The secretarial lobby was dimly lit. Crossing through the foyer, she went down a hallway to her office. She entered, flicked on the fluorescent lights, and strode directly to her file cabinets.

She had an entire file on the budgeting of NASA's Earth Observing System, including plenty of information on PODS. Sexton would certainly want all the data he could possibly get on PODS as soon as she told him about Harper.

NASA lied about PODS.

As Gabrielle fingered her way through her files, her cellphone rang.

'Senator?' she answered.

'No, Gabs. It's Yolanda.' Her friend's voice had an unusual edge to it. 'You still at NASA?'

'No. At the office.'

'Find anything at NASA?'

You have no idea. Gabrielle knew she couldn't tell Yolanda anything until she'd talked to Sexton; the senator would have very specific ideas about how best to handle the information. 'I'll tell you all about it after I talk to Sexton. Heading over to his place now.'

Yolanda paused. 'Gabs, you know this thing you were saying about Sexton's campaign finance and the SFF?'

'I told you I was wrong and—'

'I just found out two of our reporters who cover the aerospace industry have been working on a similar story.'

Gabrielle was surprised. 'Meaning?'

'I don't know. But these guys are good, and they seem pretty convinced that Sexton is taking kickbacks from the Space Frontier Foundation. I just figured I should call you. I know I told you earlier that the idea was insane. Marjorie Tench as a source seemed spotty, but these guys of ours . . . I don't know, you might want to talk to them before you see the senator.'

'If they're so convinced, why haven't they gone to press?' Gabrielle sounded more defensive than she wanted to.

'They have no solid evidence. The senator apparently is good at covering his tracks.'

Most politicians are. 'There's nothing there, Yolanda. I told you the senator admitted taking SFF donations, but the gifts are all under the cap.'

'I know that's what he *told* you, Gabs, and I'm not claiming to know what's true or false here. I just felt obliged to call because I told you not to trust Marjorie Tench, and now I find out people *other* than Tench think the senator may be on the dole. That's all.'

'Who were these reporters?' Gabrielle felt an unexpected anger simmering now.

'No names. I can set up a meeting. They're smart.

They understand campaign finance law . . .' Yolanda hesitated. 'You know, these guys actually believe Sexton is hurting for cash – bankrupt even.'

In the silence of her office, Gabrielle could hear Tench's raspy accusations echoing. *After Katherine died, the senator squandered the vast majority of her legacy on bad investments, personal comforts, and buying himself what appears to be certain victory in the primaries. As of six months ago, your candidate was broke.*

'Our men would love to talk to you,' Yolanda said.

I bet they would, Gabrielle thought. 'I'll call you back.'

'You sound pissed.'

'Never at you, Yolanda. Never at you. Thanks.'

Gabrielle hung up.

Dozing on a chair in the hallway outside Senator Sexton's Westbrooke apartment, a security guard awoke with a start at the sound of his cellular phone. Bolting up in his chair, he rubbed his eyes and pulled his phone from his blazer pocket.

'Yeah?'

'Owen, this is Gabrielle.'

Sexton's guard recognized her voice. 'Oh, hi.'

'I need to talk to the senator. Would you knock on his door for me? His line is busy.'

'It's kind of late.'

'He's awake. I'm sure of it.' Gabrielle sounded anxious. 'It's an emergency.'

'*Another* one?'

'Same one. Just get him on the phone, Owen. There's something I really need to ask him.'

The guard sighed, standing up. 'Okay, okay. I'll knock.' He stretched and made his way toward Sexton's door. 'But I'm only doing it because he was glad I let you in earlier.' Reluctantly, he raised his fist to knock.

'What did you just say?' Gabrielle demanded.

The guard's fist stopped in midair. 'I said the senator was glad I let you in earlier. You were right. It was no problem at all.'

'You and the senator *talked* about that?' Gabrielle sounded surprised.

'Yeah. So what?'

'No, I just didn't think . . .'

'Actually, it was kind of weird. The senator needed a couple of seconds to even remember you'd been in there. I think the boys were tossing back a few.'

'When did you two talk, Owen?'

'Right after you left. Is something wrong?'

A momentary silence. 'No . . . no. Nothing. Look, now that I think of it, let's not bother the senator this instant. I'll keep trying his house line, and if I don't have any luck, I'll call you back and you can knock.'

The guard rolled his eyes. 'Whatever you say, Ms Ashe.'

'Thanks, Owen. Sorry to bother you.'

'No problem.' The guard hung up, flopped back in his chair, and went to sleep.

Alone in her office, Gabrielle stood motionless for several seconds before hanging up the phone. *Sexton knows I was inside his apartment . . . and he never mentioned it to me?*

Tonight's ethereal strangeness was getting murkier. Gabrielle flashed on the senator's phone call to her while she was at ABC. The senator had stunned her with his unprovoked admission that he was meeting with space companies and accepting money. His honesty had brought her back to him. Shamed her

448

even. His confession now seemed one hell of a lot less noble.

Soft money, Sexton had said. *Perfectly legal.*

Suddenly, all the vague misgivings Gabrielle had ever felt about Senator Sexton seemed to resurface all at once.

Outside, the taxi was honking.

103

The bridge of the *Goya* was a Plexiglas cube situated two levels above the main deck. From here Rachel had a 360-degree view of the surrounding darkened sea, an unnerving vista she looked at only once before blocking it out and turning her attention to the matter at hand.

Having sent Tolland and Corky to find Xavia, Rachel prepared to contact Pickering. She'd promised the director she would call him when they arrived, and she was eager to know what he had learned in his meeting with Marjorie Tench.

The *Goya*'s SHINCOM 2100 digital communications system was a platform with which Rachel was familiar enough. She knew if she kept her call short, her communication should be secure.

Dialing Pickering's private number, she waited, clutching the SHINCOM 2100 receiver to her ear. She expected Pickering to pick up on the first ring. But the line just kept ringing.

Six rings. Seven. Eight . . .

Rachel gazed out at the darkened ocean, her inability

to reach the director doing nothing to quell her uneasiness about being at sea.

Nine rings. Ten rings. *Pick up!*

She paced, waiting. What was going on? Pickering carried his phone with him at all times, and he had expressly told Rachel to call him.

After fifteen rings, she hung up.

With growing apprehension, she picked up the SHINCOM receiver and dialed again.

Four rings. Five rings.

Where is he?

Finally, the connection clicked open. Rachel felt a surge of relief, but it was short-lived. There was no one on the line. Only silence.

'Hello,' she prompted. 'Director?'

Three quick clicks.

'Hello?' Rachel said.

A burst of electronic static shattered the line, blasting in Rachel's ear. She yanked the receiver away from her head in pain. The static abruptly stopped. Now she could hear a series of rapidly oscillating tones that pulsed in half-second intervals. Rachel's confusion quickly gave way to realization. And then fear.

'Shit!'

Wheeling back to the controls on the bridge, she slammed the receiver down in its cradle, severing the connection. For several moments she stood terrified, wondering if she'd hung up in time.

Amidships, two decks below, the *Goya*'s hydrolab was an expansive work space segmented by long counters and islands packed to the gills with electronic gear – bottom profilers, current analyzers, wet sinks, fume hoods, a walk-in specimen cooler, PCs, and a stack of

450

organizer crates for research data and the spare electronics to keep everything running.

When Tolland and Corky entered, the *Goya*'s onboard geologist, Xavia, was reclining in front of a
blaring television. She didn't even turn around.

'Did you guys run out of beer money?' she called
over her shoulder, apparently thinking some of her
crew had returned.

'Xavia,' Tolland said. 'It's Mike.'

The geologist spun, swallowing part of a pre-
packaged sandwich she was eating. 'Mike?' she
stammered, clearly stunned to see him. She stood
up, turned down the television, and came over, still
chewing. 'I thought some of the guys had come back
from bar-hopping. What are you doing here?' Xavia
was heavyset and dark-skinned, with a sharp voice and
a surly air about her. She motioned to the television,
which was broadcasting replays of Tolland's on-site
meteorite documentary. 'You sure didn't hang around
on the ice shelf very long, did you?'

Something came up, Tolland thought. 'Xavia, I'm sure
you recognize Corky Marlinson.'

Xavia nodded. 'An honor, sir.'

Corky was eyeing the sandwich in her hand. 'That
looks good.'

Xavia gave him an odd look.

'I got your message,' Tolland said to Xavia. 'You said
I made a mistake in my presentation? I want to talk to
you about it.'

The geologist stared at him and let out a shrill laugh.
'*That's* why you're back? Oh, Mike, for God's sake,
I told you, it was nothing. I was just pulling your
chain. NASA obviously gave you some old data. Inconsequential. Seriously, only three or four marine

geologists in the world might have noticed the over-sight!'

Tolland held his breath. 'This oversight. Does it by any chance have anything to do with chondrules?'

Xavia's face went blank with shock. 'My God. One of those geologists called you already?'

Tolland slumped. *The chondrules*. He looked at Corky and then back to the marine geologist. 'Xavia, I need to know everything you can tell me about these chondrules. What was the mistake I made?'

Xavia stared at him, apparently now sensing he was dead serious. 'Mike, it's really nothing. I read a small article in a trade journal a while back. But I don't understand why you're so worried about this.'

Tolland sighed. 'Xavia, as strange as this may sound, the less you know tonight, the better. All I'm asking is for you to tell us what you know about chondrules, and then we'll need you to examine a rock sample for us.'

Xavia looked mystified and vaguely perturbed to be out of the loop. 'Fine, let me get you that article. It's in my office.' She set her sandwich down and headed for the door.

Corky called after her, 'Can I finish that?'

Xavia paused, sounding incredulous. 'You want to *finish* my sandwich?'

'Well, I just thought if you—'

'Get your *own* damn sandwich.' Xavia left.

Tolland chuckled, motioning across the lab toward a specimen cooler. 'Bottom shelf, Corky. Between the sambuca and squid sacs.'

Outside on deck, Rachel descended the steep stair-way from the bridge and strode toward the chopper pad. The Coast Guard pilot was dozing but sat up when Rachel rapped on the cockpit.

'Done already?' he asked. 'That was fast.'

Rachel shook her head, on edge. 'Can you run both surface and air radar?'

'Sure. Ten-mile radius.'

'Turn it on, please.'

Looking puzzled, the pilot threw a couple of switches and the radar screen lit up. The sweep arm spun lazy circles.

'Anything?' Rachel asked.

The pilot let the arm make several complete rotations. He adjusted some controls and watched. It was all clear. 'Couple of small ships way out on the periphery, but they're heading away from us. We're clear. Miles and miles of open sea in all directions.'

Rachel Sexton sighed, although she did not feel particularly relieved. 'Do me a favor, if you see anything approaching – boats, aircraft, anything – will you let me know immediately?'

'Sure thing. Is everything okay?'

'Yeah. I'd just like to know if we're having company.'

The pilot shrugged. 'I'll watch the radar, ma'am. If anything blips, you'll be the first to know.'

Rachel's senses were tingling as she headed for the hydrolab. When she entered, Corky and Tolland were standing alone in front of a computer monitor and chewing sandwiches.

Corky called out to her with his mouth full, 'What'll it be? Fishy chicken, fishy bologna, or fishy egg salad?'

Rachel barely heard the question. 'Mike, how fast can we get this information and get off this ship?'

Tolland paced the hydrolab, waiting with Rachel and Corky for Xavia's return. The news about the chondrules was almost as discomforting as Rachel's news about her attempted contact with Pickering.

The director didn't answer.

And someone tried to pulse-snitch the Goya's location.

'Relax,' Tolland told everyone. 'We're safe. The Coast Guard pilot is watching the radar. He can give us plenty of warning if anyone is headed our way.'

Rachel nodded in agreement, although she still looked on edge.

'Mike, what the hell is *this*?' Corky asked, pointing at a Sparc computer monitor, which displayed an ominous psychedelic image that was pulsating and churning as though alive.

'Acoustic Doppler Current Profiler,' Tolland said. 'It's a cross section of the currents and temperature gradients of the ocean underneath the ship.'

Rachel stared. 'That's what we're anchored on *top* of?'

Tolland had to admit, the image looked frightening. At the surface, the water appeared as a swirling bluish green, but tracing downward, the colors slowly shifted to a menacing red-orange as the temperatures heated up. Near the bottom, over a mile down, hovering above the ocean floor, a blood-red cyclone vortex raged.

'That's the megaplume,' Tolland said.

Corky grunted. 'Looks like an underwater tornado.'

'Same principle. Oceans are usually colder and more dense near the bottom, but here the dynamics are reversed. The deepwater is heated and lighter, so it rises toward the surface. Meanwhile, the surface water is heavier, so it races downward in a huge spiral to fill the void. You get these drainlike currents in the ocean. Enormous whirlpools.'

'What's that big bump on the seafloor?' Corky pointed at the flat expanse of ocean floor, where a large dome-shaped mound rose up like a bubble. Directly above it swirled the vortex.

'That mound is a magma dome,' Tolland said, 'It's where lava is pushing up beneath the ocean floor.'

Corky nodded. 'Like a huge zit.'

'In a manner of speaking.'

'And if it pops?'

Tolland frowned, recalling the famous 1986 megaplume event off the Juan de Fuca Ridge, where thousands of tons of 1,200 degrees Celsius magma spewed up into the ocean all at once, magnifying the plume's intensity almost instantly. Surface currents amplified as the vortex expanded rapidly upward. What happened next was something Tolland had no intention of sharing with Corky and Rachel this evening.

'Atlantic magma domes don't pop,' Tolland said. 'The cold water circulating over the mound continually cools and hardens the earth's crust, keeping the magma safely under a thick layer of rock. Eventually the lava underneath cools, and the spiral disappears. Megaplumes are generally not dangerous.'

Corky pointed toward a tattered magazine sitting near the computer. 'So you're saying *Scientific American* publishes fiction?'

Tolland saw the cover, and winced. Someone had apparently pulled it from the *Goya*'s archive of old science magazines: *Scientific American*, February 1999. The cover showed an artist's rendering of a supertanker swirling out of control in an enormous funnel of ocean. The heading read: MEGAPLUMES – GIANT KILLERS FROM THE DEEP?

Tolland laughed it off. 'Totally irrelevant. That article is talking about megaplumes in *earthquake* zones. It was a popular Bermuda Triangle hypothesis a few years back, explaining ship disappearances. Technically speaking, if there's some sort of cataclysmic geologic event on the ocean floor, which is unheard of around here, the dome could rupture, and the vortex could get big enough to . . . well, you know . . .'

'No, we *don't* know,' Corky said.

Tolland shrugged. 'Rise to the surface.'

'Terrific. So glad you had us aboard.'

Xavia entered carrying some papers. 'Admiring the megaplume?'

'Oh, yes,' Corky said sarcastically. 'Mike was just telling us how if that little mound ruptures, we all go spiraling around in a big drain.'

'Drain?' Xavia gave a cold laugh. 'More like getting flushed down the world's largest toilet.'

Outside on the deck of the *Goya*, the Coast Guard helicopter pilot vigilantly watched the EMS radar screen. As a rescue pilot he had seen his share of fear in people's eyes; Rachel Sexton had definitely been afraid when she asked him to keep an eye out for unexpected visitors to the *Goya*.

What kind of visitors is she expecting? he wondered.

From all the pilot could see, the sea and air for ten

miles in all directions contained nothing that looked out of the ordinary. A fishing boat eight miles off. An occasional aircraft slicing across an edge of their radar field and then disappearing again toward some unknown destination.

The pilot sighed, gazing out now at the ocean rushing all around the ship. The sensation was a ghostly one – that of sailing full speed despite being anchored.

He returned his eyes to the radar screen and watched. Vigilant.

105

Onboard the *Goya*, Tolland had now introduced Xavia and Rachel. The ship's geologist was looking increasingly baffled by the distinguished entourage standing before her in the hydrolab. In addition, Rachel's eagerness to run the tests and get off the ship as fast as possible was clearly making Xavia uneasy.

Take your time, Xavia, Tolland willed her. *We need to know everything.*

Xavia was talking now, her voice stiff. 'In your documentary, Mike, you said those little metallic inclusions in the rock could form *only* in space.'

Tolland already felt a tremor of apprehension. *Chondrules form only in space. That's what NASA told me.*

'But according to these notes,' Xavia said, holding up the pages, 'that's not entirely true.'

Corky glared. 'Of course it's true!'

Xavia scowled at Corky and waved the notes. 'Last

year a young geologist named Lee Pollock out of Drew University was using a new breed of marine robot to do Pacific deepwater crust sampling in the Mariana Trench and pulled up a loose rock that contained a geologic feature he had never seen before. The feature was quite similar in appearance to chondrules. He called them "plagioclase stress inclusions" – tiny bubbles of metal that apparently had been rehomogenized during deep ocean pressurization events. Dr Pollock was amazed to find metallic bubbles in an ocean rock, and he formulated a unique theory to explain their presence.'

Corky grumbled, 'I suppose he would *have* to.'

Xavia ignored him. 'Dr Pollock asserted that the rock formed in an ultradeep oceanic environment where extreme pressure metamorphosed a pre-existing rock, permitting some of the disparate metals to fuse.'

Tolland considered it. The Mariana Trench was seven miles down, one of the last truly unexplored regions on the planet. Only a handful of robotic probes had ever ventured that deep, and most had collapsed well before they reached the bottom. The water pressure in the trench was enormous – an astounding 18,000 pounds per square inch, as opposed to a mere 24 pounds on the ocean's surface. Oceanographers still had very little understanding of the geologic forces at the deepest ocean floor. 'So, this guy Pollock thinks the Mariana Trench can make rocks with chondrulelike features?'

'It's an extremely obscure theory,' Xavia said. 'In fact, it's never even been formally published. I only happened to stumble across Pollock's personal notes on the Web by chance last month when I was doing research on fluid-rock interactions for our upcoming megaplume show. Otherwise, I never would have heard of it.'

'The theory has never been published,' Corky said, 'because it's ridiculous. You need *heat* to form chondrules. There's no way water pressure could re-arrange the crystalline structure of a rock.'

'Pressure,' Xavia fired back, 'happens to be the single biggest contributor to geologic change on our planet. A little something called a *metamorphic* rock? Geology 101?'

Corky scowled.

Tolland realized Xavia had a point. Although heat did play a role in some of earth's metamorphic geology, most metamorphic rocks were formed by extreme pressure. Incredibly, rocks deep in the earth's crust were under so much pressure that they acted more like thick molasses than solid rock, becoming elastic and undergoing chemical changes as they did. Nonetheless, Dr Pollock's theory still seemed like a stretch.

'Xavia,' Tolland said. 'I've never heard of water pressure alone chemically altering a rock. You're the geologist, what's your take?'

'Well,' she said, flipping through her notes, 'it sounds like water pressure isn't the only factor.' Xavia found a passage and read Pollock's notes verbatim. ' "Oceanic crust in the Mariana Trench, already under enormous hydrostatic pressurization, can find itself further com-pressed by tectonic forces from the region's subduction zones." '

Of course, Tolland thought. The Mariana Trench, in addition to being crushed under seven miles of water, was a subduction zone – the compression line where the Pacific and Indian plates moved toward one another and collided. Combined pressures in the trench could be enormous, and because the area was so remote and dangerous to study, if there were chondrules down there, chances of anyone knowing about it were very slim.

Xavia kept reading. ' "Combined hydrostatic and tectonic pressures could potentially force crust into an elastic or semiliquid state, allowing lighter elements to fuse into chondrulelike structures thought to occur only in space." '

Corky rolled his eyes. 'Impossible.'

Tolland glanced at Corky. 'Is there any alternative explanation for the chondrules in the rock Dr Pollock found?'

'Easy,' Corky said. 'Pollock found an actual *meteorite*. Meteorites fall into the ocean all the time. Pollock would not have suspected it was a meteorite because the fusion crust would have eroded away from years under the water, making it look like a normal rock.' Corky turned to Xavia. 'I don't suppose Pollock had the brains to measure the *nickel* content, did he?'

'Actually, yes,' Xavia fired back, flipping through the notes again. 'Pollock writes: "I was surprised to find the nickel content of the specimen falling within a midrange value not usually associated with terrestrial rocks." '

Tolland and Rachel exchanged startled looks.

Xavia continued reading. ' "Although the quantity of nickel does not fall within the normally acceptable midrange window for meteoritic origin, it is surprisingly *close*." '

Rachel looked troubled. 'How close? Is there any way this ocean rock could be mistaken for a meteorite?'

Xavia shook her head. 'I'm not a chemical petrologist, but as I understand it, there are numerous chemical differences between the rock Pollock found and actual meteorites.'

'What are those differences?' Tolland pressed.

Xavia turned her attention to a graph in her notes. 'According to this, one difference is in the chemical structure of the chondrules themselves. It looks like the titanium/zirconium ratios differ. The titanium/zirconium ratio in the chondrules of the ocean sample showed ultradepleted zirconium.' She looked up. 'Only two parts per million.'

'Two ppm?' Corky blurted. 'Meteorites have *thousands* of times that!'

'Exactly,' Xavia replied. 'Which is why Pollock thinks his sample's chondrules are not from space.'

Tolland leaned over and whispered to Corky, 'Did NASA happen to measure the titanium/zirconium ratio in the Milne rock?'

'Of course not,' Corky sputtered. 'Nobody would ever measure that. It's like looking at a car and measuring the tires' rubber content to confirm you're looking at a car!'

Tolland heaved a sigh and looked back at Xavia. 'If we give you a rock sample with chondrules in it, can you run a test to determine whether these inclusions are meteoric chondrules or . . . one of Pollock's deep ocean compression things?'

Xavia shrugged. 'I suppose. The electron microprobe's accuracy should be close enough. What's this all about, anyway?'

Tolland turned to Corky. 'Give it to her.'

Corky reluctantly pulled the meteorite sample from his pocket and held it out for Xavia.

Xavia's brow furrowed as she took the stone disk. She eyed the fusion crust and then the fossil embedded in the rock. 'My God!' she said, her head rocketing upward. 'This isn't part of . . . ?'

'Yeah,' Tolland said. 'Unfortunately it is.'

106

Alone in her office, Gabrielle Ashe stood at the window, wondering what to do next. Less than an hour ago, she had left NASA feeling full of excitement to share Chris Harper's PODS fraud with the senator.

Now, she wasn't so sure.

According to Yolanda, two independent ABC reporters suspected Sexton of taking SFF bribes. Furthermore, Gabrielle had just learned that Sexton actually *knew* she had snuck into his apartment during the SFF meeting, and yet he had said nothing to her about it?

Gabrielle sighed. Her taxi had long since departed, and although she would call another in a few minutes, she knew there was something she had to do first.

Am I really going to try this?

Gabrielle frowned, knowing she didn't have a choice. She no longer knew whom to trust.

Stepping out of her office, she made her way back into the secretarial lobby and into a wide hallway on the opposite side. At the far end she could see the massive oak doors of Sexton's office flanked by two flags – Old Glory on the right and the Delaware flag on the left. His doors, like those of most Senate offices in the building, were steel reinforced and secured by conventional keys, an electronic key pad entry, and an alarm system.

She knew if she could get inside, even if for only a few minutes, all the answers would be revealed. Moving now toward the heavily secured doors, Gabrielle had no illusions of getting *through* them. She had other plans.

Ten feet from Sexton's office, Gabrielle turned sharply to the right and entered the ladies' room. The fluorescents came on automatically, reflecting harshly off the white tile. As her eyes adjusted, Gabrielle paused, seeing herself in the mirror. As usual, her features looked softer than she'd hoped. Delicate almost. She always felt stronger than she looked.

Are you sure you are ready to do this?

Gabrielle knew Sexton was eagerly awaiting her arrival for a complete rundown on the PODS situation. Unfortunately, she also now realized that Sexton had deftly manipulated her tonight. Gabrielle Ashe did not like being managed. The senator had kept things from her tonight. The question was how much. The answers, she knew, lay inside his office – just on the other side of this restroom wall.

'Five minutes,' Gabrielle said aloud, mustering her resolve.

Moving toward the bathroom's supply closet, she reached up and ran a hand over the door frame. A key clattered to the floor. The cleaning crews at Philip A. Hart were federal employees and seemed to evaporate every time there was a strike of any sort, leaving this bathroom without toilet paper and tampons for weeks at a time. The women of Sexton's office, tired of being caught with their pants down, had taken matters into their own hands and secured a supply room key for 'emergencies.'

Tonight qualifies, she thought.

She opened the closet.

The interior was cramped, packed with cleansers, mops, and shelves of paper supplies. A month ago, Gabrielle had been searching for paper towels when she'd made an unusual discovery. Unable to reach the paper off the top shelf, she'd used the end of a broom to coax a roll to fall. In the process, she'd knocked out a ceiling tile. When she climbed up to replace the tile, she was surprised to hear Senator Sexton's voice.

Crystal clear.

From the echo, she realized the senator was talking to himself while in his office's private bathroom, which apparently was separated from this supply closet by nothing more than removable, fiberboard ceiling tiles.

Now, back in the closet tonight for far more than toilet paper, Gabrielle kicked off her shoes, climbed up the shelves, popped out the fiberboard ceiling tile, and pulled herself up. *So much for national security*, she thought, wondering how many state and federal laws she was about to break.

Lowering herself through the ceiling of Sexton's private restroom, Gabrielle placed her stockinged feet on his cold, porcelain sink and then dropped to the floor. Holding her breath, she exited into Sexton's private office.

His oriental carpets felt soft and warm.

107

Thirty miles away, a black Kiowa gunship chopper tore over the scrub pine treetops of northern Delaware.

Delta-One checked the coordinates locked in the auto navigation system.

Although Rachel's shipboard transmission device and Pickering's cellphone were encrypted to protect the contents of their communication, intercepting *content* had not been the goal when the Delta Force pulse-snitched Rachel's call from sea. Intercepting the caller's *position* had been the goal. Global Positioning Systems and computerized triangulation made pinpointing transmission coordinates a significantly easier task than decrypting the actual content of the call.

Delta-One was always amused to think that most cellphone users had no idea that every time they made a call, a government listening post, if so inclined, could detect their position to within ten feet anywhere on earth – a small hitch the cellphone companies failed to advertise. Tonight, once the Delta Force had gained access to the reception frequencies of William Pickering's cellular phone, they could easily trace the coordinates of his incoming calls.

Flying now on a direct course toward their target, Delta-One closed to within twenty miles. 'Umbrella primed?' he asked, turning to Delta-Two, who was manning the radar and weapons system.

'Affirmative. Awaiting five-mile range.'

Five miles, Delta-One thought. He had to fly this bird well within his target's radar scopes to get within range to use the Kiowa's weapons systems. He had little doubt that someone onboard the *Goya* was nervously watching the skies, and because the Delta Force's current task was to eliminate the target without giving them a chance to radio for help, Delta-One now had to advance on his prey without alarming them.

At fifteen miles out, still safely out of radar range,

Delta-One abruptly turned the Kiowa 35 degrees off course to the west. He climbed to 3,000 feet – small airplane range – and adjusted his speed to 110 knots.

On the deck of the *Goya*, the Coast Guard helicopter's radar scope beeped once as a new contact entered the ten-mile perimeter. The pilot sat up, studying the screen. The contact appeared to be a small cargo plane headed west up the coast.

Probably for Newark.

Although this plane's current trajectory would bring it within four miles of the *Goya*, the flight path obviously was a matter of chance. Nonetheless, being vigilant, the Coast Guard pilot watched the blinking dot trace a slow-moving 110-knot line across the right side of his scope. At its closest point, the plane was about four miles west. As expected, the plane kept moving – heading away from them now.

4.1 miles. 4.2 miles.

The pilot exhaled, relaxing.

And then the strangest thing happened.

'Umbrella now engaged,' Delta-Two called out, giving the thumbs-up from his weapons control seat on the port side of the Kiowa gunship. 'Barrage, modulated noise, and cover pulse are all activated and locked.'

Delta-One took his cue and banked hard to the right, putting the craft on a direct course with the *Goya*. This maneuver would be invisible to the ship's radar.

'Sure beats bales of tinfoil!' Delta-Two called out.

Delta-One agreed. Radar jamming had been invented in WWII when a savvy British airman began throwing bales of hay wrapped in tinfoil out of his plane while on bombing runs. The Germans' radar spotted so many reflective contacts they had no idea what to shoot. The techniques had been improved on substantially since then.

The Kiowa's onboard 'umbrella' radar-jamming system was one of the military's most deadly electronic combat weapons. By broadcasting an umbrella of background noise into the atmosphere above a given set of surface coordinates, the Kiowa could erase the eyes, ears, and voice of their target. Moments ago, all radar screens aboard the *Goya* had most certainly gone blank. By the time the crew realized they needed to call for help, they would be unable to transmit. On a ship, all communications were radio- or microwave-based – no solid phone lines. If the Kiowa got close enough, all of the *Goya*'s communications systems would stop functioning, their carrier signals blotted out by the invisible cloud of thermal noise broadcast in front of the Kiowa like a blinding headlight.

Perfect isolation, Delta-One thought. *They have no defenses.*

Their targets had made a fortunate and cunning escape from the Milne Ice Shelf, but it would not be repeated. In choosing to leave shore, Rachel Sexton and Michael Tolland had chosen poorly. It would be the last bad decision they ever made.

Inside the White House, Zach Herney felt dazed as he sat up in bed holding the telephone receiver. 'Now? Ekstrom wants to speak to me *now*?' Herney squinted again at the bedside clock. 3:17 A.M.

'Yes, Mr President,' the communications officer said. 'He says it's an emergency.'

While Corky and Xavia huddled over the electron microprobe measuring the zirconium content in the chondrules, Rachel followed Tolland across the lab into an adjoining room. Here Tolland turned on another computer. Apparently the oceanographer had one more thing he wanted to check.

As the computer powered up, Tolland turned to Rachel, his mouth poised as if he wanted to say something. He paused.

'What is it?' Rachel asked, surprised how physically drawn to him she felt, even in the midst of all this chaos. She wished she could block it all out and be with him – just for a minute.

'I owe you an apology,' Tolland said, looking remorseful.

'For what?'

'On the deck? The hammerheads? I was excited. Sometimes I forget how frightening the ocean can be to a lot of people.'

Face to face with him, Rachel felt like a teenager standing on the doorstep with a new boyfriend. 'Thanks. No problem at all. Really.' Something inside her sensed Tolland wanted to kiss her.

After a beat, he turned shyly away. 'I know. You want to get to shore. We should get to work.'

'For now.' Rachel smiled softly.

'For now,' Tolland repeated, taking a seat at the computer.

Rachel exhaled, standing close behind now, savoring the privacy of the small lab. She watched Tolland navigate a series of files. 'What are we doing?'

'Checking the database for big ocean lice. I want to see if we can find any prehistoric marine fossils that resemble what we saw in the NASA meteorite.' He pulled up a search page with bold letters across the top: PROJECT DIVERSITAS.

Scrolling through the menus, Tolland explained, 'Diversitas is essentially a continuously updated index of oceanic biodata. When a marine biologist discovers a new ocean species or fossil, he can toot his horn and share his find by uploading data and photos to a central databank. Because there's so much new data discovered on a weekly basis, this is really the only way to keep research up-to-date.'

Rachel watched Tolland navigating the menus. 'So you're accessing the Web now?'

'No. Internet access is tricky at sea. We store all this data onboard on an enormous array of optical drives in the other room. Every time we're in port, we tie into Project Diversitas and update our databank with the newest finds. This way, we can access data at sea without a Web connection, and the data is never more than a month or two out of date.' Tolland chuckled as he began typing search keywords into the computer. 'You've probably heard of the controversial music file-sharing program called Napster?'

Rachel nodded.

'Diversitas is considered the marine biologist's version of Napster. We call it LOBSTER – Lonely Oceanic Biologists Sharing Totally Eccentric Research.'

Rachel laughed. Even in this tense situation, Michael Tolland exuded a wry humor that eased her fears. She was beginning to realize she'd had entirely too little laughter in her life lately.

'Our database is enormous,' Tolland said, completing the entry of his descriptive keywords. 'Over ten tera-bytes of descriptions and photos. There's information in here nobody has ever seen – and nobody ever will. Ocean species are simply too numerous.' He clicked the 'search' button. 'Okay, let's see if anyone has ever seen an oceanic fossil similar to our little space bug.'

After a few seconds, the screen refreshed, revealing four listings of fossilized animals. Tolland clicked on each listing, one by one and examined the photos. None looked remotely like the fossils in the Milne meteorite.

Tolland frowned. 'Let's try something else.' He removed the word 'fossil' from his search string and hit 'search.' 'We'll search all *living* species. Maybe we can find a living descendant that has some of the physiological characteristics of the Milne fossil.'

The screen refreshed.

Again Tolland frowned. The computer had returned hundreds of entries. He sat a moment, stroking his now stubble-darkened chin. 'Okay, this is too much. Let's refine the search.'

Rachel watched as he accessed a drop-down menu marked 'habitat.' The list of options looked endless: tide pool, marsh, lagoon, reef, mid oceanic ridge, sulfur vents. Tolland scrolled down the list and chose an option that read: DESTRUCTIVE MARGINS/OCEANIC TRENCHES.

Smart, Rachel realized. Tolland was limiting his search only to species that lived near the environment where these chondrulelike features were hypothesized to form.

The page refreshed. This time Tolland smiled. 'Great. Only three entries.'

Rachel squinted at the first name on the list. *Limulus poly . . . something.*

Tolland clicked the entry. A photo appeared; the creature looked like an oversized horseshoe crab without a tail.

'Nope,' Tolland said, returning to the previous page.

Rachel eyed the second item on the list. *Shrimpus Uglius From Hellus.* She was confused. 'Is that name for real?'

Tolland chuckled. 'No. It's a new species not yet classified. The guy who discovered it has a sense of humor. He's suggesting *Shrimpus Uglius* as the official taxonomical classification.' Tolland clicked open the photo, revealing an exceptionally ugly shrimplike creature with whiskers and fluorescent pink antennae.

'Aptly named,' Tolland said. 'But not our space bug.' He returned to the index. 'The final offering is . . .' He clicked on the third entry, and the page came up.

'*Bathynomous giganteus . . .*' Tolland read aloud as the text appeared. The photograph loaded. A full-color close-up.

Rachel jumped. 'My God!' The creature staring back at her gave her chills.

Tolland drew a low breath. 'Oh boy. This guy looks kind of familiar.'

Rachel nodded, speechless. *Bathynomous giganteus.* The creature resembled a giant swimming louse. It looked very similar to the fossil species in the NASA rock.

'There are some subtle differences,' Tolland said, scrolling down to some anatomical diagrams and sketches. 'But it's damn close. Especially considering it has had one hundred and ninety million years to evolve.'

Close is right, Rachel thought. *Too close.*

Tolland read the description on the screen: '"Thought to be one of the oldest species in the ocean, the rare and recently classified species *Bathynomous giganteus* is a deepwater scavenging isopod resembling a large pill bug. Up to two feet in length, this species exhibits a chitonous exoskeleton segemented into head, thorax, abdomen. It possesses paired appendages, antennae, and compound eyes like those of land-dwelling insects. This bottom-dwelling forager has no known predators and lives in barren pelagic environments previously thought to be uninhabitable."' Tolland glanced up. 'Which could explain the lack of other fossils in the sample!'

Rachel stared at the creature on-screen, excited and yet uncertain she completely understood what all of this meant.

'Imagine,' Tolland said excitedly, 'that one hundred and ninety million years ago, a brood of these *Bathynomous* creatures got buried in a deep ocean mud slide. As the mud turns into rock, the bugs get fossilized in stone. Simultaneously, the ocean floor, which is continuously moving like a slow conveyer belt toward the oceanic trenches, carries the fossils into a high-pressure zone where the rock forms chondrules!' Tolland was talking faster now. 'And if part of the fossilized, chondrulized crust broke off and ended up on the trench's accretionary wedge, which is not at all uncommon, it would be in a perfect position to be discovered!'

'But if NASA . . .' Rachel stammered. 'I mean, if this is all a lie, NASA *must* have known that sooner or later someone would find out this fossil resembles a sea creature, right? I mean *we* just found out!'

Tolland began printing the *Bathynomous* photos on a laser printer. 'I don't know. Even if someone stepped forward and pointed out the similarities between the fossils and a living sea louse, their physiologies are not identical. It almost proves NASA's case more strongly.'

Rachel suddenly understood. 'Panspermia.' *Life on earth was seeded from space.*

'Exactly. Similarities between space organisms and earth organisms make excellent scientific sense. This sea louse actually strengthens NASA's case.'

'Except if the meteorite's authenticity is in question.'

Tolland nodded. 'Once the meteorite comes into question, then everything collapses. Our sea louse turns from NASA friend to NASA linchpin.'

Rachel stood in silence as the *Bathynomous* pages rolled out of the printer. She tried to tell herself this was all an honest NASA mistake, but she knew it was not. People who made honest mistakes didn't try to kill people.

The nasal voice of Corky echoed suddenly across the lab. *'Impossible!'*

Both Tolland and Rachel turned.

'Measure the damn ratio again! It makes no sense!'

Xavia came hurrying in with a computer printout clutched in her hand. Her face was ashen. 'Mike, I don't know how to say this . . .' Her voice cracked. 'The titanium/zirconium ratios we're seeing in this sample?' She cleared her throat. 'It's pretty obvious that NASA made a huge mistake. Their meteorite is an ocean rock.'

Tolland and Rachel looked at each other but neither spoke a word. They knew. Just like that, all the suspicions and doubts had swelled up like the crest of a wave, reaching the breaking point.

Tolland nodded, a sadness in his eyes. 'Yeah. Thanks, Xavia.'

'But I don't understand,' Xavia said. 'The fusion crust . . . the location in the ice—'

'We'll explain on the way to shore,' Tolland said. 'We're leaving.'

Quickly, Rachel collected all the papers and evidence they now had. The evidence was shockingly conclusive: the GPR printout showing the insertion shaft in the Milne Ice Shelf; photos of a living sea louse resembling NASA's fossil; Dr Pollock's article on ocean chondrules; and microprobe data showing ultra-depleted titanium in the meteorite.

The conclusion was undeniable. *Fraud.*

Tolland looked at the stack of papers in Rachel's hands and heaved a melancholy sigh. 'Well, I'd say William Pickering has his proof.'

Rachel nodded, again wondering why Pickering had not answered his phone.

Tolland lifted the receiver of a nearby phone, holding it out for her. 'You want to try him again from here?'

'No, let's get moving. I'll try to contact him from the chopper.' Rachel had already decided if she could not make contact with Pickering, she'd have the Coast Guard fly them directly to the NRO, only about 180 miles.

Tolland began to hang up the phone, but he paused. Looking confused, he listened to the receiver, frowning. 'Bizarre. No dial tone.'

'What do you mean?' Rachel said, wary now.

'Weird,' Tolland said. 'Direct COMSAT lines never lose carrier—'

'Mr Tolland?' The Coast Guard pilot came rushing into the lab, his face white.

'What is it?' Rachel demanded. 'Is someone coming?'

'That's the problem,' the pilot said. 'I don't know. All onboard radar and communications have just gone dead.'

Rachel stuffed the papers deep inside her shirt. 'Get in the helicopter. We're leaving. NOW!'

109

Gabrielle's heart was racing as she crossed the darkened office of Senator Sexton. The room was as expansive as it was elegant – ornate wood-paneled walls, oil paintings, Persian carpets, leather rivet chairs, and a gargantuan mahogany desk. The room was lit only by the eerie neon glow of Sexton's computer screen.

Gabrielle moved toward his desk.

Senator Sexton had embraced the 'digital office' to maniacal proportions, eschewing the overflow of file cabinets for the compact, searchable simplicity of his personal computer, into which he fed enormous amounts of information – digitized meeting notes, scanned articles, speeches, brain storms. Sexton's computer was his sacred ground, and he kept his office locked at all times to protect it. He even refused to connect to the Internet for fear of hackers infiltrating his sacred digital vault.

A year ago Gabrielle would never have believed any politician would be stupid enough to store copies of self-incriminating documents, but Washington had taught her a lot. *Information is power*. Gabrielle had been amazed to learn that a common practice among politicians who accepted questionable campaign contributions was to keep actual *proof* of those donations – letters, bank records, receipts, logs – all hidden away in a safe place. This counterblackmail tactic, euphemistically known in Washington as 'Siamese insurance,' protected candidates from donors who felt their generosity somehow authorized them to assert undue political pressure on a candidate. If a contributor got too demanding, the candidate could simply produce evidence of the illegal donation and remind the donor that *both* parties had broken the law. The evidence ensured that candidates and donors were joined at the hip forever – like Siamese twins.

Gabrielle slipped behind the senator's desk and sat down. She took a deep breath, looking at his computer. *If the senator is accepting SFF bribes, any evidence would be in here.*

Sexton's computer screensaver was an ongoing slideshow of the White House and its grounds created for him by one of his gung-ho staffers who was big into visualization and positive thinking. Around the images crawled a ticker-tape banner that read: *President of the United States Sedgewick Sexton . . . President of the United States Sedgewick Sexton . . . President of the . . .*

Gabrielle jostled the mouse, and a security dialogue box came up.

ENTER PASSWORD:

She expected this. It would not be a problem. Last week, Gabrielle had entered Sexton's office just as the senator was sitting down and logging onto his computer. She saw him type three short keystrokes in rapid succession.

'*That's* a password?' she challenged from the doorway as she walked in.

Sexton glanced up. 'What?'

'And here I thought you were concerned about
security,' Gabrielle scolded good-naturedly. 'Your password's only three keys? I thought the tech guys told us
all to use at least six.'

'The tech guys are teenagers. They should try
remembering six random letters when they're over
forty. Besides, the door has an alarm. Nobody can get
in.'

Gabrielle walked toward him, smiling. 'What if someone slipped in while you're in the loo?'

'And tried every combination of passwords?' He gave
a skeptical laugh. 'I'm slow in the bathroom, but not
that slow.'

'Dinner at Davide says I can guess your password in
ten seconds.'

Sexton looked intrigued and amused. 'You can't
afford Davide, Gabrielle.'

'So you're saying you're chicken?'

Sexton appeared almost sorry for her as he accepted
the challenge. 'Ten seconds?' He logged off and
motioned for Gabrielle to sit down and give it a try.
'You know I only order the saltimbocca at Davide. And
that ain't cheap.'

She shrugged as she sat down. 'It's *your* money.'

ENTER PASSWORD:

'Ten seconds,' Sexton reminded.

Gabrielle had to laugh. She would need only two.
Even from the doorway she could see that Sexton
had entered his three-key password in very rapid
succession using only his index finger. *Obviously all the
same key. Not wise.* She could also see that his hand had

477

been positioned over the far left side of his keyboard – cutting the possible alphabet down to only about nine letters. Choosing the letter was simple; Sexton had always loved the triple alliteration of his title. Senator Sedgewick Sexton.

Never underestimate the ego of a politician.

She typed SSS, and the screensaver evaporated.

Sexton's jaw hit the floor.

That had been last week. Now, as Gabrielle faced his computer again, she was certain Sexton would not have taken time yet to figure out how to set up a different password. *Why would he? He trusts me implicitly.*

She typed in SSS.

INVALID PASSWORD – ACCESS DENIED

Gabrielle stared in shock.

Apparently she had overestimated her senator's level of trust.

110

The attack came without warning. Low out of the southwest sky above the *Goya*, the lethal silhouette of a gunship helicopter bore down like a giant wasp. Rachel had no doubt what it was, or why it was here.

Through the darkness, a staccato burst from the nose of the chopper sent a torrent of bullets chewing across the *Goya*'s fiberglass deck, slashing a line across the stern. Rachel dove for cover too late and felt the searing slash of a bullet graze her arm. She hit the ground hard, then rolled, scrambling to get behind the bulbous transparent dome of the Triton submersible.

A thundering of rotors exploded overhead as the chopper swooped past the ship. The noise evaporated with an eerie hiss as the chopper rocketed out over the ocean and began a wide bank for a second pass.

Lying trembling on the deck, Rachel held her arm and looked back at Tolland and Corky. Apparently having lunged to cover behind a storage structure, the two men were now staggering to their feet, their eyes scanning the skies in terror. Rachel pulled herself to her knees. The entire world suddenly seemed to be moving in slow motion.

Crouched behind the transparent curvature of the Triton sub, Rachel looked in panic toward their only means of escape – the Coast Guard helicopter. Xavia was already climbing into the chopper's cabin, frantically waving for everyone to get aboard. Rachel could see the pilot lunging into the cockpit, wildly throwing switches and levers. The blades began to turn . . . ever so slowly.

Too slowly.

Hurry!

Rachel felt herself standing now, preparing to run, wondering if she could make it across the deck before the attackers made another pass. Behind her, she heard Corky and Tolland dashing toward her and the waiting helicopter. *Yes! Hurry!*

Then she saw it.

A hundred yards out, up in the sky, materializing out of empty darkness, a pencil-thin beam of red light slanted across the night, searching the *Goya*'s deck. Then, finding its mark, the beam came to a stop on the side of the waiting Coast Guard chopper.

The image took only an instant to register. In that horrific moment, Rachel felt all the action on the deck of the *Goya* blur into a collage of shapes and sounds. Tolland and Corky dashing toward her – Xavia motioning wildly in the helicopter – the stark red laser slicing across the night sky.

It was too late.

Rachel spun back toward Corky and Tolland, who were running full speed now toward the helicopter. She lunged outward into their path, arms outstretched trying to stop them. The collision felt like a train wreck as the three of them crashed to the deck in a tangle of arms and legs.

In the distance, a flash of white light appeared. Rachel watched in disbelief and horror as a perfectly straight line of exhaust fire followed the path of the laser beam directly toward the helicopter.

When the Hellfire missile slammed into the fuselage, the helicopter exploded apart like a toy. The concussion wave of heat and noise thundered across the deck as flaming shrapnel rained down. The helicopter's flaming skeleton lurched backward on its shattered tail, teetered a moment, and then fell off the back of the ship, crashing into the ocean in a hissing cloud of steam.

Rachel closed her eyes, unable to breathe. She could hear the flaming wreckage gurgling and sputtering as it sank, being dragged away from the *Goya* by the heavy currents. In the chaos, Michael Tolland's voice was yelling. Rachel felt his powerful hands trying to pull her to her feet. But she could not move.

The Coast Guard pilot and Xavia are dead.

We're next.

The weather on the Milne Ice Shelf had settled, and the habisphere was quiet. Even so, NASA administrator Lawrence Ekstrom had not even tried to sleep. He had spent the hours alone, pacing the dome, staring into the extraction pit, running his hands over the grooves in the giant charred rock.

Finally, he'd made up his mind.

Now he sat at the videophone in the habisphere's PSC tank and looked into the weary eyes of the President of the United States. Zach Herney was wearing a bathrobe and did not look at all amused. Ekstrom knew he would be significantly less amused when he learned what Ekstrom had to tell him.

When Ekstrom finished talking, Herney had an uncomfortable look on his face – as if he thought he must still be too asleep to have understood correctly.

'Hold on,' Herney said. 'We must have a bad connection. Did you just tell me that NASA intercepted this meteorite's coordinates from an emergency radio transmission – and then *pretended* that PODS found the meteorite?'

Ekstrom was silent, alone in the dark, willing his body to awake from this nightmare.

The silence clearly did not sit well with the President. 'For Christ's sake, Larry, tell me this isn't true!'

Ekstrom's mouth went dry. 'The meteorite was found, Mr President. That is all that's relevant here.'

'I said tell me this is not *true!*'

The hush swelled to a dull roar in Ekstrom's ears. *I had to tell him*, Ekstrom told himself. *It's going to get worse before it gets better.* 'Mr President, the PODS failure was killing you in the polls, sir. When we intercepted a radio transmission that mentioned a large meteorite lodged in the ice, we saw a chance to get back in the fight.'

Herney sounded stunned. 'By faking a PODS discovery?'

'PODS was going to be up and running soon, but not soon enough for the election. The polls were slipping, and Sexton was slamming NASA, so—'

'Are you insane? You lied to me, Larry!'

'The opportunity was staring us in the face, sir. I decided to take it. We intercepted the radio transmission of the Canadian who made the meteorite discovery. He died in a storm. Nobody else knew the meteorite was there. PODS was orbiting in the area. NASA needed a victory. We had the coordinates.'

'Why are you telling me this now?'

'I thought you should know.'

'Do you know what Sexton would do with this information if he found out?'

Ekstrom preferred not to think about it.

'He'd tell the world that NASA and the White House lied to the American people! And you know what, he'd be right!'

'You did not lie, sir, I did. And I will step down if—'

'Larry, you're missing the point. I've tried to run this presidency on truth and decency! Goddamn it! Tonight was clean. Dignified. Now I find out I lied to the world?'

'Only a small lie, sir.'

'There's no such thing, Larry,' Herney said, steaming.

Ekstrom felt the tiny room closing in around him. There was so much more to tell the President, but Ekstrom could see it should wait until morning. 'I'm sorry to have woken you, sir. I just thought you should know.'

Across town, Sedgewick Sexton took another hit of cognac and paced his apartment with rising irritation.

Where the hell is Gabrielle?

112

Gabrielle Ashe sat in the darkness at Senator Sexton's desk and gave his computer a despondent scowl.

INVALID PASSWORD – ACCESS DENIED

She had tried several other passwords that seemed likely possibilities, but none had worked. After searching the office for any unlocked drawers or stray clues, Gabrielle had all but given up. She was about to leave when she spotted something odd, shimmering on Sexton's desk calendar. Someone had outlined the date of the election in a red, white, and blue glitter pen. Certainly not the senator. Gabrielle pulled the calendar closer. Emblazoned across the date was a frilly, glittering exclamation: POTUS!

Sexton's ebullient secretary had apparently glitter-painted some more positive thinking for him for election day. The acronym POTUS was the U.S. Secret Service's code name for President of the United States. On election day, if all went well, Sexton would become the new POTUS.

Preparing to leave, Gabrielle realigned the calendar on his desk and stood up. She paused suddenly, glancing back at the computer screen.

ENTER PASSWORD:

She looked again at the calendar.

POTUS.

She felt a sudden surge of hope. Something about POTUS struck Gabrielle as being a perfect Sexton password. *Simple, positive, self-referential.*

She quickly typed in the letters.

POTUS

Holding her breath, she hit 'return.' The computer beeped.

INVALID PASSWORD – ACCESS DENIED

Slumping, Gabrielle gave up. She headed back toward the bathroom door to exit the way she had come. She was halfway across the room, when her cellphone rang. She was already on edge, and the sound startled her. Stopping short, she pulled out her phone and glanced up to check the time on Sexton's prized Jourdain grandfather clock. *Almost 4:00 A.M.* At this hour, Gabrielle knew the caller could only be Sexton. He was obviously wondering where the hell she was. *Do I pick up or let it ring?* If she answered, Gabrielle would have to lie. But if she didn't, Sexton would get suspicious.

She took the call. 'Hello?'

'Gabrielle?' Sexton sounded impatient. 'What's keeping you?'

'The FDR Memorial,' Gabrielle said. 'The taxi got hemmed in, and now we're—'

'You don't sound like you're in a taxi.'

'No,' she said, her blood pumping now. 'I'm not. I decided to stop by my office and pick up some NASA

484

documents that might be relevant to PODS. I'm having some trouble finding them.'

'Well, hurry up. I want to schedule a press conference for the morning, and we need to talk specifics.'

'I'm coming soon,' she said.

There was a pause on the line. 'You're in your office?' He sounded suddenly confused.

'Yeah. Another ten minutes and I'll be on my way over.'

Another pause. 'Okay. I'll see you soon.'

Gabrielle hung up, too preoccupied to notice the loud and distinctive triple-tick of Sexton's prized Jourdain grandfather clock only a few feet away.

113

Michael Tolland did not realize Rachel was hurt until he saw the blood on her arm as he pulled her to cover behind the Triton. He sensed from the catatonic look on her face that she was not aware of any pain. Steadying her, Tolland wheeled to find Corky. The astrophysicist scrambled across the deck to join them, his eyes blank with terror.

We've got to find cover, Tolland thought, the horror of what had just happened not yet fully registering. Instinctively, his eyes raced up the tiers of decks above them. The stairs leading up to the bridge were all in the open, and the bridge itself was a glass box – a transparent bull's-eye from the air. Going up was suicide, which left only one other direction to go.

For a fleeting instant, Tolland turned a hopeful gaze

to the Triton submersible, wondering perhaps if he could get everyone underwater, away from the bullets.

Absurd. The Triton had room for one person, and the deployment winch took a good ten minutes to lower the sub through the trap door in the deck to the ocean thirty feet below. Besides, without properly charged batteries and compressors, the Triton would be dead in the water.

'Here they come!' Corky shouted, his voice shrill with fear as he pointed into the sky.

Tolland didn't even look up. He pointed to a nearby bulkhead, where an aluminum ramp descended belowdecks. Corky apparently needed no encouragement. Keeping his head low, Corky scurried toward the opening and disappeared down the incline. Tolland put a firm arm around Rachel's waist and followed. The two of them disappeared belowdecks just as the helicopter returned, spraying bullets overhead.

Tolland helped Rachel down the grated ramp to the suspended platform at the bottom. As they arrived, Tolland could feel Rachel's body go suddenly rigid. He wheeled, fearing maybe she'd been hit by a ricocheting bullet.

When he saw her face, he knew it was something else. Tolland followed her petrified gaze downward and immediately understood.

Rachel stood motionless, her legs refusing to move. She was staring down at the bizarre world beneath her.

Because of its SWATH design, the *Goya* had no hull but rather struts like a giant catamaran. They had just descended through the deck onto a grated catwalk that hung above an open chasm, thirty feet straight down to the raging sea. The noise was deafening here, reverberating off the underside of the deck. Adding to Rachel's terror was the fact that the ship's underwater spotlights were still illuminated, casting a greenish effulgence deep into the ocean directly beneath her. She found herself gazing down at six or seven ghostly silhouettes in the water. Enormous hammerhead sharks, their long shadows swimming in place against the current – rubbery bodies flexing back and forth.

Tolland's voice was in her ear. 'Rachel, you're okay. Eyes straight ahead. I'm right behind you.' His hands were reaching around from behind, gently trying to coax her clenched fists off the banister. It was then that Rachel saw the crimson droplet of blood roll off her arm and fall through the grating. Her eyes followed the drip as it plummeted toward the sea. Although she never saw it hit the water, she knew the instant it happened because all at once the hammerheads spun in unison, thrusting with their powerful tails, crashing together in a roiling frenzy of teeth and fins.

Enhanced telencephalon olfactory lobes . . .

They smell blood a mile away.

'Eyes straight ahead,' Tolland repeated, his voice strong and reassuring. 'I'm right behind you.'

Rachel felt his hands on her hips now, urging her forward. Blocking out the void beneath her, Rachel started down the catwalk. Somewhere above she could hear the rotors of the chopper again. Corky was already well out in front of them, reeling across the catwalk in a kind of drunken panic.

Tolland called out to him. 'All the way to the far strut, Corky! Down the stairs!'

Rachel could now see where they were headed. Up ahead, a series of switchback ramps descended. At water level, a narrow, shelflike deck extended the length of the *Goya*. Jutting off this deck were several small, suspended docks, creating a kind of miniature marina stationed beneath the ship. A large sign read:

DIVE AREA
Swimmers May Surface without Warning
– Boats Proceed with Caution –

Rachel could only assume Michael did not intend for them to do any swimming. Her trepidation intensified when Tolland stopped at a bank of wire-mesh storage lockers flanking the catwalk. He pulled open the doors to reveal hanging wetsuits, snorkels, flippers, life jackets, and spearguns. Before she could protest, he reached in and grabbed a flare gun. 'Let's go.'

They were moving again.

Up ahead, Corky had reached the switchback ramps and was already halfway down. 'I see it!' he shouted, his voice sounding almost joyous over the raging water.

See what? Rachel wondered as Corky ran along the narrow walkway. All she could see was a shark-infested ocean lapping dangerously close. Tolland urged her forward, and suddenly Rachel could see what Corky was so excited about. At the far end of the decking below, a small powerboat was moored. Corky ran toward it.

Rachel stared. *Outrun a helicopter in a motorboat?*

'It has a radio,' Tolland said. 'And if we can get far enough away from the helicopter's jamming . . .'

Rachel did not hear another word he said. She had just spied something that made her blood run cold. 'Too late,' she croaked, extending a trembling finger. *We're finished . . .*

*   *   *

When Tolland turned, he knew in an instant it was over.

At the far end of the ship, like a dragon peering into the opening of a cave, the black helicopter had dropped down low and was facing them. For an instant, Tolland thought it was going to fly directly at them through the center of the boat. But the helicopter began to turn at an angle, taking aim.

Tolland followed the direction of the gun barrels. *No!*

Crouched beside the powerboat untying the moorings, Corky glanced up just as the machine guns beneath the chopper erupted in a blaze of thunder. Corky lurched as if hit. Wildly, he scrambled over the gunwale and dove into the boat, sprawled himself on the floor for cover. The guns stopped. Tolland could see Corky crawling deeper into the powerboat. The lower part of his right leg was covered with blood. Crouched below the dash, Corky reached up and fumbled across the controls until his fingers found the key. The boat's 250 hp Mercury engine roared to life.

An instant later, a red laser beam appeared, emanating from the nose of the hovering chopper, targeting the powerboat with a missile.

Tolland reacted on instinct, aiming the only weapon he had.

The flare gun in his hand hissed when he pulled the trigger, and a blinding streak tore away on a horizontal trajectory beneath the ship, heading directly toward the chopper. Even so, Tolland sensed he had acted too late. As the streaking flare bore down on the helicopter's windshield, the rocket launcher beneath the chopper emitted its own flash of light. At the same exact instant that the missile launched, the aircraft veered sharply and pulled up out of sight to avoid the incoming flare.

'Look out!' Tolland yelled, yanking Rachel down onto the catwalk.

The missile sailed off course, just missing Corky, coming the length of the *Goya* and slamming into the base of the strut thirty feet beneath Rachel and Tolland.

The sound was apocalyptic. Water and flames erupted beneath them. Bits of twisted metal flew in the air and scattered the catwalk beneath them. Metal on metal ground together as the ship shifted, finding a new balance, slightly askew.

As the smoke cleared, Tolland could see that one of the *Goya*'s four main struts had been severely damaged. Powerful currents tore past the pontoon, threatening to break it off. The spiral stairway descending to the lower deck looked to be hanging by a thread.

'Come on!' Tolland yelled, urging Rachel toward it. *We've got to get down!*

But they were too late. With a surrendering crack, the stairs peeled away from the damaged strut and crashed into the sea.

Over the ship, Delta-One grappled with the controls of the Kiowa helicopter and got it back under control. Momentarily blinded by the incoming flare, he had reflexively pulled up, causing the Hellfire missile to miss its mark. Cursing, he hovered now over the bow of the ship and prepared to drop back down and finish the job.

Eliminate all passengers. The controller's demands had been clear.

'Shit! Look!' Delta-Two yelled from the rear seat, pointing out the window. 'Speedboat!'

Delta-One spun and saw a bullet-riddled Crestliner

speedboat skimming away from the *Goya* into the darkness.

He had a decision to make.

114

Corky's bloody hands gripped the wheel of the Crestliner Phantom 2100 as it pounded out across the sea. He rammed the throttle all the way forward, trying to eke out maximum speed. It was not until this moment that he felt the searing pain. He looked down and saw his right leg spurting blood. He instantly felt dizzy.

Propping himself against the wheel, he turned and looked back at the *Goya*, willing the helicopter to follow him. With Tolland and Rachel trapped up on the catwalk, Corky had not been able to reach them. He'd been forced to make a snap decision.

Divide and conquer.

Corky knew if he could lure the chopper far enough away from the *Goya*, maybe Tolland and Rachel could radio for help. Unfortunately, as he looked over his shoulder at the illuminated ship, Corky could see the chopper still hovering there, as if undecided.

Come on, you bastards! Follow me!

But the helicopter did not follow. Instead it banked over the stern of the *Goya*, aligned itself, and dropped down, landing on the deck. *No!* Corky watched in horror, now realizing he'd left Tolland and Rachel behind to be killed.

Knowing it was now up to him to radio for help,

Corky groped the dashboard and found the radio. He flicked the power switch. Nothing happened. No lights. No static. He turned the volume knob all the way up. Nothing. *Come on!* Letting go of the wheel, he knelt down for a look. His leg screamed in pain as he bent down. His eyes focused on the radio. He could not believe what he was looking at. The dashboard had been strafed by bullets, and the radio dial was shattered. Loose wires hung out the front. He stared, incredulous.

Of all the goddamned luck . . .

Weak-kneed, Corky stood back up, wondering how things could get any worse. As he looked back at the *Goya*, he got his answer. Two armed soldiers jumped out of the chopper onto the deck. Then the chopper lifted off again, turning in Corky's direction and coming after him at full speed.

Corky slumped. *Divide and conquer*. Apparently he was not the only one with that bright idea tonight.

As Delta-Three made his way across the deck and approached the grated ramp leading belowdecks, he heard a woman shouting somewhere beneath him. He turned and motioned to Delta-Two that he was going belowdecks to check it out. His partner nodded, remaining behind to cover the upper level. The two men could stay in contact via CrypTalk; the Kiowa's jamming system ingeniously left an obscure bandwidth open for their own communications.

Clutching his snub-nose machine gun, Delta-Three moved quietly toward the ramp that led belowdecks. With the vigilance of a trained killer, he began inching downward, gun leveled.

The incline provided limited visibility, and Delta-

492

Three crouched low for a better view. He could hear the shouting more clearly now. He kept descending. Halfway down the stairs he could now make out the twisted maze of walkways attached to the underside of the *Goya*. The shouting grew louder.

Then he saw her. Midway across the traversing catwalk, Rachel Sexton was peering over a railing and calling desperately toward the water for Michael Tolland.

Did Tolland fall in? Perhaps in the blast?

If so, Delta-Three's job would be even easier than expected. He only needed to descend another couple of feet to have an open shot. Shooting fish in a barrel. His only vague concern was Rachel standing near an open equipment locker, which meant she might have a weapon – a speargun or a shark rifle – although neither would be any match for his machine gun. Confident he was in control of the situation, Delta-Three leveled his weapon and took another step down. Rachel Sexton was almost in perfect view now. He raised the gun.

One more step.

The flurry of movement came from beneath him, under the stairs. Delta-Three was more confused than frightened as he looked down and saw Michael Tolland thrusting an aluminum pole out toward his feet. Although Delta-Three had been tricked, he almost laughed at this lame attempt to trip him up.

Then he felt the tip of the stick connect with his heel.

A blast of white-hot pain shot through his body as his right foot exploded out from under him by a blistering impact. His balance gone, Delta-Three flailed, tumbling down the stairs. His machine gun clattered down the ramp and went overboard as he collapsed on the catwalk. In anguish, he curled up to grip his right foot, but it was no longer there.

Tolland was standing over his attacker immediately with his hands still clenching the smoking bang-stick – a five-foot Powerhead Shark-Control Device. The aluminum pole had been tipped with a pressure-sensitive, twelve-gauge shotgun shell and was intended for self-defense in the event of shark attack. Tolland had reloaded the bang-stick with another shell, and now held the jagged, smoldering point to his attacker's Adam's apple. The man lay on his back as if paralyzed, staring up at Tolland with an expression of astonished rage and agony.

Rachel came running up the catwalk. The plan was for her to take the man's machine gun, but unfortunately the weapon had gone over the edge of the catwalk into the ocean.

The communications device on the man's belt crackled. The voice coming out was robotic. 'Delta-Three? Come in. I heard a shot.'

The man made no move to answer.

The device crackled again. 'Delta-Three? Confirm. Do you need backup?'

Almost immediately, a new voice crackled over the line. It was also robotic but distinguishable by the sound of a helicopter noise in the background. 'This is Delta-One,' the pilot said. 'I'm in pursuit of the departing vessel. Delta-Three, confirm. Are you down? Do you need backup?'

Tolland pressed the bang-stick into the man's throat. 'Tell the helicopter to back off that speedboat. If they kill my friend, you die.'

The soldier winced in pain as he lifted his communication device to his lips. He looked directly at Tolland as he pressed the button and spoke. 'Delta-Three here. I'm fine. Destroy the departing vessel.'

115

Gabrielle Ashe returned to Sexton's private bathroom, preparing to climb back out of his office. Sexton's phone call had left her feeling anxious. He had definitely hesitated when she told him she was in her office – as if he knew somehow she was lying. Either way, she'd failed to get into Sexton's computer and now was unsure of her next move.

Sexton is waiting.

As she climbed up onto the sink, getting ready to pull herself up, she heard something clatter to the tile floor. She looked down, irritated to see that she'd knocked off a pair of Sexton's cuff links that had apparently been sitting on the edge of the sink.

Leave things exactly as you found them.

Climbing back down, Gabrielle picked up the cuff links and put them back on the sink. As she began to climb back up, she paused, glancing again at the cuff links. On any other night, Gabrielle would have ignored them, but tonight their monogram caught her attention. Like most of Sexton's monogrammed items, they had two intertwining letters. SS. Gabrielle flashed on Sexton's initial computer password – SSS. She pictured his calendar . . . POTUS . . . and the White House screensaver with its optimistic ticker tape crawling around the screen ad infinitum.

President of the United States Sedgewick Sexton . . . President of the United States Sedgewick Sexton . . . President of the . . .

Gabrielle stood a moment and wondered. *Could he be that confident?*

Knowing it would take only an instant to find out, she hurried back into Sexton's office, went to his computer, and typed in a seven-letter password.

POTUSSS

The screensaver evaporated instantly.

She stared, incredulous.

Never underestimate the ego of a politician.

116

Corky Marlinson was no longer at the helm of the Crestliner Phantom as it raced into the night. He knew the boat would travel in a straight line with or without him at the wheel. *The path of least resistance . . .*

Corky was in the back of the bouncing boat, trying to assess the damage to his leg. A bullet had entered the front part of his calf, just missing his shinbone. There was no exit wound on the back of his calf, so he knew the bullet must still be lodged in his leg. Foraging around for something to stem the bleeding, he found nothing – some fins, a snorkel, and a couple of life jackets. No first-aid kit. Frantically, Corky opened a small utility chest and found some tools, rags, duct tape, oil, and other maintenance items. He looked at his bloody leg and wondered how far he had to go to be out of shark territory.

A hell of a lot farther than this.

Delta-One kept the Kiowa chopper low over the ocean as he scanned the darkness for the departing Crestliner. Assuming the fleeing boat would head for shore and attempt to put as much distance as possible between itself and the *Goya*, Delta-One had followed the Crestliner's original trajectory away from the *Goya*.

I should have overtaken him by now.

Normally, tracking the fleeing boat would be a simple matter of using radar, but with the Kiowa's jamming systems transmitting an umbrella of thermal noise for several miles, his radar was worthless. Turning off the jamming system was not an option until he got word that everyone onboard the *Goya* was dead. No emergency phone calls would be leaving the *Goya* this evening.

This meteorite secret dies. Right here. Right now.

Fortunately, Delta-One had other means of tracking. Even against this bizarre backdrop of heated ocean, pinpointing a powerboat's thermal imprint was simple. He turned on his thermal scanner. The ocean around him registered a warm 95 degrees. Fortunately, the emissions of a racing 250 hp outboard engine were hundreds of degrees hotter.

Corky Marlinson's leg and foot felt numb.

Not knowing what else to do, he had wiped down his injured calf with the rag and wrapped the wound in layer after layer of duct tape. By the time the tape was gone, his entire calf, from ankle to knee, was enveloped in a tight silver sheath. The bleeding had stopped, although his clothing and hands were still covered with blood.

Sitting on the floor of the runaway Crestliner, Corky felt confused about why the chopper hadn't found him yet. He looked out now, scanning the horizon behind him, expecting to see the distant *Goya* and incoming helicopter. Oddly, he saw neither. The lights of the *Goya* had disappeared. Certainly he hadn't come *that* far, had he?

Corky suddenly felt hopeful he might escape. Maybe they had lost him in the dark. Maybe he could get to shore!

It was then he noticed that the wake behind his boat was not straight. It seemed to curve gradually away from the back of his boat, as if he were traveling in an arc rather than a straight line. Confused by this, he turned his head to follow the wake's arc, extrapolating a giant curve across the ocean. An instant later, he saw it.

The *Goya* was directly off his port side, less than a half mile away. In horror, Corky realized his mistake too late. With no one at the wheel, the Crestliner's bow had continuously realigned itself with the direction of the powerful current – the megaplume's circular water flow. *I'm driving in a big friggin' circle!*

He had doubled back on himself.

Knowing he was still inside the shark-filled megaplume, Corky recalled Tolland's grim words. *Enhanced telencephalon olfactory lobes . . . hammerheads can smell a droplet of blood a mile away.* Corky looked at his bloody duct-taped leg and hands.

The chopper would be on him soon.

Ripping off his bloody clothing, Corky scrambled naked toward the stern. Knowing no sharks could possibly keep pace with the boat, he rinsed himself as best as he could in the powerful blast of the wake.

A single droplet of blood . . .

As Corky stood up, fully exposed to the night, he knew there was only one thing left to do. He had learned once that animals marked their territory with urine because uric acid was the most potent-smelling fluid the human body made.

More potent than blood, he hoped. Wishing he'd had a few more beers tonight, Corky heaved his injured leg up onto the gunwale and tried to urinate on the duct tape. *Come on!* He waited. *Nothing like the pressure of having to piss all over yourself with a helicopter chasing you.*

Finally it came. Corky urinated all over the duct tape, soaking it fully. He used what little was left in his bladder to soak a rag, which he then swathed across his entire body. *Very pleasant.*

In the dark sky overhead, a red laser beam appeared, slanting toward him like the shimmering blade of an enormous guillotine. The chopper appeared from an oblique angle, the pilot apparently confused that Corky had looped back toward the *Goya*.

Quickly donning a high-float life vest, Corky moved to the rear of the speeding craft. On the boat's blood-stained floor, only five feet from where Corky was standing, a glowing red dot appeared.

It was time.

Onboard the *Goya*, Michael Tolland did not see his Crestliner Phantom 2100 erupt in flames and tumble through the air in a cartwheel of fire and smoke.

But he heard the explosion.

The West Wing was usually quiet at this hour, but the President's unexpected emergence in his bathrobe and slippers had rustled the aides and on-site staff out of their 'day-timer beds' and on-site sleeping quarters.

'I can't find her, Mr President,' a young aide said, hurrying after him into the Oval Office. He had looked everywhere. 'Ms Tench is not answering her pager or cellphone.'

The President looked exasperated. 'Have you looked in the—'

'She left the building, sir,' another aide announced, hurrying in. 'She signed out about an hour ago. We think she may have gone to the NRO. One of the operators says she and Pickering were talking tonight.'

'*William* Pickering?' The President sounded baffled. Tench and Pickering were anything but social. 'Have you called him?'

'He's not answering either, sir. NRO switchboard can't reach him. They say Pickering's cellphone isn't even ringing. It's like he's dropped off the face of the earth.'

Herney stared at his aides for a moment and then walked to the bar and poured himself a bourbon. As he raised the glass to his lips, a Secret Serviceman hurried in.

'Mr President? I wasn't going to wake you, but you should be aware that there was a car bombing at the FDR Memorial tonight.'

'What?' Herney almost dropped his drink. 'When?'

'An hour ago.' His face was grim. 'And the FBI just identified the victim . . .'

118

Delta-Three's foot screamed in pain. He felt himself floating through a muddled consciousness. *Is this death?* He tried to move but felt paralyzed, barely able to breathe. He saw only blurred shapes. His mind reeled back, recalling the explosion of the Crestliner out at sea, seeing the rage in Michael Tolland's eyes as the oceanographer stood over him, holding the explosive pole to his throat.

Certainly Tolland killed me . . .

And yet the searing pain in Delta-Three's right foot told him he was very much alive. Slowly it came back. On hearing the explosion of the Crestliner, Tolland had let out a cry of anguished rage for his lost friend. Then, turning his ravaged eyes to Delta-Three, Tolland had arched as if preparing to ram the rod through Delta-Three's throat. But as he did, he seemed to hesitate, as if his own morality were holding him back. With brutal frustration and fury, Tolland yanked the rod away and drove his boot down on Delta-Three's tattered foot.

The last thing Delta-Three remembered was vomiting in agony as his whole world drifted into a black delirium. Now he was coming to, with no idea how long he had been unconscious. He could feel his arms tied behind his back in a knot so tight it could only have been tied by a sailor. His legs were also bound, bent

501

behind him and tied to his wrists, leaving him in an immobilized backward arch. He tried to call out, but no sound came. His mouth was stuffed with something.

Delta-Three could not imagine what was going on. It was then he felt the cool breeze and saw the bright lights. He realized he was up on the *Goya*'s main deck. He twisted to look for help and was met by a frightful sight, his own reflection – bulbous and misshapen in the reflective Plexiglas bubble of the *Goya*'s deepwater submersible. The sub hung right in front of him, and Delta-Three realized he was lying on a giant trapdoor in the deck. This was not nearly as unsettling as the most obvious question.

If I'm on deck . . . then where is Delta-Two?

Delta-Two had grown uneasy.

Despite his partner's CrypTalk transmission claiming he was fine, the single gunshot had not been that of a machine gun. Obviously, Tolland or Rachel Sexton had fired a weapon. Delta-Two moved over to peer down the ramp where his partner had descended, and he saw blood.

Weapon raised, he had descended belowdecks, where he followed the trail of blood along a catwalk to the bow of the ship. Here, the trail of blood had led him back up another ramp to the main deck. It was deserted. With growing wariness, Delta-Two had followed the long crimson smear along the sideboard deck back toward the rear of the ship, where it passed the opening to the original ramp he had descended.

What the hell is going on? The smear seemed to travel in a giant circle.

Moving cautiously, his gun trained ahead of him, Delta-Two passed the entrance to the laboratory section of the ship. The smear continued toward the stern deck. Carefully he swung wide, rounding the corner. His eye traced the trail.

Then he saw it.

Jesus Christ!

Delta-Three was lying there – bound and gagged – dumped unceremoniously directly in front of the *Goya*'s small submersible. Even from a distance, Delta-Two could see that his partner was missing a good portion of his right foot.

Wary of a trap, Delta-Two raised his gun and moved forward. Delta-Three was writhing now, trying to speak. Ironically, the way the man had been bound – with his knees sharply bent behind him – was probably saving his life; the bleeding in his foot appeared to have slowed.

As Delta-Two approached the submersible, he appreciated the rare luxury of being able to watch his own back; the entire deck of the ship was reflected in the sub's rounded cockpit dome. Delta-Two arrived at his struggling partner. He saw the warning in his eyes too late.

The flash of silver came out of nowhere.

One of the Triton's manipulator claws suddenly leaped forward and clamped down on Delta-Two's left thigh with crushing force. He tried to pull away, but the claw bore down. He screamed in pain, feeling a bone break. His eyes shot to the sub's cockpit. Peering through the reflection of the deck, Delta-Two could now see him, ensconced in the shadows of the Triton's interior.

Michael Tolland was inside the sub, at the controls.

Bad idea, Delta-Two seethed, blocking out his pain and shouldering his machine gun. He aimed up and to

503

the left at Tolland's chest, only three feet away on the other side of the sub's Plexiglas dome. He pulled the trigger, and the gun roared. Wild with rage at having been tricked, Delta-Two held the trigger back until the last of his shells clattered to the deck and his gun clicked empty. Breathless, he dropped the weapon and glared at the shredded dome in front of him.

'Dead!' the soldier hissed, straining to pull his leg from the clamp. As he twisted, the metal clamp severed his skin, opening a large gash. 'Fuck!' He reached now for the CrypTalk on his belt. But as he raised it to his lips, a second robotic arm snapped open in front of him and lunged forward, clamping around his right arm. The CrypTalk fell to the deck.

It was then that Delta-Two saw the ghost in the window before him. A pale visage leaning sideways and peering out through an unscathed edge of glass. Stunned, Delta-Two looked at the center of the dome and realized the bullets had not even come close to penetrating the thick shell. The dome was cratered with pockmarks.

An instant later, the topside portal on the sub opened, and Michael Tolland emerged. He looked shaky but unscathed. Climbing down the aluminum gangway, Tolland stepped onto the deck and eyed his sub's destroyed dome window.

'Ten thousand pounds per square inch,' Tolland said. 'Looks like you need a bigger gun.'

Inside the hydrolab, Rachel knew time was running out. She had heard the gunshots out on the deck and was praying that everything had happened exactly as Tolland had planned. She no longer cared who was behind the meteorite deception – the NASA administrator, Marjorie Tench, or the President himself – none of it mattered anymore.

They will not get away with this. Whoever it is, the truth will be told.

The wound on Rachel's arm had stopped bleeding, and the adrenaline coursing through her body had muted the pain and sharpened her focus. Finding a pen and paper, she scrawled a two-line message. The words were blunt and awkward, but eloquence was not a luxury she had time for at the moment. She added the note to the incriminating stack of papers in her hand – the GPR printout, images of *Bathynomous giganteus*, photos and articles regarding oceanic chondrules, an electron microscan printout. The meteorite was a fake, and this was the proof.

Rachel inserted the entire stack into the hydrolab's fax machine. Knowing only a few fax numbers by heart, she had limited choices, but she had already made up her mind who would be receiving these pages and her note. Holding her breath, she carefully typed in the person's fax number.

She pressed 'send,' praying she had chosen the recipient wisely.

The fax machine beeped.

ERROR: NO DIAL TONE

Rachel had expected this. The *Goya's* communications were still being jammed. She stood waiting and watching the machine, hoping it functioned like hers at home.

Come on!

After five seconds, the machine beeped again.

REDIALING . . .

Yes! Rachel watched the machine lock into an endless loop.

505

```
ERROR: NO DIAL TONE
REDIALING . . .
ERROR: NO DIAL TONE
REDIALING . . .
```

Leaving the fax machine in search of a dial tone, Rachel dashed out of the hydrolab just as helicopter blades thundered overhead.

119

One hundred and sixty miles away from the *Goya*, Gabrielle Ashe was staring at Senator Sexton's computer screen in mute astonishment. Her suspicions had been right.

But she had never imagined *how* right.

She was looking at digital scans of dozens of bank checks written to Sexton from private space companies and deposited in numbered accounts in the Cayman Islands. The smallest check Gabrielle saw was for $15,000. Several were upward of $500,000.

Small potatoes, Sexton had told her. *All the donations are under the $2,000 cap.*

Obviously Sexton had been lying all along. Gabrielle was looking at illegal campaign financing on an enormous scale. The pangs of betrayal and disillusionment settled hard now in her heart. *He lied.*

She felt stupid. She felt dirty. But most of all she felt mad.

Gabrielle sat alone in the darkness, realizing she had no idea what to do next.

Above the *Goya*, as the Kiowa banked over the stern deck, Delta-One gazed down, his eyes fixating on an utterly unexpected vision.

Michael Tolland was standing on deck beside a small submersible. Dangling in the sub's robotic arms, as if in the clutches of a giant insect, hung Delta-Two, struggling in vain to free himself from two enormous claws.

What in the name of God!?

Equally as shocking an image, Rachel Sexton had just arrived on deck, taking up a position over a bound and bleeding man at the foot of the submersible. The man could only be Delta-Three. Rachel held one of the Delta Force's machine guns on him and stared up at the chopper as if daring them to attack.

Delta-One felt momentarily disoriented, unable to fathom how this possibly could have happened. The Delta Force's errors on the ice shelf earlier had been a rare but explainable occurrence. This, however, was unimaginable.

Delta-One's humiliation would have been excruciating enough under normal circumstances. But tonight his shame was magnified by the presence of another individual riding with him inside the chopper, a person whose presence here was highly unconventional.

The controller.

Following the Delta's kill at the FDR Memorial, the controller had ordered Delta-One to fly to a deserted public park not far from the White House. On the controller's command, Delta-One had set down on a grassy knoll among some trees just as the controller, having parked nearby, strode out of the darkness and boarded the Kiowa. They were all en route again in a matter of seconds.

Although a controller's direct involvement in mission operations was rare, Delta-One could hardly complain. The controller, distressed by the way the Delta Force had handled the kills on the Milne Ice Shelf and fearing increasing suspicions and scrutiny from a number of parties, had informed Delta-One that the final phase of the operation would be overseen in person.

Now the controller was riding shotgun, witnessing in person a failure the likes of which Delta-One had never endured.

This must end. Now.

The controller gazed down from the Kiowa at the deck of the *Goya* and wondered how this could possibly have happened. Nothing had gone properly – the suspicions about the meteorite, the failed Delta kills on the ice shelf, the necessity of the high-profile kill at the FDR.

'Controller,' Delta-One stammered, his tone one of stunned disgrace as he looked at the situation on the deck of the *Goya*. 'I cannot imagine . . .'

Nor can I, the controller thought. Their quarry had obviously been grossly underestimated.

The controller looked down at Rachel Sexton, who stared up blankly at the chopper's reflective windshield and raised a CrypTalk device to her mouth. When her synthesized voice crackled inside the Kiowa, the controller expected her to demand that the chopper back off or extinguish the jamming system so Tolland could call for help. But the words Rachel Sexton spoke were far more chilling.

'You're too late,' she said. 'We're not the only ones who know.'

The words echoed for a moment inside the chopper. Although the claim seemed far-fetched, the faintest possibility of truth gave the controller pause. The success of the entire project required the elimination of all those who knew the truth, and as bloody as the containment had turned out to be, the controller had to be certain this was the conclusion.

Someone else knows . . .

Considering Rachel Sexton's reputation for following strict protocol of classified data, the controller found it very hard to believe that she would have decided to share this with an outside source.

Rachel was on the CrypTalk again. 'Back off and we'll spare your men. Come any closer and they die. Either way, the truth comes out. Cut your losses. Back off.'

'You're bluffing,' the controller said, knowing the voice Rachel Sexton was hearing was an androgynous robotic tone. 'You have told no one.'

'Are you ready to take that chance?' Rachel fired back. 'I couldn't get through to William Pickering earlier, so I got spooked and took out some insurance.'

The controller frowned. It was plausible.

'They're not buying it,' Rachel said, glancing at Tolland.

The soldier in the claws gave a pained smirk. 'Your gun is empty, and the chopper's going to blow you to hell. You're both going to die. Your only hope is to let us go.'

Like hell, Rachel thought, trying to assess their next

509

move. She looked at the bound and gagged man who lay at her feet directly in front of the sub. He looked delirious from loss of blood. She crouched beside him, looking into the man's hard eyes. 'I'm going to take off your gag and hold the CrypTalk; you're going to convince the helicopter to back off. Is that clear?'

The man nodded earnestly.

Rachel pulled out the man's gag. The soldier spat a wad of bloody saliva up into Rachel's face.

'Bitch,' he hissed, coughing. 'I'm going to watch you die. They're going to kill you like a pig, and I'm going to enjoy every minute.'

Rachel wiped the hot saliva from her face as she felt Tolland's hands lifting her away, pulling her back, steadying her as he took her machine gun. She could feel in his trembling touch that something inside him had just snapped. Tolland walked to a control panel a few yards away, put his hand on a lever, and locked eyes with the man lying on the deck.

'Strike two,' Tolland said. 'And on my ship, that's all you get.'

With a resolute rage, Tolland yanked down on the lever. A huge trap door in the deck beneath the Triton fell open like the floor of a gallows. The bound soldier gave a short howl of fear and then disappeared, plummeting through the hole. He fell thirty feet to the ocean below. The splash was crimson. The sharks were on him instantly.

The controller shook with rage, looking down from the Kiowa at what was left of Delta-Three's body drifting out from under the boat on the strong current. The illuminated water was pink. Several fish fought over something that looked like an arm.

Jesus Christ.

The controller looked back at the deck. Delta-Two still hung in the Triton's claws, but now the sub was suspended over a gaping hole in the deck. His feet dangled over the void. All Tolland had to do was release the claws, and Delta-Two would be next.

'Okay,' the controller barked into the CrypTalk. 'Hold on. Just hold on!'

Rachel stood below on the deck and stared up at the Kiowa. Even from this height the controller sensed the resolve in her eyes. Rachel raised the CrypTalk to her mouth. 'You still think we're bluffing?' she said. 'Call the main switchboard at the NRO. Ask for Jim Samiljan. He's in P&A on the nightshift. I told him everything about the meteorite. He will confirm.'

She's giving me a specific name? This did not bode well. Rachel Sexton was no fool, and this was a bluff the controller could check in a matter of seconds. Although the controller knew of no one at the NRO named Jim Samiljan, the organization was enormous. Rachel could quite possibly be telling the truth. Before ordering the final kill, the controller had to confirm if this was a bluff – or not.

Delta-One looked over his shoulder. 'You want me to deactivate the jammer so you can call and check it out?'

The controller peered down at Rachel and Tolland, both in plain view. If either of them made a move for a cellphone or radio, the controller knew Delta-One could always reactivate and cut them off. The risk was minimal.

'Kill the jammer,' the controller said, pulling out a cellphone. 'I'll confirm Rachel's lying. Then we'll find a way to get Delta-Two and end this.'

* * *

In Fairfax, the operator at the NRO's central switchboard was getting impatient. 'As I just told you, I see no Jim Samiljan in the Plans and Analysis Division.'

The caller was insistent. 'Have you tried multiple spellings? Have you tried other departments?'

The operator had already checked, but she checked again. After several seconds, she said, 'Nowhere on staff do we have a Jim Samiljan. Under any spelling.'

The caller sounded oddly pleased by this. 'So you are certain the NRO employs no Jim Samil—'

A sudden flurry of activity erupted on the line. Someone yelled. The caller cursed aloud and promptly hung up.

Onboard the Kiowa, Delta-One was screaming with rage as he scrambled to reactivate the jamming system. He had made the realization too late. In the huge array of lighted controls in the cockpit, a tiny LED meter indicated that a SATCOM data signal was being transmitted from the *Goya*. *But how? Nobody left the deck!* Before Delta-One could engage the jammer, the connection from the *Goya* terminated on its own accord.

Inside the hydrolab, the fax machine beeped contentedly.

CARRIER FOUND . . . FAX SENT

121

Kill or be killed. Rachel had discovered a part of herself she never knew existed. Survival mode – a savage fortitude fueled by fear.

'What was in that outbound fax?' the voice on the CrypTalk demanded.

Rachel was relieved to hear confirmation that the fax had gone out as planned. 'Leave the area,' she demanded, speaking into the CrypTalk and glaring up at the hovering chopper. 'It's over. Your secret is out.' Rachel informed their attackers of all the information she had just sent. A half dozen pages of images and text. Incontrovertible evidence that the meteorite is a fake. 'Harming us will only make your situation worse.'

There was a heavy pause. 'Who did you send the fax to?'

Rachel had no intention of answering that question. She and Tolland needed to buy as much time as possible. They had positioned themselves near the opening in the deck, on a direct line with the Triton, making it impossible for the chopper to shoot without hitting the soldier dangling in the sub's claws.

'William Pickering,' the voice guessed, sounding oddly hopeful. 'You faxed Pickering.'

Wrong, Rachel thought. Pickering would have been her first choice, but she had been forced to choose someone else for fear her attackers had already eliminated Pickering – a move whose boldness would be a chilling testimony to her enemy's resolve. In a moment of desperate decision, Rachel had faxed the data to the only other fax number she knew by heart.

Her father's office.

Senator Sexton's office fax number had been painfully engraved into Rachel's memory after her mother's death when her father chose to work out many of the particulars of the estate without having to deal with Rachel in person. Rachel never imagined she would turn to her father in a time of need, but tonight the man possessed two critical qualities – all the correct political motivations to release the meteorite data without hesitation, and enough clout to call the White House and blackmail them into calling off this kill squad.

Although her father was most certainly not in the office at this hour, Rachel knew he kept his office locked like a vault. Rachel had, in effect, faxed the data into a time-lock safe. Even if the attackers knew where she had sent it, chances were slim they could get through the tight federal security at the Philip A. Hart Senate Office Building and break into a senator's office without anyone noticing.

'Wherever you sent the fax,' the voice from above said, 'you've put that person in danger.'

Rachel knew she had to speak from a position of power regardless of the fear she was feeling. She motioned to the soldier trapped in the Triton's claws. His legs dangled over the abyss, dripping blood thirty feet to the ocean. 'The only person in danger here is your agent,' she said into the CrypTalk. 'It's over. Back off. The data is gone. You've lost. Leave the area, or this man dies.'

The voice on the CrypTalk fired back, 'Ms Sexton, you do not understand the importance—'

'Understand?' Rachel exploded. 'I understand that you killed innocent people! I understand that you lied about the meteorite! And I understand that you won't get away with this! Even if you kill us all, it's over!'

There was a long pause. Finally the voice said, 'I'm coming down.'

Rachel felt her muscles tighten. *Coming down?*

'I am unarmed,' the voice said. 'Do not do anything rash. You and I need to talk face to face.'

Before Rachel could react, the chopper dropped onto

the *Goya*'s deck. The passenger door on the fuselage opened and a figure stepped out. He was a plain-looking man in a black coat and tie. For an instant, Rachel's thoughts went totally blank.

She was staring at William Pickering.

William Pickering stood on the deck of the *Goya* and gazed with regret at Rachel Sexton. He had never imagined today would come to this. As he moved toward her, he could see the dangerous combination of emotions in his employee's eyes.

Shock, betrayal, confusion, rage.

All understandable, he thought. *There is so much she does not understand.*

For a moment, Pickering flashed on his daughter, Diana, wondering what emotions she had felt before she died. Both Diana and Rachel were casualties of the same war, a war Pickering had vowed to fight forever. Sometimes the casualties could be so cruel.

'Rachel,' Pickering said. 'We can still work this out. There's a lot I need to explain.'

Rachel Sexton looked aghast, nauseated almost. Tolland had the machine gun now and was aiming at Pickering's chest. He too looked bewildered.

'Stay back!' Tolland yelled.

Pickering stopped five yards away, focusing on Rachel. 'Your father is taking bribes, Rachel. Payoffs from private space companies. He plans to dismantle NASA and open space to the private sector. He had to be stopped, as a matter of national security.'

Rachel's expression was blank.

Pickering sighed. 'NASA, for all its flaws, *must* remain a government entity.' *Certainly she can understand the dangers*. Privatization would send NASA's best minds

515

and ideas flooding into the private sector. The brain trust would dissolve. The military would lose access. Private space companies looking to raise capital would start selling NASA patents and ideas to the highest bidders worldwide!

Rachel's voice was tremulous. 'You faked the meteorite and killed innocent people . . . in the name of national security?'

'It was never supposed to happen like this,' Pickering said. 'The plan was to save an important government agency. Killing was not part of it.'

The meteorite deception, Pickering knew, like most intelligence proposals, had been the product of fear. Three years ago, in an effort to extend the NRO hydrophones into deeper water where they could not be touched by enemy saboteurs, Pickering spearheaded a program that utilized a newly developed NASA building material to secretly design an astonishingly durable submarine capable of carrying humans to the deepest regions of the ocean – including the bottom of the Mariana Trench.

Forged from a revolutionary ceramic, this two-man submarine was designed from blueprints hacked from the computer of a California engineer named Graham Hawkes, a genius sub designer whose life dream was to build an ultra-deepwater submersible he called Deep Flight II. Hawkes was having trouble finding funding to build a prototype. Pickering, on the other hand, had an unlimited budget.

Using the classified ceramic submersible, Pickering sent a covert team underwater to affix new hydrophones to the walls of the Mariana Trench, deeper than any enemy could possibly look. In the process of drilling, however, they uncovered geologic structures unlike any that scientists had ever seen. The discoveries included chondrules and fossils of several unknown species. Of course, because the NRO's ability to dive this deep was classified, none of the information could ever be shared.

It was not until recently, driven yet again by fear, that Pickering and his quiet team of NRO science advisers had decided to put their knowledge of the Mariana's unique geology to work to help save NASA. Turning a Mariana rock into a meteorite had proven to be a deceptively simple task. Using an ECE slush-hydrogen engine, the NRO team charred the rock with a convincing fusion crust. Then, using a small payload sub, they had descended beneath the Milne Ice Shelf and inserted the charred rock up into the ice from beneath. Once the insertion shaft refroze, the rock looked like it had been there for over three hundred years.

Unfortunately, as was often the case in the world of covert operations, the grandest of plans could be undone by the smallest of snags. Yesterday, the entire illusion had been shattered by a few bioluminescent plankton . . .

From the cockpit of the idling Kiowa, Delta-One watched the drama unfold before him. Rachel and Tolland appeared to be in clear control, although Delta-One almost had to laugh at the hollowness of the illusion. The machine gun in Tolland's hands was worthless; even from here Delta-One could see the cocking bar assembly had kicked back, indicating the clip was empty.

As Delta-One gazed out at his partner struggling in the Triton's claws, he knew he had to hurry. The focus on deck had turned completely to Pickering, and now Delta-One could make his move. Leaving the rotors idling, he slipped out of the rear of the fuselage and, using the chopper for cover, made his way unseen onto the starboard gangway. With his own machine gun in hand, he headed for the bow. Pickering had given him specific orders before they landed on deck, and Delta-One had no intention of failing at this simple task.

In a matter of minutes, he knew, *this will all be over*.

122

Still wearing his bathrobe, Zach Herney sat at his desk in the Oval Office, his head throbbing. The newest piece of the puzzle had just been revealed.

Marjorie Tench is dead.

Herney's aides said they had information suggesting Tench had driven to the FDR Memorial for a private meeting with William Pickering. Now that Pickering was missing, the staff feared Pickering too might be dead.

The President and Pickering had endured their battles lately. Months ago Herney learned that Pickering had engaged in illegal activity on Herney's behalf in an attempt to save Herney's floundering campaign.

Employing NRO assets, Pickering had discreetly obtained enough dirt on Senator Sexton to sink his campaign – scandalous sexual photos of the senator with his aide Gabrielle Ashe, incriminating financial records proving Sexton was taking bribes from private space companies. Pickering anonymously sent all the evidence to Marjorie Tench, assuming the White House would use it wisely. But Herney, upon seeing the data, had forbidden Tench to use it. Sex scandals and bribery were cancers in Washington, and waving another one in front of the public only added to their distrust of government.

Cynicism is killing this country.

Although Herney knew he could destroy Sexton with scandal, the cost would be besmirching the dignity of the U.S. Senate, something Herney refused to do.

No more negatives. Herney would beat Senator Sexton on the issues.

Pickering, angered by the White House's refusal to use the evidence he had provided, tried to jump-start the scandal by leaking a rumor that Sexton had slept with Gabrielle Ashe. Unfortunately, Sexton declared his innocence with such convincing indignation that the President ended up having to apologize for the leak personally. In the end William Pickering had done more damage than good. Herney told Pickering that if he ever interfered in the campaign again, he would be indicted. The grand irony, of course, was that Pickering did not even like President Herney. The NRO director's attempts to help Herney's campaign were simply fears over the fate of NASA. Zach Herney was the lesser of two evils.

Now has someone killed Pickering?

Herney could not imagine.

'Mr President?' an aide said. 'As you requested, I called Lawrence Ekstrom and told him about Marjorie Tench.'

'Thank you.'

'He would like to speak to you, sir.'

Herney was still furious with Ekstrom for lying about PODS. 'Tell him I'll talk to him in the morning.'

'Mr Ekstrom wants to talk to you right away, sir.' The aide looked uneasy. 'He's very upset.'

HE'S upset? Herney could feel his temper fraying around the edges. As he stalked off to take Ekstrom's call, the President wondered what the hell else could possibly go wrong tonight.

123

Onboard the *Goya*, Rachel felt lightheaded. The mystification that had settled around her like a heavy fog was lifting now. The stark reality that came into focus left her feeling naked and disgusted. She looked at the stranger before her and could barely hear his voice.

'We needed to rebuild NASA's image,' Pickering was saying. 'Their declining popularity and funding had become dangerous on so many levels.' Pickering paused, his gray eyes locking on hers. 'Rachel, NASA was *desperate* for a triumph. Someone had to make it happen.'

Something had to be done, Pickering thought.

The meteorite had been a final act of desperation. Pickering and others had tried to save NASA by lobbying to incorporate the space agency into the intelligence community where it would enjoy increased funding and better security, but the White House continuously rebuffed the idea as an assault on pure science. *Shortsighted idealism*. With the rising popularity of Sexton's anti-NASA rhetoric, Pickering and his band of military powerbrokers knew time was running short. They decided that capturing the imagination of taxpayers and Congress was the only remaining way to salvage NASA's image and save it from the auction block. If the space agency was to survive, it would need an infusion of grandeur – something to remind the taxpayers of NASA's Apollo glory days. And if Zach Herney was going to defeat Senator Sexton, he was going to need help.

I tried to help him, Pickering told himself, recalling all the damaging evidence he had sent Marjorie Tench. Unfortunately, Herney had forbidden its use, leaving Pickering no choice but to take drastic measures.

'Rachel,' Pickering said, 'the information you just faxed off this ship is dangerous. You must understand that. If it gets out, the White House and NASA will look complicit. The backlash against the President and NASA will be enormous. The President and NASA know nothing, Rachel. They are innocent. They believe the meteorite is authentic.'

Pickering had not even tried to bring Herney or Ekstrom into the fold because both were far too idealistic to have agreed to any deceit, regardless of its potential to save the presidency or space agency. Administrator Ekstrom's only crime had been persuading the PODS mission supervisor to lie about the anomaly software, a move Ekstrom no doubt regretted the moment he realized how scrutinized this particular meteorite would become.

Marjorie Tench, frustrated by Herney's insistence on fighting a clean campaign, conspired with Ekstrom on the PODS lie, hoping a small PODS success might help the President fend off the rising Sexton tide.

If Tench had used the photos and bribery data I gave her, none of this would have happened!

Tench's murder, though deeply regrettable, had been destined as soon as Rachel called Tench and made accusations of fraud. Pickering knew Tench would investigate ruthlessly until she got to the bottom of Rachel's motives for the outrageous claims, and this was one investigation Pickering obviously could never let happen. Ironically, Tench would serve her president best in death, her violent end helping cement a sympathy vote for the White House as well as cast vague suspicions of foul play on a desperate Sexton campaign which had been so publicly humiliated by Marjorie Tench on CNN.

Rachel stood her ground, glaring at her boss.

'Understand,' Pickering said, 'if news of this meteorite fraud gets out, you will destroy an innocent president and an innocent space agency. You will also put a very dangerous man in the Oval Office. I need to know where you faxed the data.'

As he spoke those words, a strange look came across Rachel's face. It was the pained expression of horror of someone who had just realized they may have made a grave mistake.

Having circled the bow and come back down the port side, Delta-One now stood in the hydrolab from which he had seen Rachel emerge as the chopper had flown in. A computer in the lab displayed an unsettling image – a polychromatic rendering of the pulsating, deep-water vortex that was apparently hovering over the ocean floor somewhere beneath the *Goya*.

Another reason to get the hell out of here, he thought, moving now toward his target.

The fax machine was on a counter on the far side of the wall. The tray was filled with a stack of papers, exactly as Pickering had guessed it would be. Delta-One picked up the stack. A note from Rachel was on top. Only two lines. He read it.

To the point, he thought.

As he flipped through the pages, he was both amazed and dismayed by the extent to which Tolland and Rachel had uncovered the meteorite deception. Whoever saw these printouts would have no doubt what they meant. Fortunately, Delta-One would not even need to hit 'redial' to find out where the printouts had gone. The last fax number was still displayed in the LCD window.

A Washington D.C. prefix.

He carefully copied the fax number down, grabbed all the papers, and exited the lab.

Tolland's hands felt sweaty on the machine gun as he gripped it, aiming the muzzle at William Pickering's chest. The NRO director was still pressuring Rachel to tell him where the data had been sent, and Tolland was starting to get the uneasy feeling that Pickering was simply trying to buy time. *For what?*

'The White House and NASA are *innocent,*' Pickering repeated. 'Work with me. Don't let my mistakes destroy what little credibility NASA has left. NASA will look guilty if this gets out. You and I can come to an arrangement. The country needs this meteorite. Tell me where you faxed the data before it's too late.'

'So you can kill someone else?' Rachel said. 'You make me sick.'

Tolland was amazed by Rachel's fortitude. She despised her father, but she clearly had no intention of putting the senator in any danger whatsoever. Unfortunately, Rachel's plan to fax her father for help had backfired. Even if the senator came into his office, saw the fax, and called the President with news of the meteorite fraud and told him to call off the attack, nobody at the White House would have any idea what Sexton was talking about, or even where they were.

'I will only say this one more time,' Pickering said, fixing Rachel with a menacing glare. 'This situation is too complex for you to fully understand. You've made an enormous mistake by sending that data off this ship. You've put your country at risk.'

William Pickering was indeed buying time, Tolland now realized. And the reason was striding calmly toward them up the starboard side of the boat. Tolland felt a flash of fear when he saw the soldier sauntering toward them carrying a stack of papers and a machine gun.

Tolland reacted with a decisiveness that shocked even himself. Gripping the machine gun, he wheeled, aimed at the soldier, and pulled the trigger.

The gun made an innocuous click.

'I found the fax number,' the soldier said, handing Pickering a slip of paper. 'And Mr Tolland is out of ammunition.'

124

Sedgewick Sexton stormed up the hallway of the Philip A. Hart Senate building. He had no idea how Gabrielle had done it, but she had obviously gotten into his office. While they were speaking on the phone, Sexton had clearly heard the distinctive triple-click of his Jourdain clock in the background. All he could imagine was that Gabrielle's eavesdropping on the SFF meeting had undermined her trust in him and she had gone digging for evidence.

How the hell did she get into my office?

Sexton was glad he'd changed his computer password.

When he arrived at his private office, Sexton typed in his code to deactivate the alarm. Then he fumbled for his keys, unlocked the heavy doors, threw them open, and burst in, intent on catching Gabrielle in the act.

But the office was empty and dark, lit only by the glow of his computer screensaver. He turned on the lights, his eyes scanning. Everything looked in place. Dead silence except for the triple-tick of his clock.

Where the hell is she?

He heard something rustle in his private bathroom and raced over, turning on the light. The bathroom was empty. He looked behind the door. Nothing.

Puzzled, Sexton eyed himself in the mirror, wondering if he'd had too much to drink tonight. *I heard something.* Feeling disoriented and confused, he walked back into his office.

'Gabrielle?' he called out. He went down the hall to her office. She wasn't there. Her office was dark.

A toilet flushed in the ladies' room, and Sexton spun, striding now back in the direction of the restrooms. He arrived just as Gabrielle was exiting, drying her hands. She jumped when she saw him.

'My God! You scared me!' she said, looking genuinely frightened. 'What are you doing here?'

'You said you were getting NASA documents from your office,' he declared, eyeing her empty hands. 'Where are they?'

'I couldn't find them. I looked everywhere. That's what took so long.'

He stared directly into her eyes. 'Were you in my office?'

I owe my life to his fax machine, Gabrielle thought.

Only minutes ago she'd been sitting at Sexton's computer, trying to make printouts of the images of illegal checks on his computer. The files were protected somehow, and she was going to need more time to figure out how to print them. She would probably still be trying right now if Sexton's fax machine had not rung, startling her and snapping her back to reality. Gabrielle took it as her cue to get out. Without taking time to see what the incoming fax was, she logged off Sexton's computer, tidied up, and headed out the way she had come. She was just climbing out of Sexton's bathroom when she heard him coming in.

Now, with Sexton standing before her, staring down, she sensed him searching her eyes for a lie. Sedgewick Sexton could smell untruths like nobody Gabrielle had ever met. If she lied to him, Sexton would know.

'You've been drinking,' Gabrielle said, turning away. *How does he know I was in his office?*

Sexton put his hands on her shoulders and spun her back around. 'Were you in my office?'

Gabrielle felt a rising fear. Sexton had indeed been drinking. His touch was rough. 'In your office?' she demanded, forcing a confused laugh. 'How? *Why?*'

'I heard my Jourdain in the background when I called you.'

Gabrielle cringed inwardly. *His clock?* It had not even occurred to her. 'Do you know how ridiculous that sounds?'

'I spend all day in that office. I know what my clock sounds like.'

Gabrielle sensed she had to end this immediately. *The best defense is a good offense.* At least that's what Yolanda Cole always said. Placing her hands on her hips, Gabrielle went for him with all she had. She stepped toward him, getting in his face, glaring. 'Let me get this straight, Senator. It's four o'clock in the morning, you've been drinking, you heard a ticking on your phone, and that's why you're here?' She pointed her finger indignantly down the hall at his door. 'Just for the record, are you accusing me of disarming a federal alarm system, picking two sets of locks, breaking into your office, being stupid enough to answer my cellphone while in the process of committing a felony, rearming the alarm system on my way out, and then calmly using the ladies' room before I run off with nothing to show for it? Is that the story here?'

Sexton blinked, wide-eyed.

'There's a reason people shouldn't drink alone,' Gabrielle said. 'Now do you want to talk about NASA, or not?'

Sexton felt befuddled as he walked back into his office. He went straight to his wet bar and poured himself a Pepsi. He sure as hell didn't *feel* drunk. Could he really have been wrong about this? Across the room, his Jourdain ticked mockingly. Sexton drained his Pepsi and poured himself another, and one for Gabrielle.

'Drink, Gabrielle?' he asked, turning back into the room. Gabrielle had not followed him in. She was still standing in the doorway, rubbing his nose in it. 'Oh, for God's sake! Come in. Tell me what you found out at NASA.'

'I think I've had enough for tonight,' she said, sounding distant. 'Let's talk tomorrow.'

Sexton was in no mood for games. He needed this information now, and he had no intention of begging for it. He heaved a tired sigh. *Extend the bond of trust. It's all about trust.* 'I screwed up,' he said. 'I'm sorry. It's been a hell of a day. I don't know what I was thinking.'

Gabrielle remained in the doorway.

Sexton walked to his desk and set Gabrielle's Pepsi down on his blotter. He motioned to his leather chair – the position of power. 'Have a seat. Enjoy a soda. I'm going to go stick my head in the sink.' He headed for the bathroom.

Gabrielle still wasn't moving.

'I think I saw a fax in the machine,' Sexton called over his shoulder as he entered the bathroom. *Show her you trust her.* 'Have a look at it for me, will you?'

Sexton closed the door and filled the sink with cold water. He splashed it on his face and felt no clearer. This had never happened to him before – being so sure, and being so wrong. Sexton was a man who trusted his instincts, and his instincts told him Gabrielle Ashe had been in his office.

But how? It was impossible.

Sexton told himself to forget about it and focus on the matter at hand. *NASA.* He needed Gabrielle right now. This was no time to alienate her. He needed to know what she knew. *Forget your instincts. You were wrong.*

As Sexton dried his face, he threw his head back and took a deep breath. *Relax*, he told himself. *Don't get punchy.* He closed his eyes and inhaled deeply again, feeling better.

When Sexton exited the bathroom, he was relieved to see Gabrielle had acquiesced and come back into his office. *Good*, he thought. *Now we can get to business.* Gabrielle was standing at his fax machine flipping through whatever pages had come in. Sexton was confused, however, when he saw her face. It was a mask of disorientation and fear.

'What is it?' Sexton said, moving toward her.

Gabrielle teetered, as if she were about to pass out. 'What?'

'The meteorite . . .' she choked, her voice frail as her trembling hand held the stack of fax papers out to him. 'And your daughter . . . she's in danger.'

Bewildered, Sexton walked over, and took the fax pages from Gabrielle. The top sheet was a handwritten note. Sexton immediately recognized the writing. The communiqué was awkward and shocking in its simplicity.

> *Meteorite is fake. Here's proof.*
> *NASA/White House trying to kill me. Help! – RS*

The senator seldom felt totally at a loss of understanding, but as he reread Rachel's words, he had no idea what to make of them.

The meteorite is a fake? NASA and the White House are trying to kill her?

In a deepening haze, Sexton began sifting through the half dozen sheets. The first page was a computerized image whose heading read 'Ground Penetrating Radar (GPR).' The picture appeared to be an ice-sounding of some sort. Sexton saw the extraction pit they had talked about on television. His eye was drawn to what looked like the faint outline of a body floating in the shaft. Then he saw something even more shocking – the clear outline of a second shaft directly *beneath* where the meteorite had been – as if the stone had been inserted from underneath the ice.

What in the world?

Flipping to the next page, Sexton came face to face with a photograph of some sort of living ocean species called a *Bathynomous giganteus*. He stared in utter amazement. *That's the animal from the meteorite fossils!*

Flipping faster now, he saw a graphic display depicting the ionized hydrogen content in the meteorite's crust. This page had a handwritten scrawl on it: *Slush-hydrogen burn? NASA Expander Cycle Engine?*

Sexton could not believe his eyes. With the room starting to spin around him, he flipped to the final page – a photo of a rock containing metallic bubbles that looked exactly like those in the meteorite. Shockingly, the accompanying description said the rock was the product of oceanic volcanism. *A rock from the ocean?* Sexton wondered. *But NASA said chondrules form only in space!*

Sexton set the sheets down on his desk and collapsed in his chair. It had taken him only fifteen seconds to piece together everything he was looking at. The implications of the images on the papers were crystal clear. Anyone with half a brain could see what these photos proved.

The NASA meteorite is a fake!

No day in Sexton's career had been filled with such extreme highs and lows. Today had been a roller-coaster ride of hope and despair. Sexton's bafflement over how this enormous scam could possibly have been pulled off evaporated into irrelevance when he realized what the scam meant for him politically.

When I go public with this information, the presidency is mine!

In his upwelling of celebration, Senator Sedgewick Sexton had momentarily forgotten his daughter's claim that she was in trouble.

'Rachel is in danger,' Gabrielle said. 'Her note says NASA and the White House are trying to—'

Sexton's fax machine suddenly began ringing again. Gabrielle wheeled and stared at the machine. Sexton found himself staring too. He could not imagine what else Rachel could be sending him. More proof? How much more could there be? *This is plenty!*

When the fax machine answered the call, however, no pages came through. The machine, detecting no data signal, had switched to its answering machine feature.

'Hello,' Sexton's outbound message crackled. 'This is the office of Senator Sedgewick Sexton. If you are trying to send a fax, you may transmit at anytime. If not, you may leave a message at the tone.'

Before Sexton could pick up, the machine beeped.

'Senator Sexton?' The man's voice had a lucid rawness to it. 'This is William Pickering, director of the National Reconnaissance Office. You're probably not in the office at this hour, but I need to speak immediately.' He paused as if waiting for someone to pick up.

Gabrielle reached to pick up the receiver.

Sexton grabbed her hand and violently yanked it away.

Gabrielle looked stunned. 'But that's the director of—'

'Senator,' Pickering continued, sounding almost relieved that no one had picked up. 'I'm afraid I am calling with some very troubling news. I've just received word that your daughter Rachel is in extreme danger. I have a team trying to help her as we speak. I

531

cannot talk in detail about the situation on the phone, but I was just informed she may have faxed you some data relating to the NASA meteorite. I have not seen the data, nor do I know what it is, but the people threatening your daughter have just warned me that if you or anyone goes public with the information, your daughter will die. I'm sorry to be so blunt, sir; I do it for clarity's sake. Your daughter's life is being threatened. If she has indeed faxed you something, do *not* share it with anyone. Not yet. Your daughter's life depends on it. Stay where you are. I will be there shortly.' He paused. 'With luck, Senator, all of this will be resolved by the time you wake up. If, by chance, you get this message before I arrive at your office, stay where you are and call no one. I am doing everything in my power to get your daughter back safely.'

Pickering hung up.

Gabrielle was trembling. 'Rachel is a hostage?'

Sexton sensed that even in her disillusionment with him, Gabrielle felt a pained empathy to think of a bright young woman in danger. Oddly, Sexton was having trouble mustering the same emotions. Most of him felt like a child who had just been given his most wanted Christmas present, and he refused to let anyone yank it out of his hands.

Pickering wants me to be quiet about this?

He stood a moment, trying to decide what all of this meant. In a cold, calculating side of his mind, Sexton felt the machinery beginning to turn – a political computer, playing out every scenario and evaluating each outcome. He glanced at the stack of faxes in his hands and began to sense the raw power of the images. This NASA meteorite had shattered his dream of the presidency. But it was all a lie. A construct. Now, those who did this would pay. The meteorite that his enemies had created to destroy him would now make him powerful beyond anyone's wildest imagination. His daughter had seen to that.

There is only one acceptable outcome, he knew. *Only one course of action for a true leader to take.*

Feeling hypnotized by the shining images of his own resurrection, Sexton was drifting through a fog as he crossed the room. He went to his copy machine and turned it on, preparing to copy the papers Rachel had faxed him.

'What are you doing?' Gabrielle demanded, sounding bewildered.

'They won't kill Rachel,' Sexton declared. Even if something went wrong, Sexton knew losing his daughter to the enemy would only make him more powerful still. Either way he would win. Acceptable risk.

'Who are those copies for?' Gabrielle demanded. 'William Pickering said not to tell anyone!'

Sexton turned from the machine and looked at Gabrielle, amazed by how unattractive he suddenly found her. In that instant, Senator Sexton was an island. Untouchable. Everything he needed to accomplish his dreams was now in his hands. Nothing could stop him now. Not claims of bribery. Not rumors of sex. Nothing.

'Go home, Gabrielle. I have no more use for you.'

It's over, Rachel thought.

She and Tolland sat side by side on the deck staring up into the barrel of the Delta soldier's machine gun. Unfortunately, Pickering now knew where Rachel had sent the fax. The office of Senator Sedgewick Sexton.

Rachel doubted her father would ever receive the phone message Pickering had just left him. Pickering could probably get to Sexton's office well before anyone else this morning. If Pickering could get in, quietly remove the fax, and delete the phone message before Sexton arrived, there would be no need to harm the senator. William Pickering was probably one of the few people in Washington who could finagle entry to a U.S. senator's office with no fanfare. Rachel was always amazed at what could be accomplished 'in the name of national security.'

Of course if that fails, Rachel thought, *Pickering could just fly by and send a Hellfire missile through the window and blow up the fax machine.* Something told her this would not be necessary.

Sitting close to Tolland now, Rachel was surprised to feel his hand gently slip into hers. His touch had a tender strength, and their fingers intertwined so naturally that Rachel felt like they'd done this for a lifetime. All she wanted right now was to lie in his arms, sheltered from the oppressive roar of the night sea spiraling around them.

Never, she realized. *It was not to be.*

Michael Tolland felt like a man who had found hope on the way to the gallows.

Life is mocking me.

For years since Celia's death, Tolland had endured nights when he'd wanted to die, hours of pain and loneliness that seemed only escapable by ending it all. And yet he had chosen life, telling himself he could make it alone. Today, for the first time, Tolland had begun to understand what his friends had been telling him all along.

Mike, you don't have to make it alone. You'll find another love.

Rachel's hand in his made this irony that much harder to swallow. Fate had cruel timing. He felt as if layers of armor were crumbling away from his heart. For an instant, on the tired decks of the *Goya*, Tolland sensed Celia's ghost looking over him as she often did. Her voice was in the rushing water . . . speaking the last words she'd spoken to him in life.

'You're a survivor,' her voice whispered. 'Promise me you'll find another love.'

'I'll never want another,' Tolland had told her.

Celia's smile was filled with wisdom. 'You'll have to learn.'

Now, on the deck of the *Goya*, Tolland realized, he was learning. A deep emotion welled suddenly in his soul. He realized it was happiness.

And with it came an overpowering will to live.

Pickering felt oddly detached as he moved toward the two prisoners. He stopped in front of Rachel, vaguely surprised that this was not harder for him.

'Sometimes,' he said, 'circumstances raise impossible decisions.'

Rachel's eyes were unyielding. 'You created these circumstances.'

'War involves casualties,' Pickering said, his voice firmer now. *Ask Diana Pickering, or any of those who die every year defending this nation.* 'You of all people should understand that, Rachel.' His eyes focused in on her. *'Iactura paucourm serva multos.'*

He could see she recognized the words – almost a cliché in national security circles. *Sacrifice the few to save the many.*

Rachel eyed him with obvious disgust. 'And now Michael and I have become part of your *few*?'

Pickering considered it. There was no other way. He turned to Delta-One. 'Release your partner and end this.'

Delta-One nodded.

Pickering took a long look at Rachel and then strode to the ship's nearby portside railing, staring out at the sea racing by. This was something he preferred not to watch.

Delta-One felt empowered as he gripped his weapon and glanced over at his partner dangling in the clamps. All that remained was to close the trapdoors beneath Delta-Two's feet, free him from the clamps, and eliminate Rachel Sexton and Michael Tolland.

Unfortunately, Delta-One had seen the complexity of the control panel near the trapdoor – a series of unmarked levers and dials that apparently controlled the trapdoor, the winch motor, and numerous other commands. He had no intention of hitting the wrong lever and risking his partner's life by mistakenly dropping the sub into the sea.

Eliminate all risk. Never rush.

He would force Tolland to perform the actual release. And to ensure he did not try anything tricky, Delta-One would take out insurance known in his business as 'biological collateral.'

Use your adversaries against one another.

Delta-One swung the gun barrel directly into Rachel's face, stopping only inches from her forehead. Rachel closed her eyes, and Delta-One could see Tolland's fists clench in a protective anger.

'Ms Sexton, stand up,' Delta-One said.

She did.

With the gun firmly on her back, Delta-One marched her over to an aluminum set of portable stairs that led up to the top of the Triton sub from behind. 'Climb up and stand on top of the sub.'

Rachel looked frightened and confused.

'Just do it,' Delta-One said.

Rachel felt like she was moving through a nightmare as she climbed up the aluminum gangway behind the Triton. She stopped at the top, having no desire to step out over the chasm onto the suspended Triton.

'Get on top of the sub,' the soldier said, returning to Tolland and pushing the gun against his head.

In front of Rachel the soldier who was in the clamps watched her, shifting in pain, obviously eager to get out. Rachel looked at Tolland, who now had a gun barrel to his head. *Get on top of the sub.* She had no choice.

Feeling like she was edging out onto a precipice overhanging a canyon, Rachel stepped onto the Triton's engine casing, a small flat section behind the rounded dome window. The entire sub hung like a massive plumb bob over the open trapdoor. Even suspended on its winch cable, the nine-ton sub barely registered her arrival, swinging only a few millimeters as she steadied herself.

'Okay, let's move,' the soldier said to Tolland. 'Go to the controls and close the trapdoor.'

At gunpoint, Tolland began moving toward the control panel with the soldier behind him. As Tolland came toward her, he was moving slowly, and Rachel could feel his eyes fixing hard on her as if trying to send her a message. He looked directly at her and then down at the open hatch on top of the Triton.

Rachel glanced down. The hatch at her feet was open, the heavy circular covering propped open. She could see down into the one-seater cockpit. *He wants me to get in?* Sensing she must be mistaken, Rachel looked at Tolland again. He was almost to the control panel. Tolland's eyes locked on her. This time he was less subtle.

His lips mouthed, 'Jump in! Now!'

Delta-One saw Rachel's motion out of the corner of his eye and wheeled on instinct, opening fire as Rachel fell through the sub's hatch just below the barrage of bullets. The open hatch covering rang out as the bullets ricocheted off the circular portal, sending up a shower of sparks, and slamming the lid closed on top of her.

Tolland, the instant he'd felt the gun leave his back, made his move. He dove to his left, away from the trapdoor, hitting the deck and rolling just as the soldier spun back toward him, gun blazing. Bullets exploded behind Tolland as he scrambled for cover behind the ship's stern anchor spool – an enormous motorized

538

cylinder around which was wound several thousand feet of steel cable connected to the ship's anchor.

Tolland had a plan and would have to act fast. As the soldier dashed toward him, Tolland reached up and grabbed the anchor lock with both hands, yanking down. Instantly the anchor spool began feeding out lengths of cable, and the *Goya* lurched in the strong current. The sudden movement sent everything and everyone on the deck staggering sidelong. As the boat accelerated in reverse on the current, the anchor spool doled out cable faster and faster.

Come on, baby, Tolland urged.

The soldier regained his balance and came for Tolland. Waiting until the last possible moment, Tolland braced himself and rammed the lever back up, locking the anchor spool. The chain snapped taut, stopping the ship short and sending a tremulous shudder throughout the *Goya*. Everything on deck went flying. The soldier staggered to his knees near Tolland. Pickering fell back from the railing onto the deck. The Triton swung wildly on its cable.

A grating howl of failing metal tore up from beneath the ship like an earthquake as the damaged strut finally gave way. The right stern corner of the *Goya* began collapsing under its own weight. The ship faltered, tilting on a diagonal like a massive table losing one of its four legs. The noise from beneath was deafening – a wail of twisting, grating metal and pounding surf.

White-knuckled inside the Triton cockpit, Rachel held on as the nine-ton machine swayed over the trapdoor in the now steeply inclined deck. Through the base of the glass dome she could see the ocean raging below. As she looked up, her eyes scanning the deck for Tolland, she watched a bizarre drama on the deck unfold in a matter of seconds.

Only a yard away, trapped in the Triton's claws, the clamped Delta soldier was howling in pain as he bobbed like a puppet on a stick. William Pickering scrambled across Rachel's field of vision and grabbed on to a cleat on the deck. Near the anchor lever, Tolland was also hanging on, trying not to slide over the edge into the water. When Rachel saw the soldier with the machine gun stabilizing himself nearby, she called out inside the sub, 'Mike, look out!'

But Delta-One ignored Tolland entirely. The soldier was looking back toward the idling helicopter with his mouth open in horror. Rachel turned, following his gaze. The Kiowa gunship, with its huge rotors still turning, had started to slowly slide forward down the tipping deck. Its long metal skids were acting like skis on a slope. It was then that Rachel realized the huge machine was skidding directly toward the Triton.

Scrambling up the inclined deck toward the sliding aircraft, Delta-One clambered into the cockpit. He had no intention of letting their only means of escape slide off the deck. Delta-One seized the Kiowa's controls and heaved back on the stick. *Lift off!* With a deafening roar, the blades accelerated overhead, straining to lift the heavily armed gunship off the deck. *Up, goddamn it!* The chopper was sliding directly toward the Triton and Delta-Two suspended in its grasp.

With its nose tipped forward, the Kiowa's blades were also tipped, and when the chopper lurched off the deck, it sailed more forward than up, accelerating toward the Triton like a giant buzz saw. *Up!* Delta-One pulled the stick, wishing he could drop the half ton of

Hellfire warheads weighing him down. The blades just missed the top of Delta-Two's head and the top of the Triton sub, but the chopper was moving too fast. It would never clear the Triton's winch cable.

As the Kiowa's 300-rpm steel blades collided with the sub's 15-ton capacity braided-steel winch cable, the night erupted with the shriek of metal on metal. The sounds conjured images of epic battle. From the chopper's armored cockpit, Delta-One watched his rotors tear into the sub's cable like a giant lawnmower running over a steel chain. A blinding spray of sparks erupted overhead, and the Kiowa's blades exploded. Delta-One felt the chopper bottom out, its struts hitting the deck hard. He tried to control the aircraft, but he had no lift. The chopper bounded twice down the inclined deck, then slid, crashing into the ship's guardrail.

For a moment, he thought the rail would hold.

Then Delta-One heard the crack. The heavily laden chopper listed over the brink, plummeting into the sea.

Inside the Triton, Rachel Sexton sat paralyzed, her body pressed back into the sub's seat. The minisub had been tossed violently as the chopper's rotor wrapped around the cable, but she had managed to hang on. Somehow the blades had missed the main body of the sub, but she knew there had to be major damage to the cable. All Rachel could think of at that point was escaping from the sub as fast as she could. The soldier trapped in the clamps stared in at her, delirious, bleeding, and burned from the shrapnel. Beyond him, Rachel saw William Pickering still holding on to a cleat on the slanting deck.

Where's Michael? She didn't see him. Her panic lasted only an instant as a new fear descended. Overhead, the

Triton's shredded winch cable let out an ominous whipping noise as the braids unraveled. Then, there was a loud snap, and Rachel felt the cable give way.

Momentarily weightless, Rachel hovered above her seat inside the cockpit as the sub hurtled downward. The deck disappeared overhead, and the catwalks under the *Goya* raced by. The soldier trapped in the claws went white with fear, staring at Rachel as the sub accelerated downward.

The fall seemed endless.

When the sub crashed into the sea beneath the *Goya*, it plunged hard under the surf, ramming Rachel down hard into her seat. Her spine compressed as the illuminated ocean raced up over the dome. She felt a suffocating drag as the sub slowed to a stop underwater and then raced back toward the surface, bobbing up like a cork.

The sharks hit instantly. From her front-row seat, Rachel sat frozen in place as the spectacle unfolded only a few feet away.

Delta-Two felt the shark's oblong head crash into him with unimaginable force. A razor sharp clamp tightened on his upper arm, slicing to the bone and locking on. A flash of white-hot pain exploded as the shark torqued its powerful body and shook its head violently, tearing Delta-Two's arm off his body. Other sharks moved in. Knives stabbing at his legs. Torso. Neck. Delta-Two had no breath to scream in agony as the sharks ripped huge chunks of his body away. The last thing he saw was a crescent-shaped mouth, tilting sideways, a gorge of teeth clamping down across his face.

The world went black.

Inside the Triton, the thudding of heavy cartilaginous heads ramming into the dome finally subsided. Rachel opened her eyes. The man was gone. The water washing against the window was crimson.

Badly battered, Rachel huddled in her chair, knees pulled to her chest. She could feel the sub moving. It was drifting on the current, scraping along the length of the *Goya*'s lower dive deck. She could feel it moving in another direction as well. Down.

Outside, the distinctive gurgling of water into the ballast tanks grew louder. The ocean inched higher on the glass in front of her.

I'm sinking!

A jolt of terror shot through Rachel, and she was suddenly scrambling to her feet. Reaching overhead, she grabbed the hatch mechanism. If she could climb up on top of the sub, she still had time to jump onto the *Goya*'s dive deck. It was only a few feet away.

I've got to get out!

The hatch mechanism was clearly marked which way to turn it to open. She heaved. The hatch did not budge. She tried again. Nothing. The portal was jammed shut. Bent. As the fear rose in her blood like the sea around her, Rachel heaved one last time.

The hatch did not move.

The Triton sank a few inches deeper, bumping the *Goya* one last time before drifting out from underneath the mangled hull . . . and into the open sea.

'Don't do this,' Gabrielle begged the senator as he finished at the copy machine. 'You're risking your daughter's life!'

Sexton blocked out her voice, moving back to his desk now with ten identical stacks of photocopies. Each stack contained copies of the pages Rachel had faxed him, including her handwritten note claiming the meteorite was a fake and accusing NASA and the White House of trying to kill her.

The most shocking media kits ever assembled, Sexton thought, as he began carefully inserting each stack into its own large, white linen envelope. Each envelope bore his name, office address, and senatorial seal. There would be no doubt where this incredible information had originated. *The political scandal of the century*, Sexton thought, *and I will be the one to reveal it!*

Gabrielle was still pleading for Rachel's safety, but Sexton heard only silence. As he assembled the envelopes, he was in his own private world. *Every political career has a defining moment. This is mine.*

William Pickering's phone message had warned that if Sexton went public, Rachel's life would be in danger. Unfortunately for Rachel, Sexton also knew if he went public with proof of NASA's fraud, that single act of boldness would land him in the White House with more decisiveness and political drama than ever before witnessed in American politics.

Life is filled with difficult decisions, he thought. *And winners are those who make them.*

Gabrielle Ashe had seen this look in Sexton's eyes before. *Blind ambition.* She feared it. And with good reason, she now realized. Sexton was obviously prepared to risk his daughter in order to be the first to announce the NASA fraud.

'Don't you see you've already won?' Gabrielle demanded. 'There's no way Zach Herney and NASA will survive this scandal. No matter *who* makes it public! No matter when it comes out! Wait until you know Rachel is safe. Wait until you talk to Pickering!'

Sexton was clearly no longer listening to her. Opening his desk drawer, he pulled out a foil sheet on which were affixed dozens of nickel-sized, self-adhesive wax seals with his initials on them. Gabrielle knew he usually used these for formal invitations, but he apparently thought a crimson wax seal would give each envelope an extra touch of drama. Peeling the circular seals off the foil, Sexton pressed one onto the pleat of each envelope, sealing it like a monogrammed epistle.

Gabrielle's heart pulsed now with a new anger. She thought of the digitized images of illegal checks in his computer. If she said anything, she knew he would just delete the evidence. 'Don't do this,' she said, 'or I'll go public about our affair.'

Sexton laughed out loud as he affixed the wax seals. 'Really? And you think they'll believe you – a power-hungry aide denied a post in my administration and looking for revenge at any cost? I denied our involvement once, and the world believed me. I'll simply deny it again.'

'The White House has photos,' Gabrielle declared.

Sexton did not even look up. 'They don't have

545

photos. And even if they did, they're meaningless.' He affixed the final wax seal. 'I have immunity. These envelopes out-trump anything anyone could possibly throw at me.'

Gabrielle knew he was right. She felt utterly helpless as Sexton admired his handiwork. On his desk sat ten elegant, white linen envelopes, each embossed with his name and address and secured with a crimson wax seal bearing his scripted initials. They looked like royal letters. Certainly kings had been crowned on account of less potent information.

Sexton picked up the envelopes and prepared to leave. Gabrielle stepped over and blocked his way. 'You're making a mistake. This can wait.'

Sexton's eyes bore into her. 'I made you, Gabrielle, and now I've unmade you.'

'That fax from Rachel will give you the presidency. You owe her.'

'I've given her plenty.'

'What if something happens to her?'

'Then she'll cement my sympathy vote.'

Gabrielle could not believe the thought had even crossed his mind, much less his lips. Disgusted, she reached for the phone. 'I'm calling the White—'

Sexton spun and slapped her hard across the face.

Gabrielle staggered back, feeling her lip split open. She caught herself, grabbing on to the desk, staring up in astonishment at the man she had once worshipped.

Sexton gave her a long, hard look. 'If you so much as think of crossing me on this, I will make you regret it for the rest of your life.' He stood unflinching, clutching the stack of sealed envelopes under his arm. A harsh danger burned in his eyes.

When Gabrielle exited the office building into the

cold night air, her lip was still bleeding. She hailed a taxi and climbed in. Then, for the first time since she had come to Washington, Gabrielle Ashe broke down and cried.

The Triton fell . . .

Michael Tolland staggered to his feet on the inclined deck and peered over the anchor spool at the frayed winch cable where the Triton used to hang. Wheeling toward the stern, he scanned the water. The Triton was just now emerging from under the *Goya* on the current. Relieved at least to see the sub intact, Tolland eyed the hatch, wanting nothing more than to see it open up and Rachel climb out unscathed. But the hatch remained closed. Tolland wondered if maybe she had been knocked out by the violent fall.

Even from the deck, Tolland could see the Triton was riding exceptionally low in the water – far below its normal diving trim waterline. *It's sinking.* Tolland could not imagine why, but the reason at the moment was immaterial.

I have to get Rachel out. Now.

As Tolland stood to dash for the edge of the deck, a shower of machine-gun fire exploded above him, sparking off the heavy anchor spool overhead. He dropped back to his knees. *Shit!* He peered around the spool only long enough to see Pickering on the upper deck, taking aim like a sniper. The Delta soldier had dropped his machine gun while climbing into the doomed helicopter and Pickering had apparently recovered it. Now the director had scrambled to the high ground.

Trapped behind the spool, Tolland looked back toward the sinking Triton. *Come on, Rachel! Get out!* He waited for the hatch to open. Nothing.

Looking back to the deck of the *Goya*, Tolland's eyes measured the open area between his position and the stern railing. Twenty feet. A long way without any cover.

Tolland took a deep breath and made up his mind. Ripping off his shirt, he hurled it to his right onto the open deck. While Pickering blew the shirt full of holes, Tolland dashed left, down the inclined deck, banking toward the stern. With a wild leap he launched himself over the railing, off the back of the ship. Arcing high in the air, Tolland heard the bullets whizzing all around him and knew a single graze would make him a shark feast the instant he hit the water.

Rachel Sexton felt like a wild animal trapped in a cage. She had tried the hatch again and again with no luck. She could hear a tank somewhere beneath her filling with water, and she sensed the sub gaining weight. The darkness of the ocean was inching higher up the transparent dome, a black curtain rising in reverse.

Through the lower half of the glass, Rachel could see the void of the ocean beckoning like a tomb. The empty vastness beneath threatened to swallow her whole. She grabbed the hatch mechanism and tried to twist it open one more time, but it wouldn't budge. Her lungs strained now, the dank stench of excess carbon dioxide acrid in her nostrils. Through it all, one recurring thought haunted her.

I'm going to die alone underwater.

She scanned the Triton's control panels and levers for something that could help, but all the indicators were black. No power. She was locked in a dead steel crypt sinking toward the bottom of the sea.

The gurgling in the tanks seemed to be accelerating now, and the ocean rose to within a few feet of the top of the glass. In the distance, across the endless flat expanse, a band of crimson was inching across the horizon. Morning was on its way. Rachel feared it would be the last light she ever saw. Closing her eyes to block out her impending fate, Rachel felt the terrifying childhood images rushing into her mind.

Falling through the ice. Sliding underwater.

Breathless. Unable to lift herself. Sinking.

Her mother calling for her. 'Rachel! Rachel!'

A pounding on the outside of the sub jolted Rachel out of the delirium. Her eyes snapped open.

'Rachel!' The voice was muffled. A ghostly face appeared against the glass, upside down, dark hair swirling. She could barely make him out in the darkness.

'Michael!'

Tolland surfaced, exhaling in relief to see Rachel moving inside the sub. *She's alive.* Tolland swam with powerful strokes to the rear of the Triton and climbed up onto the submerged engine platform. The ocean currents felt hot and leaden around him as he positioned himself to grab the circular portal screw, staying low and hoping he was out of range of Pickering's gun.

The Triton's hull was almost entirely underwater now, and Tolland knew if he were going to open the hatch and pull Rachel out, he would have to hurry. He had a ten-inch draw that was diminishing fast. Once the hatch was submerged, opening it would send a torrent of seawater gushing into the Triton, trapping Rachel inside and sending the sub into a free fall to the bottom.

'Now or never,' he gasped as he grabbed the hatch wheel and heaved it counterclockwise. Nothing happened. He tried again, throwing all of his force into it. Again, the hatch refused to turn.

He could hear Rachel inside, on the other side of the portal. Her voice was stifled, but he sensed her terror. 'I tried!' she shouted. 'I couldn't turn it!'

The water was lapping across the portal lid now. 'Turn together!' he shouted to her. 'You're *clockwise* in there!' He knew the dial was clearly marked. 'Okay, now!'

Tolland braced himself against the ballast air tanks and strained with all his energy. He could hear Rachel below him doing the same. The dial turned a half inch and ground to a dead stop.

Now Tolland saw it. The portal lid was not set evenly in the aperture. Like the lid of a jar that had been placed on crooked and screwed down hard, it was stuck. Although the rubber seal was properly set, the hatchdogs were bent, meaning the only way that door was opening was with a welding torch.

As the top of the sub sank below the surface, Tolland was filled with a sudden, overwhelming dread. Rachel Sexton would not be escaping from the Triton.

Two thousand feet below, the crumpled fuselage of the bomb-laden Kiowa chopper was sinking fast, a prisoner of gravity and the powerful drag of the deepwater vortex. Inside the cockpit, Delta-One's lifeless body was no longer recognizable, disfigured by the crushing pressure of the deep.

As the aircraft spiraled downward, its Hellfire missiles still attached, the glowing magma dome waited on the ocean floor like a red-hot landing pad. Beneath its three-meter-thick crust, a head of boiling lava simmered at 1,000 degrees centigrade, a volcano waiting to explode.

128

Tolland stood knee-deep in water on the engine box of the sinking Triton and searched his brain for some way to save Rachel.

Don't let the sub sink!

He looked back toward the *Goya*, wondering if there were any way to get a winch connected to the Triton to keep it near the surface. Impossible. It was fifty yards away now, and Pickering was standing high on the bridge like a Roman emperor with a prime seat to some bloody Coliseum spectacle.

Think! Tolland told himself. *Why is the sub sinking?*

The mechanics of sub buoyancy were painfully simple: ballast tanks pumped full of either air or water adjusted the sub's buoyancy to move it up or down in the water.

Obviously, the ballast tanks were filling up.

But they shouldn't be!

Every sub's ballast tanks were equipped with holes both topside and underneath. The lower openings, called 'flooding holes,' always remained open, while the holes on top, 'vent valves,' could be opened and closed to let air escape so water would flood in.

Maybe the Triton's vent valves were open for some reason? Tolland could not imagine why. He floundered across the submerged engine platform, his hands groping one of the Triton's ballast trim tanks. The vent valves were closed. But as he felt the valves, his fingers found something else.

Bullet holes.

Shit! The Triton had been riddled with bullets when Rachel jumped in. Tolland immediately dove down and swam beneath the sub, running his hand carefully across the Triton's more important ballast tank – the negative tank. The Brits called this tank 'the down express.' The Germans called it 'putting on lead shoes.' Either way, the meaning was clear. The negative tank, when filled, took the sub *down*.

As Tolland's hand felt the sides of the tank, he encountered dozens of bullet holes. He could feel the water rushing in. The Triton was preparing to dive, whether Tolland liked it or not.

The sub was now three feet beneath the surface. Moving to the bow, Tolland pressed his face against the glass and peered through the dome. Rachel was banging on the glass and shouting. The fear in her voice made him feel powerless. For an instant he was back in a cold hospital, watching the woman he loved die and knowing there was nothing he could do. Hovering underwater in front of the sinking sub, Tolland told himself he could not endure this again. *You're a survivor*, Celia had told him, but Tolland did not want to survive alone . . . not again.

Tolland's lungs ached for air and yet he stayed right there with her. Every time Rachel pounded on the glass, Tolland heard air bubbles gurgling up and the sub sank deeper. Rachel was yelling something about water coming in around the window.

The viewing window was leaking.

A bullet hole in the window? It seemed doubtful. His lungs ready to burst, Tolland prepared to surface. As he palmed upward across the huge acrylic window, his fingers hit a piece of loose rubber caulking. A peripheral seal had apparently been jarred in the fall. This was the reason the cockpit was leaking. *More bad news.*

Clambering to the surface, Tolland sucked in three deep breaths, trying to clear his thoughts. Water flowing into the cockpit would only accelerate the Triton's descent. The sub was already five feet underwater, and Tolland could barely touch it with his feet. He could feel Rachel pounding desperately on the hull.

Tolland could think of only one thing to do. If he dove down to the Triton's engine box and located the high-pressure air cylinder, he could use it to blow the negative ballast tank. Although blowing the damaged tank would be an exercise in futility, it might keep the Triton near the surface for another minute or so before the perforated tanks flooded again.

Then what?

With no other immediate option, Tolland prepared to dive. Pulling in an exceptionally deep breath, he expanded his lungs well beyond their natural state, almost to the point of pain. *More lung capacity. More oxygen. Longer dive.* But as he felt his lungs expand, pressuring his rib cage, a strange thought hit him.

What if he increased the pressure *inside* the sub? The viewing dome had a damaged seal. Maybe if Tolland could increase the pressure *inside* the cockpit, he could blow the entire viewing dome off the sub and get Rachel out.

He exhaled his breath, treading water on the surface a moment, trying to picture the feasibility. It was perfectly logical, wasn't it? After all, a submarine was built to be strong in only *one* direction. They had to withstand enormous pressure from the outside, but almost none from within.

Moreover, the Triton used uniform regulator valves to decrease the number of spare parts the *Goya* had to carry. Tolland could simply unsnap the high-pressure cylinder's charging hose and reroute it into an emergency ventilation supply regulator on the port side of the sub! Pressurizing the cabin would cause Rachel substantial physical pain, but it might just give her a way out.

Tolland inhaled and dove.

The sub was a good eight feet down now, and the currents and darkness made orienting himself difficult. Once he found the pressurized tank, Tolland quickly rerouted the hose and prepared to pump air into the cockpit. As he gripped the stopcock, the reflective yellow paint on the side of the tank reminded him just how dangerous this maneuver was: CAUTION: COMPRESSED AIR – 3,000 PSI.

Three thousand pounds per square inch, Tolland thought. The hope was that the Triton's viewing dome would pop off the sub before the pressure in the cabin crushed Rachel's lungs. Tolland was essentially sticking a high-powered fire hose into a water balloon and praying the balloon would break in a hurry.

He grabbed the stopcock and made up his mind. Suspended there on the back of the sinking Triton, Tolland turned the stopcock, opening the valve. The hose went rigid immediately, and Tolland could hear the air flooding the cockpit with enormous force.

Inside the Triton, Rachel felt a sudden searing pain slice into her head. She opened her mouth to scream, but the air forced itself into her lungs with such painful pressure that she thought her chest would explode. Her eyes felt like they were being rammed backward into her skull. A deafening rumble tore through her eardrums, pushing her toward unconsciousness. Instinctively, she clenched her eyes tight and pressed her hands over her ears. The pain was increasing now.

Rachel heard a pounding directly in front of her. She forced her eyes open just long enough to see the watery silhouette of Michael Tolland in the darkness. His face was against the glass. He was motioning for her to do something.

But what?

She could barely see him in the darkness. Her vision was blurred, her eyeballs distorted from the pressure. Even so, she could tell the sub had sunk beyond the last flickering fingers of the *Goya*'s underwater lights. Around her was only an endless inky abyss.

Tolland spread himself against the window of the Triton and kept banging. His chest burned for air, and he knew he would have to return to the surface in a matter of seconds.

Push on the glass! he willed her. He could hear pressurized air escaping around the glass, bubbling up. Somewhere, the seal was loose. Tolland's hands groped for an edge, something to get his fingers under. Nothing.

As his oxygen ran out, tunnel vision closed in, and he

banged on the glass one last time. He could not even see her anymore. It was too dark. With the last of the air in his lungs, he yelled out underwater.

'*Rachel . . . push . . . on . . . the . . . glass!*'

His words came out as a bubbling, muted garble.

129

Inside the Triton, Rachel's head felt like it was being compressed in some kind of medieval torture vise. Half-standing, stooped beside the cockpit chair, she could feel death closing in around her. Directly in front of her, the hemispherical viewing dome was empty. Dark. The banging had stopped.

Tolland was gone. He had left her.

The hiss of pressurized air blasting in overhead reminded her of the deafening katabatic wind on Milne. The floor of the sub had a foot of water on it now. *Let me out!* Thousands of thoughts and memories began streaming through her mind like flashes of violet light.

In the darkness, the sub began to list, and Rachel staggered, losing her balance. Stumbling over the seat, she fell forward, colliding hard with the inside of the hemispherical dome. A sharp pain erupted in her shoulder. She landed in a heap against the window, and as she did, she felt an unexpected sensation – a sudden decrease in the pressure inside the sub. The tightened drum of Rachel's ears loosened perceptibly, and she actually heard a gurgle of air escape the sub.

It took her an instant to realize what had just

happened. When she'd fallen against the dome, her weight had somehow forced the bulbous sheet outward enough for some of the internal pressure to be released around a seal. Obviously, the dome glass was loose! Rachel suddenly realized what Tolland had been trying to do by increasing the pressure inside.

He's trying to blow out the window!

Overhead, the Triton's pressure cylinder continued to pump. Even as she lay there, she felt the pressure increasing again. This time she almost welcomed it, although she felt the suffocating grip pushing her dangerously close to unconsciousness. Scrambling to her feet, Rachel pressed outward with all her force on the inside of the glass.

This time, there was no gurgle. The glass barely moved.

She threw her weight against the window again. Nothing. Her shoulder wound ached, and she looked down at it. The blood was dry. She prepared to try again, but she did not have time. Without warning, the crippled sub began to tip – backward. As its heavy engine box overcame the flooded trim tanks, the Triton rolled onto its back, sinking rear-first now.

Rachel fell onto her back against the cockpit's rear wall. Half submerged in sloshing water, she stared straight up at the leaking dome, hovering over her like a giant skylight.

Outside was only night . . . and thousands of tons of ocean pressing down.

Rachel willed herself to get up, but her body felt dead and heavy. Again her mind reeled backward in time to the icy grip of a frozen river.

'Fight, Rachel!' her mother was shouting, reaching down to pull her out of the water. 'Grab on!'

Rachel closed her eyes. *I'm sinking.* Her skates felt like lead weights, dragging her down. She could see her mother lying spread-eagle on the ice to disperse her own weight, reaching out.

'*Kick*, Rachel! Kick with your feet!'

Rachel kicked as best as she could. Her body rose slightly in the icy hole. A spark of hope. Her mother grabbed on.

'Yes!' her mother shouted. 'Help me lift you! Kick with your feet!'

With her mother pulling from above, Rachel used the last of her energy to kick with her skates. It was just enough, and her mother dragged Rachel up to safety. She dragged the soaking Rachel all the way to the snowy bank before collapsing in tears.

Now, inside the growing humidity and heat of the sub, Rachel opened her eyes to the blackness around her. She heard her mother whispering from the grave, her voice clear even here in the sinking Triton.

Kick with your feet.

Rachel looked up at the dome overhead. Mustering the last of her courage, Rachel clambered up onto the cockpit chair, which was oriented almost horizontally now, like a dental chair. Lying on her back, Rachel bent her knees, pulled her legs back as far as she could, aimed her feet upward, and exploded forward. With a wild scream of desperation and force, she drove her feet into the center of the acrylic dome. Spikes of pain shot into her shins, sending her brain reeling. Her ears thundered suddenly, and she felt the pressure equalize with a violent rush. The seal on the left side of the dome gave way, and the huge lens partially dislodged, swinging open like a barn door.

A torrent of water crashed into the sub and drove

Rachel back into her chair. The ocean thundered in around her, swirling up under her back, lifting her now off the chair, tossing her upside down like a sock in a washing machine. Rachel groped blindly for something to hold on to, but she was spinning wildly. As the cockpit filled, she could feel the sub begin a rapid free fall to the bottom. Her body rammed upward in the cockpit, and she felt herself pinned. A rush of bubbles erupted around her, twisting her, dragging her to the left and upward. A flap of hard acrylic smashed into her hip.

All at once she was free.

Twisting and tumbling into the endless warmth and watery blackness, Rachel felt her lungs already aching for air. *Get to the surface!* She looked for light but saw nothing. Her world looked the same in all directions. Blackness. No gravity. No sense of up or down.

In that terrifying instant, Rachel realized she had no idea which way to swim.

Thousands of feet beneath her, the sinking Kiowa chopper crumpled beneath the relentlessly increasing pressure. The fifteen high-explosive, antitank AGM-114 Hellfire missiles still aboard strained against the compression, their copper liner cones and spring-detonation heads inching perilously inward.

A hundred feet above the ocean floor, the powerful shaft of the megaplume grabbed the remains of the chopper and sucked it downward, hurling it against the red-hot crust of the magma dome. Like a box of matches igniting in series, the Hellfire missiles exploded, tearing a gaping hole through the top of the magma dome.

*　　*　　*

Having surfaced for air, and then dove again in desperation, Michael Tolland was suspended fifteen feet underwater scanning the blackness when the Hellfire missiles exploded. The white flash billowed upward, illuminating an astonishing image – a freeze-frame he would remember forever.

Rachel Sexton hung ten feet below him like a tangled marionette in the water. Beneath her, the Triton sub fell away fast, its dome hanging loose. The sharks in the area scattered for the open sea, clearly sensing the danger this area was about to unleash.

Tolland's exhilaration at seeing Rachel out of the sub was instantly vanquished by the realization of what was about to follow. Memorizing her position as the light disappeared, Tolland dove hard, clawing his way toward her.

Thousands of feet down, the shattered crust of the magma dome exploded apart, and the underwater volcano erupted, spewing 1,200-degree-Celsius magma up into the sea. The scorching lava vaporized all the water it touched, sending a massive pillar of steam rocketing toward the surface up the central axis of the megaplume. Driven by the same kinematic properties of fluid dynamics that powered tornadoes, the steam's vertical transfer of energy was counterbalanced by an anticyclonic vorticity spiral that circled the shaft, carrying energy in the opposite direction.

Spiraling around this column of rising gas, the ocean currents started intensifying, twisting downward. The fleeing steam created an enormous vacuum that sucked millions of gallons of seawater downward into contact with the magma. As the new water hit bottom, it too turned into steam and needed a way to escape, joining the growing column of exhaust steam and shooting upward, pulling more water in beneath it. As more water rushed in to take its place, the vortex intensified. The hydrothermal plume elongated, and the towering whirlpool grew stronger with every passing second, its upper rim moving steadily toward the surface.

An oceanic black hole had just been born.

Rachel felt like a child in a womb. Hot, wet darkness all engulfing her. Her thoughts were muddled in the inky warmth. *Breathe.* She fought the reflex. The flash of light she had seen could only have come from the surface, and yet it seemed so far away. *An illusion. Get to the surface.* Weakly, Rachel began swimming in the direction where she had seen the light. She saw more light now . . . an eerie red glow in the distance. *Daylight?* She swam harder.

A hand caught her by the ankle.

Rachel half-screamed underwater, almost exhaling the last of her air.

The hand pulled her backward, twisting her, pointing her back in the opposite direction. Rachel felt a familiar hand grasp hers. Michael Tolland was there, pulling her along with him the other way.

Rachel's mind said he was taking her down. Her heart said he knew what he was doing.

Kick with your feet, her mother's voice whispered.

Rachel kicked as hard as she could.

Even as Tolland and Rachel broke the surface, he knew it was over. *The magma dome erupted.* As soon as the top of the vortex reached the surface, the giant underwater tornado would begin pulling everything down. Strangely, the world above the surface was not the quiet dawn he had left only moments ago. The noise was deafening. Wind slashed at him as if some kind of storm had hit while he was underwater.

Tolland felt delirious from lack of oxygen. He tried to support Rachel in the water, but she was being pulled from his arms. *The current!* Tolland tried to hold on, but the invisible force pulled harder, threatening to tear her from him. Suddenly, his grip slipped, and Rachel's body slid through his arms – but *upward.*

Bewildered, Tolland watched Rachel's body rise out of the water.

Overhead, the Coast Guard Osprey tilt-rotor airplane hovered and winched Rachel in. Twenty minutes ago, the Coast Guard had gotten a report of an explosion out at sea. Having lost track of the Dolphin helicopter that was supposed to be in the area, they feared an accident. They typed the chopper's last known coordinates into their navigation system and hoped for the best.

About a half mile from the illuminated *Goya*, they saw a field of burning wreckage drifting on the current. It looked like a speedboat. Nearby, a man was in the water, waving his arms wildly. They winched him in.

He was stark naked – all except for one leg, which was covered with duct tape.

Exhausted, Tolland looked up at the underbelly of the thundering tilt-rotor airplane. Deafening gusts pounded down off its horizontal propellers. As Rachel rose on a cable, numerous sets of hands pulled her into the fuselage. As Tolland watched her dragged to safety, his eyes spotted a familiar man crouched half naked in the doorway.

Corky? Tolland's heart soared. *You're alive!*

Immediately, the harness fell from the sky again. It landed ten feet away. Tolland wanted to swim for it, but he could already feel the sucking sensation of the plume. The relentless grip of the sea wrapped around him, refusing to let go.

The current pulled him under. He fought toward the surface, but the exhaustion was overwhelming. *You're a survivor*, someone was saying. He kicked his legs, clawing toward the surface. When he broke through into the pounding wind, the harness was still out of reach. The current strained to drag him under. Looking up into the torrent of swirling wind and noise, Tolland saw Rachel. She was staring down, her eyes willing him up toward her.

It took Tolland four powerful strokes to reach the harness. With his last ounce of strength, he slid his arm and head up into the loop and collapsed.

All at once the ocean was falling away beneath him.

Tolland looked down just as the gaping vortex opened. The megaplume had finally reached the surface.

William Pickering stood on the bridge of the *Goya* and watched in dumbstruck awe as the spectacle unfolded all around him. Off the starboard of the *Goya*'s stern, a huge basinlike depression was forming on the surface of the sea. The whirlpool was hundreds of yards across and expanding fast. The ocean spiraled into it, racing with an eerie smoothness over the lip. All around him now, a guttural moan reverberated out of the depths. Pickering's mind was blank as he watched the hole expanding toward him like the gaping mouth of some epic god hungry for sacrifice.

I'm dreaming, Pickering thought.

Suddenly, with an explosive hiss that shattered the windows of the *Goya*'s bridge, a towering plume of steam erupted skyward out of the vortex. A colossal geyser climbed overhead, thundering, its apex disappearing into the darkened sky.

Instantly, the funnel walls steepened, the perimeter expanding faster now, chewing across the ocean toward him. The stern of the *Goya* swung hard toward the expanding cavity. Pickering lost his balance and fell to his knees. Like a child before God, he gazed downward into the growing abyss.

His final thoughts were for his daughter, Diana. He prayed she had not known fear like this when she died.

The concussion wave from the escaping steam hurled the Osprey sideways. Tolland and Rachel held each other as the pilots recovered, banking low over the doomed *Goya*. Looking out, they could see William Pickering – the Quaker – kneeling in his black coat and tie at the upper railing of the doomed ship.

As the stern fishtailed out over the brink of the massive twister, the anchor cable finally snapped. With its bow proudly in the air, the *Goya* slipped backward over the watery ledge, sucked down the steep spiraling wall of water. Her lights were still glowing as she disappeared beneath the sea.

131

The Washington morning was clear and crisp.

A breeze sent eddies of leaves skittering around the base of the Washington Monument. The world's largest obelisk usually awoke to its own peaceful image in the reflecting pool, but today the morning brought with it a chaos of jostling reporters, all crowding around the monument's base in anticipation.

Senator Sedgewick Sexton felt larger than Washington itself as he stepped from his limousine and strode like a lion toward the press area awaiting him at the base of the monument. He had invited the nation's ten largest media networks here and promised them the scandal of the decade.

Nothing brings out the vultures like the smell of death, Sexton thought.

In his hand, Sexton clutched the stack of white linen envelopes, each elegantly wax-embossed with his monogrammed seal. If information was power, then Sexton was carrying a nuclear warhead.

He felt intoxicated as he approached the podium, pleased to see his improvised stage included two 'fame-frames' – large, free-standing partitions that flanked his podium like navy-blue curtains – an old Ronald Reagan trick to ensure he stood out against any backdrop.

Sexton entered stage right, striding out from behind the partition like an actor out of the wings. The reporters quickly took their seats in the several rows of folding chairs facing his podium. To the east, the sun was just breaking over the Capitol dome, shooting rays of pink and gold down on Sexton like rays from heaven.

A perfect day to become the most powerful man in the world.

'Good morning, ladies and gentlemen,' Sexton said, laying the envelopes on the lectern before him. 'I will make this as short and painless as possible. The information I am about to share with you is, frankly, quite disturbing. These envelopes contain proof of a deceit at the highest levels of government. I am ashamed to say that the President called me half an hour ago and begged me – yes, *begged* me – not to go public with this evidence.' He shook his head with dismay. 'And yet, I am a man who believes in the truth. No matter how painful.'

Sexton paused, holding up the envelopes, tempting the seated crowd. The reporters' eyes followed the envelopes back and forth, a pack of dogs salivating over some unknown delicacy.

The President had called Sexton a half hour ago and explained everything. Herney had talked to Rachel, who was safely aboard a plane somewhere. Incredibly, it seemed the White House and NASA were innocent bystanders in this fiasco, a plot masterminded by William Pickering.

Not that it matters, Sexton thought. *Zach Herney is still going down hard.*

Sexton wished he could be a fly on the wall of the White House right now to see the President's face when he realized Sexton was going public. Sexton had agreed to meet Herney at the White House right now to discuss how best to tell the nation the truth about the meteorite. Herney was probably standing in front of a television at this very moment in dumbfounded shock, realizing that there was nothing the White House could do to stop the hand of fate.

'My friends,' Sexton said, letting his eyes connect with the crowd. 'I have weighed this heavily. I have considered honoring the President's desire to keep this data secret, but I must do what is in my heart.' Sexton sighed, hanging his head like a man trapped by history. 'The truth is the truth. I will not presume to color your interpretation of these facts in any way. I will simply give you the data at face value.'

In the distance, Sexton heard the beating of huge helicopter rotors. For a moment, he wondered if maybe the President were flying over from the White House in a panic, hoping to halt the press conference. *That would be the icing on the cake*, Sexton thought mirthfully. *How guilty would Herney appear THEN?*

'I do not take pleasure in doing this,' Sexton continued, sensing his timing was perfect. 'But I feel it is my duty to let the American people know they have been lied to.'

The aircraft thundered in, touching down on the esplanade to their right. When Sexton glanced over, he was surprised to see it was not the presidential helicopter after all, but rather a large Osprey tilt-rotor airplane.

The fuselage read: UNITED STATES COAST GUARD.

Baffled, Sexton watched as the cabin door opened and a woman emerged. She wore an orange Coast Guard parka and looked disheveled, like she'd been through a war. She strode toward the press area. For a moment, Sexton didn't recognize her. Then it hit him.

Rachel? He gaped in shock. *What the hell is SHE doing here?*

A murmur of confusion went through the crowd.

Pasting a broad smile on his face, Sexton turned back to the press and raised an apologetic finger. 'If you could give me just one minute? I'm terribly sorry.' He heaved a weary, good-natured sigh. 'Family first.'

A few of the reporters laughed.

With his daughter bearing down fast from his right, Sexton had no doubt this father-daughter reunion would best be held in private. Unfortunately, privacy was scarce at the moment. Sexton's eyes darted to the large partition on his right.

Still smiling calmly, Sexton waved to his daughter and stepped away from the microphone. Moving toward her at an angle, he maneuvered such that Rachel had to pass behind the partition to get to him. Sexton met her halfway, hidden from the eyes and ears of the press.

'Honey?' he said, smiling and opening his arms as Rachel came toward him. 'What a surprise!'

Rachel walked up and slapped his face.

Alone with her father now, ensconced behind the partition, Rachel glared with loathing. She had slapped him hard, but he barely flinched. With chilling control, his phony smile melted away, mutating into an admonishing glower.

His voice turned to a demonic whisper. 'You should not be here.'

Rachel saw wrath in his eyes and for the first time in her life felt unafraid. 'I turned to you for help, and you sold me out! I was almost killed!'

'You're obviously fine.' His tone was almost disappointed.

'NASA is *innocent!*' she said. 'The President told you that! What are you doing here?' Rachel's short flight to Washington aboard the Coast Guard Osprey had been punctuated by a flurry of phone calls between herself, the White House, her father, and even a distraught Gabrielle Ashe. 'You promised Zach Herney you were going to the White House!'

'I am.' He smirked. 'On election day.'

Rachel felt sickened to think this man was her father. 'What you're about to do is madness.'

'Oh?' Sexton chuckled. He turned and motioned behind him to the podium, which was visible at the end of the partition. On the podium, a stack of white envelopes sat waiting. 'Those envelopes contain information *you* sent me, Rachel. *You*. The President's blood is on your hands.'

'I faxed you that information when I needed your help! When I thought the President and NASA were guilty!'

'Considering the evidence, NASA certainly appears guilty.'

'But they are not! They deserve a chance to admit their own mistakes. You've already won this election. Zach Herney is finished! You *know* that. Let the man retain some dignity.'

Sexton groaned. 'So naïve. It's not about winning the election, Rachel, it's about *power*. It's about decisive victory, acts of greatness, crushing opposition, and controlling the forces in Washington so you can get something done.'

'At what cost?'

'Don't be so self-righteous. I'm simply presenting the evidence. The people can draw their own conclusions as to who is guilty.'

'You know how this will look.'

He shrugged. 'Maybe NASA's time has come.'

Senator Sexton sensed the press was getting restless beyond the partition, and he had no intention of standing here all morning and being lectured by his daughter. His moment of glory was waiting.

'We're through here,' he said. 'I have a press conference to give.'

'I'm asking you as your daughter,' Rachel pleaded. 'Don't do this. Think about what you're about to do. There's a better way.'

'Not for me.'

A howl of feedback echoed out of the PA system behind him, and Sexton wheeled to see a late-arriving female reporter, huddled over his podium, attempting to attach a network microphone to one of the gooseneck clips.

Why can't these idiots arrive on time? Sexton fumed.

In her haste, the reporter knocked Sexton's stack of envelopes to the ground.

Goddamn it! Sexton marched over, cursing his daughter for distracting him. When he arrived, the woman was on her hands and knees, collecting the envelopes off the ground. Sexton couldn't see her face, but she was obviously 'network' – wearing a full-length cashmere coat, matching scarf, and low-slung mohair beret with an ABC press pass clipped to it.

Stupid bitch, Sexton thought. 'I'll take those,' he snapped, holding out his hand for the envelopes.

The woman scraped up the last of the envelopes and handed them up to Sexton without looking up. 'Sorry . . .' she muttered, obviously embarrassed. Hunkering low in shame, she scurried off into the crowd.

Sexton quickly counted the envelopes. *Ten. Good.*

Nobody was going to steal his thunder today. Regrouping, he adjusted the microphones and gave a joking smile to the crowd. 'I guess I'd better hand these out before someone gets hurt!'

The crowd laughed, looking eager.

Sexton sensed his daughter nearby, standing just offstage behind the partition.

'Don't do this,' Rachel said to him. 'You'll regret it.'

Sexton ignored her.

'I'm asking you to trust me,' Rachel said, her voice growing louder. 'It's a mistake.'

Sexton picked up his envelopes, straightening the edges.

'Dad,' Rachel said, intense and pleading now. 'This is your last chance to do what's right.'

Do what's right? Sexton covered the microphone and turned as if clearing his throat. He glanced discreetly over at his daughter. 'You're just like your mother – idealistic and small. Women simply do not understand the true nature of power.'

Sedgewick Sexton had already forgotten his daughter by the time he turned back toward the jostling media. Head held high, he walked around the podium and handed the stack of envelopes into the hands of the waiting press. He watched the envelopes disseminate rapidly through the crowd. He could hear the seals being broken, the envelopes being torn apart like Christmas presents.

A sudden hush came over the crowd.

In the silence, Sexton could hear the defining moment of his career.

The meteorite is a fraud. And I am the man who revealed it.

Sexton knew it would take the press a moment to understand the true implications of what they were looking at: GPR images of an insertion shaft in the ice; a living ocean species almost identical to the NASA fossils; evidence of chondrules that formed on earth. It all led to one shocking conclusion.

'Sir?' one reporter stammered, sounding stunned as he looked in his envelope. 'Is this for real?'

Sexton gave a somber sigh. 'Yes, I'm afraid it's very real indeed.'

Murmurs of confusion now spread through the crowd.

'I'll give everyone a moment to look through these pages,' Sexton said, 'and then I'll take questions and attempt to shed some light on what you're looking at.'

'Senator?' another reporter asked, sounding utterly bewildered. 'Are these images authentic? . . . Un-retouched?'

'One hundred percent,' Sexton said, speaking more firmly now. 'I would not present the evidence to you otherwise.'

The confusion in the crowd seemed to deepen, and Sexton thought he even heard some laughter – not at all the reaction he had expected. He was starting to fear he had overestimated the media's ability to connect the obvious dots.

'Um, Senator?' someone said, sounding oddly amused. 'For the record, you stand behind the authenticity of these images?'

Sexton was getting frustrated. 'My friends, I will say this one last time, the evidence in your hands is one-hundred-percent accurate. And if anyone can prove otherwise, I'll eat my hat!'

Sexton waited for the laugh, but it never came.

Dead silence. Blank stares.

The reporter who had just spoken walked toward

Sexton, shuffling through his photocopies as he came forward. 'You're right, Senator. This is scandalous data.' The reporter paused, scratching his head. 'So I guess we're puzzled as to why you've decided to share it with us like this, especially after denying it so vehemently earlier.'

Sexton had no idea what the man was talking about. The reporter handed him the photocopies. Sexton looked at the pages – and for a moment, his mind went totally blank.

No words came.

He was staring at unfamiliar photographs. Black-and-white images. Two people. Naked. Arms and legs intertwined. For an instant, Sexton had no idea what he was looking at. Then it registered. A cannonball to the gut.

In horror, Sexton's head snapped up to the crowd. They were laughing now. Half of them were already phoning in the story to their news desks.

Sexton felt a tap on his shoulder.

In a daze, he wheeled.

Rachel was standing there. 'We tried to stop you,' she said. 'We gave you every chance.' A woman stood beside her.

Sexton was trembling as his eyes moved to the woman at Rachel's side. She was the reporter in the cashmere coat and mohair beret – the woman who had knocked over his envelopes. Sexton saw her face, and his blood turned to ice.

Gabrielle's dark eyes seemed to bore right through him as she reached down and opened her coat to reveal a stack of white envelopes tucked neatly beneath her arm.

132

The Oval Office was dark, lit only by the soft glow of the brass lamp on President Herney's desk. Gabrielle Ashe held her chin high as she stood before the President. Outside the window behind him, dusk was gathering on the west lawn.

'I hear you're leaving us,' Herney said, sounding disappointed.

Gabrielle nodded. Although the President had graciously offered her indefinite sanctuary inside the White House away from the press, Gabrielle preferred not to ride out this particular storm by hiding out in the eye. She wanted to be as far away as possible. At least for a while.

Herney gazed across his desk at her, looking impressed. 'The choice you made this morning, Gabrielle . . .' He paused, as if at a loss for words. His eyes were simple and clear – nothing compared to the deep, enigmatic pools that had once drawn Gabrielle to Sedgewick Sexton. And yet, even in the backdrop of this powerful place, Gabrielle saw true kindness in his gaze, an honor and dignity she would not soon forget.

'I did it for me, too,' Gabrielle finally said.

Herney nodded. 'I owe you my thanks all the same.' He stood, motioning for her to follow him into the hall. 'I was actually hoping you'd stick around long enough that I could offer you a post on my budgeting staff.'

Gabrielle gave him a dubious look. 'Stop spending and start mending?'

He chuckled. 'Something like that.'

'I think we both know, sir, that I'm more of a liability to you at the moment than an asset.'

Herney shrugged. 'Give it a few months. It will all blow over. Plenty of great men and women have endured similar situations and gone on to greatness.' He winked. 'A few of them were even U.S. presidents.'

Gabrielle knew he was right. Unemployed for only hours, Gabrielle had already turned down two other job offers today – one from Yolanda Cole at ABC, and the other from St Martin's Press, who had offered her an obscene advance if she would publish a tell-all biography. *No thanks.*

As Gabrielle and the President moved down the hallway, Gabrielle thought of the pictures of herself that were now being splashed across televisions.

The damage to the country could have been worse, she told herself. *Much worse.*

Gabrielle, after going to ABC to retrieve the photos and borrow Yolanda Cole's press pass, had snuck back to Sexton's office to assemble the duplicate envelopes. While inside, she had also printed copies of the donation checks in Sexton's computer. After the confrontation at the Washington Monument, Gabrielle had handed copies of the checks to the dumbstruck Senator Sexton and made her demands. *Give the President a chance to announce his meteorite mistake, or the rest of this data goes public too.* Senator Sexton took one look at the stack of financial evidence, locked himself in his limousine, and drove off. He had not been heard from since.

Now, as the President and Gabrielle arrived at the backstage door of the Briefing Room, Gabrielle could hear the waiting throngs beyond. For the second time in twenty-four hours, the world was assembled to hear a special presidential broadcast.

'What are you going to tell them?' Gabrielle asked.

Herney sighed, his expression remarkably calm. 'Over the years, I've learned one thing over and over . . .' He put a hand on her shoulder and smiled. 'There's just no substitute for the truth.'

Gabrielle was filled with an unexpected pride as she watched him stride toward the stage. Zach Herney was on his way to admit the biggest mistake of his life, and oddly, he had never looked more presidential.

133

When Rachel awoke, the room was dark.

A clock glowed 10:14 P.M. The bed was not her own. For several moments, she lay motionless, wondering where she was. Slowly, it all started coming back . . . the megaplume . . . this morning at the Washington Monument . . . the President's invitation to stay at the White House.

I'm at the White House, Rachel realized. *I slept here all day.*

The Coast Guard chopper, at the President's command, had transported an exhausted Michael Tolland, Corky Marlinson, and Rachel Sexton from the Washington Monument to the White House, where they had been fed a sumptuous breakfast, been seen to by doctors, and been offered any of the building's fourteen bedrooms in which to recuperate.

All of them had accepted.

Rachel could not believe she had slept this long. Turning on the television, she was stunned to see that President Herney had already completed his press conference. Rachel and the others had offered to stand beside him when he announced the meteorite disappointment to the world. *We all made the mistake together.* But Herney had insisted on shouldering the burden alone.

'Sadly,' one political analyst on TV was saying, 'it seems NASA has discovered no signs of life from space after all. This marks the second time this decade that NASA has incorrectly classified a meteorite as show- ing signs of extraterrestrial life. This time, however, a number of highly respected civilians were also among those fooled.'

'Normally,' a second analyst chimed in, 'I would have to say that a deception of the magnitude the President described this evening would be devastating for his career . . . and yet, considering the developments this morning at the Washington Monument, I would have to say Zach Herney's chances of taking the presi- dency look better than ever.'

The first analyst nodded. 'So, no life in space, but no life in Senator Sexton's campaign either. And now, as new information surfaces suggesting deep financial troubles plaguing the senator—'

A knock on the door drew Rachel's attention.

Michael, she hoped, quickly turning off the television. She hadn't seen him since breakfast. On their arrival at the White House, Rachel had wanted nothing more than to fall asleep in his arms. Although she could tell Michael felt the same, Corky had intervened, parking himself on Tolland's bed and exuberantly telling and retelling his story about urinating on himself and saving the day. Finally, utterly exhausted, Rachel and Tolland had given up, heading for separate bedrooms to sleep.

Now, walking toward the door, Rachel checked herself in the mirror, amused to see how ridiculously she was dressed. All she had found to wear to bed was an old Penn State football jersey in the dresser. It draped down to her knees like a nightshirt.

The knocking continued.

Rachel opened the door, disappointed to see a female U.S. Secret Service agent. She was fit and cute, wearing a blue blazer. 'Ms Sexton, the gentleman in the Lincoln Bedroom heard your television. He asked me to tell you that as long as you're already awake . . .' She paused, arching her eyebrows, clearly no stranger to night games on the upper floors of the White House.

Rachel blushed, her skin tingling. *'Thanks.'*

The agent led Rachel down the impeccably appointed hallway to a plain-looking doorway nearby.

'The Lincoln Bedroom,' the agent said. 'And as I am always supposed to say outside this door, "Sleep well, and beware of ghosts." '

Rachel nodded. The legends of ghosts in the Lincoln Bedroom were as old as the White House itself. It was said that Winston Churchill had seen Lincoln's ghost here, as had countless others, including Eleanor Roosevelt, Amy Carter, actor Richard Dreyfus, and decades of maids and butlers. President Reagan's dog was said to bark outside this door for hours at a time.

The thoughts of historical spirits suddenly made Rachel realize what a sacred place this room was. She felt suddenly embarrassed, standing there in her long football jersey, bare-legged, like some college coed sneaking into a boy's room. 'Is this kosher?' she whispered to the agent. 'I mean this *is* the Lincoln Bedroom.'

The agent winked. 'Our policy on this floor is "Don't ask, don't tell." '

Rachel smiled. 'Thanks.' She reached for the door-knob, already feeling the anticipation of what lay beyond.

'Rachel!' the nasal voice carried down the hallway like a buzz saw.

Rachel and the agent turned. Corky Marlinson was hobbling toward them on crutches, his leg now professionally bandaged. 'I couldn't sleep either!'

Rachel slumped, sensing her romantic tryst about to disintegrate.

Corky's eyes inspected the cute Secret Service agent. He flashed her a broad smile. 'I love women in uniform.'

The agent pulled aside her blazer to reveal a lethal-looking sidearm.

Corky backed off. 'Point taken.' He turned to Rachel. 'Is Mike awake, too? You going in?' Corky looked eager to join the party.

Rachel groaned. 'Actually, Corky . . .'

'Dr Marlinson,' the Secret Service agent intervened, pulling a note from her blazer. 'According to this note, which was given to me by Mr Tolland, I have explicit orders to escort you down to the kitchen, have our chef make you anything you want, and ask you to explain to me in vivid detail how you saved yourself from certain death by . . .' the agent hesitated, grimacing as she read the note again. '. . . by urinating on yourself?'

Apparently, the agent had said the magic words. Corky dropped his crutches on the spot and put an arm

579

around the woman's shoulders for support, and said, 'To the kitchen, love!'

As the indisposed agent helped Corky hobble off down the hall, Rachel had no doubt Corky Marlinson was in heaven. 'The urine is the key,' she heard him saying, 'because those damned telencephalon olfactory lobes can smell everything!'

The Lincoln Bedroom was dark when Rachel entered. She was surprised to see the bed empty and untouched. Michael Tolland was nowhere to be seen.

An antique oil lamp burned near the bed, and in the soft radiance, she could barely make out the Brussels carpet . . . the famous carved rosewood bed . . . the portrait of Lincoln's wife, Mary Todd . . . even the desk where Lincoln signed the Emancipation Proclamation.

As Rachel closed the door behind her, she felt a clammy draft on her bare legs. *Where is he?* Across the room, a window was open, the white organza curtains billowing. She walked over to close the window, and an eerie whisper murmured from the closet.

'Maaaarrrrrrrry . . .'

Rachel wheeled.

'Maaaaaarrrrrrrry?' the voice whispered again. 'Is that you? . . . Mary Todd Liiiiiincoln?'

Rachel quickly closed the window and turned back toward the closet. Her heart was racing, although she knew it was foolish. 'Mike, I know that's you.'

'Noooooo . . .' the voice continued. 'I am not Mike . . . I am . . . Aaaaabe.'

Rachel put her hands on her hips. 'Oh, really? *Honest* Abe?'

A muffled laugh. 'Moderately honest Abe . . . yes.'

Rachel was laughing now too.

'Be afraaaaaaid,' the voice from the closet moaned. 'Be veeeeeery afraid.'

'I'm not afraid.'

'Please be afraid . . .' the voice moaned. 'In the human species, the emotions of fear and sexual arousal are closely linked.'

Rachel burst out laughing. 'Is this your idea of a turn-on?'

'Forgiiiive me . . .' the voice moaned. 'It's been yeeeeeeeears since I've been with a woman.'

'Evidently,' Rachel said, yanking the door open.

Michael Tolland stood before her with his roguish, lopsided grin. He looked irresistible wearing a pair of navy blue satin pajamas. Rachel did a double take when she saw the presidential seal emblazoned on his chest.

'Presidential pajamas?'

He shrugged. 'They were in the drawer.'

'And all I had was this football jersey?'

'You should have chosen the Lincoln Bedroom.'

'You should have offered!'

'I heard the mattress was bad. Antique horse-hair.' Tolland winked, motioning to a gift-wrapped package on a marble-topped table. 'This'll make it up to you.'

Rachel was touched. 'For me?'

'I had one of the presidential aides go out and find this for you. Just arrived. Don't shake it.'

She carefully opened the package, extracting the heavy contents. Inside was a large crystal bowl in which were swimming two ugly orange goldfish. Rachel stared in confused disappointment. 'You're joking, right?'

'*Helostoma temmincki*,' Tolland said proudly.

'You bought me *fish*?'

'Rare Chinese kissing fish. Very romantic.'

'Fish are not romantic, Mike.'

'Tell that to *these* guys. They'll kiss for hours.'

'Is this supposed to be another turn-on?'

'I'm rusty on the romance. Can you grade me on effort?'

'For future reference, Mike, fish are definitely *not* a turn-on. Try flowers.'

Tolland pulled a bouquet of white lilies from behind his back. 'I tried for red roses,' he said, 'but I almost got shot sneaking into the Rose Garden.'

As Tolland pulled Rachel's body against his and inhaled the soft fragrance of her hair, he felt years of quiet isolation dissolving inside him. He kissed her deeply, feeling her body rise against him. The white lilies fell to their feet, and barriers Tolland had never known he'd built were suddenly melting away.

The ghosts are gone.

He felt Rachel inching him toward the bed now, her whisper soft in his ear. 'You don't *really* think fish are romantic, do you?'

'I do,' he said, kissing her again. 'You should see the jellyfish mating ritual. Incredibly erotic.'

Rachel maneuvered him onto his back on the horse-hair mattress, easing her slender body down on top of his.

'And seahorses . . .' Tolland said, breathless as he savored her touch through the thin satin of his pajamas. 'Seahorses perform . . . an unbelievably sensual dance of love.'

'Enough fish talk,' she whispered, unbuttoning his

pajamas. 'What can you tell me about the mating rituals of advanced primates?'

Tolland sighed. 'I'm afraid I don't really do primates.'

Rachel shed her football jersey. 'Well, nature boy, I suggest you learn fast.'

EPILOGUE

The NASA transport jet banked high over the Atlantic.

Onboard, Administrator Lawrence Ekstrom took a last look at the huge charred rock in the cargo hold. *Back to the sea*, he thought. *Where they found you.*

On Ekstrom's command, the pilot opened the cargo doors and released the rock. They watched as the mammoth stone plummeted downward behind the plane, arcing across the sunlit ocean sky and disappearing beneath the waves in a pillar of silver spray.

The giant stone sank fast.

Underwater, at 300 feet, barely enough light remained to reveal its tumbling silhouette. Passing 500 feet, the rock plunged into total darkness.

Racing down.

Deeper.

It fell for almost twelve minutes.

Then, like a meteorite striking the dark side of the moon, the rock crashed into a vast plain of mud on the ocean floor, kicking up a cloud of silt. As the dust settled, one of the ocean's thousands of unknown species swam over to inspect the odd newcomer.

Unimpressed, the creature moved on.

1-V-116-44-11-89-44-46-L-51-130-19-118-L-32-
118-116-130-28-116-32-44-133-U-130

DAN BROWN

THE DA VINCI CODE

'Fascinating and absorbing...
A great, riveting read.
I loved this book'
Harlan Coben

The bestselling
thriller of all time

Harvard professor Robert Langdon receives an urgent late-night phone call while on business in Paris: the elderly curator of the Louvre has been brutally murdered inside the museum. Alongside the body, police have found a series of baffling codes. As Langdon and a gifted French cryptologist, Sophie Neveu, begin to sort through the bizarre riddles, they are stunned to find a trail that leads to the works of Leonardo Da Vinci – and suggests the answer to a mystery that stretches deep into the vault of history.

Unless Langdon and Neveu can decipher the labyrinthine code and quickly assemble the pieces of the puzzle, a stunning historical truth will be lost forever...

0 552 14951 9

SPECIAL ILLUSTRATED COLLECTOR'S EDITION ALSO AVAILABLE
Go behind the scenes
of a modern classic

In this exclusive edition Dan Brown allows the reader behind the scenes of the novel, incorporating over 150 photographs and illustrations throughout the text, showing the rich historical tapestry from which he drew his inspiration. The visual sources, which provide both the backdrop and the stimulus for the novel's action, are revealed for the first time and uniquely complement the reading experience.

0 593 05425 3

DAN BROWN

ANGELS AND DEMONS

'A breathless,
real-time adventure...
Exciting, fast-paced,
with an unusually high IQ'
San Francisco Chronicle